BIG RIVER, BIG MAN

Books by Thomas W. Duncan

Novels

BIG RIVER, BIG MAN

GUS THE GREAT

RING HORSE

WE PLUCK THIS FLOWER

O, CHAUTAUQUA

Verse

ELEPHANTS AT WAR

FROM A HARVARD NOTEBOOK

HOURS FROM A LIFE

THOMAS W. DUNCAN

BIG RIVER, BIG MAN

J. B. LIPPINCOTT COMPANY

Philadelphia and New York

To
Lynn Carrick

ACKNOWLEDGEMENTS

This is a novel, not history; but there is history in it; and during the eight years spent in research, field trips and writing, I have contracted more obligations than I can well acknowledge or repay. Dead authors buried in Thwaites and live lumberjacks in the Wisconsin woods; librarians by the dozen, especially those at the New Mexico Library Commission, at Stanford University, at the University of New Mexico and at the Library of Congress; national park officials at Shiloh and Chalmette and Vicksburg; Byron McPheeters and his crew of log drivers along the Machias River; a barmaid in Portland, Maine, and a bartender in Butternut, Wisconsin; river hangers-on in Read's Landing and Memphis and Natchez and St. Louis; Mr. and Mrs. Dick Swatek in Hayward, Wisconsin, and a restaurateur named George the Turk; a Chippewa Indian who couldn't remember whether he had fathered fourteen or sixteen children, and a taxi driver in New Orleans at 2 A.M.; all have been helpful. And students of American history will understand my gratitude to Dr. Daniel Drake, author of *Pioneer Life in Kentucky,* and to Private Alvin Q. Bacon who wrote *Thrilling Adventures of a Pioneer Boy.*

My special thanks go to Miss Florence Clark of McGregor, Iowa, and to those members of the chain reaction she set off: she introduced me to Dr. H. H. Kleinpell of Prairie du Chien, Wisconsin, who introduced me to Miss Alice Smith and Mr. Wilbur Glover and Mr. Clifford Lord of the Wisconsin Historical Society, who introduced me to Professor Vernon Carstensen of the University of Wisconsin, who introduced me to Mr. Thomas Vaughan, then a graduate student in history and now director of the Oregon Historical Society, who for several years worked for me in Madison, burrowing into the magnificent collection of documents housed at the Wisconsin Historical Society.

But this is fiction, not history. Events in this book are imaginary. So are the characters, except for a few actual historical figures who appear briefly.

Finally, I wish to thank Mr. Kermit Lang, actuary with the Equitable Life Insurance Company of Iowa, who performed certain mathematical computations which were beyond me; and my cousin, John W. Buchanan, for his helpfulness and good nature as a camp mate and boat mate during our explorations of the Mississippi River, and the Wisconsin, and the Chippewa, and the St. Croix, and many smaller streams. It would be fun to record our adventures in rough waters and in still bayous, on lonely islands and in drowsy river villages; but that would demand another book as long—Heaven forbid!—as this one.

——Thomas W. Duncan

Santa Fe, New Mexico

BIG RIVER, BIG MAN

I

ALL THAT afternoon the wind had bucked them, blowing obstinately out of the south under a sky lightly streaked with oyster-colored clouds. It was wearisome wind, too warm for mid-October, that furrowed the river and slopped waves over the huge raft. Now at sundown the wind was dying, the river smoothing to olive green, and the raft lay safely moored, but he was not likely to forget that bad time in midafternoon when the raft floundered in the great eddy sweeping toward Turtle Island. For a while, Jim Buckmaster had thought they were going to break up.

Weasel Creek Eddy, Jim always said, was the nastiest stretch of water between Read's Landing and Dubuque. It was there that Weasel Creek came pouring from the Wisconsin hills, emptying its rapid current into the slower current of the Mississippi. Result of that perpetual attack was perpetual fight: those waters bubbled like beans in a pot. Weasel Creek drove itself headlong into the channel, then retreated with a wicked backdrag. Below the eddy, the Mississippi absorbed the creek and went along about its business. Below the eddy also, Turtle Island had been accumulating for a few hundred years. Now, in 1850, it was a fat, solid old island, thickly grown with elms and willows. A long sandbar reached out from its upper tip.

Toward that bar the raft had wallowed this afternoon, dragged by the current. It would saddlebag there, Jim had thought; the lines would pop, the lash-poles splinter. The devil would be to pay, then; he knew the lunacy of logs in crazy waters.

Well, it hadn't happened that way, but it had been a close thing; and even now Jim could remember how during it all he had been thinking about his meeting tonight with McSwasey, knowing that if the raft cracked up and the logs strewed themselves down miles of channel McSwasey would be madder than a timber bear with a snoot full of porcupine quills. McSwasey wouldn't explode and pound the table; he never did that; but his eyes would take on that cold look, and his quiet voice would grow even quieter. "Jim," he would say, "maybe you're not such an able rooster as I thought. That little deal we talked over in Read's Landing—let's forget that, Jim. You can go to hell, Jim."

But McSwasey wouldn't say that now. The deal, Jim knew, would stand. For he had saved every foot of that fortune in logs. Luck had helped; that and the great fact that his crew was afraid of him. When you got a raft into a tight pinch, nothing brought out the best in a crew like being plain scared of a fist in the teeth. Whiskey was also good, but not so good as a fist.

It had been necessary, while fighting the eddy, to drown a man. Leastwise, the man had gone overboard and hadn't been seen since. Jim couldn't recollect the man's last name; everybody called him Bobcat Pete. It was too bad about the Bobcat. Jim hadn't figured to drown him, although he guessed that any raftsman who could be drowned deserved drowning; a man who wasn't tougher than the river had no business on the river; a man like that ought to follow some tame occupation, like a saloon bouncer. Just the same, Jim never liked to drown a man, unless he had to.

"But he had it coming," Jim thought now, lounging there at the bow of the tied-up raft, while the lines creaked and the wind fizzled into nothingness and the bluffs of Iowa, with low sun behind them, projected their shadows on the running water. "I'd do it again," he thought, "any day. He was asking for it."

This Bobcat Pete had been working one of the six big steering oars at the tail of the raft, one of those tamarack poles tipped with a pine blade. You didn't sit down and pull on such a sweep, forty-five feet long; you spit on your calluses and pushed. You surged five steps across the raft while you pushed, the oar higher than your head. That was bucking an oar, and Jim had done plenty of that himself, in his time. You had to watch sharp to begin pushing the instant the other five oarsmen began, and to finish when they finished, and to trot back and begin pushing again in time with them. It all had to be in fine whack, like the parade-ground drilling up at Fort Snelling. But bucking an oar, Jim had been told, frazzled you more. A deserter from the fort, after working passage to St. Louis on one of Jim's rafts, had told him so.

"Jim," the deserter had said, in that St. Louis saloon, after being paid off, "if I'd known what I was getting into, Jim, bucking an oar under you, why by God, Jim, I'd have stuck by the colors."

"No hard feelings, soldier," Jim had said.

"Jim," the deserter had said, "let me tell you. That sergeant at Snelling was a terror to snakes, but he never throwed nobody into no river. He never drownded nobody."

Jim had to grin at that.

"Why, soldier," he said, "maybe you got your shirttail damp, working on that raft, but I fished you out. I'd as soon fish a man out as toss him in."

But today he hadn't fished out Bobcat Pete, and now in the shadows of sundown he stood watching the river, remembering what had happened.

*

She was a woman, that river. She could be smooth and honey you up, and next minute she'd drown you if she could, or wreck your future. But she hadn't wrecked his. Leastwise, not this afternoon.

She had been in a tantrum this afternoon, except for a stretch up beyond Catfish Bend. Up there, she flowed out of Thunder Slough and curved, running easterly for nearly a mile before turning south again at Catfish Bend. She was quieter along that stretch, snuggling against the bluffs where the south wind couldn't churn her into hysterics.

He remembered how it had been up there, with the raft sloshing along toward Catfish Bend. At the tail of the raft this rooster named Bobcat Pete stood with the other five tailsmen, waiting orders, and five hundred feet forward, at the bow, six more oarsmen waited. Jim stood behind them, watching the current and the drift, sometimes looking back along the raft to check on the complex webwork of crosslines and diagonals that knitted her together. Wider than a town street, she was a lot of raft, and his brain was the pilothouse. Every maneuver she made took place first in his brain. Sheltered by the bluffs, those tons of logs went whispering through the water like a bark canoe. Still, even there, the wind fingered the river, and amidships, beyond the two Quincy skiffs roosting on the logs, Jim could see the laundry flapping on a clothesline from the cookhouse to the crew's shanty.

He liked piloting a raft such as this, her logs floating high, not a speck of dry rot or a stick of flood trash among them. There were no better logs—damned few as good—traveling toward the St. Louis sawmills; and he had a fine feeling when he thought of how they would slice into Number 1 boards, clean of knots, giving off a sweet pine smell, blond and pretty as a naked girl. He was like that, always: when he saw logs growing in the woods or stacked in rollways or floating, he itched to feed them to the saws.

He looked downriver, wondering whether after all he should tie up. Ornery water was waiting, around the bend, and once the channel turned south the wind would rake them. But nobody ever got logs to market very fast by playing safe. A mile back they had passed a couple of tied-up rafts, the pilots leery of this wind. As Jim's raft floated by, his crew had hooted; the things they yelled were not what you would ever hear in church, although some of the words were the same. Jim hadn't yelled himself; after all, he was a pilot now; but he had thought of his wages from McSwasey, the best-paying lumberman on the river, and the squirrel-feed those tied-up pilots likely received; and he told himself that Mc-Swasey wasn't paying out cash money so that a pilot and a crew of sixteen hands would tie up for a snooze whenever a breeze threatened.

But even Jim's crew expected him to send a line to shore before the raft actually rounded Catfish Bend. He could tell that from the way the oarsmen kept giving him sidelong glances. Nobody, of course, let out a peep of advice; the only thing said came from Greasy Dick Cassidy, one of the linesmen.

Greasy Dick was an old codger, forty-five if a day, husband to a Dakota squaw and father to a flock of breeds. He had been a pilot himself; from Pig's Eye Bar to the St. Louis levee he knew the river the way a parson knew Scripture; but he was too damned old now to handle a crew of fighting roosters. Four years ago, on his last trip piloting, a little dispute had come up between him and a rooster named Kelly. Kelly had told him he smelled like an Indian. Well, that was the God's truth, but true or not it meant a fight, and Kelly had crippled him for about a year. After that, no log owner would touch Greasy Dick with a twenty-foot pike pole. He used to hang around the river front at Read's Landing, eyes mournful and tail between his legs. It was enough to make a man feel sorry for the old devil; sometimes Jim bought him a drink. And he thought of Greasy Dick when he got his first job piloting. By God, he thought, what would be wrong with hiring the Grease as linesman?

Not a thing. Fact was, it had advantages. For although Jim had known the river well enough, almost, to run a raft on a black night when it was raining cant hooks and toe rings, he hadn't known it well enough to run on such a night blindfolded. Greasy Dick had. There would be no harm, Jim thought, in getting a little advanced training from the Grease. It worked out fine. Now, after two seasons, Jim actually knew the river as well as he was supposed to when he talked McSwasey into giving him his first job piloting.

So everybody had been happy, except maybe that rooster named Kelly. Kelly had been in Jim's first crew, and it was to be expected that he would beat up on the Grease as soon as the Grease boarded the raft and announced he was shipping downriver as linesman. For the Grease smelled no better when Jim hired him than he had when that little trouble came up earlier. Kelly must have had an extra sharp smelling kit. In any case, Jim headed off trouble before it started. The day after hiring Greasy Dick, he went to a saloon in Read's Landing and found Kelly at the bar, a big rooster with red hair.

"The boys tell me," Jim said, "you've got a nose that works overtime. I'll fix it for you."

With that he landed his fist smack on Kelly's nose, another fist following to his solar plexus. It took Kelly somewhat by surprise, no doubt; he kind of caved in, going to his knees; and before he could stagger up, Jim kicked him in the jaw. Then he said:

"I wouldn't like to stomp you, Kelly, but I reckon you ought to know

16

Greasy Dick Cassidy is shipping with us as linesman. You got any objections?"

Looking dazed, Kelly wobbled his head.

"Why, no, Jim," he whispered. "White of you to ask me, but I ain't got none. I like the old stinker."

After that, Jim never had a bit of trouble with Kelly, or with any rooster. And Greasy Dick was a fine linesman. When Jim sent him to shore in a skiff he paid out the heavy line with exactly the right slack, and he always picked a stout tree around which to snub it. No tree he chose was ever yanked out by the roots when the raft tightened the line. Nor did a line he was checking ever pop apart. Jim had seen such things happen. Once when he was an oarsman a line popped, and the flying end clouted a Canuck named Roque and killed him cold dead. You needed a linesman with sense enough to check a raft to an easy stop, and with foresight enough to have a bucket of water handy when the line smoked from friction against the tree.

This afternoon Greasy Dick had sidled up to Jim, not saying anything for a spell but by his presence reminding him there were still such things in this world as lines and skiffs and linesmen. He was a lanky man, standing there working his chaw from cheek to cheek, and he was round-shouldered in an undershirt that had been white once. He kept his eyes focused straight ahead where a hundred yards away the river curved and whitecaps tossed. There was something else, too, off in the distance: a smudge of steamboat smoke whipping into the sky, its source hidden by the bluffs of the river bend.

"It might be the *Maisie Gregg,*" Greasy Dick said finally, more to himself than to Jim.

"And it might be the *Bella Cameron,*" Jim said.

Greasy Dick didn't speak further. He had performed his duty with that oblique comment, calling the smoke to Jim's notice. Not that Jim would have missed it; but voicing the fact that smoke was there gave it more significance, reminding Jim that Weasel Creek Eddy on a windy day was not an ideal place to meet a steamboat. And with Jim's reply about the *Bella Cameron,* Greasy Dick had been properly silenced. For the *Bella Cameron* no longer existed; two years ago her boilers had exploded and blown her sky high.

As the bend glided nearer, stronger puffs of wind chopped the water, and the raft danced. The oarsmen still waited for orders, their long sweeps, nicely balanced on the head-block, all aslant with handles down and blades out of water. At the bend the current quickened, sweeping the raft out into mid-channel, and the wind's big fist struck. Then Jim knew he had made a mistake. That nettled him; he hated to misjudge anything, wind, water or men.

The wind was another river flowing the wrong way up the Mississippi, whipping waves ahead of it like a pack of frothy-mouthed dogs.

17

From Turtle Island, a mile away, yellow leaves came arrowing; and above the seesawing raft a blue heron, beak pointing into the wind, hung motionless except for flapping wings. When it stopped fighting it sailed in a long arc clear over to the Wisconsin shallows.

"Pull-l-l to starboard," Jim sang out, and six oar blades dipped. With the waves smashing, the long raft hunched its back in a dozen places, caterpillar fashion.

Jim looked aft. Amidships the laundry was trying to yank loose from the clothesline, and the cook and chore boy braced themselves grotesquely while they reached to unfasten it, water foaming around their ankles. Far off at the tail, the oarsmen were toy figures waiting a signal. Jim lifted an arm, then sliced down toward starboard. The oarsmen fell to. After ten minutes, with the sweeps on both ends working, the raft straightened and pitched along parallel with the channel. Jim told the bowsmen to ship oars and signaled the tailsmen to do the same. Greasy Dick passed a jug of whiskey to the end bowsman, and it traveled down the line. Jim saw the chore boy, a blond-headed kid of fourteen, racing toward the tail with another jug. In his mental tally-book he marked one down to the chore boy's credit.

Heading into the wind, the raft wasn't getting anywhere very fast. But that was all right; Jim was satisfied to keep her straight, with now and then a few oar strokes, till that steamboat came upchannel and passed. After that, he would send Shorty the Singer, the other linesman, and Greasy Dick to the Iowa shore. The heron had the right idea; to hell with fighting the wind. He wouldn't want to be blown into the eddy.

He stared off downstream, into the pale sunshine and the wave-dazzle, eyes following the channel to Turtle Island and on between the island and the Iowa bluffs. Almost from the river's edge the bluffs swept up, thickly-wooded masses of October color that marched away endlessly till the warm golds and scarlets and rich browns blurred together in those prodigious distances. Sometimes gray cliffs showed through the foliage, like battlements the wilderness was smothering. He could see the steamboat, far away between the island and the bluffs, but he couldn't be sure who she was. Then snowy puffs left her whistle; the sound came floating in golden tones. "I'll be damned," he said, recognizing her voice, and he glanced at Greasy Dick.

"That's her," the Grease said. "The *Rough and Ready.*"

Well, that was bad news. Any time a raft met up with the *Rough and Ready,* it was bad news for the raft. For Old Man Knox, her owner and pilot, nursed a grudge against rafts which went clear beyond the routine hate of steamboat men for raftsmen. Two years ago last spring the *Rough and Ready* had been one of many boats tied up at Read's Landing in Minnesota Territory, waiting for the ice to break out of Lake Pepin; the saloons were jammed with steamboat crews and raftsmen. As could be expected, one thing led to another, and some of the boys got themselves hurt. The raftsmen, of course, won that running battle, and in so doing they found it necessary to board the *Rough and Ready,* where some deckhands had taken refuge. When they left the boat, it needed major repairs.

That little ruckus fussed up Old Man Knox something fearful. From then on he wouldn't sell passage to raftsmen, when they wished to return upriver after delivering logs to Clinton or St. Louis. And he would rather give a raft grief than swallow tanglefoot whiskey. Most steamboat pilots enjoyed giving a raft grief, but not that much. Then a year ago last August on a black night Old Man Knox was piloting the *Rough and Ready* through a chute where a raft had broken to smithereens, the channel cluttered with loose logs. She rammed a log and sank in six feet of water. They raised her, but it cost plenty, and Old Man Knox went around saying rafts should be kept off navigable rivers. So today Jim knew there was no telling what the *Rough and Ready* might do.

During the next minutes he watched her, puzzled, for although her chimneys were pouring forth smoke and her exhausts issuing steam, indicating a good head of pressure, she had slowed nearly to a stop. Engine trouble, maybe; she might have blown a cylinder-head. Greasy Dick produced another jug; Jim hooked a finger through the handle and tilted it, keeping sight of the packet while the tanglefoot coursed down his throat.

"What do you figure she's up to?" he asked the Grease, yelling against the wind, when he passed back the jug.

"No good." Greasy Dick drank. "Could be the old man's got a spyglass on us. Waiting till we fetch up by the eddy. Could be."

Jim saw it plain, then. Old Man Knox planned to crowd the raft into the eddy. He looked off to larboard, far off across the waves, his eyes following the Wisconsin shore along the cattail shallows to a point where no cattails grew. That was where a sharp coulee cut back between the bluffs. Weasel Coulee. Out of that came Weasel Creek. On a calm day you could trace its clay-colored flow into the blue-tinted Mississippi, seeing the great loop it made nearly to Iowa and then downstream on a tangent toward Turtle Island. On such a day you saw bubbles and foam and traveling whirlpools. With this wind slashing the water he could see none of that, but he estimated the raft to be about a hundred yards upstream from the eddy's hook, and ten yards to starboard, within the main channel of the river by a narrow margin but a safe one. In another few minutes the raft would drift downstream opposite the eddy, and if the *Rough and Ready* came upstream on the Iowa side her wheel-wash could swish them into those tricky currents. After that there was no predicting, because a raft could be headstrong and balky and giddy, as moody as the river itself, and everybody knew the river was the original beautiful vixen, with as many whims and notions as you'd find in a fancy house full of pretty girls.

Well, he'd better pull west, putting more elbowroom between the eddy and the raft. But not too far west, for the main channel was narrow here, the Iowa shore snaggletoothed by sawyers and flood debris, where a bank had caved in. Jim gave the order and the raft crawled sideways, bouncing with the waves. Greasy Dick grinned.

"Jim," he yelled, "that's smart. Old Knox will have to fish or cut bait now." And after a minute, jabbing a finger into the wind, he called, "See there. Here she comes, Jim. I figger if she can't crowd us into that eddy she'll try grounding us in that shore boneyard."

Jim figured that way too. It was likely to be a narrow squeak, between the eddy on one side and the boneyard on the other.

He watched the *Rough and Ready* pulling upchannel between Turtle Island and Iowa. Steam flashed from her whistle and a little later he heard those melodious tones. He admired that whistle. It was the nicest thing about her, mellow-throated and sad. All the river was in that whistle, all the big red sunrises and the lonely sloughs and the vastness.

She had blown to pass him to starboard; he frowned. For he couldn't keep the raft moving toward Iowa when the *Rough and Ready* signaled she wanted to use that water. He gave an order to ship oars, and he watched the distant boat, not much liking what he saw, for instead of coming directly upchannel she was tacking northeast in a long diagonal. Then she turned due north and after that a little west of north, aiming for the southwest corner of the raft.

That was an old dodge of steamboat pilots who wished to give you misery: to come at you obliquely, shearing off oars and striking your raft a glancing blow that would rip logs loose and slice lines and start a general disintegration, leaving the boat unharmed. It could be done, with luck and expert piloting. Jim had seen it done. But not at Weasel Creek Eddy and not in a wind like this.

"That there Old Man Knox," Greasy Dick yelled, "is a damned old devil. He'll give us a crack and then pass us to starboard, just like he signaled. He'll claim it an accident on account of the wind. We'll be scattered from here to hell's woodbox. Want a swallow of drinking whiskey, Jim?"

Leisurely, to emphasize for the crew's benefit his cold nerves, Jim lifted the jug. When he returned it he was smiling.

"We'll fox him. We won't be where he figures."

And he gave an order to pull west.

"Jim," Greasy Dick said, after a minute, "I get your drift. We're moving to starboard, and the old man will have to take that into account. He'll steer toward where we ain't now and where we ain't going to be. He'll be like a hunter aiming ahead of a running deer. And just when he pulls the trigger this old deer will backtrack. I like that, Jim. You can wrap that up for me and I'll take it home."

"No charge for it," Jim said.

20

"You'll be splitting it fine, Jim. You'll be splitting a toothpick with a broadax."

"Sure," Jim said.

"She looks good, Jim. I hope it ain't the tanglefoot that makes it look so good."

"River water," Jim said, smiling, jerking a thumb at the jug.

"It's nice to be young," Greasy Dick said.

Three hundred yards away, the *Rough and Ready* was looming plainer now, a great white swan of a packet. But Jim knew she didn't handle like a swan. She was a washtub to steer, saloon gossip said. Because of that, Old Knox might not cut the maneuver quite so fine as if he had a packet with a nimble rudder. Unless, of course, he should be beyond caring whether he bashed in the *Rough and Ready's* hull: he could always smash the raft head-on, if he didn't mind sinking his boat. He wouldn't do that. Would he? Not unless his spyglass told him this was Jim Buckmaster's raft, and unless he remembered that Jim Buckmaster had led a hundred yowling raftsmen, full of tanglefoot, aboard the *Rough and Ready* that time in Read's Landing.

"Grease," Jim said, smiling, "do you think a man's past catches up with him?"

"Not if he's fast on his feet," Greasy Dick said.

The packet was coming closer; and although Jim stood there looking amused, his big body easy and careless, he could feel his steam gauge rising. And he could sense the uneasiness running through the bowsmen. They were bucking the oars, but not as if they meant it. They didn't cotton to propelling the raft into the *Rough and Ready's* path when they would be first victims of a smash.

"Boys," Jim bawled, "you buck them oars. I know what I'm up to, boys. You buck them oars hard. But get set for a fast switch."

The closer she came the more she looked like a lot of boat, with her elegantly-scrolled woodwork and her gilded eagle perching on top of the pilothouse. In that pilothouse Jim could see Old Knox, and he could smell the smoke pouring from her chimneys and hear her engines pounding. He waited as long as he dared, and an extra second for good measure. Then he signaled the tail, and he yelled, "Pull-l-l to larboard." The bowsmen tumbled over themselves obeying.

The raft slowed, reversed. Jim watched the pilothouse. What he saw convinced him that Old Knox had hopped himself into a rage, remembering that riot in Read's Landing. For instead of holding to his oblique course, which would do no more damage, likely, than shear off a sweep, Old Knox was putting over the wheel hard, aiming to smash the raft head-on at the southwest corner. These logs were solid as granite and fatter than beer barrels; a collision would gouge open the steamboat's hull. The river was deep here.

There was one thing that might bring the old man to his senses, and

Jim did it. He danced across the raft to the southwest corner.

The outside logs were pitching with force enough to flip off an ordinary man. He made a broad jump and landed neat at the tip of the end log, with nothing but windy air between him and the river, his steel-calked boots chewing out splinters as he jigged, keeping an easy balance. He might have been in somebody's saloon jigging to a fiddle. His feet had brains of their own, back in those years; hell, there was nothing to it. He had birled logs before he could cipher and he had been a river hog; not many men as catty on their feet. Just don't look down, that's all. Never watch the water whirling. Hell with the water. Learned that when he was five. Forget it, boy; forget that damned water, else they'll fish you out with minnows wiggling from your ears.

Lot of things flew through his mind; lot of things came back, while he jigged on that heaving log, the river wind slapping his face. All the logs he had ridden, all the hell he had raised. It was like being drunk only better, jigging there on the edge of danger; he was laughing.

Suddenly he began whooping the way he used to when a drive was finished and he hit town to take it apart and find what it was made of. He yelled at the roosters to keep pulling to larboard, and when the *Rough and Ready* let loose with her whistle and kept coming straight at him he waved at the pilothouse and outwhooped the whistle. "Come on, Old Knox," he hooted. "She'll be a cold winter and hell's warm."

And for that high second at the top of life he didn't give a damn about smashups or McSwasey or the dark deeps of the river. He felt ten miles tall, then, with the sun for a watch charm and McSwasey in his shirt pocket.

Then he saw Old Man Knox spinning the wheel, and he knew he had won. Maybe the old man remembered his license and his passengers and his capital tied up in his boat; maybe it came to him it would be raw murder to smash the raft where Jim was standing; maybe he didn't want to be strung up to a tree limb, next time he put in at a rafting town like Read's Landing. Anyway, the *Rough and Ready* swerved and went swishing past like a trollop in silks, almost close enough to spit on, loaded with soldiers bound for Fort Snelling and with the wagons of movers and with oxen for the logging camps up north, her paddle box tinted with a painting of the Battle of Buena Vista.

Jim swung back to the raft just as the backwash hit. The bow reared up violently, staggering the oarsmen. Handles torn from clamped palms, three huge sweeps lashed out of control, blades flopping. One bowsman, hanging on to his oar for all he was worth, was jerked off his feet and flipped around like a whip snapper. Then the bow buried itself in the foaming river; Jim was wading to his knees; the oarsmen were drenched; the bow rose streaming; plunged again. That went on; and all the time the bow was swinging to larboard, toward the eddy. Jim let loose with so much yelling, and even a few kicks, that finally the bedraggled roosters got themselves into line, and after a couple of false starts began bucking the oars in unison.

Jim heard somebody yelling his name. It was Greasy Dick, soaked to the hide, pointing upriver. The *Rough and Ready* had slanted off toward Iowa and now was tacking toward the raft again, this time aiming for the tail.

"Get a line to shore," Jim bawled; and he was off, striking out for the tail, sometimes running uphill with the raft's pitching and sometimes down, sometimes splashing through ponds, always thinking in the back of his mind about McSwasey, always in the front of his mind remembering the eddy, never watching his feet as he ran, depending on them to pay him cumulative wages for the years he had spent as a kid learning to balance on logs, for the years as a stripling on the drives down icy rivers when he learned the treachery of logs, how they were forever conniving to grind a man's ankle to pulp, to bob, to spin, to dart, to jam, to catch a man offguard, to spill him, to pull him under their rough bellies and drown him.

Could a man's past catch up with him? Not if he was fast on his feet. Maybe he wasn't fast enough, this time. The *Rough and Ready* was part of that turbulent past, and now she was close to the tail, aiming for the starboard corner. Pull, he heard himself yelling; pull, pull, pull; although of course none of the tailsmen pulled; they pushed; you told them to pull but meant they should push; pull, you roosters, pull.

They were pulling, all right. Maybe they knew he was pounding toward them; maybe it was his fists coming with him, and his calked boots, that made them pull so hard, taking the raft to larboard, toward the eddy, but away from the pointing bow of the *Rough and Ready*. He believed by God those roosters were going to make it; the packet would miss; by inches, maybe, but a miss. Then, loud as a brass band, the *Rough and Ready's* whistle cut loose; and what happened then shot anger through his arteries.

The end oarsman at the starboard corner, hearing that whistle so close, let go his oar and ran. The oar flopped to starboard. The *Rough and Ready* missed the raft's corner but smashed the oar to kindling. Then she steamed off upriver, flirting her stern at the raft, sending back mountains of white water. The raft's tail heaved and dived; the tailsmen reeled. When Jim got there the backwash was subsiding, and the tailsmen, soaked and dripping, hawking water from their lungs, were regaining their feet.

Something was happening to the raft. Without even seeing the way the tail was swinging to larboard, without even looking toward the bow, Jim knew the eddy had got its hooks into them. He could feel the deep power of the eddy's flow; it telegraphed itself up through the logs, through his boots, up his muscular legs. They were in the eddy; that was why the *Rough and Ready* went steaming so cheerfully toward

23

Catfish Bend. Jim began to swear, and his fists throbbed with that big blind desire to smash. He could be dangerous when things got in his way, when things went against him.

The tailsmen scrambled for their oars, getting set. Jim bellowed an order: pull to starboard. They surged. All but Bobcat Pete. He couldn't; his oar was kindling. He stood foolishly at the tail-block where his oar had been, trying to look busy doing nothing. Jim stepped toward him yelling buck an oar, meaning he should double up with somebody. The Bobcat wasn't quick in the mind.

"Jim," he yelled, "I can't. Ain't got no oar."

Can't. That was a word he hated. What it had done to his father. What it could do to any man, once it landed on his shoulders and hag-rode him. Can't. Good God! McSwasey never said can't. In a flash he was remembering that talk with McSwasey in Read's Landing. That deal. Opportunity. Tremendous. McSwasey opening a door, showing him what the future could be like. Right now, today, that future could all go one way if he saved the raft, another if he lost it. "Jim," McSwasey would say, "what's a little wind, Jim? What's a little eddy? You're fired, Jim. Deal's off, Jim." He didn't want to be a river hog all his life, or a rooster either. I can't, Jim. Ain't got no oar. Can't.

He lost what was left of his temper then, and clipped the Bobcat one on the jaw. And although the Bobcat was no featherweight, it lifted him. Sent him sprawling. He never found footing again. He floundered overboard.

Jim wheeled around, yelling at the tailsmen to buck those oars harder. He could have saved his breath. They were taking no chances on his sending their clothes to the washerwoman, with them inside, as he had the Bobcat's. He struck out for the bow, his mind buzzing with too many navigation problems to give thought to Bobcat Pete.

His mind was a pilothouse with a chart tacked to the wall. Blue water showed on the chart, and Turtle Island with its sandbar, and swarms of little arrows marking the eddy's flow. A raft floated on the chart, sagging toward the bar, prisoner of those nasty little arrows. The raft's tail was swinging east. So was the bow, but not so much. If that kept up, the raft would lie crosswise of the river. The little arrows would hurry it onto the bar; it would lie in a great crescent around the head of Turtle Island. A saddlebag. The logs would writhe like fish in a net; the crosslines and the "A" lines would quiver and snap; the lock-downs would pop from their augur holes; the lash-poles would split. The whole raft would un-ravel, and logs past counting would go swimming scot-free, butting and grinding and bulling. Once McSwasey had yarned about a buffalo stampede out west. "But if I had to take wild logs or buffalo," he had said, "I'd take buffalo." Jim had said, "I'd take logs." Well, he had logs today.

Something else on the chart: a skiff rowing toward Iowa, Greasy Dick paying out the line. You could count on the Grease; he would understand the maneuver and work hand-in-glove: to get a shore-hold with that line and to get more power back to the raft's tail. Pull the tail west and hold the bow with the line. Kiss your rabbit's foot and work till you were gutted. Then work more. Raft would bounce, rear, tug, shake its tail, kick, dive, toss, yank. Raft would try to pop the line. Raft would try every trick known to logs. Logs never wanted to leave the mysterious woods and meet up with screaming saws. Logs hated to end up as houses, plain or fancy. They fought you all the way.

Jim reached the bow just as Greasy Dick was wading ashore off in Iowa, hauling the line toward a huge elm. The Grease was all right; the Grease would do. Jim yelled for the bowsmen to shag back to the tail and double up on the sweeps. All but Noisy Swanson. Noisy, you stay. The other bowsmen took off; Noisy stayed. Stayed and said nothing. Noisy always said nothing; chewed snuff and said nothing. Just over from Sweden last year, he didn't know many words to say; American words. But the boys said that at Swede Lena's in St. Louis he jabbered a blue streak. Maybe the good coffee went to his head.

"Noisy," Jim yelled, "there'll be double power at the tail. Me and you, we'll buck here and hold. And we'll pull to starboard to give the Grease slack when he wants it."

Noisy was a blond giant chewing.

"Noisy," Jim said, "you talk too damned much. Pull-l-l to starboard."

So he was bucking an oar again. Piloting also: his brain against the eddy, the wind, the raft. The bowsmen had reached the tail now, and with two men on each oar the drift was slowing. On the Iowa shore he could see Greasy Dick at the elm; the line had tightened; Shorty the Singer was lugging a pail of water from the river. Here at the bow it worked out all right with just him and Noisy Swanson bucking; they were about the same size and weight; between them they developed a fair amount of oar power. In Iowa the Grease would lift a hand, signaling, and Jim would yell pull; he and Noisy would surge, the sweeps bending against the eddy. A little slack would gather in the line and Greasy Dick would tighten her. It went on that way a long while. Fighting running water. That was what he had been doing most of his life. Preachers talked about booze fighting; mainly, they disapproved of that; but when it came to treachery booze wasn't in it with water. Pump a glass full of water and look at it. She looked meek. Nice, sweet, friendly water; that's what the tame people on the bank thought. But get a lot of that same meek stuff together and see what happened. All the white rapids he had seen; all the torrents twisting through granite; the freshets; the lakes in winter with rotten ice; the slack water hiding snags and quicksand; make mine tanglefoot, pal.

It went on. It went on.

And things happened. All the usual unexpected things. Once, for no good reason, the eddy current quickened, and the bow started jerking the line. Bucking, plunging, jerking. Jerk, jerk, jerk, threatening every instant to pop the line. And for why? No telling. Water. Just the damned strange never-know-where-you-stand-with-it way of water. Why did a coyote howl at the moon? Why did men call a boat's stern a stern, but a raft's stern a tail? Why did that half-breed Dakota gal in Emmy's place in Read's Landing always giggle, giggle, giggle, and then once, for no reason whatsoever, at an odd time, break out sobbing? No accounting. Water. Gals. Mentioned it to Greasy Dick but he couldn't explain it, even though the gal was his daughter. Make mine the same, pal; make mine tanglefoot.

It went on. With water it always went on. A dozen things happening, any one of which could smack the raft into the bar. You needed luck. You needed a lot of other things also, in the woods or on the water, but first you needed luck.

And then all at once, also for no good reason, the wind and the eddy and the raft looked at one another and said, boys, why are we scrapping so hard? Boys, they gabbed, if it means so much to that big Buckmaster rooster, getting his raft tied up, why, hell, boys, let's surprise the bastard and give him a hand. He'll flap his feathers and crow and think he's President Fillmore, but there's another day coming. Let's give him his moorage. We'll be around tomorrow. And the next day too.

The current, deflected by the head of Turtle Island, took the raft smoothly in hand and carried it to safe water between the island and the bluffs.

"Jim," Greasy Dick said, once they were tied up to the Iowa shore, "that was real cute."

Noisy Swanson said nothing.

"Wild logs or buffalo," Jim said, "and I'll still take logs."

"Jim," Greasy Dick said, "not that it means a thing to me, but where's the Bobcat?"

"He went swimming."

"I know that, Jim. But he ain't climbed back on the raft."

"Grease," Jim said, "you pass the boys some tanglefoot. And you get that spare oar mounted on the tail."

"I never wanted you to think it meant nothing to me," Greasy Dick said.

Noisy Swanson said the usual. They went toward the tail. Jim lounged his shoulders against a bow oar, a little tired, but feeling pretty good about things in general. The only trouble was, he had a meeting with McSwasey scheduled for nine o'clock tonight in New Empire, and New Empire was a town on the Wisconsin side, five miles below Turtle Island. He had wanted to moor his raft there tonight; it would have caused quite a stir along the levee, if he had been able to run that far against the wind. But no matter; he'd go in a skiff.

He stood there a long time, resting against the oar, letting his blood quiet down and his muscles take a nap, letting the air dry his sweat-soaked, river-soaked clothes, while he thought about that meeting with McSwasey. Just thinking about it made him feel nice and warm. A rendezvous, McSwasey had called it, the other evening in Read's Landing. "What the hell's that?" Jim had asked. So McSwasey, who used to be a Santa Fe trader, explained; and Jim said he guessed it was true all right that a man lived and learned.

Call it what you pleased, it was probably the oddest rendezvous a man ever had with his big push, and what McSwasey had in mind was likely the strangest job of work a push had ever given one of his hands. It promised excitement and some danger, doubtless; but the important thing was that it offered opportunity. He liked that word, opportunity. It had a shine like a gold eagle, a ring like a silver dollar. He had, Jim guessed, always wanted to get ahead more than the average man. And from the way McSwasey had talked in Read's Landing, this would mean getting far ahead, fast.

He straightened, took a good deep stretch, and stood on the logs with boots apart and hands in hip pockets. He was twenty-four years old, all bone and muscle, and he could have passed for an Indian, if you had looked only at his straight spine and his Indian-black hair. But his eyes were gray, staring off down the enormous sweep of channel. The wind was dying, the water smoothing. Along the west bank of the river, as far as he could see, the bluffs stretched away like gigantic oxen plodding into the hazes of October and coming dusk. The bluffs were gold-edged where a shaft from sunset struck across their shoulders from behind, but mainly they were lavender that spilled down their flanks into violet. The distances looked mysterious and smoky, all veiled with soft promise, like the future. Maybe that was the future down there, waiting; New Empire was there.

He thought: "She's a pretty good river, at that. Once she knows who's running things."

And he thought: "Some day I'm going to own this river, like you own a girl in a fancy house. The whole damned shebang."

II

But you couldn't own it. Big thoughts like that were just blow, he knew. You might be as rich as Caleb McSwasey, and take title to it, but you could never own the river. You couldn't own a girl in a fancy house, for that matter, or a doe deer in the woods. They were all women and they all got away. You shot the doe deer and it was yours, but what you had was no longer a doe deer with a frisky tail and soft eyes; all you had was a hunk of meat. Something had gone, like sunshine when you closed your fist. You pulled a bucket of water from the river; it was the stuff the river was made of; but it wasn't the river. Get ten million buckets and scoop the river dry and you still wouldn't have the river. Mysterious. He wondered if McSwasey thought he owned that young wife of his. He wondered why he was standing here staring off into the faraway smoke and damps, vague melancholy gathering in his mind.

He pulled his gaze back upchannel, to Turtle Island where the yellow treetops were catching the last of the sun. The wind had gone away; the river flowed glassy smooth, with here and there a red leaf floating. He glimpsed something else floating too, from upstream, and without stopping to think he took a quick step forward. But it was only a drift log, not a drowned man.

He glanced around, hoping nobody had seen him act that way. Nobody had. The crew was at the tail, some taking it easy, some helping Greasy Dick mount the new oar, two of the boys playing a game of catch. From the cook's shanty came the rattling of pans, the sound carrying sharp and hard-edged through the stillness. The chore boy was lugging a bucket of sand from shore to fix up a new firebed; the old sand had washed away.

Damn it, Jim thought, I'd do it again. He had it coming. I'd do the same thing over, but maybe easier. Trouble was, I let him have it too hard. Maybe stunned him? Maybe he was out when he went overboard, never even tried to swim, knocked out like that. Sucked under the raft? That time on the Chippewa. Spring of '45. She was a freshet all right that spring. That rapid water at Dead Oak Pitch, with a wing-jam at the downstream end. Never knew how it happened but I splashed in and closed the door on myself. When I tried to break surface I was under the jam. Boy, I thought, you'll know all the answers, if there

28

are any, in about three minutes. They'll fish you out and bury you under that dead oak and hang your boots and cant hook from a limb. Enough to give me a scare. I twisted and sort of dived and swam under water and when I broke surface there was sunshine. Jim, the boys said, you must have found you a woman down there, it took you so long, and I said yes, but the trouble was, there were three pinery boys lined up ahead of me. And I said, boys, I'll be around to hang up all your boots; and guess I just about did, at that. Now it will be the Bobcat's boots. Damn, I sure hate to drown anybody off my raft, it's no feather in a pilot's hat at all. Best way is to keep them screwed up to a scared pitch, always scared you'll deliver, so scared they jump when you spit; that way, you don't have to slug them; saves a lot of wear and tear on your fists.

He kept standing there, looking upchannel, little worms of worry boring holes in his brain. It was that way with him lots of times: he would plunge ahead into some deviltry or other, and afterwards he would remember something he wished he hadn't done. Sometimes he would brood, the way his father used to. But his mother always said, "You should have known him before his trouble. He used to laugh, then."

Hell, Jim thought, I might as well do it as keep thinking about it; and he crossed the raft and followed the plank that led ashore.

Underfoot the ground seemed to rise and fall, as always when he left the water. In his younger days he used to wonder why it should seem that way, when the ground was so solid, the water so treacherous. Once he mentioned it to Molly Fitzpatrick, who ran a house up on the Chippewa.

"Jim," Molly said, "that's what you might call an omen. You'd better steer clear of dry land. You're a river hog and you belong on the river. Dry land will bring you trouble."

He was about nineteen then, and Molly must have been nearly forty; sort of a mother to him, when you came right down to it. She had merry blue eyes and a salty tongue, and she was a big armful. Three girls worked for her, but one was horse-faced and one was half-witted and the third was a black wench Molly had bought down south; Wisconsin was free soil but the wench never heard about it. A pretty crumby outfit, except for Molly. Except for her, Jim would have passed that one up. And it was odd: he didn't go there so much for the usual reason as just to be with Molly, to eat her pie and visit. She always greeted him with a hug and a kiss, and she would say, "Jim, let's get the house-cleaning done right off. Then we can talk." And he would say, "Molly, that suits me fine. I'm lonesome for talk."

He had to grin, the time she said that about dry land bringing him trouble.

"Omens," he said. "Listen, Molly. Remember Vonnie Olson in Quick-

29

water? She read my palm once and said I'd die in a forest fire. Well, the burn came but it didn't catch me. I'm still here, Molly."

"Sweetie," Molly said, "you're a sassy young gamecock. You're pretty big for your pants, sweetie. You think you'll own the earth and you'll take what you want."

"Sure," Jim said, "that's what I figure to do."

"That's the man of it, maybe," Molly said. "I must say the ladies like it. Puts me in mind of Mr. Fitzpatrick before that dirty breed ambushed him and left me with nothing but my two legs to support myself. If Mr. Fitzpatrick had lived I'd have a carriage and coachman now. He thought the world was his oyster, the same as you. He used to say the meek would inherit the earth, but not till the strong were through with it."

"Sure," Jim said, "that's how I figure it," and he poured a tumbler of tanglefoot for each of them. Not wanting to hurt Molly's feelings, he had not gone on to say that while Mr. Fitzpatrick had sound ideas he had been an awful deadhead to let himself be ambushed by a breed. He didn't know much about keeping alive in the woods, Jim had thought.

There were woods here today, climbing the Iowa bluffs, but nothing like the Wisconsin woods where he had grown up, or the Maine woods where he had been born. No pine; just oak and hickory and sugar maple, brilliant of leaf in the fading day. He looked over the raft, deciding against walking past it along the narrow beach; some of the raft hands might guess what he was up to, and before long the story would travel about how Jim Buckmaster had drowned a man and then got conscience stricken and went looking for the body, even though the average drowned man stayed on the bottom for a spell. It would be enough to ruin his reputation.

He passed into the timber, following a deer trail that curved up the bluff through scarlet and yellow tangles; and he was no sooner on the path than his river legs left him and his woods legs came back; even in boots his step was moccasin-soft. It was his aim to circle through the timber and come out on the river above the raft, opposite Weasel Creek Eddy. If the Bobcat had drowned, one of those peculiar currents might have swept him ashore. Not much chance of that, but he wanted a look. He wanted to know. He had drowned other men but not the way he had drowned the Bobcat. Always before the man had been careless or it had been an act of God, not an act of Buckmaster. Because he was pilot he always assumed responsibility and talked as if he had done it—"I drownded Big Dan up in Crooked Slough," he would say—but never before had he knocked a man overboard without being ready to dive in and pull him out.

The path climbed, then dipped; and before following it down Jim looked through the bushes and out across the river. With dusk coming the water flowed pearl-gray and silk-smooth. That river was a woman,

30

all right, always changing clothes. Whenever you were near her you had to stop every so often and watch her swishing along. She looked drowsy now and hushed, with sleep coming on. The Bobcat was out there somewhere, so deep asleep he would never wake. Suckers and bullheads, swimming near the bottom, would wave their flippers across his eyes. A week or so and the river would give him up. That was the bad thing about drowning, that spooky business of the river holding you tight, the current murmuring in your ear, and then casting you out and waiting for some other man.

He moved on, down the dip in the path. When it reached a place where a sharp ravine notched the bluffs, it turned inland, following the ravine along a creek. In rainy weather that creek would be a torrent, but now it was only a dribble among rocks; you could cross it dry-shod. But Jim didn't cross it. He stopped, listening, staring up the ravine. From among the rich autumn smells of walnut hulls and moist earth and the sweet rot of leaves, his nose picked up a faint drift of woodsmoke coming down the ravine, sucked by the cool air currents.

It might be the camp smoke of some straggling Dakotas. Unlikely. Dakotas had more sense than to make camp where a sudden rain might drown them out. It couldn't be movers, either. No mover could get his wagon up that ravine, and not even a greenhorn would want to; movers reached shore at ferry and steamboat landings and followed established trails out onto the high prairies. No, whoever was camping there must not want to be seen, so of course Jim wanted a look, especially after that talk with McSwasey the other night.

Stooping, he unlaced his boots, leaving them in a clump of hazel brush. His heavy German socks wouldn't puncture the ground with telltale calk holes. As he moved on the scent of woodsmoke sharpened, and presently he glimpsed through the bushes the flames of a campfire on the other side of the creek. He stood letting the twilight flow thicker into the ravine, before he worked his way forward and stopped, screened by bushes. Three men were at the campfire, two sleeping in blankets, the third sitting on a log, watching a pot of coffee which had begun to release a tangy smell. A rifle lay beside him. He looked in his late twenties; he had slick black hair and big white teeth. Jim couldn't recollect him.

They might be anybody, stopping here on their way from anywhere to anywhere; the country was filling up. A few years ago a man could know, by sight at least, everybody from Dubuque up to Pig's Eye, which was getting high-toned now and calling itself St. Paul. But you couldn't know everybody any more. You could in the woods, but down here in civilization the movers were coming through in swarms, land hungry, bringing preachers and doctors, and bringing too a ragtag and bobtail of unhung murderers and thieves. Steamboats were thicker on the river than ever before; new stagecoach lines were being established;

there was even talk of railroads. Jim liked the country better the way it used to be, but once when he voiced that opinion McSwasey shook his head.

"No, Jim," he said, in that quiet voice, "you're missing the point. Where do you think those movers will live? Under the sky?"

"They'll build houses, I reckon," Jim said.

"Jim," McSwasey said, "you hit the nail that time. They'll fort up in houses built of lumber. And where will they get that lumber?"

Jim saw it then: where else would they get the lumber except from the woods up north?

"There's a lot of nice things in life," McSwasey said, "but the nicest is getting in on the ground floor. That's cream for you, Jim; that's fat buffalo meat. If this old beaver had fifty million dollars he'd sink it all in logging. If this child had a hundred million he'd spend it all for stumpage and logging kits and sawmills. This child would spot his camps on the best driving streams from the Chippewa to Lake Superior. He'd cut that white pine and float her out and saw her up, that's what he'd do. This old muskrat would skin Wisconsin slicker than a school-ma'am's leg, and he'd cash in selling lumber to those deadhead movers who think they've found the end of the rainbow when they own a farm."

That was a man of vision for you. Newspapers and Fourth of July orators meant men like Caleb McSwasey when they talked about empire builders. Words like that went to your head; they made your brain swim and your fingers itch to reach out and grab. From then on Jim felt better about the movers crowding in and ruining a nice country.

But these weren't movers here in the dusk; they weren't even stragglers turned aside from the gold trail to California. He knew that when he made out, in the campfire glow, a couple of tools. One was a pike pole, leaning against a tree, the other a cant hook. Logging tools; rafting tools.

He had learned what he wanted, so he worked his way back to the place where he had cached his boots. He guessed it was too late now to go hunting the Bobcat's body; no good would come of finding it, anyway; the sensible thing would be to forget the whole business and cheer up.

*

Dusk clustered thick along the shore and made the bluffs chocolate shadow, but the river gleamed with the last light from the sky when he stepped aboard the raft. At the bow, the water rippled in the red and green splotches from the starboard and larboard lanterns. Through the evening hush, from the island across the channel, he could hear the low hooting of an owl, and near at hand the current gurgling and the faint creak of lines as the raft swung at her moorings. Farther off, back toward the tail, Shorty the Singer had brought out his fiddle and was scraping away at "Buffalo Gals." Otherwise the crew was quiet; unnaturally so. Usually with a fiddle going somebody would have yelled "Yippee-yee-yee" and started jigging.

Amidships, he could see the cook working over the fire in the thick bed of sand outside his shanty, a blocky man with sweeping mustaches the color of his red undershirt. A fine cook, but deliberate. Ordinary thing, the crew might have administered a ducking to a cook that slow, but this cook possessed a certain fame. With a knife. He was out of the Chippewa Valley pinery, cooking in winter at logging camps. Mike Hogan. One Christmas a few years back he had tossed his knife across the room straight into the heart of the Black Frenchman. As neat a throw as Jim ever did see. The Frenchman was drunk; trouble had been gathering between them all season; but the Frenchman went too far when he found fault with Mike Hogan's beans; after that, he could expect only what he got. The boys held court there in camp and acquitted Mike Hogan in about two minutes; the Frenchman was friendless, and certainly they weren't going to string up a cook that good. In any case Hogan's action was justifiable and wouldn't have raised much sensation except for his aim. You might expect a knife, Jim thought, to strike a rib and glance off. But between the ribs. From across the room. Might have been a lucky accident, but when someone hinted as much Mike Hogan offered to try again, if anybody cared to stand as target.

Jim was hungry; it seemed Mike was slower than usual with supper tonight; probably his cooking tools had got jumbled in the blow. No use trying to hurry him, anyway. Jim lounged against a steering oar, going over in his thoughts what he had seen back in that ravine, putting that information alongside events that had happened up and down the river the past year, and fitting it all into the pattern McSwasey had sketched the other night in Read's Landing. It added up. And McSwasey's plan was excellent; bold and simple, going right to the nub of the problem. McSwasey was sharper than an old dog fox, a better man to have for friend than enemy. Jim enjoyed working for a man like that, who had knocked about the country and made a pile of money, one way or another.

And now in the quiet Jim heard a footfall on the raft behind him, and his reflexes were such that without ever thinking he dipped forward, turning, and came up ready for anything. It was done smoothly, with a lynx's economy of motion. He didn't trust anything, ever; some part of him was always on watch, the way a stag watches when the herd is feeding.

But then instantly he smiled and straightened, his fists dropping; it was nobody but the chore boy; he caught the glint of the chore boy's Danish blond hair in the firelight. The kid must have had a scare, with

Jim whirling that way, for he called out, "It's just me, Jim."

"Bub," Jim said, his voice easy and low, as always when he wasn't yelling hell at the crew, "don't you know better than to snake up on a man?"

"It was just me," the chore boy said. "I didn't mean anything, Jim."

He wasn't as stringy tall as the average kid of fourteen, but he had straight shoulders and a hard-looking jaw. He would never grow up into any six-footer, Jim judged, but in a roughhouse size didn't count for as much as you might think. A hard head to butt a bigger man in the belly counted for a lot; also speed; but most important was a fighting heart. Jim had watched this kid ever since he had joined out in July, and he figured him for a scrapper. He had some Danish name—Rolfe Torkelsen, Jim guessed it was—and he had proved up to be a good, sober, quiet, hard-working kid; not like his predecessor, who stole; Mike Hogan didn't have to threaten this kid with drowning to get him to work; Mike liked this chore boy and said he would take him to the pinery this winter and learn him the cooking trade.

"Bub," Jim said, "let me ask you. What kind of bringing up did you ever have, to snake up behind a man in the dark?"

"It was an all right bringing up," the kid said. "But it wasn't in the woods."

"No," Jim said, "it wasn't in the woods. It sticks out all over you it wasn't in the woods."

"It wasn't on the river either," the kid said.

Not the woods, not the river. Well, he guessed there were plenty of other places for a kid to be brought up, but he wouldn't know much about that. It was a big old world, so he had heard from McSwasey, with treeless plains tilting up to mountains. There were cities too. He had seen some of them, the river cities: Dubuque, Davenport, St. Louis. You would look far, he reckoned, to find a bigger place than St. Louis.

"Bub," he said, "let me ask you. Where are you ever from?"

The kid didn't answer directly, and Jim didn't crowd him. Woods etiquette, river etiquette. All the gone years were a man's own affair, to be talked of or not. Sometimes a man wished to forget, and sometimes he managed it, in the woods or on the river. There were things in his own life Jim would as soon have forgotten, if he could.

"I reckon," the kid was saying, "I'm not supposed to be on a raft at all."

Jim thought he knew then what the kid was: a runaway apprentice. Where the kid had joined out he couldn't remember; somewhere down-river, maybe; Mike Hogan had hired him. He said:

"Don't let it fret you. Half the hands on this raft are on the run from something. Trouble back east, or in the old country. And half the pinery boys in the woods, for that matter. I've always figured Mike

Hogan threw that knife once too often in Ireland."

"I'm not on the run," the kid said, faint testiness edging his voice, until it cracked, the way a growing boy's voice would, and sounded real comical.

"Anyway," Jim said, "don't let it fret you. You're here. How you got here is no matter."

"I'm not on the run," the kid repeated, keeping his voice from cracking that time; and Jim had to smile at the stubborn way he wanted that fact all settled and tied up and sealed. "I'm here because I lost my money, that's why, and I wanted to earn back what I lost."

"Why hell's fires, pal," Jim said, smiling, "if I'd known you was flat I could have staked you."

The kid shook his head, and in the dull light Jim could see his mouth set and his jaw stubborn.

"No," he said, "I lost it and it was right I should earn it back."

Jim knew one thing then: the kid would never make a raftsman, or a pinery boy either. His slant was too serious.

"Bub," he said, "you talk like a preacher."

"No," the kid said, "I'm not that and I'm not going to be. But my father—he's a preacher. Don't hold it against me, Jim."

Lounging against that oar stem, Jim slowly scratched an itchy spot, the way a moose scratches against a tree. River and sky were dark now, and evening had whetted an edge to the air. From the cook's fire there wafted a mouth-watering smell of baked beans mingled with the smoky smell of burning wood and the fishy smell of the river and the redolence of the pine logs. The kid shifted his feet and Jim's thoughts came back from their far ranging to New Empire and the business ahead tonight. When he spoke his voice was low and humorous and somehow dreamy.

"Why, bub, I used to drown preachers, whenever I could lay hold of one. There's a lot to be said for that as a pastime. You find yourself a good plump preacher, full of fried chicken, and he drowns awful nice. They used to call me Preacher Drowning Jim, up on the Flambeau. I drownded me so many it got plumb monotonous. I was younger then. Now I'm just a busted down old man."

The kid giggled. Then his face went sober again; he ran his fingers through his curly hair.

"Bubby," Jim said, "what's on your mind?"

"It's—it's about Bobcat Pete, Jim. If he came back would you drown him? Would you knock him down and stomp him, if he came back?"

Bobcat Pete again. Jim stood looking at the black water, hearing the lines creak and feeling the gentle rise and fall of the raft as the river nudged and pulled. The river. He had a sense of its mystery and a memory of how a drowned man looked when they fished him out with water weeds in his hair. He drew himself together.

"Why, bub," he said softly, "I reckon we're wasting our breath. If

35

the Bobcat comes back he'll be floating on his face. But if he'd come back on his pins, I don't reckon I'd trouble to stomp him. I never aimed to drown him. He drownded himself."

"He never did," the kid said. "He's back, Jim. He climbed over the tail a half hour since. But he's afraid to show himself, till he knows how you'll take it."

He had a sudden release from melancholy. He didn't understand himself, wholly; never had; likely never would. He knew only that he had been oppressed by some worry, but now he felt free and ready to meet McSwasey and go through with that business and wind up, some day, with a million dollars. But he didn't want to show his hand to the kid. He asked:

"And the Bobcat sent you to find out? Is that it?"

The kid nodded. For a while, saying nothing, Jim just lounged there scratching his back against that oar. The way he itched between the shoulder blades he reckoned a louse must have sneaked into his undershirt. In the old days, when he was chopping in the pinery and driving logs down the spring freshets, a louse more or less didn't bother him; but since becoming a raft pilot and an aristocrat of the logging business he tried to keep himself clean of the crumbs. He wondered whether the crumbs ever got at McSwasey. Likely not, with that young Mrs. McSwasey to keep him spruced up. McSwasey had got himself a mighty fancy wife, out there in Santa Fe when he was a trader.

"Are you, Jim?" the kid was asking. "Are you going to stomp him and drown him?"

Jim straightened then, and hitched up his pants and stretched; a good, hearty, full-bodied stretch that he could feel rippling from fingertips to toes. And he realized now why the crew had been so subdued and why Mike Hogan had been delaying supper. With Bobcat Pete back, they didn't know what might happen; they were afraid. There wasn't a tougher crew of roosters on the river, but they were afraid of him. A reputation like that was worth a mint of money to any man.

"Why, no, bub," he said gently, "I don't aim to kill him. You tell the Bobcat there won't be a word spoke or a fist lifted."

And he knew that this would be told and told again; Jim Buckmaster might be harder than an ironwood log, but he had a heart as big as the moon.

"Do you promise, Jim? Do you cross your heart on it?"

"Sure," Jim said, "I promise, bub. But I don't see why it's any bark off your log."

The kid went skipping away across the raft. Jim called:
"Bub."

The kid halted.

"Bub," Jim drawled, "you tell them I said you're some spieler, convincing me away from murder and mayhem. I reckon you ought to be a lawyer, bub."

The way the kid replied puzzled Jim, till they had that conversation after supper. For he called, "How did you know?" Then he went skipping away, warwhooping to the crew, and a minute later in the firelight Mike Hogan lifted the supper horn and blew a long flat blast. The sound echoed among the bluffs.

*

He was hungry but instead of going directly to supper he went to his own shanty near the center of the raft. Built of pine boards, with a sloping roof to shed rain, it stood on a platform of planks spiked to the logs. He stooped, entering the low door, and inside he struck a locofoco and touched the flame to a candle anchored by its own tallow to a block of wood. There was no bunk; only a pair of blankets on the floor, sodden now from their drenching when the river invaded the shanty this afternoon. The place had a sour river smell. The ceiling was so low that he had to stoop as he looked around, checking his possessions. After tonight he would not return to the raft, but he must leave enough of his things so that it would appear he had intended to return.

His calamity sack, containing his razor and a few odds and ends, hung from a spike. It was an ordinary wheat sack with a draw cord and a rope so he could carry it over his shoulder. He traveled light; always had; not since he was eleven years old had he had a home.

A scrap of mirror hung on a two-by-four; a jug of tanglefoot sat in the corner; that was about all. Hell with it, he decided; he'd leave everything. All but a swallow of that tanglefoot. He pulled out the corncob stopper and stooping lower to give himself elbowroom swung up the jug. It was raw cheap bourbon, but it had a nice burn. He dragged the back of his hand across his mouth and squatted on his heels, going over everything in his thoughts. In one lobe of his brain he could be coldly methodical; when he began an operation, whether a cruising trip into the woods or a log drive or a rafting journey, he liked to look it over from all sides, figuring everything. When he was a kid Sol Klauber had taught him that; most men drifted along half-cocked, Sol had said, sitting ducks for disaster; most men never comprehended that every minute of being alive was highly dangerous. Now that he thought of it, Jim guessed that Sol Klauber and Caleb McSwasey would have had a lot in common, except that for all his grain-of-salt slant on things Sol was sad and gentle and the kindest of men. Probably no one had ever called Caleb McSwasey kind, except maybe Mrs. McSwasey, but then she was his weakness as young wives usually were the weakness of older men.

Jim was baiting a trap tonight, he and McSwasey, and as a kid in

37

the woods he had baited enough traps to know how to cover his tracks. So far as he could judge, they were all covered. Meditatively, he scratched his jaw; he had shaved this morning but now the black stubble was tough and bristly. Finally he drank again, then patted his belly around which his money belt was strapped. It contained a neat little fortune in gold, and that was one possession he never left anywhere, least of all in a bank. One other possession he never left lying around careless: his brain. His brain, he guessed was worth a good many times what his money belt contained. It was a tool he rented out to McSwasey at the whopping figure of four hundred a month; and it was a storehouse crammed with knowledge of men and sloughs and snags and logs and deadheads and Indians and channel. He took another drag of tanglefoot, a good long one, and then he went to supper.

*

Except that there were no tables, eating on a raft was like eating in a logging camp; nobody talked. Jim wouldn't have had it any other way. Say you lifted that rule and let the boys gab while they ate; what would that get you? Big stories and disputes, and first thing you knew a roughhouse, with chewed ears and such. A roughhouse could be fun; Jim liked a roughhouse as well as the next man; but everything had its place; business before pleasure. The time and place for a roughhouse was a saloon after a job of work was finished; that way, if any of the boys got disabled, you didn't find yourself short-handed with work left to be done. On any raft he piloted there was no fighting; the roosters understood that if they fought one another they would have Jim Buckmaster to fight afterward.

The tanglefoot had warmed his blood and set his brain sparkling, but nobody could have guessed it from the way he walked. He handled his body like a Chippewa, with a light firm step. Reaching the campfire he saw that most of the crew had finished eating and had drifted off into the shadows. Arms folded, feet planted solidly, Mike Hogan stood where the iron beanpot, huge and fire-blackened, with a mighty iron spoon, sat on a block of wood. Wordlessly he heaped Jim's plate with beans and sow belly, and the chore boy added boiled potatoes, corn bread, molasses and cold venison. Jim poured himself tea and carried his food to the edge of the firelight where he squatted on his boots.

He wasn't one to waste time over victuals, once they lay on a plate before him. Hunger was a great simple reality, to be dealt with simply. Often his thoughts went blank while he ate, but tonight he kept thinking of his rendezvous with McSwasey, and now that it was so near the excitement of it was running fire in his arteries. He guessed this was another turning point in his life. There had been a lot of them and each time he had bettered himself; he had come a long way since he was eleven years old with nothing but the clothes he stood in, his family all dead.

He finished his first helping and went back for a second and by-and-by for a third; his body demanded plenty of fuel, and he could have digested rusty crosschains. Then he stood up and stretched. The crew was all through supper and the chore boy had gathered the plates and was sloshing them in a tub of yellow soap and river water.

"Mike," Jim said, "they're the best beans on the river."

"Or in the woods," Mike said.

Jim pulled out his watch.

"Seven o'clock," he said.

Mike also carried a watch, and he was proud of his ability to tell time when he couldn't read anything else. He held it where the firelight could reach its face.

"Five of."

"I guess you bought that watch at a blacksmith's," Jim said. "It's never anything but slow."

"Get on with you," Mike said.

Jim hitched up his belt, smoothed his checked shirt down inside his pants and stood with legs apart, looking toward the shadows at the tail of the raft. Inwardly he was laughing at the joke he was going to pull, but his mouth looked hard and his hands with their big fingers seemed ready to double into fists. He had the wide shoulders and narrow hard hips of a fighter. His body looked trained down to sinew, not an ounce of fat on him.

"Bobcat Pete," he yelled. "Come here."

Till then the crew had been pretty quiet, for a rafting crew, but now the silence made all that had gone before seem noisy. Everything stopped. The chore boy no longer rattled the dishes. There were only the river sounds that had been here always on October nights. From the bluffs a whippoorwill repeated its monotonous song, and in the shore weeds a cricket that would die its little death in the frosts was cheeping forlornly.

"Bobcat!"

Silence again. But the bluffs of Iowa picked up Jim's voice and flipped it across those intricate leagues of channel and islands and sloughs, clear to the bluffs of Wisconsin, and it came back disembodied and strange and mockingly thin, whittled down to size.

Then came another voice, from the tail of the raft. The Bobcat's. "All right, Jim," it said, and it sounded tired and resigned.

He could hear the Bobcat coming, scuffing over the logs, and more from habit than anything else Jim glanced back; when he faced up to a man he wanted to be sure the man's friends weren't behind him. They weren't; only Mike Hogan, looking coldly neutral, and Rolfe

Torkelsen, the chore boy. He could kill the Bobcat, for all Mike Hogan would care.

But it was a different matter, with the chore boy. He was just a kid standing there with sleeves rolled back on arms dripping soapsuds, but he looked in a temper. His hair was tousled and heat had worked into his face.

"Jim," he yelled, "you promised!"

"Keep your shirt on, bub," Jim said.

He turned and watched the Bobcat clumping into the firelight, and the Bobcat wasn't any treat to see, with his matted hair and tangled beard and hogshead chest and too-small eyes. He kept them downcast, and he licked his mouth.

"Jim," he mumbled, "don't bust me up too bad. I never meant no harm."

Till then it had been only horseplay, something for them to remember him by, something at which men would haw-haw up and down the river. But damn! Now that he saw the Bobcat so spitless scared, so ready to take a licking, Jim had to check an impulse to toss that deadhead into the river. He wouldn't; he had given his word. But he hated a man who wouldn't fight.

And then something happened that had likely never happened before on any raft, log or lumber, or on any log drive or in any lumber camp. It took his breath; the enormity of it and the spunk and damn foolishness of it left him nonplussed. For this kid—this chore boy named Rolfe Torkelsen, this crazy Dane—came darting between him and the Bobcat, and the chore boy grabbed Jim's shirt and yelled, "You promised! Not a word spoke or a fist lifted, you promised! You fight the Bobcat and you've got to fight me first!"

And Rolfe Torkelsen's face was all heated pink, and his eyes were blazing, and he shook Jim's shirt.

There was nothing to it, shutting him up. With his right hand Jim grabbed one of the kid's wrists, and he pivoted him around and pulled the wrist up behind his back, and his left palm clamped over the kid's mouth.

"Why, bubby," he said softly, "I guess you've got too much steam up. Too much pitch in your firebox, bubby."

The chore boy aimed a backward kick at Jim's shin.

Jim wanted to laugh. He liked this wild Dane; the kid had spunk and fire. He increased the upward pressure on the kid's arm, not enough to crack any bones but enough to let him know who was running the raft, and in his deep amusement he said something that showered sparks into the powder keg of the kid's racial pride; those Scandinavians were always ready to fight if you got their nationalities mixed. He called the kid Swede.

"Swede," he said, knowing it would probably make Noisy Swanson mad also, "I don't like those kicks. You and I have got to have a talk, Swede. I can't figure what's got into you. I called the Bobcat over to tell him I want him to row me to New Empire in the skiff. Him and Spaghetti Frank and Noisy Swanson. Now, Swede, you get back to that tub."

He released the chore boy. With his forearm the kid wiped off his mouth, and he said, "I'm not a Swede."

Jim broke out laughing. Even the Bobcat grinned, and all the roosters out in the shadows whooped and hollered. Somebody yelled, "Yippee-yee-yee, I eat polecats and pick my teeth with a pike pole."

But Mike Hogan didn't so much as smile. He was the most solemn Irishman you would ever meet. He glared at the chore boy and said:

"I'll skin him, Jim."

Jim stopped laughing.

"No," he said, "you won't skin him, Mike."

*

Now they stood at the bow of the raft again, Jim and Rolfe Torkelsen, but everything between them had changed. Before supper the kid had been just a kid in Jim's thoughts, one of the innumerable kids who were always turning up as chore boys. They came and went. But this kid was different; a bigger damn fool, maybe, but with more grit.

"Bubby," Jim said, "I reckon you deserve a walloping. And then a toss in the river to cool you off."

"I reckon that's what you'll give me," the kid said, "whether I deserve it or not."

In the flickering firelight Jim could see the defiance in his face and the coppery glints in his mussed hair.

"I've always been a peace loving man," Jim said. "Get me mad and I've always counted up to two before pitching in. If one of the boys reached for a chip, I've let him get it nearly to his shoulder before I've ever popped him. Yes, sir, bubby, I've hated fighting like I hate tangle-foot, and look what it's brought me. Here I was on my own raft, and the chore boy spits in my eye and wants to fight. It sure sorrows me."

"I never knew you were joking," the kid said.

"Bubby, why in hell did you want to get in my crosswalk that way?"

"You promised."

"Sure I promised. But I might have changed my mind."

"You promised. I told the Bobcat what you said. Not a word spoke or a fist lifted."

"I reckon," Jim said, "the old Bobcat must have done you a good turn some time. A man will fight for his pal."

"No," the kid said, "nothing like that."

"Then why did you want to mess in?"

"The Bobcat asked me to sound you out. I told him what you promised.

When I thought you were going back on that, I couldn't just stand there."

"Why not? A man will fight for his bunkmates, sure, but—"

"You promised. That was why."

"Bubby," Jim said, "I guess me and you are driving logs on the old Round River. Myself, I never saw that stream, but the boys say she flows in a big circle, without any headwaters and without a mouth. Driving logs on that, they always ended up at the home rollways, where they started. That's the way our talk goes."

"It was just that you promised," the kid said.

Jim saw then there was no use arguing. Somehow or other they had different slants; maybe because the kid had never been brought up in the woods or on the river. In the woods you learned early who your best friend was. Always it was you against everything. You knew where you stood; it made things simple. You didn't mix into another man's fight unless he was your pal, or unless you were full of beans and tanglefoot and just wanted to raise hell. But certainly you didn't mix in the way the kid had, driven by some foggy notion about duty. The kid sure must have clouds in his head. And yet you had to admire the sassy cuss, at that.

Jim drew a breath and looked back along the raft. In the far shadows at the tail Shorty the Singer's fiddle was squeaking, and the roosters were disturbing the quiet with a song advising townspeople to lock up their daughters because a raft was coming round the bend. It went on and on, with coyote howls after each chorus. Amidships, Mike Hogan sat by the fire, smoking a short clay pipe. Likely he was planning how he would skin the kid, once Jim went to New Empire. If the kid fought back, and he was sure to, it would be near murder. Jim reckoned he would have to take the kid with him. He said:

"I guess you know you're fired."

"I figured I would be," Rolfe Torkelsen said.

"I'll give you your time. And you pack your calamity sack. You'll go to New Empire with me."

The kid stood thinking it over.

"You're fired, and I won't have a fired hand on a raft of mine. You'll have to hit the hay trail."

"I can't go to New Empire," Rolfe said. "I'll sleep on the bank tonight, but I can't go to New Empire."

"It's growing into quite a burg," Jim said. "You might even like it."

"I can't go there till I have thirty dollars. That's what I lost and that's what I'm earning back. Even when I get my time I won't have that. I'll lack six or seven dollars."

"I could stake you."

The kid shook his head.

"I put out money at interest sometimes," Jim said. "But the risk's got to be good. Say, bubby, how did you lose your money, anyway?"

"I was a deadhead to lose it," the kid said. "I don't want to talk about it."

"Bought tanglefoot with it, I reckon," Jim said. "And blew the rest in some fancy house."

The kid looked pretty sore.

"Tanglefoot and fancy houses," Jim said. "The same old story. Drunkenness and wild living."

"Don't judge others by yourself," the kid snapped, and Jim had to smile, figuring he had picked up that old saw from his preacher father. He asked:

"Where was the fancy house?"

"I haven't been near a fancy house."

"Lena's in St. Louis, I reckon," Jim said. "Or Emmy's in Read's Landing. Got drunk and lost your pile. Went on a toot and blew your wad on the girlies."

"That wasn't it at all," Rolfe snapped. "I spent it on a nigger."

"My God! A nigger fancy house."

The kid looked hot enough to sizzle.

"Damn it, I wasn't in a fancy house! I spent it to help buy a nigger out of slavery."

"Well, by God," Jim said, and he just stood looking at the kid.

"There was a man on the boat from St. Louis and he told me about this poor old nigger named Shadrach who lived in Tennessee. His master beat him all the time, and this man said he was collecting a fund to buy the nigger and bring him north and set him free. So I gave him what I had. Thirty dollars."

"Well, I'm damned."

"Then I got the notion of going to other people on the boat and collecting for the fund. They weren't very friendly, and then the captain came and told me I was under arrest for trying to run a swindle. It made me mad."

"I'll just reckon it did," Jim said, smiling. "Did you offer to fight the captain?"

"No, I told him I was collecting money to give this man who took my thirty dollars. But when we looked for the man he was gone. He must have gone ashore at our last landing, although he told me he was on his way to Galena. So the captain said I was lying."

"And did that make you mad, bubby?"

"Well, sure. Scared me too, for I was in a fix. The captain said I'd started young to be a swindler, and he was going to turn me over to the sheriff at the next landing. But when the news got around the boat a merchant from Prairie du Chien said he'd given this same man five dollars for the fund. And a planter from Arkansas said the man must be the same one he'd given ten dollars to for a different fund. This

43

second fund was to be used to pay somebody to shoot William Lloyd
Garrison. So then we knew the man was a swindler working both sides
of the street."

"Who the hell is William Lloyd Garrison?"

"An abolitionist. My father gets a paper he edits."

"Don't tell me you're mixed up with those crazy abolitionists."

"Not exactly."

"So the captain let you loose from arrest?"

"He didn't want to, at first. He thought I was working for the
swindler. Everybody asked me a lot of questions. I told them I was
Reverend Thor Torkelsen's son from Elysian Springs, Indiana, on my
way to study in New Empire. One of the passengers said it was plain
I was honest, and he told the captain to let me loose. I guess the captain
knew him. Anyway, he let me loose from arrest. And an old lady
offered me five dollars. I wouldn't take it. I figured I'd been an awful
deadhead to get swindled that way. I was broke, but I figured I'd feel
better to earn the money back. You have to live with yourself. That's
what my father always says. I left the boat at Dubuque and worked at
what I could find. Then Mike Hogan came ashore to buy supplies and
I got this job."

"And then you got yourself fired. Picking trouble with the pilot."

"I never knew you were joking. It was just that you promised."

The old Round River again. Jim said:

"Sorry about that loan of money, bubby. But I sure couldn't touch a
deal like that. You're too risky a risk."

"What makes you think I'd be a risky risk?"

"Too young. Too hotheaded. You'd blow it all in some nigger fancy
house. And you're a preacher's son. Jails are full of preachers' sons."

"That's not true."

"They always go bad. Outlaws, river pirates. And you're a Swede in
the bargain."

"Damn it, I'm not a Swede. I'm a Dane."

"Oh, well then," Jim said, "that ends everything. You know the old
saying. Nothing crookeder than a crooked land agent except an honest
Dane."

"Damn it to hell," the kid said, "you'd get your money," and he must
have spent five minutes arguing what a fine risk he would be. Finally
Jim brought out his grouch bag and gave the kid his wages and a ten
dollar gold piece as well.

"Good-by, old pal," he said, kissing the coin. "It's against my better
judgment."

"You'll get it back," Rolfe Torkelsen said. "Every cent. When you
want to collect, I'll be at Judge Gentry's in New Empire."

"You know Judge Gentry?"

"I met him in Elysian Springs," Rolfe said. "He came there to take

44

the waters. I'm going to live at his house and read law in his office."
Jim shook his head and sighed.

"Bubby, I've been took. A preacher's son. An abolitionist. A Dane. That was all bad enough. But now a lawyer. My God!" He grinned and tousled the kid's hair. "Run along, bub, and get packed."

*

The skiff would make fast time to New Empire with the current in her favor and three men at the oars. She lay waiting now alongside the raft, with Bobcat Pete and Spaghetti Frank already aboard. Noisy Swanson squatted at the edge of the raft, a hand on the skiff's gunwale, holding her against the current. Beside him a brass lantern sat, its air holes glowing. From where Jim stood by his shanty, that smudge of light in the darkness looked mysterious, giving a secretive air to the expedition.

Rolfe Torkelsen came from the cookhouse, lugging a carpetbag flowered with faded roses. Jim saw him hesitate as he passed behind Mike Hogan, who sat staring into the fire, pulling on his pipe.

"Well," Rolfe said, "I'm ready. Good-by, Mike."

Mike didn't stir, didn't speak.

"Thanks for what you've taught me, Mike. It's all been fun."

No answer.

Rolfe trudged over to Jim and they made their way toward the lantern smudge. They had almost reached it when Jim heard a roar of disgust, back at the campfire. He looked around and saw Mike standing there shaking a fist.

"You'll never eat good beans again," he bellowed at Rolfe, "or learn the secret of their cooking. I'd have took you to the woods and learned you the song of the wind in the pines and of a stew bubbling sweet on the stove. I'd have cut off my right arm for you, and for what? So that now you leave me danglin' between God and the devil with nobody to fetch wood and water. Never cross my path or darken my door again, and may your kids all die of the pox. Now I've said my say so good-by and good luck, and you can go to the devil for all I care."

He sat down.

"All right, bubby," Jim said, "hop aboard."

Rolfe stepped into the skiff; Noisy Swanson squatted there holding the gunwale, saying the usual; and Jim looked back across the raft, held by an odd reluctance. He would never, he reckoned, come back to a raft again as pilot; he was going on to something else. It had been a fine life. Even the winds, even fighting bedeviled currents. He thought of the calm mornings with the sun warm and the river blue and turtles sitting on a log and plopping into the water as the raft drifted past. He remembered the bright noons in fine weather when you ate and felt lazy and the raft glided like a dream raft on a dream river. Now he was leaving all that. And for a second, nagged by uneasiness, he wondered whether

McSwasey's plan was so good, after all. He choked off such thoughts, boarded the skiff. Noisy Swanson followed; the current took them. The raft was a receding shadow with red and green bow lights and a distant campfire amidships.

"Good-by, boys," Jim yelled.

Then he sat in the stern, facing downriver. Facing New Empire. Where McSwasey lived. Where McSwasey would meet him at nine, in Rafferty's Saloon.

III

WHEN PERICLES ruled in Athens men were living in New Empire, Wisconsin, and when Sextus Pompeius debated in the Roman Senate, and when Geoffrey Chaucer sailed to Florence as ambassador plenipotentiary from Edward III, Rex. Only it was not New Empire then or even Wisconsin. The Turtle People called it Village-by-the-Great-Water till warriors of the terrible Ice People crossed the river by stealth and made it impossible for the Turtle People to call it anything, their hearts having been cut out. The Ice People dwelt there for three hundred moons, learning to cultivate maize and to harvest the wild rice in the sloughs. Then the Bear People attacked and there was a great victory. But after only two hundred moons the Bear People waxed fat and lazy, and the Ice People recaptured the village. That went on for thousands of moons.

Long after the Ice People had vanished, the Dakota were dwelling there, a tribe of the dreaded Sioux Nation. They called it, in their guttural tongue, Victory-in-the-Crow-Moon. They stopped that, however, after a surprise attack by their Winnebago cousins. The Winnebago didn't last long there; only about four hundred moons. They called it Place-of-the-Big-Fish. Not even the oldest crone in the village knew why; there were several legends concerning the matter, however. Then scouts from a branch of the mighty Algonquian Nation, the Fox, studied the place from the bluffs to the east and found it good. A war party attacked. They burned the Winnebago chief, a scoundrel named Peace Lover, and called the village Bluffs-that-level-out-to-the-Big-River.

The Fox did not propose to be driven out by anybody, although the Dakota, their lighter skinned enemies from across the river, made many a patriotic attempt. The Fox were a hard lot; quite matter of fact too; it took something the size of the Mississippi River to excite them. They called it *Missi-sebe,* which translated into Big River. They never called it Father of Waters. Neither did the Ice People, the Turtle People, the Bear People, the Sauk, Chippewa, Kickapoo, Dakota or Winnebago.

Joliet passed that way, and Marquette and Hennepin. *Coureurs de bois* came and went, trading whiskey for comely Fox girls. Then one fine day Nicholas Perrot took possession of the village and much other real estate in the name of Louis XIV, a chief of the French Nation. The Fox were not impressed. Another seventy years and a treaty in Paris ceded

47

the village, along with the rest of the real estate, to one great branch of the Anglo-Saxon Nation, a tribe called British. The Fox remained unimpressed. And then, as a result of tribal warfare on the Atlantic Seaboard, the village of Bluffs-that-level-out-to-the-Big-River passed from the tribe called British to the other mighty branch of the Anglo-Saxon Nation, to the restless, dangerous tribe called American. Still the Fox were unimpressed, a great error.

*

By 1850 it had become almost wholly an American tribal village, the few Indians who remained being there on sufferance. And somebody had rechristened the place New Empire. Who or when not even the oldest crone could remember, although there were several legends.

It had a tremendous future, in those days. Already virtually four thousand persons dwelt there: well, two thousand, seven hundred and sixty-eight, if you insisted on getting technical; and anybody who would have swapped a town lot in New Empire for one in St. Paul or even Madison would have been thought lacking in acumen. It had everything, almost: stage lines; fine saloons; fancy houses to fit every purse; three doctors, the best trained of whom had received his medical education as a stretcher bearer in the Mexican War; a free library, fostered by Sophronicus Gentry; a volunteer fire department; and it had the river. The Big River.

Nearly everything you might desire came by the Big River. Letters. Newspapers. Laudanum and calomel and quinine for the doctors. Newsprint for the New Empire *Chronicle*. Molasses and rum and sugar from New Orleans; whiskey and tobacco from Louisville; steamboat boilers and shingle nails from Cincinnati; blankets and shoes from St. Louis. Steamboats brought these commodities to the warehouses on the levee. And because New Empire was entrepôt for the back country to the east and north, wholesale firms were founded and prospered. Also two banks; also taverns and well-appointed livery stables.

The Fox had been correct in describing the village site as Bluffs-that-level-out-to-the-Big-River. Down from the north the bluffs came marching, following the east bank of the river, but about a mile from town they fell back from the river, curving in a great half-circle around a fertile flood plain. On that plain New Empire had grown. And was still growing. Booming, if you believed the New Empire *Chronicle*.

Booming, at any rate, seven months of the year. The other five were quieter. Toward the end of November the last steamboat would go plowing off downriver, and some morning you would waken to a day of deep blue sky and cold still air. And the first person you met would say well, did you hear the news? She froze over last night, clear to Ioway.

Winter was a long, long time, with never a steamboat whistle echoing

48

in the bluffs; only sparrows cheeping around steaming manure, and bluejays crying thief at squirrels in high bare branches. Business dropped off terribly, at the saloons and fancy houses, with the raftsmen all gone away to the woods up north, pinery boys again. Sometimes for weeks on end the sky would hang low and damp and gray, in winter. That could depress you dreadfully, if you had grown up in Santa Fe, New Mexico, where even in winter the air was thrillingly dry and clear. You could get bored, so very, very bored, in New Empire, Wisconsin, if you were a spectacular blond woman of twenty-five, married to a man in his fifties. If your name was Esperanza McSwasey.

*

She was half Prussian and half Spanish American, a combination sufficiently remarkable without the further caprice of that Apache blood from her mother and the Slavic blood from a great-grandmother on her father's side. With a family tree like that, you might have expected olives or piñon nuts or sour lemons or just plain cabbage. Instead, you got Esperanza Consuelo von Zumwalt McSwasey; Esperanza Zumwalt McSwasey, for short. Her father, Otto von Zumwalt, a romantic and a democrat, had dropped the von when he went to Paris to study painting.

God had never intended Otto Zumwalt to be a democrat, and assuredly not to be a painter. Nor had Otto's father, Heinrich Wilhelm Maximilian von Zumwalt. Old Heinrich, who owned a few estates in East Prussia, not to mention a general's uniform with a lot of tinkling medals, used to spend his time strutting and saluting around the court of Frederick William III; nothing much came of it, however, except it provided a good cover for his hobby of chasing the girls.

Otto was the seventh and frailest of nine children, and by all odds the most timid and most studious. As a boy, when his roughneck brothers were ranging the great estate, climbing the stately oaks and limes, and preparing to become commendable Prussians by dueling with wooden sabers, Otto remained inside the rambling old house studying the lessons assigned by his tutor. He did not, perhaps, take Latin with his mother's milk, but certainly he imbibed it as a chaser; and by the time he was eleven he had become so proficient in German, Spanish, English and French that his tutor reported to old Heinrich that the family had a linguistic genius on its hands. The general, always a hard man to please, only scowled and declared:

"*Ja,* but I would like it better if he would get his cowardly nose out of those books and act like a little soldier instead of some puking scholar who will grow up to be nothing maybe but a tutor already."

The tutor bowed and got out fast.

Those were difficult years for the poor general; he was a patriot and pretty mad about the way Napoleon was using Prussia as a corridor between France and Russia. A few years earlier, at the battle of Jena, he had received a bullet in the left buttock, a location which did not very well lend itself to boasting about his wound; moreover, owing to the bullet's nearness to his heart, and to his squeamishness about a surgeon's knife, he still carried the ball; so perhaps this exacerbated his temper. His wife, however, had found him difficult ever since they left the altar.

Of all foreign languages, Otto liked French best. Those irregular verbs and nasal endings did something to him. Something rhapsodic and aphrodisiac and dithyrambic. Like all good Prussians, he yearned to visit Paris, except Otto wished to make the journey in a diligence, not as a warrior. Then, after Prussia defeated Napoleon at Waterloo, with some assistance from the British, and peace came to Europe, and Otto was fifteen, he began reading Jean Jacques Rousseau, from whom he caught the notion that the noblest life was that lived in the wilderness among the uncorrupted savages. Otto, whose feet had never been within a mile of the ground, decided that was the life for him. He would go to America and become a democrat and a noble savage. First, however, a whirl in Paris.

Otto had a genius for finding idiotic books, and it was while reading Emanuel Swedenborg that he hatched the idea of studying art in Paris so that later he could paint the American savages, especially lady savages. Why reading Swedenborg should have done that to him, heaven only knew. As a lad he had shown some talent in sketching, but it had never occurred to him to become an artist. Now, however, inspiration hit and he knew what he wanted to do with his life. But when he screwed up courage to mention the matter to his father, old Heinrich was unsympathetic. Not that the general voiced objection in so many words, but he did turn purple and beat his son with the flat of a saber. Thereafter, Otto kept his mouth shut, permitting himself when the time came to be packed off to the University of Göttingen. The library and the lectures he enjoyed, but the swaggering upper classmen, their cheeks emblazoned with dueling scars, filled him with trepidation, and he lived in dread of being challenged to an affair of honor. After a few months he wrote his father a letter loaded with lies resulting from the hard thinking he had been doing about Heinrich's mental processes.

In the letter he confessed to three pieces of bad luck. First, he had received a slashed cheek in a duel. Second, he had impregnated a barmaid, who was demanding money. Third, he had lost heavily at cards. In the future he would try to be a worthier son.

His father replied with a letter bursting with parental pride and affection, if you were adept at reading between the lines. He began by calling his son a pig-dog and went on from there. But he sent a sum sufficient to pay off the barmaid and clean up the gambling debts. Next evening, Otto left quietly for Paris. And for a year he actually did study painting on the Left Bank, but he got little out of it except a case of gonorrhea. He called in a doctor who bled him regularly till he became so debilitated in body and purse that probably he would have died a pauper except for his determination to live among the North American savages. Like so many weak men he could be strong-willed about the wrong things. So summoning what remained of strength and cash he took passage for New Orleans on a wretched little ship tossed about by heavy seas, adding seasickness to his other woes. For a while it looked as if he might be buried at sea; he had never been husky and now he weighed scarcely more than a pretzel. Then one morning he wakened hungry and was able to hold down food, and during the rest of the journey he gradually gained strength. By now he was very gloomy and hence very happy. He used to stand on deck, face ashen, pale blue eyes staring off across the Gulf, thinking of himself as a child of sorrows out of some lugubrious Goethe opus.

New Orleans was a fortunate port of entry for Otto. Since gonorrhea was as common there as malaria, he found a doctor who better understood its treatment. And his fluent English, Spanish and French brought him a position in an importing house. For more than three years he worked there, saving his salary, on Sundays wandering the narrow streets with brushes and easel, stopping in some little park to paint, or more often just to sit watching the doves and the girls. Sometimes he ventured to the levee. But violence lurked there among the cotton bales and bags of coffee; for the ships from Brazil and the sugar islands, the flatboats from the Ohio, the steamboats from Pittsburgh and St. Louis, were manned by brawny men with knives, and when they eyed Otto he averted his gaze and retreated to his lodgings where he daydreamed about how he would have dealt with the ruffians if trouble had started.

At the importing house he received two promotions with pay increases, and his health returned. He was an excellent clerk and he looked it: a young man of middle height, neat and dapper, with straw-blond hair and a thin face. All day he sat on a high stool, translating letters from planters in Latin America and scratching out replies in Spanish. He was such an accomplished linguist that when exporters from Cuba or Central America turned up at the office, the senior partner would call Otto in as interpreter. On those occasions he was very stiff and Continental, clicking his heels and bowing from the waist. Probably he had a future, of some sort, in business. But he still read Rousseau. In bed he lay thinking of romance on the plains with the Indians.

And so at last, dupe of philosophers who had said that nature was good and only civilized man was vile, Otto quit his job in the spring of 1824 and took passage to St. Louis, outfitting point for expeditions into vastness. He found it a lively place, streets thronged with supple men in buckskins wearing scalping knives at their belts; with merchants in beaver hats; with steamboat men and loud tobacco-spitting mule skinners; with Spanish Americans from New Mexico and stray Osages and Kaws. His heart beat faster as he threaded his way along the sidewalk and stopped outside the drygoods and hardware emporium of Proudfoot &

51

Sons, armed with a letter of introduction from his New Orleans employers. He didn't intend to seek another job but only to ask advice about how best to reach Indian country. But after he had entered the establishment, a dusky cool place smelling of creosote and rawhide and woolens, and found fat John Proudfoot peering through cigar smoke in the dim office at the rear, Otto could not bring himself to speak of art and romance in that commercial atmosphere. It was easier to let it appear that he was simply another young man seeking fortune in the West.

"I see you speak Spanish," Proudfoot said, putting down the letter.

"*Ja*. German, French, English and Spanish. I have always been quick at languages."

"Hog Latin too?"

Otto's spine stiffened.

"Latin, of course. What it is you mean by hog I do not know. It is a noble language."

"Guess it is," Proudfoot said, smiling. "But you know, it's a funny thing. We don't get more than two or three customers a day who ask for Galena pills in Latin."

"It is a dead language," Otto said haughtily.

Proudfoot broke out laughing; Otto thought him crude. Ignorant also, as his next remark revealed.

"You Dutchmen are all alike. Serious minded."

"Please, I am not Dutch. I am Prussian. The son of—"

"Let it go, let it go," Proudfoot said. He turned to a clerk. "Tell Billy I want him." And to Otto he said, "Billy's my youngest son. He's leaving in ten days on his first trip to Santa Fe. If it's opportunity you want that's the place. I predict you'll see a big development in the Santa Fe trade. Those greasers gobble up goods. Wish I was thirty years younger."

Billy turned out to be a young man of twenty with black hair and an easy smile. When he learned Otto came from New Orleans, he wanted to know whether those Creole girls were as pretty as people said.

"Don't you ever think of anything but girls?" Proudfoot asked.

"No, do you?"

Proudfoot roared with laughter and slapped his palm down on the littered desk, raising a cloud of dust.

"By God, I do wish I was thirty years younger."

Otto was thinking of General Heinrich von Zumwalt.

"I'm sending Billy in charge of two wagon loads of goods," Proudfoot said. "But I know that Billy. He'll see those greaser girls and where will that leave Proudfoot & Sons?"

Billy winked at Otto. Proudfoot said:

"By God, Zelmer—or whatever your name is—" He consulted the letter. "Zumwalt. Well, anyway, Zumwalt, I've a notion to send you along. It says here you're honest. That makes you the second honest man I've met. Can't remember the first, but there must have been one.

52

Think you know enough Spanish to set up a store?"

"I speak it like a Spaniard."

"Well, it's all jabber anyway. French, Spanish, German—jabber, jabber. Why don't they learn American and be done with it? Billy could stay till you got a store set up—I'll want a big sign, Billy—Proudfoot & Sons, St. Louis and Santa Fe—and then he could come back with the caravan and go out next spring with more goods. Last year I sent my son Ed out with one wagon and the profits weren't bad. Not bad at all. And we sold wholesale to some greaser storekeeper and I'll bet he had a markup of a hundred percent. Maybe two hundred."

"Are there Indians in Santa Fe?" Otto asked.

"Hell, yes. Injuns everywhere. Too damned many. Government ought to clean 'em out. I'll bet if we'd run General Jackson for president he'd fix them. But don't let Injuns worry you, Zelmer. Those greasers in Santa Fe know how to deal with Injuns. They kill off all they can and marry up with the rest."

Proudfoot laughed. Otto deduced he had never read Rousseau.

"Yes, sir," Proudfoot said, "the thing for us to do is open a retail branch in Santa Fe. I'm convinced of it. Uh, Billy. Is Ed here?"

"He went down to the levee."

"Well then, is Caleb McSwasey still here?"

"He was a minute ago."

"Get him, will you?"

Billy left the office. Proudfoot said:

"McSwasey's been to New Mexico twice. He was with Captain Becknell in '22. That was when they crossed the Arkansas River and tried for a shortcut across the desert. Had one hell of a time. They were eating dogs and mules' ears before they were done with it. Think you'll like McSwasey. We're from the same state back east. He went out again last year, and he's making another trip this spring. I'm giving him goods on credit."

Billy returned with a man of twenty-eight who walked with a slight limp.

"Caleb," Proudfoot said, "shake hands with Otto Zelmer. He's a New Orleans Dutchman."

"Zumwalt. Zumwalt's the name," Otto said.

His hand, slim and soft from office work, was being shaken by a blunt-fingered hand with a hard grip.

"Come to think of it," Proudfoot said, "Caleb's been in New Orleans himself. He won the battle there, he and General Jackson."

"And I am not a Dutchman," Otto said. "I am a Prussian. The son of—"

"Zelmer here thinks he wants to kill Injuns," Proudfoot said.

"In that case," McSwasey said in a quiet voice, "I reckon the trail's the place for you."

53

"But I do not want to kill Indians."

"Then you'd best stay out of Comanche country."

"I'm thinking of sending Zelmer out with the caravan," Proudfoot said. "His main job will be to see that Billy keeps his pants buttoned, but I might put him in charge of a retail branch. All Dutchmen are good merchants. And he says he knows Spanish. Of course I don't believe him, but that's what he says. You know the lingo, Caleb. Why don't you jabber away at him?"

McSwasey smiled. He was a husky fellow of average height, dressed in thick-soled shoes, woolen trousers and a hickory shirt. His hair was dark red, his face broad and freckled, his nose bulbous above a wide mouth with heavy lips. He said:

"Como está?"

"Muy bien, gracias. Y usted?"

"Muy bien, Señor Zelmer."

"Zumwalt, Zumwalt. Otto Zumwalt. *Y no se preocupe por mi, señor. Yo leo, escribo y hablo español."*

"Wait a minute," McSwasey said, smiling. "You're too fast for me. I don't guess I know more than a dozen words."

In Spanish, very fast, Otto said:

"This old donkey Proudfoot has got everything mixed. My name is Zumwalt, not Zelmer. I am the son of General Heinrich von Zumwalt. I am not a Dutchman but a Prussian, and I do not wish to kill Indians. I only wish to meet them and be adopted into a tribe and perhaps marry a chief's daughter and spend my time painting. In Paris I was a famous painter."

"What in hell did he say, Caleb?" Proudfoot asked.

McSwasey stood thumbing his heavy jaw, head thrust slightly forward, blue eyes amused.

"I don't rightly know. Something about a jackass and killing Indians. But it's the lingo. It's just like they sound in Santa Fe. I'd know that lingo anywhere."

"Damned if I can figure why they want to jabber that way," Proudfoot said. "You'd think they'd talk so a man could understand them. Well, Zelmer, I'm inclined to hire you. I do like that idea of a branch store."

*

About two weeks later the little steamboat *Western Pride* left St. Louis, loaded with wagons, horses, mules and men, Caleb McSwasey, Billy Proudfoot and Otto Zumwalt among them. A few miles above town she nosed into the thick yellow waters of the Missouri, a vicious rattlesnake of a river coming angrily out of the high West. After several days of battling current and dodging snags, she put in at Franklin and discharged her cargo. In those early years of the trail, Franklin was the jumping off place, so considerable delay ensued while final preparations were made for the journey. The mule skinners employed by Proudfoot & Sons greased the axles of the huge wagons and rolled dice; Billy Proudfoot struck up an acquaintance with a town girl; Otto remained at camp in a pasture near the village and read Rousseau.

Before leaving St. Louis, he and Billy had bought moccasins and fringed buckskins; they were the only members of the company thus attired. Wearing those brand new garments, Otto paced about camp feeling already like a veteran plainsman, a little disdainful òf the merchants in broadcloth and the mule skinners in scuffed boots and coarse woolens. They bore up very well under his scorn, however, even commenting on his outfit.

"You know," one mule skinner drawled, within Otto's hearing, that first day in camp, "I figure this here carryvan is plumb lucky to have Dan'l Boone along."

"Boone?" another asked. "But I heard tell old Dan'l cashed in, four or five years back."

"Well, now yoù speak of it, I recollect hearing that story myself. But if that feller there ain't Boone, who is he?"

He pointed at Otto, whose spine had stiffened.

"Why, old hoss, don't you know who that is? That ain't Boone. That there is that Dutchman who learned Boone all he knew about Injun fighting."

"Why, you old beaver, I do believe you're *kee*-rect. Waugh! It's the Dutchman, sure enough. Say, this will be one carryvan them Injuns will leave alone, soon as the news gits around we've got the Dutchman to *pre*-tect us."

Whereupon the Dutchman, who was not a Dutchman at all but a Prussian of high birth, stalked out of earshot, ears red, telling himself that democracy was a beautiful theory but that it would work better in practice if the lower classes were taught their places.

Sometimes in the afternoons Otto wandered off into the timber, carrying a volume of Rousseau or Goethe or the poems of Lord Byron. Spring was at full flood, the sunlight lancing down through new foliage. There amid the calls of catbirds and the fragrance of columbine, he would sit with his back against a tree and open a book. But oddly enough, in that sylvan setting, he couldn't concentrate. He was always listening. This puzzled him, and he forced himself to read. But after a minute he discovered that his brain had refused admittance to the words; his brain was all ears. At last he had to confess that he was listening for the footsteps of Indians. That, of course, was ridiculous; the Indians in this vicinity were friendly. But were they? The mule skinners said so, but the mule skinners also said you could trust no Injun nohow, that all the good Injuns were in their graves. Otto did not believe this; once he reached Santa Fe and got Proudfoot's store operating efficiently he intended to look up some noble chief and move in on him. That was the whole purpose of his pilgrimage.

One afternoon in the timber he followed a path through bushes to a creek with a sand beach. He seated himself on a log, determined to read a few cantos of Byron. But it was the same as on other occasions, he couldn't concentrate. He tried, but presently his ears picked up a sound from back in the bushes. Footsteps! His heart labored. The footsteps were moving closer, and Otto had a vision of a naked savage howling from the bushes with a lifted war hatchet. He jumped up, yelling, ready to fling the poetry of Byron at the redskin and take to his heels. Then Caleb McSwasey stepped into view.

"What's going on?" he asked.

Otto nearly strangled with relief.

"Nothing," he said.

"What were you yelling about?"

"Did I yell?"

"Like Injuns were after you."

"Oh," Otto said, "that. A wasp stung me. Right here, on the back of my neck."

McSwasey undressed.

"I'm going swimming. There's a deep pool yonder. Do you swim?"

"Certainly," Otto said, although actually he had feared the water since that day when he was four and an older brother dunked him in the horse trough till he nearly drowned and General von Zumwalt whipped them both.

McSwasey's shoulders were broad and freckled, his rather short legs slightly bowed, his calves and biceps thick with muscles. He limped to a high place on the bank and dived in.

"Feels good," he said, after breaking surface. "Better come in."

"Thank you, but I believe I will not."

Otto thought of his own body, white and weak-muscled, as he watched McSwasey treading water and swimming side-stroke. He would have traded all his linguistic skill to be able to do that.

"You are an expert swimmer," he said, after McSwasey left the water and lay drying on the sand.

"I ought to be. I've been at it since I was knee high to a grasshopper."

"I am an expert also," Otto said. "When I was twelve we were summering on the Baltic. My older brother, Fritz, ventured out too far. I rescued the poor fellow."

"I damn near drownded myself once," McSwasey said. "I was eleven then. That was back in Massachusetts in the dead of winter."

"Swimming in the winter?"

"Fishing. Through the ice on the Connecticut River. I had a new pocketknife I'd worked hard for. I pulled up a fish through the hole in the ice and decided to clean him then and there. Damned if I didn't

56

drop the knife and it went skittering over the ice and through the hole. Well, I was a fool kid. I dived into the river after that knife, clothes and all. Waugh!"

"Waugh!" Otto repeated.

"Now this may sound like a whopper, Zelmer—"

"Zumwalt! Zumwalt's the name."

"Uh? Oh, sure, Zumwalt. Well, as I say, it may sound like a whopper, but I located that knife on the river bed and grabbed it. Fool luck. But when I tried to break surface I couldn't find that damned hole."

"Waugh!" Otto said.

"By that time I was a little cool. I needed air too. Well, I remembered hearing there was always a little air space between the ice and the water. I floated on my back with my nose against the ice and I got enough air to splash around some more. Must have done that three or four times. Then I saw a pole and grabbed it. The kid I'd come fishing with had stuck a pole down through the hole, in case I lost my bearings. He pulled me up. And by God, I still had that knife in my fist."

"Were you not very cold by then?"

"Somewhat chilly. That evening I come down with pneumonia, and something was wrong with my right leg. I licked the pneumonia but the leg's been touchy ever since. I figure them leg muscles never got quite thawed out. That's why I limp."

"You were very brave," Otto said.

"I don't know about that. I just didn't want to lose my knife."

"Is it true you fought in the battle at New Orleans?"

"Under Old Hickory? Yes, I was there."

"Did you kill many of your enemies?"

"I doubt it. I was too scared."

"I come from a long line of military people," Otto said. "My father is General Heinrich von Zumwalt. He has been often decorated for bravery. And I fought a duel once myself."

"Were you scared?"

"I? Scared?" A wintry smile curled Otto's mouth. "I ran my adversary through with my saber. *Ja*, right through the belly button. That is how little I was scared."

"Well, it's nice to be brave," McSwasey said. He stood up, brushed sand from the red hair on his legs and buttocks. "But there's no money in soldiering. My pa found that out under Washington, and I found it out under Jackson. If I hadn't joined up I might have been a rich man by now."

"You volunteered?"

"In Tennessee. When the sergeant asked why I limped I told him I'd turned my ankle and I'd be fine in a couple of days."

"But I thought you were from Massachusetts."

"From there, yes. But I left home early."

Back in camp, Otto found Billy Proudfoot bent over a wash basin. "Otto," he said as he toweled himself, "why does a gal invite a man to her house for supper?"

"Are you making a riddle?"

Billy smiled.

"No riddle about it. She invites him so she can show off her cooking. Well, Eliza Ann has invited me. That's progress, Otto. I hope the old folks get sleepy early."

After Billy had gone, Otto cooked a solitary supper, and as the long May twilight stole over the land he sat watching the fire die, invaded by a rich *Weltschmerz*. For the first time he wondered whether he had been wise in giving up a good position in New Orleans and pursuing romance. Americans and American ways he found hard to understand. New Orleans had been American also, but in spirit it was closer to Europe. Missouri was very strange. Men like the mule skinners and Caleb McSwasey baffled him. When darkness fell he crawled between his blankets underneath a wagon and lay wondering whether he should give up this journey to Santa Fe. Why had an odd shyness kept him from telling John Proudfoot he was uninterested in commerce but wished only to settle among the Indians and paint?

Indians. Who was right, Rousseau who believed the savages noble, or these crude Americans who said all Indians were better dead? He heaved a sigh and put himself to sleep by surrendering to the old daydream. An Indian village. A courtly chief. The chief's beautiful daughter, with admiration and submission in her eyes.

*

At sunrise two mornings later the caravan put out from Franklin and went rocking across the prairie, an odd assortment of wagons and carts and several dearborn carriages, straggling along without organization on this first leg of the journey. Caleb McSwasey drove his own wagon, but Otto and Billy were mounted on mules. It was a beautiful rolling land with deep grasses and brooks and groves of native timber, and Otto in his innocence expected it to continue that way clear to New Mexico. Even when the mule skinners who had traveled the trail last year told him he was mistaken he secretly believed he was right. But after a time the land changed, trees thinning, grass growing shorter, and Otto was learning about aridity. He didn't much like it. The wind blew more, the sky was more imposing, and as the distances opened out the little caravan seemed to shrink in size and importance. Otto liked it less and less. Yet he told himself that if he expected to dwell among the noble savages he must go to the land where savages were to be found, a remarkably clear piece of logic, for him. Finally the caravan reached an extensive grove of hardwood trees along a limpid stream. Other trails converged there, and more wagons were waiting. From now on, the mule skinners said, a man ran the risk of losing his hair to the Pawnees or Comanches.

"Not my hair," Billy Proudfoot said. "I brought along hair tonic." The mule skinners said this caravan would be better off if there were fewer smart alecks.

Before leaving the grove, the mule skinners repacked the freight to better advantage, and a day was spent cutting down oak and ash trees and slinging the wood under the wagons for repairs. Then an election was held to choose a captain of the caravan. Since Otto had never voted in New Orleans, this was his first experience with American politics, and he threw his support strongly to Caleb McSwasey, even going about camp and ordering the others to vote for his candidate. Whether this arrogant electioneering helped McSwasey remained an open question; at least one mule skinner declared that while he thought highly of McSwasey, he was damned if he would let a stuck-up Dutchman tell him how to vote. By then Otto felt sure the sky would fall unless McSwasey won, and he was convinced the opposition candidate was a blackguard.

On the night before the election a political rally took place, with accordion music and bibulous singing, and with stump speeches by McSwasey and his opponent. These were burlesques of political speeches back in the States; McSwasey's opponent asserted that McSwasey was a fine fellow, except for his habit of stealing horses; and McSwasey charged that his opponent was a wonderful man if you overlooked his six wives scattered about the country, two of them Injuns and one a coyote. Everyone had a splendid time, cheering and booing; everyone but Otto. Otto believed every charge McSwasey made, and if he had had his way the other candidate would have been drummed from camp. And after the balloting, when it was announced that McSwasey had lost, Otto mumbled darkly about fraudulent practices, and he doubted whether democracy was a workable form of government. And when McSwasey congratulated the victor, and said a wise choice had been made, and when the captain appointed McSwasey commander of the guard, Otto was astounded and baffled; he simply couldn't understand these Americans.

The day after the election the caravan left the grove. Entering the territory of the savage plains tribes, it traveled now under discipline, and Otto enjoyed that; it reminded him of father and fatherland. Early in the morning the captain shouted, "Catch up, catch up," the signal for the mule skinners to bring the animals into camp from the grazing grounds, and to hitch up. The first teamster ready called, "All set," and presently the entire camp resounded with those words. After a command of "Stretch out," from the captain, the teams with their jingling bells hauled the wagons to their places in the line of travel. Then the captain called, "Fall in," and the caravan moved, light from sunrise ruddy on the Osnaburg sheets covering the trade goods, the wagons casting huge shadows.

With the grove behind, the country took a turn for the worse, sweeping off endlessly in a succession of long low hills and wide valleys, dry except for an occasional creek with its cottonwoods gossiping in the wind. Fording the creeks was always a nuisance and sometimes, if the banks were steep, a major problem. Wagon wheels would be locked, mules or horses hitched on behind, to hold back, and the wagon would go slithering down the bank, threatening to topple. And to drag the wagon up the opposite bank eight or ten teams might be needed. Hours passed while the creek was being forded, and when at last the business was over and the caravan reached the next summit, Otto would gaze ahead to another green smear of cottonwoods meandering along the valley floor, and to another hill. Distances were enormous in this empty vast empire, sky and land fit for giants. On his mule Otto felt tiny as a microbe perched on an ant. He felt somehow naked and unprotected, and he grew apprehensive, not of anything so corporeal as Indians, but of some vague and unseen terror lurking behind the line where earth met sky. He began wondering just how he had got into this; perhaps it had been a mistake to hire out to Proudfoot & Sons. If he had it to do over he believed he would go north up the Mississippi and live with forest Indians.

Now and then at midafternoon clouds built into thunderheads, and while lightning crackled about the mules' ears rain pelted down. Otto had always been timid in electrical storms, and in these savage tempests on the plains he was much alarmed. He said, however, that he enjoyed the interesting display of heavenly fireworks.

But he did not enjoy what the rain did to his buckskins. With the first deluge they became soaked and mushy, and when dried by the sun they stiffened and shrank till on his mule Otto looked like a caricature of a plainsman, arms and shanks protruding from clothes too small, toes sticking through the seams of disintegrating moccasins. He was outraged. And when the mule skinners guyed him, saying they reckoned he wasn't Dan'l Boone after all, for Boone would not have been such a greenhorn as to wear new buckskins in the rainy season, Otto's spine turned stiffer than his grotesque clothes, and his face flushed. Billy Proudfoot took the ridicule with better grace; both young men, however, changed to woolen trousers lined with leather, and to tough boots.

Caleb McSwasey came to their campfire several evenings after the first rain.

"Boys," he said quietly, squatting in the flickering light, "what do you aim to do with those buckskins?"

Otto stiffened.

"Don't get mad," McSwasey said. "This ain't a joke. If you're through with them I might take them off your hands."

"*Ja*, take them! I never want to see the cowardly things again."

"They're ruined, of course," McSwasey said. "But maybe I could salvage some strips of leather for laces. What will you take for them?"

"They are no good," Otto said. "I will take what you will give."

"Hold on, Otto," Billy said.

"Four bits?" McSwasey asked.

"Four bits or no bits for the *Verräterisch Kleider!*"

And Otto stalked to a wagon and returned with the stiff garments, flinging them to the ground.

"I won't sell for four bits," Billy said.

They dickered, and in the end McSwasey paid Billy two dollars and Otto fifty cents. When Otto protested, McSwasey said a bargain was a bargain.

"He's got you there," Billy said. "You were too quick, Otto. Never take a Yankee's first offer."

McSwasey stood with the buckskins over an arm and the moccasins in his hands. A smile played over his mouth; his voice was low.

"Boys, you've bought some experience. I'll smoke these over a willow fire and knead them soft again, and once these rains are over I might make a penny or two selling them."

He limped away.

"A crook!" Otto exclaimed.

But Billy shook his head.

"Just a smart trader. Cripes, we're green. We should have known he was up to something."

In the evening after a rain there would be a wet camp, and if it was Otto's turn to guard he would pace under the muggy stars while the hobbled mules munched grass and the earth steamed. He preferred guard duty on a night when the moon was shining, for he had not quite conquered a childish fear of the dark. Yet even moonlight nights had disadvantages, for he was always imagining shadows to be creeping Indians, and he would discharge his rifle and yell, rousing everybody. When he guarded, the others lost about as much sleep as he. The mule skinners complained about this, rather pointedly; on the whole, Otto's popularity was slipping. He salved his ego, however, by telling himself that peasants had never understood the finer qualities of the aristocracy, and he freely admitted now that he had been mistaken, back in the best country on earth, when he believed himself a democrat. He had, he told himself, been very scientific in discovering this error, for had he not traveled to America and carefully studied its institutions?

As the days passed the thunderstorms grew rarer; the heat increased; and the land with its short grass flattened out. Presently it ran level in all directions. The sky was titanic. There was too much glare and there were too many rattlesnakes. Jogging along on his mule, Otto would close his eyes and remember New Orleans with its charmingly narrow streets and fountains sparkling in the civilized sunlight; and he told himself that if an east-bound party of mountain men should come along, it might be wise for him to abandon the journey and return to St. Louis.

Occasionally the caravan sighted Indians, faraway mounted figures against the sky. Otto was surprised to discover he had grown lukewarm toward his project of dwelling among the savages and painting them. His artist's supplies were packed in the wagon; he never took them out; scarcely ever thought of them. He wasn't reading Rousseau any more either. Rousseau must have been thinking of forest Indians. To hell with Indians, anyway. If they wanted Otto Zumwalt to visit them they should have chosen a pleasanter country for their home. He wondered how much farther to Santa Fe, and one evening he asked Billy Proudfoot for a look at the map. It startled him. They were not yet half way. That was ridiculous but there it was on paper. Now he was sure he wanted to go back.

"The trail gets tiresome," he told Billy.

"You think so? I'm having the time of my life."

Otto gestured at the sky, the boundless land.

"There's too much of it."

"That's what I like," Billy said. "St. Louis is too crowded. The man next door blows his nose and you know it. I've always wanted this. Let others make hen scratches in a ledger. I want to see the country before I die."

"I have seen better country," Otto said.

"Wait till we get to the mountains. Or one of those Cheyenne villages. I've heard all about it from trappers coming to the store. Those Cheyenne girls are smooth as silk. So I've heard. Friendly too."

"If they didn't live so far from everything," Otto said.

Billy laughed.

"If they lived closer there'd be more competition. Then there's those Santa Fe girls. I've heard about them too. They call them *señoritas*. They go bare-legged and wear short skirts with nothing much under them, and they wear low blouses. Waugh! And they drink Taos Lightning and smoke corn-shuck cigarettes. That's what I've heard. My brother Ed was out there last year. He told me not to get heart failure if I saw any little Mexicanos with the Proudfoot nose."

Otto smiled faintly.

"From what Ed told me," Billy said, "I guess old Caleb McSwasey is quite a hand with the ladies."

"So?"

"Sure he is. He's a quiet fellow and you'd never know it from anything he says, but he gets around. There's a story that when he lived in the South he owned a mulatto girl. She went everywhere with him. Then once in Texas he lost her at cards in Nacogdoches. They say he whispered to her before he turned her over to this old fellow who won her, and late that night she sneaked out of bed and met Caleb and they beat it back into the States."

"It is probably all a big lie," Otto said.

"Might be. And then the story goes that this gave Caleb an idea. He and the girl traveled around the South. He'd put her up for sale and get a whopping price—she was as white as you are—and a night or two later he'd meet her in the woods with an extra horse and they'd be in the next county by daylight."

"That was not honest," Otto said sternly.

"No, but one way you look at it, it was pretty funny. Think of all those old goats who bought her waking up and reaching out and finding an empty pillow."

Billy laughed. Otto looked the soul of virtue. He asked: "Were they never caught?"

"No, but I guess the South got pretty hot for them. They came to St. Louis and Caleb sold her for keeps. He bought a wagon and mules with the money, and got goods on credit from dad, and went to New Mexico with Captain Becknell. Caleb's a smart fellow. Dad says he'll end up rich."

"Did he actually fight in the battle at New Orleans?"

"Of course he did. Killed a lot of redcoats. He's a dead shot."

"He told me he was scared in the battle."

"He was stringing you along. You've noticed how he is. He talks in that low voice and underdraws everything he says. Once in the store a fellow from Virginia asked him if it was far to Santa Fe. Caleb said it was a fair piece. And when the fellow asked what the country was like, Caleb said it tended slightly on the dry side."

"But that is no better than lying," Otto said, outraged.

"Not with Caleb. It's just his way. When dad asked him if the customs officers in Santa Fe liked bribes, he said they weren't too mad if you slipped them a penny. And when I asked him about the gals out there, he said it was rumored they weren't man-haters. Of course, I'd already heard from my brother that Caleb had been stepping high with those gals. They liked his hair."

"But how was that?"

"Red hair. Injun and Spanish gals go strong for that. Think I'll dye mine red. You're lucky, Otto, with that tow head of yours. They go for blond hair too. So I've heard."

Otto felt slightly cheered.

"Maybe I'll use you for a decoy," Billy said. "You attract them and I'll take over. So I say on to Santa Fe. The life of a Santa Fe trader, that's the life for me. Ed says when a caravan pulls in those gals come running out waving handkerchiefs and calling, '*Los Americanos! Los Americanos!*' Short skirts and low blouses. Waugh! When that happens, Otto, you damned old Dutchman, don't expect me to ride on to the customhouse. You'll have to attend to all that business of bribing the officials. They call it making *diligencia*. As for me, I'll be founding the Santa Fe branch of the Proudfoot family."

"That is so long away," Otto said, with a sigh; and he lay on his blanket and tried to forget the map marked Great American Desert.

Next day was momentous, for the caravan sighted buffalo. The captain sent out hunters, Caleb McSwasey among them. Billy Proudfoot was all for going along, but the captain said this was an expedition for fresh meat, not a tea party for greenhorns. Otto would not have gone if he had been invited; he was too trail-weary. When the hunters returned that evening with meat, there was a lot of whooping and comic complaining because the buffalo livers had already been eaten. Otto gathered that as soon as a buffalo was shot the hunters sliced it open, cut out the liver, sprinkled it with juice from the gall bladder and ate it warm. His stomach had never been strong, and this made him faintly sick; he took care that his buffalo steak should be well cooked.

"McSwasey is no better than a savage," he told Billy, before they turned in. "Think of eating raw liver!"

"But they say it tastes good. I'd like to try it."

"You are not serious."

"Sure I am. They say it makes a man of you. And that gall bladder juice has a kick like a mule. Better than Taos Lightning. So I've heard."

Otto was disgusted.

"Damn," Billy said, "I'd sure like to get a bead on one of those bufflers. You're never anything but a greenhorn till you shoot your first buffler. That's what my brother Ed said. Two ways of doing it, he said, either running meat from horseback, or dismounting and walking right toward some young bull. Seems a buffler don't see too well, and if you keep on the down-wind side—"

Otto dropped off to sleep while Billy talked.

The trouble with buffalo country was that it was also buffalo-gnat country. They swarmed by the million, clustering on the whip-wounds of the mules, pestering the tossing heads of the horses, crawling up inside Otto's pants and down his spine and into his nose and eyes. Everything else had been bad but the gnats were too much. Adventure and romance on the plains had never been like this, in Otto's daydreams. He longed for an east-bound party of mountain men, thinking what a paradise it would be to return to St. Louis and maybe to East Prussia, which now seemed a wonderful land. But the caravan didn't meet mountain men. The glare was endless, the gnats were endless, the trail was endless.

Late one night during the third watch, when Otto was standing guard, he was startled by a figure stepping from behind a wagon into the moonlight. He gripped his rifle; then, recognizing Billy Proudfoot, lowered it.

"Sh-h-h," Billy said.

"What are you about?" Otto whispered.

"I'm going for a mule ride."

"You are doing what?"

"I'm going out to shoot me a buffler."

"No," Otto said. "You must not."

"Why not?"

"I cannot permit it. It is against the rules."

"I figure to sneak up on a herd about daybreak. Or maybe even in the moonlight."

"But the rules—"

"Damn the rules. Just look the other way, Otto. I've got to get me a buffler."

Billy winked, and his teeth flashed in a grin.

"I do not think you should."

"I'll be back by breakfast. You just keep making your rounds. You haven't seen or heard a thing."

With bridle and rifle, Billy went stealing off toward the hobbled animals.

Otto was troubled. In his Prussian soul he worshipped rules, any rules, and certainly his friend was doing a foolhardy thing. But if he fired his gun and wakened the camp everybody would be annoyed; now that he was a more experienced guard he was learning to control his perpetual apprehension and not sound the alarm whenever he glimpsed a jackrabbit. Still, he shouldn't allow Billy to go. Yet he didn't know how to stop him, short of rousing the camp. If he did that, Billy would be in a huff.

He stood scowling, trying to make up his mind; and then, off in the moonlight, he saw Billy on his mule, riding away bareback. Billy waved his rifle. Otto waved back. There were muffled hoofbeats, growing fainter toward the southwest, and Billy had been swallowed by the vast ghostly land. Otto continued on his rounds. He felt uneasy and guilty but he didn't know what he could have done to stop Billy. Decisions were hard for him, and taking firm stands. When the next guard relieved him he did not mention the incident.

At daybreak Billy had not returned, nor was he in camp for breakfast. He was missed. Staring at the horizon, the captain swore and declared that if Billy were not John Proudfoot's son he would let him shift for himself, but as it was he reckoned they had better find him. This wasn't western Missouri; this was Comanche country. Young blood, the captain said, was impatient, and that fool Billy must have sneaked off alone to hunt buffalo. So now Caleb McSwasey, as commander of the guard, began an investigation, questioning each of the four watches of the night before.

He was a very different McSwasey from the man Otto had watched swimming in a Missouri creek. His voice, if anything, was quieter, but it had a cool, deadly quality; the pupils of his blue eyes were needle points. Otto, with his paler blue eyes, found it hard to meet his questioner's gaze; he denied everything. Billy had certainly not left camp during his watch.

"Was he in his blankets when your watch began?" McSwasey asked.

"Ja, I think so."

"Was he there when your watch ended?"

"I did not notice."

McSwasey stood with his head slightly forward, in the listening attitude of a deaf man. But his hearing, Otto knew, was sharp. Sometimes with a blunt thumb he scratched his jaw. The captain joined them.

"Learn anything?"

"No," McSwasey said softly. And he added, "This could be serious."

"Hell, yes, it's serious. One man out there alone. Even the Kaws would risk taking on one man. None of the guards saw him leave?"

"They say not."

"Think they're lying?"

McSwasey stood in that listening attitude.

"Could be they're a little forgetful."

The captain fixed steady eyes on Otto, whose ears began to burn. He drew himself up stiffly.

"Please, I do not lie."

"Well, we've got to find him," the captain said, and he appointed three of the best trackers to follow Billy's trail. Several guards were sent too, and when Otto insisted on going along, the captain consented.

Mule tracks led off to the southwest, and the mounted men jogged along with eyes fixed on the ground. Already the sun was well above the horizon, and the cloudless sky promised another burning day. An hour passed before they reined up and dismounted, silently, where Billy Proudfoot lay prone, his back a quiver of arrows.

"Comanches," somebody said.

Otto gaped at Billy's scalped head, then turned away, sweat breaking out on his brow. His stomach turned over and he lost his breakfast; he felt faint. One of the party said:

"That's Injuns for you."

Suddenly Otto hated Injuns. Comanches, Pawnees, Cheyennes, Kaws, Osages, Kiowas; he hated them all. And he hated this land where Indians roamed; this immensity of flatness with its gnats and buffalo grass and buffalo wallows and buffalo skulls white in the sun. He wanted to go home.

They buried Billy as best they could, in a shallow grave, and stood awkwardly with hats off.

"Friend," one of the men muttered to Otto, "somebody ought to say a few words. Why don't you?"

Otto knelt.

"Oh, God," he began, but the prayer piled up in his throat. At last he went on. "He wanted to see the country, God, and maybe you will let him do that now. He wanted to see the girls in Santa Fe, and maybe you will let him do that too. He was cut down in the flower of his

youth, God, so he will always be young, riding these plains. Amen."
Putting on their hats, the others stared curiously at Otto. He never
realized he had prayed in German, to the God of Martin Luther.

Before they turned away from the low mound, one of the party said:
"Wish there was rocks to pile on it."

"No good would come of it," another replied. "Wolves will get him
tonight, if not before."

Otto didn't want to be sick again.

After that the days blurred together like heat mirages. Dust, glare,
gnats. Wagons broke down, were repaired, dragged on. Once a band
of Pawnees attacked, but the wagons wheeled into a circle and the men
lay flat, rifles cracking. Otto had never been so frightened; his hands
shook wildly, loading his gun. From the battle he carried a memory
of Caleb McSwasey under the next wagon, taking a long cool aim and
pressing his trigger. Otto looked where the gun was pointing and saw
a paint-smeared warrior pitching from a horse. As he reloaded Mc-
Swasey was smiling. Otto aimed at a warrior; the gun kicked his
shoulder; the warrior continued riding and fitting arrows to his bow.
In the entire battle nobody was killed except Pawnees. That would
learn them, the captain said, not to fool around with a strong caravan
of dead shots.

Once in the night a party of Comanches tried to stampede the hobbled livestock, but the guard sounded the warning. Men sprang up
from sleep, grabbing their rifles, and the Comanches vanished. The
trail went on, on, coming finally to the Arkansas River, a flat expanse
of sand veneered with water. The caravan followed its north bank for
days, before crossing it and striking off southwest toward Raton Pass.
The buffalo-gnats were fewer now, but the heat continued. Days were
bright hell, nights dark hell, because of the dreams. In the dreams men
pointed accusingly at Otto, yelling that he had sent Billy Proudfoot to
his death. Sometimes Caleb McSwasey limped through the dreams with
a mulatto girl, and sometimes Billy came back, laughing weirdly as he
sprinkled hair tonic on his bloody scalp. Indians warwhooped through
the dreams, out to get Otto Zumwalt.

It was all endless, the days as nightmarish as the dreams. Once Otto
Zumwalt had been a stripling reading Swedenborg in Prussia; once he
had sat in a sidewalk cafe; once he had presented a letter to a man in
St. Louis who peered through cigar smoke. Long ago. He would have
liked returning to that cool emporium with its smells of creosote and
rawhide, but he had given up hoping for an east-bound party or for anything good, ever.

But then another change came over the land, so subtly that it might
have been imagined, at first. Yet gradually it became unmistakable:
the country was rolling more, and there was a feeling of altitude; the
nights were cooler. One morning Otto noticed faint clouds on the west-

67

ern horizon; they didn't move; by late afternoon they were more distinct, silvery pale.

"Them there," the captain announced, "are the Rocky Mountains of North America. Boys, you're lookin' at the Spanish Peaks."

*

Otto was living now with a single goal, to reach the mountains. It took a long-time. At daybreak he would stand amid the stirring camp, with its smoke from breakfast fires rising in perpendicular threads, and gaze at those remote peaks sparkling in the thin air. All day he watched them, day after day, as he rode his mule. With Billy dead, he had no friends in the caravan, not even Caleb McSwasey; for ever since the morning of Billy's disappearance McSwasey had been cool and distant. He did not, it was evident, believe Otto's denials of letting Billy ride off alone. Nor did the others. They avoided Otto; if he joined a group at a campfire they acted as if he didn't exist; if he asked a question nobody answered; on one occasion two mule skinners, ignoring his presence, talked acidly about how correct the Injuns were when they said some people were bad medicine. Otto was in the caravan but no longer of it; he felt an outcast; and although he told himself over and over that Billy's death was not his fault, there was a secret part of him which no more believed this than did Caleb McSwasey.

Sometimes he thought of going to McSwasey and confessing everything, but his vainglory would not permit it; nor would his fondness for his own skin. The shameful truth was that he feared that these rough plainsmen might string him up by the neck from a wagon tongue if they ever learned for certain he had permitted Billy to leave camp. Americans were strange; they not only lacked respect for their betters but seemed utterly unaware that they had betters. Even for the captain of the caravan they showed scant respect, by Prussian standards; when he gave an order they didn't snap to attention and salute. Not these noodleheads. They would think over the order and drawl, "Well, I reckon you're right about that. I'll git at it."

So Otto was much alone, and sometimes as he rode his mule or moped in the dusk he muttered to himself, in German. Once he overheard somebody calling him that loco Dutchman. Although fresh game was plentiful now his appetite languished and his thin face became thinner. He never smiled. His blond skin refused to compromise with the burning sun and winds; it turned lobster-colored and kept peeling.

Often now the caravan met Indians, but since they were Cheyennes and considered friendly there was no fighting. Otto regarded them coldly, wondering how he could have been so callow as to believe savages noble.

Once the caravan came upon a Cheyenne village and camped for a day and two nights. There were many barking dogs, the youngest and tenderest of which were presently roasted and eaten; there were yipping small boys and wrinkled old women; there were many braves and old Cheyenne politicians smoking the council pipe; and there were, of course, the giggling maidens. Otto's lips curled and he thought, "They are no better than Parisian whores." Only one girl interested him at all, perhaps because she noticed him, pointing at his hair and speaking some outlandish tongue and laughing. Recalling what Billy had told him, Otto said, in German, "*Ja*, it is blond, and maybe you like it. You are pretty enough but you have an awful smell. Maybe if you would bathe I would walk with you into the willows." The girl did not respond, for at that moment she glanced beyond Otto and gave a squeal of delight. Otto turned to see her greeting Caleb McSwasey, who fondled her like an old acquaintance. Otto stalked away, asking himself how any white man could be interested in an Indian girl. That night he lay under a wagon, sounds of wassail drifting to his ears. He thought how Billy Proudfoot had looked that morning lying with ants crawling over his body and buffalo-gnats swarming round his skull; he shuddered. He hated Indians, and if only he would have confessed it he feared them too. He was glad when the caravan moved on.

His life was empty. For years he had been ruled by the single purpose of reaching the wilderness and the savages, and all that striving had brought him something he despised. He felt lost and drifting, his spirit as barren and sun-shriveled as the plains. *Ja, ja*, he was truly a child of sorrows. At night in his blankets sleep refused to come, even though he ached from the saddle, so he fell into the habit of taking a nip of whiskey. Sometimes after a second or third drink he felt almost cheerful, and he told himself everything would come out all right after all; he pictured himself returning to Prussia with tales of his bravery as an Indian fighter. And his older brothers who used to bully him would say, "*Ach*, Otto, you have done better than any of us," and old Heinrich would listen spellbound as he told about tracking down and slaughtering the Comanches who had murdered Billy Proudfoot.

Opportunity to return east presented itself at last, when the caravan reached the foothills and camped where a trout stream tumbled whitely. From the Pass, following that stream down its canyon, two dozen men came into camp, bound from Taos to St. Louis. Some were Mexicans, some Indians, but mainly they were sinewy Americans in greasy buckskins and moccasins.

Otto could have joined that party. Theoretically, it would have been possible. They wouldn't have wanted him but they wouldn't have refused. His mule could have endured the return journey. He could have gone back.

But when he thought of the trail across endlessness, of the gnats and glare and heat and Pawnees and Comanches, he recoiled. Now that he had reached the mountains with the pines and cold sweet water and green grass he couldn't bring himself to leave. Yet even to his secret ego he would not admit that fear of Indians was chaining him to the caravan. So he rationalized. If he turned back, who could be trusted to look after the Proudfoot interests? Certainly not the mule skinners. McSwasey?

"He would skin old Proudfoot out of his teeth," Otto thought. "I cannot trust him. Billy is dead and all the responsibility for Proudfoot's goods is on me. My duty leads to Santa Fe."

And while some of this may have been true, it was actually only pretext. Otto was doing the right thing for the wrong reasons, just as he had often done the wrong thing for the right reasons.

That evening by firelight he wrote John Proudfoot, telling of Billy's death and announcing his determination to open a retail store in Santa Fe according to plan. "I believe this is what you would wish," he wrote, "and what poor Billy would wish. I miss him very much. He was the best friend I ever had. I watched over him like a brother, but alas! He slipped from camp while I was sleeping."

When the men in buckskins rode away next morning, they carried that letter. Otto watched them go. As they passed around a bend in the canyon, he realized the full implication of his decision to remain. He would remain forever, he thought with panic, prisoner of the vast wastes he could never bring himself to cross. He wanted to cry out for the horsemen to wait; he wanted to leap to his mule and gallop after them. He didn't. But that was what he should have done, on that summer morning in 1824.

*

Up from the plains, up the rutted canyon trail, up through the sweet smell of pines and the spicy smell of sage, up through the aspens which were showing an occasional yellow leaf, the caravan of heavy wagons and winded animals dragged itself, to the summit of the Pass; and from that eminence Otto Zumwalt, thin and heartsick, stared off at the Continental Divide. Those imperial mountain chains with their limitless forests staggered his brain.

"Plenty of beaver out there," the captain said.

"And Injuns," somebody added, "to lift a man's hair."

That night Otto stood guard over the sleeping camp, under the most brilliant stars he had ever seen. The cold air turned his breath to frost as he crunched back and forth, gripping his rifle, stopping now and then to listen, hearing the horses stamping and snorting, and the blanket-wrapped men sighing in slumber. Beyond the dying campfires the shadows under the pines fluttered and rustled with living things. Otto thought of Indians and his scalp tingled.

Once he heard footsteps and made out a man between himself and the red coals of a fire.

"Halt! Who goes there?"

"Friend."

McSwasey's voice.

"Advance and give the password."

After complying, McSwasey asked how the watch was going. Everything quiet, Otto said. He thought that probably McSwasey, as commander of the guard, was checking to make sure he was not asleep at his post. If so it was wasted energy, for falling asleep was the last thing Otto was likely to do, in Indian country.

They talked about such matters as the nippy mountain air, and then McSwasey said:

"You fooled me, Zumwalt. I thought you'd never stick it to Santa Fe."

"But why should you think that?"

"I thought you hated the trail, the way you've acted. I figured you'd go back east with that party from Taos."

"But it is my duty to go to Santa Fe. I am working for John Proudfoot. I could not go back on my agreement."

"You'll have a big advantage over the rest of us," McSwasey said quietly, "once we get to Santa Fe."

"But how is that?"

"You know Spanish."

"*Ja,* that is true."

"I reckon," McSwasey said, "that next to you I know more Spanish than anybody in this caravan. And I know twelve or fifteen words, at the most."

"How then do you do business?"

"Some of the greasers know a little American, so we make out. But it's not very satisfactory."

"*Ja,* I can see that."

"It works out fairly well in selling goods, but Spanish would help a man at the customhouse. You know, in making *diligencia.*"

"You mean bribery?"

"Yes. If a man knew Spanish he could make a better deal. That's where you'll have the jump on the rest of us."

"*Ja,* true, true."

In the darkness Otto squared his shoulders. McSwasey was a shadowy figure with his head forward, in that listening attitude of a deaf man. He said:

"Maybe you and I could make a deal, Zumwalt."

"So?"

"That's right. I could learn you the ropes of trading, and you could help me at the customhouse. When you dicker to get Proudfoot's goods through, you could get mine through too."

"*Ja,* that could be done," Otto said slowly.

"Shake," McSwasey said, extending his hand.

"Ja, shake."

When McSwasey spoke again, his voice was so quiet that Otto also stood with head forward, to catch the words.

"I see no reason for cutting in the rest of these traders on a deal like that. Do you?"

"No," Otto said, "I do not."

"Life's a fight, Zumwalt. If they don't know Spanish they shouldn't have started for Santa Fe. We'll have an advantage, with the collector of customs, and I say let's keep it. We might even sweeten him up with a little extra *diligencia,* if he'd agree to hold the rest of the goods in customs for a day or two."

"But why?"

"Don't you see, Zumwalt? Nobody can sell a thing till they're cleared by customs. Those greasers are hungry for American goods. If we're through first we can charge dearer prices. Even the skim milk is rich enough, in the Santa Fe trade, but the cream is richer." McSwasey's low voice had a lip-smacking quality, as if his tongue were dripping saliva. "Once we're out of customs, those greasers will crowd around our wagons there on the plaza, fighting to buy. Hell, we'll be sold out before any other trader is through customs."

"Ja, ja," Otto said, "you will be sold out. You have only one wagon. But I have two. Besides, John Proudfoot wants me to open a store already. I could not do that if I were sold out of goods. Proudfoot said with a store we could mark the goods higher next winter after the other traders have gone, and the profits would be better in the long run than if we sold from a wagon. And with a store we will be an established firm with regular customers."

"He's foxy," McSwasey said. "He looks sleepy and he's fat, but not in the head. Well, let's deal anyway, Zumwalt. You get me through customs first, and I'll cut you in on two percent of my profits."

It was Otto's moment. Not since leaving Missouri had he felt so fine.

"I want none of your profits," he said. "If I do what you wish it will be because you are my friend. But how can we be friends when all the time you are thinking I am a no-good loafer of a guard who permitted Billy Proudfoot to leave camp? I was asleep in my blankets when he left. He did not slip through my guard."

"Why Zumwalt," McSwasey murmured, "you know I never thought any such thing. I told the boys I knew Billy didn't get by you. I told them you're the best guard on my staff."

"You told them that?"

"Sure I did. I've always liked you since we met in Proudfoot's office. Anybody can see you're a good many cuts above the rest of us coyotes."

"Ja, ja," Otto agreed, with enthusiasm, "it is true I come of a noble family. My father is General Heinrich von Zumwalt. Myself, I am an artist and not used to the ways of trade. In Paris I was a famous painter.

Ja, sure, sure," he added magnanimously, "I will get your goods through ahead of the others. Anything for a friend. It has never been charged that Otto Zumwalt has failed a friend."

"Shake on it," McSwasey said.

"*Ja,* shake."

*

"So!" Otto told himself, after McSwasey had limped away. "So! Maybe I am not the best swimmer in the world and maybe that time the Pawnees attacked I did not kill as many as I might if I had had a decent gun. Maybe that Cheyenne girl liked red hair better than blond—I would not have slept with her anyway because she needed a bath—and maybe those *dummkopf* mule skinners made fun of me because my buckskins were new, but now they will laugh from the other side of their mouths. When I rattle off Spanish in Santa Fe and they know nothing of what to say except their filthy English they are going to be sorry they treated me so bad."

Rifle on shoulder, Otto marched furiously back and forth, smiling in the darkness.

"*Ja, ja,*" he thought, nodding his head, "even Mr. Smarty McSwasey with his lies about jumping through a hole in the ice is now my friend. He would not believe me when I told him Billy did not sneak through my guard. He went whispering behind my back and tried to get those cabbage-headed mule skinners to hang me maybe already, but now he sings a different song. *Ja,* sure, now he needs me and I showed him how a real aristocrat acts toward his friends."

For perhaps ten minutes Otto's exultation lasted, and he daydreamed of meeting some beautiful girl in Santa Fe, and every man in the caravan would be mad for this charmer, but without knowledge of Spanish they could only blush and gulp. But Otto—*ach,* Otto Zumwalt—would he blush and stammer? Not he! From his worldly tongue musical Spanish would flow, he would be courtly and masterful, and the lady would all but swoon into his strong arms. And certainly she wouldn't quibble about such trifles as whether he could swim. They would marry and go sailing back to Prussia—

Ja, but how would they get to a seaport? Only by crossing deserts and Indian country. This detail seriously interrupted Otto's honeymoon. He became aware of the darkness, alive with imaginary redskins, and he stood listening, gripping his rifle.

Toward midnight the moon rose, white and old, and the distant peaks glimmering in that pale light looked timeless and secretive. Somewhere down the mountain the moonlight touched off yearning and melancholy in a pack of coyotes; their yipping and wild hallooing was like an outcry from the great lonely soul of the West; and Otto hated the West. He was glad when the next watch relieved him.

Change came into the landscape when the caravan wended its way down from the Pass and out onto the rosy beige expanses of New Mexico. Color was everywhere. For days on end the sky was a miraculous turquoise, promising everything; mesas reared up boldly from the tawny plain, complex with shifting tints of mauve and peach and dark purple; the flanks of nearby hills were veined with sulphur-yellow and rich reddish brown; even the dust rising from the caravan shimmered at sunset in delicate tans and pinks. It was like living in a water color, and Otto's fingers would have ached for his brushes, if his impulse toward painting had ever been anything but a stray seed sprouting in the hothouse of his romanticism. As it was, he didn't even think of his palette. He rode his mule, bandaged in self-pity, blaming his New Orleans employers for giving him a letter to John Proudfoot, blaming Proudfoot for enticing him into this expedition, blaming McSwasey—who was the best friend he had in all the world, since Billy's death—for calling him a liar behind his back and urging that he be lynched, blaming the mule skinners for not using stronger arguments to convince him, back in Missouri, that the trail was long and hideous. At last he found refuge and comfort in resignation. That was the Slavic strain from his mother's mother, a pale Latvian girl whom Otto's wild grandfather, a soldier, poet, gentleman and cabbage connoisseur, had married to everybody's great regret, especially his own and his bride's.

"All is lost and hopeless," the Slav in Otto said.

"*Ja,* and it is all John Proudfoot's fault," the Prussian added.

"I will live and die in this alien land," the Slav said, "a plaything of destiny. New Mexico is my Siberia."

And the stalwart Prussian added:

"*Ja, wahr, wahr.* And that Proudfoot is the big pig who exiled me. I would like to Proudfoot him a kick in his fat hind end."

Although there were copious springs in this land, and clear streams from the mountains, the air remained arid, but it was not the depressing aridity of the buffalo plains. This was high plateau country, the air clean and light, a tonic to the lungs. The mules perked up their ears and regained their sense of comedy, more life came into the trail-weary horses, the mule skinners whistled at their chores, only Otto remained disconsolate.

And so day by day the caravan journeyed deeper into New Mexico, land of the cross and the *conquistadores,* of the banners of Spain and the horses of Spain, of Mendoza and the Seven Cities of Cíbola. This was the land of the sky stones, of the irrigated corn patch, of the lash and the arrow, of the Apache and the Pueblo, of the dry and bloody ground. And this was the land newly lost by Spain, to be ruled for a time by the manifestoes and pronunciamentos of a young and faintly comic Republic.

Sometimes the caravan kicked up the dust of a village, where from

74

mud houses dark eyes looked with wonder and trepidation upon this loud, creaking manifestation of free enterprise; upon the Yankee and the Kentuckian and the Missourian, those restless ones. The trail swung into the mountains again, after Rio Gallinas, following a pleasant open canyon where sheep and cattle grazed on the slopes among the piñons and cedars. The days were brilliant and matchless. Sometimes the caravan met a swarthy man in sombrero and sandals, leading a burro laden with faggots; sometimes it passed an adobe house with ducks waddling in the dooryard and goats bleating. Then at last came an evening when the camp busied itself with shaving and hair trimming; fresh clothes were unpacked; boots were polished and horses curried; mule skinners manicured their fingernails with pocketknives and yarned about fandangos. Tomorrow was the time; tomorrow would bring Santa Fe.

To the Proudfoot wagons that evening came Caleb McSwasey, cheeks razored clean, dark red hair slicked down.

"Could you spare me a minute?" he asked.

Otto followed him up the mountainside among the junipers, where they sat on a boulder. Through the crisp darkness they could see campfires flickering in the canyon below, and hear an accordion playing while the mule skinners sang:

> *I jumped on a mule and started west,*
> *Started west, started west,*
> *I jumped on a mule and started west,*
> *Bound for Santy Fee.*

> *The mule was neither horse nor mare,*
> *Horse nor mare, horse nor mare,*
> *The mule was neither horse nor mare,*
> *But he took me to Santy Fee.*

"Well," McSwasey said, "it's almost over. She's been a long slow trip, but on the whole a pretty good one. Except for losing Billy."

"That was not my fault. He did not slip through my guard."

"Nobody's blaming you, Otto."

"He was my best friend. When I saw him lying with those arrows in his back I was very sad."

"Nobody's blaming you."

"Once he said maybe he should dye his hair red because the Spanish girls like red hair. When I saw his head all red with blood I thought of that. I have a strong stomach, but it made me sick."

"Better to forget it," McSwasey said.

"*Ja,* better. But he was my best friend and sometimes I dream about it. Do you think the cowardly wolves dug open his grave?"

"A man had best not think about such things," McSwasey said. "I remember how it was with me after the battle at New Orleans. Old Hickory ordered the crack riflemen to take position right behind the cotton bales. Don't know how I got into that front line."

"But you are a good shot. I saw you kill a Pawnee."

"Injuns don't count. But a white man is something else. Lord, I can remember how it was. The British came marching like they were on parade. Our boys were from Kentucky and Tennessee and had fought Injun style since they could hold a gun. I got a bead on a kid who didn't look sixteen. He had rosy cheeks. I drilled him. And you know, I always remembered how he looked. So damned surprised. I used to think about it when I was going to sleep. That surprised look. I reckon it's hard to die young."

"The British in any case are a pack of cowardly hyenas," Otto said.

"Maybe they are. But not the ones we fought at New Orleans."

"Have you killed many men?"

"Injuns, of course. I had to kill a nigger once too."

"I mean white men."

"I reckon so, in battle. You can't always be sure. Too much smoke. Once in a duel I killed a man."

"A duel! *Ja,* I too have fought duels. A man of honor must fight many duels."

"This wasn't exactly honor. It was about a girl. And she wasn't worth it. I was jealous, of course. Jealousy is one of my faults. It's got me into a lot of trouble. But the other fellow was the one who challenged."

"You fought with sabers?"

"Oh, no. Hell, no. Pistols."

"I too killed my man," Otto said. "But with a saber. I ran him through. Like that. Right through the belly button."

"Is jealousy one of your faults too?"

"*Ja, ja,* I can be a jealous fiend. A girl was involved between us, but she was only a little peasant barmaid not fit to lick our boots. After I had avenged my honor I fled to Paris and never saw her again."

"You'll never guess what I did."

"No?"

"After the duel the girl eloped with a third man. So I bought me a nigger gal."

"A black nigger?"

"Not so black. Matter of fact, not black at all. Color of coffee with cream."

"You mean," Otto said, *"café au lait."*

"Do I? Well, anyway, I bought her."

"Ja?"

"And I paid a fancy price."

"So," Otto said, "you owned her good all for yourself. What did you do with her?"

"What do you suppose?"

"I mean, how did you dispose of her?"

"Sold her, in St. Louis. To a Frenchman."

"*Ach,* the French. They are a pack of cowards."

"Are they?"

"Oh, *ja,* sure. And their women are all whores already and diseased also."

"And I used the Frenchman's money to buy me a wagon and mules. Thought I'd settle down to a legitimate business. So I took to the Santa Fe Trail. A funny way to settle down, when you come to think of it."

From down in the canyon the singing drifted:

> *I found me a gal in Santy Fee,*
> *In Santy Fee, in Santy Fee,*
> *I found me a gal in Santy Fee,*
> *Pure as the driven snow.*

"Didn't know they came that way, in Santa Fe," McSwasey said.

"I have heard the girls there are very beautiful," Otto said.

"They are. All of them. In the dark. Well, tomorrow's the day. Is it still a deal you'll get me through customs first?"

"*Ja,* sure. You and I will be first through. I said I would and I will. My word is as good as gold."

"Most men's ain't."

"*Ja,* they are awful liars, most men."

"When we get there tomorrow, the fellow to look for at the customhouse is the collector. He's a short fat fellow—I can't place his name— but he's the key man. He handles everything for the governor."

"I will attend to it all."

"I've been thinking over what you said about opening a store," McSwasey said. "It's a good idea, of course, to get established and build up customers, but on the other hand if you'd sell from your wagons on the street you'd do a whiz of a business."

"*Ja,* but with me it is a delicate matter. I am a *Junker* and it is shameful enough I should go into trade. In a store maybe with some dignity, *ja,* but selling from a wagon to a pack of cowardly peasants, no. I will open a store. That will be more fitting for a man of my position. But I will get your wagon through right along with mine."

"Well, I'll be in your debt," McSwasey said. He stood up. "Shake on it."

"*Ja,* shake."

They picked their way down the mountain, the singing growing louder:

> *She fed me corn and she fed me beans,*
> *Fed me beans, fed me beans,*

77

She fed me corn and she fed me beans,
Till I left old Santy Fee.

"See you in the morning," McSwasey said.

Long after Otto had gone to his blankets the singing continued; there was whooping too, and laughter. Otto lay thinking about that liar, McSwasey, how back in Missouri he had said he doubted whether he had killed anybody in the battle at New Orleans because he was too scared, and how tonight he claimed to have killed a boy with rosy cheeks. "He is nothing but a big liar," Otto thought, "and probably a coward as well. I do not believe he ever fought a duel any more than I did. If he were not my best friend I would tell him so too, right to his freckled face."

Otto twisted and tossed, finally getting up and swallowing a jolt of whiskey. In his blankets again he thought of Billy Proudfoot, wondering whether he was in his grave tonight, at peace with God, or whether the wolves had dug him out. Perhaps his ghost was here now, mournful because his poor bones lay far away on the plains. At last the camp quieted and Otto slept, deeply and dreamlessly, in the cold mountain air.

He wakened to a flawless morning, the camp already astir. After breakfast, for the last time, the captain called, "Catch up! Catch up!" The mule skinners raced for the livestock; soon came the cry, "All set! All set for Santy Fee!"

"Stretch out!"

The wagons lumbered into position.

"Fall in! Fall in, for Santy Fee!"

And so presently, in the brilliant sunshine under a bright sky, the long caravan with its pillar of rosy dust, with its creaking wheels and jingling bells and cracking whips, jolted out of the mountains and down across the lion-colored tableland to the Royal City of the Holy Faith of St. Francis of Assisi; to trail's end, to the city of destiny, where the houses were golden-beige adobe with blue-painted doors to scare away evil spirits; where fruit trees grew in sideyards; where chickens fled squawking; where ragged dogs were barking and ragged urchins shouting; and where, just as Billy Proudfoot had predicted, bare-legged girls in low blouses waved handkerchiefs and called musically, *"Los Americanos! Los Americanos!"*

✳

During the next hours in the Royal City of Santa Fe—which was no longer royal and had never been of city size—Otto cheered up. It wasn't his fault; he tried not to; but the place was too much for him. The thin air was heady, the lavish sunlight an elixir. In that altitude his lungs cried out for oxygen, so he breathed more deeply; his blood

78

flowed faster. But it was something more that banished his gloom.

It was the lighthearted spirit of the town, reminding him a little of Paris and New Orleans; it was the dark grogshops where the renowned Taos Lightning was served; it was the less potent but still ardent *tequila;* and it was the sunny *plaza publica* with the flag of Mexico above the governor's palace, and the sweet tones of the cathedral bells, and the crowds around the monte games on the sidewalks, and the girls with willing eyes. Otto's new-found authority also cheered him.

After being a timid lad in Prussia, a vagabond in Paris, a minor clerk in New Orleans and a faint-hearted nobody on the trail, he discovered that in Santa Fe, as factor for the important firm of Proudfoot & Sons, he was treated with deference. A little deference went a long way with him; it roused the arrogance in his blood; he squared his shoulders. What raised his spirits most, however, was his advantage as a linguist. Even the other merchants, who had ignored him all the way from Missouri, became friendly and asked his help, when they saw how his Spanish obtained the release from customs of the McSwasey and Proudfoot wagons.

As soon as the caravan rumbled across the plaza to the customhouse, Otto learned that knowledge of Spanish was indeed power, in Santa Fe; for of all those merchants and adventurers he alone could put together a fluent sentence and deal in the equivocal shadings of phraseology so soothing to the self-respect of officials trafficking in *diligencia.* Scarcely had he dismounted from his mule, there at customs, before he received a wink from McSwasey, who indicated a plump brown bean of a man with noble mustachios and eloquent eyes who wore that complacent air of authority peculiar to medium grade bureaucrats. Otto went over to the fellow, clicked his heels and bowed.

"Excellency," he said, "a thousand pardons, but is it my honor to address the Collector of Customs of the Royal City of the Holy Faith of St. Francis of Assisi?"

"It is, *señor*. But the honor is mine and the pleasure this gives me is boundless."

"I am enchanted beyond measure," Otto said, "to encounter a civilized gentleman in this civilized and beautiful city after so many weeks in the company of the *Americano* pigs."

"You are not an *Americano, señor?*"

"I am a Prussian, Excellency. The son of General Heinrich von Zumwalt, at your service."

"*Señor.* I am transported. Major Manuel Delgado, at your command."

He bowed, gave Otto an *abrazo,* bowed again. And he said:

"If I may ask it, *señor,* how is it that a *caballero* finds himself in such a company?"

His pudgy brown hand gestured toward the wagons.

Otto thought fast.

"It is my *wanderjahr,* Excellency. I set out to see the world. Paris, New Orleans—"

"Madrid, perhaps?"

Since Otto had never visited Madrid, his impulse was to say he had, but he decided to remain on safe ground.

"Sadly, no. But I hope to visit the cafes of Mexico."

"Ah, *señor,*" murmured Major Manuel Delgado.

"In St. Louis, friends introduced me to Mr. John Proudfoot. I arranged to travel by this route to Mexico, with his son. But a sad thing occurred. His son fell victim to the savages."

"Ah, sad," said Major Delgado. "One's heart bleeds."

"So I find myself saddled with the responsibilities of business."

Otto grimaced; Major Delgado shuddered sympathetically.

"If I can be of service," he murmured richly.

"Now that you speak of it, Excellency, there is a trifling matter. Could I persuade you to join me in a dram?"

The major's reply, boiled down, was that he had never been known to refuse.

"Excellency," Otto said, "with your permission I shall invite a friend to join us. *Señor* Caleb McSwasey."

"By all means."

Otto signaled McSwasey. At his approach, Major Delgado's eyes lighted.

"But I know this *caballero,*" he said, "from his visit to us last year. *Señor.* This is a delight."

He bowed, gave McSwasey an *abrazo,* bowed again.

"What did he say, Otto?" McSwasey asked, in English.

"He's glad to see you."

"Tell him I'm glad too."

"*Señor* McSwasey," Otto said, "presents his compliments and wishes you to know, Excellency, that he is overcome with pleasure."

By now several merchants from the caravan were clamoring in English for attention.

"What is it they say?" Major Delgado asked Otto.

It was then Otto fully realized the power he enjoyed by knowing both languages.

"They are in a great hurry and are demanding that you push them through customs at once."

Major Delgado's eyes turned cold.

"Tell the donkeys I am not a bale of hay to be brayed at."

"He says," Otto told the merchants, "that you do not seem very eager to get your goods through. I believe him to be hard of hearing. You must speak louder."

The traders began shouting.

80

"In the name of Christ on Calvary," the major said, "tell the jackasses to stop."

"He says," Otto told the merchants, "that he does not believe you have enough money to pay customs duties. If you show him your money he will see that you get action."

Still other merchants had arrived now, and all joined in the uproar. Some held up American gold pieces, and those who knew a little Spanish were calling, *"Diligencia, diligencia!"*

"Mother of God," the major exclaimed. "Do the fools want to ruin an honest man's reputation? Shut up, you coyotes, or I will order you locked in the pillory on the plaza."

It was then that Caleb McSwasey, smiling broadly, lifted an arm.

"Take it easy, boys. The major wants a drink before he talks business. Leave everything to us."

Flanked by McSwasey and Otto, moving with dignity, his belly floating before him like a captive balloon, resplendent in his martial uniform, Major Manuel Delgado waddled along the *portales* of the plaza and turned in at a *cantina*. The floor was earthen, the adobe walls uneven and stained. At the crude bar, when *tequila* was served, Otto lifted his glass.

"To our mutual success and prosperity, in all our business dealings."

The major smiled, the brown fat of his face nearly slitting shut his eyes.

"Si, to our mutual prosperity."

"Good luck," McSwasey said. It was the toast of mountain men and of the trail.

At the importing house in New Orleans, Otto had learned the amenities of Spanish commercial life, so now he kept a flow of small talk going.

"It is admirable," he said, sipping his *tequila,* "that you are an officer of the distinguished army of the great Republic of Mexico. I too come from a military family."

"Ah, *si, si.* It is a brave life."

"It happens my father is General Heinrich von Zumwalt."

"So you said, *señor.* Alas, I am not so fortunate in my ancestry. I was born of the *pobre* and was obliged to make my own way."

Otto thought, "He is nothing then but a peasant." He said:

"The more then you honor yourself by achieving so high a rank."

"Gracias, señor. Would you believe it? I was born in Santa Fe and as a poor lad I herded sheep in the mountains. But I was ambitious. I was only eleven when I made my way to the City of Mexico with a caravan. I knew nobody there and it was not easy for a boy of that age to maintain himself. But I survived. I even prospered."

"Let us have another *tequila,"* Otto said, "and drink to your continuing prosperity."

"That is an agreeable suggestion."

"Good luck," McSwasey said, when the drinks were poured.

81

"At what age," Otto asked, "did you take up the sword?"

"Not at an early age, *señor*. I maintained myself by dabbling in various interesting affairs till I was thirty-three. Then came the sixteenth of September, 1810. On that bloody Sunday the terrible revolution of Hidalgo and Allende was begun. Well do I remember that morning. The revolution broke out in the town of Dolores, and I was there. I was a patriot, so naturally I did not join. I hurried to Mexico City and placed my life at the disposal of General Trujillo. He was pleased to commission me a captain, and I do not believe he ever had cause to regret it."

"I am sure not, Excellency."

"I was wounded at the Mountain of the Crosses. Alas, during the remainder of the revolution I could not serve in the field. But when my wound healed I served with honesty and industry in Mexico City. It is a charming place. One never lacks for pleasures in Mexico. After the revolution was crushed, I stayed on in the army. Then in 1817 the treacherous Mina arrived in the country and the revolution broke out anew. I served with distinction at San Miguel. It was I who tracked down the rascal Mina's second in command and killed him. In reward I was made a major and given the customs post at Santa Fe."

"My father too has slain many rascals," Otto said. "And I have often acquitted myself with valor on the field of personal honor."

"But although I was anti-revolutionary," the major said, "do not think my heart did not go out to the *pobre*. I am a humanitarian."

"I am too, so am I," Otto said.

"And although I served with the loyalists in 1810 and 1817, do not think I did not welcome the blessings brought by the great revolution of 1821. That was another matter entirely."

"It was successful?"

"Gloriously so. Ah, the great Agustín de Iturbide! What a leader! What a savior of the masses! It is too bad he became such a bad emperor and had to be exiled. And it is sad he returned to the country and had to be shot. But as a patriot I am convinced it was all for the best. *Viva Mexico!*"

"*Viva Mexico!*" Otto and McSwasey said.

"*Dios y Libertad!*"

"*Dios y Libertad!*"

"My stomach would welcome another *tequila*," the major said.

"Mine also," Otto said.

It was during their third drink when business chanced to intrude itself into the conversation, and once this had happened there was nothing to do but deal with it, although Otto as an aristocrat and the major as a patriot both exhibited an admirable delicacy in the discussion. The major declared it pained him beyond measure to collect customs duties from *Señors* Zumwalt and McSwasey, both upholders of *Dios y Libertad,* and Otto suggested that the major, as a man of the world and a friend of

God and Liberty, might be able to think of another way to handle the matter. One thing led to another; McSwasey offered pertinent suggestions; and by the time their fourth *tequilas* had been swallowed everything was arranged on terms satisfactory to themselves, tolerably satisfactory to the government, and not at all satisfactory to the other traders, whose wagons would be ordered to the camp at the edge of town and whose merchandise would be impounded till tomorrow.

"*Caballeros*," said Major Delgado, "you may rely upon me. Your goods shall be cleared immediately."

And they were, back at the customhouse, after a proper number of gold coins passed into the hands of Major Delgado. It was then that the other merchants implored Otto's help.

"No," he snapped, "I can do nothing. The collector is putting the goods through alphabetically."

"But your name begins with Z, and you're first through."

"*Ja.* He is beginning at the end of the alphabet."

With that he about-faced and marched away, spine like a poker. Old Heinrich would have been proud of him.

*

In one of the Proudfoot wagons a strongbox had traveled from the States, containing Otto's savings and a larger sum belonging to Proudfoot & Sons. After Major Delgado had been paid, a considerable amount remained, and Otto fretted about its safety. Thus far it had been safe enough, with the mule skinners to protect it; but now that the Proudfoot merchandise had cleared customs the mule skinners were impatient to visit the grogshops; they would carouse all night; and Otto disliked guarding that money in the camp at the edge of town. He decided to ask McSwasey's advice.

But McSwasey was hard to reach, now that his goods were cleared, for he was making the most of his advantage over the other traders. While they fumed, he had started doing business on the plaza; Otto saw him standing on the tailgate of his wagon, auctioning a bolt of calico. Presently the high bidder, probably a storekeeper from some village, made his way through the crowd and paid for his purchase.

Otto edged into that crowd, with its reek of unbathed bodies and garlic, glad indeed that he had decided against selling goods this way; he disliked associating with the common run of humanity.

"Please," he commanded sharply, "let me pass."

As he elbowed and squeezed, women stared at him curiously over the *rebozos* partly covering their faces. Then McSwasey held up another bolt of goods and bidding began; Otto was jostled in a trap of bodies, pressed by hips and bosoms. Smoke from somebody's corn-shuck cigarette drifted past his nostrils; a sombrero, embroidered with silver, brushed his cheek; a boot crushed his toes. He was outraged. Then he had an idea.

"In the name of Major Delgado," he commanded, "make way. I am sent by Major Delgado."

Magically, a path opened.

"From Major Delgado," people murmured. "A messenger from Major Delgado."

Shoulders squared, Otto marched to the wagon, where the sale had been concluded.

"What's the trouble?" McSwasey asked, squatting so they could speak confidentially. His work as auctioneer in the dazzling sunshine had flushed his face.

"What am I to do with my strongbox?" Otto whispered.

McSwasey stared off across the crowd. His hair was rumpled and sweat-globules hung from his red eyebrows.

"You might leave it with Hod Kite."

"Who is he?"

"He owns that saloon over there. He's from the States by way of Texas. I've never heard of him touching a cent anybody left in his safe."

"Is there no bank?"

"This isn't St. Louis."

"You think my money will be safe with him?"

"I use a money belt."

"But I have no money belt."

"I've got an extra one you could use."

Otto imagined himself attacked by thugs, and he said hastily:

"No, no, I do not like a money belt."

"Then Hod is your best bet. Tell him I sent you."

"And he is honest?"

"I never like to pass on another man's honesty, but next to a money belt he's your best bet."

"Thank you, I will hunt up this Hod. Will I see you later today?"

"It ain't unlikely. I understand Hod is throwing a fandango tonight, and I might drop in to listen to the music."

Otto faced the crowd.

"In the name of Major Delgado—"

At the wagons, when he wrapped the strongbox in a blanket, one mule skinner asked:

"What do you aim to do with it?"

"I shall leave it with Mr. Hod Kite."

"Well, now, that there is a good idea. I hear tell Hod used to be in the banking business, back in Pennsylvania, before he went to Texas for his lungs."

"A consumptive?"

"Naw, I hear tell he was plumb afraid of gitting bullets in them lungs of his. Seems he was in the wrong end of the banking business. The robbing end. But he turned honest in Texas, so they say. A right peculiar place to turn honest."

A bank robber! *Mein Gott!* But then Otto told himself the mule skinners were all big liars. McSwasey had recommended Hod. With the box under his arm he crossed the plaza to Kite's Saloon. It was a huge place, its floor hardpacked earth, like nearly every floor in town, its gambling tables busy, its proprietor a cheerful little man with a gray-fringed bald head. "That lying mule skinner," Otto thought, "trying to bamboozle me into believing this mouse a bank robber!" When the safe door closed on the strongbox he felt relieved, and at the bar he ordered his first drink of Taos Lightning.

"Have one with me, *Herr* Kite," he said.

"No, Sport, I'm a temperance man. A preacher converted me in Arkansas Territory. Every time I serve you I shorten your life by five minutes. Now I've done my duty so here's your drink."

"Your health," Otto said.

"Thanks, Sport. I'll remember you in my will. So Caleb McSwasey sent you. How is Caleb?"

"Well and prosperous."

"Now ain't that fine. A prince of a fellow. A quiet prince."

"You have known him long?"

"A dozen years, off and on. I met him first back in Maryland. We were both out to see the world, for reasons of our own. So we throwed in together and went to Virginia on a little deal in niggers. Turned out very nice too. Must have been about four years after that when our trails crossed in Texas. That was in Nacogdoches. Caleb had been mixed up in something over in the States, and he was cooling off."

"A duel, perhaps?"

"No, it warn't no duel. Kind of seems niggers was mixed up in it, but I ain't sure. Nothing serious. One of them kettles of trouble any young fellow will get into."

"Was that when he owned the nigger girl?"

"Ha! He told you about that? No, he didn't have the gal that first time. It was later when he came to Nacogdoches with the gal. I was running a place there. Not a layout like this, you understand, just a hole in the wall."

"Was the girl beautiful?" Otto asked.

"Yes, sir, Sport, that gal was all right. I wouldn't have scolded if I'd won her myself. But some old planter won her at cards, and I reckon you've heard what happened. Late that night she lifted the planter's bankroll and met Caleb in my place. They were on their horses and over the Sabine before the planter ever woke up. Caleb stayed out of Texas, after that. When he turned up here in Santa Fe we had many a laugh about the old days."

"He said you were friends and my money would be safe with you."

85

"Safe as in a bank, Sport."

Otto ordered a refill.

"Five more minutes chopped off," Hod said.

Taos Lightning, Otto thought, deserved its reputation. As he stood there with his vitals glowing, watching the heads of pretty girls passing the windows, remembering how McSwasey was now in his debt and how he had struck up an acquaintance with a consequential official like Major Delgado, he felt a man among men, a far-wandering adventurer, and he thought that perhaps after all this royal old capital, a thousand miles from anywhere, was worth the journey across those dreadful plains.

"I shot a buffalo in Comanche country," he heard himself saying.

"Yeah, but did you shoot a Comanche?"

"Five. *Ein, zwei, drei—*" He counted them off on his fingers. "They killed the best friend I ever had. But I got even. And now McSwasey is my best friend."

"Don't ever get him jealous," Hod was saying, his voice sounding muffled and distant. "He likes the ladies awful well, so don't go tickling his women."

"He is an expert swimmer too. Like me. Once I saved my brother Fritz from drowning. *Ja,* it was nothing. Fill my glass, *bitte. Gracias, señor.* What tongue are we employing, *Herr* Kite?"

Hod's bald head had a white gleam.

"Taos Lightning," Otto heard him saying. "The only lightning that strikes twice in the same spot. Five more minutes. It eats the lining right off your kidneys. You know that, don't you?"

Otto drew himself up.

"We will not discuss my kidneys, *bitte.* Once I ran a man through with a saber. I too can be a jealous fiend. It was an affair of honor. I fled to Paris and since then I have been an exile. I am a famous painter also."

"You won't find much of that work out here, Sport. You take this adobe, it don't demand paint like them houses back east."

"And now I am a merchant. What you call a merchant prince. My father is a general. *Ja.*"

"Mine shot a general, in '79. Least he always claimed to."

"And in New Orleans," Otto said, "I lived the life of a gentleman. I had an estate on the sugar coast with fifty niggers. And a house in town."

"Say, Sport, tell me about them Creole girls. Are they as lively as I've heard?"

Otto pointed at his empty glass.

"Attend, *bitte.* Then I will tell you about your Creole girls. I knew them all."

*

He was waking and he didn't want to. Something told him returning consciousness would only bring problems. He was lying on his back with a forearm across his eyes, his tongue feeling swollen and his throat parched. He didn't know where he was and he preferred not finding out quite yet.

He dozed; but then the darkness started whirling. To stop that he opened his eyes; he saw gray boards. Then he knew where he was. He was lying under a wagon in the camp on the outskirts of Santa Fe. Bit by bit he recalled incidents of the night before, and he thought, "*Mein Gott!*"

In memory a fandango was going full blast in Kite's Saloon. The gambling tables had been shoved aside, and on the earthen floor people were dancing to the music of fiddle and guitar. Candles flamed in wrought-iron brackets stuck into the adobe walls, and in the soft light mule skinners and trappers and traders and the brown Mexican men of Santa Fe were waltzing with eight-year-old girls and with fifteen-year-old girls and with handsome young matrons and plump older matrons and toothless grandmothers. The *Americanos* yelled Woo-yoo-yoo and Waugh!

It was all smoke and flakes of color in Otto's memory, but then everything snapped into sharpness as he saw himself crossing the *sala* to a bench along the wall where Major Manuel Delgado stood drinking *tequila*.

"Ah, *Señor* Zumwalt. You must meet my family."

He made fluent and elaborate introductions. Otto clicked his heels and bowed over the hands of the ladies.

One hand was dry skin and bones like a bird's claw. It was attached to a wasted forearm which was attached to an old body as ugly and twisted as a tree at timberline. The thin white hair scarcely covered a dark old skull; the nose was thin and hooked; the mouth showed three teeth as yellow as the fangs of an old she-wolf; the eyes were black and evil.

That was Major Delgado's mother.

His wife was a mass of brown fat, his daughters the same. Then he presented his niece, *Señorita* Consuelo Delgado. Otto's lips touched the back of a slender warm hand, the skin olive smooth. When he lifted his head he saw a young brown face with high cheekbones and dark brows above eyes as black as a blackbird's wing. The hair was also black, drawn back to reveal exquisite ears with cheap glass earrings. In her hair were several combs glittering with brilliants. She wore a scarlet skirt, a black blouse cut low to display charms which were not present in any abundance, and a scarlet *rebozo* draped over her shoulders. When she arose to accept Otto's invitation to dance, he saw that her waist was almost too slender, as if she were underfed. Then he noticed her feet. They were long and slim, without stockings or shoes. He felt oddly shocked and disdainful. Santa Fe! A thousand miles from anywhere and ten thousand miles from civilization. He told himself it should be easy to seduce a girl dressed so skimpily.

They danced, and it was like dancing with a girl of wind.

"Señorita," he said, "permit me to say you are light on your feet."

She murmured something. It might have been, "*Gracias, señor.*"

She did not smile.

"You are *triste* tonight?" he asked.

Her shoulders moved in a faint shrug.

"Do you never smile?"

"Is it so important, to smile?"

The music from fiddle and guitar was thin and sad as night wind blowing from a mesa through the wheel spokes of an abandoned wagon. The fandango was a shifting mass of tight leather trousers with silver buttons, of bare shoulders and whirling bright skirts. Otto glimpsed Caleb McSwasey smiling as he whispered to his dancing partner, a beauty with high-piled hair and a voluptuous body. Americans kept yelling and dancing so enthusiastically that they jostled Otto.

"They are pigs, the *Americanos,*" he said.

"You are not an *Americano, señor?*"

"I am a Prussian."

"And what is that?"

"Certainly you must have read of the brave deeds of the great Prussian race."

"But I cannot read, *señor.*"

Her dark eyes were unfathomable in her thin sad face.

"You cannot read? You do not know your letters already?"

"Naturally not, *señor.*"

Ignorant! Otto experienced a vast superiority. It roused his concupiscence.

"Please," she said, "you are hurting my fingers," and he realized that in his passion he had been gripping her hand hard.

"I will tell you about the Prussians," he said, there in the crush of the fandango. "They are the greatest race in Europe and in all the world."

"Europe, *señor?* Is that in Spain?"

"*Gott im Himmel,* no, no. The Prussians live in their own land with their own king. My father is a general in the Prussian army."

"Does he fight?"

"Fight! He has done nothing but fight all his life. He still carries a ball near his heart. My father is a warrior. *Ja.*"

"My uncle Manuel is a major. Is a general better than that?"

"A major! Bah! A major in Prussia does nothing but exercise a general's dog."

Otto had nearly stopped dancing, so absorbed was he in teaching geography and militarism; and now a drunken mule skinner, dancing acrobatically, bumped into him.

"Pig," Otto muttered. "They are all pigs, the *Americanos*."

"They are strange and wild, *señor*. Their ways are not ours."

"Pigs and pig-dogs. Cowardly pigs."

"I do not believe them to be cowards, *señor*. But they are most strange."

Otto guided Consuelo Delgado toward the bar.

"Taos Lightning," he told Hod Kite. "Two, *bitte*."

"Coming up, Sport. Lightning forked."

They drank.

"*Tequila* I have tasted," she said, "but never this. It is as hot as a little yellow pepper."

"It will make you smile."

She placed her empty glass on the bar.

"If you wish it," she said, "I will smile."

Hot and mysterious, her black eyes met his. Then she smiled. The effect was radiant, although her front teeth were stained and her wide mouth showed several back teeth missing.

"*Señorita*, you are lovely!" Otto turned to the bar. "Two more, *bitte*."

"Sport, I can't make 'em more bitter than they are. Two coming up. Forked lightning strikes twice."

The music was playing again and the Americans were noisier. Otto had another glimpse of Caleb McSwasey, still dancing with the full-bodied girl. She was dressed with even less modesty than Consuelo, wearing only a thin chemise above her waist and a carelessly draped *rebozo* permitting a fine view of her rich bosom. Her flowered skirt was short. She did, however, wear low black slippers. As Otto watched, a brown young man with greased black hair touched McSwasey's arm. McSwasey shook him off and with the girl in his arms danced deeper into the throng.

From her skirt pocket Consuelo Delgado produced a pouch of tobacco and a slip of corn shuck. Dexterously, her fingers rolled a cigarette, her tongue licking the edge. When the ends were pinched, she brought out a roll of raw cotton, slim as a goosequill, bound with calico and projecting from a short tin tube. With flint and steel she struck fire to the cotton and lighted the cigarette. Then she drew the cotton into the tube and held her forefinger over the end till the flame went out. Smoke came from her mouth and nostrils.

"The *señorita* plays with fire," Otto said.

"Also the *señor*," she replied.

*

They were dancing again and the fandango was quite mad now, the air thick with smoke from cigarettes and candles. More *Americanos* had arrived and the whooping was continuous. One mule skinner was jigging, and every now and then he leaped high and kicked his boots together, yelling like a Comanche. Another was dancing alone, arms placed as if he were embracing a partner, being the life of the party. Otto thought the whole town must have turned out for the fandango, everybody drinking and packing the floor of the brown-walled room. The air smelled of whiskey and chewing tobacco and bodies and cheap perfume. Sometimes the boots of other dancers kicked Otto's heels and their elbows struck his ribs. His dislike of crowds prevented him from enjoying dancing, and when he observed a group of Mexican young bloods conferring in a corner, eyes angry, his caution warned him that perhaps trouble was gathering; he had heard tales of fandangos ending in free-for-alls. So once more he guided Consuelo to the bar.

It was thronged with men who kept yelling for Taos Lightning. Otto yelled too. Hod Kite and two helpers were working frantically, but they couldn't keep pace with the demand. Men were always slamming down coins and roaring, "Lightning! God damn it, Hod, I'm parched." Only occasionally could Otto hear the music through all that uproar.

At last they were served.

"Why did you say," Otto asked, "that I also play with fire?"

Her smile was genuine now.

"You have insulted my aunt Natalia and my fat cousins and my grandmother as well."

"I do not understand."

"The custom of our country demands that first you should have danced with my grandmother and next with my aunt Natalia. After that with either me or my cousins. Probably with my cousins first, because they are rich and I am poor."

"I had no wish to dance with your grandmother."

"She is a witch," Consuelo said. "Half locoweed and half tarantula. I think she is a witch who will never die."

"You cannot mean she is an actual witch who bargains with the devil."

Consuelo shrugged.

"Who can say? She has knowledge of many obscure matters. She is a *curandera*."

"And what is that?"

"An herb woman. Since I was a child I have gone with her to the mountains to gather roots to remedy the sick. She has many secrets. When a baby gets itself born my grandmother assists."

"I have been treated by many famous doctors myself," Otto said. "In Paris and New Orleans. Does your grandmother practice phlebotomy?"

"Who can say? She is an old wasp who does not buzz her secrets."

"A phlebotomy," Otto said, "is the letting of blood to rid the veins of disease. It is practiced by famous scientists in the capitals of the world. I have known many of these great men."

"I do not believe my grandmother does that."

"In any case," Otto said, "I had no wish to dance with your cowardly grandmother."

"Oh, but she is not a coward, *señor*. She is perhaps a little touched in her head, but she is fearless as a rattlesnake."

"Nor did I wish to dance with your fat cousins or your aunt."

Consuelo giggled.

"My aunt is cursed with a certain itch. It is deliciously scandalous. She cannot keep her fingers away from young men. And best she likes young men like you, with skin and hair the color of a wheat field at harvest. Hair like yours is sufficiently rare with us, *señor*. My aunt sits against the wall like a she-goat in season while we dance. My poor uncle. He has horns—this long."

Consuelo placed wrists against her temples, forefingers extended. Then she rolled a cigarette.

"Do you not smoke, *señor?*"

"*Ja,* of course. In New Orleans I smoked the best cigars from Havana."

"Then this is for you."

She put the cigarette between his lips and gave him fire. The smoke tasted sweet. Consuelo rolled another.

"Your fingers are clever, *señorita.*"

"Sufficiently so."

"It is too bad you cannot read."

"But I have no need of such an accomplishment."

"Does your grandmother read?"

"Naturally not."

"Then how did she learn her magic?"

"From her mother. And from the Indians."

"Indians! *Ja!* I have killed many Indians in my time."

"When my grandmother was a woman in her twenties," Consuelo said, "the Apaches raided Santa Fe. They came not to kill but only to steal horses and grain and women. It was the way of the fierce Apaches to allow the people of Santa Fe to live so they would raise food and breed horses which could be stolen. When they wished to carry away my grandmother Jesus objected so of course they had to kill him."

"Jesus?"

"*Sí,* Jesus Delgado. He was my grandmother's husband, and in the nature of the matter he objected. So what could they do but kill him? They carried off my grandmother and she learned much Indian medicine. After two years she put together a charm which helped her escape and return to Santa Fe. I have seen the charm, *señor*. It was a wooden Saint Anthony, carved and painted by my grandmother's very fingers. It also had symbols of the Apache gods which I could not understand. But it was a powerful charm. It took her safely across the desert."

Otto smiled.

"*Señor,* you must not make fun. It was a charm so powerful that it even protected my uncle Manuel while my grandmother was a captive. He was not yet a major or a collector of customs then, but only a boy of eight. After my grandmother was stolen he greatly feared being sold into slavery. So he fled to the mountains and found refuge with a sheepherder who tended the flocks of a rich *caballero*. And although the charm had not yet been put together it was already in my grandmother's mind, so it protected my uncle."

"Does your uncle read?"

"Of course, *señor*. In his work at the customhouse, naturally. My grandmother says he was always sharp as a prickly pear. And a schemer like a coyote. When he was a boy herding sheep he would sometimes separate a few sheep from the flock into a flock he called his own. After a while he drove the small flock to a distant village and sold them. This gave him his start in the world."

Consuelo snuffed out her cigarette. Otto considered ordering more drinks, but perhaps lightning had struck often enough: his feet and hands were tingling, and the fandango was a blur of whirling red and yellow skirts. The din was awful.

"Now I am ready to dance again," Consuelo said.

Otto clicked his heels and bowed. She rewarded him with a dazzling smile. They moved toward the dancing, then stopped.

"Mein Gott," he said, "what sort of monkey business is this?"

Out among the dancers some kind of eruption was taking place. It seemed to be centering around Caleb McSwasey and the full-bodied girl. Otto caught sight of the Mexican young bloods he had noticed earlier; he saw McSwasey landing a fist blow. Knives flashed in the candleshine; women screamed. At the bar the mule skinners and trappers let loose with warwhoops and charged into the fray with knees pumping high. Everything was happening fast. Otto grabbed Consuelo's arm and hurried her to the door and out into the cold night air of high country. In the light from a half moon the thick-walled buildings of the plaza were shadow-pocked. They stopped, hearing the uproar from inside the saloon.

"They are fighting, *señor*," Consuelo said, breathing with excitement.

"Ja, the cowardly pigs."

A man given the bum's rush came hurtling out the door and skidded on hands and knees in the dust.

"Come," Otto said.

"But *señor*, do we wish to miss the brave sights?"

"I will run you a race," he said.

He seized her hand and they bounded along the roofed sidewalk of the plaza and through the white dust of a narrow street where shadows from *alamo* trees were sketched black on the mud walls of courtyards. At last they halted, panting. The pure air was streaked with a sweet scent of piñon smoke. Everything was still except for their hard breathing and the distant sounds of brawling. Against the northeast the peaks of the *Sangre de Cristo* gleamed faintly.

"It is too bad to miss seeing the hot fighting," Consuelo said.

"*Ja*, but it is no matter."

"One would be amused to see my uncle Manuel crawling to hide behind the skirts of my aunt Natalia."

"Is your uncle not a brave man?"

"As brave as a squawking hen. I believe he loves his own ribs better even than money. I have heard him say it is better to have a reputation for bravery than to be brave."

"But he told me he fought for the government during the Hidalgo revolution."

"*Si*, he was in that affair. He fought on both sides, if one can call it fighting."

"You mean he was a turncoat already?"

"Hardly that. It was just that he was always supporting only the great cause of Manuel Delgado. My aunt has told the whole story to my grandmother. When the revolution broke out my uncle was in the town of Dolores, as he is fond of telling, but he was there against his will. He was in jail."

"*Mein Gott!* Why was he in jail?"

"Who knows? A great mystery cloaks those years of his life. Perhaps he was a bandit or a card sharp. But he was in jail, *por cierto,* that Sunday when the revolution broke out. The rebels stormed the jail and invited the prisoners to join their cause. My uncle gladly joined, and he assisted in looting many towns. My aunt was then a girl living in Guanajuato, some miles away. When the rebels sacked ʳhat town her parents were killed and she fled to the mountains. She wished to avoid what one could only expect if one were a girl of fourteen in a revolution."

"I am opposed to revolutions," Otto said. "Look what it did to the cowardly French. I am for a strong government such as we have in Prussia. *Ja*."

"But my aunt learned the truth of what the priest has said: often one will rid oneself of a heavy cross only to find one must bear a heavier cross. So with my aunt. For after my uncle had looted his fill, he realized the revolution could not succeed. He wished to be on the winning side. So he went into the mountains and made his way toward Mexico City. In the mountains he came upon my aunt, half starved and in tatters. She was not so fat then. Nor was my uncle. He told my aunt he was himself a loyalist and would guide her to Mexico City."

"A stable government is best," Otto said. "A strong, stable government with a disciplined army. That is what we have in Prussia."

"If one is a girl of fourteen," Consuelo said, "traveling through wild country with a bold young man, one can expect certain things. Such things happened. In Mexico City my aunt and uncle were married, and a child was born in eight months. With the gold he had looted my uncle bought a commission under General Trujillo. He was wounded at the Mountain of the Crosses."

"My father has suffered many wounds. But you may be sure he has inflicted more. *Ja.*"

"But my aunt has told my grandmother the wound was not quite so serious as a needle prick. Yet it served my uncle well. After that he fought the war in luxury in Mexico City. My aunt did not learn for many years that he had been a revolutionist."

"But he told me," Otto said, "that he fought like a Prussian at San Miguel and killed the second in command to the pig-dog, Mina."

"*Si,* but that was the second battle of San Miguel, seven years after the first revolution. My uncle was there in the loyalist army. He was given a promotion and a medal.

"My father has many medals. They cover his chest."

"I believe my uncle has only one. And my aunt has told how he obtained it. When the fighting began he ran and hid in a hen house. When somebody else came in my uncle was so frightened that his pistol went off. It was his luck that the bullet killed the intruder, and his greater luck that the man he killed was a high officer on the other side who had also sought refuge among the chickens. My uncle's story was that he had tracked the officer to the hen house and killed him. My aunt heard a different story from my uncle's body servant. But my uncle was a hero, and in reward he was made Collector of Customs at Santa Fe. He loved the City of Mexico, but he knew the opportunities for *diligencia* would be many in a customs post. His reputation for bravery is high."

"My motto," Otto said, "is that it is better to be brave than to have the reputation for bravery."

They had walked beyond the sounds of brawling; everything was quiet. Consuelo stopped.

"Where are we going, *señor?*"

In German, Otto said:

"We are going where I can seduce you."

"I do not understand."

Still in German, he said:

"You will understand soon enough, my little peasant, when I go to work on you."

"Please, *señor,* what are you saying?"

"Only that you are beautiful and desirable."

As they walked on, Otto put an arm around her waist, and he said, in German:

"I wish you were plumper. I can feel your ribs standing out like a hungry little dog's. I wish you were plump as a dumpling in the chest and in the seat like that girl who was dancing with that liar, McSwasey. You are too skinny."

She laughed.

"*Señor,* you are teasing me by speaking in that odd language I do not understand."

"In Prussia," he said, still in German, "the peasant girls are like noodles, and when you want one in a field you throw her down in a haycock."

Consuelo was giggling.

"*Señor,* when you speak those fierce words so deep in your throat you sound like a dog growling."

Otto stiffened. In Spanish, he said:

"Let me remind you, *señorita,* that you are casting a slur on the language of my fatherland."

"But *señor!* I did not mean—"

"I am a patriot. I am the son of General von Zumwalt. Once I ran a man through in an affair of honor. On the plains I killed five Comanches because they had killed the best friend I ever had. No more slurs."

"*Señor,* do not be angry."

He drew her to him and kissed her.

"*Ach!* You are as hot as a little yellow pepper."

"I think I am tipsy, *señor.* I think the whiskey you call lightning has made my head whirl. It must be very late. Where are we going?"

"To get one more little drink."

"But where? We are at the end of town."

"To my wagon in camp."

"I think I had better not."

"*Ja,* you are coming along."

"No, *señor.* It is late."

He gripped her wrist. And he learned she had fortitude: it was quite a while before she cried out that he was hurting her.

"Are you coming along?" he asked, his cheeks hot.

"*Si,*" she said, in a small voice.

*

They passed an adobe house where a dog was barking, and a field of squaw-corn rimmed by an irrigation ditch. Otto still gripped her wrist, leading her along the road and into waste land among the mesquite and nopal. When they reached an open place they moved among the animals of the caravan and on into camp where the wagons were scattered in the moonlight. A solitary man doing guard duty lifted his rifle; Otto called out, identifying himself; they passed on. In the shadow of a Proudfoot wagon Otto pulled her toward him; she resisted; so he yanked hard and embraced her and kissed her bruisingly.

"Señor," she whispered, "you said we would have a little drink."

"Whiskey is in the wagon," he said.

He led her past the huge wheels and at the front pointed toward a step in the shadows.

"Now we will climb in."

"It is so high," she murmured, "and I am weak tonight as a little jackrabbit. You will have to go first and pull me up after you. Are you strong enough for that?"

"For a man who has lived in the open it is nothing," he said.

He climbed to the driver's seat, his breathing quick and shallow.

"Now if you will give me your hand," he said, turning.

She was not there.

"Señorita."

No reply.

"Señorita! I am ready to pull you up."

Silence.

She had run away. It struck him like a blow. He plunged down, in his agitation missing the step and tumbling, skinning his palms. Yelling, he scrambled up, looking around wildly. Off at the edge of camp he glimpsed a shadowy figure disappearing into the chaparral, and he struck out in pursuit, shouting, *"Señorita!* Stop! Halt! I order it! *Señorita!"*

But she didn't stop.

Among the horses and into the mesquite he floundered after her, filling the moonlight with curses and pleas, shouted in the German he always used when overwrought. When he reached the road to Santa Fe he saw her again, a far tiny figure racing fleetly through the night. She turned a corner and was lost in the mazes of a foreign town. Otto slowed to a walk, panting.

"You would not have been so smart and got away," he shouted, "if you had not been a dirty little peasant full of tricks already and beneath my notice. But I will catch you yet, you little Mexican whore, and give you a good lesson. You are a little savage going barefoot to a ball and playing your filthy tricks on the son of General von Zumwalt, but one of these days I will catch you and take it out on your hide. *Ja, ja,* sure you outrun me when I wear boots and you wear nothing on your dirty feet and not enough on your skinny body for decency. You are nothing but a whore with your lies that you were weak as a young jackrabbit, and then you outrun me and make me a big jackass."

Suddenly his invective was cut short by a stream of hot Spanish from a dark window:

"In the name of Christ and Mary how can a man sleep when you drunken *Americanos* howl the moon? In the name of the good God—"

Otto choked and plodded on, muttering. Well beyond the house, he stopped and shook a fist.

"Grease-eating swine," he bawled; and then he took to his heels.

On the plaza, tramping toward Kite's Saloon, he stumbled over a drunken man. Otto swore and drew back a boot to kick the pig. Then he desisted; the man might not be so drunk as he seemed.

No music came from the saloon; only dim light and loud voices. Otto peered through the lattices. The *Americanos* had broken up the fandango and now they thronged the bar. Caleb McSwasey was there, hair mussed, face bruised, shirt torn, but looking happy as he fondled the full-bodied girl. Otto's loins were brimming with unquenched desire, and he wanted the consolation of a drink. But he turned away, telling himself they were cowardly ruffians, no fit associates for a *Junker*. He wandered across the plaza, coming upon a man in the pillory suffering public punishment. The man was an old peon, head bowed. When he heard Otto his eyes fluttered open and he lifted a toothless mouth.

"*Señor,*" he whispered, "in God's name a drop of water."

Otto stared.

"In the name of *Nuestra Señora de Guadalupe*, a drop of water."

Otto stepped forward and delivered two hard slaps to the old fellow, once on each cheek. Then he spat on him.

"There is your drop of water," he said.

Then, feeling better, he staggered off toward camp.

*

Near the plaza, on a street so narrow that two wagons could hardly pass, and so twisting it must have been engineered by a wandering burro, there stood a low adobe house, flush with the hard dirt sidewalk. The house was the warm golden brown of New Mexican earth, and the turquoise-blue door was the color of New Mexican sky. In accordance with Santa Fe custom, the windows were latticed but without glass; on cold nights, however, inner shutters could be closed. When Otto arrived in Santa Fe, the house belonged to a recently-widowed woman who wished to return to her relatives in Chihuahua; Otto had been less than a fortnight in town when he bought it at a bargain, using the American gold dollars he had saved.

Till then, he had found no storerooms for rent on the plaza, and he had been perplexed as to where he could set up shop.

"Why don't you buy a house?" Hod Kite had asked, one afternoon when Otto was drinking. "You could use it for a store and live in it too."

"Who would come to a house to buy goods?"

"I would. So would everybody else. Santa Fe ain't like them cities back east. Anything goes here. You buy a house and rent it to Proudfoot. You'd take in enough rent to pay your keep. Use your head, Sport."

Otto had never thought of that possibility.

"This town," Hod went on, "has got a future. She'll boom some day. And do you know why? Because she's the crossroads of commerce. Three trails end up right here on the plaza. You've got the trail from the States. You've got the trail from Chihuahua and Mexico City. You've got the trail from Taos with all that rich fur from the Rocky Mountains. And you might even say you've got a fourth trail, on to Californy. And on top of all that, you've got a perfect climate. Sure, she's a little hot in summer, but the shade's always cool and you need a blanket every night. And our winters ain't nothing to complain about. She may snow in the night but she's all melted by noon. Seldom a day the sun don't shine. I'll admit we get a little wind, but what's wrong with wind? I've roamed in lots of places, but you can't beat the climate right here. That's why I come here, among other reasons. No, Sport, you'd never go wrong owning property in Santa Fe."

"But where could I find a suitable house?"

"Well, now," Hod said, massaging his bald head with his palm, "it just so happens I keep in touch with what's going on. I might be able to snort around and find just the place. You give me five percent of the buying price, and I'll get you a real bargain."

Otto scowled.

"Back in the States, *Herr* Kite, the buyer of property pays no commission. Only the seller."

"That's back in the States, Sport. Ain't it worth five percent if I find what you want at a bargain? Ask anybody. Ask Caleb McSwasey."

"But he has gone to Taos."

Hod smiled.

"I know. He went to buy beaver pelts. First man through customs, first sold out, first to Taos. That's Caleb. Now that his wild days are over he'll make a fortune."

"I was the one who got him through customs," Otto said.

"You were? Well, now, that's mighty nice, because it means you've made a friend. Caleb always shoots fairly square, with his friends. Unless, of course, you should wink at one of his women. Where the ladies is concerned, he's the most jealous buffalo I ever did know. But we were talking about a house. I'd find you something nice, for five percent."

"Oh, well, *ja, ja,*" Otto said. "That would be agreeable with me."

He stood drinking, but instead of mulling over this new business venture he kept thinking about *Señorita* Consuelo Delgado. He had not seen her since the other evening when she gave him the slip, but he had brooded considerably. His emotion toward her was hardly tender, but it was close to love, as close as hate could ever be. He said:

"What about that girl I was with the night of the fandango?"

"What girl what night of what fandango? We throw a fandango in this joint damn near every night, when a caravan is in."

"Her name is Delgado. Consuelo Delgado."

"Oh, her. Well, what about her? You tell me. I've never been in bed with her. Have you?"

Otto flushed and started to go Prussian on Hod. Then he sighed.

"No," he said, "I haven't. But I thought I was going to. She seemed to change her mind. I told her if that was how she felt to get along home. I was sleepy anyway. What is her reputation?"

"Great God, how should I know? I ain't her confessor. Off hand I'd say she might, but then again she might not. You never know with these Spanish gals. Trouble is, you traders come out from the States where the ladies cover up everything interesting, and when you see the way these gals dress you start panting and think they're easy. Well, some are and some ain't. But the ones that ain't dress just like the ones that are, and they're all natural flirts. So there you are. Now about this house. You come here at eleven tomorrow morning and I might have something to show you."

Otto said:

"She is very poor, I understand."

"What do you mean, poor? Why, her pappy is one of the richest men in Chihuahua. I'll get the best deal I can, but she ain't so hard up she'll take beans for money. How did you know about her anyway?"

"Who are we talking about?" Otto asked.

"Don't know who you're talking about, Sport. I'm speaking of this widow lady who owns the house."

"No, no. I mean Consuelo Delgado."

"Oh, her. Well, I suppose she is poor. Ain't many rich families here. Those that are rich are awful rich, and the rest starve along. She lives with that old granny of hers, and they must make out somehow. I hear tell the old lady is a pretty good doctor. A little loco, but she knows her herbs. I don't reckon she takes in much real money for tending the sick, but she probably takes in plenty of beans and eggs."

"I understand Major Delgado is rich."

"No, not really rich. He makes a nice little thing out of the custom-house, but he ain't a rich man."

"Then Consuelo was only lying when she said her uncle is rich."

"He likely seems rich to her. Probably he gives them a peso now and then, and the gal thinks he's rich."

"I think," Otto said, "she is nothing but a little whore in any case."

"You ought to know, Sport. I sure as hell don't."

Otto finished his drink and left, wandering across the plaza where chickens were scratching and pigs sauntering, where the open air monte games were flourishing outside the *feria,* where teenagers were jeering at prisoners in the stocks and the pillory. Street vendors cried their wares, and Otto bought a tamale wrapped in a wet corn shuck, munching it as he watched the strolling girls. He did not see Consuelo.

He wondered why he kept thinking about her. She was not beautiful. Her face was attractive enough, but not her body. Many of these *señoritas* displayed full bosoms in low blouses, and their bright skirts swayed from voluptuous hips; their night-colored eyes were seductive, meeting his, and they smiled. He remembered what Billy Proudfoot had said about their preference for blond men; if he were to cock an eyebrow, he believed he could strike up an acquaintance with any one of them. Why didn't he? Why couldn't he forget the skinny little peasant and go strolling with one of these willing beauties? Physically he wanted to, for with all the trilling voices and delicious laughter and swelling calves there was desire in the very air. Yet he did not cock that eyebrow. He had unfinished business with the little peasant. Before he could go ahead and enjoy these lavish daughters of sun and night he would have to give the skinny little whore a fine lesson.

But how? Well, he didn't know. But he was devoting his talents to the problem. Certainly he did not intend to chase after her. He had done that; his ears burned at the memory. He had treated her wonderfully and she had made fun of the language of his fatherland. He had offered her a fine drink of whiskey and she had fled. He had been courteous, kindly, gallant. And what had it brought him? The ears of a jackass! No more of that. Next time he would not treat her so fine. Next time she would not get away.

"*Señor* Zumwalt," somebody was saying. "This is an unexpected pleasure."

Otto came out of his trance and recognized Major Manuel Delgado. "Excellency! I am delighted."

That went on for a while. Then the major said:

"I have not seen you since the fandango. Did you enjoy yourself?"

"Sufficiently so, Excellency. Except for the presence of the *Americanos.* They are swine."

"*Si, si,* swine." Major Delgado looked downcast. Then his eyes warmed and a lump appeared on his cheek as a result of his pushing at it with his tongue. His great belly, pregnant with beans and *enchiladas,* heaved in a chuckle. "But rich swine, *señor.* Profitable swine."

"Swine and swine-dogs."

"Ah, well . . ." Major Delgado's shoulders moved lightly and eloquently. "If one wishes bristles and lard, one must have dealings with swine."

"Excellency," Otto said, "I fear I am in disgrace with you."

"*Al contrario, señor—*"

"You are very kind, Excellency. But I owe you the deepest apology. At the fandango I did not know that the custom of your country demanded that first I should have danced with your distinguished mother."

"Ah, well, ah, well. One cannot be expected to know the customs of strange lands."

"And with your beautiful daughters, and with your lovely wife."

Major Delgado sobered.

"With my daughters, *si.* But with my wife . . . Well, *señor,* that unfortunately is another matter. My wife, sadly, suffers from a weak heart.

She will not admit this woeful defect, but it is true. Dancing is most injurious to her heart."

"In view of that, Excellency, I shall ignore the custom of your country and never invite her to dance."

Smiles returned to the major's brown-moon face. As they stood talking, Otto kept asking himself how he could bring the conversation around to Consuelo. Finally he said:

"Your niece, Excellency, is a charming enough girl, but if you will permit my saying so she is not so beautiful as your daughters."

"*Si*, charming enough. But she is only my half niece."

"I did not know that."

"Her father and I were only half brothers. My father was Jesus Delgado, while his—who knows?—his was some unbaptized Apache."

"An Indian?"

"None other. When I was but a lad the Apaches came to pillage and steal. My father was slain, God rest his soul, and my mother stolen. After many hardships she made her escape and returned to Santa Fe, carrying my half brother, Alfonso, in her womb. Is that not a sad tale, *señor*? Alfonso took the distinguished name of Delgado from my mother, but he was half Apache. He lived and died a Christian, but his blood was darkly mixed. My half niece, Consuelo, has a fourth of her blood from the Apaches. Her father was the fruit of rapine, *señor*, in an Apache lodge long ago. And she is the fruit of rapine, once removed. She has a certain strangeness, *señor*, a certain dolor and endurance. It is impossible to tell what she is thinking or what she will do next. The Apaches are a wild fierce nation. Three hundred years have not been enough to tame them. Their fibers are as tough as the ocotillo, and they are brothers of the desert winds."

"An Indian!" Otto exclaimed.

"Si, *señor*, an Indian. At least the fourth part of her."

"An Indian!" Otto thought, after he and the major had parted. "A savage little Indian peasant! Her father was the son of rape. And she is nothing but the granddaughter of rape. She cannot even read. She thought that Prussia was in Spain already! And yet she ran away from a general's son and gave me the long ears of a jackass!"

Ach! Ach!

*

Promptly at eleven next morning Otto called for Hod Kite at the saloon, and the two men set out for the widow's home. It was another radiant day, and even at this hour the pretty girls were strolling around the plaza, manifestations of that perpetual motion contraption, the life urge. In counterpoise, brown old men in *serapes* squatted against the façades, unmoving, watching the ever-shifting but ever-the-same flow of business and desire. Vendors cried; small boys scuffled; old hens fertilized the dirt sidewalks and dogs irrigated the adobe fronts; the flag of the young Republic of Mexico hung limp on its staff; the monte games were raucous; beggars importuned; fat old women haggled with other fat old women in the open market, where mocking birds sang in *amole* cages and Mexican parrots squawked, where flies buzzed and deposited their eggs in newly-butchered slabs of pork, legs of mutton, sides of beef.

Otto did not see Consuelo. She was doubtless in bed, he told himself, selling her charms. The little Indian whore!

"Do they think life is always a day at a fair?" he asked Hod. "Does nobody ever work?"

"Not if they can get out of it, Sport. Just like you and me. Their demands ain't much. And they don't have no taxes. That's one advantage you'll have, owning a house."

"No taxes? But how is that?"

"They don't like property taxes. Since they wouldn't pay them anyway, the government don't bother with a levy. We're a long way from Mexico City. If the governor here in Santa Fe did collect taxes, likely none of the money would get to Mexico."

"They are a strange people," Otto said.

"Ain't we all, Sport?"

Otto felt oddly comforted to learn that Consuelo came of a race so lackadaisical, so thriftless, so devoid of civic responsibility as to refuse paying taxes.

They left the plaza and followed *el Camino del Chamiso.* Cottonwoods grew there; the deep dust of the roadway lay undisturbed; tranquility flowed from the thick-walled houses; and with its twisting narrowness and heavy shade the street seemed protected and intimate, a refuge from the sweeps of New Mexican landscape. The sky remained to remind Otto of vastness, but even it was only a narrow slice.

When Hod stopped and knocked at a door, Otto cast a glance at the front of the house. It was small, and it looked weathered and shabby; he was disappointed. A woman opened the door and murmured, *"Caballeros."* She wore a black shawl and earrings of sky stones. "Please come in," she said. "My house is at your disposal." Otto bowed and entered his first Santa Fe home. Inside, Hod took a pinch of corn meal from the prayer bowl and scattered it, blessing the house. Otto, uncompromisingly Lutheran, did not follow his example.

There were but three rooms, all nearly bare. On the beige wall of the living room, above the corner fireplace with its wooden *santos,* a silver Christ hung crucified; the floor was packed earth, the air cool, almost dank. No chairs or tables were to be seen, but a thick mud bench ran around the wall, draped with vivid blankets.

"I would get chairs," Otto thought, "and of course a wooden floor."

The adjoining room was much like the first; the kitchen had earthen shelves for pottery, and another corner fireplace with a pothook and a turnspit.

"Where do they sleep?" Otto asked Hod, in English.

"Where did you sleep on the trip from the States?"

"Under a wagon on the ground."

"They sleep under a roof on the ground."

"No bed or chairs?"

"Lumber is scarce in these parts," Hod said. "And it costs like sixty to bring furniture from Mexico or the States."

Otto thought of the caravans crawling across arid infinities, and he asked himself what he was doing here, half a world away from home. And what was this madness of buying a house? He said:

"Furniture I would have to have."

From the kitchen they went to the patio, a place of intimacy and charm, with its asters and hollyhocks blooming within the high adobe wall. A spring bubbled in one corner, and from a tree-well in the center a young cottonwood grew among petunias.

"I would want geraniums also," Otto thought, remembering the potted plants on Berlin windowsills.

On top of an outdoor oven, which looked like a little brown igloo, a lizard was sunning, head immobile, jeweled eyes brilliant. A chipmunk scampered across the hard earth and climbed a stack of piñon wood under the overhang of the house. On its haunches, it lifted tiny paws and begged cracked corn from the *señora*.

Otto asked the price of the house; Hod quoted it in pesos; and certainly it was reasonable enough with the favorable rate of exchange for American specie. Otto paced slowly around the patio, looking thoughtful and somewhat out of place in that Spanish setting, with his Teutonic hair and skin, his pale blue eyes, his mouth with cruelty drowsing in the corners, his Prussian suspicion of some funny business in this deal already, his plodding trail boots, his endemic megalomania, his obstinate head set stiffly on squared thin shoulders, his seriousness.

"*Ja,*" he was thinking, "I could make out here. But no chairs or even a bed. That little Mexican whore who thought she was so smart and ran off from me, maybe she has never slept in a bed herself."

Shiftless, shiftless.

Suddenly a thought struck him, and he turned on Hod in almost jeering triumph.

"The roof! What about the roof? *Ja,* I would want to know about that."

"Well, now, Sport," Hod said, in slow puzzlement, "I don't rightly know what's got you so excited. It's just a regular Santa Fe roof."

"*Ja?* So! I would want to know about the roof. Once I heard my father say no house is better than its roof. He is a general and there is no monkey business about him."

"It's just like all the roofs out here, Sport. Them *viga* rafters with willow branches laid crosswise and dirt on top. Same kind of roof I've got on my own saloon. Won't find a better roof than that."

"*Ja?* And what good are willow branches and dirt? When it rains maybe you get crowned with a mud pie already."

"No, Sport, you'd be surprised. She sheds rain pretty good. And if she ever does spring a leak, you just climb up and dump on more dirt. Nothing to it."

"*Ja*, climbing, climbing. Climbing with the rain pouring. And with big puddles on the floor."

He wondered whether Consuelo Delgado had ever wakened in the night with the roof leaking. He hoped so.

"She is nothing to me in any case," he thought. "She is only a little Indian with a lying old grandmother making up big lies about being raped."

He stopped by the tree-well, staring at the little cottonwood, as if it could tell him what he should do. But in the windless morning its topmost leaves, scarcely higher than Otto's head, never so much as whispered.

"If I buy a house," he thought, "I will take root like the tree and never go back."

He turned to Hod.

"What is the price again?"

"Same as before. That there is a rock bottom price."

"I will think it over," Otto said. "I will let you know tomorrow."

Hod laughed.

"Looks like Santa Fe has got you. You're a regular native now. *Mañana.* Always *Mañana.*"

*

"It is not true," Otto told himself, late that night. "Santa Fe has not got me and it will not."

He was lying under a wagon, wooing sleep. But sleep was a fleet-footed girl who ran away through the moonlight. By now he was pretty mad at sleep.

And he was annoyed at Hod Kite for putting into his head this idea of buying a house. By itself, of course, the idea was sound. And the house was a bargain. If he were an ordinary young man, content to go into the Santa Fe trade and perhaps marry a Santa Fe girl, living out his life here with occasional trips back to the States, it would be sensible to buy the house and use the living room as a store. But he was not an ordinary young man. Blood from the old Prussian knights flowed in his veins. *Ja,* sure, he had been wild, running off to Paris and America, killing Indians and buffalo, making love to beautiful women, fighting duels; but now at twenty-three he wished to return to his fatherland

104

and marry some tow-headed maiden, plump full of dumplings and *kuchen*, and sit in the evenings wearing carpet slippers. *Ja*, that would be the life.

But he could not do that unless he crossed the plains. There was the rub. In the past years he had made a series of decisions, each one taking him closer to Santa Fe; and Santa Fe was a trap. There was no escape except across Indian country.

Finally he slept, tossing and muttering, and during sleep he reached his decision. He would buy the house and work for Proudfoot & Sons till next summer. Then he would return to Missouri and Prussia. Next summer he would be strong and brave; he would laugh at the dangers of the plains. And in the meantime he would find a way to give a good lesson to Consuelo Delgado.

The following day he wrote two letters, one to John Proudfoot, a long, thorough and wholly admirable report of the financial standing of the Santa Fe branch of Proudfoot & Sons. Written with a sharp quill, the words small and precise, the letter might have been printed from copperplate. He told of the lack of rental space, and how he had decided to buy a house with his own money and set up shop there. "I will leave it, sir, to your fairness and business judgment as to whether you should pay me rent for the portion of my house used for commercial purposes, and if so how much. I remain, sir, your faithful and obedient servant, Otto Zumwalt, Resident Manager, Santa Fe Branch, Proudfoot & Sons."

The second letter was addressed to General von Zumwalt, and it contained scarcely a word that was true. Up from the German script floated an Otto Zumwalt never seen on land or sea, a resolute young man who had struck out for himself and killed seven Comanches to avenge the murder of his best friend. By the time Otto had finished the letter and read it several times, he half believed its contents.

On the night before the caravan left Santa Fe, he gave the letters to McSwasey, who had returned in high good humor from Taos, where he had bought beaver pelts at a price which would yield him an excellent profit in St. Louis. It was Otto's first evening in his new home, and in celebration he had invited McSwasey for supper. After the meal, the two men sat in the patio, cigars glowing.

"Don't you think I was a smart fellow to buy the house?" Otto asked.

"I doubt if you'll rue it."

"At least I showed that Hod Kite a thing or two. When I wanted to sleep on the idea, he made fun of me and said Santa Fe had got me. '*Mañana*,' he said, 'always *mañana*.' But I showed him I could make up my mind fast without any nonsense."

"Hod was likely just joking," McSwasey said.

"*Ja*, always jokes. But now the scoundrel will joke from the other side of his mouth. Is it true he used to be a bank robber?"

"I wouldn't doubt it."

"Was he robbing banks when you knew him in Texas?"

"Not that I know of."

"In any case," Otto said, "I bought the house and taught him a fine lesson not to make jokes at me."

"You fooled me, Otto," McSwasey said. "I never thought you'd stay in Santa Fe."

"But I had given my word to John Proudfoot that I would work for him, and I am not one to go back on my word. I will get his store established good, and then next year I will resign and go back where there is green grass. Maybe even to Prussia where the cows have big udders and the grass grows as high as their bellies."

"If you went back you might not like it."

"*Ja,* sure I would. It is the best country on earth."

"You might not. I went back to Massachusetts once."

"And you didn't like it?"

"Everything seemed smaller. I had changed. A man can't go back."

"I will if I want to," Otto said.

"I went back in the fall of '21. My older brother has a store, and I figured I might buy into it and settle down. I didn't last a month. People would say, 'Why, hello, Caleb. You've been away for a spell.' I'd been gone eight years, but I'd say, 'Yes, I had a little trip.' And they'd say, 'Well, I reckon it seems good to get back.' I'd say yes, there was no place like East Bainbridge. But I'd remember how the Mississippi runs like hot gold past the Natchez bluffs at sundown, and the smell of whiskey mash in a limestone hollow in Kentucky, and the spooky feel of a Louisiana swamp when you're hiding out at night and hear some old 'gator coughing, and I knew I couldn't stick it. My brother had been to Boston once. My other two brothers hadn't even been to Springfield. When I told them how the sun comes up in Texas they didn't know what I was talking about."

"*Ja,* sure, sure," Otto said, "I know how it is. My brothers are all loafing stick-in-the-muds."

"I remember," McSwasey said, "how one night I took a walk alone, there in East Bainbridge. There's only one street that amounts to anything, and I walked south along it. It was a nippy November night with a white moon and a smell of leaves burning, and there was white mist rising from the bottoms of the Connecticut River west of town. I passed the house where I'd been born and raised, but I didn't belong there any more. My dad and mother and my Grandpa Seasongood were all dead, and the house had been sold. One of those white houses with a shed attached to the kitchen and a barn attached to the shed. My dad had had a shop out in the barn. He liked to tinker. Once he tried to invent a collapsible horseshoe. I never did figure why any man would want a collapsible horseshoe, and maybe he didn't know either. But he liked to set his mind to such things. He used to sit out there by the hour in a broken down old chair he'd wired together, and smoke his pipe and drink whiskey. He never got drunk more than a couple of times a year, but when he did it was a pretty good bender. 'Frosty McSwasey's off on another toot,' people would say, and they'd click their tongues and enjoy the scandal. He never was what you could call a leading citizen in that town. But folks couldn't help liking him. He was a tubby little beaver, and there wasn't a stopped clock he couldn't make run or a fiddle he couldn't repair, if you gave him time to think it over in his own way."

"My father is a general," Otto said.

"Well, mine was a soldier too, for that matter. He fought right through the Revolution, and he knew so much about guns people used to bring them to East Bainbridge from miles around to be fixed. His first wife died when he was off fighting. After the war he got a job as hired hand on my Grandpa Seasongood's farm. He met my mother there and married her. None too soon either. My older sister was a seven months baby. The boys around town used to say it was the only time Frosty McSwasey had done a job of work before he was supposed to."

"My father is always on time," Otto said. "*Ja,* right on the dot. He makes things march."

"That's like my grandpa. He lived with us, when he got too old to work his farm. He had a Roman nose and a white beard and he used to say he'd never even tasted hard cider. My dad would say, 'Well now, father Seasongood, that's too bad. You've missed a lot.' Then they'd be off to an argument. I remember they always used to argue as to whether the Nineteenth Century began on January 1, 1800 or January 1, 1801. They never did settle it. It usually ended with my mother having one of her headaches. Her name was Harmony, and I reckon she had her hands full keeping harmony between my dad and my grandpa."

"*Ja,* sure, my mother had headaches too. Those cowardly women are always having headaches."

"Folks used to say I took after my father. But my brother, Paul, he was different. He was ten years older than me, and he set himself up in a store when he was only twenty. He had the Seasongood nose and he was sure a hustler. Still is. You can buy anything in that store of his, from sand in the sugar to worms in the flour. He was sure my grandpa's pride. But I always had a sneaking notion my father didn't care much for Paul. If so, the feeling was mutual. I never liked Paul none too well myself. He pushed too hard. They set me to working in his store when I was fifteen, and I might as well have been in jail. Well, he'll end up rich, but maybe I'll end up richer. I figured out early I'd never get rich by rubbing two pennies together to make them hatch a third. When I make it I have to make it in hunks, and have fun doing it.

"Well, on that night I took my walk in East Bainbridge, I did a lot of thinking. I asked myself did I want to be like Paul and never see Spanish moss again. And as I walked around town, maybe I was hunting for a lost kid, the kid I'd been. Well, he'd gone away, but I remembered a few things about him. I remembered how when he was ten years old he'd been a pretty fair marble player. He started out with maybe six marbles, and before long he had twenty-five or thirty. Then he got a crazy kid notion of cornering the whole marble supply in East Bainbridge. And by God, he practiced so much and got so expert he damn near did it. Agates, taws, white alleys, potters—Lord, he had hundreds. He'd swap them back to the other kids for something he wanted. With a start like that he might have pyramided his holdings and kept swapping till he owned the whole town, except for a sissy who minded his mamma and wouldn't play for keeps. Of course, none of us was supposed to play for keeps. God wouldn't like it. God used to live up in the steeple of the Congregational Church, with the pigeons. When a grownup came along past a marble game, we always said we were playing giveaway.

"Well, I decoyed this sissy into a game. After I'd won his marbles he wanted them back. He even tried to grab them, and I had to bloody his nose. He went screaming home, and the whole story came out and the town sort of rocked, when all those good church goers found their sons had been gambling. There were quite a few sore hind ends among the younger generation that night."

"Mine has often been sore, living with my father," Otto said.

"Mine was supposed to be, but it wasn't. Old Grandpa Seasongood wanted to attend to the matter himself, but my dad said he guessed he could handle me. So he took me out to his workshop and locked the door, and he sat down and had a nip from his bottle. 'Caleb,' he says, 'when us boys fought for liberty or death, we didn't fight all the time. I passed some of my time in ordinaries, and some of it in the prettiest arms in the colonies, and some of it rolling dice. Caleb,' he says, 'this great country was founded by boys who knew how to roll them, whether they were girls or dice.' He took another swig. 'Caleb,' he says, 'start howling.' So I howled while he sat grinning at me over his bottle. 'That's enough,' he says finally. And he asks, 'Caleb, did you do a pretty good job on Malcolm Penwick's nose?' Malcolm was the sissy, and I says, 'I think a pretty fair job.' 'Good,' he says, taking another swig. 'It was old Eb Penwick who had me arrested that Sunday when I went fishing. I guess,' he says, 'I never should have sold my bounty land after the war. I guess I should have gone out west.'

"When the whole marble scandal was boiled down, all the parents decided Caleb McSwasey was to blame. By the time I got into a scrape and left East Bainbridge a few years later I was the town black sheep, and I reckon it all started with that marble business. But I didn't mind. I was always a little too much for East Bainbridge."

"*Ja, ja,* I know how it goes," Otto said. "I was a regular black sheep myself."

"So this night when I took the walk I remembered about the marbles, and I remembered the summer of the big watermelon. I must have been twelve or thirteen then. Old Eb Penwick, this sissy's father, ran the bank. The old bastard was built like a rake handle and he had one of those lemon-sucking faces and he was tighter than Noah's pants after the big rain. Well, he was proud of son Malcolm, and he was always telling what a fine garden Malcolm had and what an industrious little man he was. So one spring the old bastard offered a prize of one dollar to the East Bainbridge boy who would grow the biggest watermelon. I reckon he figured Malcolm would win and that fortune in prize money would stay in the family.

"Thinks I, 'If that sissy can grow watermelons so can I.' So I spaded me ground and put in seed. And I had a talk with my dad. He sat rocking, there in his shop, and scratching his head—his hair was red, like mine, only sprinkled with salt—and finally he says, 'I guess if you do like I say, you'll have a nice melon.' And he told me what to do.

"First off, I was to dig a trench around each watermelon hill and keep pouring buttermilk into it. That was easy, for we had an old cow and there was plenty of buttermilk after my mother churned. Next, I was to dig an outer trench and fill it with cow chips and keep it watered down. Then when the vines flowered, I was to pinch off all the blooms on each vine but one good one. And when the melon came, I was to pinch off all the runners except the one with the melon I was coddling. I did it all.

"Man, I had melons. They were all big, but the one I picked as winner and gave special attention to, that one swelled up like a nigger with dropsy. I'd water it every day, and feed it buttermilk and cow chips. Pretty soon it weighed twenty pounds. Pretty soon I couldn't lift it. I won that contest hands down with a melon that weighed forty-three and a half pounds. Malcolm's old tightwad father paid me the money, but I don't reckon he ever recovered. He sort of slowly wasted away, after that. And he spread the story that I'd been up to some trickery in winning. He couldn't figure what, but he said the Lord had never intended watermelons to grow that big. He was a great one, anyway, to explain what the Lord thought about various matters."

"What was your scrape when you left town?" Otto asked. "A duel?"

McSwasey smiled.

"I reckon it was a sort of duel, at that. Malcolm was mixed up in that too. So was a girl. I was turned seventeen then. The girl's name was Florence, and she had yellow hair. I liked her and so did Malcolm. I was so jealous I bloodied his nose again. Well, this time we were both older, and next day I was tipped off that Malcolm and his father had driven to the county seat to swear out a charge of assault with intent to kill. I decided I'd best leave town.

"That was when I was working for Paul in the store, and when I told him I was lighting out he gave me a lecture. It was in the evening after closing time, and I can see him yet, pacing back and forth with his beak nose ahead of him. He was only twenty-seven himself, but he seemed old to me. He even looked old. Born old, maybe. His shoulders were round from so much hunching over accounts, and his voice sounded like a preacher's. He told me to be a man and stay and face the music. I couldn't see it. 'I'm lighting out,' I said.

"He stopped pacing then, and looked at me quite a while. Then he asked, 'Where will you go?'

" 'South,' I said, 'and likely west. Kentucky, maybe.'

"He turned his head, and I could see his nose in profile, and for a minute he looked tired and maybe even sad. He heaved a breath. And his voice wasn't like a preacher's when he spoke, but low and sort of yearning. 'I wish you luck,' he said. 'You'll see a lot of country.'

" 'I aim to,' I said.

" 'They say it's a big country,' he said. 'Sometimes I've been tempted . . .' His voice died away. Then all at once he took a breath, and he was the old up-and-at-'em Paul. 'I've got the best business in the county,' he said. 'And the most economical wife. Just remember one thing, young man. A rolling stone gathers no moss.'

"My dad didn't do any lecturing. I told him I wanted to talk with him private, so we went out to his shop. He lighted a candle and had a nip, and when I told him I was leaving he said he was going to miss me.

" 'Lord God,' he said, 'we've had fun. That watermelon . . . Where do you figure to go?'

" 'I'll take a scow,' I said, 'and float down the river. Then I'll cut across country. Into Virginia, I reckon. And then out the Wilderness Road to Kentucky.'

" 'By God,' he said.

" 'I've hated that store,' I said. 'I want to see the country.'

" 'The old Boone trail to Kentucky,' he said. 'I've read about that. You'll have fun.'

" 'More fun than in jail,' I said, 'if the Penwicks can make that charge stick.'

" 'Hell,' he said, 'they can't. I know the state's attorney. We was in the army together. But you go anyway. God, yes, boy—you go. You stay here and first thing you'll get some girl into trouble and there you'll be. You go and see those fields of cotton. You find out what it's like where there's flowers in January. You keep out of trouble if you can, but if you can't, why by God have a good time.' He took another nip. 'I should have taken up land out west,' he said. 'Or gone south, after the war. I've never watched the geese go over in the fall without thinking about it. She's a big country. Tommy Jefferson bought Louisiana and you should have heard them howl. Eb Penwick, and his likes. All that Louisiana stretching off to the sunset. She's all yours, Caleb. You take her. I'm too old.'

"I left that night, by scow. And when I came back eight years later the house was sold and my dad was in what the preacher calls his long home, and my mother and grandpa too. And those charges against me were forgotten. Malcolm came into the store the first day I was back and shook hands. He was getting a banker's belly and a banker's fat hind end. I was crazy ever to think of going back and settling down. A man can do a lot of things but he can't go back.

"So that night when I took my walk I got to thinking of the hot biscuits with honey they feed you for breakfast in Tennessee, and of the possum hunts in Kentucky, and of how before I left St. Louis I talked with Billy Becknell and he told me he was going to try for New Mexico next spring, and if I wanted to go along . . . Waugh! Next day I left East Bainbridge, and I've never been back."

"And will you never go back, now?" Otto asked.

"On a visit, maybe. After I've been gone so long nobody can say I've been gone just a spell. Or after I've made my first million. It might be fun to hear them say they always knew I'd be a rich man, ever since I cornered the marbles and grew the biggest watermelon."

"*Ja*," Otto said, "that would be good to go back rich and get even. And now I will tell you about the summer I grew the biggest cabbage already."

*

And so there in the patio under the brilliant New Mexican stars the evening wore away, with yarning and cigars and occasional drinks of Taos Lightning. Otto told of his boyhood and of how he had sailed to America with the intention of living among the Indians, and he told of how when the Comanches killed Billy Proudfoot his feelings toward the savages underwent a complete reversal from romantic sentimentality to repugnance and hate.

"Billy was my best friend," he said, "just as you are now my best friend. After his death I no longer wanted anything to do with them, even with the Indian girls."

"I see what you mean," McSwasey said, "although you're making a mistake in passing up the Injun gals. Some of them are nice armfuls."

"*Ja?*"

"Wild as antelopes," McSwasey said, "under a blanket."

"Have you had many of them?"

"Well, I've lived in the West, and I'm a man."

"Are they better than niggers?"

"Niggers are all right too. I'm not running down niggers. But I think the Santa Fe gals top them all. Now you've got a house, maybe you should get you a gal."

"You mean get married?"

"I wouldn't go so far as to say that. But you'll need someone to do the cooking and chores. Maybe you should buy a slave."

"A slave!"

"Sure. She could fill in for you till you find a gal."

"But where would I find a slave?"

"Maybe Hod Kite would sell you one of his."

"He has slaves?"

"Four or five. Didn't you know?"

"But how much do they cost?"

"Different prices. If you didn't want to spend a lot of money all at once, you could probably rent one. That way, you wouldn't have a lot of capital tied up. And when you do get married, if your wife didn't like her, you could always take back a rented slave and let your wife pick one she did like. Sometimes women are fussy about their slaves."

"*Ja,*" Otto muttered, "*ja, ja,*" and his heart was thumping with the excitement of new vistas opening out. A slave!

"Have you found a gal yet?" McSwasey asked.

"I found me one I do not like."

"Then you'd better find another,"

"First I have a little matter to settle," Otto said. He finished his drink; and suddenly, there in the hushed and shadowed patio, with the whiskey and the cigars and the lateness of the hour all fostering the exchange of confidences, Otto experienced the universal need of humanity to share its perplexities and its woes, and he told the whole humiliating story of his evening with Consuelo Delgado.

"So she made me a big jackass," he said bitterly, "and I am going to teach her a good lesson she will not forget so soon."

"How?"

"*Ach,* that is it, I don't know how. I have been beating my brains for some way to teach her, and I have thought of nothing. What is your advice?"

The tip of McSwasey's cigar brightened and dulled. At last, in his habitually quiet voice he said:

"I'd forget the whole thing."

"But I can't! I have had many beautiful women, but never one who treated me so bad."

"Good Lord, man. If that's the worst treatment you've ever had from a woman, you're lucky."

"Lucky!" Otto growled. "Lucky! *Ja,* I go around with the long ears of a jackass and you say I am lucky."

"Find another gal. Forget the little slut. Maybe she's a teaser. There's nothing worse than that. Forget her, Otto. What the hell!"

"Forget her, forget her! *Ja*, that's what I would like. But I cannot forget. She is nothing to me, I tell you, but I cannot forget. I want to get even with her." In his excitement Otto jumped up and paced, cigar waving. "I want to take off my jackass ears and pin them on her. I want to make her sorry and cry and know better next time. *Ja!* Making fun with me and running away! She is a dirty little whore of a Mexican-Indian, and it is time she had some sense knocked into her. *Ja!*"

"You're sure you don't love her?" McSwasey asked quietly.

"Love her! Me? Me love an Indian already when maybe some relation of hers killed Billy Proudfoot?"

"Hold on, Otto. You're getting hysterical. She's only a fourth Injun, if her grandpa was an Apache, and it was the Comanches who killed Billy, not the Apaches."

"*Ja*, well it was Indians who killed him, and she might as well be all Indian as a fourth. And I am going to find some way to get even."

"Otto, don't you know you can't win?"

"Why can't I? *Ja*, sure I can win! I will teach her one fine lesson."

"You can't win a fight with a woman, Otto. They'll always top you somehow. You ought to know that."

"I can win and I am going to!" Otto nearly shouted. "Of course I can win! Didn't my father who is a general always win his fights with the old lady? *Ja*, he had her scared, I can tell you! She would think twice before she opened her jaws. Dogs and women, my father always said, the more you beat them the better they love you. *Ja!* He knew how to treat the old lady, I can tell you that. Once at table she waggled her tongue just once too often, and my father dashed a stein full of beer into her face. *Ja!* He would stand no monkey business. The old lady shut her jaws quick enough then. I wanted to bust laughing at her sitting there with all that beer running down her face and dripping onto her dress. It was funny, I can tell you that."

"It must have been," McSwasey said, not laughing.

"*Ja*, sure, sure. So you see, I am my father's son and I also will stand no monkey business. I am going to get even somehow so there is no need for you to try to talk me out of it. The little whore needs a lesson and I am the one to teach it. Would you like another drink?"

"One more. Just a shorty. Then I've got to go. We're off to an early start in the morning."

The subject of Consuelo was dropped. They sat talking of other things, mainly of business, and of the bright future McSwasey saw in the trade between Santa Fe and the States.

"We're in on the ground floor, Otto," he said when he rose to leave. "If we use our heads we'll end up rich."

"*Ja*, that will be nice, too."

"On this trip alone, I'll clean up enough to pay my debts and buy another wagon and more mules. I'm keeping my credit A-1 with Proudfoot. Next spring I'll be out here with two wagon loads. And the year after that with three or four. It's a big gamble because of the Injuns, but I like to gamble. Nothing risked, nothing gained. I'll pyramid my winnings and some day I'll have a mansion in St. Louis with a dozen nigger wenches to give me a bath. Waugh!"

"Waugh!" Otto said.

Carrying a candle, he lighted his guest through the kitchen and into the two front rooms, piled now to the ceiling with the goods that had traveled up the Missouri to Franklin on the *Western Pride,* and from Franklin to the hardwood grove and across the arid plains to Raton Pass and the land of turquoise sky and turquoise sky stones.

Outside the front door, McSwasey extended his hand.

"Well, Otto, it's been a great trip. Thanks for the meal and the drinks and for getting me through the customs."

"That was nothing. Anything for a friend."

"Take care of yourself."

"Ja, you do the same. I hope you have a safe trip."

"We'll make out, I reckon. *Adiós."*

"Ja, adiós. Auf Wiedersehn."

Whistling cheerfully, McSwasey limped off down the Street of the Chamiso.

"Ja, ja," Otto muttered, "I will teach her a good lesson and teach you that I can teach her a good lesson. I will show you how we treat women in Prussia already."

*

As yet Otto had no bed, so that night he slept on the ground in the patio, wrapped in his blankets. Now that he had made his decision to remain in Santa Fe till next summer, he was untroubled by insomnia, and he dropped at once into deep slumber.

"Well," he thought, when he wakened next morning, "the caravan is on its way," and he considered himself lucky to be here on his own premises instead of starting a long dangerous journey.

After breakfast he went to Kite's Saloon for his strongbox. Home again, he locked the door and counted the money; every cent was there; and he spent the rest of the morning hollowing out three separate cavities in the thick adobe walls. He divided the money into four stacks. Three of these he wrapped in canvas, putting each bag into one of the cavities. With thick brown mud he plastered shut the holes, smoothing and patting this native cement. The fourth pile he returned to the strongbox, and this he buried in the patio near the corner outhouse. Now if bandits should break in and torture him, he could always show them where to dig for the strongbox; they would never know about the money in the walls.

The next days he spent cleaning his house and unpacking the trade

114

goods; soon the rooms were a jumble of cambrics, velvets, hats, knives, hatchets, shawls, gunpowder. But without furniture there was no place to display this merchandise, except on the mud bench against the living-room wall; so he went to the trouble of sending native workmen into the mountains to fell pines and whipsaw the logs into rough boards. The work dragged, but he had resolved not to open his store till everything was *recht.* At last the lumber came from the mountains, and with the help of a native carpenter, a friend of Hod Kite, he built chairs and display tables and a bed of sorts. He understood now why most Santa Fe homes lacked furniture and wooden floors. Still, he resolved to have a board floor. He would attend to it one of these days. *Mañana.*

Last of all, he nailed boards together and lettered a sign which he hung above the front door. It said:

PROUDFOOT & SONS
St. Louis and Santa Fe
Otto Zumwalt
Resident Manager

Of that sign he was exceedingly proud; several times a day he stood in the street admiring it.

*

So finally he opened his store, to excellent business, for merchandise was scarce in Santa Fe, and the goods sold by the other traders had only whetted the demand. To the store came the brown-bean people from the country and the brown-bean people from the town; the *pobre* came, and the *ricos,* and many *señoritas.* Chattering with a great trilling of *r's,* these young women pawed over the merchandise, smiling at themselves in looking glasses, snapping open and shut the scissors, fingering the calicoes and cheap jewelry, and always flirting with Otto. He did not respond, because of the score he had to settle with Consuelo Delgado.

Except for that unfinished business, he was not unhappy with his lot. The store was his life; sometimes a week passed without his venturing as far from home as the plaza. He kept busy, arranging and rearranging his merchandise, dusting and scrubbing, swatting flies, chasing spiders, buying fruit and meal and jerked beef from the vendors who passed his door; all the comforting humdrum which gives life a sense of continuity and stability. The mornings and evenings were sharper, now that autumn had arrived, but the noons were warm. In the patio the yellow juices of October infiltrated the leaves of the little cottonwood; dusk came sooner.

One day a stray cat wandered into the store, took a liking to Otto and decided to remain. On the crisp evenings he would sit in the living room with the shutters closed and flames crackling in the fireplace, stroking the cat, which he had named Hilda, and computing how much he was likely to make from the store when, in accordance with his agreement with Proudfoot, he added five per cent of the profits to his salary.

Often on those evenings he brooded about Consuelo Delgado; he couldn't forget her. He was still wearing the jackass ears she had pinned to his head, and it enraged him to remember how she had led him on and then insulted him by running away. And now she was compounding insult by never visiting his store. Other girls came and came again; other girls admired his hair; other girls flashed him smiles and gave him invitations with their eyes. Not Consuelo. She needed a lesson.

But what kind? He didn't know. Day after day he devoted his best thinking to the problem; still he didn't know. If only he could force her to chase him as he had chased her! If only he could compel her to visit his store!

"*Ja*, little Hilda," he used to murmur, stroking the cat, "I would like to teach her one fine lesson she would never forget."

And then at last, after all those weeks of brooding, a magnificent idea for humbling her sprang full-grown from his brain.

IV

OFTEN IN Otto's store Sunday was the busiest day, for church brought the whole countryside to Santa Fe, on burros and in *carretas,* and after Mass the throngs were eager for the pleasures of shopping, of gaming, of gossiping, of drinking in *cantinas,* of jeering at the prisoners in the stocks and the pillory, of strolling, always strolling, round and round the plaza, till late afternoon brought the even more exquisite pleasures of a cockfight, a chicken pulling, or an exhibition where a dozen starved dogs were turned into a cage with a mountain lion.

None of these activities tempted Otto. Being the only Lutheran within a thousand miles, he could hardly attend the church of his choice. The church of Santa Fe's choice, with its opulent ritual, he suspected darkly, for no good reason; never had he stepped inside a cathedral, and never did he intend to. Of gambling he was likewise suspicious, believing it morally wrong and financially painful.

As for the cockfights and other amusements where animals were tormented, Otto was outraged, for he liked animals and was kind to them, even to mules. On the trail to Santa Fe, and in the town at trail's end, this marked him as an oddity. More zoophile than homophile, he preferred in general the company of animals to that of men, if only because with animals his superiority was indubitably established. With them he could lower his guard and relax. Animals did not question his courage. Next to Caleb McSwasey, he considered the cat, Hilda, his best friend.

On this November Sunday both cockfights and a cougar baiting were scheduled, and as Otto puttered around his store while the cathedral bells rang he was infuriated to think of these strange brown people cheering and laughing while some beast suffered.

"I would like to turn old Delgado into a pit with a cougar," he thought, "and a few more of these dirty Mexicans."

Even perhaps Consuelo. Not, however, till he had taught her a fine lesson. But what lesson? That was a problem still unsolved.

Toward noon on that momentous Sunday customers began entering the store and business grew brisk. There were the usual pretty girls, chattering like Mexican parakeets, the usual witticisms, the usual disarranging of neatly arranged goods. Then the door opened and two corpulent people waddled in, wearing Sunday best and a having-been-to-church air. They were Major and *Señora* Delgado, so for a time the store was as full of amenities as a diplomatic reception.

"You have not been in much lately," Otto told Major Delgado. "I have missed our pleasant chats."

"Ah, yes, so have I. But I have been indisposed. Little pains have chased themselves from here to here."

On the great globe of his abdomen his forefinger traced a voyage from the Tropic of Capricorn to the Tropic of Cancer.

"I am sorry to hear that, Excellency."

"It was nothing," the major's wife said.

"But pet, begging your pardon, it was most painful," the major said.

"He eats too much," *Señora* Delgado told Otto. *"Frijoles, empanadas, biscochitos*—he is a sinful glutton."

"But my dear. With your permission, I eat no more than do you."

"I eat like a bird, only enough to support life. Besides, I do not suffer from *dolor de estómago."* She turned to Otto. "To hear him groan one would suppose him suffering labor pains."

"Your blessed tongue, my dear, is betraying you into exaggeration."

"One would suppose him giving birth to twins."

"Hardly twins," the major said.

"Triplets."

"Twins or triplets," the major said, shrugging, "it is no matter. Although the pain was great, I believe I bore myself with soldierly stoicism."

"Passersby supposed I was bearing another child, God forbid," *Señora* Delgado said.

"En todo caso," the major said, "it all ended well. I sent for my blessed mother, who has great skill as a *curandera*. She applied a hot poultice of silver sage and administered *sabadilla*. I am now as good as new."

Fondly, he patted his *vientre*.

While his wife looked over the merchandise, the major inspected the other customers, his mustachios spruce, eyes pleasantly alert.

"You are busy today, *señor,"* he said.

"Always on Sunday, Excellency."

"If your business continues so brisk, you will be needing a clerk."

It was an idle remark, mere chaff. But the chaff contained a seed. A clerk!

"Si," Otto said, trying to control his excitement, "I have been thinking of hiring a clerk. Of course, I could not pay much."

"Naturally not."

"But I do need a clerk. *Ja, si,* I need one."

"Certainly in that case you should hire one."

"Si, si, I believe I should."

"By all means, *señor.* Your talents are too large to be used in the mere selling of needles."

"But where," Otto asked, "can I find a clerk?"

"Where not? That should offer no difficulty."

"*Ja*, but I would want a good, efficient one. Somebody young and quick."

"A *señorita*, perhaps?"

"*Si*, perhaps. Somebody like your niece perhaps. What is her name? Consuelo? *Si*, not necessarily her, but some girl who would like to earn a few pesos."

Across Major Delgado's countenance, vast affability broke.

"Permit me to say, *señor*, that she would be an excellent choice."

"*Si*, good enough, doubtless. At least I might give her a try."

"She is an excellent girl, *señor*. The daughter of my poor dead brother, God rest his soul. She should have been married long since for she is all of seventeen, but God has willed otherwise. It has been a drain on my purse, *señor*, offering support not only to my blessed mother but also to my blessed niece."

"I can see that," Otto said savagely. "A strong young girl like that should not expect you to support her."

"Ah, well, I am the head of the family and her protector. But at times I have wished the itch to marry would overcome her. She has had suitors, but always something has gone amiss. She is fierce and wild and independent, and perhaps she has held her chastity in too great esteem."

"*Ja*, they get silly notions, those girls."

"Do you wish me to speak to my niece, *señor?*"

"Perhaps it would do no harm."

"When would you wish her to enter upon her duties?"

"There is no hurry, Excellency. But if convenient, tomorrow morning at nine."

"She will be here. And now, my friend, there is the painful subject of *salario*. What will you be pleased to pay?"

"What she is worth. I will try her for a few days. Then the matter of salary can be settled."

The major shrugged.

"*Si*, a mere detail that can be settled later to the satisfaction of all. And *señor*. She is but a girl with no thought of the value of money. So with your permission, you will pay her salary to me and I will see that it is spent wisely on her behalf."

"*Ja!* That will be fine."

"Then it is settled. She will be here at nine tomorrow."

"But Excellency. Suppose she gets a silly notion she does not wish to work in my store."

The major sobered. And for a moment, Otto glimpsed a Major Delgado of whose existence he had been unaware. There was an instant of ruthlessness in his eyes, of *fiereza* on his mouth. The brutality passed; polished affability returned.

"She will not get such a notion, *señor*. Of that I can assure you. She will be here at nine."

*

"*Ja*," Otto told the empty store, that evening after the last customer had gone, "now we will see who laughs last. Now you will find, you little whore, that it is a long road that has no turning. You will be sorry now that you treated me so bad."

All the time he prepared supper he talked aloud, sometimes addressing the cat.

"*Ja*, little Hilda cat, you have noticed maybe how in the dumps I have been. You have wondered perhaps what kind of fellow I am, to let an Indian spit on me and jeer at me and make me a big jackass already. Well, little Hilda, now you will see how the son of General von Zumwalt attends to such matters. She will be sorry now."

He was too excited to eat much. And too angry. The sound of his own voice fueled his rage.

That night he slept poorly, twisting in bed and thinking of Consuelo across town somewhere.

"*Ja*," he muttered, "we have a little appointment in the morning. You will work for me and take orders from me. If you are lazy I will report you to your uncle. If you run away I will never chase you but simply report the matter to him. I think he is as greedy for money as for food, and he will not like it so well to have you running away from a fine job in my store. Maybe you are thinking of this right now and wishing you had not been so smart with a general's son."

He was up at daybreak, washing and shaving. After breakfast the long waiting began.

Seven o'clock.

"In two more hours you will be here. I wonder what you are doing now. Maybe you are a lazy little slattern still snoring away the minutes. But you cannot sleep forever."

Eight o'clock.

"By now you are surely up. *Ja*, you have overslept, but now you are rushing about. Maybe this will give you a good lesson not to be so lazy."

The minutes dragged. Otto kept fussing over the trade goods. Then he chased those cowardly spiders that ran so fast across the adobe walls, nearly always eluding him. Then he sprinkled water on the earthen floor and used his grass broom, telling himself he must arrange for lumber to lay a wooden floor; an earthen floor was not fit for a civilized European. He would see about that within a day or so.

It was ten minutes till nine.

He wandered out to the patio and back again, then went to the street. Its rich dust lay undisturbed in the morning sun. Cottonwoods stood motionless. Everything was silent. Overhead the unclouded sky was a glorious turquoise, as serene with expectation as a sky in spring.

He looked up at the sign he had painted, brilliant in yellow and purple. Proudfoot & Sons. St. Louis and Santa Fe. A fat man had peered through cigar smoke and said, "I'll want a big sign, Billy . . ." That was half a year ago, but it seemed longer. Now Billy was a heap of bones on the plains. Wind would be blowing, cold wind by now, maybe carrying snow. The long trail would be desolate, empty ruts from Missouri to Santa Fe. McSwasey would be nearing Missouri by now, if the savages had not scalped him.

"I am well off here," Otto thought. "If only it wasn't so far from everything. If only the trail were not so long. But maybe I will go back anyway. Next year."

It was five minutes till nine.

He returned to the store, smiling slyly, and looked at himself in a mirror. He wandered out to the patio again, and back, and out, and back, his heart beating rapidly.

It was nine.

His hands trembled when he returned his cumbrous watch to his pocket.

Nine o'clock. And where was she?

He wanted to go to the door and peep along the street. But if she were coming she might see him. A minute passed. Another. No girl. No Consuelo. No clerk. The seconds ticked away. At last he seized the broom and went to the door, brushing an imaginary speck across the sill. In so doing, he glanced both ways along the street. It was empty. Angrily, he flung the broom into a corner and stalked to the patio. Why wasn't she here? It was now five after nine. Otto paced the patio, eyes furious. Was this another of her tricks? Seven after nine now. What kind of clerk was this, not arriving on time? How could she expect to get ahead in the business world, acting like this? Punctuality! A tremendous virtue! In New Orleans he had always arrived at the office on the dot. *Ja!* Never a minute early or a minute late. Always! *Ja!*

Ten after nine.

Great *Gott!*

He knew what he would do. He would stride over to the cutomhouse and accost fat old Delgado. "How is it then," he would demand, "that you lazy Mexican savages bring up your daughters already without punctuality?"

He strode into the house. And stopped.

She was standing inside the front door, her poor cheap *rebozo* concealing her lower face, her black Indian eyes inscrutable, her head lifted warily, her body suggesting a little cottontail frozen to danger but ready to flee. Otto was glaring, and her gaze dropped.

His glance swept her, from black hair to feet which now were wearing shabby *huaraches,* and for a moment all the heat rushed out of his hate and his anger. He felt disappointed, frustrated, cheated. For weeks he had raged about her, calling her whore, liar, teaser, peasant, and now that he saw her in the flesh, his clerk, his property really during business hours, he felt like a man who had lunged with great force to batter down a door only to find the door ajar. Often he had shouted she was nothing, beneath his notice, and now he realized he had been right. For a second he almost pitied her, she was so thin, so timid, so humble. But then his manly qualities asserted themselves; and dragging out his watch he pointed at the shameful time of morning.

"So! Your uncle orders you to be here at nine and now it is long after. Is that any way to start a fine new job?"

"*Señor,*" she whispered, "I do not understand."

"Not understand! You do not understand that nine o'clock means nine o'clock and not ten minutes after already?"

"But *señor,* with your permission, I have no watch. And in any manner I cannot read the time."

"Do you not have a clock at home?"

"But no, *señor.* We have no need of such a contraption."

"No need for a clock!" Otto shouted. "*Mein Gott!* How is it that you live? Like chickens on a roost?"

"*Si,* that is right. The chickens waken in God's good time, and so do we."

Otto nearly choked. Thrusting his watch back into his pocket, he said, "Well, do not let it happen again. Now that you are here I will explain your duties. But first take that thing away from your face so I can hear what it is you say."

She dropped her *rebozo.* And he realized again she was no great beauty. Yet her young dark face with its high cheekbones and eyes set at the slightest possible slant was interesting. It was complicated. It was challenging.

"First of all," he thought, his libido rising, "I will teach her to be punctual."

But he never did.

*

Although Otto needed no clerk, he did need a woman, for he had obstinately kept his resolve not to woo any girl till he could settle matters with Consuelo. This had encumbered him with a plethora of desire, more than he realized. Yet for several days after Consuelo began working in the store, he manfully resisted succumbing to passion, chiefly because of vanity. After the way she had humiliated him the night of the fandango, he certainly did not intend to give her the satisfaction of being thought desirable. Indeed, he kept telling himself she was not desirable: too skinny, too many stains on her teeth. Moreover, she was probably a whore and indubitably a peasant, an Indian, a Mexican. *Ja,* and not a Lutheran but a Catholic already!

The Catholic faith he scorned quite as much as the Methodist, and nearly as much as the Quaker and the Reformed Lutheran, for he had his prejudices. Never having studied dogma, his understanding of these denominations was hazy, his grudge against the Catholics and Methodists being rooted in his notion that both churches baptized by total immersion. The Quakers he thought a cowardly lot because of their opposition to efficiently-organized mass murder; not a general or even a corporal in the whole sect! As for the Reformed Lutherans, he simply could not find words to express his loathing. So far as that went, General von Zumwalt had also believed the languages of civilized man too prudish in this regard. Mentioning a Reformed Lutheran to the general was about as perilous as mentioning an anarchist to a czar.

With Consuelo afflicted by so many shortcomings, it was surprising that she interested Otto at all. Yet she was, of course, a girl. And a girl who had rebuffed him, eluded him, humiliated his proud *Junker* spirit. At the fandango that first night, if she had decided he was the man for her and she must have him, she could have hit upon no surer way to his heart than through his wounded vanity. And when she arrived late at the store, and stood looking submissive, receiving his abuse meekly, she could scarcely have roused him more if she had stripped off her clothing.

After lecturing her about punctuality, during which—except for a tightening of her lips—she received his tongue-lashing with the humble endurance of a beaten squaw, Otto conducted her on a tour of the merchandise. Never had he carried himself more like a soldier. His blond flesh was flushed, his neck stiff. Consuelo might have been a little dog following him around and hoping he wouldn't kick her. Rapidly, curtly, he announced the optimum price of each article as well as the lowest offer which could be profitably accepted. During this stern indoctrination, Consuelo's meekness gradually gave way to animation; the bright buttons and gauds and gay calico enlivened her interest and brought back some of the girlish charm that had shimmered about her the night of the fandango. Noticing this, Otto thought, "*Ja,* you are thinking maybe I have forgiven you for treating me so bad and that you will have an easy time of it here. We will see about that."

"Now that I have told you the prices," he said, sitting down on one of the crude chairs he had designed, "we will learn if you have been paying good attention."

"Oh, yes, *señor.* I have listened with sharp ears."

She went to the other chair, regarding it curiously.

"Ooo, how funny-looking it is! The boards are sawed so crooked and it has a short leg. I wonder if it will hold me."

Laughing, she seated herself.

123

Otto's ears turned scarlet.

"Get up!" he ordered.

"But *señor*, it is quite strong. Observe how it does not collapse." Consuelo thrust out her pretty legs and rocked back and forth, eyes merry. "It is most *extrano*, but it is better than it looks."

"Get to your feet!"

"Do not worry, *señor*. I believe it will hold me. And the short leg makes it a rocking chair."

She demonstrated this.

Otto jumped up, looking wrathful enough to hit somebody.

"When I order you to stand up," he shouted, "you are to obey. It is a good chair. I will bet it is better than any chair in your house."

"But *señor*," she said, remaining seated, "we do not have such *guarniciónes*."

"No chairs and maybe no bed already," he shouted. "And I will bet you live like swine with only a dirt floor."

"How not? Our floor is the same as yours."

"*Ja, ja*, first you laugh at the fine chair I design so I can live like a civilized Prussian, and now you jeer at my floor. Is it my fault it is dirt when it came that way with the house? One of these days I will have a good wooden floor. I will have the finest floor in Santa Fe, and the governor will come to admire it."

"Ooo, that will be a great honor."

"Honor! What is honor to me? I care nothing about honor. It is the floor that matters. *Ja*, sure," he added reasonably, "if the governor wishes to inspect it I will let the fellow in, but I do not propose to lay a floor merely to impress him. Maybe out here at the end of nowhere the governor is considered a great man, but I can tell you I have known greater men. In Prussia my own father is a greater man."

Otto glared down at her. She lowered her gaze; in her lap her hands were loosely clenched. He felt masterful, standing over her, and he resisted an impulse to touch her hair. When he spoke his voice had dropped, but it was stern.

"Now we will see how well you remember what I told you about my fine merchandise. How much is this spool of thread?"

"Who knows, *señor*?"

"What kind of answer is that! I know."

"If you know, then why is it you ask me?"

"*Mein Gott*, you noodlehead, because you are supposed to know."

"I did not realize that, *señor*."

"But I told you the price. You were not paying attention!"

"Ooo, but *señor*," she murmured, gazing up with round and elaborately sober eyes, "with your permission, I was paying close attention."

"Lying will get you nowhere. I told you the price and now you do not remember."

"But *señor*. I thought you were naming prices in case I wished to buy. Since I am very poor, I could not buy if I wished. So naturally I did not listen to the prices."

"*Gott im Himmel!* You did not listen!"

She shrugged.

"You are my clerk and supposed to know prices when a customer asks."

"But *señor*. Why should I burden my head when you know prices so much better than I could ever learn? The customer could ask you."

"A noodlehead!" he exclaimed. "Nothing but a noodlehead!"

She shrugged again.

Nearly incoherent, he turned and paced between store and bedroom, muttering. Consuelo rolled a cigarette. He ignored her, the *dummkopf!* But when with flint and steel she lighted the cigarette, he swung around, glaring. Lost in girlish musings, she sat enveloped by smoke, by indifference, by the luxury of New Mexican indolence.

"*Mein Gott!* What is this? Smoking in business hours!"

And he stormed toward her and struck the cigarette from her hand. Sparks showered over her blouse and skirt; with a cry she jumped up, brushing them away.

"I will not have it," he was shouting. "During business hours it is forbidden."

Eyes angry, she shot him a glance; he had the impression of strength coiling in her body. Roughly, he seized her wrists.

"Not—in—store—hours," he said heavily. "Forbidden! Forbidden! Do you understand?"

She tried to jerk loose; his grip tightened; he could feel the tendons of her forearms squirming as her hands clenched.

"You will have to do as I bid you," he said, his heart thumping with an excitement beyond anger.

Her black eyes were curiously opaque now; he had seen such eyes, inscrutable and deadly, in the faces of Cheyenne braves.

"If you do not obey me I will tell your uncle," he said.

Her wrists went limp and he released her; he was breathing hard.

"Now," he said in a strained voice, "I will teach you prices, and you are to pay strict attention."

So the happy hours passed, while he made love to Consuelo.

*

All that day and the next Otto worked at teaching her punctuality, prices and arithmetic, and although he enjoyed his work more than he pretended he accomplished only hoarseness. It was not, as he insisted, that she was stupid but only that she had never been intended for a career in retail merchandising. Her lack of interest was overwhelming. She had never, she admitted happily, spent one day in school; she knew neither alphabet nor multiplication tables.

He stamped about the store, storming her ignorance with ridicule and words brutal as clubs; she remained bland and artless. On Tuesday morning nine o'clock was twelve minutes lost to eternity when she arrived at work, on Wednesday fifteen minutes lost. When they debated some momentous question, such as Resolved, That Consuelo Delgado Should Learn the Price of a *Vara* of Calico, she flouted all rules of logic, begging the question, ignoring the question, or shifting the question, so that presently Otto found himself arguing the usefulness of clocks or the merits of a wooden floor. Nothing was ever settled. She remained incorruptibly herself. When a customer asked about prices she shrugged and said, "Who knows? Perhaps *Señor* Zumwalt could tell us." Despite the ban on tobacco she persisted in sneaking a few puffs, when Otto went to the outhouse; returning, he sniffed suspiciously. At noon she went home, and Otto was lucky if she returned as early as two. Why the delay? Her siesta. A custom of the country, *señor*.

"No wonder you never get any place and live in houses without floors," Otto said, on Wednesday afternoon. "Sleeping all the time!"

"Not all the time, *señor*. Only at night and in the afternoon."

"Do not dispute me."

"But I am not. I am only telling you when we sleep."

"*Ja*, sleep, sleep! Where would we have got in Prussia if we had slept our lives away?"

"Who knows, *señor*?"

And she picked up the cat, Hilda, and murmured charming nothings. Otto watched sullenly. He felt excluded from that feminine colloquy, on the far side of the chasm separating sex from sex.

"Maybe then," he said, "you just want to remain a know-nothing all your life and never learn to add and subtract and give a customer the right change."

They looked at him, girl and cat, with the dark eyes of Spaniard and Apache, with the green eyes of feline mystery. He felt more ostracized than ever. Consuelo said:

"Such knowledge is not for girls."

And even Hilda, purring melodiously, seemed content to have him banished from that cincture of femininity, with its ancient enigmas, its dusty magic, it cunning snares, its baffling metaphysics. Otto felt defeated and dejected; muttering, he tramped to the patio, where the advancing season had robbed the little cottonwood of its leaves. They lay dry and yellow on the packed earth, crackling underfoot as he paced.

It had been such a brave idea, hiring Consuelo; such a superb opportunity to humble her. And it had failed. Or he had failed. *Ja*, he would face it: he had failed. Always with the girls he had failed. Once he had mooned about his cousin, Gretchen, when she visited the estate, but it was his older brother, Fritz, who stole kisses. At the university with that pretty barmaid he had not even tried, except in imagination, because the upper classmen who were expert duelists were always monopolizing her. In the cafes of Paris he had seen lovely girls, but they were always in the company of other men. So he picked up a cocotte. One did not fail with a cocotte, but it had been a purchased victory followed by disease and pain. That experience taught him to avoid such adventures not only in Paris but also in New Orleans, for the doctors there had warned him that some of the prettiest girls from the nicest families were infected. So he had gone up the big river and west across the plains, dreaming of making love to Indian maidens with gleaming bronze legs, but he had turned against Indians after Billy was killed, and besides, the Cheyenne girls offended his fastidious nostrils. Then Santa Fe. Then Consuelo. Then humiliation. Then opportunity for retribution. She became his clerk. He could order her around. He could make her life miserable. Only he couldn't. Or hadn't. His scorn and contempt only glanced off her self-composure.

It could not go on like this. He would not permit it. If she thought he had used his final weapon she was mistaken. He was stronger than she. Any time he pleased he could take her into his arms and whether she liked it or not would make no difference because he was stronger. *Ja.* He had hoped it would not come to that. He had hoped he could recover his self-respect by humiliating her with words alone, discharging her as a final blow. That would have assuaged the wounds his honor had suffered the night of the fandango. Then he could put her out of his thoughts and try his luck with *señoritas* lovelier than she could ever hope to be. But no. The choice had been hers; she had continued forcing him to wear long jackass ears. So now he would show her and show her good.

He called, "Consuelo."

She did not reply.

"Consuelo!"

Silence. Insubordination!

Angrily, he strode into the store. She was not there.

"Consuelo!" he shouted; but it was no use; she had gone; the bird had flown.

"What kind of monkey business is this!" he bawled, glaring at his watch. "Only four o'clock and she quits work! What kind of success can she expect in business if she leaves as soon as I turn my back? *Ach,* the noodlehead! The *dummkopf!*"

Without her the store seemed empty.

*

That night in sleep he was following the trail back to Missouri with Caleb McSwasey and Billy Proudfoot, who had returned from the dead. Just as in the old days Billy rode his mule, but he no longer laughed, and the strangeness of death was upon him. In the dream Otto tingled with

127

excitement because here was opportunity to learn the secrets of the great shadow world, but Billy would not speak or meet his gaze. The caravan stretched out across the endless plains, but instead of summer it was winter, the sky full of evil green and purple clouds, the flat land contaminated with odd light from the heavens. Suddenly Billy lifted his rifle, waving, and went galloping away swift as a phantom. Otto called for him to wait and solve the great riddle, but Billy did not heed. On his own mule Otto struck out after him, only now he was not riding the mule alone. Mounted ahead of him sat Consuelo, her naked body jouncing against him in delectable unison with the rhythms of the mule. He clutched her but all at once she slid from the mule and laughed and ran, a naked girl with flying hair. Otto dismounted and gave chase. Now it was snowing thickly, the flakes whirling in a tempest. He plunged through mounting drifts, calling, "Consuelo, Consuelo, do not run, please do not run." The drifts kept growing till they were mountains of snow, toppling to bury him. "Consuelo," he called weakly, "I am lost."

He wakened, shivering, in the blackness of 3:00 A.M. Dank cold had filled the house and the wind was blowing a gale. Or was the wind a residue of the dream? Groping for reality, he lighted a candle, and when he was wide awake he still heard the wind. The fine weather of the past weeks had ended. In some savage glen of the high mountains the wild horses of autumn had roused and stampeded down from the peaks, an invisible *caballada* galloping over the mesa and across the roofs of town. In the patio when Otto went for wood the wind was flinging sand among the bare branches of the cottonwood, and the dead leaves whirled. After kindling a blaze in the fireplace he poured Taos Lightning and drank it neat. He poured more. The dream had been only a dream and not worth his attention. The dead did not rise to ride the plains. Man suffered enough tribulations during the years of his mortality without the further woe of cracking the earth above his resting place and returning to the sad world of the living.

"*Ja,*" Otto thought, "he is dead, he is dead. I should never have let him ride off to hunt buffalo. But I was afraid if I stopped him he would be mad with me."

He fell to thinking of that part of the dream which concerned Consuelo. In his arms she had felt wonderful, all soft and brown and naked. Till the dream he had not realized how really attractive she was.

"*Ja,* she was very nice," he thought. "It is too bad she is nothing but a little Indian whore."

But she ran away. Always she was running away.

"I wonder if she likes me a little," he thought, after returning to bed.

When he wakened it was already half past eight. He scrambled from bed; she was due to arrive in thirty minutes and he wanted to be scrubbed and shaved. He felt oddly happy; he had grown to look forward to her coming. The wind was still howling, and when he peeked outside he saw not blue sky but only a ceiling of tan dust.

"So Hod Kite says this is the perfect climate!" he thought. "He is nothing but a liar making up big stories so people will buy houses. I wonder what he is thinking now about his perfect climate."

Nine o'clock arrived but not Consuelo. Ten o'clock. Eleven. By then Otto was pacing furiously; he kept glaring at his watch.

"So! When the wind blows she does not work! A fine piece of cheese! I have never known a girl so lazy and useless. Maybe though it is not all her fault. She comes from a race of lazy Mexicans, and of course those cowardly Apaches never worked a day in their lives. I would like to take them all to Prussia and teach them a thing or two about how civilized people manage matters."

No Consuelo, and no customers either. The store was lonely and dim; against the closed shutters Otto could hear a constant ticking of blown sand. By eleven-fifteen he could tolerate his own company no longer; he jammed on his hat.

"I will report her to her old swine of an uncle," he was thinking. "Then she will be sorry she was so lazy."

El Camino del Chamiso was confusion and madness. The wind lashed around buildings, whipped the bent spines of cottonwoods, flung up dust by the shovelful. Clutching his hat, eyes slitted, Otto stumbled along to the plaza. It was all but abandoned. Only a tethered burro with head hanging and tail miserable, only the forlorn prisoners in the stocks and the pillory. The air was choked with the dry beige fog. Otto groped to the customhouse but the door was locked. He beat it with a fist. Nobody answered. The wind howled, and the plaza might have been the ghost plaza of a town that had died in some earlier century.

"Lazy swine," Otto muttered. "Afraid to step out in a dust storm. They are all huddled in their miserable houses, living on dirt floors like pigs in a sty."

His lips and ears stung from the hurled sand, his nostrils burned. Shielding his eyes with a forearm he tottered toward Kite's Saloon. The shutters were latched, the door closed but unlocked. When he opened it the wind propelled him inside; he leaned on the door to close it.

In the saloon it was like night, candles smoking. The gambling tables were shadowy and abandoned. But Hod stood behind the bar.

"Hello there, Sport," he called. "Ain't this a fierce one?"

Otto rubbed at the dust in his eyes.

"*Ja,*" he said, "but it isn't so bad."

"Damn the wind, anyway," Hod said. "Day like this I want to throw her all up and go back to the States."

"And get into snow already? And ice underfoot and cold to freeze your feet. I will have Taos Lightning, *bitte.*"

Grumpily, Hod reached for the bottle. He looked smaller than usual today, his eyes guarded and doleful, the skin of his sharp little face a duststorm-brown in contrast to his white bald cranium where highlights shifted and shone. Otto could hear the wind screeching under the *portales* outside; somewhere a shutter was banging. Hod poured the drink.

"Five minutes chopped off your life, Sport," he said with a sigh.

"*Ja. Danke schön.* Your health."

"Thanks, Sport. I'll remember you in my will. Damn the wind to hell, anyway."

"*Ja, Herr* Kite, but you take it all in all, this is a pretty good climate. *Ja*, sure, a little wind now and then, but *ach*, the days of sunshine. Myself, I have traveled all over the world, and I have seen many countries. I am what you call a globe-trotter, *Herr* Kite, and I can say the climate in Santa Fe beats them all. Another Lightning, *bitte*."

"Ten minutes off your life," Hod said; and he rolled a cigarette. When he lighted it he cupped his palms; drafts carried the smoke in hurried currents.

"The climate is better than the people," Otto said presently. "Now you take my experience as a man of business. I hire a clerk. And what do I get? A lazy, shiftless little whore."

"What whore is that, Sport?"

"Consuelo Delgado."

"Has she turned professional?"

"*Ja*, sure, sure, just a whore."

"That's where the ladies has got it all over us, Sport," Hod said. "A lady has a run of bad luck and she can always make a living."

"It's a funny thing though, *Herr* Kite. You can say what you please against Consuelo, but she is still a pretty enough little Indian."

"Most of them are, when they're young. I remember once I had me a squaw in Nacogdoches. That was the winter after I was converted to Christ. I had to get rid of her though. She liked her liquor and she drank up my profits. So I bought me a nigger."

"Of course," Otto said, "you take me, coming from a *Junker* family, I would never look twice at a girl like Consuelo Delgado. I have had many women in my time, and to marry a little whore in Santa Fe is the last thing I would ever do."

He remained in the saloon till afternoon, and when he left he was quite drunk, wavering across the dust-blinded plaza. Sometimes he reeled and struck his shoulder against the adobe façades; once he fell. In his own house he staggered aimlessly from store to kitchen and from kitchen to bedroom, sprawling at last on the bed. He dozed, breathing heavily, and it seemed he went floating into a land-that-never-was where Consuelo Delgado was waiting among blossoms. "I should not call her a whore," he thought vaguely, "but if she keeps giving me trouble I will grab her in my arms and show her how strong I am. *Ja, ja*, only an Indian . . ."

And as he dropped into sleep, he was telling himself she needed to be humiliated and given a fine lesson; she needed to be taught never again to start a Prussian on the warpath. *Ja,* here at last was one Indian of whom he was not afraid. It never occurred to him that she might be the most dangerous Indian of them all.

*

Next morning the wind had gone away to pester other people, and Consuelo astonished Otto by arriving ten minutes early.

"What is this?" he demanded, tapping his watch. "Will you never learn punctuality?"

She smiled, and he thought she looked radiant and surprisingly attractive.

"I do not believe I will," she said happily.

"First you come late, always late. And now early."

"But *señor,* that is one of those matters beyond my control. My grandmother has a rooster that is very old. Our other chickens are speckled but he is pure white, and my grandmother says he has much magic about him. By watching him she reads many omens. It is his habit to crow under the window at a certain hour and waken us. If I am early it is because he crowed earlier than is his custom. So you can see none of it is my fault. When the rooster crows is his own affair."

"*Mein Gott!* Am I to understand I should open my store according to the notions of a cowardly rooster?"

"*Si, señor,* that is right. But the rooster, with your permission, is not a coward. He is the bravest chicken of the flock. You should see him chasing the hens."

"That is no test of bravery," Otto said loftily. "All over the world I have known many roosters and always they chase hens."

"White roosters?"

"White, black, red, green, yellow—it makes no difference. *Mein Gott,* why are we talking about roosters already? Why can't we keep talking about what we are talking about?"

"Who knows, *señor?*"

"What are roosters to me? About roosters I care nothing. We were talking about punctuality. I want you to learn it good. This morning you are early already. Do not let it happen again."

And he pivoted and stalked to the patio, but once there he remembered how the other afternoon she had slipped away, so he returned immediately to the store. A fine state of affairs, he thought, when the proprietor dare not turn his back lest his clerk take wing.

He found her seated with the cat on her lap. He took the other chair and watched, stiff-spined as a cadet. Below the hem of her full yellow skirt, he could see her slender feet in their dilapidated *huaraches,* the smooth skin gleaming where it was taut over her ankle bones. Her hands fondling the cat were also slender, the fingers long. Her black hair was lustrous. But her face interested him most, with its complexity of high cheekbones and generous red mouth, her skin a delicious blend of beige and faint rose, like her native earth, with a warm hint of Indian copper. She must have felt his gaze, for she glanced up. Her eyes were night, all the mysterious depths and seductiveness and danger of night. She smiled. And Otto, sitting so stiffly, permitted an answering smile to sweeten the prussic acid of his mouth.

"I believe maybe you like the cat already," he said.

"*Si.* I like to hear her purr. Such a nice soft song she sings."

"*Ja,* she is a fine singer, that little Hilda cat."

"And her fur is so silky. Listen to it snap."

Consuelo drew her palm lightly from Hilda's head to tail, and in the quiet store Otto could hear the faint crackling of electricity. Consuelo laughed in delight. She said:

"Her fur sounds like a piñon fire on a frosty night."

"*Ja,* it is always that way with cats."

"Why do you think her fur snaps and crackles?"

"It is a long story," Otto said. "Some day I will explain it to you. She is a fine mouser too, that little Hilda."

"Ooo, *señor,*" Consuelo trilled, half laughing, "I cannot believe this gentle little cat would wish harm to the mice."

Otto became stern.

"The mice are nothing but thieves. *Ja,* all the time stealing from honest people. But when they came here they stole once too often. Hilda taught them a fine lesson."

"Did you do that, Hilda?" Consuelo crooned.

"*Ja,* I can vouch for her that she did. She is a good efficient cat."

"And so pretty too."

"*Ja,* and not the only pretty one around here."

As he watched Consuelo, whose gaze had dropped, he thought the rosy tones of her flesh warmed, the way he had seen a beige mesa shifting its tints from nude-pink to old rose when the morning sun appeared. Then she glanced at him in shy coquetry.

"But what do you mean by that, *señor?*"

"I mean," Otto said, "that you would not stop a clock yourself."

She smiled; her voice was teasingly low.

"Ooo, no, *señor.* I would never do that. I do not like clocks, and I would not meddle with one in any manner."

"Why are we always talking about something we are not talking about!" Otto exclaimed.

"*Señor,*" Consuelo said, slowly shaking her head, "I do not understand any of it."

"Well, let us see that you do better in the future. What I was saying is that you are a pretty girl yourself."

"*Gracias, señor.*"

The cat absorbed her full attention. Otto cleared his throat.

"And maybe you like Hilda's master a little, *ja?*"

"Who knows?" she murmured.

"What do you mean by that? Don't you know what you know?"

"How can I know, *señor?* How can I know anything when only the other day you said I was a know-nothing?"

"*Ach,* that was all a joke."

"It has all been a joke, *señor?*"

"*Ja,* sure, sure. I am full of jokes."

"Then *señor,* you did not mean it that I should be here at nine and bother my poor head about prices?"

"Not mean it!" he shouted, jumping up. "Of course I meant it, you noodlehead! Maybe you think I was just talking to hear myself. Maybe you think—"

The arrival of a customer cut him short.

*

It was late that afternoon when he tried to take her by force. Why not, he asked himself, force the issue? Wasn't she only a little Indian whore? Hadn't she teased him and wronged him the night of the fandango? To wrong her in return would be only fair and just. By imposing upon her the ultimate embrace, wouldn't he also be imposing the ultimate humiliation?

During the long noon hour while she was home enjoying her siesta he laid his plans. When she returned he greeted her almost politely, but distantly. Customers drifted in, and of course she was totally useless in serving them; while Otto quoted prices and eulogized the merchandise she distracted prospective buyers with comments and questions wholly extraneous. Once Otto ordered her to stop chattering but this proved to be a mistake, for there followed one of those divagating conversations, in which the customer now took part, which strayed far from commerce and ended in a debate as to the proper way to prepare *carne adobada,* the result being that the customer lost her buying mood and left without spending a *centavo.* For this Otto reproved Consuelo, but as always she only shrugged and replied with comments and questions which in their simplicity had the annihilating effect of Socratic irony.

"*Ja,* but just the same you spoiled the sale," he said, stamping toward the patio. But he didn't go beyond the kitchen, because again he remembered how the other day she had left work early. That must not happen today; he had other plans for her today. So he returned to the store where he pointedly ignored her while he gratified his passion for order by rearranging the merchandise. She stood gazing out the window, humming.

How useless she was! If she had common sense, he thought, she would realize that, and if she had any pride she would resign. Not that he would accept her resignation, but it would be a noble gesture. She was good, he thought, for only one thing, and that was not retail merchandising.

He stole glances in her direction. At the window she stood with her back to the room, and he feasted his eyes on her hair, so dark, so rich, so girlish with its braided plait ending in a red ribbon. Her waist, round and slender, was tightly engirdled by a rawhide belt below which her yellow skirt rippled over winsome hips. Her legs were hidden inside the skirt, but he could imagine them straight and tight-skinned with delicate dimples in the smoothness behind the knees. He thought how delectable it would be to caress those dimples with a finger. Smooth, smooth. He might even brush them with his lips while she lay languid. His tongue had grown dry; his heart was pumping. He stepped behind her, clamping a palm on each shoulder; under his hands she stiffened.

"*Señor*. What is it?"

With a palm he encircled her plaited hair, near her scalp, tightening his grip, as if he intended yanking her off her feet and dragging her to bed.

"*Señor*. You are pulling my hair."

"*Ja.*"

"Please do not do that."

"Why not?"

"Because I do not like to have my hair pulled."

His grip loosened. With his palm still encircling the braid he followed that lustrous plait down her back to the hair ribbon. He lifted it, inspected it. Below the ribbon the hair curled out briefly. He bent and brushed the hair ends across his lips. A faint fragrance reached his nostrils, the scent of a young girl's hair.

"*Señor*. Why do you do that?"

Before he could reply a customer entered the store. *Ach!* He dropped the braid, nettled, and tramped into the next room. Why couldn't those cowardly customers stay home where they belonged? This customer was a fat young matron, and as Otto watched he compared her with Consuelo. And Consuelo survived that comparison very well. The customer's nose was coarse, her lips thick, her hair greasy, her body shapeless. Beside her, Consuelo looked dainty and virginal. Even beautiful. Those high cheekbones, those dark eyes, that supple body. Why had he always told himself she was not beautiful? She was lovely. Maybe not pretty, but such an interesting face, so complex, enigmatic! He thought she was like some wild little woods animal, of obscure species, delicate of bone and fleet of foot, that had been snared in the mountains and brought to Santa Fe and only half tamed.

"But I will tame her," he thought, with a secret smile.

*

134

The customer had gone; it was late afternoon. From the low sun, shafts of light fell across the town of mud houses. Inside the store the corners were filling with shadows. Otto's hand trembled as he consulted his watch; his voice quavered.

"It is almost time to close."

"*Si, señor.*"

"Before you leave I wish to show you something in the patio. Go out there, please."

"To the patio?"

"*Si.* I will be there in a moment."

When she left the store, Otto closed the front door and swung the heavy bar into place.

"*Ja,*" he muttered to the darkling room, "that will keep out those nosey customers."

For a moment he hesitated, there among the trade goods, his breathing shallow, his lips oddly stiff. Then he went toward the patio, pausing inside the kitchen door. In the beginnings of dusk he saw her standing by the little cottonwood, a girl alone, pensive. Otto drew a breath. Then, walking stiffly, a peculiar smile on his mouth, he went to her, faced her, seized her shoulders.

"This time," he said, "you will not run away."

In the fading light he was looking full into her eyes. The dark eyes of Spain, of maidens in the dim forgotten halls of the Montezumas, of the Apaches that sword and cross had never vanquished.

"*Ja,*" he said softly, pulling her toward him, "I think that this time—"

He did not finish. The rest of his words were knocked down his throat. For, as unexpectedly as a kick from some pretty little animal, a blow landed on Otto's mouth, delivered swiftly and accurately by Consuelo's fist. It flattened his lip against his teeth, cutting the skin. Otto yelped, in astonishment and outrage. Then he gasped, his body jack-knifing, as she buried her other fist in the pit of his stomach.

"*Mein Gott—!*"

It was not as he had planned. He was not assaulting her; she was assaulting him. Treachery! A low, cheap Indian trick! In the surprise of her attack his hands had been torn from her shoulders, but when he bent nearly double he managed to clutch her skirt above the hem. Now she was trying to run, but Otto, on his knees in the dead leaves, kept his fingers clamped on her skirt. Scalding Spanish poured from her tongue; she whirled and attacked his hands with her fingernails, scratching like a cat. Otto clutched one of her wrists, and when she clawed that hand he let loose her skirt and grabbed her second wrist.

"Consuelo, my little sugar plum, do not run away."

Still on his knees, he yanked her arms, trying to drag her down.

"Don't you want to lie down beside me and rest, my sweet Consuelo?"

Apparently not. For with no warning she jabbed out a knee, delivering

135

a hard blow on the side of his face. It jarred him; he released her wrists. She fled.

"Consuelo! Halt! I command it!" he bawled, scrambling up and chasing her. "Halt! It is my order!"

He plunged into the house, gloomed by dusk. At the front door, where she was fumbling with the bolt, he overtook her, grabbing her braided hair near the scalp. She cried out.

"*Ja,* now it is different already. Always you have treated me so bad, but now that I have caught you it is very different. Maybe you love me, *ja?*"

"I hate you!"

"*Ja?* Well, we will see about that."

By the hair he pulled her against him, the back of her head nearly touching his chest, her spine arched. Then with his free hand he slapped her face.

"Maybe you love me better now."

"You are a rattlesnake."

He slapped her some more. Her body went limp. She crumpled in a heap on the floor.

"Little Consuelo," he murmured tenderly, "what is the matter? Maybe you do not feel so well."

In a faint voice she said, "Where am I, *señor?*"

"You are with the man who loves you," he said.

"If I would stand on my feet would you kiss me, *señor?*"

"*Ja,* sure. I would be glad to."

"Help me up, *señor.*"

When they stood facing each other, Otto once again placed his palms on her shoulders.

"Always you have run from me," he said. "Is that any way to treat me? Now I will give you a nice kiss."

He drew her toward him. And then once more, without warning, she attacked, jabbing a knee into his groin.

He howled.

"I hate you, hate you!" Consuelo screamed; and with both arms stiff before her she rammed against him, knocking him over backwards. His head struck the table loaded with merchandise; he was unconscious before he collapsed on the floor.

*

That was Friday. And although Saturday and Sunday were usually days of flourishing business, on that week end the Santa Fe branch of Proudfoot & Sons remained closed, the door bolted. Consuelo Delgado, the clerk, never came near. Otto Zumwalt, the resident manager, was ailing; all day Saturday he remained in bed. On the back of his skull a lump could be seen; his body ached; his soul ached. The Prussian legions had tried to invade Apache territory and had been repulsed by Apache treachery. It was monstrous. Otto was so mortified he could scarcely face his cat. He kept the shutters closed, and he lay in the dull light with a forearm across his eyes. When he so much as twitched, he groaned with pain. He hated Consuelo. And yet he loved her. He had told her so and he did. He couldn't understand why. Nor could he understand how Consuelo could hate him. Yet she had said she did. Perhaps she had only been leading him on. *Ja,* that must be it. Doubtless she was actually as mad for him as he was for her. But why did she express her love in such a violent manner? Because she was nothing but a cowardly Indian, that was why.

"Anyway," Otto thought, "I showed her a thing or two when I slapped her. I showed her how in Prussia we deal with Indian whores."

Sunday morning he got up, dressing slowly and painfully, his loins feeling like a cluster of boils. After breakfast he sat sunning himself in the patio while the cathedral bells pealed and the cat played with a yellow leaf. Sometimes he stretched out his hands, fingers spread, and stared at the long scratches with their red scabs. Her work. McSwasey had said Indian girls were wild as antelopes, under a blanket.

"*Ja,*" Otto thought, "that liar McSwasey thinks he knows about the girls. But I will bet Consuelo could teach him a thing or two."

In a certain fashion he took pride in Consuelo's wildcat ways. What a spitfire! What sons a girl like that could give a man!

The morning wore away. The cat wearied of playing with the leaf and dozed; Otto dozed. About noon he was roused by loud knocking on the front door.

"Go away!" he shouted. "The store is closed."

The knocking continued.

"Why do you keep up such a racket?" he shouted, hobbling into the house. "I am unwell and the store is closed."

More knocking.

"The store is closed, I tell you," he shouted, unbolting and throwing open the door. Then his manner changed, for Major Delgado stood outside.

"Ah, *señor.* I trust I have not disturbed you."

"Excellency! A tremendous pleasure."

Gold epaulets jiggling, the major waddled across the threshold. Otto asked about his health and the health of his distinguished family. All first rate, the major said, devotedly patting his stomach. Then he asked:

"And your health, *señor?*"

"On Friday, Excellency, I suffered a fall. I have been in pain ever since."

"*Señor,* I am desolated. Friday is a treacherous day. How did you happen to fall?"

"It was nothing, Excellency. But I have been unable to work."

"*Si*, it is well to rest. Work in any case is a great curse. I have often wished that Adam had refused to taste the apple."

"*Ja*, he should have had more sense. But it was all his wife's fault. She should have stayed home where she belonged instead of running around talking with cowardly snakes."

"Ah, *si*. Women are weak vessels."

"*Ja*, that is right. In my travels around the world I have known many women, and they have brought me nothing but trouble."

"That is man's lot, my friend. On the other hand . . ." The major smiled and shrugged. "There are compensations, *señor*. Especially when they are young and blooming. I should like being your age again, so that I could make use of the knowledge I have acquired. One muffs many opportunities when one is callow."

Otto nodded, scowling.

"And now to the painful and degrading subject of business," the major said. "Since my niece has been in your employ for a week, I thought no harm would come from calling to collect her wages."

"Your niece is no longer working at my store, Excellency."

"*Señor*, what are you saying? You discharged her?"

"Naturally not, Excellency. I have been most patient. Her lack of interest in business saddens me, but I have done my best to teach her. In due time I believe she might learn. But she has no idea of punctuality. She is always either too late or too early, and sometimes she leaves without my permission."

"Ah, well, *señor*." The major smiled indulgently. "A few minutes either way is no great matter."

"*Ja*, but on Thursday she did not come at all."

"Thursday? But that was the day of the blowing dust. Surely you did not expect her then. I did not myself go to work that day. I sat by my fire and dreamed of the brave campaigns of my youth."

"*Ja*, well, maybe not on Thursday. But yesterday and today already. She did not come either day. I believe she never intends to come back."

"She will come back, *señor*. I will strongly persuade her to do so."

"*Ja*, but there is yet another matter, Excellency. Perhaps I should not mention it. But certainly you are a man of the world."

"If not that, nothing. Have I not for many years been an officer? Have I not lived in the City of Mexico?"

"Your niece is young, Excellency. And certainly my blood is not cold."

"Nor mine, *señor*."

"On Friday afternoon, Excellency, I attempted to steal a kiss."

"Friday? But why did you wait so long?"

"And she wounded me, Excellency."

"She wounded your feelings?"

138

"More than my feelings. Look at my hands."

"Ah, your poor hands, *señor*. The ugly scratches! My niece is a little wildcat, as I have good reason to know. It is the furious Apache blood."

"*Ja*, and look at my head already. She gave me a push and I struck my head on the table when I fell. It left me *inconsciente*."

"What a pity! There is dried blood on your head and a lump the size of a hen's egg."

"But that is not all, Excellency. She wounded me in a more vital spot."

"More vital than your head?"

"*Ja, si, si!*"

And Otto explained.

"*Señor, señor!*" Vicarious agony crossed the major's face. "I am racked on your behalf. I shudder."

"She might have injured me permanently."

"Let us hope not, *señor!*"

"I do not think she did, but she might have."

Major Delgado sighed.

"It is her wild Apache blood, *señor*. I see I must give her a sound thrashing."

"*Ja!* Good, good!"

"It is the only way, *señor*. With her one must overlook certain things because of her Apache blood, but I cannot have it said my niece is going about using her knees in such a manner. It would give my whole family a bad name. I believe you can rely on it, *señor*, that after my persuasion she will return to your employ."

"Maybe you can teach her punctuality too. Tell her she should be here at nine tomorrow morning. Nine, right on the dot!"

"Hardly tomorrow, *señor*."

"But why not? She has been lazy long enough."

"But *señor*. If I thrash her today she will hardly be able to come tomorrow. Even, perhaps, not Tuesday. I shall tell her to come Wednesday. And she will be here. I can assure you of that."

"Then Wednesday. At nine. Right on the dot. Be sure to tell her that."

"Ah, well, one must not be unreasonable. What are a few minutes either way? And now to the painful subject of wages."

They discussed that matter for quite some time. Otto thought the major overvalued Consuelo's services, and the major thought Otto undervalued them. At last they struck a compromise. And Otto paid out a full week's wages, even though Consuelo had worked but four days. Since the major was going to punish Consuelo, Otto decided he should not be mean about the matter.

Consuelo did not appear at the store either Monday or Tuesday. But she came Wednesday morning. Right on the dot. At a quarter after nine.

By then most of the soreness had left Otto's body, although his hands were still scratched and his head was still swollen. He was waiting for Consuelo, holding his watch, and he expounded the virtues of punctuality. She listened meekly enough, but when he had finished she mentioned the interesting fact that the white rooster had crowed belatedly that morning. Otto said he would like to wring the rooster's neck.

"Ooo, no, *señor!* You must never do that. The rooster is full of magic."

So once again they were lost in a dialectical labyrinth, and everything was the same as last week.

Yet not quite the same. Try as he might, Otto could not summon as much insolence as he had formerly used in training the girl. This did not mean he loved and hated her less, but only that he respected her more. Like all Indian fighters, he had learned caution.

As for Consuelo, she seemed more detached than he remembered, more veiled in feminine mystery and Apache mystery. Sometimes she sat in vast girlish lassitude, stroking the cat. Customers came and went, but she made no move to serve them. Her indifference was immeasurable. When asked the price of merchandise, she would only shrug. And Otto, the resident manager already, the scion of *Junkers,* would have to wait on the customers himself. A fine keg of pickles! Paying a clerk who did nothing but stroke a cat! Feeding a cat that did nothing but sit to be stroked! And when he rebuked Consuelo she sat dumbly, as if he were employing a language she did not understand, and in which she had not the faintest interest. Or worse, she would reply with one of those devilishly simple questions which lured him into involved arguments.

"If she is not careful," Otto thought, "I will report her to her uncle and he will thrash her again."

Again? Had the major actually thrashed her? As the morning wore away, Otto began to doubt it. Where were her bruises? She did not handle her body as if it were sore.

Wednesday afternoon, when she returned late from her siesta, Otto screwed up his courage and asked:

"Why did you not come to work Monday and Tuesday? I have been meaning to ask you that."

"I was indisposed, *señor.*"

"You were indisposed already! What do you mean by that?"

"By that, *señor,* I mean I was indisposed."

140

"Gott im Himmel! Here we are again going round and round like a cowardly dog chasing his tail!"

He stamped into the next room and flopped down on the bed. He was in despair. Could he never teach her a fine lesson? Would she always get the better of him? There was no way to attack her, no way to reach her, by words or actions. *Ach,* she was like the tough, scrubby vegetation growing in this desert land, with its sweet little flowers guarded by needles.

As he lay there he heard the voice of a newcomer in the store; a familiar voice. *Señora* Delgado's. Otto went to greet her.

"May I have the honor of serving you, *señora?*" he asked.

"No, you may not," she said coldly. "I am here only because my husband sent me."

"Your husband is well, I trust?"

"My husband is not well. He is home groaning like a pig bearing shoats. This is his third day of indisposition."

"I am grieved to learn that. Did he eat unwisely?"

"He always eats unwisely, but it is not that. It is what she did to him."

And *Señora* Delgado jabbed a finger at Consuelo.

"But I do not understand," Otto said.

"You should. Oh, I have heard how you have carried on with the little slut. And I have heard how the little wildcat dealt with you. Last Sunday my husband went to the home of his blessed mother to administer a sound whipping to his blessed niece. But he had got in only a few licks when she flew at him and scratched his face and used her knee on him in a certain manner. Not once but three times. And when the clumsy fool doubled in agony she pulled his hair and kicked him in the stomach."

"You do not tell all the truth, my blessed aunt," Consuelo said.

"You say that I lie?"

"I say that if you tell it you must tell it all. I did not kick him because he beat me. I kicked him because he tried to do certain other things."

"You lie."

"I do not lie. Ask him."

"I have asked him, you little fool. Do you think I have lived all these years with Manuel Delgado for nothing? I asked him if he tried to kiss you and he denied it."

"Then he is lying," Consuelo said. "He has often tried to kiss me, and last Sunday he tried to do certain other things."

"Then I will deal with him when I get home. I came only because he sent me to find if you had come to the store as he commanded. I told him of course you would be here, that I have the brains to know you are setting your snares for *Señor* Zumwalt. Now I am going and leave you two to your sinfulness. I spit on you both."

And *Señora* Delgado waddled out.

*

Otto stared at Consuelo. She was utterly tranquil, sitting with hands loosely clasped in her lap, her head slightly bowed, her black hair rich, her yellow skirt flaring lavishly, her ankles pressed together. A faint smile curved her lips.

"*Señorita* . . ."

"*Señor?*"

"Did your uncle make an outcry when you kicked him?"

"*Sí*. A great outcry."

"He is a brave warrior, your uncle."

"*Sí*, such is his reputation."

Their eyes met, and they smiled.

"Perhaps," Otto said, "we should drink to your uncle's recovery."

"Perhaps no harm would come of it," she said.

When Otto returned from the kitchen with Taos Lightning, he saw that an amazing phenomenon had taken place during his absence. The front door had closed itself and bolted itself.

He thought, "*Mein Gott!*"

And he thought, "I will never understand her."

And later, much later, after dusk had swirled into the bedroom, he was thinking, "It was all lies, lies. Hod Kite and Caleb McSwasey saying she was nothing but a little whore! The liars! The liars!"

*

"Why do you cry?" he asked, later yet.

She did not answer.

"Is it then that you are sorry?"

"No, *señor*. I am not sorry."

"I wish you would call me Otto."

"Otto," she said tentatively.

"*Ja*, that is my name. Otto. It is one of the few names that spells backward the same as forward."

"I know nothing of spelling, Otto."

"That is all right. I would not love you more just because you could spell."

"But you do love me?"

"*Ja*, very much."

"I love you, Otto. Ooo, it is all so strange."

"When did you begin to love me?"

"Who knows? Perhaps that evening at the fandango when you asked me to smile and I gave you a cigarette. That was an evening most romantic."

"*Ja*, but you ran off from me."

"Of course. I was not a little roadside weed any rooster could peck at."

"Let us leave roosters out of it."

"Besides, I thought perhaps you might catch me."

"You ran too fast."

"*Si*, my feet have always been swift. When I was a child I used to run races with the wind."

"The other day why did you scratch me?"

"It was all part of making love, *señor*. Otto. I cannot seem to remember to call you Otto."

"And why did you kick me?"

"Because you pulled my hair and slapped me. I was not a slave to be won without wooing. But I did not kick you so hard as I kicked my uncle. He is a wicked one, my uncle. My father was otherwise. When he died I cried. I did not cry when my mother died because I was too young to know. I was but a year old when the great plague carried her to her grave. But I was eleven when they brought home my father's shoes."

"But how was that?"

"I do not want to talk about it now, Otto. I want to be happy now. I have not been very happy in my life. The other children used to torment me because of my Apache blood. Sometimes I would run, and sometimes I would fight back. I learned to scratch and kick. No, I have not been happy. Have you been happy, Otto?"

"*Ja*," he was going to say, "sure, sure. At home my father always called me his happy little bumblebee."

But oddly, he did not say that. He said:

"No, I have never been happy. When I was six I dropped a beautiful vase and broke it. My father was furious but he was just leaving for Berlin and could not stop to beat me. But he promised me a hard beating when he returned. He was gone a month. It was always like that. My brothers played tricks on me and I used to cry myself to sleep. I have often been lonely. I have been a homeless one wandering the earth."

"Otto, poor Otto. You are not lonely now?"

"Not now," he murmured. "Not now, my little desert flower."

*

For the next weeks Otto was not himself at all. No longer did he wait, watch in hand, to rebuke Consuelo when she arrived tardily. No longer did he call her noodlehead and cabbagehead, or upbraid her because she could not remember prices. Everything had changed. Selling merchandise had dwindled to unimportance. He moved in a nimbus of delusion and enchantment.

143

"*Ja, ja,*" he thought, "I am in love. I am in love with Consuelo Delgado. That is a pretty name."

He marveled at how stupid he had been that first night he met her to suppose she was not beautiful. She was ravishing. *Ja,* maybe her teeth were tobacco-stained and several back teeth were missing, but that only gave her piquancy.

And he was aghast at the depravity of those character assassins, Hod Kite and Caleb McSwasey, who had said she was nothing but a little Indian whore. Slander! How could a girl be both a whore and a virgin already?

Consuelo had also changed, or so it seemed to Otto. The wine and meat of love agreed with them both. Her hair was glossier, richer, so electric with life that it crackled when he stroked it. Her skin glowed. Her eyes were more tender, merrier, more seductive, and sometimes they were brimming with such sweet heartbreak that Otto could have cried out, if customers had not been present.

Customers had become a tremendous nuisance. Otto and Consuelo would be embracing, or holding hands, and then a confounded customer would arrive.

"*Ja, ja,* what is it that you want?" he would demand testily.

"Only to look, *señor.*"

"Always looking!" Otto would say to himself. "You have all of Santa Fe to look in, but you must come here when we are busy."

And while the customer disarranged the merchandise, Otto's gaze would meet Consuelo's and they would smile; or perhaps he would bring a stifled giggle to her throat by lifting his brows and rolling his eyes and drawing a long breath.

Sometimes the customers were girls of Consuelo's age. It made no difference; they were as tiresome as anybody else; with them he was also gruff, even when they became coquettish. Just silly girls. Probably whores. Too plump. Too greasy. Quite unattractive. In these days he had eyes for only one girl.

Consuelo especially disliked customers of her own age and sex. When they were in the store her eyes were pure Apache, watchful and deadly. Sensing her dangerous mood, Otto stepped carefully, keeping all conversation with those flibbertigibbets on a high business plane, as Platonic as a promissory note. And when he and Consuelo were alone again, she would be somber and estranged. This dismayed him, but it also charmed and flattered him. Jealous! *Ach!* What a girl! What a dark flame of a girl!

Late in November the weather turned cold; wind blew from the mountains, driving clouds of dust before it, and homeless tumbleweed. One morning Otto wakened to a day of turbulence, the air swimming with debris; he did not expect Consuelo to turn up at the store. Yet she came. Late, to be sure, but she came. And what a different reception he gave her from those in the bad old days!

"Consuelo! I didn't expect you."

"I wanted to come, Otto. My grandmother forbade it, in this storm, but I had to come."

They embraced. And after the door was bolted Otto led her to the bed in the second front room.

*

He would carry it always in memory, that day so foul and fair. That day when love was still new enough to be full of wonder and surprise, but not so new as to be maladroit. It was their day, gift of Aeolus and his mad horses of wind galloping over the royal city of mud houses and brown-bean men. The world left them alone, that day. Customers stayed away.

They loved. And they laughed and talked and ate and loved again. In the patio they braved the wind together to fetch more wood for the fire. In the kitchen they played at keeping house, as if they were married, but the food was woefully late in getting itself prepared because they stopped so often to kiss. It was that day, very likely, when Consuelo conceived.

She also talked. It was as if she had some compulsion to turn her mind inside out, bringing to her liege lord all the treasures and rubbish of her years. The treasures were so humble that once Otto would have been disdainful; now he pitied her. When he looked back his own life seemed threadbare enough, but compared with hers it was cloth of gold. He had traveled half the earth; she had traveled scarcely a dozen miles from Santa Fe. As a boy he had learned to read German, Latin, French, Spanish, English. She had read nothing, ever. Yet she was not stupid. Uninformed, yes; but her mind was sharp and agile.

Always she had known poverty, the bitter poverty of the peon. And her mother and father had gnawed the same bitter rind. Yet somehow when they married her father had managed to buy land at the edge of town, and using his own earth for material he had molded adobe bricks and built a house and planted cottonwoods and fruit trees. A garden had flourished, and chickens. He had been a dark one and a silent, this Alfonso, born of Apache rapine. For weeks he would work faithfully, cultivating his chili peppers and Indian corn, or hiring himself out to the rich, but a time always came when restlessness seized him and he would go off alone to the mountains, armed with bow and arrow.

Consuelo was the first born, a baby with the silky black hair and jet eyes and Mongol cheekbones of the Apache. Another child was on its way when the wife of Alfonso perished in the plague. Even La Luz Delgado, Alfonso's mother, had been unable to brew a potion whose steaming magic would vanquish the plague. After the death of her

145

daughter-in-law La Luz abandoned her own hovel and moved into her son's house, to prepare his meals and rear his daughter.

An ugly one, La Luz Delgado. A bag of bones, a cracked voice. People feared her. And they said she had never been the same since that long-ago day when the Apaches pillaged the town and murdered her husband and carried her away into mysterious lands. Some said she was half mad. Some said she had sold her soul to Belial in exchange for hidden knowledge of herbs, and some said that during her exile she had renounced Jehovah and worshipped the powerful Apache gods who dwelt in the vast mountains somewhere far to the west. In any case she had suffered sadly on her desperate hegira from the Apache Nation, a woman whose tongue was swollen with thirst and whose womb was swollen with Alfonso.

Yet if people feared her they also summoned her in time of sickness. Through the years her reputation as a *curandera* grew. And her ugliness grew also. From earliest memory Consuelo feared her, for she had a wicked way with a switch.

After the death of his wife Alfonso never remarried, although there were whispers that he had carnal knowledge of women. People said there was a sheepherder's wife in the mountains who gave him love, and there were rumors about him and a slave girl belonging to a rich man. But the rumors ceased when Consuelo was seven and her father became enamoured of religion. Nearly every day he went to the cathedral, and presently it was known that he had become a novitiate in the Third Order of St. Francis. This was a shadowy and secret society umbilical to Europe and the middle ages, and even though the priests and the bishop and the pope himself inveighed against it, the order persisted in obscure crannies of the mountains. One Friday night early in Lent Alfonso was gone from the house, but in the darkness before Saturday's dawn he returned in exhaustion and agony. Although supposedly asleep, Consuelo watched while Alfonso took off his shirt and revealed for La Luz's ointments a lacerated back. Six sharp cuts were to be seen at his waist, three horizontal and three vertical; and the rest of his back was a mass of marks from the lash. The child heard him babbling about the meaning of the stripes, and as the years passed she learned he had received seven stripes for the seven times Christ spoke from the cross and five for the Saviour's five wounds and forty for the forty days in the wilderness.

By the time she was eleven her father's back was nothing but scar tissue and fresh wounds; he bore them gladly, as if by humiliating his flesh he could bring harmony to his soul, that battleground where Spaniard and Apache fought unceasingly; and it was that year, on Good Friday, when he was chosen by lot to take the leading role in the clandestine Passion Play off in the secret mountains. Good Friday was cold that year, and in the mountains snow was blowing. Long afterward

Consuelo pieced together what had happened. From the *morada* of the order Alfonso had staggered along a high mountain trail, shoulders bent under a huge cross, while lashes fell on his back and on the backs of all the Penitentes in the procession; and to the howling of the wind was added the high, unearthly skirling of the *pitero's* flute. At the appointed place Alfonso, naked save for a loin cloth, dropped the cross and lay down upon it, arms spread. Nails were driven through his hands and feet. Then the cross was erected. He hung there in the blowing snow till life slumped from his body.

Next day three men arrived at the house, bringing a pair of shoes. They had belonged to Alfonso. When she saw that token of death La Luz screamed curses at the men and sometimes her words were those of the Apache tongue. The men fled. And La Luz, cackling to herself like some mad old witch, prepared a secret brew and dropped the dead man's shoes into the steaming cauldron. Presently she dipped a ladle into the scalding brew and flung the liquid upon the crucifix hanging above the fireplace.

"That will bring him back," she screeched at the wide-eyed Consuelo. "Wait and see. On the third day he will arise from the dead."

But he never did. They never saw him again. They never even found his grave, lost somewhere in the mountains.

*

That was the story Consuelo told Otto on the day of the great wind, her voice low and utterly resigned to the tribulations of life and the fluctuations of human destiny. Her eyes were dry and stoical; she was without self-pity. Indeed, as she ranged back in memory through that swamp of morbidity and superstition, she brought to the telling a certain dignity and even poetry, the dignity and poetry perhaps of the Apache, that nation of far mysterious deserts and remote high country. When she had finished, Otto held her in his arms.

"And what did your uncle think," he asked, "about those cowardly Penitentes killing your father?"

"He did not live in Santa Fe then. He was still a brave warrior in the cafes of Mexico. It was the summer after my father's death when my uncle and his family moved to Santa Fe. Often I wished they had never come."

"But did he not relieve your poverty?"

"*Si*, greatly. In words."

"Not in deeds?"

"Very little. The *huaraches* I am wearing are castoffs from my aunt's feet. That is how my uncle has helped."

"On the night of the fandango your feet were bare."

"*Si*. My aunt's feet are bigger than mine and it is clumsy to dance in her shoes."

147

"How is your uncle's health by now?"

Consuelo smiled.

"I am not greatly concerned about it. But my grandmother has been treating him and she reports him much improved. Soon he will return to work, doubtless to his sorrow. He is a lazy one, my uncle."

"And wicked?"

"Very wicked. I would not have kicked him so hard if it had been the first time his hands had misbehaved with me. One's hands should have a sharp conscience with the daughter of one's brother. But he is going about town proving himself a man. Some years ago he ceased being a man with my aunt. So at least the whisper goes from my aunt to my grandmother. My aunt asked my grandmother to prepare a tonic to restore my uncle's gallantry. That was last spring. With my grandmother I went to the mountains to gather roots for the medicine. I do not believe my grandmother knew what she was about, but for good measure she gathered a little of everything. *Sabina macho* for colic, *contrayerba* for dysentery, *oshá* for a cough, *capulín* to cleanse the blood, *escoba de la víbora* for rheumatism, *yerbabuena* and *yerba mansa*—a little of all the herbs. I wished to include a bit of poison in the mixture, but my grandmother restrained me. However, when we returned home and my grandmother was brewing the potion I watched my chance and sprinkled in a substance of my own gathering. 'There, my blessed uncle,' I thought, 'that will give you the strength of seven.' I do not believe, however, that it helped, for my aunt still complains and makes eyes at the young men."

"What was the substance?" Otto asked.

Consuelo smiled.

"I asked myself what animal had the greatest strength where my uncle was weakest. What animal but the bull? So I gathered the dried chips from a bull and sprinkled a bit into the potion my uncle was to drink. But even it did not help my poor uncle. Is that not sad?"

"You are a vixen," Otto said.

"*Si*, I am a vixen fox no man can catch unless I wish it."

"I have caught you."

"Only because I wished it. Watch me, Otto." She stood up, smiling, and suddenly exclaimed, "Now you will not catch me."

And she whirled and fled through the kitchen and out into the blowing dust and eddying leaves of the patio, Otto pursuing her. Fleet and graceful, she danced always out of reach, round and round the little wind-bent cottonwood, her hair streaming and her skirt billowing, till it seemed to Otto she was some mythical and lightfooted daughter of the wind. At last, laughing, she permitted herself to be overtaken. Strong sap was running in his veins, and he swept her into his arms and carried her into the house.

"Otto, Otto," she murmured, shaping the vowels with rounded lips,

148

"I did not really wish to escape you, Otto. I never wish to be beyond your reach."

*

It was late that evening when she said she must return to her grandmother's house.

"I will go with you," he said.

"There is no need of that, Otto."

"*Ja*, I will go. I do not want harm to befall you."

In the candlelight he saw tears glisten in her eyes; she threw her arms around him and began to cry.

"Otto, *vida mía, amor mío* . . ."

"Do not cry, *pobrecita*. Why do you cry?"

"Because it is over. It has been a beautiful day, but now it is over."

"There will be other days."

"*Sí,* but never this day again. The day is old now and soon must die. The minutes have been beautiful, but they have died and dropped away like leaves from a tree. They are as dead now as they will be in a thousand years. And some day, *muy amado mío,* we too must die, and the memory of this day so beautiful will be forever lost. I am frightened, Otto."

"Do not be frightened. I will protect you."

"Even you cannot protect me from time."

"*Pobrecita,* you are tired."

"*Sí,* tired and sad. But happy too."

"We will have a little drink for our little journey to your grandmother's house. You will feel better then."

He poured Taos Lightning. And that fiery liquid from the town in the high mountains fulfilled the great mission of whiskey among the race of mortals, dulling the ache that lives like a shadow in the spirit, bringing to the blood the fertility of earth and the heat of the sun, capsuled in the summer grain and set free in the sorcerous worms of the distillery.

They kissed and kissed again, before going forth into the black torrent of wind pouring over the huddled town. Dust assaulted them, and clouds of withered leaves. Clinging together they toiled along like two weak figures on the floor of some unfathomable stream, while overhead the mighty river roared. Sometimes they paused to take breath, backs to the wind, twigs and sand and the husks of squaw-corn flying past them.

"Otto. You should not have come. A storm so bad . . ."

"Easier for two than for one alone . . ."

"*Sí.*" She huddled close to him. "Perhaps that is why God wills that man and woman should face life together. Always easier for two than for one alone . . ."

At the town's end they reached her grandmother's house, set back from the road under the tossing cottonwoods, shadowy and humble, thin strips of candlelight shining through cracks in the shutters. As Otto watched even that light faded behind an intervening whirlwind freighted with the loose earth of New Mexico.

They fumbled toward the house, and when they stopped Consuelo whispered:

"It has all been wonderful and beautiful, this day. It has been the most beautiful day of my life."

"Of mine too. *Ja, wunderbar und schön.*"

"May you dream of beautiful things, *amor mío.* May you walk in dreams through the freshness of spring and stop when you are thirsty to drink from a sparkling mountain stream. May you walk where the goats always give milk, and the wine vats are brimming, and the hives are rich with honey, and the kernels of wheat are fat and heavy on the stalk. And may I dream the same dream, *vida mía,* and walk into the mountains, and may we meet each other in our separate dreams."

"*Ja,* I think that will happen when we are sleeping."

"Good night, Otto. It is a knife in my heart, to say good night. Good night, my life."

"Good night, Consuelo. My pretty little one."

And then he was alone, reeling back into town through turbulence; and when he reached his house it seemed an empty chrysalis without her. The fire had burned low; frigid drafts leaked through the shutters. The wind screeched and rushed and rattled, ceaseless and elemental as surf. And he was depressed because the golden day had ended in the dustbin of time and because there could never be another like it. He poured a drink, standing in his store with the trade goods, staring at the floor which was still packed earth but which one of these days would be of fine boards. Aloud, he said:

"*Ja,* I am in love. She is wind and fire. I didn't mean it to be like this but I am in love. I love her enough to marry her tomorrow, if only she were not a cowardly Indian."

* * *

They never had another day like that, not ever. Next morning the wind had died, bequeathing a legacy of beige dust to the merchandise in Otto's store, and a legacy of slate-colored clouds to the skies. Now and then the sun tried to shine, but the rays were feeble; the clouds thickened; the patio looked bleak; and with the shutters closed against the raw air the store was gloomed. In the heavy atmosphere the fireplace chimney did not draw properly; sometimes smoke puffed into the room. Otto wakened in a lugubrious mood which breakfast only partly dispelled, and as he dusted the merchandise he brooded about the imperfections of a universe in which a high-born Prussian found himself in love with a

Mexican-Indian. Where would it all end? *Ach,* where?

He felt better when Consuelo arrived; even though she was a half hour late he did not chide her; he kissed her.

"Have you missed me, Otto? I have missed you, *vida mía.* Sleep would not come to me last night because I longed for your arms. I lay wide awake hearing the wind and thinking of you."

"*Ja,* it was that way with me also."

"When I entered the house last night my grandmother was waiting up for me. She was angry."

"Because you came to the store through the dust storm against her wishes?"

"*Si.* And because I was so late returning home. I believe we have come under her suspicions, you and I."

"So? What did you tell her?"

"I told her we are in love."

"*Ja,* good. That is true."

"She did not think it good. It made her more angry."

"*Ja,* well maybe she would do better to mind her own business. Tell her to keep her nose out of our affairs."

"Ooo, no! That would make her more angry and she would object to you more than she does."

"She objects to me?" Otto asked, thunderstruck.

"*Si, vida mía,* I believe she does."

"To me? You mean she objects to me?"

"I should not have told you, Otto. My tongue is clumsy this morning."

"To me she objects? *Mein Gott!* Maybe you should go home at once and tell her I am the son of General von Zumwalt."

"I have told her that. I have talked much about you, *vida mía.* When we are apart I want only to think of you and speak of you."

"You mean you have told her my father is General von Zumwalt and she still objects?"

"*Si,* she still objects."

"But why?"

Consuelo did not answer.

"Why? *Ja,* that is what I want to know. Why?"

"You would not be happy if I told you."

"So? Well, maybe you think I am happy now. Maybe you think I am braying with happiness because the old woman gabbles she does not like me."

"Otto, do not be upset."

"Do not be upset?" Otto exclaimed, pacing the floor. "Who is upset? I am not upset. What is it to me if some lice-bitten old ostrich with all her feathers molting away flaps her wings and clucks that she does not like me? Why should I care? I do not care. Better people than her have disliked me. *Ja,* I have been disliked by some of the best people in

151

Europe. So what is it to me if a foul old woman living like a filthy pig in a house without a floor dislikes me already? I will tell you what it means to me. Nothing! I snap my fingers at the old pig-bitch. Why should she dislike me? Haven't I always spoken well of her? How could she dislike me when she has never seen me but once that night of the fandango?"

"Otto, please do not get so excited."

"I am not excited. It is the ugly old woman who is excited with her lies about being raped by some Apache. I am as cool as a pig on ice."

"Otto, *amor mío*. My tongue is clumsy today. My tongue has betrayed me. It is not that she actually dislikes you. I think she is fond of you."

"So? Well, I am fond of her too, but it makes me mad when I hear the lying old hyena is going about town howling she dislikes me when she is really fond of me."

"Otto, Otto, she has not told anybody except me."

"Nobody but you! So! She whispers her lies behind my back and tries to make you stop loving me! That is the worst of all!"

"Nobody could make me stop loving you, *amor mío*. Nobody except you yourself and maybe not you. For I have become part of you, Otto. Alone without you I am only half a person. Without you I am the apricot tree that has suffered blight and stands dead in the noonday heat. Without you I am the doe stricken down by the hunter's arrow. Be calm, *amor mío*. It is not that my grandmother dislikes you but only that she objects to your beliefs."

"But how does the old woman know what my beliefs are? Sometimes I hardly know myself."

"Dear Otto, she objects to you because you are not a member of our faith."

"You mean because I am not a Catholic?"

"*Si,* that is what I mean."

Otto stood staring at Consuelo, and the store became so still that he could hear the low purring of the cat. He sat down. Quietly, he said:

"It is true that I am not. I am a Lutheran."

"I have never heard of that religion, *vida mía.*"

"You mean," he asked slowly, "that you have never heard of Lutheranism?"

"I do not believe I have."

"*Ach,* what am I doing in New Mexico?" he said, in German. "In Prussia the fields are green. In Prussia the cows wade in rich pasture. In Prussia all men have heard of Martin Luther and General von Zumwalt. What am I doing lost in this dry land of waste places? What am I doing owning a house and half mad with love for a beautiful little Mexican-Indian? *Gott im Himmel,* help me. How did it all come about?"

152

"Please, Otto, my dearest. Do not talk in words that are beyond my understanding."

He stared at her.

"Otto, Otto. You are to me the sun on the *Sangre de Cristo*. You are to me a spring day in the mountains when the little flowers are blooming and the clear brooks are rippling in the sun. Otto, *vida mía,* I am in despair with worry. Last night I could not sleep. I love you, Otto, and I do not wish you to suffer through all eternity in the flames of hell. Do you not think, *amor mío,* that you could embrace my faith and be saved?"

"You mean I should leave the Lutheran Church already?"

"What else?"

"No," he said, "no."

"But Otto—"

"Never. Never that. *Mein Gott,* I was brought up a Lutheran. My father and mother are Lutherans. No, no, I could never leave the Lutheran faith."

He saw her stricken face, her dry stricken eyes.

"Then it is not *hasta luego,*" she said. "It is *adiós.*"

She went to the door.

"Consuelo! Wait!"

Outside the door she broke into a run, her fleet feet taking her beyond pursuit down the Street of the Chamiso.

Otto returned to the store.

"Always she has run away," he said, in German. "But this time it is different. She is a part of me and I am also a part of her. *Gott, Gott,* why did I ever come to this land of Mexicans and Indians?"

✳

Consuelo did not return that day. Otto kept going to the door and peering along the street, but he did not see her. His melancholy deepened. Darkness fell early; he barred the door and poured whiskey and sat staring into the fire.

"It is a terrible experience," he thought, "this falling in love. It has made me happier than I have ever been, but also more dismal. I never guessed it would be like this. When I used to read in *The Iliad* about those warriors fighting I thought the fighting was good but it was silly to go to war because of some woman. But now I understand."

He sighed.

"Maybe she will be here tomorrow. *Ja,* of course. I would like to wring the neck of her lying old grandmother."

He sat there a long time while the fire burned low. Once he thought he should go to the kitchen and prepare food, but he was not hungry. The cat padded over to rub against him; he picked her up.

"Hilda, Hilda, I do not feel so well. It is because of the little Mexican-Indian. Maybe she will come back tomorrow. I will never go to her,

153

little Hilda cat. That would be giving in to her girlish notion that I should leave the Lutheran faith. A man cannot give in to every silly notion those girls get into their pretty heads. I will never go to her but maybe by and by I will take a little walk past her house to see what I can see."

The idea of doing that gave him solace and hope. Perhaps he would encounter her on the street, and in the darkness they would fly into each other's arms.

When he opened the door he discovered that it was snowing, and he exclaimed, "*Ach!*"

Snow! Outrageous! The final indignity!

"So this is the perfect climate!" Otto thought. "Here it is hardly December and we get snow. We never got snow in New Orleans. I would like to have Hod Kite here and wash his face in the stuff."

He stood muttering; at last he plunged into the storm. The flakes were large and wet; they worked under his collar; soon his boots were sodden and his feet grew cold. Nobody else was abroad; he crunched along with head lowered, scolding the weather; and when he reached Consuelo's house he stood staring at the light shining through the shutter cracks. He listened, hoping to catch the sound of her voice. But all was quiet.

*

When he wakened next morning it was still snowing. Always in a bad mood before breakfast, he puttered about the kitchen carrying on long imaginary arguments with Hod Kite concerning the Santa Fe climate. Breakfast improved his temper, and he told himself that perhaps Consuelo would come today. She didn't. He spent the morning scooping a path across the patio to the outhouse, and from the front door to the limits of his property. The work finished, he leaned on his shovel and scowled at the unscooped sidewalks of his neighbors. Lazy Mexicans! By now the snowfall had ceased and the sun was promising to shine. He consulted his watch. Nearly eleven.

"Now we will see," he thought, "if that lying Hod Kite was telling the truth when he said the snow in Santa Fe always melts by noon."

An hour later Hod stood convicted as a liar; Otto was outraged. And although the skies cleared that afternoon, the ground was still white at dusk. Both business and Otto had been wretched that day; he could not face another evening alone; so after supper he went to Kite's Saloon. And even though it was Saturday night business was slack, owing to the weather. But Hod was cheerful.

"A fine snow, wasn't it, Sport?"

"What was so fine about it?"

"The moisture. You'll see millions of wild flowers this spring."

"*Ja?* Well, that is a long time away, and I need moisture myself. Lightning, *bitte.*"

"Five minutes chopped off your life."

"Your health, *Herr* Kite."

"Thanks, Sport. I'll remember you in my will. How's everything? You look kind of peaked. Ain't been sick, have you?"

"I am never sick. I have a rugged constitution."

"So does the U.S.A., Sport. Has to have, with a president like Monroe. Sure wish we could hear some election news. General Jackson was running, last I heard. If I was back in the States, he'd be my man."

"*Ja,* McSwasey has told me about the general. I understand he fights like a Prussian."

"I doubt it, Sport. I don't think Old Hickory fights like anybody but Old Hickory. I'd bet on him, if I was back in the States."

"I wouldn't. I am not a betting man."

"You're not? Lord Almighty, Sport, you're passing up some fun."

"*Ja,* and I'm passing up losing money too."

"So you never bet! Well, I'm damned. You would, though, if you had a sure thing."

"There are no sure things."

"Caleb McSwasey rigged a sure thing once. And how he cleaned up! Matter of fact, so did I. We were in it together, although I can't rightly take credit for the idea. That was McSwasey's. I was running a joint in Nacogdoches in those days. Not much of a place, you understand, but good enough if you wanted to get in out of the wind for a drink or a gal. Well, one day old Caleb blows into town, fresh from New Orleans, and heading up toward the Comanche Nation on business of his own. He was always coming and going in those days. I never asked him what he was up to, because in the first place it warn't my business, and in the second place if he'd told me it wouldn't have been true, and look at all the breath we both would have wasted.

"Nacogdoches was kind of lively at that time. It's not far into Texas across from Louisiana, and you know how it is with a border town. Sometimes she'll doze like a cat in the sun, and the next thing she's rocking. There was some nigger smugglers laying over with me just then. Things had tightened up along the Louisiana coast, so they'd landed their niggers in Texas and were fixing to cross the Sabine and sell their haul in the upcountry. They must have had twenty niggers with them, fresh from Africa by way of Cuba. Kept them in a lean-to out back of my joint. Chained, of course. Them niggers made an awful racket, day and night. You'd hear their chains clank, and then they'd start singing. Not in American, of course. Sort of a moaning song. I didn't like it. Not my kind of music. But that's neither here nor there.

"Well, what with them nigger smugglers and various gents from the States, business was good just then. That was one thing about Nacogdoches, it was close enough to Louisiana so that if a gent got into trouble in the States he could come over and pass away the time with a greaser gal till things calmed down. Well, when Caleb blew in from New Orleans, some of the gents wanted to know who was likely to win the election for mayor. Caleb said that when he left the two candidates was running neck and neck, but he had a hunch who would win. They wanted to know who that was. And in that quiet way, Caleb smiled and said, 'The man who gets the most votes.' Everybody laughed. Caleb said he'd best turn in, since he was leaving at daylight heading northwest.

"With all them nigger smugglers and various sporting gents, I didn't have no kind of bed for Caleb, but he said he'd sleep in his blankets. Before he left, he come over to the bar. 'Hod,' he says, keeping his voice down, 'I'd like to talk to you. I'll be camping down by that blazed live oak. Come and see me, when business simmers down.'

" 'Lord God, man,' says I, 'with this bunch of sports that may be three in the A. M.'

" 'If I'm asleep,' he says, 'wake me up.' And he limps out.

"Well, I guess it must have been near three in the A. M., at that, when the joint goes quiet. It seemed a shame to wake a man who'd had a hard day in the saddle and another hard day ahead, but I knew Caleb well enough to know that when he said he wanted to see me he meant he wanted to see me. So I went. East Texas ain't like West Texas. It's all trees and skunks in East Texas. West Texas has got the skunks but no trees. It was the black of the moon that night, as I recall, and them trees cast black shadows. Quiet as death at that hour, except now and then one of them niggers would clank his chains and kind of yowl. Then another would take it up and after that the whole coffle of them, like a pack of hound-dogs. That sound followed me all the way down the road, and I didn't much like it. Too mournful. Reminded me of when I was in jail once in Maryland. You likely know how men in jail will break out singing some sad song late in the night.

"Them yowling niggers excited the coyotes too. There was a pack over on a hill, and they'd listen to them niggers and then they'd bust out yapping. After a while they'd stop to listen to the niggers again.

"She was a black night, but I saw the coals of Caleb's fire and headed for them, thinking what a shame it was to wake the man. But when I got nearer I saw old Caleb laying in his blankets propped on an elbow with his pistol pointing in my direction. I yelled it was me and he lowered his gun.

" 'Lord, man,' I said, 'I thought you'd be asleep.'

" 'I was,' he said, 'but I woke up. It's how I've trained myself. I always wake up when anybody comes near.'

" 'A habit like that,' I said, 'could be worth a lot to a man.'

" 'I've found it valuable,' he said.

"And then he told me his plan. He's a quick thinker, that Caleb. The scheme had come over him in a flash, there in the saloon, when he sized up the crowd and they asked about the New Orleans election. His idea was to fade out of town before daylight. Everybody would think he had gone northwest, but he'd head back to Louisiana. He'd go to a little steamboat landing he knew about, on the Mississippi, and leave his horse with a planter and take the boat for New Orleans. I've forgotten his timing, but it was neat. He knew the steamboat schedules, and he figured one boat would put him into New Orleans on election day, and another would take him back upriver right after the votes was counted. He'd get off at that landing and ride hard to Nacogdoches. It would be a long trip—more than two hundred miles—but there warn't no stage routes in them days, and he figured he'd beat the election news back to Nacogdoches.

" 'Lord, man,' I said, 'that's going to put you to a lot of trouble.'

" 'Hod,' he said, 'making money is always trouble. Leastwise if you do it honest, like we're planning. I'll get to Nacogdoches during the night and I'll circle in from the northwest, if I'd happen to be seen. I'll leave my money belt with you and the name of the election winner. You can bet all my money and as much of yours as you want. I'll fade west from town and come back later to collect. Are you in?'

" 'Sure I'm in,' I said, 'but I'm out of breath keeping up. You move fast.'

" 'Sometimes a man has to,' he said.

" 'Caleb,' I said, 'I'm kind of touched. I mean the way you're letting me in on this, and trusting me to bet your roll.'

" 'You needn't be,' he said. 'I'm letting you in because it takes two to work it, and as for my money, I guess you know what I'd do if you skinned me.'

" 'Caleb,' I said, 'I guess I do.'

" 'There you are,' he said. 'So where's the risk?'

"Then he rolled up in his blankets and said, 'Hod, I reckon I'll get another hour's sleep. I'll see you in a couple of weeks. You might as well keep the boys' interest stirred up in that election. Don't drag it in by the tail, but you might drop a remark now and then. Good night.'

" 'Good night,' I said. And I'll bet he was asleep before I'd walked thirty paces.

"Well, sir, during the next couple of weeks I did just what Caleb ordered. When the boys was at the bar I'd speak of that New Orleans election, mentioning how a lot of money was sure to change hands. With a crowd of sporting gents that was all I needed to say. They all wanted to bet, but they was somewhat handicapped because New Orleans was so far away, and most of them had never heard of either candidate. I hadn't myself till Caleb told me their names, and now I've forgotten what they were. But you know how it is with real sports. They'll bet on anything. They would ask me who my money was on, and I'd say I was thinking it over. I kind of liked Tweedledee, I'd say, but on the other hand Tweedledum might nose him out. That stirred up their sporting blood something fearful, and even the nigger smugglers caught the fever. You take the average nigger smuggler, he ain't much of a sporting man. He wants a sure thing. When he lands niggers in the States he's got the officials all bribed, and if things have tightened up he lands them in Texas. It's a sound business, smuggling niggers, but kind of dull. You buy black meat in the Antilles and sell it in the States at a thousand percent profit. Nothing sporting about it. The average nigger smuggler just goes along in his rut, smuggling niggers, and not giving a damn about what numbers are turning up on a roulette wheel. But these smugglers was getting tired of their own company, laying out there in Nacogdoches till the time was right to cross with their niggers into the States. For that matter, I was tired of their company too. Any time of the day or night you'd hear them niggers clanking their chains and yowling, till sometimes you couldn't sleep.

"On the evening before Caleb was due back, I let fall the word that I'd about made up my mind which candidate to bet on. I wanted to think it over during the night, I said, but I'd announce my choice in the morning and take all bets. Well, sir, those gents were excited. There's something about an election or a horse race that stirs up a gambling gent. I remember one gent calls out, 'Hod, I'll bet you three hundred dollars even money.'

" 'On which candidate?' says I.

" 'Either one,' he says.

" 'No,' says I, 'that ain't the way I do business, Sport. I've a reputation for a fair and square house, and I aim to keep her spotless. I'll think this matter over tonight, and maybe pray for a little guidance, and I'll announce my man tomorrow.'

"By now I was getting jumpy about the whole business. Maybe, I thought, Caleb wouldn't get back that night. Or maybe somebody would see him riding in from the southeast before he could circle the town and come in from the northwest. If we were ever caught cold-decking that election, our numbers would be double zero. In a deal like that a lot of things can go wrong. But I shouldn't have worried, with Caleb as my partner.

"He came that night. It was in the small hours of morning, and I don't guess he stayed more than a minute. 'Here's my money,' he said. 'Bet it all.' And he told me the winner's name.

" 'Did you have a hard trip?' I asked.

" 'Middling so,' he said. 'Wore out three horses. Luck.' And he left.

"And there I was with all that specie shining in the candlelight, and them niggers out back moaning like they was in jail.

"A man will take awful chances in his life. I decided to play it big. Hell, I was the house, and I'd never welshed on a bet yet. I had a good reputation. Sometimes when things was tight I'd paid off in counter-feit U. S. bank notes, but counterfeit or not it's all just paper. I knew a printer who used to bring me his output to pass. But these sporting gents was sharp. They weren't greasers. They'd been around, and they weren't taking paper money. They'd want to know they'd be getting specie, if they won. So next morning I showed them a box full of specie. I wouldn't let them heft it, and they understood that, because you let a sporting gent heft your money and he may palm off an eagle or two. But I put that box on the bar and let them look at it. It was heavy too, although between me and you it was three-fourths full of sand, with Caleb's money and mine on top. U. S. gold and Spanish gold and milled Spanish dollars. 'The house is good for it, boys,' I said. And I told them I'd take all bets even money, with me backing Girard, or whatever the winner's name was. I've forgotten. Some frog-eater. Well, sir, before I was through I'd taken an awful sight of bets. And them nigger smug-glers had bet me their whole coffle of niggers down to the last toenail.

"Then the waiting began, for the New Orleans papers. We sent a fellow on horseback over to the Mississippi to get them, and till he got back that joint of mine was pretty quiet. It was full of gents, but no-body said much. You'd hear a glass tinkle, or cards being shuffled, but not much else, from inside. From outside, of course, you'd hear them niggers moaning and howling and clanking. It had a jail-y sound, and I didn't like it. And sometimes, to pass away the time, a nigger smuggler would go out and unlock a wench from the coffle and take her into one of my cribs. Your average nigger smuggler always figures exercise is good for a wench. And if she's going to whelp he'll get a better price for her.

"It all came out fine, of course. My man had been elected, and those gents weren't ones to welsh. The sporting gents drifted back over to the States and the nigger smugglers left for the Gulf Coast. And there I was with all them niggers on my hands. They was a sorry lot. Two or three were sick, and none of them seemed to like Texas. By God, they was a real problem. They couldn't speak American, and I couldn't speak African, and the whole thing was a bad situation. That was my first deal-ing in niggers and my last. I mean in niggers raw from Africa. Damn, how they howled. Then one morning I went out and found that one had died in his chains during the night. By God, by then I was pretty dis-gusted. That lean-to was filthy as a backhouse. The smell was fearful. The others were taking on and howling worse than ever, all except for one who was too sick to do more than groan. You take a bunch of niggers like that and have a corpse chained among them and they take on terrible.

"I don't know what I would have done, if old Caleb hadn't showed up that day. He knew just what to do. I kind of had the feeling, from the way he took hold, that he must have done a little nigger smuggling himself, some time or other.

" 'Why, hell, Hod,' he says, when he looks them over, 'these niggers ain't in good shape at all. Especially,' he says, pointing at the corpse, 'that one there.'

" 'Caleb,' I says, 'I know the jack of diamonds from the ace of clubs, and I know the banking business, but I sure as hell don't know the nigger business.'

" 'No,' he says, 'it don't appear that you do. We've got to get that boy there buried. We've got to bring a little order out of this mess.' He stands looking them over, and then he says, 'That boy there is going to die. Blood poisoning from chain-chafe, I reckon. We've got to get the chains off these niggers and give them some fresh air or we'll have a shed full of dead niggers.'

" 'We take off the chains,' says I, 'and they'll skedaddle.'

" 'No,' he says, taking out his pistol, 'I don't believe they will. I don't like to do this, Hod, but that boy with blood poisoning will be dead by sundown anyhow. I don't like to do this, but I've got to show them I mean business so they won't skedaddle once they're unshackled.'

"Well, sir, old Caleb walks up to them niggers with his pistol cocked, and he points the barrel at first one and then the next, like he's picking them out by lot. Howl? You ain't never heard howling like them niggers howled. They all dropped to their knees, men and women, and clanked their chains and rolled their eyes and just plain howled. I remember one gal who was going to have a kid kept kissing Caleb's boots. After he had pointed that gun at each and every one he started over again. When he reached the sick boy he took careful aim and shot him through the heart. The boy gave a few kicks, like a rabbit when you've shot him, and it was over. He might as well have stayed in Africa, for all the good travel did him.

" 'Hod,' Caleb said, while he reloaded, 'I didn't like to do that, but that boy would have died by sundown. Now if you'll get a couple of spades, we'll give these boys some exercise grave digging.'

"It really pleasured me to see how Caleb took hold with them niggers. After I'd scared up the spades he sent me for a buggy whip. Lord God, you should have heard them niggers when they saw that. He whished it through the air a few times, so they could hear it sing, and then he un-chained the biggest buck nigger and handed him the whip. And he said a few words to him in a lingo that was new to me. It must have been nigger lingo, for this big buck boy grinned and nodded. From then on I was certain old Caleb must have done a little nigger smuggling in his time, else how did he know the lingo? Then he unlocks the rest of them dismal niggers, and we had a pair of graves dug in no time.

" 'Hod,' he says, 'the best guard for a bunch of niggers is another nigger. It's also dirt cheap guarding. You remember that, next time you're in the nigger business.'

"'There won't be no next time,' says I. 'The saloon business is good enough for me.'

"'I see what you mean,' he says. 'The nigger business has its drawbacks. But I reckon every business has.'

"Next day Caleb set out for the States with them niggers. I made a deal with him so he'd get seventy per cent of the profits instead of fifty. That extra twenty per cent was for taking charge. He hired three greasers to make the trip and help guard. He said a white man with a pistol and a nigger guard could handle a coffle of that size in a place like Nacogdoches, but where he was going he'd feel easier with the greasers along. Not that a greaser is much good guarding, but them niggers didn't know that.

"He headed northeast, up through Arkansas Territory, with that coffle of niggers. When he hit the Mississippi he sold them in river towns. That far from the Gulf Coast, nobody asked questions as to whether a nigger was smuggled. So the deal turned out all right, although I always suspicioned that Caleb may have upped that seventy per cent of his to maybe eighty or eighty-five. But I didn't kick. I was too glad to get them niggers off my hands."

"*Ja*, sure, I can see how you felt," Otto said. "I was in the nigger business once myself, but I didn't like it. They howl too much, those cowardly niggers."

*

Next day, Sunday, was warm and fair, but Otto arose with a heavy heart. His head ached from too much Taos Lightning and his stomach felt queasy. Breakfast set him right physically but not emotionally. Although only two days had elapsed since Consuelo ran away from the store, it seemed weeks ago. As he tidied up the merchandise his feet dragged, and sometimes he stood staring at the wall. The ringing of the cathedral bells jangled on his nerves, for they reminded him of his quarrel with Consuelo. He thought, "Maybe she will never come here again. Maybe I will never see her again."

The snow actually had melted by noon when Major Delgado waddled into the store on his first visit in some time. Sight of that man, who had dared lay hands on Consuelo, nettled Otto, but he tried to be civil.

"How is your health by now?" he asked.

"Improving, *señor*. But I had a painful time. Where is my niece? Is she not in your employ today?"

"Of course she is. It is only that I have granted her a few hours' freedom."

"Do not be too easy with her."

"I am attending to the matter," Otto said coldly.

He was vexed. On that other Sunday he had been delighted when the major said he must punish Consuelo, but now everything had changed.

"She may be your niece," he thought savagely, "but she is my girl and you are to keep your hands off her. Maybe we had a little quarrel, but I am heartsick to see her and we will patch things up."

"If she fails to do her duty," the major was saying, "report her to me."

"No," Otto snapped. "She is a good girl and I am satisfied with her. I do not want you beating her again," he added, amazed at his audacity.

The major's brows lifted; there was heat behind his eyes. Then he shrugged.

"Ah, well, perhaps it is better for you to deal with her yourself. I am growing older, alas. Once if I had slipped and fallen when chastising a wayward girl I would have regained my feet in an instant. Now I am not so agile."

Customers entered the store and Otto turned to serve them, his neck stiff and his face unsmiling. They said they were only looking, and Otto rejoined the major, whose face was also unsmiling.

"I wish to talk with you privately, *señor*," he said.

Otto led the way to the patio, followed by Major Delgado in his gold-braided uniform, and by the cat, Hilda, with her tail in the air. Out there, puddles of snow-water had collected, but the sunshine was spring-like. The major stood patting his belly, affectionately but absent-mindedly; his mustachios were martial. But his voice was velvetly chocolate.

"There are two small matters, *señor*. First, we must degrade ourselves by speaking of money. It pains me to mention it, but I wish to collect my niece's *salario*."

Otto paid him.

"*Gracias, señor*. It is a sad thing when business dealings must take place between friends. At such times there is always the victor and always the vanquished. With commerce it is the same as with affairs of the heart. *Si*, in love itself one is the winner and one the loser."

He waddled about the patio, picking his way among the puddles, sometimes lifting his broad nose and sniffing the benign air. With his gross belly he looked topheavy; it was as if he remained erect only because he was filled with gas. He paused where the little cottonwood grew from the tree-well, its bark damp from melted snow.

"The other matter, *señor*, concerns news I have had from my blessed mother. She is persuaded that Consuelo finds herself in love."

"So?"

"Exactly. One is aware, of course, how women chatter about these matters, but my blessed mother believes the girl has formed a sentimental attachment for you. This is a delicate question, and save for the firm friendship between us I would not voice it. But as head of my family and the girl's protector, I must ask whether it is your opinion that she is in love."

"What is in the wind now?" Otto asked himself. "It is no business of this old bandit."

He said, "How is one to know the heart of a girl?"

The major's lips were pursed, his eyes as dark and worldly and worn as the history of Spain. Then, coyly and lasciviously, he smiled.

"There are ways by which one knows."

"*Ja,*" Otto said irritably, "maybe she does love me. Whose business is it but hers? Once she said she hated me, but that was all a big joke. I think she no longer hates me."

The major burped, daintily patted his mouth.

"And now, *señor,* may I ask a question of even greater delicacy? With your permission, what are your feelings toward her?"

"You wish me to tell you my private business?"

"Please, *señor,* do not be offended. It is only that I am the head of my family and have been like a father to the girl. And nothing would please me more than the glorious news that a man of your distinction and valor has found my niece a worthy object of your love."

"*Ja,* it is true I come of a distinguished family. My father is one of the greatest men in Prussia."

"Who can doubt it, *señor?*"

Otto heaved a breath.

"*Ja,* well, it will do no harm to tell you. I love the girl. She is a little Indian but I love her. I will never know how it all came about, but I do. When she is not near me I am sad. She is such a funny little Indian. She is as pretty as a little rabbit and as swift when she runs. She is all strange and new and shining. I am hollow in the chest when she is gone. She is like a girl of wind. *Ja,* like the wind coming soft over spring fields."

The major was smiling, eyes slitted, the grossness of his face like that of some corrupt idol carved by Aztec priests from rotten brown stone. He chuckled.

"Ah, my young friend, she will make you a lively bride. It is said that when a man takes a Spanish bride a tempest tosses the counterpane, but when a man takes an Indian the bridal chamber is rocked by an earthquake."

Otto drew himself up.

"We will not discuss her in this way, please."

"As you wish, *señor.* But now that you are almost my nephew there can surely be no objection to an uncle's natural interest in a merry wedding night. She has a fourth of her blood from the untamed Apaches, and you will find that a touch of savagery in a young virgin is as challenging as the wildness of an unbroken mare."

Otto flushed.

163

"*Ja, ja,* maybe that is so, but this is not the time or place for such discussions."

The major's tongue, looking oddly small in his fat face, grazed his lips.

"I have heard cavalry officers say, my blessed nephew, that a lean mare makes good colts."

"Enough! She is not a horse already that I should go around the town talking about her. You will watch your words. I have often engaged in affairs of honor, and I will not have you calling her a horse!"

"But my dear nephew—"

"I am not yet your nephew already so fast. When I am married I will be the head of my own family and of my own house. Like my father, already. *Ja!* He would stand no monkey business. Once my mother's old father came to visit us. He had been a wild head of cabbage when he was young, marrying my grandmother who was one of those cowardly Latvians. But he was not wild when he visited us. He had a long white beard and his hand shook so he could hardly lift a stein of beer to his mouth. The first day when we sat down at the table my father asked him to say grace, but he mumbled so bad he could not be heard. My father broke right in and shouted, 'Speak up! Speak up! You are mumbling like some cowardly recruit. If we cannot hear you, how can *Gott?*' *Ja,* that taught the old scoundrel a fine lesson not to mumble so. My father is a general already, and with him everything must march."

And Otto himself kept marching, there in the patio, back and forth, shoulders squared, his stern expression masking his uneasiness at having ordered the major to watch his words.

"*Mein Gott,*" he was thinking, "I came close to challenging him to a duel! If the old bag of wind has any honor he will demand satisfaction. I should have governed my tongue, but he made me mad calling Consuelo a horse."

As for the major, he observed Otto with the peevishness of a man who has found a cockroach in his bowl of chili.

"*Señor* Zumwalt," he said, "did I understand you to hint at an affair of honor between us?"

"*Ja!* I will challenge any man who calls Consuelo a horse. Sabers, pistols, bayonets, stones, it makes no difference to me. At the university I often fought duels. If a man insulted me we met at daybreak. Our sabers clanged. And I would go through his guard and slide the blade up to the hilt right through his belly button. Otto the Swordsman, that was my nickname. In New Orleans, of course, it was different. We met in the dueling oaks and used pistols. But sabers or pistols, to me it is all the same. I shoot once and my opponent drops. In New Orleans they nicknamed me One-Ball Zumwalt."

"Ah, New Orleans," the major said, good nature breaking over his

164

face. "I have heard much of that city. You must tell me about its wonders."

Otto's heart leaped with relief, but his voice remained stern.

"Some other time. But now I must ask you if you meant it when you called Consuelo a horse."

.."*Señor, señor!* My dear friend! There has been some misunderstanding. I would be the last man to call her a horse."

"You would be the next-to-the-last," Otto said. "I would be the last."

"A wonderful girl. All the feminine virtues have combined in her. She will make you a splendid wife, my dear nephew, and I congratulate you. When do you plan to go to the church and take your vows?"

"I will never go to the church to take my vows."

"*Señor!* What are you saying? That you love her and yet will not marry her?"

"I will marry her and nobody can stop me. But I will not marry her in your church. I will not have a priest marry us."

"But my dear friend. My dear nephew. How else will you marry her?"

"In any other way. By what they call the common law, or by a preacher already. And I mean a Lutheran preacher and not a Reformed Lutheran."

"But my dear nephew. No other way is possible. I am an officer of the army. I am a civil servant. I cannot permit it to be said that I scandalously permitted my niece to be married outside the church. You will naturally have to become a Catholic."

"I will have to do what!"

"Become a Catholic, *señor*. How long would I hold my position if the governor learned I had permitted my niece to marry a heretic? He is a religious man. Between ourselves, I am not. If you repeat what I am saying it will go hard with you, but I am indifferent to all religions, *señor*. But one abides by the custom of the country if one is to hold office. So if you marry my niece I will see to it that first you join the church. After that, I do not care. To me it is nothing. As I have said, I am indifferent."

"But I am not," Otto said. "I am a religious man. I am a Lutheran. It is the religion of Prussia, which means it is the best religion in the world. I can never become anything else, Quaker or Catholic or Methodist or one of those atheistic Reformed Lutherans."

"It will not be necessary, *señor*, for you to become any of those others. Only a Catholic."

"No. I never will."

"But what do you have against the Catholics?"

"I have nothing against them except they are not Lutherans. I am a Lutheran and I will remain a Lutheran."

"I believe you will change your mind."

"No."

165

"I believe you will, *señor*, in good time."

And the major left.

*

Consuelo did not come to the store that afternoon. Otto kept hoping, but to no avail. At four o'clock, when cockfighting was scheduled in the plaza, business dwindled to nothing, and he stood outside the store watching for her. But the street lay quiet. From the plaza he could hear the sound of Sunday's humanity, a low far surf, with now and then a crescendo of cheering.

At last he tramped into the store, bolted the door, poured Taos Lightning, drank it down, poured more, and carrying his glass paced between house and patio, muttering to himself. Dusk came. The hullabaloo from the plaza had ceased. The town lay silent on the silent desert, inked by the hemicycle of darkness that hours ago had crossed the wintry Atlantic to invade the shores of the young Republic far to the east, that Republic of dreams the dreamers had dreamed. At Monticello Mr. Jefferson stirred in his sleep, coughed an octogenarian cough and slept again, while the darkness went spinning across the great Louisiana of his dream, across the big river and the buffalo plains, across Texas where men were already dreaming another dream of a proud and solitary star, across the silences of deserts and the silences of mountains unscaled and ungutted, across the sage and the rattlesnake rocks and the dead lake and the dry lakes, toward the blue ocean creaming the sunset shores. In Santa Fe, Otto Zumwalt lighted a candle and moodily poked the fire. "I should eat," he was thinking, "but I am not hungry."

He finished his drink, flung himself down on the bed.

"*Ja,*" he muttered, after a time, "that is what I will do. I will wait till tomorrow and if she does not come I will go to her. I cannot stand it much longer, not seeing her."

He felt better; presently he dozed.

He was roused by tapping on the front door.

"Some cowardly Mexican," he muttered, "who has not the brains to know I am closed for business. *Ja, ja,*" he called, "I am coming. Have a little patience."

Holding the candle, he unbolted and opened the door. Consuelo stood there, eyes sad and dark above her *rebozo.*

"Otto," she said, "I could stay away no longer."

*

They did not quarrel again that night or during the days that followed. They had been two people walking a sunlit road when unexpectedly they had come upon a great encumbrance, cowled and shadowy, with which they must deal before they could pass on and with flowers woven in their hair dance in the meadows of Arcady. And they had fled their separate ways, through the briers fringing the road. Now they were scratched and wounded but they had gained the road again and found each other, and they pretended it had never happened. The sunshine was still very nice, although not quite so clear and golden. Nor were they ever alone. They made believe they were, but the encumbrance was with them. They did not mention it.

They were happy, nevertheless. Sometimes their happiness had an almost frantic quality, as if they were snatching all they could while they could. Yet even so their happiness was not much more frantic than that of all lovers who harken the clock of eternity ticking off the minutes that never return.

Loving and quarreling and loving again had mellowed and improved Otto, till sometimes it seemed he had never been born a *Junker*. As for Consuelo, he thought she was growing more beautiful with every day that passed, and perhaps she was, for after all she was undergoing the sort of beauty treatments which women have always found efficacious. Her hair shone with a rich, dark luster; color warmed her beige-and-copper skin; her body seemed winsome, to him; and he never tired of her melodious voice.

But there were days when she was moody and not in the least talkative, and at such times she seemed not Spanish at all but the silent Indian girl Otto used to imagine when he was a clerk in New Orleans. Once it occurred to him that in a large measure he had achieved all that he used to daydream about as a boy in Prussia: he had crossed the ocean and followed adventure into the American West and had taken an Indian girl as mistress. Yet the actuality was very different from the way he had imagined it would be, and he wondered whether other men, upon attaining their goals, encountered such divergences.

Winter set in, with all the surprises of a place where mountains reared up from desolate plateau country. There were days bright and fine, when a lagoon of warm air would accumulate in the patio; there were days of gales and dust from the desert; there were days of sloppy snow and of freezing rain; there were days when clouds shrouded the mountains. It was not a perfect climate; Hod Kite had lied. It was a violent land. The nights were Arctic with frigid air sliding down from the snow fields of the *Sangre de Cristo;* Otto bought burro-load after burro-load of wood. But the days, on balance, were flooded with tremendous sunshine.

One morning Consuelo did not arrive at her usual hour of a quarter after nine, nor did she come at ten or eleven or twelve. As always, he was restless when she was not with him. All morning he kept pulling out his watch and going to the door. Noon passed; the siesta hour passed; midafternoon found him outside the store, watching for her. A futile business. Now that he thought of it, he never remembered having seen her during one of these vigils. Always she slipped in quietly, when his back was turned.

"I will go inside and keep busy," he thought. "Maybe that will bring her."

He cast one last look along the street. And the incredible occurred. He saw her. She was racing fleetly down the middle of the street. He smiled and waved.

When she reached him she was panting, and her eyes looked swollen and harried.

"Otto! Get inside! We must get inside and fasten the door."

"But what is the matter?"

"Get inside, Otto, please. Then I will tell you."

Her apprehension was contagious. He thought, *"Mein Gott!* Perhaps it is an Indian raid."

He hurried after her into the store, slamming and bolting the door.

"Is it Indians coming already?" he asked.

"Indians? No, no, not Indians. Not Indians, Otto, not that."

Tears welled into her eyes and she flung herself to the bed, sobs racking her shoulders.

"Consuelo! What is it? You must tell me."

"Otto, Otto . . ."

Her voice sounded strangled.

"Consuelo, my little one, why do you cry so hard?"

Her shoulders quivered.

"It is too bad, too bad," he murmured, lying beside her and stroking her hair. "I am sorry the sobs are tearing you so apart."

She lifted her head.

"Did you fasten the door?"

"Ja, sure I did."

"She will be here. Promise you will not unbolt the door when she comes. I outran her but she will be here."

"Who?"

Consuelo broke into more sobbing.

"Who, my little one? Who will be here?"

"My . . . grandmother . . ."

"Your grandmother! But why would the old crone come here?"

"Otto! You must promise. You will not unlock the door and you will stuff your fingers into your ears. I do not want you to hear it from her."

"Hear what from her?"

"Otto, I do not want . . . to tell you now. There should be peace and love when I tell you."

"But *mein liebchen—*"

There sounded a tremendous racket at the front door.

Consuelo jumped up, her hair mussed, her face tear-streaked, her hands moving helplessly.

"Otto! Do not let her in. Do not listen to her. I will tell you now. I did not want it to be like this, but I will tell you because I should be the first to tell you. Otto, my life, I am going to have a baby."

"*Mein Gott!* You are going to have a what?"

"A baby, Otto. A little one. I am the soil where a seed has been planted."

"A baby," he said, staring, while all the time fists were thumping the door and an old voice was screeching to be admitted. "You are going to have a baby. Can it be possible!"

"*Si, si,* it is possible. It is true."

"*Ja, ja,*" he said, pacing the earthen floor, "of course it is possible. *Ja,* I can see that now. Like my mother and father. They had babies, already. It is what happens. There is the sowing and the sprouting and the harvest."

The knocking and screeching were louder. Otto stopped, as if hearing it for the first time.

"Shut up out there, you filthy-legged old one! Drag your snake tongue back into your mouth and close your slobbering lips."

There was a moment of silence, as if the disturber of peace had been rocked back on her heels.

"A baby," Otto said gently. "*Kinder. Ja,* a man in the days of his youth finds the soil sweet for the planting. *Ja, ja,* it is the way of life. A carpenter can make a table and a stonemason can build a wall. But only the flesh of man and of woman can make a baby." He stared wonderingly at the blond flesh of his hands, at the Spanish flesh of his woman. "*Ja,*" he said, with a sigh, "and the seed traveled far. The seed crossed the ocean and traveled up the big river and across the big plains. *Ja, ja,* a long voyage for the planting in New Mexico."

The knocking had resumed, and the demands for admittance. His thoughts had also traveled far, but now the racket impinged on his hearing.

"*Mein Gott!* Has the filthy old she-goat no patience? Quiet, quiet, shut up, you are making of yourself a great nuisance," he shouted, striding to the door. "Go away! You are not wanted here. Go home to your white rooster and cackle to him. Your voice is a stench in my ears like sewerage in my nose. Go home to your filthy house where you live like a sow on a dirt floor. I will stand no more of this nonsense."

"Seducer of maidens!" screeched the voice from beyond the door. "Scum of gutter scum! I will kick down the door and scratch out your eyes!"

"Scum! Me, scum! I will have you know my father is a general—"

That went on for some time, Otto and La Luz Delgado flinging the vilest of insults, the way two hysterical dogs will froth at each other when separated by a stout fence.

Tossed about on that torrent of words, Consuelo threw herself between Otto and the door, begging him to hold his tongue, begging her grandmother to go home, and when neither heeded her wishes she dropped into a chair, sobbing into her arms; and when the invective continued she sprang up, thrust fingers into her ears and fled to the patio, returning almost at once to plead for peace.

Peace came at last, but only because Otto and the old woman had exhausted themselves.

"You will pay for this, you gringo rapist," the cracked voice called.

"*Ja?* Well, so will you, you lying old whore, running away with Indians already."

From beyond the door came an exclamation of fury and detestation. Then silence.

*

In the kitchen, when he poured drinks for Consuelo and himself, his hands trembled so violently that the Taos Lightning spilled. He swallowed one drink fast and raw, poured another, and by an effort of will nearly succeeded in carrying the two glasses into the bedroom without spilling a drop. Consuelo sat on the bed, her swollen eyes dry and staring.

"*Mein liebchen,* I am sorry I lost my temper."

"*Si,*" she whispered. "I am also sorry."

"It was only that the old sow made me mad. In such matters I take after my father. I will stand no monkey business."

"Your tongue is like scalding water," Consuelo said drearily. "How do you think of such things to say?"

"It is easy. I have a talent for it."

"*Si,* I believe you do."

"But if you think I am good you should hear my father when he is mad. If he walks through a pasture the grass withers."

Consuelo sat holding the whiskey, still staring.

"Drink what I brought you, *mein liebchen.* It will make you feel better."

She seemed not to hear. He finished his own drink and sat beside her, taking her glass.

"Please, my loved one, take a sip. I will hold it to your lips."

She drank then, obediently.

"That is good," he said. "You will feel better now."

"I do not believe I will, Otto."

"*Ja,* of course you will. You must not let a little tiff upset you. Fighting is nothing. In Prussia we do it all the time."

She sat staring.

"I will get you another drink," he said. "And another for myself. It is just what we need."

When he returned from the kitchen, he found her as he had left her. She took the glass but did not drink, till he sat beside her as before and held it to her lips.

"Do not be sad, *mein liebchen*. We will have a good life together."

"Will we?"

"*Ja*, of course. As soon as you move in I will send men into the mountains to cut wood for a proper floor. It is no way to live on a dirt floor like swine. It is too hard to keep clean."

"The floor makes no difference, Otto. I would live with you in a sheepherder's hut in the mountains."

"That would be very foolish, to move into a hut when we have such a fine house. The floor, of course, is a filthy dust trap, and I would rather have a house with shingles already, although I will say for that lying Hod Kite that he told the truth when he said it would shed water. Except for the floor and the roof, it is as good a house as a young couple like us deserves. It keeps out the rain and the wind."

"It does not keep out the unhappiness, Otto."

"Maybe not, but it does as good a job as any house. Are you unhappy, my dear one?"

"*Si*, I believe I am. But I was happy yesterday. I was happiest of all on the day of the great wind when only you and I were in this house together."

"*Ja*, that was a happy one, that day."

"But today everything went wrong. When I wakened I was strangely sick inside my stomach. And when I was standing in the kitchen the sickness made the room whirl and the night come. It was like a little death. When I wakened I was lying on the floor and my grandmother was holding a cold cloth to my temple. And at once she began asking many questions, some of them of the most intimate sort."

"She is a prying old long-nose," Otto said.

"I did not want to tell her, Otto. I wanted to turn my face to the wall and sleep and maybe die. But she gave me no peace. I did not tell her about us till this afternoon, but at last she had the truth. She was in a fury."

"A bad disposition," Otto said.

"She started off toward this house to tear out your hair. She seemed to have lost her sanity. But I have always been a swift runner. I overtook her and raced to reach you. I did not want her to be the first to tell you of the little one."

"Why did you not tell me before?"

"Because I was not sure. But it is true. My grandmother is a *curandera* and a midwife and a woman herself. There are certain signs, and she knows them as well as she knows her own kitchen."

171

"That is where she should stay, in her kitchen."

Dusk had gathered in the bedroom; they lay side by side.

"What will become of us, Otto?" Consuelo whispered.

"Do not worry, my pretty one. I will take care of us both."

"Now that I am a field plowed and planted, do you love me still?"

"More than ever now."

"Otto, Otto. Do you intend to marry me?"

"Of course I will marry you."

"You will marry me so that I am married like the other girls? In the church?"

"As I have told you before," Otto said, "for me that is impossible. But there is a marriage they call the common law. You will live with me here and I will call you my wife and you will call me your husband. And then some day we will find a Lutheran pastor and be married also by him."

"It would be living sinfully, married by what you call the common law."

"No, it would be a good marriage."

"That I could not do, Otto. With me it would have to be a marriage in the church, or I would be a sinner. I have talked about the matter secretly with the priest. He is a good man and a kind one, and he gave me much comfort. He does not believe it would be sinful for you to be married according to your beliefs. But for me it would be sinful because my beliefs are otherwise. He does not believe you should join my church unless you feel it in your heart. He told me there was something said once by Saint Augustine, that man could not believe otherwise than of his own free will."

"*Ja*, well, I would like to have that fellow in Prussia and we would see what he would believe. He would change his tune then."

"I do not believe he would, Otto. He told me it is his opinion that conversion by the sword or the fist is not conversion but only submission. Those were his words."

"*Ja?* Well, I will tell you one thing, I will never—"

A knock fell on the door.

*

In his arms, Otto felt Consuelo stiffen, then begin to tremble.

"Otto! It is my grandmother again! Ooo, will I never know peace?"

There was more knocking.

Otto's hackles lifted.

"Go back to your sewer and wallow in your filth, you whelp of a mangy jackal," he shouted.

"Otto! Please, please do not begin it again."

He jumped up, groped through the darkness to the front door.

"Go back to your gut-wagon, you outcast buzzard and eater of snakes

172

and carrion. Go back to your grave-robbing and your boneyard, you insane old ghoul."

Silence from beyond the door.

"Did you hear what I told you?" Otto shouted.

"*Si, señor,* but why do you call me a buzzard? Am I not your friend?"

Major Delgado's voice!

"*Mein Gott,* Excellency! Why did you not say it was you? I thought it was your filthy old mother."

He lifted the bolt and flung open the door.

"Excellency, I am honored. My house is at your orders. This is a delight. How is your health?"

The major was a squat silhouette, crossing the threshold to merge with the darkness inside.

"I am well, *señor,* except for my eyes. Either they have suddenly failed me or there is no light in this house."

"*Ja,* I will admit it is dusky. Let me light a candle."

The flame transformed the room from chocolate to golden, disclosing the splendid mustachios of Major Delgado.

"*Gracias, señor.* It is a cheering thing, the light of a candle."

His eyes moved, roving the store and the adjoining bedroom, halting when they discovered Consuelo. She sat on the bed, gaze downcast. The major's eyebrows cocked rakishly; his tongue produced a lump on his plump cheek; his smile was infinitely cynical.

"Ah, my blessed niece. You are working late. And in the dark. Ah, well, I believe that often a girl will do her most satisfying work in the dark."

Her gaze shot up and struck like a rattlesnake. The major chuckled.

"I regret disturbing you at your work, my little virgin niece. But one should not work constantly, no matter how pleasant and absorbing the task."

Consuelo stood up.

"I have heard it said, my blessed uncle, that there are those who lack the power to work in the dark."

The major's mustachios twitched.

"I should have sold you into slavery when you were young, my little virgin. In Mexico there are third-rate houses of love which might have been induced to pay a bag of beans for you."

"Of the prices paid in those affairs I know nothing, my blessed uncle. Such knowledge is only for pimps."

The major's cheeks were the color of red wine spilled on banquet olives.

"*Ja, ja,*" Otto broke in, "maybe that is all true. But what is past is past and all water under the bridge. Let us have no more quarreling."

The major gave him a sidelong glance.

"Blessed is the peacemaker, *señor.*"

"*Ja,* I agree with that. Myself, I have always been a peacemaker. When everything is said and done peace is a good thing."

"We are in agreement, *Señor* Zumwalt. May we always agree. And this brings me to the object of my call. I have a matter of considerable import to discuss with you. Alone."

He looked at Consuelo.

She returned his gaze, steadily, for a full second, then went to Otto. He kissed her.

"You are my life," she whispered.

He held her close.

"And you are my pretty little flower blooming in the land of great sunshine."

Then she was gone, soundlessly as the shadow of a soundless Indian.

*

The house had grown cold; Otto rekindled the fire and brought Taos Lightning from the kitchen. The major heaved a great sigh, eased himself into one of the crude chairs, lifted his glass.

"To the successful outcome of our conference, my friend."

"*Ja,* I will drink to that."

They drank; the major absently massaged his belly.

"The whiskey is good, my friend, but the subject is painful. All my life I have sought to avoid pain. It is a sad affair to be a living thing. Every inch of one's skin is exposed to pain. Also every inch within the body. By comparison there are so few parts of the body to bring pleasure. The tongue, the stomach, a few more. But the cards are marked against man's pleasure. That is why I rejoice when I hear a man has found pleasure and taken it. That is why I rejoice with you, my friend. The body of a young girl is a pleasurable thing. Alas, the years go swiftly. Presently the only pleasures remaining are those of swallowing food and evacuating the waste. My friend, with your permission I will have another drink."

Otto poured it.

"*Gracias, señor.* Tonight my mood is one of melancholy and I am weary. It is a burden to lug this thing around with me." The major slapped his belly. "But I cannot resist the pleasures of the table."

"*Ja,* it is fun to eat."

"I am being frank with you tonight, my friend. Soon I must speak of a painful subject, and it is well to be frank from first to last. Perhaps my blessed niece has told you of my boyhood."

"She has mentioned it, that is right."

"I was born of the *pobre.* But what can such a statement mean to you, one born of the rich? As a boy were you ever hungry? I do not mean hungry when a steaming meal was awaiting your pleasure. I

174

mean hungry with no food to be had. Were you ever hungry in that fashion, my friend?"

Otto scowled, wrestling up an answer. He wanted to top the major and say that once he had all but starved to death, but how would that square with his tales of a bounteous Prussia swimming with beer and pig's-knuckles? He said:

"*Ja*, once I nearly starved, but that was when I was a nigger smuggler in Texas and I would prefer not talking about it."

The major's pudgy hand gestured acquiescence.

"*Si, naturalmente*. With us all there are episodes that do not bear looking into. We are all of us villains."

"*Ja*, that is true. I have been quite a villain in my time."

"When the Apaches slaughtered my father and stole my mother I fled to the mountains, *señor*. I did not wish to find myself sold into slavery. Perhaps my niece has told you how I nearly starved before a sheepherder gave me shelter. He was a loco one. Quite *rabioso* in his preference for young boys. At first I did not understand his fondness. And when I understood—well, what would you? Was I to starve? Was I to return to Santa Fe and suffer the fate of orphans?

"*Si*, a loco fellow. And most strong. And not a believer. His history I never learned, beyond a few scraps. He had been born in Spain and shipped off in disgrace to the New World. It is my opinion he involved himself in scandals in Mexico and took flight. He was fond of sheep. Very fond of sheep. Also of books. It is *extraño* to find a sheepherder with a small library and able to read. Perhaps in Spain he had studied for Holy Orders before disgracing himself. I do not know. Always I had been curious about black printed letters, and in Santa Fe I had received some instruction from the priest. The sheepherder taught me further. Soon I was reading his books. There was a Shakespeare and a Cervantes. Also several that argued against God. The sheepherder—his name was John of God—also argued against God. I can see it now, our campfire in the mountains with the stars overhead. He would stand and preach mock sermons. It was his opinion that the devil had slain God. He believed the devil ruled the world. It was a theory *fantastico,* but logical enough when he argued it. And I must say he practiced what he preached and served the devil to the best of his ability. For a time even I was converted to his beliefs. Later I dismissed them as nonsense, but I never recovered a belief in God."

"You are an infidel, already?"

The major shrugged, held out his glass, and after it was refilled he said:

"That is dangerous knowledge for you to possess, my friend. If you ever repeat it I shall see that you are put to death. Painfully."

"I am not in the habit, Excellency, of tattling confidences."

"It is well that you are not."

"Your secret is safe with me," Otto declared, with great emphasis. "Perfectly safe. And is it true you stole sheep and sold them so you could go to Mexico?"

"Of course. One must get on in the world. But I had a more impelling reason to leave John of God. As time passed he grew more loco. One day he seized me by the throat and choked me till my face must have been purple. The sun vanished and all was black. When I recovered my senses he was most kind. But he told me he had dreamed I went to Santa Fe and announced that John of God believed God had been slain by the devil. That was why he choked me. If the vision came twice again he would know it as a warning. Then he would choke me to death. I did not wish to wait till he had dreamed the vision twice more, or even once. Choking is painful, *señor*. I can well believe the noose and the garrote are unpleasant ways to die."

Otto's throat tingled.

"So I left him, *señor*, and went to the City of Mexico. A beautiful city. Men say it is the loveliest of world capitals."

"So? Paris too is beautiful, and Berlin—*ach!*"

"All the pleasures are to be had in Mexico, *señor*. But money is necessary. I supported myself, one way or another. For a time I wandered the provinces selling pieces from the true Cross of Calvary. You may imagine with what religious fervor I cloaked my cynicism. I did many other things also. They are better not mentioned. Then came the troubled waters of the revolution, and I fished to my advantage. *Sí*, I got on. But I should have remained in Mexico instead of taking this post in Santa Fe. Coming here was the mistake of my life."

"Of mine too, Excellency."

"Ah, well, it is a bed of downy feathers. And I have the pleasure of much authority. It is not the best of positions, but neither is it the worst. I should not like to herd sheep again. Mutton is one dish that turns my stomach. With life being what it is, *señor*, I should not enjoy being dislodged from my position. Which brings me to the point of my visit. You have probably deduced that my mother called on me this afternoon."

"*Ja*, the old woman was here too."

"She can be difficult, *señor*. When I returned to Santa Fe after so long an absence it was a surprise not wholly pleasant to discover my mother alive, and my niece. A man in public office is held accountable for the actions of his family, especially when he is head of his family. The more family, the more chances for scandal. Especially if there are many girls under his protection. My blessed niece is under my protection, if no longer under my authority except in name. Do I make myself clear?"

"*Ja*, I think maybe you are angry with me because Consuelo is going to bear a little one."

"Angry?" The major smiled. "With your permission I will have one more drink on that. Thank you. A brave statue should be erected to

176

the benefactor who discovered how to concoct whiskey. I believe I am a little drunk. And that is good. I wish to be no more drunk nor no less. I wish only to maintain the pitch. As for my being angry, *señor,* undeceive yourself. I am delighted. My niece will now pass from my protection to yours. To me she has been a great burden. I am cursed with daughters. My only son died in infancy, after stuffing himself on green peppers. Sometimes I wish I had died in infancy, *señor.* Perhaps God lives. Who knows? If he lives I will suffer. If he does not, think of the trouble I have put myself to, pretending to be a believer. Ah, well, it is a truism that life is not easy. But I am not angry with you. On the contrary. But I am angry with my mother, screaming outside your door. I know Santa Fe. I know the gossiping tongues. The news doubtless is known now in every kitchen. I have permitted my niece to conceive. I will be censured. As if I, a poor mortal with a burdensome belly, could cool the itch of youth. Ah, well, the damage will be repaired. As soon as you marry her I will be praised instead of blamed. I will have done my duty. I will have made of my niece an honest woman, and I will have converted the angry young man of the yellow hair to the true religion."

"*Ja,* I will marry her. As soon as a Lutheran pastor can be found there will be a ceremony. Till then we will live by the common law. But I will not of course enter the cathedral for marriage or for worship."

The major sat slumped in his chair, watching the reflections of the firelight in his whiskey.

"Please, *señor,*" he said, "do not be difficult. Do not force me, an infidel, to the final irony of compelling you, a follower of your own blond gods, to become a true believer."

"I am a Lutheran. I will always be a Lutheran."

"*Señor, señor.* You are my friend. You are to be my nephew. I have been frank with you. I am fond of you. You give me much amusement with your brave tales. Do you have a father? And if so, is he actually a general?"

"Do I have a father!" In his excitement Otto leaped up as if stabbed by a needle. "*Mein Gott!* Of course I have a father! Do you think I was hatched from an egg like some white rooster? And is my father a general! Are you mad? Of course he is a general! And no cowardly American or Spanish general either, but a Prussian general already. Maybe I did not kill seven Comanches. Maybe I lied. *Ja!* I lied. I killed only five. But when I told you my father is a general I did not lie. That is the greatest thing that has ever happened to me, and about that I would not lie."

"Be calm, my friend, be calm. You have converted me. I do not believe in God, but I believe in General von Zumwalt."

"*Ja,* that is more like it already!"

177

"Do not pace the floor, my friend. It wearies me, watching you. Sit down. Take your ease."

"My father not a general! *Gott im Himmel!* He is such a warrior I was always afraid of him. My brothers too, and also the old lady. He made us march!"

"In any case, *señor,* he is not here tonight and you do not need to keep marching. Sit down, sit down. I am dizzy watching you."

"Not a general!" Otto muttered, dropping into a chair. *"Mein Gott!"*

Major Delgado drained his drink.

"I have become mellow, my friend. I feel as ripe as a peach. I do not wish to argue any matter with you. I wish to be kind. I wish you to take an urbane view of the matter. Surely if all these years I have pretended to be a believer, you could also pretend to be one and join my church to make matters easy for yourself. You will do that in the end, I can assure you. You will do it because I cannot have it said that Major Delgado, an officer of the government, permits his niece to marry an infidel."

"But I am not an infidel! I am a Lutheran. You are the infidel."

"True, my friend, true. I am not arguing the right or wrong of the matter. I am arguing only expediency."

"Ja, well, I am not so expedient as all that. I will take your niece into my house and treat her fine because I love her. We will be man and wife. And some day a Lutheran pastor will come over the trail and marry us. But I will not join your church or be married in the cathedral. That is the end of it."

For a long time, Major Delgado did not reply. Eyes heavy, he sat slumped, staring at his empty glass. At last he sighed.

"Then, my friend, you have my pity. I should not do it, but I will give you till sundown tomorrow to change your mind. Sleep on the matter, my friend, and kneel and pray to your furious blond gods. Do you think they will hear you, in their northern fastnesses of snow and ice? I do not believe they will. I do not believe the gods have been slain. I believe they never lived. Now let us drop the matter and have a final drink. I will drink to the little one you have planted in the warm soil of my niece. The little one has my sympathy, for the wind from the mountains blows cold, and the rocks are sharp on the path underfoot, and the midsummer sun can blister, and the belly is always hungry, and the lash is cruel, and the little one will be born naked and helpless. It is a sorry thing to be born, my friend. Often I have wished it had never happened to me."

"Ja, sure, I have wished the same thing at times," Otto said. "But I will drink with you to the little one. And then I will tell you my plans for a fine board floor."

*

178

Next day the sky was a confusion of clouds dumped from some celestial ragbag and blown about by the wind. It was not a dust-storm wind, but a wind raw and sneaking and intermittent, striking unexpectedly and darting away like a pickpocket. Consuelo did not come to the store, and Otto moped and brooded, his mind littered with worries. Perhaps again today she had wakened sick and had fainted.

"I am going to put an end to this monkey business," he thought, "and see to it that she moves in with me. I do not like thinking of her under the thumb of that foul old grandmother. We could be happy if they would all leave us alone. We could live married under the common law, and maybe next fall we would go back to St. Louis with the caravan and find a Lutheran pastor. I would not be so uneasy about Comanches if I had her by my side. *Ja,* I think when a man has weaker ones to protect he forgets dangers to himself."

During the morning he thought back on his conversation with Major Delgado. He couldn't remember it in detail, because too much Taos Lightning had fuzzed his brain, but the parts he did remember evoked his contempt and a vague uneasiness.

"He has been a wicked one," Otto thought, "living with that sheepherder and reading books that attacked God. He is a big chunk of brass, telling me what church I should join when he is an infidel. But I do not like the way he gave me an ultimatum to make up my mind. When he comes at sundown he will maybe challenge me to a duel. *Ja,* well, I will take care of him properly. I am not worried about that hippopotamus. Besides, how can he come at sundown when the sun is not shining today? This is a fine climate indeed with its clouds and wind, and I am going to tell Hod Kite what I think of it."

Otto had fallen into the habit of holding Hod responsible for bad weather.

The pattern of that day was the pattern of all the days when Consuelo did not appear. He was restless, restless, plodding on endless round-trip journeys from house to patio. With customers he was short-spoken, impatient. A greater number than usual drifted into the store, most of them just looking. Their eyes were wickedly amused, their smiles secretive; they cast knowing glances at one another, and sometimes for no good reason they giggled.

"I will bet I know why they are here," he thought suddenly. "They heard about the commotion that filthy old woman caused, yelling outside the door, and they have come expecting more fireworks and to see how I am taking it. And they giggle whenever they catch sight of the bed. *Ach,* they are filthy and low-minded. I am sick of Mexicans. All except her. I wish I could gather her into my arms and carry her far away and we could begin all over. I have made a mess out of everything. I cannot understand why always things go with me so badly. It has always been the same. Never could I make friends easily or keep the ones I made. I do not think I am very well liked, and I do not know why. But that lying Hod Kite is a good friend. He may be a bank robber and no gentleman, but he is my friend. Also that lying McSwasey. Growing the biggest watermelon already! I will bet he never grew so much as a gooseberry. But I believe he likes me. I hope so because he is my best friend now that poor Billy has been all eaten up by the wolves. Consuelo is the best friend of all, and more than a friend too. Maybe the little one when it is born will be my friend. I hope so. I hope the little one will like me."

Dusk came early that day; the customers left; Otto lighted a candle and poked at the fire. Then he had a drink. He was ready for another when he heard a knock at the door. Major Delgado stood outside.

"Excellency! I am glad to see you. My house is yours. Come in and have a drink."

"*Señor,* it is with regret I must refuse. My mission is not a pleasant one, and I cannot accept your hospitality until I learn your decision. Have you decided to embrace the church?"

"Please, please," Otto said, stiffening, "let us not argue the matter further. I am a Lutheran. A Lutheran I have lived, and a Lutheran I will die. I am tired of the monkey business. Let us forget it. I wish you would let me pour you a drink."

Major Delgado shook his head.

"I am leaving now, *señor*. If you should at any moment change your mind let me know and I will help you."

He turned.

"But Excellency! One drink. I am lonely tonight and you are my friend. You are almost my only friend."

The major heaved a sigh, and in the candlelight his eyes were mournful, disenchanted, worn.

"I am sorry, my nephew. Whatever happens remember that I am sorry. Remember the urchin who was hungry, and who learned early that the first law of life is self-protection. Now I must go. I wish you a good night."

He left.

Otto stood staring at the closed door. Outside the wind sniffed around the house like a starved dog. He turned back to the Taos Lightning.

But before he could pour a drink another knock sounded.

"*Ach,* he has changed his mind," Otto thought, opening the door.

Three soldiers entered the store, wearing the shakos of the Santa Fe garrison.

"*Señor* Zumwalt?"

"*Ja.*"

"Come with us."

"Where?"

"Come with us."

"What are you saying?"

"Come with us."

"Why should I come with you? I have done nothing. Get out of my house. I order it. March!"

Otto's arms were seized.

"Stop it!" he cried, in German. "How dare you, you cowardly privates, put hands on the son of General von Zumwalt!"

He gave a great jerk; he kicked.

In the candleshine he saw a smooth brown face, smiling. He saw a brown fist drawing back.

"I will tell my father!" Otto yelled, in German.

The fist swung toward him.

*

He came to his senses gradually and imperfectly. Cold wind was blowing through the evening; his arms were outflung, each hand imprisoned painfully; he was partially erect and being dragged and walked along a street, supported by a man on either side. His uncovered head wobbled every which way, his chin hammering.

Words formed in his brain, but they expired somewhere along his phonetic nerves.

"Wait!" he cried mutely. "What is this? There is a mistake. I do not understand. I am the son of General von Zumwalt."

He fought toward consciousness. And the nearer he approached it, the more aware he grew of pain. His jaw ached. His nose felt swollen and sore. His feet, in being dragged, encountered obstructions; his boot-toes snagged rocks and his feet were twisted till agony leaped along his ligaments.

Then he achieved consciousness; his feet began to walk. His captors halted. Somebody said:

"The *señor* has finished his siesta."

Otto was aware of dim lights swimming in a scene familiar and strange.

"*Ach,*" he thought, "it is the plaza. But what am I doing here?"

Aloud, he mumbled:

"What is this? Why have you seized me? It was not my fault. I tried to stop him but he wanted to kill a buffalo. He waved at me in the moonlight, but he wouldn't stop."

A figure wearing a shako appeared between Otto and the bleared lights.

"*Señor* Zumwalt. Have you decided to do what Major Delgado wishes?"

Otto remembered then, everything.

"*Mein Gott!* What are you saying? Of course not."

When the fist struck his sore jaw he experienced the quintessence of agony; then more darkness.

He was a thing of bruises, of sprains, when consciousness returned.

Something harsh was sawing at his medulla oblongata; something harsh sawed his wrists; something harsh sawed his Adam's apple. Slowly he realized that the sawing resulted from the weight of his slumping body. His feet were unfettered; he could feel them scrambling far away, dancing an absurd jig. At last they gained solid support; the sawing ceased. He closed his eyes; the darkness was whirling.

"What is it?" he moaned. "Where am I? What has happened?"

He could not move his hands; when he tried to move his head it encountered something hard and rough. It was as if his hands and head had been locked into openings too small to permit their withdrawal.

Ja, that was it, that was exactly it, he realized, when he opened his eyes; he was standing bent over, locked in the pillory on the plaza.

*

He knew terror, the ancient terror of the kingdom of animals; the trap-terror, the snare-terror. By comparison, fear was nothing. Fear could fight back; fear could flee.

"*Mein Gott!* Let me out of this contraption!" he yelled, in German. Nobody responded.

"Let me out of this! Let me out!"

He yanked his arms in panic, trying to jerk his hands free. But the holes confining his wrists were too small to permit escape. He drew back his head, grinding his skull and his jaw against the encircling wood; again, the hole was too small. His feet danced and kicked; it was all futile. And the full shock of his predicament struck. He thought he couldn't endure another moment of standing with his spine curved and aching, his wrists pinioned, his neck sawed by the wooden collar. And yet he had to endure it.

"I can't!" he shouted. "Not another minute! *Mein Gott—*"

That was a mistake, filling the windy evening with his despair, for his cries attracted several boys in their early teens who, after the manner of adolescents, had been idling on a street corner, telling dirty stories. Otto heard them pounding through the shadows, shouting the glad news that somebody was in the pillory; and he saw them halt, not far away, dim figures conferring in whispers. Presently one boy shambled to the pillory, giggling.

"Go along about your business, you cowardly puppy," Otto ordered.

"Oyee! It is old yellow hair. It is the stiff-necked *Americano.*"

"I am not an *Americano.* I am a Prussian."

"Oyee, it is the gringo! The *yanqui* with the stiff neck."

"I am not a Yankee, you unlicked *hündchen.*"

"Oyee! Oyee!" the boys shouted, capering about the pillory, calling Otto filthy names. Otto responded with names just as filthy, but in his excitement he employed German, so his tremendous talent in vituperation was wasted. But the uproar, which could be heard for several blocks, attracted other young people, boys and girls, and before long twenty or thirty congregated there, screeching, dancing, jeering.

"Go home to your mud houses," Otto yelled, "and live on your dirt floors like squealing pigs."

His voice was lost in the bedlam.

"I am sorry I ever came to this barbarous town," he shouted. "You are ignorant savages. You are worse than the Comanches."

"Oyee! Oyee!"

"If I had known what you were like I would never have left St. Louis."

"Oyee! Oyee! Oyee!"

"I would have turned back that morning at Raton Pass," he shouted hoarsely; and then his voice broke, and almost in a sob he added, *"Ach, I was free then. I could have gone back. Why didn't I? Mein Gott, why didn't I?"*

The hubbub died down, after a while, and Otto saw his tormentors gathering in a conspiratorial circle. He heard whispering, sometimes a laugh came from the circle; and finally a girl shrilled, "Let me do it. I will do it well."

Laughing, she skipped over to where Otto's unprotected head was thrust through the pillory; her companions gathered round. In the dull light he recognized her as one of the girls who used to smile at him flirtatiously in the store.

"Ah, look who is here," she trilled sweetly. "It is the great *Señor* Zumwalt, I believe."

"Ja," he said, with as much dignity as his position could afford, "that is right. And I wish to tell you one thing. I am tired of this monkey business—"

"The *Señor* Zumwalt whose father is a general?"

"Of course he is a general! He is the greatest—"

"The *Señor* Zumwalt who has conquered the Apaches?"

At this, a great hooting and catcalling soared from the throng.

"We will leave her out of this!" Otto said.

"But *señor,* with your permission, I do not believe it possible to leave her out of this."

"You hussy," Otto said. "I will not have you talking about her this way."

"Ah, *señor,* what pretty hair you have. Has she not admired it?"

"It is none of your business what has taken place between us."

The girl thrust her fingers into Otto's hair and yanked his head from side to side.

"Stop it! I order it—"

"Ah, *señor,* do you not like to have your hair admired? It is such beautiful hair."

"Ja, sure, sure, but I wish you would leave your greasy fingers out of it."

"Very well, *señor.* I am at your command."

"Then go home to your filthy house and sleep like a pig-bitch under your dirt roof without any shingles already."

The girl swung her open palm and slapped Otto's cheeks.

"Stop it!"

She slapped him some more.

"Stop it! I order it! I will not have it! Only a coward will hit a man when he is down."

She kept slapping him while her companions yelled rapturously and Otto danced and kicked and yanked his wrists against the holes imprisoning them.

"*Señor, señor*," she said sweetly, "how can you object to my caresses?"

"I do object," he shouted hoarsely.

She stooped and came up with something in her fingers.

"What is it?" Otto demanded.

"Only a blade of grass. A beautiful blade of grass. Let us call it *Señor* Zumwalt."

"I will not have any cowardly grass named after me."

"But *señor*, it has already been christened. It is such a nice blade of grass. So long and nice."

"Not as long as we grow in Prussia."

"I believe it is Prussian grass, for its name is *Señor* Zumwalt. And let us call this nose Consuelo."

The girl reached out and pinched Otto's nose between thumb and forefinger, twisting it and yanking it.

"Stop it! I will not have you naming my nose after Consuelo."

The onlookers were bending double in laughter.

"Oh, but *señor*, that is its name."

The girl drew back her hand as if to strike Otto's face. He yipped. And then amid cries of amusement and derision she permitted her hand to float slowly toward him. When it was near his face she held the blade of grass daintily and brushed it across his lips.

"*Cosquilloso, señor?*"

"Stop it! Sure I am ticklish."

She tickled his lips again.

He blew away the grass.

She slapped him hard.

"*Señor*, with your permission, I must slap you when you blow away the grass."

She tickled his lips more, then brushed the grass across his nostrils. He wrinkled his nose. And while the young people laughed and hooted, she probed his nostrils with the grass blade, producing a sensation so excruciating that tears came to his eyes and he snorted and blew. So she slapped him. Then she hawked and spat into his face.

"*Ach!* Stop! *Ach—*"

She spat again and again, and all the happy throng surged forward and followed her example.

Then suddenly a yell went up and they took to their heels.

Otto opened his eyes. A shadowy man in a shako stood there.

"*Señor* Zumwalt. Major Delgado sends his compliments and wishes to know whether you have become convinced that his way of thinking is best."

"No! No! Never!"

Pain thudded against his jaw; he slumped.

*

He was unconscious a long time, yet not so deeply unconscious but that his brute will to survive took care of him. Always he dreamed mad dreams of being choked, and when his windpipe closed his body would thresh and sway, tethered by his imprisoned wrists and head; his feet would kick convulsively; and then for a while the pressure on his throat would be relieved and he would breathe. Presently he would slump again, his throat crushing down against the wood of the pillory, cutting off air to his lungs, and once more his body would thresh.

The wind had become sharp and icy, when finally he regained consciousness, and he felt stupefied with pain and cold. A sob racked him. Far away his feet were floundering, leaden and half-frozen; his wrists had been chaffed raw; his jaws ached; and his face felt unclean where the spittle from many mouths had spattered.

And he had a vision of the hot mineral waters at Baden-Baden, and of himself soaking in a steaming bath till all the aches and cold and corruption were boiled from his pores, till he was clean through and through with the blond cleanness of the Prussian; and he thought of how it would be to swallow glass after glass of the cleansing waters, and to lie on a rubbing table while a masseur kneaded any lingering soreness from muscles grown supple; and then alcohol would be applied, and he would be anointed with sweet oils; and he would sleep pleasantly and waken refreshed and sit in a cafe with a ravishing girl.

"*Ach,*" he mumbled, "Europe, Europe . . ."

"Otto," somebody said gently. "Otto, my life."

He unlidded his eyes to the blowing dust, the shadowy plaza in the Royal City of the Holy Faith of St. Francis of Assisi.

"*Ja,*" he whispered vaguely, "once I was there. My father took me to Baden-Baden once. I was ten already. Just my father and I. A young widow lived there. He had met her in Berlin. The masseur was a cowardly Austrian from Salzburg. He called me Young Master Zumwalt. I used to buy sugar plums from a shop on the *Lichtentaler Allee.*"

"Otto, I am sorry. You must remain no longer in the pillory. Otto, you will catch cold and die."

His eyes had drooped shut; with effort, he opened them.

185

"Is it a dream already?" he mumbled. "Is it a dream I am having of Consuelo?"

"No, no, it is no dream. I am with you, Otto. My uncle came to my house to boast of what he had done with you. I wanted to come at once but they would not let me. But after my uncle left and my grandmother slept I came."

"*Ja*, she is a filthy old one, your grandmother. And once your uncle hid with hens. He does not like mutton. I lied about the Comanches. Not seven. Only five. They killed my best friend."

"Otto, listen to me. Can you hear me, Otto?"

Her breath was warm in his ear.

"*Ja, ja,* I can hear. I am very tired."

"Do you know me, Otto?"

"*Ja*, sure, sure. You are a funny little Indian. As pretty as a little rabbit."

"Otto, you must do what my uncle wishes. Promise to do what he wishes and I will race to his house and you will be released."

"*Ach,* that would be good. But I am a Lutheran. I remember the Sunday when I was confirmed. I wore new shoes that squeaked."

"Otto, my life, listen. Terrible things will happen to you unless you are released."

"Terrible things? I think they have happened already."

"No, Otto, no. Nothing like what will happen. You do not know my uncle. He is wicked and cruel. You must not blame my religion for this. The priest does not even know. It is all my uncle. Otto, you must yield. You will die if you do not yield."

His eyes had closed. Her whispers seemed to come from far infinities. He heard himself mumbling:

"*Ja, ja,* anything. I am very tired. I will do what he wishes."

Then she was gone; he hung in utter exhaustion. His brain was black and whirling. He thought he walked on a vast plain carrying a candle in windy darkness. It seemed very important to shield the candle from the wind.

"*Ja,*" he thought feebly, "but not in my heart. In my heart I will be a Lutheran till I die."

And he always was.

V

CORRESPONDENCE RECEIVED by Otto Zumwalt in June 1825, after having been carried from Missouri by a party of hunters and adventurers, traveling light and fast:

From John Proudfoot:

St. Louis, Missouri
March 28, 1825

Mr. O. Zumwalt, Mgr.
Santa Fe Branch
Proudfoot & Sons
Santa Fe, New Mexico

Dear Sir:

Your letters received and contents noted. Must say I was glad to find enclosed your financial statement, also inventory of merchandise, all in good order. Can't say I feel it wholly wise for you to buy real estate in Santa Fe, never know with the greasers what market conditions will be, I reckon them an unstable lot, however it's your money and since you could locate no rental property am glad to know our branch now so well situated. As for rent, it's hard for me to figure, not being on the ground, but would suggest $7.50 per month, wish I could pay more but business is slow.

I plan to send you three wagons of merchandise leaving here in May. Caleb McSwasey will also have three wagons, all six being under his charge and care.

Great blow to learn of Billy's passing. Know you did all anyone could. Your condolences and report of giving him Christian burial greatly appreciated by Mrs. Proudfoot and myself. Also appreciate the way you took charge of matters and got my goods through customs and set up a store.

Reckon you haven't heard how they stole the presidency from Old Hickory after he was elected. Would like to wring Henry Clay's neck for his part in the sorry business. Old J. Q. Adams took office March 4. If I'd wanted to live under Adamses would never have left Massachusetts. The country can hope for little relief from the Indian problem now. Gen'l Jackson was my man. Bet we'll elect him next time. Then the damn redskins had best look sharp.

Believe me, sir, your obed't. etc. etc.
John Proudfoot

*

From Caleb McSwasey:

St. Louis, Missouri
March 28, 1825

Friend Otto:

Will hasten to drop you a line as I understand the Butler party is leaving tomorrow bound for New Mexico. I believe they will likely get through, but must say I don't covet them the trip so early in the season.

Had uneventful trip back last fall. Pawnees quiet except for one hunting party, we dealt with them to our satisfaction. Two or three brushes with the Comanches, they are a sort of ornery bunch. We lost a mule skinner to their arrows, you might remember him, fellow name of Hall.

Will say my profits from the trade last year were middling good, better than I expected, those beaver pelts from Taos sold well. I could have disposed of many more than I had. Will arrive in Santa Fe with three wagons this year. Am not too long on cash at present because I have bought a couple of business lots here in St. Louis. Week after buying same could have disposed of them to my profit. St. Louis remains lively, no question but it has a future, though will not say what kind. I bought three niggers late in December from Kentucky gent embarrassed for ready funds, sold two of them at a profit but have kept the third, a likely wench. May trade her for another business lot before hitting the trail west. Nice thing about unimproved real estate is it don't get sick on you or run off when your back is turned.

Otto, hope you have kept in touch with that greaser at the customhouse, that was a real favor you did me last year and I am much obliged. I have put in a good word for you with Proudfoot. Would be obliged if you could see your way to smooth things for me when I hit Santa Fe next August. If we work together and sleep with one eye open we have a chance to end up with a potful of pennies.

I hear from Proudfoot he is offering you $7.50 per month rent. That is stealing it. Will talk it over when I see you. Know you can get at least $10.

Fair amount of interest here in the election. General Jackson received the most votes but due to some horse trading in Washington they have put in Adams. I would bet the hole in a doughnut the general is mad. So God help Adams and the rest of them. In the army we used to say that if a flea bit Old Hickory when his dander was up, the flea would die of hydrophobia.

Give my best to Hod Kite, and take care of yourself.

Yours, etc. etc.
Caleb McSwasey

*

Letter from Otto Zumwalt to John Proudfoot:

Santa Fe, New Mexico
August 25, 1825

Mr. John Proudfoot
Proudfoot & Sons
St. Louis, Missouri
U. S. A.

Dear Sir:

It was a great pleasure to receive your letter of last March. I am enclosing herewith an inventory of all merchandise in your Santa Fe Branch, as of August 15, inst., as well as an accounting of all funds. I trust you will find these in good order.

The caravan from the States has not yet arrived, but we are expecting it daily. I am looking forward to getting the new merchandise, as well as to seeing Caleb McSwasey, who is my best friend. I will do my best to get our goods and his through customs quickly and cheaply; however, the man who was Collector of Customs last year is no longer in Santa Fe. Perhaps McSwasey has told you about him, his name was Major Delgado. Last spring, owing to some political changes in Mexico City, Major Delgado was relieved of his position, and in June he left Santa Fe with his wife and daughters, going to Mexico, where he hopes once more to find employment with the government. I believe, however, my knowledge of Spanish will enable us to make a good deal with the new Collector of Customs here.

As you will see from the enclosed accounts, the store has prospered, and perhaps you will be interested to know that I am now a married man. My wife is from one of the most aristocratic families in New Mexico. After a whirlwind courtship we were married last winter. She is a splendid girl, well-versed in all the arts and letters, and she has been a great help to me, clerking in the store. Just now, however, we are expecting a little one, so the burden of selling merchandise is mine alone.

As for rent, I believe $7.50 per month is too low. I have discussed the matter with Mr. H. Kite, one of the leading businessmen of Santa Fe, and he believes $10 per month would be a fair price.

My health has been good except for a touch of pneumonia last winter as a result of being exposed one evening to the elements. This is not a perfect climate.

Thanking you again for past and future favors, I remain, sir, your obedient servant,

Otto Zumwalt, Manager
Santa Fe Branch
Proudfoot & Sons

PS. September 6, 1825

The caravan arrived a few days ago, but Mr. Proudfoot, something terrible has happened, I am nearly out of my mind and hardly know what I am writing. At five minutes of eleven last night my pretty little wife gave birth to a daughter, but oh, Mr. Proudfoot, everything went wrong, it was too much for my wife, and at four this morning she passed away. What am I to do? Caleb McSwasey and Hod Kite are with me but I am like a crazy man with grief. Most of the night I was on my knees praying, but God took her from me, she has run away for the last time, and I do not know which way to turn. But I will carry on as best I can with the store.

O. v Z.

VI

"And if it is a girl," Consuelo had said, "let us name her Esperanza."

"*Ja*, but it will be a boy. Then we will name him Heinrich after my father."

"But I believe it will be a girl."

"It will not be a girl," Otto said. "But if it is, let us name her Hedwig. What kind of name is Esperanza? It sounds like some Mexican living on a dirt floor."

"But Otto. She will be a Mexican and an Apache too."

"She will not be. She will be a Prussian. Except it will not be a girl at all. It will be a boy."

But the victory was Consuelo's, achieved at great cost. Weeks later, on a September afternoon, when, after the cool dusk of the cathedral, and the dryness of the burying ground with its sun-blistered wooden crosses, Otto shambled through emptiness, back to the Street of the Chamiso, accompanied by a red-headed man who limped, and a perky little man who had once served drinks in Nacogdoches—when Otto stood in the patio, and Caleb McSwasey gripped his shoulder in that ageless gesture of consolation to the inconsolable, and repeated the ageless banalities, and reminded him of the child, the new life that must be nurtured—when these things were said and done, Otto spoke at last as from a far land.

"*Ja*, the child. But for the child I would go home. But for the child I would take the trail back to Missouri. I do not think I would be afraid of Comanches now."

"You never were afraid of them," McSwasey said. "No more than anybody."

"*Ja*, except maybe Billy Poudfoot. And maybe Billy too, at the end. First Billy. And now Consuelo. My best friend and my wife both in the ground."

"There's the baby," McSwasey said again. "She's a fine baby. What are you calling her, Otto?"

"*Ja, ja,*" he muttered vaguely, "it is true she will need a name. I do not think I will call her Hedwig. I think I will call her what my wife wanted. Esperanza. It is a Spanish name. It is a name meaning hope and expectation. Esperanza."

"Esperanza," McSwasey said, for the first time speaking that name he would speak so many times, down the years.

*

During her earliest childhood there were persons in her life she could not remember at all by the time she was twelve. But she heard about them from her father. There had been, it seemed, a witch named La Luz Delgado who had cared for her till she was twenty months old. The witch had been her great-grandmother, an evil one who quite uninvited had moved into the little house on *el Camino del Chamiso*. According to the baby's father, the witch had tried to murder the baby by feeding it queer Spanish foods and administering strange nostrums brewed from wicked herbs. But then the witch had died. And when the old wives prepared her for burial, they had discovered a concealed weapon on her person. A knife. Razor-sharp. It had given the baby's father pause, he said, when he imagined how the witch must have intended to slide that knife from its sheath and plunge it into his vitals while he slept. He still had that knife; occasionally he would take it from a shelf in the kitchen and exhibit it.

The baby's father had not attended La Luz Delgado's funeral, inasmuch as the service took place in the cathedral.

"We are Lutherans," he often told his daughter, in the German he was taking pains she should learn. "Some day a Lutheran pastor will come over the trail and you will be confirmed. I remember the day I was confirmed. It was in East Prussia—"

And he spoke at length of that halcyon land he had lost.

After the death of La Luz Delgado, peace came to the Zumwalt house, and also a slave. Having saved his earnings, Otto was able to pay Hod Kite a good price for the girl. She was seventeen, an attractive wench named Lilith, with a soft tongue and a skin not much darker than brown sugar. Long ago in Texas Hod had bought mother and child, and he assured Otto that Lilith, according to her mother, was a descendant of a First Family of Virginia. That clinched the transaction, for if Otto was going to have a slave, he wanted an aristocratic one.

Less than a year after becoming Otto's slave, she presented her master with a son; they named him Wisdom.

"Now ain't that fine," Hod Kite said. "Didn't I tell you Lilith would be a good breeder? That nigger boy would fetch two hundred dollars right now, in Texas. You've made yourself two hundred dollars without no work at all, to speak of."

"*Ja,* but I will bet he will be a big eater."

"Feed him table scraps, Sport."

Soon after Wisdom's birth, Otto bought another piece of property, a house adjoining his on the way to the plaza; it had belonged to a family named Garcia. Workmen came and carved a gateway in the wall between the patio where Consuelo used to whirl in the wind and the new place. Presently Lilith and Wisdom were installed in the Garcia house. It was larger than Otto's first house, and perhaps this was the first instance in history when slaves occupied finer quarters than their master. But he liked it that way. He had grown fond of the little house with its memories of Consuelo, and besides, his store was there. To live where he could watch over his business satisfied some deep racial precept; he was like a diligent general-director living beside his *fabrik*.

*

From childhood Esperanza could not remember Caleb McSwasey either, for after her second birthday his trips to Santa Fe ceased. He had, it seemed, accumulated enough capital from all the goods he had freighted to New Mexico, and from all the beaver pelts he had carried back, to buy a partnership in Proudfoot & Sons, and after that he remained in St. Louis. To Esperanza he was a legendary figure, her father's best friend, a magnifico as hazy as that other colossus, General Heinrich von Zumwalt. Letters from the general never reached Santa Fe, but from McSwasey they arrived with some regularity; these Otto would read over and over, and in the evening he would spin tales for his daughter about the hardships he and McSwasey had shared on the trail.

"I gave him his start. When I first knew him he was nothing but a poor young man, trying to get ahead. On the trail I nearly elected him captain of the caravan, but those *dummkopf* mule skinners swindled him out of that. He had a wagon full of goods, but in Santa Fe he could not get them through customs so quick because he did not know the language. I got them through for him. And not third or fourth, but first! And that was the beginning of his fortune. That is the kind of friend I am."

She considered her father quite a fellow, in those years. As a badge of maturity he was cultivating a mustache, rich, luxuriant, golden, and she enjoyed watching him apply wax to persuade the ends to bristle upward. After such applications he looked deliciously bellicose, more like a lieutenant than a tradesman. But for some reason, perhaps because of the dry climate, the mustache persisted in turning down, an hour or so after being waxed. The effect was to give Otto's thin face a woebegone appearance, like a starveling poet's. He formed the habit of seizing the ends and twirling furiously, but the mustache continued to droop, till he waxed it again.

Esperanza's earliest memories went back to the burgeoning days of the mustache; perhaps earliest of all to a spring afternoon. A week before, plainsmen had arrived from Missouri, bringing mail; and now she toddled through the front door and saw her father on a barrel, putting up a new sign announcing this the Santa Fe Branch of Proudfoot & McSwasey, Otto Zumwalt, Manager.

"Now we will sell goods," he said, stepping down from the barrel and admiring the sign. "More goods than ever. That is what McSwasey wants. In his letter he said that now he is a partner everything must march. It has been a sleepy firm, but with McSwasey in the business it will go forward like a cavalry charge."

The old sign lay in the dust; he picked it up. Once it had been brilliant, but now it had been dimmed by sun and wind. He stood in silence, staring at the faded letters; then abruptly, he disappeared into the house. Esperanza followed, through store and kitchen to the patio, where she found him pacing, tears on his cheeks, in the shade of the little cottonwood that was not so little any more.

She did not understand his tears; she would never understand them. She toddled back into the house, where, a few minutes later, Otto discovered that she had snitched a pair of scissors from the counter.

"*Ach,* not scissors, my little one! No, no, the Zumwalts do not play with scissors."

He snatched them.

She tried to snatch them back.

He put them beyond reach on the counter; their glances met. Her eyes were dark, as dark as her mother's had been; and now, as so often when her will was thwarted, they became curiously opaque and as expressionless as black glass.

"*Ach,*" he murmured tenderly, "you are a little Apache. Sometimes I wish you would cry more instead of giving me that look that reminds me of her and of more than her. *Ja,* I think you are more Apache than she was. Sometimes, little monkey, when you look at me like that I think of Indians and remember poor Billy the way he was that morning so long ago. Four years it has been; four years dead. Maybe some day we will go back to St. Louis and even to Prussia, when all the Comanches have been killed."

Esperanza was trying to climb after the scissors.

"No, no, little monkey," Otto said, taking her into his arms. "Let us go find your doll."

When he carried her to the patio, she yanked his mustache.

"No, no. Not my mustache, little one."

He took her hand, tiny, beautiful, the color of fine tan sand faintly flushed with rosy light. He marveled at its perfection: the exquisite fingers and flawless skin. And when he set her down in the patio, and she toddled from the shade of the cottonwood into the full brilliance of the New Mexican sun, he caught his breath at the beauty of her hair, silken, halo-like, golden blond.

"It is true then," he thought, "that a child of love is the most beautiful of all. I wonder if she likes me. Sometimes I think so, but then sometimes when she looks at me with those Apache eyes—"

Aloud he said, "No, no, do not chase the lizard. We Zumwalts do not waste our time fighting lizards."

*

He was not happy, during those years when Esperanza emerged from babyhood into early girlhood, but he was seldom acutely unhappy either. La Luz Delgado was dead for all time and out of his house: that was something. Major Delgado was long gone from Santa Fe. And the wounds left by Consuelo's death had pretty well healed. Yet sometimes when the year was old and the great winds came from the mountains and the sand rattled against the shutters he would be driven nearly out of his mind. But he managed somehow to endure those days, as men must.

The store kept him busy and for this he was grateful. It was trade; it was beneath a man of his high birth and talents; it was humdrum; but it was also forgetfulness. Then too he could always visit the saloon operated by his second-best friend and banish his melancholy. He could scold Lilith about her slackness at housekeeping and boast about how some day he was going to have a wooden floor. It all helped.

Lilith really wasn't much of a housekeeper. Not by Prussian standards. The spiders adored her; the ants and flies believed her kitchen and the millennium to be identical; and if Mistah Otto disapproved of her sanitary methods, well, you couldn't please everybody.

Two virtues, however, she did possess. Just as Hod Kite had predicted, she turned out to be a fertile breeder. By that old black magic she produced another child for Otto, a daughter named Perpetua, about a year after Wisdom's birth. And she was a superb cook, taught by her mother who still kept house for Hod. None of that vile Mexican food either, such as Consuelo used to prepare. At Otto's request, McSwasey had shipped out a table and chairs from Missouri, and Esperanza and her father, on fine evenings, used to dine in the patio. Tableware had also come from St. Louis, and Otto patiently taught his daughter—his white one—the social graces. He was almost happy on those evenings. And he used to reflect that his slave's cooking was compensation enough for the expense of installing her in the Garcia house.

Santa Fe could not understand why Otto permitted his slaves to live in better quarters than his own. But Santa Fe had never understood any of the aberrations of the *alemán,* that furious blond man from the north.

"I believe the poor fellow is a little loco," the town said, shrugging. "Ah, well, he is quite harmless. But it is a scandal how he is rearing his daughter. He is teaching the *pobrecita* to read what is written in books and to speak that odd language."

And those charges were true. Even when Esperanza was a baby Otto had spoken to her in German alone, and after she learned to talk he was

195

determined to rear her without knowledge of Spanish. English he was forced to teach her, because Lilith employed that language. And misused it, Otto declared. If his daughter was going to learn English at all, she must learn it in all its purity, so that some day, when perhaps she would be presented at court in London, they would not say she spoke like a lazy nigger.

"It is a Teutonic language in any case," he told Esperanza one afternoon in the store, when she was five. "The English, of course, are nothing but thieves, the black sheep of the German race, sailing across the channel and stealing our language. But we still have our language, and it is the best in the world. It is the language your grandfather uses. He is a—"

Otto broke off at the sound of customers approaching.

"Into the patio, little one," he whispered. "I will not have you hearing Spanish."

It was an intention, of course, wholly quixotic; probably no one but Otto would have attempted it. Against Spanish as a language he had nothing, except he thought it simple and frivolous; but he had everything against it as a key Esperanza could use to the life of the town. After that, who knew what might follow? Mexican playmates, certainly; into her very bones would seep all the folkways and superstitions, spiritual and secular, of Spaniard and Aztec. She would want to attend cockfights, to play strange games on the plaza; and when she was older she would want to stroll round and round the plaza, arm in arm with giggling brown girls, fair game for the ruffians from Missouri and the trappers from the north; and she would flirt with brown boys. Some day she might marry a brown boy. *Ach,* that he could not endure. All the great destiny of the von Zumwalts crumbling to naught in a mud town on a remote desert.

Certainly life must hold something better for her than that. Better for him too. In those years when she was five and six and seven, he used to dream of how it would be when she was twelve and fourteen. By then, surely, the plains Indians would be exterminated; by then he could face the journey back to St. Louis. He would sell his slaves and his real estate, and with the money from these and the money he had saved he would have a tidy sum. So back to civilization they would go, father and daughter, to Paris sparkling in the sunshine, to Berlin. By that time Esperanza would be a young lady, and there would be upstanding young men, large, blond, of military erectness, to pay her court. Then she would be glad he had forbidden her the Spanish language.

But she was not glad now, and as she grew older she became less glad. It was the old story, Otto thought, the forbidden was the tempting. Even at five she used to linger in the kitchen to eavesdrop on the Spanish spoken by customers in the store. A willful child. By the time she was six and seven she was always running away to strike up friendships with brown children, her preference even then being for boys. Lilith was supposed to watch over her, while Otto attended to business, but that arrangement never worked out well; Lilith would doze, and next thing you knew Esperanza would slip out the door and go racing away with that fleetness of foot inherited from her mother. Sometimes she would be gone for hours, doing heaven knew what. Then Otto would be angry, but always at Lilith, never at his daughter. Once, hoping to please her master, Lilith trailed Esperanza to the plaza, where she found her among a horde of children jeering at somebody in the pillory. Lilith scolded her and Esperanza scolded right back, the situation going from bad to worse, till losing her temper Lilith switched the child. Humiliated, murderously angry, Esperanza kicked and scratched, breaking away at last to race home and report what had occurred. Otto was furious. He closed up shop right then. When Lilith returned he ordered her to disrobe, and when she was naked he held her fast while Esperanza punished her with a switch. Lilith screamed, begging that the punishment cease, and in the excitement her son, Wisdom, and her two-year-old daughter screamed also. But Esperanza was relentless. After that, there was never the slightest doubt who was mistress at the *Casa Zumwalt*. Henceforth, Esperanza did what she pleased, for Lilith occupied a position of responsibility without authority. After that, when Esperanza gave an order, Lilith jumped. So did the two slave children, for that matter.

Otto never punished Esperanza for anything, that poor motherless child. He wanted her to like him. For her frequent misconduct he always found excuses, even when she stood on a chair and from the kitchen shelf pilfered that villainous knife that had belonged to La Luz Delgado. After all, he told himself, the knife was a fascinating plaything, and, so long as it was sheathed, a harmless one. Esperanza, of course, learned fast enough how to unsheath it: as she slid the blade from its leather scabbard her fingers trembled and she was invaded by unaccountable excitement. On the hilt mysterious hieroglyphics had been inscribed, symbolic birds and beasts of the Apache Nation; she would study these, entranced. Then, stealthily, as if indulging in a secret vice, she would stroke the cool flat of the blade and finger the sharp point, her lips oddly dry and curved in a strange smile, her black eyes opaque.

Sometimes, in childish play, she would frighten Wisdom by brandishing that wicked blade. It was great fun. But Wisdom lacked the stoutheartedness of the other Zumwalts; he didn't hold with all that parrying and riposting nonsense of his father; Wisdom believed the best defense to be a good fast retreat. Get him scared enough by that knife and he could outrun even Esperanza. Once she chased him clear to the plaza: that boy was covering ground. Thereafter, Otto hid the knife in the wall with his money, humiliated that a son of his should sink to such cowardice.

As for Esperanza's running away, Otto thought she couldn't be blamed: she only wanted to see what lay in those forbidden vistas beyond her little universe of store and patio. *Ja, ja,* he could understand. He wished his property might be a fortress to shield her from the town, the rowdy, vulgar town, and from the whole world and from the sadnesses of life itself. *Ja,* but it could not be. Even he could see that. So he sought to satisfy her wanderlust by taking her on expeditions about the town, when she was seven and eight. Sometimes they dropped in at Kite's Saloon, where the proprietor welcomed them warmly and exclaimed about the beauty of Otto's daughter.

"*Ja,* I come from a family of beautiful women."

"If I'm any judge, Sport, she didn't get them eyes from your side of the family. Them's Injun eyes."

Esperanza took a great liking to Hod, that nimble little man, who was never too busy to spin great tales about his adventures in Texas and in the States. Many of these yarns Otto had heard years before, and he had borrowed certain incidents and interpolated them into narratives of his own past, but if Esperanza suspected plagiarism she almost never mentioned it. Sometimes Hod became quite animated in reliving his rich life; he would scurry from behind the bar and enact little dramas.

"So there's this big fellow behind the bushes, see? He's got a knife. And here I come walking down the path—"

As she listened to those stories of violence in remote places on the American map, Esperanza's eyes were rapt and hot; and it was disillusioning, after they left the saloon, when Otto declared they were all lies. This was unfair, for at least half Hod's stories were based on incidents that had really happened, not to him, perhaps, but to somebody.

On one expedition when Esperanza was ten Otto took her beyond the town, along the beginning of the trail to Missouri. Wheels of the freight wagons had carved deep ruts in the earth, and they followed these to the tablelands. From there, Santa Fe was a mere incident, a casual collection of golden tan houses and green trees, on the vastness of the valley. To the north, Otto could trace the start of the trail to Taos and the mountains beyond, where the trout streams tumbled and the beavers were at work and the men who trapped the beavers. To the south, across glaring immensities of brown and gold, the trail toward Mexico straggled away through the chaparral. To the west he could see no trail at all, only the wasteland sweeping up and down and on and away to a distant range of mountains. He stood there bleakly, watching a far whirlwind pursuing an aimless quest, a sad-eyed man with sagging shoulders and a mustache too heavy for his thin face, with hair that had been wheat-colored once but that now the years were dulling to the shade of old rope; dulling and thinning, at the temples and the crown.

*

Ultimately, of course, he lost his battle to prevent Esperanza from learning Spanish, for she had a rapid mind and the language was in the air she breathed; by her twelfth year she spoke Spanish as fluently as English or German; perhaps she inherited her father's talent as a linguist. He would not, however, teach her to read that language; by this refusal he salved his defeat. Esperanza didn't mind. There were no Spanish volumes in Otto's little library, anyway.

English and German she read with facility, and later French. When she was five, and the caravan from Missouri rolled into town, and teamsters stacked the boxes and barrels of trade goods in the warehouse room of the Garcia house, (which the family now called the Other House), Otto ferreted into the merchandise and came up with a half dozen English and German readers which he had asked McSwasey to send.

"Now," he told Esperanza, "we will learn to read. Little black marks on paper, that is all. But they are little horses that will carry you to a wonderful land. *Ja,* some day the little horses will carry you to the great ones."

So every morning, day after day and year after year, Otto taught his daughter. It was her only schooling. When the weather was fine they sat in the patio, with the cat dozing nearby and the voice of Lilith floating from the Other House, calling admonitions to Wisdom or Perpetua, or singing lullabies to the new baby, Faustina, while the pages rustled under Otto's fingers as he taught his daughter to harness the little black horses that would whisk her off to lands enchanted. He was very patient, always. In his patience and tenderness it was as if he were atoning for all his old intolerances, his old furies.

Esperanza was a brilliant pupil, and presently, with her rapid progress, these sessions were largely devoted to her reading aloud from the textbooks, at first from the pages with large print and banal narratives. Later, the narratives grew more complicated, the sentences longer; and later still, as the years slipped by and more textbooks rode from Missouri, the cat and an occasional lizard heard that Patrick Henry desired liberty or death, and that men are created equal. That passage was followed by an address from the teacher who, with many more than a few well chosen words, impaled its absurdities on the saber of logic.

"*Ja,* but that is all a lie," he would declare, stroking his mustache that by now, long past any hope of bristling, drooped as luxuriantly as a weeping willow. "Are you and Wisdom equal already? Are you and that lazy Lilith? No, they belong to us and must do what you say. And is a Frenchman the equal of a Prussian? Is a loafing Mexican—?"

Warming to his discourse, Otto would spring to his feet and pace, while Esperanza, who after all these years was accustomed to her father's harangues, and bored by them, and somewhat contemptuous of them, would sit silent and unsmiling, hair glorious. Like Consuelo's, her face was complicated, the high cheekbones almost Mongolian. Her nose, straight as an arrow, had thin and faintly arched nostrils. At the ends of her mouth, which was wide with full lips, there lingered some ghostly hint of brutal ancestors in warpaint and in armor. Her jaw was long and willful.

"So now you see," Otto would say, "what nonsense is all that monkey business about equality. Read on, *bitte*."

Esperanza's favorite stories were to be found in the German readers, those stirring, bloody, lugubrious tales of a mighty Siegfried, wrapped in his magic cloak, brandishing his magic sword, guzzling beer and striding forth to slay a dragon under dark and thunderous skies. She reveled in the way mighty Siegfried waded in blood and smote the fire-breathing beast. After the study sessions were over, she used to pretend a stick was a magic sword and that one of the patio lizards was a dragon. But the lizards were not so valiant as their hippopotamic cousin of legend; the lizards darted from reach. Stalking them, Esperanza looked less like a daughter of Siegfried than a daughter of the Apache, as on bare, high-arched feet she crept toward her prey.

Sometimes she pretended that Wisdom was a dragon, but this role the lad did not enjoy.

"I ain't no dragon, Miss Esperanza," he protested, backing away. "Don't dragon me, Miss Esperanza."

"Yes, you are. You're a nigger dragon and I'll slay you."

"Ain't no dragon. Ain't no dragon. Don't slay me. No, no!"

The first time they played that game it ended badly for Wisdom. She chased him into the patio of the Other House, where after being cornered several times and escaping, he fell and was smitten cruelly with the magic sword. He howled. This brought Lilith and Otto to the scene, and when Esperanza explained that it was merely a game, and that Wisdom had spoiled the fun by his undragon-like behavior, Otto scolded the boy. Thereafter, when Esperanza started that game, the dragon retreated nearly as fast as the lizards, racing off down the street with his playmate close behind, whipping his bare legs with her magic sword. It was Wisdom's bad luck that Esperanza was so fleet-footed, although sometimes, by various low ruses such as ducking into somebody's patio and over the opposite wall, he would postpone the inevitable for quite some time. But she always caught him, finally, and whacked him enthusiastically. Like an Indian tracker she was shrewd and persistent and given to employing ruses herself.

Compared with the stories in the German readers, those in the English readers were dull and tame, namby-pamby tales with pointed morals, contrived by clergymen on Beacon Street. Esperanza hated moralizing.

Actually, she couldn't understand it. She did as she pleased and her conscience never bothered her. When she read about some inhibited little New Englander who was a bad boy because he played hooky from school, or held back a penny from the collection plate, and whose conscience tormented him till he confessed and made amends, she thought the fellow a fool. In the English readers, the only stories she could tolerate were those celebrating the triumph of American arms in the Revolution and the war of 1812. These stories interested Otto also, and he would launch into military criticism.

Growing older, Esperanza daydreamed about how some day she would marry a man not unlike Siegfried, a big-fisted, square-headed man who would stand no nonsense in a *frau*. He wouldn't be anybody with such a craven spirit as Wisdom, or somebody you could wind around your finger, like her father. She didn't, the horrid truth was, have much respect for Otto. Even when she was bad, and knew she was bad, and needed punishment, he scarcely rebuked her. Weak! And she despised weakness. When she married she wanted a man with a more brutal spirit than her own, somebody she could look up to, somebody who would knock her around and make her behave.

But those were ideas that heated her up at thirteen and fourteen; in the years when Otto taught her, such thoughts were still hazy.

During those earlier years, she learned not only reading from her father, but history as well, in a version unencumbered by footnotes, original sources or authorities; and so it was that her understanding of mankind's long savagery was even more chauvinistic than most children's. And Otto taught her Biblical history too, according to his lights. Thus she learned that Abel was doubtless the first Prussian, Cain the first Comanche, and that the Garden of Eden had been situated not a great distance from the Elbe.

As for mathematics, Otto was overjoyed to discover that Esperanza had a natural aptitude for that subject which her mother had always found difficult. At six she could rattle off the multiplication tables; she thrived on long division and fractions; at eight she was outstripping her preceptor; at eleven she would turn the pages of those books from St. Louis and solve problems that Otto considered insoluble. Her achievements filled him with pride, but also with chagrin. She was his daughter; she was brilliant and he enjoyed the reflected glory; but after all she was nothing but a woman.

"*Ja,*" he would mutter, scowling down at the paper where the problem, in her neatly-penciled digits, lay conquered. "*Ja, ja.*"

Lips pursed, rich mustache professorial, neck stiff, hair brushed to conceal his expanding bald spot, he looked very dignified. With inscrutable eyes Esperanza observed him, a faint, harsh smile hovering at the corners of her mouth. Presently, Otto dropped mathematics from the curriculum, although Esperanza throughout the remainder of her girlhood amused herself with decimal points and cube roots; she even wrote a letter to Mr. McSwasey in St. Louis, asking him to send along an algebra and a geometry. After these arrived, she used to have fun pretending bafflement and beseeching her father for aid. Then, when he was bogged and floundering, she would exclaim, "I see it now, father. Give me the pencil." And while Otto, a man in early middle age, definitely bald now, pulled his mustache and silently cursed that cowardly Euclid, Esperanza solved the damned thing and, in a voice of innocence and sweet reasonableness, elucidated it. The rest of the day, to regain his daughter's respect, he would repeat for the thousandth time some of the brave episodes from his lost youth, pacing about the store and poking a phantom saber through a phantom adversary's umbilicus.

"So you see, that taught the fellow not to—"

His voice trailed away; he stood wistful and round-shouldered and crestfallen; he sighed. His daughter was lost—or pretended to be—in one of those silly French novels from St. Louis.

*

He never knew how it happened, his losing his daughter's respect. It was a slow process, that terrible loss, a seepage over the days and years. Looking back, trying to puzzle it out, he blamed Major Delgado.

"I was never the same after that night in the pillory," he thought; and this was true. Never after that night had he been quite so haughty or domineering. He still told as big stories as ever, and did his best to act like a Prussian, but he had changed. As a result of that horrible night, when he had learned that in Santa Fe the dignity of his person was at the mercy of bureaucratic tyranny, he had permitted La Luz Delgado to move into his house, for he had been afraid that if he refused she would go to the authorities and somehow bring pressure to bear.

And after her death, when he bought Lilith, he was a very different Otto from the arrogant *Junker* who had bullied Consuelo when she began working in his store. Lilith received fairly decent treatment, and for this she could thank the pillory. He railed at her, of course, but that was all right: often during his tirades she was thinking of something else entirely. Just so he didn't whip her, that was all she asked. And chastened by his experience in the pillory, and by his dawning suspicion that life sometimes seized a man's weapons and used them against him, he seldom gave her so much as a swat, till Esperanza was old enough to demand it. And then he was only an accessory, holding the slave girl so she couldn't run while Esperanza made her howl. Lilith respected her young mistress more than she respected her master; indeed, she respected him not at all.

And by the time she was twelve, Esperanza no longer respected her father. Nobody respected him; he hardly respected himself. Nevertheless, carried along by the momentum of braggadocio, he still attempted the role of aristocrat and duelist, One-Ball Zumwalt, the terror of New Orleans, the scourge of the plains. He was the laughingstock of the town.

Yet despite these personality difficulties, his store flourished and he prospered, during those years when Esperanza was growing up. Every summer the caravans arrived with more goods, and even though Major Delgado had long since vanished from the customhouse, his various successors were quite willing to listen to reason. With Otto it was a point of pride that the goods consigned to him should go first through customs, even though there was no real advantage in this, for like all men he clung tenaciously and fondly to his little victories. Perhaps it cost more in *diligencia* than if his merchandise had gone through fourth or eighth, but it made him happier to be first so it was money well spent, especially since the money belonged to Proudfoot & McSwasey.

After the merchandise had been cleared, it was very exciting to hear the wagons rumbling along the Street of the Chamiso. They were mainly drawn by oxen now, and the mule skinners had become bull whackers. At the old Garcia house, while they unloaded, they told all that had happened on the way out, and all the news from the States. Good old Andy Jackson had taken office. St. Louis was growing like sin. The town of Franklin had been gobbled up by the Missouri River; go there now and you would see nothing but yellow water. You stayed on the boat clear to the new town of Independence now. Things were changing, year after year. Old Hickory had had an awful row with John C. Calhoun. South Carolina, angry about the tariff, had threatened to nullify, but Old Hickory's fury had risen and South Carolina's had gone down. John Proudfoot was a sick man. Bladder ailment. But Caleb McSwasey was fine and getting richer every year; McSwasey would never die in a poorhouse. Latest thing he had done was to take a boat up to Wisconsin Territory and buy a lot of pine timber land. Stumpage, he called it. Why would a smart fellow like McSwasey do a fool thing like that?

"It is odd he has never married," Otto said, making conversation.

"No, but he has him plenty of women. He's a stepper, that Caleb. I've often seen him in a flashy carriage with a pretty gal on each side, and up front a nigger man in a plug hat driving a pair of matched bays. He has all the women he wants, and he don't meet them at church."

"*Ja,* he is my best friend. In the old days we used to carouse all night, singing drinking songs and kissing the girls. That is the kind of friends we were."

With the trail from Missouri now an established trade route, one of the imperial roads of the continent, caravans were numerous and mail service improved. Now Otto was likely to receive letters from Caleb McSwasey several times a year. These were filled with such news as the decline of John Proudfoot's health, the election of Van Buren, the growth of St. Louis and the increasing value of those business lots Mc-Swasey had bought some years before. They were always filled too with urgings that the Santa Fe branch sell more goods.

"Seems to me," McSwasey would write, "that your '35 sales fell short of what we have a right to expect. Otto, are you pushing the merchandise as hard as you can? You've got to keep pounding away, Otto, for the cream is off the pail and we're down to the skim milk. More traders are heading west every year, there's more competition now and there will be more all the time. John Proudfoot is not well at all. When the expected happens, I may buy the other half of the firm. Ed Proudfoot left the business a few months ago and has gone into banking, he likes that better than retailing. He has indicated he will sell out his interest in the firm to me when old John is no longer with us. I took a trip upriver a while back, there's a lot of virgin wealth in those northern forests for a man who knows how to grab it. I may get into lumbering. But I'm not in lumbering now, so push your sales, Otto."

"Push!" Otto thought. "All the time he wants me to push! If I had him here I would push him one in the nose!"

And while perhaps this was not a very charitable way of thinking about one's best friend, still Otto did have his troubles, for McSwasey kept sending more merchandise from St. Louis than could well be sold by the Santa Fe branch. In the mill towns of New England new factories had been built and the latest machinery installed, and from these flowed an increasing torrent of goods. Capitalism was off on one of its binges. Times were good, mill owners said; Jackson was a dangerous radical but times were wonderful; so the spindles hummed and the flywheels flew. Throughout the Republic new banks were opening and spawning tons of paper money; men were reaping fortunes, on paper, by speculating in land and canals and steamboats. Possibly even that shrewd firm, Proudfoot & McSwasey, had increased its inventories more than was prudent; perhaps that was why Otto found himself engulfed by merchandise, the wareroom in the Other House packed to the ceiling.

Esperanza was beginning to give him more trouble too, as the mid-thirties became the late thirties. Boys were her trouble; *ja,* boys already. One boy especially, when she was fourteen. But even as early as 1835 Otto suspected her of curiosity about biology; at least one afternoon, on going into the patio of the Other House, he surprised her and Wisdom playing a game of tag, without their clothes. This was doubtless very innocent, but Otto disapproved. He said so too, using his native tongue, as always in crisis. Esperanza, in a pleasant way, told Otto to mind his own affairs; the day was warm and if she wished to cool off by going bare she intended doing so. This angered Otto so much that he switched Wisdom.

All that racket brought Lilith from the Other House. Still in a rage, Otto waggled a forefinger at his slave and asked why she was not more up and coming, why she did not keep better watch over his daughter and chase spiders more industriously.

At that moment, he was not much concerned about spiders, but in upbraiding Lilith he always mentioned them, and ants too. And she always replied that she did her best to rid the premises of such varmints. So now, as soon as she heard the word, spiders, her response was automatic.

"I chases them, Mistah Otto, right fast. But I don't know, seems them spiders is too spry for me."

"Spiders!" he shouted. "Why are we talking about spiders? What I want to know is why you let my dear daughter and that cowardly Wisdom take off their clothes."

Lilith looked at Wisdom.

"She wanted to," Wisdom said, pointing at Esperanza, who was ten years old to his seven.

Whereupon Otto, quite beside himself with the perplexities of domesticity, strode over to Lilith, seized her hair and prepared to switch her.

"Don't hit me with that thing," Lilith yelled.

Otto didn't, but Esperanza did. Happy with all the excitement, dancing like a naked little Apache, she begged Otto to give her the switch, and since he could never refuse his daughter anything he complied.

"That is enough," he shouted finally. *"Mein Gott,* you've made her bleed."

But Esperanza kept flailing away till Otto released Lilith, who ran screaming into the Other House, chased by her young mistress.

"Ach! Niggers!" Otto cried out, against the screeches from the house. "How did I ever get mixed up with niggers? I am going to sell them all."

He didn't go quite that far. Late that year, however, he did dispose of Wisdom and the two smaller slave children, selling them to a *ranchero* from far down the Rio Grande. Really, there was nothing else to do; he could not permit that sneaking Wisdom to corrupt his daughter. But he had a pang the morning the rancher called for his chattels. It was December by then, a day of blowing dust, and Otto stood outside the store while the rancher led his purchases away down the Street of the Chamiso.

"It is not a good thing after all, slavery," he thought. "Those Mexicans should enforce their laws."

For of course the central government in Mexico City had abolished slavery, but the decree was only words on paper in a faraway capital; Santa Fe did as it pleased.

Lilith too seemed opposed to slavery, that morning when she stood in the street with Otto, watching their flesh and blood going away to some ranch. After the little slaves had trudged from sight, she still stood staring; then, throwing her hands above her head, she ran sobbing into the store.

Otto sighed. Esperanza giggled.

*

In Santa Fe 1837 began like any other year. Esperanza would be twelve in September. Lilith was pregnant again. So was Hilda, for about the twentieth time. The store continued doing well, although not so well as McSwasey wished. Out on the plains the Comanches were still doing what Comanches enjoyed doing. Esperanza amused herself with Byron and Tacitus, with mathematics and French verbs, those same irregular verbs that long ago in Prussia had fascinated her father and catapulted him into action whose consequences would never end. It had been with reluctance that he taught his daughter French.

"It is an unclean language used by diseased people," he had told Esperanza, several years before. "French I will not teach you."

So he taught her French. It was the last subject he ever taught her, for by 1837 she knew more than her father, or thought she did. All the books in his library she had read, and all the books McSwasey sent at her request. A brilliant child. And, her father thought, beautiful. She wasn't, actually, but certainly she was striking. Her beige skin had a faint coppery glow, like her mother's. And her body was developing nicely, giving promise of being lovelier than her mother's had ever been. Her delicious coloring deceived most persons into believing her a great beauty. Esperanza herself was so deceived. Not, however, Lilith, although she pretended to be.

Early that year in St. Louis the fine old firm of Proudfoot & McSwasey became Caleb McSwasey & Co. The "& Co." was mere window dressing; there was no company. Only McSwasey was in control; McSwasey and the bank that held his loans.

Several momentous events took place in Otto's life that year, beginning late in January when Lilith gave birth to twins.

"Ain't that fine!" Hod Kite said. "Them baby girls are worth two hundred dollars apiece easy. Didn't I tell you Lilith would be a good breeder?"

"*Ja*, but I bet they will be big eaters."

"Feed 'em table scraps, Sport. You've got a little money-making fool in that Lilith. I always knew she'd be a good breeder."

This was not quite true, for years ago Hod had experimented with Lilith and concluded she was barren; but he was not one to begrudge Otto his good fortune.

"What are you calling them?" he asked.

"Winola and Viola."

"Them's good nigger names. You raise them girls right and when you're ready to sell you'll make yourself some money."

206

At the bar Otto scowled into his glass.

"I may not sell them. When they are older I may set them free, if my daughter will let me. I have been doing a lot of thinking, *Herr* Kite, and I am not so sure slavery is a good thing. It is not good for the slaves or the master either. It is all inefficient, and I do not think Pastor Moeller back in Prussia would like the way I have been acting. And I do not think, *Herr* Kite, that one person can own another."

"That's a funny notion."

"*Ja,* but do I own my daughter? No, she does as she pleases. Do you know what she has done now? She has moved into her own bedroom in the Garcia house. Well, she is growing up and maybe she is too old to sleep in the same room with her father, but I can tell you it is lonesome some nights there in the store all by myself when the wind blows. And she has written McSwasey to send out next summer a wooden bed and chairs and a dresser already, so she can have furniture in her bedroom like those girls she reads about in books."

"Women are expensive," Hod said.

"*Ja,* but she is a smart girl and a good worker, helping me sell to customers, and I am not complaining. I am only saying what I have been thinking, that slavery is not right."

"I couldn't say about that, Sport, but you've sure made yourself four hundred dollars worth of nigger babies mighty easy."

"Sure, I know, but it embarrasses me with my daughter. Since the twins came she has been in a bad mood, and she has taken to smoking cigarettes like these filthy Mexican girls. And when I forbid it she only smiles and blows smoke in my face. Sometimes she is very cross with me. She is getting to be a woman now, and once I had Lilith explain to her how it is that babies come. So now she knows what I am up to when I visit Lilith at night, and since the twins came she looks at me in a way I do not like. Sometimes I do not understand my daughter any more. Sometimes I think she does not like me."

"Women are queer," Hod said.

"*Ja,* you take a man of the world like myself, I have had many women, but I have never understood them."

"But they're kind of nice to have around."

"*Ja,* I agree with that."

"Sometimes," Hod added.

It was true that Esperanza was a great help in the store, now that she was almost a young woman. With her quick mathematical mind and Prussian efficiency she was a far better clerk than her mother had been, and one day Otto told her so. Not much of a compliment, perhaps, for after all Consuelo had not been a successful merchandiser, never having sold so much as a pin, but Otto meant it as praise and his daughter accepted it as such. But for those kind words she showed no gratitude; mouth sullen, she just stared at him with smoldering eyes.

"Why are you so cross, little one? Do you not like your papa any more?"

With a long-suffering sigh, she turned her back.

"Have I not been a good father to you?"

Teeth clenched, she whirled and uttered a low, intense exclamation.

"Arrgh! I wish you would leave me alone!"

Otto stood bewildered.

"*Ja, ja,* I know," he said at last. "It is hard, this growing up. First you were a little girl and soon you will be a woman. But now you are on a bridge between the two, and the bridge is wobbly and you are frightened of falling into the torrent of life underneath. I remember how it was with me. I was a great problem to my father when I began to feel my oats."

But she had her moments of geniality. Sometimes boys accompanied their parents to the store, and on those occasions, when she displayed the merchandise, her voice was unusually cordial; she moved vivaciously, her waist slim and pliant, her bright skirt swirling about her fine legs. And Otto noticed scornfully how the boys were flushed, tongue-tied, gawky.

One boy, however, was not so affected. A year or so older than Esperanza, tall, thin, with an oval head and black, dry, mussed hair, with intelligent merry eyes and a pleasant mouth, he stood watching while his mother completed her purchase. Oddly, Esperanza seemed less at ease than usual; color showed in her cheeks.

As the boy and his mother were about to leave, the cat entered the store. She looked ready to give birth to kittens at any moment, which was a fact, and none too happy about it, also a fact. The boy stooped to pet her. Esperanza did the same. Hilda looked cynical.

"What do you call her?" the boy asked.

"Hilda."

"She's going to have kittens."

"Yes."

"*Ja,*" Otto put in, "that is a wonderful little cat."

Esperanza shot him a certain look.

"We have a cat too," the boy said. "But he is a *gato.*"

"A *gato?*" Otto said. "*Ach,* a tomcat is no good. All they want to do is roam. But little Hilda is the best mouser in the world. She stays home and attends to business, and there is not a mouse within earshot of this store."

"We must go," the boy's mother said. "The sun lowers itself."

"Could I interest you in a fine watch?" Otto said. "Then you would not have to tell time by the sun."

"*Gracias, señor,* but with your permission, no. The sun serves."

"*Ja,* but when the weather is cloudy—"

"*Gracias, señor,* not today."

They left. At the door Esperanza stared after them. Then she whirled and glared at her father.

"What are their names?"

"How am I to know?"

"You should know the names of your customers."

"Me? What are you saying! I am a Prussian. Why should I know the names of these Mexican loafers?"

"Arrgh!"

"What is the matter, little one?"

"Why did you tell the boy his tomcat is no good?"

"Because he should know it and be rid of the coward. No tomcat is any good. All they do is howl outside my store and get little Hilda excited so she is always having kittens."

"Arrgh! Why did you have to mention watches and shame me so?"

"But I always mention watches. McSwasey sent them and it is what he wants. I am to create a demand."

"Arrgh!"

She left angrily for the patio.

"But my little one," Otto called, starting after her. Then, sighing, he stopped. And to Hilda he said:

"Everything I do is wrong."

Aloof, tail up, Hilda padded to the kitchen and her box.

That very night while Otto slept the pains of labor seized her. Always she had been an amorous cat and a fruitful one, but now she had grown really too old for such goings-on, and at this accouchement she perished in the cause of love, three of her six kittens losing their lives before they could be born. Early in the drab dawn Otto found her in her box, already cold and rigid, the three surviving kittens meowing thinly. Still in his nightshirt, he cried out and stumbled toward the Other House.

"It is Hilda, Hilda," he moaned, in German, when he reached his daughter's bedroom. "It is little Hilda who has died."

Esperanza lay looking up at his puckered face.

"You must help me, you must stand by me, my dear daughter," he cried. "It is little Hilda who is dead."

"I'll get up," Esperanza said. "I wish you wouldn't make such a racket. She was an old cat, anyway."

He knew then she didn't share his grief or understand it, and as he paced about the patio, quite beside himself, nearly wringing his hands, tears glistening on his outsize mustache, he felt more alone than he ever had since swift-footed little Consuelo eluded him for the last time.

"I am acting terrible," he thought. "I have gone all to pieces and my dear daughter thinks I am a fool and weak as some woman, but I cannot help it. *Ach,* Hilda, poor Hilda. She was such a pretty little cat."

They buried her in the patio near the wall, where now the chipmunks could scamper unafraid across her grave. By then Otto's eyes were dry, but infinitely sad, for he buried more than Hilda that morning. He buried nearly all that was left of his daughter's respect, for how could she honor a father who broke down and cried? And he buried a link with his past. Hilda had come to him when he was still a young man and a bachelor; she had been his confidante on the long evenings even before Consuelo came to work in his store; she had arched her back against the villainous calves of Major Delgado; she had been present, silent and broadminded, when Otto made love to Consuelo. She had witnessed much, heard many secrets, and she had never told.

*

The following August Otto lost what little remained of his daughter's respect. A man named Armijo brought this about, quite unintentionally, for he knew nothing of Otto Zumwalt. In the whole affair *Señor* Armijo's purpose was simple enough: he was a politician who wanted to become governor of New Mexico. Unfortunately, however, the governor's chair was already occupied by one Col. Albino Perez, duly appointed by the central government and sent from Mexico City to rule the province. With him he brought many newfangled ideas, most interesting of which was a scheme to raise money by direct taxes on real estate. Death in Santa Fe had been as certain as anywhere else, but taxes had not; and since Colonel Perez's arrival people had been discussing his innovation with lively interest. Otto, with his knack for turning up on the wrong side of nearly any question, favored the plan.

"*Ja,* they will be a good thing, taxes," he told Hod Kite. "In Prussia we are taxed nearly out of our teeth, and what do we have for it? A fine army, that is what! And that is what is needed here, a larger and better disciplined army. Maybe if they collect taxes we will have a stronger army to protect us from the Indians."

But Otto was a minority of one. Sensing the discontent, *Señor* Armijo, whose heart bled for the people as readily as any other politician's, decided to run for governor. The only trouble was, this was not an election year; no year was an election year. But that did not dismay *Señor* Armijo. Believing with other political philosophers that a ballot is only a flattened bullet, he determined that an election should take place in August, 1837.

Oddly, he did not announce his candidacy or mount the hustings or kiss a single baby. Indeed, his campaign was conducted so secretly that the opposition did not know a campaign was in progress. For voting strength he relied on the Pueblo Indians living north of Santa Fe. In early August these independent voters, having been treated to strong waters by *Señor* Armijo's ward heelers, assembled in a mass meeting at a village some twenty-five miles away. *Señor* Armijo was not present, for he wished to remain unknown should the election go against him. Actually, the assembled voters knew even less about their candidate than do most voters. They did not know his name; they did not even know there was a candidate. Even of the issues many had not heard. They knew only that things had been dull lately, and that now they were going to march on Santa Fe, where they could anticipate shooting and rapine and liquor and plunder.

*

Couriers brought news of the mass meeting to Santa Fe. In the governor's palace, when Colonel Perez heard of the impending election, he was startled. But not so startled as Otto Zumwalt, who heard the news in Kite's Saloon.

An Indian uprising!

"And the governor," Hod said, "is calling out every able-bodied man to march north and fight them."

"What is that you say?"

Hod repeated the news, adding, "It will be a great chance for you young fellows to collect a few scalps."

Otto felt the blood draining from his cheeks.

"But I am not so young any more," he said. "I am getting to be an old man, *Herr* Kite."

"Young enough to stop an arrow, Sport."

Otto put down his glass.

"I must go home now," he said, "to see that my daughter is safe. Then I will join the militia. *Ja,* the very thing to do! Indians have never bothered me. On the plains I often picked off a Comanche before breakfast. A man can only die once. And I am a dead shot. In New Orleans they called me One-Ball Zumwalt."

Hurriedly he left the saloon and made his way among the crowd in the plaza. Everybody was chattering about the coming invasion. When he reached his own street he broke into a run. Luckily, no customers were in the store; only Esperanza reading about seduction in the court of France. He slammed and bolted the door, closed and locked the shutters.

"What's the matter?" Esperanza asked.

"Quick! Go and lock the Garcia house."

"Why?"

"Do as I say! Quick!"

He had never spoken so harshly to her; she obeyed. When she returned, with Lilith at her heels, she found Otto on his knees in the bedroom, digging a hole in the wall. He jumped up.

"Go back to the Garcia house and stay there," he ordered Lilith.

Lilith looked bewildered.

"Do as I say or you will be scalped. It is an Indian attack that is coming."

"A which, Mistah Otto?"

"Indians, you *dummkopf!* Hurry and protect the twins."

211

"How am I going to protect them, Mistah Otto?"

"How do I know how until you do it! Just protect them, that is all. Hurry!"

Lilith shuffled away.

"Indians," Esperanza said, eyes shining. "How do you know they are coming?"

On his knees again, digging at the adobe bricks, he repeated what he had heard. Presently he reached into the hollowed wall and brought out a leather sheath.

"The knife!" Esperanza said. "So that is where you hid it."

"*Ja,* that foul old La Luz kept it razor-sharp and it was nothing for a child to play with. But you are almost a woman now. Keep it and if you need it, use it."

Esperanza pulled out the blade. Her eyes had turned opaque and shallow; her lips were curved in a strange smile. With the flat of her palm she stroked the blade, languorously and voluptuously; her fingertip tested the point.

"Ooo, it is sharp!"

"*Ja,* the edge too."

"Ooo! I will wear it under my blouse near my heart. When I wish I will bring it out, and I will go like this."

Knife aloft, she took a few quick steps, sketching out deftly the movements of assassination. It was graceful as a macabre ballet, and in the dusky room she might have been an Apache maiden.

"When I poked it at Wisdom," she said, smiling fondly, "he used to run."

"*Ja,* that Wisdom was a terrible coward. Worse than my brother, Fritz."

"I would go like this," she said, whirling and slicing the knife toward Otto.

"Stop it!"

"I am only showing you how I scared Wisdom."

"I understand how you scared Wisdom."

"Or like—this."

She laughed, crouching and launching herself toward her father in a leap as fluent as that of a girl on a frieze.

"Stop it, I say!"

Esperanza was thoroughly enjoying herself, but then a knock sounded on the door.

"*Mein Gott!*" Otto whispered. "It must be the soldiers."

The knock sounded again.

"Come," he whispered, and he fled to the patio, his panic increasing as he remembered what had happened the other time soldiers had pounded the door. Near the adobe outhouse he stopped, speaking fast.

"I think it is soldiers to drag me away to fight the Indians. I cannot go. You will need me."

"I will not need you, now that I have the beautiful knife."

"You will need me. My store needs me. Even Lilith and the twins. Go and tell those soldiers I have gone to meet the caravan which is almost due."

"But father—"

"Do as I say! Please!"

And Otto hurried into the outhouse and locked the door.

"I am a family man," he told himself, as the minutes passed. "I cannot go chasing after Indians. If they were Comanches, *ja,* then I would. But not these cowardly Pueblos. Maybe when I was a young man, but not now."

Presently Esperanza's voice drifted sweetly from beyond the door.

"You may come out now, my brave father."

"They have gone?"

"They have gone."

"How many were there?"

"Only two."

"Two! Did they ask for me?"

"No, father."

"They did not ask for me?" Otto demanded, somewhat outraged, despite himself, at the inefficiency of the Santa Fe military.

"No, father."

"Then what did they want?"

"It was not soldiers, father. Only two women who wished to buy calico."

"Women! *Ach!*"

And there in the outhouse, he realized how he had bared his soul to his daughter; he dreaded facing her.

When the militia marched from Santa Fe to meet the enemy, Otto did not accompany them. Soldiers never did call at his store. In the excitement of meeting the invasion, nobody in authority happened to think of that loco storekeeper, *Señor* Zumwalt.

*

"Hold it higher," Esperanza said. "No, that's too high. Down a little."

"Yes, ma'am."

And Lilith lowered the candle so that her young mistress could receive full advantage of the mellow light.

In her bedroom in the Garcia house, Esperanza was seated upon a packing case, a mirror in each hand, inspecting the results of Lilith's hairdressing. They were excellent. Heretofore, Esperanza's coiffure had consisted of two dangling braids. Now the braids had been wound in a coronet on her head.

Esperanza continued her inspection, turning this way and that, dark eyes observing the bedazzling contrast between her coppery-beige skin and her wheat-and-honey hair. She looked almost adult; girls with Apache and Spanish blood ripened early. During these past months she had grown taller; her body had the pleasing roundness of a swelling bud; and she had poise, usually. In the candlelight, which painted everything with soft golds and soft charcoals, her face was exceedingly complex. Beneath dark brows, her eyes were set at a slight slant, the dark lashes fringing them thickly; her high cheekbones cast faint smooth shadows. She was wearing low black slippers, a voluminous yellow skirt, a low black blouse. Within that blouse, hard against her ribs, she could feel the sheathed knife that had belonged to La Luz Delgado.

Several days of revolution had become history. The great expedition which had marched north to quell the uprising had ended with most of the militiamen deserting to the enemy. And Colonel Perez, governor of New Mexico, proconsul of the Republic and tax expert extraordinary, had joined his ancestors. This very afternoon his distinguished head had been severed from his distinguished body. Then, high at the tip of a lance, his head had been paraded about the plaza. Afterward the insurgents had used it as a football. Nearly everybody favored the revolution now. To the ranks of the Pueblo Indians had flocked the *mestizos*, the *mulatos*, the *zambos*. The town was thronged with strange people. Runaway slaves, village idiots, sheepherders, ranchers, beggars, thieves: all were there. Esperanza had seen them in the plaza this afternoon; she had heard them roar disapproval of taxes when Colonel Perez's head paraded on its lance. But another head, attached to a pair of careless shoulders, had interested her more.

"I saw the boy this afternoon," she told Lilith.

"You seen Wisdom?"

"No, stupid. I saw the boy who was in the store that day."

"Boy," Lilith said, "in the store. What boy, Miss Esperanza?"

"I've told you about him. He has a tomcat."

"I recollect now. He still have the tomcat?"

Esperanza sighed, the thin ends of her otherwise rich mouth turning down.

"I didn't talk to him, *dummkopf*."

"How come not?"

"Too many people between us. Everybody was yelling."

"He see you?"

"I don't know. Maybe. I think so. He smiled. I think he smiled at me."

Lilith cackled ripely.

"First he tell you he have a tomcat. Then he smile. Lordy Lord! What you say his name is?"

Esperanza's eyes narrowed.

"I don't know his name. I thought my brave father knew. But he didn't. He could have asked. The *dummkopf!*"

Still holding the candle, which dripped an occasional pearl of tallow, Lilith stood on one foot, reflectively scratching her calf with the other.

"Your papa a brave man?"

"He says he's brave."

"He tell me the same thing, Miss Esperanza. He say he often fit white men in duels. One-Ball Zumwalt they call him, he say."

Lilith laughed. Esperanza smiled, unpleasantly.

"That what he say. One-Ball Zumwalt. Ain't that something?"

Lilith laughed again.

"I might see him tonight," Esperanza said.

"See who?"

"The boy."

"Boy with the tomcat? Where you figure to see him, Miss Esperanza?"

"Oh, somewhere. Anywhere." Her smile was sweeter now, her eyes dreamy. "On the plaza, maybe."

"Um-m-m," Lilith said. "You sure itch for that boy."

Smiling secretly, Esperanza replaced the two mirrors on the barrel-head which served as dressing table. Any day now, as soon as the caravan arrived, she would have real furniture.

"I'll see him," she said, "somewhere. He has nice hair. Dry. Not greasy."

"Reckon you'll tousle his hair for him some day," Lilith said, smiling. "Reckon he'll tousle yours too."

Esperanza touched her hair. She looked cool, aloof, self-satisfied.

"Of course," Lilith added, "you're a little young for actual tousling."

"I'm not young!" Esperanza said sharply.

"Didn't mean you was, Miss Esperanza. No, ma'am. You as old as I was, very near. Always remember what my mama told me. 'Daughter,' she say, 'up till now you been thinking, daughter, that your legs is for walking purposes merely.' That what she say. 'But daughter,' she say, 'from the way Mistah Kite been looking you over, you going to learn damn different damn quick.' And Lordy Lord, mama was right!"

She cackled.

"Hod Kite?" Esperanza asked.

"Yes, ma'am, the same. He owned me then."

"But he's old."

"Sure he's old. But don't you never go judging no man by his age. No, ma'am. That Mistah Kite figure he going to outlive Methuselah. He tell me all about it. He pick up five minutes here, five minutes there, just by not swallowing liquor. Yes, ma'am. I say, 'Lord, man, you any younger and I never see nothing but the ceiling.' Laugh? You ought to hear Mistah Kite laugh. Things like that don't hurt a girl none to say—that's what my mama told me—and they please the gentlemen.

215

Specially the older gentlemen. With Mistah McSwasey now, that was different. I was getting along toward sixteen then. Last time he was in Santa Fe he rented me out from Mistah Kite to take me on a trip up to that place they call Taos. He was nowhere near as old as Mistah Kite. No, ma'am. A right spry man, that Mistah McSwasey. I was kind of sweet on him. I went all the way with him in his wagon up to that Taos place. He was going for to fetch beaver furs. Wild country up there. Yes, ma'am, very wild. Mountains and canyons and such. Took us a good spell to reach that place, and we camped out on the way. I was sort of sweet on Mistah McSwasey. You get yourself a redheaded man, Miss Esperanza, and you got something. Yes, ma'am. But when we gets to Taos he go out at night and finds himself an Injun gal. Mad? I was sizzling. Would have scratched that squaw's eyes right out of her face, if I could have got hands on her. Know what I done? I was there all alone in the wagon, so I sneaks out and finds me an Injun man. He was on the old side too. I don't know, my luck seem to run to older men in them days. Wore his hair in two braids, like a woman. But he wasn't no woman. No, ma'am! When I sneaked back to the wagon there was Mistah McSwasey. He asks where I been and first thing you know he fetches the truth right out of me. He's a tough man, that Mistah McSwasey. My experience, it don't pay to tell the truth too true to no man no time nowhere. 'Lilith,' he say, 'I ain't so delighted to hear you been prancing with an Injun. Lilith,' he say, 'I know niggers.' Then he wallops me. Then he tousles me. Then everybody feels better and is friends again. I say, 'Mistah McSwasey, why don't you buy me and take me to St. Louis?' He say, 'Why, Lilith, the first Comanche you'd see you'd wave it at him.' He was a real gentleman, that Mistah McSwasey."

"He sends me books," Esperanza said.

"Reading books? There you are! Yes, ma'am. A real high class gentleman. But he's tough."

"I don't remember him."

"If you was older when he was here you'd remember him. Yes, ma'am. I ain't never forgot him. When he left Santa Fe I cried my eyes raw. 'Daughter,' my mama say, 'it's me and Mistah Fairburn all over again.' I asks, 'Who is Mistah Fairburn?' 'Why,' my mama say, 'you little fool, Mistah Fairburn is your daddy, and he was a fine Virginia gentleman. Daughter,' my mama say, 'you carry good blood. You is chuck plumb brimful of fine Virginia blood.' I say, 'Mama, all that fine blood ain't doing me no good now.' And my mama say, 'Daughter, it is hard, sure enough, being a nigger. And daughter,' my mama say, 'it is hard being a woman likewise. Of the two,' my mama say, 'I sometimes think it is harder being a woman.' Which conversation done nothing in no way whatsoever to bring Mistah McSwasey back. I say, 'Mama, you reckon maybe I will have a baby by Mistah McSwasey?' 'Daughter,' she say, 'if you don't it will be a greater miracle than the loaves and fishes. But daughter,' she say, 'you have a baby and how you know he is Mistah McSwasey's? Maybe that baby will be the offspring of Mistah Kite or that Injun gentleman in Taos.' But I never did have no baby till I had me Wisdom out of your papa. He was a caution, that Wisdom, but I still think about him. Sometimes I wake up at night grieving for that boy. You reckon he's still at that ranch, Miss Esperanza?"

Esperanza shrugged. She was holding the mirrors again, and she said: "I want a rose for my hair. Get me one."

"Yes, ma'am," Lilith said, shuffling off toward the patio.

*

With her full swishing skirt, her updone hair with its red flower, her eyes dark with the old wisdom of the Spaniard, the Aztec, the Apache, she looked fifteen or sixteen when she reached the plaza on that night of blood and music. A black lace *rebozo* masked her lower face, and her hauteur concealed the uneasiness beginning to assail her.

On the Street of the Chamiso, white in the moonlight, she had been the only pedestrian, but the plaza swarmed with vaster multitudes than she had ever seen. Pitch pine torches flamed and smoked, casting a ruddy, savage glow over the boiling expanse of close-packed shoulders and bobbing heads; the racket was dreadful. Under the *portales,* the sidewalks were glutted with a dense, elbowing, sluggish flow of peons in tight leather trousers, ranchers in glazed sombreros, lost bawling children, giggling girls, squaws with nursing papooses, warriors who had daubed black paint around their eyes and white paint on their throats, vendors hawking tamales, love birds, *santos.* So far as Esperanza could tell, nobody knew where he was going but everybody wanted to get there; so they shoved and shouldered, grunted and scolded, sometimes jamming into the entrances of buildings where they trampled the beggars who squatted against the doors. On top of the *portales,* men roosted like buzzards in the moonlight, staring down at the turbulence.

She paused where the Street of the Chamiso debouched into the plaza. Three blind old musicians stood scraping at fiddles and twanging a guitar, the music losing itself in the din. In a cracked voice the guitar player sang an interminable ballad about the career and death of Colonel Perez, mournfully recounting how he had imposed taxes on a suffering people and how he had lost his head and tonight was roasting in hell. Three small boys squirmed giggling through the slow-moving sidewalk legs and picked up stones. These they hurled over the heads of those on the sidewalk, into the masses in the plaza beyond. Whether the stones found targets was impossible to see or hear, for the yelling was constant in any case.

She hesitated to wedge her girl's body into the thick jostle on the sidewalk, and she asked herself whether her father might have been right after all when he pleaded that she remain tonight behind locked doors. She had thought him a coward and by her manner she had intimated as much, taking pleasure in rubbing his nose in his own cowardice when she described in lurid detail the misfortune that had befallen Colonel Perez this afternoon. Lying a little, she had said that the revolutionists intended slaughtering all citizens known to favor real estate taxes. Otto had turned pale. And in a dry, small voice he had asked whether she had heard his name mentioned.

"Only once or twice, father. I do not think they will bother you."

It was truly comic the way he had then pleaded with her to stay home tonight. He had said that by her blond hair she would be conspicuous as the daughter of *Señor* Zumwalt, the supporter of taxes. Himself, he was not afraid to die. But he wanted to meet death in honorable combat. In, for example, a duel. Not at the hands of revolutionists. Revolutionists he despised. Never a revolution in Prussia! In Prussia there was order, authority, taxes! Not that he favored taxes for Santa Fe! Santa Fe was a different matter. Taxes here would be a curse. He, a property owner, had naturally always opposed taxes here. Anybody who thought he had favored taxes had misunderstood. Esperanza must tell everybody how he despised taxes. She must also stay home tonight.

She had refused; but now she experienced misgivings. The mob looked grimmer tonight. This afternoon a carnival spirit had shimmered in the sun, although even then, when Colonel Perez's head wobbled high on a lance, she had heard mutterings that the affair had been mishandled; he had been permitted to die too quickly. But men had said in consolation that a dozen other government officials remained alive and could be dealt with more deliciously.

But how could she hope to witness any of the dying in this swarm? Even this afternoon in the crowd-choked plaza she had not seen the actual beheading. One would need great luck to squeeze so deep into the throng as to reach the stocks and the pillory where the punishment of the wicked tax mongers would take place. And one would need luck even greater to catch sight of the boy with the dry, mussed hair. And luck greater yet to be jostled near enough to ask about his tomcat and perhaps learn his name and whether he lived in Santa Fe or in some village so distant that he visited the capital but rarely.

So she stood hesitant, a dark and golden girl in the red torchlight, while the blind musician twanged his guitar and sang of Colonel Perez in the furnaces of hell, and starved dogs barked and a vendor tried to sell her a souvenir of this rapturous day in the shape of a hair plucked from the head of the wicked Colonel Perez. She gestured him away. And all the while her eyes were intent on the moving crowd, seeking the boy with the dry, mussed hair.

Had he really smiled at her this afternoon? Had he remembered her from that day in the store as she had remembered him? Always from that day onward she had been watching for him, thinking when she strolled to the plaza that perhaps this time she would see him, thinking when she rose in the morning that perhaps today he would come to the store again. And then at last this afternoon the moment came. There in the sunny plaza amid the stench of peons and the yelling and the hooting she had seen his head among so many heads. Her throat had tightened, and she thought she couldn't stand it if he looked her way, and she thought too she couldn't stand it if he did not. Jostled and shouldered by the mob, she stood staring. He too was being jostled and swept along by the crowd. He was also laughing and waving his fist at the high-riding head of the governor emeritus. Then, as if feeling her gaze, he glanced toward her. She caught the smile on his face and then, involuntarily, looked away, her cheeks burning. When she looked again she saw the back of his head tossing and bobbing as the torrent of moving bodies swept him along. She tried to follow, to squeeze and claw her way among the multitude, but it was hopeless. And now she worried lest when she glanced away he had thought she wanted nothing to do with him, and she also worried lest he had thought she had been staring at him, trying to attract his attention.

If she saw him now, what should she do? Smile? Wave? Call out and inquire about his tomcat?

"*Señorita,*" somebody said.

It was a man she had never seen before. He was thirty perhaps, his scraggly black hair dripping to his shoulders where it was matted with burrs like the hair of an animal that had lived in wild places. His toothy mouth with its flabby lips wore an idiotic grin such as the imbecile grin on the gills of a scavenger fish. On his face she could see several sores swollen with pus, and instead of mustache or beard there sprouted from his oily skin a sparse growth of coarse black hairs, each particularized and curly. Although grease-soaked, his leather trousers were in the fashion: open side-seams lined with buttons. Many of the buttons were gone. His shoes were bright yellow, and now he pointed at them, then at Esperanza's hair.

"Same color," he said, his tongue laboring against a speech impediment. Then he laughed idiotically.

"Go," she said sharply.

He was about her height, and he stood grinning, exhaling *tequila* fumes, staring with unblinking moronic eyes.

"Same color," he repeated, laughing again.

"Go, simple one," she said.

His mouth hung loosely open; she could see his thick gray tongue.

"*Zapatos y pelo,*" he said. "Same color."

His cumbrous hand floated toward her hair. She struck it sharply.

"*Idiota!*" she snapped; and she darted toward the plaza where, squeezing among the pedestrians, she lost herself in the slow-footed throng.

She did not look back. Girls who did not wish to be followed never looked back. Presently, carried along by that sluggish wash of humanity, she forgot the encounter. She did not see the boy who owned the *gato,* but she kept watching.

Occasionally, as she worked her way deeper into the plaza, she recognized girls of her own age who were customers of the store. Always they moved in groups. Sometimes they spoke to her, politely, briefly, never inviting her to join them, for tonight she remained what she had always been in Santa Fe: the alien daughter of that odd, boastful, *alemán.* Among those girls she had no friends. When she was younger that had not much troubled her. But during these past months her body had been invaded by change, by odd caprices, by urges erratic, tantalizing, extraordinary and yet tentative as the far flickers of lightning before storm, and lately she had yearned for friends with whom she might whisper, speculate, giggle, exchange secrets. Some of those girls might know the boy who owned the tomcat. One of them might be his sister. In that case, if only she were the girl's friend, she might drop in at her home. Whereupon, family life being what it was, the boy himself would be apt to turn up. And the girl would ask, do you know my brother? And Esperanza would pucker her brows and say, why, he does look familiar, haven't you been in the store? And the boy would say, yes, I've been there, you have a cat. And she would say, yes, I remember now, you have a tomcat.

Nothing to it!

And after that, who knew? Things had ways of happening. Sometimes in the course of human events introductions ripened into jolly good friendships. In her daydreams that part of it was all peach-tinted and vague. She was very young. Lilith's detailed instruction in biology had left her informed but inexperienced.

But she did not know the boy's sister. If he had one. Nor did she know any girl well enough to confide that there was a certain boy whose name she would be gratified to learn. Her only confidante was Lilith, who was decidedly not a girl. Lilith's mind was not delicate. If one thought a boy interesting and wished to learn his name and perhaps chat with him about cats, Lilith smacked her lips and discussed biology.

In recent weeks Esperanza had tried to strike up friendships with girls of her age, but nothing came of it. A little polite chit-chat and the conversation lagged. Possibly she had inherited her father's lack of finesse in making friends. Yet it was more than that. She was always the girl *diferente.* Her hair was blond. She could read, divide, rattle off the multiplication tables. Her life was not like theirs. Even the food she ate was not like theirs. They worshiped in the cathedral, prayed to saints whose names she scarcely knew. With the folkways of Santa Fe they were in perfect accord. And who was she? Daughter of that loco Zumwalt. Daughter too of the strange Delgados. For her mother's soul never a Mass had been said. Her great-grandmother, one heard, used to entertain the devil in her bed. So the mothers of the town whispered no, no, Maria, do not speak more than necessary with Esperanza Zumwalt. No, no, Dolores, no, no, José and Esteban, she is not of us.

She knew she was not of them. And she wanted to be. They were the herd, she the rejected, the alone. And yet, being even then a person very complicated, she disdained them all. Had not her father perpetually sneered at their likes as dirty, cowardly Mexicans? Could they read? Had they ever heard of algebra and that charmingly handy little symbol, *x*? Did they count a general among their ancestors? And in their veins did Prussian blood flow?

Into her ears, since she could remember anything, had been drummed the superiority of the Prussian race. Well, she was Prussian. *Ergo,* she was superior.

And she was Apache also. From Otto she had not heard much about that. Yet from one source and another, she had learned that the Apaches were the fiercest of the fierce, a kind of Prussian Indian Nation. Up from Mexico the Spaniards had marched, grandees on steeds in cloth of gold, and before them had fallen one pueblo after another. But never had the Apaches bowed before them. Never! Unconquered after all these centuries, proud, deadly, they lived their hot free lives off to the west. And she was of their blood. On summer nights she used to stand in the patio, gazing into the western heavens, thinking of her kinsmen off there somewhere, dim, sinewy half-gods, expert with arrows, war hatchets, knives. Knives! Doubtless the very knife belonging to La Luz Delgado had been cunningly shaped by Apache craftsmen. And perhaps it was the Apache ghosts in her blood that caused her breath to quicken and her fingers to tingle when she glimpsed that beautiful knife.

So with that Apache blood, that Prussian blood, with her hair so gloriously blond, with her books and her distinguished grandfather, should she be troubled because the girls of the town shunned her? Certainly not! She was, though. Especially since that afternoon when the boy with the dry hair visited the store.

Would she see him on this night of revolution in the plaza? Deep now in the multitude, she kept watching. It was thrilling to reflect that somewhere among these thousands he must be shouldering his way and yelling and laughing. Any moment she might spy him. Sometimes she stood on tiptoe, her gaze hurrying among the teeming heads that wobbled and bobbed like a cargo of shipwrecked coconuts on a dark sea. Once she glimpsed a head that might have been his; she caught her breath. But she couldn't be sure. The head was some distance away, separated from her by a dense wall of bodies, and the flickering torchlight was uncertain.

Then, making itself heard above the continuous low roar of the assemblage, a great outcry soared from the far side of the plaza. Something was happening over there near the governor's palace. The outcry swelled. All the people jam-packed around Esperanza took it up, hooting and screeching and brandishing fists. From the direction of the *calabozo* soldiers were forcing entrance into the massed humanity, clubbing a path as energetically as the vanguard of troops cutting through jungle. In the close-woven carpet of people a rift appeared, ripping out wider, then rushing together and mending itself after the soldiers passed. As the procession sliced deeper into the plaza, those in its path fought in panic to remove themselves. They screeched, swore, butted, kicked, leaped. Their agitation sent deep, powerful waves of energy through the congestion. The crowd swayed, stumbled, clawed. Around Esperanza the press was awful. The multitude exuded heat like a great furnace. The noise was deafening. An elbow glanced along her cheek. A knee thudded against her spine. Anonymous feet crushed her toes. Nearby a desiccated old woman, screaming supplications to divinity, sank from sight as if into a tossing sea. Her prayers were lost underfoot and expired. Caught in that rip tide but managing to keep her feet, Esperanza found herself swept along without volition, wedged tight among the bodies of strangers, the vile crowd odor thick in her nostrils. Then presently the crush eased as the soldiers with their prisoner reached the stocks in the center of the plaza.

Necks craned. A vast outpouring of insults flowed from raw throats. Fists raged. In the torchlight Esperanza could see the prisoner, a slim gray-haired man with a hawk's nose. He was Spain. He was the Moors in Toledo and Toledo steel. For a moment he stood looking out at the Goya-dark assemblage, on his mouth a cold smile. Then they locked him into the stocks. Then they began to work on him. Then he began to scream. The mob went insane. Esperanza's fists were doubled and she shouted hotly with the rest. Oyee! Oyee! Give it to him! Give it to him hot! Even at a distance people tried to spit on the prisoner. Around Esperanza there was a constant powerful surge and recoil. The din was terrific. And in the midst of it she felt fingers in her hair and a voice sounded from lips close to her ear.

"Same color. *Zapatos y pelo.*"

The voice came from behind. As hard as she could she drove both elbows backward; she kicked. Then, without looking over her shoulder, she pried and pitched and scratched her way among the throng. It was slow going. Sometimes people yelped angrily at her; once a woman slapped her. But she was in panic now to elude the man with yellow shoes, and she burrowed savagely. Now and then, when for a moment the uproar subsided, she heard the wavering, ghoulish screams of the prisoner in the stocks. Then the mob poured out its ecstasy. People shouted urgent advice to those who were working on the prisoner. Women screamed that he should not be killed too swiftly. Babies were bawling. Esperanza kept fighting her way through the thick smells of stale whiskey and sour sweat and the leather clothes of ranchers giving off the odor of horseflesh. Then at last the crowd thinned and she knew she had reached the edge of the plaza. Breathing hard, her hair hanging, the rose lost, her face unclean with the spittle that had been aimed at the prisoner, her blouse torn, her feet sore from being stepped on, she paused to take bearings. She had emerged from the plaza on the side opposite the Street of the Chamiso. And when she looked back she saw the man with yellow shoes coming through the ragged edge of the mob. She ran.

Through the dust of a street leading away from the plaza she ran, where moonlight creamed road and walls. Her panic subsided, now that she had disentangled herself from the mob. Always she had been fleet of foot. In the open she could outrun the wind. But then as she ran her panic returned. To run was a pain tonight. Her toes had been bruised by the many-footed mob. Try as hard as she might, she could not skim over the ground as swiftly as usual.

At a corner, deep in the shadow of a moon-silvered *alamo,* she paused, gasping. She listened. In the distance she heard roars surging up from the plaza. Once, high, thin, tremulous, she thought she heard the prisoner. And it occurred to her that perhaps her father was not such a fool to conceal himself from the revolution. Then she forgot all that when she heard somebody pounding hard along the street. She waited, poised, till she saw his mouthful of teeth gleaming in the moonlight. Then she broke from the shadows and fled.

She went racing along a winding road where the houses had become infrequent. Once as she passed a wall a dog let loose savage barking from inside. But she saw no lights in houses and she encountered nobody. The town was in the plaza. And her feet felt burning raw. She tried to run faster but her feet were on fire. When she cast back a glance she caught sight of the man with yellow shoes. The plaza noise was very distant now; it might have been a far cataract. In the whole world she and the man with yellow shoes might have been the only creatures alive under the ghostly moon. Then a rock in the road tripped her. She pitched forward awkwardly, her stride broken, and in the end she could not save herself from a fall.

She was up in a twinkling, but she knew it was too late. She could never outrun him now. Suddenly she was calm, knowing what to do. She saw him pounding toward her and she turned her back, so he could not catch the gleam of the blade when she slid it from its sheath.

"*Señorita,*" he mumbled thickly, panting.

She did not respond, did not look over her shoulder.

"Same color," he said; and he was so close she could hear his labored breathing and smell the cloud of *tequila* fumes from his mouth.

Easily, almost demurely, she pirouetted, the knife in her fist.

His flabby lips twitched in a grin; his hand floated toward her hair.

"Same color," he muttered.

One step took her close to him. She plunged the knife into his belly. Then she danced back.

He stumbled toward her, one step, two steps. She backed beyond reach. Then he went down, mumbling incoherently. His hands were threshing the air trying to locate the knife and remove it.

Esperanza stepped behind him, found a rock, slammed it against his skull. He stopped moving. He lay on his side, knees drawn up, like a baby with colic. Esperanza seized his hair, slick with grease and matted; she yanked his head and kicked at his knees, till he lay on his back. Then she withdrew the knife. He was breathing with great difficulty. His mouth looked very fishlike. Her own breath came fast as she stared down at him. Then she leaned over and probed his shirt, on the left, with the point of the knife, till she found a place between his ribs. Then, suddenly, she drove in the knife to the hilt. From the depths of unconsciousness he groaned, once, and his legs jerked. Then he lay still. Presently she withdrew the knife. The fluid on the blade looked black in the moonlight. She wiped the blade carefully on his shirt before returning it to its sheath in her bosom. Then, walking fast, she moved on. She would make a wide circle of the plaza to reach her father's house. Half way there she began to tremble. Then she cried.

*

During the next days the revolution kept itself busy putting to death all the officials of the old government. It was pleasant work but quite exhausting, emotionally; and possibly that was why, after electing José Gonzales of Taos governor, the revolution dispersed itself without sacking the town. Only the homes of the dead officials were looted. In addition to the members of the old government, quite a few persons were slain during the great election, but that was the way of elections. Several of the dead were never identified, among them a man in yellow shoes. A peon living near the spot where this man was killed gave him fairly decent burial, after stealing his shoes. Nobody had any idea who had stabbed the fellow, and nobody cared.

When *Señor* Armijo learned that *Señor* Gonzales had been elected governor, he spoke in excited Spanish for several minutes. After all, it was in *Señor* Armijo's brain that the scheme of holding an election had been hatched, and the gist of his remarks was that he had been double crossed. Forthwith he retired to Albuquerque and spent several months raising a force to quell the revolution. Rumors of this reached Santa Fe, where both *Señors* Gonzales and Zumwalt were disquieted. During the autumn following the revolution Governor Gonzales had imprudently allowed his army to disintegrate, and now when he summoned them back to the colors they yawned. More fighting? Ah, but they had already done that. Last August.

So when *Señor* Armijo marched on Santa Fe, Governor Gonzales betook himself north, leaving the gubernatorial chair vacant. Like nature, *Señor* Armijo abhorred a vacuum, so he sat in it. And to Mexico City he dispatched a valiant communique describing his patriotic activities in behalf of law and order. It made such brave reading that the government in Mexico not only confirmed his self-appointment but also sent dragoons to his aid. After these arrived and refreshed themselves in Kite's Saloon, (which had been prospering mightily, revolting and counter-revolting being thirst-rousing occupations), they marched north and won a glorious victory over the remaining insurgents. Ex-governor José Gonzales fell before a firing squad. In Santa Fe, Otto Zumwalt breathed easily again. But he looked older.

*

After that night when she was forced to deal roughly with the man in yellow shoes, Esperanza followed her father's example and stayed home behind locked doors during the remainder of the revolution. This pleased Otto. It just went to show, he thought, that if one was patient with a growing girl, and let her have her head, why after a while she would realize that one's way of thinking was best.

All in all, the revolution exerted a salubrious effect on Esperanza. It subdued her, reminded her that there really were a few grains of wisdom in the Second Commandment. And whereas the revolution added several years to Otto's life, it seemed to subtract a year or two from hers. Not for a long time, after that momentous night, did she put up her hair. And she no longer cherished the beautiful knife. The very next morning after she had so effectively used it, she came into the patio behind the store, carrying it gingerly. She found Otto repairing that rotten old ladder he had so often climbed to heap more dirt on the roof when rains threatened.

His carpentry was no more skillful than when he had helped construct those chairs which so amused Consuelo, and as Esperanza approached he suffered the misfortune of smashing his thumb. She saw him leap up and fling the hammer in a throw which Hercules might have envied; she heard him cursing. He looked haggard and pathetic, that round-shouldered, bald, long-mustached man, nursing this latest wound in his life of not-so-quiet desperation.

"Did you hurt yourself?" she asked.

He started, removed the injured thumb from his lips.

"It is nothing," he said. "I only hit my thumb with that damned hammer."

"Let me see."

"It is a worthless hammer," he said. "Why I use it instead of taking a new one from stock I do not know."

"Ooo, it is going to be black and blue. That is too bad. I will kiss it for you."

And she did. And Otto was amazed at her sympathy, and somewhat suspicious that it might be ironical. But her face was sober, her eyes solicitous. They were also swollen.

"Have you been crying, little one?" he asked.

She looked away; her voice was low and hesitant.

"I think I cried last night in my sleep."

"Were you having an *Alpdrücken?*"

"*Ja, vater,* a terrible nightmare. A man was chasing me. It woke me and I was crying."

"*Ach,* little one," he murmured, patting her head.

When she looked at him her eyes were swimming.

"You are good to me, father, and I love you," she said.

Otto was startled and, like all men, tremendously gratified at this unexpected armistice in the war of sexes.

"I wish I had been in that nightmare," he said, "and I would have taught the fellow not to pick on my daughter. I would have fixed him."

"I fixed him, father."

"*Gut!* How did you fix the coward?"

She hesitated; then, with a faint smile, she said:

"I woke up."

"*Ja,* that is the only way to deal with those nightmares. Wake up. I have had some terrible nightmares myself in my time, but I always fix them good by waking up."

Her gaze was on the ground; she murmured:

"Even after I woke up I was very frightened."

"*Ja,* that is the way it goes with those nightmares. Of course myself, after I wake up, I am never frightened. I know it was only a ridiculous nightmare. But you are only a child."

"I lighted the candle," Esperanza said, "and left it burning. All night it burned, father."

"*Ja,* well, that is all right. A candle is not so expensive, especially getting them at wholesale. A candle or two will not break me up."

"I did not want to sleep in the dark," she said.

"But little one. You have never been afraid of the dark."

"I know."

"No Prussian is afraid of the dark. Except that brother of mine, Fritz. He was always afraid of the dark. It became a scandal in the family."

"I will not be afraid in the dark again," she said. "But if I am I will light another candle."

"*Ja,* the very thing to do. Of course, even at wholesale they run into money."

"I do not think I will be afraid again. It was the affair in the plaza last night that gave me the nightmare. They pulled out a man's tongue

226

and waved it in his face. They pulled out his eyes and chopped off his legs one by one."

"*Ach!* They are savages! Why I ever came to this land I do not know!"

"It gave me a nightmare," Esperanza said. "I do not like nightmares. That is why I am not going to the plaza again."

"That I am glad to hear!"

"I should not have gone last night. You were right about it, father."

"Little one," he said, "dear little one. I only hope they will not break into my store and drag me to the plaza. Death on the field of honor is one thing, but—"

"They will not bother you, father."

"I hope not," Otto said.

"They will not, father. I have told everybody how you hate taxes. I have said you would be in the plaza waving your fists with the rest, except that you have gone to meet the caravan."

"*Ja, wahr!* True, every word of it!"

"They will not come here."

"If they do," Otto said, "we will fix them with the ladder."

"But how is that?"

"If they try to break down the door we will all of us climb to the roof and pull up the ladder. We will lie flat on our stomachs with never a squeak. Then the cowards will think we are not here and will go away."

"I do not think they will bother us. They are too busy with the officers of government."

"*Ja,* well, if they do they will not find us. Myself, I do not like this idea of hiding from anybody, but the rascals have no idea of honor. And even kings have sometimes had to flee and hide during revolutions. So I have been thinking, and I do not believe the outhouse is such a good hiding place. If I were a revolutionist—and of course I am, in a way, for I loathe taxes—the first place I would look for a storekeeper would be in the outhouse. But would I look on the roof? No, that would never come into my head. I think the roof will be a better hiding place. More comfortable, also."

Otto crossed the patio and picked up the hammer.

"Do not smash your thumb again," Esperanza said.

"If I smash it again I will break the hammer in two and use it for kindling. I will have nothing more to do with this hammer if I smash my thumb once more."

Esperanza watched him pounding. At last she said:

"Father."

"*Ja.*"

"I have brought you the knife. I believe it would be well for you to hide it again."

"But little one, maybe you will need it."

"I am not going out again, father, till the dreadful revolution is over. I hate it. I wish it had never happened."

"*Ja,* well, so do I, although of course one cannot blame those sneaking Mexicans for revolting against such an outrage as taxes. Anybody who thought I liked taxes just did not understand. Sometimes my Spanish is not so good and I express myself badly."

"Here," Esperanza said, handing him the knife, "I wish you would hide it."

"You are sure you will not need it?"

"No! I never want to see it again."

Otto stood looking down at the sheathed weapon.

"*Ja,* I will hide it. How I ever escaped being stabbed by that filthy old La Luz I do not know."

"Hide it, father, right now."

"Before I finish repairing the ladder?"

"Please, yes. I do not like to have the knife where I can see it."

So Otto carried it into the house and returned it to its place in the wall. Then he found a sheet of paper, ink, a quill. And he lettered a sign. Presently he peered outside, then tacked the sign to the door. It said:

Closed For One Week
Señor Zumwalt Has Gone To
Meet the Caravan
Long Live the Revolution!
Down With Taxes!

*

Deep in Otto's nature, however, he continued to wish for taxes; he was a unique businessman. But even after *Señor* Armijo took office as authentic viceroy of the central government, taxes did not come. Inasmuch as the central government, through thick and thin, had been just as enthusiastically in favor of taxes as Otto, this was perhaps odd; but by now the situation had become quite confused, what with *Señor* Armijo's plotting both against and for the government; and the rulers in Mexico must have decided to let matters drift. Not till 1847, when the United States grabbed New Mexico, was Otto's desire for taxes fulfilled; after that he had all the taxes anybody could wish.

The caravan arrived shortly after José Gonzales took office, and Otto told the bull whackers about the revolution. They were only mildly interested. Greaser politics, they said, were beyond understanding.

As for the news from Missouri, stirring events were happening. With business something had gone awry. Also with finance. Also with real estate. Capitalism had been off on a wonderful spree; now the hangover. Letters reaching St. Louis told of workers marching in New York, demanding bread; of mills closed in New England; of inventories jamming

228

warehouses. Money was very scarce. Hard money: paper money was all but blowing about in the gutters. Bank doors had done what bank doors always did at such times.

"How is McSwasey making out?" Otto asked.

"Well, you know Caleb," the bull whacker said. "He admits money is a little tight. He's got some whopping bank loans and a lot of deadbeats on his books. But he'll keep afloat, if anybody does."

Four wagons stuffed with goods had arrived for the Santa Fe branch of McSwasey & Co. An inundation! Heretofore, one front room in the Garcia house had served as warehouse; now the merchandise filled two rooms.

"*Mein Gott!* Why did he send so much?"

"Reckon he figured the stuff might as well rot here as in St. Louis."

Among the cargo was the furniture for Esperanza's bedroom, the uncrating of which produced great excitement. Several bull whackers lent a hand in this work, possibly because Esperanza had developed into such an attractive girl. She supervised proceedings, rewarding them with her dazzling smile. Otto was there with his hammer, and Lilith also was in the bedroom, observing the bull whackers from the ends of her eyes. But the competition was pretty keen: so long as those Missouri boys could flirt with Esperanza, they weren't likely to get any idea of buying Lilith and taking her to St. Louis. In any case, Otto would have refused to sell her, for she had become more wife than slave.

*

That evening Otto sat in the store, re-reading a letter McSwasey had sent with the caravan. It said:

St. Louis, Mo.
May 2, 1837

Mr. O. Zumwalt
McSwasey & Co.
Santa Fe Branch
Santa Fe, N. M.

Friend Otto:

Will dash off a line to send with the merchandise. Hope you and your daughter are enjoying good health. Am sending the books she wanted, I'm not very good at picking out books but the clerk in the store thought they would fill the bill. Hope the furniture gets to you in good shape. Invoice on same is enclosed.

Glad to get your letter of last January. That was good news about Lilith having twins. I remember seeing her at Hod Kite's some years back, she seemed a likely wench, you can't go wrong breeding niggers. Quickest money I ever made was in the nigger business.

Business here has slowed down somewhat, think it's only temporary, there should be a good pickup in the fall. Real estate prices have shaded off from their peak, also the nigger market is dull here in St. L. although I understand prices are holding well further south. I own a couple of young wenches and three field hands I bought on speculation last November, if the market here don't pick up soon I may load them on a boat and take them to Natchez, there's always a good demand there. Niggers usually balk at going south but I don't anticipate any grief with mine, I know fairly well how to handle niggers.

Believe I mentioned some time back about how Ed Proudfoot had bought into the Mechanics & Pilots bank. With Ed in that bank it was not difficult for me to swing a little loan when I bought the business from the Proud-foot estate. Well, the bank along with many others has headed into adverse currents and isn't making the headway expected. I believe it will eventually open again and nobody will lose a great deal, but just now the depositors have the fidgets and there is a few hard feelings, the receivers would like to have the loans repaid, etc. etc. The mischief is that prices have dropped somewhat, so if a man used a bank loan to buy merchandise he could not repay his loan because he can't sell the merchandise even at retail at anywhere near what he paid for it at wholesale. This is all a little flurry that will be over before you can say Jack Robinson, but in the meantime businessmen are not getting as much sleep as in better times. I have had to let my city lots go, however I'm holding tight to my Wisconsin stumpage for I believe big money will be made in lumbering, I may go into that, once my affairs are straightened out.

You are a good businessman, Otto, you will understand how it is that the currency issued by a bank that has since closed is not sought out eagerly by the average man. Hard money is greatly in demand. If I had $20,000 in hard money I could buy most of St. L. and end up in a few years with a potful of pennies, that shows you how dear hard money is. So I will say that if you will send all profits of the Santa Fe branch in gold or silver, all you can spare and maybe a little more, just retain enough capital to squeeze through on, I will appreciate same. Also Otto, I am willing to pay ten percent on any specie loaned me, I wonder if you have some savings you would like to reap ten percent on, I'm talking about gold money of course. For security you have my reputation as an A-1 credit risk, also I would be willing to put up as security the Santa Fe branch with all inventory, good will, etc., if you could send me a loan of two thousand dollars in hard money, and you would be getting ten percent interest, Otto, that is two hundred dollars a year on two thousand, think it over, Otto, such op-portunities do not knock more than once in a lifetime, besides we are old friends and when I first met you I figured you as a man who would never let down a friend. Think it over, Otto, if you can see your way clear to do the undersigned this favor send it in gold back with the caravan, it will be much appreciated, I can assure you.

Give my best to Hod Kite and your daughter, also you might ask Lilith if she ever gets up to Taos to renew old friendships among the Injuns.

Think over that loan proposition, Otto, you are too good a businessman to pass up a golden opportunity like that.

Believe me ever your friend,
Caleb McSwasey

*

Now that he thought about it, Otto was surprised that he had fared so well that he could consider lending his employer two thousand dollars. Never had his salary or commissions been large, nor had the rent from store space, but they had flowed in steadily, year after year, and in Santa Fe his expenses had been small. His greatest capital outlays had been in buying his house, the Garcia house and Lilith. After thirteen years, the store-space rent had paid for his house several times over; he had charged his employer a small monthly rental for warehouse space in the Garcia house; and Lilith had been obliging about bearing valuable children.

Always the money he saved had been in gold, and with pack-rat astuteness he had hidden it in the walls of his house. During the revolution, he had worried lest the money be stolen; and with civil affairs still unsettled perhaps he acceded to McSwasey's plea for a loan because he felt the two thousand dollars would be safer in Missouri than in Santa Fe. But that was only one reason. The interest was another, but activating him most powerfully was the balm to his self-esteem: when McSwasey found himself in a tight squeeze it was to Otto Zumwalt he turned for help.

"We are like Damon and Pythias, McSwasey and I," he told Esperanza. "*Ja,* we are such friends as you do not often find. 'Otto,' he has often said to me, and now you can read it in his own handwriting, 'Otto, you are a man who would never let down a friend.' *Ja,* and the fellow is right about that. Never let down a friend: that has always been my motto. I only hope the gold reaches him without being stolen by those Comanches."

He fretted about that considerably during the fall and winter, but in the spring he received a letter from McSwasey reporting safe arrival.

"Money stays awful tight," the letter said, "and that specie from you saved my neck."

"See what he says," Otto told Esperanza. " 'You saved my neck.' *Ja,* and this isn't the first time either."

Esperanza looked tired of the whole subject of friendship. But she let him crow. Probably a year before she would have said something to wound her father, but since the revolution she had quieted down. Sometimes she looked troubled, but Otto ascribed this to adolescence. She was a great help in the store, working long hours, as if by absorbing herself in business she was seeking forgetfulness of some kind. She managed the household well too, slave-driving Lilith more relentlessly than Otto ever had. Esperanza liked value received from a servant. Lilith had her hands full, with the cooking, the cleaning and caring for the twins; and if she sat down she was supposed to start sewing for her mistress. She was a pretty good seamstress too, except she found it hard to stay awake. Her needle would shuttle slower and slower and first thing you knew she would doze. Finding her like that, her mistress would awaken her in quick painful ways.

Otto had never given away Hilda's last three kittens, and by now they had matured into vigorous cats, Wilhelm, Konrad and Alberta. Even from kittenhood the brothers, Wilhelm and Konrad, were always tussling; and presently, as rivals for Alberta, they dueled all over the place. When Alberta was ready for kittens Otto lugged her in a box to Kite's Saloon, for he feared that if the litter were born at home Konrad and Wilhelm might murder them. By and by, behind the bar, Alberta gave birth to five; Hod presented these to various customers; and Alberta returned home, primed to repeat the cycle.

With the revolution months behind, things moved along normally in Santa Fe. The depression which troubled the more civilized world never touched New Mexico, and Otto's store flourished; slowly, steadily the stacks of merchandise in the Garcia house diminished, to be replenished —and more than replenished—when the caravans arrived in 1838 and 1839. As for the interest on the loan Otto had made, McSwasey wrote that although times were hard he was determined to pay it, and he suggested that his creditor subtract the two hundred dollars from the store's profits. There was a friend for you!

Growing older, Esperanza helped Otto keep accounts in the store, sometimes joyously unearthing errors he had made in addition; and she was like McSwasey in that she wished to reckon up greater sales in each month that passed. She schemed and plotted against the customers as if they were enemies; she had none of Otto's lingering shame that he, a *Junker*, should be in trade. And she was always hoping that the boy who owned the tomcat would return to the store. One evening in 1839 she mentioned that it was odd he had never been back.

"But he has," Otto said. "He and his mother both."

"They have returned to the store?"

"*Ja*, certainly. Several times."

"When were they here? I remember them only once."

"Well, they have been here, I can tell you that. They were here not a month ago. You were in the Other House with Lilith trying on a new skirt."

"Did you learn their names?"

"Of course not. What are the names of these filthy Mexicans to me?"

232

"Arrgh!"

"What is the matter, little one?"

"You should have called me! Did they ask about me?"

"No, they asked about a saw. I sold them a saw for the boy."

"Arrgh!"

"But what is the matter?"

"You should have called me!"

"But you were busy with that lazy Lilith. When you are trying on a skirt you are cross if I interrupt."

"Arrgh! When they come again you must call me."

"Even if you are measuring a skirt?"

"Even if I have nothing on!"

"Ja, well, I will call you, but only if you are properly clothed."

Esperanza's eyes blazed, and with an exclamation of disgust she strode from the store.

Otto looked baffled; he sighed. He sat pulling his mustache, the candlelight gleaming on his bald head and on the gray beginning to show at his temples. And to the empty store he muttered:

"I do not understand her. She can be very sweet when she wishes. Why is she now mad with me?"

Late that night, when he sneaked from Lilith's bedchamber, he glimpsed light under his daughter's door, and he surmised that another of her frequent nightmares had made her cry in her sleep and she had lighted a candle. He wanted to knock and offer comfort. But then she would know he had been after Lilith again, and she would look at him as Pastor Moeller might. Besides, he didn't wish to embarrass his daughter by disclosing that he knew she had inherited from Uncle Fritz a humiliating fear of the dark.

*

"Little Alberta," Otto said, one morning the following spring, as he sat in the store stroking Hilda's daughter. "More kittens coming. Well, soon I will take you to Hod Kite's."

"She is having kittens too often," Esperanza said.

"It is not her fault, living with two tomcats already. And when we try to shut her in, that lazy Lilith is very careless in such matters."

"Lilith should be taught better."

"Ja, but a nigger will be a nigger till he dies. I have often heard McSwasey say those very words. But even before I had Lilith poor little Hilda was always having kittens."

"Didn't you shut her in?"

"Ja, but she would sing in a sad way to break my heart and I would let her out. Poor Hilda. Always having kittens in a house with a dirt floor. If I had had a proper floor she might be with us yet. But some day I will have a fine board floor."

"When?"

"I don't know when. But soon, in any case. I would have had it long ago if these loafing Mexicans were not so lazy."

"I think you will never have it."

"*Mein Gott,* that is no way to talk. Of course I will have it."

"When?"

"How do I know when, already? When I can get those Mexican loafers to work, that is when."

"Have you tried to get them?"

"Of course I have tried. Do you think I am a liar? I have often tried."

"When?"

"*Ach,* all the time. Maybe not lately, but I have tried many times and I will try again."

"When?"

"I will try tomorrow."

The corners of Esperanza's mouth turned down; she sighed.

"Always *mañana,* my father," she said.

With Otto, *mañana* had been a fighting word ever since Hod Kite used it so long ago; now he jumped to his feet.

"*Mañana!* No, that is not it at all. I have tried and I will try again. I will try today. I will try this afternoon. No! I will try this morning. I will try right now! That is the kind of fellow I am. When I decide a thing, it happens. Like that. With me everything must march. *Ja!* That is what my father, the general, taught me!"

He squared his shoulders and he actually did march, out of the store and toward the plaza. Within thirty minutes he found workmen willing to go to the mountains and saw pine logs into lumber. This astonished him. For so many years he had declared that Mexicans were unobtainable for this work that he had come to believe it.

*

"More of his lies," Esperanza told Lilith, after Otto returned with the great news that he had hired workmen. "He will never have a board floor. He will talk about it, that is all."

But she couldn't have been more wrong. Matters did not precisely march, however, in obtaining that floor. Days elapsed and then weeks with no news from those loafers who had disappeared into the mountains, and Otto grew tremendously impatient. He had, he said, dreamed for years about a board floor, and now that he had ordered it what happened?

"No floor is what happens," Esperanza said, with her quietly arrogant smile.

"*Ja!* Exactly! These good-for-nothing Mexicans—"

During that long waiting, Otto could scarcely keep his mind on business; he paced; he stood in the door scowling along the street, muttering in his mustache, while his daughter carried on the immemorial usages of retailing, or, if trade was slack, sat reading the Memoirs of the Margravine of Baireuth, her hair in two flaxen plaits. With a long breath Otto would turn back into the store, where he puttered futilely; and often he dissertated upon the virtues of wood as flooring material.

Always the Prussians had dwelt on wooden floors, he said. *Ja,* even when they were still savages, long before the Romans came, they would go out into the middle of some lake and drive piles and build houses so that their enemies who were always picking on them would drown trying to march out and butcher them. And what kind of floors did those houses have? One kind and one only! Wood! *Ja!*

Usually Esperanza continued reading, for she had grown accustomed to those background noises, the way dwellers in all windy regions become inured to rush and roar; but now and then she glanced up and with some oblique remark let him know she didn't for a moment believe he had hired men to get lumber.

"Be patient, my pretty one. One of these days we will have the best floor in Santa Fe."

And then amazingly, one fine May morning, a dilapidated wagon piled with lumber and pulled by burros squeaked along the street and wobbled to a halt outside the store. The driver, a brown man in a sombrero, sat rolling a cigarette.

"*Mein Gott,* you are here! But what took you so long?"

"*Señor,*" said Pedro Salinas, shrugging, "there were many difficulties."

Otto urged him to unload the lumber, but Pedro said that with *Señor* Zumwalt's permission he would first finish his cigarette.

"Esperanza!" Otto called, rushing to the patio. "The lumber is here!"

"What lumber?"

"*Gott im Himmel!* The lumber for the floor!"

Proudly he led the way through the store, followed by his daughter, by Lilith, by Winola and Viola. When Lilith saw the wagon she cackled, and the twins played tag around their father's legs.

"How long will it take to lay the floor?" Esperanza asked the driver.

"Who knows, *señorita?* More lumber is waiting in the mountains."

She turned to Otto.

"If I'd known we were going to have a floor I would have made plans."

"But my daughter! I told you—"

"Yes, I know. Well, everything will be torn up, and you certainly can't sleep in this house. You'll have to move to the Other House while they work."

"*Ja,* the very thing. You are a good organizer, little one."

"And we can't sell goods from here while they're working. We'll have to move the store over there too. Winola and Viola! Stop that noise!"

"You heard what the lady say," Lilith warned the twins. "Shut that squealing or she'll give you something to squeal for."

The twins desisted.

235

"*Ja*, she is a good organizer and she understands discipline," Otto told the driver. "She is like my father, the general. With her everything must march."

The lumber was stacked next to the house, and the lumber that arrived three days later, and the final load that arrived four days after that. An impressive pile. And if it blocked the sidewalk and nearly blocked the street, nobody minded. One could always detour around it. Everybody in town had heard of this latest caprice of the mad *alemán,* and in the evenings whole families strolled by to see the lumber for themselves; children clambered over the stacks.

By then, the store and the adjoining bedroom were bare, the move to the Garcia house having been accomplished. One front room had been cleared to serve as store, its inventory of merchandise crammed into the second front room and even into the kitchen.

Since the Garcia house had but two bedrooms, and Esperanza occupied one, Otto had to sleep with Lilith and the twins. To this he raised objections: the twins wakened at dawn and were given to pranks, such as tickling his nose with a feather; and he declared that as master of the house it seemed hardly fitting for him to sleep with slaves. But Esperanza squelched him.

"You've slept with Lilith before, I believe."

Ach! She knew, she knew; *ja,* of course she knew. And she did not approve, any more than Pastor Moeller back in Prussia would have approved. So far as that went, he did not approve himself. But, he asked himself, what else could he have done? He was a man, already. And like all men he must occasionally return for peace and renascence to the labyrinthian ways whence he came. Better this way, he thought, than to have married another Mexican girl and reopened those old religious wars.

"*Ja,* sure, it is nothing," he said. "I will sleep with the niggers. But I only wish those twins would not tickle my nose. It gives me bad dreams. But it is all a temporary arrangement in any case."

He was almost as afraid of Esperanza as were Lilith and the twins.

*

For ten days the lumber stood outside the store, and nothing happened. Except for Pedro Salinas, superintendent of transportation in the great project, Otto had not laid eyes on the workmen since he had hired them. Mystery of mysteries, they had not even called for their wages.

"But *señor*," said Juan Archuleta, the head workman, when Otto finally found him in a *cantina,* "we returned from the mountains only last night. The hunting and fishing were good there. You may pay me now if you wish and I will pay the others. Is the floor in any hurry to get itself laid?"

Otto spoke for several minutes.

"Ah, well," said Juan Archuleta, "we will begin the work *mañana.*"

"I will expect you then tomorrow morning at seven o'clock sharp."

"*Sí,* seven or thereabouts. One sometimes oversleeps."

Otto mentioned the virtues of punctuality and even advised the purchase of one of the watches which could be bought at his store.

Señor Archuleta, a tall man of forty, with a lean face and vague eyes, replied that he preferred learning the time by consulting the sun.

Next day no workmen arrived. Nor the next.

After nearly sixteen years in Santa Fe, Otto still had no difficulty recalling the amazing diligence of Prussian workmen, and he spoke of this to his daughter. She was furious.

"All you do is talk," she said. "The whole household is upset and the store is a rat's nest. If they're not here tomorrow I will go after them."

So next morning, eyes angry, she set forth to visit the Archuleta house and bring pressure upon *Señor* Archuleta through his wife. She had great faith that a woman's tongue could move mountains.

At the market in the plaza, she received directions for reaching the Archuleta house, which, she was told, found itself sitting out beyond the mother irrigation ditch which brought the blessed water from the mountains.

"*Gracias,*" she said, and on high-arched Indian feet, shod in low slippers, she strode off with the directness of an Apache arrow.

It was mid-May, the sky turquoise, the sidewalk cool with blue shadow under the *portales,* checkered with sunlight under the cottonwoods. She passed garden patches of chili peppers and beans, where families were hoeing and purple grackles were feeding. High overhead a hawk wheeled; from beyond a patio wall she heard a wren's song. But she was out of sorts, exasperated with her father, discontented with the course of her life. She was nearly fifteen. Girls married at fifteen; yes, and at fourteen and thirteen, in Santa Fe. And girls enjoyed friendships with other girls and with boys. But did she? Never! Her father's fault. It was, she thought, as if like the ancient Prussians he had built a life for himself and his daughter on piles in the middle of a lake, the lake of their alienism.

Houses thinned, the sidewalk gave way to the road, its thick dust pinkish yellow in the hot sun, and presently she crossed the irrigation ditch where poplars grew and weeping willows trailed their branches in the smooth-flowing water and blackbirds were singing. Beyond, she came upon three children forking the back of a tatterdemalion burro, and to her inquiry about the Archuletas they pointed along the road toward a vast old cottonwood shading a low golden house encompassed by vineyards and orchards. She evoked alarmed clucking from a hen with peeping chicks when she turned in at the gate. Outside the door, taking the springtime air in its soap-root cage, a parrot with chartreuse and cobalt feathers screeched insults at her approach. The door stood open and she knocked on the jamb, but no response came from the cool dim interior. The parrot's squawks increased in vehemence. She was turning from the door when somebody rounded the corner of the house.

"*Señorita,*" he said pleasantly, "our house is yours."

It was he. It was the boy of the tomcat.

"*Gracias,*" she managed to say.

After her first glance at his dry tousled hair and thin face her gaze fell; his long legs were clad in faded trousers rolled above his knees and his feet were bare and streaked with dried tan mud.

The boy addressed the parrot.

"Be still, roguish one."

The parrot replied with something that sounded like thief.

"Her manners are bad," the boy told Esperanza.

"It is no matter," she said.

The boy poked a finger into the cage. The parrot tried to bite it. The boy laughed.

"It is said she is very old and has had many owners," he said. "She did not learn her manners from us."

"I am sure she did not, *señor.*"

"She came over the trail from Mexico. I am sorry she called you thief."

"It is no matter," Esperanza said.

"Thief!" the parrot squawked.

The boy shrugged. He wore no shirt; his torso was long, his muscles fluid under brown skin.

"Is it your pleasure to enter the house?" he asked Esperanza. "Or shall I carry in the bird? One cannot think in her presence."

"It is no matter."

"Then I will carry her in. She has had enough air in any case."

Esperanza watched his easy shoulders and straight gleaming spine as he disappeared with the cage.

"A very wicked bird," the boy said, grinning, when he returned.

Esperanza smiled. Her heart was racing and she felt breathless and a little tipsy. In the sun her hair seemed to bedazzle the air with a fine, dry dust of gold. The brilliant light had contracted the pupils of her eyes to black pinpoints. Her lashes and brows looked black as a crow's feather.

"We are all of us in the field irrigating," the boy said. "I had returned to the house for a certain shovel when I heard the parrot. I am sorry she scolded you."

"It is no matter."

Silence fell. Esperanza felt she must break it at all costs, but she could think of nothing to say. A faint rosiness blended itself with the copper and beige tones of her flesh. She looked virginal and shy as she stood gazing out at the road. Then she heard herself saying in a small, tight voice:

"That is a large cottonwood."

"*Sí,* it is very old."

"Perhaps it is older than the parrot."

"I believe perhaps it is. But the parrot is very old."

She glanced at the boy and glanced away. Her tongue felt dry when she spoke.

"We also have a cottonwood."

"*Si*, I remember it."

"Then you know I come from the store?"

"Of course, *señorita*. One recalls you because of your hair. Perhaps you do not remember, but one day long ago I visited your store and you were there. Also a certain cat."

"Her name was Hilda," Esperanza said.

"*Si*, perhaps it was."

"She is dead now."

"Once I had a *gato*," the boy said, "but he is also dead. Do you believe a cat has nine lives?"

"Perhaps some cats. Hilda did not."

"Nor did my *gato*. When he died I cried."

"*Si*, the death of a cat is a sad affair. When Hilda died I also cried."

Another silence. Off in the distance a crow was cawing, and from the cottonwood a warbler whistled. At last the boy said:

"A day will arrive when my father and I will come to your store to lay the floor."

"There is no hurry," Esperanza said.

"When we have finished the irrigation. We find ourselves late with this work because we were in the mountains cutting wood for the floor. We sent the lumber to the store in the care of Pedro Salinas. He owns a wagon and we do not. Besides, the mountains were pleasant and we stayed on to enjoy them. Did the lumber reach the store?"

"*Si*, it is there."

"I am glad to hear that. Pedro said he had delivered it but sometimes he is forgetful when he pours too much *tequila*."

"It is nicely stacked outside."

"Felling the trees was a tremendous task," the boy said. "Many difficulties presented themselves. But it was fun camping in the mountains. We hated to leave."

"*Si*, mountains are most enjoyable."

"In the mountains," the boy said, "there are many piñon nuts. I found a heap which a squirrel had hidden. My father would not let me take them all. He said that squirrels too have to live."

Silence again. Esperanza said:

"I had better be returning to the store."

"Why so soon?"

"I had better go. My father will need me."

"*Si*, perhaps mine will need me too, with the irrigation."

Another silence.

"Well," Esperanza said finally, "I had better go."

"I hope you will honor our house again," the boy said. "I am sorry the parrot raised such a racket."

"It was nothing."

"She is very old," the boy said. "She came from Mexico."

"Well," Esperanza said, "I believe I will be going. *Hasta luego.*"

"*Hasta luego.* You can find your way back?"

"*Sí,* I believe I can."

"Straight down the road and over the bridge."

"*Sí.*"

"That will take you directly to town."

"*Sí, gracias. Hasta luego.*"

"*Hasta luego.*"

Without looking back she moved through the dust of the drive to the dust of the road. Her feet felt far away. At the road, quite without intending to, she looked back. The boy was standing where she had left him. He waved. She waved. Then, also without intending to, she broke into a run and raced fleetly clear to the irrigation ditch. When she slowed, panting, she was exhilarated and also covered with shame because of all the inane things she had said and all the things left unsaid. She had not even asked his name or told him hers. What would he think of her, that exquisite boy?

*

For days she moved in a dream. When she wakened in the mornings she lay staring at the peeled-pine *vigas* of her room, smiling softly, thinking perhaps this would be the day when the boy would come with his father to put down the floor. She thought she could not wait for that to happen, but at the same time she dreaded it because the pleasure would be so delicious as to approach pain. Just to think of it set her heart to beating wildly and brought sweet suffocation to her lungs.

"What will I *say* to him?" she asked Lilith, at breakfast in the patio. "What will I *talk* about?"

"Don't you worry none 'bout that. A girl don't have to talk. A girl just is. That what my mama say, and she been in bed with some of the leading gentlemen of Virginia."

"But I can't just stand there like a *dummkopf.*"

"Might ask his opinion. Might say, 'Boy, how come you think I ain't got nothing to say 'bout all these matters? Boy,' you might say, 'how come you think the cat's got my tongue so sudden with you around?' Question like that might start things off and before you know it you end up in bed with the boy."

Lilith cackled.

Esperanza flushed.

"I wish," she said, "you wouldn't always talk about bed."

"Ain't nothing wrong with bed. Some of the nicest times I ever had has been in bed."

"This boy is different."

"He is? That case, maybe you don't want him."

"I want him," Esperanza said. "And I'll have him."

"My, my," Lilith said, "sometimes I think I been lucky being a nigger. With a nigger gal it ain't no question of *if*. No, ma'am. It only a question of *when*. White man see a nigger and he either buy her or rent her, or he don't. If he don't, you just think he's no-good trash. If he do, there ain't no question what he's up to."

So Lilith was not much help, and of course Esperanza did not mention the boy to her father.

"*Ja*, maybe you know now I wasn't such a big liar after all," Otto kept saying, as the days passed without the workmen coming. "I have always said they were all loafers, those filthy Mexicans."

She let him rail. And without the checkrein of her reproof, he carried railing to extremes unconscionable even for him, as he tramped from the temporary store to the old store, bare to the walls, and stared gloomily at all that fine space being wasted, and ruminated upon the slackness, the blundering, the incompetence which prevailed in the non-Aryan world; as he brooded through the door and contemplated the lumber stacked in the street; as he wandered back to the temporary store which even the orderly hands of one Prussian and one half-Prussian had been unable to save from untidiness, confusion, a chaos of trade goods. It was all so monstrous, so monumental an example of the cowardice, the filth, the—well—the inefficiency of the Latin race that at last words failed even Otto, and he lapsed into silence, or near-silence.

Esperanza was mainly silent also, but hers was a soft-smiling, dreamy, anticipatory silence. Everything lay before her. She lost interest in keeping the accounts and in selling goods to those who did not want or need them, that very heart's core of salesmanship; and in bed at night she no longer needed a candle to banish remembered horror. The nightmares had abandoned her bedchamber. At last, she thought, she was forever rid of the midnights when through grotesque streets of her brain a man with a fish mouth pounded after a poor fleeing girl. She was free of that moment—so much more hideous in memory than in actuality it had ever been—when she plunged the knife into his belly. How he had looked, stumbling toward her, hands threshing in the moonlight! With what awful labor he had breathed! And how his idiot's body had jerked when she drove the knife into his heart! What a mad little Apache she had been! To withdraw the knife and see it dripping black in the moonlight! To wipe it on his shirt! Awful, awful!—why had she done it?

"I loved that knife," she thought. "I wanted to use it. I loved using it. It was the Apache devil in my heart. I was a savage when I used it. I liked it when he jerked. I liked it when the knife dripped. I was an

241

Apache and I would have danced a victory dance if I had known one."

So she used to torment herself when the nightmare, in one of its many forms, wakened her and she was shaking and crying.

But now it was over. Now she was free. Worry, fear, horror, dread: all had been banished. She was different now. She had talked with the boy who had once owned a tomcat and she would talk with him again and she was different. The child who took such voluptuous delight in the knife was dead; dead as the man with the fish mouth. She was different. Existence was sweet. The future lay all before her in sun and turquoise and running water.

*

And then one day they came to begin work, Juan Archuleta and his son; came at the outrageous hour of 10:30 A.M. by Otto's watch; and once there they did not instantly fall to, but stood in the street amiably regarding the lumber and reminiscing pleasantly about their adventures in the mountains when they manufactured it.

"*Ja*," Otto said, "that is all very well, and I am glad you enjoyed yourselves in the mountains, but that is all over now and the time has come to begin work."

"Father," the boy said, "tell him about Pedro and the *mapurite*."

"Now is not the time," Otto said, "to hear about Pedro and some cowardly skunk. Now is the time for work."

"But you will enjoy this story, *señor*," Juan Archuleta said. "One evening when Pedro—"

From the door of the Garcia house, Esperanza's head occasionally appeared for an instant, then disappeared, as she stole glances at the trio.

"Lilith," she breathed, "I'll die if I don't go over there."

"Never you mind about that dying, Miss Esperanza. Don't you go chasing that boy. You wait a spell."

"I'll die."

Again she peeked out the door. Juan Archuleta and his son were laughing; Otto was pulling his mustache. Then they disappeared into the little house. Minutes passed. Esperanza stared. At last she said: "I'm going."

"That ain't smart," Lilith called after her.

Archuleta and son were examining the floor with considerable interest, Otto was discoursing upon the remarkable strength of Prussian joists, and the three cats were pondering the eccentricities of man when Esperanza entered the store.

"Father," she said, "where is that box of pongee handkerchiefs?"

"How should I know? *Mein Gott,* the store is so untidy—"

Esperanza had been frowning in puzzlement, staring straight at her father, but now she chanced to notice the two workmen.

"Ooo," she trilled, "*buenos días!* You have come to lay the floor?"

"*Si, señorita,*" said Juan Archuleta, sweeping off his sombrero. "I am Juan Archuleta, and I believe you have talked with my son, Gilberto."

"*Si,* we have talked," Gilberto said, smiling. "Good morning, *señorita.* You did not tell me you have three cats."

"*Ja,*" Otto said, "the best three cats that ever lived, except Hilda. Not a mouse—"

"How is your parrot?" Esperanza asked.

"She is well."

"Of course," Otto was saying, "I do not like them to chase lizards, because lizards catch spiders, but—"

And Juan Archuleta was saying:

"The parrot, *señorita,* is very old. How old one often wonders—"

In the hubbub Gilberto was smiling when Esperanza's glance met his; she also smiled and looked hastily away. A vein was hammering in her throat and her cheeks felt heated.

"Now what was it, little one, about the handkerchiefs?" Otto asked.

She reeled off a facile lie that stamped a worried frown on his brow and sent him off to the temporary store. Gilberto picked up the cat, Alberta, who purred contentedly in his arms. Juan Archuleta was explaining that although his fondness for cats was unequaled save by his fondness for wife and family, still it was now impossible, with a parrot in the household, for the Archuletas to harbor a cat, owing to the proclivity of cats for stalking birds.

"How old is this little Alberta?" Gilberto asked.

"She is three."

"That is not very old."

"No, it is not."

"They were in plain sight, already," Otto announced from the door. "One dozen pongee handkerchiefs in their box on the table."

"But father. Are you sure they are pongee? I looked—"

"*Ja,* sure I am sure. If they had been a spider they would have bitten you. Well, the time has come to lay the floor. *Ja.* Let us go right to work and make matters march without more monkey business."

"*Señor,*" said Juan Archuleta, "your mention of monkeys reminds me of a story. When I was a boy a traveler from Mexico brought a monkey over the trail—"

"*Ja,* I have also known many monkeys but this is not getting the floor laid."

"It is a story most droll, *señor.*"

"I am sure it is, but perhaps you could tell it while you work."

"Oh, no, *señor,* I do not believe I could. I cannot work while I talk."

"*Señor,*" said Esperanza, smiling, "one would be delighted to hear the story."

"*Señorita,* I am sure you will laugh till you weep. When I was a boy a traveler from Mexico brought a monkey over the trail—"

At that story, and at the many others touched off in Juan Archuleta's memory, Esperanza laughed in delight, and sometimes her gaze happened to meet Gilberto's. And although he must have heard the stories before, he was a most appreciative member of his father's audience. He kept saying, "Father, tell us the one about—" Otto pretty well controlled his own mirth.

Then—how the minutes passed!—it was noon and time to knock off work.

*

Laying the floor proved to be an enterprise nearly as protracted as expelling the Moors from Spain. In theory, Pedro Salinas and Carlos Garrido, who had helped the Archuletas manufacture lumber in the mountains, were to follow right through in bringing the undertaking to a triumphant conclusion; but Carlos, for reasons beyond understanding, never did show up on the job, and on the few days when Pedro came he was so drowsy with *tequila* it was decided wiser to let him sleep in the shade. The Archuletas themselves were faithful toilers, arriving almost every day at mid-morning and working till noon, when they adjourned to the stacks of lumber and spread out lunch. Following this they enjoyed their siesta, also on the stacks of lumber, and usually by about two-thirty they resumed work. June came and then July before the store found itself with a new floor. "My patience," Otto kept saying, "is exhausted," but perhaps the languid progress was all for the best: certainly the lumber, green when delivered, had a splendid opportunity to cure during those long, dry, golden days. "It is better not to hurry matters," Juan Archuleta was fond of saying. When Otto sought to spur him on, *Señor* Archuleta was quite imperturbable; he smiled, shrugged and pointed out that after all this was the first floor he had ever laid. And when Otto declared that he would rather live like a pig on a dirt floor than go through all this again, *Señor* Archuleta replied that those were his sentiments precisely.

"Think of the trouble you have had," he said gently. "I believe you would have been happier to continue living on your blood floor."

"Blood! What is that you say?"

"*Si, señor,* of course the floor is of blood. Of pig's blood mixed with earth. It makes a very nice floor."

"*Mein Gott!* Blood, already! I did not know that all these years I have been living like a pig on a pig's blood floor!"

"*Si,* pig's blood or sheep's blood, both are good. It is said that cow's blood also makes a very satisfactory floor, but I believe I like pig's blood best."

"Blood!" Otto kept repeating. "Me, a Prussian on a blood floor! No wonder we have had ants so bad!"

Señor Archuleta shrugged.

244

"Always ants, *señor*. They mean no harm."

The floor-laying attracted many sightseers, and often they asked questions of *Señor* Archuleta, who, because of his policy of working when working and talking when talking, stopped whatever he was doing to reply. Sometimes an hour slipped by before he again reached for hammer and nails. The sightseers, being also wellwishers, occasionally offered advice in construction matters, and although *Señor* Archuleta was grateful for counsel he usually preferred his own carpentry methods, so long confabulations ensued, with everybody joining in, including Otto. His opinion carried no more weight than anybody else's, which was singular, inasmuch as he was paying for the work and since he was the only person in the group who had ever seen a board floor. He lost his temper now and then, greatly to the mystification of all, for those discussions, except for his contributions, were always well-mannered and affable, being carried on in the subjunctive mood. But since he was the loco *alemán*, for many years an institution in Santa Fe, they only smiled and shrugged when he denounced them for idling and insubordination and stalked to the patio, where he paced and muttered.

Esperanza did not share his distress at the project's longevity; quite the contrary. When her father grumbled that the task, with Prussian workmen, could have been finished in three days, she merely shrugged; nor was she agitated by his alarmist's prediction that the work might drag out all summer, that when the caravan arrived in August it would find the floor unfinished and the temporary store a helter-skelter of shovels and axes entangled with necklaces and shawls.

"*Mein Gott,* where will we stack the new merchandise? Already we are stuffed full like a sausage."

Esperanza couldn't be bothered; other matters engrossed her; she lived in perpetual excitement. "Gilberto will be here today," she thought upon awakening, and the last thing at night she thought, "He will be here tomorrow." With Lilith she held long, confidential conferences at which, in elation, she reported what he had said, how he had looked at her; and occasionally, if affairs had gone adversely, she shed angry tears and belabored herself as a bungler in the skill which every successful girl must know. Lilith delivered many sage recommendations, often quoting her mother. Nub of this advice was that, under physical law, it was impossible for two corporeal bodies to chase each other at the same time. One must pursue, one take flight, although not so rapidly as to preclude capture. One must not fling oneself at a boy. Might scare him off. One must tempt, beguile, beckon without seeming to beckon, lure, promise much, deliver less. Fundamental! Yes, ma'am.

And although like all girls Esperanza had been born with this knowledge, although she freely affirmed it as a standard to which wise women should repair, she had learned that, with Gilberto on the premises, theory often succumbed to the urgencies of reality. She simply could not keep away from the construction activities. This left the business without a clerk, for Otto, in his efforts to speed the work, haunted the old store, diverting Archuleta and son with travelogues concerning the Rhine and the Vistula, with little journeys to the homes of great Prussians, with comments on the prevalence of disease in Paris, the exigencies of sugar planting in Louisiana and slave smuggling in Texas, the tactics of Comanches, the technique of blade and pistol, and with panegyrics on friendship. All this retarded progress, for *Señor* Archuleta disliked working while he listened nearly as much as working while he talked; and besides, when Otto yarned of the beautiful girls he had won and discarded in New Orleans, *Señor* Archuleta would be reminded of a story. And when Otto wasn't talking he was getting into somebody's way. Like so many workers in wood, the Archuletas dropped more nails than they drove, and Otto, with exemplary Prussian thrift, was always bending over to glean these. Lumber scraps he also picked up, to be stacked for kindling, and after *Señor* Archuleta's saw wandered through a board, Otto fetched a broom and swept up the sawdust: this kept the place more tidy, and the sawdust too could be burned.

"*Ja,* all my life I have been a thrifty fellow," he said. "That is how I have got where I have got. But once when I was courting a French countess I forgot thrift. You would not believe me if I told you the flowers I sent her."

"*Si,* a few flowers," said Juan Archuleta, "the ladies like them. I am reminded—"

"But I never should have done it. Her husband challenged me and I had to kill the poor fellow. In any case that French nobility is beneath one's notice. They went too far with their taxes and there was a great revolution already."

"As great as our revolution, *señor?*"

"Perhaps not quite, but fairly great. And please do not misunderstand me about taxes. I am opposed to them from reveille to taps. They are no good, those taxes. Not right!"

"Who can doubt it, *señor?*"

"Not me! You have never heard me favoring taxes, and anybody who says I did is just making up big lies to cause me trouble."

Archuleta and son looked baffled at this insistence on the obvious, and when their glances met their eyes showed sympathy for the poor mad *alemán*.

During lunchtime and the siesta, Otto returned to the temporary store where he labored over accounts; Esperanza, however, usually joined the Archuletas at the lumber stacks. Her pretext was the serving of hot chocolate, a beverage rare in the Zumwalt house, for Otto, whose worship of coffee approached religious zeal, believed the Spanish preference for chocolate indicated some essential flaw in their character. That very first day when the Archuletas spread out their lunch, Esperanza, who was certainly a thoughtful girl, offered to fetch something hot to drink.

"*Gracias, señorita,* you are too kind," said Juan Archuleta. "With your permission, a cup of chocolate, perhaps."

A crisis! Not a speck of chocolate in the house! But Esperanza did not admit this; she retired through the old store to the Other House and to the street again, along which she raced toward the plaza market. The Archuletas, chewing contentedly on the lumber stacks, chanced to glimpse her flying feet; they thought it most strange.

"Ah, well," said Juan, "perhaps she discovered the larder is bare of chocolate."

"Out of chocolate! Well, perhaps. But why did she run? And why did she run that day when she left our house?"

Juan shrugged eloquently.

"*Quién sabe?* Perhaps in that country her loco father speaks of they always run. It wearies one to think of it."

"There she is, father, returning," Gilberto said presently. "And she is running."

"To be believed it would have to be witnessed," said Juan, sighing. "Through the heat of the noon too!"

"Her hair is very pretty," Gilberto said.

"*Si.* But there is more to a woman than her hair."

"I like her waist," Gilberto said. "It is slim and yet round like a young coyote's."

"*Si.* But her *tetas* are too small."

"Not so small. And they are young and saucy. And her hips are pleasant."

"For my taste, too narrow."

"*Acaso.* But they are trim and yet nicely plump."

"My son," said Juan Archuleta, "do not forget the trouble I have had arranging with Sebastian Ortiz that you should marry his daughter."

"I have not forgotten."

"There is nothing small about the *tetas* of Concepcion Ortiz. I took them into account when I arranged the marriage."

"*Si,* but there is also nothing small about the nose of *Señorita* Ortiz." Juan shrugged.

"In the dark, who notices a nose?"

"Also, she has the figure of a bear."

"True, she is built generously. But her dowry is generous too."

"*Si.*"

"And it is nice her father's lands adjoin ours."

"*Si.*"

"So do not permit yourself to dream about the figure of *Señorita* Zumwalt. Besides, she is an infidel and will doubtless end up as mad as her father."

"But she is not mad now."

"I am not so sure, my son. Who but a mad girl would run through the heat of noon? I knew her great-grandmother, La Luz Delgado. She also was mad. It is said she sold her soul to the devil and he used to visit her in her bed. But she was a fine *curandera*. When I was a boy she cured me of warts."

"*Señorita* Zumwalt has amazing hair," Gilberto said. "It is as golden as wheat straw in the sun."

"All hair looks alike in the dark."

"And she has a fragrance when she passes near. She smells fresh as a mountain columbine after a shower."

"Doubtless she bathes too often and perfumes herself with scented waters. Women, my son, have many tricks."

"*Acaso.*"

"A young man," said Juan Archuleta, "should not permit his thoughts to wander when he has been promised to so fine a girl as Concepcion. After your marriage, that will be different."

"My thoughts do not wander," Gilberto said.

Presently Esperanza appeared with the hot chocolate.

"It is delicious," Juan said. "I hope you did not put yourself to trouble."

"Ooo, no!"

"It is the best chocolate I have ever swallowed," Gilberto said.

She smiled.

"*Señorita,*" said Juan Archuleta, "is it possible for me to believe what I saw? Did I see you running?"

The wine of confusion flowed red in her cheeks.

"Not very fast," she said.

"In the heat of noon," Juan Archuleta said, "one should not run. It brings on diarrhea."

Esperanza did not look at Gilberto, whose cheeks were also flushed.

"So avoid running in the heat or you will find yourself compelled to run," Juan said.

"With your permission," Esperanza said, "I must now excuse myself and help my father in the store."

After she had gone Gilberto said:

"You are a devil, my dear father."

Juan Archuleta's eyes were humorous and wickedly wise.

"When a young man's thoughts wander," he said, "it is well for him to be reminded that there is more to a woman than her hair."

Not again that day did Esperanza visit the stacks of lumber. That evening she held a sober conference with Lilith.

"How come you think he say that?"

"I don't *know,*" Esperanza breathed. "I could have died."

"Watch that old man. Yes, ma'am. He ain't on your side. He just trying to cool off that boy. But in a way it's good. If that boy ain't all het up, the old man wouldn't have no call to cool him. Tomorrow you let me lug over that chocolate. Don't show yourself. And if I gits a chance, I'll spill some of that hot chocolate on the boy's papa."

So the next noon Lilith served the chocolate.

"But I didn't spill any," she reported. "Kick my hide, I didn't. Got scared of trying, at the last minute."

When siesta time came, Esperanza stole through the patio to the old store. Stealthily, she peeked out the door. On the lumber Archuleta and son lay, sombreros over their faces. The day was brilliant, hot, still, murmurous with flies. Esperanza cleared her throat. The Archuletas did not stir. She coughed. No movement from the stacks.

"Gilberto," she called softly.

His sombrero stirred. Esperanza glided back into the store. And in her low, sweet, girlish voice she sang one of the songs from her father's brave youth:

> *"I jumped on a mule and started West,*
> *Started West, started West . . ."*

Presently Gilberto appeared in the door, hair mussed, eyes sleepy. *"Señorita."*

"Ooo!" she exclaimed, keeping her voice low. "You surprised me."

"Did you call?"

"I? Call? No, I do not believe I did."

"Perhaps I was dreaming. But I thought your voice called."

"No, I did not call."

"I think I was dreaming," he said.

He stood looking at her, eyes bemused. Esperanza lowered her gaze and with the toe of her slipper traced hieroglyphics in the sawdust. Her breath was shallow. The store and the street and all New Mexico lay drugged in siesta silence. Her young breast rose and fell, and she wondered if he could hear her heart thumping.

Gilberto glanced over his shoulder, through the door. Then in a low voice he said:

"Let us go to the patio and look at the cottonwood."

"*Si*, it is a lovely cottonwood."

She felt light-headed and light-footed and yet languorous when she moved through the kitchen to the patio. And when Gilberto halted and gazed at the cottonwood wonderingly, as if he had never seen a tree before, she stood closer to him than she had ever before dared. In her body, which looked so graceful and willowy, she was aware of tremendous dynamics swaying her toward him. He was naked to the waist, his skin browned by many suns and by many races of the sun. Mingling with the fragrance of her own Eau de Cologne she could identify his male smell of dried sweat and the stable.

"An old tree," he said.

249

"*Si.* It is older than I."

"And how old is that?"

"Soon I will be fifteen."

"I am sixteen," he said.

The cat, Alberta, padded over to investigate, and Gilberto picked her up. In the great sunny silence Esperanza could hear her rich purring and Gilberto's breathing and the low humming of bees.

"She is a pretty cat," Gilberto said. "Her fur is an unusual color. Is it gray or blue?"

"A little of both, perhaps."

"*Si.* And if I may say so, your hair is also unusual, *señorita.* And very beautiful."

"*Gracias,*" she murmured.

He was staring at her hair, his eyes full of wonder.

"I remember it from that first day I visited the store so long ago. It is the color of sunshine on the golden aspens when October comes to the mountains."

She felt as if her veins were running with yellow wine; her brain was light and giddy.

"*Gracias,*" she whispered.

Idly, he stood stroking the cat. Closer to him now, so close that their bodies nearly brushed, Esperanza felt she had passed under the sway of some sweet opiate; her legs felt heavy and lassitudinous, as if she were hip deep in a pool of warm water through which sluggish and amorous currents flowed. Overhead the sky arched vast and somnolent; the sunshine was tremendous.

"How still it is," she breathed. "Not a leaf moving. One could hear a feather whispering to the air as it floated along."

"*Si.* Always at the siesta it is quiet. Do you not in your house observe the siesta?"

"I do not believe we do. My father says it is a waste of time. That is not my belief. With many of his ideas I do not agree."

"Is it true his father is a general?"

Gilberto was smiling faintly; she also smiled.

"Who knows?" she said.

A lizard scampered across the patio and climbed the wall. In Gilberto's arms Alberta snapped alert and sprang to the ground. An exclamation broke from his lips.

"What is it?"

"Only her sharp claws. She meant no harm."

Several red scratches showed on his wrist.

"Ooo!"

"It is nothing. When I had my *gato* he was always scratching me."

"Let me see," Esperanza said, and her fingertips brushed his hand.

It was like touching some source of primary energy. She thought an invisible and cataclysmic current streaked up her arm and hurled itself in an instantaneous lacework to all parts of her body. Her hand jerked back. Her legs were trembling and her cheeks felt fiery. She could hardly breathe. For an instant she looked full into his face; he was blushing furiously.

"Cats are always scratching people," he said, his voice strained.

Esperanza's throat felt swollen shut; her heart hammered. She found herself drifting across the patio and pausing at a bed of poppies. Absently she picked one and stood in indecision staring down at the yellow petals. She sensed Gilberto at her side.

"I think," she said in a queer tight voice, "I had better go. My father will need me."

"*Si,* I suppose he will."

Her gaze remained fixed on the flower as she revolved the stem between thumb and forefinger. Her body felt heavy and pregnant with all the light and heat and drowsiness of the afternoon.

"I had better go," she said.

"And perhaps I had better return to the lumber," he said, "before my father wakens."

"*Si.*"

"Perhaps I will see you tomorrow at the siesta hour," he said.

"*Si,* it is possible."

"If I am dozing call to me and I will waken."

"Perhaps your father will waken too."

"No, I do not believe he will. He is a heavy sleeper."

"*Hasta luego,*" she said.

"Then I will see you tomorow?"

"Perhaps. *Hasta luego.*"

When she walked toward the patio of the Garcia house it seemed she was almost floating. Not till she reached the door did she look back. He was standing where she had left him. He waved. She waved. Then she ran into the house and on to her bedroom and flung herself on the bed and burst into tears.

*

Slowly, slowly, the work on the floor progressed, despite interruptions, despite the Archuleta habit of declaring holidays on the birthdays of Gilberto's brothers and sisters, nine in all, and his uncles, cousins, second cousins and occasionally some dear friend of a second cousin. And slowly the friendship between Esperanza and Gilberto progressed; too slowly, she thought. Those patio afternoons, while Juan Archuleta slept on the lumber, were exceedingly pleasant but also amazingly circumspect. Esperanza and Gilberto talked, but that was about all. This was not the way matters went in those French novels she had read. In the company of the fair, those Frenchmen were great ones for coming to grips with cosmic forces; conversation was fine up to a point, but thereafter actions spoke louder than words.

Now and then—too seldom, really—Gilberto mentioned the beauty of her hair, or how her smooth skin in sunlight glowed with a faint tint of copper underneath the beige, or how her eyes were the purest black he had ever seen; and the conversation perked up.

"Why do you tell me such things?" she asked, touching his arm.

"I just happened to notice them. Look at Alberta. She's caught a beetle."

Arrgh! What a Frenchman would have achieved after such an opening!

"Mean to say," Lilith asked, during an evening council of war, "that he ain't even kissed you?"

"No!"

"Uh! You is almost fifteen and never been kissed!"

"It's not my fault."

"Didn't mean it was! No, ma'am! Boy's fault wholly. You reckon that boy ain't got what it takes?"

"It's not that. He wants to. I know he wants to. But something holds him back."

"Never seen the like," Lilith said, frowning. "Maybe the thing to do is not show up at that lumber tomorrow."

"Ooo, but he will be expecting me."

"There you are. Just let him expect. More the boy expects more he will heat up."

But Esperanza was far too headstrong to follow such advice. The next afternoon she roused Gilberto from his siesta, and on nearly every afternoon. Always she moved through the patio with Indian stealth and tiptoed into the old store where she paused at the front door, her heart rapid, her nerves tingling, everything silent save for the twittering of a goldfinch in the *alamo*, or the whir of a hummingbird among the buttercups, the air pungent with the scents of new sawdust and sand verbena and the cool faint mustiness of old adobe. Usually Gilberto was already awake when she arrived, but once he did not rouse even after she had called several times. It was mid-June by then, summer at full flood, and on soundless squaw feet she stole out to the lumber and lightly removed the sombrero from his face. How exquisite he was! How black his hair! How dry and boyishly mussed! In repose his lashes curved; downy fuzz showed on his cheeks; the faintest of smiles parted his lips. His naked torso gleamed golden brown. Sunlight, summer, a beautiful boy. Some day he would kiss her. Perhaps today. Her hands wanted to touch him but she forced herself to wait. She stood smiling with her dreams, laved by a happiness almost unbearably sweet. Then she reached to waken him. But in midair her hand halted, poised, then fell to her side. And she nearly cried out at the thought which, all unbidden, sneaked on moccasin feet across her mind.

She was thinking how easy it would be, while he slept, to lift a knife and drive it into his heart.

She was dumfounded. She was utterly shaken. With a palm clapped over her mouth, she stood dazed, staring off down the street where the dust lay thick and hot in the pitiless sun. Little whirlwinds of sickness curled in her stomach; icy little devils leaped along her spine. Not looking at Gilberto, she crept noiselessly into the old store where she sank to the earthen bench along the wall. Much of the floor was now wooden, sugared with sawdust and littered with scraps. Through the latticed window a bee flew in, buzzed in circles, departed. She stood up, wearily, and moved through the store and the patio toward the Other House.

Why had such an awful thought entered her head? Why? In her bedroom she went to the mirror and stared at a girl with black unknowable eyes and lips parted in shock. Grains of sweat hung on her forehead. "I hate you," she whispered to the girl in the mirror. Then she lay on the bed, dry-eyed, staring at the ceiling. And always she asked why, why?

Yet she knew why. The man with the yellow shoes was why, the man with the fish mouth. He had also lain with chest upturned. But by what grotesqueries in the dark bottom of her mind had Gilberto become identified with the man of the yellow shoes? Why had that thought, unexpected as an Apache attack, raided the fiesta of her happiness? Why had she thought of the knife? She hated the knife. She loathed the knife. Why had she thought of using it on Gilberto? Gilberto she loved. Gilberto she lived for.

"I do not understand," she thought. "I do not understand myself."

And there came to her a vision of herself as a land as vast and unknown and mysterious as the deserts of the Apache Nation, as the arroyos choked with ocotillo and cholla, the violet mesas, the plateaus of blowing sand, the pine-dark mountains where nameless cataracts roared through nameless canyons and the Apache gods lived.

Not again that day did she see Gilberto. And that night she slept with a candle burning by her bed. But no nightmares came, and next morning she felt fine again. Everything was as it had been before, almost.

*

Esperanza became somewhat difficult to live with, as the floor neared completion and Gilberto dawdled. Poor Otto suffered. And Lilith suffered too, although not because of bad treatment from her mistress. Indeed, now that the problem of ensnaring Gilberto had arisen, Esperanza's manners with her slave had improved; she never whipped her any more. They were leagued together against Gilberto's happiness, and Lilith's suffering was the vicarious sort undergone by all women who serve as seconds in matchmaking. Lilith had fully expected that by early

253

June Esperanza and Gilberto would be thicker than two in a bed. And here it was late June! What was the matter with that boy? She decided it was high time to call in consultation.

"I'd best talk with my mama," she said; so one hot morning early in July, arrayed in her salmon-pink silk dress, her scarlet stockings and green shoes, (Christmas presents from Otto), she waddled from the store with the twins, also presents from Otto, bound for the living quarters behind Kite's Saloon. From the door Esperanza watched them swishing off down the street, the twins much excited about visiting grandma, their buff-colored legs bare, their matching yellow dresses all starched and frilled, big red ribbons bobbing at the ends of their pigtails. Out of sorts this morning, Esperanza considered calling that the twins could not, after all, accompany their mother; on former occasions when she issued such a dictum the twins had shrieked in disappointment and Esperanza, a strict disciplinarian, had taken deep satisfaction in thus strengthening their characters for the rigors of life; but today she decided to sacrifice the twins' best interests for her own; she did hope that old nigger of Hod Kite's would come up with some bright idea. Lilith turned around once, flashing back a toothy grin and cackling. Esperanza smiled faintly, the ends of her mouth bitter. And as she watched Lilith's receding figure, she was idly interested in how the years had filled her out. Within Esperanza's memory Lilith had been plump in the customary places, but her belly had been pliant and her legs attractively girlish. Now all had changed. Lilith had ballooned out all over the place, especially since the twins' birth; she was, Esperanza thought, a big fat two-fisted wench.

Esperanza turned back into the store, where her father, whom the years had also changed, stood bald and graying, stroking his sweeping mustache, eyes worried because it was ten o'clock and the Archuletas had not yet arrived, (certainly a worry about something that could not be helped, for the Archuletas never arrived before ten-thirty), worried also lest he was falling down on his tremendous destiny of being a Prussian by granting Lilith the day off. This too was a useless worry: Esperanza, not he, had granted the holiday; but of course Otto maintained the fiction that he headed the household. Under these cares and stresses, and numberless others, his shoulders sagged; it would have been difficult to imagine that this middle-aged man in baggy pants and carpet slippers had ever, when the trail was young and the world was young, set out for Santa Fe clad in buckskins, his neck too stiff for comfort, his shoulders erect, his fine squarish head bristling with tow hair, such a figure of a plainsman that he had been mistaken for *Herr* Boone.

"Three minutes after ten," he muttered, watch in his palm, staring gloomily at the second hand busy pilfering the treasure of life from all who lived. "I wish they would come."

."Well, they won't," his daughter snapped, "till they get good and ready."

"Mexicans," he muttered. "Dirty, lazy, ignorant. They will never learn punctuality."

He sighed, and the Teutonic gloom in that store, thick as the fumes of beer in a rathskeller, would have dulled the sword of Frederick the Great.

Esperanza rolled and lighted a cigarette, and its sharp sweet smoke reminded Otto of another girl, another cigarette, at a fandango.

"It is all like a cigarette," he muttered vaguely. "It burns and goes into smoke and air and you wonder where it went."

"What are you talking about?"

"*Nichts, nichts* that would interest you, my little one," he said, sighing; and with hands clasped behind his back, like a strolling professor, he moped to the street where he stood gazing wistfully for carpenters who were ever tardy, before plodding on to the original store.

"*Ach,*" he muttered when he entered the little rooms, rooms that looked too small to have harbored all the ecstasy and sorrow they had known, "I only hope the work is finished before the caravan comes. If those bull whackers would find us in such a mess they might tattle to McSwasey that it is hurting business. Then he might discharge me. And then what would I do?"

*

"That mama of mine knows men," Lilith said. "Yes, ma'am. That mama of mine been in bed with more men than Solomon had wives. So when my mama say what to do you do it. Yes, ma'am."

Night was far advanced; Lilith had returned late from her conference, clutching a bottle of Taos Lightning which Hod Kite had given her for old times' sake. Some of the bottle's contents had already unfettered genii in her brain. Now, with the twins put to bed, Lilith sat in Esperanza's room, the bottle uncorked, openly defying a time-honored edict against mixing slavery with alcohol. Esperanza frowned, watching her tilt the bottle. She had, she decided, been too easy with Lilith these past weeks. Give a nigger an inch. She would have to attend to that. But first she wanted to know what scheme Hod Kite's old nigger had concocted.

"Coming to it," Lilith said. "Yes, ma'am. Had a great day, Miss Esperanza. Mistah Kite a fine man. Mistah Kite let my mama have a nip whenever she can sneak one. It oil my mama's tongue and loosens up her memory. She tell me all 'bout her and Mistah Fairburn back in Virginia. He my papa, you know. He lose my mama in a bet on a running-horse race. Yes, ma'am. Gentleman name of Ridgeway win her with me in her belly. He sell us South. I was born in New Orleans, my mama say. She can't recollect just when. We was then sold to another

255

gentleman heading for Texas. Yes, ma'am. And he sell us to Mistah Kite."

"Hod Kite's a fool to give you whiskey," Esperanza said.

"Yes, ma'am, he sure is. But a mighty wise old fool. He got his start robbing banks. He tell my mama all 'bout it, one night in bed. Man likes to talk at such times. And it's safe talkin' to us niggers account of we can't stand up in court and say nothing. No, ma'am. They won't let us. 'Cause we's niggers. Saves us a lot of lying, my mama say."

Lilith tilted the bottle; Esperanza watched with deadly eyes.

"So I tell mama all 'bout you and the Mexican boy. I tell her how you meet him in the store and how you go looking for him that night of the revolution when they kill all them high government personages. And how you never see him. But he must have been there. Yet you never see him. No, ma'am. Neither hide nor hair. What you do that night, anyway?"

Like a young cat Esperanza sprang to her feet and pounced on that stray conversational lizard.

"Why did you ask that?"

"Miss Esperanza! What the matter? Why you look at me like that? Leave go my hand! Don't spill that drinking liquor!"

"*Dummkopf!* I'll break that bottle over your head!"

"No, ma'am! Don't do it. That liquor too hard to come by. You spill my liquor and I won't tell you what my mama say."

Esperanza's grip loosened on her slave's wrist. Her eyes were glitteringly opaque. Her voice was low, smothered with fury.

"Why did you ask that?"

"Ask what, Miss Esperanza?"

"Do you know something? How could you?"

"I don't know nothing about nothing, Miss Esperanza. 'Cepting what my mama tell me."

"Then why did you ask?"

"I ain't sure what we is talking of. What did I ask, Miss Esperanza? Kind of hot in here. Yes, ma'am. I'm sweating like a nigger in July. Liquor, maybe. Why you think liquor make you feel so fine? If I had me all the liquor I could drink I'd never do nothing but drink and love and sleep. He used to give me a nip in the wagon. On the way to Taos. Made me wild, he say. He likes 'em wild. Reckon he the only man I ever love. Red-headed. Get you a red-headed man and you got a wild one."

Lilith cackled. Esperanza stood watching her narrowly.

"Why you look at me like that, Miss Esperanza? Ain't I your friend? Ain't I ask my mama how to git that Mexican boy? Ain't I make your papa rich giving him valuable little niggers? But I sure wish he never sell that Wisdom. The gals, yes. The gals, I don't sorrow so much. But Wisdom

256

She tilted the bottle.

"You're drunk," Esperanza said.

"Sure I is drunk. Yes, ma'am. I is drunk as a nigger. But I ain't all nigger. No, ma'am! Chuck plumb full of fine Virginia blood. But all that fine blood never done me no good. I is like a chicken. Some of me's white meat and some dark. But I ain't like a chicken neither. Me, the dark meat spoils the white. It's hard being a nigger but the liquor helps. Give me enough liquor and I sing like a crow. But I'm good in bed. Ask your papa."

She tilted the bottle; she seemed trying to put its contents beyond the possibility of being spilled.

"What did your mama say?" Esperanza demanded.

"I'm comin' to that. Yes, ma'am. She say . . ."

Esperanza listened. And to her surprise, the plan sounded excellent.

"Ain't I a good nigger, Miss Esperanza? Ain't I git from my mama a way to git the boy?"

"Lie down on the floor," Esperanza said.

"No. Don't! Please!"

"Lie down on the floor and pull up your dress."

"No! No! Please! Miss Esperanza!"

*

Next morning, sore-legged from the punishment and sore-headed from the Taos Lightning, Lilith had the sulks when she served her mistress breakfast in the patio, but Esperanza scarcely noticed. It was a beautiful summer morning, the dishes and linen dappled with cottonwood shade, the patio tinted with lavender shadow and sunlight, and while she ate Esperanza examined the scheme concocted by Lilith's mother. It looked foolproof. With a cigarette she lingered over coffee, daydreaming. A wren sang. From the old store she could hear her father puttering with a broom; from the Garcia patio came the twins' voices; sometimes they giggled and screeched gleefully.

"Lilith!" Esperanza called sharply.

"Yes, ma'am."

"Tell the twins to shut up that noise."

"Yes, ma'am."

Lilith waddled off, moving awkwardly, because of sore legs. The noise ceased. Presently Otto emerged to the patio laden with scrap lumber, which he stacked neatly.

"Father," Esperanza called.

"*Ja.*"

"I thought Hod Kite was your friend."

"*Ja,* that is true. He is my second-best friend. McSwasey," Otto continued, warming to a favorite subject, "is my first. Would you believe it? I lent the fellow two thousand dollars and always he has paid the interest. *Ja!* Right on the dot! That is the kind of friends we are!"

"Hod Kite gave Lilith a bottle of whiskey."

"*Ja,* I know, the coward shouldn't have done it, but you cannot blame him too much. He is nothing but a retired bank robber."

"I want you to tell him not to do it again."

"*Ja,* sure, I will, but of course it is a delicate matter to discuss with my second-best friend. In any case you gave that drunken Lilith a good lesson, only perhaps you used her too badly. Her howling woke me up, and after she came to bed she kept me awake with her groaning. Well, perhaps it is what I can expect, sleeping with lazy niggers. But the floor will be all nicely laid in a day or two and I can move back into my own bedroom. Then I will sleep as a Prussian should on a board floor. I have looked forward to it for years."

He returned to admire the new floor; Esperanza finished her coffee.

"I'll want a bath at eleven," she told Lilith; and, humming happily, she moved through the Garcia patio, where the twins maintained utter and wide-eyed silence, and on to the temporary store, where she studied accounts and waited on a few early customers. At 10:43, when the Archuletas arrived, a slow, powerful excitement pounded in her wrists, but she didn't show herself. She left the store at eleven, and went to her bedroom. For once, Lilith was right on time with a kettle of steaming water; Esperanza stripped and sponge-bathed. By now she had forgiven her slave's tippling, and she chattered happily about the net she would weave to ensnare Gilberto, but Lilith's responses were monosyllabic: still sulking! Niggers, Esperanza thought, were a great trial.

"You may go," she said, after she had toweled herself; and Lilith, looking sullen, lugged out the bath water. Esperanza lay naked on the bed, blowing cigarette smoke at the *vigas,* her shining hair enriching the pillow, her body enjoying the smooth counterpane and the warm air which flowed through the high, latticed window. Sometimes she lifted a leg, smooth and beautifully-shaped, and admired its classic lines and rich caramel color. As the minutes passed she became more aware of the excitement singing through her body; she felt hollow in the stomach; and when in imagination she rehearsed her coming activities she experienced the familiar sensation of invisible thumbs choking her windpipe. But it was a delicious choking. At twelve Lilith knocked and said food was ready.

"Lilith," Esperanza sang out, "I'm too excited to eat."

"Yes, ma'am," Lilith said, standing in the doorway on one foot, gently massaging her calf with the other.

"Do you think it will be all right?"

"Yes, ma'am."

"What's the matter, Lilith?"

"Ain't nothing the matter, Miss Esperanza."

The door closed. After another cigarette Esperanza sat on the bed brushing her hair, which fell nearly to her waist, richer than all the lavish treasure of which Spain had ever dreamed. Under her brush strokes it crackled. Then she wove it into two girlish plaits, and these she wound on her head. Naked before her mirror, she looked queenly as some brown and gold empress from fantasy.

From the dresser she selected a needle and returned to the bed. With a fingertip she tested the point. Sharp! Till now all had been pleasure, but this she dreaded. Her palm caressed the inner flesh of her right leg, some distance above her knee; smooth, smooth, tender. She hesitated, then, her long jaw resolute, she stabbed the needle into her flesh. She winced, waited a moment, withdrew it. A drop of blood showed against the creamy beige. She rolled a cigarette.

Early afternoon had come when she scented her nakedness with French water, stepped into low slippers, engirdled her waist with a crisp linen skirt, of peacock blue and brilliant orange, and her bosom with a blouse of *bois de rose*. She was ready. And breathing rapidly. In the hall she heard Otto's voice from the temporary store, discussing with Lilith the folkways of ants. Esperanza glided into the Garcia patio, dazzling after her shadowy bedroom, and stole noiselessly toward the old store. Lilith's mother, she thought, had hatched her scheme none too soon, for the wooden floor had triumphantly laid itself in both front rooms and had marched more than halfway through the kitchen. On the balls of her feet, Esperanza moved to the front door. The stacks of lumber had diminished to a few boards, but they served well as a siesta couch for Archuleta and son. Juan was snoring. Gilberto lay still. Esperanza cleared her throat. Gilberto's sombrero moved; silently he arose and came tiptoeing, grinning boyishly.

"I was awake," he whispered. "I was waiting for you."

On this of all days she wished to avoid disturbing Juan Archuleta, so with only a smile for reply she led the way through the kitchen, her full skirt dipping and swishing, her breathing fast. She paused in the shade of the cottonwood, caressing him with her eyes. She felt very female.

"Gilberto," she said, "it is good to see you."

"I have been thinking about you all morning," he said.

She looked away. Somewhere a warbler chirped in the heat. The patio was filled with a low monotonous humming of bees in the flowers.

"The floor is almost laid," she said.

"*Sí.* We should finish tomorrow."

"It has seemed so short a time," she said. "It is like yesterday when I went to your house and the parrot squawked. How is your little parrot?"

"She enjoys good health."

"When you no longer come to lay the floor I will miss you," she said.

"I will miss you too. When the siesta comes I will remember other siestas on other days. I will remember the girl with the bright hair."

"It is sad to think about," she said.

"*Si,* when I think of it my heart is heavy."

Esperanza's heart was hammering. Her feet felt light as a floating cobweb when she drifted slowly toward the wall where flowers grew. Picking a poppy, her fingers shook. She stood twirling the stem, pensively staring at the blur the revolving petals made. Then suddenly she gasped, dropped the flower, seized her skirt and shook it.

"But what is wrong?" Gilberto asked.

"Something stuck me. It was like a needle."

"But what could it have been?"

"Look!" she exclaimed, pointing. "A bee! It buzzed under my skirt and stung me. And now it is buzzing away."

"Esperanza," he said, "I am sorry the bee stung you. Does it hurt?"

She bit her lip; her eyes looked pitiful.

"I am afraid it does a little. But it will be all right."

"You are very brave."

"It will stop hurting after a time. Let us talk of something else and I will forget it."

"*Si,* a wonderful idea."

"I will tell you about my furniture. Did I ever tell you how it traveled all the way from St. Louis?"

"I do not believe you did."

"Ooo," she said, "it is very fine furniture. There is a bed, a dresser, a mirror and two chairs. It is most handsome."

"I am sure it is."

She stared off toward the Garcia patio.

"I will do something nice for you, Gilberto. I will show it to you."

"Do you think you should?"

"But why not?"

He was blushing.

"During the siesta," he said, hesitantly, "when everybody is sleeping, perhaps we should not go to your bedroom."

"But in my house we do not observe the siesta."

"*Si,* that is true. I had forgotten."

"Everybody is awake in my house. It will be quite proper."

"*Si,* perhaps it will."

Her skirt trembled over her hips and rippled and swished as she led the way. Once, in the center of the Garcia patio, where Lilith sat dozing over her needlework, Esperanza stopped suddenly, wincing, as if in pain.

"But what is the matter?" he asked.

"It is nothing," she said. "It is only the place where the bee stung my leg. For a moment I felt stabbed again. Perhaps the stinger is still in my flesh."

"I am sorry," he said. "The sting of a bee is painful."

She started on, then paused when he did not follow. He was smiling, regarding Lilith, who sat in the shade with her mouth open, her head lolling, lost in sleep.

"It is plain that some in your house observe the siesta," he whispered. Esperanza's eyes narrowed.

"I will waken her," she said.

"Do you think you should? She seems very tired."

"It is only that she is suffering a hangover. Last night she was a bad nigger and drank too much."

"In that case it would be better to let her sleep. I have never suffered from a *sobrante* but now and then my father has. He says it is enough to drive a man from drink."

"I will waken her," Esperanza whispered, "in a manner that she will believe a bee stung her. Then we will run."

"Do not bring her pain," Gilberto said.

Esperanza tiptoed to Lilith's chair, plucked the needle from the sewing in her lap and jabbed it into her arm.

"Yow-ow!"

Leaving the needle where she had inserted it, Esperanza scampered lightly to the back door.

"Hurry!" she urged Gilberto.

And she fled into the hall and on to her bedroom. Inside, with the door closed, she yielded to giggling. Gilberto was smiling dubiously.

"I hope you did not hurt her too much."

"You can't hurt a nigger," Esperanza said. "Their hide is very tough."

"But if you did not hurt her, why did she jump?"

"She always jumps. But she hardly feels the needle because her hide is so tough."

In the bedroom, with its thick adobe walls and solid door, all was dusky and quiet, and Esperanza spoke in whispers as she conducted Gilberto on a tour of the furniture. He had, he said, never seen furniture like that before; he stood looking curiously at the bed.

"Do you really sleep on that?"

"*Si*," she whispered.

"Is there not danger of its tumbling down?"

"Ooo, no! See how strong it is?"

She sat on it, bouncing up and down.

"I wonder why it does not collapse," he said.

"Because it is made to be strong. It would even hold us both."

"Is that possible?"

"*Si*. Sit beside me, Gilberto, and you will learn its strength."

He hesitated. She extended her hand. He took it and she pulled him down beside her.

"*Si*," he said, "*si*." He spoke with difficulty, as if he had been running. "It is strong."

Silence. Esperanza still clutched his hand, which felt feverish.

"Suppose," he whispered, "the door should suddenly open. It might look odd to somebody finding us sitting like this."

"The door will not open," she said. "When I close it nobody dares open it unless I give permission."

"But suppose your father would come looking for you."

"He will not. But if he did he would see the door closed and think I was bathing. He would not open it."

Silence again. Esperanza's tonsils felt dry; her heart was racing. She still held Gilberto's hand. Suddenly she clutched it tightly and gasped.

"What is the matter?"

"It is the place where the bee stabbed me. I think he left a stinger in my flesh."

"*Si*, if it keeps hurting perhaps he did."

"Gilberto."

"*Si?*"

"Would you do something for me?"

"What is it you wish?"

"Would you find the place where the bee stabbed me and squeeze out the stinger?"

She could feel his hand shaking in hers. His voice also shook.

"Do you think it would be proper?"

"*Si*," she said.

*

In the patio Lilith sat rubbing her arm, face sullen. Presently she stood up and shuffled to the back door of the Garcia house, staring along the hall. Then, moving painfully with her sore legs, she turned back into the patio where she stood scowling.

"If I dared," she muttered.

After a minute she started for the patio behind the original store. Paused. Returned. Scowled.

"If I only dared do it."

She stood rubbing her arm. At last she started again toward the other patio, and this time she proceeded into the original store and out to the street where Juan Archuleta lay under his sombrero.

For a full minute she stood staring down at him. Then she shook his shoulder. He came awake reluctantly.

"*Señor*," she said, racking her brain for her scanty Spanish, "your son—"

But she couldn't remember the Spanish words.

"What about my son?"

"Gilberto," she said, "and Esperanza."

He was wide awake now, and he knew a little English. At last, by means of his meager English and her meager Spanish, and a generous use of sign language, she secured his promise never to say where he had heard what she would tell him. Then she told. He sprang to his feet and, following Lilith's directions, strode through the original store and on to the Garcia house and to Esperanza's bedroom door, which he flung open.

*

The scandal was very great. By nightfall half the town knew it; by morning all the town. Not since that long-ago era when La Luz Delgado hammered the door of Otto's store, screaming insults, had the town been so titillated. Like tumbleweed the rumors rolled along the streets, picking up dusty gossip and the debris of conjecture. It was hard to separate the true from the false, so hard that nobody tried.

Señor Zumwalt had challenged *Señor* Archuleta to a duel: false. When *Señor* Archuleta opened the bedroom door he had surprised his son and Esperanza in a questionable situation: true. He had raged: true. Esperanza had hurled a chamberpot which had shattered against *Señor* Archuleta's skull: false. She had thrown a pillow: true. He had slapped her: true. She had flung a pitcher which had struck his temple: true and false: he had successfully dodged. The disturbance had brought *Señor* Zumwalt from the temporary store, and he had objected to *Señor* Archuleta's calling Esperanza a harlot: true.

So it went: so difficult to know precisely what happened.

But a few facts were incontrovertible. *Señor* Archuleta had indeed discovered those heedless teen-agers up to something; he had received scratches, and he had, in the melee, blackened *Señor* Zumwalt's left eye. Then he had kicked his son's fleeing rear-end from the bedroom to the original store, where in high dudgeon he had collected his carpenter's tools, demanded and received his wages, and gone stalking homeward, lecturing his son.

Incontrovertible too was the fact that during the following week the proposed alliance, by wedlock, between the Ortiz and Archuleta families was gravely threatened. *Señor* Ortiz took the reasonable position that if a betrothed young man wished to dally with a girl of dubious morals he should at least have the common sense to lock the door. *Señor* Archuleta agreed that such a precautionary measure was basic, but he excused his son on the grounds of youth and inexperience. *Señor* Ortiz was not so sure this exonerated the lad: he thought Gilberto's negligence might indicate an innate carelessness not desirable in a son-in-law. At last, however, a compromise was struck: it was agreed that *Señorita* Ortiz's dowry should be reduced, and that Gilberto should journey with a caravan to Mexico City, marrying upon his return. If he actually were of a flagrantly careless nature, he would probably be surprised and scalped by Apaches on the trip; if not, his safe return would be acceptable evidence of his prudence. So about ten days after the flurry in Esperanza's bedroom, Gilberto left Santa Fe. By then his father had forgiven him, and his parting injunction was that if Gilberto found he simply must succumb to the temptations of Mexico, why by God boy lock that door!

Among the inconveniences resulting from Lilith's treachery was the harrowing fact that *Señor* Archuleta had walked off the job without completing the floor. Otto's black eye, with assistance from raw beefsteak, healed itself; but the floor made absolutely no move to lay itself. Nearly half the kitchen was still without wood. During those first days when his eye was swollen and his spirit anguished, Otto used to stand regarding the unfinished work, sighing, taking a swig of Taos Lightning, which helped a little in anesthetizing his sorrow; and so deeply did he yearn for a completed floor that he even considered asking *Señor* Archuleta to return with his tools. But he couldn't do that: it simply wasn't in the nature of a *Junker* to beg favors from a cowardly scoundrel who had blackened his eye. So in the end Otto himself went to work with hammer and saw. And he was amazed at how simple the task proved. A morning did it. He didn't even smash his thumb.

"*Ja*," he thought, "I am as good a carpenter as that Archuleta. He needn't think he is so smart, going around breaking into bedrooms and blacking people's eyes."

So he had his floor. But it didn't, after all, bring unalloyed happiness or even inner peace. Otto, the truth was, knew no more about what had occurred in Esperanza's bedroom than did the town, and he hesitated to ask: he feared she might tell him. So long as she avoided the subject, so did he; and she avoided it conspicuously. For that matter, she avoided her father and the customers, remaining in her bedroom for hours at a time, sometimes emerging to wander about the patio or to go walking late at night when the town slept, her eyes swollen, her disposition plumbing new depths. Lilith, in excellent spirits again, brought the latest gossip back from market: thus Esperanza learned that Gilberto had departed for Mexico, to be gone months, perhaps years, perhaps forever.

Otto most feared that a day would come when she would bring him news of approaching grandparenthood. *Ach,* a baby with beady black eyes, swarthy skin, inky hair. Spain, the Aztecs, the Apaches absorbing and obliterating the blondness and the bravery of the proudest family in Prussia.

"I couldn't stand it," he thought, but he knew he would stand it if he had to, the way he and all humanity had always stood so much.

The scandal injured business, not because customers lacked, for the whole town kept flocking to the Street of the Chamiso, in anticipation of *Señor* Zumwalt's black eye, and in hopes of seeing his daughter; but Otto had closed the store. Closed for remodeling, *ja!* That would show those dirty scandal eaters! It was a valid excuse too, for with the floor laid Otto and Lilith were busy lugging the trade goods from the Garcia house back to the original store. It took a long time; the midsummer weather was blazing and they rested between trips. Sometimes Otto shared a nip of Taos Lightning with Lilith, providing she would promise not to tell Esperanza. She promised vehemently. Once he whispered to Lilith his worry about Esperanza's possible pregnancy, and out of the wisdom of long racial tribulation she advised him not to go hunting trouble, no sir, not even to meet trouble half way. She didn't, she said, have much idea what actually had happened in the bedroom, for Esperanza had clammed up, but as she judged the situation Gilberto was a boy given to taking his time, so she doubted whether he had moved with much more celerity than molasses in January. This comforted Otto, although he was still dazed that his daughter—hardly more than a child—had been victimized by one of nature's livelier instincts.

"What you've got to expect," Lilith said. "That girl has been panting for some time now. You ask me, that girl will always pant. She see a man she want and ain't nothing will stop her."

*

The store's reopening, in its original quarters, was a smashing success, for although Otto's black eye had returned to normal the town wished to verify this for itself, just as it wished to inspect the wooden floor and to check on the circumference of Esperanza's waist. But she disappointed everybody by keeping to her room. Her absence fueled the gossip and also increased business, for customers kept returning day after day hoping she would appear. She didn't, for several weeks. In her room, or in a secluded corner of the patio, she sulked and sorrowed and daydreamed and read; and sometimes, to while away the hours, she turned to algebra or geometry. As for the circumference of her waist, there had never been the slightest hazard of its increasing, for Lilith had been wholly correct in her estimate of Gilberto's capacity for delay; when the bedroom door flew open the fool had still been searching for the bee's stinger.

With the passing weeks Esperanza recovered quite nicely from her grand passion, for nature had liberally endowed her with Spanish and feminine realism in such matters: Gilberto had gone to Mexico and that was that; but her dejection persisted because she saw no future in Santa Fe except living on with Otto, clerking in the store and reading about love instead of participating in it. Always the town girls had avoided friendship with her, and she suspected that now they were snickering at her failure to enmesh Gilberto. As for the boys, her good sense told her that the bedroom episode would doubtless whet their interest in strolling with her along some dark lane, but not in forming any enduring partnership. Archuleta had called her a harlot, and Lilith reported that now the town was calling her that. She was finished in Santa Fe. Even back when her reputation was sullied only by her father's eccentricities and her great-grandmother's association with Satan, achieving marriage would have taken a bit of doing, for in New Mexico marriage was oftener than not arranged by parents; and what parents would have sought out the mad *alemán* as a future father-in-law for a son? Now it was hopeless.

So she read and reread Byron and Moliere and Tacitus and the Restoration dramatists, looking forward to the arrival of this year's caravan with new volumes; and thinking about the caravan reminded her of the bull whackers. Some were young. But they all chewed tobacco. Still, they were men. But lumpkins, drifters, penniless ne'er-do-wells. It would be nice, she thought, to marry a man of means.

By August, even reading and geometry palled, so out of boredom she returned to her duties in the store. This gave business another shot in the arm. And when customers said they were just looking they certainly told the truth: Esperanza's willowy waist, the most interesting and finest piece of merchandise in the place, was the cynosure of all eyes, even of Otto's. And he did more than look; he was always inquiring about her health. Had she chanced to experience sickness at her stomach on arising? Were her bodily functions maintaining an efficient Prussian schedule? Did she ever feel faint?

His solicitude earned him only her contempt, for she instantly deduced what occasioned it; so for a couple of weeks she had fun inventing horrendous symptoms that brought anxiety to his eyes and set him to pacing and pulling his mustache. Finally she wearied of the game and asked:

"Why so interested? Do you think I'm pregnant?"

A wave of crimson suffused his ears and bald head.

"Pregnant! *Mein Gott,* what are you saying! No, of course not! You aren't, are you?"

"Father! I think that's insulting! You should be ashamed!"

"*Ja,* sure, of course, I am ashamed. Asking my innocent daughter such a thing. But maybe if you would tell me I would sleep better."

"You'll find out," she said.

Long before Otto stopped fretting, the town regretfully concluded that no more scandal would ensue from that midsummer afternoon's scheme, and business subsided to normal.

One hot August day during the siesta, when Otto was puttering with his flowers in the patio, and Esperanza sat reading *Venus and Adonis* in the store, she heard the hoofbeats of a horse, and at the window she watched a man dismounting. Not a Mexican; not anybody she knew. A carbine bristled from his saddle-sling; his trail boots were dusty, his blue shirt sweat-splotched. He tied the reins to a cottonwood across the way and patted the horse, then turned toward the store.

She was lost in her book when his boots scuffed over the threshold; the pungence of horseflesh and sweat wafted into her nostrils. She glanced up. From the window he had looked young, but now she saw he was probably in his forties, a tough-muscled man with heavy shoulders and a chest powerful above a tight belt with a holstered knife. His thumbs were hooked in his belt, and his thick hands were freckled and stubby-fingered. She noticed his blocky jaw and bulbous nose and red eyebrows; his skin was sun-reddened under its film of dust; his blue eyes were cool with self-assurance. His lips were thick and weather-cracked, the lower lip protruding, as if his false teeth had been fitted cumbrously; he was smiling.

"You're better looking than your mother," he said, his voice low with almost a wary quality, as if adventuring in many tight places had taught him to speak softly. "And I don't see your father in you at all, except your hair."

She was taken aback and not displeased. And she thought she had never encountered a man so quietly sure of himself. He made her feel childishly young and yet intensely feminine; she didn't know what to say.

When he took off his hat she saw that his short red hair, unruly as wire grass, was salted with gray. His eyes had shifted to her book.

"Shakespeare," he said. "I've seen his plays on the stage. They're all right. But I thought Shylock got a raw deal. And that nigger who married a white woman. He was quite a fellow. He wouldn't have liked it in Mississippi."

"On the stage! You've been in a theater?"

"They're mainly firetraps," he said. "Tell your father Caleb McSwasey is here."

*

McSwasey! *Mein Gott!* Oh, friendship!

Otto's enthusiastic greeting lasted several minutes, and before it was over tears welled into his eyes. McSwasey in Santa Fe! Imagine! But when did he arrive? Why was he here? Was it possible! After all these years! *Ach!*

Through it all, Esperanza noticed how amusement twinkled in the visitor's eyes and how a smile quirked his dusty lips. He was not, she decided, a handsome man, for his face with its tough jaw looked hammered inexpertly from rock and battered by its assaults on existence, but certainly he exuded maleness the way a stallion on a frosty morning exuded steam. One could not imagine him hiding in an outhouse during a revolution, or putting up with monkeyshines from a daughter, or blundering away precious minutes searching for a bee's stinger. He looked, she thought with odd excitement, as tough as a buffalo, capable of slugging it out with rebellious mule skinners and of mastering fractious horses and women.

"You seem glad to see me," he said, when Otto paused for breath.

"Glad to see you! *Gott im Himmel!* My best friend!"

These sounds of celebration carried even to the Garcia patio, where Lilith had been dozing; now her bare feet slapped through the kitchen.

In the doorway she paused, blinking; then recognition burst over her.

"Mistah McSwasey! Eee!"

And with arms outstretched she hurtled forward.

"'Member me?" she shrieked. "You ain't forgot Lilith? You ain't forgot that trip to Taos?"

Lilith had grown as big as a cow; her sheer weight would have knocked over most men; but McSwasey hardly budged. After disengaging himself he said:

"Those Taos Injuns are real lady killers."

Volcanic laughter erupted.

"Eee! Mistah McSwasey! You be the death of me yet! No, sir! Them Injuns ain't got no shine like a high class gentleman. Them Injuns all right in a pinch, but that's all. Eee! 'Member how you wallop me? 'Member how mad you was?"

He smiled.

"Hod Kite would have raised the rent," he said, "if he'd known there were two."

Lilith bent in almost convulsive mirth.

"Mistah McSwasey," she gasped, "you is always saying the damndest! You is always got me laughing."

"I know niggers," he said; and that statement of obvious fact nearly did her in.

A polite smile flitted beneath Otto's mustache; Esperanza's eyes looked opaque.

"That will do, Lilith," she said.

"Eee . . ." Lilith backhanded laughter-tears from her eyes.

"You may go."

"Eee . . . Yes, ma'am. Eee . . ."

Reluctantly, she splay-footed it toward the kitchen. In the door she turned, almost coquettishly.

"You like to see my twins?"

"Injun?" McSwasey asked.

She nearly collapsed. At last she was able to speak.

"I'll get 'em scrubbed and dressed. Yes, sir. I make fine little niggers. Wish you could have seen my boy, Wisdom."

After she had gone, Otto looked expectantly at McSwasey, as if willing to have the jokes explained. But his best friend only said:

"You must eat well here."

Otto looked baffled.

"Ja, sure, that is true. I like plenty of food. Are you hungry?"

"My throat is dry."

"Ach, what is the matter with me! Ja, of course, after the saddle. I will get Taos Lightning."

"I'll get it, father," Esperanza said; and, obedient daughter that she was, she glided to the kitchen, hips swinging in honor of the guest.

And in further honor of the occasion, even Esperanza sipped a little Lightning, despite her father's scowl. Glass aloft, Otto proposed a lengthy toast. At its conclusion McSwasey nodded, said "Luck," and tossed down his drink. Esperanza hurried to pour him another.

"You came with the caravan?" Otto asked.

He had ridden in ahead of it, McSwasey said; it would be along in a day or so. Yes, a good trip out. A little trouble with the Comanches, of course. They bothered more than they used to. Nothing, however, to worry about.

Ach!

"How's Hod Kite?" McSwasey asked. "I didn't stop at his joint on the way in."

"He is the same old Hod. A wonderful fellow. My second-best friend, just as you are my first. We will have him to eat with us tonight and it will be a fine reunion. *Ja,* and of course you must plan to stay right here with us."

"You have room for me?"

"Room for my best friend? *Ach!* I will give you my bed here in the store and I will sleep with the niggers."

"No need of that. I'll put down a blanket in the patio."

"*Ach,* no! In my bed. I do not mind sleeping with the niggers."

"No," Esperanza put in, "he has slept with Lilith before."

McSwasey looked at her. They both smiled.

*

The party that evening in the *Casa* Zumwalt was a radiant and joyous occasion, one long glorification of friendship. Upon inviting Hod, Otto did not tell him of McSwasey's arrival, so the affair among its other ecstasies achieved surprise-party status. Otto was waiting outside the store when at six-thirty Hod came trudging along the street, clean-shaved and fresh-shirted; the host shook the guest's hand warmly, quite as if he had not talked with him three hours before, then ushered him into the store where McSwasey sat grinning, all bathed and shaved and clean-clad, smelling of bay rum.

"I want you to meet a friend of mine," Otto said.

"What was the name again?" McSwasey asked.

Hod stared, then vaulted into the air, kicking his heels together and letting loose a whoop that was part Injun and part ancestor of the rebel yell. From the kitchen door Lilith's suppressed mirth exploded, and her mother, Panthea, a lively little ninety pounder, who had been secretly lured from Hod's living quarters to aid in preparing the banquet, and who looked as wrinkled and wise as an old monkey, added to the merriment. The twins, pigtails flying, shrieked with joy and cakewalked. Otto was saying something about friendship; only Esperanza remained silent.

In his astonishment, Hod repeatedly took the Lord's name in vain and called McSwasey an old nigger stealer; but it was all in fun. Presently the host, his daughter and his guests adjourned to the patio, where Lilith served drinks. Hod started to refuse; then, in honor of the tremendous occasion, he declared that by God he would have one: it would be, he said, pretty small of a man to think of longevity at a time like this. This example of what friendship could do brought a lump to Otto's throat; he was so carried away that he told Lilith she and her mother might each have a short one. As it happened, they had anticipated his generosity, but in her gratitude Lilith did not mention that. Esperanza also drank; by the time supper was served only the cats were wholly sober, for even the twins had been given a few spoonfuls equally compounded of sugar and Lightning.

With the cooks toasting each other in the kitchen, supper was delayed, but nobody minded, not even Esperanza. Her intention had been to swallow drink for drink with the others, because then Mr. McSwasey would realize she was a young woman of the world, but after the second round she decided there were doubtless other ways to gain his approbation, and she nursed her third glass; she didn't want to pass out. As the long summer twilight waned and dusk filled the corners and the first stars sparkled, she sat smiling sweetly, quiet as a flower and as fragrant, wrapped in as much universal mystery as the cat at her feet and the stars glowing out beyond the light-years. Now and then she sipped her drink. Odd how it burned when it slipped down her throat. Like drinking sunlight. Her thoughts were large, far-wandering in past and future. Once I stabbed a man. Long ago. He breathed and then he did not breathe. I brought that about. I am always remembering it. Why? He shouldn't have chased me. He made a mistake when he chased a girl with Apache blood. A skull now and bones dry in the earth. And they sent Gilberto to Mexico. Because of me. Where are you tonight, oh foolish Gilberto? By a campfire on the southern desert? Thinking of me? I am not thinking of you. Not really. You are nothing to me now. The world is a great world, Gilberto. There are many men, Gilberto. The world is more than Santa Fe. The world is Fontainebleau in a book and a forest called Arden and golden isles by a wine-dark sea. The world is Rome in blazing sunlight and men with golden beards in the Black Forest and a city called St. Louis. It is a trail from Santa Fe to St. Louis. There are theaters and restaurants with wine and canvasback. Look for me when you return, Gilberto, and I will not be here. I think I am going to St. Louis, Gilberto. He does not know it yet but he will take me. He keeps looking at me, Gilberto. He has false teeth but he is very strong. He has much money, Gilberto. He is St. Louis and a world of silks and lights and lovers.

So she sat sipping her drink, her thoughts befuddled and bedazzled, while from the kitchen floated an occasional peal of laughter mingling with her father's declaration that Billy Proudfoot certainly did not sneak past his guard, and with Hod Kite's recitals of brave deeds in the long ago. Darkness had fallen now and Caleb McSwasey was a shadow. Once her father launched upon a disquisition applauding friendship, and Hod interrupted to assert that in honor of McSwasey's visit he would arrange a fandango tomorrow night in his saloon, and would everybody come? *Ja*, sure, her father said, he would attend if nothing prevented it, he had always enjoyed fandangos because they afforded fine opportunity to rough up these filthy Mexicans who were so lax they preferred an inefficient soldiery to paying taxes—not that he favored taxes!—a curse!— but it was undeniable that without taxes one could not properly equip troops—

"Can you come, Caleb?" Hod asked.

"I might drop in to hear the music," he said. And he addressed a question to the patio at large. "Will Esperanza go?"

She replied instantly, the words shaping themselves deep in her brain and springing from her tongue without conscious volition.

"I have never learned to dance. I will go if you will take me and teach me."

There was a moment of silence, broken only by the uncontrolled laughter from the kitchen, and then in the darkness McSwasey spoke.

"It's time a pretty girl like you knew how to dance."

She realized then that she had been all but holding her breath, and suddenly gladness flared in her brain and she knew that despite his worldliness he was only a man like her father who could be twisted to her wishes and led by the nose and used. And she had a swift vision of the world far beyond Santa Fe, the world she had found in novels and in the memoirs of royal courtesans: the gay world of brilliant balls where champagne flowed and soft-throated violins murmured dulcet songs and men—countless, endless men—men handsome and polished and boundlessly rich—flocked around a vivacious girl begging the next waltz.

"*Ja*," her father was saying, "I should have taught her to dance, but if I had done so she would have been chasing off to those dangerous fandangos with these Mexican boys who are so hot-blooded it worries me. But for you to teach her is different. You are my best friend. You I can trust. *Ja*, and if there is fighting you are handy with your fists so it will be safe enough for her to go."

"And you will also be there, father, to protect me from the Mexican knives."

"*Ja*, of course I will be, that is if I can make it. But we are very busy just now with the store—we are hardly settled on our fine new board floor—the best in New Mexico if I do say so myself—so it might be I could not attend much as I would like to, but you people go and have a good time."

"We'll work at it," McSwasey said.

"Ooo, yes! It will be a great honor to attend as the partner of a man like Mr. McSwasey."

"The honor is not the point," Otto said. "It is the teaching you to dance that is important. *Ja,* it is time you knew. I was once the best dancer in New Orleans. Fairy-footed Zumwalt, they called me. You should be very happy that a busy man like my best friend is willing to do it."

"Ooo, I have never been so happy about anything."

Hod Kite, who had flung to the winds any hope of outliving Methuselah, broke into laughter.

"Listen to the gal! I've never known it to fail! Old Caleb and the ladies! How do you do it, Sport?"

"What is he talking about, Otto?" McSwasey asked.

"*Ja,* well, I think he has had too much to drink."

"Ha!" Hod exclaimed. "*In vino veritas,* as that preacher used to say. But let me tell you, Esperanzy. Don't get him jealous. He's killed men on account of the ladies."

"Only one," McSwasey said.

"One! More like twenty. Don't let his quiet talk fool you, Esperanzy. That muskrat's got ice for a brain and he can out-scheme a Chinaman. And nerves like steel wire. Once in Nacogdoches I seen a bastard pull a gun on him. 'I'm going to drop you,' the bastard says. 'No,' Caleb says, 'I don't think you are.' The whole barroom separated them, and damn if old Caleb don't walk right up to him and take his gun and slap his face. And then buy him a drink. Remember that, Caleb?"

"I didn't buy him a drink."

"Anyway, you get the idea. So watch yourself, Esperanzy. The ladies all like him."

"Hod should sober up or else have another shot," McSwasey told Otto.

"*Ja,* well, of course it is true, the ladies have always liked you and me. I think it is our hair."

"What hair, Sport?" Hod asked.

"Sure, *ja,* I know, mine has thinned, but you should have seen the girls chase me when I was young. Blond hair and red hair the ladies like. It was nothing in Paris for me to ride along the boulevards in a carriage with a pretty girl on each side. *Ja,* but those French women are all diseased. Anyway it has been my experience that friendship lasts longer than love. Friendship is—"

A few minutes later Lilith, gleefully unsteady, lighted the candles on the table and announced supper. Esperanza finished her drink and took Mr. McSwasey's arm, following the example of great ladies in Parisian novels, and as she drifted along beside him toward the table she thought his limp was fetchingly romantic, like the limp of Lord Byron, and she wished those vixenish Mexican girls could see her now, escorted to supper by a man of wealth and vast experience in the great world. She indicated his place at her right; he flourished out her chair at the head of the table; and she sat there looking slender and virginal and desirable, her skin golden brown and coppery in the candleshine, her hair spectacular, her black eyes bewitching, her face vivid as a gypsy girl's and complex with many races. In her ears, which were crisply and beautifully stamped out of beige flesh, she wore turquoise jewels, the sky stones of her native land, and a necklace of turquoise and silver encircled her lovely throat and lost itself between the swelling smoothness of her breasts. She felt on the threshold of great events. What was Gilberto to her now? How callow he seemed, how bungling, how mawkishly young when compared with the soft-spoken man on her right! She felt as heedless and tipsy as some golden-winged moth which the sun-soaked nectar from Taos had released from the chrysalis of her girlish uncertainty. She touched Mr. McSwasey's sleeve; she leaned toward him, surrendering utterly her gaze to his; her voice was low, honeyed, intimate.

"Tell me about St. Louis," she said.

*

Late that night after the rest of the household had retired, Otto and Caleb sat in the patio with bedtime cigars and drinks, discussing business and friendship and Comanches.

"I suppose you're wondering," McSwasey said, "why I've come to Santa Fe."

"*Ja,* I have thought of it."

"It's because I've sold my business."

"You have done what?"

"I've sold the business in St. Louis. Gave possession May first."

"*Mein Gott!*"

"I'm going into lumbering."

"Lumbering, already! But you will not like that! If I told you how long it took to get those few boards for my floor—"

"Lumbering's different, in Wisconsin. A man can make a potful of pennies in the pineries."

"But—but—"

Otto felt dazed.

"So I sold out."

A terrible suspicion slithered through the garden of friendship in Otto's mind. Sold out! The business in St. Louis, *ja,* and maybe the business in Santa Fe also! His best friend selling him out like a lazy nigger!

"You sold the Santa Fe branch too?" he asked slowly.

"Do you think I'd do that without consulting you?"

"*Ach,* no, of course not. My thoughts are all tangled tonight like recruits at drill. Maybe I have had too much Lightning."

"I kept this business, Otto. And I've come to give you a chance at it."

"But what do you mean?"

"To give you first chance to buy it."

"Me? Me own the whole Santa Fe branch already so it is no longer a branch?"

"Why not?"

"*Ach,* me run it all alone without my best friend to depend on?"

"You've been running it sixteen years."

"*Ja,* I know, but I have been the general in the field and you have been the king. You have told me what to do."

"I sent you watches you couldn't sell."

"Not my fault! These Mexican cowards—"

"Of course it wasn't your fault. That's what I'm driving at. You're on the ground and you know what merchandise will move. You can run it better alone. You'll make a potful of pennies."

"*Ja,* sure, but—"

"That loan you made me will help you buy it."

"*Ja,* it isn't that I don't have capital. I have been a thrifty fellow, saving my money in gold eagles and in Spanish doubloons."

"Gold, eh?" McSwasey said softly.

"That is right, I like my money in gold. I have plenty hidden around the house, so I could buy the store if I wished, but without my best friend to guide me—"

"The caravans will still bring you goods. You own the building. You know the trade. What's stopping you?"

In the darkness Otto scowled; his mustache was taking a terrible pulling.

"I think maybe," he said hesitantly, "it is the responsibility. It is not that I am afraid of running it alone, but—but—well, maybe I am a little afraid. All my life when I have done anything by myself it has turned out badly. I buy a nigger and after a while I have a stable full. I chase a girl in the moonlight and before long a cowardly old buzzard is living with me and will not move out even when I hint I wish she would. I run away from the university and before I know it I get a dose of clap in Paris. *Ja,* and I start for Indian country and poor Billy Proudfoot is killed. When I touch something it gets all tangled like a ball of yarn when my dear little Hilda used to play with it."

"Who was Hilda? One of your nigger kids?"

"A nigger! What are you saying! *Mein Gott,* no! Hilda was my little cat I loved so much."

"You'd make good profits," McSwasey said.

"*Ja,* but I think I like it better working for wages."

"You could put up a new sign over the door. It would look nice. Otto Zumwalt & Company."

"That is true, *ja.* It would show these lazy Mexicans a thing or two, except of course most of them cannot read. Even my dear wife was so ignorant she could not read. But my daughter reads all the time."

"And you'd be helping me out, Otto. You'd be helping out a friend."

"Helping you? That is different, already! By buying the business I would be helping my best friend?"

"I could use the money," McSwasey said. "I'll need plenty where I'm going."

"*Gott im Himmel!* Why didn't you say so in the first place? Nobody can say I ever failed to help a friend. I do not want to run the business all by myself, but if it means so much to you to sell it maybe I will buy it. What do you want for it?"

"We can go into that later. I've got another proposition too. How would you like to be my partner?"

"Partner with my best friend! *Mein Gott,* I can think of nothing so wonderful! But I thought you wanted to sell the branch—"

"I mean in the lumber business."

"Lumber, already! When it takes so long to get a few boards—"

"In Wisconsin. I've been up there. She's loaded with opportunity, Otto. Lord, we'd end up rich. White pine. Acres of it, hundreds of acres, thousands. Rich and virgin. Just waiting to be grabbed. It would make your mouth water. It would make your tongue drip. You can walk all day through those woods, and all the next and all the next. You can keep walking for a month and never leave them. Pines as straight and true as a ship's mast. Pines so big at the base that two men couldn't reach around them. Pines without a branch till you climb a hundred feet. And rivers to float 'em out. God! Talk about money! Talk about opportunity!"

"*Ja,* I know, but I am in Santa Fe—"

"I'll be in Wisconsin. We could organize as McSwasey & Zumwalt. With times what they are back in the States, if I'd take your specie into the woods I could buy anything. Those pinery boys would fight to work for me. McSwasey & Zumwalt. Lumber barons."

"McSwasey & Zumwalt," Otto said, his voice awe-struck. "Two lumber barons. Two friends . . ."

*

Otto slept on those proposals for several nights, but this was merely a formality. Actually, there was never any doubt that he would follow McSwasey's advice and buy the Santa Fe branch and go into partnership with his best friend.

Nor was there ever any doubt that he would grant a third request, this one propounded by his daughter. About a week before the caravan was scheduled to leave for the States, she informed him that she had decided to go to St. Louis for a bit of post-graduate work in a female seminary. Lilith could accompany her as chaperone.

Mein Gott! What an idea! No, of course not!

So it was all decided, and in the end Otto granted consent. Not, however, till he had discussed the matter with McSwasey, to whom it came as no surprise.

"You might as well let her," McSwasey said. "If she stays here she'll likely marry some greaser. Do you want that?"

Ach!

So at last, after sleeping with the problem, and storming about it, and muttering its pros and cons to his mustache, Otto told his best friend:

"*Ja,* maybe I will let her after all, if you will promise to take care of her."

McSwasey said he assuredly would take care of her.

And to Esperanza her father said:

"I have about decided to let you go. But you must promise that as soon as you reach St. Louis you will find a Lutheran church and talk to the pastor so that you can be confirmed. *Ja,* and I want it understood I do not mean one of these Reformed Lutheran churches either. Will you do that for your papa?"

"Maybe."

Lilith, of course, was ecstatic about the journey, although she too presented a request: that the twins go along. Certainly not, Otto said. It was going to be lonely in Santa Fe, and he wanted the twins for company, even if they did persist in tickling his nose so that he had nightmares. But one evening shortly before the scheduled departure McSwasey advised Otto to reconsider.

"The nigger market's pretty good in St. Louis," he said. "Especially for a couple of cuties like those twins who will be coming prime in a few years. Those twins would buy us a lot of stumpage in Wisconsin."

"*Mein Gott,* but they are my own flesh and blood! Their skins are nearly as light as Esperanza's."

"That's why they'll fetch a good price."

"*Ach,* no, I could not think of it. Prussian blood on the slave block! *Gott, Gott,* how did I get all mixed up with niggers? There is something about slavery that is not right. I have thought it over a great deal. I buy a nigger and pretty soon there are little niggers. They are my children and they will grow up and some day I will have grandchildren who are niggers, and it will go on and on. It will never stop. All because I came to América. All because I killed a fellow student in a duel and ran away from the university. In two hundred years there will be niggers with von Zumwalt blood all because I read a book by Rousseau. Sometimes I think I should have stayed in Prussia."

The twins, of course, joined the company bound for the States.

*

A September evening: clear, serene, star-spattered. In the morning, before sunrise, the caravan would depart for the States. Now its wagons lay scattered among the nopal and greasewood in the camp at the edge of town, the same site where another caravan had encamped sixteen years

276

before. Campfires flickered; somebody was strumming a banjo; men sang. An air of expectancy hung over the huge-wheeled wagons which in a few hours would begin rolling across the tableland and through the mountains toward the vast plains.

Around one campfire a little group had congregated, four females, two males. Everybody seemed exceedingly happy and excited, except one male of *Junker* extraction. Oddly, since he was not leaving with the caravan, he seemed the only member of the group anxious about the hazards of the journey. He kept mentioning an Indian Nation called Comanche. It would be prudent, he advised, to guard the caravan vigilantly against these cowards.

"We'll manage, I reckon," McSwasey said.

"*Ja,* I hope you have no trouble. Everything I hold so dear except of course my cats is going with this caravan. My beautiful daughter and my niggers. My best friend. The money I have saved."

"We'll manage. The Comanches don't like to fool around with a caravan as strong as this one."

"*Ja,* the cowards."

Lilith and the twins seemed as gladly anticipatory about the journey as any other of the wayfarers. From their gaiety it might have been supposed they were migrating toward freedom instead of toward one of the last great strongholds of chattel slavery in civilization.

"Them Comanches ain't going to pester us," Lilith assured Otto. "Not with Mistah McSwasey to shoot 'em dead."

The twins had gleefully discovered that a freight wagon was an excellent object around which to play tag. They raised such a racket that Esperanza dispatched an order, through channels, for them to desist or suffer the consequences.

"Hush up that squealing," Lilith called. "You hear? Hush that up or Miss Esperanza will take after you."

The twins quieted.

So the evening wore away, and presently it was time for Otto to return to his fine store.

"I would like to see you a moment alone," he told his daughter.

He led the way into the shadows of a wagon. Everything was quiet there, except for the music of the distant banjo and the voices of bull whackers lifted in song.

"I hope you have a good trip," he said.

"Thank you, I believe we will."

"Do not study too hard at that seminary but do not waste your time either."

She was silent.

"If you were a boy," he said, "and going to a university I would be worried. I mean because you would be fighting duels. It is in the von

277

Zumwalt blood not to accept insults. Like father, like son. *Ja*, I was always fighting the cowards in my student days."

"Were you?"

"*Ja*, sure. And in New Orleans also. They used to call me One-Ball Zumwalt."

"Did they?"

"Sure they did. Because I was such a dead shot. I hope you will be a good girl and study hard and maybe come back next year with the caravan."

No response.

"Or the year after," he added. "Do you think you will?"

"Who knows?"

"Another thing. I believe McSwasey would like to sell the twins in St. Louis to raise more money to buy stumpage. I would like it better if you would keep the twins and perhaps some day set them free."

"But father. That would be throwing away good money."

"*Ja*, I know, but there is something not quite right about slavery. If I had it to do over I would not buy a single slave. It is like Hod Kite says. You get one and you end up with a stable full. But in any case if you have to sell the twins I hope you sell them together and perhaps into a Lutheran family. And you understand I do not mean Reformed Lutheran."

No response.

"I hate to see you go," he said.

"It is better, father. There is nothing for me in Santa Fe."

"*Ja*, true, I would hate to have you stay here and marry some filthy Mexican. But I will miss you."

"Will you?"

"*Ja*, of course I will. Do you think a man likes to see his daughter go away after so many years? It makes me feel all twisted up inside the way it did when poor little Hilda passed away."

"But you have other cats."

"I know, I know. And they are fine cats also. Not a mouse within earshot. But they are not Hilda."

He sighed.

"Father," she said, "I think you should be going. We are starting so early in the morning and we will need our sleep."

"*Ja*, that is true. Perhaps I had better. What is an hour or two longer when I must say good-by in the end? *Ja, ja.* But there is one more matter."

He fumbled in his belt, grasped something, pressed it into her hands.

"Keep this," he said. "And if the Comanches attack, use it."

"Father! It is the knife!"

"Sure it is the knife."

"I don't want it."

278

"Whether you want it or not you must take it. You might need it."

"But—"

"Unless you take the knife you cannot go at all. I will not have my daughter going unarmed into Comanche country."

She was silent; then, at last, in a small voice, she said:

"I would rather not."

"Do not be a silly goose. If you need it, use it."

She hesitated, there in the shadows; then slipped the sheath inside her blouse.

"That is better," he said.

Back at the campfire, Otto kissed the twins and even Lilith, and he shook hands with his best friend. Then, eyes glistening, he embraced his daughter.

"*Lebe wohl*," he whispered. "*Lebe wohl,* my little one."

And he turned and hurried from the campfire.

On his way to town he paused, stared back at the flickering fires. The banjo still played, the singers still sang:

> *She fed me corn and she fed me beans,*
> *Fed me beans, fed me beans,*
> *She fed me corn and she fed me beans,*
> *Till I left old Santy Fee . . .*

He hurried on, stumbling a little.

*

The following spring he received his first letter from Esperanza. It contained the tremendous news that his daughter and his best friend had been married in St. Louis, in January.

VII

THE SPANKING new Western Exchange Hotel, in St. Louis. The bridal suite. Spacious. High-ceiled. Elegant. Tall polished doors leading to a corridor, a sitting room. Gold and silver wallpaper, imported from France, stamped with plump cupids and kissing scenes.

From the town outside, with its shouting teamsters and rumbling drays, January sunshine speared between the rose damask draperies; and in the low Napoleonic bed, expansive with fine linen, its walnut posts carved with acanthus leaves, the bridegroom wakened. The clock on the white marble mantel showed nearly nine.

Warm beside him under the silken counterpane, his bride still slept. Moving cautiously, resisting her tempting lips, he stole a fond and almost fatuous glance at the thick-braided golden hair, the smooth black brows, the curved black lashes, the delectable coloring of her skin. My wife, he thought; Mrs. Caleb McSwasey. Quite a girl, quite a girl. Three times her age. Why me? Always have been lucky. And it's all legal.

He lay back on the voluptuous pillow, nostrils titillated by the fragrance of powders and scented waters and almond bath paste drifting from her dressing table to mingle with the perfume from a great basket of yellow roses on a gilded tripod. In the huge cheval glass he could see the bridal bower mirrored and expanded: the glow of cannel coal in the grate; the rosewood and satin chairs freighted with girlish ribbons, frivolous gauzes, dainty chemisettes, Irish laces. He smiled, almost dotingly, his thoughts lingering on this madness of his middle years. The word was a four-letter word; the word was a not uncommon word in the English tongue; the word was love. He had fallen in love. At forty-four. The bridegroom cometh. Waugh!

And—oh, quintessence of miracles!—she had fallen in love. She had said so. I love you, Caleb. I do, I do. Since that hot afternoon. You were very dusty. Your throat was dry. I got you a drink. Even then I loved you.

Never before had it been like that with any girl, red, black, white, or interesting combinations thereof. Others had loved him, and said so, and he had loved, and said so; but never had love come simultaneously to him and a girl. Not till now. Not till Esperanza Consuelo Zumwalt.

He had not, actually, fallen in love with the flattering speed which his bride asserted she had experienced. Back on that August afternoon, entering the store in Santa Fe and encountering his bride-to-be, he had thought, "Well, look at this pretty catbird." When she went to the kitchen for drinks, her skirt lyric, he had told himself that the catbird was blessed with a very handsome tail. When she smiled he had thought, "That peach is getting ripe. A man might pick that peach, except it's growing in the Dutchman's orchard." And when, at that historic supper apotheosizing friendship, she had agreed to attend the fandango providing Mr. McSwasey would escort her, he had thought, "Dutchman's orchard or not, when a peach falls into your lap . . ." But he had been liquored then. Next night at the fandango when he taught her to waltz he was not yet in love, but certainly he was tremendously stirred by her lovely young body. He had, however, counseled himself against any rashness that might upset the business deal pending with the son of General von Zumwalt. He needed those Zumwalt gold eagles for the lumber operation he was planning.

"Mr. McSwasey," she had said, when they left the guitar music and strolled slowly and circuitously homeward, "will you do something for me?"

"I might."

She touched his arm.

"Will you take me to St. Louis?"

Memory brought it back: the crooked street heaped with shadows, a dim adobe wall, the far faint music from Kite's Saloon.

"Why?" he asked.

"There's nothing here," she said, her voice low, *triste*. "I want more than this. I've never been anywhere. Everything's stupid here."

"The climate's pretty good," he said.

Her fingers tightened on his arm.

"Take me to St. Louis. Please."

Women were odd people. He asked:

"What do you figure to do in St. Louis?"

"I could go to school."

He was aware of obscure disappointment. Men were odd people too. School! For a moment he had thought her words meant more than they said. Natural mistake: after all, she had been flinging herself at him ever since he arrived.

"What would your father think?" he asked.

"He'll let me go. Lilith could go along. To protect me."

Girl, he thought, you have odd ideas about bodyguards.

"Will you take me?" Esperanza was asking.

"We might manage it."

"Ooo!"

Impulsively, she flung her arms around his neck, her bosom smooth against him for a tantalizing instant. Then she darted from his enclosing arms.

"I think you're wonderful!" she said.

He was baffled; she was something new in his experience. With her, all his technique, pleasantly acquired through the years in the Southern backwoods and in gay Southern cities, in St. Louis and in Cheyenne tepees, was going for naught. If she weren't the Dutchman's daughter . . . But she was. Nevertheless, he decided to experiment; when they reached the Street of the Chamiso he slipped an arm around her waist.

"Mr. McSwasey," she murmured, "why do you do that?"

Well, my God! His voice was dry.

"I need support in my old age."

"Ooo, I do not believe you are telling the truth. You seem to me very strong and very attractive."

So he could not be actually displeased, even when she took his hand and, giving it a parting squeeze, removed it from its treasure hunt.

The household had gone to bed; quietly, Esperanza edged open the door of the store and lighted a candle. Then, in the room where he would sleep, she turned back the covers of his bed and patted the pillow.

"I hope you sleep well," she said. "You were sweet to take me to the fandango. I had never been before."

Her first fandango. Just a bud. He told himself she didn't realize what she had been doing to him; his exasperation vanished.

"It was a nice evening," he said.

"Ooo, yes! I felt very proud. All the girls envied me."

He stood thumbing his jaw, head slightly forward, in that listening attitude of a deaf man, odd for somebody with ears as sharp as his.

"I reckon they'll survive," he said. "They're likely whispering you were there with a man old enough to be your father."

"You must not *say* such things."

"It's the truth that hurts," he said.

"Poo, poo! I think any girl would be proud to dance with such a man of the world. You must have known many girls, Mr. McSwasey."

"A few."

"I believe you are too modest. I have heard all about you from my father."

Great God, he thought.

"But I do not care. I am proud that from all the girls in Santa Fe you chose me to take to the fandango. My father says you have often fought duels and in battles. Have you killed many men?"

"Not a great number."

"How many?"

"Injuns," he said, "don't count. As for niggers—"

"I mean white men."

She had seated herself in one of the chairs designed by her father so long ago; deftly, she was shaping a cigarette, dark eyes looking up into his as she licked the edge.

"War," he said, "is one thing, and peace another. Two for certain, in battle, and likely a third. I was with Old Hickory at New Orleans."

"But that is wonderful! I have read about that battle. Wasn't it very exciting?"

"It was pretty noisy."

"How did it feel when you killed your enemies?"

Through the cigarette smoke he noticed that her eyes had taken on a quality shallow and opaque: Injun eyes. Injun blood would always out. Hard to tame. Impossible, maybe. He said:

"It felt all right."

"After the battle what did you do?"

"I cleaned my rifle."

"I mean—did you celebrate? Were there balls in New Orleans in honor of the victory?"

"Quite a few. For the officers. I was a private in a hunting shirt. They weren't inviting the likes of me. I didn't mind. I was scheming to buy cotton. Peace was coming and the blockade would be raised. I figured cotton prices didn't have nowhere to go but up."

"Ooo, that was long-sighted!"

"Just common sense," he said. "I bought me all the bales I could handle. Maybe a few more. It worked out pretty well. I pyramided on the way up—borrowed on the bales I held to buy more. I did all right. After I was mustered out I lived like a gentleman. Then they invited me to balls."

"And you fought duels?"

"Only one."

"Weren't you afraid?"

"You're damned right. It was at ten paces. That's a little close, but it's how the other fellow wanted it."

"And you killed him?"

"Well, they buried him and he didn't raise no complaint."

Her gaze had dropped; her voice sounded small, hesitant.

"Do you ever think about it?"

"I'm thinking about it now."

"I mean—worry about it."

"What would be the good of that?"

"Do you ever dream about it?"

"I haven't yet."

"Sometimes I have nightmares," she said. "Do you ever have nightmares?"

"Not that I recollect."

The opaqueness, he noticed, had left her eyes; in the candleshine they looked softly Spanish. Faint shadows lay in the hollows of her face beneath the high cheekbones; she sat pensive, cigarette smoldering, her yellow hair reminding him of a pawpaw leaf in October. The room was very quiet. Her lavish skirt of brilliant red cotton was hemmed in black and worked with golden flowers; red-throated flowers bloomed in the fabric of her white blouse. The neckline was low, leaving her coppery shoulders half-naked and gleaming. A shadow of golden-beige nestled where her bosom began.

"It is late," she said. "I had better go to bed."

She dropped the cigarette to the new floor and crushed it beneath her dainty slipper. Caleb watched the candlelight shifting on the bare skin of her pretty ankle. Then she stood up, smoothing her blouse and tucking it more snugly beneath the waistband of her skirt. Her every move was graceful and utterly feminine; he thought he had never known such an attractive girl.

"I had better go to bed," she repeated. Her face was sober, her eyes unfathomable. "It was a lovely fandango. When we waltzed I closed my eyes and thought I was a whirlwind on the desert. I never wanted to stop. I wanted to go on and on, whirling across the mesquite and over the mountains and into the sky till I was lost in the stars." She drew a long breath. "I read in a book that waltzing is wicked. Do you think it is wicked?"

"I reckon it is. Most things are, if they're fun."

"Do you think kissing is wicked?"

"I've never worried none about it."

She looked him full in the eyes.

"I am very happy you will take me to St. Louis. I am so happy I believe I will kiss you good night."

That time, he was ready for her.

"Ooo!" she breathed, when at last she broke away. She clapped a palm over her mouth and stood wide-eyed, cheeks flushed. "I feel so strange."

He was not unaffected, himself.

"Ooo, my heart is racing. I wonder why." She stood staring, then added, "It was the first time I have been kissed."

Suddenly he felt a cradle robber.

"You'd better run along to bed," he said.

"*Si*, perhaps I had." Unexpectedly, she smiled. The effect was dazzling. "I will go to bed and dream about the fandango. I will dream about dancing with you. Good night, Mr. McSwasey."

She whirled and ran. A faint sweet scent of her Eau de Cologne lingered in the candleshine.

*

He was not a fool, even in that realm of human activity where the most canny man is vulnerable; and after going to bed he lay asking himself what the girl was up to. He knew he was no Apollo; his success with women had been spectacular mainly when his ambition had been confined to Injuns, black girls, tan girls, girls in the better fancy houses, and to free and easy girls in the half-world of cities; only twice had he aspired higher. And both times the affairs had ended in violence. In East Bainbridge he had smashed Malcolm Penwick's nose because of Florence Abbott, and in Natchez he had dueled because of Triphena Huckins. After that he had decided that polite courtship was simply too much trouble, a parlor game for gentlemen of wealth and leisure; and it was impractical too, and full of waste motion: planters' daughters never believed that a straight line was the shortest distance between two points. So in Mobile he had bought Yvonne. Without benefit of Dr. Johnson he had concluded that maidenheads were for plowboys, and for men less occupied with the accumulation of money.

By and large, this policy had served him well. Yet here he was in Santa Fe on a money-getting mission, sleeplessly engaged in that most futile of meditations: trying to decipher feminine motive.

Nearly from the moment of his arrival the girl had showered him with flattering attention. Why? He was no longer young. He was anything but rich; after years of scheming he was worth, in addition to his Wisconsin pine lands, only about five thousand dollars. He had overreached himself in the 1830's; the panic had all but cleaned him. Yet the girl was leading him on, quite as if he were a millionaire and not a man who had been compelled to borrow two thousand from her father.

Hopelessly wakeful now, he got out of bed and went to the patio, where with a cigar he sat considering the enigma. And gradually, the completely obvious explanation forced itself upon him: the girl found him attractive. Well, by God! He sat smiling at the darkness, basking in the scented zephyrs of remembered flattery whispering through his brain. And he permitted himself to muse about the future. He thought of how it had been when he kissed her. And before leaving the patio he stood staring at the shadowy Garcia house, where she lay sleeping. He thought: I could fall in love without half trying.

*

During the rest of his visit in Santa Fe they were thrown much together, and when they were apart she was seldom out of his thoughts. He daydreamed. He lived with illusion. He consorted with miracle. The years ahead rose before him in immaculate mirage. He found himself planning how, once he had snatched her from beneath her father's nose, he would marry her, and with her by his side he would chop a fortune from the pineries of Wisconsin. Yet sometimes from deep in his tough old brain a voice whispered that he was plunging into folly. He listened but did not heed. His life had not been devoid of folly, and if this were folly supreme he had journeyed too far into tinted daydreams to turn back.

285

He felt younger; and when, preparing to shave, he saw in the mirror the same old face—the wiry red hair beginning to frost, the bulbous nose laced with purple veins, the carrot-colored brows and the guarded blue eyes, the blocky jaw and thick lips, the skin which looked faintly powdered with brick dust—he was quietly outraged that all trace of the gone years had not been erased. He stropped his razor to a mad-nigger edge and shaved close. With his pocketknife he cleaned every speck of dirt from beneath his nails. And he belabored himself for not bringing to Santa Fe his city clothes.

But he had brought his memories, and at table in the patio he astonished himself by verging perilously near boasting about his adventures. It was unlike him. But Esperanza hung on his words and asked questions and sometimes exclaimed, "Ooo, weren't you afraid?" Otto looked even more impressed than his daughter; he pulled his mustache as he listened to those thrilling tales, and the admiration on his face seemed to say that when he became the best friend of Caleb McSwasey he had builded even better than he knew.

So in the noonday sunshine or by candlelight, while Lilith served the best food west of Virginia, and the cats washed their paws or listened cynically, he told again how he had dived through a hole in the ice to rescue a jackknife, how he had grown a famous watermelon, how he had smashed Malcolm Penwick's nose and had left East Bainbridge in the night, floating by scow down the Connecticut River, buying food from farmers when it was inconvenient to steal eggs or lift a pullet from a hen house or to sneak into a pasture and milk a cow; how at Hartford he sold the scow and struck off across country, southwest through Connecticut and New York State and Pennsylvania, sometimes working a few days for a farmer, sometimes sleeping in haystacks. The South and the West—those had drawn him. He had wanted to see cotton snowy in the boll, redbud in the spring, laurel and rhododendron in the Virginia mountains. He had wanted to hear the mockingbird in the magnolias, to taste the whiskey in Bourbon County and the pralines on Bourbon Street. A young man from a land of gray winter skies, he had yearned to soak in the lazy Southern Decembers. And after that the West: all the immensities of butte and mesa and greasewood and mesquite.

He told how one September day in Maryland, when he was five months out from home, a farmer in a lumber wagon gave him a lift. The farmer was a spruce little man with a knack for getting information, and after he had heard Caleb's story he confided that he was not a farmer after all but a fortune seeker from Pennsylvania who had broken jail while awaiting trial for seeking fortune in unorthodox ways. Sport, said the little man, maybe me and you should team up. There's a free nigger lives over yonder . . .

So that night they accosted the free nigger who thereafter was not free at all but a gagged and bound bundle of outrage in the wagon bed. At dawn they crossed the Virginia boundary, and a few days later they sold the nigger after threatening him with castration if he made a fuss. One nice thing about nigger stealing, the nigger couldn't stand up in court and testify.

Caleb and Hod Kite parted company, after disposing of the nigger, and not till Nacogdoches did their trails cross again. By then he had seen a lot of the South: Charleston Harbor and the indigo coast; rutted roads in the Carolina upcountry; the Wilderness Trail through Cumberland Gap to the fair land of Kentucky. He had wandered, drifted, adventured. Then in a Tennessee court town he lied to a recruiting sergeant about his bad leg, and with other young men in hunting shirts he floated down the Cumberland to the Ohio, down the Ohio to the biggest river of them all, down that into a broad swampy land of alligators and Spanish moss. He was part of something big, then; part of General William Carroll's division of Tennessee militia; they were going to kill a lot of British if ever they got rifles. On the flatboats half of them drilled—with cotton-wood sticks—while half of them manned the oars, and everybody cussed the government for calling up militia without providing guns. But then one day on the big river they overtook a shipment from the War Department, and after that they drilled with rifles. He felt like a real soldier then, with bullets in the pockets of his copperas-dyed pantaloons, a powder horn dangling from his shoulder, a war hatchet and a scalping knife stuck in his belt. Five days before Christmas they landed in New Orleans; the air was like June in Massachusetts; everywhere you heard ripe nigger laughter; oranges hung ready to be picked; oleanders and roses and magnolias and crape myrtles smothered the wrought-iron filigree of the pink houses; this, Caleb thought, is for me. But it wasn't, till after the necessary fighting.

That took place below the city on land that mushed underfoot, with the river on their right and the earthworks and cotton bales stretching off to their left, and an open field before them. The fighting was very noisy, very smoky, with cannons making a lot of widows and orphans every time they belched, and with bullets humming like skeeters. Paken-ham's men were natural targets, marching across that field in scarlet coats. He never did see old Pakenham. But he saw Old Hickory, for about thirty seconds, when the battle smoke was thick. That was an experience, he judged, about like seeing the whole United States of America striding around long-legged and blazing-eyed, no more scared of singing bullets than if they'd been cream puffs, a gaunt-faced, raw-boned man who was telling a colonel that by the eternal something-or-other . . . and who disappeared into the smoke. Caleb was eighteen, then.

So they licked the redcoats, he and General Jackson, and in March when he was mustered out he stayed on in the city of grilled balconies and humid fecundity, spending the easy money he made buying and selling cotton. Next year he went north, up the river, and returned with four niggers. He kept them in line by telling them he would set them free, in New Orleans. When he sold them instead, to his profit, those niggers were a little disappointed. He had made a lot of money off and on through the years in the nigger business. Most of it legitimate money too. But on the whole nigger dealers weren't very refined men—they didn't stand high in the social scale of the South—so he decided to turn planter, after meeting Triphena Huckins in New Orleans. She was an olive-skinned beauty with hair the color of a moonless night and three nigger maids and a figure that would have depopulated a monastery and a drawl so lazy with honey and molasses that she could hardly talk at all. He followed her home to Natchez and damned if her cousin, Pemberton Huckins, didn't challenge him. Those southerners were forever falling in love with their cousins! Well, he killed her cousin in that damn fool duel, which flattered the hell out of Triphena—it was the sixth or seventh duel inspired by her promontories and bottom lands—and then by God she eloped with a Georgia planter. Caleb was disgusted. And in his disgust he drifted downriver and over to Mobile where a French sea captain who needed money, and who was about to sail anyway, offered to sell him Yvonne. You'd scarcely think her a nigger; her blue-black hair fell to her waist without a kink, and her coffee-with-cream skin was whiter than Triphena's. He sold her at last in St. Louis and returned to East Bainbridge. It was autumn; he had been gone eight years; he was twenty-five; high time he settled down.

East Bainbridge on a day of cobalt November sky and thin yellow sunshine. The flash of white houses amid bare elms and maples. The Connecticut River flowing in cold blue from that corner of the universe where Vermont and New Hampshire met Massachusetts. Nothing had changed; everything had changed. His brother Paul looked older, the skin tighter over his beak, his hands dry and stingy. When they were boys Grandpa Seasongood used to have them hold their palms up to the window, fingers glued together, and although Caleb's fingers leaked light like a rusty bucket, you never could see a gleam between Paul's. That proved Paul was a true Seasongood, Grandpa said; no pennies were going to slip through his fingers. Well, none had. By scrimping and working Paul had saved damn near half as much money as Caleb had possessed at eighteen, after selling his New Orleans cotton . . . Caleb, Paul said, you've seen a lot of country, how did you like it? I liked it fine, Paul. It's a big country, Paul, a damned fine country . . . Caleb, I used to think maybe I'd like to go west . . . You never will, Paul, you'll never go anywhere, except to the burying ground.

And as he looked around Paul's general store and sniffed the familiar smells of coffee and salted codfish and bolts of muslin and oil of peppermint, it gave him an odd trapped feeling to think that this was where Paul had spent those eight years. A free nigger had been kidnapped out of Maryland; the palmettos had rattled in a wind off Charleston Harbor;

288

the dogwood had bloomed on Virginia hillsides; Old Hickory had strode gigantically through battle smoke; on a Louisiana sandspit across from Natchez the cousin of Triphena Huckins had doubled over with a bullet in his liver; and where had Paul been? In his store.

Coming back was a mistake, Caleb thought. I'm a ghost here.

He wandered to the place of ghosts in the Congregational churchyard on a day of wild skies and whirling leaves. Six feet away—and an eternity away—Grandpa Seasongood lay hidden in the Massachusetts earth, and Harmony Seasongood McSwasey and Frosty McSwasey himself. He wondered whether the argument had ever been settled as to when the Nineteenth Century began. Dry eyed, he stared at the slab lettered Harmony Seasongood McSwasey, remembering the perpetual worry stamping her forehead, remembering her thin round-shouldered figure, her large knuckles and fingers twisted by rheumatics. The steamy kitchen on a freezing winter Saturday, and he a boy setting forth with skates. You be careful, Caleb, don't fall in. . . . How she had watered his sinful head with tears at the time of the marble scandal; how dubious she had been when he announced he would grow the biggest watermelon; how troubled she was at Frosty McSwasey's bouts with the bottle. Every week or so her cares would pile up into a splitting headache, and she would lie in a darkened bedroom, her suffering sponged away by laudanum sleep. One way to escape East Bainbridge.

Next day he escaped. And the next spring he struck out for New Mexico with Captain Becknell. And never regretted it, not even when the party staggered and wavered across the Cimarron Desert, canteens long empty. Not a buffalo, not an Injun, not a water hole, not a creek. Except in mirages. Plenty of sun, however, and withered land. Then somebody sighted a buffalo. Thought it a mirage, at first. But a bullet had no effect on a mirage, and on this old bull a bullet had great effect. They cut him open; his stomach was sloshing full of tepid water. A drink had never tasted sweeter. And they knew then that a river must flow not far away.

So his life had been not without its follies, its adventures; and he wondered why, when he sat at supper in the Zumwalt patio, he talked so much. But he knew why, really.

*

Perhaps those stories aided in the founding of that mighty firm, the McSwasey & Zumwalt Lumber Company. Perhaps they convinced the son of General von Zumwalt that here was a man—a friend!—in whose keeping one's savings would be not only safe but fertile. Or perhaps Otto would have invested anyway. In any case, he invested.

It was a partnership, simple and fairly pure. As his share, Caleb put up all his Wisconsin stumpage, easily worth, so he said, ten thousand dollars. And Otto put up a like amount in gold, indubitably worth ten

289

thousand dollars. As for the Santa Fe store, Otto bought it. How could he have done otherwise and remained a sterling friend?

So as the caravan jolted eastward, Caleb could not doubt that his trip to Santa Fe had been successful beyond hope. Specie in the strongbox; his debt to Otto cancelled by the sale of the store; in his wagon the three Zumwalt niggers and the Zumwalt daughter. He was in his prime; the Wisconsin forests waited; Esperanza waited. Waugh!

But of course true love—and how else could such a mutual grand passion be described?—never ran smooth; and sometimes on that eastward journey he tormented himself remembering the drops of bitters Hod Kite had sprinkled into the wine of his enchantment. On his last afternoon in Santa Fe he had dropped in at Hod's saloon, exultant at how trustingly Otto had accepted his valuation of the Wisconsin stumpage, the sun of his fortunes rising, his head full of dreams; and as he drank his Taos Lightning, and memory flashed him bewitching pictures of Esperanza, he experienced a compulsion, odd for him, of sharing his bliss. He felt as warm and bursting with happiness as an oven-browned rooster bursting with rich wine dressing; he lighted a cigar—one of his aromatic Cuban Pelions—and blew smoke at the ceiling; and as he watched Hod refill his glass he said:

"It's been a great trip, Hod. I'll end up with a potful of gold eagles."

"Sport," Hod said, "I don't doubt it. I could have told you that back in Maryland. The way you took hold when we nabbed that nigger. Cracked him over the skull and he dropped like a preacher's pants."

"Stumpage," Caleb said. "Pine stumpage. The best pine stock in Christendom. She's a pretty land, Hod. You go up the Chippewa and you come to the Whiskey River flowing in from the north. And you go up the Whiskey and what do you see?"

"God, Sport, how do I know?"

"Pine," Caleb said, saliva glands dripping. "Not a branch for a hundred feet of trunk. Straight as the road to hell. They'll scale out at twelve hundred board feet. More than that, some of them. And I damn near own that river, Hod. Section after section, on both sides. And I've got me sections checkerboarded in the back country. Enough to give me a talking point when I cut on government land. It's all in my croaker bag, and I'll skin it like a nigger skins a possum."

"Sport, I hope you ain't planning to steal timber."

"Hod," Caleb said, eying the ash on his cigar, "you know I've never been a stealing man. There's laws against it. But this land's different. This is government land. And Washington City's a long way from the Whiskey River. A man might cut uncle's timber by mistake. Everybody makes mistakes."

"Is Zumwalt in with you?"

"He thinks he is."

"Ha!" Hod said.

"A thrifty Dutchman," Caleb said. "Well, that's fine. Somebody's got to furnish the capital for developing the country. Me, I never could breed a nickel to a dime and get penny pups."

"Have you pretty well cleaned him, Sport?"

"He's my partner, Hod."

"Ha!" Hod said.

"He's still got the store and that extra house. He'll make out. I'm taking his niggers to St. Louis. They think they're going for the ride. They think."

"Hold on to them nigger twins," Hod said, "and you'll double your money. Them's the color a gentleman would buy, in a few years."

"There's certain gentlemen in St. Louis," Caleb said, "who will buy them now."

"God damn everybody," Hod said.

"Lutheran gentlemen, I'll tell the Dutchman. He won't mind."

"God damn us all," Hod said. "That preacher was right. Brother, he used to say, the human race ain't fit to live. It stinks worse than a skunk, it's sneakier than a weasel and meaner than a catamount. It acts tame but it ain't. It's got a wild heart and a killer panther's eyes. Flood the last time and fire the next. Let 'er come, I say. And maybe the Dutchman's right, too. You can't own 'em. You think you do, but you don't. Want another Lightning, Sport? It'll shorten your life by five minutes."

"Not my life, it won't. I'm going to live forever, the way I feel today. Were you ever in love?"

"Back in Pennsylvania. But I got cured. Married her. A good wife too. She slept with the sheriff's deputy and snitched his keys. That jail was nothing but a crackerbox, anyhow. Told her I'd meet her in Baltimore. But I borrowed a farmer's team and wagon and lit out. Are you in love?"

"I might get married," Caleb said, "when I land in St. Louis."

"God damn us all. Who's the gal?"

"Can't you guess?"

"I don't try no more. Not since the day I guessed the sheriff was in York. Damned if he wasn't behind the partition with the cashier talking a loan. Nabbed me like a lizard nabs a fly. No, I can't guess."

"Esperanza," Caleb said.

Hod just looked at him.

"The Dutchman's daughter," Caleb said. "Esperanza."

"I heard you the first time, Sport."

Caleb stared into his drink.

"It sneaked up on me," he said softly. "I was going about my business, behaving myself, and then there it was. I'm taking it hard. Maybe I'm a damn fool. I'm forty-four. She's fifteen. But she seems eighteen. Twenty, maybe. Or a thousand. Hell, she's Eve. She's got me dizzy. I don't sleep so good any more. I talk business with the Dutchman and I'm thinking about his daughter. What's a man to do?"

"You can always jump on a fast horse and run."

A smile hovered over Caleb's lips; his eyes were far away.

"Maybe I don't want to. Maybe I'm ready to settle. Forty-four. I feel about sixteen. And it's nice to get a woman for once that no man's been at before."

"Get 'em a day old, Sport, and you ain't the first. No man ever lived that didn't take another man's leavings."

"I'm the first," Caleb said. "The Dutchman's watched her."

"Ha!"

"Don't you think he's watched her?"

"Like that sheriff's deputy watched the jail. You can watch a woman twenty-three hours and fifty-nine minutes a day. And in the other minute she'll fool you."

"I reckon," Caleb said, "you ain't known the right kind of women."

"There's only one kind, Sport. What do you think the Dutchman's been running? A convent?"

"She didn't even know how to waltz. I taught her. She's innocent."

"Not the way I heard it, Sport."

"And sweet," Caleb said. "Puts me in mind of lilacs in May. They grew in our yard. Back in East Bainbridge. A spring shower would come and you could smell the new grass and the lilacs. And hear the robins."

"You're hearing robins, Sport, that's for sure. Sweet! Lord God of hosts! I've never seen you like this. What's happened?"

Caleb smiled.

"I'm in love, that's what," he said.

"By God. I believe you mean it."

"I'll have another Lightning," Caleb said. "Of course I mean it."

"Well, by God."

Caleb smiled.

"I believe you mean it," Hod said. "By God! Sweet! You ought to talk with that old nigger of mine. With Panthea. Sweet! Like lilacs! Like a wildcat, you mean."

"Hod," Caleb said, "I don't think I like that."

"An Apache," Hod said. "Those eyes. And a greaser. You'll never know where you're at. And the Dutchman's daughter. That mouth. Those thin ends! Mean!"

"I don't like it, Hod."

"And innocent. God on his throne! Two months ago she had the town rocking. When them greasers laid that floor. There's a greaser named Archuleta. He popped open the door and found his kid in bed with her."

Caleb reached across the bar, spilling his drink, and grabbed Hod's shirt near the throat. His ears were humming, his head felt full of blood.

Faint sickness went racing through his veins. His vision blurred and swam with Hod's bald head bobbing like a balloon.

"Don't do it, Sport," Hod said.

They stood that way for what seemed a long while; then Caleb's fingers relaxed and he withdrew his arm. On the bar he righted his glass. Hod's damp towel swabbed at the spilled Lightning. When Caleb spoke his voice was scarcely audible.

"What did you say the greaser kid's name was?"

"Archuleta. Gilberto. Why? You aim to beat him up?"

"More than that."

"You always were lucky," Hod said. "You kill the son of a bitch and they'd cut your eyes out. You're in New Mexico, Sport. And you're a gringo."

"Where does he live?"

"Besides you're liquored. Although I've seen you act the same without a drop. Glad I wasn't born jealous. I'd still be in that jail. But you're in luck. The kid's gone to Mexico. And there's no call for you to go after his old man. The old man was as mad as you are."

Caleb could feel a vein pumping in his throat; his cheeks felt hot as a sizzling buffalo steak. He stared at his cigar, soggy and chewed; he dropped it, ground it under his heel. Hod's voice sounded far away:

"Ain't good for a man to be as jealous as you are. I've always said it would bring you trouble. I recollect that time in Virginia when you picked up that tavern wench. Anybody could see she was taking 'em as they came, but you had to get jealous—"

Caleb's stubby fingers curled round his empty glass; he stood staring into it.

"But I've never seen you like this," Hod was saying. "By God, I believe you're in love. I've seen you jealous but never in love. A bad combination. God help you, Sport."

Caleb drew back his arm, hurled the glass. Hod dipped from sight. The glass smashed into the bottles ranked behind the bar.

"That'll cost you, Sport," Hod called.

"Charge it," Caleb said, and pushed outdoors to the plaza, legs unsteady, limp more noticeable, stocky body shoving among the young blades in leather trousers, the strolling girls, the brown humanity clustered about the monte games. He walked for a long time, without purpose, without destination, along streets of beige dust under the empty turquoise sky, while the sun lowered in the west and in the mountains slits and gulches filled with mauve shadow and the cliffs turned golden tan and ashes of roses.

Remembering other times, other jealousies. Florence Abbott of the East Bainbridge Abbotts. Pale hair, pale skin, slender small-boned body. Lamplighting time in February, the windows of Paul McSwasey's store thickly frosted, and Florence entering from the purpling evening, her

293

cute little nose faintly rosy from the icy air; a delicate girl of filigree and silvery voice, with hands that made aimless little gestures. He had started attending Sunday evening services, gaze fixed on her lovely head two pews away while the parson tried to throw a scare into those rock-headed Yankees by evoking the fierce Yahweh of a few obscure and scattered tribes in Asia Minor. Caleb was shaking, not because of the hell-flames issuing from the parson's mouth, but because tonight he was going to ask Florence if he might see her home . . . Why, yes, Caleb, she said in the vestibule. As they crunched toward her house through the snow-blue moonlight he touched her elbow occasionally, but that was all he ever touched with her, on the half-dozen Sunday evenings she accepted his invitations. Maybe her thoughts were less angelic than her face, maybe she thought this isn't getting anywhere fast, or maybe her father said I don't want a daughter of mine getting mixed up with Frosty McSwasey's son. In any case, one Sunday evening in April, she passed up Caleb in the church vestibule and accepted Malcolm Penwick's invitation. That was about the last time he'd been inside any church anywhere, and that night he tossed sleepless in the feather bed in the room with the slanting ceiling. I ought to beat up that Malcolm, he thought; I ought to punch the bastard's nose. (Not that Malcolm, a child of his parents' respectable middle years, was a bastard!) Next morning in the store Paul asked, what's the matter with you today? And Caleb said nothing is the matter except Malcolm Penwick walked Florence Abbott home from church . . . Well, Paul said, mouth grinning under his beak nose, competition is the life of trade . . . I ought to slug him one, Caleb said.

Whereupon Paul, who had been born old and conservative, a Federalist and a Seasongood, who had believed that Thomas Jefferson was a dangerous radical and a spendthrift to boot, wasting the people's money in that unconstitutional Louisiana Purchase, hastily pointed out that the Penwicks were excellent customers, excellent Federalists, excellent conservative people; and besides probably Florence Abbott was only trying to rouse his jealousy.

So he had a name for how he felt: jealousy. He smashed Malcolm's nose and left town. In East Bainbridge, Massachusetts, smashing a rival's nose wasn't done, unless you were the shiftless son of that shiftless Frosty McSwasey who drank and loafed and fished—and maybe worse—on the Sabbath.

It was different in the South, life was melodramatic there. The South was another country, and he liked it a lot better than old lady Massachusetts corseted in granite. He remembered the blackness of 4:00 A.M. in Natchez, wisps of fog curling past yellow streetlamps. It was October, the pre-dawn air clammy, tomorrow at this time he might be dead. His nigger man Jed moped along at his heels like a lugubrious hound-dog, but his second, Dr. Wherry, was brisk. As they groped down from the bluffs to Natchez-under-the-Hill, where the fancy houses and gambling houses were going full blast, the fog thickened. They would never find their way in this pea soup, Dr. Wherry said, but Caleb said they'd try, he didn't want to show up late. They shoved off in a scow; everything was dripping wet; must have taken the good part of an hour to cross the river and locate that sand beach. Nobody was there. He paced slowly in the sand, wishing the thing were over because then he could eat a square meal: last night he had skipped supper and this morning he had swallowed only coffee, because Dr. Wherry had said it would work out better if his bowels were flat. He kept thinking of Triphena Huckins, probably still asleep in her canopied bed.

When at length the other party arrived, Pemberton Huckins' second apologized to Dr. Wherry for being late; the fog had delayed them. It was thinning now, swirling in translucent white; Pemberton Huckins, a supple young man with a face sallow from malaria, had brought a leather case lined with red velvet in which nested the pistols, their silver mountings etched with thistles. Caleb thought of him in love with Triphena, maybe kissing her, and he thought of the way Triphena's bosom billowed out under a dress of shell-white lace, and that familiar jealousy poured through his body. He knew it wasn't acceptable practice, what he was going to do, but he couldn't help himself: he limped over to the little group and with his open palm smacked Pemberton Huckins' cheek.

Rage followed, and outrage. They had to hold Pemberton Huckins and he was screaming that Caleb McSwasey was no gentleman. Well, he had never claimed to be. The entire party—even Caleb's nigger man— was aghast. The seconds conferred, sought vainly for precedent in the complicated code; to a Massachusetts Yankee it seemed as frivolous as arguing whether ten thousand or nine thousand angels could stand on the head of a pin. They decided that in view of the—er—unfortunate—er— breach of punctilio, Pemberton Huckins had a clear right to name the number of paces. He screamed: ten! That's pretty close, Caleb said, you'll be so scared you'll wet your pants. Pemberton Huckins flew into such rage that he danced like a fighting cock; his second gave him a swig of brandy to calm him; ten, he kept screaming, ten!

So they decided the question at ten paces, and Pemberton Huckins was shaken by such gigantic rage that his shot went wild. Caleb put a ball into his liver. By then the rising sun had broken through the fog; the river rippled past all silvery and blue and olive; the bluffs of Natchez gleamed. Word was whispered around town that Caleb had slapped that usually sure-shot, Pemberton, just to get him rattled. That evening, as they strolled a brick path among the oleanders, Triphena was arch. For a few minutes. But Caleb had learned she had no defense against flattery. The thicker the better. Honey and molasses and taffy and chocolate cream: he poured it on. I couldn't help myself, honeychild.

You're so beautiful you turn me insane. When I saw him I thought of your eyes and I flew mad . . . Nothing to it; within a quarter of an hour, in the summerhouse, he had the front of her dress unbuttoned.

She astonished everybody, except her favorite personal maid, by eloping with that Georgia planter a few days later. Caleb drifted to Mobile. And when he bought Yvonne, and in the months that followed sold her to various lecherous old Southern gentlemen, and stole her to sell her again, he felt obscurely that he was evening things up with Triphena and the whole kit and caboodle of the gentility. Occasionally, looking back on that duel, he wondered whether the scheming part of his mind had figured that if Pemberton Huckins' temper were roused his aim would be shaky. But he didn't let it worry him. He was alive, wasn't he?

He grew pretty fond of Yvonne, and his jealousy used to kick up something fearful when he sold her and waited in a pine copse or a cotton field or a mosquito swamp while she fulfilled her wench's destiny, especially if the man who bought her chanced to be younger than usual. No two ways about it: jealousy like his was a handicap. He used to ask her if it had been good, when she met him after sneaking away from her latest purchaser. Why, honey, she always said, it ain't never really bad.

So as time passed he sold her less and less often. Not that he loved her, actually; but she was his woman and it was too damned painful to share her, even for the greater good. The South was no place for a man to get caught in dealings like that; they had some close calls; his jealousy kept getting worse; he told himself he ought to settle down; so finally in St. Louis he sold her for good and all. On the boat to Cincinnati he missed her fearfully, but he was on his way to East Bainbridge and a life of humdrum respectability. He should have known himself better than to imagine he could ever be contented in a tight little village like East Bainbridge. A man made some awful damn fool plays in life, just by not knowing himself.

And now in Santa Fe his jealousy had returned, and as he limped along headed for nowhere, his shadow long in the sundown, he had a notion to announce that he would not after all take Esperanza Zumwalt to St. Louis: let her stay here and kiss the greasers. Then it occurred to him that so far as her father knew, and so far as Esperanza or he himself had ever said, she was traveling to St. Louis only for the upright purpose of attending a female seminary. He had gone to work and fallen in love with her, but he had never told her so. She acted pretty sweet on him, but she had never yet said she loved him. He had no claim on her; not yet. Besides, maybe that story of Hod Kite's was nothing but gossip. Maybe if he took her along in the caravan, he could catch her unawares, spring the story on her when she least expected it, and see how she reacted.

Of course it was only gossip. Must be. But even if it was true, he guessed he couldn't bring himself to leave without her.

*

He knew the trail east like the palm of his hand. Santa Fe, Glorieta, Pecos, San Miguel. Pink dust rising from hoofs and wheels. Whip crackings, shouts, whickerings, brayings. Into the mountains with their juniper and piñons, along a white-tumbling stream, past mountain meadows white-dotted with sheep. And overhead the cloudless sky, the sky of New Mexico, pure and young and fair as the sky in a dream, promising everything.

He rode his horse, never straying far from his wagon pulled by six mules, for he preferred mules to oxen. His driver was a gangling mule skinner named Tad Weesener, a young man with hay-thatch hair, a negligible chin sloping toward a long neck with a wobbly Adam's apple, a face where yellow pimples bloomed. In the bed of the wagon, wrapped by canvas, covered with Mexican blankets, rode the money chest containing the Zumwalt specie—the McSwasey & Zumwalt specie now—the good, round, hard gold coins for which, in Wisconsin, men would go into the pinery and chop down the best timber in Christendom.

In the wagon bed three niggers also rode, and sometimes a girl of beige and blond. Caleb liked it better when she rode there, seated on the money chest; but usually she sat beside Tad Weesener, who wore a bashful, sickly grin and perpetually blushed and sneaked looks at Esperanza's low blouse.

Caleb was not actually jealous of Tad Weesener; even his stupendous jealousy had limits. Still, he could see no harm in watching developments. And he failed to grasp the necessity of Esperanza's prattling so much with Tad, and smiling. Nor did he approve when, occasionally, on an easy stretch of trail, Tad's scrawny hands with their bony knuckles relinquished the reins to Esperanza's dainty ones. From his saddle Caleb watched her sitting very straight, her jaw resolute, staring ahead over the mules' ears. He had a notion to forbid her driving; still, when she drove, she couldn't flirt—virtually—with Tad.

He guessed the truth was that he didn't want her to look at anything that wore pants, his pants excepted. For that matter, he liked it none too well when she became friendly with something male that didn't wear pants, such as old Rover, the caravan collie. Maybe, he thought, as he watched her fondle Rover, a man could carry jealousy too far; he'd have to curb that tendency, if he ever found himself going to extremes.

Except for his worry about the gossip Hod Kite had mentioned, those first days on the out-trail were golden and enchanted. Love was young then, even if he wasn't; and sometimes he could imagine that even he was young, that his years in a St. Louis store had never occurred, that he was about twenty-nine, returning to the States with a ravishing

297

Mexican bride. Then he would become conscious of his false teeth. But except for them—and many a man lost his teeth early!—he couldn't see that he had slowed down much. His eyesight was damn near keen enough to make out the fleas on a mile-away sheep dog. He had ears like a fox. His muscles were hard, his tendons rawhide, his rifle-aim steady. A day in the saddle didn't tucker him much. His freckled hands were broad, stubby fingers thick and powerful, and he could double them into as effective weapons as ever: just let that gawky Tad Weesener try something with Esperanza and the son of a bitch would be coughing up teeth for a week. He was a long way, he guessed, from becoming a cast bull.

He had always liked the trail and this trip was the best of all. I'll never forget it, he thought; and he never did: at odd times in the after-years it would come back to him: on drab November afternoons in New Empire when the river flowed slag-gray; in the woods with snow blowing; that night when he went to Rafferty's Saloon to meet Jim Buckmaster. It was something special, that trip, something nobody could ever take away. It was the brilliant New Mexican air, the mountain mornings when he snapped awake to a world of sparkling frost, to the sound of a creek rushing and to the smells of sage and piñon smoke and boiling coffee. It was the hot sun when they nooned, the good healthy fatigue when he swung from the saddle at day's end. And it was Esperanza. Esperanza in the mornings still asleep in her blankets, looking like an Injun despite her golden hair; Esperanza kicking off her slippers and wading in a trout stream, skirt held up, legs shapely invitations to delight; Esperanza's spitfire fury that night east of Wagon Mound when she was returning to camp after being off on feminine business and an old fool bull whacker tried to steal a kiss, and the way she had rewarded Caleb after he had knocked the bull whacker down, and kicked him in the kidney, leaving him in such poor shape that for days he urinated blood; Esperanza that evening on the Cimarron Desert when they had sighted Comanches at sundown, and when by firelight she showed him the knife that had belonged to her great-grandmother and whispered that she would use it on any Comanche who came sneaking around her; Esperanza that night soon after they left Santa Fe, when they were still in the mountains, and she put to rest all his worries about Hod Kite's gossip. That was the night she whispered, for the first time, I love you, Caleb . . . Waugh!

It was the high point of the journey, that night was, and maybe the high point of his life. No matter what happened in the years to come he could always close his eyes and go back to that canyon in the *Sangre de Cristos,* and hear again the rush of Pecos Creek among the boulders, and smell again the sweet smoke of the cedar campfires mingling in the frosty air with the good sharp odors of horseflesh and leather harness and manure and the dark aroma of piñon. Off in the shadows you could hear the oxen lowing, and the horses and mules stamping and munching the bunch grass and sometimes blowing softly. Lilith had tucked the twins into their blankets in the wagon, and now she was puttering at such camp chores as washing supper dishes. Esperanza sat on a boulder, hands clasped over her drawn-up knees, staring at the tiny flame-blue wraiths that danced among the hot gold coals of the campfire, maybe listening, and maybe not, to the Missouri twang of Tad Weesener who squatted on his heels, ungainly hands dangling, and sniveled out a long, pointless yarn about the flatboat voyage his pappy had once made from the Falls of the Ohio to New Orleans. Caleb watched her, noticing how the firelight, when it struck her hair, seemed to aerify into a soft lucent nimbus of spun gold; how the flickering light called forth the latent coppery tones of her flesh and brought into relief the high cheekbones and willful jaw and smooth fine forehead; and he noticed the long mouth, in repose now, with the red passionate lips and thin ends. Cruel? Hod Kite had said as much. That didn't bother him. He reckoned he was capable of keeping a gal with Injun blood gentle. What bothered him was the memory of Hod's gossip. Not that he believed it, actually. Still, he wanted to know, he wanted to be sure, so far as a man could be sure of anything with any of them. He cast his cigar into the fire, got to his feet. Tad Weesener broke off talking; Esperanza looked up inquiringly.

"I want to show you something," Caleb told her.

He enjoyed the way she handled her body, when she stood up. Most gals, even the prettiest, had moments of clumsiness. But hardly ever an Injun gal, and never Esperanza. She moved like a cat, springing smoothly to her feet, and it excited him to imagine how, hidden by her skirt, her legs must look when they accomplished that maneuver, the tendons taut and yet fluid of line like the tendons on the bold bronze leg of a statue.

He guided her into the shadows and up the mountain, among the spruce and scrub cedar and chokeberry, into the pure high air where the duck hawk nested and the pack rats hid. It winded him somewhat, that climb, more than it would have twenty years ago, but he told himself that was only because long residence in St. Louis had left him unaccustomed to high altitudes. Part way up he stopped.

"It's a nice sight," he said. "I wanted you to see it."

He gestured toward the floor of the canyon, where the campfires were tiny blazes scattered along the creek. Figures of heel-squatting or lounging men showed in diminutive silhouettes. Subdued and distant, the sound of the trout stream came floating up in silken whisperings. Across the canyon the opposite mountains loomed solid. It was like a summation of the trail, of the West.

"All my life," Esperanza murmured, "I have wondered what it was like, going to St. Louis. I love it."

They were standing close; he took her hand.

"I want to see it from higher up," she said; and she broke away, climbing smoothly among the yucca and the jack pines, her slippers sending back a rattle of pebbles. Following, he heard an accordion striking up down at camp, and when he gained the summit he found her singing to its music, her voice low-pitched:

> *She fed me corn and she fed me beans,*
> *Fed me beans, fed me beans . . .*

The accordion, elfin in those infinities of silence, swung into other trail songs; Esperanza sat on a flat outcropping of granite, humming, her voice girlishly sweet; and once she leaned back on her elbows, breathing deep, staring into the vast heavens where Orion strode across the centuries.

"Happy?" Caleb asked, sitting beside her.

"*Si*, very happy."

He sort of hated to break it up, but he figured she was as off-guard now as he would ever find her. He drew a long breath.

"What's this I hear," he asked, "about you and a greaser kid named Gilberto Archuleta?"

She stopped humming. Silence poured in upon them, from the dark immensities of mountain, desert, sky, faintly broken by the merry tiny music from the accordion. She sat up.

"What did you hear?" she asked, her voice low and dark.

He didn't answer; and there in the night with her hair faintly luminous he felt quietly and joyfully brutal, punishing her for the hells of uncertainty he had been suffering.

"I want to know what you heard," she said sharply, her fingers steely on his wrist.

"I wouldn't like to repeat it," he said. "Did you love him?"

She broke out laughing.

"Did I love him! Did I love him! You are making a joke."

He held his tongue and waited, like a hunter waiting for a rabbit to thresh and entangle itself in the toils of a snare.

"He was *malvado*, that Gilberto," she said bitterly. "I knew it the first day he came to lay the floor. I begged my father to dismiss him but he can be very stubborn. And you ask if I loved him! Arrgh!"

She shuddered.

"Maybe I shouldn't have mentioned it," he said.

"And why not? I have nothing to hide. What did you hear? Who has been repeating the lies of the town?"

"Hod Kite said something about it."

"What did he say?"

"I don't like to repeat it."

"Something that bad," she whispered. "And you listened. And perhaps you believed it."

"I don't believe everything I hear," Caleb said.

"But you wondered. I thought you were my friend. You of all people I thought I could trust. Now I am alone."

She buried her face in her hands and began to sob.

He realized then he had made a terrible mistake. His old enemy, jealousy, had betrayed him. He felt like a man who in a misguided moment has kicked a kitten.

"Hold on," he said. "Of course I didn't believe it."

He put an arm around her racked shoulders; violently, she shook free and sprang up.

"Gilberto Archuleta indeed!" she exclaimed, her voice pouring fire. "A *malvado,* a tarantula, an *araña del sol!* From the first I hated him. My father laughed but I am a girl with a girl's wisdom in such matters. I loathed him for a snake. His eyes were cruel and hot. His hands were always reaching for me."

"By God!" Caleb declared, as in imagination he pictured that sneaky, oily greaser with rapine in his eyes. He thought: I should have tracked the son of a bitch to Mexico and cut him.

"One day in the patio," Esperanza was saying, "he caught me alone. He told me I must be nice to him or he would spread gossip about me. He would tell lies to his cronies that I had entertained him in wicked ways."

Caleb jumped to his feet, fingers doubled into fists.

"Why that horny bastard! Excuse my language, but—"

"I do not care what you call him. You cannot call him names low enough to reach him in his gutter. I slapped him that day, in the patio."

"Good! By God good for you! If I'd been there I'd have—"

"Then one afternoon," she said slowly, "during the siesta, I was sleeping in my bedroom. He must have been watching his chance, for he sneaked in. When I wakened his hand was inside my blouse. I screamed. I fought and scratched but he was very strong. When I screamed again he slapped a palm over my mouth. I struggled as best I could but my strength was going fast. Then just in time the door banged open and his father and my father rushed in. They had heard my screams. It was a scandal, of course. What stories he told about me before they packed him off to Mexico I do not know, but I can guess."

Caleb stood shaken by rage, stung by remorse, oppressed by the injustices of the world.

"That is what happened," she said, "and I was helpless against the stories he set afloat. I am sad to think that Hod Kite would repeat them and sadder to think that you would believe them."

"But I didn't!"

"I believe you did. Perhaps you still do."

She sank to the boulder in tears.

"Esperanza! Honeychild! Listen to me, Goldilocks! I never believed that gossip. I don't believe it."

He sat beside her and enfolded her in his arms.

"*Si, si,* I believe you do. My happiness is over and my dark star rises. They should have named me Dolores because I am a girl of many sorrows. I am in love with a man who believes I have been bad. I love you, Caleb. I do, I do. From the moment you entered the store—"

Then he was kissing her and whispering endearments; and while far below in the canyon the accordion music died away and the camp slept to the rush of mountain waters and the stars wheeled on their immemorial courses across the New Mexican heavens Caleb McSwasey in his bewitchment and his enchantment encountered proof incontrovertible that he was taking no man's leavings.

*

After that, of course, he was a gone buffalo, a skinned beaver. There was no help for him, after that. Years later, he used to look back on that night and think, "Maybe it wasn't her dark star rising. Maybe it was mine. Still, I reckon I would do it again."

For he always loved her, even after he had grown to hate her.

So the caravan crossed the plains, with Esperanza more desirable and charming every day, with his jealousy such a cocked pistol that no bull whacker dared so much as to say good morning to her; and in St. Louis they were duly married, although by a cowardly Baptist minister instead of a Lutheran, and the twins were sold, although not to a Lutheran family.

One afternoon soon after the wedding Caleb accompanied his bride on a shopping expedition. It was a sunny day of January thaw, and as they proceeded along the wooden sidewalk, often pausing to gaze into store windows, they were an affluent-looking couple, Esperanza fashionable and willowy in a beribboned purple bonnet and a black fox pelerine, her shapely hands forever darting from her muff to point at some costly importation from Paris; Caleb dressed like a city gentleman, and a wealthy one at that, in his fawn-colored overcoat with a velvet collar, his gray beaver hat, his gray trousers strapped beneath polished black shoes. They would not have looked out of place in the Bois de Boulogne or in Piccadilly, unless you had chanced to remark the girl's almost naive animation at the wonders of this city, or unless you had observed the memories of Indian country in the man's sharp blue eyes, and the rough red wind-burn of his knurled face.

"That fan!" Esperanza breathed, her index finger prodding the show window, within which a creation of black ostrich feathers, with a diamond-set handle, reposed on gray velvet.

"Like it?"

"Ooo, I like everything! I never knew there was so much in the

302

world. I want to do everything, and buy everything, and see everything—"

"Not sorry you married me?"

She made a face at him, wrinkling her nose and sticking out her tongue, then seized his arm and snuggled against him.

"I have never been so happy," she said.

Waugh! He had never been so happy, either. You could say what you wanted to in favor of fancy houses, and helling around with fantailed pigeons, but the fact remained that marriage had advantages too. You married a girl and the law said you were one. Till the last few days he had always thought that an odd legal fiction; now, however, he understood. Mrs. Caleb McSwasey. Esperanza McSwasey. Mrs., Madam, *Señora, Frau.* Your name looped out like a lariat and enclosed the two of you. She was yours—all legal! Mrs. Caleb McSwasey—all branded, tagged, signed, sealed and delivered. Property of Caleb McSwasey. This seat is reserved. No trespassing, no poaching, posted, keep out by God!

"And that goes for all you sons of bitches," he thought, his jaw belligerent as his gaze flicked the male pedestrians of this frontier town, the shuffling Negroes, the roustabouts from the levee, the plainsmen in buckskins, the merchants in broadcloth, the moping, bewildered Osages and Kaws.

They moved on, pausing outside a red-brick façade with many-paned show windows which displayed an opulent array of *nonchalantes* in gay pastels, dainty riding boots with silver spurs, silk parasols, gold-mounted opera glasses, wispy gauzes, feathery boas. It was the establishment of Madame Letourneur, a modiste recently of Paris; and after they had opened the frosted glass door, stamped with green fleur-de-lis, Madame herself came sweeping from a conference with several seamstresses and greeted them in all her snake-eyed, arch-nostriled, bespangled-fingered, tremendous-busted glory.

"By God," Caleb thought, "if she ever goes broke at this I'll bet she'll open a fancy house."

Esperanza said she had come in to look, and Madame Letourneur indicated a gilded chair and suggested that perhaps the customer's father would like to be seated while his daughter tempted herself.

Caleb would have let that pass, although he liked it none too well, but Esperanza informed the Madame that the gentleman wasn't her father, whereupon all the Latin wisdom of the ages showed in the Madame's eyes, and a fair amount of the lasciviousness of the ages on her mouth, and in strongly Gallican English she apologized for calling mademoiselle's friend her father.

"He's my husband," Esperanza said.

Whereupon the Madame made a beeline for the most expensive merchandise.

Removing his overcoat, Caleb sat with both feet planted on the lavish pearl-colored carpet, in the gilded chair by the gilded table bearing fairly recent issues of the *Gazette des Salons* and the *Journal des Dames et des Modes,* fingering the gold watch chain looped across his flowered mauve waistcoat, in his nostrils the scents of powders and furs and perfumes and fine fabrics and femininity which always linger in such modish haunts. This was a new adventure in that unexplored country of so many flowery meads and leafy bowers and quicksands and pitfalls called matrimony. He saw that matrimony could be a full time job, if a man let it. He guessed that tomorrow he'd better get to work, talking business with lumber wholesalers.

Esperanza had removed her pelerine and bonnet, and as he sat there Caleb took pleasure in her beautiful hair, her exquisitely complicated face, her body in a tight-bodiced dress of pale gold velvet which flowed out from a narrow black belt to fall in lovely lines over her outstandingly handsome tail.

"By God," he thought, "I've always been lucky. She's got more style than a river packet, and three times the steam and dash."

In this lair of voiles and satins, foulards and chiffons and kidskins, he was an innocent, but his native Yankee sense kept flashing him warnings: he was as wary in the interests of his pocketbook as he used to be for the safety of his scalp when he encountered Indian sign. Still, he could understand that a fine bird like Esperanza needed fine feathers, and even if the feathers came at a dear price he reckoned his bride was worth all she cost. As he sat contemplating her fine waist and illustrious buttocks he was filled with a rich sexual satisfaction when he reflected that his money, earned by his brain, had bought the clothes she was wearing. He didn't, he told himself, want to let the tightfisted Season-good blood gain ascendancy in his life; stingy people like Grandpa Seasongood and Paul McSwasey hoarded up a wall of pennies between themselves and the pleasures of living. Yes, and between themselves and opportunity. Well, he had found plenty of opportunity, up there in Wisconsin Territory; from those forests a torrent of money, golden and musical, would pour into his coffers, more than enough to satisfy even a luxury-loving wife.

Back at a counter, Madame Letourneur and Esperanza were engaged in scrutinizing some object which Caleb couldn't see, and presently his bride turned, face vivid with pleasure, and beckoned him. Going to join them, he looked as stocky and knotty-muscled and tough as an old bull buffalo.

Esperanza's eyes flashed with excitement.

"Look!" she whispered. "Aren't they lovely?"

On the counter, nesting in black velvet, lay a string of pearls. Caressingly, Esperanza picked them up and displayed them; then, with Madame Letourneur's aid, the necklace circumnavigated the young bride's throat. Ankles together, body pert as a catbird's, head cocked, Esperanza gave Caleb an enchanting smile. Then she fluttered to a long mirror, where she struck regal poses, and poses of girlish simplicity, sometimes lifting her willful jaw and regarding herself archly, sometimes bending forward and smiling roguishly at herself.

"By God, she's a handful," Caleb thought dotingly.

When she returned to her husband she exclaimed, "Aren't they beautiful!"

"My dear creature," Madame Letourneur said, "there's nothing like a necklace to draw attention to the bosom."

"Lady," Caleb thought, "I don't reckon that's a problem for you."

"Chic," the Madame said.

Thumbing his jaw, Caleb stood regarding those consequences of ill health among bivalves.

"How much?" he asked.

Madame Letourneur said the necklace could be bought at only seven hundred and ninety-nine dollars and ninety-five cents. Caleb didn't stir a hair. But he was thinking his thoughts.

"I'd love to have them," Esperanza said. She went to the mirror again. When she returned she said, "I'd love to have them."

"We'll think about it," Caleb said.

Even after the necklace was returned to its black velvet, Esperanza kept favoring it with covetous glances; her mouth drooped; once she sighed.

Madame Letourneur said that while the necklace was being thought about, perhaps her customer would enjoy inspecting material for gowns. Esperanza interposed no objections.

"Something for a ball, perhaps?" the Madame asked. "Let me look at you, my dear creature." She sailed majestically from behind the counter, regarding her customer intently, even circling her, as if Esperanza were a young mare. "If you don't mind my saying it," she said, "that frock is not your color."

Already Caleb had learned that his bride's temper was unreliable, and he half expected a flareup. But nothing of the sort! Esperanza accepted this criticism with the same objectivity and scientific devotion in which it was offered.

"Why not?" she asked.

"The gold is too pale in tone. When you wear gold or yellow or orange, they must be toned to the exact intensity of your hair. And you must stay away from blue. Never blue with your black eyes and caramel-colored skin. Blue is for schoolgirls in any case. And never pink! To see you frilled in pink would send me to bed. But turquoise, yes! By all means! And possibly sea-green, although never silver. But you'll always be stunning in white. And in black and in the wine reds."

Esperanza, Caleb noted, was listening carefully. So was he, with considerable wonder. Never till now had he realized the niceties of judgment

305

involved in the intricate business of being a woman. By God, you went to more trouble dressing a woman than in harnessing a horse!

"And now your hair," Madame Letourneur said. "Mmm-m-m. Let me call my husband." She looked toward the rear of the establishment. "Oh, Octave!"

Octave came. Caleb didn't cotton to him, even though the Madame declared that he had been the most dextrous *artiste en coiffure* in Paris, the very favorite hairdresser of the Marquise de Mouchy.

"Mon lion," said the Madame, "what would you?"

And she waved a hand at Esperanza's hair.

Octave's countenance wore an expression of pain and amusement as he regarded the simplicity of Esperanza's coiffure; he sighed, shook his head; it would not do; it really wouldn't. Lovely hair; *oui*, like silken sunlight; like spun gold; like a jonquil in an April garden; but how it was dressed!

"I like it the way it is," Caleb said.

"What does it need?" Esperanza asked.

It needed, Octave said, the expert fingerwork and artist's touch of Octave Letourneur. It needed a low chignon at the back, perhaps enmeshed with a black net and diamonds, perhaps held by a decorative ivory comb; it needed curls at the temples like bunches of golden grapes; it needed the sorcery of lacquer, and perhaps the pretty conceit of silvery snowflakes scattered amid the sunny tresses—

"I like it the way it is," Caleb repeated. "Besides, I won't have any man fussing with my wife's hair."

Octave looked startled. And when he protested, and Madame Letourneur protested, and Esperanza looked disappointed, Caleb shook his head.

"If you want to show her something to wear, go ahead," he told the Madame. "But I won't have any man working on my wife."

"Monsieur is a jealous husband?" the Madame asked airily.

"You're damned right he is."

"Ah," she said coyly, "you had better not take her to Paris."

"I wasn't aiming to."

At last Octave retired in some bewilderment; Caleb stood with feet apart on the carpet, bison-like, his jaw looking bigger than Plymouth Rock. Madame Letourneur smoothed the ruffled atmosphere with a flow of honey, mentioning a gown which had been ordered for a ball and never called for. She billowed over to a rack, producing a shimmering creation in white satin.

"I believe it's your size exactly," she told Esperanza. "Let's try it on." And after Esperanza had been conducted by a seamstress to a fitting room, the Madame told Caleb:

"The child adores that pearl necklace."

"The price is too dear," he said.

306

"Pearls on a lovely throat," the Madame said. "The child is really extraordinarily beautiful. Pearls were made for youth and beauty."

"That may be," Caleb said, "but I won't buy it at your price. For that money I could buy me all the glass beads in St. Louis and trade them for all the gals in the Cheyenne Nation."

"You are a realist."

"If I hadn't been, I'd have lost my hair twenty years ago."

"You will pay—what?"

"My price wouldn't interest you," he said. "Not for those. But I'll do this. We'll tell my wife I've bought them but you won't let us take them now. Something's wrong with the thread or the clasp and you have to restring them. So you scare up some good imitations and string them up to look like these. Send them to my hotel tomorrow. She'll not know the difference, once they're away from the store. And I'll pay you a hundred dollars."

Madame Letourneur's eyes were disenchanted.

"That I could not do."

"Then we'll drop the matter."

The Madame sighed; her voice was resigned.

"In France," she said, "we heard great tales of America. St. Louis was a French city and one could reap a fortune in a year. But it is not a French city. It is a muddy town full of trappers who need baths and Germans who prefer beer to champagne. You Americans drive shrewder bargains than fishwives." She shrugged. "You may have these pearls for a hundred. They too are imitation."

Again, Caleb didn't stir a hair. He was seated in the gilded chair when Esperanza returned from the fitting room; at sight of her he stood up, thinking, "Waugh!"

Madame Letourneur had been correct; white was for her. The golden hair, the black eyes and brows and lashes, the skin tones of warm beige and copper, the girlish breasts trying to peer over the edge of the low-cut bodice, the round willowy belly unconfined by stays, the luscious, shining white satin, cascading and swishing in the full skirt—she was stunning. And when, going to her at the mirror, Caleb encircled her warm throat with a pearl necklace known to be priced at seven hundred and ninety-nine dollars and ninety-five cents, she crooned, "Ooo-ooo," and her face lighted with all the glory of a beige mesa at sunrise, and she flung her arms around him and rewarded him with a kiss. Waugh! And after they had left the shop, where she ordered more dresses and purchased many feminine accessories, and returned to the hotel, she rewarded him further, Lilith having been directed to remain in the living room of the suite.

*

307

She wore the pearls and the satin gown that evening when they took supper in the dining room of the hotel, a place of terrazzo and iron pillars and tall windows with velvet draperies. When they entered from the lobby an orchestra was playing Viennese waltzes behind potted palms, and as they followed the head waiter in his boiled shirt to the table with its gleaming silver Caleb became conscious of half a hundred stares fixed upon them. He didn't like that; he preferred slipping through life without attracting attention, because a man might be engaged in a piece of business whose success required secrecy; but he guessed Esperanza would always cause a stir wherever she went, especially when sheathed in a gown as daring as this one. Even after they were seated they didn't sink from public scrutiny, for Esperanza shaped a cigarette and blew smoke at the goblets: from the way the men ogled her, and the women looked down their noses, she might have been some vivid popular actress.

"Mistah McSwasey, suh, good evening, suh," their waiter said, a soft-voiced old Negro with a touch of misery in his joints. " 'Spect you don't 'member me."

"You must be Toby," Caleb said.

"No, suh, excuse me, suh, but I ain't Toby. Me, I'm Skip. Used to belong to Miss Nettie. She sell me after that there panic."

Caleb remembered him then, but inasmuch as Miss Nettie, before the panic, had operated the most resplendent fancy house in town, with Skip as butler, he didn't care to reminisce about the old days.

"I'm married now," he said.

"Yes, suh, so I hear tell. That what your Lilith tell me, out in the kitchen."

Caleb ordered dry sherry, to be followed by Burgundy, and after the wine was poured, and Caleb said, "Luck," he sat enjoying the sight of Esperanza across the linen, a sparkling girl lifting a sparkling glass.

"Happy?" he asked.

"Ooooo!"

"Glad you married me?"

Her eyes were soft as a kitten's, her smile intimate.

"I think you like to tease me," she said.

And I own her, he thought, she's my property, it's all legal. By God, marriage is all right.

He had never been happier, sitting there with the joyous stringed music caressing his ears, his legs sometimes brushing his bride's under the table, the wine running in his veins. He felt so overflowing with enchantment, so stuffed and replete with the pleasures of matrimony, so voluptuously contented, that he thought he must look as full of well being as a great fat Buddha enjoying the salaams of Chinese maidens and the slow-rising sensuous incense. Idly, while Esperanza chattered about the dresses she had ordered, he reflected upon the capriciousness of existence, how a boastful Dutchman named Otto Zumwalt had come upriver from New

Orleans with a letter to John Proudfoot, how if John Proudfoot had not hired him the Dutchman would likely never have gone to Santa Fe and married a girl named Consuelo Delgado and fathered a girl named Esperanza. His mind was staggered at the bewildering complexity of the patterns human beings stitched, at the incalculable number of minor miracles that had gone into producing this beautiful miracle who sat across from him, slowly turning the wine glass in lovely fingers.

The waiter poured more wine, elaborately avoiding the briefest glance at Esperanza. Niggers, Caleb thought, his jealousy dozing, were all right: a nigger boy learned early not to stretch his eyes at a white girl. Roast beef came, juicy and rare, the way he had learned to like meat on the plains, when he used to sink his teeth into liver that had been part of a living buffalo, a minute earlier; and while he ate he fell to thinking in a large, warm, cloudy way about this new adventure soon to engage him: logging. His plans were laid; he was on guard against his natural tendency to extend himself too much, spread his capital too thin, to try to pyramid a fortune in a year; this time he would proceed methodically, always keeping capital reserves against the contingencies inevitable in business; the panic had taught him a lesson. He was unaware of the food on the plate before him, and for the moment he had forgotten even his bride, for visions had risen in his brain of a land arched by blue northern sky, threaded by hurrying creeks and by wide copious rivers which he would burden with miles of floating logs. In imagination he could see the forest itself, stretching away for leagues uncharted, raw wealth waiting. Stumpage. Long-legged, massive trees striding gigantically in a virgin country. The Whiskey River, its transparent water arrowed by speckled trout. It would be his river: his to use till he had skinned the country. And after that there would be other rivers. The Chippewa. The Eau Claire. The Flambeau. Their very names brought back to him the crisp tang of pines, the gleam of running water. And there were other forests, beyond and back of beyond, endless, limitless, inexhaustible, at least in his time.

So intense was his concentration that he remained unaware that two persons had stopped at the table; Esperanza spoke his name. He looked up to see muttonchop whiskers framing the face of a bank president named Alonzo Henderson; he got to his feet; there were introductions; chairs were brought. Accompanying Alonzo Henderson was his son, Alonzo, Jr., a boy of seventeen. And while Alonzo, Senior, told Caleb he was glad to encounter him, fresh back from Santa Fe, and to learn the state of business in New Mexico, in order to guide him in lending to traders going out there this spring, and while Caleb answered his questions, he was less interested in the subject under discussion than in the conversation between Alonzo, Jr., and Esperanza. He caught snatches of their chitchat; he noticed how brilliantly she smiled. And instantly he was suffused by that old, familiar, bile-colored feeling, so intense as to approach physical sickness, and he knew that if he were a dog he would be curling his lip and growling, and if he were a bull buffalo he would be pawing the sod and lowering his head. Here in a fashionable dining room he did not, of course, fling a wine bottle at Alonzo, Jr., but by God he felt like it; and after father and son departed he sat regarding his bride narrowly. Behind her cigarette smoke her eyes were innocent, meeting his; she asked what was wrong. Nothing, he said; but everything was wrong. His lemon sherbet felt like a clammy tadpole sliding down his throat, and it lay cold in his stomach; his cigar tasted flat; the apricot brandy burned him. And after they had returned to their room he came out with it: he failed to see the necessity, he said, of her acting as she had with Alonzo, Jr.

She was offended; didn't he want her to be civil to his friends? Yes, he said, but she needn't act like a hustler.

It developed into a first-rate quarrel, before it was over; he accused her of having smiled too sweetly at that hairdresser, Octave; of having showered too much charm on that mule skinner, Tad Weesener; she really was offended, then; and he announced his disapproval of the way she regarded with interest handsome strangers on the street and in the lobby. About that time she began stamping her foot and exclaiming, "Arrgh!" Finally, goaded into a frightful Apache rage, she rushed at him with scratching fingernails, and he cuffed her around. Then he seized her shoulders and shook her till the hairpins flew. She was sobbing by then, and begging him not to dig his fingers so hard into her flesh: he was hurting her.

"You're damned right I'm hurting you," he said.

And he hauled off and smacked her with his open palm.

She flung herself on the bed, crying like a child, beating the counterpane with her fists.

"I know Injuns," he said, looking down at her. "Now get up."

When she didn't obey he yanked her to her feet; again his hands grappled her shoulders.

"Injuns don't hurt that easy," he said. "It's temper."

Her face was streaming; her lips quivered.

"You're going to be true to me," he said. "Aren't you?"

She tried to break away.

"Aren't you?"

"Y-yes."

But her eyes avoided his.

His voice, habitually quiet, was now deadly so.

"I'll kill any son of a bitch," he said, "who comes poaching. And I'll do with you what a Cheyenne I once knew did with his squaw. I'll firebrand that pretty face of yours. Is that plain?"

310

"Y-yes."

"It had better be," he said.

*

In April when they took the steamboat *Gypsy Lady* to New Empire the honeymoon showed signs of exhaustion. As it had been in the beginning so it was now and ever would be: Caleb's narrow-minded convictions concerning monogamy in an attractive young wife seriously interfered with Esperanza's intentions that marriage should be a gay round of balls and parties and flirtations leading to what always came to pass in those French novels. Like her father before her, who had discovered that the only place savages displayed much nobility was in the pages of Rousseau, Esperanza learned that life after all did not invariably imitate art. Not, in any case, life with a husband so ridiculously jealous that you suspected him of deliberately refusing invitations to levees in the most fashionable St. Louis homes simply because gay young dogs might be there, wagging their tails and bringing you punch.

Till Caleb, her experience with men had been principally confined to Otto, who was not precisely a strong, silent man, and to Gilberto, who was not the masterful type. Looking on marriage as an escape from Santa Fe, as a stepping stone into a carriage that would whirl her along gay boulevards with confetti and band music and kisses, she found herself wholly unprepared to cope with a tough-minded husband in whose matrimonial decalogue the most popular commandment advised against the wife's wearing the pants. He could be the gentlest of men, the most considerate of lovers, the most generous of husbands, so long as she behaved herself; but inasmuch as behaving herself went contrary to everything she had ever stood for, it was inevitable that occasionally their wills should cross. And crossing Caleb's will had its unsafe moments. He expected obedience and got it, even at the cost of physical coercion. With her Apache, Prussian and Slavic blood, this increased her respect for him, and doubtless would have increased her love, if there had ever been a morsel of love to increase; so it might have turned out a really ideal marriage if only he hadn't been so captious about her interest in other men. Men, men, men—St. Louis was simply swarming with fascinating men; sinewy young fellows in buckskins; gay blades in broadcloth; blond Germans; Irishmen with the devil in their eyes; a banquet feast of men! But did she dare talk with them, even smile at them? She did not. So of course she felt defrauded, as frustrated as a little dog dragged summarily past a butcher shop. She often planned to venture forth on her own, when Caleb left the hotel on business, but he was forever returning unexpectedly and catching her in street garb. Then he would ask questions which, early in the honeymoon, she answered defiantly, and later, having learned better, she parried with easy little fibs, a talent for which she had inherited from her father.

311

As the honeymoon waned, Caleb fell into the practice of taking her along when he made business calls, a custom which vitiated efficiency, for if you were the proprietor of a lumber yard or of a sawmill, or if you were a county official who might be buying lumber next year for a plank road, and a blocky hard-bitten man entered your office to discuss a proposal whereby your mill would saw his logs on a percentage basis, or a deal whereby, if your palms were anointed, you would spend tax money for planks, you found it trying to keep your attention riveted on business when he brought along a bewitching young thing whose bright hair filled the room with blond light and whose dark eyes were will-o'-the-wisps beckoning toward a bedroom and who, when she sat with crossed legs, displayed a lacy white froth of petticoat and a glimpse of pretty ankle. Nevertheless, Caleb persisted in this unbusinesslike habit, for it was his mad intention not to let her out of his sight.

"Don't you trust me?" she asked once, when they were an old married couple of six weeks.

"No."

And while that rejoinder demonstrated his sound common sense, still it did lack tact, and it sharpened Esperanza's growing realization that when she had promised to love, honor and obey this intractable man she had placed ankles and wrists in invisible fetters. Hence, like even the best-behaved members of a chain gang, she began dreaming of escape, if only for an hour. She managed escape too, one morning in March, by complaining of a headache and by covertly gagging herself with a forefinger, so that she threw up: perhaps, she said, she was coming down with cholera. Caleb didn't look greatly worried, but he did leave the hotel without her. After a few minutes she scrambled from bed, snatched on her clothes and, having warned Lilith to hold her tongue, set forth to enjoy the city. But how could one enjoy a city without money? Her purse contained only a couple of dollars: Caleb handled the money in that family, even the money received from the sale of the twins. Esperanza resented this, and perhaps with justice, for certainly the twins, a product of those excellent brood animals, Otto and Lilith, had come into the world without Caleb's so much as lifting a finger.

That morning, after strolling about for a few minutes, never dreaming that her husband might be shadowing her, Esperanza bought a ticket and entered Huppard's Museum, an establishment which smelled like a cross between a taxidermist's shop and a zoo. American eagles, somewhat moth-eaten, perched atop glass cases containing arrowheads, war clubs and insects preserved in amber; and in a canvas pit rattlesnakes lay regretting their assumption that a forked stick was an ineffectual artifice of capture. Esperanza found it pretty dull, till a couple of soldiers from Jefferson Barracks wandered in. She didn't really flirt with them, at first, but she didn't exactly ignore them, either, and certainly they didn't ignore her; and after they had opined that they would just bet she would skedaddle if one of them rattlers took out after her—well —she felt she had to uphold the Zumwalt honor by replying that she just bet she wouldn't. Many a witty remark followed, and much laughter, but it was all perfectly harmless. Caleb, however, didn't think it so, when he found her strolling from display case to display case, squired by those defenders of the flag, and he lost no time in rescuing her and, back in the hotel, in upbraiding her. That was the day, between spasms of crying, when she glared up from the bed and announced she regretted ever marrying him. It frightened her, the way he received that news, his eyes turning icy, his smile wintry.

"You're my wife," he said, his voice so low she could scarcely hear it, "and I propose to keep you. If you ever run away I'll bring you back, if I have to trail you to Timbuktu."

"Maybe I'll get a divorce," she said.

"I don't think you will," he said, with such complete conviction that a shiver scampered along her spine. "If you try, you'll regret it."

She remembered then his old threat to firebrand her, leaving her face a hideous mass of scar tissue that would repel all men; and as she lay there exhausted by weeping she found her thoughts hovering about the sheathed knife that had belonged to her great-grandmother. And a horrible little scene flashed through her imagination: Caleb coming toward her with a flaming brand, and her sliding the knife from the sheath in self-protection. But she knew she could never manage to sink the knife into his belly as she had sunk it so long ago into the man with yellow shoes. Caleb was too strong; he had survived too many barroom knife-frays; he knew all the tricks. Sometimes, however, in the nightmares which were pestering her again, when she was chased not by a man with yellow shoes but by her husband brandishing a fiery stick, she managed to stab the knife into his bowels, and after that she was a terrified girl running home and sobbing hysterically in her father's arms, begging him to bury the knife forever.

Lilith was beginning to enjoy St. Louis more, now that Mistah Mc-Swasey was learning what she could have told him all along. At first she had been pretty miserable, kissing the twins good-by and watching them depart in the company of that fox-eyed old gentleman, and being barred from the bedroom of the suite, as she had been most of the time after that preacher made everything legal; but as the weeks passed, and Mistah McSwasey found it necessary to tame his little spitfire's spirit, Lilith delighted in lingering outside the bedroom door, silently but enthusiastically cheering Mistah McSwasey on.

"That's right, give it to her, man!" she would think. "I always knowed she wouldn't fool you for long."

She had always been devoted to Mistah McSwasey, ever since that halcyon journey to Taos; sometimes she hoped that he would tire of his bride, and realize that good old Lilith was still mighty spry in a tousling match; but whether or not that happened she was still on his side in any squabble; and once when Esperanza was in her bath, Lilith volunteered her services to him as chief intelligence officer in a domestic spy network. Handsomely clad in black broadcloth, wiry hair bristling from his big round skull, wiry eyebrows bristling above his sharp blue eyes, thick lips parted in what might have been a smile, he stood thumbing his obdurate jaw. When he spoke his voice was low.

"You're a good nigger," he said.

"You ain't goin' to sell me, is you? You'll keep Lilith?"

He gave her rump an affectionate pat—it thrilled her so much she wanted to cry, "Eee!" and fling her tremendous breasts against his chest —and he pulled out his chamois moneybag and handed her a silver dollar.

"You keep your eyes open," he said, "and your mouth shut and I won't sell you."

*

In the glass cage of the *Gypsy Lady's* pilothouse Caleb's pupils were pinpointed against the brilliance of April sun ricocheting from running water and from a gilded ball suspended between two lean chimneys pouring forth plum-colored smoke streaked with sparks. The smoke smelled of pitch pine—in the South, he remembered, they called it fat pine—and its redolence thickly overlaid the rich brown odor of plug tobacco from the cud of Mr. Pickens, the pilot, and the sweetness of powder and French water from Esperanza.

"Another half hour," Captain Willard said, "and we'll be there." He smiled down at Esperanza. Caleb watched them narrowly. He was standing close behind his bride in the cramped pilothouse and hence he couldn't see her face, but from the movement of her poke bonnet—a flaring creation of springtime straw with daisies and with white ribbons tied beneath her chin—he suspected that she looked up at Captain Willard and flashed him a smile.

That she considered the captain an interesting man Caleb had learned from Lilith; also that she thought him handsome in his blue jacket with brass buttons. That Captain Willard, who was young for a steamboat master, shared this opinion was apparent from the dandyish way he touched his silky chestnut mustache and used his languishing eyes. Caleb would have liked to pop him.

"This," Captain Willard said, gesturing easily, "is Muskrat Bend. Now we'll make a crossing. Although at this stage of water we could cross anywhere. Isn't that so, Mr. Pickens?"

Maybe it was and maybe it wasn't, Mr. Pickens said. He shot a thimbleful of tobacco juice into the spittoon and put over the wheel, a tall beautifully-carved thing of polished walnut. Mr. Pickens, Caleb thought, managed admirably to control his enthusiasm for visitors in the pilot-house.

"Anyway," Captain Willard said, "it's a good stage of water."

Yup, very fair, said Mr. Pickens, although he had seen better.

The great white boat, a stern-wheeler, sparkling new this season, followed the channel toward the Iowa side, Mr. Pickens sighting their course by means of the jackstaff and a far shore sycamore.

"Did you have rivers like this out there in New Mexico?" Captain Willard asked Esperanza.

"Ooo, no!" Her laugh came musically from the poke bonnet. "I have never seen so much water. And the trees and grasses! Everything so green!"

Captain Willard chuckled; Caleb felt as if his heart were stuck full of porcupine quills. No two ways about it, jealousy like his was a hair-shirt. Especially when he was married to a luscious girl who attracted men the way a sweet hyacinth attracted bees. And especially when flirting came as naturally to her as chasing moonbeams to a moth. Sometimes he almost wished he had never met her. Sometimes he disliked her. And that was odd because at the same time he loved her more passionately now than even in the early days of marriage.

So he was in a pretty pickle; and occasionally he thought that maybe it had been a mistake to make that deal with Lilith whereby she would keep a sharp eye on her mistress and fish for information and report any infatuations. Not that there had been any infatuations; not yet. But he was perpetually uneasy lest there might be. He didn't know—not for certain—what action he would take if Lilith should report that Esperanza had actually fallen in love with some man, but he had a fair idea what action he would take, and it worried him. This wasn't the South; this was more like Massachusetts, the way people frowned on duels; and if he bumped into a situation where he had to remove a rival it might demand a little doing to make sure he didn't end up in considerable trouble. Still, it would be a pretty narrow-minded jury that would blame a husband for putting a home-breaker into a coffin.

Captain Willard was smiling and telling Esperanza that if he were pilot of this steamboat and not merely the captain he would let her take a turn at the wheel. That was supposed to be a joke, about his being merely the captain, and it was also a hint to Mr. Pickens. Esperanza laughed and declared she would like nothing better. Mr. Pickens ignored the whole business. And Caleb, to remind all concerned just who was married to whom, inched closer to his bride and rested his hands lightly on her waist, as if to encircle it.

Her dress was of biscuit-brown muslin, the provocative bodice narrowing to her supple waist, the skirt full and free-flowing. Beneath his fingers Caleb could feel the roundness of her body, unprotected by stays, soft and warm as the belly of a pretty little fox. As always, to touch her was to desire her; with some effort, he forced his hands to remain casual.

"Now then," he thought, regarding Captain Willard, "I reckon you know whose woman she is, you son of a bitch."

"Would it be possible," the captain was asking Mr. Pickens, "for Mrs. McSwasey to take the wheel?"

"Nope," Mr. Pickens said.

"On my responsibility," Captain Willard said. "As owner."

Caleb wanted to snort: everyone knew it was Captain Willard's father who owned the boat. Mr. Pickens did not deign to answer.

"Ooo, I would love to!"

Caleb could feel her getting ready to step over to Mr. Pickens and exert her charm: he had never known a girl so determined to have her own way. She was harder to break than a mustang, and she wouldn't stay broke; you could ride her and spur her till you thought you had tamed her at last, but next day she would buck and kick and bite with as much spirit as ever. Now, his hands tightened on her waist.

"Don't," she said, trying to wiggle free. And when she couldn't manage it she turned her head. Her face, framed by the scoops of her bonnet, and by clusters of curls at her temples, looked stormy. "Let me loose," she demanded.

"You're all right where you are."

Her eyes turned opaque; his gaze met them; there was a moment of connubial infighting; then her lashes dropped and he had won. When she looked at him again her eyes were submissive as a lodgepoled squaw's.

"You're mussing me up," she whispered.

He released her then; she smoothed her skirt over her waist and elegant buttocks. But she didn't attempt going to Mr. Pickens. And thereafter Captain Willard, looking baffled, avoided the subject of her taking the wheel. Jaw brutal, Caleb stood wrapped in enigma, but his eyes were victorious and his soul rejoiced as jubilantly as if he had knocked Captain Willard downstairs. Subtly, the balance of male power there in the pilot-house had shifted from Captain Willard back to the husband, where it belonged. If he knew his wife, Caleb thought, her interest in the captain would wane, now that he had failed to carry his point. She liked a winner. Well, by God, she had picked one in him.

Captain Willard, who was fundamentally, Caleb reflected, a mule's west end, smiled easily and touched his mustache.

"Twenty minutes and we'll be in New Empire, eh, Mr. Pickens?"

"That's up to the Lord," Mr. Pickens said.

The captain winked at the McSwaseys. It was evident he considered his pilot quite a card. Esperanza murmured something about going below to make sure that Lilith had finished packing all the valises and portmanteaus and bandboxes in their cabin; but Captain Willard urged her to stay; with the amount of freight to be unloaded at New Empire, there would be ample time for disembarking.

"We'll stay," Caleb said.

From the height of the pilothouse, he watched the Mississippi sweeping toward the bow like an immensely wide highway, blue-tinted and sparkling, the Iowa bluffs stretching off to the north in foliage and in limestone, gray and castellated, the bluffs of Wisconsin softly mauve and mysterious beyond a flood plain choked with cattails and lotus and wild rice, where redwings were feeding. When the boat steamed past islands he could look down on the topmost branches of sycamores, their feet wading in the high April water, their trunks entwined and their limbs festooned with the prolific endlessness of wild grape and honeysuckle and Virginia creeper. Behind the islands sloughs wandered, brown and sluggish, havens for mallards and teals, for cranes and herons and wild swans; and beyond the first sloughs more half-drowned islands, more sloughs, brimming with the overplus of water that six weeks ago had lain in snowdrifts along the Chippewa, the Yellow, the St. Croix, the Whiskey.

And while he kept a weather eye on his wife—who, as he had anticipated, no longer seemed to find the captain so fascinating—he fell to thinking of his stumpage along the Whiskey River and of his plans for camps and tote roads and rollways, for logs afloat on the freshets of spring, next year. Down the Whiskey to the Chippewa, down the Chippewa to the Mississippi, and after that rafts on the way to the mills.

Sudden happiness ran through him: he couldn't miss. The Panic of '37 had caught him with his britches down, but now he had capital again. And he was in a new country in the prime of life. Waugh!

And as he gazed out on the main channel steadily pouring its tonnage of water past the islands it was forever piling up and gnawing down, swinging powerfully around mile-long bends, from Iowa to Wisconsin and back again, bearing on its vastness a flotsam of bobbing stray logs, scraps of bark, bubbles, foam, hurrying whirlpools and even a mighty tree with half-grown leaves and sun-clawing roots—as he gazed at that big river of the American heartland, draining the trout streams of Minnesota Territory and the cranberry bogs of Wisconsin, fed by snow brooks from the pineries and by creeks from the high prairies of Iowa, hurrying toward many a whirling rendezvous with waters from the plains and bad lands and remote glaciers of the West, from the Alleghenies in the East, from Kentucky hills and Illinois meadows and Indiana pastures, from canebrakes in Tennessee, from carp creeks in Missouri, from springs in the Ozarks and from sluggish mud creeks and swamps and bayous in Louisiana, he felt suddenly bigger than life, bigger than his blocky, tough-muscled self, a giant of a man who would use that river for his own purposes, master her, possess her, as he mastered

317

and possessed his bride. He thought, "Yippee-yee! Bring out the brass band, boys, here comes Caleb McSwasey!"

Esperanza was tugging his sleeve. Feeling like a man jerked from dreams of empire, he looked where she was pointing and saw, on the Iowa side, where the bluffs opened out into a coulee, a Dakota village with hide tepees, innumerable dogs, tumbling and racing children, staring squaws, breech-clouted braves. A half dozen boys jumped into dugouts and paddled into the channel. One boy, older than the others, exhibited his prowess by grasping the gunwales of his dugout. Then, with a quick side jerk, he overbalanced the round-bottomed craft; it rolled like a barrel, coming up with the boy laughing and dripping, still grasping the gunwales. He performed the maneuver again and again, sinewy body gleaming like animated bronze. Esperanza laughed in childish delight, and Caleb noticed that she kept looking back till the dugout was a speck bobbing in the wake. He also looked back, over the continuous snowy foam of the stern wheel with the spray-rainbow above it; and he realized he had been imagining rifle sights fixed on the boy and how a bullet would take the starch out of him.

"I'm getting ridiculous," he thought, as it came to him that he was being jealous of that Injun. And yet he kept right on being jealous, for several minutes, worrying himself with the reminder that the boy in the dugout was about her age, and that she had inherited Injun blood, and that under the right circumstances—perhaps if he was off in the woods and the boy knocked at the kitchen door peddling catfish—she might invite him into the house and they might end up in the bedroom. By God! He could feel his face flushing, and he imagined himself coming home unexpectedly and how he would deal with that Injun son of a bitch. Scalp him! It wouldn't be the first Injun he had scalped. He wished he weren't so jealous. Hod Kite had been right; it could get him into a peck of trouble. He couldn't go on like this, wanting to biff every man he saw; it was slashing him up inside; it was taking his mind off money-making.

Presently Mr. Pickens pulled the whistle rope; the pilothouse shook with a sound as palpable as a fist-blow; and the *Gypsy Lady* steamed round a bend, bringing into view a magnificent piece of river. Dead ahead, a sandspit widened into a heavy island populated by elms and willows; Mr. Pickens put over the wheel and the steamboat nosed into a deep-looking back-channel between the island and Wisconsin.

And Caleb saw New Empire floating toward him in the soft April morning, a town of romance today because he came not as a St. Louis businessman speculating in stumpage but as a conquistador establishing a beachhead against the defenseless forests in the North. He had a swift vision of those pines crashing under the axes of the men Otto Zumwalt's money would hire; his spirits rose. And as he watched New Empire gliding nearer, with Front Street paralleling the river, its warehouses imposing, its sandstone and wooden façades displaying signs announcing the Rivermen's Rest Hotel, the Back Channel Bar, Rafferty's Saloon; as he saw Winnebago Street coming from the east to the river which suckled it; as he made out the distant cupola of the courthouse rising among the fine old maples and locusts, he realized that the actual reason this expedition seemed drenched in romance was because his woman was with him. She might be a handful but with her by his side existence was sharpened. With her along life had tang, like buffalo liver sprinkled with gall juice.

Bells chiming, the *Gypsy Lady* nosed toward shore, where horses hitched to buggies waltzed on hind legs, when Mr. Pickens gratuitously yanked the whistle rope. From Rafferty's Saloon a rowdy came staggering, clambered into a lumber wagon, bowed low; dogs were far lost in hysteria; from the cobbled levee longshoremen shouted jovial insults at roustabouts on the main deck; and townsmen in beaver hats waved at Captain Willard in the pilothouse. At least, Caleb assumed it was at the captain they were waving. It had better be at him and not—the sons of bitches!—at Esperanza.

*

At first they lived in a hotel, the Commercial House on the north side of Winnebago Street, pretty wretched pickings after the Western Exchange in St. Louis. The rooms were cubbyholes, the food unmentionable; but worst of all Esperanza had nothing to do but sit in their room and brood about God knew what: Caleb prohibited her sitting alone in the lobby, of course. He used to drag her along to his office, after he rented one in the Gentry Block, a brick building on the northwest corner of Court Avenue and Winnebago Street; but taking her there was unsuccessful—he wanted to sit planning his plans, and she interfered with concentration—so presently he came to depend more and more on Lilith to chaperone her. With his permission, the two women used to go on long walks to the grassy bluffs east of town or to the river. Lilith proved a wonderful guardian, perhaps because she enjoyed her work, and Caleb rewarded her with a dollar now and then.

Sometimes Dexter Yarlow, the Negro janitor at the hotel, accompanied the women, along with his fishing pole. He was grizzled and fiftyish, although Lilith considered him a pretty fair lover in a pinch, which this certainly was; and he it was who theorized that since Wisconsin was free soil Lilith was no longer a slave. That seemed dubious; and besides, with her affection for Mistah Caleb, and the possibility that he might tousle her, she wasn't going to leave the McSwaseys and marry Dexter; but nevertheless, as time went on, all that talk about freedom incited her to become somewhat uppity with her mistress. One of these days, Esperanza told herself, she would have to teach Lilith a fine lesson.

To reach Caleb's office, a single shabby room, at the northeast corner

319

of the building, you climbed wooden steps to the second floor of the Gentry Block, picking your way among spatters of tobacco juice to a door that said: "McSwasey & Zumwalt Lumber Co." The furnishings weren't much: a wall-map of Wisconsin Territory, a pine table, hard chairs, a spittoon. But Caleb didn't mind; the real office was inside his head.

Hardly anybody went there, during April and May, but in late spring after the lumber camps closed up north, and the log drives ended, pinery boys drifted down to New Empire with checks for their winter's work. The checks were post-dated October 1, for most of the logging companies did business on a credit shoestring, and not until autumn would they harvest money from the sale of their logs. But the pinery boys needed cash. To get it they were glad to sell those checks for twenty percent less than face value; for twenty-five percent, if the cash was in gold. When the boys began hitting town they learned in Rafferty's Saloon that a newcomer named McSwasey stood ready to discount their checks and pay in gold dollars; so by June, with gold still scarce after the panic, calked boots tramped to Caleb's office, and the coins that friendship had lured from the walls of Otto Zumwalt's store passed into palms calloused by ax helves.

Caleb did not, of course, accept every check. The logging company had to be good for it. But by June, after exhaustive inquiries in saloons and banks, and especially from his landlord, Sophronicus Gentry, he had a brain packed with cold-blooded information about every operator in the pinery.

Knocking about the country, he had learned to judge men, and as those pinery boys clumped in, their calks dotting the bare floor with loggers' smallpox, he sized them up shrewdly, and when he encountered intelligence and reliability he asked:

"How would you like a boss who would pay wages in cash?"

"Ain't none such."

"You're looking at one now," he said; and he advised them to get in touch with McSwasey & Zumwalt before hiring out in the fall. Thus he culled the best brains and brawn for his first camp on the Whiskey River. And thus he found Amos Peabody.

Peabody was a State-of-Mainer who had learned his logging along the Penobscot, which meant a deerfly could swallow anything he didn't know about timber. It was sheer luck, people said, that McSwasey & Zumwalt was able to hire Peabody as camp foreman: what the boys called a push. Caleb let them say what they pleased, but he knew it wasn't luck.

"You stick with me," he told Peabody, "and you'll end up with a potful of pennies. We've got capital. My partner's one of the richest men in New Mexico." At the wall-map he flipped his hand against the Whiskey River country. "We're starting small here, but ten years from now—"

His hand swept the map.

He delegated Peabody full authority to hire a crew and buy all the oxen and chains and axes and salt pork and beans that made up a logging kit. Assured of cash payment, and in gold at that, the New Empire merchants shaded their prices considerably; and in August, when the foreman and a cadre of men left by steamboat for the woods, to cut tote roads and to build camp, Caleb felt affairs were off to a good start.

"I'll be up in October," he told Peabody.

And back in his office, staring through cigar smoke at the map, he dreamed of next year, when he would have two camps cutting timber, and of the year after, when he would have four, and of the year after, and the year after, and the year after.

The front portion of that second floor in the Gentry Block was occupied by the law offices of Sophronicus Gentry—Judge Gentry, people called him, although he no longer sat on the bench—and one of Caleb's first moves was to retain the judge as attorney for McSwasey & Zumwalt. In the outer office of that fortress of law, its walls stockaded by shelves of hidebound books, its redoubtable safe defending the whereases and wherefores of many a tape-tied document, several of the judge's student clerks sat at a long table, poring over Chitty and Blackstone, or scratching industrious pens across sheets of foolscap, and when Caleb limped in one of those future counselors would rap on the judge's door, announce the visitor and wave him into the inner office, a place of faded raspberry carpet, a marble fireplace, green-shaded lamps, and a revolving bookcase loaded with Addison, Dryden, Shakespeare, Gibbon, Fielding, Plutarch, Vergil, Voltaire, Tom Paine and Thucydides, together with Greek and Latin dictionaries. A white marble lion prowled atop a black marble pedestal; a moose head grinned sardonically from the wall; a stuffed owl, looking old enough to have been an owl of Attica, perched on a second bookcase; a glass case held a collection of coins from the ancient world.

The judge, a large man in his early fifties, with a massive head and a mane of white hair, would be sitting at his desk puffing a pipe and reading Goldsmith or Thomas Jefferson or Plato. Seldom had even his student clerks caught him studying a deed or a brief, yet surely he must have spent a few minutes daily on legal matters, for he was almost never bested in court and he could quote endlessly from decisions by judges whose brains had long since been provender for worms. His clerks thought him an intellectual Goliath, and they may have been right: certainly the judge, who was in a position to know, wouldn't have argued very heatedly against that hypothesis. And if less biased evidence were demanded, there was always his diploma hanging on the wall, stating in plain Latin that he had been graduated *summa cum laude* from Transylvania University, Class of 1810.

Nor were the judge's talents confined to matters legal and intellectual, for unlike so many attorneys he was an excellent businessman.

"Gentlemen," he sometimes told his clerks, "the weakest department in any law firm is usually its collection department. Watch collections. If you can't get cash, get land, and if you can't get land, get a horse or a bushel of potatoes. Gentlemen, any pecuniary success I may have enjoyed is due to my realization that collections are of overweening importance."

And he would go on to point out that the very land where the Gentry Block stood had been taken on a debt, and that its mortar had been spread by a brickmason unable to pay cash for a murder acquittal. Even his desk had been constructed by a cabinetmaker who in a thoughtless moment had stolen a mule.

Three pictures adorned the office walls, one an oil portrait of the judge himself, showing a huge man in legal robes standing beside a globe of the world. In the background, marble colonnades stretched into misty infinity. Looking at that portrait, you received the impression that the subject must have sat, at the very least, on the bench of the United States Supreme Court, and that the marble columns must enclose some celestial Hall of Fame where the spirits of Solon and Coke sought out Judge Gentry for advice.

The remaining pictures were steel engravings, one of General Jackson at New Orleans, showing a battle much more sanitary and heroic than Caleb remembered; and the other of Henry Clay. Oddly, since Clay was still alive and talking, this portrait was draped with black crepe, its huge bow bearing the gilt numerals: 1825.

On Caleb's first visit, when he came inquiring about office space, he regarded the funereal decorations of that portrait with some curiosity, and the judge—who, his clerks averred, possessed almost Jovian omniscience—seemed to deduce instantly what his visitor was thinking.

"I don't know your politics, sir," he declared in a voice like distant thunder on Olympus, "but as for me I used to be a Clay man. It was my privilege at Transylvania University to study under Harry of the West. But sir, the Clay I knew and revered lost his honor in 1825, when he betrayed a statesman whose backside he is unworthy to kiss."

"I voted for Jackson in '24," Caleb said. "And in '28 and '32, for that matter."

"Sir, let me say you voted for the greatest statesman this Republic has known since the founding fathers."

"He was a pretty good general too," Caleb said. "I fought under him at New Orleans."

Hunched in his chair, fingers peaked, head forward, brown eyes smol-

322

dering, the judge stared hard at Caleb, then slowly rose, looking gigantic, his big feet pacing over to his visitor.

"Sir, I wish to shake your hand." He did so. "The greatest statesman since Jefferson." Another shake. "The greatest general since Washington." Another shake. "I fought, sir, under Governor Shelby. It has been the regret of my life that I did not serve under Old Hickory. But I met him once. I shook his hand as I am shaking yours. And I broke bread with him in the White House."

"I take it you're a Democrat," Caleb said.

"I am a Jacksonian. Some people tell me I am actually a Jeffersonian. But first of all, sir, I am a citizen of the Republic."

"By God," Caleb thought, "I'll bet the eagle squeals when he orates."

And yet, despite the judge's words, which would have sounded bombastic in a lesser man, Caleb found himself brushed by the stuff of dreams when the judge, in such a tone as Seneca might have employed in speaking of Burrus, pronounced the word, Republic. It brought to mind Valley Forge and the Blue Ridge Mountains seen across a wheat field in the Shenandoah Valley; it made you think of lonesome nigger songs in Tennessee and the flag carried through battle smoke; you remembered the trail across buffalo country and Split Ticket Whiskey and all the proud rivers you had traveled; it brought to mind, strangely enough, Frosty McSwasey dead in the Massachusetts earth.

Back in his chair, the judge asked how much office space McSwasey & Zumwalt would require. Not a great deal, Caleb said; his lumber operation would be modest, at first. But the firm would grow. The judge was nodding; Caleb, he said, had come to the land of opportunity . . . this Great Northwest . . . blessed by the largess of a bountiful Providence.

"I have a vacant room," he added. "Used for storage now. Books, chiefly. I haven't been eager to rent it. But you fought under General Jackson. Do you play chess?"

Caleb shook his head.

"A pity. I'm hard put to find opponents, although I insist that my clerks learn chess with their Blackstone." He waved toward a table where a chessboard displayed carved figures. "That's a game I'm playing by post with Senator Hale." He looked down at the board, a commanding figure with a smooth-shaved face and shaggy brows. "The Senator, you will note, brought out his queen early. His third move. Madness. I trust he will live to regret it . . . I'll show you the vacant room," he added, turning. "Were you closely associated with the general?"

Caleb told what there was to tell, and perhaps a little more, as they left the office and moved along the hall to the future headquarters of McSwasey & Zumwalt.

*

It was from Judge Gentry, in June, that Caleb bought a house. A couple of blocks south of Winnebago Street, in a shaded yard with snowball bushes and bridal wreath, the house stood on the northeast corner of Blackhawk Street and Gentry Avenue, the avenue having been named after the judge, of course, for he was the leading citizen in the community and one of the leaders in the whole Territory. As a young man, coming to New Empire after being appointed sub-Indian agent on the recommendation of Henry Clay, the judge had bought a number of acres in what was then a wooded meadow at the edge of town, later platting the area and putting in streets. Now it was the best residential district, with the judge living west across the street from the McSwaseys in a house which had first come into being on his own drafting board. If Francis Bacon could take all knowledge for his province, so could Judge Gentry; if Thomas Jefferson could draft architect's plans for Monticello and for a great university, the judge felt he could do the same for his own house and for the Fox County courthouse. Hence, back in the thirties, he had ordered books on architecture from the booksellers in Cincinnati and New York where he kept open accounts, and after the books arrived his thirsty mind sponged up all the knowledge they contained. Then, with a tumbler of Kentucky bourbon at hand and with Kentucky burley in his pipe, he set to work. Results were felicitous if not strikingly original: the Fox County courthouse, in a grassy square on the east side of Court Avenue, resembled the statehouse in Richmond, Virginia, while the judge's residence was not dissimilar to Mr. Clay's Ashland in Lexington, Kentucky.

As a student in Transylvania, already bent on conquering all knowledge, and consequently a great favorite with his professors, Sophronicus had been invited to a supper party in Mr. Clay's home, and at table the talk had turned to his unusual given name.

"Very classical," Mr. Clay had said easily. "You must have been christened after one of the Roman consuls."

"No, sir, after my grandfather. He came through the Gap with Boone's party."

"A Long Knife named Sophronicus," Mr. Clay mused. "But surely *he* must have been named after a classical hero."

Whereupon Sophronicus, who took his classics seriously, and who deplored Mr. Clay's penchant for such errors as confusing Sallustius Crispus with his great-uncle, Caius Sallustius, shook his head and declared:

"No, sir, after a race horse back in Virginia."

Mr. Clay was titillated: that man who never forgot a constituent's name certainly wouldn't forget this one. Some years later, when he received a letter from Sophronicus Gentry—a veteran of that war so dear to Mr. Clay's heart—requesting a political appointment of some sort, he replied with a charming note, inquiring after the health of Mrs.

Gentry—who had been Lucretia Randolph, daughter of Lexington's distinguished Dr. Damon Randolph—and promising to do something for Sophronicus.

"I am sure," Mr. Clay wrote, "you must be champing at the bit to get on in life, and I am equally sure you will pull ahead of the field and come down the stretch with colors flying. *Expede Herculum!*"

Sophronicus thought Mr. Clay might have selected a happier figure; besides, imagine a man of his attainments spelling the word Herculum instead of Herculem!

But the appointment came through.

Back in those days, soon after the War of 1812, New Empire was a raw village in the wilderness, and the Gentrys dwelt for a few years in a log cabin. Sophronicus didn't mind—after all, he had been born in a log cabin, back in Kentucky—and Lucretia said she didn't mind either, although the possibility existed that she occasionally remembered the fine town house, only a stone's throw from the Transylvania campus, (with all those handsome students!), where she had spent her girlhood.

"But once I saw your father," she told her daughters, "I never looked at another boy."

"Never? Did you close your eyes when you met them on the street?"

"Well," Lucretia said, "not exactly."

Sophronicus's appointment as sub-Indian agent brought great unhappiness not only to his immediate superior but to the Indians themselves and eventually to the entire Office of Indian Affairs. As a lawyer—an officer of the court, sir—he took the outlandish position that laws were written to be enforced: that when Washington City said no redskin should be sold redeye, Washington City meant it. Washington City, said his superior, meant no such thing; and of course it didn't; but Sophronicus had already fallen hopelessly in love with that other woman in his life: that dream woman who was a misty merging of a draped figure holding aloft the scales of Justice and of the woman, America, radiant-limbed and sword-brandishing, who in his imagination went striding across the new continent, patron goddess of the Republic. The Indians got mighty thirsty and the Indian agent mighty worried about jail conditions, while Sophronicus held office; and the letters he wrote while still an official, and after his discharge, threatened to disrupt the entire Era of Good Feeling: fortunately, however, the politicians in Washington City, as always, were equal to the crisis.

"Well, honey," Lucretia asked, upon learning that her husband had been dishonorably discharged, "what do we do now?"

"We stay," Sophronicus said. "I'll hang out my shingle."

It was a rough go for a while; but after all Sophronicus was the grandson of a Long Hunter, and the son of Margaret Kincannon who had migrated to Kentucky from the Waxhaws of Carolina, (her parents had been neighbors of the Jacksons!), and the son too of Daniel Gentry, who had distilled the best whiskey in Bourbon County, and shot a Shawnee or two in his time; and while that beautiful strawberry blond, Lucretia, might exhibit a surface giddiness, and say the wrong thing at the right time, such as once when Sophronicus was still sub-Indian agent, and a Fox called at the cabin, and she invited him in to have a drink of bourbon, still she didn't come from any race of weaklings either: her father had been an Albemarle County Randolph, and her mother an Albemarle County Littlepage, before they up and married and took the Wilderness Road to Kentucky.

For a year or two, there in New Empire, Sophronicus planted a truck patch in addition to practicing the law, and milked a cow and went off to the river bottoms with a long-barreled rifle and brought back venison and rabbit for pie and squirrel for stew; but with the town growing, and steamboats appearing on the big river, it wasn't long before neighbors started quarreling, and assaulting and battering, in which case they turned to that intellectual engine, Sophronicus, from whose mouth six-syllable words tumbled as easily as corn from a sack, and who, because of his tremendous reputation for honesty—gained at the cost of a soft job with the government!—had only to tell a jury what the facts were as he saw them, and where the right lay, and the jury would vote another victory for Sophronicus Gentry.

So presently the Gentrys moved from the log cabin into a clapboarded house, and then, as the daughters kept coming and finally a son, into a larger house; and at last, after he was a circuit court judge, (appointed by no less a man than General Andrew Jackson, president of the United States of America), and a mighty prosperous lawyer and holder of rich real estate, Sophronicus designed his present house, the one which resembled Ashland, although not precisely, because after all he hadn't been taken on a tour of the Clay home, that night he ate supper there, and hence in planning his house he had to resort to his imagination and, as he termed it, to the logic of space.

"Lucretia," he used to say, when the house was nothing but marks on paper, "the logic of space puts the library in this wing."

"Well, I do declare," said Lucretia, who had never quite become accustomed to the miracle of being wife to this Jove of jurisprudence.

The house was completed in 1835, a gracious dwelling of red brick, two stories high and with one-story wings wandering off to the north and south, its lines mainly Georgian with here and there a touch of Greek revival and of Kentucky race horse. Sophronicus couldn't resist adding a cupola—cupolas were his weakness, as the Fox County courthouse attested—and while the house would have fared very well without one, still the whole effect was ingratiating. A fine lawn swept east to Gentry Avenue, south to Blackhawk Street and north to Gentry's Alley, for the grounds occupied a quarter of a block, and a brick-paved drive circled to the one-story Doric portico and back to the commodious stable, also topped by a cupola, as well as by a weather vane with a gilded horse trotting. With its handsome beeches and locusts and maples, its orchard and flower plots, the Gentry residence—some intrepid souls even called it a mansion—was good enough for anybody; and perhaps one reason Sophronicus resigned his circuit court judgeship, soon after moving in, was because he disliked leaving it to travel about the Territory. Perhaps also with a fine house to support, as well as a wife, servants, daughters, a son, horses, two canary birds and several goldfish, he desired what he would have termed the more opulent emoluments of private practice. Yet these couldn't have weighed heavily in his decision, for he told Lucretia—and he seldom lied to her—that his conscience was often troubled at judging his fellow human beings, that he thought no man wise enough or pure enough to judge another.

"Not even Solomon?" she asked, with her refreshing habit of hurling tangentials into a discussion.

"My dear," he replied, "I haven't given Solomon sufficient thought to answer your question."

In any case, Judge Gentry did resign; and it was rumored that in 1836, when Wisconsin Territory was organized out of Michigan Territory, President Jackson offered to appoint him governor, but that he deferred to his friend, Henry Dodge. Whatever truth the rumor may have contained, the fact was that in the mid 1830's, following a visit to their native Kentucky, Judge and Mrs. Gentry went on to Washington City where they were entertained at the White House. They must have been received with great cordiality too, for in after years the judge often mentioned this visit; and as for Lucretia, when asked about Old Hickory, she always said, "He's *such* a sweet old man."

Life in Wisconsin Territory, what with the rigorous winters and the absence of racing stables and distilleries, wasn't much like Kentucky; but nevertheless at Lexylvania—as Sophronicus had named his estate—there were abundant bourbon and cognac and charm and Burgundy and books and lovely ladies; people lucky enough to be entertained there said it was the most beautiful house north of St. Louis, and as for the hospitality, you would have to travel to New Orleans to find its equal. Certainly Mrs. Gentry was a delightful hostess, just as cordial now as when she lived in a log cabin and invited an Indian buck to have whiskey. Back in those days, it had been generally acknowledged that she possessed the most shapely figure that had yet pioneered in the Northwest, and the coloring of her skin and hair looked the way strawberries with sugar and cream tasted. They had been a striking couple when they were young, she so feminine, he so stalwart and black haired and strong. They had met in Lexington when he, a Transylvania freshman, had come to Dr. Damon Randolph's house to ask, sir, whether he might withdraw books from the circulating library of which the doctor was secretary. A sober young adult of fifteen. Lucretia, a gangling thirteen-year-old, sandy-haired and freckled, had interested him not at all.

"But who *is* he?" she had asked her father after Sophronicus departed with the first volume of Gibbon.

He was, it seemed, a protege of the Presbyterian pastor, the Rev. David Walker, who had once filled the pulpit at the village of Callaway in Bourbon County. While there, he had undertaken to school the young fry, and Sophronicus had proved not an apt pupil, not merely an eager one, but a positively voracious one. He could scarcely wait for Mr. Walker to teach him Latin and Greek. In that village, through which Finley's Branch flowed with pretty little waterfalls from limestone ledges, school was held all of three months during the winter, but even in summer, when Sophronicus worked hard at home, he was forever coming to the log parsonage, lighted by tallow dips, for instruction.

His own cabin stood on the east side of the pike that wandered through the village, and just north of the stone bridge crossing Finley's Branch. His father had built it when with his bride he left Boonesborough and came to that region of hills and hollows and rich corn bottoms. Across the road, where a spring bubbled sweetly from limestone, his father had also erected a modest distillery, the mellow product of which he decanted at eighteen pence per quart, if you brought your own jug. Sophronicus used to tote along a quart when he called on the Rev. Mr. Walker, and the two would drink it neat while they resurrected the glory that was Greece on a summer's evening, while the skeeters hummed and a whip-poorwill called from a buckeye tree and sheep bells tinkled far away and hound-dogs yelped a distant coon.

With Mr. Walker's congregation liking Gentry's whiskey just as much as he did, the distillery flourished, and some years it was all Daniel Gentry could do to raise enough Indian corn to supply it, even with the aid of his two older sons, Todd and Sophronicus. Not that a corn famine ever actually occurred, although there were summers when the family went light on the roasting ears, and times when the hogs subsisted mainly on acorns, and even winters when Daniel's wife, Margaret, declared that the supply in the crib was dwindling so fast she doubted whether the family would have sufficient hominy and johnnycake to last till next season.

"You reckon I'd best shut down the stillery for a spell?" her husband asked.

Being a public spirited woman, from whom, indeed, Sophronicus had inherited his civic consciousness, Margaret declared emphatically against such a drastic measure whose results might have doomed pore puny old ladies and even pore little children to go to bed thirsty.

"We ain't just about to shut down that stillery," she said. "Not even if we have to fetch through the winter on pumpkin stew and possum."

Next season the Gentrys put in yet more corn, Daniel breaking the ground with a shovel plow while Sophronicus rode and guided the mare. After the soil was harrowed with a locust limb, and the wild cucumber vines cleaned out, Todd and Sophronicus dropped seeds into the furrows, their father following with a hoe. Then, till the sprouts pushed up, somebody had to guard the fields lest the squirrels and crows gobble the seeds; a chore that fell to Sophronicus, and one which he relished, for he could sit in the shade of the brush fence, pebbles heaped by his side, a book from Mr. Walker's library in hand. Every minute or so, while he read *Robinson Crusoe* or *Roderick Random*, he would let out a mighty whoop, to scare the crows, and when those birds decided that whooping couldn't hurt you, he would scramble up and pelt them with pebbles.

When Sophronicus was fourteen the Rev. Mr. Walker was called by God, who used the presbyters as mouthpiece, to the Presbyterian church in Lexington; and before departing he dropped in at the Gentry cabin for a sip of bourbon and a solemn talk with Sophronicus's parents. He said that while farming and whiskey-making were occupations necessary to the happiness of mankind, still it would be a waste of brilliant brain power for their second son to spend his life mixing mash; and he proposed that next year the boy be sent to Lexington and Transylvania University, where he could live with the Walkers free of charge, although if the Gentrys didn't feel right about that—as he knew they wouldn't—they could always pay for their son's keep with an occasional barrel of whiskey: the best he had ever tasted, even better than that of his native Scotland; he often wondered about Daniel's recipe. Daniel looked pleased, although he wasn't telling even a preacher his recipe, which, really, was simple enough: when a batch was finished, just sprinkle in a goodly amount of wood ashes. It was, Daniel said, mighty fine of the Reverend to make that offer, but he wondered how he could make out with his son gone off the place.

Margaret said they could make out right well, for Todd was now able to do a man's work, and there were three younger sons to swingle the flax and sow the timothy and jackknife a hickory sapling into broom splits; and Permelia and Eliza were big enough now to churn and to pound the hominy block. Anybody with eyes in his head, she said, looking steadily at Daniel, could see that Sophronicus was cut out to be a famous man: he was always quoting Shakespeare to old Brindle when he toted her fodder, and spouting Latin—or was it Greek?—when he slopped the pigs and split the kindling. It wouldn't surprise her in the least, she said, if the people of the United States would haul off and vote in Sophronicus as president some day.

"She never did surprise easy," Daniel said, fetching more whiskey. And he added, "If you think it's the Lord's will, Reverend, I reckon I can spare the boy."

So the next year, in a wagon with a box-trunk and a barrel of whiskey, Sophronicus rode with his father to Lexington, a sober-faced boy in a homespun suit dyed black by walnut hulls; in a shirt of India muslin and socks from the wool he had helped shear off bleating sheep; on his large, powerful head a white Roram hat.

"I reckon you'll be all right," his father said, when they parted outside Mr. Walker's house, across the street from the campus. "Don't take no man's lip or no man's paper dollars. If a gal offers to sell it you'll catch the pox for sure, and if she offers to give it away just recollect that nothing comes free in this world except cockleburs and bedbugs. If you don't like it here you can always come home and no questions asked. Keep your bowels open. Giddap."

Sophronicus stood watching while the wagon creaked off down the street, pulled by old Ned and Molly, his father hunched on the seat. A lump had accumulated in his stomach and another under his Adam's apple; and he was remembering how his old shep-dog, Prince, had wailed to come along, and how he used to go into the timber to gather seeds from the coffee trees, and how the bees had hummed among the blossoms of the buckwheat patch, and how early of a summer's morning a certain catbird had perched in a sugar tree, sometimes meowing and setting old Prince half-crazy. And suddenly he had half a mind to light out after that wagon and go home to Callaway and let some other boy grow up to be voted in as president. But just then he sensed somebody by his side; it was that short-legged old Scot, David Walker, who said that the roads from home were ever sad, but that the good Lord had vouchsafed whiskey for times like this. So presently they were sitting in the parsonage study where the Rev. Mr. Walker, between swallows from a tumbler and puffs on his pipe, read aloud from *She Stoops to Conquer*.

He was homesick for months, and yet, once matriculated in such courses as belles-lettres and natural philosophy, he didn't actually want to go home; and when finally he did go, the following spring, for a short visit, he was troubled to discover that the actual village of Callaway was not the village he had been yearning for in his memory. The cabin with its cats-and-clay chimney, its straw ticks, its puncheon floor, its fireplace with a tea kettle hanging from a lug pole and a johnnycake baking on an ash board, looked smaller and meaner than he had remembered. His mother was grayer, his father more squint-eyed. Tell us about gittin' educated, they said. He tried . . . On the last afternoon of his visit he wandered off through the timber with Prince, who wasn't so spry any more, passing the snake fences whose rails he had split, lingering at the old charcoal pit with its dark acrid odor of burned hickory, staring at the rotting log which had once been a sycamore tree. He had axed down that tree, to get the sweet treasure bees had stored in its hollow center. He had had a devil of a time finding it: he remembered how he had heated a flat stone and melted a piece of honeycomb, the sweet smell attracting the bees. Then he had followed them to the sycamore. That night the family had drooled honey on their mush and milk.

Leaving home after that visit was sadder, in a way, than his first leaving. That first time, he had thought a sure cure for homesickness lay within his power: he could always go home. But now he had done that and he was still homesick. He wanted to cry when Prince, whimpering with rheumatics, limped over and licked his hand. His mother said, "Don't you go gittin' so educated you'll forget your kinfolks."

And when he returned to the university it too seemed strange. His spirit was sorely troubled, and one evening in the parson's study he told David Walker how wherever he went any more he felt lonely inside. That, David Walker said, was man's portion; and as he stared into the tobacco smoke, glass in hand, he quoted Holy Writ.

" 'All things are full of weariness; man cannot utter it: the eye is not satisfied with the seeing, nor the ear filled with hearing . . .' Sophronicus," he added, "you're growing up. Could be you need a gal."

But it cost a sight of money to roister with the young bloods in taverns, where you might find a gal to tumble in the hedgerows; and if you started sparking the other kind you might find yourself all tangled up like a tomcat in a skein of yarn, wedded before you knew what had hit you and farming again, your hopes for getting educated deader than last year's flies. So he was mainly lonely at Transylvania, and the best anodyne for that was hard work. His candle burned late; he was the faculty's pride, the most honorable of honor students. When he became a lawyer, they predicted, he would bring renown to Transylvania, for he would not be one of these fly-by-night one-galluse shysters, but a counselor with a brain full of sound classical learning. He sat under Henry Clay, whose brain was not precisely full of that, although with his silver-dipped tongue everybody thought it must be.

"Gentlemen," said Mr. Clay, "two words will make any man of sound intellect a lawyer, industry and application, and the same words with a third, economy, will enable him to make a fortune."

That went into Sophronicus's bulky notes, along with the comment: "So sayeth Harry of the frog mouth. Does he not know that Dame Rumor whispers of his evenings at brag, with stakes running into the thousands? Economy! Still, they say he is a consistent winner."

And then one April afternoon when his college years were ending—years twice interrupted by bouts of backwoods teaching—he went to Dr. Randolph's to return *Candide* to the circulating library. He had turned twenty, a large young man with coal-black hair sweeping back from an imposing forehead, brown eyes serious, jaw and nose strong. Lucretia Randolph had just returned from Mrs. Keats's School for Females in Mason County, and that afternoon it struck him that she was no longer a gangling freckle-face but a young lady with hair like the golden sands of Hellenic shores, her mellifluous figure sheathed in chamois-colored silk. Recently he had won a cash prize offered to the student composing the best Vergilan georgic with a Kentucky setting, and he was glad now that he had squandered the money with a tailor: his dark-green jacket sported metal-plated buttons and a black velvet collar; his waistcoat was pale yellow; his trousers Indian nankin. What, he asked Miss Lucretia, had she studied at Mrs. Keats's school? They had wandered into the brick-paved garden where English ivy climbed the mellow walls and the fragrance of a flowering catalpa mingled with the perfume of honeysuckle and sweet alyssum. She had studied, Lucretia said, how to walk across a drawing room without unbalancing three books perched atop her head, as well as street manners and dining room manners and all about those old Greeks, Cicero and Charlemagne, and that old Trojan, Homer.

"Homer?" Sophronicus asked, smiling. "Homer who?"

"I don't rightly recollect," Lucretia said. "I always did get him mixed in my head with Hannibal crossing the Rubicon on an elephant."

Sophronicus sighed; her eyes were sea-green; his big hands could have encircled her lovely waist; and he was stunned at his obtuseness in spending years in Lexington without getting better acquainted with Lucretia. Dr. Blythe, president of Transylvania, had half promised him a minor faculty post, after he attained his degree. A young man could probably support a wife on the honorarium.

When he suggested as much to Lucretia, several weeks later, one evening after he had taken supper at her home, she said:

"Honey, I do think the honor is wonderful, but we'll need a little money too."

They were married in August, with Dr. Blythe officiating, and that man was as good as his half-promise: Sophronicus became professor of moral philosophy, with one class in contract law. Dr. Blythe could scarcely have done otherwise, what with Sophronicus's tremendous scholarship and with Lucretia's father being such a community leader and a member of the board of trustees. Sophronicus felt a little ornery about asking Dr. Blythe to speak the ceremony, instead of David Walker, but Mr. Walker understood and was delighted to serve as best man. For a wedding present, Lucretia's father gave them a cozy little house, and Daniel Gentry dowered them with two smoked hams, a half dozen cakes of maple sugar and fifty gallons of Bourbon County whiskey.

Daniel and his wife had driven all the way from the home place to attend the swank garden wedding, and Sophronicus secretly upbraided himself for feeling ashamed of his back-country parents. They looked older, much older; Margaret's hair was white, her face weather-beaten; Daniel had lost his teeth; his squint was more pronounced, his gnarled body gangling. They acted ill at ease, like people at a funeral. But once the knot was tied, and the great occasion celebrated by a wedding reception, with the gleam of silver and snowy linen, and black servants carrying trays, Dr. Randolph decided to tap the barrel of whiskey his new son-in-law's father had been neighborly enough to bring, and he pronounced it the most sublime he had ever tasted. Others sampled it, even Dr. Blythe, and before that reception was over it was generally acknowledged that Lucretia had married the son of a genius.

"I kind of had an idy you'd like it," Daniel said. "Though it ain't the best I've ever stilled, by a long shot."

The reception, one of the merriest in Kentucky history, lasted longer than scheduled, because Daniel's whiskey had a way of blurring one's sense of time; and before it was over Dr. Blythe was standing with his arm around Daniel's shoulders, telling him what a smart son he had bred over there in Bourbon County; and the Rev. Mr. Walker entertained the company by dancing the Highland Fling.

The newlyweds were very happy, with Sophronicus working at the university by day, and enthusiastically founding a family by night. You might have supposed that Lucretia's occasional errors in classical reference would have distressed him, but they didn't: he did, however, try to set her straight. But nothing ever came of it.

"But honey," she would say, "I'm just certain Socrates was a Roman senator. Mrs. Keats told us all about it. He was killed in one of those sanctuary Pubic Wars."

"Mrs. Keats! *Ex nihilo nihil fit!*"

"That's right, darlin'," Lucretia beamed. "He fit 'em in Africa. Only now I recollect it better, I don't believe they dropped him in battle. They captured him prisoner and made him drink the hemorrhoid."

Not that Lucretia lacked soundness of intellect! She loved to read and she remembered what she read too; the only mischief was, she remembered the right things about the wrong people. On a more workaday level, however, she was always astonishing Sophronicus with her shrewd estimates.

"The trouble with Mr. Clay," she said, one day in 1812, after reading a speech he had delivered in Washington City, trumpeting war, "is that he wishes to be president."

"What in the world makes you think that?"

"I don't know, honey. The way he wears his hat, I reckon."

Yet with all her charming vagueness, and her languid air of having whiled away the hours in a garden sniffing flowers and chasing butterflies, she surprised everybody by turning out to be an excellent housekeeper and superb cook. So far as anybody could recall, Lucretia had never so much as peeled a potato, at home; so in the interests of his son-in-law's stomach Dr. Randolph had offered the newlyweds the loan of one of his nigger girls. But Lucretia shook her pretty head.

"I want to do it all by myself," she said. "I reckon I can cook for my man better than any old nigger."

She wasn't quite that good; still, her fried chicken and corn fritters wouldn't have given even a dyspeptic indigestion; and one Sunday when

333

the Randolphs were dinner guests of the Gentrys, Dr. Randolph asked: "Daughter, where did you learn to cook such delicious food?"

"Why, daddy, I reckon I've always known how to cook. It runs in the family."

The doctor renewed his offer of a nigger gal, at least to help with the housework, but Lucretia still declined.

"Sophronicus," she said, "is set against owning niggers."

It was true: slaves had been uncommon in Callaway, and Sophronicus, that logical young stalwart, did not believe that a man who breathed the heady airs of a free Republic and dreamed of eagles soaring in Equality's bright skies should own bondsmen. In this regard, his thinking had been buttressed by Mr. Clay's theories, but not by that slave-owner's practice.

Mr. Clay's war came at last, in 1812, a few months after the birth of their first daughter, Achilla; and Sophronicus, being a disciple of Mr. Clay, (with reservations), and a Kentuckian, itched to get into the scrap, although if anybody had questioned him closely he would have admitted that he considered the Peloponnesian War of greater significance. Being a Kentuckian also, Lucretia wouldn't have had him not want to go, but this didn't mean she was actually enthusiastic about his marching away and getting slain. She kept finding excellent reasons why he should not go at once; she coaxed him to delay enlisting till next year; she cajoled; she even secretly urged her father to advise Sophronicus to let the boys without families enjoy military honors first; and he yielded finally, thus saving himself the discomfiture of being massacred at the River Raisin.

But when the survivors of that battle made their broken way back to Kentucky, ragged men who told how the redcoat commander had persuaded General Winchester to surrender, and how the command, when disarmed, had been fallen upon and scalped by the Injuns while the redcoats stood watching, the state seethed. Even Lucretia became a War Hawk then, although a reluctant one. Remember the River Raisin. Remember the scalps of Kentuckians drying in front of Injun campfires. Sophronicus was elected a lieutenant; the fifes shrilled and the drums boomed, fading into the distance along the Frankfort pike; Lucretia looked haggard. But she refused to move in with her parents, refused even the loan of a nigger girl to keep her company; she lived on with her daughter in the little house across whose threshold Sophronicus had carried her as a bride.

"Daughter," her father said, "you're looking poorly."

"I reckon," she said, "it's because I'm feeling poorly."

She hated Mr. Clay.

Autumn came, soggy with September rains, bright with October leaves, and sometimes at night wild winds blew along North Limestone Street, whistling under the eaves of a shadowy house where a young Kentucky wife lay staring. Then, on a soft sunny noon, a messenger from Frankfort brought tidings of a magnificent victory along the Thames River, off to the north; Tecumseh had been defeated and killed; presently a letter arrived from Sophronicus; and then Sophronicus himself. Lu-. cretia thought she just never would stop crying, once she was in his arms, she who had endured the months of his absence dry eyed.

*

She never forgave Mr. Clay for being such a War Hawk, (only she called it a War Eagle); and in 1825 when belated newspapers arrived in New Empire with accounts of how Mr. Clay had betrayed that sweet old General Jackson, and Sophronicus, in a rare rage, crumpled the newspaper and flung it across the room, Lucretia said, "I never did trust that man, honey. He just wishes to be president."

And a decade later, at supper in the White House, with Lucretia sitting on the president's right, she brought Mr. Clay's name into the conversation, thereby rousing the fears of the whole table that the general might suffer apoplexy.

"Sophronicus was *so* furious the way he schemed against you in 1825," she said. "Weren't you put out about that?"

The general's knuckles had turned white, his dark face crimson; his lips were trembling.

"Well, goodness knows you had a right to be," Lucretia prattled on, "although nobody would have ever known it. But I'll tell you what's wrong with Mr. Clay. He danced with me at my first ball back in Lexington, and I knew right off what was wrong with him."

"Madam," the general said, "you would be doing your president and your country a great service if you would tell us what's wrong with Harry Clay."

"He wishes to be president," Lucertia said brightly.

There was startled silence; then the company roared.

"Well, he does," Lucretia added; and the general laughed himself into a coughing fit.

"Madam," the general said, when he had recovered sufficiently to speak, "perhaps you could tell us what is wrong with Mr. Calhoun. You must have seen him in the senate."

"Indeed I did," Lucretia said. "His trouble is that he's puny."

And she couldn't understand why everybody roared again, when after all she had only mentioned the obvious, that poor Mr. Calhoun was on the frail side.

Next morning in the president's office, Judge Gentry reached a hard decision: he refused the governorship of Wisconsin Territory.

"Although, sir, if you order me to accept, it will be my patriotic duty to accede, but sir, it is my hope you will not so order."

"Well, by the eternal!" the general said.

And when the Gentrys left, President Jackson asked permission to kiss

335

Lucretia good-by. His eyes, so bitter and tortured, were suddenly moist when she said she would love it.

"What would you think," Sophronicus asked his wife, when they reached Pennsylvania Avenue, treading on air, "if I told you I refused the governorship of the Territory?"

"Why, honey, I reckon I'd think you did just right. But why did you refuse?"

"It's hard to explain," he said, but he tried, while they moved along that imperial avenue of grunting pigs and clucking chickens. Life was short, ambition a disease, draining and withering a man while the books—books by the hundreds—gathered dust on the shelves of a forsaken library. He wanted to be the best educated man of his era. But of late he had felt the tug of ambition—political ambition—judge—governor—senator—and then? Mr. Clay, eating his heart out; Mr. Calhoun, withered, embittered, yes, puny; Mr. Van Buren, a red fox scheming away the mortal minutes; and General Jackson, the incomparably great General Jackson, at the very pinnacle of fortune, a lonely old man. Ambition was noble only when it operated in the Republic of the intellect. He sighed.

"I'm probably a fool."

"Why, honey, don't you dare say you're a fool! You're the smartest man since Hiberius Africanus, or whatever that old Greek's name was. I knew it that first day you came to daddy's library and took out *The Rise of the Roman Empire.*"

*

Offspring had come easily to Lucretia and Sophronicus, and by the late 1820's they had launched five daughters and a son into American history. For a while it had looked as if no son were going to appear, a prospect which distressed Lucretia, for she knew that her husband wanted a male heir to carry on his name. Sophronicus, however, drew upon his learning and consoled her, repeating the legend of Robert Bruce and the spider. They were lying in bed, but his voice was as oratorical as if he were addressing a caucus.

"Twelve times the spider attempted the desideratum," he declared, "and twelve times the *aranea diadema* failed ignominiously. But the thirteenth time his efforts were crowned with success."

"I just don't know where we'd ever put twelve daughters," Lucretia said.

"My dear, that is merely an illustration of the power of pertinacity. I do not deem it improbable that the procreative processes will yield us a son long before a baker's dozen of attempts."

"It's *so* nice," Lucretia sighed, "to be wedded to an intellectual man. But I do wish we'd have a son for a change. Do you reckon those recreative processes will give us one next time?"

He thought it worth a try; and so at last, in 1828, a son was born to

326

these Kentucky expatriates. With Sophronicus's admiration for Old Hickory, there was nothing to name the boy but Andrew Jackson Gentry, although Lucretia, in a merry moment, did suggest they might call him Robert Bruce Gentry.

Those were good, happy years, with the family all together, living in the house which was later bought by Caleb McSwasey. Sophronicus was making plenty of money from the law and the sale of land; and once he even took a flier in the steamboat business, buying half interest in a new boat, a speculation so profitable that he could hardly believe the figures: before the season was over the boat had paid for herself, and next season she cleared thousands. Such a harvest, he thought, was too good to last; so he went into financial conference with himself. Then he understood why the return on his money was so great: because steamboat owning was hazardous. Forthwith he sold his interest in the boat, at a fine profit, and the very next season her boilers exploded. Many lives were lost and lawsuits followed. Sophronicus might have garnered whopping fees, representing the plaintiffs, but this he refused to do, for his fastidious professional conscience boggled at bringing suit against his former business associates. Nor would he represent the defendants, after learning that the boat had been racing with her safety valve tied down.

"Not all the wealth of Croesus," he told Lucretia, "would tempt me to barter my honor."

Even in those years when Andrew Jackson Gentry was an infant, Sophronicus kept musing about the new house he would build, and wishing to goodness he had been invited to a slumber party at Ashland so that he might have picked up architectural hints as to the arrangement of upstairs rooms. On Sunday afternoons he used to stroll across the street to the lot where he intended to build, accompanied by Lucretia with the baby boy in her arms, and by his five daughters, Achilla, Cerelia, Delicia, Fayme and Helice. All were lovely girls, laughing and chattering and looking up to their father as a fount of all wisdom and of many new clothes; and on those pleasant afternoons, wandering among the burdock and sweet williams of the vacant lot, Sophronicus was steeped in the rich, fruity satisfactions of the paterfamilias who had cornered more than an average portion of society's money supply and could afford to indulge his dear ones. He carried a hickory cane, to demonstrate his support of President Jackson; and often on those strolls, like a stallion showing off for his mare and fillies, he would utter scarcely a word not Greek or Latin.

In 1830, when Achilla was a young lady and Cerelia almost one, Sophronicus escorted them by steamboat and stagecoach, back to Kentucky and Mrs. Tevis's Science Hill School at Shelbyville. On that trip he visited Lexington. Mr. Clay was also in town, examining political fences, and when he heard that Sophronicus was a guest in the home of Mrs. Gentry's sister, he sent an invitation for supper at Ashland.

"There is always," Mr. Clay wrote, "a welcome stall at my stable for an old friend in the blinders of the law. I hear you kicked up your heels considerably in that sub-Indian agent pasture, and that now you are treading rough shod over your legal opponents. Can you take supper with us Wednesday? Don't say me neigh!"

When he read that note Sophronicus flushed, and with nostrils distended and statesmanlike mane tossing he really did look a little like a Kentucky thoroughbred.

"Inform your master," he told Mr. Clay's nigger man, "that it will be impossible for me to come."

He would have enjoyed visiting Ashland again, if only to pace off the dimensions of the dining room, but he was not a man to sup with an enemy of General Jackson, even if Mr. Clay had promised to throw in a set of architect's drawings with the brandy and cigars.

*

When Mr. and Mrs. Caleb McSwasey were first invited to Lexylvania, all the Gentry daughters had married or were away at school; only Lucretia and Sophronicus, with their son, were left to entertain. By then young Andy was thirteen, so subdued by bashfulness that throughout supper the nearest he came to joining in the repartee was when he said please pass the mashed potatoes; not even Caleb succeeded in being jealous of him, although he tried. Certainly, however, Esperanza gave him no cause for jealousy in that quarter; she had turned sixteen, she looked eighteen or twenty, and having inherited from warrior ancestors a dislike of wasting ammunition, she shot young Andy scarcely a smile. Nor was Caleb really jealous of Sophronicus, even though Esperanza, at table, flattered him with charm and attention.

Like most persons who encounter a lawyer on a social occasion, she seized the opportunity to obtain free legal counsel, asking whether it was true that her nigger woman, Lilith, was no longer a slave. Yes, madam, he said, in his opinion the wench was free, the Missouri Compromise having prevailed for some two decades. And might the soil of Wisconsin, he added, ever remain free, and might the day arrive when every Ethiope should be transported from this great Republic and colonized happily in tropic climes. Not, madam, that he harbored prejudice against the blackamoor; quite the contrary; but the institution of chattel slavery, so out of place in a free Republic, had been viewed with trepidation by the founding fathers, who feared it might lead to dissension within our midst, an opinion in which he concurred, would you care for more chicken, madam?

"He's *so* smart, don't you think so, Mr. McSwasey?" Lucretia asked.

"He's my lawyer," Caleb said.

338

"But he just never would own a nigger. I recollect how daddy wished me to have Hyacinth Ann, but Sophronicus said no. Have you owned many niggers, Mr. McSwasey?"

"Not to any extent."

"Dear me, I don't see why people want to get so disturbed about a few old niggers." She sighed, smiling, and addressed her husband along the candlelit table. "Honey, didn't those old Greeks and Romans own slaves?"

"If we can believe Gibbon and Plato and Thucydides," he replied, "and in my opinion we can believe them, if not *ad unguem,* at least in *bona fides,* it is correct that the Ancients held slaves."

"Then why do these abortionists want to turn the niggers free?"

"Abolitionists, my dear!"

"Well, whatever they call themselves."

"Autres temps, autres moeurs," Sophronicus said.

"I know, honey, but our niggers are Moors too. Leastwise, they're black as Moors. I heard you say that a little time ago."

"Blackamoors, my dear."

"That's right!" Lucretia exclaimed, smiling brightly. "I just knew we were talking about the same thing."

"Please pass the mashed potatoes," Andy said.

*

The McSwaseys were often guests of the Gentrys, as time went on, for both families were Democrats in a period when the Whigs had come into power, and this was a common bond. Moreover, Caleb had fought under Old Hickory, and Sophronicus could never quite get over the wonder of it all: he was forever asking just how General Jackson had acted when the battle smoke was thick. And on some evenings, perhaps once in six months, Sophronicus would read aloud a letter he had received from the Hermitage, the handwriting wavering with age but the comments still sharp. He took it pretty hard when the letters stopped coming in 1845 and would never come again.

Among other attainments, Sophronicus practiced what he called the horticultural arts, (Lucretia called it the hortatory arts), and on evenings when politics grew stale he would reveal his latest scheme for outwitting the potato bugs and rose beetles that pestered his garden.

"My roses last year were beautiful," he would say, "until the *macrodactylus subspinosus* appeared."

"And the rose beetles bothered them too," Lucretia said.

"Sir," he told Caleb, "the entomological enemies of man are among the most vicious he has to contend with."

"I don't doubt it," Caleb said.

"He knows *so* much about etymology," Lucretia said, sighing. "A bug's just a bug to me. But," she added, with her bright smile, "some of them are mighty pretty."

Judge Gentry's enthusiasm for gardening did not overwhelm him to the extent that he performed manual labor; his yard man did that, just as the yard man's wife and niece attended to household chores. This did not mean, however, that the judge contemned manual labor, for he never delivered a Fourth of July oration without mentioning the tremendous dignity of the same, and without recounting how as a youth he had "guided the quadruped which pulled the plowshare, stood vigilant guard over the embryonic maize, lest the ravens of the air and the rodents of the arboretum purloin it from the bosom of Ceres," and sometimes he even hinted that as a lad he could mix up a pretty potent batch of corn liquor; but now that he had attained his fifties and a good bank account he disliked the stiff muscles following a bout with the hoe. Hence, he practiced the horticultural arts as he practiced politics: as a strategist and a Nestor rather than as a toiler in the vineyard. On a fine spring afternoon, following a hard day in court, where his oratory bedazzled the jurors, his logic ensnared his opponents and his jurisprudence baffled the hell out of the bench, he liked to pace among the flower beds of Lexylvania, hickory cane in hand, white mane flowing, big body clad in a white suit, high stock rising from a snowy ruffled shirt. In the late sunshine the lawn rippled away in smooth green gold, shade-dappled by the beech and sugar trees; the house with its ivy and graceful fanlight delighted his eyes; the potato plants in the truck patch behind the stable had been dusted with his newest experiments in insecticides; along the alley to the north the apple and cherry trees were thriving; the shaded avenue passing his home bore his name: he was full of honor and erudition and contentment, glad he had had the good sense to refuse a career in politics.

And yet—well—he would have been scarcely human not to let his thoughts occasionally wander among the marble columns of the career that might have been his; the career that might still be his. One of these days Wisconsin would be admitted as a state; probably, by stretching out a hand, he could close his fingers on the toga of a senatorship. He loved making speeches. But after such soul-searchings he always decided against seeking higher honors. His was the good life, the full life; by employing about a fourth of his energies he captured abundant fees; and the rest of his energies could be devoted to the quiet joys of musing over coins from ancient Syracuse and Thebes, over problems in chess, over Shakespeare and Swift and Horace.

But perhaps his most impelling reason for avoiding a career in politics was his suspicion that the actuality would shatter the Republic of dreams that lay shining and immaculate in a secret place in his mind. From the speeches of Washington, Jackson and especially Jefferson he had caught the vision of a Republic purer than Plato's and more felicitous than the

Athens where Socrates and the young athletes sought truth; a Republic on a new continent unshadowed by the scepters of tyrants. Here beneath the soaring eagle in the bright sky man would be governed by his own consent; here man would seek counsel of his intellect and select as rulers the giants of his kind. Here—

But of course, as he would have been first to admit, such a Republic did not yet exist. But the dream existed. In the most eloquent papers of state you could sometimes find it, and in the Declaration and the Constitution, those shining documents. And in the minds of men. Some men. Dropping off to sleep, he could always seek out that Republic of fantasy, with its American rivers flowing bright and clear, its sunlit and untarnished palaces of justice and of council, its eagle-guarded headlands. It was his America: for it he had marched out of Lexington on the Frankfort pike; for it he had triggered his rifle at the Battle of the Thames; for it, as sub-Indian agent, he had written those outraged letters that had so discomfited the politicians of the Era of Good Feeling.

*

Strangely, Caleb never did become jealous of Judge Gentry, nor was this an instance when the husband suspected his wife of infidelity with every man except the guilty one, for Sophronicus treated Esperanza with great circumspection. He had never been much of a ladies' man, any-way; he never doubted his powers as a lover any more than his powers as a Demosthenes; so he had never been reduced to reassuring his ego by hopping into strange beds. Lucretia had kept him pretty busy in that regard in any case, and of course anybody could see they were a devoted couple. Hence, Caleb was surprisingly broad-minded when on a summer day he came home and found his wife and the judge chatting on the front veranda, the judge having brought over roses or some luscious straw-berries; and even on winter afternoons when Caleb surprised them in the living room, deep in chess, he never called the judge a son of a bitch and ordered him from the house. He didn't even think of him as a son of a bitch. Certainly it would have been most unfair if he had, for Sophronicus, that Houyhnhnm of rectitude, concentrated so powerfully at a chessboard that all awareness of time, place and partner was effaced from his brain.

Chess was his passion; it sluiced out and refreshed his mind; and he loved teaching the moves. Early in the Gentry-McSwasey acquaintance-ship, Caleb had feigned interest in learning, although really he could see little point in any game not employing chips; he had learned only to please the judge, because the judge was a power in the Territory and one never knew when one might need a friend at court. Esperanza's interest in the game, however, was not feigned; she took to it as she had taken to long division and geometry. It was mock warfare, with elaborate grand strategy, so perhaps from her Grandfather von Zumwalt, (a general already!), she had inherited a fondness for sending pawns to slaughter; and it was also a game of ruses, cunning snares and ruthless attack, arts which her Apache forefathers had not neglected. She developed rapidly into an excellent player, although not for quite some time was she able to checkmate Sophronicus. At her first victory he was delighted, for now he had an opponent worthy of his mettle. Only one other player in New Empire had ever beaten him.

That other player, amazingly, was Lucretia; amazingly, because she simply didn't play right. Of the philosophy of the game she had not the slightest conception; of its great historic principles, its complicated openings, its debates as to queen-side versus king-side castling, its premeditated sacrifices she remained in charming ignorance. Yet she won! Like as not she would open with some weird move, such as advancing her queen's rook's pawn; like as not she would ignore development and keep moving that damned pawn, or move it in conjunction with, say, the king's knight—unorthodox!—dreadful!—and like as not, having thrown her husband into such perturbation as an astronomer would experience if some morning the sun should rise in the northwest, she would chatter brightly about household matters and checkmate him. Whereupon he would exclaim, "Rats!"

"What's the matter, honey? Isn't that a legal move? I believe it is. I believe you're checkmated, honey."

"I'm checkmated, yes, but—but—you don't play properly, my dear."

"I don't? What did I do wrong, honey?"

"Not any specific thing, perhaps, but—but—my dear, you must understand that a chess player's first goal is to develop his men. Development and mobility are to chess what logistics are to an army. Neglect development and you'll never win."

"But I *did* win, honey."

"Yes, but in the wrong way. The end never justifies the means."

"Dear me," she sighed, smiling in that every-cloud-has-a-silver-lining-it's-such-a-big-wonderful-beautiful-world way, "I reckon chess is just too deep for me."

When Esperanza won—and as her skill developed she was able to win one game in three—Sophronicus felt he was fairly beaten; and often he would congratulate her upon some ambush she had laid.

Having fostered such a dangerous opponent, he was eager to join battle often; so on winter evenings the two families spent many cozy hours together in the library which occupied the south wing of Lexylvania, a spacious and beautiful room, comfortable with deep chairs, lighted by whale-oil lamps, warmed by a huge fireplace whose iron-sheeted back-wall bore embossed figures of Roman charioteers, and upon whose mantel a bronze Greek athlete stood poised with a discus.

Sometimes while Esperanza and Sophronicus were locked in silent combat, Lucretia and Caleb would set up another board, but their games were never the deadly Apache-versus-Kentuckian duels of their spouses, for chess or no chess Lucretia enjoyed talking, her pleasant voice with its soft Blue Grass accents rippling in the lamplight like a limestone creek while she reminisced upon such variegated subjects as the time her daddy, although not a veterinarian but an M.D., had been called in to save the life of Major Crittenden's blooded mare, Kentucky Belle, and of how in gratitude the major presented daddy with the mare's foal, and how the foal matured to win many a race and wager for its owner, all of which led her to remember their early days in New Empire, when Sophronicus was sub-Indian agent, and of how once in a Fox village he diplomatically consented to play straws with the warriors, and won all their wampum but gave it back, much to their bafflement.

"Is it my move, Mr. McSwasey? Oh, I *am* sorry—here I've been thinking it was your move. Am I white or black? No, don't tell me, I recollect now, I'm black, and I think I'll just move this little old knight."

And the knight's move having been accomplished, she went on to tell how those Fox Indians in those early days were *such* quaint persons, mighty afraid of Americans, much more so than ever they had been of the French or British: why, with her own ears she had heard a chief say that from their enthusiasm for battle the Americans deserved to be called white Indians. And they did so love whiskey, those Fox Indians did, and so far as she was concerned she had never seen the harm in giving them a dram or two—just enough to mellow them and to promote their digestion, which was probably bad, they ate so many beans and dogs—but Sophronicus was very stern about withholding bourbon from the savages because he said they didn't drink like gentlemen.

"Is it my move? Well, now, let me see."

Playing with Caleb, she won two games out of three, but this was not surprising because his mind was no more on chess than hers, for in those years his thoughts were endlessly involved with the rising fortunes of the McSwasey & Zumwalt Lumber Company: money-making was his favorite game.

About midevening Lucretia would repair to the kitchen where, the maids having gone out dancing or to a church social or to bed, she would prepare a large bowl of popcorn, running with butter, and presently fetch it to the library along with sweet red apples. Like as not Esperanza and Sophronicus, both concentrating as if their lives depended on the game, would be unaware she had been absent.

"Dear me," she would say to Caleb, her face smile-wreathed, "some people would rather play chess than eat."

About that time Sophronicus would look up and say, "Why, my dear, you've popped corn."

"Indeed I have, honey, and if you don't watch out it's going to be all eaten before you've had a bite."

"Um-m-m, yes," he would reply, sinking back into his trance; so

343

Lucretia would fill two small bowls and set them where Sophronicus and Esperanza could nibble while they played.

And while Lucretia rambled brightly through her conversational Arcadia, perhaps telling how once when Sophronicus spent the night in a Fox village the chief offered to supply him with a pretty young bed-fellow—those Indians were always *so* hospitable—and how of course he refused, Caleb would peel and quarter an apple, and munch popcorn with some care, so the grains wouldn't lodge in his false teeth, and observe Esperanza at the chess table, her hair magic in the firelight, her eyes opaque, her face pure Apache as she stared at the checked battle-ground.

On some evenings Andrew Jackson Gentry was present, although he cared nothing for chess, preferring to sit in a corner with the *Youth's Companion* or with some such book as *One Hundred Useful Objects a Boy Can Build,* poring over plans for kites and iceboats. He had a workshop out in the stable, and according to his mother he was right handy with tools. Being the judge's son, it was perhaps singular that he preferred a chisel to Pindar's odes, but of course he might have taken after his grandfather Daniel Gentry, who had not only distilled the best drinking liquor in Bourbon County, but who could then turn right around and cooper a barrel for his product.

Thirteen-year-old boys have a way of becoming fourteen-years-olds, then fifteen and sixteen-year-olds, and Young Hickory did not deviate from the pattern; and as this took place, and he grew into a husky-voiced stripling, with his mother's sandy hair, and his father's long body, Caleb observed him closely. But during an entire evening young Andy, who was even less suave than most adolescents, addressed scarcely a half-dozen words to Esperanza. Yet now and then Caleb caught him sneaking a glance at her. Absorbed by chess, she was unaware of that scrutiny; or was she? After the game, when conversation became general, she would occasionally say something to the lad, who would immediately color. So Caleb wasn't too happy, the way the situation seemed shaping; but then that worry was abruptly ended when, in the summer of 1844, Lucretia and Sophronicus accompanied their son to Lexington, where he would enter Transylvania, and where they would attend the wedding of their youngest daughter, Helice, who had found Kentucky every bit as good a hunting ground as had the Long Knives several generations before.

*

Fortune favored McSwasey & Zumwalt, during those years of the 1840's when one of the great historic migrations of peoples was occurring on the North American continent. The Panic of '37 was only a bad memory now; the West was beginning to boom; and if you owned an established business in the Mississippi Valley, and enough capital so that some wildcat banker couldn't get his hooks into you, and if you used the brains that God gave you, you would have been hard put to it to end up bankrupt. Some men managed to go broke, but it took more effort than it was really worth; and as for men like Caleb McSwasey, they prospered like foxes in a henhouse.

Expansion was in the air, in those years, and Caleb fell easily into his old habit of pyramiding his winnings; he was always opening more logging camps. "You can't win it if you don't bet it," he used to say. Even Otto Zumwalt benefited to a modest extent from the business in which he was partner, for Caleb thought it only fair and expedient to send him now and then a few dollars of profits, but on the whole he preferred to pocket for himself most of the money left over after he had plowed back into the business at least half the returns from any given year.

Although he steadily acquired, in his own name, great tracts of standing timber, he thought it wiser to hold these in reserve, for usually they straddled creeks or encircled lakes of great strategic value to a lumberman: some day, he told himself, his holdings would be spotted so astutely that no man in his territory could get a log to a driving stream without first dealing with Caleb McSwasey. For immediate cutting, he favored skinning the land which belonged to the people of the United States. Nobody much blamed him; everybody was doing the same.

Cutting on Section 37, people called these raids on the public domain, and everybody laughed at the joke because of course no American township had more than thirty-six sections. Now and then, some trouble-making bureaucrat in a government land office—doubtless a socialistic sorehead out to interfere with private enterprise—would raise a feeble protest, but usually if you slipped him a few dollars he developed a convenient blind spot. If he persisted in his Un-American activities, and ordered the poor business lambs to stop plucking hairs from the government wolf, there were ways to get rid of him and send him back where he came from. You simply spoke to your lawyer, who yanked a wire; and presently, in faraway Washington City, a congressman would go into action, steaming into the central land office and demanding fair treatment for his constituents who were building up the country by cutting down the trees. A good lawyer, Caleb always said, came in as handy to a man as a civet-bladder to a skunk.

Oddly enough, however, although Judge Gentry was certainly a good lawyer, he refused to reach for that political wire, the first time Caleb needed it yanked. If McSwasey & Zumwalt had cut on government land by mistake, the judge said, he would gladly defend the firm; but sir, if the cutting had been intentional he would have nothing to do with the matter. Caleb said he reckoned the boys in Camp Number Five had stolen the timber, right enough, although he had known nothing about it. In that case, the judge said, McSwasey & Zumwalt should offer the government a fair price for the skinned land. Caleb thanked him and left. But instead of following that advice—imagine buying land already cut over!—he visited the *New Empire Chronicle,* whose editor enjoyed considerable political influence; so the wire was yanked after all.

"Sophronicus is an idealist," the editor said with a smile.

Caleb nodded; but privately he concluded that Sophronicus had refused to act because the amount of money involved had been picayunish; let McSwasey & Zumwalt become entangled in a big lawsuit, he told himself, with a substantial fee in the offing, and Sophronicus would forget his ideals.

Presently McSwasey & Zumwalt built its own sawmill up on the Whiskey River; and after that, in addition to rafting raw logs to market, the company rafted finished lumber down to New Empire where it had established a yard. Caleb was a busy man in those days, with his affairs prospering, but although he hired a young fellow to manage the lumber yard, and camp foremen to work under Amos Peabody, his general woods superintendent, he didn't employ so much as one clerk in his Gentry Block office. It looked much the same as when he first rented it, an almost bare, one-man office. But the real office remained in his head; he didn't like to share an intimate knowledge of business affairs with anybody.

Of all his enterprises, his marriage alone had fallen short of success, perhaps because Esperanza was a more vexatious partner than her father. But in Lilith, Caleb had a major-domo who kept him accurately informed of his wife's activities, and who cooked just as many delicious concoctions for Mistah Caleb as ever she had for Mistah Otto. Like all superior cooks, Lilith loved eating—she was forever sampling food in preparation, and licking the icing from spoons—so as the years passed her figure expanded enormously; dresses she had worn during her first days in New Empire now lacked inches of encircling her girth. She never fretted about gaining weight, however, for Dexter Yarlow, that hotel janitor, liked them plump.

As a servant, Lilith's principal shortcomings occurred in the department of sweeping, dusting and spider extermination, just as back in Santa Fe before Esperanza replaced Otto as slave driver. Now, however, Esperanza's commands had no effect, for Dexter had convinced Lilith she was indeed a free nigger who could theoretically quit the household if she chose. Not that she intended leaving, with her devotion to Mistah Caleb and her eternal hope that he would replace Dexter as her lover, but she often told Esperanza that she might.

"No, ma'am, I ain't going to waste no time with that feather duster. I am free now, that's what I am, and you ain't making me do nothing I don't want to."

This insubordination distressed Esperanza, but there was no way to remedy it, for she had grown a bit afraid of Lilith ever since an incident soon after the McSwaseys moved into their Gentry Avenue house. On that occasion, she had told Lilith she was tired of her uppity ways, and she ordered her to fetch a switch. Instead, Lilith spat into Esperanza's face.

What followed sounded like a clash between a bear and a wildcat. When it was over, Lilith bore nary a scratch, but Esperanza's hair hung in shreds, and her blouse was torn and her face scarlet from being slapped.

"Just you wait till Caleb comes home," she screamed, insane with rage. "He'll take a cowhide to you."

Lilith's eyes went dreamy, but Caleb disappointed them both.

"She's a good nigger and we're keeping her," he told his wife.

The affair was only one of those common domestic misunderstandings, for Caleb suspected that his wife suspected that Lilith had been set to spy on her, so of course this increased his already lively suspicions; and while under ordinary circumstances he wouldn't have had an uppity nigger in the house, he certainly wasn't sending away such an excellent detective as Lilith.

During those first years of marriage, Caleb thought that children might increase his wife's happiness, so he worked diligently to beget them. But the little fellows have a mischievous way of trooping into households where they are not wanted, and avoiding homes where the latchstring is always out; so many a wedding anniversary came and went with the McSwaseys childless. At last, Esperanza did bear Caleb a son, although it wasn't his.

But that was far in the future during those years when the McSwaseys lived on Gentry Avenue, and Caleb worked so hard to become a lumber baron. Even though he trusted his superintendent, Amos Peabody, as far as he trusted anybody, he still deemed it prudent to go into the woods himself several times each logging season, and this brought him face to face with the inconvenience of having an unreliable wife. If only she were pregnant! But she wasn't. So that first October when he boarded a steamboat to visit his first camp, he took Esperanza along. They were still virtually bride and groom then, and they didn't yet hate each other, so Caleb could always look back on that voyage as tinted with the enchantment of love, and comparative youth, and the fresh beauty of a business venture when it is new and rosy with hope. The weather was sublime, autumn at its most bewitching, the big river winding lazily among its countless islands and miles of bluffs, where the foliage was a feast of wine reds and butter yellows. Early one morning, just before the steamboat reached the Chippewa River at the foot of Lake Pepin, they stepped ashore on the Wisconsin side at a trading post operated by Stub Flannigan. They were the only passengers for Flannigan's Landing, and they had hardly set foot on the bank before the boat backed away and steamed off into the thick mist hanging over the glassy water.

Amos Peabody had promised to send Chippewa Injuns with canoes to meet them, but the landing was deserted, the log store asleep. Caleb pounded the door. It inched open, finally, and a sloe-eyed girl, Flannigan's squaw, peered out.

"Howdy do," she said.

While Caleb explained his business, she listened, wary as a weasel, then asked:

"Dakota with you?"

"Just us *Chee-moke-o-mon,*" he said.

"You see Dakota?"

"Hell, no. They're all across the river."

"Sometime they cross. Dugout. They out there?"

"Look, Pocahontas," he said, "I'm McSwasey. Hell with Dakotas. I'm rendezvousing with Chippewas here. You a Chippewa?"

She nodded and said:

"But I no Pocahontas. I Coppa-mo-ba."

"All right, Coppa-mo-ba, I'm looking for Chippewas from the Whiskey River. Peabody was to send them."

"Come in," she said.

The dim store smelled of fish, stale whiskey, gun oil and blankets. Having bolted the door, Coppa-mo-ba explained that the party of warriors Peabody had sent were encamped a couple of miles away in the Chippewa bottoms. They were brave warriors but too few to risk ambush by their mortal enemies who lived across the river. Walking Wind, their leader, had been visited by a dream which warned him of ambush. Coppa-mo-ba would escort the McSwaseys to their hiding place.

Injuns and their damned dreams! Caleb said:

"We'll want breakfast first."

In the dimness she was a silent shadow.

Caleb brought out a fifty-cent piece, flipped it, caught it, rang it down on the sawed log counter.

"I get," she said.

Outside, the mist was turning from mouse gray to ash gray, and as light oozed through the window Caleb made out a man slumped in a corner on the puncheon floor. It was Flannigan, hog fat and hog dirty. He stirred, when Coppa-mo-ba brought coffee, fried catfish and cold johnnycake; and while the McSwaseys stood eating at the counter he sat up and stared, legs sprawled like a monstrous baby's.

"Who the hell you?" he mumbled, after a minute. And he sat there staring, lips flaccid, eyes glazed, talking to himself. Once he raised his voice and bawled, "Gentlemen, gentlemen, I demand the right to be heard. As pretty a mare as ever ran, an' I'll wager the whole estate from me sainted father that she'll carry me colors across the finish first. But the jockey was a bastard and doped her. Oh, the bastard, the bastard . . ."

Silent in deerskin moccasins, Coppa-mo-ba carried him coffee. He took a gulp and sprayed it out, swearing.

"And now they're cuttin' me whiskey with slop from the jar," he bawled, splintering the cup against the wall and swaying to his feet. "I'll fight any man in the place." His fists waved uncertainly. "Do you hear me, you rogues, I'll fight any man in the place." His fists dropped. "Gentlemen, gentlemen, never travel steerage to America. She died, gentlemen, she died. Food for the whales . . . I never swung a pick an' shovel, I told the bastard, an' I ain't starting now. Take your canal an' stick it, I told him, I'm heading west . . ."

He stood with eyes closed, rocking on wide-planted feet. Then his lids snapped up and he was staring at Esperanza.

"Little Christ Jesus on Christmas morn! As pretty a squaw as ever wiggled her tail. Her hair like a popple leaf when the frost kisses it gold, and her skin, gentlemen, her skin—"

He lurched forward. Caleb drew a pistol, grasped it by the barrel and smashed the butt into Flannigan's jaw. He dropped. Caleb stood over him, lifted a foot, drove the heel down into Flannigan's mouth. Then he lighted a Cuban Pelion.

"Shall we go?" he asked.

*

The sun had burned away the mist, the sky was deep blue, when Esperanza and Caleb followed Coppa-mo-ba along the marshy path through the water pepper and cattails toward Walking Wind's camp in the swamps.

Short of the camp, Coppa-mo-ba halted.

"Far enough. I go. I come back soon."

She left them; Caleb eased from his shoulders the possible sack he had packed for the trip, and grounded his rifle.

"Why did she have us wait here?" Esperanza asked.

"She's telling them we're coming. If we busted in we'd give them a scare. They're jumpy about the Dakotas. But the Dakotas ain't much for swamp fighting. They're hoss Injuns. The Chippewas are ducks on the water and foxes in the woods."

"But if they're scared of the Dakotas why did they come at all?"

"I reckon Peabody promised them whiskey. An Injun will do anything for whiskey, except talk to his mother-in-law. But Walking Wind had to have a damned dream. They're spooky about their dreams. Think you can handle a paddle, Goldilocks?"

"I think so. But I can't swim."

He had to grin, at a gal with Injun blood who couldn't swim.

"Don't let it fret you," he said. "I can."

Coppa-mo-ba returned.

"Howdy do," she said. "Walking Wind ready."

The four Chippewas had bivouacked on a tongue of land jutting into the cinnamon-hued water of the slough. Among the bulrushes Caleb saw three canoes, their calking-stripes of pitch-and-charcoal black against their eggshell-colored bark.

"Howdy do," Walking Wind said.

He wore moosehide moccasins and leggings worked with stained quills; a brass cross dangled from his flat nose; his head, shaved with flint, was naked save for his scalp lock, glossy with bear grease and tufted with roaches of deer hair and an eagle's feather dyed scarlet and blue. A war hatchet and a hunting knife hung at his belt; he carried an old smooth-bore musket.

"Whiskey?" he asked.

Caleb shook his head. And in what he knew of the Chippewa language, he told Walking Wind there would be whiskey when they reached the lumber camp. Walking Wind stuck out his tongue and touched it.

"Thirsty," he said. *"Nee, nee, minniquah."*

Caleb gave him tobacco.

Two of the other warriors wore white men's pants; the third wore only a buckskin breech clout.

"All right, boys," Caleb said, "let's get the hell going before the Dakotas find us."

Mentioning the Dakota proved a mistake, for at that key word Coppa-mo-ba took to her heels and the warriors dived into the bulrushes. Caleb looked over the canoes, selected the tightest, loaded his gear on the cedar flooring amidships and steadied the craft while Esperanza picked her way into the bow, where the man-board was brilliantly decorated with geometric zigzags. Then, shoving off, he sprang into the stern.

"Are we leaving them?" Esperanza asked.

"They'll be along."

The canoe was light and coltish, frisking like a waterbug, till Caleb got the hang of it. Every bark canoe had a feel and a disposition of its own, like every rifle and every horse. And every gal, for that matter. Esperanza tried her hand at paddling, while they whispered along through the sloughs. Migrating blackbirds shrilled in a slippery elm; once their approach sent a flock of mallards whirring upward. At last the watery maze opened out into the Chippewa, a silent, deep, smooth-flowing river sweeping down to its meeting with the Mississippi; and presently, glancing back, Caleb saw his guides trailing along.

The willows were yellow, the sumac scarlet, and in the lazy autumn weather the Chippewa flowed so bright and clear you could see sand bottom and pickerel darting among the speckled rocks. Caleb paddled along easily, taking pleasure in the sight of his wife sitting in the bow, hair shining in the sun, body moving rhythmically with the dip and flash of her cedar paddle. Once when they rounded a point they saw a deer poised against the yellow foliage; another time a herd of elk trotted to safety; and in the late morning they surprised a bear swimming. The Injuns halloed and sent their canoes in chase, but the bear made shore

350

and disappeared. When they nooned on a sand beach Caleb noticed that the Injuns were still watchful; Dakotas, Walking Wind said, in essence, were ornery bastards; Red Wing's band had slain his father and Wabasha's band his brother; and he kept fingering his necklace of eagle claws: the eagle was his Manitou. Caleb patted his pistol and his rifle: they were his Manitou.

But no Dakota appeared; probably, Caleb told Esperanza, they were having bad dreams of their own, and making their own medicine against unexpected attacks by the Chippewa; although all things considered, he reckoned the Dakota and the rest of their Sioux brothers were better all-round scrappers than most Injuns.

That night, the Chippewa camped on one island, he and Esperanza on another, and that was one of the happiest interludes he had known since traveling the trail from Santa Fe. He portaged the canoe back into an alder thicket, for even good Injuns were silly people and these might decide that Walking Wind's dream indicated they should make off with the canoe and leave their white friends stranded. Then he kindled a fire, drying and warming the earth where he and Esperanza would sleep, and after the fire had burned down he scooped aside the coals and gathered cedar branches for a browse bed to mattress their blankets. Squaw-like, Esperanza worked at the campfire, boiling the coffee water and roasting spitted-venison from a deer he had killed in late afternoon.

After they had eaten, Caleb lounged with his cigar, full of contentment, glad he had chosen the river route to the lumber camp instead of the tote-road trail from Lake Pepin. Across the fire he watched his wife smoking her cigarette. As always, the firelight did magical things to her hair; and her eyes, staring into the flames, were black deeps of inscrutability. She looked enough like an Injun tonight, he thought, to be a breed, if she had sooted her hair. And that was fine with him; Injun gals did right well by a man, if you understood handling them.

"Happy?" he asked.

She gave him a swift and almost startled glance, maybe because it had been so long since he had asked that; then she smiled.

"Sí, I believe I am."

"Damn it," he thought, "I've given her a rough time." But he couldn't figure how else he could have dealt with her, since she carried Apache blood.

"You're not very happy in New Empire, are you?" he asked.

She shook her head.

"Sorry you married me?"

"Perhaps sometimes. But not tonight. It has been a wonderful day. The mist when we left the steamboat, and breakfast in that odd store, and the way you hit that fat man."

"Flannigan's all right," Caleb said. "But he can't carry liquor."

"Why did you kick him in the mouth?"

351

"Well, he was down. I figure the best time to kick a man is when he's down. Leastwise, that's what everybody does. Did it bother you when I kicked him?"

"I liked it," she said. "And the way you shot the deer from the canoe. I thought you had missed him, the way he went bounding away."

"Your average deer," Caleb said, "don't have brains enough to know when he's killed through the heart. He'll always take a few bounds, even when he's dead on his feet."

"And I liked paddling the canoe. It was like floating on a cobweb."

"Maybe," Caleb said, playing with ideas, "we ought to start out, just you and me in a birchbark. Find out where the Mississippi comes from, and portage over to the Red, and trap for a living and to hell with stumpage."

"Ooo, I would like that."

"So would I," he said, "but we'd die in the poorhouse."

Night had fallen on the river; the stars were frosty; the Big Dipper sparkled in the north, and Polaris winked like a beacon calling a man to the bonanza forests. Caleb poked the fire, tossed on a hunk of squaw wood. Off in the hills a coyote was yapping. He thought of the nights innumerable he had sat by a fire and heard the coyotes, in Texas, New Mexico, the Rockies, on the Trail. Probably, he told Esperanza, those fool Injuns would suspect the coyote of being a Sioux from Red Wing's band, signaling his comrades to be ready to attack at dawn, when the spirits no longer walked. Injuns were as skittish as spooky ponies. They and their dreams.

"Sometimes," she murmured, "I have dreams that are very bad. They waken me and my heart is pounding. Why do you think we dream?"

"God knows," he said.

"Do you think our dreams foretell what is to come in our lives?"

"I doubt it."

"Sometimes," she said, her voice hushed, "I dream I am back in Santa Fe at the time of the revolution, and a man is chasing me. It wakens me and I feel sick, and all the next day my thoughts are black. And one day in our own house I came downstairs in broad daylight and thought I saw the man crouching in the hall."

"A man in our house?"

"There was no man. It was only a shadow. He was there and then he was gone. His face was covered with sores and he wore yellow shoes. It was the first time he had ever dared show himself except in my dreams. I wanted to scream and burn down the house to chase him away. But it was only a shadow."

"If I'd been there," Caleb said, "I'd have slugged the son of a bitch."

"You wouldn't have seen him," she said drearily. "I think nobody could have seen him except me."

And unexpectedly she began to cry. He jumped up and went to her,

352

holding her in his arms and calling her Goldilocks. She sobbed like a child, and once she said, "I don't want him to come back. I don't want to see him again, ever. Oh, Caleb, Caleb . . ."

He held her close, and he felt tremendously protective, ready to shield her from whole regiments of men in yellow shoes. He thought, "She's just a kid. Reckon I've been too rough with her." And he was amazed at the realization that locked inside her pretty head there existed a whole universe of terrors and desires that he could never know.

*

Before daylight when the mist was thick the clock in his mind wakened him. He tucked the blanket around his sleeping wife, brushed his lips across her forehead, and arose to feed the fire and measure out coffee and slice bacon with his hunting knife. Somewhere in the darkness a few cold-sounding frogs lamented the lost summer, and the bird which the Chippewa called *muck-a-wiss* sang whippoorwill. Squatting on his heels while the foliage dripped and the bacon sizzled, he smiled as he dreamed out the day ahead: the day in the Moon of Migratory Game when he would reach Camp Number One of McSwasey & Zumwalt.

When the bacon had crisped and the wet air was fragrant with coffee, he went to the browse bed and looked down at Esperanza, asleep in the flickering gold light, her brows and lashes black as charcoal against her coppery-beige flesh. He touched her.

"It's daylight in the swamp," he said. "This is the day to make the fortune, honeychild."

Her lids stirred; and as always he experienced mild wonder when he saw her eyes, so unexpectedly black and Injun-like with her fair hair.

"Ooo," she murmured sleepily, "I do not think it is daylight yet."

"It will be," he said, "if the Lord's tending to business."

The mist was pearly bright and lifting from the running water when, with breakfast over and their gear packed, Caleb steadied the canoe while his wife took her place in the bow. She was like the canoe, he thought, as light-footed and gracefully curved.

Upstream a quarter of a mile he made out through the thinning mist two canoes beached on the island where the Injuns were camping, but he saw nobody.

"Goldilocks," he said, "don't let me scare you. Keep us nosed into the current while I rouse them Injuns."

He yowled like a coyote; and then, bringing up his rifle, put a bullet through the branches of the island trees. And he had to laugh when he saw Walking Wind leaping up and crashing into the underbrush.

"Howdy do, you brave sons of bitches," Caleb yelled. "You'll never get rich this way."

Silence from the island.

"It's daylight in the swamp," he yelled, "and we're off to make the fortune."

"Howdy do."

"Howdy do yourself, brother."

"Dakota?"

"No Dakota. We're going ahead. Get a move on your red tails or you'll never catch us."

"Whiskey?"

"Not for breakfast. It would give you the snakes."

An hour later, when the mist had vanished and the day was brilliant and the river blue, Caleb looked back and saw them following, their canoes far specks with flashing paddles.

"Them Injuns," he said, "are more trouble than a flea in church."

But he didn't give a damn: he was riding high, that day, off to the woods and his first million, with his woman where he could watch her and a canoe that could float on a heavy dew. The mosquito season was gone; the woodticks were dead as a pine with center-rot; frost had killed the deer flies and no-see-ums. He was smiling as his paddle dipped and flashed.

The Chippewa was a handsome river, with its sweeps and bends, but he liked the Whiskey River better because he thought of it as his. They reached it at midmorning, a sparkling stream rippling in from the north, with cold transparent waters that made him think of trout.

"Goldilocks," he called, as they paddled along its lower reaches fringed with cattails and wild rice, "what do you think of it?"

"Ooo, I like it."

"It's all yours and mine," he said. "At least, in a way of speaking."

Sometimes they passed the mouths of creeks and spring-fed brooks, pouring into the Whiskey, and his thoughts were busy with plans for dams up those inlets, to hold back reserves of water for his log drives. Peabody would know about that. When he hired Peabody he had bought the use of the best logging brains in the Territory.

"He's the woods brains," Caleb thought, "and the pinery boys are the hands. I'm the pocketbook."

And he ruminated upon the oddness, when you came to think of it, of commerce and merchantry, how the hand that held the pocketbook ruled the world, and the brain that owned the pocketbook ruled the hand. The trick was to have the sort of brain that could fill the pocketbook in the first place; after that, everything was simple. You could always buy first class brains like Peabody's for less than they were worth to you.

He never knew precisely when it happened, but at some moment that morning as they glided along the Whiskey River they crossed an invisible boundary into the North. The sunlit air was crisp; in the meadows of wild hay an occasional boulder showed itself; now and then, among the oak openings, a rugged old hemlock stood lonely against the sky. Once they passed a creek suckled by a cedar swamp; a stand of white birches flashed from a hillside; clumps of beggarly jack pine appeared, wandering among the cranberry brambles of an old burn; rocks began cluttering the stream bed, creaming the accelerating current. Then they reached Hangover Rapids, and from one of the other canoes Walking Wind called:

"*Onúggemeg.*"

"*Waýgonin taŕnin?*" Caleb called back.

"*Onúggemeg.* Portage."

"Long?"

Walking Wind shook his head, held up a finger.

"*Opugidpewinon.*"

"One pause?"

"One pause, you bet."

Caleb indicated that Walking Wind should shoulder the McSwasey canoe.

"Whiskey?"

"At camp."

Walking Wind touched his tongue.

"Thirsty. *Gwotch. Nee, nee, mínniquah.*"

"At camp."

They followed the ancient moccasin path among wild raspberry brambles and choke cherries. At the pause, which showed the ashes of old campfires, Caleb said:

"Maybe Dakotas here?"

Walking Wind's thick lips curled in a smile; he patted his necklace of eagle claws, fisted his chest.

"I kill 'em all, you bet."

So they were out of the neutral hunting ground along the Chippewa.

They nooned at the end of the carry, eating pemmican with their coffee. By then, white pines were appearing, solitary at first, or in scanty groups crowning the ridges, too scattered to be worth the chopping.

"Your white pine," Caleb told Esperanza, "grows best in a crowd. The thicker the better, for them and for us."

After lunch they took to their canoes again, and about an hour later they brought up at the Jigger Rapids portage.

"Now we're getting there," Caleb said. "Noggin Lake is just up yonder, at the head of the rapids. Now you'll see white pine, Goldilocks."

Leaving the canoe for Walking Wind to carry, he led Esperanza along a path through the alders and the kinnikinnick. The roar from the rapids grew louder; spray had sponged the path and daubed the rocks with slippery footing; by the path a puddle had accumulated in the hole from an uprooted popple tree. Caleb stopped, pointed among the bushes to the rapid water churning over the boulders.

"Come spring," he said, "and those rapids will be buried under a head of water that will float logs as easy as a spaniel carries a duck. Back yonder at Hangover I'll build me a mill. I'll skin this country slick as a schoolma'am's leg."

And when they reached Noggin Lake, he swept his hand in a large gesture.

"There you are, Goldilocks. There's your pine."

Immaculate, smooth, sky-blue, the lake lay brightly cupped by low hills, its sparkling waters stretching off to far shores with pretty little coves and points. Among the lily pads and swan potatoes of the near shore, ducks were quacking; off in mid-lake a heron flapped through the still afternoon, trailing long thin legs; the wickiups and beached canoes of a Chippewa village showed on a distant finger of land. But Caleb ignored the Indian lodges, the wild rice marshes, the bulrushes, and all the other evidences of a nicely-balanced primitive economy. He saw the pines.

They were dark, thick, rich; the clean air was aromatic with their fragrance; the eagle nested in their lofty crotches; the porcupine climbed their centenarian boles; the wild turkey bowed their branches; the fox played with its cubs in their shadows; the elk ranged there, and the moose, the bear, the wolf, the lynx. Caleb saw the pines, the board feet. From the far shore they stretched off to infinity, over ranges of hills, leaping across tamarack swamps, skirting other jeweled lakes, they and the sandy loam of the North anchoring each other in natural symbiosis.

"Goldilocks," Caleb said, voice low and saliva-dripping, "I'll go through them pines like a sickle through grass. I own every section fronting this lake, so no other son of a bitch can boom a log in these waters. And I've got me sections spotted off there—and there—and there. And those I don't own belong to uncle, and Caleb's his favorite nephew. He won't mind what I take, so long as I leave him the stumps."

"Uncle?" she asked.

"Striped pants and chin whiskers," Caleb said. "A blue coat and a vest with stars. Uncle Sam, Goldilocks."

"I think you may get into trouble," she said.

"I reckon not. Why, a man would be a fool kind of hoss not to grab them while they're there to grab. If I didn't grab them, some other bastard would. Uncle don't care, Goldilocks. He lives in Washington City."

"I think it will bring you trouble."

"Trouble?" he said, smiling. "Why, Goldilocks, I reckon not. But if uncle gets snoopy, the son of a bitch will wish he hadn't. I've got me a lawyer, Goldilocks. I own his brain like I own Peabody's. Nothing will stop me now, honeychild. I'm in on the ground floor, and that's better than fat buffler steak. Waugh!"

*

"Whiskey?" Walking Wind asked, when they had crossed the lake and beached where a tote road wandered back into the woods.

"At camp," Caleb said.

He stood there a minute by the canoes, imagining how that shore would look next spring with his logs piled in rollways. He was smiling; his eyes were far away.

"Goldilocks," he said, "we can't miss. It's better than a shipload of Congo niggers."

His salivary glands were leaking when he shouldered his possible sack, took up his rifle, and led the way along that tote road through the wild plum thickets and raspberry tangles and sumac burned red by autumn. Under his boots the road was crunchy with sand, its ruts fringed by frost-withered goldenrod and asters. They passed a marsh choked with tamarack and swamp milkweed, a brake where the grape leaves seemed stamped from translucent gold and the bittersweet clustered in handfuls of fire; and once, after the road had left the marshy places and snaked through scrub jack pine and popple, a Canada jay alerted the woods with cries of thief. Somewhere a crow answered, far and forlorn.

White pines stood lordly and aloof among the balsam and cedar; the road was epigraphed with oxen droppings; and when they reached a fork Caleb hesitated only a second, remembering the operations map Peabody had sent, before he took the left turn. It led to a clearing.

He stopped when he saw it, his first camp, chopped out of the wilderness beside a trout brook sparkling from the dark woods beyond. By God, he thought, smiling; and excitement tingled in his veins. Across the fresh stumps he saw the huddle of log buildings, chinked with reindeer moss and clay, roofed with shakes: the stable, the bunkhouse, the blacksmith shop, the cookhouse with woodsmoke curling from the stone chimney. That smoke smelled light and sweet, redolent with memories of all the campfires in his life, long burned to ashes and scattered, as it mingled with the fragrance of the pines.

"Goldilocks," he said softly, "this is it. McSwasey & Zumwalt Number One."

"It seems so small," she said.

He saw what she meant; those low buildings looked dwarfed by the pines.

"Why, honeychild," he said, "it's snug. Those loggers ain't choosey beavers. They'll never see it by daylight anyhow, except Sundays. A bullet is small too," he added, "but it can drop a moose."

As they crossed the clearing Caleb sighted a blocky man in a red undershirt beyond the far end of the bunkhouse. His mustaches were sweeping, and he was somberly engaged in balancing a knife on his palm and flinging it at a crude bull's-eye marked on the bark of a birch tree. It pierced the target and stuck there, hilt quivering.

"Friend," Caleb said, "is anybody around?"

"Mike Hogan's around," the man said. "He was alone and happy for it, till four Injuns snuck in with a pair of whites."

"Are you Hogan?"

"And what's it to you?"

"I'm McSwasey."

Mike Hogan yanked the knife from the target, examined the point, ran a thumb along the edge. Then he marched back to a line marked in the dirt and balanced the knife again.

"There's coffee in the pot," he said. "But you'll wash your own cups and I'll have no Injun heathens in my kitchen. Supper's when I blow the horn and my beans is the best in the woods."

He flung the knife; it pierced the center of the bull's-eye; again he yanked it out and took his stance.

"Friend," Caleb said, "I reckon you've got a pair of bunks in the cookhouse."

"And would I be sleeping on the floor?"

"I wouldn't like to guess about that," Caleb said.

Hogan's ears turned as red as his flannel-colored lips.

"A bunk for myself," he said, "and one above it for my cookee, once we get a full crew."

"You'll sleep in the bunkhouse tonight," Caleb said.

"And that I will not."

"Friend," Caleb said, "I reckon you will. My wife and I will use your bunks."

Hogan's eyes were cold; the knife lay balanced on his palm. Caleb's thumb was hooked in his belt, near his pistol. They looked at each other.

"That's a neat toss you've got," Caleb said softly. "I've seen better, but yours ain't too bad. But I like this one best of all."

He stepped forward unexpectedly, took the knife. Instantly, it flashed back over his shoulder and pierced the bull's-eye.

"Sometimes," he said, "a knife comes in handy, if a man knows how to use it. You keep practicing, friend. You're doing right well."

Mike Hogan went to the target and stood squinting.

"Did you plan to stab through my last cut," he asked, "or was it the devil's own luck?"

"Why, friend," Caleb said, "I reckon I'll let you puzzle about that."

Hogan yanked out the knife and sheathed it.

"It's like I've always said," he said, "a man sleeps as well one place as another, if he's at peace with God. Now would you be liking coffee? Or maybe hot tea?"

Caleb looked at Esperanza.

"Coffee," she said.

"I'll have tea," Caleb said. "But first fix up these Injuns with a couple of jugs."

358

"Straight, or cut, Mr. McSwasey?"

"Why, friend," Caleb said, "I reckon you ain't done much Injun trading. Cut it with water and pour in some pepper."

"Whiskey?" Walking Wind asked.

Caleb nodded.

Walking Wind touched his tongue.

"Thirsty," he said.

"God, man," Caleb said, "why didn't you say so before?"

"Kill many Dakota," Walking Wind said, thumping his chest.

"Leave a few for breeding stock," Caleb said.

When Mike Hogan emerged from the cookhouse with the jugs, the Injuns started to mob him.

"Back, you dog-eatin' heathens," he bawled, "or I'll cut out your oysters and cook me a stew."

"If I was doing it," Caleb told him, "I'd decoy them back to the canoes before I'd give them a drop."

Silence sneaked out of the woods, after the Injuns followed Hogan from sight. Caleb stood looking after them. Then he shouldered his possible sack and with Esperanza crossed to the covered dog-trot between the bunkhouse and the cookhouse.

"That man Hogan," he said, "talks a mighty fine meal. I hope he cooks one as good."

The cookhouse smelled of fresh logs and baked bread; whiffs of fragrance drifted from the fireplace, where pots steamed and beans bubbled in molasses and salt pork. New oilcloth gleamed on the two long tables, set with pewter ware and thick crockery cups. Caleb dumped his possible sack into the cook's bunk with its cedar-browse mattress to discourage gray backs.

"I didn't know you could throw a knife," Esperanza said. "You're better than Hogan."

"I wouldn't like to be worse."

"When did you learn?"

"Why, honeychild, that's been longer than I like to think. I got me a Barlow knife when I was a kid who didn't know spit from vinegar. Our barn door was all chewed to splinters from my practicing."

"Did you ever kill a man with a knife?"

He shook his head, then said:

"Maybe an Injun or two. I sort of favor a knife. It don't misfire, or run out of powder and balls. But that man Hogan should learn to draw and toss in one move. I've known places where they'd lug him out feet first, if he'd stand like he does and take a slow aim. If you ain't fast with a knife you'd best not fool with it."

They left the cookhouse and looked in on the bunkhouse, a dull-lighted rectangle lined with sleeping cubbies in tiers. Beneath a hole in the roof, a thick bed of sand held ashes from last night's fire; German socks dangled from an improvised clothesline.

"Peabody's a good man," Caleb said, when they emerged to the clearing. "I couldn't have laid out a better camp if I'd done it myself."

High in the pines, a current of air trickled among the sun-tipped needles; the forest stirred and soughed. Like an old dog sniffing strange premises, Caleb moved among the raw new stumps, the heaps of slash; and at the creek he turned and stared at the log buildings.

"I'll have me a dozen camps," he said, "some day."

They followed the creek into the pines, where everything was shadowy and cool, the ground clean of underbrush. Moss clung to the trunks that rose like tremendous pillars, straight and boldly cylindrical. A squirrel would climb a long way, Caleb guessed, before he reached the first branches. Sometimes, dazzling in the dimness, a streak of sunshine slanted across those limitless colonnades, but mainly everything was dusky and hushed, as if the remote boughs roofed a vast temple where the ancient forest gods communed with measureless time. Soft underfoot, the needles of ten thousand moons velveted the earth.

Once their passage was blocked by a huge windfall, rotting under its encrustation of moss and toadstools; once they came upon a partly exposed root, keg-size, that anchored a magnificent and patriarchal pine, so deep-girthed that its bole could have housed a whole nunnery of dryads. Caleb tapped the trunk, peeled away bark, jabbed his knife into the firm, resinous flesh.

"Sound as a thousand-dollar nigger," he said.

"How old is it?" Esperanza asked in a whisper.

"Why, Goldilocks, this one's old. They're all old, but I judge this one's been here a couple of centuries."

His voice, habitually low, sounded almost loud in that place of cached millenniums; and for an instant he felt small, of less consequence in the sweep of eternity than one of the numberless needles on the forest floor. And as he stood there in the silence an odd fancy flashed through his thoughts as he imagined how he and his woman would look, viewed from the topmost heights of that tree: a couple foreshortened and shriveled to specks.

"Maybe two hundred years," he said softly, "and maybe older."

His gaze followed its trunk, up, up, up, till his neck cricked.

"Will you cut it too?" Esperanza whispered.

He grinned; saliva runneled his tongue.

"Why, Goldilocks," he said, "a year from now this tree will be lumber. I wouldn't like to figure how many board feet it will scale. But enough to build a lot of backhouses."

*

360

Twilight had charcoaled the woods and crisped the air when Peabody and his crew of road-swampers and bull whackers trooped into camp; and before supper, while oxen lowed from the stable and the pinery boys cupped creek water in their palms and scrubbed their faces, Caleb talked things over with his woods superintendent. They sat in the kitchen, Caleb mainly listening.

By next week, Peabody said, they would finish swamping; the week after, with a full crew on hand, they would throw a dam across the outlet of Noggin Lake, and build driving dams on the various creeks emptying into the Whiskey River. That way, when they were floating out logs next spring, they could always open the gates of those dams and have a good head of water where they needed it. After the dam-building, say in another month, they would start real logging. He hoped for early snow and lots of it.

He was a burly man of forty, with steady eyes and dependable shoulders and a scar that zigzagged from his left temple to the hinges of his jaw. He called that his "Bangor mark," for he had received it in an Exchange Street grogshop when he was young and wanted to fight every man who got in his crosswalk.

Mike Hogan lighted the table candles with a pitch pine sliver, took up the long tin supper horn, went to the door, blew a stout blast. The pinery boys came tumbling in around him before he had paced in sturdy dignity back to his fire. Instantly they sat on the puncheon benches and fell to.

Peabody sat at the head of the table, with Esperanza on his right and Caleb sitting between her and the next pinery boy. No erudite and scintillating conversation here, such as in Sophronicus Gentry's dining room. No conversation at all. Only the sounds of rattling dishes, of sucking lips. Mike Hogan, wearing an apron, patrolled the table, armed with a huge coffee pot. And Caleb approved the rule of silence, for otherwise those pinery boys might have engaged in raillery with Esperanza. As it was, their gazes sometimes slid in her direction, but when that happened they had Caleb's eyes to deal with.

They were a muscular crew, shirts checked and faces neglected by the razor, with ears of cauliflower, noses smashed in old brawls, fingers minus joints, broken knuckles, cheeks scarred by calk marks. But one was younger than the others, a boy of fifteen. Caleb kept noticing him. His hair was black as gunpowder, his eyes a shrewd, cool and yet humorous gray in an Injun-colored face. When the meal was over he stood up and stretched, handling himself like a smooth-muscled lynx, and he glanced Caleb's way with an easy and faintly cocksure smile. His long body was slim but his frame was large, and he looked all hickory and rawhide. Caleb glanced sharply at his wife, but her eyes were on her plate.

Later, over their cigars, he asked Peabody about the fellow.

361

"That's Jim Buckmaster," Peabody said, "and he's going to make a logger. I've put him at swamping, but he'll be a chopper by spring. He handles an ax like Boone handled a rifle. Easiest swing I've ever seen. That ax bites where he aims it."

"He looks part Injun," Caleb said.

"No, he ain't a breed. He's Maine stock. I used to hear tell of his pa back on the Penobscot. They said his pa could swing an ax so slick it would shave the whiskers off a hopping flea. The kid does damn near that good now."

"Where did you find him?"

"He found me. Seems he worked as a chore boy in camps over northeast of Quickwater. But after the drives last spring he went off into the woods by himself. Ended up in this Chippewa town on the lake. When we got here he had him his own wickiup and squaw. Well, he hits me for a job. 'Hell, boy,' I told him, 'logging's a man's work.' 'So I've heard tell,' he says. 'Boy,' I says, 'you run along and play with your bow and arrows. Logging's a man's work,' I says. 'Mister,' he says, 'you wouldn't happen to have an ax in this camp?' 'Why,' I says, 'there might be a rusty one around. An ax,' I says, 'comes in sort of useful now and then, in a logging camp.'

"Well, he looks over our axes and hefts one or two till he finds a helve that he likes. Then he says, 'All right, mister, try me out.' This is when we're building the bunkhouse, so I point at a log and tell him to swing away. He goes through that log like an eel through water. I know right away he'll make a logger, but I say, 'Well, boy, I've seen worse chopping, but what about your wind?' He says, 'Why, I reckon the beans will take care of that.' 'Boy,' I says, 'you think you're good.' 'Hell, mister,' he says, 'I know I'm good.' 'Boy,' I says, 'you work along with grown men and where will you be?' 'A jump ahead of them,' he says. 'Boy,' I says, 'I've a mind to call you on that one. I've a mind to hire you for a day just to watch you wilt.' He just looks at me and grins. So I hire him and by God the chips fly. End of the day comes and he says, 'Hell, mister, there's a moon tonight. Let's go loggin', mister. Let's work up a sweat and tucker ourselves so we can sleep.' I says, 'Boy, you think you're good.' 'I know I'm good,' he says. I says, 'Boy, I reckon you're right about that. A touch of the rooster never hurt anybody,' I says, 'when he's young. Life will take the starch out of you soon enough.' 'Well,' he says, grinning, 'life's tried a few times already, but it ain't got no place.' So I knew I'd found me a logger. That boy will make a foreman one of these days. You keep an eye on that boy, Mr. McSwasey."

"I intend to," Caleb said.

*

So Caleb did just that, during the rest of his visit in camp, but he never caught Esperanza and Jim Buckmaster in anything like a flirtation. So far as he saw—and in such matters his eyesight was unmatched —their gazes never met head on. Yet the next day, when with his wife he trudged along the logging road to trail's end, and encountered the crew chopping off limbs, and watched Jim Buckmaster swinging his ax so smoothly and rhythmically and effectively, the highly-sensitized tentacles of Caleb's jealousy quivered and twitched as they encountered—or seemed to encounter—some invisible and powerfully-charged current racing between Esperanza and that boy. But maybe not. Maybe it was only the atmospheric disturbances to be expected when you took a desirable woman into a camp of healthy males. Caleb guessed bringing his wife to the woods was a mistake; on his next trip, he would leave her in Lilith's charge.

He tried to trap her, one evening on their return journey to New Empire. With supper over, they were lounging by the campfire, and Caleb said:

"Peabody has picked a good crew. Couldn't have done better myself. I like the way that boy, Jim Buckmaster, swings an ax."

Nerves tight, watching Esperanza, he awaited her comment. If she said nothing, it would be suspicious. If she asked which logger was Jim Buckmaster, it would be doubly suspicious. But she said:

"Ooo, yes, it seemed the ax was part of him."

Hell! What could you make out of that?

"I'm going to make him a foreman," Caleb said.

"Are you? But isn't he very young for that?"

She seemed quite indifferent, really.

"I'll wait a few years," Caleb said.

He dropped matters there. And in the months that followed, when he tossed Buckmaster's name unexpectedly into a conversation, he never tricked her into revealing more than casual interest in the fellow. And Lilith reported that she never mentioned his name. The next spring, when Caleb announced he was going up to Noggin Lake, to catch the beginning of the log drive, Esperanza evinced neither disappointment nor elation when he said she should remain in New Empire. And as the years passed, and McSwasey & Zumwalt became a two camp outfit, a four and an eight camp outfit, he nearly forgot he had ever been jealous of that cocksure boy. Then Andrew Jackson Gentry returned to New Empire from the Mexican War, and Caleb had his hands full being jealous of him, without giving a thought to that camp foreman, Jim Buckmaster.

*

One morning several thousand years before, a tree uprooted by flood waters came whirling down the big river and lodged itself near shore about a half mile north of the village called Place-of-the-Big-Fish. Driftwood accumulated in the tree's snags, along with twigs and weeds, so that presently this mass of debris offered obstruction to the flowing water. Spinning in hesitation, the water dropped bits of silt. By and by, the place where the tree had lodged became an agglutination of rotten wood, topsoil, dead fish, bird guano; water weeds and wild rice rooted there; a cottonwood sprouted; and all the time, while on the other side of the world men boiled their fellow creatures in oil, or drew them and quartered them, or roasted them at the stake because they threatened civilization by believing the earth round and the universe old, the embryonic island near the Place-of-the-Big-Fish stayed right at home and minded its business and like all American entities strove to grow bigger. In the 1840's Caleb McSwasey bought it.

By then, it was an island more in name than fact, separated from the mainland by a thin neck of water where Croton bugs skated and cottonwood fluff drifted and frogs dwelt among the lotus and munched mosquitoes during intermissions between the lesser known works of Bach and Beethoven. From tip to toe the island ranged for half a mile; at its widest it measured two city blocks; and during the centuries it had improved its property with a fine growth of elms, swamp oaks, black walnuts and sycamores. Caleb said it was a fine place to build a house, and it was, for on the hottest summer nights a breeze sucked up the river channel, air conditioning the bedrooms and blowing away the mosquitoes. And it offered another advantage, more obscure but even more telling, if you were cursed with a jealous nature: when you left your wife at home in your new house, you left her on an island, moated against sons of bitches. This advantage, to be sure, was largely symbolical, for if love had always laughed at locksmiths it certainly wouldn't let that neck of water halt it, especially since the water was bridged, but after all if Caleb felt comforted to think of his wife cut off from the mainland, well, it was his money that bought the island and built the house.

But it was Sophronicus Gentry, that sometime architect, who designed it, complete with a cupola so commodious that it really deserved to be called a widow's walk: a glassed-in little tophouse where Esperanza, if so minded, could spend many a wistful hour watching for Caleb's steamboat to bring him back from the pinery. She never took advantage of the opportunity, but certainly that was not the cupola's fault.

"What sort of house do you plan to build?" Sophronicus asked, one winter evening in 1846, soon after the island had joined the growing company of McSwasey property.

"What would you advise?" Caleb asked.

They were seated in the Gentry library, eating popcorn and fudge; it was one of those evenings when Sophronicus had bested Esperanza at chess, so he was feeling that God was right where he should be and that there was nothing wrong with the world that a few more such victories couldn't cure; and now he launched into a learned discussion of architecture. Before it was over he offered to design the house, and Caleb gladly accepted.

So next day Sophronicus unearthed his drawing board and his books on architecture, and during the rest of that winter hardly an evening passed without the McSwaseys' going to the Gentry library for conferences on such matters as whether the house should be equipped with its own gas plant and whether Caleb wanted to experiment with such dubious contraptions as running water and central heating. He told Sophronicus to let his conscience guide him; what he wanted was a fine imposing mansion. What he really wanted was a house twice as palatial as the Penwick residence back in East Bainbridge; and to achieve that, if left to his own devices, he might have built a peacockish wooden castle with seven gables and a half dozen cupolas. But Sophronicus, that natural child of Kentucky and Greek civilizations, worshipped purity of line, whether in a façade or a race horse, (cupolas always excepted), so by spring, when he presented Caleb with a drawing labeled, "Residence of Caleb McSwasey, Esq., Front Elevation, Judge Sophronicus Gentry, Architect," the sharply-inked lines showed a creation as lyric as a clipper ship and much less given to seesawing, its portico equipped with the handsome pediment and lofty Doric columns not unheard of on the Acropolis.

"Looks fine," Caleb said.

"And do you like the cupola?" Sophronicus asked.

"Can't see a thing wrong with it."

"I must confess," Sophronicus said, "I'm rather partial to that cupola myself."

"Dear me," Lucretia murmured, "I just don't see how he does it."

"And you madam?" Sophronicus asked Esperanza.

"Ooo, it is beautiful. I think you are a wonderful architect."

"The well rounded citizen of a free republic," Sophronicus told his admirers, "should strive to improve himself in all branches of the moral, philosophical and scientific arts."

"He's a dead shot with a squirrel rifle too," Lucretia said.

He sobered and said:

"Before this affair with Mexico is over, we may all need our squirrel rifles. Sir, in my opinion President Polk has shown more patience with the sovereign government of Mexico than is consistent with the honor of this Republic. If I were president, our legions would be encamped this very night on Mexican soil."

"It shouldn't be much of a trick to lick the greasers," Caleb said.

"I hope you are correct, sir. Remember the Alamo!"

"I'm no Whig," Caleb said.

Sophronicus stood up and slowly paced in front of his audience, like an orator on the senate floor.

"Sir, the destiny of this Republic is plainly manifest. From the Atlantic littoral to the California surf our citizens must be able to stride unafraid beneath the protection of the eagle."

"We'll have to convince the Injuns of that first," Caleb said. "But they don't convince so hard, if a man's powder holds out."

"Sir, heaven has destined us to be a continental power. A Republic embracing—"

And for the next minutes, Sophronicus sketched the history of republics, actual and utopian, and outlined the policies this Republic should follow with those unreasonable Mexicans. When he had finished, Lucretia smiled and nodded.

"That's right, honey. If they won't sell us that territory I think we ought to march in and take it."

"Ah—well, my dear—that isn't *quite* what I've been saying—"

"We'll lick them without much trouble," Caleb said. "I know greasers."

When news reached New Empire that General Taylor's troops had crossed the border, Sophronicus's delight was complete except for the fact that the general was a Whig.

"Mark my words," he told Lucretia. "If this man Taylor is successful, he will emerge a hero, and I fear for the Democratic Party in '48. A general in the White House! But it is a possibility we must face, for as Gibbon has said, mankind is always more ready to applaud its destroyers than its benefactors."

"Wasn't General Jackson a general?" Lucretia asked.

"That, my dear, is a different matter entirely. General Jackson was not a professional soldier."

After congress got around to announcing that a state of war existed—certainly no great news to anybody—a letter came from Andrew Jackson Gentry, reporting that he had enlisted for a year with Kentucky troops, and expressing confidence that he would send many greaser souls into eternity.

And although Lucretia was mighty proud of that boy, she broke down and cried, and even Sophronicus's eyes were humid. War, after all, had its drawbacks.

*

But its advantages, as any fair-minded man had to admit, greatly outweighed those drawbacks, for how else could an up-and-coming young country, short of gold but with plenty of manpower, buy so much new territory so cheaply? On the other side of the scales, of course, Texas had to be admitted to the Union, and the United States couldn't very well crawl out of taking Southern California, but nothing is perfect, and even at the risk of ending up with a general in the White House the opportunities were so beguiling that a real-estate-minded and warlike nation simply couldn't afford to pass up invading its southern neighbor. Besides, most significant of all, war lodged a bur under the tail of the business mare: profits of McSwasey & Zumwalt zoomed to a new peak in 1846, although Otto never heard about it. Caleb's conscience, however, being a good old New England conscience, didn't trouble him on that score, for he felt that if the simpleton was fool enough to trust a Yankee, he deserved everything that didn't come to him. Moreover, most of Otto's share of the profits went into building the new house, so his daughter would benefit.

Construction of the house began that first summer of the war, the workmen promising to complete it by the following March. On the strength of that, in November, Caleb sold his Gentry Avenue house, agreeing to give possession April 1, but as always in such projects delays piled up, what with the severe winter and human slothfulness, and when spring came the workmen admitted they had been over-optimistic, although undoubtedly the house would be ready for occupancy by June, or perhaps July or August. The buyer of Caleb's old house was eager to take possession on schedule, so it looked as if the McSwaseys might have to make do by moving into the Commercial House, but the Gentrys wouldn't hear to that.

"You must stay with us," Sophronicus said. "Our domicile is commodious beyond our needs."

"And we have *plenty* of room," Lucretia added.

So after auctioning off their old furniture—for the new house was to be adorned with the latest rosewood and ormolu and brocatelle—Esperanza and Caleb, with Lilith, were guests at Lexylvania. Lucretia made them feel completely at home, even telling Lilith it seemed like old times in Kentucky, having a nigger around; and Lilith, who recognized quality when she encountered it, and perhaps quiet authority, grinned and said yes, *ma'am,* and pitched in with the housework and never once peeped about being a free nigger who no longer needed to chase flies.

Caleb had misgivings about the living arrangements, although he couldn't say why, for certainly from first to last the Gentrys were the soul of southern hospitality, and Esperanza remained on good behavior, never flying into those vixenish rages which had more and more tarnished her deportment the last few years.

In the Gentry house, the only possible cause for jealousy came with the letters received from Private Andrew J. Gentry, Second Kentucky Infantry, U.S.A. Sophronicus read these aloud. But after all, he had been reading Andy's letters to the McSwaseys ever since the boy enlisted, long before they had vacated their old house. Caleb observed his wife narrowly, while the letters were being read. She seemed engrossed, but admittedly the letters were exciting, with their romantic datelines such as "On Board the Brig *Louisa,* En Route from New Orleans to Mexico." With each new letter Sophronicus would open an atlas and trace Andy's wanderings to Matamoros and up the Rio Grande to Camargo and then to Monterrey.

At first the letters had been brimming with patriotic enthusiasm, as

Andy told of enlisting and going to Louisville, where the regiment boarded steamboats for New Orleans and an encampment on the field where General Jackson had defeated the British. But after Andy reached Matamoros at the mouth of the Rio Grande, a certain mordacity flowed from his quill. He liked the lemon trees and the scented evenings, and his shock at seeing "the fair daughters of Mexico bathing unclad in the river" was not unmixed with enjoyment; but the flies swarmed in clouds, the mosquitoes were bigger than owls, fleas infested the camp, the heat and the boredom were oppressive, and he did wish that sloppy old General Taylor would get a move on and lead them into battle.

In one letter, still from Matamoros, he told of going to the Resaca House and sampling a drink called the Rough and Ready, "which set my head to whirling in a manner quite amazing"; he had attended a play presented by Mr. and Mrs. Hart's dramatic company from the States; Yankee enterprise had sailed a ship loaded with ice from Boston, sold in Matamoros at a dollar per pound, "too dear for my purse"; and a daguerreotypist from New Orleans had opened a studio. "I enclose one of his products, which will probably be his last, as I fear my physiog wrecked his equipment."

The daguerreotype, which Caleb thought his wife scrutinized longer than necessary, showed a uniformed young man, silent looking, with a long, lean face.

"He's *so* handsome," Lucretia sighed.

He wasn't actually; but he was young; and Caleb didn't like to think of Andy watching those fair daughters of Mexico bathing naked, and perhaps being reminded of Esperanza, also a fair daughter of Mexico.

A letter from Camargo, in December 1846, told of his slow recuperation from dysentery. "I am better now, though quite weak. Our men have been dying like flies. This is a torrid and filthy place, very unhealthful with miasmas from the San Juan river. You hear the dead march every hour bearing the corpse of another brave fellow to a grave in the chaparral, far from loved ones. I wish I had come upriver in time for the capture of Monterrey. Now I fear I will never smell gunpowder before my enlistment is up next May. I am not going to re-enlist. None of us are. Thoughts of home are ever with us."

Tears were rolling down Lucretia's face; and Sophronicus's voice nearly broke, reading that one.

Caleb thought: "Maybe the son of a bitch will never get back."

But the next letter was more cheerful. His health was better, although "the Camargo quickstep still bothers some," and he had marched with his regiment to Monterrey, for garrison duty. "There are rumors of big doings in the offing, so maybe I will see the elephant before my enlistment is up. I believe our boys will fight stoutly, if well led. This is a very beautiful city, with many mountains. In the plaza women and girls sell delicious oranges, pomegranates, grapes and bread. I have learned to speak passably in the Spanish tongue, and I have struck up an interesting acquaintance with a handsome girl named Inez Hinojo. She works with her mother in the plaza, selling fruit. I believe she likes me."

And ten days later:

"Did I mention a girl named Inez Hinojo who sells fruit in the plaza market? Her mother and father have a small *rancho* near this city with several goats. Her father leads the goats to the encampment at nearby Walnut Springs and milks the goats on the spot to sell to our men. Every morning Inez and her mother bring fruit into the city. When I am off duty in the evening I escort them home, because some of the wilder ones among the volunteers have committed outrages against the inhabitants of this place. Feeling is bitter between the army and the natives, several times when one of our men has been drunk at night in a gutter his throat has been cut. But the Hinojo family feel no bitterness toward me. Inez is a very pretty girl, I wish you could meet her, she is really a wonderful girl with a good singing voice. Last night the moon was nearly full and the Mexican landscape looked like an enchanted place with the white moonlight on the mountains. Everything was deathly still. Inez showed me about the *rancho* and sang some quaint little Spanish songs. Her voice is very sweet. I would like to have you meet her."

And then, in a letter dated February 17, 1847:

"This letter may be my last. The enemy under Santa Anna is on the march, and we are ordered forward to Saltillo which General Taylor has already occupied. Rumors are rife of a big battle coming. I know I shall fight with the bravery of recklessness, because I do not care now what happens to me. It is almost more than I can bear to write, but a horrible tragedy has been enacted here. Little Inez is dead, and by her own hand! Many of the volunteers with this army are a lawless and undisciplined lot, the officers little better, things have been out of hand. Three nights ago when I was on duty in Monterrey a group of drunken volunteers went to the Hinojo ranch and broke down the door, in a drunken rage because one of their number had been slain by a Mexican during a brawl in town. None of the Hinojo family had anything to do with that, but these ruffians killed Inez's father and mother and then committed such outrages upon the poor sweet girl that she plunged a knife into her own heart. The ruffians have not been apprehended, their officers make no move because when their enlistment is up they will be back home with their men and maybe want to run for public office and need their favor. Things are disgraceful with this army, General Taylor is as slovenly as a teamster who hasn't had a bath in a year. Now I must close. If I am buried in a soldier's grave remember I love you both. Your heartbroken son."

Andy was just turned nineteen.

*

369

Late in March, rumors of a battle in far off Mexico rode the spring winds across the United States. Sophronicus haunted the post office in New Empire, shuffling through his mail for a letter in a familiar hand, searching the newspapers for mention of that vague battle. He found only rumor and rumor of rumor. He looked older, plodding along Gentry Avenue through the blowing leaves; he looked as if one of these days he might really be needing that hickory cane, till now only a jaunty symbol of a devout Jacksonian. And Lucretia's face looked drawn, beneath the serenity of her innocence.

At last in April the news broke in the press: A Great Victory. General Taylor Leads Our Troops to Triumph at Buena Vista. Santa Anna Repulsed. Official Dispatches Reach Washington From Old Rough and Ready. "A little more grape, Captain Bragg."

Sophronicus read the news stories aloud, his words dropping into the silence of the library with the fatefulness of clods onto a coffin. General Wool had selected *La Angostura*—the Narrows—as the battle site. Santa Anna came marching with his banners bright above twenty thousand men. American strength: 4,759. The Second Illinois. The Arkansas Cavalry. Dragoons. Bragg's Battery. Lieutenant George G. Meade. Second Lieutenant George B. McClellan. New American names tasting printer's ink and glory.

"On the morning of February 22, about 11, a flag of truce approached from the enemy's lines, bearing an order to surrender from Santa Anna. General Taylor, gallant leader that he is, declined. Soon thereafter the battle was joined . . . With dusk the last of the firing ceased, and our troops rested on their arms. In that high altitude the night was cold, but no fires were permitted. With the dawn . . ."

Casualties were mentioned, although not, naturally, of private soldiers. But Colonel William McKee, commanding the Second Kentucky Infantry, was slain. Likewise Lieutenant-Colonel Henry Clay, Jr., second in command.

The Second Kentucky.

Sophronicus finished reading; the paper rustled loud.

"Oh, dear," Lucretia said. "Dear me, dear me."

Sophronicus sat staring.

"Harry Clay's son," he said. "I'm sorry to hear that."

*

One bright May afternoon an elegant surrey pulled by a pair of matched chestnuts left the Gentry drive, glittered north to Winnebago Street, proceeded west to Front Street and again turned north. Caleb held the reins. Beside him sat Judge Gentry, eyes haunted by the perpetual worry of no letter from Andy. Once the judge turned and addressed his wife.

"Feeling better, my dear?"

"Of course I am, darlin'. Fresh air is just what I needed."

And she smiled. But her eyes didn't smile. No question about it, war had its drawbacks.

Not even the fourth member of the party looked very happy. She was a young matron of twenty-one, the age for love in woman, like thirty-one and sixty-three and seventy-nine. A parasol of apricot silk shaded her leghorn hat adorned with lilies-of-the-valley; her body, shapely in a cambric frock, looked heavy with ennui; her mouth drooped.

The carriage, leaving the pavement of Front Street, followed a sandy lane through the songs of meadow larks and the fragrance of river marshes. Presently it turned west, the hoofs of the horses booming on a new bridge that crossed a narrow brown bayou exhaling the sweetness of bee-balms and the good mucky richness of stagnation. The carriage gained the opposite shore and followed the road leading north on Mc-Swasey's Island through a wildwood of blooming locust trees and red-haws and wild cherries.

Till their anxiety about Andy had grown acute, the Gentrys had often visited Caleb's house under construction, for Sophronicus enjoyed watching the product of his brain taking shape in brick and lumber. Now, however, two weeks had elapsed since their last trip to McSwasey's Island. Tomorrow Caleb was leaving for the woods, to be on hand for the great spring log drives, and he had asked Sophronicus to inspect the new house today to make sure the workmen were faithful to the architect's plans.

Where the island was broadest, the road reached an open space littered with piles of brick, lumber, heaps of earth and gray-coated mortar boxes. To the east, beyond the vine-tangled thornapples and June berries, Caleb glimpsed the slough moating his premises, and beyond that, off on the mainland, the Wisconsin bluffs bold against the afternoon. To the west, perhaps a block away, the Mississippi flowed blue as the sky it mirrored. A fine site for a home. An island!

And a fine house it was too. Or would be. The Penwick house in East Bainbridge couldn't hold a candle to it. Caleb sat for a moment admiring the long Doric portico, its columns supporting a second-story gallery grilled with ornamental iron. The high entablature, with its richly-sculptured frieze and crowning cornice, would make the Penwick place look like two cents.

He alighted, tied the horses, handed his wife down from the carriage. He was past fifty, all the red pepper of his hair turned salty, face battered by the years, mouth deeply-set into its false-teeth look, lower lip protruding. Esperanza, with her slow-swaying skirt and angelic hair, looked young enough to be what strangers sometimes thought her: his granddaughter. But of course he looked old for his years, he had lived so hard.

The Gentrys looked old for their years too, moving toward the house. Once Caleb heard Lucretia's low voice:

"A letter *might* go astray. Don't you reckon it might?"

And Judge Gentry's soothing murmur:

"The most likely thing in the world, my dear."

The walls of the house, of plaster-covered brick like the huge columns, filled the portico with the scent of fresh lime.

"And what color will you paint it?" Sophronicus asked Caleb.

"What's your advice?"

"Shell-white, if it were mine."

"Sounds fine," Caleb said.

They entered the vestibule, still lacking doors, and passed into the central hall, lofty-ceilinged and wide, which ran clear through the house to the back portico, with its unexcelled view of the river. The fragrance of new plaster lingered here too, along with the mingled odors of putty and sweet sawdust and wood shavings. Everything was on a scale spacious and monarchial: when they walked through the music room and the dining room, flanking the hall on the north, and through the front and back drawing rooms on the south, their voices echoed in those vast, bare rooms with a peculiar hollow quality.

"Have you thought about furniture?" Sophronicus asked.

"Just that I want the best money can buy."

Sophronicus stood musing, there in the center of the front drawing room, staring at the windows, with sashes yet to come, which extended from floor nearly to ceiling; and sometimes, contemplatively, he tapped the hardwood floor with his cane.

"A carpet in pale cream," he said, "with a thick pile. Perhaps garlanded with roses. And a rosewood sofa upholstered in blue velvet. Valenciennes lace at the windows. And as for a table—"

Caleb couldn't keep track of it all; he wasn't much interested in such details anyway; he just wanted a luxurious lair that people would say was finer than a seven-story fancy house. He said:

"Why don't you order the furniture? Or go to St. Louis and buy it, if that would be better. My credit's good. And by God if it ain't, I'll pay cash."

Sophronicus said of course he would be glad to help select furnishings; his interest in architecture had led him into decoration; but he didn't want to seem presumptuous, furnishing another man's house.

"I'd be much obliged if you'd do it," Caleb said. "I'm busy with logs."

From the central hall, the stairway to the second floor rose lyric as birdflight, with its fluted newels and walnut banister; and up there, while Sophronicus consulted with carpenters, and the women wandered from room to room, Caleb stepped to the west gallery and stood with fingers on the wrought-iron railing, his gaze following the tremendous sweep of river toward the north. He was thinking of logs, and of how he had done all right these last few years. The money was rolling in.

372

And it would roll faster, from now on: snowballing, pyramiding; nothing could stop him now.

The scent of French water sifted up his nostrils, and he saw that Esperanza had joined him.

"Like the house?" he asked.

She nodded, moodily.

"Happy?"

She flashed him a quick look, eyes shallow obsidian; and her shoulders lifted in the faintest of shrugs.

"If you're not happy with a place like this," he said, "I reckon you never will be."

She kept staring at the river, as far away from him as the Spanish Peaks.

*

He was gone two weeks in the pinery, conferring with Amos Peabody, looking over his holdings, watching his logs float down the freshets of spring. As always when he steamboated north, and disembarked at Flannigan's Landing, and canoed up the Chippewa, he remembered that first wilderness journey with Esperanza and regretted her absence now. Yet not really; she had changed, somehow, for the worse. He reckoned she didn't like him any more, if she ever had; certainly he didn't like her. Yet he still loved her. Sitting alone by his fire on that island where the two of them had camped so long ago, he thought that maybe it had been a mistake to marry her. White blood and Injun, he guessed, didn't mix so well when everything was legal. Maybe he should have just squawed with her. But if he had done that, he would never have had any legal authority over her; first pair of fancy pants she saw, she might have up and left him.

He felt now that she was in pretty safe hands, back there in New Empire, with both Lilith and the Gentrys to watch over her. Lilith was worth her weight in sawlogs, all two hundred and fifty pounds of her. You watch the Missus like a hawk, he always told her.

The Whiskey River and the Noggin Lake country, where McSwasey & Zumwalt had first cut logs, was now only an incidental part of the company's operations; mile after square mile had been skinned, and the pine fed to the sawmill at Hangover Rapids. A few more seasons, Caleb figured, and there wouldn't be enough timber left in those townships to keep the mill busy. But that was all right; he'd simply yank out the mill machinery and move it into virgin country. His main operations now lay further up the Chippewa anyway.

On this trip he paddled up the Whiskey to the mill and spent the night, then returned to the Chippewa and headed upstream. The river was high, the current swift, with twigs and bubbles hurrying. In early afternoon, rounding a bend, he saw something bobbing toward him;

373

then something else; then a lot of somethings. Logs. Good, big, tough-hearted pine logs. By God! He had met his drive. He hung there in the current, wanting to cheer. Saliva oozed along his tongue and trickled over his grin. Logs. His. Maybe they had belonged to Uncle Sammy a few months back, but they didn't belong to uncle now. They belonged to Caleb McSwasey. Yippee-yee! He paddled to shore, beached the canoe, and stood watching the head of his drive. Those logs came swimming in profusion now, rolling and bobbing, riding the current toward the booms down in the sloughs at the mouth of the Chippewa.

A bateau came into sight, manned by river hogs with pike poles. Then another bateau. When a log took a notion to nose into an alder thicket, a pike pole hooked it and sloshed it back into the current. When a log thought maybe it would like to be a deadhead, and dragged its tail to rest on a buried sandbar, with doubtless some idea of starting a center jam, a pike pole jabbed it and nudged it. Keep moving, bub, those pike poles said. The country wants lumber, they said.

Bateaux and logs swept on past, and Caleb put out in his canoe again, paddling upstream. Occasional stray logs came coasting with the current, and he swerved to avoid collisions, but for the most part the river was empty. Must be a jam, he thought, somewhere upstream. Logs always gave you a lot of grief, when you turned them loose to frisk down a spring river.

Afternoon was well advanced when he sighted the jam, heaped in midstream with wings stretching toward shore. He had seen worse plugs, but this was sizable enough, and he wasn't taking chances on its giving way suddenly and flopping downstream to bury him, so he banked his canoe high and safe and followed a gig trail through the willows and huckleberries.

Out in midriver, yelling-distance from shore, men were picking at the jam without accomplishing much, and Amos Peabody, boss of the whole drive, was spitting disgustedly into the reed grass at water's edge when Caleb came up behind him and said quietly:

"Quite a few toothpicks mixed up out there."

Peabody whirled.

"Well, I'm a son of a bitch! How did you get here?"

"That ain't important," Caleb said. And he asked, "What are those logs trying to do, send me to the poorhouse?"

Those logs, Peabody said, were acting ugly as bears in rutting season. But the bastards would learn a thing or two, as soon as the jam crew got here.

"Appears to me," Caleb said, "that the jam crew should have been here hours ago."

So Peabody explained. The drive stretched along thirty miles of river; nobody could be everywhere at once. And seven miles upstream, another jam had formed. That was jam number one. Well, while Jim Buckmaster and his jam crew were working on that, this second plug had formed. Damn logs to hell anyway. Nothing but trouble.

"That's business," Caleb said. "Trouble. No trouble, no business."

Anyway, Peabody said, as soon as he learned of this jam, he sent word back to Buckmaster to shag down here: hell would be to pay if that upstream jam busted and those logs came flocking to clutter things more here.

From upriver, a few minutes later, two bateaux appeared, carrying men with cant hooks and pike poles. And Caleb noticed somebody else aboard one bateau. A plump woman with sandy hair.

"Looks like Molly Fitzpatrick," he said.

"You can't never keep a whore away from a log drive," Peabody said.

"I don't know as I'd even want to," Caleb said.

He watched the bateaux going to the upstream lip of the jam; Buckmaster and his crew sprang to the logs like tomcats.

"You be careful, sweetie," Molly Fitzpatrick called.

And Caleb saw Jim Buckmaster grin back at her.

The bateaux came poling toward the bank, pushing through pickerel weeds and arrowheads. Skirts lifted, Molly Fitzpatrick stepped ashore, light on her feet despite her plumpness. Her ankles were well-formed, her calves provocative in silk stockings. She wore a hat with a white plume, and there were sweat splotches at the armpits of her green taffeta dress. Her nose was faintly curved like the beak of some genial bird of prey, but in her merry blue eyes an odd innocence persisted. She was in her forties.

"Caleb McSwasey!" she exclaimed, her voice twangy as a ripsaw. "Well, chop me down for a jack pine! Why haven't you dropped in?"

"Now, Molly," Peabody said, "don't pick on Mr. McSwasey. He just got here."

"Hello, Molly," Caleb said. "How's business?"

"I can't complain in the least," she said. "It's always lively when Jim Buckmaster is around."

"You let Jim be," Peabody said. "That rooster has got work to do. That boy's the best hog on the river."

"Now, Amos," Molly said, "you know that boy's like a son to me. That boy means more to me than anything that ever wore pants. Except Mr. Fitzpatrick, and he was my husband. But he's dead now, as it were. Ambushed by a dirty breed."

"Injuns are tricky," Caleb said.

"So if Jim likes my pie," Molly said, "I'm not slamming the door. Better he should come to me than to some of these joints where they'd slug him and roll him and pitch him in the quicksand. I run an orderly house, as it were. Ain't that right, Caleb?"

"Orderly as a church," Caleb said.

375

"I don't know about that," Molly said, "but there's never any slugging. What are you grinning about, Amos?"

"At anybody slugging Jim Buckmaster. That boy's hard."

"And you don't know the half of it, sweetie," Molly said.

*

You never blasted a jam with powder if you could help it. Ruined too many logs. Caleb liked the way Jim Buckmaster took charge, setting his crew to work dry-picking the logs, heaving them with cant hooks and rolling them into the river. You could always tell whether a man knew his business, watching him work for a minute, and Caleb could see Buckmaster knew his.

After an hour, those cant hooks had eaten a big bite from the wings and the center of the jam, and Caleb knew then what Buckmaster had in mind: to rip open the center so the current could sluice in among the tangle and buoy it. Maybe that wasn't the safest way to break a plug, for with the river flood-full you never knew when the waters might bulge up under the massed logs and the whole tonnage would give; but it was quick.

With Buckmaster in charge here, Peabody went back upriver, but Molly Fitzpatrick stayed.

"Caleb," she said, "you watch that Jim. Those logs start to move and he'll be the last man off."

"I wouldn't doubt it."

"That Jim's a cat on a log," she said. "You watch."

When Caleb brought out a fresh cigar, Molly asked if he had an extra he could spare, so he gave her one of his Cuban Pelions. She puffed luxuriously.

"By God," she said, "that's good. That's a gentleman's cigar. So what were you doing with it?"

She laughed and whacked his shoulders. He grinned, but he kept his eyes on the jam.

Men with cant hooks had finished dealing with the wings that stretched shoreward from the tangle; now the jam was an obstinate island with logs upended and thrust out at odd angles, all snarled together like sticks in a buzzard's nest. Yanking out logs was going slower, now that the crew had burrowed into the core of the hodgepodge; sometimes, for minutes on end, nothing seemed to be happening. That must mean, Caleb thought approvingly, that Buckmaster was using his head as well as his muscles, figuring how a tap here, a jerk there, might unlock the whole muddle.

A half hour passed with no apparent progress; the afternoon was slipping away. Then Molly Fitzpatrick caught her breath, and even Caleb's heart skipped a beat, for unexpectedly a sigh seemed to go through the clotted logs, and the unwieldy mass shuddered. A sound of cracking wood came over the water; the jam moved. And, after about two inches, stopped heavy in its tracks.

The crew started to skedaddle, when the logs shifted, but they stopped sheepishly when Jim Buckmaster vaulted from the burrow where he had been working. Caleb heard him swearing. Boys, he was bawling, I thought I had me a jam crew of real river hogs. My mistake, boys. You're just a bunch of shoats.

Caleb had a notion the crew wouldn't skedaddle next time, till Jim gave the word.

Afternoon was waning; midges swarmed over the river; cliff swallows zigzagged after mosquitoes; and the low sun, swimming red in the hazes, bathed the logs and the crew in ruddy light. Caleb saw Jim cast a look at the sun, as if it were a watch, before swinging to the downstream side of the jam.

"Look at the damn fool," Molly Fitzpatrick said. "He wants to bust it before dark, so look what the sweet bastard's up to. That's a hell of a way to make a living."

"There're no good ways," Caleb said.

"The damn fool, he'll kill himself sure," Molly said.

"That's every man's privilege."

But Caleb's nerves tightened as he thought what might happen to a man on the downstream side of the jam, with all those tons of logs bulking above him. The Chippewa, swirling and gurgling in the guts of the tangle, might heave blindly, snapping a hidden trigger, and that wall of logs would topple. In that event, a man's chances would be slimmer than afoot in a buffalo stampede.

But if Jim Buckmaster had such misgivings you would never guess it, Caleb thought, as he watched him teeter from perch to perch along that log overhang, splinters and bark falling into the river from his calked boots. He was squatting now at the tip of an out-thrust log, cool as a jaybird on a branch, using his cant hook to probe the plug. He must have found what he was looking for, because after a minute, balancing himself like a wire walker, he catfooted it along the face of the jam and climbed to the top, where he gave orders.

The bateaux went poling out to the logs, and Jim waved all the crew, except two men, into one boat. It pulled away. The other boat stayed at the upstream end of the jam. Then Jim lowered himself to the downstream end, teetering along the base of that cliff of logs. And while on top of the jam the two men pried with hand spikes, Jim thrust his cant hook into the tangle.

"Caleb," Molly Fitzpatrick said in a choked voice, "I can't look. I can't stand it."

She buried her face in her palms, then ran screaming to the water's edge.

"Jim Buckmaster! You get the hell back on top of that jam!"

Her voice carried across the water, and the crew was laughing. Jim waved at her, then thumbed his nose.

Molly came squealing to Caleb and buried her face in his chest.

"The sweet bastard," she said, almost sobbing. "God damn the sweet bastard."

Then she broke away and strode back and forth, stamping the earth and swearing.

"There's men like that," she was wailing. "Think they're the biggest thing in pants. Eat cannonballs for breakfast and call them eggs. Thumb their noses at all creation and knock a chip off God's shoulder."

"Molly," Caleb said, "if you know any more like that, send them around. I pay cash wages."

"Look at the damn fool," Molly yelled. "Look at him buying a ticket to hell."

Caleb watched Jim perched at the tip of that out-thrust log, ferreting with his cant hook. Then he tugged. A faint quiver ran through the heaped logs. Caleb thought this was it. But Jim remained there, poised, listening. Then he yelled, "All right, boys." And the top men on the jam pried and Jim tugged again.

Another quiver. Then a deep shudder. And then, fluid as a water snake, the logs moved, with a swelling sound of crunching, thudding, rumbling. Caleb saw Jim Buckmaster, poised like a squirrel on that out-thrust log. The tip described an upward arc. And at the precise instant for a jump, Jim jumped; jumped into what had been the face of the jam and what now was a convulsive turmoil of logs. Powerful legs pumping, he climbed those spinning logs as easily as a man climbing steps. He was smiling when he topped the jam, and as it broke wide open, grinding and crashing, timbers flopping every which way, he went dancing across that bobbling mass and sprang into the bateau as neat as a cat to a cream shelf. And when the bateau shored, and Jim stepped out, Molly Fitzpatrick flung her arms around him, sobbing.

"You sweet damn fool," she howled.

He stroked her hair.

"Why, Molly," he said, smiling, "what's come over you?"

"Son," Caleb said, "that was nice jam busting. I couldn't have done it better myself. What are we paying you?"

And when Jim told him, Caleb said he would throw in some extra dollars, come payday.

Jim smiled. But Caleb had an uneasy feeling he had made a mistake, mentioning wages at a time like that, when he noticed Jim's eyes. They were gray, and they had a look in them that made Caleb feel suddenly cheap and a tame pinch-penny, talking about money to a man who had been teetering on the brink of something vaster than tangled pine logs on a northern river.

"That's nice of you, Captain," Jim said. "I'll remember it when you're working for me."

*

It was June, the afternoon blue-skied and hot, the levee radiant with sunshine, when Caleb left the boat on his return to New Empire. He had written Esperanza when to expect him, so he counted on a rig to be waiting at the landing, but there were only a farmer's buggy, a dray and a couple of democrat wagons, horses switching flies. At the southeast corner of Front and Winnebago Streets, loafers sat outside Rafferty's Saloon, spitting and whittling.

In his woods clothes, possible sack over his shoulder, needing a shave, Caleb might have been a loafer himself, or an out-of-work drifter from the log drive. Yet there was that about him—the set of his underslung jaw, the way he limped along like a man who knew where he was going—that announced money and power to the world. The loafers made way for him when he entered the cool duskiness of Rafferty's for a beer. Rafferty wasn't there; maybe upstairs with one of his girls; and Caleb didn't know the bartender. But the bartender called him sir.

Caleb stood with a foot on the rail, out of sorts because he would have to walk home, beset by the usual after-journey weariness and slight surprise at the strangeness of familiar sights. He wondered how his new house had progressed—he would drive out there in the cool of the evening—and whether there had been important mail and how Esperanza had been behaving. To think of her filled him, as always, with intense sexual excitement, but at the same time he dreaded resuming the workaday ordeal of marriage. By God, she was a handful.

He had another beer before shouldering his sack and starting for Gentry Avenue. At the levee the steamboat still lingered, unloading freight, steam from its escape pipes hissing whitely in the sun. Caleb turned east and limped past the lodging houses for rivermen and the fancy houses that weren't very fancy. Then came a stretch of vacant lots, with broken bottles among the horse nettles and tansy. Then the more respectable business houses of town, aloof from the rowdy river front. Through opened doors drifted the scents of shoemaker's leather, of ink and paper from the *Chronicle* office, of chemicals from a drugstore.

When he turned south on Gentry Avenue, with its elm branches intertwining high above the brick pavement, his eyes welcomed the shade and the pleasant lawns. A robin sang; from an open window came the tortured blatting of a boy practicing the cornet. A grocery wagon went clop-clopping along. In the fruit trees bordering the Gentry place, cherries hung in green clusters that would redden soon, if the robins didn't steal them.

He thought the house looked unusually quiet, when he walked along

379

the brick drive; the women were napping, probably. The front door stood open. Inside, the house was dim as a cave and nearly as cool, with shutters closed against the heat; it smelled of furniture polish. He went upstairs to a guest bedroom, where he expected to find Esperanza. She wasn't there. He dropped his possible sack; and at the dresser mirror he stood fingering the salty stubble on his jaw. He'd have to shave; whiskers aged him; and God knew he looked old enough at best, married to her. You old bastard, he thought, eying his bristling brows, his bulbous nose, his thick protruding lips. He could smell the fragrance of his wife's French waters and powders, hovering about the dresser like the ghosts of fair women.

Downstairs again, he went toward the kitchen to raise somebody. But part way across the living room he stopped, making out a shapeless bulk snoring on the sofa. It was Lilith, mouth wide, yellowed teeth agleam in the dull light. She looked, he thought, like a great sow; God, how niggers ate. He shook her. She groaned; a hand floated up and brushed at him ineffectually, as if he were a fly. He shook her again; her eyes opened.

"Oh, God," she mumbled. "I was dreaming of Wisdom."

"Who the hell's Wisdom?"

She came full awake then and scrambled to a sitting position, the sofa creaking.

"Mistah McSwasey! You're back!"

"Where's everybody?" he asked.

"You're back! Thought perhaps you wouldn't git back so soon. You have a good trip?"

"Where's Esperanza?" he asked.

He could always tell when a nigger was stalling, and he watched her narrowly as she closed and opened her eyes, curled her tongue over her teeth, yawned heavily.

"Why you think," she asked, "it's so hard for me to git awake?"

"Where's Esperanza?"

She sat staring dully at him; then her face puckered, her body rocked, and she flung herself down on the sofa, moaning.

"Go git you a buggy whup," she wailed, "because you'll need it. Git you a buggy whup and whup me and git it over. But Mistah Caleb, it warn't my fault. I tell them you won't like it, but they say Lilith, you damn old nigger, shut your black mouth. I tell them I want to go too, but they is real ornery about it, yes, sir, I tried, I did so, but they ain't listening to nothing pore old Lilith say. Mistah Caleb won't like it, I say, but they just laugh and go anyway and let their other servants have time off and I have to stay alone in this here house that sometimes I think may be haunted about midnight when the boards creak. You believe in haunts, Mistah Caleb?"

Niggers! My God, niggers, niggers!

380

"Where did Esperanza go?"

"Yes, sir, she go all right, just like I say. She go to St. Louis with Mistah and Mis' Gentry, that's where she go. But they ought to be back any day."

"You let her go to St. Louis alone?"

"No, sir! I ain't letting her go nowhere alone. She go with Mistah and Mis' Gentry. They say it will be all right. They say you don't care. They say they watch over her and not let nothing git her."

He stood staring.

"Don't look at me like that, Mistah Caleb. I say I got to go along but they say God damn you, Lilith, you black bag of pork, shut your mouth or we shut it for you, they say. It will be all right, they say, because Mistah McSwasey say he want Mistah Gentry to pick out the fine furniture and such-like for the new edifice on the island, and Mistah Gentry say he feel better about it anyhow if your wife is along to say no, by God, I won't have that measly old 'hogany table in my house nohow, I bust a vase over your head, judge, if you buy that."

Lilith cackled.

"They went to St. Louis to buy furniture?" Caleb demanded.

"Sure enough they did. Mistah Gentry say you tell him to go buy a houseful. Was he just lying about it? Would a man that's sat his hind end on a judge's bench lie?"

"No," Caleb said, "I told him to buy the furniture."

"That's what I been saying, Mistah Caleb. That's why they went to St. Louis along about a week ago. Reckon they'll be back in no time. You going to whup me, Mistah Caleb?"

"God damn it, Lilith," Caleb said, "you're a fool."

"Yes, sir! Ain't no doubt of that at all. I'm sure a fool about you, Mistah Caleb. You want to whup me like that time in Taos, it's all the same to me. I am now a free nigger, they tells me, but it's all right. I tell Mistah Gentry he better wait till you gits back before they go chasing off to St. Louis, but of course he's real hot to git there after he gits them letters."

"What letters?"

"Them letters from his son. His son been off somewhere fighting Mexicans, and they think perhaps he got a belly full of lead bullets and died on account of they ain't hear from him. But then one day the old judge comes prancing in like a turpentined hound. He git three letters at the same time. Listen, he say, our offspring is not even nicked by a Galena pill, our offspring is in New Orleans waiting to be mustard, he say. Why you think they put a mustard plaster on that boy if he is in such fine shape? And the boy is going to come up the big river and reach St. Louis by such and such a date, and I hear the judge say the boy asks why don't they meet him there and open a bottle of drinking liquor. So the judge say we will kill two birds with one stone. That what he say. We will meet our offspring, he say, and buy furniture for the edifice and perhaps you had better come along madam—he call your wife madam—and help me decide on that fine wood furniture. And your wife say yes, *sir,* I will do just that, she say, and we will leave pore old Lilith here for the haunts to git her. That what she say. She is mighty excited, seem to me, about buying that furniture . . . Why you look at me like that, Mistah Caleb? Ain't you feel well? Mistah Caleb! Where you going? Why you burn up that carpet for the front door? Mistah Caleb! Come back, man! Ain't I a good nigger? Have you forgot all about that fine trip we made to Taos?"

*

He couldn't remember walking to the business district; his senses had blanked. When he came awake he found himself standing quite aimless at the corner of Gentry Avenue and Winnebago Street, hatless in the summer sun, staring at the façades of brick and sandstone. He thought: I'd best pull myself together. Cool off. People see me this way, they'll start talking.

He looked something like an old bull buffalo, standing there with jaw down, hair mussed, eyes rancorous; it demanded all his strength of will to take hold of himself and pretend he was an ordinary husband, tame as a puppy, not in the least disturbed to find his wife gone to St. Louis on the pretext of selecting furniture but probably switching her tail at that son of a bitch, Andy Gentry.

But he'd have to act normal. Keep a cool head. Throw the town off guard and Esperanza off guard. That way, he would stand a better show of learning the facts. It would never do to bust Andrew J. Gentry in the nose the moment he stepped off the boat. People would talk. It might be that ultimately he would have to do worse than bust Andy in the nose, and if it came to that he didn't propose to leave a back trail. This wasn't the raw West. This was civilization. You kill a son of a bitch here and you might get into trouble, if you left a back trail.

So he pulled himself together and crossed the street, calling at the post office for mail. He had not realized he had been hoping for a letter from Esperanza, till none appeared; then he was furious. But he smothered his fury. Keep cool-headed. At the post office writing counter, he went through his letters a second time, just to be certain she hadn't written. She hadn't. But there was a letter addressed to her: one he had sent her from the pinery. It gave him an odd feeling, finding it there.

He reckoned it was never too early, if you wanted to throw trackers off your trail, to start leaving false sign; so he went to the *Chronicle* office and told the editor of his trip to the pinery, and of how many logs his crews had driven, and—for sure-fire copy—of how this Great Northwest was entering a period of tremendous prosperity and everybody would end up with a potful of pennies; and then he mentioned how, with his approval and blessings, his wife had accompanied Judge and Mrs. Gentry to St. Louis to buy furniture and to meet Andrew J. Gentry.

"That boy is the finest young man I know," Caleb said. "He's a hero, the way he acted at that battle of Buena Vista."

For all Caleb knew, the son of a bitch had probably wet his pants and run, but it never riled people to call a home boy a hero.

"What did he do?" the editor asked.

"Reckon you'll never hear it from him," Caleb said, "because he's a modest beaver, but I understand that boy was in the thick of the fighting. And when Old Glory fell, he picked it up. And the troops rallied there and countercharged."

The editor looked impressed.

"We ought to give that boy a royal welcome," Caleb said. "This town ought to meet his boat with a brass band."

"We sure had, Mr. McSwasey. What boat is he coming on?"

"Soon as I hear, I'll let you know."

The editor thanked Caleb for the suggestion; he would speak to the leader of the New Empire Military Band and get plans for a celebration under way.

Before going to his own office, Caleb stopped in and asked one of Judge Gentry's student clerks when the Gentrys were returning. Letter this morning, the clerk said; they would arrive Friday evening on the *Vox Populi*. Today was Tuesday; three days till he saw her. He felt suddenly forlorn, aware of an ache under his ribs. But he smiled, and spoke of the celebration that was being planned, and suggested that the clerk go to the *Chronicle* with the news of when the Gentrys were arriving.

In the northeast corner of the building, his own office greeted him with stale air, heat and loneliness; he flung up the windows and stood looking out at an alley, a vacant lot and Court Avenue running north into tree shade. A block away, on the east side of the avenue, the courthouse cupola rose above the highest foliage. He thought of the courtroom beneath that cupola, with a witness chair. In the South, if some bastard stole your wife, you could shoot him at high noon and be acquitted, or challenge him and cross a state line and have it out. But this was New Empire and Judge Gentry was a leading citizen. You put a bullet into his son's liver and people might not like it.

Cigar cocked, he limped back and forth in that little office, sometimes halting to look at the wall-map marked with his holdings, thinking how in those labyrinthian sloughs at the mouth of the Chippewa his men would be sorting logs today and stitching together log rafts. Probably, he thought, he should start thinking about buying a mill or two somewhere downriver; it would be more profitable for McSwasey & Zumwalt to saw everything, instead of selling raw logs. An integrated operation, from forest to retail yards.

Usually when he stared at that map he saw more than lines on paper; he saw dark kingdoms of pine, rivers running full of pine. But today he saw Esperanza. Esperanza switching her tail at a soldier just back from womanless camps, from a womanless transport. He remembered how goaty the boys used to be just in from New Mexico, after that long womanless aridity from the Cheyenne Nation to Missouri. They would see a skirt and go crazy. He thought of Judge and Mrs. Gentry in one hotel room; Andy in another; Esperanza in another. And no Lilith to guard her. By God! He flung his cigar into the spittoon with such force that sparks geysered up. Maybe he should grab a boat for St. Louis.

But where would that get him? They would be on the river coming up while he was going down. Making a damned fool of himself. No, the thing to do was play it close to his chest. Smile. Spread the geniality thicker than bear grease on an Injun. Jealous? Caleb McSwasey jealous of a young fellow like Andy? Great God, no! Fool them all. Even Esperanza, maybe. And watch. And set Lilith watching. And wait. See what happened. If he had to kill the son of a bitch he would, of course, kill him; but there were more ways of doing that than shooting him full of lead in broad daylight on Winnebago Street. No point in killing him and ending with a noose around your neck and your wife wagging her tail at the hangman.

*

Things gathered momentum, and by Thursday afternoon, when the weekly issue of the *Chronicle* appeared, you would have thought Private Andrew J. Gentry had done just a little more toward winning victory at Buena Vista than had General Taylor. Well, likely he had.

Not that the editor didn't give General Taylor some credit for the victory. But journalistic integrity compelled him to hint that it was New Empire's own Andy Gentry who had saved the day. The hero of Buena Vista: that was what the editor called Andy; and in his news story, which would have felt more at home in the editorial columns, he implied that anybody who did not come to the celebration at the levee Friday evening was probably an unpatriotic kicker and whiner, the sort of traitor who sometimes turned up in the local land office and tried to prevent honest businessmen from stealing timber.

Full credit in that news story was given Caleb McSwasey, "one of our most enterprising citizens," for dredging up the idea of welcoming Andy.

"Mr. McSwasey tells us that at a crucial moment in the battle Andy snatched up the fallen flag, rallied his comrades and led a countercharge against Santa Anna's hosts, which goes to prove what we have always maintained, that this Great Northwest which has everything, including a bracing climate, produces not only beautiful and virtuous women, but men whose bravery is equaled only by the purity of their lives and their business integrity."

Caleb read that paragraph with considerable satisfaction, for it just didn't stand to reason that an enterprising citizen would call a young man a hero and foster a celebration in his honor if he had any idea of killing the son of a bitch.

Nobody knew exactly at what hour the *Vox Populi* would arrive Friday evening, although Sophronicus in his letter had said it would probably reach town about nine. Steamboat schedules, however, were erratic, and the leader of the New Empire Military Band, at rehearsal Wednesday evening, told his musicians they should be uniformed at the levee and ready to toot by 6:00 P.M. This gave his wife an idea. She was president of the Methodist Ladies' Aid, and before the Baptists knew what was happening she arranged with the mayor to rope off the corner of Front and Winnebago Streets, so the ladies could set up tables and serve supper and make money to hide in calico the charms of distant Polynesian girls. The Baptists retaliated by organizing a Young People's Marching Brigade, complete with transparencies lettered with such mottoes as "Welcome Home, Andy," "Hail to the Hero," and "New Empire for Christ." The Presbyterians, into whose faith Andy had been baptized, were understandably vexed at all this, till their pastor conceived the idea of having the janitor hike from levee to church, as soon as the *Vox Populi* hove into sight, and ring the bell. A fine idea, but it misfired, for the damned janitor got drunk.

Not that you could blame him!—quite a few well-meaning persons did the same. This resulted from the proximity of the church supper to Rafferty's Saloon. Pat Rafferty wasn't any too happy about that church supper, serving meat loaf on Friday and competing with his free lunch, so he was quite ready to make a deal whereby Caleb McSwasey would pay for several barrels of whiskey to be set up outside the saloon and served free of charge in Andy's honor, compliments of the McSwasey & Zumwalt Lumber Company.

"You must be fond of the lad," Pat Rafferty said.

Caleb nodded.

"He's like a son to my wife and me."

*

The *Chronicle* must have had nearly half the circulation the editor claimed for it, because word of the celebration certainly got around. By six o'clock, with the June sun still high, Winnebago Street was choked with rigs, horses, mules and even several yoke of oxen, for farmers had driven in from the whole countryside. Rivermen attended, and pinery boys, and nearly everybody in town. The Methodist Ladies' Aid served hundreds of persons and thousands of mosquitoes. The band serenaded the celebration with patriotic airs, then ate, then played every piece they knew and several they didn't. Even Lilith attended, all decked out in rose-colored silk and a picture hat, squired by Dexter Yarlow from the Commercial House. Caleb paid for their supper; and the Methodist ladies, in accordance with one of the unrecorded precepts of the Nazarene, directed these future black angels to go sit on a log and eat, away from the white folk.

By seven-thirty everybody had eaten, the brass band was pretty well winded, all the various dogs in attendance who were going to fight had fought, and with the arrival of the *Vox Populi* still an hour and a half away, the multitude might have succumbed to boredom, except for Caleb's foresight in furnishing free whiskey. The Methodist ladies, out of respect for John Wesley and the need for doing the dishes, did not drink, but nearly everybody else had a nip, so it wasn't long before arguments flared into fist fights, with a good deal of side betting, and thus the minutes passed quite pleasantly. As dusk came on, a number of couples, including Lilith and Dexter, drifted away into the shadows, although for what purpose it was difficult to imagine, since the celebration was taking place right here at Front and Winnebago.

Once the Methodist ladies had cleared away the dishes, and their husbands had dismantled the trestle tables, the area was unroped, and a team of mules hauled in a dray wagon. This would serve as speakers' platform when Caleb introduced Sophronicus and Sophronicus introduced his son. By now, here and there in the crowd, spots of actual rowdiness, more ominous than the friendly fist fights, were developing, owing to the free whiskey and the hint of saturnalia in the soft June evening: the town marshal, looking worried, mentioned this to Caleb. Those pinery boys get liquored up, he said, and they might be hard to handle.

"I'll take care of it," Caleb said.

In the crowd he located several pinery boys from his last winter's camps.

"I want twenty men," he said, "who would like to earn a dollar apiece and have some fun."

And when the men had been rounded up, he led the way to the edge of things and explained what he had in mind. There were certain bastards present tonight, he said, who might try turning the program into a roughhouse. Against that contingency, he was deputizing this group to stand in a cordon around the speakers' wagon. If anybody started trouble, pop him.

"I'll be in that wagon," he said, "so watch me and do what I say. Come to my office tomorrow, and I'll pay you off. If any of you jacks don't want in on this, say so now and we'll bust you up and get it over."

They all wanted in.

"All right, remember you're law and order for a change. This is my town tonight and you're my roosters. You can have as much fun beating up bastards from the side of the law as from the other side, else why would any son of a bitch ever run for sheriff? Now do what I say or I'll bust your bones and blacklist you. Get it?"

They got it.

"Now shag your hairy asses over to that wagon," Caleb said, "and do what I tell you."

When he reported what he had done, the marshal said:

"That beats! Hiring trouble makers to keep down trouble!"

"It's an old trick from the nigger business," Caleb said. "The best guard for a crowd of tough niggers is the toughest nigger of the lot."

When nine o'clock came, the band tuned up and played, but it was wasted breath for the *Vox Populi* was nowhere in sight. Nine-fifteen. Nine-twenty. People were consulting their watches and talking about the long drive home. Now and then, over by the whiskey barrels, some ringtail roarer whooped it up for trouble, and Caleb sent a couple of pinery boys to quiet him. The band played again.

It was after nine-thirty, during a pause in the concert, when a steamboat wailed from downriver. Anticipation ran through the crowd. Then came another wail, closer now, echoing from the bluffs of Wisconsin to the bluffs of Iowa, filling the summer evening with music gallant and yet sad, the sadness of drowned men and foundered steamboats and smashed rafts and smashed hopes and lost time. For a moment, there in the throng, an almost unbearable nostalgia washed over Caleb, as he thought of the boat bringing the precious freight of Esperanza. And in that bleak instant he saw himself as a man far journeyed into his middle years, setting snares for that which could never be caught again. The band began to play.

Torches crackled; candles flamed within transparencies; and dogs barked and people cheered as the *Vox Populi,* lovely river witch, all white gingerbread and lighted cabins and swishing wheel, came gliding shoreward, sending a forewash up the levee.

What so proudly we hailed . . .

The crowd surged down the levee, Caleb among them, accompanied by a half dozen pinery boys to clear a path for the hero of Buena Vista.

Whose broad stripes and bright stars . . . through the perilous night . . .

Caleb saw Sophronicus, rising to the occasion like a thoroughbred hearing the sweepstakes bugle. And then, coming along the plank behind Lucretia, he saw Esperanza, hair golden in the torchlight, lips vivid, a girl tantalizing as thirst. Through the crowd he thrashed toward her like an old bumblebee to a flower.

"Hello," she said.

His arms shot around her and he buried himself in her young femininity, for a blurred moment of fragrance and breasts soft against his chest and lips twisting under his.

"Don't," she snapped. "You're mussing me."

"Damned right, you little hustler," he muttered.

Land . . . of the free-e-e-e . . . and the home . . . of the . . . brave . . .

*

The mules hitched to the dray twitched ears at the commotion, but the driver had calmed them by the time the McSwaseys and the Gentrys were perched on improvised seats in the wagon. Now Caleb stood up and lifted an arm. But that silencing gesture only brought more cheers from the multitude, and the band kept tooting "General Andrew Jackson's Presidential Grand March." Caleb stood looking out over the wobbling torches, wigwagging transparencies and fluttering handkerchiefs; and with all the shouting he saw more tonsils than even a popular throat specialist was apt to see in a year. The *Vox Populi* had delayed its departure, in honor of whatever this was in honor of; passengers clustered the decks like flies on an angel-food cake.

Caleb tried to speak, but the crowd wasn't having any yet; so, smiling in resignation, he turned back to his wife and friends. He was feeling fine now, less jealous than usual, and mighty relieved too, because he was beginning to doubt whether it would be necessary to kill Andy. Till tonight, he had not seen the boy in several years, and in imagination he had pictured him as a rough-tough buck private, loud-mouthed and brazen, pawing the sod whenever he sighted a skirt.

Andy wasn't like that at all. Caleb glanced at him now, sitting there in the wagon, elbows on knees, eyes on his interlaced fingers, long body thin in civilian clothes, face longish and narrowish, a hint of sallowness in the skin weathered by Mexican sun and winds. In the flickering torchlight his hair looked the blond of bronze. He had uttered, Caleb reckoned, all of a half dozen words since leaving the boat: a couple of yesses, a couple of noes, and a vigorous, "Oh, hell!" when told the celebration was in his honor. Andy was not, Caleb told himself, the sort of young man with much appeal for Esperanza. She would prefer the rough-tough soldier, callous and even brutal, body full of button-popping vitality. She liked a winner.

"Just think, honey," Lucretia was telling Andy, "those cheers are all for you."

A smile sweet as etcher's acid crossed his silent mouth.

"Andy isn't feeling well," Sophronicus told Caleb, *sotto voce*. "His dysentery has been kicking up."

Caleb nodded sympathetically. And he thought, "Better a pain in his guts than a bullet." He asked, "When did it come over him?"

"On the boat from New Orleans to St. Louis. He's been in pain since we met him."

Yippee-yee! A sick man wasn't a skirt chaser. The chances were excellent, Caleb thought, that in Esperanza's hotel bedroom, and in her stateroom on the boat, nothing had occurred except a night's sleep. Certainly she looked and acted sulky enough to have been getting her full quota of sleep.

He turned back to the tailgate of the dray, and this time the band stopped playing and the crowd quieted.

"Ladies and gentlemen," Caleb said, "let me present Judge Sophronicus Gentry who will introduce the guest of honor."

The multitude gave Sophronicus what the *Chronicle* editor called in his notes a "trem. ov." And Sophronicus repaid them with fifteen minutes of the best oratory since the Second Catilinarian. Silvery mane flowing, gestures eloquent, he spent the first few minutes of his discourse mentioning the virtues of General Andrew Jackson, and after that he traced the interesting steps in the real estate deal which culminated in the Mexican War. He also lined himself up solidly behind "that great statesman, the Honorable David Wilmot of the great Commonwealth of Pennsylvania, who has proposed that not an inch of territory which this Republic may receive from Mexico shall be permitted to bear the impress from the pedal extremities of a vassal Ethiope."

People were not sure what he was talking about, but they cheered.

In his peroration, the judge spoke of military glory which, he begged leave to say in all modesty, had never been unknown in the Gentry family; and he worked his audience into a fighting pitch, describing the way Mexican aggression had been repelled. Like spectators at a boxing bout, the audience felt themselves vicarious combatants: if Santa Anna had attacked New Empire at that moment, nobody would have invited him to sit down for a bowl of chili.

"And now my fellow patriots, let me introduce a young man who proudly bears the given name of our greatest statesman since Jefferson; a young man who has enjoyed the high honor and priceless privilege of serving with the Second Kentucky Infantry; a young man who in the second lunation anno Domini 1847 stood in battle on the field of Buena Vista—my son, Andrew Jackson Gentry."

The crowd went mad; they tried to reach the wagon to paw the hero, but that cordon of pinery boys held them back; and in the pilothouse of the *Vox Populi* the pilot yanked the whistle rope.

Smiling proudly, forcing back the tears, Lucretia told her husband: "It's like one of those old Greek Triumphs."

"Roman, my dear," he said.

Even one of the mules brayed, till cussed into silence by the drayman.

Watching Andy, Caleb thought, "Here's where he falls on his nose."

A reasonable expectation, for surely a boy of nineteen could not hope to outshine Judge Gentry. He just stood there, Caleb noticed, gaunted by dysentery, thin face unhealthy and unsmiling.

"Thank you," he said, when the noise subsided.

They cheered again.

"I don't reckon," he said, "I should say anything after that speech my

389

father made, but it came to me while he was talking that maybe you home folks would like to hear what it's really like down there in Mexico. A war comes along and you get to thinking that everybody on your side is angel pure, and everybody on the other side is a mean varmint; that all the right is over on this side, and all the wrong over on the other. Well, it's not always that way, exactly."

"Hell with the greasers!" somebody called from the crowd, and people laughed and cheered.

"I didn't notice who said that," Andy said.

"I did." A man's arm waved in the throng.

"Have you been in the war?" Andy asked.

"No, sir, I ain't, but my second cousin is down there. So I say to hell with the greasers!"

More cheers.

Andy's face looked dark and sober.

"It's not always the way you read about it in the papers," he said. "Myself, I don't call them greasers any more. Some of the nicest people I've met were Mexicans, and some of the boys on our side were pretty wild. I'm not talking about the regulars, the regulars know what discipline means, but some of the volunteers got out of hand. There at camp in Matamoros some of the volunteers from one state used to start fighting volunteers from another, even shooting at each other, and the situation was real bad."

"Boys will be boys," the man in the crowd yelled.

People laughed; somebody else shouted, "Hooray for Old Rough and Ready!"

"Well, now," Andy said, "you don't hear much of that among the troops. Much cheering for General Taylor, I mean. You talk to the troops and they say he's a sloppy old bungler."

An appalled silence. Then several men began yelling. Who's a bungler? Hey, what do you mean by that, running down General Taylor? Hooray for Old Rough and Ready! Why, I read in the papers that he—

"Everything was a mixup from the start," Andy said. "At Matamoros we hauled drinking water from the Rio Grande and it was half mud. The town was nothing but grogshops and gambling halls. Troops kept landing from the States and short-term volunteers were always coming down the river on their way home, and there was nowhere to put them. Everything was disorganized and there wasn't any discipline. The boys would get drunk and beat up the Mexicans."

"Hooray!"

"Civilian Mexicans, I mean."

"Hell with the greasers!"

"Camargo was worse," Andy said. "Going up there the steamboats burned green mesquite and couldn't get much steam in the boilers. The town was on the San Juan River and it smelled something fearful. A flood

390

in the spring had left mud all over town, and by the time we got there the dust was a foot deep. You ate dust and you drank dust. The river was mainly sewerage and you drank that too. Our boys fell sick and died like chickens with the pip. It never rained there, the sun was a white ball of fire, baking down on those bare rocks till they were hotter than frying pans, and then the wind would blow and the dust choked everybody. We camped along the river with all those miasmas. That's where I came down with dysentery. I used to lie there and hear the dead march and think I'd be next, and sometimes I hoped so. But I got on my feet and we marched more than a hundred miles across the desert to Monterrey. I liked it there. I liked the people too, they were friendly and gentle. But some of our boys, I mean the volunteers, did things they should have been ashamed of. They would beat up Mexicans and rob them and sometimes kill them."

"Thought that's why you went, to kill greasers," somebody yelled.

"Civilians," Andy said, "that's what I mean. They'd kill old men."

"Hooray! Mop up the damned greasers!"

"They would kill women too," Andy said, "and assault the girls and kill them."

"Our boys did that?" somebody yelled.

"The volunteers," Andy said. "And the officers never punished them and old General Taylor just guzzled his mess and didn't care."

Out in the crowd, six or eight men with whiskey voices were yelling such things as you're crazy, our boys don't pick on ladies, what's the idea of talking that way about Old Rough and Ready? Caleb could see Andy's face dark with anger as he shouted:

"General Taylor is a stupid old bungler who would have lost at Buena Vista except for—"

The roar of the crowd, swelling heavily, drowned out his words. Caleb saw Sophronicus step quickly to his son and take his arm. Andy broke free and shouted at the increasing din. Caleb thought the crowd looked like a mob of milling buffalo; men drunk on free whiskey were yelling for Andy's scalp. Caleb told the pinery boys:

"We're leaving. Clear a path."

Rocks and clods were flying, women were squealing, and Sophronicus was trying to shut up his son as Caleb limped across the dray and told the driver to whip up his mules.

"I ain't certain I want to," the driver snapped. "By God, a young feller talk like that about Old Rough and Ready and—"

Caleb's fist struck the driver behind the ear. Then he dumped him into the mob. Then he grabbed the reins and the whip.

Those pinery boys did all right, clearing trail, and the dray went rumbling east along Winnebago Street. Caleb looked back once and saw a dozen fights erupting like smallpox on an Injun. Pinery boys would rather swing fists than make love, almost, and tonight, being on the side of law and order, they would let themselves go.

As the dray skidded around the corner and the mules galloped south along Gentry Avenue, Caleb was smiling. Like old times! Besides, he had saved Andy from mob anger; once people had cooled off they would remember that, and never suspect him if he should have to kill the bastard.

In the Gentry living room, Andy looked drained and unwell, pains of dysentery shadowing his tight mouth.

"Son," Sophronicus said, "tonight you committed the unforgivable sin of a speaker. You told the truth."

*

The following week Esperanza, Lilith and Caleb left by upriver steamboat on a business trip. Very likely McSwasey & Zumwalt would have continued prospering without that trip, but Caleb wanted to get his wife away from the Gentry house. Try as he would, he had been unable to figure the situation—if a situation existed—between Esperanza and Andy, but he told himself that in any case no possible good could result from her living under the same roof with a boy of nineteen; better that they should travel till their new house was ready to move into.

As a result of illness, and exhaustion following the great welcome, Andy had remained in bed, and Caleb didn't much like his wife's sudden compassion for the sick. At odd times he returned from his office to find Esperanza at Andy's bedside, perhaps reading to him or just watching while he slept; and even though Lilith sat there too, she was given to dozing, and Caleb might have become an illegitimate father several times a day without her knowing. Not that he really worried about that, for indubitably Andy was a sick boy, cheeks hollow and yellowish-brown, eyes bitter with all he had seen in Mexico. Dr. Washburn kept him dosed with calomel and laudanum, so he slept a lot, and sometimes when he dreamed he twitched and sobbed. Ten to one, Caleb used to think, it was the memory of that Mexican girl that had him down; he acted like a fellow who didn't care whether he lived or died. Well, Mexican girls could do that to a man.

Lucretia and Sophronicus, of course, were half sick themselves, with worry, and Caleb thought that all things considered it was time to pull stakes. If he had announced he was moving to the Commercial House the Gentrys would have protested, and probably Esperanza likewise; so he had simply said he had business to attend to, up and down the river, and had left town. Sophronicus promised to oversee work on the new house, and to keep Caleb informed of progress.

They went first to Read's Landing in Minnesota Territory, a raftsmen's town on the west bank of the Mississippi, opposite the mouth of the Chippewa. Leaving Esperanza with Lilith in a hotel room, Caleb would walk past the saloons and gambling houses to the river and take off in a canoe, paddling across and finding his way into the innumerable sloughs where his logs were boomed and where, under Amos Peabody, men were at work with augers and lash poles and plugs, brailing them into rafts. He didn't see Jim Buckmaster; Peabody said that Buckmaster had already gone downriver, bucking an oar on a raft.

"He has a pretty good opinion of himself," Caleb said.

"Wouldn't you, if you were him?"

"I have anyway," Caleb said, "and I'm not even him."

"That boy is a stud-horse for work," Peabody said. "He may like fighting and the gals, but work comes first."

"That's a mistake," Caleb said, "that many a young man makes."

"And now he wants to be a raft pilot."

"If he wants to," Caleb said, "I reckon he will."

Although Caleb enjoyed Read's Landing, it was so wide open and rip-roaring, Esperanza found it dull, for of course he refused to take her into the gambling palaces; so presently they boarded a downriver boat, bound for St. Louis, never even stepping ashore at New Empire, when the boat stopped there in the night. Testing his wife's temperature, Caleb asked whether she would like to stop for a day or so, to see how work was coming on the new house, and to learn how Andy was feeling; but she said no, it would be more fun to get to St. Louis. That really cancelled his worry about Andy, unless she was being foxy. But he doubted that. When Esperanza wanted anything she wanted it right now, like a four-year-old howling for candy.

"By God," he thought, pacing the deck late one night, "I'm just as glad it turned out like this. I'd have been put to a sight of trouble, killing the son of a bitch."

Then, flipping his cigar into the river, he went to his stateroom and made love. She fought him off—that had been going on for a year or so—but her young nakedness roused him savagely and he got what he went after, as always. Injun gals took crazy notions, but Caleb believed possession was nine points of the law.

*

When they returned to New Empire in August, Caleb had acquired a fine new sawmill in the St. Louis area, powered by steam and equipped with gang saws and edging tables and all the other modern machinery for slicing forests into lumber. With the Mexican War not long for this world, the owners of the mill had foreseen lean times ahead, and they had been glad to sell for a modest payment in cash, the balance secured by a mortgage on the property. Let the buyer operate the mill during slack times, the owners figured, and let him go broke; at the end of two years they would foreclose, and the down payment and the deficiency judgment would be velvet.

Caleb figured otherwise. Peace or war, the country would keep growing; nothing could halt the westward flood of movers. And where would those movers live, once they had settled the prairies? In houses. What kind of houses? Wooden houses. And where would they get the lumber? From McSwasey & Zumwalt. It was his favorite tenet.

"Nothing can stop me now," he told Esperanza, on the upriver boat. "The North Star Mill up on the Whiskey can supply all the lumber we'll need in the New Empire yard. And the Missouri mill can wholesale to the St. Louis trade. I'll have me more mills some day, and a string of retail yards. My men will cut the pine and my men will drive the logs. My men will raft them to my mills. From log to farmer every board foot will be my operation. Every markup will be mine. I'll have a potful of pennies before I'm through."

She looked bored, but he didn't notice; he had been using her only as a sounding board, anyway.

Letters from Sophronicus had reported Andy's health better and the new house completed, at last. Should he, Sophronicus asked, have the furniture moved from the warehouse to the magnificent edifice on Mc-Swasey's Island? Sure, go ahead, fix it up finer than a seven-story fancy house, Caleb had replied, in substance.

Sophronicus met their boat, the morning they returned to New Empire, but Andy was not there; his recuperation was slow. The dysentery had been vanquished, his father said, but not the melancholia, the jumpy nerves. He couldn't, it seemed, forget the battle of Buena Vista; he had really been in the thick of the slaughter, although he had not snatched up the flag and led a countercharge: how that story had got started Sophronicus couldn't imagine.

"Neither can I," Caleb said.

And after Esperanza and Lilith had been seated in the carriage, and the drive begun to the island, Sophronicus told how sight of a horse bothered Andy, because horses reminded him of other horses, in Mexico, when the battle was gallant. Memory of wounded men was harrowing enough, Andy had told his father, but to think of those wounded horses was more than he could bear. Screaming, slavering horses, galloping riderless across acres of dying men.

"When he sees a horse now, he remembers," Sophronicus said. "He stays much at home, in the house. Sometimes he walks to the river and sits by the hour. He never goes downtown. The unfortunate disturbance at the welcoming program left him in a state of shock. He avoids people. But he's getting better. In both mind and body. I'm sure he's getting better. For a while, I don't mind telling you, I was deeply concerned lest he had contracted some obscure brain fever. I thought he might lose his reason. But he's better, even though his outlook is still dark. He'll forget that battle, gradually, and his sorrow at the tragic circumstances surrounding the demise of the Mexican girl."

"Did he love her?" Caleb asked.

394

"Oh, unquestionably."

"Sounds to me," Caleb thought, "like he lost some wheels from his brain in that battle. At that welcoming program we should have presented him with a horse."

Just at this time, Sophronicus said, idleness was very bad for Andy. If only he had work, light work, to occupy him, he might recover more quickly.

"I had hoped," he said, "that he would enter my office and read law. But that's out of the question now."

The carriage crossed the bridge and followed the sandy road north on the island. As the foliage thinned and Caleb caught sight of the house, he said:

"By God, Judge, that looks fine! You're a good architect. Couldn't have designed it better myself."

"The cupola came out well, don't you think?"

"Looks fine. And it's all paid for. Don't owe a nickel on it."

"And you, madam?" Sophronicus asked, turning to the back seat.

"Ooo, it is lovely!"

Well, it was. And should be, Caleb thought, for what it cost. All the builders' debris had been cleared away, and the front yard leveled and seeded; a driveway circled to the portico. The walls and pillars of plastered-over brick had been painted a soft shell color, the entablature and wooden trim glistening white. Curtains showed at the tall windows.

Not in a long time had Caleb seen Esperanza so animated. She stepped lightly from the carriage and went skipping ahead to the portico, bubbling with quick little laughs, eyes bright.

And after Sophronicus presented Caleb with the key, Esperanza was first into the magnificent central hall, where Kashan throw-rugs in silken green and gold lay on the polished cypress floors.

"Ooo, it is beautiful, beautiful," she murmured, gazing up at the chandelier, intricate with tear-drop crystal, which hung from a plaster medallion.

She pivoted slowly, admiring the black and scarlet wallpaper, with its Oriental scenes of mosques and barges where slaves waved great plumed fans over lolling nude courtesans. Cinquecento chairs stood stiff against the wall; black-walnut pedestals were topped by bronze busts of Quintus Fabius Maximus and Caligula; there were gold and blue vases of Chinese origin; and a carved oak seat from the Italian Renaissance was ornamented with grotesqueries of mermaids half-smothered by flowery seaweeds.

Smiling, smelling the fragrance of new furniture and rich fabrics and fresh paint, Caleb watched her during the next minutes, as they toured the music room with its oatmeal-colored wallpaper stamped with chamber-music scenes from the court of Louis XV; the dining room, floored with geometric parquetry and hung with oils showing ripe fruit and dead mallards; the back drawing room south of the hall, papered in sunny gold and opulent with rosewood and ormolu and yellow brocatelle.

"Ooo, I love it," Esperanza said, as they entered the front drawing room where an expansive pier mirror—nearly as tall as the ceiling, and framed in gorgeously-curled gilt with love birds perched vis-a-vis—reflected the deep carpet, the tapestried roses and festooned vines of the Louis XV fire screen, and—above the white marble mantel—the copy of Rubens' "Judgment of Paris" with its fruity full-blown nudes.

"By God," Caleb thought, "it's better than a fifty-dollar fancy house."

"Be lots of dusting around this mansion," Lilith said. "All them bric-a-bracs. Lots of cleaning. I'll need me help."

"You'll have it," Caleb said.

*

What with all the excitement of getting settled in such sybaritism, and hiring servants, and learning to sleep in a bedroom tinted in flesh-pinks and champagne-yellows, with a satinwood bed vastly canopied by silk, Esperanza was metamorphosed into an almost perfect wife, for several weeks, and Caleb told himself the house was worth the expense.

But it didn't last. By September the girl was nearly herself, by October wholly so. Then, late in October, a magnificent reception took place, to warm the house and possibly to show it off, and preparing for that Esperanza turned sweet once more. Everybody in town who could wangle an invitation—not a difficult feat—attended the reception; even Dexter Yarlow was there, for at Lilith's insistence Caleb had recently hired him as butler and coachman.

Naturally the Gentrys attended, for Sophronicus wished to be on hand to receive the plaudits regarding design and decoration; and—*mirabile dictu!*—Andy also came, his first venture into society since the welcome at the levee. This marked real progress in his recovery, so his parents were happy that evening, and grateful to Esperanza for making a special trip to their home to urge Andy to come.

Having known nothing of this, Caleb was astonished when the hero of Buena Vista turned up with his parents. Because they were to stand in the receiving line, the Gentrys were the first arrivals, coming in from the fine frosty evening smelling of cold and leaf smoke.

"Look who we brought!" Lucretia sang out.

It was he—none other than the son of a bitch!—saturninely handsome in his black Inverness cape and evening clothes.

Caleb limped over and shook his hand, feeling a twinge of old jealousy as he observed the healthier color in Andy's long face and the absence of pain in his sardonic eyes.

Then Esperanza came swishing along the hall, elegant empress of an empire builder, bejeweled and deliciously décolleté, hair shining in the candlelight, bodice full of promise that any offspring of the House of McSwasey would not starve.

"Ooo, it's Andy!" She clasped his hand. "Now I know it will be a brilliant reception."

"Why, you little slut!" Caleb thought, feeling as if a whip had been lashed across his face. But he stood looking as usual, heavy lips smiling over his false teeth, salty brows bristling, jaw big as two doubled fists, head forward in that listening attitude.

Esperanza gushed and posed and flirted her tail and picked an imaginary raveling off Andy's lapel and in general, Caleb thought, carried hospitality beyond the bounds of decency. He addressed Andy.

"Been doing any horseback riding lately?"

Something intangible crossed Andy's face.

"No," he said.

Both Sophronicus and Lucretia began talking about nothing in particular but anything to change the subject, and Caleb thought:

"Reckon I showed my hand that time. Got to watch it."

The doorbell pealed. Dexter Yarlow, also in evening clothes, and wearing a pair of tight misery called shoes, ushered in the members of a stringed orchestra, carrying shrouded cellos and violin cases. They had been imported especially from St. Louis; so presently, from the music room, there drifted tuning-up sounds, and then the conductor's "One, two, three, *spiel*," and the semibreves and crotchets of the "Overture to Oberon." Caleb thought "Home Sweet Home" would have been more appropriate, and "Bright Shines the Moon" livelier. Guests began arriving.

One nice thing about that receiving line, he had Esperanza under scrutiny. Andy, refusing his hostess's invitation to stand by her side, had wandered away somewhere into the vastness of the house; and while Caleb shook hands with elite and canaille, and thought how far he had climbed since kidnapping a nigger in Maryland, it occurred to him that perhaps he had been premature in writing off Andy as a threat to the marriage of McSwasey and Zumwalt. It might be necessary to kill the bastard after all, although he really hoped not.

"Thank you," he kept saying when people told him they liked the house. "The credit belongs to Judge Gentry. He designed it."

It did no harm to let it be known how thick he was with the judge; news traveled.

And when a banker came along the line and congratulated him, Caleb said:

"Glad you like the place. One thing, I don't owe a nickel on it."

That sort of news traveled too.

Along about nine-thirty, after the receiving line broke up, and the orchestra conductor was all but dislocating his arm, and people with the aid of champagne were discovering how clever they were and what a fine old world it was after all, Caleb missed his wife. Nor did he see Andy. And with that arithmetic peculiar to a husband believing himself teetering on the edge of cuckoldry, he feared that one plus one equaled one. Immediately he set out to find her. But guests kept stopping him, as he looked in on the music room, with its gleaming Steinway; on the dining room with its crystal and Sheffield silver; on the blaze of candles and bare shoulders in the back and front drawing rooms. She wasn't anywhere in the throng.

"God damn it," he thought, limping toward the stairs, twice halted by windbags. And he thought, "Have to be nice to the bastards. Play it smooth."

He broke away at last and gained the stairs, carpeted in Turkish red, climbing past the tremendous Louis Quinze tapestry with amorous shepherds and shepherdesses in rococo frolic; up past the bronze mask of Medusa; to the landing with its stained-glass rosette, its massive cassone with lion's-claw feet and embossments of fauns and satyrs, and its tapestry where urbane and licentious birds fluttered among tangles of grapevines and amaranths; and finally to the upper hall.

Guests lingered there, admiring the intaglios, the girandoles, the bas-reliefs, the Sèvres vases with gold and black mountings, the Saracen poniards, the antique urns on a gilded *bombe* commode of tulip and Amboina wood.

He brushed past them, heading like a bullet for the master's suite at the southeast corner of the house.

Both doors stood ajar; his glance showed nobody in the bedroom. He limped along fast to the second door, opening on the sitting room of the suite. And he saw them.

Not that they had become one, but they were alone and that was the next thing to it; alone in that room of lavender and soft French gray, where wallpaper girls coquetted in swings and flowery bosquets. They were standing at the east wall discussing—of all things—a piece of furniture, an elaborate Boulle cabinet inlaid with lapis lazuli, blue marble and shells. Caleb felt his fists clenching.

But then luckily, just before they heard him and turned, he caught sight of himself in the huge mirror between the south windows. In that magnificent glass, ornamented with gilded floral sprays and urns, he saw a bull buffalo of a man, an old bull but not yet a cast bull by any means, and with his blocky shoulders and dangerous jaw and doubled fists that mirrored man looked ready to charge.

"Smooth, smooth," an inner voice warned. "Play it close to your chest."

Not the South, not the West.

"Oh," Esperanza said poutily, when she turned. "Hello."

"Hello, Goldilocks," Caleb said easily. "Sorry to butt in, but folks are starting to leave. You'll be needed downstairs."

She sighed elaborately.

"You've got a fine house here, Mr. McSwasey," Andy said.

"Why, son," Caleb said, giving his shoulder a pat, "I'm glad you like it. Come see us often."

*

One gray afternoon a few weeks after the reception, Caleb sat in his office reckoning accounts, rolling his cigar from side to side of his thick mouth. His steel-rimmed reading glasses gave him an oddly clerical appearance, quite at variance with his tough old face, and when with a stubby-fingered paw he clutched a pencil and jotted down figures, the whole effect was as if an animal trainer had dressed some grizzled old bruin in man's attire and taught him tricks.

Among the papers on the table several bankbooks lay, loaded with money, for McSwasey & Zumwalt found it prudent to hoard quick assets not only in New Empire but in such financial centers as Chicago and St. Louis as well. The business was expanding, not beyond Caleb's dreams, for they were boundless, but certainly at a smart clip. Up in the pinery ten camps were chopping down pine, and he could have told you—but probably wouldn't, being a close-mouthed man—just how many board feet each camp had cut last season and was likely to cut this. In his two mills saws were screeching through logs, and he had plans for more mills, more stumpage, more everything. People were beginning to say that Caleb McSwasey was a big man; perhaps the biggest on the big river.

He spittooned his cigar, removed his glasses and sat staring at the wall-map. He would, he thought grudgingly, have to start thinking about a larger office and hiring a clerk or two. He enjoyed paper work; it had become, indeed, a sort of solitaire in which he could bury himself and his matrimonial worries; but the last year or so it had increased and encroached on the hours he could better spend on overall strategy.

Lighting a fresh cigar, he hooked on his glasses and reached for pen and paper, beginning a letter to Mr. Otto Zumwalt, Santa Fe, New Mexico, Dear Friend Otto, explaining that business had been slow of late, "but we'll win through yet, Otto, just be patient, if you need it I could let you have a couple of hundred from profits although it would be better, Otto, to plow the money back into the business and—"

The door edged open and Lilith peered in.

"You busy, Mistah Caleb?"

"Come in," he said.

Wearing a spark-blue coat trimmed with rabbit fur, and a scarlet bibi-bonnet with yellow ribbons, Lilith sank into a hard chair, wheezing.

"Whew! Them stairs gits me. Puffing like a bride. Why you think them stairs do that to me?"

"You're getting old," Caleb said.

"Ain't that! No, sir! Dexter is slowing down considerable, but I am just as lively as on that trip to Taos."

399

She cackled.

"You're looking younger every day," Caleb said.

"Eee! That sounds mighty fine, Mistah Caleb. Younger every day! Yes, sir! How you like my new raiment?"

She stood up, turning. Niggers and money, Caleb thought. He had given her a good sum after that reception, with instructions to watch Esperanza closer than ever, and to set Dexter watching. It had been money well invested, for it had brought him the information that Andy Gentry had called several times at the house on McSwasey's Island. According to his spies, nothing alarming had occurred, but he didn't like it, his jealousy was boiling, and he had been weighing various oblique schemes for ending those visits.

"Dexter say I am pretty as a plate of pork chops in this bonnet," Lilith said.

"Looks fine," Caleb said. "What's on your mind?"

"Yes, sir, coming to that. And it ain't good. You hear what I say and you are going to be mad. Yes, sir, reckon you'll sizzle when you hear Andy has been to the house again."

"This afternoon?"

"No, sir, this morning. Them visits of his is gitting closer all the time. I go to the door and there he is. 'I was taking a little walk,' he say, 'and first thing I know I was on this here island. Is your mistress in?' he say."

Caleb sat staring at Lilith.

"So?" he said.

"So I go upstairs and tell your wife she got a gentleman visitor down in the parlor. She is looking a sight, but my, my, you should see her rush around. She mighty het up about that gentleman caller, seem to me. Reckon no gal ever changes clothes as fast as she does. And she pick up that high class perfume you give her last Christmas and rub the stopper on her hair."

"What did she say?" Caleb asked.

"She say, 'Lilith, you damn old nigger, why you stand there gawking? Git on about your work,' she say. She ain't telling me things like she used to in them bygone days. Reckon she don't trust pore old Lilith no more. So I git out of there but I has a word with Dexter. 'Dexter,' I say, 'stop that dozing and move your black hinder off that chair. Wake up, man,' I say, 'and pay attention to what I tell you. You take that feather duster,' I say, 'and go to work in the hall. Keep your ears open and listen.' He say, 'With you around, I ain't never caught up on my sleep since I left that fine janitor position at the Commercial House.' I say, 'You can sleep when you're dead, man, but you ain't dead now except in your head and feet. Move, man!' I say. 'I want to know,' I say, 'what is said by way of high class conversation when the judge's son call on Mis' McSwasey. So you listen,' I say, 'and tell me.' I figure perhaps Miss

400

Esperanza say things to that young man when Dexter is around that she won't say if I am there. Don't think she trusts me no more. Don't know why, neither.

"Well, old Dexter he whishes that feather duster in the hall, all the time listening, and what you think he hear? Nothing, that's what! On account of they talk too soft, perching there together on that love seat in the front parlor. Why you think they call that a love seat, Mistah Caleb? Mighty small for much loving, seem to me. Dexter tell me he sneak a look now and then into that parlor, and they is sitting looking in each other's eyes like they do wish that love seat was a bed. 'Man,' I say, 'maybe they is just sitting there thinking high class thoughts. Just because you never think about nothing else,' I say, 'ain't no proof that quality like a judge's son go around thinking what you is always thinking.' Old Dexter he laugh and say he don't know what a judge's son think, but he say it plain what Miss Esperanza have in mind, else why when they sit there would she sometimes reach over her hand and touch him? 'Leading him on,' Dexter say. 'If that judge's son ain't never had nothing but high class thoughts,' Dexter say, 'why that boy's got some nice surprises coming.' Yes, sir."

"How long did he stay?" Caleb asked.

"About an hour. And when he leave, old Dexter is still whishing that duster over them statues of dead men in the hall. He sneaks a look at them standing in the vestibule by the front door, and Dexter tell me Miss Esperanza is edging closer and closer to that boy, yes, sir, shoving it right at him, and puckering up her lips in the air so they'll be handy if that boy take a notion to kiss her. But there weren't no kissing that Dexter see. Might have been some he didn't see, but he claim not. He say though that ain't Miss Esperanza's fault. 'Ain't going to be long now,' he say. 'They is gitting ripe for it,' he say. 'Love seat today, bed tomorrow,' he say. Yes, sir."

Fifteen minutes after Lilith left, Caleb stepped from his office, plans laid and composure recovered, and moved along the hall for a conference with Judge Gentry. He told the judge what a high opinion he had of Andy, and how he was always on the lookout for young men of promise, to take into his business.

"I'm getting along," he said, "and if I can find the right young man I'll push him fast. In a few years he'll have an interest in the company. I've been watching Andy for some time, and he looks good to me."

Sophronicus beamed.

"No point in starting him at the bottom," Caleb said, "in a logging camp. The work's too hard. Might bring back his dysentery. But if he wants a job with a future, I'll start him measuring lumber and keeping accounts at my North Star Mill. I'm going up there tomorrow, and if you approve I'll take him along. He'll end up with a potful of pennies."

401

"Capital!" Sophronicus said. "Time has been heavy on his hands, and a job is the very thing to make him forget Mexico. Capital!"

*

Caleb found his wife in a temper when he returned from the North Star Mill, for of all those concerned with the activities of Andy, she alone had been uninformed of his taking a job with McSwasey & Zumwalt. Why, she demanded, hadn't Caleb told her he was packing Andy off to the woods? Never thought of it, he said; he hadn't supposed she would be interested in such trivial business details as adding another name to the payroll.

"If you had asked me I'd have told you," he said. "How did you find out about it, anyway?"

That cooled her down; and it amused him to observe the wariness shuttering her eyes. She had, she said, just happened to meet Judge Gentry on Winnebago Street, and he had told her. Caleb figured that was a lie, from the way she kept staring at the cigarette she was rolling, but he let it go.

It was dusk of a November day; candles had already been lighted in the sitting room of the master's suite; Esperanza, gazing into the fireplace, lay curled on a chaise longue of lavender silk woven with gold flowers. Drinking his bourbon, Caleb diverted himself by recounting the smallest details of his trip without mentioning Andy. Finally she asked:

"Did he say anything about me?"

"Who?"

"Andy."

"No," he said slowly, "not that I recollect."

This was not quite accurate, for Andy had mentioned Mrs. McSwasey a number of times, and had especially asked that Caleb convey his apologies for not getting to the island to say good-by; but Caleb wasn't mentioning that, even if telling the truth might have put Esperanza into better humor. By now, he was used to her sulkiness; indeed, her rare good moods he found suspect.

Next day he told Sophronicus how much Andy enjoyed his work at the mill, how well he was looking, and what a fine future lay before him in the lumber business; and after a few well directed questions he learned that Esperanza had not heard about Andy's job from the judge on Winnebago Street, but in his home, where she had called to discover whether a recurrence of dysentery had kept Andy from McSwasey's Island. That settled it: if Esperanza would lie about meeting the judge, something more than friendship had been brewing with her and the judge's son; and Caleb told himself he had done well to place Andy beyond reach. And so smoothly done too! Much cannier than killing the bastard.

Winter came early that year, the river frozen solid, the snows deep, the mercury low and Esperanza's spirits lower. Returning from town in his cutter, Caleb would find her in the upstairs sitting room, lost in some French romance or pouting at the cheerful fire, hardly giving him a hello when he entered. He used to wonder what she was thinking, during those weeks when the bitter cold kept her imprisoned on the island, and he wished he might manacle her spirit and command its submission as effectively as he subjected her body, but he reckoned no man could do that with a moody woman, not even if he owned every stick in the pinery, every nigger in Christendom, every pot in the nation filled with all the pennies.

People were always getting up dances during the winter, to be held in the Masonic Hall or in the dining room of the Commercial House, and sometimes Esperanza hinted it would be fun to attend. He hardly bothered to put his refusal into words: a man would be a fool kind of hoss to take a young wife to such affairs, where God knew how many men would flock around her. But leaving that out of it, his dancing days were about over, he reckoned; he had other things to occupy him on these long evenings of his middle years, such as figuring board feet, stumpage, logging campaigns.

Even games of chess with the Gentrys had become infrequent, now that the McSwaseys no longer lived a few steps across the street from Lexylvania, for on evenings of biting cold Lucretia and Sophronicus disliked the long sleigh ride to McSwasey's Island, and Caleb wasn't eager to take Esperanza to the Gentry house, with its memories of Andy and all the talk of Andy up there in the pinery getting a start in the logging business.

As the cold increased and the snows deepened, Caleb's jealousy gradually dulled, for with Esperanza marooned on the island and Andy marooned at the North Star Mill, he felt he had effectively precluded the cuckoo from attempting its meddlesome nesting habits. And if as the days passed his wife seemed ever remoter from him in spirit, he told himself women were indecipherable, especially Spanish and Injun women, and it was time wasted to try fathoming their thoughts.

Yet he was tempted now and then to try, such as on that 3:00 A.M. in January when he was wakened by Esperanza's threshing and screaming in bed beside him. It was one of her habitual nightmares, the worst he remembered. In his flannel nightgown he scrambled from bed and lighted a candle, for from experience he knew that regaining consciousness in the dark only frightened her the more; then he shook her shoulder.

"Goldilocks. Wake up. It's all right, honeychild."

She clung to sleep like a blind puppy to a teat, but at last she came awake, shivering, brow damp, hair mussed, tears shining on her face.

"Honeychild," he said, "what's the matter?"

Her eyes were wild and black, like an Injun's seeing ghost warriors galloping on ghost pintos.

403

"You're all right," he said. "Sure you are."

But she wasn't; not yet. The insanity of nightmare still showed in her eyes as she shrank from him and went scuttling like a fleeing animal across the bedclothing. Before he could catch her she sprang erect on the carpet and dashed into the sitting room of the suite. When he followed carrying the candle he found her at the vitrine against the north wall, rummaging in that glass-front cabinet among the Chinese porcelain dragons and cats and bronze dogs; her fingers curled on the hilt of a sheathed knife. He hadn't seen that knife in seven years, not since she had shown it to him on the trail from Santa Fe and told how it had belonged to her great-grandmother. Suddenly now she dropped it, as if it had turned hot, and racked by sobs she sank to the floor, beating the carpet with her fists.

He knew then she must be still asleep; he put down the candle, lifted her, shook her and slapped her back into consciousness.

"Ooo, don't, don't," she choked, crying. "What have I done?"

"Honeychild," he said, "you've been asleep. But you're all right now. You were dreaming."

Lips apart, she stared at him; then buried her head in his chest and cried heartbrokenly. And after he had smoothed her hair and patted her and told her everything was fine, everything was legal, they were in their own house in New Empire, Wisconsin and didn't owe a nickel on it, she begged him to light every candle in the suite.

"What's the good of that?" he asked. "We'd best get back to bed."

But when she insisted he humored her, and after all the candles were blazing he stirred up the fire and poured bourbon for them both.

"Luck," he said.

She gulped the whiskey so eagerly it set her to coughing, so he pounded her back and told her whiskey and Sunday throats didn't agree, and when the coughing fit had passed he fetched another drink and declared, not without pride, that by God she was a handful.

She smiled.

"Goldilocks," he said, "what set you off like this?"

"Ooo, it was terrible. I dreamed a man was chasing me."

"Any man chase you when I'm around," he said, "and I'll kill the bastard."

"It was only a dream," she said.

He stood watching her curled on the chaise, staring into the fire, body soft and young in the nightgown of peach-colored silk. His thoughts were husbandly; he sat beside her, fondled her.

"Caleb," she whispered, "I don't like it here."

"It's a little crowded," he acknowledged.

"I mean—in New Empire. Can't we move away?"

"Why, Goldilocks," he said, "I reckon you don't know what you're saying. We've just built the house. Business is pretty fair. We're in on the ground floor. We stay here and we'll end up rich. Hell, we're rich already. We've stumbled on a beaver valley that's never been trapped. We've hit a pay streak. It beats driving a coffle of nigger wenches into a town without a fancy house. Where would we go?"

"Somewhere. Anywhere. Once you said we could take a canoe and go up the river and never come back."

He grinned.

"Reckon that's the Injun in you. Maybe you ain't house broke."

"And leave Lilith," she said. "I don't like Lilith any more."

"Lilith's all right," he said, "except her brains are in her pants."

"Maybe we could sell her," Esperanza said.

"Not in Wisconsin. Wouldn't be legal. Lilith's all right."

"Sometimes she scares me," Esperanza said. "The way she looks at me. I think she hates me."

"Hell," he said, "niggers all hate the whites. Kill us all, if they had the gumption. You're just upset, honeychild, with that dream."

Her head, cradled on his shoulder, nodded.

"Santa Fe was in the dream. Sometimes I think I would like to see Santa Fe again. The sunshine and the mountains. And my father. He was very good to me. It has been a long time."

"That's the Apache in you," he said, "wanting the desert."

"*Si,* perhaps. But I am not all Apache."

"Enough of you is," he said, "to keep a man humping."

"My grandfather was a general. In Prussia. His name was Heinrich von Zumwalt. He must have killed many men, in battle."

"If he was a general," Caleb said, "I doubt it."

*

She said she didn't want to return to bed, perhaps to dream again, and while they lay there together on the chaise, sipping bourbon and smoking, she recounted many of the stories Otto had told her long ago about the greatness of General von Zumwalt. Most of those stories Caleb had himself heard from Otto, and he did hope Esperanza wasn't going to fall into her father's habit of dragging the estimable old general into every conversation.

Toward dawn, after the fire and their glasses had been replenished several times, they made love, on the chaise to begin with, but soon adjourning to the carpet, for Lilith's summation of the impracticality of love seats held good also with a chaise; and on this occasion Esperanza rewarded his understanding and patience concerning the bad dream with much of the enthusiasm she had brought to the early nights of marriage. And although, with their seventh wedding anniversary behind them, everything was indubitably legal, the hour and the place sharpened the experience to extra-legal piquancy, and it did Caleb's heart good to think of Andy Gentry up there in the frigid pinery, huddled alone under his

405

blankets in the office of the North Star Mill. And when, on the chaise again with refilled glasses, Esperanza told him he was wonderful, that he was mainly good to her and that she was sorry the devil sometimes entered her soul and made her a vixenish wife, he felt he had won a great victory over Andy and over all the sons of bitches who considered a woman fair game if her husband was thirty years her senior.

"Love me, Goldilocks?" he asked.

"*Si.* I think I always have and always will."

Waugh! Show the bastards!

"Honeychild," he said, "you mean more to me than all the pine in the Chippewa Valley."

She grew drowsy, and before carrying her in to bed he poked the fire and went to a window, parting the draperies, his blunt thumbnail scratching a peephole in the thick rime on the glass. Through the hole he could see the dawn, trees black and bare, snow cold blue. And for a high moment he experienced a satisfaction rich and sensuous, standing there warm in his nightshirt, the heavy carpet cushioning his toes, a man rich and independent enough to sleep till noon if he chose, while far away in the north the crews from ten camps were already assaulting the pine.

"It beats nigger stealing," he thought, "or running a store in East Bainbridge."

Esperanza was fast asleep now, under the opiates of love and bourbon, and he stood looking down at her, eyes and smile tender. What a handful! But an armful, too, of warm fragrant woman. His. All legal. Waugh! And with voluptuous pleasure his gaze circled this cozy lair his money had provided: the fireplace with wreaths and rosettes chiseled in its white marble; the gilded walnut furniture, the girandole clock with its gilded winged victory, the cabinet whose brass mounts were wrought in lovely girls' heads.

Then, on the bud green carpet patterned with yellow primroses, he saw the knife which Esperanza had dropped; he picked it up and withdrew the ugly blade. Respectfully, he thumbed the sharp point and the razor edge; typical greaser-girl weapon. Quiet, deadly. He balanced it on his palm, thinking idly of Andy Gentry, then sheathed it and returned it to the knick-knacks in the vitrine.

*

All marriages, he reckoned, had their ups and downs, and the fortunes of his graphed upward, for a few weeks after that night of Esperanza's bad dream. But he might have known Hod Kite had been right, about a woman fooling you the one minute in twenty-four hours when you turned your back. He might have known something was going on out of his sight, like moths eating silently and ruinously in a bale of beaver pelts.

Late in February Lilith turned up at his office with a letter. That morning, she said, before Miss Esperanza was up, a man brought it to the house. He was a teamster who picked up a frosty-nosed and miserable livelihood by sledding supplies to the pinery, and carrying a bag of mail. This letter, however, had not traveled in the mail bag from the woods; at the North Star Mill Andy Gentry had put it into his personal care, with instructions to deliver it directly to Mrs. McSwasey. Lilith had assured him that an excellent way to get his hair torn out by the roots would be to tramp upstairs with the letter and wake Mrs. McSwasey; she had promised to deliver it the moment Mrs. McSwasey ordered breakfast.

"But I did no such thing. No, sir. Figured you'd want that letter yourself."

Caleb gave her five dollars and told her he wished to be alone.

The letter said:

> North Star Mill
> Wisconsin Territory
> February 16, 1848

Dear Madam:

It is beyond my powers of description to tell you the happiness that overcame me when the mail arrived this morning with the missive from you. I can well understand your wounded feelings upon learning last November that I had departed for the pinery without calling to bid you farewell, but I assure you this breach in deportment was not of my choosing. My father returned from his office one afternoon with the news that Mr. McSwasey had offered me a start in the lumber business, with a splendid future, but that I must be prepared to leave for upriver bright and early the next morning. I had, madam, no time to spare, and it was impossible for me to say good-by. But I told your husband to explain to you the circumstances of my departure, and to give you my very best. I am surprised you did not receive the message.

Believe me, madam, when I tell you that since my arrival at this place (I almost said God-forsaken place), my thoughts have often returned to New Empire and to a certain house on a certain island. Sometimes, alas, I have been alarmed at how often I have thought of you and of your many kindnesses, for perhaps the world would say that one in my position has no right to dream of the loveliness of one already wedded to another. My only retort would be that one cannot always control the flight of his fancy, *no matter how much he tries,* and I assure you that I have tried, yet often I have recalled our hours together when, if my hopes did not deceive me, our eyes spoke of that which our lips dared not. Perhaps my boldness in that last sentence will affright you. If so I humbly apologize, but I cannot bring myself to blot out the words.

Life is very dull here, one day like another. The work is so light that I am led to suspect Mr. McSwasey made a place for me out of friendship for my father. I have learned to measure the board feet of sawed lumber—scaling is the technical term—and to record the day's cut. Sometimes also I serve as offbearer, that is, carrying the planks from the saw to the drying stacks south of the mill. The mill, as perhaps you know, is located on the east bank of the Whiskey River, at the foot of Hangover Rapids, so we have usually a swift flow of water to revolve the mill wheel, although often on the coldest nights ice forms at the dam and our work is hung up. We have two muley saws and on a good day each is capable of producing four thousand feet of lumber.

Mr. Olinick, the mill foreman and head sawyer lives in a nearby cabin with his wife, he is an old man in his forties who suffers asthma. Francis Quinn, the assistant sawyer, lives in another cabin with his wife and five small children. There is also a third cabin that serves as bunkhouse for Hank Underwood and Lem Voland, they bring logs into the mill from the boom and also work as offbearers. I have fixed up the mill office as living quarters. I have a bunk and a small stove. Some nights are very cold, the mill walls are only of clapboards and the wind whistles through the cracks, but the office is in the southeast corner so I am somewhat protected from the rude north winds.

I like the lumber business fine so far, although there are lonesome times when I feel farther from civilization than during my service in Mexico. Perhaps a day will come when Mr. McSwasey will need me to work in New Empire and I will be nearer my friends.

Madam, it is almost too much to hope that you will favor me with another of your charming epistles, but nevertheless I am full of hope for such a "consummation devoutly to be wished," as the bard put it. I think of you often in your beautiful residence. It seems only justice to tell you—although perhaps you will deem me too bold—that I owe you a debt of gratitude for helping me drive out the melancholy humors that afflicted me upon my return from Mexico, when I couldn't forget my dear friend who perished there by her own hand, Inez Hinojo. In some strange fashion you remind me of little Inez, it is almost as if you were she, although more beautiful. Alas, I fear I write with a boldness that may offend your gentle sensibilities, and if so I can only say that you may burn this letter and put from your thoughts forever your devoted friend,

Andy.

Caleb sat as if at the core of some vast numbness. When he lighted a cigar his fingers trembled.

*

He neglected business, the rest of that sick day, but when he returned to the island in late afternoon he looked much as ever, except for a certain absent-mindedness about his eyes. And his feet dragged, when he entered the vestibule and hung up his beaver hat and fur-lined great-coat.

At supper he dawdled with his food, every bite tasteless, his stomach flashing messages that it wanted nothing. The Burgundy sloshed sour in his mouth. In the master's chair at the head of the table he looked more slumped than ordinarily, his bison shoulders sagging, as if he were uncommonly tired, weighed down by all the timber he had stolen and all the years of roistering and pirating. Once when he reached for wine his sleeve knocked over his tumbler of water; it made quite a mess on the fine linen cloth and came dripping over the table edge. Generally at a time like that he would have jumped up and righted the glass; not tonight; he just sat there while Esperanza tapped the bell and one of the Swedish hired girls hurried in to clean up after his clumsiness. Hell with it.

When everything was set in order again, he noticed Esperanza regarding him curiously. He avoided her eyes.

"Don't mind me, Goldilocks," he said. "I've got a headache and I'm working on a big deal."

"I think you work too hard," she said.

"There may be other ways to make money," he said, "but I've never run across them."

He lingered long with his cigar and brandy, and when Esperanza mentioned a book she was reading he told her to run along, not to wait for him. She came to him and kissed the top of his head. He watched her leaving: how the taffy-colored silk of her dress shaped itself to her handsome waist and flowed in womanly lines.

There had been a man named Hod Kite: "I've seen you jealous but never in love. A bad combination. God help you, Sport."

There had been a man named Otto Zumwalt: "Esperanza. *Ja.* It is a Spanish name. It is a name meaning hope and expectation."

There had been a girl named Esperanza Zumwalt: "I love you, Caleb. I do, I do. Since that hot afternoon."

And there had been a boy named Andrew J. Gentry who had loved a Mexican gal and the gal stabbed herself and the boy returned a restless veteran to New Empire and began mooning around property that didn't belong to him, warm, shapely property; sweet-breathed property; smooth-legged, soft-breasted property.

Cigar ash dropped onto Caleb's vest.

Ashes, he thought, you've got the right idea: close to the vest. Smooth. Play it smooth, smooth as smooth warm legs in smooth silk. You kill the bastard at high noon on Winnebago Street and you might get into trouble. You might anyway but that's the risk a man runs.

He finished his brandy; two blond-headed hired girls, old country

409

fresh, cleared the table, replaced the cloth with a center lace doily; the bare mahogany gleamed.

"Tell Lilith I want her," he told the girls.

He kept sitting there, feeling old, bleak, grizzled as a buffalo bull cast out by the herd to wander off somewhere across the windy plains till the wolves sniffed him. A cast bull. Young cows didn't want him no more.

His lips curled, looking thick and ugly; his jaw toughened.

Just too damned bad. For the young cows. For the young bull too.

How to get rid of the bastard. Well, he'd figure it. Might take time, since smoothness was desirable, but he'd figure it.

Lilith entered.

"Sit down," he said, voice dead quiet.

"Mistah Caleb," she whispered, "you looks terrible. Glad I ain't never crossed you up in no way whatsoever."

He stared at her; more ash dropped to his vest. He regarded the cigar, half smoked, then tossed it to the bare mahogany table. There was a faint scent of scorched varnish.

"Eee!"

Lilith snatched up the cigar, wet her thumb, rubbed the blemished wood.

"You shouldn't never do that, Mistah Caleb. That there wood ain't never going to be the same."

He grinned, watched Lilith hurrying the cigar to an ashtray.

"Man, you is sure acting awful," she said. "What's come over you?"

"Sit down."

She obeyed, asking, "You read that letter old Lilith brung you?"

He nodded.

"Reckon it made you mad," Lilith said. "Reckon that why you act like this. You going to take it out of Miss Esperanza's hide?"

He stared at her.

"You want to whup her," Lilith said, "and I'll hold her down for you. Yes, sir. Whup her naked meat and learn her. If I was you I'd do that."

"God damn it, Lilith," he said, "you're a fool."

"Sure is! Yes, sir. No question 'bout that."

He brought the letter from his pocket, neatly sealed. And he told her that tomorrow morning she should hand that letter to her mistress with the information that it had just been delivered by the teamster.

"Yes, sir, but I sure don't understand, Mistah Caleb. Miss Esperanza read that letter and she's going to sizzle till she sets her chair on fire. She going to write that boy. And he going to write back."

Caleb nodded. And from his wallet he fished a bill and flipped it to the table.

"When the next letter comes," he said, "see that you get it first and bring it to me."

*

410

Two days later Lilith reported that Esperanza had walked through the snow to town, presumably to the post office. And in March the teamster again appeared at the McSwasey door with a letter. But luck was against Lilith, that morning: when the teamster arrived Esperanza happened to be downstairs and took the letter in person. And when the third letter came in April, she was enjoying the spring sun in the yard and intercepted the teamster.

No matter, no matter. Andrew J. Gentry wasn't to die at noon on Winnebago Street, but he was to die just the same. By accident. By the accident of a boy's deciding, long ago on an estate in Prussia, that he would enjoy studying art and migrating to America and dwelling among the noble savages.

*

That was a lovely spring, drenching McSwasey's Island with the fragrance of wild blossoms and bloodroot and spicy arbutus. Caleb, always a quiet man, grew quieter, smoking a contemplative cigar as he paced slowly about his estate in the tender twilights. Sometimes Esperanza took the air with him, and he thought her as young and pulsating with the life-demands of posterity as the sweet white violets and the fawn lilies. He looked older, that spring, with his sagging shoulders and white hair and deliberate movements. Well, he felt older.

West of the house, flanking the brick path leading to the river, a garden had been laid out, with many winding walks, and upon advice of Sophronicus Gentry a fountain had been ordered. This arrived on the first spring boat from St. Louis; by late April the pipes were laid and the fountain set up in a circular sanctum hedged by privet; Caleb liked to go there and observe the wet nude marble of a river nymph and her goat-footed lover perpetually showered with fine spray.

When Dexter Yarlow had been engaged as butler, he had agreed to serve also as gardener, but the March winds had scarcely stopped blowing before Caleb realized that Dexter's abilities lay in beds other than horticultural; so presently an old German named Ferdinand Vogler came marching every morning from town to teach the weeds fine lessons and to drill the peppermint geraniums and the sweet basil. When Caleb encountered him diligently spading and hoeing, Ferdinand removed his hat; when Esperanza appeared he all but dropped a curtsy, for—using her father's native tongue—she had told him about General von Zumwalt, and although Ferdinand had departed from the homeland to avoid military service, he still had as much respect for a general as for a pig's-knuckle.

Now and then, returning early from his office, Caleb would go exploring remoter parts of his island, sometimes accompanied by his wife. Since striking up a correspondence with Andy, she had become a much more agreeable helpmeet, vivacious as a butterfly. On those strolls, when she picked violets and Dutchman's breeches, or found a swamp buttercup to pin in her hair, he used to study her covertly, amazed that so much deception could be flourishing in her pretty head, and amazed too that a smart girl like Esperanza could be so obtuse as to believe she could deceive an old hand like himself.

"Goldilocks," he thought, "you're prancing for a fall. I'll give you all the rope you'll take, and then—"

One May afternoon, warm with sunshine, sweet with all the woodsy odors of spring, melodious with robins and yellow throats, they wandered to the north tip of the island, following a dim path through a ferny wildwood of shellbark hickory and honey locust to the water's edge. In the slough between the island and Wisconsin, pickerel weeds and arrow-heads grew in profusion; the dead water, ripe with backwash smells, was covered with the olive-green pads of Indian lotus. Redwings fluttered and sang. Esperanza snuggled by his side, arm linked through his.

"Caleb," she said.

He knew by her tone that something was coming. He said, "Yes?"

"Are you going up north this spring to the drive?"

"Reckon I will. Next week, likely."

"Will you do something for me?"

"I might."

"Will you take me along?"

"Goldilocks," he said, "you take odd notions. Why would you want to visit the drive?"

"I don't know," she said. "I just thought I'd like to. Will you take me?"

He hadn't expected that, although he realized now that he should have; and as he stood there staring off across the lily pads he asked himself how her presence would affect his plans. They were carefully laid, microscopically examined for pitfalls. Then it occurred to him that she was handing him Andy's head on a platter. With her at the North Star Mill, he might have to exert a little extra caution, but taking her would be playing it smoother than smooth, for how could the world suspect he was jealous of Andy when he took his wife into Andy's territory?

"Will you, Caleb?"

"No."

He sensed her stiffening.

"I won't take you to the drive," he said. "Nobody but whores go there. But I'll do this. If you want a trip I'll leave you at the mill while I'm off on the drive."

"Ooo—Caleb!"

She flung her arms around his neck and kissed him passionately.

*

It was like their trip to the pinery years ago, with a few differences. That was October, this was May. Injuns met them then and guided them; no Injuns now. But they camped on that same island in the Chippewa, and Esperanza if anything was sprightlier, lovelier, eyes shining with expectation, on tiptoe with the joy of living, like a girl escorted to her first ball.

Caleb himself acted affable, although he wondered how he managed it, for that was a voyage of heartbreak and anger. Not the anger of fire— that had passed weeks ago—but the frozen anger of a glacier grinding and bulling.

Sitting late by the island campfire, unable to sleep, chewing his cigar, he asked himself what she took him for, a complete idiot? And what did Andrew J. Gentry take him for? And he resolved that when the time was ripe, long after Andy became something that wouldn't interest even an undertaker, he would drop an occasional hint to let his wife know that she had never duped him for a moment. He wished he might let her know now. He wished he might waken her and say, "Goldilocks, remember that bastard Andy Gentry? Well, Goldilocks, he's got in my crosswalk. I'm going to put him out of his misery."

He wondered what had been said in those letters Lilith had failed to intercept. What endearments, what planned trysts? Son of a bitch! Why did the bastard have to be Judge Gentry's son? If he'd been an ordinary rooster or river hog a man could have shot him through the heart on Winnebago Street. Through the heart? No, they died too fast that way. Through the guts. Let him groan and moan a while, knowing a coffin was coming; let him serve as example to any other wife-stealing bastard, the way a dead hawk hung rotting on a chicken-yard fence to warn off other birds of prey.

He grew drowsy at last, very late, and slept two or three hours, dreaming weirdly, but he was out of his blankets before the cat-owls stopped their screeching, before the thrushes and bunting birds twittered hymns to the dawn. Blowing steam from his breakfast coffee, he looked as tangle-haired and red-eyed as a bull buffalo. His mouth tasted of insomnia and stale cigars.

At midmorning their canoe entered the flood-full Whiskey River, and he watched Esperanza up there in the bow, dipping her cedar paddle or trailing fingers in the water. Her hair, uncovered to the sun, had been pulled high and fastened with a decorative comb, revealing the lovely curve of her neck, the flesh looking as sweet for kissing as brown sugar. Sometimes she glanced back and flashed a smile, but he knew her smiles were not for him.

He forced geniality into his eyes and sent a smile to his own lips when, in early afternoon, he beached the canoe on the east bank of the river. A rod upstream he could see the mill, a long gray-boarded building, water splashing from the turning wheel and churning out of the tailrace, water hurling itself over the face of the dam to the boulders below, where it dashed in circles, black and deep and foam-flecked, and exhaled bright vapors which jeweled the scouring rushes and bog willows that waded along the shore.

He dragged the canoe high on the landing, safe from the swollen current, and picked up Esperanza's portmanteau. She glanced at his possible sack, left in the canoe.

"Aren't you staying till morning?" she asked, voice lifted against the racket from the dam.

"Why, no, Goldilocks, I thought you knew. I've got to get to my drive. By tonight I'll be miles from here."

They climbed the bank and made their way among the stacks of drying lumber, fragrant and resinous, sweeter to Caleb's nostrils than a hundred flower gardens; and when they emerged at the mill he pointed toward the nearest of three log cabins among the stumps off to the east.

"That's Elmer Olinick's. He and his wife will put you up."

He put down the portmanteau and led the way into the mill office, with its high stool and sloping desk by the east window, its neatly-made bunk against the west wall. Andy's quarters. Even here in the office the mill noises intruded, floor and rafters quivering under the assaults of raw power from the revolving undershot wheel. And when Caleb opened the door into the mill room, pandemonium greeted them: all the rattling of cogs, the clamor of whirling shafts, the creak of pitman against noddle pin and stirrup, the chewing of saws, the thud-thud of log carriages.

Caleb stopped for a moment, unseen and unheard by the mill hands, the strong prosperous smells of sawdust and grease swirling around him; and for a half second, heart lifting at sight of those rough big logs forced against the saws, being sliced into pristine lumber, he forgot his purpose here.

"This is it, Goldilocks," he said, tongue swimming in saliva. "This is what it's all about. All them pines growing, all them camps working— just for this. Planks. Board feet. They come in as raw logs and leave as something a farmer will pay money for. By God!"

Maybe she didn't hear him, in that clamorous place, and maybe she wouldn't have understood anyway. But it was a fine romantic vision he had in that moment, when in a flash he saw all his stumpage, all his camps, all his rivers with logs on the move, his mills, his retail yard: McSwasey & Zumwalt, growing, acquiring, expanding.

Then Elmer Olinick, head sawyer and foreman, turned and saw him there.

"Billy God in Jerusalem! If it ain't Caleb McSwasey!"

Lanky, black-haired, cheek full of chaw, he came wiping his hands on his pants.

Esperanza smiled prettily, but after the introduction, while Caleb explained how his wife would be the Olinicks' guest till he returned from the drive, he noticed that her interest had been snagged by the wide north door. Out there, three men had pike-poled a log from among its countless fellows in the boom pond, and with cant hooks were rolling it toward the mill. One man was Andy Gentry. And after the log had come grumbling in toward its rendezvous with building up the country, Esperanza lifted a hand and wiggled her pretty fingers. Andy responded like a trained dog.

He looked healthier, huskier, striding across the mill floor; Caleb stepped to meet him, hand outstretched.

"Glad to see you, son. You remember Mrs. McSwasey?"

Of course, certainly! And Esperanza said hello and gave him her hand, and her smile, and her eyes. Caleb was very hearty, and all smiles himself, but it was all he could do to keep from jumping astraddle the son of a bitch then and there.

The four of them went through the office into open air, where they could hear themselves think, and Elmer Olinick said Caleb had better stay till morning. He shook his head.

"I want to get to my drive. I'll be miles on my way by tonight."

Elmer lugged the portmanteau off toward his cabin, to tell his wife about their unexpected guest, and Caleb, leading the way to his canoe, told Andy his parents were fine and had sent love.

"Well, son," he said, shaking hands, "I'll be seeing you before long."

"Have a good trip," Andy said.

Caleb kissed his wife.

"Good-by, Goldilocks. Keep out of mischief."

He shoved off, into the swift blind power of the current from the dam; and he looked back, once. Esperanza didn't notice. He carried with him the memory of her hair in sunlight and her face in profile, smiling up at Andy.

*

Half a mile downstream he angled the canoe toward the east bank where a gap appeared in the willows and alders. That marked the mouth of Witch Creek, a placid stream no wider than a country lane, flowing from a chain of tamarack and cedar bogs off to the east. The canoe was light as a shadow, venturing into the creek, nosing softly upstream through the watercress and wild celery. Weeping willows leaned from the banks, their limber branches brushing Caleb as he paddled along, eyes alert against submerged sticks. Whirligig beetles fled before the canoe; underwater coontails waved languidly in its wake.

Fifty yards upstream he found what he was hunting: a meager sand beach on the north bank, with a deer trail leading away through the tall wool grass and joe-pye weeds. The canoe nosed softly into the beach and hung there in the apathetic current. Before landing, Caleb opened his possible sack and brought out doeskin moccasins. He put them on, stowed his shoes in the sack. Then he stepped ashore and dragged the canoe after him. In days to come, if anybody chanced on this place, no shoe tracks would tattle in the sand: only marks of a canoe and Injun moccasins. He had planned it all weeks ago, thinking of everything.

His watch showed three-thirty; he spread a blanket and settled to wait, chewing a cigar but not permitting himself the luxury of smoke. Chances were a million to one against his being detected here, except by the pee-wees chirping in the button bushes, and the dragonflies circling endlessly; but if anybody should happen along, say a stray Injun, he would instantly change his plans. He would return to the Whiskey River, punch a hole in his canoe, beach it, and walk back to the mill.

"Reckon I'll stay over night after all," he would say. "My canoe needs patching and I'm tired."

And Andy Gentry would enjoy a reprieve.

He stretched out on the blanket and dozed. But his ears were trusty sentinels. Beyond range of the thumping mill with its noisy dam, he lay at the bottom of vast silence, broken only by the usual wilderness sounds: a white-throat singing, the low music of a mourning dove, the subdued gurgling of the creek, an occasional fish splash. His ears discounted them and permitted him to sleep, lightly. Long years agone he had trained his ears. He could trust them, because they were part of him. That was what life boiled down to: you could trust yourself and nobody else. It was you against the universe. So you'd better be strong. Grab what you wanted and then guard it, ignoring the law in either operation, so far as possible. The law, he thought, dropping into deeper sleep, was only a conspiracy of the multitudinous weak against the strong. Against their betters, their superiors. Against the rare few in any generation who towered over the ruck-muck of ordinary men like a half-ton moose over pine mice.

The sun had set and mosquitoes were singing in the beginning of twilight when he came full awake, abruptly, and sprang to his feet. His ears had caught a sound on that path through the wool grass, and now he stood staring into the moist, naked muzzle of a buck deer, velveted antlers like sprouting twigs. The deer reared and whirled, bounding off along the path with a flirt of snowy tail. Caleb grinned, rubbed his jaw, stowed his blanket in the canoe and brought from his possible sack a thick woolen sock loaded with a rock the size of two eggs. He whirled the weighted sock, smacked it into his open palm.

Moonrise would come at nine tonight. Weeks ago, poring over an almanac in his office, he had debated the advantages of both full moon and black moon, and full moon won. More risk perhaps, but he hadn't favored floundering through brambly darkness, perhaps getting bogged in a marsh, on his getaway from the mill. Risks either way. At his age he reckoned he weighed risks more than he used to.

He waited a little longer, standing there by the creek, going over everything, and suddenly he sucked in his breath and thought, "By God!" In disgust he pulled off his hat and flung it into the canoe. A man was always apt to overlook something. Say he'd not thought of that hat and had worn it. Say there'd be a scuffle and it would be knocked off and he'd leave without it. Might hang him.

Moccasins. Rock in sock. Wallet and pencil and cigars and everything else from his pockets left in the canoe. Reckon he was ready. Dusk was deepening as he started along the path.

It twisted through the swampy grasses of the creek valley, then climbed dimly northwestward toward the higher ground along the bank of the Whiskey. Caleb moved along easily toward that higher land, cranberry bushes and witch hazel shrubs swishing past his shoulders. When he topped the low hill where pin cherries grew, and where birch and popple trees were slim ghosts, he stopped and took his bearings. Stars were coming alight, the Big Dipper pointing at Polaris and Polaris hanging over the North Star Mill. He moved on, hearing the crash of water at the dam. The woods smelled moist and fragrant. A few more minutes and the sound of the dam had increased to a roar; he wondered why rapid water always sounded louder at night. Then from another low hill he sighted the mill, a shadow black as Egypt, and he saw the lights of the three log cabins scattered to the east. Within pebble-toss, he could make out the shadowy stacks of drying lumber and smell their resinous wealth. He stood watching.

Nothing happened for a while. Then the door of the middle cabin opened and one of Francis Quinn's brats came out, hooting like a coyote and accompanied by a shepherd dog. They were dim shadows in the starlight. Then suddenly the dog began barking, as if it had caught a strange scent. It came rushing toward Caleb's hilltop, then stopped and retreated, then came closer. Caleb gripped his loaded sock but thought better of it; he stood motionless among scrubby jack pines. "Here, Shep, here Shep," the Quinn brat was yelling; but Shep came barking to within inches of Caleb's ankles.

"Go home, Shep," Caleb said quietly.

The barking stopped; tail-wagging began.

"Go home. Go home, Shep."

Now the brat was coming toward the hill, calling his dog. Caleb held his breath. And for a while Andy Gentry's life hung in counterpoise, till finally the dog went romping to his master and they both returned to the cabin and the scales swung against Andy. Caleb sighed. And he marveled at the intricacies of life, at the myriad casual encounters and trifling decisions that at every watch-tick altered the quicksilver flow of existence. Men you would never know, men on the other side of the earth perhaps, were by their ceaseless activity, or inactivity, shaping events that would come to pass next year in your life, or next decade. A half century ago a certain General von Zumwalt had made love to his *frau,* and tonight Caleb McSwasey stood watching under the stars and next week a certain Judge Gentry would look drained by grief.

On the eastern horizon, beyond a hill where spruce tips pointed toward the stars, peach-colored light was beginning to show, fanning out in soft luminosity, and as Caleb watched the moon peeked over the hill, ripe and corpulent and red-faced. Soaring free of the horizon, it sent light into the brambles, and Caleb sought the deepest shadows. Somewhere an owl hooted; off on a hill a fox barked. And a few minutes later the door of Elmer Olinick's cabin opened, and in that lighted doorway Caleb could distinguish two persons, Andy Gentry and Esperanza.

Despite the perpetual roar from the dam, he could hear her laugh floating through the evening, and he caught most of her words as she told the Olinicks she would return soon but if they were sleepy not to wait up for her: Andy had promised to show her the dam.

Caleb's face felt hot, his heart was laboring, as he watched Esperanza and Andy strolling through the moonlight, her arm linked in his. Once they paused; Esperanza threw back her head, as if breathing deep of the springtime fragrance, and gazed rapturously up into the sky magical with silvery-blue light. Andy put his arms around her but she broke away and went chasing toward the stacked lumber. Before she reached it he overtook her, and this time when he embraced her she did not run. They kissed.

Caleb stared, lips twisting, fists clenched, ears roaring, blood throbbing in a swollen vein at his temple. And when they moved on, into the shadows of the stacked lumber, where he could not see what was occurring, it was with the sheerest physical effort that he made himself stay hidden. Faint sickness, as if from tainted food, curled in his stomach and agitated his bowels; his blood seemed to have curdled; his lips and tongue were fever dry. Under his breath he kept emitting a constant slaver of invective; his nerve-ends tingled; muscles he had not realized he possessed kept twitching in his face; and he clutched that sock with the rock inside and ached to use it.

Then he saw Andy and Esperanza again, emerging from the stacks of lumber and going to the river. They stood on the bank, Andy's arm around her. Caleb could see their figures dim in the moonlit mists rising from the crashing water. At last they turned and drifted back toward the Olinick cabin, but they didn't go far. As if slowed to a halt by some elemental tug, they stopped at the door into the office of the mill, Esperanza leaning against the jamb. As Caleb watched, seeing her hair shining in the moonlight, glimpsing occasionally the flash of her teeth when she smiled, he fought an almost uncontrollable impulse to burst into tears, he who hadn't cried in forty years. Then his anger returned, pouring through his arteries, when he watched them disappear into the office of the mill, the door closing behind them.

He waited for a light to show on the office window. None showed.

He stood with shoulders heavy, jaw hanging, thinking of Andy's bunk. He wanted to go crashing through the underbrush to the office door; he would kick it open and smash his rock against Andy's skull, beating it to a mass of blood and bones. But he remained rooted there in the jack pine thicket, telling himself he must play it smooth, he must follow his carefully laid plans. And as the minutes passed and the moon climbed higher, a tremendous lassitude stole through his body; his legs trembled and chills poured along his spine; the sickness returned to his stomach. His fingers felt stiff and icy. My God, he kept muttering, my God.

It was happening. Nearly eight years since he had met her, nearly eight years of keeping her fenced in from sons of bitches. Maybe in some part of his being, even when he was most jealous, he had always nourished the hope that he was mistaken, that when the chips were down she would slap the face of any poaching bastard and say a light flirtation was one thing but kissing was another. Maybe he had hoped that at such a moment she would say sir, I'm a married woman and I love my husband; sir, never darken my door again; get the hell out, you son of a bitch.

"God damn it," Caleb muttered. "God damn it."

An Apache, Hod Kite had said. Those eyes. And a greaser. You'll never know where you're at.

In his stomach the sickness was whirling faster now, and at last he could resist it no longer; he bent, retching, but nothing came except swallowed spit and mucus, he hadn't eaten for so long; and while he retched his bowels moved slightly.

That snapped him out of it. A few minutes later, having attended to himself as best he could, using his woodsman's knowledge in such matters, he stood watching the mill again, jaw like the rock in the loaded sock, brain clear and cold.

The moon had climbed into midnight skies, the mist from the dam had thickened, when at last he saw the door open and two persons emerge from the office, pausing outside to kiss, then moving languorously, as if walking through a river of honey, toward the Olinick cabin. They stopped to kiss again. Caleb picked his way down the hillside, scrooching low, and darted into the ambush of the lumber stacks. He heard himself breathing hard as he reached the stacks nearest the mill and peered toward the Olinick cabin. Through the mist he could make out two figures embracing deeply. At last they moved on toward the cabin.

Caleb withdrew into his ambush, planning how he would step from hiding, when Andy returned to the office door, and swing the loaded sock against his skull.

A minute passed.

Lovers' kisses, Caleb thought.

Presently he peered toward the Olinick cabin again, and this time he

419

saw Andy coming through the mist alone. Caleb ducked back into the shadows of the stacked lumber. His fingers clutched the sock.

A footfall. Caleb went tense.

But instead of entering the mill, Andy swung on past. From ambush, Caleb saw him going deeper into the bright mist, toward the river, where he stopped, unbuttoned his pants and began to urinate.

Caleb drew a breath and plunged toward him, into the mist and the noise of crashing water.

*

Three days later Elmer Olinick, canoeing up the Chippewa, reached the drive. He brought bad news. Thursday morning Andy Gentry had turned up missing. Thursday afternoon searchers set forth. Not till Friday had they found his body, two miles down the Whiskey River, caught in a tangle of driftwood. In some odd fashion he must have fallen off the dam, struck his head on the boulders below, and drowned. Lucky his body had got mixed up with the driftwood, or they wouldn't have recovered it yet.

"My God," Caleb said, "that's terrible. How could he have fallen off the dam?"

Olinick shrugged.

"High water. Things happen."

"What about the body?" Caleb asked.

"The boys knocked together a coffin and packed it with ice and saw-dust. They're on the way to Flannigan's Landing to catch a steamboat. We kind of thought the judge would want him buried in New Empire."

Caleb sighed. "Be hard on the judge," he said. And he asked, "How is my wife?"

"Fair to middling. Upset, of course. She took on terrible at first. Guess we shouldn't have never let her see the corpse. You know how women are."

*

Two hundred and seventy-seven days later, Esperanza gave birth to a baby. A boy. He looked, strangely enough, like a tiny, red, wrinkled edition of Sophronicus Gentry.

420

VIII

CALEB PASSED the cigars, the day after Esperanza's baby was born, and set up drinks in Rafferty's Saloon, and accepted congratulations with good grace, quite as if he had been responsible; and when nice old ladies stopped him on the street, and asked if the news was true, that the stork had visited McSwasey's Island, he never once said: "Not the stork—the cuckoo." And when, in the government land office, the deputy register—who with that special talent of impecunious men had fathered eight—said that children were a great blessing, Caleb handed him a cigar wrapped in a fifty-dollar bill, and only a low-minded, suspicious, objective observer could have deduced that the fifty was a bribe for future favors.

By then it was February, 1849, and McSwasey & Zumwalt had moved into its new offices in a fine brick building, two stories high, down at the northeast corner of Front and Chicory Streets, a block north of Rafferty's Saloon. Caleb had built it the summer before, on ground occupied by his retail yard. The first floor was given over to retail business, and the second to the larger and ever-growing affairs of the parent company. From the north and east windows of his private office, Caleb could look out over the yard with its stacks of pine boards and shingles, and from the west window he could look beyond Front Street to the river that had carried the rafted lumber from the North Star Mill.

Those were views he enjoyed more than the courthouse cupola, although really he had nothing to fret about, so far as courts were concerned, because nobody, not even Esperanza, suspected that Andy had been beaten over the head and thrown into the Whiskey River. He had planned Andy's death as successfully as he had planned his own life. His thoughts seldom returned to that May evening up on the Whiskey, except when he saw his son, who certainly looked remarkably like Judge Gentry, save for his blond hair, or when he encountered the judge himself. But that didn't happen much these days, since McSwasey & Zumwalt no longer headquartered in the Gentry Block. And even when he met Sophronicus on the street he hardly recognized him, the judge had aged so much: a gaunt old scarecrow with a hickory cane. He wasn't an old man, either; only fifty-nine; but he had been harrowed by grief, and by the election of a Whig general to the White House.

During the past months McSwasey & Zumwalt had acquired more retail yards, in river towns, and it was dickering for yet others; so what with all the reports pouring into company headquarters, from the yards, from sawmills, from raft pilots, from logging camps, Caleb really had need of the clerks who sat in the outer office, perched like drab sparrows on high stools at sloping desks, neat, careful, meek men, grateful to peck away their lives under the aegis of an empire builder.

While a necessary measure, and one he never regretted, murdering Andy Gentry did not really promote Caleb's domestic tranquility as much as one might have expected, probably because of what Andy had left Esperanza to remember him by. As this souvenir of friendship and spring-time became more apparent, Caleb's jealousy raged in secret, and during Esperanza's pregnancy he formed the habit of returning to his office in the evening, where he would sit blowing cigar smoke at the green-shaded lamp, scheming new coups and conquests. On his desk, serving as paper-weight, sat a rock about the size of two eggs, and when his jealousy seethed he used to calm himself by fingering that rock. And if this was tinged with morbidity, he didn't consider it so, any more than does a nation when it hauls the artillery which has murdered its enemies into places of honor around the statues of its dead heroes.

On the night when Esperanza's baby was born, in the bedroom of the master's suite, Caleb slept soundly across the hall. If the child had been his, he might have paced and lost valuable sleep, but as it was he felt the whole affair was Esperanza's problem. Unreasonably, she resented his attitude, so while the child, with excellent judgment, fought against ven-turing into a dubious world, Esperanza yelled louder than necessary, in the hope of disturbing her husband's repose, but all she accomplished was to make the nurse, Lilith, exceedingly happy, and to worry poor fumbling old Doc Washburn. He had begun his career as a veterinarian's assistant back east, interning in a barn, but now he was as fine a physician as could be found in Wisconsin, and like all members of his profession a splendid conservative, pretty skeptical of the theories propounded by that man Harvey.

Caleb considered that naming the child, like bearing it, was wholly Esperanza's affair; his only request was that it not be called Caleb. That, certainly, had been the furthest from her intentions; she wanted to call the boy Andrew, but she didn't dare, quite. So at last she settled on Heinrich von Zumwalt McSwasey, honoring her grandfather, of whose valor at the Battle of Jena she was growing prouder all the time.

When Otto, months later, learned that a son had been born to his daughter and his best friend, and named after the general, he replied with a rapturous letter, saying many fine things about friendship, and about Americans as well, who had at last come to their senses and elected a general president, and who were imposing some wonderfully efficient taxes on Santa Fe, and keeping troops there. He would, he said, enjoy meeting his grandson, and if *Herr* General President Taylor discharged his duties honorably, and slaughtered all the cowardly Comanches, perhaps some day he would visit Wisconsin. Not, of course, that he would let the Comanches prevent his making such a visit, but just now he was very busy with his store.

By the time Otto's letter arrived, Esperanza was less interested in Heinrich von Zumwalt McSwasey than in another male, a fellow named Jim Buckmaster. And Caleb was much less jealous of Heinrich than of Jim, although nobody would have suspected him jealous of either.

*

She had grieved for Andy about as long as she had grieved for Gilberto Archuleta, who, for all his carelessness, had been in the final analysis the less careless of the two. Other similar qualities linked Gilberto and Andy in her memory: neither lad, for instance, would have been tolerated for one minute in a French novel. Time and again, when Andy called at McSwasey's Island, she had invented opportunities with a fertility of imagination which would have brought a French author urgent invitations to join the Academy, but Andy, the deadhead, only went on talking about that dirty little Inez Hinojo. Inez, Esperanza thought privately, had been no better than necessary, and was well off dead.

She was bitterly offended when Andy took off for the North Star Mill without so much as a good-by kiss, and although ordinarily her opinion of her charm and beauty was high, his abrupt departure jolted her as much as she thought it jilted her, and during that cold, dull winter she used to stare at herself in the glass and wonder why Parisian women were forever enjoying flirtations at the Opera and clandestine meetings at the Champ de Mars races, while she, a general's granddaughter, found herself manacled to a jealous, lecherous old man.

Not that she objected to his lechery or his age; it was his jealousy, so unreasonable, so Un-Parisian, that ruined their marriage. She was even fond of him, in her fashion, and the only reason she ever fought off his caresses was because like all Apache and Prussian women she enjoyed being conquered. But by more than one sweet enemy! Heavens, the way things were going she might live out her years without ever being in love.

She had not, she realized, actually loved Gilberto; only a girlish infatuation; and after she recovered from the shock of Andy's death, and from the tremendous cost of their evening in the mill office, she was forced to admit that she had never loved him. He was too—well—juvenile, tentative, unsure of himself; too polite and considerate; too gentlemanly, actually. In a drawing room gentlemanly behavior had merits, but not in a mill office. What woman wanted a man to ask whether he might kiss her? Well, perhaps some women; but as for her, she wanted a man who would take what he wanted when he wanted it. Caleb was like that, and it was, of course, his tremendous virtue; but she was used to Caleb, he was her husband for goodness sake, he had grabbed her young before she had found much opportunity to experiment with her power, his jealousy had kept other men at bay, and by no stretch of fancy could she ever love Caleb.

Love. Her thoughts were forever flitting around that scented word. Love. It must be wonderful, the real thing, because the counterfeit was splendid enough. Love. Sometimes she whispered the word, gazing at herself in the mirror. And on gloomy, headachy days, curled on the chaise before the fire in the upstairs sitting room, she used to fear she would never know it, except at second hand in books.

*

She found little Heinrich dull company, his vocabulary limited to "Goo" and "Waaaa," his personal habits less gentlemanly than his father's; so she was delighted to farm him out into Lilith's care. Lilith also enjoyed this arrangement; not since Wisdom had she possessed a male baby all her own; and Lilith liked males. Moreover, having fallen into the common error of assuming that a child has inherited the chromosomes of the man whose surname it bears, Lilith thought herself privileged to wait upon a son of Mistah McSwasey.

And so it was that after the baby came, Lilith turned over all kitchen duties to the Scandinavian girls and devoted her working hours to Heinrich, singing the Virginia lullabies she had learned from her own mother as she rocked him to sleep. One thing, it was a sitting-down job, advantageous to a woman whose weight kept increasing and whose feet gave trouble; and when Heinrich slept in his bassinet, Lilith could doze in her chair; so, like an executive advanced from seventh to sixth vice-president, she felt she had been promoted and that without her indispensable services all would go to pot.

Free from the cares of motherhood, Esperanza was eager to try it again; and in late winter, on thawing afternoons, she would dress herself in the latest fripperies and fal-lals, figure mature but not too mature, face so striking that people thought it beautiful, and with Dexter driving she would ride from the island to town in one of the family's handsome carriages. Always she felt, like all hunters, keyed-up and expectant, stepping into the carriage; and as she sat on the morocco upholstery, ears and throat bejeweled, fingers smoothly gloved in the finest kid, head ornamented in a wide-brimmed hat of black velvet, luscious with ribbons, she looked aristocratic and yet dashing, ready for anything, like some faintly déclassée marquise from Balzac.

Often the carriage paused at the lumber yard and Esperanza swept into the retail office, moving quickly—but not too quickly for a glance at the men, clodhoppers mainly—up the stairs to the counting room of McSwasey & Zumwalt, her swishing femininity bringing glamour to that workaday place. Heads of clerks snapped around to a man: if mental rape had been a crime, Caleb would have lost his whole force to the sheriff.

Poised and queenly, she waited at the counter while some man in sleeve protectors slid from a stool and came smiling.

"Is Mr. McSwasey in?" she asked, her voice not unfriendly but still reserved, for she didn't want word to travel that she would enjoy sleeping with anything in pants: that was a damned lie.

"One moment, Mrs. McSwasey."

And the clerk would hurry to Caleb's door, rap discreetly, and announce, although not in so many words, that the most delicious armful in Wisconsin awaited audience. And upon returning he would flourish open the gate and bow, nostrils blissful with her perfume and seductive powders, eyes popping as he drank in the slow, rhythmical flow of her skirt, swishing from left to right, right to left, in the popular mating nautch of certain semi-civilized peoples dwelling along the Mississippi River in North America.

She found Caleb at his desk, involved with reports from his landlookers, or at the mahogany table in the center of the room, thumbing through stacks of enormous maps showing sections of pine lands, or at the great colored map of Wisconsin dominating the wall. Usually a cigar was cocked up from his mouth, like an exclamation point emphasizing the power in his pugnacious face; his hair was mussed; and his thick hands that had quelled so many refractory mules and niggers, that had swept in so many winnings, looked too rough-tough for the starched cuffs encircling his heavy wrists, just as his whole body looked too muscular and charged with violent energy to be contained within the punctilio of his business leader's suit, with its finely-tailored gray coat and trousers, its flowered satin vest.

"Hello, Goldilocks. What's on your mind?"

"I just stopped by. I'm going shopping."

"Need money?"

She shook her head, smiling, and kissed the lobe of his ear, the gray tufted hairs tickling her nose.

He softened slightly.

"When you need it," he said, smiling, "come to McSwasey & Zumwalt. We grow it on trees."

"You work so hard," she said.

"Honeychild," he said, puffing his cigar and staring at the wall-map, "we're getting rich. By God, sometimes it even surprises me."

"You're wonderful."

Their gazes met, and she was aware of a quality she had observed in his eyes the past year: a cold, blue, appraising quality, sharply skeptical. It made her uneasy. But he couldn't have known about her affair with Andy. How could he? He had left her at the mill, up there on the Whiskey River, and had hurried on to the log drive. It was that evening when Andy fell off the dam. Not even a husband as jealous as Caleb could have imagined that events had happened so swiftly. He didn't know about the letters she had exchanged with Andy, or about Andy's visits to the island. Unless Lilith had tattled. But obviously Lilith hadn't, because if she had, Caleb would have forbidden Andy the house.

"How's Heinrich?" Caleb asked.

"He was napping when I left."

"He's a sober baby. Looks just like a little judge."

Her heart stopped, although not permanently.

"You think so?" she said.

"Hadn't you noticed?"

"Noticed what?"

"How sober he is."

"Oh. Yes. He's a good baby."

Relief swept her. She too had observed Heinrich's resemblance to Sophronicus, and while she was prepared to maintain that such resemblance was purely coincidental and accidental, still it was a subject she preferred to avoid.

"You're busy," she said. "I'll run along."

She kissed him lightly.

"By God, honeychild, you're a handful. Keep out of mischief."

From the door she blew him a kiss. But as she swept through the counting room she was frowning. She had come to the office and told him her shopping plans because she had learned he was happier that way, less inclined to suspect her of a tryst than if he heard from Dexter or some acquaintance that she had been out shopping. Once, early in marriage, she would have defied him. But she had learned; she too had grown careful. Especially since Heinrich's birth. She had never forgotten his long-ago threat to firebrand her face. She thought he might do it, if he took the notion. A resolute man. And what troubled her now was his saying Heinrich looked like a little judge.

And yet, in the carriage again, she dismissed that worry. Her sense of adventure returned. Perhaps on this shopping tour she would meet a man. She liked to play with firebrands.

*

But she didn't meet a man; at least not a Man. Figures from French literature were uncommonly scarce in New Empire. At this time of year, with the pinery boys off in the woods, even bachelors were scarce. Not that she would have given a pinery boy a second look. Well, at least not a third look. The man she was hunting would be polished, urbane, witty, wise, the glass of fashion, rich, and probably the bravest man in the world. He would have to be, to stand up to Caleb and tell him he was snatching his wife.

In her endless daydreams she pictured that scene, Caleb furious and the Man drawing a rapier and running him through. *Ja,* right through the belly button. Who had said that? Well, anyway, run him through. And Caleb would die and the Man would sweep her into his arms and they would take flight, two cloaked figures riding fast horses through a night of windy moonlight and witch clouds. The daydream became hazy about there, but it ended happily in world capitals with luxury and champagne and balls and the honeyed music of fiddles and other Men, Men, Men.

Esperanza sighed, standing at a counter in Durham & Co., Gen'l Mdse., fingering a bolt of silk, while old Mr. Durham asked if she thought it would do. She didn't think so. She had not expected to find any suitable dress goods at Durham & Co. A shopping expedition was only a subterfuge for hunting, the way a man's hunting expedition is often only a pretext for poker. She preferred shopping in St. Louis, and she would have preferred hunting there too, where game was more abundant, if only Caleb on their trips together hadn't kept her under such close scrutiny. Eight years married and he guarded her like a bride.

She left Durham & Co., drifting along Winnebago Street, casting a quick glance into a barber shop, entering a drugstore for a glass of soda water; no Men; only men; New Empire was dull in winter, with the river locked in ice. Sometimes the younger married set organized skating parties in the evenings, with light from bonfires flickering where pretty wives skated arm-in-arm with other husbands. She would have enjoyed that, gliding off into the shadows for harmless kisses. But the younger married set never invited the McSwaseys to skating parties or any parties; Caleb was too old for the younger married set. He would have refused such invitations anyway.

The afternoon was wearing away; she returned to her carriage. As it wheeled back toward the island, her eyes were black and flat and dispirited, staring out at the snow, cold violet in shadow, warmly primrose where great shafts of light struck across it from the lowering sun. The air was frigid when the carriage crossed the bridge to the island and moved among the bare trees. Another day nearly gone; she was twenty-three; her best years slipping away; if she tried to leave him he would follow, perhaps with a firebrand, and drag her back. He would live forever; he was indestructible; all he thought about was keeping her prisoner and piling up money to buy more stumpage which would bring more money.

*

March came with its gusts and rare quiet days when the warm sun coaxed the skunk cabbage into flower and brought tentative croaks from intrepid frogs. Then a two-day blizzard. Then a thaw with rivulets everywhere. Then cold wind with the frozen slush crunchy. March was a blow-hard fat man guffing endlessly about a lovely girl named April coming from the South.

But what was spring to Esperanza? By mid-March she had given up. Days passed without her venturing forth to seek adventure. Spring could break your heart. Spring could send you to the enormous walnut bookcase in the lower hall, to finger volumes by Keats and Byron and the Shakespeare of the Sonnets. Spring was Lilith calling that little Heinrich was breast-hungry. Spring was one of the Scandinavian maids announcing she was quitting to get married but she had a friend Olga who would like the job.

Esperanza saw her first robin on the morning of Tuesday, March 20. That was a day and date she always remembered, although not because of the robin. The day began windless and bright, with Ferdinand Vogler raking dead leaves from the flower beds and all but saluting the real, live granddaughter of a general gloriously wounded at the Battle of Jena. She paused to talk with him, there in the garden by the dry fountain, mentioning her father who lived in Santa Fe and had slain so many Comanches. Ferdinand had never slain a Comanche, but he recounted bravely how he had emptied a shotgun into the pants of some juvenile delinquents raiding his watermelon patch last September. *Ja,* and the cowards never returned. He was also a terror to mice and aphis. As Ferdinand and Esperanza exchanged these tales of valor it sounded as if they were gargling sore throats, but this was only because they were employing the native—although not the favorite—language of Frederick the Great.

She wandered on, following the brick path west to the river. Ice still choked it; soft, rotten-looking ice. Soon the steamboats would return, coming from the South like the spring. The air this morning was as sweet and warm as a lover's breath. She thought idly of Gilberto Archuleta, wondering if he had safely negotiated the round trip between Santa Fe and Mexico. She thought of Andy Gentry, beyond reach of the sun in the graveyard east of town. Some day she too would lie in the earth where the sun would never find her. A handful of sweet spring mornings and then the dark. She felt big with *Weltschmerz.*

By early afternoon, March being March, the wind came frolicking from the west, bringing a froth of clouds; and in the garden all Ferdinand Vogler's neatly-piled leaves went scurrying along the paths, whirling like dogs chasing their tails. Esperanza lounged on the chaise in the upstairs sitting room till she finished a novel; then, like Lilith and Heinrich, she slept. It was three when she came awake and heard March whistling under the eaves; Lilith was snoring. Esperanza stared at her, there by the bassinet, sprawled in an armchair, head lolling. Once she would have jabbed her with a needle or a cigarette. She would have enjoyed doing that today. But Lilith had grown very brawny, very uppity; and Caleb, unlike Otto, sided with Lilith.

428

Esperanza stood up, glimpsing herself in the mirror. Hair mussed, wearing an old black wool dress, she thought she looked a sight. It didn't matter. She went downstairs to find another book.

Even with the highly experimental central heating Sophronicus had specified in his architect's plans, the downstairs was chilly, what with the wind trying to get in and Dexter Yarlow's forgetfulness about furnace chores. Caleb ought to whip him. But he was free. Wisconsin was a mad place, expecting niggers to behave themselves without whipping. Last May it had entered the Union as the thirtieth state, free of course. Sophronicus had been much excited about its statehood, till Andy departed from the Union.

Esperanza was at the hall bookcase when the doorbell pealed. She kept fingering books; the bell pealed again. Really! Five servants and nobody to answer doors. Caleb should whip them all. She flounced into the vestibule and yanked open the door.

A man stood there.

And she looked a sight!

A man. Maybe even a Man. Her heart was pounding.

His long legs were clad in snug black pants; lean boots, with gray German socks showing at the tops, reached nearly to his knees. His Mackinaw was bright-checked in red and black, thrown open to show a woolen shirt, checked in blue. He wore a muskrat cap with a jaunty tail dangling.

"You're Mrs. McSwasey," he said.

She nodded, staring up at his Injun-colored face.

"I'm Jim Buckmaster. Met you years ago at Camp One. Where's your husband?"

"Have you been to his office?"

He snapped his fingers.

"By golly! Never thought of that!" Then his mouth and gray eyes were humorous. "They told me," he said, "they didn't know where he was. He'd stepped out. So I thought I'd try here."

"Come in," she said.

In the hall he took off his cap; his hair, thick and mussed, looked black as shoe blacking.

"I don't know where he is," she said. "Maybe he'll be along. Maybe you should wait."

He stood with boots apart, lips pursed, eyes thoughtful.

"Might be in a saloon, I reckon," he said. "No, I'd best not wait. I'll scare him up somewhere."

"Is it important?" she asked.

He had turned and reached the vestibule; now he stopped, humor in his eyes.

"I don't know as I'd go so far as to name it important," he drawled, voice soft. "I'm foreman at Camp Seven. I left there yesterday morning and footed it to the Falls of the Chippewa. Hired me a team and cutter and drove down the Chippewa on the ice. One horse was spavined and the other had the heaves. Hired me another team at Read's Landing. Got me a bite of supper there too, though I can't figure what came over me to be so hungry—it wasn't long past midnight. It's cold up there and the sledding's good, so I started down the Mississippi on the ice. But this morning, eight miles north of here, I had a little accident. Remember that piece of river where the *Nellie McGurkin* blew her boilers last June? No, guess you wouldn't. Anyway, the ice turned soft there, and the horses drownded themselves and the cutter. I hadn't had a bath since my birthday in July, so I guess it was all right. Thought I might have to swim on down here under the ice, but I managed to climb out. I built me a couple of fires and thawed out between them, though I hated to waste the time. Got here an hour ago and went straight to the land office. Took up three thousand acres of stumpage for McSwasey & Zumwalt, but I couldn't pay for it. The monkey at the land office promised to hold it till six tonight, so it might be as well to locate your husband—there's an outfit in Quickwater wants that same stumpage. Not, you understand, that it's important, but your husband might think so."

He was smiling when he opened the door and went striding across the porch.

Esperanza flew after him.

"Did you really fall in the river?" she called.

He was in the driveway by then; he stopped.

"Why, no, lady," he said, smiling, "I've been on a drunk and dreamed up the whole thing."

She stood with the wind blowing her skirt, watching his long legs eating up the yards toward town; he went swinging along with the loose-jointed, ground-covering stride of a woodsman. He didn't look back.

*

She shivered suddenly, from the wind, and plodded back into the house, moving along the hall to the bookcase and standing there uncertainly, not wanting to read now, feeling as restless as the wind, as rudderless as the blowing leaves. He had said he remembered meeting her at Camp One. She remembered too. That had been long ago when she was hardly more than a bride; she hadn't thought of him in years. But she would think of him often from this day forward; already she realized that.

She wandered into the front drawing room, pacing slowly and aimlessly, coming at last to a halt beneath the imposing chandelier of Waterford crystal. Pressing her flushed cheeks, the tips of her fingers felt cold. She turned, dully, and dragged across the thick-piled carpet to the huge mirror between the front windows, staring at her mussed hair, her black Apache eyes, her figure unflattered by the old wool dress.

Remembering all the afternoons she had togged herself out in her finest. All those fruitless trips to town. Always the same men. And today she had napped in her clothes and looked it. Frowsy. Arrgh! She stamped a foot and whirled, wanting to seize one of the dragon vases and hurl it at the mirror.

She didn't, but her anger sent her pacing again, and she upbraided herself for not detaining him here at any cost. But how? He wasn't like the clerks in the counting room, those pallid men kowtowing to Caleb McSwasey's wife. If she had ordered him to wait while she sent somebody searching for Caleb he would have laughed at her. He had anyway, really. Lady, his attitude had been, you're a kind of simple little piece. You're just delaying matters, lady, with your silly questions. It's a man's world, lady, big things are stirring, out of my way, lady, leave hold of me.

He hadn't even looked back; by now he had forgotten her, probably.

She sank to the rosewood sofa and cried, lying with fists clenched, thinking her life was a hash. She had everything and she had nothing. Her grandfather had been a general but she bungled everything she did. As a girl she had been cornered into killing a man but he wouldn't stay dead; he came back to haunt her dreams. Once—oh, ghastly memory!— she had seen him in broad daylight. And she had married a man who kept her in subjection. When she gave birth to a boy he looked like her lover's father. She couldn't do anything right.

Her tears ceased but she kept lying there, flaccid, her spirits plumbing fathomless nadirs. Even the daydreams she had enjoyed seemed stale now. Who wanted a polished, oily, courteous lover? No better than a dancing master! Who wanted a foppish, glass-of-fashion lover? Popinjays! She heaved a long breath, thinking of cold swift rivers in the North, of blue lakes among dark pines, and of a canoe dreaming across those waters with a girl in the bow and a lean man with an Injun-colored face dipping the paddle. Night would overtake them deep in the wilderness; she would gather wood for a fire, cedar for a bed, and she would cook supper while he lounged with a pipe. If the coffee was too bitter he would give her a backhanded clout alongside the jaw, to learn her to do better. They would sleep under the crackling stars; she would curl against him and feel the sinewy tendons of his long legs. She would be up before dawn and have bacon sizzling before he stirred. Then they would take off again in the canoe, threading through chains of undiscovered lakes, deeper into wilderness uncharted. Somewhere he would build a cabin, swinging an ax with herculean accuracy, and when she bore him a son the child would not look like some chess-playing judge; it would look like its father, sleeping in its cradle-board of embroidered bead-work, warmed by mosses and cattail down.

But she had a husband already, and a son.

At last, eyes swollen, face astringent with the dried salt of her tears, she pushed herself up from the sofa and climbed the stairs. Lilith was awake now; Heinrich was crying.

" 'Bout time," Lilith said. "This here young one's hungry."

Esperanza took her son, sat listlessly on the chaise, gave him her breast.

"Your eyes look like you been crying," Lilith said.

Esperanza stared at the floor.

"Why you been crying?"

"A man was here," Esperanza said quietly.

"Man? What man?"

Esperanza hesitated; the fire crackled; Heinrich made contented sucking noises.

"Why that man come here and make you cry?"

Esperanza stared at Lilith, remembering her excellent counsel long ago in Santa Fe. Could she be trusted? Had she tattled about Andy's visits? If she had, wouldn't Caleb have ordered Andy to stay away?

"What's the matter with you, Miss Esperanza? You act like you been brained with a club."

She stared down at her son, drawing life from warm secret springs of her being.

"Something has happened," she said.

"What has done happened? They ain't arrested Dexter? He told me he give up stealing long ago."

"To me," Esperanza said. "Something has happened to me. I never felt like this before. I think—I think I'm in love."

*

Dusk had fallen but the wind still blew when the rig halted in the driveway and the nigger man opened the door. Jim stepped from the carriage and stood looking at the house.

"Captain," he told McSwasey, "you've got a nice little place here. When you're ready to sell, let me know."

But he felt kind of uneasy, entering that house; he would have preferred eating supper at the lodging house where he was putting up, and then early to bed. He hadn't slept since night before last, and he had covered a good bit of ground the last two days; he was beginning to feel tired. But McSwasey was pleased as a bear in a honey tree, beating the Quickwater Log & Lumber Company to that stumpage, and he had insisted that Jim come home with him to supper. "I want to talk with you," he had said.

Well, Jim wanted to talk with him too. After what he had done for McSwasey, the least McSwasey could do in return was set him to work piloting a raft. Logging was all right, but piloting a raft was what he had been aiming for. So had a lot of other roosters. Only difference was, when he aimed for something he got it.

But hell on wheels, he wasn't in no shape to go eating fancy at Mc-

Swasey's, wearing boots and a checked shirt, face unshaved since night before last. He'd never put his feet under a table in a house that fine, and he had a depressing premonition that there'd be more forks and spoons than a man would know what to do with. He'd about as soon go through a hole in the ice again, and drown a good team, as to grub with the McSwaseys.

In the vestibule, McSwasey took his cap and Mackinaw and hung them up, waiting on him like a nigger, and Jim knew then that he sure as hell must be mighty pleased to get that stumpage. A big push like McSwasey didn't go around waiting on his hired help every day.

"Come on in," McSwasey said. "Want a drink?"

"Captain," Jim said, "me and you talk the same language."

McSwasey yanked a rope of twisted red velvet, with a gold tassel at the end, and from somewhere deep in the house Jim thought he heard a bell tinkle. A minute later a yellow-headed Swedish girl, dressed in black with a white apron and about half a white nightcap, appeared in the hall.

"Lena," McSwasey said, "Mr. Buckmaster and I will have whiskey in the back parlor."

Jim stood there in the hall, smiling, thumb and forefinger cupped around his jaw.

"Captain," he said, "that's real neat. Yank a rope and you've got you a gal. *And* whiskey. By God, Captain, I like that."

McSwasey explained about the wires strung through the walls, with bells in the kitchen, while he led the way toward the back drawing room. And Jim knew then he was going to see some real sights tonight in this mansion. Just yank a rope. Slicker than an otter slide!

The hall was wide and long, with a high ceiling, but just the same Jim felt sort of too big and awkward for the place, fearful that if he moved real sudden he might knock over statuary, or that he might forget himself and stretch and send a chandelier crashing. He knew now how an antlered moose must feel, getting through a jack-pine thicket. But he negotiated the hall without mishap and stepped into the back drawing room, where he stood smiling, looking things over.

"Say," he said, "this is all right. This beats a bunkhouse in a logging camp."

"Jim," McSwasey said, "ten to one there ain't a fancy house could touch it."

"Captain," Jim said, "you win that pot."

"Leastwise," McSwasey said, "not this side of New Orleans."

Jim couldn't deliver no judgments on that; he'd never been in New Orleans. And the houses he'd known in logging towns, and even in St. Louis, had been ramshackle things, catch-penny traps baited for river hogs.

He looked around the room, papered in sunny gold, carpeted in thick

433

leaf-brown with a tapestry pattern of yellow roses. From the chandelier dangled crystal pendants shaped like clusters of grapes; grapevines were chiseled in the white marble fireplace. Must have cost a lot of sawlogs to furnish such a room.

"Luck," McSwasey said, after a tray had been set on a rosewood table inlaid with lime and pear wood. And he added, "Sit down, Jim."

Jim eased himself down real gentle, onto the gold brocatelle sofa.

"It will hold you," McSwasey said.

Jim smiled, and he felt more at ease once the whiskey warmed his stomach; it was the one familiar thing in all the room's unfamiliarity.

"Captain," he said, "that there is good whiskey."

"Should be," McSwasey said, "for what it cost. Have another."

"I don't care if I do," Jim said.

McSwasey refilled his glass, waiting on him again. Like he was President Taylor, or somebody. Getting that stumpage sure must have meant a lot to McSwasey, that he'd start waiting on a man hand and foot.

"It's none of my business, Captain," Jim said, "but who are those roosters?"

He pointed to the north wall where, on two waist-high pillars of blue marble, rescued from Pompeii, sat marble busts of Julius Caesar and Claudius.

"Damned if I know," McSwasey said.

"Thought they might be friends of yours."

"Friends of Sophronicus Gentry, I reckon," McSwasey said.

Jim settled his shoulders back against the sofa; it was real comfortable, and stronger than it looked. He accepted another drink. And he felt as easy now as in a saloon.

"You know," he said, "I'm going to have me a place like this some day."

"Might as well," McSwasey said.

Jim pointed at the south wall where an engraving, heavily-framed in gilt, showed a Christian fighting a lion in the Roman colosseum.

"What's that rooster up to?" he asked.

"God damn it, Jim," McSwasey said, "that's from the Bible. That's Daniel in the lion's den."

Jim fingered his jaw.

"Must have been a pretty good man, to tackle a lion."

"He had the Lord on his side," McSwasey said.

"That would help," Jim said.

He was working on his fourth drink, and feeling a little drowsy, he'd lost so much sleep, when a swish of skirts sounded from the hall and McSwasey's wife came into the room. McSwasey stood up; he was active as a squirrel tonight. Jim stayed where he was.

"You know my wife."

"Evening, lady," Jim said.

Mrs. McSwasey said hello, she was glad to see him again, glad he could come for supper.

"I hope it won't put you to no trouble, lady," Jim said.

*

He was sure glad he'd been fortified with whiskey, once he was sitting at the supper table, for just as he'd expected there were enough knives, forks and spoons to outfit a jobber's camp. He sat on the east side of the table, with McSwasey at the north end and his wife on the south, with the chandelier blazing overhead and those Swede girls building up to a lot of kitchen work, the way they gave a man a new plate every time he so much as chewed a mouthful.

He was hungry tonight, like always, and he lit into that food, uneasy lest those hired girls grab away his plate before he was finished. At first he figured on watching the McSwaseys, and following their lead in using the table hardware, but when he tried that he found he wasn't getting the victuals into his system with any regularity. So he thought the hell with it—if a man didn't sit at a table to eat then what did he sit there for?—and he ignored all those silver forks and different knives: he just picked one good efficient knife and one good spoon and started logging with them.

He'd always let wine strictly alone, himself. Way he figured, you stick with whiskey and you had solid footing. Drink it neat or with branch water, you knew where you were at. He liked to know where he was at, in a saloon or in the woods.

But he drank wine tonight. Couldn't very handily get out of it, for McSwasey seemed very proud of the bottle, saying it was Burgundy imported from France. But McSwasey forgot his manners that one time, after he pulled the cork: he started filling his own glass first. Then he caught himself and remembered his company manners, for with his glass only a third full he handed the bottle to the hired girl and she filled Mrs. McSwasey's glass, and Jim's, and then finished filling McSwasey's.

"Ooo, it's a lovely bouquet," Mrs. McSwasey said, sniffing her glass; but Jim didn't see any flowers. Wouldn't have been room for any on her dress, it was cut so low. He figured the Missus must have had one snifter too many, there in the parlor, to be talking about bouquets.

McSwasey said yes, and its body was just right. Give it a try, Jim. So Jim tossed his down. And he said:

"Why, yes, it's all right. Usual thing, I like a tanglefoot with a little more burn, but this here's all right."

But he was just being polite. For all he cared, the French could keep their wine to home.

The roast and the baked potatoes were very tasty, but he'd have enjoyed that meal more if the McSwaseys had let a man eat in peace, if they hadn't kept asking questions. If Mike Hogan had been here with all that talk at the table, he'd have batted somebody. Jim ate, answering yes and no, and of course he finished first, so while waiting for dessert he told them what they wanted to know, although McSwasey had heard the story before, and his wife part of it.

Camp Number Seven, he said, where he was foreman, was located on the north side of the Medicine River up in the Chippewa Valley. The Medicine River flowed into the Chippewa from the west.

"Here's how it is, lady," he told Esperanza, marking knife-lines on the tablecloth. "Your husband owns a hundred-and-sixty acres of prime white pine right here. We built us our camp on that, about five miles west of the Chippewa. Everything around us is government land, with pine that will stump out at about seventeen thousand feet to the acre. I've cruised all that congress land, and you wouldn't want a better logging chance. The Medicine River flows through Mud Hen Lake, away back here, and that means we're sure of a good head of water on the Medicine to float out our cut.

"Way I figure, it will take four or five years to clean all the pine out of the Medicine River drainage. Some of them trees stand two hundred feet tall, and they'll run four-and-a-half feet through. None of them is shaky, and you won't find a hollow-gutted stick in the lot. So we've got years of good logging ahead of us on that land. And the quarter-section the company owns is a real talking point, if Washington City ever wants to make trouble."

McSwasey said:

"Washington City won't. I know a congressman."

"There you are," Jim said. "She's all ours. We can cut clear on west of Mud Hen Lake and boom our logs there, after another year or so. The company will walk out of there with its fists full of dollars, before the last of that pine is cut.

"All right, lady, there's the layout. But now let's go east from Camp Seven. It's five miles to the Chippewa, as a pickerel would swim it down the Medicine, but the stumpage on east don't add up to much. Some white pine, but she's scattered. It's mainly hemlock and spruce and jack pine, nothing worth sawing. And as you come nearer the Chippewa, you run into cranberry marshes and swamps. Add it all up and it don't amount to as much as two Norwegians in a skiff. The good pine don't begin till you get back where we located our camp.

"Down here," Jim said, pointing with the knife, "is where the Medicine empties into the Chippewa. And a half-mile north, on the west side of the Chippewa, a friend of mine runs a sort of place. Her name is Molly Fitzpatrick and she runs a sort of tavern."

"It's a fancy house," McSwasey told his wife. "It's called the White Water House, and Molly Fitzpatrick is a whore."

"Well now, Captain," Jim said slowly, "maybe she is, at that. Anyhow, anybody who is up in that country is going to stop in for a drink and a meal. She's a fine woman and she runs a square place. What I mean, there's no slugging. She may clean the boys, but nobody cracks the back of your skull. I've known Molly since I was a kid in Quickwater. She used to hold me on her lap. She was a fine woman then, before her husband was killed. Hell, she's still a fine woman. She's done what she had to, like all of us, I reckon.

"Well, lady, you'd never guess what happened at three o'clock yesterday morning. Somebody began pounding our bunkhouse door, and it was Molly. She'd walked all the way to camp from the White Water House to tell me a piece of news, which shows you the kind of friend she is.

"Now you take a woman from the average quail roost and she's flighty. And if she ain't flighty she don't know a porcupine from a cat-faced log. Molly ain't that way. She's level-headed. So when she hoofs it through the snow in the middle of the night, whatever she's got to tell is worth listening to.

"She told me that the day before a couple of cruisers had turned up at her place, just in from the woods. Molly served them drinks, and it wasn't long before they let drop they'd been out landlooking for the Quickwater Log & Lumber Company.

"Well, that made her cock her ears. In the first place, she hates the Quickwater outfit, because years ago her husband was a partner with Dan Stoughton in that company, and after Molly was left a widow, Dan crooked her out of her share. And in the second place, that outfit has never had a camp so far south. Their operations are all up beyond the Flambeau fork of the Chippewa. So she wonders what them landlookers are doing down in McSwasey & Zumwalt territory.

"But Molly's too smart to start asking questions. She just serves them drinks and keeps her ears open. Well, liquor's funny. Sometimes it goes to a man's legs and they fold, and sometimes it goes to his fists and he wants to slug. And sometimes it goes to his tongue and his brains run right out of his mouth.

"That's how it was with these cruisers. One of them laughed and said McSwasey & Zumwalt would have a surprise next fall, when the Quickwater outfit built a camp at Mud Hen Lake. 'Why, boys,' Molly says, 'how is that? McSwasey & Zumwalt has been cutting along the Medicine, and I think they figure to clean out that whole valley.' Sure, the cruiser said, but McSwasey & Zumwalt was in for a surprise. And he told how him and his pal had been back around Mud Hen Lake, estimating timber. They'd given us at Camp Seven a wide berth, so we wouldn't get wind of what was happening, and they'd landlooked everything around the Mud Hen and beyond. They had it all marked up in their platbooks, and they had the minutes all wrote out for quarter-sections spotted around Mud Hen Lake and on west. Next fall they could build a camp back there and clean out those congress lands and boom their logs in Mud Hen Lake.

"Well, Molly knows a few things about logging, and she saw that would finish us in the Medicine drainage. Where would we be, owning one quarter-section for a campaign base, against them owning three thousand acres spotted just right? As I say, she's a friend of mine, and she sure as hell hates the Quickwater outfit, so when them cruisers sit down to supper she pours them each a stiff drink of tanglefoot and loads it with chloral. That means lights out for them landlookers. As soon as they're snoring, she goes through their tussocks till she finds their platbooks and minutes.

"Molly's husband was a surveyor, before he got mixed up with Dan Stoughton, and she used to help him when they was first married. So land descriptions were nothing new. She copied out those minutes and brought them to me at Camp Seven.

"'Jim,' she says, 'you make tracks for the land office at New Empire and take up them lands. Them cruisers figured to start down there at sunup, but with them knockout drops they'll sleep late and wake up with gongs in their heads. You'll be six jumps of a rabbit ahead of them. You file on that land in your own name. If you need money I'll stake you. With all that merchantable pine in the Medicine drainage, you can sell out at your own price.'

"What she said was true, of course. But I reckoned I'd play it straight. 'Molly,' I says, 'I'm much obliged. But I'm working for Caleb McSwasey and I'll file on that land for him.'

"'Why,' she says, 'you lunkhead, you're passing up something big. McSwasey will grab that land and slit your throat for your trouble.'

"'No, Molly,' I says, 'you've got him figured wrong. I'm entering that land for Mr. McSwasey. Reckon he needs it worse than I do, and besides, I'm figuring to pilot a raft, come spring. If I enter that land for Mr. McSwasey,' I says, 'he couldn't do much else than let me pilot a raft. He's always been square with me, and he'll put me to piloting a raft sure as sap rises.'

"Soon as I'd grabbed a bite of breakfast, I set out for the Falls of the Chippewa. Things went all right till my second team of horses went through the ice up in the Winneshiek Bottoms. Well, you've got to expect things like that this far south, if you drive a cutter over ice in the month of March, and I'd kind of got ready for it. I'd wrapped them land descriptions in oiled silk, and my friction matches was in a waterproof case. And I'd remembered some advice my father had passed along to me once, about traveling over ice, so I'd cut me a long pole and I carried it on my lap in that cutter. When the bottom dropped out of things, that pole reached to solid ice on either side of the hole, and I got out. It delayed me, but I got to the land office before they shut up shop, and I found Mr. McSwasey in time to pay for those entries. Them cruisers never did show. Be here in the morning likely. In my opinion, they're going to be put out."

Listening, Esperanza had been leaning forward, there at the end of the table, smiling at Jim and giving him an eyeful. Now she said: "I think it's wonderful, what you did."

"Well now, lady, let me tell you. When I work for a man I work for him."

Her smile was dazzling. And she would have been a magnet for any male eyes, with her bare brown shoulders and her dress cut so low. But for some odd reason, sight of her didn't really heat up Jim's boiler. She wasn't, somehow, his type. He would never have picked her out, in the parlor of a fancy house.

Dessert came—mince pie with yellow cream—and Jim went after it, and he swallowed two cups of coffee while the McSwaseys were drinking one.

"Jim," McSwasey said, grinning from the head of the table, "I never knew you wanted to pilot a raft."

"You know now," Jim said.

"Think you could handle one?"

"Blindfolded," Jim said.

*

He felt higher than a flight of Canada geese when he left the house. And not from the brandy, either. McSwasey offered to have his nigger man drive Jim back to town, but he said no, thanks just the same, a walk is just what I need. The wind had died, the sky was full of stars, and the night smelled of early spring when Mr. and Mrs. McSwasey told him good-by. Everything was settled by then; he was going to be a raft pilot.

"Much obliged for everything," he said at the door. "You set a good table, lady."

She gave him her hand, and a funny thing happened. He didn't imagine it, either: she pressed his hand with a few quick squeezes, as if flashing him signals, the way men visited over wires with the dots and dashes of those telegraph contraptions he had heard about.

Well, whatever she was trying to say, he didn't understand it.

On his way to town he stopped once, while still on the island, and looked back at the house. Quite a wigwam. Some day, he guessed, he'd have him a house like that. He'd save him up a stake from rafting wages and hire a timber crew and start logging. Make a million dollars. The future looked easy and all his, the way he felt tonight.

"Hell," he thought, "some day I'll buy and sell McSwasey."

Walking on, he had to smile when he thought how wrong Molly Fitzpatrick had been, saying McSwasey would grab the pine and slit his throat. Molly should have known McSwasey would play square with one of his crew. Square as a die? Well, maybe not. Maybe square till you got in his way. Fair enough; Jim understood that. Not many people in this world put your interests ahead of theirs. Molly Fitzpatrick was one, and Sol Klauber had been another.

On the way to his lodging house he passed Rafferty's Saloon, only he didn't pass it, right away, for although he was tired and wanted bed, yet he felt elated enough to make a big jump and grab a star and go swinging around the heavens, from one star to another. Whiskey would calm him.

When he entered, the place was quiet, with a grumpy poker game under a shaded lamp, with three or four soaks clinging to the bar like drone bees, with Pat Rafferty, a thin-shouldered man of fifty, staring at the ceiling. Inside the door Jim stopped, looking things over. He always enjoyed livening up a place; so, smiling, he patted his palm against his lips and let out a timber-wolf howl. Everyone jumped.

"Come on, boys," he yelled, striding through the sawdust. "It ain't as bad as all that. The treats are on me, boys."

Half an hour later the place was crowded; by some mysterious instinct, like blackbirds congregating for migration, every thirsty man in town found his way to Rafferty's. Hearing the excitement, the upstairs girls came swinging down in their red dresses; Pat Rafferty was on the jump, behind the bar. In the lamplight, smoke drifted thick as breath from oxen on a zero morning.

"Boys," Jim yelled, "I'm a raft pilot now. Just you watch me, boys. I'll own the whole damned river, one of these days."

*

He could read and write, and that would be helpful in keeping track of his possessions, if he ever owned the river. An ax had taught him his ABC's; an ax handle. The ax hung pegged on the wall of the cabin in Quickwater, and burned crookedly into the helve were the words: Lorne Buckmaster. That was his father's name; and Jim, at five, learning to duplicate the letters by marking a pine board with a burned stick, used to wonder why this ax was so special; his father never used it.

"You mustn't ask why," his mother said. "Don't you ever mention that ax, when your father's around."

The cabin was a snug home against the three-day blizzards whirlpooling across that northern land. Maybe it was a mite too snug: only one room for his father and mother, for Jim and his older sister, Harriet, and for Alice and May and Dobner, when they came along. Still, it was a good cabin with a puncheon floor and windows of oiled deerskin and a shake roof tight against the frozen January stars.

"Better than I deserve," Lorne Buckmaster used to say.

"Bosh," Myrtle would reply. Myrtle was his wife and she was the cheerful one of the pair, always trying to lift his spirits.

Uphill work. Some time or other life must have got him down and pounded him, maybe even stomped him with calked boots.

"The poor always get the hind tit," he used to say.

"Fight for the front one," Myrtle said.

But he never did, within Jim's memory. Too weary, with a weariness more than physical. He was a man who might have been tall, if only he had straightened up and squared his shoulders, and who might have been handsome. But he always looked doleful, hair coffin-black, skin sallow, eyes blue and gentle but suffering from some inner hurt.

"You should have known him before his trouble," Myrtle used to say, when Jim was nine and ten. "He was carefree, then. I thought moving to Wisconsin would help, but he brought himself right along."

He worked in the lumber mill on the east bank of the Chippewa River in Quickwater, Wisconsin. Not the state of Wisconsin, in those days; not even Wisconsin Territory, at first. On a map it was lettered Michigan Territory, but everybody called this neck of the woods Wisconsin. It had a great future, everybody said, and Quickwater had one too: in those days every cabin where two paths crossed expected to grow into a metropolis.

But Quickwater consisted of more than one cabin, even as early as 1829 when the Buckmasters arrived. They came in a two-wheeled cart pulled by a yoke of oxen, creaking along the sandy, stumpy road through the woods, all the way from Green Bay. All the way from Maine, actually, although not by ox cart.

Jim's memory of that cart, heaped with household possessions, was never more than a dim haziness of huge wheels and the warm, thick smell of the oxen, but his mother liked to recount how they had obtained it. She was proud of the way Lorne had risen above himself there in Green Bay, showing his old spunk. She had thought the move really was helping him, that it was bringing back the man she married. But that flash of spunk had been the last upflaring from the ashes of his spirit, not the herald of brave new fires.

Travel from Maine had gobbled money faster than they had figured, and on that May afternoon in Green Bay, when they disembarked from the lake boat, their resources were low. Nobody in Green Bay had ever heard of Eliphalet Hoyt who operated a sawmill in Quickwater; few had even heard of Quickwater. It was off through the woods somewhere; a long way off, if it was a Chippewa River town. A man would need an ox cart to transport his family there.

In his purse, Lorne carried a clipping from the weekly *Federalist* of Juniper Falls, Maine; Eliphalet Hoyt had written his home-town editor that he was doing fine out west; he had a sawmill in Quickwater where the white pine was thicker than blueberries in Penobscot County. But he needed experienced timber hands. So did all the other sawmill operators, all the logging companies. "Come on out and make your fortune, you Maine lads," Eliphalet had written. "Just say you're from Maine and you'll have a job."

Well, that was true enough; Maine men were born with an ax in one hand and a cant hook in the other; a Maine birthright was recommendation enough in the Wisconsin pinery. So the Buckmasters were eager to reach Quickwater and make a fortune, but after a few days in a Green Bay tavern, with board and room so costly, Lorne's purse contained only a dollar and twenty-seven cents. And Myrtle didn't even own a purse.

That wasn't any situation to write home about, to the *Juniper Falls Federalist*. Myrtle was scared, sitting in that sleazy tavern room, with five-year-old Harriet looking wide-eyed and sober, having caught her parents' worries, and with little Jim playing noisy games on the floor: he never seemed to catch anybody's worries.

Myrtle's husband had gone walking, to puzzle out what they could do, and Myrtle sat white-knuckled and white-faced, two months pregnant again, wishing they'd never left the Penobscot Valley. She was only twenty-two herself, a big, magnificently-formed girl with ginger-colored freckles and rich chestnut hair.

Lorne returned to the room, scarcely ten minutes after leaving, and Myrtle knew at once that something good had happened. She had been whispering a few prayers concerning fiscal matters, but even though her God was a kilted Presbyterian several generations a resident of Maine, and hence not so celestial as to ignore money, still it seemed dubious that he would give ear to pleas from Green Bay, the town so obviously had been platted by the devil.

Yet when she saw her husband she thought perhaps her prayers had been heard after all, for Lorne's eyes had regained their old mischievous snap, and even though he was still rail-thin, he had pulled his shoulders square and his feet weren't dragging.

"What is it?" she asked.

"Myrt," he said, "I'm going to make us some money."

He picked up his long Pennsylvania rifle, patting the curly maple stock.

"You're not going to sell it!" she exclaimed, for Lorne was a crack shot and she couldn't imagine how they'd get fresh meat in the wilderness, without that rifle.

He laughed.

"I'm not that crazy," he said. "Now don't you worry, Myrt."

But she did worry, naturally, after he had gone. She didn't think Lorne would hold up anybody and steal his money, for whatever his faults Lorne was honest; still a man desperate with trouble sometimes lost his wits and did daft things. Presently, through the open window, she heard shooting. She looked out but she didn't see anybody. Then more shots. That settled it; she took Harriet by one hand and little Jim by the other and went downstairs and out into the afternoon.

More rifle shots, now. She hurried in the direction from which they came, Jim leaping and cavorting by her side. And after a few minutes, beyond the edge of town, she reached a pasture where a target could be seen on a hemlock tree and where men were thronging. She knew then that Lorne had got wind of a shooting match.

That would mean putting money into a pot, the best marksman taking the winnings. It would mean side bets. That might have shocked Myrtle, if she had come from a part of New England less robust than Maine. As it was, hurrying toward the match, she asked God to keep Lorne's rifle steady and to strike his competitors with ague.

A cheer went up, following a rifle report, and she glimpsed Lorne's pleased face. She edged nearer, into the sharp smells of burned powder and charred wadding. Then somebody yelled: "Here comes Red!" And other men were exclaiming that Red was the best shot in the Territory, and the stranger had better look to his shooting now.

She saw a stringy man crossing the pasture with a rifle; his hair, not surprisingly, was red. And while the crowd cheered Red's coming, Myrtle caught her husband's gaze.

Face flushed, eyes bright, Lorne joined his family, clutching a purse heavy with silver.

"I'm hot," he said, and she knew he wasn't talking about bodily temperature.

"How much?" she asked.

"Something over fifty dollars. But I don't know about this new man, Red. They say he's good."

"You're good too," she said.

"Better keep this," he said, handing her the purse. "I'll take a dollar for the pot."

He hurried off.

Myrtle stood hefting the loaded purse, hearing men offering two to one odds on Red, and other men demanding three to one. From the confusion of voices she gathered that the next round was to be a match between Red and the stranger. The stranger: that was Lorne. Calmly, Myrtle approached the crowd.

"Fifty dollars on the stranger," she said, "but I'll have to have three to one odds."

A man with diamond shirt studs said:

"Taken."

Her fingers were utterly steady, counting out fifty cartwheels, and she stood holding a purse filled with little more than air.

Lorne's rifle went to his shoulder; the long barrel didn't waver; the rifle cracked. A babble rose from the crowd; men trotted toward the bull's-eye, forty yards away; the shot, Myrtle gathered, had been excellent, but it could be improved upon, by hair's-breadth shooting.

Myrtle held Jim in front of her, to calm his liveliness, as the man named Red lifted his rifle and took careful aim. The silence was painful. Eyes fixed on Red's trigger-finger, Myrtle's hand wandered to little Jim's ear. And just as she sensed that Red's finger was ready to squeeze, she pinched Jim's ear as hard as she could.

"Waaa-ow-ow-ow!" Jim yelped.

Nearly simultaneously, but not quite, the rifle cracked. Remembering the slight start she had seen Red give, Myrtle knelt to comfort her son, telling him it was a shame his ear was aching.

In that crowd, most of the money had been on Red, so there weren't many cheers for the stranger's superior marksmanship.

*

So that was how Mr. and Mrs. Lorne James Buckmaster, refugees from disgrace in Maine, were able to buy cart and oxen and set forth from Green Bay. On that journey through the woods, hope burgeoned in Myrtle's heart, for it seemed possible that her husband's old cockiness and dash would come back, after the boost of winning that shooting match. But self-confidence lost wasn't that easily regained; you couldn't buy it in a store. And certainly you couldn't migrate from the bad old past if you insisted on bringing the past along, epitomized in an ax with your name burned on the helve. Myrtle guessed Lorne was punishing himself by keeping that ax in sight; it must have satisfied some black compulsion in his Welsh blood and in the Scottish part of his Scotch-Irish blood.

Still, she kept hoping; and gradually she lost her homesickness on that journey to Quickwater, probably because the Wisconsin woods, fragrant with spruce and balsam, so closely resembled Maine. Even Quickwater reminded her of Maine, when they reached it in late June, on a morning of bright, crisp air. The Chippewa, flowing south past the west edge of town, might have been the Penobscot, it was so sky-blue, so clear, so northern when it mirrored the spruce and silver birches along its far shore. A dam had been thrown across the river, with a sawmill on the east bank, and below the dam you saw the rapids frothing among the granites and swirling in sea-green around the feldspars.

"Lorne," Myrtle said, "I love it here. It's Maine all over again, but it's a new country, Lorne. We'll be fine here."

And standing there on the bank of the Chippewa, wind molding her gray homespun dress against her fine big body, skin fresh with the spray from the rapids, she looked capable of coping with that heroic country, and of bearing sons who could conquer it. Still, it had its tricks, that land did.

Lorne looked worried, telling her how at the mill he had just learned

444

that Eliphalet Hoyt, two months since, had sold the business and moved on west. Myrtle would have liked giving Hoyt's ear a good hard pinch, for thus throwing Lorne into the panic of a stranger in a strange land. You could work a month, trying to rebuild his confidence, and then some trifle would shatter it.

"Maybe the new owner will hire you," she said.

"Maybe."

"There's one way to find out," she said briskly, "and that's ask. Did you ask?"

"He's not at the mill. His name is Dan Stoughton and he runs the trading post and the Northern Saloon. They told me to ask there."

He avoided her eyes, staring down at the fountain mosses waving in the rapids. Since his trouble he could hardly bear accosting strangers.

"I'll go to that saloon," she said, "and ask him to give you work. That is, if you're afraid to."

She knew she had hurt him, but she had to, sometimes.

"Afraid?" he said. "What's there to be afraid of? I'll ask."

"Tell him you're good," she said.

"I used to be."

"You're still good," she said.

She loved him, and maybe that was why she worked so hard, bucking him up. She'd always loved him, even through the blackest days of his trouble, when people were whispering that Myrtle Dobner drove her ducks to a mighty poor market, when she married Lorne Buckmaster. And bucking him up bucked her up too; she wasn't always as cheerful as she seemed; but she wasn't going to let his sickness infect her and perhaps her children; already she had high hopes for Jim.

So now, smiling confidently, she shepherded Harriet and Jim back to the ox cart standing near the mill. Looking grim, Lorne turned the oxen around, and the cart creaked east along Chippewa Street. The sawdust paving, aromatic as pine needles, was resilient under Myrtle's feet.

Earlier, on their way to the mill, she had noticed the saloon at the northwest corner of Chippewa and Squaw Streets, a block east of the river; and now, keeping leisurely pace with the oxen, holding Jim by one hand and Harriet by the other, Myrtle watched it coming closer. "Northern Saloon," tall letters announced, on its false front; and on the store adjoining the saloon on the west, another sign said: "Stoughton & Co. Trading Post. A Square Deal For All."

The oxen halted; Lorne stood rooted, brow furrowed; Myrtle could almost see his spirit shriveling. Without looking back to make sure he was following, she crossed the street to the board walk. Several old Chippewa bucks stood outside the store, sodden and speechless; she felt their blank gazes as she climbed the three shallow steps.

"Them's Injuns," Jim told his mother.

"Sh-h-h," she said.

Inside she paused, still not looking back, smelling the pleasant, mingled odors of sweetgrass baskets, rawhide, ground coffee, pungent spices. The store was cavernous and dusky; on the floor squatted hogsheads of sugar and flour, barrels of salt pork and red horse, kegs of gunpowder jacketed in burlap. Hearing a footstep behind her, she turned to smile at Lorne, then moved on. The damp odor of beer and the sharpness of whiskey wafted through the connecting door from the saloon, where Frenchmen were clicking dominos on round-topped tables. A Chippewa woman materialized from the shadows at the rear of the store, padding toward Myrtle on moccasined feet, her corpulence engirdled by a purple velvet skirt and a green velvet blouse.

"Is Dan Stoughton in?" Myrtle asked.

The woman grunted and disappeared into the saloon. Myrtle patted her husband's arm. After a minute she saw a broad-chested man of medium height coming through the connecting door, eyes and hair black, skin the color of twist-tobacco. He wore high boots and a checked shirt; he looked about fifty-five. And on his right shoulder, amazingly, rode a monkey wearing a red fez. The man said good morning; the monkey chattered in some jargon it had never learned in the north woods. Myrtle was remembering her girlhood in Bangor and sailors on Exchange Street just in from the Indies, with monkeys and brilliantly-feathered parrots. Harriet hid behind her mother's skirts, when she glimpsed the monkey, but Jim strode right up to the man, smiling and pointing.

"Take care, sonny," Dan Stoughton said. "He bites."

Myrtle pulled Jim away; he was a lively tadpole. And she saw Lorne looking bony-shouldered and miserable, sweat misting his forehead. He tongued his lips, and finally said:

"At the mill they told me to come here."

"Why does he bite?" Jim asked.

"He's a grouchy cuss," Dan Stoughton said, "when he's sober. Most of the boys leave him a drop of whiskey in their glasses, but not these Frenchmen." He jerked his head toward the saloon. "So he's cold sober this morning and he's sore."

"Why?"

Stoughton smiled; two deep wrinkles ran from his nose to the corners of his mouth.

"Sonny," he said, "if I knew that I'd know why a partridge drums. I'd know why a raccoon washes his food, and why an Injun can't carry liquor."

Jim was pointing again; the monkey scolded.

"See there?" Stoughton said. "He's grouchy."

"My father wants a job," Jim said.

Stoughton smiled; Myrtle made a grab for Jim; the monkey removed its fez and scratched its head. Jim pointed.

"Why?"

"Fleas," Stoughton said.

Lorne looked stricken, and Myrtle could see him gathering strength as if for an ordeal.

"Reckon my boy's told it all," he said at last. "I'm just in from Maine and looking for work."

"From Maine, you say?"

"Juniper Falls."

And Myrtle could tell Lorne was bracing himself for the question that might follow. A question such as why did you leave Juniper Falls? But Stoughton didn't ask that.

"Maine, eh?" he said softly, looking Lorne over. "Well, the Territory's filling up. And this town's growing. When I come here seven years ago there was nothing here. Just Injuns and porcupines. I laid out the town and look at us now. How did you come to pick Quickwater?"

"I knew Eliphalet Hoyt back home. We worked in sawmills together."

"Friend," Stoughton said, "why didn't you say so in the first place? Can you run a gate saw?"

Lorne nodded.

"Well," Stoughton said, "I can't. I don't know a headblock from a tailrace. But Eliphalet wanted to sell. I told him he was making a mistake, leaving Quickwater. 'We'll grow,' I told him, 'you just watch.' But he would go on west. Me, I've got faith in this town. Must be a hundred people here already, not counting the Chippewa over east in Injun Hollow. I could use another man at the mill. Six to six at sixteen a month."

"He was the best sawyer on the Penobscot," Myrtle put in.

"Now, Myrt," Lorne said.

"It's the truth," Myrtle told Stoughton. "You'll be getting a sharp sawyer and a millwright in the bargain. He could do it for twenty."

"Twenty?" Stoughton said. "Why, lady, twenty's a lot of money. I might go to seventeen."

Myrtle shook her head.

"Twenty or nothing. He knows logging and he knows mills. You break a ratchet wheel and he'll make you a new one. He's clever with tools. And he sawed the straightest planks in Maine. And with the least kerf."

"Eighteen," Stoughton said.

"Twenty," Myrtle said. "You want you a bateau and he can make it. He's good. Back in Maine we feed the young ones sawdust and they cry for more. So it's twenty or nothing. We've got an ox cart outside and we can always move on."

"Friend," Stoughton told Lorne, "I don't like to argue with a lady. I'm a man of few words. You're hired."

"At twenty?" Myrtle asked.

447

Stoughton nodded.

"Why does he bite?" Jim asked.

*

So it wasn't such an ordeal after all; and later that day Myrtle said their luck was certainly turning. And she told Lorne she was mighty proud of him, the way he had stood up to Dan Stoughton and demanded a good job and got it. Life gave you what you demanded, she said, if you spoke as if you meant it; the race was to the swift, life's prizes to the strong. Lorne acknowledged that it did look as if their luck was turning, but his voice sounded unconvinced. Sometimes Myrtle wanted to grab him and shake him, but she never did, loving him so much and understanding the hells he had been through.

After hiring Lorne, Dan Stoughton asked where they were going to live. That, Myrtle said, was the least of their worries; they had been camping out for a month and they'd keep right on, till they found a piece of land at a reasonable price where they could build a cabin. Stoughton said camping out was all right, but how would they like buying a fine cabin they could move into immediately? That, Myrtle said, depended on the price. Stoughton said he'd like to show them a cabin he had for sale; one moment, please. He disappeared into the saloon, where he left the monkey, and presently he returned wearing a battered old beaver hat. And on the street, looking over their cart and oxen, he suggested that if they wished to buy the property he was about to show, a trade might be worked out.

"I buy, sell and trade," he said. "A square deal for all."

"Including Dan Stoughton?" Myrtle asked.

He smiled. And he told Lorne:

"With a wife like yours, I'd own the earth and eighty acres on the moon."

At the corner, Lorne hawed the oxen north, and the cart creaked along past town lots which were vacant save for surveyors' stakes and weeds. But some day, Stoughton said, this town would boom. How otherwise? This was the best mill site on the Chippewa River, and stretching off in all directions grew the pine. The Buckmasters, he said, had made no mistake in selecting Quickwater.

"If there's a way to make a mistake," Lorne said, "we'd find it."

Myrtle would have liked to kick him.

After two blocks, the oxen turned east on Yew Street at the edge of town.

"There it is," Stoughton said, pointing toward a log cabin on the north side of the street. "When I bought the mill, Eliphalet threw in this place on the deal."

"He built it?" Myrtle asked.

"With his own hands."

Well, any cabin built by a Maine man was certain to be weather-tight; and outside the rail fence Myrtle stood looking it over. She didn't dare ask the price, just yet, but suddenly, when she thought that a place like this might be theirs, she was aware of a lump in her throat and a great yearning in her breast. Even from the road she could see that the logs had been closely-fitted and neatly-chinked; a handsome stone chimney climbed the east wall; in the front yard a fine old Norway pine towered. She said:

"It looks run down."

Stoughton denied that; and after conducting them along the path to the front door he pointed out how snugly the wooden pins fitted into the cross bars, how the door swung without sagging on its green hickory hinges, how the floor puncheons had been adzed smooth. Myrtle could have cried, she wanted it so much; already, in imagination, she was installing her big spinning wheel in the southeast corner and her Dutch oven on the hearth.

"It's small," she said.

"Easier to keep warm," Stoughton said. "Our winters are nippy. And you could always add a loft."

Outside, northeast of the cabin, Myrtle looked over the well with its long sweep in an upright fork, and the log shed that could shelter hens.

"Four acres go with the place," Stoughton said. "And plenty of good oak and maple wood."

"What are you asking?" Myrtle asked.

Stoughton named an outrageous figure; Lorne went shuffling beyond earshot, leaving the dickering to her; she could see him round-shouldered and forlorn among the burdock and goosegrass, staring off at the woods, dark and deep, that beleaguered the town. Stoughton offered to take their cart and oxen in swap, and to accept a note on the fifty dollars to boot. She said she wouldn't think of it; she said they'd just camp out and build their own cabin; she didn't much like this place anyway, she said. She wore him down, finally, to only ten dollars to boot, and that in silver, right now: she'd had enough of notes. Then she went to get Lorne's approval.

Avoiding her eyes, doubtless ashamed he'd let a woman do a man's dickering, Lorne listened. He said:

"You've made a smart deal, Myrt. I like the place."

*

The following Monday Lorne went trudging off to his job in the mill; to the job which, Myrtle maintained, was to be only a financial breath-catcher. He wouldn't always be working for wages, she said. Come winter, maybe he could make money trapping, although how a man could follow a trap-line while working from six to six was obscure. They would raise chickens, a truck patch, perhaps a pig. And some day Opportunity would come striding up to the door and bang with loud knuckles.

They raised the truck patch, right enough, and the chickens and the pig, but Opportunity never did locate that cabin. Funny thing, too, for wasn't the West the land where Opportunity lived and bred young ones? Could have been, maybe, that Opportunity never did go round knocking on doors. Could have been that Opportunity was as elusive as a doe deer, loitering in protective coloration beyond the by-paths. Maybe if a man plodded back and forth between home and a mill job, eyes on the ground, he never would glimpse her.

Jim heard enough about Opportunity, in those years, to last a lifetime.

"Jim," Myrtle used to say, "you go after the money. You get the money and everything else will fall into place. You'll be a rich man."

Well, sure. He never doubted that.

"And don't go trusting every man and his dog," she used to say. "You make friends, but don't you trust them too far. Don't make the mistake your father did. You watch out for yourself, Jim. Nobody else is going to."

He knew that already; seemed he'd always known it.

*

She was born in Bangor but when she was nine she moved with her family to the woods, for her father said he was fed up with the carpenter's trade, building houses for men grown rich in shipping: they were always coming around and interfering with your work, telling you how they wanted something done and calling you a stubborn Scot if you refused. "A man's a man for a' that," her father used to say; it was his favorite quotation, sufficiently all-embracing and indefinite to deal with any contingency. He was not, however, actually a Scot, except by descent and in appearance: a wiry man of medium size with sandy hair and a long, homely Scottish face. But he had been born right here in Bangor.

It was probably true that he had a dash of Scottish stubbornness, although, in his remarkably deep voice, he would argue all day that he was not stubborn. Resolute, yes; determined, yes; persistent, yes; not stubborn. He readily confessed, however, to a love of independence. All they had to do, to get him to enlist in the Revolution, was call it the War for American Independence. He was only fifteen at the time, and he fell in with Benedict Arnold when that man was still a patriot, marching clear to Quebec. That wasn't a very bright campaign and the British took him prisoner. They soon learned their error; he was always throwing up to them how England had been unable to conquer Scotland, how the only way the Scots could be brought under the British flag was by placing King James of Scotland on the throne in London.

In August, 1776, the British turned Newcomb Dobner loose, along with the rest of those Quebec prisoners. They said they had paroled him but this was a damnable canard: he wouldn't sign a parole. All the other

450

prisoners did, but not Newcomb Dobner. He was, however, such a thorn in the lion's paw, and so young and amusingly spunky, that one of the lion's lieutenants, himself a Kirkcudbright man, forged Newcomb Dobner's name. That was on a vessel bound from Quebec to the New Jersey coast. In army life Newcomb had encountered some slight infringements on his independence, so once he was free he made a beeline home to Bangor without further effort to defend his country. Just as well: if he had rejoined the army and served in battle, he might have felt that stubborn feeling coming over him at a crucial moment, and lost the war for the colonies. From his father he learned the carpenter's trade.

The day he turned twenty-one he married, chiefly because his father had argued against it, and fifteen years later there were five children to mourn his first wife's death. Since nobody forbade his marrying again, he took his time about finding another bride; not till age thirty-nine did he propose to Vanora Woodberry. She refused; at eighteen she had been engaged to a boy lost at sea, and at thirty-one she remained faithful to his memory; she would never, she declared, marry now. A month after her refusal she became Newcomb Dobner's bride, and ten months later she gave birth to a son. But the son died. So by the time Myrtle, the second child, reached the age of nine, she was the only young one in the household, her half-brothers and half-sisters having scattered.

Vanora was quite contented in Bangor, so when Newcomb, voicing a hazy daydream, said it might be fun to chuck the carpenter's trade and begin a new life in the wilderness, she opposed the idea. That, of course, settled it: mighty lucky for all concerned that Newcomb hadn't said it might be fun to move to the Fiji Islands. Within a month he had sold his Bangor place and bought forty acres of wooded land far up the Penobscot River, where he built a one-room cabin. The next summer he added more rooms, the original cabin serving as kitchen. Myrtle loved it up there. Newcomb said he loved it and thought he loved it, but only the Lord knew whether he actually did: having made the move, he would have loved it even if he had hated it.

Vanora wasn't so complicated: she liked nothing about Moose Meadows, as Newcomb called the place, just as if it were a village instead of a one-family clearing; she wanted to return to Bangor. Nope. So after a couple of years she up and died. Smothering with pneumonia, she begged Newcomb to bury her up here, not to take her body back to Bangor, and it worked out precisely as she had hoped: Newcomb nailed together a coffin and went to a lot of trouble, hauling her remains down the frozen Penobscot to a Bangor churchyard. Although dry-eyed, he was devastated by grief, but against contrariness he was as helpless as a chip of pine in rapid water.

The Dobner house, built of hemlock logs mortared with clay and moss, stood on rising ground a stone's throw from the west bank of the Penobscot. It was a long, solid house with a tight roof and a connecting

451

shed on the south leading from the kitchen to the log barn. Above the front door, which gave on the kitchen, a pair of moose antlers branched; steel traps hung from pegs; and sometimes you saw beaver pelts curing there on oval hoops. Newcomb had partitioned off five rooms with cedar splints, so even indoors you smelled the sweetness of the forest. Outside you saw the forest itself, darkening the river hills with rich stands of spruce and pine and balsam fir.

Newcomb's affairs were flourishing, by the time his wife died, for hard work didn't scare him and a dollar had no more chance of escaping from his purse than a bear from a deadfall. In summer he cut wild hay from the marshes to sell to the logging camps; in winter he trapped a cash crop of furs. He kept bees; he grew potatoes and beans and Indian corn; in his barn two cows yielded milk by the bucketful. For fish and fresh meat he had only to go to the river with his pole or to the woods with his gun; and responding to his musket's invitation, wild ducks and geese were always dropping in for Sunday dinner.

With her mother dead, Myrtle had taken hold of things in fine shape, for she was a strong healthy girl without a lazy bone in her body: might as well have tried catching a weasel asleep as to find her idle. When the sleepy winter sun peeked a red eye over the eastern hills, it saw cedar smoke rising tall in the frosty air from the kitchen chimney, and when it peered through the windows of that large room at the south end of the house, it saw Myrtle bustling to set the breakfast table, an attractive girl in the delicious haze from frying ham and eggs and from steaming buckwheat cakes. After breakfast she swept with a broom of cedar twigs tied to a stick, and during the day she kept busy rolling out dough, churning, gathering eggs, spinning, sewing, and—if her father was late from his line of traps—swilling the pigs and forking hay to the team of horses. In summer she added weeding the truck patch to her other duties, and sometimes she allowed herself such recreation as gathering huckleberries or going fishing with her father.

Every fall the loggers went striding past the Dobner place, bound for the woods, and every spring the logs came floating down the Penobscot, herded by brawny men with pike poles. They used to stop at the Dobner house, to buy a drink of spruce beer and a wedge of blueberry pie, so almost before he knew it Newcomb found himself operating a casual tavern; by the time Myrtle was sixteen that business provided a nice trickle of cash, and the pinery boys called the house Dobner's Tavern. But there was, of course, no bar—the atmosphere remained always that of a hospitable farm kitchen—and no pinery boy would have dreamed of roughhousing there or pinching the barmaid. For one thing, although Myrtle's well-proportioned body offered plump opportunities for pinching, she was not a barmaid at all but a good, wholesome girl in clean-smelling clothes; for another, if you had pinched her she would have grabbed a stick of firewood in her large, capable hands and batted you.

But those events never happened; in those days, the loggers were just good, healthy Maine boys, a little wild in a saloon, perhaps, but well-behaved in a respectable home, young fellows you might meet at church, or at least at a church party. In Myrtle's presence they watched their language, and none of them so much as touched her, except Lorne Buckmaster, and he didn't till she had promised to marry him.

Lorne was about the most quiet-spoken pinery boy on the Penobscot, but he carried a big wallop in his fists. He was tall without being skinny, and he had muscles like tawed leather, although he never felt called on to flex them under anybody's nose. His eyes didn't miss much of what went on, whether in the woods or in a saloon, and usually they twinkled. He had been born and bred right down at Juniper Falls, son of Adam Buckmaster and his wife, Nettie, she who had been Nettie Harrison. Ever since the first white settlements there had been Buckmasters and Harrisons in the Penobscot Valley; no girl could go wrong setting her cap for a Harrison or a Buckmaster. Old Adam's word was better than money in the bank; about his only shortcoming was being subject to seasickness. At fourteen he had sailed away to fish for mackerel and cod off the Newfoundland Banks, but it wasn't too happy a choice of oc-cupation; the crew said he fed more fish than he ever caught. That, however, must have been exaggeration, because ship owners kept signing him on. Finally, having saved enough to buy the old Cottner farm a mile north of Juniper Falls, he married Nettie and swapped seafaring for farming. Although the farm was mainly woodland and pasture granite, he managed to make a comfortable living. But he still liked boats. He said if he couldn't sail them he could at least build them; so presently in Juniper Falls, on the north bank of the river—which curved from west to east as it flowed through town—he established a modest boat works. Because Juniper Falls was above tidewater, or maybe because the very thought of oceangoing vessels brought on seasickness, he didn't build sailing ships; he built bateaux.

The bateau was a V-bottomed boat, sharp-pointed at bow and stern, tougher than a gar pike, designed to shoot rapids and to take abuse from boulders. You couldn't sink a good bateau, unless tricky currents sucked her in under the splash from a dam and she filled. If she sank then, you couldn't blame anybody but God. But in ordinary white water, if a bateau rammed a niggerhead and the river gushed in and drowned you, you could blame the builder, and you were unlikely to return to his shop for another boat. So Adam Buckmaster must have known a keel from a gunwale when he built bateaux, and he must have used well-seasoned wood, for loggers kept ordering more of his product and the business prospered. He was a long-legged, stoop-shouldered man with hair black as the inside of a chimney and with plenty of salt in his spit. He wasn't anywhere near as stubborn as Newcomb Dobner, but he did have a certain independence of spirit not uncommon in that part of the Republic, and when he built a bateau he took his time. You could no more hurry him than you could hurry frost out of the ground.

"Why, squire," he used to say, when some impatient tomnoddy wanted fast delivery, "if you're in such a rush to reach the churchyard you'd better hire a hearse."

The boat works was a long, shed-like building, pungent with the smells of new boards, fish scales, chewing tobacco, tar, turpentine and the clouds of steam employed to shape ribbing. To reach it you crossed the covered bridge from the business district and turned east on a footpath through burdock and nettles. Mirroring the bridge, and the alders and willows, and the white town hall on the opposite bank, the river flowed deep and smooth on its way to the sawmill dam several hundred yards downstream. Even as a little shaver Lorne was always turning up at the boat works, and at twelve he was hanging around the place every minute he could spare from such home chores as pulling turnips and harvesting the fresh crop of rocks from last winter's frost. Adam was right glad his sixth child took to boat building, instead of hankering for the sea like the older brothers.

"Ever get seasick?" he used to ask them, when they returned infrequently, bringing yellow China silks and smelling of East Indian spices. And when they said no he said they must have taken after his wife, who had been sick hardly a day in her life.

Lorne's interest in boat building, actually, was mild; what decoyed him to the shop were the men who came for bateaux. Loggers, log drivers. Red-shirted men with spiked boots. River hogs who could stand erect on a stick of timber and travel through smooth water and rough, as easy as a farmer standing in a lumber wagon. He wanted to do that, some day. Meanwhile, humoring his father, he learned to construct the bateaux those men would use. He took to tools; at sixteen he was the best bateau builder in those parts, except for Adam. But young blood was restless, and one day he told Corky Ingram that maybe the time had come for them to hire out in a lumber camp.

"What I've been thinking," Corky said.

Corky's actual name was Ulysses, but nobody except his parents and the schoolmaster called him that. If you wanted a quick fight, without a lot of buildup concerning chips on shoulders, just call him Ulysses. He was a month younger than Lorne, and the two had been friends since they were little sannups with hardly enough muscle to bloody each other's noses. But after about the age of five they never tore into each other, more than twice a year; they did, however, make common cause against anything else in pants. Even those Irish kids from shanties down in The Patch thought twice before yelling Ulysses and hurling brickbats at Lorne and Corky.

"You get him low and I'll get him high," Lorne used to say, and those were redoubtable tactics.

Although short for his age, Corky was a dependable ally, solid as a pasture wall and gritty as sand in sugar. He looked something like a woodchuck, the way his sturdy shoulders supported his head without any neck to speak of; but unlike a woodchuck he was never scared of his shadow and he never used his teeth in a fight unless a real emergency arose. His hair was the color of sun-dried grass, his sassy nose freckled, his eyes impish; and his oddly small mouth housed the most humorous tongue in Maine. Some people, especially at apple-stealing time, used to predict that Corky would end in state's prison, instead of following in the footsteps of his cobbler father, but he lost no sleep over such forecasts.

With his sprightly wit, Corky was mighty good company; even as a boy he was always composing limericks about such natural enemies as schoolmasters and tattle-tales and Old Man Perkins who sprinkled ashes on the icy walk sloping past his home, thus ruining sledding. And in school, Corky was a caution. Once when he couldn't recollect the capital of France, and the schoolmaster inquired how long his memory was, anyway, he replied that he had never measured it. And when the schoolmaster whaled him, Lorne, always a loyal friend, peppered the fellow's shiny dome with ammunition from a beanshooter, so he got whaled too. That night the boys stuffed the schoolhouse chimney with old rags, and when the schoolmaster kindled the morning fire it smoked something fearful; no school could be held. Even under whaling neither boy would snitch on the other, but the town had a laugh and fairly strong suspicions that Lorne and Corky had been up to their usual tricks. It was well-known, of course, that they were the culprits who tracked Deacon Lovejoy one evening when he left his wife and children and strolled over to pay his weekly call on Prudence Wingate. She was a maiden lady living with her father, and from the hedge the boys watched the deacon take a ladder from the stable and climb through the May moonlight to Prudence's second-story bedroom. After the deacon disappeared through the window, the boys returned the ladder to the stable. The deacon, when he was ready to leave, couldn't very well go downstairs and risk encountering Prudence's father, so he hung from the windowsill and dropped, spraining his ankle. The story leaked out, but when Adam Buckmaster heard it, instead of punishing Lorne, he only said that the deacon should have acted with more caution and less prudence.

When the spring drives came down the Penobscot, delivering logs to the mill at Juniper Falls, there was no keeping Lorne and Corky from the river; even at the penalty of smoking britches school could go hang. Watching the drivers cuffing the logs, the boys, at eight and ten, used to say that would be the life for them. And when summer came with its swimming weather they would find some log left high and dry, roll it into the river and practice birling. They took a good many duckings, learning the quirks of floating timber, but they were fish in water. Balancing himself with a pole, Lorne grew adept at birling; once when he was eleven he rode a floating log from Elbow Island clear down to the sawmill booms. It gave him a fine feeling of freedom and power, sailing along with the current, bare feet sure as a cat's on the rough bark. He waved at Corky, trotting along the bank; and when he looked off across the bright blue water toward town, seeing the stone foundations of stores rising from the river bank, and the flash of the church steeple among green maples, everything seemed intensified to extraordinary significance, the way things looked brighter and better on your birthday.

That was a sensation Corky never experienced; he couldn't get the hang of log birling. Nor could he match Lorne's axmanship; he lacked the easy knack. Splitting kindling, the boys used to pretend they were loggers in the woods, and by the time he was fourteen Lorne could make an ax do anything he wished, except stand on its hind legs and recite the Lord's Prayer. On Saturday mornings in the fall, right after breakfast, Corky would show up at Lorne's, and the two of them, munching fried-cakes, would go to the wood lot east of the house where the grass was slick with hoarfrost and the hardwoods were yellow. Lorne would work for an hour or so, chopping fireplace lengths, and then with Corky's help he would cart the wood to the pile near the kitchen door. It was a huge pile, round as a haystack, with the sticks neatly arranged at a slant like the spokes of a buggy wheel. "Better to have more wood than we need," Adam Buckmaster always said, "than to need more than we have." Sometimes Lorne's twelve-year-old sister, Susanna, would come out and help. But only when Corky was there. After the wood was stacked, Mrs. Buckmaster would invite them into the kitchen for slices of hot johnny-bread with strawberry preserves, and then the boys would tramp down the road past Corky's house to the boat works in the village, accompanied by Lorne's rabbit-hound, Buster, and Corky's shepherd dog, Ned. The road ran mellow and tawny under the high bright foliage, and usually before they reached the curve where it jogged east past a bubbling spring, the dogs scrambled over a stone fence and went yipping across a meadow after a cottontail.

Now and then came a Saturday when a tree was to be felled—they called it "falled" like real loggers—and that was always exciting. The day before, Adam Buckmaster would have earmarked some old-growth rock-maple as victim, and now Lorne would study it carefully, taking into account the way it leaned, and whether the wind was blowing, for it was a point of pride with him to bring a tree to the ground exactly where he wanted it to fall. Then he whetted his ax and went to work. His swing had a fine, steady rhythm, and the blade bit where he aimed. It looked easy. So Corky would give it a try, spitting on his palms and gripping the helve, looking in his determination more than ever like a woodchuck, with his thick chest and small, close-set ears. He heaved a mighty swing, but the blade usually missed its target by a good eight inches.

456

"You try too hard," Lorne said. "Loosen up."

But Corky kept swinging and hacking wildly, muttering such comic imprecations that Lorne was doubled laughing long before his friend, in disgust, flung the ax to the ground. Then Corky laughed too, and brought out his harmonica. Already he was planning how some day he would buy an accordion; his natural talent for music offset his miserable performance with an ax. He could wiggle his ears too.

When Lorne had chopped some more, and the tree began giving little creaks and snaps, Mrs. Buckmaster and her three daughters would come from the house to watch the excitement, and to hold Buster and Ned by the collars. You could hardly hear the ax strokes, because of the barking; usually too the girls were giggling at Corky's jokes. Then a deep shudder would pass along the trunk, and for a second the old maple would stand balanced. "Timber!" Lorne would yell, dancing back out of range, in case the tree should jump its stump; and then all the tonnage of branches and trunk would go crashing. And Lorne's mother, who had watched without once warning him to take care, would tell him he was getting to be a real woodsman. And Buster and Ned would go lift their legs on the new-fallen branches.

Some people—prigs and gossips—used to say that Corky was a smart aleck, and a wild and woolly young one, and they wondered what the Buckmasters were thinking of, letting Lorne run with a boy like that: he'd get Lorne into trouble, sure. It was even rumored that Corky sometimes sneaked into Sullivan's Saloon and listened to the rough talk of river hogs. This was true, although it was the pickled eels and salted cod at the end of the bar, rather than the talk, that attracted him. He did, however, pick up some interesting variations of taking the Lord's name in vain, and once he heard a big tale about a logger up in New Brunswick who was so expert with an ax that he could chop between the outstretched fingers of somebody's hand on a stump and never nick the skin. Next morning in the Buckmaster wood lot Corky repeated the story.

"Bet you could do that," he said.

Lorne just smiled.

"Sure you could."

"Yeah," Lorne said, "and with whose hand?"

"With mine."

"You'd be scairt."

"Want to bet? Look."

And Corky knelt at a smooth old stump and slapped down a pudgy hand, fingers spread wide.

"You're crazy as a bedbug," Lorne said.

"Who's scairt now?" Corky said. "Not me. Go ahead."

Lorne started to lift the ax, then dropped it, remembering all the advice his father had given when teaching him to use an ax. "Son," Adam had said, "there's three things in this world you got to respect—a loaded gun, a woman's tongue and a sharp ax." And on another occasion: "Never be careless with a full purse or a sharp ax." And on another: "A sharp ax has no conscience."

This was a very sharp ax.

"Crazy as two bedbugs," Lorne said. "I'd likely chop off your hand."

"It's my hand," Corky said. "We could practice and make money doing the stunt."

"I don't see how."

"Sure we could. We could do it for the pinery boys and win bets. We could pass the hat."

Lorne shook his head.

Corky brought out a pencil and traced the outline of his hand on the stump.

"There," he said. "If you're scairt to swing at my hand, swing at those marks."

"I guess I'd better not."

"You're scairt just to swing at those pencil marks?" Corky demanded.

"I'm not scairt," Lorne said. "I just don't even want to think about a stunt like that. If I could do it between the pencil marks, next thing you'd want me to do it with your hand."

Corky kept arguing but Lorne held firm. Still, all the rest of the day he kept thinking about that stunt, knowing that if he had a mind to try it he could carry it off. And early next morning, alone, he went to the stump. He was carrying the ax. A couple of times he started to swing, then checked himself; but he kept standing there thinking. Finally he tried one swing. The blade flashed into the stump between the outline of Corky's thumb and first finger. He swung three more times, between the other fingers. If Corky's hand had been on the stump it wouldn't have been nicked.

"But I'll never do it with his hand," he told himself; and he didn't, either, till the following spring, when one day Corky caught him in a weak moment and wore him down. And it was just as Corky had predicted: the stunt went off without a nick. But after it was over Lorne began to shake; he was scared in reverse for days; and not for another six months would he try it again.

Nearly every young fellow in Juniper Falls, when he felt his oats sprouting, hired out for a season or two in the woods, unless he liked the smell of salt water better than fresh; so when Lorne, at sixteen, told his father he planned to take a job cutting pine, old Adam didn't keel over with surprise.

"Son," he said, "maybe it ain't a bad idea. Leastwise you won't get seasick. You stay here and next thing you'll be catching crabs at Goat Gertie's. I reckon Corky's going with you."

That, Lorne said, was the plan.

"Then I pity the foreman," Adam said. "With you two in camp it will

458

be Halloween every night and April Fool every morning. Don't know what I ever done to get a son like you. Lived a blameless life, I reckon."

And he feinted at Lorne, who dodged and laughed, and Adam nearly smiled himself.

So in the fall shortly before Lorne's seventeenth birthday, he and Corky shouldered their calamity sacks and footed it up the valley toward jobs with the Liberty Lumber Company. Being green hands, they were put to work swamping roads, but Lorne was such a fine axman that before many snows he was promoted and spent the rest of the winter limbing trees. Corky, however, still couldn't get beyond a speaking acquaintance with an ax, so after the roads were swamped he was shifted into a job skidding logs by ox-power from stump to rollways. In the evenings he brought out his harmonica, and to his accompaniment the crew would sing mournful ballads about faithless women and drowned rivermen and faultless mothers and pinery boys who went to Bangor and lost their wages to saloon keepers so mean they would steal the pennies from a dead man's eyes.

When the boys came down with the spring drive, Lorne had been promised a chopping job next fall. Hard work and camp victuals had added fifteen pounds to his weight, all of it sinew. Corky had gained weight too; he looked almost tubby. But he wasn't soft.

Lorne helped in the boat works that summer, but Adam could tell he was only marking time till October when he could return to the woods; he loved logging. Any more, the only tool that pleasured him was an ax. He drew a picture of the axhead he wanted, and hired a blacksmith to forge it, the sides concave, the poll tapering just so, the bit tempered like a barber's razor. That axhead weighed upwards of six pounds. For the helve, Lorne was choosey as a man picking a wife; he looked over scads of ironwood till he found a stick with a grain he liked, then draw-knifed and whittled and sanded it till he had a four-foot handle, slim and flaring. Presently he ordered a second axhead, with a different balance, and carved out another helve. Thus armed, he left for the woods that fall, predicting he would make the chips fly.

He must have, too, for season after season he went back to the woods, always at better pay, and the winter he turned twenty-two he was foreman of a camp. By then he was working summers in the Juniper Falls mill of the Liberty Lumber Company, and nearly every woman in town was angling to become his mother-in-law. You couldn't blame them; any girl who married Lorne would have a good provider by the ears. He had, of course, sowed his share of wild oats, but all young men were full of the Old Boy, if they were worth the vinegar to pickle them; if they didn't sow those oats early they were likely to sow them late, like Deacon Lovejoy.

Corky Ingram trailed along with Lorne, to the woods every fall and down with the logs in the spring, but not many mothers plotted against his bachelorhood: five years after going to the woods he still worked skidding logs, and on a drive he was always losing balance and splashing a hole in the water. Some people said that except for Lorne's influence he couldn't have held down a woods job. Maybe not; but then again, maybe so: he was just the sort of comical cuss a crew needed to keep its spirits high. In the bunkhouse on Saturday night he unlimbered his accordion, and like as not he would sing a humorous ballad he had made up right out of his head when he should have been working, the tune catchy and the words not always fit for women or preachers. By midnight all the porcupines within a mile would be hearing that ballad, sung by the whole camp; and a month later boys in camps all over Maine would be singing it. Sometimes, to finish off the Saturday festivities, Lorne and Corky performed their ax trick: it was a real jim-dandy. When they did that trick, the bunkhouse turned deathly quiet, except for the snapping fire and the sound of wind in the pines. But some nights Lorne refused to risk the trick, if he had swallowed one drink too many.

*

He was the best man on the Penobscot, in those days, and the best in the pinery, and in the after-years Myrtle liked to remember him as he was then, striding into the kitchen at Moose Meadows, long legs booted, blanket-coat thrown open as he stood blowing on a cup of coffee, hair black, laughter wrinkles around his eyes. Even at fourteen she was half in love with him, and at sixteen more than half. In those days people said he would go far, he would make his mark, you couldn't keep a good man down. One of these days, they said, he would likely strike out for himself in a logging operation of his own, hiring a crew and sluicing his logs down the river to Juniper Falls, making a smart profit and the next year doubling his operations. Even Newcomb Dobner, that habitual dim-viewer, expected Lorne to end up rich, and although he was contrary about most things he offered no objections when Myrtle reported that Lorne had asked her to become his wife.

"Daughter," he said, "you'll never regret it."

Well, she never did, actually.

She was just turning seventeen when they were married, in the white church down in Juniper Falls, on a June day melodious with the cooing of pigeons and the trilling of robins. The drive was down; Lorne would spend the summer as head sawyer in the lumber mill; he had rented a house on Winthrop Street; if ever a marriage began auspiciously, it was that one. One of Lorne's sisters served as maid of honor, and Corky Ingram stood up with Lorne as best man, face sober for once, brow crinkled and gleaming with sweat. Myrtle looked lovely in her bridal gown, not really beautiful maybe, but young and healthy and robust. And although people called Corky the best man, that was only in a way of speaking: Lorne was easily the best man in the place, hands steady when he slipped the ring on Myrtle's finger.

Newcomb Dobner would have liked throwing a wedding reception, but Moose Meadows was too far off in the wilderness for that, so after the ceremony everybody piled into rigs and drove north from town to the Buckmaster place. There were so many guests that the house couldn't have held them, but the afternoon was fine and tables had been set up on the lawn. Even Deacon Lovejoy and Prudence Wingate attended, although not together, and all the pinery boys and river pigs who had worked with Lorne were there. Corky had brought his accordion; after the early supper he struck up the music and people sang. It was then that Nettie Buckmaster, Lorne's mother, touched Myrtle's elbow and told her she wanted to talk to her, alone.

Nettie was a short, plump woman with iron-gray hair, the nose of a Roman matriarch, and a warm voice nearly as deep as a man's; Myrtle felt like a child, following her into the house and up the narrow stairs to a front bedroom. Through the window she could hear the accordion and the singing, and she could see the sunset fading beyond the wooded hills off to the west.

"Sit down, Mrs. Buckmaster," Nettie said, smiling.

It was the first time Myrtle had been called that; it made her feel warm and choked-up and happy.

They sat together on the edge of the high old walnut bed with its checkered quilt, and Nettie explained she had brought her here because of a prank the pinery boys were planning: they intended kidnapping Lorne when he drove back to the village with his bride. Corky had got wind of these shenanigans and had tipped off Lorne.

"It will be fun to outsmart them," Nettie said, and there were sparks in her black eyes. "They were watching you. They figure Lorne won't stray far from where you are. But by now he's in the wood lot. I'll take you there, and you two can sneak through the south meadow. There's a team tied down the road that Corky got from the livery stable."

Nettie went to a window and looked down at the side yard. When she came back to sit by Myrtle she said:

"Corky's a friend worth having. He'll keep them busy singing for a spell yet. When Adam and I were married they snatched him on our wedding night. He didn't get home till the next noon. He spent the next year making up for lost time. Now that you and I are alone I suppose I should give you a regular talking-to. There's more to marriage than the wedding cake."

Myrtle felt embarrassed and a little scared and eager to steal from the house so Lorne wouldn't be kidnapped.

"We've time," Nettie said. "But maybe you won't thank me for advice."

"I'd like it."

"Maybe it's not much," Nettie said, "but it's worked with Adam and me. Once you're a wife you've got to be four things. I mean if you want to keep him happy. You've got to be his mother. You've got to be his cook. And you've got to be his friend. What I mean, if you're washing windows and the stew's on cooking and he comes in and says he'd like you to go along with him to catch a mess of trout, you go. The windows can wait and so can the stew. And the fourth thing you've got to be is a Goat Gertie."

"What's a Goat Gertie?"

"Goat Gertie," Nettie said, "runs a house over in The Patch. Adam calls it a house of ill shape. She's our bad woman."

Myrtle said, "Oh." In the gathering twilight she could feel her cheeks flushing.

"You be a Goat Gertie," Nettie said, "and you can forget everything else I've told you. I'm a plain-spoken woman. I guess Seth Lovejoy would never have sprained his ankle if his wife had been a good Goat Gertie. The place for an icicle is hanging from the eaves, not in a feather bed. I think you and Lorne will be all right. I expect he'll turn out a pretty good husband, although nobody can ever know how far a frog will jump. One thing you'll learn, he has his moods. Black as his hair. Adam's father was that way too. Scotch-Irish. That blood has streaks like the black veins in granite. Now we'd better go."

Twilight was thickening and Corky's accordion was playing "Barbara Allen" when Nettie and Myrtle slipped out the kitchen door and stole along the path to the wood lot. It was a fine evening with a sound of distant frogs and the buzzing of June bugs; dew was falling. When they reached the gate into the south meadow Lorne stepped from the shadows.

"All right, children," Nettie said. "It's up to you now. You be good to each other."

"Well, I guess," Lorne said.

Nettie kissed them both and rustled back along the path.

*

The accordion music grew fainter, the sound of frogs louder, as they picked their way on a diagonal across the meadow. Down in the draw, where a brook flowed, mist was rising, and they passed through a cool current of air that was sweet with wild thyme and bayberry. When they came to the stile over the wall, Myrtle could see a phaeton on the other side of the road, the team tied to a choke-cherry tree.

"Just where Corky promised," Lorne said. And after handing Myrtle into the buggy he added, "I trust him like a brother, but maybe I'd best look things over."

She could see him, a dim shape in the evening, examining the wheels and the traces. Then he untied the team and climbed in beside her.

"Everything's all right," he said. "Not that I don't trust Corky, but a man's fair game on his wedding night. Sometimes a wheel drops off a buggy, and sometimes the horses walk right out of the shafts. But Corky wouldn't do that to me."

And as they started toward the village, he explained how Corky had listened to the river hogs in Sullivan's Saloon planning to kidnap the bridegroom. That was yesterday. Their scheme had been to snatch him after the wedding reception and leave him tied all night in the sawmill. Corky had said sure, count him in. But he had warned Lorne, and they had schemed that Corky should hire this rig from the stable.

"We've always stood together," Lorne said. "And now it's you and me together, Myrt." His hand touched hers, clasped in her lap; it made her feel weak, and set her heart to beating.

Stars were shining in the summer heavens; the evening smelled of earth and growing things and blooming things, all mingled with the good honest smell of horses and leather; she always remembered everything about that drive. Once a small owl fluttered up from the soft dust, and the horses shied; peepers were singing in the grassy ditches; and when the buggy drew near the covered bridge she could hear the distant roaring of water at the sawmill dam. But near at hand everything was quiet.

The bridge was a velvety tunnel looming ahead, and Lorne told how when he and Corky were boys a nest of hornets had hung in the rafters.

"We stoned it," he said. "The hornets swarmed all day in the bridge. Nobody could cross. We were always in everything."

She had never lived in that town, but something must have told her the covered bridge had uses beyond roofing out rain and snow, for when the horses rumbled onto the floor boards and everything was black she expected Lorne to do what he did, pull on the reins. Maybe those livery horses knew from experience what would happen, for they stopped willingly. Lorne took her into his arms.

"Mrs. Buckmaster," he said.

He had never kissed her like that in courting days, and her mind went floating away and she never wanted it to end. But then she thought of those river pigs who wanted to kidnap him, and she broke away; she couldn't stand the thought of his being kidnapped away from her tonight. But he laughed.

"Why, Myrt," he said, "they'll never catch me now. Corky will give them false leads. They'll be hunting me in the barn and the chicken house." But he unwound the reins from the whipstock and said giddap.

Beyond the bridge, a whale-oil lamp stuck on a wooden post was burning at the corner of Center and Water Streets but no pedestrians were out; that was a small town. On the northwest corner the brick store of Lovejoy & Osgood looked lonely, the windows black. South across the street, Sullivan's Saloon showed a dim smudge of light, but his customers were at the wedding supper. The buggy kept wheeling south along Center, past Doc Rider's apothecary shop with its huge bottles of colored water, and at Winthrop Street, opposite Warren's Temperance House, it turned west. That was a nice part of town, a street with fine old elms and rock-maples, and with heavily-shaded yards and comfortable houses. Roger Fiske lived there, and Lawyer Porter, and Thayer Nash who owned the Liberty Lumber Company. The neighborhood was better than the house Lorne had rented, although there was nothing really wrong with it. Myrtle wouldn't have swapped it for any she had seen.

It stood beyond Rudd Street on the north side of Winthrop, a white clapboard house with a one-story kitchen wing; an apple tree grew in the little front yard, and vines screened the porch. Between the brick walk and the street an iron hitching post stood, shaped like a horse's head, and Lorne tied the team there, where Corky could get it later and return it to the livery stable. Then he helped his bride down from the rig.

"We're home, Myrt," he said.

"It's a good home," she said.

And she must have known, for already she had spent several nights there, with her father, after they had come down from Moose Meadows for the wedding. Tonight her father would sleep in Lorne's old room at Adam Buckmaster's.

They stood for a minute on the shadowy sidewalk, and Myrtle felt unreal.

"Some day," Lorne said, "I'll build you a mansion like Thayer Nash's."

"This one's fine," she said. "I don't want anything better than this."

*

She used to wonder, that first summer of marriage, what Nettie Buckmaster had been talking about when she said Lorne had his black moods, for he was riding high in those days, whistling when he set out for the sawmill in the mornings, smiling when he came home. When she looked back on that summer, it was all dreamy and honey-tinted; and she could think that in those days Lorne was the way all men should always be, sure of himself, on top of life, with the future all planned. If she had told him, that summer, that she wanted the moon in her kitchen, to slice like a muskmelon and serve with stardust for salt, he would have thought he could reach and get it for her. As for such a thing as becoming the richest man in Maine, there was nothing to it. They would save up a stake and he would strike out as an independent logger: easy. Nothing could ever stop him except death, but they never gave death a thought that summer, they were such willing flumes through which life poured so abundantly.

They had been married on a Wednesday, so every Wednesday they played a game of wedding anniversaries. "It's been a week," Myrtle would say. "It's been two weeks. We're getting to be an old married couple." And Lorne would say yes, it was a caution, but he couldn't see that they were cooling down. Then Myrtle would blush. He always had to grin at that, and sometimes he told her the plain words men used in describing the great preoccupation of all hot young marriages, and she would hide her head in the pillow. But in those weeks they thought they had discovered something nobody else had known about, and they celebrated their discovery ecstatically.

They liked to go out too, to parties and to church on Sundays, partly because it was such delicious torment to be near each other but unable to touch hands or kiss, and partly because somebody would be sure to call Myrtle Mrs. Buckmaster, and those words were delectable in their ears.

They had their quarrels, of course, and their times of making up, all sweet and poignant as a sword dipped in sugar. They thought they were quarreling about the usual things, such as jealousy or food cooked wrong, but what was really being decided on that immemorial battlefield was who would wear the pants. And the issue was decided to their satisfaction: Lorne wore them.

One night when they had been two months married, and the moon flooded through the bedroom window, Myrtle told her husband of the advice Nettie had given. She blushed when she told it, although not so hotly as if it had been earlier in their honeymoon. Oddly, Lorne was surprised to learn that nice women spoke of such things, but finally he laughed and said his mother needn't have worried about his bride's being a Goat Gertie. Whereupon Myrtle burst into tears. And after he had comforted her, and assured her he hadn't meant it the way it may have sounded, she asked him if he had ever visited Goat Gertie, in his bachelor days. He came near telling the truth, but some ancient masculine wisdom must have been his guardian angel, warning him that a few secrets did no harm to even the best of marriages, and he said no.

She had been a regular backwoods girl, living up there in Moose Meadows since the age of nine, so even a quiet village like Juniper Falls seemed populous to her, and it took some getting used to. Right at first, when anybody walked past the house, she would say now who can that be, and hurry to the window. Or at nine of an evening, when the curfew bell rang in the town hall steeple, to scare the young ones off the street, she would say, "What's that?" He used to have some good laughs, and tease her. And it took her a long while to learn that if you ran out of sugar or flour it wasn't a major catastrophe; it wasn't the woods miles from anybody; you could walk right down to the store.

Sometimes when Lorne got home from work she would have food in a basket and they would go to the river, carrying fishing poles and wearing old clothes.

465

"I look a sight," she said. "If anyone sees me, you'll be ashamed."

"Well, I guess not," he said.

So they walked right over to Center Street and across the bridge to the boat works, where an old scow was moored among the eel grass. In the twilight the river flowed glassy smooth, except when a bass splashed. Lorne manned the oars and sculled upstream, the sound of the sawmill dam growing fainter, while the stars came out and the lights of town were yellow specks in the blue evening. Boy and man, he had fished or swum or skated or log-driven every foot of these waters, and after they had pulled ashore at Elbow Island, or pushed the scow across the sandbar at the mouth of Juniper Stream, and followed that cow brook up through the meadows to the waterfall, he would tell her of the adventures he had had, growing up in that country, such as the time when he and Corky were seven, and had shinnied up a red maple there at the waterfall, and how in imitation of a squirrel he had leaped with outstretched arms from one limb to another, and missed his grab, and fallen.

"It shook me up and that night I wasn't hungry for supper. When my folks found out what had happened, they hurried me in to Doc Rider. He couldn't find anything wrong, but he grinned and said, 'Adam, the biggest mistake I ever made was leaving this young one at your house. I should have locked him in my satchel and thrown the satchel off the bridge.'"

And he went on to tell how Doc Rider's wife, so people suspected, was an opium eater, she was such a yellow sackful of skin and bones; and how Clint Warren, who ran the Temperance House, had never worked since he married a woman with enough inheritance to build the hotel; and how Lawyer Porter would lock himself in his office and stay drunk for days, making speeches to phantom juries; and how Thayer Nash, that thin, cobwebby old man, who never missed a prayer meeting, had always been mean to his son, Frank, breaking his spirit so that although Frank was now a man of forty he had never married but lived at home under the old man's thumb.

"I'd like to see Thayer Nash best Seth Lovejoy on a deal," he said, smiling, "and then see Seth best Thayer. They'd both die of broken hearts."

It was after one of those fishing expeditions, on a fine September night in the bright of the moon, that Myrtle saw how he could handle young bloods who thought they were tough. She was five weeks pregnant by then, and their marriage had slipped imperceptibly from one phase into another, the first headlong passion tempered by gentleness; but he was not gentle with those bully boys from The Patch. She could think he was less gentle with them than he might have been, because she was along and might get hurt.

Coming down the river in the scow, Myrtle and Lorne heard yells

466

and whoops from the bridge. And when the scow passed through the shadow under the bridge, they could hear boots thudding on the floor boards overhead, and a wild tangle of voices.

"Sounds like The Patch," Lorne said, and after he moored the scow he picked up a length of heavy chain.

Summer was gone by then; the frosty air made her shiver when they picked their way along the path to the road, where a team and buggy had been halted by the bridge entrance. In the moonlight she saw Doc Rider, an old man now with a short white beard, lame from a ball in his leg received fighting the British years ago.

"Lorne," Doc said, "I don't know what this town's coming to. I'm just in from a call and they won't let me across."

Myrtle saw a pile of brush blocking the road, and in the darkness of the bridge dim shapes that yelled things. Then she heard the chain clank and Lorne went into action, jumping over the brush pile like a buck deer and knee-pumping into the bridge with the chain swinging. There were yelps of surprise and pain, and a great scurrying of feet. She never saw most of those troublemakers, for they fled through the bridge and scattered in the village, but one—older than the others, maybe, and harder—grappled with Lorne and the two of them came tumbling out onto the dusty road. Myrtle didn't have time to be scared, it was over so fast; Lorne had him on his belly and applied a toe-hold that made him squeal. Then he pulled him to his feet and marched him to one of the windows midway across the bridge. There was a screech and a splash, and Lorne came back and cleared away the brush.

"Lorne," Doc asked, "can that boy swim?"

"He said not," Lorne said, "but a rotten egg will always float."

"I'm much obliged," Doc said. "How are you feeling, Mrs. Buckmaster?"

As well as could be expected, Myrtle told him, except in the mornings.

"It's a natural process, just remember that," Doc said. "But complicated. If I wasn't a religious man I'd say I don't know what the Lord was thinking of when he planned it out. I could have done better myself. Well, you're built for it. If it's a boy he'll be a fighter. I'd bet on that. Can I give you a lift?"

The Buckmasters said they would walk.

"Well," Doc Rider said, "I'm much obliged, Lorne. Remember that time Bert Hawkins was driving pigs past my house, and you and Corky whooped and scared them through my petunias?"

Lorne said he guessed so.

"I could have killed you both," Doc said, "but now I'm just as glad I didn't. I'm much obliged. If it's a boy I'll bet he'll be a humdinger."

There were no reports of anybody's drowning that night, so the fellow Lorne heaved from the bridge must have been a swimmer after all.

*

In October Myrtle began to understand what Nettie had meant when she said Lorne had his black moods, for as the time approached for him to leave for the woods he grew moody. In other years he had looked forward to going, but now of course he was leaving a wife in Juniper Falls, and in the evenings he sat pulling glumly on his pipe. Myrtle could hardly blame him, for his logging camp was so far away that he wouldn't get back all winter; she felt sad too, although she tried to hide it. Pshaw, she said, cheer up, it will be spring before you know it. His dejection made him unreasonable and her cheerfulness only irritated him; once he even accused her of being glad to get him out from under foot. That led to trouble, for she was a spunky piece, and in the end she cried and admitted she was as sad about his leaving as he was.

"That settles it," he declared. "I just won't go."

Having lived with her father, she knew all about the stubborn stands men could take, so she didn't argue. But she asked:

"What will you do if you don't go?"

"I'll stay on at the mill till the ice hangs us up. Then I'll build bateaux with my father."

"Whatever you decide," she said.

He was lighthearted the rest of the evening, but after sleeping on the problem he grew troubled again. After all, logging was his career, and his job as camp foreman meant a lot to him. The Liberty Lumber Company had plans to open more camps, and he hoped to be appointed general woods superintendent. In the sawmill he had gone as far as he could, and he didn't want to spend his life building bateaux for other men to use. His brain and body were highly skilled tools in the logging business; he didn't want them to rust away.

"I reckon," he said at breakfast, scowling, "I was too hasty last night. I'd best go to the woods after all. But one thing's understood, I'll be back for a visit in April."

It was in April when she expected her child.

"Whatever you think, Lorne," she said.

So one frosty morning long before sunup Corky came to the house, and Lorne shouldered his calamity sack and kissed her good-by. His eyes were dry and so were hers; in that part of the world, for generations, men had been kissing their women good-by and going to the woods or to sea. After he had gone, the house seemed deathly quiet, and Myrtle understood why he had been so disconsolate, for something had ended that would never come back again. They would never be bride and groom again.

Lorne's family were good to her, that autumn and winter; Adam used to come and bring in wood and shovel paths through the snow; and on zero afternoons Nettie helped sew for the baby. Myrtle would have been welcome to spend the winter with Lorne's parents, but she knew no kitchen could hold two women. But she and Nettie were friends. When the baby came, Nettie would help out, for she knew a thing or two about midwifery, although of course Doc Rider would also be on hand. Some women were prissy about having a man doctor, but not those Maine realists.

"The way I figure," Nettie said, one howling March afternoon, "it's a man who gets a woman into the family way, so let a man get her out of it."

Taking all the data into account, Doc Rider calculated the baby would be born the last week in April. And he was right, although it was a close thing: another half hour and the child would have come on May first. Lorne wasn't so punctual, although through no fault of his own, for on his long walk down from camp a freak snowstorm tried to get him lost and freeze him. But he knew the woods and how to cope with that hard climate; he built him a lean-to and a roaring fire and holed in. Needing a shave and hungry, but otherwise in good fettle, he walked in on the afternoon of the second of May. He was disappointed that the child was a girl, but he never let on, and when Myrtle said she was naming her Harriet, after Aunt Harriet in Bangor, that was fine with him.

"You two," Doc Rider said, "make good young ones. And you don't let any grass grow under your feet. I wouldn't give a continental for a June marriage that didn't bring a spring baby. That's a gritty wife you've got, Lorne. Hardly a peep. Let me know when you need me again in this house."

But when the next child was born, a boy named James, Myrtle and Lorne had moved up to Moose Meadows, and he no longer worked for the Liberty Lumber Company, and the black mood had moved in on him permanently.

*

After a two days' visit Lorne returned to the woods, but this time his leave-taking was more cheerful, for it wouldn't be long now till the drive started down the Penobscot; he'd be back in six or seven weeks. Myrtle was up and around, by the time the frost had cooked out of the ground, and Adam spaded her a garden patch and fenced her a chicken yard. She was seventeen, with energy to burn now; and she planted vegetables and set some gray Dominique hens and sang as she swept. Summer was coming and the drive was coming down from the woods and Lorne was coming. She had been terribly lonely for him, last winter.

The sun smiled down on the Penobscot, bringing a roar from the saw-mill dam, and the ice went out of the river. Of an evening the frogs were singing again; boys were beating carpets and girls were playing jacks; and one day in June the news raced through the streets of Juniper Falls that the head of the drive was coming. People turned out as at a festival, to watch those first sawlogs bobbing along in the current;

small boys even climbed to the roof of the covered bridge, where they stood pointing upriver, ignoring old Bill Mellen, the constable, who upbraided them for clambering over public property; but the boys in that town had been climbing the bridge every June for years; old Bill had done it when he was a boy.

The logs came and came. And kept coming. They filled the booms at the mill, they filled the auxiliary booms at Elbow Island. They had a strange wild look, those logs freshly-torn from the wilderness, like new-killed deer. Standing at the bridge, Harriet in her arms, Myrtle could smell their piney fragrance; it was a stirring and exciting smell, reminding her of Moose Meadows and cold blue lakes and green mosses and wind-scoured granite and endless miles of forest.

When the drive was at its height she saw Lorne a few times, but only for hasty minutes, for as river boss he had to be everywhere at once; he would kiss her and the baby and be off, back upriver, to make sure the logs didn't plug. But finally the rear came floating in, sacking crews and all, and the drive was down. That was a late afternoon in mid-June; she and Harriet, waiting at the sawmill boom, saw Lorne and Corky step from a bateau, calamity sacks hanging from their shoulders. Old Thayer Nash, gray and lean and dry, stepped across the landing and shook hands.

"A pretty clean drive," he told Lorne, his voice, as always, more a whisper than a voice, as if he had laryngitis. "I'd have liked it better if you'd finished up sooner, but I'm not complaining. In my day we did it with half the crew, but I'm not complaining. You ain't listening. You're just thinking about kissing your wife. All right, damn it, kiss her."

So Lorne kissed her, and later, as they walked with Corky toward Center Street, Myrtle was scornful about Thayer Nash. What did he mean, that Lorne should have finished sooner? This drive had set a record. Everybody was saying so.

Lorne just smiled; Corky said:

"When old Thayer dies, he'll show the devil how to get twice the heat with half the fuel."

That was a brilliant afternoon, with dandelions yellow on grassy banks, and the air sweet with linden blossoms. She could remember how fine Lorne looked; and she could look forward to that evening when they would make love for the first time since he left for the woods last October. His long legs in driving boots and tight pants, his lean belly with a wide leather belt, his strong arms and shoulders—all seemed to give off a current of male vitality; and as she walked by his side toward the business district her legs felt heavy and dreamy; and now that she had thought of how it would be tonight she could think of nothing else. But at the corner of Water and Center Streets, where the town hall thrust its white steeple toward the sky, he came to a stop. Diagonally across the street Sullivan's Saloon was jumping with river hogs celebrating the end of the drive; she could hear shouts and singing.

"Myrt," Lorne said, setting down his two axes, "you go along home. I'll be there in ten minutes."

She was surprised.

Corky grinned and jerked his head toward the saloon.

"You can't," he said, "expect a river pig to end a drive without wetting his whistle."

"We've spirits at home," she said.

"Well now, Myrt," Lorne said, "that wouldn't be quite the same. I bossed the drive, and the boys expect me to set them up. I've just about got to drop in at Sullivan's. Those boys risked their necks more than once. If I pass up the celebration they'll wonder."

She felt disappointed and vexed.

"I wish you'd come home with me," she said.

"I reckon," Corky put in, grinning so she would know he was joking, "that a river pig should never marry. He ain't a domesticated animal. But don't worry, Mrs. Buckmaster. I'll send him home in time for supper."

Lorne patted her shoulder.

"Don't you fret, Myrt. What kind of push would the boys think me, if I'd pass up the treats?"

He picked up his axes; she watched him striding across the street, Corky hurrying by his side. When the saloon received them a cheer went up.

Feeling piqued and bereft, Myrtle walked homeward past lawns where robins were pulling earthworms; and when she reached her own kitchen she cried. Yet she couldn't blame him entirely; if you were river boss you had to buy drinks.

But Corky broke his promise; Lorne did not get home by supper time. Not even by dark, and that was nearly the longest day in the year. The curfew rang; ten o'clock struck; no Lorne. She was angry, furiously so, when he fumbled open the door at ten-thirty; and there in the candlelit living room she delivered a tongue-lashing she hoped he would never forget. He stared at her, saying nothing; he looked in a drunken stupor; and while she talked he slipped the calamity sack from his shoulders and put down his axes. Then he sat with hands dangling. Finally she ran out of words and out of anger and began to sob. But he didn't go to her and comfort her; he just sat there staring. At last she ran out of tears as she had run out of anger. Then he spoke. He seemed to have difficulty making words.

"I'm not drunk, Myrt. I've had a few, but I'm not drunk."

All at once, contrary to all reason, she believed him. Something was wrong, terribly wrong, but he was sober.

"Maybe you're not," she said slowly.

"No, Myrt, I'm not. If I was drunk I'd be happy. I'm not drunk."
In the candleshine he looked another man from the one she had met at the sawmill. His face was drawn, the eyes deep set and stricken; his whole body was limp.

"What is it?" she asked. And when he didn't answer she repeated the question, her voice rising. "Lorne! What's happened?"

His gaze met hers, then dropped to his hands. He tongued his lips.

"It happened at Sullivan's. I didn't want to go. I wanted to come home with you. But the boys expected me. Corky expected me. Old Corky. Old Corky said to me yesterday, 'Now just because you're married,' he said, 'you ain't going to pass up the celebrating. The boys won't like it,' he said. What could I do, Myrt? I never meant to stay away so long. Sullivan's was jammed tonight. All singing. All laughing. Well, I set them up, Myrt. Then Corky he set them up. Then somebody else and somebody else. I forget. I had a few. But even then I wasn't drunk. Why, Myrt, I could drink them all under the table if I had a mind to. I've done it, other years. But not this year. Not this year, I told them, because I'm a married man and she's expecting me. That's the God's truth, Myrt, that's what I said. But then old Corky, old Corky he said, 'One more round. One more round I want to buy,' he said, 'for the best push on the river.' They cheered then. They were cheering me, Myrt. What could I do? I heard the curfew ringing but what could I do? So we drank one more round and I said boys, I've got to go."

Myrtle saw that his mouth was a tight line now, his head was bowed, his hands were twisting together.

"Then, Myrt, somebody yelled that maybe they'd best let me go, with my beautiful wife waiting. That's what he said, Myrt—my beautiful wife. And Corky, old Corky pipes up and says, 'If she was mine, I wouldn't have waited this long.' I was standing right by him, Myrt, and that's what he said. And know what I did, Myrt? I slapped him. Talking about my wife in a saloon full of pigs. I slapped him. I slapped old Corky. We've been friends since I can remember anything but I slapped him. We would have fought too, but Long Mike steps in. Old Long Mike, he was my best white water man, Myrt. And Long Mike he says, 'You boys don't want to fight. Hell,' he says, 'you're friends.' And he kept that up till he had us laughing, Myrt. And Corky says he'll buy me a drink to show there's no hard feelings. Could I leave then, Myrt?

"So we made it up, old Corky and me, and I bought a round to show the boys there was no hard feelings. What else could a man do, Myrt? I bought them a round and then I says boys, now I've got to go. And Long Mike he says, 'Why, sure, if your wife's waiting, but first do us the ax trick.' That's what he says, 'Do us the ax trick.' But I says no, not tonight, boys. I've had one too many, boys, with no victuals in my stomach. Not tonight, I says. Then Long Mike says, 'You're still mad at Corky. You're mad at Corky or you'd do the ax trick.' And Corky he's near crying. He says he never meant nothing when he said that about my wife, and he says it's terrible to have me mad with him after we've been friends since we can remember. Come on, Lorne, he says, and let's do the ax trick like old times.

"What could I do, Myrt? Could I walk out like I was mad at old Corky? So the boys bring in a chopping block and I pick up my best ax. They clear a space for us to do the trick, and old Corky kneels and slaps down his right hand. I wasn't drunk, Myrt. But the candles were swinging and the faces in the crowd were queer. A man's nose would turn to tallow and run down his face. And my ears were singing, Myrt. I could hear wind singing in my ears louder all the time. But I swung. And I swung neat, Myrt, right down between Corky's thumb and first finger with never a nick. The boys cheered and somebody yelled, 'He ain't drunk.' I asked, 'Who said that?' Nobody peeped and I couldn't see the boys very well, Myrt, they were all running together like soft candles in the sun. I took me a grip on the ax, Myrt, and I swung again, and the blade landed clean with never a nick. Right between old Corky's fingers with never a nick. The boys cheered again and I thought two more swings and I go home. But the next swing, Myrt, that next swing was no good. Something went wrong, Myrt, on the next one. I swung good and hard too, but it was no good. It never landed between his fingers, Myrt. That's a broad blade and a sharp one, Myrt. And it landed on his hand and wrist. It was pretty bad, Myrt. Somebody yelled, 'You son of a bitch, you've split his hand.' 'Who said that?' I yelled, but nobody paid attention. Corky, old Corky, he was crumpled up there on the floor, and there was blood. The boys were milling and somebody was running for Doc Rider. And Sullivan, Tim Sullivan, he ripped off his shirt and wound a strip around Corky's arm to stop the blood. 'Boys,' I yelled, 'somebody jostled me, boys,' but they wouldn't pay attention. 'Boys,' I yelled, 'I was jostled,' and Tim Sullivan boomed at me, 'Shut up, you drunken fool, you was mad at him and you've cut off his hand.' Old Tim. The money I've passed across his bar. 'I wasn't mad,' I yelled. 'I bought him a drink and I wasn't mad.' But they all kept milling around, Myrt, and those that heard never said nothing. They just looked at me, Myrt.

"Doc Rider came and stopped the bleeding. And he says, 'This hand's got to come off. Get a blanket and poles,' he says, 'and carry him to my place.' Old Corky. His right hand, Myrt. 'How can he play his accordion?' I yells. 'If you cut off his hand he can't play.' Doc Rider just looks at me and he doesn't say nothing. Nobody says nothing except Tim Sullivan. 'As vicious a thing as I ever did see,' Tim says. 'A fair fight is one thing,' he says, 'but to chop off a man's hand because you're mad at him!' But I wasn't mad at him, Myrt. Do you think I was mad at him?"

473

She said, "No. No, Lorne, you weren't mad at him."
And she went to him and tried to comfort him.

*

But there was no comforting Lorne, that night or the next day or for many days and nights. He was a man stricken by some black disease of the spirit in those weeks; nothing she said ever reached him. He might have been a sleepwalker, shambling through broad daylight.

She could look back on that time and see her mistakes: she should have made him do the things he shrank from doing, such as go to the Ingram house the morning after the accident and pay a sick call on Corky. She should have taken him by the arm and gone with him. The town didn't much like it, when word got around that he never went to see Corky.

And she shouldn't have let him skulk there at home, never leaving the premises except late at night, when he walked alone through the sleeping town. She should have made him go to Sullivan's Saloon and to Eaton's Livery Stable, to the veranda of Warren's Temperance House and to the crackerbarrel forum in Lovejoy & Osgood's store, to all the places where men congregated and public opinion was shaped. It didn't look good to the town, the way he acted; it was easy to believe he had been mad at Corky.

And certainly she made a big mistake not to protest more when, the day after the accident, he took the ax that had chopped Corky's hand and went to the back yard. He built a fire out there, and heated a poker, and burned his name into the helve of the ax. She should have said, "Lorne, what's past is past. Water over the dam, Lorne. No good comes from brooding. Drop that ax off the bridge, Lorne, where you'll never see it again." But he seemed to take some twisted satisfaction in the sight of that ax, and his name in black, crooked letters on the handle. His satisfactions were few enough in those days, so she let him sit staring. But she never thought he would keep that ax for years.

She was still young then; she didn't know the world very well; how even a friendly town like Juniper Falls abided by wolf-pack law, whirling with bared fangs to rip and destroy anyone wounded beyond fighting back. But she learned how the town felt when she went shopping. People working in their yards looked the other way when she walked by, and on the street other people spoke to her briefly or not at all. When she entered Lovejoy & Osgood's store everybody stopped talking. She was still proud in those days, so she carried her head high and gave them as good as they sent.

Blood was thicker than water, so Lorne's father and mother and sisters came to the house on Winthrop Street, to show him they were on his side and to try cheering him, but nobody else came. Not till nearly a week after the accident. And then the caller was the last person Myrtle would have expected, old Thayer Nash. And he came not out of friendship but on business, asking why Lorne hadn't come to work on schedule as head sawyer at the lumber mill.

Lorne was sitting on the porch in the dusk, shielded from the street by vines, and he stared at Thayer Nash.

"I thought," he said, "you might not want me now."

"Pish posh," Thayer said, in his whispery voice. "Are you talking about what happened in Sullivan's Saloon?"

Lorne didn't reply.

"Pish posh. Juniper Falls!" His pale lips curled and he hissed in his teeth like a disgusted old tomcat. "Talk! This town! After a drive river pigs will always wallow in the muck. There will be fighting. Somebody always gets hurt, after a drive."

"I didn't mean to hurt him," Lorne said. "I was jostled."

"Likely you were," Thayer Nash said. "Some people say one thing, some another. Me, I don't care. You've still got two hands. You can still saw a straight plank. If I'd let this town run my affairs I don't know where I'd have got. The town didn't like it when I started pulling ahead. In '89 I let Elijah Harper have three hundred pounds on a year's note. He was killed by lightning and I took the farm from Electra Harper. You should have heard the talk. My boy Frank wanted to marry Constance Eaton. I wouldn't have it. And there was talk. Talk never caught a fish or sawed a log or put a penny in a man's purse. Pish posh! You come to work in the morning."

So Lorne went back to his old job in the mill, but even then he didn't face up to the town the way he should. He got up far earlier of a morning than there was any need, and sneaked to the mill through alleys; he came home soft as a shadow in the dusk. And he wouldn't go see Corky Ingram, convalescing with a raw stump where his hand had been.

*

In the end it was Corky who made the first move to patch up the friendship. That was in September, after his stump had healed; he went to the sawmill to see Lorne. Myrtle heard about it that evening.

"He don't look so well," Lorne said. "He looks peaked. We shook hands, Myrt, and it nearly killed me. I mean the way he has to shake hands with his left hand. He tried to crack jokes, the way he used to, but his jokes aren't so funny any more. I tried to laugh, but they aren't funny. What's he ever going to do, Myrt? He can't work with only one hand."

"There're things he can do," she said. "He'll find them."

"He can't play the accordion now," Lorne said, "and he can't go to the woods. He can't learn cobbling from his father."

"He'll find something," Myrtle said.

"A man with one hand," Lorne said. "He'll ask for work and they'll shake their heads. But one thing, Myrt, he don't blame me. 'I was jostled,' I said, and he said, 'Sure you were. We were both crazy,' he said. I said, 'Corky, I reckon I should have come to see you.' And he said, 'That's all right, Lorne. Think nothing of it.' I kind of wish I'd gone, now. He's not mad at me, Myrt. The town has been saying things behind my back, but not old Corky."

"Lorne," Myrtle said, "you just face up to this town. You stop that sneaking through alleys. It was an accident. Accidents happen. You straighten up your back and square up your shoulders. You walk right down Center Street, Lorne. We'll go to church again, and you stop in at Sullivan's for a nip. Wear a chip on your shoulder. You face right up to this town."

"Sure," he said. "That's what I'm going to do, Myrt."

But he never did.

In October he left for the woods. But it wasn't like other years. Other years, Corky had gone with him, cracking jokes as they strode along the old gig trail. Now he walked alone, eyes on his toes and shoulders bowed. Seeing him off, Myrtle wondered how long he would last as camp foreman, in that mood.

Yet something—the habit of years, maybe—must have snapped Lorne out of it, up there in the woods, for he stayed on as push of his camp. If the monthly figures of timber cut had dropped below other years, Thayer Nash would have got rid of him fast. Maybe hard work was forgetfulness; maybe he threw himself into the job for eighteen hours every day so that he would sleep dreamlessly the other six.

But a black mood like Lorne's wasn't anything for a man to take to the woods, where you needed luck; a mood like that attracted calamity. And so it was that late in January, when they sent somebody from Camp Number Three to Juniper Falls, to tell Myrtle that Lorne had been injured, she was alarmed but not actually surprised. She realized she had been expecting something like that, all along. Once bad luck moved in on a man, it usually made a long visit.

*

They had taken Lorne to her father's house at Moose Meadows, and she and the baby rode up there with Doc Rider in his sleigh. That was the zero season, the Penobscot frozen into a glassy road, the sky cold blue, the hills white-robed, the wind a thin buggy whip. Myrtle was only eighteen, but the news hadn't sent her into hysteria; she had grit. Any tears that came to her eyes on that trip were just wind-tears.

According to the man who brought the news, the accident had been in no way owing to Lorne's carelessness; it was one of those unexpected strokes of ill-fortune that were always happening in the woods. Two choppers had been felling a lofty white pine, with Lorne supervising;

476

when the tree began cracking, all three retreated a safe distance; it was all routine. The afternoon had been windless; there was no real reason why the pine should have swerved slightly, striking a hemlock; but of course a falling tree was skittish. Lorne had been standing in the deep snow under the hemlock; when he saw the pine swerve he backed away, keeping well out of its path. But up in the hemlock hung a widow-maker, which was what the pinery boys called a loose limb. That widow-maker was the unexpected: the falling pine jarred it loose. One of the choppers yelled warning, and Lorne glanced up in time to see it falling. And he used his head; he never could have run fast enough to get out of its way. Instead, he flung himself face down into the snowdrift. The widow-maker landed on top of him, hurting his back; except for the cushioning snow, it probably would have struck him dead.

On that long sleigh ride to Moose Meadows, Myrtle kept wanting to ask Doc Rider what he thought; she wanted him to tell her the accident was probably nothing, that Lorne would be up in a few days; but she had sense enough to know that no doctor was going to give an opinion till he had examined the patient. Doc Rider was a fur cap and a fur coat and a woolen muffler, with only a red nose and a pair of wind-watery eyes visible. Once he gave her the reins and fumbled under the buffalo robe for a bottle of whiskey, but when he offered her a swig she refused.

"Nonsense," he said. "Do you want to catch the pneumonia?"

So she drank.

He held the bottle to his lips for a long while; and after he corked it again he said:

"It's a hard country, Myrtle. If I had it to do again I reckon I'd go to sea as a ship's doctor. Last time he was home Lorne's brother Enos was telling me about the East. Islands where they've never seen snow and where the girls wear flowers in their hair. I've seen frost here on the Fourth of July. Not often, but I've seen it. Well, a hard country makes a tough people. We live a long time. Lorne comes from a tough stock. Whatever that tree did to him, I reckon he'll pull out of it."

And the Doc was right; Lorne did pull out of it; but it took months. The falling limb hadn't actually broken his back, but it hadn't done it any good, either; always after the accident his neck would get stiff in cold weather, and he developed a kind of dowager's hump. All the rest of that winter he lay in bed, in Myrtle's old room at the northwest corner of her father's house, and when summer came he sat out in the sunshine wrapped in a blanket. By then Myrtle had turned the house in Juniper Falls back to the landlord and had moved bag and baggage up to Moose Meadows. So she was right back where she had started from, two years ago, except now she had a baby and a husband no better than an invalid. But she was spunky; she wouldn't let Lorne speak of himself as an invalid; and she always talked about how when he got well he would return to logging. But his logging days were over.

*

By the following autumn when Newcomb Dobner laid out his line of traps Lorne was up and around more than he was down, and although sickness had hollowed his cheeks and gaunted his chest he was able to do light chores. He used to fork hay to the horses, that winter, and carry swill to the pigs and even chop a little wood, but he tired out easily. Much of his time, on freezing afternoons, he sat in the kitchen, in one of the slat-back chairs facing the huge fireplace, his face cadaverous with its sallow skin and black hair. Sometimes he limped over to the front windows, staring out through the wavy, bluish panes at the overhang of icicles and the snow-buried Penobscot. Maybe he'd see a Canada jay, flashing among the boughs of the white pines in the front yard, or a gray squirrel; or maybe his eyes, blue as a lake and full of hurt and gentleness, would follow a flight of crows toward the woods, and his ears would pick up their wild coarse caws.

Myrtle was pregnant again that winter, and happy about it, both because she wanted children and because she had developed a theory that any man who could father a child must be essentially healthy. Some people might have thought it unwise for a family to increase itself when the husband was unable to bring in money, but she always had faith that things would be better. She believed, or pretended to believe, that by next fall Lorne could go back to his old job as camp foreman, and if not that certainly he could set a line of traps.

"Don't you worry," she always told Lorne. "We'll get along."

Spring came reluctantly that year, as usual, with brief thaws followed by low skies and tons of snow; and it was then, with the fur season over, and with Newcomb Dobner no longer following his trap-line, that Myrtle's father and husband began getting on each other's nerves. Like all convalescents Lorne could be irritable, and of course Newcomb had the Scottish passion for dialectics, so as winter hung on and hung on, wearing out a welcome that had never been warm, the two men would neglect their cribbage and sit in front of the fire by the hour, arguing over trifles. Since both were ardent Jacksonians, politics was not in dispute, but everything else was, especially the weather. It was Newcomb's hypothesis that this year might turn out like the one a decade ago, when New England had no summer; he believed the climate in those latitudes was gradually changing for the worse. Lorne said nonsense: he had seen a robin yesterday, and last evening he had heard two owls hooting at each other, a sure sign of thaw. Newcomb puffed his pipe and shook his head.

"I'd rather meet the devil on Exchange Street," he said, "than see a robin in March. And what do owls know about the weather?"

478

As much as anybody, Lorne replied, and more than some; and after that the discussion grew heated. Myrtle used to break it up by telling Newcomb to go milk the cow and Lorne to fetch in wood; and once she declared that two women in a kitchen were doves of peace compared with two men in front of a fire.

Being so contrary, Newcomb would have preferred a blizzard at the summer solstice, rather than lose the argument: he looked pretty glum when spring came at last, right on schedule, about the end of May, and he couldn't forgive his son-in-law for being right. Lorne's health was better by then, as certainly it should have been, nearly a year-and-a-half after his accident, and that summer he helped Newcomb cut marsh hay to sell to the logging camps. If he had made a trip down to Juniper Falls, and asked Thayer Nash to hire him again, as sawyer in the mill for the summer, and as foreman of a camp come fall, he probably would have got those jobs and would have been able to fill them, but when Myrtle suggested as much he hemmed and hawed and said he reckoned he'd best wait another year. She began to suspect then that he would never return to the mill and the woods, that in his memory the mill and log driving and the woods and Juniper Falls were all darkly entangled with cutting off Corky Ingram's hand. She could look back on that spring and know it was then she should have been firm; she should have made him go see Thayer Nash; but her pregnancy was far advanced and she didn't have the strength to harry those black ghosts from her husband's spirit.

The baby was due late in July, and at mid-month, when the time came for somebody to go down to Juniper Falls, and bring back Nettie Buckmaster and Doc Rider, if he could leave his practice long enough, Myrtle learned how stubbornly the black ghosts clung to her husband. No road led from Moose Meadows to Juniper Falls, only a trail, and the plan was that Lorne would walk down and bring back his mother and the doctor on horses from Adam Buckmaster's barn. The night before he was to leave, however, Lorne turned sick; he threw up his supper and his old back injury turned his spine into a hot poker. It was not malingering; he lay in bed suffering an agony too obviously genuine to be feigned; but yet—well—it seemed strange that his illness should coincide so neatly with his scheduled departure. He could not go, of course; Newcomb Dobner went. After that, Lorne's recovery was swift. And Myrtle knew then that at the altar, when she had repeated those words about in sickness and in health, she had been promising more than the average bride. Sometimes she wondered whether he would ever return to Juniper Falls; perhaps always at the last moment those dark forces in his spirit would turn him sick. But life always made people do the things they could not; and a time came when Lorne had to return to Juniper Falls. But that was two years in the future.

*

Myrtle's new baby didn't keep anybody waiting very long; he was born with the sunrise on July 25 a couple of days after Nettie Buckmaster and Doc Rider arrived with Newcomb Dobner.

"You've got yourself a son, this time," Doc told her, there in that northwest bedroom.

"Is he all right?" Myrtle asked, for she had been fretting lest Lorne's indifferent health might after all impair the baby.

"A fine husky boy," Doc Rider said, "full of fight and vinegar. He kicked me in the stomach first off, and then he tried to biff me in the nose."

Myrtle smiled and sank into sleep; and presently she was lying in a half-dreamy world with her son at her breast, thinking that his life would be always fair and honorable and gallant, not the jumbled thing his father's life had become. But no man could have lived a life as victorious and unerring as the one Myrtle dreamed on that summer morning in 1826.

With the baby successfully delivered, Doc Rider decided to give himself an outing, up here in the wilderness, so he remained several days, much to the sorrow of the rainbow trout over in Spirit Stream. On the evening before his return to Juniper Falls he gave Lorne a medical examination, and next morning in Myrtle's bedroom he sat looking from the new baby to its mother to its father. The door was closed, for this was a family conference; Myrtle lay propped in bed, her chestnut hair hanging in two thick braids, her warm gray eyes serious; Lorne stood staring at the floor.

"You'll be all right," Doc Rider told Myrtle. "Up and around in a few days. But don't hurry it. You've earned some rest. As for Lorne here," the Doc went on, "he'll be all right too. I put my ear to his chest last night and his heart's still beating. He may have a backache now and then, but I've had a backache for fifty years myself. Carried too many babies in satchels, I reckon. Between ourselves there's nothing to that story about the stork."

Myrtle giggled.

"No," the Doc told her, "it's not you I'm worried about, and it's not that young one. He's a husky. I'll bet a nickel he could beat up half The Patch right now. But don't let him try it. He might wander into Goat Gertie's, and he's too young for that."

Myrtle giggled again and even Lorne smiled.

"The only one in this family I'm worried about," the Doc went on, "is Lorne. And I don't mean his health. I mean his spunk. Where it's gone to I don't know. You get that spunk back, Lorne."

"Well, sure," Lorne said, not looking at anybody.

"You used to have enough and maybe too much," the Doc said. "You and Corky. I know you don't like to have me mention Corky, but that's something you've got to get over. Let's say you were both

480

damned fools. Well, who hasn't been a damned fool? It's not uncommon. You've both paid the price of damned foolishness, so why not wipe the slate clean? You ought to go back to the woods, Lorne."

Lorne nodded vaguely, staring at the open window through which came the sound of Nettie Buckmaster talking with her granddaughter, Harriet, and of hens clucking out in the chicken yard.

"A life like this," the Doc said, "here at Moose Meadows, is all right for a man of Newcomb Dobner's age. It's quiet and it's slow. But you've got a wife and two children. You've got a fortune to make. You make you a fortune and I'll guarantee you one thing—everybody in Juniper Falls will laugh over everything you and Corky ever did and think it was fine. They'll say, 'Recollect that night Lorne chopped Corky's hand? I always said that boy was a smart one.' "

Myrtle could see Lorne wincing, but maybe that was what Doc Rider wanted, to lance open that festered old wound and clean it out.

"You make you ten thousand dollars," Doc said, "and they'll put a marker on that schoolhouse chimney you and Corky stuffed. You make you fifty thousand and they'll elect you governor. You make you a hundred thousand and Deacon Lovejoy will set up in a booth at fairs and charge for sight of that ankle he sprained when you stole the ladder. I'm minded of the night it happened. He came hopping to my office on one foot all the way from Pru Wingate's. I thought I'd heard all the cuss words there were during my army days, but he had a few new ones. 'Deacon,' I said, 'I've heard of men being hopping mad, but never till now have I seen it.' "

"We didn't steal the ladder," Lorne said. "We just carried it back to the barn where it belonged."

"Anyway," the Doc said, "you get that spunk back. Wherever it's gone, you go after it. A man that can father a boy like this one can do anything. By the way Myrtle, what are you naming him?"

"James Lorne Buckmaster," she said. "His father's name, only turned around."

"Jim, eh?" Doc Rider said, standing up. "Well, Jim, you behave yourself while I'm gone, you little devil."

"He's not a little devil," Myrtle said.

*

An amazing thing happened in September. By that time, of course, Nettie Buckmaster had returned to Juniper Falls and Myrtle was up and around and the baby, Jim, was getting to be a person in his own right, with his father's black hair and his mother's gray eyes.

"The best baby I ever had," Myrtle always said of him; and it was true that he was good-natured, lying there in the kitchen in his cradle hollowed from a popple log, eyes bright when somebody attracted his notice with a gourd rattle.

Despite Doc Rider's advice, Lorne had made no move to get a logging job, and oddly enough—for he had always been energetic—he didn't hurt himself working around the place there in Moose Meadows. If Myrtle asked him to fetch a bucket of water he did it willingly, or if Newcomb Dobner told him to milk the cow; but he had lost the knack of finding work that needed doing. Maybe he had got the habit of sitting doing nothing when he recovered from his accident; in any case that was what he mainly did nowadays; Myrtle would look out the front window and see him down on the little wharf, watching the river flow past in the September sunshine. Maybe the sight of running water, and the sound of the river gurgling around the pilings, and the autumnal feel in the air, with the hills faintly hazy and milkweed gossamer floating, all helped soothe his spirit; she hoped so.

Now and then he used to take down his rifle and go hunting, but nothing came of it. Odd: he was an excellent shot. But on those soft days when the leaves were yellowing and the sumac was turning red he would forget all about game; he just went wandering along moose trails wrapped in his own thinking, and like as not he would end up sitting on a stump, rifle across his knees, while overhead the geese honked southward and the white-throats sang, and near at hand the season's last dragonflies buzzed past his ears and from the underbrush a porcupine watched him or maybe even a bear.

More than two years had wasted past since he chopped Corky's hand; nearly two years since he hurt his back in the woods. But time meant nothing to him any more. How much longer, Myrtle used to ask herself, would it go on like this? Would he end up as a backwoods loafer, good for nothing except fathering a flock of shirttail young ones? Yet she tried to be patient, tried to imagine herself in his place, with that dark streak in his blood that demanded atonement.

Newcomb Dobner was not so patient; privately, he told Myrtle that Lorne was acting like a damned fool. He never said that again, for she was a woman of fierce loyalties, and all Lorne's trouble had hardened her. If Newcomb didn't want them, she said, living here with him in Moose Meadows, why they would just pack up and leave this very day.

"Where could you go?" he said; and at that she broke into tears.

He comforted her then, saying he was sorry and that she and her family would always be welcome under his roof; he was a stubborn man but not a mean one. And he went on to say that perhaps some day he would go back to Bangor to live and be a carpenter again; he was tired of the woods, anyway. But she wouldn't hear to that. If he left, she would feel she had moved her family in on him and they had taken over and driven him out. She wasn't very happy in her marriage any more. Except for her children. When nobody else was around she used to look at Jim in his cradle and say, "You'll show them all. You'll be a rich man, Jim. You'll be able to buy and sell them all." He was too young to understand talk like that in those days, but he waved his fists and smiled. "All right, laugh," she would say. "It's true, though. You'll be rich." She always looked beautiful, talking like that to Jim.

Late in September the weather turned cloudy and the autumn rains set in, with gusts of wind that sent the maple leaves whirling; and on the third afternoon of bad weather Newcomb Dobner and Lorne sat before the fire discussing without too much amiability whether the almanac had been prescient or merely lucky in predicting rain on this day. Newcomb was puffing his pipe and looking the way he always did when that stubborn feeling stole over him: he had, he declared, been following the almanac for years; it was usually correct; and when it wasn't, he implied, the fault was less the almanac's than God's.

"You're arguing in a circle," Lorne said.

"I'm doing no such thing. I've never argued in a circle. What would be the sense of that?"

On the floor several kittens were tumbling, pretending the soft panther rug was a live catamount; their mother sat on the hearth, washing a paw; the hunting dog, Zippy, who was mainly coon hound, lay stretched between Newcomb Dobner and Lorne; and the watchdog, Duke, an old shep, lay by the front door. Myrtle was stuffing a hen for supper; Jim lay asleep in his cradle; Harriet was taking a nap in the bedroom. Overhead the rain drummed the roof; the windows were gray and spattered. Then the amazing thing happened.

First off, the dog Duke stirred himself and started barking; Zippy joined in. Myrtle tried to shush them, because the children were napping; Newcomb Dobner said somebody must be coming, and started for the door. Before he reached it a knock fell. Myrtle always remembered the startled look—it was almost panic—on Lorne's face, because she knew then that like a painfully shy child he wanted to run and hide; and she told herself it was doing him no good, living up here away from people, for he was only coddling his humiliation.

When her father opened the door Myrtle saw a man on the stoop, blocked against the rain; a stocky man with freckles and a grin and a turned-up nose. When he shook hands with Newcomb Dobner he used his left hand. Corky Ingram!

"Well I'm damned," she heard Lorne say; and he was smiling when he hurried to the door.

There was a lot of laughing then—pretty nervous laughing, some of it—and Lorne took Corky's cap and coat and after shaking off the water hung them on the deer antlers topping the silver-birch hat tree. Corky kept saying it was great weather for ducks, and a long time between drinks, and why didn't Lorne ever come down to Juniper Falls, anyway?

For a moment, before she went over to say hello, Myrtle was aware of an altogether unreasonable dislike of Corky Ingram. "He's trouble," she thought. "He's always been trouble for Lorne." Then, seeing the steel hook Corky wore where his right hand should have been, she was ashamed.

"It's good to see you," she said. "Sit down and I'll get hot drinks."

Corky was in great form; while she prepared hot toddies, and arranged doughnuts on a plate, she saw him go to the mantel and pick up the birch-bark moose-call that always stood there, between the Bible and the square-faced clock; he put the call to his lips and blew.

"Am I man or moose?" he said, grinning.

Everybody laughed, except Newcomb Dobner, who had never much liked Corky anyway; he sat hunched down in his chair pulling on his pipe, his long face brown and homely.

"You'll stay for supper," Myrtle said, when she served the second round of drinks.

Corky nodded vigorously.

"I wouldn't miss a chance at one of your meals. And I'll spend the night, if I can rout out the dogs and use their bed."

"We've the northeast bedroom," Newcomb Dobner said. "You're very welcome to it, I'm sure."

"Aw, now, Newcomb, you know you won't let me use a bed. I might give you fleas. You'll make me sleep in the sugar barrel with the dogs."

Again everyone laughed, except Newcomb; he drank down his toddy and said it was time to do the chores. It might have sweetened his grumpiness, Myrtle thought, if Lorne had offered to help, but of course this was a reunion of old friends and Lorne couldn't be blamed for wanting to sit visiting. The rain had settled to a steady, hard downpour and shadows were gathering when Newcomb buttoned his India rubber slicker and left by the south kitchen door, which took him through the shed, with its smells of fish lines and seines, to the barn.

Preparing supper, Myrtle kept wondering what had brought Corky to Moose Meadows. Certainly he couldn't be on his way to a winter in the woods, with one hand. She was mainly glad he had come, for surely the visit was good for Lorne: he hadn't laughed so much since the old days. And yet—well—something kept telling her Corky always brought trouble.

It was not till after supper, when the children were asleep, and Myrtle's hands were in dishwater, and the men sat by the fire smoking, that the reason for Corky's visit came out.

"Lorne," she heard him say, "maybe you're wondering why I'm here. It's to talk something over with you, Lorne. I'm going into business."

"I'm glad to hear it," Lorne said.

"I haven't done much, the last couple of years," Corky said. "A few odd jobs. I sold my accordion, and that brought some money. But I've just monkeyed around. Still, I've done a lot of thinking. I've thought of this business and that. I didn't want to rush into anything."

"You've had it hard," Lorne said.

"I didn't mean that. I don't want anybody to think I'm complaining. Nobody can say I've ever complained. But I've done a lot of thinking and—well—you know—I've thought of this business and wondered about the money in it, and of that one. And do you know what's one of the best businesses in Juniper Falls?"

"Lovejoy & Osgood," Lorne said.

"They do well," Corky said. "Yes, they do all right. But it's mainly credit. And Roger Fiske does all right with his hardware, but it's credit too. A fellow like me, just starting out, you can't have a lot on your books. Harley Eaton does all right with his livery stable too, but I don't much cotton to horses. So what does that leave? I don't mean businesses like Arnold Ulin's carriage shop and a blacksmith business like Fred Jackson's—I'm no good with tools any more. Never was much good with them, for that matter. I mean a business I could handle. What have you got left?"

"There's Sumner Alloway's grocery," Lorne said, "and Clint Warren's Temperance House."

"The grocery is a credit business, Lorne, and I can't handle that. Not enough capital. And it would take a sight of money to buy out Clint Warren. Besides, he wouldn't sell. So what have you got left?"

Myrtle could see Lorne scowling and wetting his lips. But he didn't say anything.

"I'll tell you what," Corky said. "You've got Tim Sullivan's place. You've got Sullivan's Saloon. *He* don't do no credit business. No, sir! Cash on the barrelhead, that's a saloon for you. I could handle a business like that. I could make a living out of it. If Tim can support a wife and eight kids and hire his nephew to help tend bar, why it looks to me like I could make a living."

"You figure to buy him out?" Lorne asked.

Corky shook his head.

"He wouldn't sell. Or if he would, he'd want a fortune. No, I figure to start in competition with him. I'm well liked if I do say so myself, and Tim's not. Last few years he's got grouchier and grouchier. He's not well liked, Lorne. I think I could do all right, in competition with him."

"Where would you locate?" Lorne asked.

"As close to him as I can get. That way, if Tim gets grouchy with the boys and they leave mad, why they'll stop in at my place. Remember that vacant lot west of Sullivan's? Well, Thayer Nash owns it. All it's doing is laying there and costing taxes. Thayer will build to suit the tenant. He's got plenty of lumber at his mill and plenty of money to hire help—he'll build. He told me so."

"You've been to Thayer Nash?" Lorne asked.

"I've not been just sitting whittling—I've been thinking and I've been figuring. And I've talked to Thayer Nash. He'll build me the kind of

485

building I want and give me a lease. I've got his word for that. And no matter what they say about Thayer, nobody can say he goes back on his word. So I'm all set, except I don't have enough capital. Not near enough. My father's promised me two hundred dollars, but I'll need more. Fixtures come high. So does stock. I'd like to have a thousand to feel comfortable."

Myrtle had stopped rattling the dishes, and nobody said anything; the rain sounded louder than ever.

"With a thousand," Corky said finally, "and with the two hundred from my father I could make a go of it. It would be something for me to do."

From the end of the kitchen Myrtle could see the three men there at the hearth, shadowy except where the glow from the fire lighted them. Then her father stood up, reached toward the fire with a resinous splinter, and after it had ignited moved the flame back and forth across the bowl of his pipe. He asked:

"Have you had business experience?"

"Well," Corky said slowly, "not exactly. No, you might say I haven't."

"Then my advice is to stay clear of it. Running a saloon is for the ragtag, anyway."

Corky turned to Lorne.

"What do you think?"

"I can't say that I agree with Newcomb," Lorne said. "No, I don't agree with him. A saloon might be all right. If I had a thousand I'd give it to you tonight, Corky. But I don't have. I don't have a hundred. I don't have fifty. We're poor up here. I got hurt too, Corky. That widow-maker. I saw it falling but there was no time to run. I dropped in the snow. Might have killed me. I haven't worked for near onto two years. I wish I could help you. I've thought about you, Corky. I've worried. If I could help you I would."

"You'll work again," Corky said. "Some day. You'll have you a job again."

"My back's not what it used to be," Lorne said. "It gives me misery. I fag out too. I was strong once. Where all that strength went I don't know."

"I'm as good as new," Corky said, "except for my hook. When they're hiring they don't want a man with a hook. But I could tend bar. And I can take in the money with one hand. And if anybody wants trouble I can bat him with my hook. It's steel. Strong. It's as good as a club for batting a customer over the head."

Newcomb Dobner said:

"If you want my advice you'll stay out of a business like that."

"Lorne," Corky said, "I can get the thousand. I can get it tomorrow. That building won't take three months to build, and I can be in business by the first of the year. Thayer Nash will build it and lease it to me, and he'll lend me a thousand."

"Thayer Nash? I don't know," Lorne said, "as I'd want to be in his debt."

"Who else is there? Seth Lovejoy, maybe? He drives a dearer bargain than Thayer. But Seth might not have a loose thousand. Thayer, he has. And he stands ready, Lorne, to let me have it. A two-year note at eight percent. 'Mr. Nash,' I said, 'make it six percent.' Old Thayer just shook his head. 'No,' he said, 'eight or nothing. You shop around,' he said, 'if you think you can do better than eight. Eight percent on a two-year note,' he said. 'Just you sign your name to that note, Corky,' he said, 'and get Lorne Buckmaster to sign with you. Then the thousand is yours.' So I told him I reckoned he'd made a deal. And I brought the note up here with me, Lorne. With the business I'll do there'll be nothing to paying it off. Here it is, Lorne, you can look it over yourself. I've signed already and after you sign I'll get the money."

Corky rustled out a sheet of folded foolscap; Lorne carried it over to the supper table where candles were burning. Newcomb Dobner said:

"It's been a rule of my life never to go on a note with any man."

Lorne made no reply; he was reading through all the legal phraseology.

"If you want two years to go by fast," Newcomb said, "just sign a note. A year will seem like a week and a week like a minute."

Lorne was reading; Myrtle went to the table and looked over his shoulder.

"Thayer Nash and I," Newcomb said, "have had no dealings. But I know his sort. I worked for men like that in Bangor and there was no pleasing them. Everything had to be done their way."

Lorne finished reading the document.

"It sounds all right, I reckon," he said. "I'm no lawyer, but it sounds legal."

"Oh, it's legal," Corky said. "C. E. Porter drew it up. It's legal."

"Lorne's got nothing," Newcomb Dobner said, "so what's the good of his name on a note? I'll tell you what. Thayer Nash must have figured his father and his brothers would make it good. That will be gilt-edged, with Lorne's name on it, because of his father and his brothers."

"It's gilt-edged anyway," Corky said. "I'll make enough to pay it off inside a year."

"And there's me," Newcomb said. "His father and his brothers, Thayer Nash must have figured, and Newcomb Dobner too. A saloon business! I'll have none of it. You can tell Thayer Nash I said so."

In the candlelight Myrtle could see the blood working under the skin of Lorne's face; on the table his fist was clenched.

"If I sign," he said, "and I'm going to, nobody will have to make my promise good. I've stood on my own feet before, and I will again. It's my own doing. Nobody will be called on to help. Where's the ink and a quill, Myrt?"

*

He had to sign that note; she could understand. He and Corky had been friends always, but it was more than that: it was atonement, and it was a demonstration that he had not been piqued at Corky that night in Sullivan's, and it was an affirmation of his manhood. She wanted to kick her father for going on and on about how Lorne had nothing, about how Thayer Nash wanted his name on the note because Adam Buckmaster and Newcomb Dobner and Lorne's brothers could be expected to make the note good if Corky should fail. Lorne may have been floundering in the muck at the bottom of life, but he still had pride; and she knew that now he would never let anybody make the note good, if he and Corky couldn't. But she could hope Corky would make a success of the saloon business.

She thought Lorne never forgave her father for the way he talked that night. For that matter, she never forgave him either. There had been no call, she told herself, for rubbing Lorne's nose in his poverty and his failure. Yet, as she thought it over during the next weeks, she realized Newcomb Dobner had been only trying to prevent Lorne from making a mistake. He had spoken vehemently, and said more than he should, but that was only because he was of Scottish descent, with the Scot's dread of debt and general hysteria about parting with money. For days after the signing of that note Newcomb was lost in gloom, and he got on less and less well with his son-in-law. Myrtle lived in the hope that by the time another logging season came around Lorne would take a job in the woods and move his wife and children to a house down in Juniper Falls.

The time came for Newcomb to follow his trap-line, and for the next several months life was happier at Moose Meadows; a trapper had to be up and gone before daybreak, and usually he didn't return till dusk. Sometimes, even, he was gone several days at a stretch. During the trapping season, it was almost as if Myrtle and Lorne had a house all their own; if Lorne wanted to come up behind Myrtle in the kitchen, and put his arms around her and kiss her ear, and maybe lead her to the bedroom, he was free to do so. They still loved each other and they were still lovers. Harriet, of course, was getting to the age—she would be three in April—when they couldn't be too demonstrative before her; but little Jim was no problem in that regard.

Or in any regard, really; Myrtle said she was sure he must be the best baby that ever lived. And the smartest. And the healthiest. Lorne used to help when she gave Jim a bath, and they both admired his deep chest and chubby arms. Even at that age he loved the water; he liked to sit in the washbowl splashing like a gosling.

"He'll be a river pig," Lorne said.

"A millionaire, that's what he'll be," Myrtle said. "He's a smart one."

She knew a mother shouldn't have favorites among her children, but Jim was always hers even when she had five. She loved the way he looked at her with his gray eyes; a sharp, cool and yet humorous gaze, as if he pretty well saw through this thing called life.

"Well," she used to say, when he was still a baby, "you needn't look at me like that. I'm not going to steal any of your dollars, you old money-bags!"

He always laughed then.

He saw his first log drive and met his first river hogs when he was not yet a year old, for of course the whole season's cut of the Liberty Lumber Company came floating down the Penobscot past the house at Moose Meadows, and Jim, secure in his mother's arms, was on hand to watch.

"Wave at the men," Myrtle would say.

Maybe that was why he always felt so at home and yet so nostalgic on a drive, and maybe that was why a drive always made him want a woman. Maybe in some dusty corner of memory that first drive remained: sawlogs swimming on the freshets of spring, and the smells of pine sap and pine bark and a fishy river and the rank vegetation of shore. And the smell of Myrtle's clean clothes and skin must have been mingled with the log smells, and the faint odor of the dried lavender leaves from the pomander she wore on a chain between her breasts.

As always, the river pigs that year used to stop at the Dobner place, for a slice of pie and coffee, and perhaps in his mind there remained some recollection of those log drivers, of their unshaved, cocky faces, their big-knuckled fingers, their sweat-sodden and river-sodden garments, their clanking cant hooks. Anyway, he never wanted to be anything but a logging man.

With the drive going past, Lorne managed to make himself scarce by wandering off to the woods on the pretext of hunting. Myrtle begged him to stay and talk with the boys, even to drop the word that he had signed the note with Corky. "They'd think I was bragging," he said. Men! Male pride and male bullheadedness!

She wasn't too squeamish to tell the boys how Lorne had signed the note: she wanted the news to get around. And she asked how Corky was doing in the saloon business. They were evasive, saying they had been in the woods all winter. But one river pig who had recently come up from Juniper Falls to join the drive said well, ma'am, it was this way, Tim Sullivan was a pretty popular saloon keeper, his free lunch was very tasty, and of course the boys were used to going to Tim's.

"But Corky's doing all right, isn't he?" Myrtle asked. "He's making money?"

"I reckon so, ma'am. The boys still go to Tim Sullivan's, but they drop into Corky's too. Only trouble is, Corky likes a drop himself. Maybe I would too, if I'd lost a hand. Maybe I'd drink up my profits too. if I was in Corky's shoes."

*

Two-and-a-half years since Lorne's accident; his recovery was as complete as it would ever be; yet still he made no effort to get his old job back. The drive was over and the river silent again, except for the screams of fish hawks and the cries of loons; summer was at full tide, with bats flittering in the twilight and myrtle-birds singing in the dawn; among the bellflowers and the poke milkweed in the marshes honey bees were buzzing; but Lorne was little better than a drone. He still helped cut hay, of course, and he would weed the garden till his back began hurting, but for the most part he puttered. Maybe he would sit in the sun whittling out a bobber for a fishing line, or using oily rags to clean his rifle, or carving out a finely balanced canoe paddle of rock maple, but none of that was actually work in Newcomb Dobner's book. Nor in Myrtle's, for that matter.

In August a timber cruiser, returning to Juniper Falls, stopped for a meal, and at Myrtle's request he agreed to deliver a letter to Thayer Nash. She marched Lorne to the bedroom and shut the door and made him write the letter, asking to go to work that fall as a woods foreman. But some of Lorne's defeatism must have seeped between the lines; September and October came with never a reply.

When the pinery boys straggled past that autumn, going to the woods, Myrtle kept asking how Corky Ingram was doing in the saloon business, for in another year his note to Thayer Nash would fall due and she was worrying. Their reports were not encouraging. Tim Sullivan, as it turned out, was more popular than Corky had estimated; his long-established saloon still did the bulk of the thirst-quenching in Juniper Falls.

"It's soured Corky," one pinery boy said. "When you do go to his place he's got a grouch on because you ain't been there before. He's not the way he used to be. And he's drinking more than a man should."

If Corky couldn't meet the note Thayer Nash would be after Lorne for the money. A thousand dollars. Lorne had hardly a thousand cents. That fall and winter, long after Lorne had gone to sleep, Myrtle used to lie awake worrying. This couldn't go on forever, this living with her father; it wasn't fair to anybody, least of all to Lorne, for when a man didn't buckle down and support his family some of his manhood dribbled away. Sometimes in the darkness, while the house creaked in the January cold and the frost crept over the pane, tears would roll down Myrtle's cheeks. What kind of start, she used to think, would it be for Jim, having a father who was a loafer? In that part of the world, in public estimation, a loafer was right down there at the bottom of society, hardly better than a drunkard.

490

Now and then, far past midnight, she would slip from bed and steal to the kitchen, stirring up the coals in the fireplace and brewing herself a cup of spicebush tea. She was hardly more than a girl in those days, but worry had given her face a drawn look, and her hands were rough from so much hard work. Wrapped in a quilt, huddled before the fire, she used to hear the night voices of the wilderness: a porcupine gnawing at the corner of the house; wolves howling the glittering stars; a panther's scream. She used to think that Lorne's life had become something like a log jam on a river, all plugged and tangled, and she would cast about in her mind for some way to find the key log and get him moving again.

Now and then when she returned to bed Lorne would waken and take her into his arms and they would make love: their passion was always wild and wonderful; she could forget everything then. Some women might have used the ultimate feminine weapon and held out on him, until he got work, but she had a strain of integrity which would have blocked her using that weapon if she had wanted to, and she never wanted to.

Another spring came and another log drive; this year Jim had outgrown being held in her arms; he stood by her side watching, learning the words for logs and cant hooks and driving boots and bateaux and calks. He was a great favorite among the river men, when they came to the kitchen. "Want to fight?" they used to say, kneeling and waving their fists and letting him punch them.

So another drive swept past the house in Moose Meadows, with Lorne finding excuses for going to the woods so he wouldn't have to face the river hogs; and when the bateaux of the rear crew went downriver Newcomb Dobner rode along, to buy supplies in Juniper Falls. When he returned, a week later, he brought startling news. As usual, with the drive over, the river pigs had raised merry hell, roistering in Sullivan's Saloon and in Corky Ingram's; and along about three in the morning a gigantic roughhouse had shaken the foundations of Corky's place. Corky had been drinking and had batted men with his hook; one thing led to another; somebody—it was never determined who—knocked Corky over; his head struck the corner of the bar, and it killed him.

*

When Lorne heard that news, in the kitchen at Moose Meadows, his face went pasty.

"Corky?" he said. "Corky Ingram? You're sure?"

"Sure I'm sure," Newcomb said. "I went to his funeral."

Without another word Lorne stood up and went shambling out the front door; Myrtle caught up with him on the path to the woods. His eyes were those of a man desperately wounded; his lips in the sunshine were bloodless.

"Myrt," he said, "leave me be. Leave me be for a spell."

She always remembered how he looked, walking off toward the hemlock and spruce woods, his pants bagging, hands dangling, shoulders humped, feet stumbling over pebbles. He was gone all day, all night, and till late afternoon of the next day. That was mosquito time but he must not have built a smudge, wherever he had been, for his hands and face were savagely bitten. His shirt had been torn by thorns; his hat was missing. When he got back he walked through the kitchen without a word and in the bedroom she found him lying face down.

"Lorne," she said, "where've you been? I worried, Lorne."

He just kept lying there.

"Lorne," she said. "I'm sorry. Tell me about it."

He couldn't bring himself to speak, for quite a while, and then he said it was his fault Corky Ingram was dead.

She said sharply:

"Lorne! This has gone far enough. Too far. How could it be your fault?"

His fists were clenched; he lay prone, talking to the bedclothing. Talking about old Corky.

"Dead, Myrt. Dead and buried and I never knew. I chopped his hand, Myrt, and they had to cut it off. He wore a hook. He tried to laugh like he used to but it was no good. He wore a hook. They didn't want him, Myrt, in the woods or in the mill. They didn't want him any more, a man with one hand. He had to shake hands with his left, Myrt. He sold his accordion."

"You helped him," she said. "You signed his note."

"And I never should have, Myrt. I should have got a job and turned over half of my pay, but I never should have signed that note. It allowed him to open a saloon, Myrt. I chopped off his hand so he had to open a saloon, and it was in his saloon he got killed. He'd be alive today, if I hadn't signed that note."

"Lorne," she said, "you've got to take hold of yourself. You've got a wife, Lorne, and two young ones. You've got to take hold."

"I know it," he said; but he just kept lying there.

*

That was a sick summer, with Lorne shambling through futility, with Newcomb Dobner looking down his nose, with Myrtle feeling like a girl alone in a bateau swept along by rapid current toward a waterfall. The date in September when the note fell due—that was the waterfall. Her father had been right; if you wanted time to race by, just sign a note.

A letter came that summer from Thayer Nash, sent up to Moose Meadows by one of his landlookers. Written with a sharp goosequill, the letter stated that Thayer Nash expected Lorne Buckmaster to pay in full the one thousand dollars, plus accrued interest, owed by one Ulysses Ingram, deceased. When Lorne read the letter he sat staring, and after a while he said:

"He never liked it if you called him Ulysses. He'd fight anybody who called him that."

September came, and the dread date when the note fell due. But oddly, nothing out of the way happened on that date. Myrtle had been bracing herself, but the blow didn't fall. A week or so later, some pinery boys on their way to the woods stopped in with another letter from Thayer Nash, demanding payment; if he didn't receive his money by November 1, he said, he would have to take further action. But that deadline also came and went with nothing happening.

"Let him fume," Lorne said. "He can't get blood from a turnip."

That was a gloomy autumn, with Myrtle losing sleep about what action Thayer Nash might take. Her face thinned and there were dark places under her eyes; her nerves were jumpy. She was always expecting bad news to come up the river and knock portentously on the door.

But when the bad news came it wasn't so very dramatic after all: just old Bill Mellen, the town constable, shuffling in on a soft, gray, unseasonably warm afternoon in December, complaining about how hard on his feet the walk from Juniper Falls had been. He was a lean old man with a white mustache and faded eyes, not much account even for scaring the young ones off the streets after curfew; the town hired him out of charity, mainly. Still, he was the law, with a warrant and everything; upon the demand of Thayer Nash he had come to take Lorne to debtors' jail.

*

Down by the south river bank in Juniper Falls, among the weeds and junk of Musquash Street, out of sight of respectability, sat the town jail, a squat stone building. Lorne was the only prisoner; he remained three weeks. It was an antique law, jailing a man for debt; it would be abolished before long; and even now such imprisonment was mainly a token punishment: Bill Mellen left the door unlocked and Lorne could have come and gone at will, so long as he remained within the limits of the town. But he did not come and go; he stayed inside. Maybe he hated to face the town, or maybe it satisfied some dark demand of his nature for penance, being in jail.

Adam Buckmaster could have got him out in a minute, by paying Corky Ingram's debt to Thayer Nash; but Adam said Thayer had enough money now and besides Lorne had never seen a cent of that thousand dollars.

"I don't propose to pay another man's bills," Adam said. "If I started that, I'd end up in jail myself."

But he might have paid that note, if there had been no other way to get Lorne out. But there was another way. With the genius of a self-governing people at finding ways around the laws they have imposed upon themselves, the people of the state of Maine had discovered a loophole in their bad old law. They could throw you into jail for debt but they couldn't keep you there, if you were willing to take a pauper's oath.

The only trouble was, Lorne wouldn't take that oath. Too proud, maybe.

But then Lorne's brother Enos returned from sea, and when he heard what was going on he said nonsense, he'll take that oath after I talk with him.

And Lorne did. He couldn't do much else, with Enos threatening to use his savings to pay Thayer Nash. And it was Enos who happened across that letter from Eliphalet Hoyt in the *Juniper Falls Federalist,* urging Maine boys to come west to Wisconsin and make their fortunes, and it was Enos who offered to stake Lorne if he wanted to move out there with his family.

"I don't know," Lorne said vaguely. "We'd be among strangers."

"Bosh," Myrtle said. "We'll go."

494

IX

It was better in Wisconsin, not so good as Myrtle wanted, but at least they owned a cabin, and Lorne had a job. Maybe he would never set the Chippewa River on fire, but he supported his family. Dan Stoughton couldn't have found a more faithful worker to saw his logs.

On winter days when the mill wheel was frozen Lorne went to work anyway, arriving at six and staying till six, except for the hour when he went home at noon. He always kept busy, tinkering with belts and pulleys, sharpening saws, repairing the log carriage; and at odd times he would build a bateau for Dan Stoughton to sell. When he got his pay he never went to the Northern Saloon to blow it; he went home. In that free and easy country where most men worked only to get money for a bender, Lorne was one in a thousand, and if he had demanded it doubtless Stoughton would have doubled his wages or given him part interest in the mill. But he didn't like to risk losing his job. Fear of losing it snapped him awake in the darkness of a winter morning and sent him shambling toward the mill, anxious lest he be thirty seconds late. He could have been an hour late and Stoughton would never have known, for after the habit of successful men Stoughton enjoyed sitting up late and sleeping late and perhaps making love to one of his Chippewa girls before breakfast.

That first year or two there in Quickwater, Myrtle used to keep after Lorne to ask more wages from Dan Stoughton, but it was like nagging a boulder, she couldn't move him.

"You square your shoulders," she used to say, "and go into his trading post and walk right up to him. Tell him you need more money. Tell him you want a share in the mill."

"He'd never do that, Myrt."

She used to want to scream, but then she would notice the gray old fear showing in his face, and she'd want to cry. He lived with fear; he was a tanglefooted, round-shouldered, hump-backed embodiment of apprehension. He fretted about all kinds of things: that the mill might burn down and throw him out of work; that the Chippewas over in Injun Hollow might take to the warpath; that there might be a flood or a forest fire or a slack market for lumber; that news of his disgrace might travel from Maine to Wisconsin. Especially about that. And it was the silliest worry of all, for in Quickwater nobody would have been much interested; up in that country people were willing to let the sleeping past lie.

*

"That's impossible," he used to say, about projects that were not impossible at all. "It can't be done."

"Can't never could," Myrtle told him.

But he was far gone in self-doubt. If he nicked a chisel or cut his finger, he said things like that were always happening to him. Maybe he believed that the forces controlling the universe had singled him out as the butt of creation; whether they had or not the result was the same, so long as he believed it.

Still, he was a good husband, as husbands went in this world. He never kicked a dog or threw a tomcat into a well or cuffed his children. He dragged himself to that sawmill job every day, even when his bronchial tubes were clogged with mucus and his thin body was racked by coughing. In the spring, after working hard all day, he spaded a garden patch and planted vegetables. He chopped wood for the fireplace, he fixed up a pen for a pig and a chicken yard for Myrtle's hens. And in October, on bright Sunday afternoons, he would take his family to the woods to gather walnuts and hickory nuts and hazel nuts; sometimes they all went fishing.

When the Buckmasters had been three years in Quickwater Dan Stoughton donated land for a school, down on Chippewa Street a block east of the Northern Saloon, and when men gave their labor to raise the log building Lorne was right on hand to help. Lack of a school had worried him, for he had that New England passion for education; he wanted his children to have advantages. But actually, Jim learned more from his father than from any teacher at a desk.

Lorne taught him to use an ax, to make indelible ink from sumac juice, and how it was prudent to lock up axes and hammers at night, because otherwise porcupines would be certain to come and gnaw the handles to get the salt that had oozed from sweaty palms. He taught him to use a rifle and to treat all guns with respect, especially empty ones, and how when he went hunting he should bite his thumb when he saw his first deer, to keep buck fever away. He taught him trapping and how to build lean-to shelters and how, if he got lost in the woods, he should never panic.

"Climb a tree and look around," Lorne said. "Locate a stream. Follow it to a bigger stream and follow it to a river. A river will always lead a man to a cabin or a town."

He taught him to drain turpentine from tamarack to rub into aching muscles; to apply hemlock bark to burns; to chew the bark of slippery elm and use it as a poultice for wounds. And on Sunday afternoons in spring, when Lorne sat whittling in the sun, he told Jim about fighting.

"The other man," he said, "will always look at the place where he figures to hit you. Watch his eyes and beat him to it. If he's an Injun smack him on the nose; an Injun can't take it on the nose. But if he's white, Jim, don't let him have it on the nose. And not on the mouth, for that matter. You get a white man drinking his own blood and he goes wild. You can't hurt him then. What you do, give him a smack on the jaw."

Lorne seemed a different man when he talked about fighting.

"If he's shorter than you," he said, "he'll want to go into a clinch. All right, let him. But then give a twist and throw your left side into his body. Lever your elbow under his chin and pry up. He'll break his hold then. If he don't his neck will break. When you feel his hold breaking you jerk back and wham your fist into his chin. He'll fold then. But after you hit him, you step back. He may be down but not out. He may try kicking. If he does, you grab his heel and give a jerk. He'll land on his head. After that you can walk away and set up the drinks."

Lorne taught his son to swim too; Jim could hardly remember when he couldn't swim. On warm Sundays the two of them would leave their place and walk west along Yew Street, (which everybody called Shin-Tangle Street because the Canada Yew was nicknamed shin-tangle), and go to the swamp north of the sawmill along the Chippewa River. They would stop there, hearing the croak of frogs, while Lorne pointed out which plants were wire grass and squaw weed, and which were good to eat, such as swamp turnips and sour dock. Cattails grew there in jungles, along with tall bulrushes and sedge cane; there were pools like green ink and violet ink; and the whole place reeked of fish and rot and wild peppermint and the clean scent of the pine sawdust which the mill dumped there. Jim loved those wild smells; but best he liked the sweetness of sawdust. It was a smell he always associated with his father, for when Lorne came home from work there were grains of sawdust clinging to his shoes and scattered in his hair.

On those Sundays Jim and his father would pick their way through the swamp and go to the river, walking north to a swimming hole with a sand beach. Few people went there; you could go into the water two-finger. Without his clothes Lorne looked shockingly thin, shoulder blades and collar bones sticking out, but even as a little tad Jim had a fine body. In those days the Chippewa was a bright clear river, and when you waded you could look down through the wavy water and see your toes on the white sand bottom. After Jim had learned to swim and tread water and float and dive, there came a day when Lorne found a sawlog the sacking crews had missed, and rolled it into the river and taught his son birling. Right away he could tell that Jim was going to make a riverman, and he was proud. On those Sundays he was almost happy; it was like living his own boyhood again. Later, he used to take Jim to the booms above the sawmill and let him practice jumping from log to log and riding a single log around the boom pond. And he taught him the quirks of logs.

"Give me white pine," he said, "and you can have the rest. White pine floats high and dry, and she's steady. You've got to peel hemlock or she won't float worth a damn, and once she's peeled she's cranky. Cedar's cranky whether you peel her or not—you ride a cedar log and you'll float out from under your hat. As for oak and hickory, you might as well try to float a stone."

Once at the mill Lorne taught his son how to make a dog-raft out of slabs; he showed him how to use a cant hook and a pike pole. And in the fall when they spent a day in the woods, he showed him how if you wanted to climb a tall tree you could make a ladder from a smaller tree by chopping off the branches but leaving the stubs on; he taught him to make a turkey call from the hollow bone of a wild turkey's wing, and to get chewing gum from black spruce by cutting off the resin blisters, and to pick up the horns shed by deer because they were valuable for knife handles. They had fun on those Sundays; in those days Jim thought his father a remarkable man.

*

But perhaps the most valuable thing Lorne passed on to his son was that quality which in any man is a good servant but a poor master: a sense of caution. Lorne had grown to have too much and his son had been born with too little, but after their Sundays together, although Lorne still had too much, Jim had just enough. He would need it, in that vast land.

"It's you against everything," Lorne used to say. "A lake may look solid with ice, but down at the bottom there are warm springs that cause air holes—watch for them. Watch out for everything all the time. Swallow the wrong mushroom and you'll double with cramps and die. Step on a rotten log a hundred miles from nowhere and you'll break a leg. When you're in the woods, you watch and you listen. There might be a string across a deer trail that you would never notice—walk into it and you'll pull the trigger of a set gun. An ax can glance and take off your foot and even a cornered deer will fight. Nothing's safe."

Some sumac, he said, was harmless and some poisonous; you could tell the poisonous by its white fruit and smooth-edged leaf. As for poison ivy, if you ever got your hands tangled up with it wash them in soap suds and then whiskey, finishing the treatment by powdering them with wood ashes. A bug might crawl into your ear while you slept: he'd come crawling out toward the light if you held your ear near a lantern. For an aching ear, go to a marsh and dig up a bulb of wild garlic, heating the heart of the bulb and putting it into your ear.

"But worst of all in the woods," Lorne said, "is the toothache. A fellow back home had good teeth, but he paid the barber to yank them all before he ever set out on a winter's trapping. Maybe he was smart. If you get a toothache find a prickly ash tree and put the berries in your mouth. If it ain't berry time, use the bark. If she still aches, put some hot sand in a buckskin bag and hold it to your jaw."

Myrtle seldom talked to Jim about being careful; her talk was about getting ahead. Even before Quickwater had a school she taught him his letters and a little arithmetic, and after the school was established she saw to it that he attended every term. "Knowledge is power," she used to say.

But book learning wasn't what he wanted; he never took to school. He was six years old when Dan Stoughton gave the land for a schoolhouse, and as soon as he heard about it he knew it was bad news. It was exciting, of course, to go down and watch his father and the other men building that children's jail, with its puncheon floor and two log backhouses, with its blackboard daubed with lampblack and its windows so high that only the teacher could look out, but he was uneasy. He liked nothing about it; give him the woods every time. A carpenter built a long desk in the center of the room, with sloping boards and bench seats, and at the sides of the room were other long desks and benches. The teacher would sit on a platform near the box stove. By October the building was ready, but school couldn't be held because there was no teacher. Maybe there never would be one, Jim used to hope.

But in December a man named Alexander Castleman drifted into town carrying a hand-bell and a globe; the globe, he said, proved the world was round. His pants bagged, his big belly bagged, and trickles of tobacco juice fertilized the soft stubble on his chin. After a couple of drinks in the Northern Saloon, he announced he had heard this thriving little city was looking for a teacher; well, here he was.

"I was a successful pedagogue back in York State," he said.

"That may be," Dan Stoughton said, "but can you teach school?"

"Examine me," the stranger said.

Stoughton stood there thinking, then took the globe and went to a corner. Over his shoulder he asked:

"What color is the British Empire?"

"Pink."

Stoughton nodded admiringly.

"That clinches it," he said. "Looks like we've found us a teacher."

So school took up, with its smells of sweaty woolens, of stale air, of asafetida, of Alex Castleman's tobacco-and-whiskey breath. Jim studied in Noah Webster's *Elementary Spelling,* in Murray's *English Reader,* in Kilbourn's *Columbian Geography;* from Dillworth's *Arithmetic* he learned to cipher, scratching a shale slate with a piece of soapstone. Later he was given a copybook, a goosequill and an inkstand made from a sawed-off cowhorn. For two terms each year school was held; Jim didn't like it. He used to envy the Chippewa boys; nobody made them go to school.

*

Long afterward he could look back and see it all in memory: the cabin on Shin-Tangle Street with a deer carcass hanging frozen on the north side; the bench on the south with a gourd wash basin and a wooden bucket; the door with a leather latchstring; and inside, over the door, his father's rifle and powder horn hanging on forked cleats. It was dim in the cabin, with its windows of oiled deerskin, but the fireplace sent out flickers of gold light. Maybe his mother would be sitting by the fire, teaching his sister Harriet to darn a sock over a gourd, or nursing his younger sister Alice, or, later, his youngest sister May, or, later still, the baby brother, Dobner. He would have been nine years old by then, nearly ten; but time was always jumbled in those memories.

There were blank spaces, as if river mist had drifted across his mind, but he could remember everything about the cabin. In the northwest corner stood a pole bed, and at first, when he was little, he must have slept in it with his parents; but at some hazy time his father built a loft with a ladder of jack-pine poles: Jim and Harriet slept up there. Snow sifted in, on blizzardy nights, and the wind howled and Jim knew what the wind was, for he had heard about it from Chippewa boys: it was the Windigo, spectral and homeless, out on his rounds collecting dead men's souls. Harriet used to hide her head under the covers, but Jim wasn't scared, very.

He must have learned the Chippewa tongue nearly as soon as he learned English, for he couldn't remember a time when he didn't know that *keemeechawich* meant you stink, and that *mackquáh* was bear. His mother encouraged him to make friends with the Chippewas, for she said that Chippewa country would be Jim's country, and it might come in handy for him to know the language. By the time he was six he was always trudging over to their village in Injun Hollow; he liked them and they liked him; he would have made a good Chippewa, one old man said. Except for his gray eyes he even looked somewhat Injun, with his black hair and his skin coppery from being outdoors so much. It was from the Chippewas he learned to handle his body like an Injun, walking softly in the woods, practicing the art of leaving no sign.

Years later he could remember everything as it looked then, all shining and enchanted. The path to Injun Hollow was soft with brown needles, and the bright air smelled of fresh water and of balsam and pine. Usual thing, in those memories, the sky was cloudless blue and the sunshine brilliant but crisp, and the stream which flowed through Injun Hollow—Snowshoe Creek, it was called—came rushing whitely over boulders from around a bend where spruce grew thick. The water was icy clear and teeming with trout.

500

Not again would the Chippewas have a place like that to live, with the forests uncut and lakes strung along trout streams like blazing blue gems on a chain. You'd hear partridges drumming and wild turkeys gobbling and quail whistling, and you'd see flight after endless flight of wild geese and wild ducks heading south in the Hunter's Moon. Panthers were in those woods then, and herds of moose; there were beaver dams and beaver marshes. He could see it all, looking back.

Maybe some of it, in memory, looked better than it had actually been; certainly that Chippewa village must have been dirtier than he remembered. Yet always in his thoughts that village was a place of enchantment, its wickiups trim and tidy with their walls of brown cedar bark and their roofs of canoe birch. Slender girls were there with black shining hair; girls who chattered and laughed and sometimes, in astonishment or maidenly chagrin, clapped palms over their mouths. But in those days he thought girls silly.

He remembered boys of his own age with names like Nekeek and Shángwoitch; boys with black unreadable eyes and unexpected grins, with lithe, tricky bodies when you wrestled them; boys fast in foot races and accurate with bow and arrow. They taught him things he never would have known: wrestling holds, and how to make a bow of hickory or ash, with a bow-string from the neck of a snapping turtle; a string like that would never stretch or shrink. But by then bows and arrows were only playthings; the hunters of the tribe used guns from Dan Stoughton's store.

Sometimes he was invited into a wickiup with its smells of cedar and furs and popple smoke; he remembered the sweetgrass baskets and baskets of willow withes; the mats of woven rushes; the bags of soft buckskin with beads and quills. He learned to build a fire Injun fashion with the wood wheel-spoked; he ate wild rice stewed with chunks of rabbit and venison; a time or two he ate dog. It nearly choked him, but he wanted to be polite.

Nekeek's mother said Jim was one of her sons; she gave him a pair of moosehide moccasins with pucker tops, and taught him to make his own; after that in Quickwater moccasins were his footgear. She showed him the Injun way of tanning hides too; how you soaked a hide in a mixture of water and the animal's brains; how you smoked it over a cob fire to give it a soft golden color. He used to watch her sewing rabbit-skin blankets, and doeskin leggings for her daughters, and buckskin mittens for her sons; but she would never let him see how she prepared the fragile skin of unborn fawn; that was mystery and medicine; ceremonial herbs and shells were wrapped in that, and then tucked away in the beaver-skin medicine bag. But he could watch when she dyed porcupine quills, and so he learned of the bright red latent in bloodroot and alder; of the purple in rotting maple wood; of the yellow in lichens.

He may have hated school, but he loved the things he learned in

Injun Hollow: how to gather nettles for snares and fish nets; how to make snowshoes with green ash frames and rawhide netting; how to get twine from basswood bark and tough thread from deer sinew. He learned the wonders of birch bark: how you could use it to make watertight kettles and pails for blueberries; how in June, when it peeled easiest, you could harvest it in great sheets and build a canoe. He never did build one himself—it took two weeks and demanded skills beyond his years—but after he was a grown man he traveled countless miles in Injun canoes, and it was handy to know how to waterproof the seams with spruce gum and charcoal.

Looking back, he could see he owed the Chippewa Nation a lot; more than he could ever repay, and more than he ever did repay, with anything good. But when he was six and seven he kept faith with them all; he said he wished he'd been born a Chippewa. Their enemies he took for his own: he used to declare he hated the Dakotas, although he had never laid eyes on one. He even said he hated Dan Stoughton just because the Chippewas did, for Stoughton had bamboozled them in a hundred ways, corrupting them with rotgut and decoying their daughters to his fancy house; Quickwater itself had been a Chippewa village before Stoughton mulcted them out of the land. But in later years Jim could see Stoughton's side of the matter: a man had to get ahead.

*

Because they were poor getting ahead became the great goal in his life; by the time he was eight or nine he took it for granted he would make wagonloads of money. All over America, in those days, boys were dreaming how they would strike it rich: money fever was one of the commonplace childhood diseases of the Nineteenth Century. Jim could see his father had taken the wrong fork in the road, and sometimes—although it gave him a guilty feeling—he secretly scorned him for it, especially after his mother told him the whole story about Lorne's trouble.

"Jim," she said, "don't you go signing notes for friends. Promise me you won't."

"I guess I'd never do that," he said, smiling.

"You save your pennies," she said. "After while you'll have a dime. After while you'll have a dollar. After while you'll be rich."

Years later he could remember that advice and smile: nobody got rich that way. There were many ways to turn the trick, some of them honest, but nobody got rich hoarding pennies.

Yet he tried it for a while, when he was a boy; he worked at anything, and he saved like a miser. He used to go to the Chippewa River and gather the bark which floated in the pokelogans; it made a hot fire, once it was dried, and he peddled it for kindling. Dan Stoughton turned out to be his best customer for that, and for the cranberries he gathered in the woods, and for wild strawberries and walnuts. Right at first it stuck in Jim's craw, dealing with a Chippewa enemy like Stoughton, but Stoughton paid cash on the line, and Jim wanted money. He paid well for errands too; once Jim earned a whole nickel going over to Injun Hollow. That was when Slim Willow, one of the Chippewa girls who lived behind the Northern Saloon, was suffering great pain in her stomach; she wanted to be treated by Hole-in-the-Day, the medicine man. But Hole-in-the-Day refused to go to the saloon; Slim Willow, he said, had become a *matchee móyamee,* a bad woman. She died that night, which was kind of too bad, for she was only sixteen and very pretty, one of Stoughton's best money-makers.

One Sunday Jim's father taught him a river song from Maine, and Jim happened to sing it for Stoughton. It was a fine rollicking song composed by a Maine pinery boy named Corky Ingram; Stoughton liked it and gave Jim a penny.

"Jim," he said, "you come to my place some night when the boys are here. I want you to sing it for the boys."

By then Jim no longer thought of Stoughton as his enemy, so the next Saturday evening he slipped away from home and crunched through the snow to the Northern Saloon. That was in the dead of winter when he was eight, and he could remember how white the half moon looked in the icy sky, how the stars glittered, how silvery the snow looked with inky pencilings of shadow, how black were the woods hemming in the town. He heard timber wolves howling, away over east; his breath was a cloud of silver; the cold tingled in his nose; underfoot the snow squeaked. Hurrying south along the west side of Squaw Street, he passed the long wooden building attached to the rear of the Northern Saloon; some of the windows were black and some showed rose light. That was where Stoughton kept his Chippewa girls; and for a moment, as he remembered his friends out in Injun Hollow, as it came back to him how the girls laughed when they winnowed wild rice, some of his old loyalty to the tribe returned. He almost stopped and ran back home. But up in that country nobody would ever get anywhere stringing along with Injuns; he remembered how Hole-in-the-Day had once said a white settlement was like a drop of raccoon grease on a blanket; at first you hardly saw it, but it would spread and take everything. Nobody in his senses chose the losing side. Besides, Dan Stoughton had said he might make some money, singing that song.

Years later he could remember how the town looked that night. It had been growing, the last year or so; Xenophon Yates had built a hotel called the Shanghai House, on the northeast corner of Squaw and Chippewa Streets; and on the southeast corner Jim could see the frosted windows of Gentleman Steve's Woodsman's Friend Saloon and Parlor of Chance, A Good Time For All.

But the Northern Saloon there on the northwest corner still had the most business; when Jim opened the door it was crowded, and he never forgot the blissful warmth, and the cheerful blaze of candles, and the smells of sawdust and tobacco mingled with the good yeasty smell of beer and the whiffs of bourbon and rye. The woods were endless and full of cold and death, but the Northern Saloon was dazzle and life. Old magic glowed in the polished wood of the bar and glistened on the glasses pyramided in front of the plate-glass mirror. Stoughton's monkey was perched on the bar, begging drinks; and the Chinese bartender, Mon-Fah Lee, looked resplendent in a white coat. You had a feeling of fine things about to happen.

He could remember how self-conscious he felt, standing there in his muskrat cap and moccasins stuffed with deer hair; but then Dan Stoughton came shouldering through the crowd, his black eyes friendly and amused.

"Jim," he said, "I'm glad you could come. Would you like a drink?"

"I don't care," Jim said.

He had never tasted liquor, and he knew he would catch it if he went home smelling like the town drunk, but he was always game.

Stoughton patted his shoulder and guided him to the bar.

"Jim," he said, gesturing toward Mon-Fah Lee, "meet my great-grand-father. He's one of the Virginia Lees. They called his son Light-Horse Harry."

Men were laughing; Mon-Fah Lee, who was about thirty, bowed and smiled.

"You serve Jim a Sarsaparilla Mead," Stoughton said. "Jim's the smartest young one in this town. Some day we'll all be working for him, like as not."

Jim thought he had never tasted anything so delicious as that Sarsa-parilla; he drained his glass, getting the last drop; and then Stoughton told him there were some newcomers he wanted him to meet, and took him to a round table of polished cherry wood where a man and a woman were sitting. Their names, Stoughton said, were Mr. and Mrs. Lew Fitzpatrick; Mr. Fitzpatrick was a surveyor, here on a business deal that would make great news.

They were rich people; Jim saw that at once. And they were from a world about which he had only dimly heard: a world of cities lighted at night, of fine suppers, of music. Mr. Fitzpatrick, who looked about thirty-five, was a long-legged, reddish-blond man with an angular face, a narrow mustache and sharp eyes; he talked fast in a clipped voice. His waistcoat was of black sateen, and on his left hand he wore a skull-and-crossbones ring of heavy silver with diamonds for eyes.

But it was his wife, Molly, who interested Jim most; he had never seen a woman like her. She looked much younger than Mr. Fitzpatrick and much jollier. In the candlelight her hair was the color of golden buckskin, her eyes blue and merry; she wore a white satin turban bespangled with flakes of gold and decorated with a white aigrette; long gold pendants dangled from her ears. Her nose was faintly Roman and her body looked soft and plump, as if she had eaten much whipped cream and many aromatic spices and pink sweet bonbons and pink lobsters; her lips were red as if stained from wine. But she was drinking whiskey.

She held out a hand when Stoughton introduced Jim; it was a soft warm hand with a firm grip; several bracelets flashed and jangled on her wrist with operatic effect.

"Honey," she said, "you'd better take off that coat. It's warm in here and you might catch cold when you leave."

His mother might have said that. But his mother's voice was often tired and sometimes edged; Molly Fitzpatrick's voice had zip and tang and the pleasant harshness of a catbird's. And he couldn't imagine his mother having a free and easy time in a saloon full of men.

Jim didn't much want to take off his blanket coat, thereby revealing his old hunting shirt of greasy deerskin, but Molly insisted and draped it over a vacant chair.

"Jim," she said, "I wish I had a boy like you. How old are you?"

"I'll be nine in July."

"Come sit on my lap, Jim," she said.

It was a soft lap, with warmth and roundness; she had a fragrant aura.

"You smell nice, ma'am," Jim said.

Mr. Fitzpatrick threw back his head and laughed; Molly was chuckling.

"Jim," she said, "that's not me you smell. That's Jockey Club perfume, four dollars an ounce in New Orleans. You ever been in New Orleans, Jim?"

"Where?" he asked.

"I can tell you haven't," she said, "or you wouldn't ask where. Mr. Fitzpatrick surveyed for the Pontchartrain Railroad. He surveyed and I lost his wages at roulette. But I made it up at the races. A filly named Creole Princess paid forty to one. I was rolling in catnip that day."

"Roulette's not her game," Lew Fitzpatrick said, "but she can pick horses. Could I buy you a drink, Dan?"

No, Dan Stoughton said, the drinks were on him; and he summoned Charlie Usher, the man-of-all-work at the Northern Saloon. He was small and on the gray-haired side of sixty, but very nimble.

"Charlie," Molly Fitzpatrick said, "Dan here tells me you write poetry, as it were."

Yes, ma'am, Charlie said, that was true; only he had never got the poem finished; he had been working on it for years, but had never made much headway.

"But I've got the first line," Charlie said. "It starts off, 'Oh, the beauties of Nature!' But I can't seem to go on from there."

Dan told Charlie to bring the whiskey bottle and a Sarsaparilla for Jim; and quite some time later, when the whiskey in the bottle was much lower, Dan stood up and called for quiet.

505

"Boys," he said, "we've got a surprise tonight. We've got entertainment. But first I want you to meet a couple of strangers. I want you to meet Lew Fitzpatrick. He was up here nine years ago surveying this townsite, and he bought himself ten thousand acres of pineland. He's a surveyor, boys, and he's been everywhere—he knows a good thing when he sees it. Now he's back, and I reckon he'll stay. You'll be knowing him better, boys."

Lew stood up and waved a careless hand; the crowd clapped.

"That was fine, boys," Dan Stoughton said. "Me and Lew are on a deal that will make your ears thump against your head. You'll be hearing about it, boys. And now meet Mrs. Fitzpatrick."

You could almost hear that crowd catch its breath when she stood up, she was such a voluptuous piece of woman-flesh; her taffeta gown rustled and whispered and shone.

"Boys," she said, in that strong voice with its delicious rasp, "I'm pleased to meet you. Timber country is right down my tote road, boys. I was born in the New Brunswick woods."

They cheered and stamped and whistled.

"Boys," she yelled, laughing, "that was real nice. I hope you live forever and I live to see you die."

They raised the roof then.

She sat down, beaming; the cheering kept on; so she jumped to her feet again.

"Boys," she yelled, "I like to see you happy. Have a round of drinks, boys. The treats are on me."

It was pandemonium in that saloon, for a while. Usual thing, at that hour on a Saturday night, you might have expected trouble breaking out here and there, but not now; it was as if some strong current of bonhomie flowed inexhaustibly from Molly Fitzpatrick and made everybody love everybody else. At one point an old Canuck named Pierre Somebody-or-Other edged through the crowd and declared that *Sacre!* he too had come from New Brunswick. What part of that country was Molly from?

"The Oromocto River," she said, "below Fredericton. A settlement called Pigeon Grove. My folks were fresh over from Ireland when I was born. Pappy worked cutting masts for the royal navy. His name was Grady Lanagan."

Pierre shook his head; he had never known Mr. Lanagan.

"Well, maybe not," Molly said. "My whole family was massacred by the goddamned Abnaki Indians when I was five. I'd gone to the woods that evening. We didn't have a water closet, see? Pappy had never got around to digging one. So I'd gone to the woods and the Injuns came and wanted whiskey. Pappy never liked Injuns, and he was quick with his fists, as it were. They massacred my whole family."

"Gar!" Pierre said.

"I ran through the woods to the Prouts', and Reuben Prout raised the alarm. The settlers tracked the Injuns and killed every one of the bastards. But that didn't bring my folks back. The Prouts raised me. They didn't have any kids of their own. You ever know Reuben Prout?"

One of Pierre's ears had been frozen; it was swollen twice as big as an ordinary ear. He stood scratching it, shaking his head.

"Nice folks," Molly said. "I lived with them till I was seventeen. Then Pappy Prout decided to build a new barn. He threw a barn-raising frolic and Mr. Fitzpatrick came. He was a stranger in that country, there on business, but everybody was welcome. A week after that Mr. Fitzpatrick and I were married. We left for the States and I've never been back."

Lew Fitzpatrick said:

"You've been drinking too much. What does Pierre care whether your pappy built a backhouse?"

"A backhouse," Pierre said seriously, "she is ver' handy."

Molly slapped her thigh and laughed. Then she drained her glass and said:

"They were good to me, those Prouts. Reuben was nice but Sadie was nicer. Sadie, she was his wife. She was so nice I couldn't bear to tell her when old Reuben started bothering me. I was fourteen then. I never even told her when I was going to have a baby, but then I slipped and fell on the back stoop and I didn't need to tell her. I was a sick girl."

"Molly," Lew Fitzpatrick said.

"Hell, Lew, it's all between friends. It was a long time ago. I was fourteen, and now I'm twenty-seven. What the hell. All in a lifetime, eh, Pierre?"

Pierre nodded pensively.

"You happy tonight, Pierre?" Molly asked.

He shrugged.

"I lose too much at euchre."

She patted his hand.

"Easy come, easy go—that's what I always say. You cheer up, Pierre. I like to see you happy. I always want to see the boys happy."

The racket in that place was deafening; people were singing. Dan Stoughton banged the empty whiskey bottle on the table.

"Boys!" he kept yelling, "boys!"

When at last they quieted, he said he wanted them to behave long enough to hear Lorne Buckmaster's son sing a song called "The Ballad of Faithful Nellie."

"It's not a hymn, boys—you'll like it." And he told Jim: "Better stand on the table so everybody can see you."

Jim's knees were quivering, after he stood on that table, and his tongue was dry. He wanted to jump down and streak for the door, he was so scared. But Stoughton had told him they would pass the hat, once he had finished, and he wanted to earn money. So he made himself sing.

"One day in the springtime when snow was no more,
And the logs in the river were ten million strong ..."

It had a rousing good tune, and the lines flowed along like a river in freshet; you could close your eyes and see white rapids and whirlpools and shallows swarming with minnows. Spiked boots were in that song, and cant hooks and pike poles.

He hadn't sung a half dozen lines before he knew it was going to be all right; he was scared no longer. Everybody was listening; he could look down from that table and see checked shirts and snow pacs and Mackinaws and plaid caps; he could see rheumy eyes and grizzled jaws and cocky young faces and faces with ruddy noses. And over by the door that led back to the fancy house, he could see pinery boys with drinks in their hands and with arms around Chippewa girls. They were all listening and Jim felt fine.

Years afterward he could think how he looked that night, a kid needing a haircut, his pants patched and his wrists rough and red from the weather. But there must have been something about him even then that got a hold on people; they always liked him. Some day he would be a legend up in that country; he'd have his hands on its throat, some day; but they always liked him. They'd always vote the way he said.

Their feet were tapping before he was through; it was their kind of music.

"Oh, drive the logs down, boys, drive the white pine,
Drive 'em and ride 'em down to the boom,
Where my Nellie is waiting in raiment so fine,
She'll be my bride and I'll be her groom."

They shouted and whistled and stamped, once he was through, but he didn't remain on that table to take any bows. Dan Stoughton looked pleased and patted his shoulder; and Molly Fitzpatrick, who maybe had swallowed too much whiskey, grabbed up her husband's beaver hat and dropped in a silver dollar. Then she went among the crowd passing the hat, her skirt rustling and swinging. She was plump as a partridge but light on her feet, in her dainty winter boots of gray velvet ornamented with fur.

They had all been kegging up, and when Molly yelled they should shell out they dug into their pockets; that hat harvested a lot of money. Jim's blood was racing and his pockets jingling when he left; he ran all the way home. But he wasn't a hero at home; not at first. His parents said they had been worried; they wanted to know what he had been up to, staying out till all hours. But he had a trump card; it was a good idea, he always thought after that, to hold a trump card.

"I've been earning money, that's what," he said; and he emptied his pockets.

They changed their tune then; Lorne looked at him with a sort of awe. Myrtle counted the money.

"Jim," she said, "that's a lot of money. That's five dollars and sixteen cents. You're a money-maker, Jim. You're going to be a rich man."

"I know it," he said.

Up in the loft he was too excited to sleep. And when drowsiness finally came it was not the money he was thinking of; it was of Molly Fitzpatrick. Remembering her was like remembering the taste of candy; he felt warm and strange and filled with pleasure. Remembering her was like swimming in warm water and having a mosquito bite where you couldn't reach to scratch.

*

The Fitzpatricks stayed at the Shanghai House, and Jim used to see them occasionally on the street; in that frozen town they looked dashing and warm-blooded and cosmopolitan.

"Why, it's Jim," Molly would exclaim. "How are you, Jim?"

He would say he was fine, and he would stand there smelling Molly's perfume and the fragrance of Mr. Fitzpatrick's bay rum and expensive cigars. They certainly must be wealthy, he thought; their clothes alone must have cost a fortune. Mr. Fitzpatrick wore high boots of gleaming black leather and a gray tweed cape with a black beaver collar and beaver lining; across the chest it had a gold cord and tassels; his beaver hat rode at a jaunty angle. Molly's dove-gray witzchoura was likewise lined and trimmed with beaver, and she carried a huge beaver muff.

"Jim," she said, late one afternoon in February, "do you like oysters?"

"I don't know," he said.

"You've never tasted oysters, Jim?"

He felt oddly ashamed but he confessed he hadn't, so she told him to come to the Shanghai House and have supper with them; a teamster had arrived that day, bringing oysters in his sled-load of supplies.

He ran home through freezing light; he scrubbed his hands and face; he put on his best homespun pants and his newest shirt of soft deerskin sewed with whang strips. His mother looked dubious about that invitation to supper, for it was rumored that Mrs. Fitzpatrick smoked cigars; but nothing could have stopped Jim from going.

The Shanghai House, two stories tall, was built of pine lumber, not logs; Quickwater was forging ahead. Twilight had turned the snow blue and the woods black when he climbed the steps to the hotel veranda and opened the door with its thickly-frosted pane. The Fitzpatricks stood at the hotel desk where Molly was matching pennies with Xenophon Yates, the proprietor; they were laughing.

"Here's Jim," Mr. Fitzpatrick said, and Molly wheeled lightly around.

She was the only woman he had ever known who dressed in elegance and high fashion; compared with her his mother seemed drab. He

509

watched her coming toward him, her gown low on her shoulders and tight in the bodice and full-skirted; it was of rich brocade that looked the color of liquid copper in the candlelight. She stooped and kissed him; he caught a whiff of whiskey.

"You're right on time," she said. "You'd be out of style in New York, Jim. The dandies there think they have to keep you waiting."

Everything was better than he had anticipated; he remembered the hotel dining room with Chippewa girls bringing on the food; he remembered his first taste of oyster stew. In the white bowl yellow islands of butter floated on its steaming surface, and flakes of pepper; little round crackers, delectable beyond belief, were heaped in a dish; he liked to scatter them in the stew and push them under with his spoon.

"Baltimore is the place for oysters," Molly said once. "Washington, too. I was eating blue points there in '29 and found a pearl. We'd taken three congressmen to supper—Mr. Fitzpatrick was pushing a land claims bill. It was worth a fortune to all concerned, so I had to be nice. When I found that pearl old Congressman Acker wanted it for his mother. *He* said. So I had to give it up. I'll bet he never had a mother. Congressmen are pigs."

She laughed, and added:

"But never eat oysters in a month without an 'r,' Jim. Once at the Sulphur Springs we ate oysters on May first and Mr. Fitzpatrick was sick. Not me, though. Me, I can eat anything. Mr. Fitzpatrick says it's my goat blood, as it were."

She laughed again. Lew Fitzpatrick asked:

"How about that time at Rockaway?"

"Why, damn your soul!" she exclaimed, in great good humor. "Yes, there was Rockaway. I'll have to take that back, about eating anything. We went to the trotting races at Rockaway with these friends of Mr. Fitzpatrick. I forget their names. A couple of switch-tail actresses and a pugilist and a waxworks owner. I'd picked a string of winners at the track, so I blew them to a supper at the Marine Pavilion. We had champagne and headcheese. I was sick then, all right. But after that Mr. Fitzpatrick took me to the United States Hotel at Saratoga. I drank the waters for a week and they fixed me up."

"And never sick a day since," Lew said.

Much of that talk Jim didn't understand, but it left him with an impression of whirling gaiety and the careless scattering of money; he thought it would be fine to grow up and dress like Mr. Fitzpatrick in starched and ruffled linen and a roll-collar waistcoat. Upon finishing his meal, Mr. Fitzpatrick produced a silk case and selected a cheroot; he used a pearl-handled penknife to cut off the end, and he lighted it at one of the table candles. Then he unfolded a copy of a newspaper which must have reached town by today's supply sled, and studied an inside column. His hands holding the newspaper were buff-colored and smooth, the fingernails clean with half-moons showing. Jim had never seen a man with hands like that; his father's were rough-skinned and battered.

"Molly," Lew said, from behind the paper, "they're quoting Wabash Canal at eighteen."

"Well, skin me for a squirrel," she said.

Lew put down the paper, tilted back and blew smoke at the ceiling.

"I headed the survey on that canal," he told Jim. "They offered me three dollars a mile cash or ten dollars a mile in stock. I took stock."

"Cows?" Jim asked, and Mr. Fitzpatrick broke out laughing.

"Pieces of paper, Jim. Ownership in the company. Cows have to be fed, but you put commercial stock in a safe and forget it. Movers come in and settle the country and the company booms. Pretty soon the stock goes through the roof. I'm about through surveying, Jim. There're easier ways to make money."

"He's got the golden touch," Molly told Jim. "Back in '24 he bought Illinois bank notes at thirty cents on the dollar. He took a satchelful east and sold them to speculators to pay off their taxes on prairie land. That's how I met him. Richard Vedder of Boston had come to New Brunswick and Mr. Fitzpatrick followed him there. What did he pay you for those notes, Lew?"

"Sixty-two cents on the dollar," Mr. Fitzpatrick said. "No, wait a minute. He paid sixty-five."

"Anyway," Molly said, "we had a nice honeymoon with all those profits. We stayed at the Cataract House at Niagara Falls." She glanced around the dining room, then touched her husband's arm. "Honey, give me a drag."

So he passed over the newspaper and the cigar; Molly unfolded the newspaper and hid behind it; a cloud of smoke issued from her ambush. She was laughing richly when she handed back the cigar. Mr. Fitzpatrick winked at Jim.

"Best-natured woman alive," he said. "Just keep her in tobacco and spirits and satin and velvet, and she purrs like a cat. She's ready for anything and she takes things as they come."

"I've had to," she said, "married to Mr. Fitzpatrick," and now she winked at Jim. "When he went out surveying he wouldn't leave me— afraid I'd be gone when he got back, I guess. I've seen some rough country, as it were. I've waded in Louisiana swamps and I've heard the mosquitoes sing in the Arkansas Country. I slept on the ground and I wore pants just like a man."

"Not *just* like a man," Lew said. "Not with that rear end of yours."

She drew back a fist as if to hit him, but she was laughing.

"You!" she exclaimed. And she told Jim:

"Except for hunters and squatters, surveyors are the first ones into a new country. A surveyor is bound to run across minerals and salt licks and good mill sites, so he can pick up a little money on the side, as it were. Mr. Fitzpatrick was never squeamish about that."

Lew shrugged.

"A man's a fool," he said, "if he doesn't capitalize his information."

"Anyway," Molly said, "it was a rough life. I used to cook for the crew. And once in the Illinois Delta a damned Injun killed one of our flagmen, and Mr. Fitzpatrick put me to work lugging flags and rods. But those days are over. I hope."

"They're over," Lew said.

When they left the dining room, Molly asked Jim if he liked candy; he said he liked it. So the Fitzpatricks took him upstairs and along a bare cold corridor that smelled of raw pine boards. But their bedchamber was warm from a small stove, and it smelled fragrant from all the cut-glass bottles of perfumes and lotions cluttering the dresser. The door of a tall oak press stood ajar, and Jim caught sight of enough dresses to start a store. Piled in a corner of the room were gay bandboxes; a leather trunk stood with its lid up, overflowing with plumes and silk mittens and ribbons.

Once the door was closed, Lew Fitzpatrick poured two glasses of brandy, and Molly bit the end off a slim cigar and puffed with satisfaction.

"Don't tell on me, Jim," she said. "Not that I care, but Mr. Fitzpatrick says it would give the wrong impression here in Quickwater. Folks would think he married a high-stepper, as it were. Well, maybe he did." She laughed. "We went back to Fredericksburg, Virginia once. His father runs an apothecary shop there. The family thinks he married beneath his station."

"They'd think that," Lew said, "if I'd married Princess Victoria."

"We've had fun, anyway," Molly said, and she rummaged in the trunk, bringing out a glass jar packed with stick candy. "Here you are, Jim."

When he got home he passed the candy to his sisters and his parents; chewing it, Lorne sat staring at the fire, looking worried.

"Did Fitzpatrick say anything about me?" he asked.

Jim was surprised; he shook his head.

"Something's afoot," Lorne said. "He and Stoughton keep coming to the mill. Maybe he's going to buy the mill and fire me."

"Bosh," Myrtle said. And she asked whether Mrs. Fitzpatrick had smoked.

"No," Jim said, "she didn't."

He was like that, always; he stood by his friends.

*

Early in March Dan Stoughton and Lew Fitzpatrick announced the formation of the Quickwater Log & Lumber Company; the two men were equal partners. They had great plans for the company, such as replacing the slow old gatesaw in the mill with a muley saw, and installing a second muley. Lew Fitzpatrick, it was announced, had put much fresh capital into the company, as well as his extensive holdings of pine stump-age up along the Flambeau.

The great news broke in the *Quickwater Mercury,* a weekly paper which Dan Stoughton had encouraged Nora and Emerson Tate to establish the previous year. Some people said Stoughton had put up the dollars for the venture, and that every week dozens of copies were sent to newspapers and capitalists in the East to induce big money to find its way to the Wisconsin woods. That must have been the case, for surely Quickwater could never have supported an unsubsidized paper.

Reading the *Mercury,* you hardly recognized the town; it always called the lumber mill "that bright jewel among our factories, the magnificent milling works"; it spoke of somebody's ordinary log cabin as a "palatial residence"; it called Alexander Castleman "the distinguished pedagogue who is superintendent of our matchless school system"; and in nearly every issue there appeared references to the salubrious climate with which Quickwater was blessed. When the thermometer registered thirty below the *Mercury* mentioned "the beautiful bracing weather we have been enjoying"; when a blizzard buried the town the paper mentioned "the pulchritudinous effect of spruce and fir decorated with millions of sparkling diamonds"; and when the snow melted in April and everybody waded in slush it said, "Spring with all its beauties of balmy airs and bird song has arrived." It never criticized or took a dark view. If a man caught pneumonia it reported him slightly under the weather; if he died it usurped the judicial bench of the Almighty and said he had passed to his reward. And it never called Three-Cent Olson by his nickname; it called him Mr. Knut Olson and sometimes Reverend Olson, although he had never been ordained.

Mr. Olson was a blacksmith and wagon maker whose shop stood on the southwest corner of Chippewa and Squaw Streets; Jim liked to drop in there and watch sparks showering from a horseshoe on the anvil. Some years earlier, a river pig named Ed Wheeler had drowned, and when a collection was taken up for his widow, Knut Olson gave three cents. After that he was always Three-Cent Olson, even on Sunday when he held divine worship in the schoolhouse. He was in his late fifties with a narrow head and prominent teeth; and he must have been a better blacksmith than a preacher, for his shop drew more customers than his church services. He was married to a woman named Vonnie; she was in her forties and his second wife.

The Olsons were the Buckmasters' nearest neighbors; they lived a block east in a log cabin on the south side of Shin-Tangle Street. Three-Cent Olson kept a cow and Vonnie Olson kept chickens; the *Mercury,* in reporting a birth, always called her Dr. V. Olson. Actually she was not a physician but an excellent midwife; if a baby was reluctant to become a citizen of Quickwater, Vonnie loaded a goose quill with snuff and blew the powder up the nose of the patient. In the sneezing that followed, the baby came into the world expeditiously.

"I'm too busy a woman," she always said, "to waste time waiting till some snot-nose kid decides to be born."

She was tall and rangy, and as a healer she specialized in diseases of women, which she called the afflictions of the ladies. In the spring you would see her going to the woods in search of yarrow and snakeroot. And in addition to her other talents, Vonnie thought herself psychic, being given to premonitions and odd dreams; moreover, she could read palms. Once she followed the life line of every member of the Buckmaster family and came forth with the prediction that they would all die by forest fire. It scared the children, and of course it gave Lorne something else to fret over, but Myrtle was too practical to worry about a thing like that. She just laughed, after Vonnie had gone.

"Bosh," she said; and she pointed out that few of Vonnie's prognostications ever came true, except those predicting a cold winter for Quickwater with several drunken Injuns freezing to death in snowdrifts on the way home from the Northern Saloon.

Molly Fitzpatrick must have heard about Vonnie's clairvoyance, for late one afternoon in April as Jim was returning from the woods he saw the two women coming out of the Olson cabin. Molly waved and Jim entered the yard. She was beaming.

"Jim," she exclaimed, "I've got great news. I'm going to have a baby." That made him blush.

"Mrs. Olson read it all in my hand," Molly said. "In about a year I'll have a baby boy. And after that three more. It's all in my palm, as it were. I've always wanted a boatload of kids. I've swallowed a ton of Brandreth's Vegetable Universal Pills, but nothing's happened."

He could remember that afternoon; it was about the first warm day in that land of reluctant springs. In the woods he had seen Johnny-jump-ups and violets; blackbirds and robins were singing. And here in the Olson yard he could hear the lowing of a cow fenced in the east lot.

"That cow," Vonnie said, "drives a body to distraction. Mr. Olson is weaning her calf and she's lonesome."

Molly wanted to see the calf; after all, she said, she had been brought up on a farm; the smell of a haymow always reminded her of Reuben Prout, as it were. So Vonnie Olson led Molly and Jim to the back yard, where chickens were clucking, and on past the woodpile to an enclosure beside the log barn.

The calf was a heifer with the friendliness of a puppy and a sagacious suspicion of the predatory habits of two-legged animals.

"By God," Molly said, "she's cute. I want to pet her."

She unlatched the gate and picked her way lightly among the pancakes of manure. Her skirt, of ankle-length taffeta, cascaded over her hips with much swishing; she was wearing a bibi-bonnet with a white plume. The calf, after a certain amount of head-lowering and feinting as if it had horns, permitted its face to be stroked. In the warm light from the western sun its silky hair was glossy red and white.

"This," Molly said, "is the way to live. Eggs from your own hens and milk from your cow. We've never had a home. Ever since we were married it's been hotel rooms and lodging houses. Living in a trunk. Mr. Fitzpatrick's work has kept him on the go, and he has trouble with his feet. They itch. Maybe we'll settle down, some day."

She scratched the calf's forehead and it nuzzled her fingers; she laughed. "It thinks they're tits," she said.

From the chicken yard came the singing of hens, and high overhead a flight of wild geese went honking northward, bringing the spring from smiling lands Jim had never seen. The air was scented with pines and young grasses and the warm, moist odor of cow.

"Are you happy?" Molly asked the calf. "I like to see everybody happy."

She was turning to go when a man appeared from beyond the barn; it was Three-Cent Olson.

"Mrs. Fitzpatrick," Vonnie said, "this here is my man, Reverend Olson."

"Pleased to make your acquaintance," Three-Cent said.

"That goes double, Reverend," Molly sang out. "Do you do baptizing?"

Three-Cent Olson's face was all angularity and high cheekbones and yellow horse teeth. He said he guessed he could do anything any other blacksmith or preacher could do.

"I may have a job for you," Molly said. "Your wife tells me I'm to have a baby."

"You don't look it, ma'am."

"I don't mean here in the cow lot," Molly said, laughing. "I mean in about a year."

"If the Lord hasn't called me home," Three-Cent said, "you bring that baby to church. I'll give him the best baptizing a young one ever had, and it won't cost you a penny."

"That settles it, Reverend. You're hired."

"Of course," Three-Cent added, "if you want to put something in the collection plate I can't stop you . . . Well, I guess I will feed the calf."

Molly wanted to stay and see that; presently Jim saw Three-Cent coming from the house with a pan of warm milk into which he had put cold boiled potatoes.

"Mr. Olson," Vonnie said, "do you know what you're doing, feeding potatoes to a calf?"

Certainly he knew what he was doing, Three-Cent said; he always knew. The calf was well weaned now; it would drink. The next step was to teach it to eat solid food.

He placed the pan on the ground and the calf buried its muzzle in the milk and slupped; then it gobbled the potatoes. But those potatoes were large and they must have taken it by surprise, for it began gasping.

"Mr. Olson," Vonnie said, "that critter's in trouble."

"I think it will be all right," Three-Cent said.

But it wasn't all right; the calf stood choking with head lowered and sides heaving. Then it ran around the lot, gasping. Finally it sank to its knees and flopped over on its side, horrible rasping coming from its throat.

By then Three-Cent was excited; he ran over to the calf and slapped the back of its neck.

"Do something, somebody," he yelled. "Jim, why don't you do something?"

Jim stood watching, thinking fast.

"You save this calf," Three-Cent yelled, "and you can have her."

Potatoes, boiled potatoes, Jim was thinking. You put them on a plate and mashed them with a fork.

He whirled, ran out of the cow lot and returned with a length of firewood. He dumped it on the ground beside the calf, pushed Olson aside and stood astride the animal's neck. It was still heaving and gasping, but more weakly. Jim's hands met under the calf's neck and he tugged, lifting its head and placing its throat over the round length of firewood. Then he pushed down on the calf's neck and rocked; the wood rolled back and froth. All at once the calf gave a snort; then another and another; and finally it scrambled to its feet; Jim had to be quick to jump aside. It stood drawing great gulps into its lungs.

"By God!" Molly sang out. "Excuse my language, Reverend, but wasn't that smart?"

"Jim," Three-Cent Olson said, "you are a good boy."

It was easy, Jim said; boiled potatoes would mash; just mash the potatoes in its throat and they would no longer block the air passage.

"A good boy to save my calf," Three-Cent said.

The calf was sufficiently recovered now to go to the pan and lick up what was left of the milk. Jim patted it. And he asked Olson if he could borrow a rope, to lead the animal home.

"To do what?"

"It's mine," Jim said. "You said I could have it."

"Now, Jim, you know I was excited when I said that. You knew it was a joke."

Jim stood looking at Three-Cent Olson; his jaw was hard.

"It's mine," he said. "I saved its life and it's mine. It's my calf."

"He's got you there, Reverend," Molly said. "You wouldn't go back on your word."

Nothing but a joke, Three-Cent was muttering. The calf would have come out of it.

It was Vonnie Olson who settled the argument.

"Mr. Olson," she said, standing with fists on hips, "I never heard the

516

like of you. A man that will go back on his word to a boy will deny
his Lord. Next thing we'll be hearing the cock crowing three times, just
like it did with Judas."

"It wasn't Judas," Three-Cent said. "It was—"

"I don't care if it was Moses," Vonnie said. "I don't care if it was
Jonah and the whale and Goliath. You said Jim Buckmaster could have
this calf and he can. Jim, there's rope in the barn. Fetch it and I'll fix
a halter. You lead this calf home."

The story spread; it tickled the town's fancy; pinery boys chuckled
about it in camp. They were still repeating it up in that country a half
century later when he was long gone from Quickwater and had grown
to giant's stature.

*

It caused a sensation when Jim came leading the calf home; Myrtle was
delighted.

"Jim," she said, "you'll get ahead in the world. You'll be a rich man."

"Sure," he said.

"Don't let them get you down, Jim. Don't let them stop you."

"They won't stop me."

He could remember how chesty and important he felt, owning that
calf; he could sense the deference of his sisters and even of his mother.
He was hard at work nailing together a temporary pen for the critter
when Lorne came shambling from the mill, looking fagged and stooped
and vanquished in the falling twilight.

"What's this?" he asked.

He stood there in the yard, gangling and hollow-chested, a worried
look on his sallow face, listening to the story.

"I don't know," he said, when Jim had finished. "I don't know as I'll
let you keep it."

"What!"

"I don't know as you ought to. It don't seem exactly honest, some way."

Jim was flabbergasted; he could feel the blood sweeping into his ears.
"I'm going to keep it," he said. "It's mine."

Even then he had a strong property sense, and he could be obstinate;
that was the Newcomb Dobner in him, maybe.

"Olson is our neighbor," Lorne said. "It's a bad practice for a man to
get his neighbors down on him."

"It's mine," Jim said.

"We don't want hard feelings with our neighbors. We don't want the
town to turn against us. You're young, son, and you don't know what it
means to have a whole town turn against you. You say hello and they
never answer. They never see you. You walk past a house and the folks
on the porch quit talking. You hear your own footsteps loud as a clock
in an empty house. We don't want that here in Quickwater, son."

517

Myrtle spoke up then.

"Father," she said, "this town won't turn against Jim."

"I don't know," he said, standing there with hands dangling. "Towns are funny. People you've known all your life look right through you. Never see you or say hello."

Myrtle slipped an arm around his humped shoulders.

"Father," she said quietly, "you're tired. You need your supper. Quickwater won't turn against Jim. Quickwater will laugh. They call him Three-Cent Olson, don't they? They know he's close. They'll think Jim is smart. I think he's smart."

"Oh, he's smart," Lorne said quickly. "No question as to that. He's a smart boy. A good son. Better than I deserve."

"Jim earned the calf," Myrtle said gently. "It would be dead now, but for Jim. Three-Cent Olson told him he could have it if he saved it, and he did save it. It's his. It wouldn't be right not to let him keep it."

"I'm going to keep it," Jim said.

Lorne heaved a breath; you could almost hear his ribs rattling against one another and his joints creaking.

"Well, maybe so," he said. "Maybe you're right, Myrt. I hope you're right."

"I know I'm right, father."

"I hope it lives," Lorne said. "I hope it don't take sick."

*

It not only lived; it prospered and waxed fat, munching the grass in the Buckmaster wood lot. Jim named it Bossy, and he guessed no cow was ever better cared for; he remembered how he used to go to the woods and the swamps that summer, cutting Indian grass and reed-meadow grass. With his father's help he built a small log barn and a two-wheeled cart; gripping the shafts, he hauled his hay crop home and stored it. Those were busy months when Bossy was growing up, for that fall Jim began trapping in earnest and selling the pelts to Dan Stoughton. His trap-line did not, of course, extend very far, but he caught a good many muskrats and even some beaver and otter. Lorne helped him make drying boards and taught him how to set a trap on a floating log or to stake it in deep water so the animal would drown fast before it could gnaw off its paw, and he showed him how to skin a muskrat with the fur side out and an otter with the fur side in. Jim was nine years old that fall and winter, a big boy for his age, long of arm and leg, lean in the flanks, with large hands and feet. Outdoors as he was in all weathers, his hands became so chapped that sometimes they bled; Myrtle told him to rub bear's oil into his skin, but he seldom did: those rough hands made him feel grown up.

In the spring, when Bossy had been a Buckmaster cow for about a year, Jim led her away one day without saying a word to anybody; that evening Myrtle missed her and asked where she was.

"I took her to Perry Roquemore's," Jim said.

Roquemore ran a livery stable and feed store down on the corner of Chippewa and School Streets; Myrtle wanted to know why Jim had taken her there.

"I'm having her bred," Jim said. "He's got a bull."

Myrtle and Lorne looked at each other.

"How did you know about that?" Myrtle asked her son.

"About what?"

"About—well—you know. About taking her to Roquemore's."

"Why," Jim said, "she won't come fresh unless she's bred and has a calf. Everybody knows that. Perry Roquemore's been telling me to watch her and to bring her down when she started acting frisky. She's been swinging her rump and mooing and—"

"That will do, Jim," Myrtle said.

Lorne sat staring at the floor. He had been supposed to tell Jim about where calves and babies came from, but he had never got around to it; afraid he'd be embarrassed, maybe, and couldn't pull it off. Now, more than likely, Jim had picked up that information at the livery stable. Sometimes his son was too much for Lorne. It worried him, the way Jim went plunging into this and that money-making scheme; he was afraid the boy would stumble and skin his nose.

But worrying, of course, had long been a habit with Lorne; even when things turned out well he was still apprehensive. And things did turn out well for him, sometimes: for instance, the newly-organized Quickwater Log & Lumber Company had kept him on as head sawyer at the mill and had hired another man to work under him, in addition to Earl Martin and Watt Prothero; Lorne was the mill push now. And best of all, his wages had been raised. Could have been that Molly Fitzpatrick said to her husband something like look here, Lew, Jim Buckmaster's a nice boy and his family's having it hard, why don't you give his old man more money? Could have been; there was no proof. Anyway, Lorne got his raise. Goodness knew he deserved it, for he was a crackerjack sawyer, and he was trustworthy in keeping mill records and in his stewardship of money received for lumber. But he always expected the worst.

"Don't get your hopes up, Myrt," he said, when he bought home news of his raise. "It may be a fluke. It may not last."

With the mill sawing more lumber than could be sold locally, somebody had to go down the Chippewa to take orders; that was Lew Fitzpatrick's job. He did well at it too, for he had all the nervous energy and camaraderie that made a good salesman. Sometimes he and Molly were gone for weeks; once she reported they had been clear to St. Louis. They had never established a home of their own in Quickwater; just lived on at the Shanghai House.

"Mr. Fitzpatrick is a bird of passage," Molly told Jim. "A rolling stone for sure. He says a house would tie us down. Well, maybe, but I'd sort of like a home."

Never yet had she given birth to that baby she had been so elated about, when Vonnie Olson predicted it, and that was strange. But one day in the livery stable Jim heard a loafer say that somebody had reported that Mrs. Fitzpatrick had told somebody that as a boy Lew Fitzpatrick had contracted the mumps and they went down on him and that maybe he could never father a baby, although he could keep going through the motions. If true that was kind of too bad, Molly wanted a baby so much.

One thing was sure: that bull of Perry Roquemore's had never had the mumps; his union with Bossy produced the prettiest little bull-calf Jim had ever seen. After it was weaned he sold it, and he used to peddle the milk Bossy produced so abundantly, the proceeds going into the drawstring bag where he kept his money. By the summer of his tenth birthday he had more than fifty dollars in that bag, harvest of all his errand-running and trapping and what-not. That cache was his secret; his parents knew he earned and saved, but he could be vague when they wanted details. He kept the bag hidden up among the rafters of the barn, and sometimes he would latch the door and count his riches, a conglomerate mess of coppers and silver and currency. He liked the feel of that money; he liked the way the bills rustled and the coins tinkled; that little hoard seemed to glow and warm his fingers.

And then Jim came upon another way to earn money and it led him into trouble.

*

Quickwater was beginning to boom now, just as Dan Stoughton had predicted on that day long ago when the Buckmasters first met him. The more orders Lew Fitzpatrick took for lumber the more logs the mill needed, and that meant more camps in the woods, more pinery boys to man the camps, more supplies to be teamed in from outside. By the time Jim was ten there must have been upwards of four hundred persons living there, counting drifters and timber speculators and sharpers of various kinds, but excluding Injuns and Injun dogs. Farmers were beginning to move to the area too, buying cutover land and hauling lumber from the mill to build barns and houses. Yet another saloon was built, called the Widow Maker; that made three, and they all prospered. New children were always turning up at school; it kept Alexander Castleman tired out, whaling them.

The sawmill, of course, was the throbbing heart that sent prosperity through the arteries of trade in that town; everything depended upon plenty of logs being sliced into planks and those planks being transported to market. And in those days, long before the hoot of a locomotive was dreamed of in that country, there was one good way to send lumber downriver: by rafting it. And the way to do that was by build-

520

ing the individual planks into a basic unit called a crib.

A crib measured sixteen by thirty-two feet, on the Chippewa, the planks piled across one another in alternate layers. Each layer was called a course, and the average crib was twenty courses deep, the whole unit cinched tightly together by runners and binder-planks and grub pins. When you had seven cribs you lined them up end-to-end on the river and coupled them together: that was a string. When you had four strings you coupled them together side by side and you had a Chippewa raft. You had, in fact, a floating lumber yard. And a flexible one. At a narrows on the river you could uncouple the strings and float them through one by one. At a retail dealer's you uncoupled one string or two, one crib or two, as many or as few as he needed. At a dam you sluiced the strings through on a slide, and this took some doing; for if the river was high and the current swift those strings went racing through at arrow speed and dived heedlessly into the spinning waters below: the raftsmen would have been flipped overboard, except for the sucker-line. This was a safety rope rigged down the center of the string; the raftsmen clung to that. Occasionally, somebody lost his grip and then he probably drowned, but it was understood that a man who wished to die with dry feet should avoid the rafting profession, either lumber or logs.

In those years of expansion, the Quickwater Log & Lumber Company built a slide with sluice-gates in the dam there at the sawmill, and on the river bank north of the mill it built a shed called a rafting dump where the cribs were put together. To do this work it imported a lean, cold-eyed Irishman named Pete Casey, and Jim used to go there and watch him stacking the planks and using a big auger to bore holes through the frame of the crib. Casey didn't much like children, possibly because he had eleven of his own, and he used to chase away the boys who wanted to hang around; all but Jim. Not that he liked Jim any better than the others, but after all Lorne Buckmaster was in charge of the mill and might have resented his son's being batted over the head with a two-by-four. So Jim was tolerated; and thus he learned about a highly-marketable commodity called a grub pin.

The grub pin was forty-two inches long and two inches thick, its function being to go through the auger holes in the framework at the bottom of the crib and then—after the planks were laid—through corresponding holes in the framework at the top. A sapling of hickory or white oak made the best grub pin; these young trees were cut off three feet above the ground with a blob of root left on: this knurl could not be pulled through the two-inch hole in the bottom framework. When the crib was all lumbered up, and the other end of the grub pin had been threaded through the hole in the top framework, Pete Casey used a powerful lever called a witch to yank the grub pin tight. Then he pounded in wedges to grip it in the hole.

Building cribs and coupling them together in strings consumed hundreds of grub pins; they were a very specialized and most essential device in the rafting of lumber. No grub pin, no crib; no crib, no string; no string, no raft; no raft and the lumber would remain unsold in Quickwater. Nor were grub pins to be found lying around loose in the street; to get them you had to go to a lot of trouble finding the right sapling and cutting it down and grubbing out part of its root; too much time and trouble to attract a grown man, for the going price per grub pin was only ten cents. Yet for a boy who wasn't afraid of work it offered opportunity.

Jim wasn't afraid of work, or of much else; so when he learned of the demand for grub pins he set about supplying it. He ranged the woods spying out saplings two inches in diameter; and when these lacked he would chop down a tree with a thicker trunk and whittle it to size. Slow work; but the market for the finished product was lively and the pay in cash.

School irked him more than ever, that winter and spring when he was ten, he was so busy with his trap-line and his cow and his grub pins; he wanted to chuck book learning, but his parents would have none of that; he had to go. He used to say it was a waste of time, and he may have been right, for Alexander Castleman wasn't much of a teacher, being unable to cipher beyond the rule of three, and always confusing the nominative and objective cases of pronouns. Forever needing a shave, forever drooling tobacco juice, forever wearing socks with holes and shirts with egg stains, sometimes sneaking a nip during school hours, Castleman sat on a platform with his sloppy belly and his dirty fingers, picking his teeth and scratching his ribs and yawning, staring vacantly out the window while some child recited and forty others studied aloud, for that was a blab-school and you could hear it a block away. The only time Castleman snapped out of his lethargy was when some scholar needed a whipping, which was often. Occasionally he kept bad boys in after school; Jim heard some odd tales about what happened then; people were beginning to say maybe they should send Castleman on his way and hire another teacher. But who?

One spring day Jim had all the school he could stomach, so after noon dinner instead of returning to his studies he wandered off toward Injun Hollow. At home his absence wouldn't be reported, for both his older sister Harriet and his younger sister Alice, notorious tattle-tales, were laid up with colds; what would happen tomorrow when Alexander Castleman asked for his written excuse he didn't know, and, at the moment, didn't much care. He thought he would cruise the woods and locate grub-pin saplings for later cutting. It was a fine May afternoon, except on the dry side—snow had been oddly sparse last winter and the spring rains hadn't materialized—but it was still indubitably spring with the flickers hammering and bobolinks singing.

The moccasin path, fringed by catbriers and star grass, seemed to take him through the very essence of spring, the sunlight warm and scented with chokecherry and wild plum and the drugging sweetness of locust. The air was humming with bees darting on golden zigzags; high overhead, in a sky the pure blue color of blueberries, a bald eagle sailed and soared; a white-throat sang; and when the path skirted a tamarack swamp, where limbs were putting forth young needles like pale green lace, Jim could see red-wings chasing May flies and balancing themselves on slim branches.

Spring soaked him to the bone; suddenly he didn't want to hunt for grub pins and make money; his blood felt thick and lazy. Moving softly in his moccasins, he followed the path to a ridge and lounged on a granite boulder, looking off to the north where to the limits of eyesight he could see the pine forests sweeping away over glacial hills, covering those endless reaches with blue-greens and yellow-greens and spruce-blacks. He daydreamed. He thought of school, of how all the scholars were busy as ants while he loafed; and he imagined what he might do if Alex Castleman licked him for playing hooky. He might, for instance, butt his head into the fellow's soft belly; or in a wrestling maneuver learned from the Injuns he might dive for the teacher's ankle, jerk, upset him, and twist. Probably he wouldn't; probably he would take the licking. Still, he believed he was stronger than Castleman, and when you were growing up a time came when you refused to acknowledge any authority save that of superior strength.

Looking off at the forest, he thought of the pinery boys up the Chippewa; already the spring drive had begun; the head of the drive would be reaching Quickwater any day now. When it came, he guessed he'd play hooky again; he liked it. He brought out his knife and sat whittling a popple stick; it was jacketed in bark like birch only grayer; the wood was soft and sliced off in thin white shavings, releasing a moist wild odor. Finally he wiped the knife blade on his jean pants, snapped it shut, and lounged there thinking maybe he would go on over into Injun Hollow, although he didn't know what kind of reception they'd give him, it had been so long since he had stopped in to see them. Injuns knew when you were their friend and when you were just pretending, and he had thrown in his lot with Dan Stoughton. Usually he didn't regret that, but something in his mood today made him want the company of Injuns; he thought he'd like to move in with the tribe and wear a hair roach and beaded leg bands and dance to the music of a cedar-log drum.

He heard soft clucking and remained very still, smiling, as he watched a hen partridge stepping daintily from the underbrush with a brood of spring chicks. Brilliant-eyed, head twisting this way and that, she sacrificed alertness every now and then to peck up a bug. Jim had learned to bark like a fox and hoot like an owl; he considered giving her a scare, but decided not to. Then she had a scare anyway, for somebody was coming along the path from Injun Hollow; the partridge squawked and chattered, spreading her wings and mothering her peeping brood into the undergrowth. Jim stood up. He didn't know the man on the path, but he guessed he must be a peddler, for over his shoulder he carried a bag of stout canvas which looked heavy; he was long-legged in a rusty black suit with a shabby long-tailed coat cut away to show a dark blue waistcoat sprigged with yellow flowers.

"Hello, cousin," the man said, smiling, for lots of times you addressed an Injun that way.

"Bon jour, chief," Jim said.

A ginger-colored beard grew from the man's chin, matching his straggling mustache, and even when he smiled his liquid brown eyes were somehow melancholy, the way a deer's eyes were melancholy from being hunted and scared.

The man eased the pack to the ground and said, "Whew! I thought I was coming to the frozen north." He took off his wool hat and fanned himself; sweat glistened on his forehead and on his large, aquiline nose. Then he sat on the rock and took off his shoes.

"You an Indian, son?" he asked, smiling.

"No," Jim said, "are you?"

The man laughed, sitting there stretching his toes. He said:

"That all depends. If Aaron Levi was right and the Indians are the lost tribes of Israel, then I suppose the obverse is true and I'm an Indian."

"What's the obverse?"

"It's the other side of the question."

Jim looked the man over; his thick ginger-colored hair was sprinkled with gray; he looked gentle and wise.

"No," Jim said, "I don't guess you're Injun, mister. For one thing you make too much noise coming through the woods. You been over in the Hollow selling them trade goods?"

"Trying to," the man said. "They're mainly broke."

"Dan Stoughton keeps them that way," Jim said. "What's your name, mister?"

The man said it was Sol Klauber, and Jim told him his name; they shook hands. Mr. Klauber's hand was large and warm, his handshake firm.

"How old are you, Jim?" he asked.

"I'll be eleven in July."

"You're big for your age," Sol Klauber said. "I've got a boy about your size and he's twelve. His name's Isaac. Maybe you'll meet him in the fall. He's in Boston now, but I'll go get him this summer and we'll be here in September. I'll make the logging camps next winter. This is just a trip looking over the possibilities."

"Boston," Jim said. "I was through there once. On our way to Wisconsin from Maine. I was too little to remember."

"That's where Isaac is," Sol Klauber said, "with his grandma and grandpa. I'm anxious to see him. I've been away since last fall."

"Well," Jim said, "that's a long time."

"Too long." The man looked sad. "But Isaac will be with me," he added, "when I come back in September. He'll learn peddling and maybe we'll have a store some day. I hope he's better at business than I am. What are you going to do when you grow up, Jim?"

Why, Jim told Sol Klauber, he reckoned he'd go into logging, that was what. Some day he'd have him a jobbing camp.

"I hope you make a go of it, Jim," Sol Klauber said.

"I aim to," Jim said.

Mr. Klauber put on his shoes, stood up, and with a long breath tugged the pack to his shoulders.

"Now I'll try the houses in town," he said. "Maybe my luck will be better. Glad to have met you, Jim. You and my Isaac are about of a size."

He started off down the path, bent under the pack, walking splay-footed.

"Mister," Jim called.

Sol Klauber stopped.

"If you go to the Buckmasters' place on Shin-Tangle Street," Jim said, "I'd like it just as well if you don't say anything about meeting me. I'm supposed to be in school."

Sol Klauber's face was amused.

"Jim," he said, "I've never seen you before. You're a stranger."

He waved and disappeared along the path.

Jim liked that man.

*

At this time of year Snowshoe Creek should have come tumbling bounteously through Injun Hollow, frothy in the sunlight when it leap-frogged over boulders, fluid bronze in pools of hemlock shadow. Coming down the ridge, Jim should have heard it prattling and tittering like half-grown squaws. But not today. Drought had sobered it.

Drought had sobered the village too; Nekeek's mother looked older, speaking of the dryness; the seeds of corn and squash and beans, she said, lay ungerminated in the earth. Hole-in-the-Day's medicine had failed; the Corn Dance had failed. The spirits were angry; the East Wind was angry; *Kitchee Mannitoo,* the Great Spirit himself, was angry; he had abandoned the tribe to *Matchee Mannitoo.*

"*Sánnegat,*" she said.

"*Sánnegat,*" Jim said.

They were sitting in her lodge, empty now of children, for Nekeek had gone with his father on a journey of many sleeps to fish for sturgeon on the Ontonagon River; thirty moons ago her son Warbeshance had been slain on an excursion against the Dakotas; her daughter Jônia Squissow had gone with her husband to dig for copper far to the northeast; her daughter Thurensera was as one dead, as one long in the ground beneath the burial totem, for she had departed to dwell in Quickwater behind the Northern Saloon.

"I didn't know," Jim said.

"Now you know," she said.

It was dusky in the lodge, with occasional streaks of sunlight piercing chinks in the birch-bark roof; the cedar-bark walls smelled of dry resin. On the floor the mat of woven rushes looked dry and old.

"*Acquoisee nin,*" she said. "I am sick with great weariness. The corn does not sprout. *Matchee Mannitoo* has his way with us." She sat staring, then added that Hole-in-the-Day had carved a cedar effigy of Dan Stoughton and had hung this crazy medicine to flip about in the four winds, but Dan Stoughton lived. *Kitchee Mannitoo* had looked upon the tribal ways and found them not good. Customs of the forefathers had been forgotten; skills lost; warriors no longer fashioned arrowheads of flint; they traded furs for guns and *mackcutty pingo;* they traded furs for *scótaywábo* which made them drunk; Hole-in-the-Day was saying perhaps the tribe should abandon their village and move many sleeps to the north. Herself, she thought him right. He had always been right. A drop of raccoon grease on a blanket, that was the Big Knives . . . And now Jim, she said quietly, was wholly of the Big Knives. Once he had been her son.

"I still call you mother," he said.

She shook her head. That was long ago. Everything good had been long ago. She held no enmity against him, but he was her son no longer. It was the way of things. Once as a little girl she had rescued an owlet fallen from the nest. She had warmed it and fed it. Then came a morning when it feared her shadow and refused food. Then came a dusk when hootings sounded from the forest and the owl that had been so tame it would cuddle between her breasts spread its wings and fluttered into the shadowy air. It never returned. Jim who was once her son, she said, had answered the call of his kind. *Sánnegat,* she said, *sánnegat.* But it was the way of the forest and of the world.

He could remember how melancholy he felt, taking his leave of her lodge and trudging through that village; he felt alien there now; when he spoke to Hole-in-the-Day squatting outside his lodge, ancient as human sorrow, wrinkled as a last year's apple, the medicine man did not respond. Hanging from a cedar pole Jim noticed a tiny wooden figure; that must have been the crazy medicine Hole-in-the-Day had fashioned against Dan Stoughton. It looked forlorn and pitiful and impotent, dangling in the spring sunshine. Jim went on to Snowshoe Creek but he didn't linger there; it too looked forlorn, trickling among dry rocks.

He turned, followed the path up the ridge, stopping at the summit; he could see Hole-in-the-Day still squatting outside his lodge; he could see the village corn patch without any green sprouts; overhead the sky arched vast and cloudless.

Jim stood there a while longer, thinking he probably wouldn't be returning to that village very often, telling himself that if Dan Stoughton hadn't come to these woods some other Big Knife would have. At last he started back toward town, silent in his moccasins, his stride easy and long like an Indian's, his toes pointed straight ahead. Presently, opposite the tamarack swamp, he saw a boy of his own age kneeling on the path, using a skinning knife on a dead porcupine that lay belly up. It was Trout Face; his crude pogamoggan lay beside him; he must have killed the porcupine with that war club. Jim moved so soundlessly that Trout Face never heard him coming, till he chirked like a squirrel; then Trout Face sprang to his feet; Jim laughed.

"*Jour,* cousin," he said.

"Cousin," Trout Face said. His eyes were lusterless slits.

Jim said he guessed Trout Face's family would be eating roast porcupine tonight; Trout Face nodded; the meat, he said, was sweeter than young mutton. Jim had never tasted it; he was waiting to do that when he was lost in the woods without gunpowder; you could always walk right up to a porky and brain him, for porky had an exaggerated opinion of the defensive power of quills.

Trout Face resumed work, peeling the skin off the porcupine like a glove. Jim stood watching, smelling that raw odor which always came from freshly-killed meat. The pogamoggan lay on the path; it had been made from hickory, with a ball-shaped head. That started Jim thinking.

"Cousin," he said, "do you want to make some money?"

"*Cawween nee stoticee.*"

"Money, cousin," Jim said. "A nickel. Many nickels. *Cunner kee stóotewar?*"

"*Kee, kee, nóneydone,*" Trout Face said.

"Listen well, cousin," Jim said; and he described a grub pin, telling how Trout Face should search the forest for hardwood saplings and how he should cut them and grub out the roots with the crowns left on. For each pin he would pay Trout Face a nickel. Would Trout Face do that?

"*Nangaýmer.*"

"*Meegwoyack, neejee,*" Jim said. "Bring them to my house in Quickwater. You know my house?"

Trout Face knew.

"A nickel for each," Jim said; and as he walked on toward town he felt fine, thinking how he would double his money on any grub pins he bought from Trout Face. It never occurred to him that such dealings could bring him trouble.

*

That evening he felt a little guilty, letting his family suppose he had spent the afternoon in school, although he didn't have to lie, for playing hooky wasn't mentioned. At supper Lorne reported that the log drive was getting close to town; probably the head of the drive would reach the Quickwater booms tomorrow morning. Jim considered playing hooky again tomorrow, but decided that might be crowding things. Day after tomorrow, maybe. It all depended on how hard Alex Castleman licked him. One thing, when he got a licking at school that was that; Myrtle and Lorne didn't hold with meting out a second licking at home, the way some parents did.

"I bought some needles today," Myrtle said. "There was a peddler here and I bought needles and a paper of pins. I wanted some scissors but they were too dear."

Jim let his face go blank, but evidently Sol Klauber had kept his word about not snitching.

"You bought from a peddler?" Lorne asked.

"That's what I was saying," Myrtle said. "I bought needles and pins."

Lorne sat staring at his johnnycake; in the light from the tallow dips his face looked dark and worried, his brows black as charred sticks.

"I don't know, Myrt," he said. "If Dan Stoughton hears about that he won't like it."

"Stoughton's high on his pins," Myrtle said. "And on everything else."

"It might cost me my job, Myrt. He might send me packing."

"Now, father," she said, "you stop. You know that mill couldn't run without you. They raised your wages."

"I don't know," Lorne said, "it may not last."

That went on through the rest of supper; Jim scarcely listened; he had heard it all before, and besides, he was thinking about the log drive. When he left the table he went outside and hurried through the spring evening toward the river, where frogs were gallumping and peepers cheeping. Lack of rain hadn't much affected the Chippewa, maybe because up north at its source, among countless lakes and swamps and spring-fed rills, more snow had fallen last winter than in the Quickwater area. In any case, the river flowed dark and strong tonight with a good head of water, its surface star-spattered; Jim could hear a loon wailing upriver, and from the dam came the roar of thunderous waters. He stood there looking north; and just thinking of those sawlogs on their way to the booms set his heart to beating faster. It was always that way with him; and he was always like a compass needle when it came to which way his attention swung; his magnetic pole was in the North. With most Americans it was the West; they could get a little drunk thinking about trekking toward sunset; not Jim; he never gave a damn about going west.

Tonight he left the river reluctantly; in the loft of the cabin he dreamed of sawlogs; and next morning his feet dragged on the way to school.

"James," said Alex Castleman, "you were absent yesterday. Do you have an excuse, James?"

Jim shook his head.

"James," said Alex Castleman, "you will remain after school this afternoon."

But Jim didn't, and for an excellent reason: he played hooky again the second afternoon in a row. Not to postpone the licking—he always figured his backside could stand it longer than Castleman's arm—but because the head of the drive had reached Quickwater at ten o'clock that morning; he spent the afternoon along the river. And spent it well: all his life he carried in his head pictures from that afternoon. And smells. And sounds. Logs carpeting the river as far as he could see; logs bobbing, rolling, butting; logs being herded into the booms on the far bank; logs perfuming the afternoon with the tangy scent of pine. He could remember blue sky and silver birch backdropping those moving logs; he could remember men in driving boots and red-checked shirts looming big as heroes cast in bronze; magnificent sinewy men; deep-chested, lean-bellied, strong-legged men with pike poles and cant hooks; and other men in bateaux. Once a bateau came poling in close to shore where he was standing; he remembered a red-headed giant named Matt Moriarity waving and calling. "Hey there, bub. Ain't you Lorne Buckmaster's boy?" Yes, he was Jim Buckmaster. "Thought so," Matt Moriarity said. "Thought you was the one who sang that song . . . Say, Jim, why ain't you in school?" Jim grinned. The man said, "Played hooky, I bet." Jim kept grinning. "Say, Jim," Moriarity called, "will that Castleman feller lick you for that?" Jim said he reckoned so. "All right, Jim," Matt Moriarity called, "you pass him some advice. You pass him the advice to lay off, see? Tell him to lay off, Jim, else he'll have me to deal with. Else he'll get a licking from me. And if I ain't man enough to do it alone, I'll get you to help . . . That was a song, Jim . . . Ride the logs down, boys, ride the white pine . . ." His voice came booming across the water in a rhythm like the upsurge and downswing of floating sawlogs.

*

Dan Stoughton, that friend of education, had donated a banjo clock to the schoolhouse; it hung on the wall behind Alex Castleman's desk; Jim, sitting at the common desk which ran along the center of the room, could hear its loud ticking and see the picture of Niagara Falls which adorned its neck; he thought it would be quite a trick to drive sawlogs over those falls.

Ten minutes ago school had been dismissed, but in the silent room, despite the high windows opened on the fine afternoon, the fusty smells of unwashed scholars still lingered. Up on his platform Alex Castleman sat at his desk chewing twist tobacco and rustling the pages of a copybook; not, Jim hoped, his copybook, for he had never caught the knack of pothooks and hangers, and his spelling was open to criticism. Leisurely and rhythmically Castleman's jaws were working; now and then he spat into a sand box; as yet he had made no move to select one of the switches which stood in the dunce corner. The dull light gleamed on the hand-bell sitting on Castleman's desk, and on the globe beside the desk. A fly came buzzing through a window, reconnoitered Castleman's head with its mussed brown hair and dandruff, found it unappetizing, and flew to the north end of the room where, by the door, its interest was roused by the wooden water pail on the wooden bench. It lighted on the gourd dipper, left a speck on the edge, and then departed through a window, bound for the school backhouses.

At last Castleman closed the copybook and stood up, his belly looking pregnant; and he shuffled over to the box stove which served as his liquor cabinet during warm weather. Opening the door, his hand darted inside and came forth with a bottle which he held under his coat. Then, pants sloppy, belly wagging, he shuffled to the door, bolted it, and ladled the dipper a third full of water, adding a two-thirds portion of whiskey; he drank it in two gulps. As a chaser he took a nip of whiskey undiluted. Then he returned the bottle to the stove. Then he came over and stood beside the long bench where Jim sat.

"James," he said, "you have been absent two afternoons in a row. You have brought no written excuses. You know the penalty."

"Sure," Jim said.

"James, when you address your teacher the correct form is yes, sir."

"Is it?" Jim said.

He could feel stubbornness working in his soul.

"You know it is, James. Say yes, sir, James."

Jim clammed up; it was the Newcomb Dobner in him.

"James," Castleman roared, "say yes, sir."

Jim remained silent.

"I shall have to punish you, James."

"What's stopping you?" Jim said.

He knew now he wasn't going to lean over and clutch his ankles and let Alex Castleman whale him; he was going to fight. He might get a licking before it was over, but he wasn't going to submit to one.

"James," Castleman said, and his voice had dropped to a purr, "why are you this way? You know I like you, James."

Jim sat staring at the puncheon floor; he felt Castleman's hand touching his head, stroking it, patting it.

"I like you, James," Castleman repeated; and he sat down on the bench, his hand fondling Jim's shoulders, his biceps.

"What hard muscles, James. Quite a little man. Are the muscles in your legs hard too?"

Jim could smell Castleman's breath; an odor compounded of whiskey, tobacco, rotten teeth and catarrh; he could smell the dried sweat in Castleman's armpits, and the reek of his feet.

"Yes," Castleman was murmuring, "your calves are bulging with muscles, and your thighs . . . yes . . . your . . . your . . ."

Castleman was breathing like a team of oxen skidding a heavy log.

About seventeen seconds later, Jim Buckmaster could have been seen clambering through a schoolhouse window and dropping to the ground and racing west along Chippewa Street. He hadn't waited to unbolt the door although really he had plenty of time, for Alex Castleman, jolted by the fist-blow, had toppled off the bench like a hogshead of sow belly, and Jim had kicked him in the appendix.

*

He didn't go directly home, for he felt unclean; he made his way to the swimming hole north of the swamp, where he peeled off his clothes and splashed in. Compared with the warm air, the water seemed icy, but that was all right, for he could imagine his skin hot where Alex Castleman had fingered it and he wanted to be clean as an icicle. After his swim, he went over himself with cupped hands, flicking off the water, and he lay drying in the sun.

Well, he was through with school. No matter what his parents said or did he wasn't going back. No matter what anybody did he wasn't. On that point his mind felt like a mule with legs braced. If he had to he would run away from home; he would go deep into the northern forests, leaving no back trail, searching out some far band of Chippewas and becoming an Injun. He didn't want to leave home; thought of never seeing his mother and father again, and his sisters, and his baby brother Dobner, lumped his throat; but his mind was made up. He had heard of boys running away and being found a day later, weeping, clothes torn, and of their being glad to return. With him it wouldn't be that way. He didn't want to leave but he certainly would, if they tried to force him back to that schoolhouse and Alex Castleman.

That decision made him feel calm; he only smiled when he walked into his yard and his sisters chanted:

"Jim got a licking, Jim got a licking. . ."

His mother asked:

"Did you get a licking, Jim?"

"Not a hard one."

"What did you do, Jim?"

He told her he'd played hooky yesterday to watch the log drive. She couldn't scold much about that; after all, back in Juniper Falls, the log drives always depopulated school.

"I wish you wouldn't do things like that," she said, but she didn't look mad. And she added, "Well, the drive's ended up. Your father said the rear was due in this afternoon."

Jim guessed that was true; at the river today he hadn't seen any bateaux; in those years the drives for the Quickwater Log & Lumber Company were short affairs, both in distance covered and time consumed. Tonight, he reckoned, the river pigs would be taking the town apart. He wanted to see that, so after supper, without announcing his intentions to his parents, who could be narrow-minded about his owling around, he made his way toward the business district. It was a fine evening in the dark of the moon; moths were fluttering through the warm air looking for pickups; Jim saw several bats swooping and flitting about their shady business; from the woods a whippoorwill was calling. He whistled in answer; the bird responded enthusiastically; he was good at imitations. Once in the woods with his father's gun he had imitated the squeal of a terror-stricken rabbit, and before long a coyote had come loping, thinking the rabbit had been trapped. That coyote certainly had looked surprised, seeing instead a boy with a rifle. Jim could have shot it except he broke out laughing; besides he didn't care about killing wild things unless he had use for their fur or meat; the Chippewas had taught him that. The Chippewas said every animal and bird had a spirit, and you shouldn't go around killing them aimlessly. Jim remembered one time when he had been hunting with Nekeek and Nekeek's father; after shooting a bear, Nekeek's father took its paw in his hand and shook it, saying something like, "Oh, *Mackquáh,* I am very sorry I had to kill you, my good cousin, but my lodge needs your steak and your warm fur."

Things were happening, when Jim reached the corner of Squaw and Chippewa Streets; he never remembered the town so lively. Every shade in Dan Stoughton's fancy house was flushed with light; the Northern Saloon was bursting at the seams with accordion music and whoops and hollers; kittycornered across the street Gentleman Steve's place, the Woodsman's Friend, was giving forth snatches of song and shouts and the scraping of a fiddle; and west of the intersection, on the south side of Chippewa Street, even the Widow Maker Saloon was doing all right, judging by the sounds. Jim stood on the corner smiling, wishing he were old enough to go shouldering up to a bar and ordering whiskey for everyone in the house.

Once while he stood there he saw a half-dozen river hogs bursting from the Widow Maker; they linked arms and came staggering along the street singing; at the intersection one fellow pawed the deep sawdust paving and howled like a timber wolf; then he bellowed, "Brethern and sistern, we are gathered here in the sight of God for the purpose of—"

And then he preached a humorous sermon, beseeching the Almighty to prevail upon Dan Stoughton to lower his fancy-house prices; and his companions cheered and shouted amen, and more river hogs came to augment his congregation. Then somebody told him he needed a text; it was sacrilegious to preach without a text; and the mock preacher exclaimed why, you son of a bitch, you wouldn't know a text if I gave one; and then a fight started, everybody pitching in, kicking and biting and gouging; but those riverjacks were tough and nobody was much hurt, especially since it was against the unwritten law for anybody but a cook to pull a knife; so before long men who had been slugging each other stood with arms around shoulders, speaking of undying friendship and lifting voices in song. It had been going on this way since afternoon; it would go on all night and maybe all day tomorrow and tomorrow night, till money ran out and even those magnificent physiques were dropped in their tracks by sleep.

When the melee had calmed, the river pigs went scattering into saloons of their choice, and Jim thought he would enjoy seeing the inside of the Woodsman's Friend; he had never been there. He remembered how soft and springy the sawdust of the intersection felt under his moccasins as he crossed the street; he remembered the odor of beer and tobacco flowing in a seductive river from the blaze and uproar of that saloon. He peeked under the swinging doors and saw a forest of boots and pants, and even some bright skirts, for Gentleman Steve had imported dance-hall girls to give Stoughton's squaws a run for their money. Jim had a pretty accurate hunch that his parents would not approve of his entering, but recklessness was in the air that night, so presently he slipped in and worked his way through the throng to the gambling tables located beyond the end of the bar and on the near side of a dancing floor where a fiddler's music sent couples spinning and jigging, calked boots pocking the pine boards and chewing out slivers.

Gentleman Steve himself, a squat, pudgy, benevolent-looking man in silver-rimmed, square spectacles, stood behind the crap table watching, while one of his employees, thin and shirt-sleeved, a dead cigar aslant from his tight lips, said in a metallic voice such things as the dice are coming out, and little Phoebe, and it's the lady's roll.

The lady was Molly Fitzpatrick.

Standing there with her husband, ear-pendants sparkling, a thin cigar in her fingers, (she must have decided that a roaring town like Quickwater wouldn't hold smoking against her), Molly looked as much in her element as any pinery boy; you could hear her twangy voice above the whoops and the fiddle music. When she rolled the dice she seemed to put everything she had into it, shaking them near her ear and crooning admonitions, swinging back on her heel and then forward, giving them a long roll so they would obey house rules and strike the bounceboard.

"Look at that!" she exclaimed once, but without anger. "Just look at that, boys. Crapped out!"

"Stick to the ponies, precious," Lew Fitzpatrick said.

"By God," she said, "yes. What I should do." She took a swig from her glass. "But there's not a horse race within a thousand miles of this burg."

She saw Jim then.

"Why, Jim," she exclaimed, "it's you. Hello, Jim."

She put down her cigar and her glass and came sweeping over to Jim in a rustling of silks, giving him a hug, enclosing him in an aura of perfume and sweet powders, her body soft and resilient with all the juices of a fine, healthy woman.

"Jim," she said, "are you happy tonight?"

"Well, sure," he said.

"Jim," she said, "I like to hear you say that. I like to see everybody happy." She patted his head. "Are you thirsty, Jim? Would you like a drink?"

"I don't care."

So Molly went shoving toward the bar, clearing a path by yelling, "Gangway, boys! Let the little lady through!" Even in the uproar she made herself heard, she was so big-voiced. Lew Fitzpatrick stood watching her, smiling, eyes perhaps a little ironical.

Now she was booming her way back through the crowd, but without a drink.

"No Sarsaparilla," she said. "Can you beat that?" And she called across the dice table to Gentleman Steve: "Hey, Steve. What kind of place are you running without Sarsaparilla?"

"That's for Injuns," Steve said, and behind his glasses his eyes crinkled nearly shut and he slapped his thigh and laughed and laughed. Finally he took off his glasses and wiped the humor-tears from his eyes. "Oh, my!" he said, and then he added, "That's for Injuns," and laughed again.

A faint smile flitted around the dead cigar in the crap dealer's mouth, but nobody else seemed amused, except Molly. She laughed and called, "Steve, you're a clown." That sent him into another fit of mirth. One of his dance-hall girls, a skinny woman in a sleazy gold gown, stood looking as if she'd bitten into a choke cherry.

"Steve," Molly said, "we'll go over to Dan Stoughton's. He carries Sarsaparilla."

Gentleman Steve said he didn't doubt it. And he added, "You tell him I said Sarsaparilla is for Injuns. Tell him to feed it to his Chippewa gals."

His laughter followed Molly and Jim and Lew to the door. Outside, Molly said:

"Say, what was the joke?"

"Damned if I know," Lew said. "You were the one laughing."

"Well," Molly said, "I couldn't hurt his feelings, could I?"

"She's got a heart as big as Lake Superior," Lew told Jim.

"Only warmer, I hope," Molly said.

"A hundred degrees warmer," Lew said. And he told Jim, "If she ever does me wrong it will be because she's big-hearted. She hates to say no."

Molly linked her arm through his and cuddled against him.

"I'll never do you wrong, sugar-pie."

"At least not while I'm around," Lew said.

They paused outside the Northern Saloon, listening to the racket. Molly threw back her head and took a deep gulp of the spring evening.

"By God," she said, "this is living. Life always ought to be like this. Music and people laughing and everybody happy. Like a lake steamer with a nigger band. Remember that amusement park at Lake Pontchartrain? Remember that time in Havana when we saw the cock fight and went to Pedro's and drank rum? Lew, I'm thirsty."

"You drink too much," he said. "You're not a whale, precious."

"What the hell," she said. "We're only human once."

Molly went ahead, running interference, when they entered the Northern Saloon with its candles blazing and somebody playing an accordion. Elbowing to the bar, she told Mon-Fah Lee they were all dying from thirst; Jim was given a Sarsaparilla. While he was draining the last of that sweet syrup he heard his name spoken; it was the peddler, Sol Klauber.

"I didn't tell on you, Jim," he said.

"I know it," Jim said. "Thanks, mister."

"You two know each other?" Molly asked. "Jim, you get around."

"Sure," Jim said.

"Well, it's a small world," Molly said. "Mr. Klauber is staying at the Shanghai House and we've been eating at the same table. Sol, what do you think of my boy here?"

"He's big for his age," Sol said. "As big as my Isaac."

"And he packs a lot of brains under his hat," Molly said. "I wish he was mine. But I'm going to have a boy. Some day. A palm reader told me all about it. It was all in my palm, as it were. I'm going to have a baby and a house and stay home and behave myself. You won't know me then—I'll be a different woman. I'll have me a carriage and a coachman and a nursery full of babies. And I won't farm them out to any Reuben Prouts for raising. But the Prouts were all right except he bothered me, as it were. I'd hardly come around the first time before he started. 'I'll tell Sadie,' I said. Sadie was his wife. 'You wouldn't do that, Molly,' he always said. 'You wouldn't make Sadie cry.' Guess he knew me better than I knew myself. I almost told her a couple of times, but I liked her. I couldn't make her unhappy, could I?"

"Molly," Lew said, "that's enough."

"You mean it's too much," she said, "and maybe you're right. Too much tanglefoot and too much talk. But I'm Irish, sugar-pie. I'm Irish and you get me to drinking and I *will* talk. First born daughter of Grady Lanagan. He could charm a bird down out of a tree, but I guess he was shiftless. He would have built a backhouse, if he hadn't been shiftless, as it were."

"You're drunk, precious," Lew said.

535

"No I'm not, sugar. Not very. How many have I had tonight? It's hard to keep track. I never was good at numbers. Never could remember nine times seven."

"We're going now, precious. Going home."

"Home?" she said, and she laughed. "We don't have a home. You know that."

"Home to the hotel, precious. I'll put you to bed."

"Just like a man. Always thinking of bed. Not that I've ever complained. Have I ever complained, sugar-pie?"

"Never. You've been wonderful."

"See there?" Molly exclaimed to nobody in particular. "Married more than twelve years and he says I'm wonderful. And I've never done you wrong, sugar. I've never kicked over the traces. You know, I'm pretty proud of that."

Lew Fitzpatrick asked Sol Klauber to give him a hand; flanked by those two, Molly went unsteadily toward the door.

"Jim," she called once, "are you coming, Jim?"

"I'm right behind you," Jim said.

Outside, Jim stood watching while Lew and Sol guided her across the street. Once she stopped and looked around.

"You coming, Jim?" she called.

"I've got to go home," Jim said.

"Tell your mother she's lucky," she called. "Tell her she's lucky to have a boy like you. But you wait, Jim. Wait till you see my son. You won't know me. I'll never touch another drop. You happy, Jim?"

"Sure," Jim said.

"That's nice," Molly said. "I like to see you happy."

Jim watched her going unsteadily up the steps of the hotel porch; he couldn't say why, but he felt sort of sad.

*

He stood on that corner thinking he actually should be going home but hating to miss any excitement. Once he watched laughing while a dozen river pigs came bursting from Gentleman Steve's and played leap-frog in the street; a little later a group from the Widow Maker Saloon came marching down Chippewa Street singing "Yankee Doodle." One of the men carried a metal chamber pot which he used for a drum; now and then he yelled, "To arms, to arms! The British are coming." When the group reached the Northern Saloon the man hurled the chamber pot across the street where it banged against the door of Olson's Blacksmith Shop.

"I'm Paul Revere!" he yelled.

But he wasn't Paul Revere; he was a riverjack named Matt Moriarity; when he noticed Jim he let out a whoop.

"Jim," he bellowed, grabbing his hand and slapping his back, "it's good

536

to see you. I'm drunk, Jim. Drunk as a lord. After while I'll be drunk as a king. To hell with kings. The British are coming, Jim, but we'll lick 'em. If we can't we'll get you to help."

Jim laughed.

"When did I say that before?" Matt Moriarity said. "Now *when* did I say that before? No, no—wait—don't tell me. I've got it now. It was on the river. We were talking about that schoolmaster feller. Did he lick you, Jim?"

Well, not exactly, Jim said. In fact, he didn't lick him at all. In fact, he . . . he . . . well . . .

"What did the son of a bitch do, Jim?"

Well, Jim said, it wasn't so much what he actually did as what he seemed intending to do; he . . . he . . .

"What did the bastard do, Jim? Did he—?"

Well, Jim said, you couldn't really say he . . . oh, hell . . . it was what his hands . . .

And Jim told what happened.

"Oh, the bastard!" Moriarity bellowed. "The fat British bastard."

"He's American," Jim said. "I popped him and he went down."

"Well done like the fine Irish lad you are!" Moriarity exclaimed. "I've always said one Irish lad could lick three Englishmen."

"Well," Jim said, "I'm not exactly Irish and Alex Castleman is an American, but—"

"Sure you're Irish, Jim. The way you use your fists proves it. Hell's afire. A poor helpless lad like yourself! What he'll do to you when you go back to school!"

"I'm not going back," Jim said.

"You'll have to, Jim. They'll make you, my lad. My old man always said, 'One thing, I'll never hang.' But they hanged him high, Jim. The British bastards hanged him high. Did it when all he had done was knife a lime-sucking grenadier. Slit his throat and they hanged him for it. There ain't no justice, Jim. You'll have to go back."

"I'm not going back," Jim said.

"They'll send you back and it will be murder or worse. By God. We Irishmen have always had their boots on our necks. But those days have ended, Jim, my lad. We may be Irish, you and me, but we're Americans now. Where does the bastard live? Where does the beef-eating son of a bitch live?"

Jim said Castleman had a room at the Shanghai House.

"Thought so, Jim. Sitting there in his room and gloating about how they hanged my old man. All he did was cut the limey's throat, Jim. 'I'll never hang,' he said, 'I'll die first.' But they hanged him, Jim, the pudding-eating bastards."

Jim said he was pretty sure Castleman must be an American; at least he always claimed he had been born in York State.

"I thought so, Jim—a lying bastard! A lying, gloating, British bastard. He murdered my old man, Jim, sprang the trap and sent poor Aloysius Moriarity to hell. 'Aloysius,' my mother used to tell him, 'you keep knifing grenadiers and they'll be getting mad. They'll hang you, Aloysius.' 'Get on with you, woman,' my father would say, 'a man has to have his recreation. I'll never hang.' But Castleman sat there on the judge's bench and sentenced him, and then sprang the trap. And now he sits in his room gloating."

Brandishing a fist, Moriarity went reeling toward the Shanghai House, then pulled up short at the sound of a commotion over by Olson's Blacksmith Shop, where a number of riverjacks were using a log as a battering ram against the door. They were all laughing and hallooing.

"Wait, boys, wait," Moriarity hollered, stumbling over to join them. "Let's hang the British bastard first. He spit on the flag, boys, that's what he did. Saw him with my own eyes."

His voice was lost in the uproar; more river pigs came trotting; above the laughter and singing and hooting Jim heard wood splintering; the door sagged; a score of men plunged into the shop and came out pulling a breaking plow. Somebody fetched a rope and tied it to the tongue; whinnying like horses men grabbed the rope; somebody gripped the plow handles and set the share; and after that the plow was dragged east and west along Chippewa Street till for several blocks the street was furrowed from wooden sidewalk to wooden sidewalk.

"And now to the feed store," somebody yelled.

The uproar in the street had emptied the saloons; there must have been a hundred men trooping east along the street; and Jim was right in there with them. At Roquemore's Livery Stable and Feed Store the mob shattered the glass windows and kicked in the door; men came out lugging burlap bags heavy with oats. These were ripped open; everybody dipped out oats and ran along the plowed sawdust of Chippewa Street scattering the grain and shouting that no man could say now they had never sowed their wild oats. Now and then a fist fight broke out; there were more games of leapfrog; and when Jim returned to the corner of Chippewa and Squaw Streets he saw Matt Moriarity on the porch of the Shanghai House haranguing a cluster of riverjacks who stood panting from all their exertions.

"He hanged my father, boys, and spit on the flag—"

More river pigs kept turning up; in the light from the hotel windows they were a roiling mass of checked shirts and waving fists and mussed hair.

"So I say let's give him what he gave my father, boys. Let's get him and hang him high."

Jim yelled for them to wait; but that mob of heaving shoulders and pumping boots flowed up the steps to the hotel porch and into the lobby with the force of some fabulous, many-footed beast; Jim tried to crowd through the door but was flung aside; Xenophon Yates ran from behind the hotel desk but they sent him spinning; up the stairs to second floor they clumped, their calked boots lacerating the steps. When Jim managed to get inside he yelled for them to listen, but nobody heard him, there was so much racket; and then from upstairs came laughter and yelps of pain and Jim saw Alexander Castleman being dragged down the steps, his belly ballooning out his dirty nightshirt, his oddly thin shanks flopping.

Jim flung himself across the lobby and grabbed Matt Moriarity, yelling wait, God damn it, wait, listen to me; but big Matt was blind drunk now; clutching his biceps was like clutching pigs of iron; he flipped his arm and Jim found himself thrown violently backwards, losing balance and skidding across the floor on the seat of his pants, his head whacking a table leg so that something seemed to explode like dynamite in a log jam and inside his head the logs erupted and banged the inside of his skull and he was crying while boots went tramping from the lobby and in the street men were whooping and shouting hang the British bastard.

He must have lost consciousness; he remembered crawling toward the door, his head feeling as big and full of stinging pain as a nest of hornets; and then he was outside, pitching down the steps and running after the hooting toward the schoolhouse. He heard voices yelling we need light, and other voices answering we'll give you light; and by the time he reached the edge of the mob something unbelievable had happened: men had kicked in the schoolhouse door and set the place on fire; flames were beginning to lick across the dry shakes on the roof and to cast red light over the mob marching Alex Castleman toward a hemlock in a vacant lot east of the school.

Pain kept hammering inside Jim's skull and his stomach felt curdled, but he knew he couldn't get sick now, he had to do something to bring them to their senses because maybe Alex Castleman was a filthy scalawag but he didn't deserve lynching, and if they lynched him Jim would always remember he had started it. So he dived and wriggled through the mob, reaching that hemlock while they were tying the rope around Castleman's neck; he always remembered how in the light from the burning school the teacher's face looked green as vomit, how his eyes rolled and his tongue lolled over his loose lips.

"Make him kiss the flag," Jim heard himself yelling, because that would delay matters till he could think what to do. "If he spit on the flag make him kiss it before he dies."

"But we ain't got no flag," Moriarity shouted.

"There's one at the hotel," Jim told him. "Xenophon Yates keeps one behind his desk. I've seen it. I'll get it. Don't let him die without kissing the flag."

That's right, men were bellowing, get the flag, make him kiss it, make the bastard kneel and—

539

Jim had never run so fast as on the way to the hotel. His head still throbbed but his thoughts had cleared and he knew who could handle this; Molly Fitzpatrick could. He raced through the hotel lobby and upstairs to the Fitzpatricks' room, banging the door. Lew opened it and Jim poured out his story.

From the darkness he could hear the bed creak and Molly's voice, groaning that she was sick, oh, God, she was sick; all that noise of boots in the hall had made her sicker—

"You've got to come," Jim shrilled. "They're going to hang him."

"All right," she said. "All right, Jim. Don't know what I'll do, but I'll do something. Lew, where's your pepperbox?"

She was carrying that seven-shot pistol when they left the room and hurried along the hall; going down the stairs she clung to the railing; the world was tipping, she said, but she guessed she'd make out; in the lobby you could see the bare curves of her bosom at the lacy neckline of her nightgown; she was wearing a blue peignoir over the nightgown and blue silk mules.

"My God," she said, as they hurried along the street, "they've set the school on fire. They'll burn us all up."

Jim was afraid Matt Moriarity might have had his way and they would find Alex Castleman dangling, but he was still standing green-faced in the light from the blazing school. Molly yelled, "Gangway, boys! God damn it, let me through!" When she reached the hemlock with the rope over a limb she stopped and looked over the situation, then wheeled.

"Boys," she said, "fun's fun. I'm Irish myself and I don't care what you do with this pouch of bear's grease, but first you've got to put out that fire. The woods are like tinder, boys, and they'll catch if you don't get buckets of water. Now God damn it get going or I'll shoot your pants off."

They looked at one another.

"Get going!" she yelled. "I'm just drunk enough to shoot out your lights."

She brandished the pepperbox.

They began melting away, toward the river. But Matt Moriarity hesitated.

Molly's voice shot out from the corner of her mouth.

"Are you going to move that no-good Irish ass of yours," she demanded, "or do I have to shoot off your—?"

He moved.

"Got a jackknife, Jim?" she asked, after the last of the riverjacks went trotting down Chippewa Street. "All right, give it to Lew. Lew, cut this gazoon loose."

Alex Castleman started to stammer thanks; Molly cut him short.

"Shut up, school teacher. Save your wind. I've never liked you from the first day I laid eyes on you slobbering soup. Now get the hell out of

540

town and keep going. Find a farmer and get him to give you clothes and send me the bill. Now move."

Molly swung down the barrel of the pepperbox and pulled the trigger; the bullet kicked up the turf near Castleman's feet. He moved.

*

The burning schoolhouse roused the town, and all the good citizens like Myrtle and Lorne Buckmaster came to help put out the fire. By then it was too late to save the building, but when sparks shot up and went sizzling into vacant lots men hurried to prevent new blazes. Lucky there was no wind that night, people said, or the woods would have caught, everything was so dry.

Fire fighting sobered the riverjacks somewhat, and by the small hours of morning, when the school was a mass of glowing coals, nobody asked where Alex Castleman had gone; probably those pigs were beginning to feel ashamed. Certainly they were ashamed by the next afternoon when, as a result of an edict by Dan Stoughton and the other saloon keepers that no more liquor would be served till things quieted, everybody was cold sober.

"Things got a little out of hand," the river pigs said.

By then they were contrite, passing the hat to pay Three-Cent Olson and Perry Roquemore for damage; and they promised to cut logs and rebuild the school. And they were grateful to Molly Fitzpatrick, they said, for preventing them from stringing up Alex Castleman; they weren't really lynchers at heart; lynchers were weak men who needed to be part of a mob to feel strong; those river pigs weren't like that; they just enjoyed pranks.

Talking over what happened, they couldn't quite figure what had come over them to pick on Castleman that way; when somebody said it was Matt Moriarity's fault for stirring them up, Matt was sure there was a mistake somewhere, although he had no clear recollection of the night's events.

"You told us Castleman was a British bastard," they said.

Matt scowled, trying to remember.

"Boys," he said, "the fellow may be a bastard for all I know. I wasn't there when his ma and pa got together. But hell, boys, I wouldn't hold that against anybody. And I don't think he's British. Seems like I heard somewhere he was born in York State."

"And you told us," the river pigs said, "that he hanged your old man back in Ireland."

That made Matt mad.

"I'll fight any man who says my old man was hanged," he declared. "He's never been in Ireland in his life, and he's alive and well, God keep him, back in Connecticut."

It was all mysterious.

On the second day after the fire, a stump-land farmer drove in and quietly picked up Castleman's belongings from the Shanghai House, and Xenophon Yates sent word to the school teacher that nobody was mad at him and he'd better return and hold school in a tent till a new schoolhouse could be built. Yates felt a good deal worse about the fire than, say, Jim Buckmaster, for he hated to lose a steady customer; but Castleman wasn't having any; as soon as he got his clothes and his carpetbag he left the country.

Jim Buckmaster was just as glad things turned out that way. It had given him a good scare, that near-lynching, but now his conscience was spotless. A new schoolhouse, he figured, would take quite some time to build, and after that more time would be needed to find a teacher. Meanwhile, summer was coming in full flood; he could go swimming every day.

*

It just wouldn't rain that summer; not in the Quickwater area. In June and July through the long hot days great cumulus clouds used to go floating overhead, but instead of peppering down raindrops those clouds were regular leeches, filling their snowy bellies with moisture the sun sucked up from the river and the woods. Sometimes in the afternoon the clouds ran together like purple sealing wax and you saw lightning and heard the sky-drums rumbling, and everybody said thank God, it's going to rain now for sure; but damned if it would. Not in Quickwater. You were always hearing how fifty miles away in the north or northeast there had been a soaking rain; how off to the west the woods had been drenched by a cloudburst; but in the Quickwater region the creeks had shriveled with dead fish stinking; the swamps were drying out; even the frogs sounded thirsty; and the Chippewas in Injun Hollow and Three-Cent Olson and the mourning doves all prayed to their various gods.

"Weather's always freakish," Dan Stoughton used to say. "And it always keeps on doing what it has been doing. It always carries everything too far."

"An unusually pleasant summer," the *Quickwater Mercury* said. "A little rain would be welcome, but meanwhile we are enjoying the copious sunshine."

"Damn but it's hot," Molly Fitzpatrick said. "If it weren't for beer we'd dry up and blow away."

"Even the wells are going dry," the stump farmers said. "And a man dassn't burn his brush."

"It's bad for business, that's what makes me mad," Xenophon Yates said.

"The Great Spirit is angry with his children," Hole-in-the-Day said.

"Never have saw the like," Pete Casey said, down at the rafting dump. "She keeps raining around us, but damned if she'll rain here."

542

"Oh, it'll rain," Myrtle Buckmaster said. "I wouldn't be surprised to see a shower this afternoon."

"I don't know, Myrt," Lorne said. "It looks like we're in for it. So far the well's all right, but if this keeps up—"

By August the *Quickwater Mercury* no longer commented on the weather, concerning itself with the higher things of life, such as how the price of town lots had doubled in three years. Nor did Molly Fitzpatrick comment, for late in July she and Lew left on a trip combining business with pleasure, heading for St. Louis and Cairo and the Atlantic Seaboard. Nor did the peddler, Sol Klauber, comment; he was long gone from Quickwater on his journey to Boston.

One advantage, Jim thought, of that hot dry weather was that it drained away community spirit; people kept talking about rebuilding the school, but nobody made a move. On dog-day afternoons Jim enjoyed walking down toward the school ruins, the deep sawdust of the street mushing dry and hot between his bare toes. Smiling, he would enter the school yard and look with deep satisfaction on the charred timbers with their burned-wood odor. Burdock and nettles and pig weed grew around the old foundation, and Alex Castleman would never return. Oddly, the two log backhouses had not caught fire; they stood like malodorous tombstones on the grave of pedagogy; sometimes passersby stopped to use them. Come Halloween, Jim thought, and he'd organize an expedition to topple them.

*

Like Molly and Lew Fitzpatrick, Jim made many trips that summer combining business with pleasure, but his were shorter: only from the Buckmaster cabin west to the Chippewa River, where he pastured Bossy. Before tethering her along the river, he used to examine the vegetation; he didn't want her eating poisonous musquashroot, or mixing wild garlic with her cud and spoiling the taste of her milk. Fat and sleek, she was a good industrious cow whose udder gave plenty, but her intelligence quotient was not high, and if you didn't watch her she would flavor her product with wild licorice or get the scours from eating horsetail rushes. While she grazed Jim went swimming, but he always kept her within sight. Sometimes he led her into the river and splashed her to discourage the moose flies and no-see-ums.

What with delivering Bossy's milk to a half-dozen families, and chopping wood against next winter's need, and manufacturing grub pins, Jim kept busy that summer; his savings increased; and by his eleventh birthday in July he had nearly a hundred dollars in the buckskin bag hidden in the barn. It had been a good stroke of business to offer Trout Face a nickel apiece for grub pins; Jim's only worry was that Trout Face might learn that Pete Casey paid ten cents apiece. One afternoon in August Jim had a scare, for after paying the Indian for six of those pins, and carrying them to the rafting dump, and getting his money, he saw Trout Face in the middle distance on River Street, watching. Jim waved but Trout Face turned and ran. Well, Injuns were funny. A few days later when Trout Face turned up at the Buckmasters' with fifteen·pins he wanted eight cents apiece; it seemed that upon learning the ultimate use for those pins, and the price paid at the rafting dump, he had decided to be difficult. Jim took a chance and refused; a week later Trout Face came back and settled at the old price. Jim figured he must have tried to sell directly to Pete Casey and that Casey, who had less use for Injuns than for children, had chased him away. In any case, Jim was delighted to remain in the place of power traditional to the entrepreneur, right smack athwart the supply line between producer and consumer.

"Where did you get these?" Pete Casey asked, when Jim delivered the pins he had bought from Trout Face.

He didn't want Casey to discover he was enjoying a markup of a hundred percent; that man might overcome his prejudice and buy pins at five cents and charge them against the company at ten. So he answered vaguely that he had got them out in the woods. Casey gave him a long stare before tossing the pins into a pile in the shed and paying him off. If he seemed oddly curt, Jim ascribed it to the heat and drought, which by then was getting on everybody's nerves.

Lorne, naturally, was doing enough worrying for a drought twice as bad as it was; from his lined face and the gravity of his eyes you might have thought it had never rained in Quickwater and never would. Every night he stared at the sky, hoping for clouds, and every morning. Down at the mill he coopered two barrels and lugged them home and filled them with water, in case of fire.

"We're living in a tinder box," he used to say.

In early September he hired Three-Cent Olson to forge a netting of grilled iron, and he climbed to the cabin roof and fastened this over the chimney as a spark arrester.

"These shakes are dryer than cured hay," he announced from his perch. "One spark from this chimney and we'd go up in smoke."

"Don't worry, father," Myrtle said. "Worry never brought rain."

"Hold the ladder, will you, Myrt?" he said, preparing to descend. "I'd hate to slip and break my neck."

That sounded odd from a man who used to be such a cat on logs. But he wasn't, of course, the same man any more. Even in summer he coughed a great deal, and sometimes he had asthma attacks; his chest was more concave than ever, the hump on his shoulders more apparent; his hair was turning gray.

September brought relief from the heat but not from the dryness; you wondered how the roadside goldenrod and asters and black-eyed Susans found enough moisture to bloom; their flowers were dusty. Winds blew, dreary September winds, whirling the sawdust on Chippewa Street and rattling the dry needles of the pines. Cloudless though the sky remained, it was not such a clear azure as in summer, for strange haze showed on the southern horizon and spread; sometimes the heavens looked yellow. There were reports of scattered fires off to the southwest; farmers' brush fires out of control; fires set by half-breed settlers to burn blueberry bushes for a bumper crop in the future; you didn't get blueberries without a burn. The *Quickwater Mercury* made oblique references to these fires, but added there was nothing to worry about.

Not for several weeks had Trout Face come to the Buckmasters' with grub pins; Jim was wondering whether the tribe had followed Hole-in-the-Day's advice and moved. Then one murky morning when you could smell smoke in the still air Trout Face came with a great haul, two dozen pins; Jim paid him and that afternoon carried them to the rafting dump. The smoke had thickened like fog, cutting visibility to a few hundred feet; your eyes smarted and you coughed. Pete Casey said a teamster had reported a pretty good blaze twenty miles south, although they were getting it under control. He wished it would rain. His eyes were watering from the smoke when he counted the pins and paid Jim off.

The weather had turned warmer again, and the heat added to everybody's discomfort, although the air cooled with twilight. But it didn't clear. Through the smoky darkness of evening you could see a red glow on the southern horizon, as if a volcano were there. At supper Lorne looked more worried than Jim had ever seen him; he was seized by coughing spells; his hand trembled, passing the hominy.

"What's wrong, father?" Myrtle asked. "Does the smoke bother you?"

He sat staring at his plate.

"The smoke, and other things," he said at last. "Jim, I want to talk with you."

"Sure," Jim said.

"Not now. After supper, in the yard."

Myrtle looked from her son to her husband and back to her son.

"Jim," she said, "have you been into something?"

He looked squarely into her eyes, gray and steady like his own. He shook his head; his conscience was clear.

"Not a thing," he said.

She kept looking at him, in that way of mothers.

"I haven't," he said. "Not a thing."

She smiled then.

"All right, Jim, I believe you." And she patted his hand. "You've been a good son, Jim. You've given me a lot of pleasure."

He felt embarrassed, remembering ancient sins he had never confessed; fights; beanshooters; all those lapses that any boy finds it wiser not to mention.

"A good son," she repeated. "And you'll be a rich man."

"I know it," he said.

Years later he could look back and be glad she had said that, about his being a good son, and he could remember leaving the cabin with Lorne after supper. In the yard the air was like the inside of a smokehouse; you could hardly make out the stars. Jim's eyes stung and his nose itched; in the barn Bossy was lamenting the way she did when her udder was painfully full, but Jim had milked her dry before supper. When they reached the well Lorne was seized by a fit of coughing; he bent nearly double, hawking and spitting. When he could speak his voice was thin, trying to form words through the mucus in his throat.

"I don't know, Jim," he said, "I hate to bring this up. I'd rather take a licking. But this afternoon a man told me you'd been stealing."

Lorne's voice trailed away; Jim stood scowling, hearing Bossy's forlorn mooing and seeing the red glow in the southern sky; he tried to remember what he'd been up to lately that might have given anybody that notion.

"Have you, Jim?"

"No," Jim said. "I don't steal. Who said I'd been stealing?"

As always when troubled, Lorne had brought out his jackknife and had picked up a stick; he stood there whittling.

"I don't know as I should tell you," he said. "I don't like to cause hard feelings."

"Who said that?" Jim asked sharply. "I've got a right to know."

"A man ought to keep on good terms with everybody," Lorne said. "You have to live with people, and when they get down on you it's bad. They don't speak to you on the street, and you know they're talking behind your back. That happened to me once. Corky Ingram was the best friend I ever had. We never even fought, except when we were little sannups and I called him Ulysses. It was his name too, but it made him mad. We were good friends, but when an accident happened they said I'd done it on purpose. It sort of bothered me."

"Who said I'd been stealing?"

"I don't know, Jim, as I should say. Still, I reckon you've got a right to know. It was Pete Casey."

"Then he's a liar," Jim said. "If he says I stole he's a liar."

"Oh, he said it, Jim. He come into the mill just before quitting time and said it. He said you'd been stealing grub pins."

"I never did," Jim said. "That's a lie."

"He took me out to the rafting dump and showed me," Lorne said. "Showed me the pins you sold him this afternoon. Each one had a little knife-notch in the stem. He said that proved you'd stolen them."

"Why, the son of a bitch," Jim said.

"I'm just telling you what he said, Jim. He said about a month ago you sold him fifteen pins, and they looked familiar. He began to suspicion you right then, Jim. He figured you sneaked down to the rafting dump at night and stole pins and then sold them back to him."

"The bastard," Jim said. "The Irish bastard."

"Now wait, Jim. Don't go calling names. You've got to live with people, Jim, and they don't like it if you call them bastard, even if it's true. Especially if it's true. So Pete said he figured to lay a trap for you. He never kept them pins locked up because there'd been no trouble about stealing, and he didn't lock them up now. What he did was to notch the stem of every pin with his knife. That way, he'd know it if you were stealing them and selling them back. Well, this morning he noticed the pile of pins seemed smaller, and this afternoon you brought in two dozen pins and sold them. And every one was notched, Jim. Every last one. He said he wouldn't go to Dan Stoughton about it unless he had to. Everybody steals a little now and then, he said, and he didn't like to make trouble. He said if you'd give back the money he paid you for the stolen pins he'd forget the whole thing."

"He's crazy," Jim said.

"I don't know, Jim, I don't think he's crazy. He's a right smart fellow, when you come down to it."

"It must have been Trout Face," Jim said.

"Trout Face? I don't guess I know who that is."

"An Injun kid. I've been paying him a nickel for every pin he brought me. Then I'd sell them for ten cents. He never knew, I reckon, what I wanted them for, till one afternoon he followed me to the dump. Then he must have asked around. He must have found out I was getting ten cents apiece. Well, Pete Casey hates Injuns, and maybe he wouldn't buy pins from Trout Face at that price. Maybe not at any price. Maybe he just chased Trout Face away. So Trout Face must have stolen those pins and sold them to me. And I sold them to Pete. That's what happened."

"Jim," Lorne said, "that's a load off my mind. I never thought you'd steal. But can you prove it?"

"Mother's seen him coming here," Jim said. "She never asked what was going on, but she's seen him. So have Harriet and Alice."

"That might be good enough for Pete," Lorne said, "and it might not. He might figure your family was covering up your tracks for you. Maybe you ought to make Trout Face tell Pete about it himself."

Jim could remember how surprised he was at his father's shrewd figuring about that; he had fallen into thinking his father wasn't too sharp, because he had never made a lot of money; now he could recognize that Lorne was nobody's fool.

"That's what I'll do," Jim said. "I'll go to Injun Hollow in the morning and drag Trout Face down to the rafting dump and make him tell the truth. He's likely spent the money. I guess I'll have to make that up to Pete out of my own pocket. But after he hears Trout Face he'll know I'm no thief. He should have kept those pins locked up. If I was Stoughton I'd fire him for being careless."

"That Injun might give you trouble, Jim. Could be he won't come along like you want."

"He'll come," Jim said. "I know an Injun hold. He knows it too, but I'll grab his hand before he guesses. Then I'll turn his hand palm up and yank his arm over my left arm. When I lever down it'll hurt. If I keep levering I can break his arm with that hold. He'll march along where I want, once I've got that hold. If he's spent the money I'll make him gather me enough pins to pay me back what I'm out of pocket to Pete Casey. If he won't do that I'll take it out of his hide till he promises. I can lick Trout Face. I've done it before."

"Don't go so far as to break his arm," Lorne said. "You might get into trouble."

"Trouble over an Injun?" Jim laughed. "I guess I could kill an Injun and nobody would care."

"Don't kill him," Lorne said. "You'd live to regret it."

"I won't kill him," Jim said. "I won't have to."

"Don't kill him, Jim. And don't break his arm. Life's sort of funny. Sometimes you do something to a man's arm or his hand and you pay for it always. It's an open account on the ledger that's never paid off. Just make him confess. And get back your money."

"I'll get it back. If not in cash in grub pins."

"But make it up to Pete Casey right away. Then he won't mention the matter to Stoughton. It would never do for Stoughton to get ideas. You might need him some day. Have you got enough cash to make it up to Casey?"

"I reckon I have," Jim said. "I've been saving."

"I'm glad to hear that, Jim. You save you up a stake and you're out ahead of most men. Most men blow it as it comes in. But you get you a stake and first thing you know you'll see an opportunity. You can move in then and hire men to work for you. You work for yourself and you've got just two hands. But you hire a man and you've got four hands working for you. You hire three men and you've got eight hands, counting your own. It's the way to get ahead. I used to figure that's what I'd do. But things sort of went against me, Jim. A freshet hit my logs, so to speak, and swept them all downriver and scattered them on the banks. I had a lot of trouble, Jim, and it took the heart out of me. It used up my stake and more too. A lot more. It's none of my business, Jim, but how much have you got saved?"

"Nearly a hundred dollars," Jim said.

It must have taken Lorne's breath; he just stood there in the smoky darkness for a moment. Then he said:

"A hundred dollars. Are you sure, Jim?"

"Sure," Jim said. "I'm always counting it."

"A hundred dollars. That's a sight of money for a boy of your age. Or for anybody, when it comes to that. A hundred dollars. I never would have thought it."

"I've saved," Jim said. "I've watched the pennies."

"And it counts up," Lorne said. "It sure counts up. A hundred dollars. That beats. I don't know, Jim, that makes me sort of proud of you. A hundred dollars."

And he reached out and patted Jim's shoulder. Jim always liked to remember that.

*

Next morning when Jim started for Injun Hollow the smoke was thicker than ever; you could hardly see across the road. His eyes kept smarting and his breathing was shallow: if you took a deep breath your lungs filled with the stuff and you nearly strangled. Overhead the sun looked like a red-hot penny. The morning was hot for September, the air forebodingly still. Silent too, except for the mooing of Bossy which followed him down the road; she hadn't carried on like that since he weaned her calf. Jim guessed that after he settled matters with Trout Face he would lead Bossy to the Chippewa and they would both go into the water and cool off.

He hadn't expected to encounter anybody on Shin-Tangle Street, but when he approached Three-Cent Olson's place he caught sight of two figures blurring toward him, a man and a boy. The man walked splay-footed and leaned forward under the weight of a pack. It was Sol Klauber.

"Jim," Sol Klauber called, "is that you, Jim?"

"Sure," Jim said.

"I couldn't make you out for certain," Klauber said. "Isn't this a fright?"

"Kind of smoky," Jim said. "When did you get back?"

"Yesterday, Jim. If we'd known what it would be like, Isaac and I would have stayed in Boston. Jim, I want you to meet Isaac. He's new in this country, and maybe you'll show him around."

In that roiling smoke, Jim couldn't get much of a look at Isaac, except to see that he was black-haired and about his own height.

"Is it always like this?" Isaac asked. "If it is I'd rather live in a chimney during a cold winter."

"She'll clear," Jim said.

"We came in with a teamster," Sol Klauber said, "from the east. Nothing's burning over that way. But I hear they've got a couple of good blazes south of here."

"Breeds set fire to the blueberry lands," Jim said.

"They shouldn't do it," Sol said. "This country's too dry for setting fires."

"That's breeds for you," Jim said.

"Is your mother home?" Sol asked. "Maybe we'll stop in and see what she needs."

Jim said she was home.

"We'll say hello, anyway," Sol said. "Then we'll go back to the hotel. It's too smoky for selling. The customers can't see the merchandise. All I could sell Mrs. Olson was some snuff."

"She uses a lot of it," Jim said, "when she quills. She quilled my mother when my brother Dobner was born. They made us kids go down to her house and stay, but when I came home to do the chores I could hear my mother sneezing in the cabin. Then Vonnie Olson came out and said I had a baby brother."

"We'll get on, Jim," Sol Klauber said. "Come down to the hotel some time and get acquainted with Isaac. You two boys should get on fine."

"Sure," Jim said, and he watched Sol Klauber go toiling away till he looked like a splay-footed ghost in the smoke with a smaller ghost beside him.

It was a good thing, Jim thought, that he knew the way to Injun Hollow as well as he did, else he'd have got lost a dozen times; even as it was he made slow progress, turning south on Goosefoot Street and fumbling along till he located the path leading east. He had never groped through such thick smoke, not even when he was a small boy and used to cavort in the smoke from autumnal heaps of leaves; he remembered how that bonfire smell would stick to his clothing. But the smell of this smoke was different; he didn't like it; for the fragrance of burning pine had been heavily tainted by the acrid reek of burning weeds.

The sun had been obliterated, visibility reduced to a few feet, when he passed the dried-up tamarack swamp where branches and needles were sere as a Christmas tree in mid-January. Off in opaqueness he could hear the plaintive cheepings of forest birds; and once, amazingly, a horned owl hooted. At this time of day that owl should have been dozing in a hollow tree; hearing it now gave him an uncanny feeling. But what bothered him most was what happened when the path started climbing the ridge. Something rustled from the withered underbrush and he saw a wolverine go sneaking across the path toward the northeast, bushy tail between its hind legs and short ears laid back along its head. It was close enough, almost, to kick. Jim jumped back, for a wolverine wasn't anything to meet up with unarmed; its legs were powerful as a bear's, its claws scimitars; but today that vicious killer went crashing off through the brush as if in flight. Jim didn't like that. And he liked it even less when, almost immediately, eight or ten white-tailed deer came bounding across the path, heading northeast, following the wolverine. No herd of deer in their right minds ever went toward a wolverine; that was as unlikely as a minnow chasing a black bass. Jim listened, expecting to hear the death scream of a hamstrung deer; it didn't come. That would be something to tell Dan Stoughton about, except Stoughton wouldn't believe him; nobody would believe him.

At the crest of the ridge the smoke swirled so thick it gagged him, and he dropped to hands and knees till he was half way down the slope to

Injun Hollow, and then he scooted along stooped, for the air was purer near the ground. And as he dropped down into the hollow visibility increased; he could see maybe a hundred feet ahead; he could see the lodge of Nekeek's mother, and he went there. But it was empty; cooking utensils gone, everything gone; only the reed matting on the floor. It gave him an odd feeling, and he went from lodge to lodge; they were all abandoned. In front of Hole-in-the-Day's lodge, still dangling from the cedar pole, the little carved effigy of Dan Stoughton remained; smoke drifted around it.

The tribe must have followed Hole-in-the-Day's advice and gone away to better lands. Knowing they were leaving, Trout Face must have stolen those two dozen grub pins night-before-last, making a final good haul. Jim thought that except for this smoke he would have tracked the tribe and found Trout Face and marched him back. Useless to try that now. He had been duped and rooked. He'd be out of pocket more than a dollar, after paying Pete Casey for the stolen pins. And maybe Casey would always think him a thief; maybe he'd tell Dan Stoughton. Well, the thing to do would be to get to Stoughton first with the story. Damn Injuns, anyway.

The morning had grown hotter; Jim was thirsty suddenly; and he went to Snowshoe Creek. It wasn't there. Only a trail of rocks where water used to foam and sing. No wonder the Chippewas had left the country, with their creek drying up. He stood tracing moccasin patterns in the arid sand, feeling alone and bereft, as if he were a ghost that had wandered back. Then something happened that gave him a real scare.

He had never been scared by rabbits before; he would have laughed, if anybody had told him he'd ever be scared of those timid creatures This was different; this was part of the eeriness of deer following a wolverine. For while he stood there in the dry creek bed he saw, coming from the southwest, thirty or forty cottontails, bounding along with ears back as if chased by a thousand foxes, so terrorized by what was behind them that they never swerved when they sighted Jim but darted past him as if he were a stump, running right through the streets of the Chippewa village and on out of sight into the thick haze. Jim looked to see what might be chasing them. But nothing was chasing them.

Then it came to him, what he should have figured out before, except he'd been so absorbed in his strategy of catching Trout Face and marching him to Pete Casey. He knew then that those rabbits were not fleeing anything of flesh and blood; they were fleeing fire. Maybe the smoke had warned them, or maybe some instinct. And instinct must have warned that wolverine and those deer. They were all getting the hell out of here while the getting was good. Perhaps instinct had warned the Chippewas too.

The silence suddenly was appalling; Jim heard his own breathing; and the smoke smarted his eyes so that tears kept running down his face.

He started back toward town; at the summit of the ridge the smoke was suffocating even when he crawled along with his nose scraping the pebbles. He was coughing; his eyes felt as if pepper had been flung into them. The trail rocks cut his hands and knees. When he reached the bottom of the ridge the smoke cleared slightly and he lay gasping, but he felt like a smoked slab of venison.

Then he heard something else and for a moment he was glad, thinking the air would clear. It was the soughing of the tall pines in the start of a breeze. And the air did clear, in patches; once the smoke swarming around him suddenly whirled in an odd upsuck; he could see trees and bushes; he got to his feet and filled his lungs with gulps of purity. But after a minute smoke poured around him and he couldn't see farther than his nose. He ran, bent low, hurrying along the path till his lungs were bursting; then he dropped prone and breathed close to earth. Far overhead the wind in the pines sounded louder. Then the air cleared suddenly again and he sluiced his windpipe full of pure oxygen and ran.

He was nearing the tamarack swamp when the wind swabbed across it from the southwest, cleaning away the smoke the way Alex Castleman used to obliterate figures on the blackboard with a wet cloth. For an instant Jim could see maybe a quarter of a mile out through those drought-browned tamarack limbs and needles. He even saw sky once, with spruce tips serrated against it. And then something happened which he hoped he'd never see again. Nobody would believe it when he told them. For all at once, off to the south of the swamp, those spruce trees changed from green spires to red torches. Instantly. One second they were green and growing, the next towers of flame. Like a wisp of dry grass when you touched it with a flaming sliver. Like a miller moth ignited by a candle. And then, racing from those burning spruce, he saw a long scarlet snake of flame, darting across the tamarack tips. And the air exploded, as if swamp gasses had been set off like gunpowder. One moment brown tamarack; next moment a seething wall of flame. He didn't wait to watch; no buck deer had ever run much faster. Behind him, back at the swamp, a hellish racket filled the air; crackling, snapping, popping like firecrackers on the Fourth. Once he flung back a glance; the wind had freshened more, and he saw a red vortex whirling out of the swamp and across the path where he had been, crackling into the thirsty timber. Whole trees, whole gigantic white pine trees, broke into flame, sending pillars of smoke sky high. Birds were circling and screaming; Jim ran on.

The wind was howling like forty tribes of Sioux when he reached Goosefoot Street on the east edge of town, and the air was cluttered with blazing hunks of debris, some of them sailing high toward the woods to the north, some dipping and rising and dipping again, to fall into weeds and start fires; and off toward the business district vast flame-streaked puffs of smoke whirled skyward till the wind flattened them and they flapped along like blown blankets. Quickwater was burning; the Northern Saloon was burning; Dan Stoughton's fancy house and the Shanghai Hotel and Gentleman Steve's Woodsman's Friend Saloon and Parlor of Chance, A Good Time For All—every one of them was burning. The streets themselves were burning, all that packed dry sawdust, everything was on fire. In the distance sounds could be heard above the roar of the conflagration; yells, screams, oxen lowing, horses neighing. Perry Roque more must have turned his animals loose from the livery stable, for as Jim went scooting across vacant lots, avoiding the bright rivers of hell that the sawdust streets had become, he heard louder neighing and once he saw through the smoke a gigantic Clydesdale plunging insanely.

He had had some idea of making it to Shin-Tangle Street and his cabin; of dousing gourdfuls of water on the roof; of rescuing Bossy; but now he knew all that was futile; Quickwater was a town in hell now, with demons riding the wind; the woods were forests of hell; and there was but one possible place of safety, if he could make it: the Chippewa River. Gagging with smoke, eyes like coals, tongue dry as maple punk, he thought of the river as he fought his way across lots, how he could swim out to the middle and go under water and come up for air and go under again.

When he reached a street—he didn't know which one—he saw a hedge of flame from that damned sawdust; he stopped short and turned but in the wall of smoke behind him he could see darting tongues of crimson; so he catapulted forward, right through those flames, singeing his hair; and his pants caught fire; so beyond the street he rolled and dug handfuls of earth—hot earth—and smothered out the flames. By then he was so done in he thought his lungs would collapse; he wanted to lie there; Nekeek had said once that his grandfather had told him if he was ever burned at the stake by the Dakotas that he should inhale smoke and thus lose consciousness and avoid flame torture; Jim had a notion to inhale a little more—it wouldn't take much—and pass out and maybe some time or other men would come from outside to poke in the ruins of Quickwater and find him, a skeleton broken and charred. But the will to live always flowed strong in him, so he went crawling in what he hoped was the direction of the river, and after a while he was running again, stooped; and then he came to another street, on fire like the one he had already crossed, they never should have used sawdust for pavement, it burned, it caught fire, that was the trouble with sawdust. He guessed he plunged through that street too, for he was rolling again and digging up earth, his skin hurting where firebrands had arrowed him and where the flames had seared. He lay longer this time, mightily tempted to inhale that smoke, wondering why he had ever broken off wild grapevine and dried it and run a wire through it and smoked it, pretending it a cigar; if he lived through this he would never smoke grapevine again; he would only breathe air as sweet and pure as water and dive into swimming holes and be cool. But again, something in him made him crawl and then run, through smoke and screams from people he couldn't see and from horses he couldn't see; and then he came to yet another street where the flames were higher and the smoke thicker; afterward he figured that must have been River Street with the sawmill and lumber piles sending northward flame dragons and smoke dragons.

He dreaded to go through those flames; he had done it before and it was painful, he hated to tackle it; but then his legs propelled him forward, he was burning, he was burning, he was a faggot; but then he wasn't, he was something rolling and digging handfuls of earth hot as ashes and smothering his clothes; and by then he was tired, tired. He lay prone, breathing what oxygen his nostrils could scrape together; and he began feeling nice and comfortable; a little warm, maybe, and with a few smarting places on his skin but on the whole pretty comfortable; and he was thinking of water flowing cool and clear, water rippling along your flanks, he liked water, someday he'd be a river pig.

Somebody let out a yell above him; he was too tired to look; he was sleepy; let them yell; and then he was lifted bodily and carried, his feet dragging sometimes; he didn't like that so he worked his feet; and all the time somebody he couldn't see kept dragging him along; and then all at once he was in water. And it wasn't a dream, either; it was real; he went under and came up snorting and spitting; and in the yellow light with the white background of smoke he saw he was waist-deep in the river and a man with a ginger-brown beard and mustache was standing there in the water with him, gaping. And all at once the man's eyes showed terror and he yelled:

"You're not Isaac! You're Jim! You're not Isaac!"

The world had gone mad, some time back, but not so mad that Jim thought his name was Isaac.

"No," he told Sol Klauber, "I'm not Isaac. I'm Jim."

"Isaac fell," Sol Klauber was yelling. "He fell down. I picked him up. But you're not Isaac! You're Jim! You're not Isaac!"

"No, mister," Jim said. "I'm Jim."

"Isaac," Sol Klauber yelled, splashing toward shore, "Isaac," and he went groping into smoke. After a while he came back, without Isaac, and his eyes were streaming, probably not altogether from the smoke.

X

WHEN HE looked back on those days most of what he saw was smoke-blurred and scrambled, and he could never be sure how much was fact and how much delirium. Fragments came back to him like charred pictures, but all were scattered and jumbled. It was a long time ago; the gone years flowed across his memory and distorted what he saw. He remembered how people came reeling to the river, gagging in the smoke or screaming because their clothes were blazing, but some fell in the marsh where the sawdust was burning, and some suffocated in the clouds rolling from the piles of lumber, and some who pitched head-long into the river sank like rocks; for days after the fire men were always pulling bodies out of the Chippewa, maybe a dozen miles down-stream. One of those bodies might have been Sol Klauber's, for he couldn't swim, but Jim found a drift log and told him to grab that. Sol didn't want to; he wanted to go blundering into those hells of smoke and heat, searching for his son; but Jim made him hang onto that log. Then he towed him out into mid-river. Even that far from shore the air was bright with heat; Jim kept going under water and splashing Sol.

Later that day they were lying on the far bank of the Chippewa, too done in to wiggle a toe. Over there, the birch and fir had caught fire early and now were smoldering. On to the west, beyond a wasteland of ashes and smoking rubble, green trees were standing unharmed, for the conflagration had been driven by a southwest wind and the flames had flowed with it, not against it.

Night came, with its distant cries, with the Chippewa flowing red from the sky-glow. Lying there on the bank, or crawling to a sand-spit where he drank from the river, Jim felt as if his body too were glowing, all fevered from the splotches where his skin had burned. His eyebrows had been scorched away, his hair seared. Sometimes he tried to ease his pain by lying in the shallow water near shore, or plastering his burns with mud.

He thought of his family. Maybe they had pulled through; maybe not; he felt utterly resigned and suffused with an emotion beyond grief; grief was too small to cope with what had happened. Tears came later; not that night. And he remembered thinking that if he was the only Buckmaster to survive, he wasn't going to let busybodies put him into no orphanage. He would disappear; he would find him a Chippewa band or a logging camp. But maybe deep down he never thought the fire had snuffed out his family; maybe that was why he kept calm.

Along toward morning he thought he must be crying, for his cheeks were wet; only they weren't wet from tears but from raindrops. He sat up. The raindrops fell faster; before long they turned into a downpour. But that rain was a day late.

*

Men were a long time piecing together what had happened, for in those days the government did not maintain socialistic agencies like a forest service and an efficient weather bureau; that was a golden age for persons who disliked government interference; individuals could die ruggedly then. In any case, it seemed that those fires south and southwest of Quickwater had been burning along nicely but conservatively, like a banker's cigar; but then a storm front moved in. That meant wind; in the Quickwater area it meant perhaps a baby tornado. So the fires whipped out of control, and after that it was every rabbit for himself. When at last the rains began they fell steadily for hours and intermittently for days; rains of the autumn equinox.

Cruising the woods during the next weeks, men discovered that the fire had kept to the east side of the Chippewa, destroying timber in a long strip to the northeast shaped somewhat like a salamander. But nobody worried about ravaged timber; in those days the pines were going to last forever.

But that holocaust did teach men a great lesson: that where there's smoke there's fire. Beyond that, nobody learned much. In north woods towns sawdust remained a favorite paving material, and when a jobber logged over an area he left the tops and branches of fallen trees to dry out and become fire breeders. People kept right on burning blueberry lands, and lumber was always stacked beside sawmills, and men were forever knocking live coals from their pipes. It was a free country, wasn't it?

*

Quickwater looked dreary in the rain; what was left of Quickwater. Nothing, actually, was left, except stone chimneys. The streets of town were ashes, the trees of town smoking stumps. Weeks later, even after those soaking rains, men would see smoke wisping from the ground, and a few minutes' work with a spade would reveal bright fragments of the forest fire still eating along the involuted root systems of old trees. Some people said the ground had been burned three feet deep.

Wandering through the ruins, men discovered that people had done all sorts of damn fool things when the fire came roaring in. Vonnie Olson had jumped into the well beside her cabin and drowned. Gentle-

556

man Steve had hiked to the privy behind his establishment and locked the door. His bartender had jumped into a full barrel of whiskey. One whole family had taken refuge in a root cellar where they had been suffocated and roasted. Survivors reported that Perry Roquemore, after releasing his horses, had climbed to the roof of his livery stable with a bucket of water; the roof collapsed flaming. Mr. and Mrs. Emerson Tate, who edited the *Quickwater Mercury,* had gone crying through the streets telling everybody to be calm, it wouldn't be much of a fire; a minute later they were running torches.

Dan Stoughton survived, although not his monkey or his Chippewa gals or Charlie Usher, his man-of-all-work; that poem about the beauties of nature would never be finished now. When the wind freshened, Dan had been walking toward the sawmill, and he broke into a run, heading for the dam, when he saw the woods south of town flame up, and a ball of fire detach itself and come sizzling toward Chippewa Street like some huge spark-dripping sphere from a gigantic Roman candle. The very air, he said, seemed to explode, as if gasses had been ignited. The hairs were singed from his forearms when he reached the sluice-gate out in the middle of the dam. He saved himself by swinging down into the sluiceway and picking his way to the face of the cribwork where he stood in the splash; when the fire was at its worst, he said, the water flowing over the dam ran hot. All that day he stayed there, and all that night; but when the rain began he returned to town and told anybody who would listen that Quickwater would be rebuilt; a Felix from the ashes, he kept saying; he must have meant a phoenix. Xenophon Yates and his wife had also saved themselves, and they announced they would rebuild the Shanghai House.

But Quickwater could never be rebuilt; Jim knew it never could. A new town, maybe; not the old town. By then he knew his family must all be dead, although nobody had seen them doing any of the fool things some people did. He was glad of that; he was glad he came of a stock that kept its head even when dying in a forest fire.

*

It was all muddled in his memory; he never could be sure how long he remained in what had been Quickwater; four or five days maybe. There was nothing to eat in town but the survivors did not complain; nobody was hungry; they just wandered through the ashes looking for bodies. Sometimes they found bodies too and wished they hadn't. But for the most part that fire did a thorough job, consuming flesh and bone as if they were pine needles; Jim never found anything that could be buried and prayed over. He remembered shuffling along what had been Shin-Tangle Street and turning in at what had been the Buckmaster place, where the cabin chimney still stood and the fine old Norway pine in the front yard was a jagged stump. He touched it and got his fingers black, and he remembered the swing his father had fixed for the children from a limb of that tree.

What had been the barn was sodden ashes, and Jim didn't even go poking for the money he had saved; maybe he was afraid he would find some relic of Bossy. In any case the currency would be ashes and the silver blackened. Money didn't seem so important now; he wished he had spent those savings.

Some time during those first days food was sent to Quickwater from more fortunate communities down the Chippewa, and Jim ate. But he couldn't say he enjoyed it; still, it helped a little, making him feel less like a drifting ghost. Sol Klauber ate too, there at the rude commissary by the dam, and he told Jim he was going to a town called New Empire where he would replenish his peddler's stock; before leaving Boston he had shipped extra merchandise to New Empire, planning to pick it up as he needed it. Did Jim want to go with him?

Jim thought it over, suspecting some large plot to plunk him into an orphanage, where men like Alex Castleman would be in charge; he was wary, now that he was alone.

"I don't know about that, mister," he said. "Aren't you mad at me?"

Sol looked haggard, his eyes sunken and his beard burned half away. He shook his head and said gently:

"Why would I be mad at you?"

"Well," Jim said, "because—because I wasn't Isaac."

"I'm not mad at anybody," Sol said. "You'd better come."

So they left town together, footing it through mile after mile of desolation where occasionally a charred tree stood like a cenotaph mourning the forest. Jim might have been a beggar boy with his grimy hands and sooty face, his shirt and pants scorched, his feet bare; he had lost his moccasins in the river. But his soles were tough and he tried to be tough. The burned spots on his arms and legs had turned to blisters, and they hurt, but he didn't complain; he didn't want Sol taking him to some doctor and the doctor saying this boy should be in school or in an orphanage.

After a while an occasional green tree appeared, and presently they had left the burned land and were following a trail through a sweet-smelling forest; when they reached a village Sol bought food. Jim had supposed they might have to beg it, but Sol wore a money belt containing gold eagles. Jim had never seen a money belt.

"Mister," he said, "that's pretty sharp. That's better than hiding it in a barn. Some day I'll have me one of those things."

Sol bought blankets too and they slept in the woods; and when they reached the Mississippi they hired a man to ferry them across to a town called Read's Landing, where a downriver boat was ready to leave. They boarded that, sleeping in their blankets on the boiler deck.

It was quite a river, that Mississippi; Jim took to it right off. He liked the daybreak mists and the sweep of river in the afternoon with the bluffs marching away into far hazes. He still cried now and then, when he could get a minute alone, but he was always resilient, landing on his feet like a lynx, and seeing the Mississippi River helped salve his grief; he could even laugh again; short laughs. And although he liked Sol Klauber, he slept with his mind at half-cock, just in case Sol should summon men to drag him to an orphanage. He didn't trust anything or anybody.

*

New Empire seemed the biggest town on the biggest river in creation. There was a courthouse with a cupola; there were brick-paved streets and stores; Sol took him into a store and outfitted him. By then most of his suspicions had evaporated, Sol was so gentle, although it did occur to him that those new clothes might be in preparation for an orphanage; he was still careful; he had his plans all laid as to how he would make a break for it if anybody tried to put him where he didn't want.

But nothing of the sort. They rented a room in a lodging house on the north side of Winnebago Street, a half-block east of the river, where in bed at night you could hear the sad *woo-hooing* of steamboat whistles far away. It was a two-story house built of lumber, not logs; Jim had never lived in a place so fine; their room had a chamber pot decorated with gold vines, and even the outhouse was of lumber. After Sol bought a peddler's license they used to go through the residential district selling goods. But sometimes they didn't sell; once an old crone said she wouldn't buy nothing from no dirty Jew.

"What's a Jew?" Jim asked Sol, after they left that woman's house.

Sol was looking sort of troubled, but then he smiled.

"Why, Jim," he said, "a Jew is somebody who is like everybody else only more so. If he's mean he's meaner, if he's good he's better, if he's kind he's kinder, if he's dirty he's dirtier, if he's smart he's smarter. If he wants money he goes after it harder, and if he wants learning he'll never rest till he's read every book ever written. And if he's just an average sort of fellow he'll be more that way too."

"Are you a Jew?" Jim asked.

"With this nose and you ask me that?"

By then Jim almost never cried any more about what had happened in Quickwater, and Sol was more cheerful too, although when he spoke of Isaac tears came to his eyes. Jim kept trying to figure just what a Jew was, and Sol kept trying to explain, although he said there was no neat answer because so many strains had blended and intensified to produce the Jewish people. The more they talked about it the more puzzled Jim became, because it seemed that Jesus Christ was a Jew, and his mother, and his foster-father, and his disciples; and the sect which called itself Christian had a high opinion of Jesus and the rest of those estimable old

559

Jews, even calling them saints and using the book which the Jewish God had dictated, when he wasn't destroying cities or flying into a rage about petty matters; but despite the fact that the Christians had cabbaged onto everything Jewish, in a religious way, still they held the Jews in low esteem.

"You're expecting people to be consistent," Sol said.

That was one evening in their room, and Jim asked:

"What's consistent?"

So Sol explained, and then one thing led to another and he told Jim about his life.

*

More than a hundred years before, in Munich, there had been a boy of fourteen named Abraham Klauber whose parents were arrested by the police and charged with murder. Things must have been dull at police headquarters just then, or perhaps the police chief had a wife who picked on him and he wanted to restore his ego by picking on somebody else; in any case the Klaubers were arrested for a crime that had been committed many centuries before when a young carpenter was crucified in one of the less important colonies of the Roman Empire. The Munich police accused the Klaubers of this Christ-killing, and to hear them tell it you would have thought crucifixion must have been some strange and unusual punishment instead of just a routine way of rubbing out thieves and intellectuals. By the time the Munich police were through working on the Klaubers they were dead and glad of it; and their son Abraham was on his way to Amsterdam, traveling by night.

Compared with Munich, Amsterdam was an enlightened city with a prosperous Jewish colony, so when Abraham Klauber arrived hungry and ragged he was fed and clothed and given a few guilders; all of which, from a Christian standpoint, was reprehensible, for it came under the heading of how the Jews always stuck together. After a few days the Amsterdam Jews shuttled Abraham across the channel to London, also an enlightened city, where many rich Jews were living, having migrated there some years before to escape the Portuguese Inquisition, which could be unpleasant. Abraham Klauber, who had red hair and even then a big craggy nose, looked up these wealthy Portuguese Jews and said something like you'll never know the trouble I've seen and what are you going to do about it?

They were not entirely glad to see him, for the mischief was that he was an Ashkenazic or German Jew and they were Sephardic Jews who thought of themselves as aristocrats. They did, however, possess a certain compassion unknown to the Christian aristocracy, so they couldn't very well boot Abraham Klauber down the stairs; they kept him in funds and sent him to live with other Ashkenazic Jews of London while they tried to figure out what to do. Then somebody thought of James Oglethorpe.

Oglethorpe, a rich non-Jew, was just then engaged in being a traitor to his class, for he harbored advanced ideas in economics and penology, wishing to spring unfortunates from debtors' prison and send them to North America; and by much talking and wire-pulling he succeeded in getting the colony of Georgia established, sending thence many paupers and jailbirds to settle and raise silk and found the proud Southern Aristocracy.

To the Sephardim this looked like a pretty good dish of krupnik; why not, they thought, get these damned Ashkenazim off our necks by dumping them in North America? So they chartered a vessel and wished them luck, and with a sigh of relief went back to being aristocrats; and that was how Abraham Klauber happened to migrate to Georgia, landing in the Savannah area in the mid 1730's.

About this time the Inquisition in Portugal was kicking up again, and not every Jew wished to be burned alive, so those with money escaped to London where hearing about Georgia they too chartered a ship and sailed to the New World, buying land and settling down as planters.

But although Georgia lacked the fogs of London and the thumbscrews of Lisbon, it was still not really Utopia, for all the pilgrims who had migrated there, Jews and Gentiles alike, were human beings, with the boundless capacities of this odd species for raising hell with one another; so almost at once the persons who had been rescued from debtors' prison back in England were announcing that they were better than those Sephardic Jews, and the Sephardic Jews maintained that they were really the chosen people and too good to associate with those schnorrers the Ashkenazic Jews.

None of this bothered Abraham Klauber. Energetic as a bumblebee, he talked himself into a job on a plantation operated by a Sephardic Jew, where he worked cultivating silk and indigo and grapes for wine; he saved his wages; at twenty he was business manager of the plantation; and at twenty-two he quit to establish a small store on the river front in Savannah. It prospered. At twenty-four Abraham remembered something Jehovah had said about being fruitful, so he went to work and fell in love with Miriam Salvador, a gentle, intellectual girl of Portuguese descent who had been born in London and who had migrated with her family to Savannah. Her parents, of course, objected to the match, for they were proud Sephardim, but Abraham Klauber wasn't one to take no for an answer, or Miriam a girl to give no for an answer when she was so much in love; so after all the tears and handwringing and tumult and even a little shouting the inevitable happened and Miriam and Abraham became one, with the result that before long the Klaubers were the parents of two children with bright wise eyes. And although Miriam's family had objected to the merging of Sephardic and Ashkenazic blood, the mosquitoes from the swamps thought it very tasty, so after being nibbled in the romantic southern dusk by a hungry anopheles the children contracted malaria and perished and being non-Christian doubtless went forthwith to hell. Soon thereafter, in 1750, a third child was born and named Benjamin, and although he was a fine little fellow, with a gentle, dreamy and even poetic nature, inherited from his mother, the mosquitoes didn't care for him and he lived, which was perhaps a mixed blessing, for life was always a little too much for poor Ben.

Meanwhile, Abraham Klauber was making a thumping success of his business, expanding it till he had not only a store on the south side of Bay Street fronting the river, with a fine home and a pleasant garden adjoining the store at the rear, but also, on the north side of the street, a great warehouse which presently flaunted a sign: A. Klauber & Son, Importers. Planters used to haul in their indigo, rice, silk, wheat, corn and peltries, and Abraham bought these and shipped them to foreign parts; and he imported such fine merchandise as cheeses, damasks, velvets, laces, earthenware in crates, Scotch snuff, Osnaburgs and ticklenburgs; as well as casks of wine from Madeira; and from the sugar islands such goodies as lime juice and Barbados rum.

"My son," Abraham used to say, "you will have a rich business to carry on after I die. So why do you keep writing poetry?"

Ben couldn't give a reasonable answer; why did a mockingbird sing? When he was fourteen, upon orders from his father, he used to cross the street to the warehouse and in the counting room go through the motions of learning the business, but he was always thinking about Dryden's essays or Herrick's poetry or something from Donne, and about the only attraction the business world had for him was when he could stroll through the gloom of the warehouse and smell the mingled exotic odors from tropical fruits and pipes of wine and crates of oilcloth unbrellas; and he used to enjoy standing in the wide warehouse door and looking at the Savannah River, dazzling in the sunshine, with its wharfed brigs and schooners and its sharp odors of rank water, fish, pitch, tar and hemp, and its gulls wheeling in brilliant light.

He would never make a good businessman, at that rate. He did, however, keep trying, to please Abraham.

In the 1770's, when that argument about taxes arose between the American Colonies and their English mother, and the colonies decided to pinch the old girl where it would hurt, in the pocketbook, and declared an embargo against imports, people in Savannah said such things as now we'll see the true colors of that damned old Jew, Abraham Klauber, he'll never stick by that embargo, Jews care nothing about anything but money, damn the old kike anyway. But Abraham fooled everybody, for it turned out that he loved America as much as anyone did, and perhaps a little more; he stuck by that embargo as if it had been Mosaic Law, refusing to import so much as a needle; and when the colonists turned out to be a bunch of wild-eyed radicals and declared their independence Abraham was all for it and went around repeating passages from that agitator

Patrick Henry. Naturally this roused suspicions, because some people said Jews lacked patriotism, their only loyalties were to the kingdom of finance; and the persons who said this oftenest were those in Savannah who were Royalists and wished to see General Washington's little army cut to shreds.

The war worked its way down the Atlantic seaboard, reaching Savannah in 1778, the American troops ready to fight but wishing they might collect some of their back pay and grumbling about how they had a notion to light out for home and deprive their descendants of membership in the Daughters of the American Revolution. Not wanting such a catastrophe to take place, Abraham Klauber conferred with the paymaster of American troops in Georgia, offering to advance $10,000 in hard money to the revolutionary cause. The paymaster grabbed that money and wrote out a receipt, but after his benefactor left the tent he said he'd never seen the like, there must be a catch somewhere, for of course Jews loved money above everything including patriotism, maybe that money was counterfeit. But it wasn't, and the paymaster never got over it; it likely hastened his death.

The American general leading the army in Georgia was no shrewder than the average general, although not actually feeble-minded as his troops believed; and while the redcoat general was no brain wave either, still his I.Q. was in the upper forties, which made him an Alexander the Great by comparison; and when late in 1778 he landed troops early one morning at Girardeau's Plantation east of Savannah considerable excitement ensued, what with the militia marching out to McGilvray's Creek, Abraham Klauber and his son Ben with the rest. The battle took place in swampy land, scaring the bullfrogs and turtles half to death; and when it was over Abraham Klauber lay with a ball through his heart and Ben was a British prisoner along with nearly two hundred others. So he didn't celebrate New Year's Eve in Savannah but aboard the prison ship *Nancy* where food and entertainment were third rate. The ship sailed away to the West Indies. Ben could have extricated himself from that predicament if he had been willing to swear allegiance to the British king, but he wasn't, preferring to swear at the king; and not till almost a year later was he paroled and permitted to return to Savannah, where he found the warehouse of A. Klauber & Son, Importers, nothing but charred rubble, the enemy having fired it. The store, however, had been spared, along with the house behind it, and Ben settled down to a good life of reading Chaucer and Shakespeare, and writing an occasional lyric, and planning a five-act tragedy in blank verse which he eventually completed, except for the dialogue; and sometimes he sold tea or dress goods but without enthusiasm; it was lucky that his mother Miriam had buried a chest of specie in the garden when those redcoats invaded the city. She had saved the receipt too which the paymaster had given Abraham Klauber, and she said that as soon as General Washington won the war and established a responsible government the chances were that the $10,000 would be repaid.

Ben had his mother's Portuguese dark hair and olive skin and fine nostrils; he was really a handsome dog; but he had never done much with those good looks till he met Rachel Rose, an Ashkenazic girl of twenty, whom he married because she reminded him of Shakespeare's Rosalind. This was one of the most egregious cases of mistaken identity in history. Rachel had more business acumen in her thimble than Ben had in his whole body; she moved right in with Ben and his mother and proceeded to stimulate both business and her husband, so that presently the store yielded a decent living and Rachel yielded four children, the youngest of whom was born in 1793 and named Solomon. By then the store no longer dealt in objects of art and fine cashmeres; it was little better than a second-hand clothes shop; but it supported the family nicely, and there was always that receipt for $10,000 which certainly the government would repay. Congress, however, always had more important matters pressing for attention, and this Republic shared with those of history a tendency toward ingratitude, although the congressman from the Klauber's district regularly introduced a bill for payment and orated while his colleagues napped or drifted out for ale.

Solomon's two older brothers, and his older sister, were sharp as quill pens, having inherited business instinct and drive from their mother and from grandfather Abraham; but Sol never took to trade; he was more like his father Ben and his grandmother Miriam, who by now was a white-haired old lady weighing all of a hundred pounds. She used to read aloud to Sol, when he was little, and tell him stories, and escort him around the garden with its paths of crushed oyster shells and its luxuriant and almost tropical vegetation; he could remember the rattling palmettos, the China trees, the fragrance of magnolias and cape jessamines.

When Sol was twelve his father died of a disease that mystified the doctors and hence was diagnosed as stomach gout, and after that Sol's mother said it was high time he worked in the store and learned something of business. He hated it, but his mother—who had grown less and less like Rosalind—was nobody to cross wills with. During those years his sister Rebecca made a good marriage to a doctor in Savannah, and his brother Jake sailed away to New York and a career in finance, and his other brother Mordecai clerked in the store and became skilled in buying old clothes cheap and refurbishing them and selling them to sailors and such; but Sol always thought business dull and faintly degrading, which was odd indeed for he came of a people supposedly expert at it, and he belonged to a nationality which some day would believe there was no god but Business and that Profit was his only prophet.

When the second war with England broke out in 1812 Sol was nineteen; he thought it offered adventure, and certainly it offered escape from the store; so he took a ship for Baltimore where he signed up for service on a letter of marque, the *Star of Maryland*. She was a swift ship with an audacious captain, so Sol enjoyed some of the adventures he had been wanting, but one day in August 1813 she had a brush with an even swifter ship and was captured. Sol was carried off to England and fought the rest of the war in Dartmoor prison. When he returned to Savannah in 1815 his grandmother was dead; she had left him her books, which was all right with everybody, and that receipt for $10,000, which exasperated everyone except Sol. Mordecai and Rachel were running the store; Sol could have re-entered the business, but he had had enough of prison; he used to sit in the garden and wonder what he was going to do with his life. At last Dr. Liebman, the husband of Rebecca, came up with a fine idea: his brother Joseph owned a store in Boston; how about Sol's going there and learning the business?

Business again. But at least business in different surroundings, far from his mother's tongue; so he sailed to Boston where Joseph Liebman hired him and gave him board and lodging. And although he liked retailing new merchandise no better than retailing second-hand coats and pants, he told himself it was time he settled down and he did his best, especially after Joseph's daughter Isabel promised to become his wife. She lived up to that promise too, and bore him fine children, although the eldest, named Miriam after her great-grandmother, died of pneumonia when only a baby. But Leah and Isaac and Abraham were healthy; Isabel was a good wife, without a shrewish hair in her head; Sol liked his mother-in-law and his father-in-law; he should have been happy. Well, he was; as happy as any square peg in a round hole. And he always had hopes that the congressman from Boston would have more success in collecting that $10,000 than had the congressman from Savannah.

Joseph Liebman's store was a three-story brick building on Atlantic Avenue, the Liebmans dwelling on the second floor and the Klaubers on the third; customers were mainly sailors and waterfront workers. That store, being so close to the wharves, was very handy for the microbes of cholera when after traveling from Asia to Europe they migrated to the New World in 1832; among their first victims were Sol's wife Isabel and his daughter Leah and his son Abraham; when it came to killing Jews, those microbes worked faster than the Inquisition, although less painfully. Nor did they have race prejudice; they killed Gentiles just as cheerfully as Jews, moving quite uninvited into Beacon Street houses and dropping the descendants of Cromwellian riffraff faster than a dowager could gobble beans; and presently those microbes, tiring of Boston and a New England diet, moved on to more vulgar cities, killing so many persons that business was bad that summer, retail sales off frightfully.

After that epidemic Sol didn't much like the hub of the universe, or the universe itself, for that matter. He didn't want to go on living, but he had to, because of Isaac. He never knew what he ate; all food tasted like dust, even such specialties of the house as Grandmother Liebman's holishkes and stuffed kishke. In his grief, and his exhaustion following grief, he neglected to needle his congressman about collecting that $10,000 loan; the receipt lay half-forgotten in his lawyer's safe. At last, a couple of summers after the epidemic, he made out a will leaving the receipt to Isaac; then, while Isaac stayed with the Liebmans, Sol took to the road with a peddler's pack, traveling through New England. He liked that better than the store, and during the next two years he sold notions from Maine to northern Virginia. But competition was lively in that long-settled part of America; he decided to try his luck in the West; so that was how he happened to encounter Jim Buckmaster one May afternoon on that path to Injun Hollow.

*

Those weeks in New Empire with Sol Klauber always came back to Jim as a sad white time when everything he had to be homesick for was nothing but rubble and ashes. He learned about grief in those weeks; not the first smash of grief with its outrage and incredulity, but the knife-jabs that outlasted shock, and the ache that stayed a long time. And yet, looking back across the gone years, he could find a melancholy pleasure in those weeks, maybe because he had been brave.

He didn't always go peddling with Sol; sometimes he went to the bluffs east of town and sat doing nothing in the October sun while the box-elder bugs clicked through the warm air and puffballs lay rotten-ripe in the millet grass. Sometimes he whittled; sometimes he stood for minutes at a time looking out at the immensity of river. Up there, he could see for miles: the roofs of New Empire sharp and shining in the foreground below him; far islands whose trees looked no taller than a clipped lawn; the bluffs of Iowa mauve in the distance and blurred with autumnal scarlets and yellows; and for leagues uncounted, from north to south, the sprawling magnitude of the river meandering down its valley, flowing in tones of water-blue and water-green, of liquid mulatto and sunfish-gold, coming from lavender hazes and going out of sight in the south where the air was misty and smoked. Sometimes he saw a float of lumber or logs, looking tiny; or a speck of steamboat; or a fleet of Injun canoes like so many water fleas; but for the most part that river flowed in majestic emptiness. And even then he could sense she was a woman, all lure and surprises.

There were sunny noons when he wandered along Front Street like any river loafer, staring at the wavy reflections of warehouses or watching the excitement of a steamboat's arrival; but in those sad days he felt detached, removed from reality; and when anybody spoke to him he answered briefly and shuffled on. Once he visited an island upriver from town; some day it would be called McSwasey's Island and a mansion would stand there; he would live there some day; but when he first went there McSwasey hadn't even moved to New Empire; it was a tanglewood then.

Business wasn't so good for Sol Klauber in New Empire; for one thing, there had been a financial panic in cities and people were hard up; for another, there was too much competition from retail stores; Sol said a peddler did best in the economic backwaters. So late in October he and Jim packed up and took a boat south, stopping to peddle at the Fever River settlement in the lead-mining region and then taking another boat, keeping ahead of winter. January saw them headquartering in St. Louis and working the surrounding country; by February they were in Arkansas, traveling up the river to Little Rock. Some nights it froze down there or even snowed, but the weather was very different from the hard winters Jim had always known; he missed Quickwater; and he used to wonder whether Dan Stoughton had rebuilt the town. In June they worked their way up the Mississippi again, peddling to farmers on both sides; but although they went right past the mouth of the Chippewa, Sol wouldn't go up that river to Quickwater; he said he couldn't yet face returning to the scene of the fire. That winter they followed the Mississippi clear down to the Natchez area, where Jim saw oranges growing and black men driving mules; and the next summer they traveled way up to the Falls of St. Anthony; he saw a lot of country in those two years traveling with a peddler. It was a hard life sometimes, slogging along raw roads in the mud; barked at by dogs; sleeping on the floor of a crowded tavern, or in barns or haystacks, or in the woods; eating grease and drinking vile coffee; yet Jim thrived on that life, his body getting longer and his shoulders wider, his hands and feet bigger, his voice deeper.

Knocking around that way taught him about the world, and Sol taught him too. Sol would never be a big money-maker; in that he reminded Jim of his father; but Jim guessed money wasn't everything, quite. Sol used to say it was only a necessary nuisance, the getting of which distracted a man from his proper occupation of trying to unravel the mystery of the universe. Well, maybe so; Jim never worried about the mystery of the universe. On steamboats, or in hotel lobbies, or on fine noons when they lunched by the roadside, or in their room at night, Sol used to read such authors as Pascal and Epictetus; and just so long as he read to himself, and not aloud, that was all right with Jim. Once Sol said he wished he could have attended some great university and spent his life teaching philosophy; fine; but Jim certainly wanted to be counted out of anything like that; he'd rather go logging.

Yet for all the clouds in his head Sol had a certain Jewish realism; he was seldom overcharged, and never taken in by the confidence men and gamblers infesting river packets, or by some farmer trying to buy a brass clock with wildcat money; centuries before, the imperatives of survival had obliterated any strain of gullibility or stupidity from the

Jewish people. And although he had a basic universal pessimism, it was not like the dreary pessimism of Lorne Buckmaster; he was cheerful company; it was as if long ago he had concluded that man's lot was hard in an indifferent universe, and had gone on from there to be optimistic about little matters within the great pattern of pessimism. Once he told Jim that a man should always live as if the next minute would be his last. Jim could agree; that was just woods caution stated in a different way; although it was possible Sol meant a little more than Jim understood. And Sol said it was pitiful and absurd how most people went through life, without any grand strategy, or basic philosophy, or alternative tactics if things turned against them; he hoped Jim wouldn't be like that.

"I reckon not," Jim said.

He didn't elaborate, but already he was thinking he couldn't go on like this, traveling with Sol and living off him; he was lonesome for the woods and eager for the fortune he planned to cut out of the woods; it was about time, he figured, to get a job in a logging camp and learn the business; he was thirteen by then and big for his age.

But Sol had been good to him and he hated to leave him cold-bloodedly; he might have stuck with him another year or so, if Sol hadn't kept fretting because Jim was missing being educated. On their travels, whenever they passed a school, Sol would say that was where Jim should be, and an argument would follow.

"I'm not doing right by you," Sol would say. "You're smarter than a Philadelphia lawyer, but your brains will go to waste if you're not educated. It worries me."

But Jim shook his head and said he was through with school.

One day in September, about two years after the forest fire, they landed in New Empire on their way downriver, and that evening in their room Sol talked long and earnestly about the future, saying Jim was like a son to him and he planned to make him his heir; and then he sprang a surprise, sitting there in the candlelight looking tired, his shadow huge on the wallpaper.

"Jim," he said, "it's time I visited Boston. I ought to see my lawyer and the Liebmans, and I ought to go to the wholesalers and buy instead of ordering. Do you think you'd like Boston?"

Jim said he didn't know about that; but he very well knew; he didn't want any Boston; he wanted the woods.

"I think you'll like it, Jim. It smells of salt water and it looks like an English town. You'll see ships in from China and you'll eat lobster. The streets are so crooked you'll get lost, but first thing you know you'll come to the Common in the dusk and see sailors with their girls. And over there in Cambridge you'll smoke a pipe and drink ale and get drunk on ideas."

"I don't know about that," Jim said.

Well, maybe not right away, that part about Cambridge, Sol said. First there would be some tutoring; several years of it, maybe. Jim could live with the Liebmans and go every day to a rabbi who ran a school and be taught Latin and Greek and geometry and whatever else the authorities at Harvard required for entrance. That rabbi was a learned man and Jim had a mind like a steel trap; it shouldn't take too long, preparing for college. Not if Jim would buckle down.

"I can't have you growing up like a timber wolf," Sol said. "There's more to the world than these river towns. Maybe they'll teach you French so you can read Rabelais and roll on the floor laughing. You'll find out what an adventure Shakespeare is, and you'll sail with Homer on the wine-dark seas. You'll be a gentleman, Jim, before those gray-beards at Harvard are through with you."

Jim had gone cold all over, and he knew this was it. This was good-by to Sol Klauber. But he didn't want Sol seeing a lawyer and getting guardianship papers, or whatever it was adults called those legal instruments they used in their conspiracy against the young.

"Why, yes," he said, "maybe you've got something there. I've never tasted lobster, that I know of. Maybe this Boston will be an all right place."

He felt ashamed when he saw how pleased that made Sol.

*

But Sol should have known he'd never go along with any crazy notion like traveling so far from the woods and wasting his time on books in a place like Boston. He didn't even want to be a gentleman. After they were in bed that night Jim lay awake, waiting till Sol's breathing was deep and regular, and then waiting more, going over in his mind just which of his possessions he could handily take with him, and where they were in the dark room, so that he could find them without undue noise. At last, in the silences of deep night, he slipped out of bed and into his clothes; he wasn't five minutes leaving that room. But after he eased open the door, just before he stepped into the hall, something odd happened, taking him by surprise. He found he had stopped, and all at once he gave a sob.

And for about a minute he considered sticking by Sol and going to Boston and becoming drunk on ideas and ale in Cambridge. Yet he couldn't; his compass needle always pointed north. But it was hard leaving; Sol had been like a father, not a gentleman, maybe, but certainly the gentlest of men, saving him from burning up in that forest fire and then never holding it against him that he was Jim and not Isaac. He could hear Sol's regular breathing and imagine how his face looked, sad because about everybody he had ever loved was dead, his beard and hair grizzled. It seemed almost like stabbing him in the back, this sneaking off while he slept.

There were times, years afterward, when Jim looked back and saw that was one of the big decisions of his life; he used to wonder how his life would have gone if he had stuck by Sol. Maybe he really would have liked Boston and that rabbi and those graybeards at Harvard. He might even have become a gentleman; no telling; his life might have been better. But of course it was all futile, thinking what might have been; it was all water down the Mississippi and out into the seven seas.

Jim took hold of himself and sneaked into the hall and down the creaky stairs and out into the cool September night. On the porch, in the light coming from a whale-oil streetlamp, he spread out his blanket —one of those blankets Sol had bought long ago after the forest fire—and rearranged his few possessions, rolling them in the blanket and tying the ends and carrying the blanket over his shoulders. Then he left, going east along Winnebago Street. At the corner he came to a halt and looked back, wanting to cry, remembering the presents Sol had given him on Christmas and on his birthday; remembering how Sol had nursed him the time he caught the chicken pox in Arkansas; how Sol never scolded even when he got into fights with kids in the towns they visited and came limping back to their living quarters with torn pants and swollen lips. Remembering all that sent a wave of sadness over him and he wanted to go back. But something wouldn't let him.

At that hour Winnebago Street was a deserted stretch of streetlamps and darkness, but Jim didn't want to chance meeting a watchman; he turned north and followed Marquette Avenue past black sleeping houses where sometimes dogs heard him and sounded alarms; once a shaggy shepherd dog came growling at his heels. He spoke to it and extended a hand; a minute later that dog was letting him scratch its ears; dogs always took to him. With its tongue lolling out in dog laughter, it followed him clear to the edge of town and along the road leading north; he kept telling it to go home and at last it obeyed. He felt lonely, after that, but he didn't want to steal anybody's dog.

The road he followed was the river road, soft with dust and fringed with choke cherries and nannyberries, tuneful with the night songs of peepers and crickets and swamp frogs; sometimes it dipped to cross a creek and he was walking through sweet-smelling mist. To the east he could see the solid shadows of bluffs, and pretty soon those bluffs moved in, crowding the road close to the Mississippi bottoms. He didn't want to keep following the river, for on its way toward the Chippewa at the mouth of Lake Pepin it swung northwest, and he was bound for Quickwater in the northeast; besides, Sol Klauber might send word up the river that he had run away, and people would be on the lookout for a boy of his description. So he kept watching for a road fork and at last, when daybreak was beginning to gray the east, and the mist had thickened over the river bottoms, he came upon a road leading back from the river into a coulee. So he said good-by to the Mississippi River for a while, but he would be back some day; he could feel it in his bones he would; he liked that river.

Everything smelled fragrant and woodsy along that coulee road; he could hear a creek trickling along a rocky bed; a couple of times he passed farmhouses and smelled pigsties; from up among the oaks and hickories on the steep side of the coulee he could hear a cowbell bonging. The road kept winding and climbing, and just before sunup it humped itself out of that coulee and went wandering northeast across a deeply rolling upland. Jim was hungry and sleepy by that time, so he wiggled through a snakerail fence into an oak opening. Red haws grew there, as big and luscious as cherries on their thorny branches, and he feasted. And he found hazel nuts in their bolls on bushes; they tasted as delicious as filberts after he cracked their shells with his teeth. Wild plums, sweet and meaty, and foxgrapes, so plump and purple they were almost black, rounded out his breakfast; then he spread his blanket in a witch hazel thicket.

Usual thing, when his head hit the pillow he was asleep, but now he had no pillow and besides there were thoughts in his head. He kept wondering if right now, at this very moment, Sol Klauber was waking up and calling his name . . . Jim . . . Hey there, Jim . . . Where are you?

Sol would ask the landlady if she had seen Jim this morning; and after that he might go to the sheriff; word would spread; people would be watching for him; if they found him they would make him go to Boston or perhaps pop him into an orphan asylum. Even Boston would be better than that; he had heard tales about orphanages. Still, Sol wouldn't let them put him into an orphanage. But maybe Sol couldn't keep them from it; maybe by running away he had broken some law or other. Anyway, he would be hunted now; he'd have to lie low till he reached Quickwater. After that everything would be fine; he'd get a job in the woods and the woods were beyond the law.

The sun was up now and Jim was tired, but he kept squirming on his blanket; and somewhere deep in his chest there was a feeling he didn't like, as if his heart had turned to a heavy bag of sand. And flitting through his mind were many pictures of a sad-faced man toiling along with a peddler's bag over his shoulder, walking splay-footed . . . Jim, you're like a son to me . . . I can't have you growing up like a timber wolf . . . What would you like for your birthday, Jim? You'll be a gentleman, Jim . . .

He knew he was going to cry and he fought it, the way you fought throwing up after eating goose plums and sour apples, even when you knew that throwing up would make you feel better. But he was too old to cry; damn it, he was thirteen, he looked fifteen; too old to cry.

Yet he did cry at last, bitterly. Then he slept.

*

571

When he wakened the sun had plowed its way well into afternoon, and he felt lonesome and lost, thinking how by now Sol Klauber knew beyond any doubt that he had run away and left him. He didn't cry any more, not with his eyes, but somewhere inside some part of him was crying. He lay there staring at the sunshine slanting through the witch hazel, hearing a blue jay scolding and a squirrel chirking, half thinking he'd go back to New Empire and tell Sol he was sorry. But that would mean Boston and school books.

No, he couldn't go back. But he guessed he wouldn't go sneaking through the countryside like an escaped criminal, either. He had a little money; enough to buy food; and he'd walk along the roads in broad daylight and when he came to a farmhouse ask to buy a meal. If the sheriff had sent out word to nab him all right, he'd be nabbed. If not, he'd get to Quickwater. Let it go by luck.

So he folded his blanket and crawled through the fence and took to the road; an hour later he came to a farmhouse and walked up to the door as big as you please and asked to buy a meal. The farmwife put him down at her kitchen table and served him corn dodgers and cold stewed pigeon and friedcakes and apple pie and tea, never even asking whether he was a runaway boy; maybe he looked too old for that, or maybe his decision to face up to whatever happened had given him an air of confidence. He paid her for the meal and walked on, stopping at another farmhouse that evening and eating again and sleeping in the haymow.

By the time he reached the Chippewa River a few days later, he had talked with dozens of people, telling them his name and that he was heading for a winter in the woods, and not once did anyone look suspicious or try to nab him. It came to him then that maybe Sol had never reported his running away to the sheriff; maybe Sol had just heaved a sigh, his sad face even sadder, and had thought well, if Jim doesn't want to be educated I can't make him. That would be like Sol. Now and then, perversely enough, Jim was a little disappointed that he hadn't been nabbed and taken to New Empire. Not that he had changed his mind about going to Boston, but it would have been nice to see Sol again and maybe talk him out of wanting to stand the expense of a college education; Jim missed him.

*

It gave him the willies, returning to Quickwater, for the new town looked just enough like the old to seem familiar, but everything was different. The woods themselves were different. Maybe unconsciously Jim had been expecting the woods to look as they had before the fire, pine and spruce and hemlock; or maybe he had thought they would look charred and stark as they had that rainy morning when he left Quickwater with Sol. Well, they didn't look either way; they looked like the enormous seedling lot of a tree nursery, with saplings about waist high. But not evergreen saplings; these were quick-growing soft woods like popple and elm. Jim felt strange walking through that Lilliputian forest; those little trees were so rank and enthusiastic, growing there in the graveyard of their betters, that even in their gay autumn colors they seemed like some faintly sinister manifestation of nature; you caught the feeling of enormous fecundity, the woods taking everything back. If they had only been pine seedlings Jim would have felt all right; he couldn't understand why the pine let this no-account popple crowd in.

Lack of pine forests gave Quickwater a naked look; there was too much light; you looked at the horizon expecting to see the dark woods and they weren't there. Coming in from the south, he stopped on the new bridge crossing Snowshoe Creek, but even the creek had changed; it used to foam and sparkle, and trout lived in its clear water; now the water was clay-colored and it flowed sluggishly; maybe when a heavy rain fell there was nothing to hold back the runoff, with the big trees gone; maybe the downpour went rushing into the creek, washing soil with it, flooding the creek for a few hours and leaving a deposit of mud; in the old days a rain soaked into the soil and fed the creek gradually over a period of weeks, or fed springs which in turn fed the creek. Anyway, Jim thought, a trout would have choked to death in that creek today.

He walked on north and turned west on Chippewa Street, but the familiar landmarks were gone. Roquemore's Livery Stable, the office of the *Quickwater Mercury,* Gentleman Steve's place—all gone. But the rebuilt Shanghai House was there, on the northeast corner of Squaw and Chippewa, only now it was called the New Shanghai House; and across the street the rebuilt Northern Saloon was labeled the New Northern Saloon. Jim couldn't see why they were so proud of being new; the old had been good enough.

He didn't enter that saloon right away but walked on west past the trading post, also labeled new, and followed Chippewa Street to the river, where a bigger and better sawmill was loud with the agony of logs being converted into lumber. He saw offbearers lugging planks from the mill and stacking them, but those workmen were strangers; he didn't know them from Adam's off ox. Probably they had never heard of a man named Lorne Buckmaster who had been such an expert sawyer.

Jim stood looking at the water flowing over the dam and frothing among the boulders; he felt tired and sad; and at last he turned and went north along River Street, past the fragrant stacks of lumber and past the place where a swamp had been. Now the swamp had vanished beneath heaps of yellow sawdust. When he turned east on Shin-Tangle Street he was wondering about the spirits of the dead; whether, as old wives said, they returned to linger where their bodies used to live. Maybe so; but he didn't see any spirits on that street where Lorne used to shamble, or on the site of the Buckmaster cabin. Only a stark chimney and weeds growing.

It came to him then more than ever before that he was alone in the world; he could have died and nobody would have cared, except Sol Klauber, and he had run away from Sol. Alone; adrift like a strayed sawlog. And suddenly he couldn't stand it; he wanted to be with people.

There weren't many people in the New Northern Saloon when he entered; a stranger tending bar; a couple of French Canadians playing cribbage; a man who needed a shave with a boot on the rail, carrying on a low conversation with two raddled strumpets wearing limp evening dresses although it was still afternoon. The saloon had been rebuilt on the old floor plan; Jim walked back to the connecting door and on into the trading post; Dan Stoughton was sitting deep in papers at a desk in a railed-off space. And if he had changed, Jim couldn't see it; his hair was as black as ever, his skin as swarthy, his eyes as black and steady.

"Yeah?" he said, looking up.

"Mister," Jim said, smiling, "do you need anybody to sing about faithful Nellie?"

"Well, I'll be damned," Stoughton said, getting to his feet. "Jim Buckmaster! Jim, you've grown like the gourd of Jonah. Where in hell have you been?"

"Places," Jim said.

"My God, boy, you've grown. Where did you go? I figured to take care of you after that fire, but you turned up missing. What have you been doing?"

"This and that," Jim said. "I've got along."

"And you've grown. You've filled out. Say, I don't think I'd want to tackle you now, in a rough-and-tumble. You're going to make a big man, Jim."

That went on for a while, Stoughton asking questions and Jim telling a little about his travels; and finally Stoughton said:

"Jim, I don't know where my manners are. You're thirsty, I'll bet. Come on and have a drink."

They entered the saloon; Stoughton asked what Jim would have; and instead of ordering a Sarsaparilla Mead, Jim said he'd have whiskey. Stoughton didn't bat an eye; just took it for granted that Jim had grown up enough for a man's drink. But he had never tasted whiskey.

It surprised him, the way it burned, and for a moment he thought he might strangle and spoil Stoughton's good opinion of him, but he always had pretty good control over his body; he stood there smiling. But after that he didn't gulp so fast. He heard Stoughton saying have another, and himself saying sure; he liked it; he kept thinking my God, how long has this been going on, I like this.

He stood at the center of a warm nimbus, his sadness washed away, the world a very good place. He had run off from Sol Klauber but by

574

now Sol would have forgiven him; Sol would be all right; everything would be all right. Once he heard himself saying Dan, have one on me, that is if you'll charge it, you can take it off my wages. Dan was smiling; he asked, what wages? Why, hell, Dan, Jim heard himself saying, I came back to go to the woods and work for you . . . Dan laughed; he said Jim, you're a fast worker, how do you know I'll give you a job? Jim said, because you're a Boston gentleman, Dan, that's why . . . Dan laughed again. And he said well, Jim, there's an opening at my Teal Feather Camp, how would you like to go up there and bull-cook? Jim said, bull-cook? A bull cook's just a chore boy, ain't he? Sure, Dan said, but what did you expect? Did you expect to be the push? Sure, Jim said; there was a lot of laughing.

So he had him a job of sorts; he would eat and learn logging; everything would be all right. He thought his bones must be air-filled like a bird's, his body felt so light; in the bar mirror he saw himself smiling, his hair rumpled; and then in the mirror he saw those two strumpets in evening dresses; they looked younger now and prettier; they were smiling at him; before long they had hip-swung over to stand beside him.

"Hello, handsome," one said. "Where've you been?"

"Places," he said. "But I wouldn't go to Boston."

"Flo," Dan Stoughton said, "cut it out. You and Billie drift."

"Oh, gee," Flo said.

"You drift," Dan said. "Jim here ain't as old as he looks. I don't guess he's more than fifteen."

"Have a drink, girls?" Jim said, and they giggled.

"God damn it," Dan Stoughton said, "this is the last time I'm going to speak to you about it. You drift."

So they drifted, back toward the door leading into the fancy house, and Jim watched their hips swinging.

"You used to have Chippewa gals," he told Dan.

"Wish I still did," Dan said. "Easier to handle. These no-goods will give you the rot, Jim. You keep away from them."

He might not have, except he wasn't used to strong spirits, and his head kept ballooning lighter and bigger till finally it floated up to the ceiling and on through. It must have been dark outside by then, for after that everything was black oblivion. He woke up next morning in Dan's living quarters behind the trading post, and that day he left for the Teal Feather Camp with a bull whacker who was hauling in supplies.

*

If you wished to become a rich lumberman that was a good way to do it, starting young as a cook's helper in a logging camp. They called you a chore boy, or a bull cook, or a shanty boss, or a flunky, and if you were the sort of kid who let people pick on you, which Jim wasn't, they made you the butt of jokes; but you had your revenge at 4:00 A.M. when you marched through the bunkhouse banging a pan and yelling, "It's daylight in the swamps, boys. Roll out, tumble out, any way out. This is the day to make the fortune, boys."

You chopped firewood and carried out ashes and washed dishes; and in those early days of small camps you were also the cookee, or cook's first assistant, meaning you peeled potatoes and set the table and rushed reinforcements when the hands were eating; and at noon you lugged the flaggins, which was what they called victuals, into the woods where the crews were working. You were always busy, but if you kept your eyes and ears open you learned a lot about logging.

The great mystery was how you managed waking up at 3:30 A.M. so as to get the fires stoked and to wake the cook at three-forty-five. Well, you had to, that was part of the job; if you were a sleepyhead they'd fire you. Those first few nights at camp Jim didn't sleep so well, thinking how he had to be up at three-thirty; he kept waking up every hour and looking at the clock; but after a week or so he slept like a hibernating bear and snapped awake at three-thirty exactly. There were occasions when he wanted to roll over and dive back into sleep, but he never succumbed; he used to grit his teeth and tell himself that if he wanted to get ahead in life he'd better be about it; so he would swing his feet out of the bunk and jump into his clothes. In the depths of winter, with the thermometer registering twenty or thirty below, he had no inclination to dawdle over dressing.

Before he ever left Quickwater for the Teal Feather Camp, he heard from Dan Stoughton how Lew Fitzpatrick was no longer a partner in the Quickwater Log & Lumber Company.

"Lew had some hard luck last winter," Dan said. "A breed killed him. Wanted his watch."

The breed's name, Dan said, was Henry Crow; when Henry brought the watch to the trading post, wishing to exchange it for liquor, Dan had become suspicious.

"That looks like Lew Fitzpatrick's watch," Dan said.

Well, he never should have said that; the breed knew then he'd made a mistake in killing Lew and he took off for Canada or somewhere. Leastwise, he'd never been caught. Dan bought out Molly Fitzpatrick's share of the company, and she had gone down the Chippewa a few miles and had started a kind of tavern on the west side of the river.

That was Dan's version.

There were other versions in camp that winter, for men would gossip; even hints that perhaps Dan Stoughton had not been unaware of the breed's intentions before he ever killed Lew. But that must have been just scandalmongering. It seemed fairly well substantiated, however, that once Lew was dead, and Molly carrying on with grief and maybe drinking too much, Dan Stoughton had got her really drunk and then had bought her share of the company for a pittance. That, of course, was only good business, although it did seem kind of too bad that Molly had been crooked out of thousands of acres of valuable stumpage. According to one man, who may have known, because he had slept with her, Molly was nothing but a whore now. When Jim heard that he didn't like it and it led to trouble. But that was two full weeks after he arrived at camp.

*

Up the Chippewa to the mouth of the Flambeau and up the Flambeau through mile after mile of magnificent pine—that was the way to the Teal Feather Camp. With three yoke of oxen pulling the supply wagon, it was a journey of eleven-and-a-half days. Jim could have made it faster walking alone, but he was in no hurry, for his wages from Dan Stoughton began the day he left Quickwater. It was a fine season of the year in those timbers, late September and early October, the nights frosty and the noons warm, the Flambeau running yellow and crimson with the reflections of willows and maples, flocks of crows cawing at day-break and dusk, lakes cluttered with numberless ducks and geese; Jim loved it. Looking back, remembering how it had been and how he had loved it, he sometimes thought it curious he had done so much to destroy it; but he guessed he'd do it again; whenever he saw a pine tree, something in him made him want to chop it down. And whenever he saw a whole stand of pine from across a marsh or swale, looking so feminine and mysterious against the sky, and so defenseless, and so beautiful and dark, he was oddly stirred with a power-urge completely male; he felt big and long-legged; he wanted to swing an ax and convert all that whispering beauty into something less troubling and more easily understood, such as numerals on the credit side of a bankbook.

On that journey up the Flambeau he kept remembering that afternoon in Dan Stoughton's saloon, how Dan had thought he was fifteen instead of thirteen; how whiskey had waved a magician's wand over everything and made it shining; how he had felt when those strumpets swung their hips and smiled. He had never had a woman, but he could see that the future had much to recommend it, with whiskey and girls waiting.

By later standards that Teal Feather Camp wasn't much; a bunkhouse with the kitchen at one end and a rock-and-sand firebed in the center of the room beneath a hole in the roof. No chimney; smoke was supposed to climb straight up through the hole, but it didn't, always. No windows; low eaves; a scoop roof; a puncheon floor; bunks mattressed with balsam; wind sniffing at the moss-and-clay chinks between the logs, or howling all night when a blizzard came; it wasn't much for twenty men. But Jim never wanted to trade it for a room at Harvard College.

Along with a hovel for the oxen, that bunkhouse stood in a cleared space about a rod from the south bank of the Flambeau; on the noon when Jim and the bull whacker reached it you could see the river sparkling beyond the silver birches. That early in the season a full crew hadn't arrived and they weren't really logging yet, just swamping; and Nels Quist, the push, a husky Swede with a toothpick in his mouth, was standing beside the bunkhouse door. He had a high bald forehead with mouse-colored hair, but his eyes were blue and steady, and he looked like a square dealer. His palm felt like sandpaper, when they shook hands.

"Jim," he said, "I heard you sing once. You've grown. Where've you been, Jim?"

"Here and there," Jim said.

"You've grown," Nels Quist said, "and I know how it is with growing boys. Everything you see, you either want to fight it or go to bed with it. Well, Jim, I won't have no fighting in my camp. We're here to cut lumber, and I can't have my crew laid up from fights. Do you like Danes, Jim?"

"Sure," Jim said, "I like everybody."

"The cook's a Dane, Jim. Me, I don't like Danes. Norwegians, yes. A Norwegian's just a Swede who lives too far west. But you take a Dane, you never know what he'll do next. The cook's a Dane named Red Erik Larsen, and by Christmas he'll likely poison us all." Nels Quist cupped his great hands around his mouth and bellowed, "Erik! Hey, there, Red Erik!" His voice was mighty as a moose's; the woods resounded.

An answer came from toward the river, and presently Jim saw a middle-aged man of medium height lugging a bucket of water. His hair and beard were fiery red, and a white apron was tied around his heavy belly. He said:

"Swedes are too loud. Opinionated and loud. I worked for a Swede once but he died. I hated to cut his throat that way, but his voice got on my nerves. Oh, hello, Nels."

"Erik," Nels Quist said, "shake hands with Jim Buckmaster. I've been telling him about Danes, and his blood's running cold. Jim's your bull cook."

When they shook hands Jim could tell he was being sized up, and something told him he had passed muster.

"Jim," Red Erik said, "I've got two rules. One, no talking at the table. You hear somebody talking and you bat him with a fry pan. And the other rule is we work twenty-five hours a day. You might as well start now peeling potatoes."

But he didn't work twenty-five hours a day; only about seventeen.

*

All that season and all the next he worked under Red Erik Larsen at Teal Feather Camp, and during the intervening summer he was given the soft job of remaining at camp as watchman, seeing that the oxen, which were turned loose to forage, didn't wander too far, and that no Injuns sneaked in to steal tools. About the only drawback to that watchman job was that he missed the spring drive down the Flambeau to the Chippewa and down the Chippewa to Quickwater. But by staying alone in camp he had plenty of time to practice using an ax, applying the techniques he had heard discussed around the winter fire. He practiced birling too, going to a little lake and chopping down a pine, limbing it and rolling it into the water with a cant hook, and then, a pike pole in his hands, riding that log all over the lake. He hunted and fished that summer too, for his skillet, and his body grew bigger and tougher. Those were months well spent; he could see that, looking back; but he never wanted to do it again; it was too lonely. From mid-May till mid-September he never saw another person, not even an Injun; he might have forgotten how to use his tongue, except he fell to talking to himself and to the oxen. He liked people, and it didn't do you any real good, talking to yourself. He turned fourteen that summer but he wasn't sure when, for there was no calendar, and along in June he neglected to notch down the passing days.

He had a lot of time to think, lying in his bunk or walking along logging roads, and he used to plan how he would go down with the drive the next spring, and celebrate in Quickwater. Maybe he would see Molly Fitzpatrick, although probably not in Quickwater, for the boys said she was too mad at Dan Stoughton to go there; if he wanted to see her, he'd have to go to her fancy house on down the Chippewa. He guessed it was true that she had become any man's woman, although when he first heard that it had gone down hard and he had made a fool of himself defending her name. That was when he first started working as a chore boy; his cheeks burned when he remembered what a fool he had been. It was one Saturday night in the bunkhouse when the crew sat up later than usual, not drinking, for Nels Quist ran a dry camp, but telling stories and jigging to a fiddle and saying that since this was Jim Buckmaster's first season they would have to initiate him by tossing him in a blanket. Jim, they said, bring us your blanket.

Having been brought up in a logging family, he knew what was coming; how a half dozen men would grab the blanket and shake it, testing it to be sure it was strong, before tossing him. So when he went to the kitchen for his blanket, he scattered a handful of pepper in the folds. And sure enough, the men tested it, but not for long; the air was thick with pepper and sneezing; everybody ran for fresh air. So he wasn't blanket-tossed that night, or ever; loggers liked a joke, and if you could turn it against them they laughed and gave you credit for outsmarting them.

After the air had cleared in the shanty they went back inside, and later that evening a chopper named High-pockets Fred was telling of his adventures in walking up to camp from Read's Landing, one incident being his stopping at Molly Fitzpatrick's place for a drink and a game of craps and a session with Molly. "As you know," he said, "she's a whore now."

He didn't, as it turned out, mean to malign Molly, but was just stating a fact, the way you might say John Jones is a grocer now. But Jim hadn't heard about Molly's new career; he thought High-pockets Fred was slandering a friend of his; and he always stood by his friends. It touched off his temper; and although he was no match for Fred he flung himself at the deacon's seat where Fred was sitting, relaxed and filling his pipe. The deacon's seat was a bench running along in front of the bunks, so when the attack landed Fred toppled into a bunk, Jim on top of him, slugging. It was most unexpected, especially to Fred, so Jim got in some pretty fair licks. But then Nels Quist was yelling to break it up, and Jim was grabbed by the boots and pulled out of that muzzle-loader bunk; Quist took hold of his shirt and yanked him to his feet.

"Jim," he said, "it's against the rules to fight. You want to fight, you wait till the season's over. The woods ain't no place for fighting, Jim, the woods is for logging. You fight in a saloon."

"He called Molly a whore," Jim said.

"Well, now, Jim," Nels Quist said, "what's wrong with that? That's what she is. She's a whore and a damned good one."

He always remembered the incredulity of that moment when he was still thinking of Molly as she used to be, one man's woman, her husband's; a woman earthy and full-blooded and a little gayer than average, perhaps, but nothing like the girls in Dan Stoughton's fancy house.

"She's not," Jim said.

"How about it, boys?" Nels Quist asked; and all those loggers responded with confirmations.

It took the fight out of him; they couldn't all be lying. He remembered his chagrin as he looked at them, thronged there in checked shirts and suspenders; their faces came back to him: the olive-skinned faces of Canucks; the grizzled beard of Pop Smith, barn boss and blacksmith, the oldest man in camp; faces flannel-mouthed with Irish blood and ruddy with Scottish; Swedish, German and just plain American faces, some with mustaches or stubble or scars or boils.

Sure she's a whore, they were chorusing, she took my money, she cleaned me at dice and went to bed with me on credit, she's got a nigger working for her and—

Jim swallowed, and he could feel his ears burning. And somehow he felt she had gone back on him; it probed him where it hurt.

"I never would have thought it," he said.

"Hell, Jim," Nels Quist said, "you never know what a damned woman will do. They're worse than Danes."

"I resent that," Red Erik Larsen yelled, but he was smiling; it was all sham warfare, between him and Nels.

"She was always good to me," Jim said.

"To all of us," Nels said, and the boys laughed.

That lighted Jim's temper again and he swung his fists, but Nels Quist still held him by the shirt and the blows went wild.

"Jim," Quist was saying, "you've got to learn I mean what I say. No fighting in camp. That's the rule. I'm not mad, Jim, but I'll have to learn you. I won't bust no bones, but you'll remember the rule."

Jim had been feeling pretty cocky the last few months, with all those belligerent male juices working in his glands; he thought he knew about fighting. But he wasn't in a class with Nels Quist. Nels gave his face an open-handed slap and whirled him around and marched him out into the autumn moonlight, all the shanty boys trooping after them to stand in a circle like men at a cock fight.

"Jim," Nels Quist was saying, "I'm push of this here camp."

Then his fist came smashing, a ham-size fist that was rock hard; it was like being hit by a catapulting log; Jim went down and Nels yanked him up and knocked him down again. Then he kicked him in the buttocks with his spiked boot; Jim rolled away and sprang up and went charging in, head low, catching Nels in the diaphragm with his head; it was like butting a blacksmith's anvil; Nels stepped back and smashed him in the nose; that brought blood; and from then on it was like being whirled in a tornado full of flying debris.

"Had enough?"

Jim was down on one knee then; he yelled, "No!"

And he jumped up and lunged at Nels, giving him one in the jaw.

After that Nels really started logging. Now and then Jim must have landed a good one, for the next day Nels showed some marks, but for the most part it was a punishment, not a fight. But whenever Nels asked if he'd had enough, his voice far away, Jim just clenched his teeth; pretty soon, through whirling pain, he heard men urging Nels to let it go at that and other men urging Jim to say yes, he'd had enough; but he could be stubborn. He passed out, finally; they undressed him to his woolens and put him into his bunk.

Next day was Sunday when everybody could sleep, but out of habit Jim wakened at 3:30 A.M., stiff as a frozen deer and sore all over. He knew it was Sunday but he crawled out anyway, fumbling into his clothes, and he went tottering through the bunkhouse yelling it was daylight in the swamp. His lips were so bruised and swollen he could hardly make words, but it roused those shanty boys and they rolled out and dressed. Then Jim said:

"Today's Sunday, boys, and breakfast is at eight, but I didn't like to see you falling into lazy habits. Me, I'm going back to bed."

They blinked and growled; then they laughed. The kid, they said, had spunk.

"Jim," Nels Quist said, "did you have enough, last night?"

"Enough?" Jim said. "What do you mean, enough?"

"All right, Jim," Nels said, "once you get healed we'll have another go."

"Sure," Jim said. "Any time."

But Nels never went through with that threat. Maybe, being a good push, with the knack of sensing how the wind blew, he could tell he would only turn his men against him if he kept beating up on young Buckmaster. And in a camp like that, if your men turned against you, tools would be mysteriously lost and broken, and the season's cut would fall way below expectations. Discipline was one thing but slave-driving another; loggers weren't slaves.

*

For a day or two Jim was a sight, one eye swollen shut and the other nearly so; lips puffy; purple bruises on his skin. But he was healthy and he healed fast. He guessed that licking was the best thing that could have happened; it taught him to wait till he packed more sinew before tackling grown men; it showed him he didn't know everything about rough-and-tumble fighting. During that season and the next, there at Teal Feather, he was always asking well-thought-of fighters to show him their bag of tricks; even Nels Quist taught him punches and parries.

But one wound didn't heal so fast; the one that started hurting when he learned Molly Fitzpatrick had turned whore. Once he was a grown man he could smile at how hard he had taken that news, telling himself that women had dozens of ways of hurting men, and that a man was a fool to put much stock in any of them; but at Teal Feather Camp he kept remembering how sweet Molly had smelled and how she had wanted babies and what a gallant sort of couple she and Lew had been; he wished she hadn't started taking the men as they came. Could have been that with his mother dead he had fallen into thinking of Molly as a sort of mother; she used to call him her boy; anyway, he hated to think of her running a fancy house.

During his first winter at Teal Feather, a load of supplies was sledded in from Quickwater, and the teamster brought mail. Jim wasn't expecting any—letters weren't sent from where his family had gone—and he thought it was a mistake when they told him he had a letter. Then he saw Sol Klauber's handwriting on the envelope.

Looking back, he could see he had been a funny sort of kid then, passing through the awkward age; he remembered how his fingers were shaky, holding that letter, and how instead of reading it at once he stuffed it into his pocket and went back inside the shanty. It was mid-afternoon; he sat peeling a mountain of potatoes, and apples for pie, feeling ashamed because he had run away from Sol Klauber, and feeling too some of his old uneasiness about being put into an orphanage. Only about four months had passed since he left Sol, but it seemed years, his way of living had changed so much. He set the long table; the crews came stamping in from the woods and sat shoveling in the grub; he ate his own supper and washed the dishes and brought in wood; and all the time he was conscious of that letter in his pocket. Finally, at bedtime, he sat on the edge of his bunk, turning the letter over and over, dreading to read Sol's anger or his resentment. Well, he couldn't wait forever; he fingered open the letter.

But no anger or resentment came from the handwriting; only affection and sad resignation. Sol had written it before leaving New Empire and had sent it care of Dan Stoughton in Quickwater, figuring that was where Jim had gone. Nothing in that letter about going to the sheriff or chasing Jim; nothing about orphanages or guardianship papers; just Sol saying it was likely his fault that Jim had run away; he was sorry he had pushed so hard for education; he should have known, he said, that if Jim didn't want to be educated there was nothing he could do; he supposed Jim had got a job in the woods and he hoped he'd be happy.

"I miss your company, Jim," he wrote. "You're the only son I have. I made a mistake in trying to live your life for you; I might have known you'd never stand for that. I think whatever you do will come out all right, for you have the mark of success on you. I leave for Boston tomorrow but I'll be back some day and look you up."

Jim kept thinking about that letter long after lights were out, and when he slept he dreamed of Sol, confused and troubling dreams whose details eluded him next day but whose mood persisted. Sol had asked him to write and he fully intended to, but before he got to it the teamster returned to Quickwater. Now and then, for months afterward, he would decide to write Sol, but he was busy, and putting thoughts on paper came hard.

The Teal Feather Camp banked a lot of logs, those two seasons he worked there, and in memory those days all blurred together. He never could be sure whether it was his first season or his second when he began shaving, buying a razor from the chest of supplies which Dan Stoughton sent in from outside, purchases being deducted from wages. Anyway, the boys joshed him about shaving, but it was good natured; they liked him; he had shown what he was made of, that night he refused to say he'd had enough punishment from Nels Quist. In some ways it was a monotonous life, but the days slipped along and at season's end you wondered where they'd gone. He remembered dawns when the air was feathered with falling snow, and nights of such intense cold that you would hear trees frost-cracking with a report like a rifle. A winter in the woods was always the same: at bedtime the men hung up their snow-drenched socks, and the smell was fearful; from bunks you'd hear snoring and tired bodies shifting in sleep; you'd hear wind in the pines and owls hooting and wolves howling. He remembered how his breath was a silver cloud, when he carried flaggins to the crews at noon; how icicles dangled from mustaches and from the eaves of the bunkhouse; how the snow squeaked and the woods rang with the sound of axes.

After his summer as camp watchman, when the crews returned, he was no longer a greenhorn; there were new faces. Pop Smith had died during the summer; High-pockets Fred had drowned on the drive; some of the boys had hired out to other camps. But Red Erik Larsen came back, after a summer of cooking on a river packet, and Nels Quist. Jim, Quist asked, did you pick many fights with yourself, alone up here? If you did I'll have to lick you . . . Sure, Jim said, I fought every day.

Logging camps were all alike, essentially; years later when he had camps of his own, and dropped in for over night, he would smell beans simmering and bread baking and feel like a chore boy again at Teal Feather.

*

At the end of his second season he went down with the drive, and it was the best of logging. A camp might be monotonous but never a drive; it was excitement from rollways to booms. Spring was in the air, on a drive; you heard frogs and saw violets blooming among patches of die-hard snow. At that season the rivers flowed full of snow-water; rapids were white and powerful; and always the air was bright with danger.

Danger hovered over the rollways, those great stacks of logs banked along the river, for when calked boots climbed those stacks, and men pried and yanked with cant hooks, nobody knew what might happen. Snow would have sifted among those logs, and ice would have formed, gluing them together, so that sometimes when the rollways were broken out, and the logs went cascading into the river, two or three logs would roll as one, pitching and wobbling and maybe knocking a man off his feet and he would be buried in that cataract of rumbling timber. Or he might just slip, or perhaps a log, for no reason that a physicist could ever explain, would suddenly leap up and go hurtling, smashing a man's head or his spine. Logs were great ones for pulling surprises; they seemed to come alive on a drive; maybe they knew it was now or never; if they didn't make their getaway now they would be fed to the saws sure.

All the way down you herded them like a drove of unruly bulls. They strayed to shore and into pokelogans; they piled up in jams; they thrust their noses between boulders in midstream and reared up their hind ends; they thought they were muskies and dived to the river bottom; they swished their tails like minnows and rubbed together like lovers and darted when you thought they would balk and balked when you expected them to swim free. And sometimes, just to fool you, they floated along as sedately as swans.

Like boats, and like running water itself, they had the souls of light ladies; and often they conspired with their cousins, the goose girls of spring weather, to repay man for ancient wrongs against their sex. Rain pelted the usual log drive, and hail, and unseasonable snow; damp winds blew; or the weather turned sultry, hatching out mosquitoes and swarms of no-see-ums. You slogged in drenched boots; you slept in wet blankets under a leaky tent; and you loved it, if you were Jim Buckmaster.

Not that he used a cant hook or a pike pole on that first drive; he was still the cook's helper. But that wasn't any soft snap; it took a lot of beans and pie and potatoes to float sawlogs down a river. He and Red Erik got up earlier than usual, cooking in the open where the tents were pitched beside the river; and at midmorning and midafternoon huge lunches were served, and it was Jim's job to deliver that food to prearranged places; he had a scow for that. The jam crews and the rear crews were strung along a dozen miles of river, working both sides, so it kept Jim humping, but he always delivered those lunches on time. He would have a fire blazing and hot tea ready when the men came poling shoreward in their bateaux.

"Jim," they used to say, "this tea's strong enough to float an ax. You'll be a better cook than Red Erik, some day."

He grinned; but he knew he'd never be a cook.

Nels Quist was boss of the whole drive, and when he slept Jim never knew; the last thing at night, when most of the river pigs were in their blankets, Nels would be squatting by the fire, talking in a low voice to one of his jam crackers, and maybe drawing maps in the sand; and he was up in the morning even before Jim. He drank gallons of coffee; that was the Swede of it; most loggers preferred tea.

All the way down jams kept forming, wing jams stretching out from shore, and center jams in midstream, but usually the jam crews pounced on those obstructions and broke them up. Only once was there a serious plug; they were nearly a day untangling that. Jim would have traded half interest in hell to have helped at that untangling, but Nels Quist made him stay on shore. It was a sight to remember when finally the plug gave way, all those thousands of logs rumbling free and hurling themselves blindly through boiling rapids. One log struck a jam cracker in the head and knocked him out; he drowned. His body was pulp when they found it; they buried him in a pork barrel beneath a tree and hung his boots and his cant hook over a limb.

"Glad now you stayed on shore?" Nels Quist asked.

"No," Jim said.

But he kept thinking how that man's body looked; if you were going to be a white water man, you'd better be a good one; he could see that.

Rain was falling, when they reached the Chippewa River. The Chippewa was flowing full and so was the Flambeau; it was quite a sight to see those two rivers coming together in a wide, whirling, churning mass, the logs rolling and turning end-to-end in the crazy currents. Through the rain-slant you could see men in bateaux out among those logs, herding them along. That evening the crews huddled close to the fires, steaming out, and in their tents at bedtime men stuck cant hooks into the ground and hung their boots on top of them, upside down; next morning they poured hot water over their boots before pulling them on.

"If you're going to have wet feet anyway," they said, "you might as well have warm boots."

Those spring rains kept falling all the way down to the booms at Quickwater, and Jim had to smile at how the river hogs hated rain. You might have thought a little more water wouldn't have mattered, they were wading in the river so much of the time, often to their belts. But they said the rain peppered into the bowls of their pipes; a man couldn't even have a good smoke, on this drive.

And so at last, nearly three weeks after breaking camp at Teal Feather, Nels Quist and his pigs brought the drive down into Quickwater, herding the last of the logs into the booms. By then the rain was easing off, but the Chippewa was running high, the dam spillway roaring with the gate wide open. People lined the river bank watching the drive come in, and when Jim stepped ashore he couldn't help feeling pretty chesty and superior to those tame landsmen; he had been nearly two years in the woods and he had followed a log drive. Over in the west the sun was trying to break through the clouds, and the Northern Saloon was waiting with the magic of whiskey and fancy women. He'd soon be fifteen; he could have passed for eighteen; he was almost a man. He'd been in a scow since noon, and when he stepped ashore the land seemed unsteady, he was so accustomed to river rhythms. And shore seemed a kind of inconsequential place, cramping him in, he was so used to wide waters.

In his absence Quickwater had kept growing, new buildings standing where charred foundations had been. Just east of River Street on the north side of Chippewa, a raw plank office was lettered Quickwater Log & Lumber Co., Dan'l Stoughton, Pres. The men were trooping in there for their winter's pay, and Jim went along. It looked like a bank inside, with clerks wearing sleeve protectors busy behind grills. And just inside the door Dan Stoughton stood. When he saw Jim he stepped forward with his hand out.

"Jim," he said, "I'd hardly know you. My God, but you've grown. I hear good things about you, Jim. Quist tells me you're the best bull cook he ever had. He tells me when he fought you you wouldn't say enough."

Jim stood smiling.

"I guess not," he said. "Maybe I didn't know enough to say enough."

"You've got gravel in your craw, Jim, that's what Quist says. You'll make a logger. Quist has a notion he'll let you start swinging an ax next fall. Don't tell him I told you, but that's what he figures to do. Think you can handle an ax, Jim?"

"I just might," Jim said.

"Quist tells me you'll go places, Jim. 'Dan,' he says, 'I've got a future push working for me as bull cook.' That's what he said, Jim."

Life had never seemed better than when he stood in that lumber office with its smells of new planks and wet clothes and pipe smoke; he felt a little drunk already. Nobody would ever think of popping him into an orphanage now, he looked so grown; nobody could ever make him go to school again. Youth was running in his veins that day, and when he looked toward the future he felt bedazzled; it was like looking at the sun.

"Dan," he said, "it's good to see you. By God, it's good to get back. You've got a new office."

"We're growing, Jim," Dan said. "They're buying all we can saw. Would you like to raft lumber this summer, Jim?"

"Sure," Jim said, "why not?"

"There's a job waiting," Dan said.

His check was for nearly two hundred dollars, when a little bald-headed man rustled it through the grill; for nearly two years he had drawn no cash wages.

"Mister," Jim said, "I'd like to turn this into genuine money."

"Next window," the man said.

So Jim stood in line there.

But the man at that window wouldn't pay the face amount of the check, because the check was postdated October 1.

"Glad to discount it though," he said. "Twenty percent discount."

Jim had a notion to tell him to stick it, but he wanted money. And he saw then why the Quickwater company was growing; if you paid your hands in June with postdated checks, and turned around and cashed them at twenty percent discount, you couldn't help coining money.

The sun had broken through when he left that office, his fist full of currency; and he headed for the New Northern Saloon as naturally as a log toward a pokelogan. The clearing sky had a deep June-blue color; a white-throat was singing; his shadow stalked long ahead of him on the wooden sidewalk, and his calked boots chewed out slivers of wood. Whiskey and girls were just ahead; he had waited a long time for this.

But when he reached the saloon entrance a cluster of men were talking about a drowning down at Snowshoe Creek. The creek, they said, was flood full, and about an hour ago when a man started across, the bridge gave way and pitched him into the creek. Several persons had seen it happen; the man had drowned, right enough; but his body, instead of going to the bottom, had been caught in a tangle of snags.

"Come on, boys," somebody said. "We'd best go help."

Jim didn't exactly hanker to see another drowned body, so soon after watching them bury that jam cracker, but he went along with the rest; after all, when your profession was outwitting running water, you did well to learn all the tricks that water used to grab victims.

The sun was low, when they reached Snowshoe Creek, and the air had that moist feel of early June after a spell of rain, with robins singing about the long fine summer ahead. The creek was over the road in places, and it had sheeted out over the adjacent lowlands, the water clay-colored and rank with flood smells. The bridge had gone, only the abutments standing, and a couple of hundred feet downstream three men in a rowboat were untangling a body from snags. After a time the boat came sculling upstream and across the flooded lowlands to the road. Men lifted out the body and laid it face up on the ground.

The drowned man had been well into middle age, with hair and beard mainly gray. Mud smeared his face and his clothes. He looked tired in death, and sort of sad.

"Thought it was a white man," one of the rescuers said. "If I'd known it was a Jew I'd have let him rot."

Jim recognized the drowned man then; it was Sol Klauber.

*

He always wished, afterward, that he had had presence of mind enough to slug the man who said that about letting the body rot. But it rocked him, recognizing Sol. He remembered letting out a yell and pushing through the crowd and dropping to his knees, grabbing Sol's water-logged shoulders and shaking him. And he remembered yelling something like Sol, hey, Sol . . .

There was a babble; he caught snatches: say, Jim Buckmaster knows him . . . Say, Jim, he a friend of yourn?

"Yes," Jim said, "sure. He was a friend of mine."

"Sol," his mind was saying, "my God, Sol, I meant to write. I hated running off like that, Sol, and I meant to write."

Well, it was nothing but foolishness, talking to the dead; everybody knew that; a dead man had no ears. Whether you burned in a fire or drowned in a freshet you didn't hear so good any more.

"Sol," his mind was saying, "I guess you were sort of a second father to me. But I couldn't stomach going to Boston. You catch a whiskey-jack, Sol, and cage him up and take him to Boston and he'll molt and die, you know that. But I hated to run away."

Sol looked so dead; that was what got Jim; he looked so damned dead.

He knelt there a little longer, knowing he'd be disgraced forever if he cried, but he was crying inside.

Then he stood up, jaw hard, eyes dry, and took charge. Somebody fetched a blanket and they made a stretcher from poles and carried Sol Klauber to a carpenter's shop.

"Mister," Jim remembered saying, "I need a coffin. Can you put a coffin together, mister?"

"When's the funeral?" the carpenter asked.

"Right now," Jim said. "The funeral's right now and right here," he said, tapping his forehead. "And I'm the only mourner, mister, and to hell with this town. This town's death and sorrow, mister, and I'm pulling stakes."

The carpenter gave him an odd look, as if he'd wandered off his skid trail; well, maybe he was not quite himself, thinking of how Sol had been good to him and of that son of a bitch who had said they should have let him rot.

Darkness had come, by the time that carpenter finished the coffin; some neighbors came over and helped lay Sol inside. They were scandalized, when Jim said they would bury him right now, without a funeral or anything. Besides, where would they bury him?

"On the Buckmaster place," Jim said, "that's where. Get lanterns and I'll show you. I'm the only Buckmaster left so I reckon I own that ground."

Much later that night, Jim stood alone by a mound where the Buckmaster cabin had once been.

"Good-by, mister," he was thinking. "Give my regards to Isaac, mister."

Then, shouldering his calamity sack, he strode along Shin-Tangle Street and south on Squaw, past the New Northern Saloon with its hoots and singing. He didn't enter; there was a time for hell-raising, but this wasn't that time. He went to the river and found the scow he had used on the drive and rowed across to the west bank. When he stepped to shore he looked back at Quickwater across the dark water, then started south through the woods to find Molly Fitzpatrick.

XI

He always thought he finished growing up when he went from Sol's grave to Molly's place. For months he had been making forays into adulthood, but that night he consolidated his gains. Molly added to his education, during the time he spent with her, but that was only incidental and postgraduate.

Below Quickwater the Chippewa River went tumbling down a chain of rapids, and as he made his way through the woods in the darkness he could hear those waters roaring off to his left. Last night at this time, he kept thinking, Sol was alive. He was, he supposed, responsible for Sol's death; probably Sol had been peddling this area thinking he'd come across Jim Buckmaster; but damn it, he never should have tried crossing a bridge weakened by a freshet. Some instinct told Jim not to let thoughts of guilt get their hooks into him; that had been his father's trouble.

Daybreak came early at that season, and today promised to be fine. Dew glistened in the first light; thickets were coming alive with the chirps of indigo birds and the trilling of marsh wrens; the owls and night hawks were shutting up shop; everything smelled damp and sweet with early summer. The roaring of rapids had stopped; and among the birches and alders Jim could see the Chippewa flowing broad and smooth, the color of creamed coffee in the dawn; an island in mid-river looked new-minted. When he came to a spring-fed rill sparkling among ferns he knelt to drink; and just then, for no reason he could fathom, except maybe that part of him was unexplored country which he would never understand, he thought that Sol would not be seeing the sun come up today or any day ever again, and he let loose with a sob.

He felt shamefaced, kneeling there crying like a girl, and before long he got control. Then he drank and splashed water onto his face and felt better.

Off to the east low hills molded themselves against June sky, and the sun was edging above them when Jim sighted Molly's place. By then he was following the gig trail along the river, and he had to hand it to Molly, she had picked a nice spot, her place facing east with a grassy meadow sloping to the cattails wading along the west shore of the Chippewa. She even had a crude sign hanging from a post at the trail side, with a finger pointing. "The White Water House," the sign said. "Molly Welcomes You."

The place looked sound asleep as he followed the path through the dewy grasses; and he stopped once, some masculine sense of protocol telling him this was the time of day to be leaving a fancy house, not going to one. But this wasn't just any old fancy house; this was Molly's; and he walked on.

At the south end, the house was one-story and built of logs nicely chinked, with a puncheon bench beside the door where a cat was dozing; but the north end was of unpainted lumber and two stories tall. The cat watched him approaching, then vanished in a slate-gray streak around the house, so fast that Jim laughed. After he pounded the log-slab door nothing happened for quite a while; he knocked again. Finally the door was opened by a young black wench winking sleep from her eyes.

"Kind of early, white boy," she said.

"I'm looking for Molly," Jim said.

"Miss Molly, she's asleep. Anything I can do for you, I'd be pleased to oblige."

"Sure," Jim said, "you can let me in."

And he stepped past the girl who looked comical in a white nightcap and nightgown with her rangy arms and legs in such black contrast.

It was dusky in there with the shades drawn, but he made out a bar faced with log slabs, and he smelled last night's beer and whiskey and tobacco. At the west end of the room he could see a crap table and a roulette layout.

"Bedrooms is this way," the girl said, indicating a door in the north wall. "They pay Miss Molly but sometimes the logging gentlemen give me a mite extra. Anything you want I'm pleased to oblige."

"What's your name?"

"Philantha."

Jim brought out a quarter, thumb-flipped it toward the log rafters, caught it and tossed it to the girl. She was butter-fingered; it tinkled on the puncheon floor; she scrambled after it.

"Philantha," he said, "don't wake Molly. I'm a friend of hers and I'll wait. Is there somewhere I can catch a nap?"

"My bed's mighty soft," she said.

"All right, Philantha, you get back into it."

After she shuffled away, Jim spread his blanket on the saloon floor. A minute later he was in deep sleep. That was where Molly found him.

*

It was a pleasant way to be wakened, having your forehead lightly stroked and your lips lightly kissed and your nostrils becharmed with the fragrance of powder and perfume. Right away he knew where he was; he knew he had found Molly; he opened his eyes and smiled.

"Jim," she said, her voice honeyed, "you've got a sweet smile. You'll have the girls trotting after you like bitch pups, with a smile like that."

In the dimness he could see Molly on her knees beside him, all softness and cream, her hair the golden color of buckskin. She wore it this morning in two dangling braids, long and heavy, but where it framed her face there was a charming disorder of stray wisps and ringlets. He lay there smiling like a young prince, contented to soak in her aura of womanness. She touched his arm, and a delicious tingling skimmed along his nerves.

"Jim," she said, "you've grown. You've lengthened out and muscled up. You've got a fine body, Jim."

"It takes me where I want to go," he said.

"Where the hell have you been, Jim? What have you been up to?"

"Here and there," he said. "Logging. What have you been up to?"

The light was dull, but he thought she colored. Then she broke out laughing, and when she spoke her voice had its old zip and twang.

"Damn you, Jim. You know damned well what I've been up to."

He took a deep stretch, like a healthy young animal, and sat up. He could feel the ripple of strength in his biceps, the power in the long sinews of his back.

"I've been thinking about you," he said.

It pleased her; he could tell that.

"Have you, Jim? I thought you'd forgotten me."

"I don't forget my friends," he said.

He stood up, moving with the smoothness of a woods cat. For a moment Molly remained kneeling, looking like early morning in her green silk peignoir.

"That reminds me," she said. "A man was here looking for you. Day before yesterday. It was that peddler, Sol Klauber, and he wondered where you were. Did he find you?"

It hit him; he stood staring, mouth tight. Then he became very busy folding his blanket.

"What's wrong, Jim? Do you owe him money?"

"I'd as soon not talk about it," he said. "Yes, I reckon I owed him plenty. But he never found me. I found him. He got drownded in Snowshoe Creek."

"Jim," she said, "that's too damned bad."

She was standing beside him, her hand on his shoulder, and he corked up his grief by thinking idly that yes, he sure as hell had grown, she used to seem like a tall woman, a fine, tall, robust figure of a woman. She was still robust but no longer tall.

"A lot has happened, Jim," she said. "God damn, but a lot has happened. That fire. I heard about it, Jim. I heard about your family. And Mr. Fitzpatrick passing away. A lot has happened in four years."

She began to cry, snuggling her head against his chest; he put his arms around her and patted her. Her body felt smooth against him, and warm. Before long he forgot Sol Klauber and everything else except Molly; when she looked up he kissed her. Then she broke away.

"Jim," she said, "all these years I've been thinking of you as a boy. But you're a man now, damn near."

He smiled.

"And you'll be hell on wheels with the ladies," she said.

"Think so?" he said, reaching for her.

*

All the poetry of running water went rippling through his mind, and all the lure of the woods. Her bedroom was a pink and silver place fragrant with rosemary and thyme, the air dusky behind drawn silken curtains, the bed a fantastic and lovely conceit of a gondola with carved ivory swans. He was with her but sometimes his mind went far away, on the Mississippi at sunset with everything red gold, in the winter woods with blue shadows on sugary snow. Then sweet fatigue benumbed his body and he slept. Much later her voice wakened him.

"Jim. You must be hungry, Jim. Look what I've fixed you."

His nose picked up the aroma of steaming coffee and crisped bacon, and in the dim light he saw Molly putting a tray on the bedside table. He hadn't eaten since yesterday noon; Molly arranged great pillows behind him.

"Jim," she said, "I like to see you eat. Are you happy, Jim?"

He smiled.

"I put you to sleep, Jim. Do you still like me, Jim?"

"Sure," he said. "I wouldn't have come to see you unless I'd liked you."

"How do you feel, Jim?"

He smiled again; he felt triumphantly male; he could have caught two wolverines in his bare hands, feeling like that, and tied their tails together and eaten them for lunch; he could have logged off a whole section of white pine between sunup and dusk; in one stride he could have stepped across the Mississippi from the bluffs of Wisconsin to the bluffs of Iowa.

"I feel fine," he said.

"Damn," she said, "but you'll be hell on wheels. You're hell on wheels already. As good as Mr. Fitzpatrick. Better. You made me feel like a girl."

"Fine," he said.

"Could I ask you something, Jim?"

"Anything you want to know," he said; for it seemed he knew the answers to everything then.

"Was it your first time, Jim?"

"I reckon it must have been," he said. "I don't remember any other times, and I'd not be likely to forget."

593

She broke out laughing.

"God damn it, Jim, I like you. How old are you, anyway? I never can remember ages."

"Seventeen," he told her, and that was accurate, within a couple of years or so.

"You look older. And you seem older, in bed. You're a real logger, Jim. But something made me think it was your first time. A lady has hunches. I wish I was seventeen too, Jim. I'm thirty-three. Does that seem old?"

He shook his head, but even twenty seemed old to him in those days.

"I wish I was seventeen," she said, "and a virgin. And you'd chase me through the woods and throw me down in a thicket of ferns. Then you'd have to marry me."

"Sure," he said; but he never planned to marry. It tied a man down.

"Know what I've done, Jim? I've put a closed sign on the door. Nobody will bother us. All day today and all tomorrow and all the next day, if you want it. Just you and me. The hell with all the others. Their whiskers scratch or they've got big bellies. Just you and me, Jim, like a honeymoon. We'll keep the curtains pulled and hide out like lovers."

"That suits me," he said. "Suits me fine."

"I wish I was seventeen," she said. "You'd marry me then, and I'd always be true to you. I sort of guess I love you, Jim, but don't let it scare you. I'm just dreaming, Jim. We'd get married and I'd give you a dozen kids, every one a boy and hell on wheels. They'd all be millionaires and we'd own the earth."

"Hell," he said, "I'm going to own the earth anyway."

*

He remembered those days as a misty, fragrant time when Molly treated him like her lord and master, doing any wonderful thing he asked and some he didn't. Downstairs, the Negro girl cooked their meals and Molly fetched them up on a tray; it was all a festival of loving and eating and drinking and loving, just the thing for a growing boy. In the afternoons and in the evenings men would bang the door, but the Negro girl sent them away; a pretty good nigger, Molly said; she had bought her in Kentucky on the trip east with Mr. Fitzpatrick the year of the forest fire.

That had been a time of financial panic so Molly picked up the girl at a bargain for a personal maid, and on the return trip, in Cincinnati, she had also bought furniture and draperies to put in the house Mr. Fitzpatrick had promised to build in Quickwater.

"This bed," she told Jim, "was out of the best fancy house in Cincinnati. The business went broke in the panic. I bought it for a song and sang it myself. Mr. Fitzpatrick laughed at me, for buying a bed from a fancy house. But I thought it was pretty."

All that furniture had traveled by river steamer to Read's Landing and by pole-boat and ox wagon up the Chippewa to Quickwater. But Mr. Fitzpatrick never built a house. He could have afforded it; being long-sighted, or perhaps just lucky, he had sold his securities and had plenty of specie when the panic hit; but when they returned to Quickwater he was too busy getting the lumber company on its feet to think about a house. They stayed in the rebuilt Shanghai House. Then he was killed.

"I went a little crazy, as it were," she said.

She had tried to wash away grief with whiskey; it was no good; after months of that she became, she guessed, a nuisance in the New Northern Saloon. Her whiskey usually tasted of the salt tears that fell into her glass. She didn't eat; kept alive on whiskey; drunk from one midnight to the next. Men used to walk her over to her hotel room and put her to bed; especially Xenophon Yates, who owned the hotel. Sometimes he got into bed with her; being so drunk, she didn't know what she was doing. With her mistress in that condition, the nigger girl Philantha had seized the opportunity to make a little pocket change; before long Molly and Philantha had drifted into being, as it were, whores. And the New Shanghai House was getting a fancy reputation. So Mrs. Xenophon Yates told Mr. Xenophon Yates that this had gone far enough. Either those harlots go, she said, or I go.

Along about then—it was all hazy in Molly's memory—Dan Stoughton offered her a cash deal on Mr. Fitzpatrick's share of the lumber company. In her sodden condition she would have sold out for a kiss, but Dan wanted it legal, he wanted something to show he had bought it. Therefore, although his buying figure was low, it wasn't absolutely ridiculous, as rumor said; it was a thousand dollars. Molly said sure and signed anything he wanted. And next day she sobered up. Funny thing: having that cash money and being afraid Philantha would steal it, had sobered her when nothing else would. She knew then she had been taken by Dan Stoughton. Business is business, he said. She read him the riot act, in his saloon with the pinery boys listening; business is business, he kept saying.

She never forgave him. She came down the Chippewa with Philantha and bought a log cabin—what was now the saloon end of the house—and set up in business. Located on the trail men used going to the woods, and on the Chippewa with its lumber rafts, the business flourished. She enlarged the house; she wrote a friend in New Orleans and ordered a crap table and a roulette wheel. She didn't drink so much any more; just a little social drinking; she was out for the money now. Some day she would have a houseful of girls and reap the just rewards of the alert businesswoman. No Injun girls, though. Injuns had brought her nothing but trouble, killing her family that evening in New Brunswick, and a breed killing Mr. Fitzpatrick. What she wanted was to get a pile of money together and use it to ruin Dan Stoughton. I'll ruin you, Dan, she had screamed, that time in his saloon; God damn you, Dan, I'll ruin you.

She had, she supposed, grown harder; she told Jim in great secrecy that her roulette wheel was gaffed, and she had learned to switch dice; but there was no Mr. Fitzpatrick to care for her now; when a woman was left with nothing, as it were, but her two legs to support herself she had to be hard. But she would never take money from Jim.

*

She cried when he left, but he thought he'd best be on his way.

"You'll be back, Jim?" she asked. "You'll come again?"

"Sure," he said. "I'll be around."

"You need money, Jim? Glad to lend you a few dollars."

He shook his head; he was flush with two years' wages.

"You never should have cashed that check with Stoughton," she said. "You should have gone to New Empire. The boys say there's a new operator who will cash your checks for gold. Name of Caleb McSwasey. The boys say he's opening a camp next fall at Noggin Lake, and he'll pay cash wages."

"McSwasey," Jim said. "I'll remember that name. Sounds like my man."

So he left Molly and went down the Chippewa, taking his time, sleeping in the woods. When he reached the village of War Bonnet he met an old friend at the trading post: Nekeek, the Chippewa boy he used to play with over in Injun Hollow. And it transpired that, despite their flight, Hole-in-the-Day and Nekeek's mother and many other members of the old band had been burned in the great fire; it had walked faster than they, Nekeek said. But he was fine and living now up at Noggin Lake; why didn't Jim make him a visit?

So, in addition to other supplies, Jim bought fancy goods that a young squaw might like, in case he found one; and he did, and was her husband for several months; and he was right on hand there at Noggin Lake when men started building Camp Number One of the McSwasey & Zumwalt Lumber Company. He talked himself into a job, and that October he saw Esperanza Zumwalt McSwasey for the first time. She was an attractive girl, he could see that, but not his kind somehow; he never did really take to her.

*

He went up fast, working for McSwasey & Zumwalt. It was a young company, right on its toes and expanding rapidly, with a woods superintendent who would promote a young fellow who had it in him; and Jim had it in him. Swamper, chopper, river driver, jam cracker, log raftsman, camp push: he climbed right to the top.

It was a fine time in his life; the best of all, he sometimes thought.

Every autumn he went to the woods and every spring he followed the drive; heaven only knew how many pines his ax sent crashing; how many bushels of beans and sowbelly he shoveled into his mouth; how many times he rolled out of his bunk on sub-zero mornings, to pull on three pairs of German socks and two pairs of pants. He got his growth in those years, and it was mainly gristle and sinew and cartilage. Handling an ax thickened his calluses and broadened his shoulders and deepened his chest; he was a lot of man. In camp the boys were always getting up contests in jumping or lifting or Indian wrestling, but after a time they barred him from competition, for it was freely acknowledged he could outstrip anybody.

He was always glad when camp broke in the spring, for he liked driving logs better than anything in the lumber business. Logs didn't bar him from competition; they challenged him; they thought they were as tough as he was. Well, maybe; but he was nimbler. He had some close calls, on those northern rivers; once on the south fork of the Eau Claire, breaking out a rollway at the start of a drive, he almost cashed in. That rollway was a mass of logs rising forty feet from the water's edge, with snow and ice packed in the crevices; for two days they had been working trying to get it to break, and he had grown careless. When it gave, without warning, he and Dutch Kellenburg were perched away up there at the edge, yanking on a trip-rope; all at once the rollway became a landslide of tumbling logs. Jim thought this was it, but he was only nineteen, with lots of fight in him, so he kept jumping from log to log as they rumbled underfoot, and he saved himself. Dutch Kellenburg wasn't so lucky; the logs opened under his boots and he dropped into a hole; they closed on top of him and rolled him into the river. The boys found him later headfirst in the water, boots pointing skyward from among the logs.

After incidents like that you didn't mind the routine discomforts of a drive, such as being drenched to the hide most of the time from spills or wading in icy currents. Sometimes hunks of ice floated among the logs and Jim's legs went numb, but he never caught cold any more than a muskrat.

"Come on, boys," he would yell, wading into the water, "it won't burn you."

In those days his vitality was so abundant that he squandered it, and something made him flirt with danger. At the head of a stretch of rapids he used to enjoy spotting a log coming downstream and jumping onto its back, digging in his calks. It came alive then, like a young stallion, and he knew there was fun ahead. Balancing himself, using his pike pole as a rudder, he stuck with that log as it swam with the quickening current. He could see the pitch just ahead, a frothing piece of river, with rocks and spinning eddies and waterfalls, and he knew death might be thirty seconds away, but he was tipsy with something you couldn't buy in a saloon. He always whooped like a moose in rut, as the rapids snatched the log and it went shooting forward, sometimes racing along buried in foam, sometimes leaping clear like a horse hurdling a fence. How he managed to ride it he never could have explained; his brains were in his boots then; the rest of his body just went along for the fun. Shore sped past in a blur; everything was spray and splash; sometimes Jim was dancing, sometimes squatting like a man on skis; and always the log bobbled and squirmed, trying to toss him, until it reached smooth water and knew it was licked.

On a drive, in his blankets at night, he used to dream about shooting rapids and cracking jams; torrents roared through his sleep, and mountains of logs buried him; his drowned body went sinking through watery greens into watery blacks, where the eel grass waved and the mud puppies swam; dreaming that way, it was like working twenty-four hours a day.

Compared with those drives, bucking an oar on a Mississippi raft seemed just plain hard work, although it had its excitements. That was one thing about those years with McSwasey & Zumwalt, life was never dull. Even his pleasures—especially his pleasures—were lively. He took them where he found them, in lumber towns and river towns, and they were simple and intense and fundamental: hard liquor, hard fighting, hard women. His drink was whiskey, cheap, raw forty-rod, and he couldn't have kept count of the glasses he tossed down. Nor of the women he bedded with, for that matter. But none of it meant anything. At that period he was never within a hundred miles of being in love.

Fighting he took more seriously, although he was never one to go looking for quarrels, and if a man wasn't his match he couldn't be bothered; he never fought just for the fun of pulping somebody's mouth. But there were always bullies wanting trouble, and he used to clean their rudders for them. Once when he was twenty, in Read's Landing, everybody was talking about Bulldog Ryan, a logger from the St. Croix waters who was in town with his crowd, and as Jim stood there at the bar in the Catfish Saloon he had the hunch he'd likely be fighting Ryan, who had the habit, the boys said, of swaggering along the plank sidewalks and kicking people in the shins with his calked boots. And sure enough, before long the door bounced open and in came Ryan, leading a crowd of bully-boys and dragging his Mackinaw, daring any man to step on it. Jim stood with his back to the bar, lounging on his elbows, smiling.

Ryan was a big red Irishman who looked as if he considered the Marquis of Queensberry a decadent Britisher; Jim thought he could lick the fellow, although he wouldn't have bet. Anyway Ryan kept stamping around the saloon, making more noise than the devil at a wake, and something must have told him Jim was the best man there, for he came dragging over his Mackinaw and giving forth with dares. Jim knew then he'd have to make a true believer out of him.

"Why, Paddy," he said, "I don't step on your Mackinaw because I don't want to dirty my feet."

Ryan let out a yell and charged with head lowered, aiming to butt Jim in the belly. Jim stepped aside and Ryan butted the bar. That made him mad, and he called names. His bully-boys licked their lips and egged him on; they were a hard crowd. Jim didn't propose to have one of them bash his head with a bottle while he fought Ryan; he said:

"Sure, Paddy, I'll fight you. But I need elbowroom. First we'll clear out this place and lock the door. Then I'll fight you."

Ryan didn't take to that idea; he did a lot of God-damning. Jim shrugged.

"If you're afraid to be alone with me, Paddy, forget it."

You might have thought Jim had said there were still snakes in Ireland, from the way those bully-boys reacted; and Jim's friends were yelling too. For a while it looked as if a general roughhouse might break out. Then Butch Patterson, who owned the saloon, and who may have been worried about his fixtures, made himself heard; Jim's idea was a good one, he said; the boys could all wait outside and lay bets as to whether Ryan or Jim would walk out winner. That appealed to their sporting blood; they tramped out; Jim and Ryan faced each other alone.

"Me boy," Ryan said, "I'm going to gouge out your eyes."

"If you're man enough," Jim said.

On the street outside the crowd kept growing, for the town was full of raftsmen and steamboat crews. At first Ryan's cronies boasted the fight wouldn't last two minutes, telling about their man's prowess in chewing off ears and noses, in thumbing eyeballs from sockets, in stomping an opponent once he was floored. If Jim survived at all, they said, he would be crippled for life; and they were free with their wagers. Five minutes passed; ten minutes; the crowd grew quiet. Occasionally they could hear, from inside the saloon, the thump and thud of bodies, or the crash of a table. Then, after a long while, one of the fighters— they couldn't tell which—let out an ungodly howl, as if from agony, followed by short screeches. After that, quiet. The crowd looked at one another. Then the door opened and Jim stood swaying on the threshold, his shirt torn to shreds, his undershirt ripped half off his scratched torso, his face puffed and purpling, his lips swelling, his nose bleeding. A cheer went up and he managed a smile.

"Boys," he said, "I had to bust his arm. He was after my eyes. I stomped him too, boys."

He lurched forward and the crowd opened a path; with his friends tagging along he went staggering toward the river, where he waded into the shallows and dropped to his knees, splashing his face and chest, giving his head quick shakes, as if to clear his thoughts.

"His bones were tough, boys," he said. "I got me a hold on his arm, but I thought I'd never break it. Cracked it, finally. He doubled up then and I stomped his hands."

"You hurt, Jim?" somebody asked.

"Sure," he said, "sure I'm hurt. But I walked out. They never should have fired them blueberry lands, boys. And a bridge in a fresh, she'll give way sure. He couldn't swim."

Jim was on his feet in the shallows; he staggered to shore and fell in the sand.

*

By next morning his thoughts had cleared; a week later you would hardly have known he'd been fighting. Bulldog Ryan fared worse, for with no doctor in Read's Landing a steamboat captain set his broken arm, and set it crooked; he would never fight again. His hands had been pretty badly used too, when Jim stomped them with his calks, the fingers mashed and lacerated; he couldn't fight any more. When he was able to travel he left Read's Landing and went somewhere. He never should have picked on Jim Buckmaster, people said.

That fight didn't do Jim's reputation a bit of harm; various logging companies offered him jobs; but he stuck with McSwasey & Zumwalt, when the woods superintendent matched every offer and made him a camp foreman. He never had to do much fighting, after licking Ryan; other bullies stayed out of his crosswalk. When he entered a saloon everybody wanted to buy him a drink and he let them; but he bought plenty in return, during those years. He was a free spender, up to a point; the boys thought he spent himself broke the way they did, but not for nothing was he the grandson of Newcomb Dobner and Adam Buckmaster. He had a streak of Scotch interwoven with a streak of Maine thrift, and all that ambition his mother had pounded into his head stayed with him. So he bought him a money belt like Sol Klauber's and turned part of his wages into gold eagles and tucked them into the belt. He always thought the time would come when he would see opportunity and that money would be useful.

He spent a lot of time planning his future, after he became a camp push and a raft pilot. To get ahead a man needed capital, he could see that; with capital your powers were multiplied; you could buy stumpage and hire men and make a profit off the work of each man. The more men, the more profit. He figured that by the time he was twenty-five he'd have capital enough to go into business for himself.

But that wasn't the way, after all, he reached the top. He got there all right; he became the biggest man in New Empire, and later the biggest man on the big river and the biggest man in the woods; finally he was one of the biggest men in the U.S.A.; but he didn't do it because of his savings. It was something else; his smile, maybe.

*

Looking back, he could see his real career began when he traveled from Camp Seven to New Empire carrying the minutes Molly Fitzpatrick had copied from the field notes of those cruisers for the Quickwater Log & Lumber Company. It pleased McSwasey, getting that stumpage in the Medicine River Valley when the Quickwater outfit wanted it; and when Jim hit him for a job as raft pilot the answer was yes. From then on, he was traveling a path bound to lead to success, unless he blobbed things terribly.

Not, however, an easy path. Quick, comparatively, yes; not easy. It took him through underbrush and into a swampy labyrinth, and before he was through he was floundering in quicksand, but he saved himself finally, although the price of deliverance was high. Too high, maybe, he sometimes thought.

But the future looked easy, that night he left McSwasey's Island and set up drinks for everybody in Rafferty's Saloon. He didn't get drunk, because he had a strong head for liquor, but he might have been a little drunk on the future, telling the boys he would own the river one of these days.

"Sure," they said, "sure you will, Jim," but they thought he was just another rooster flapping his wings.

He remembered how he felt that night, standing there with his boots apart, tossing down whiskey; the future could never have been as shining as it looked then. No doubt about it, he was too big for his britches that night. When he looked at Pat Rafferty behind the bar and at the saloon hangers-on and at the fancy girls from upstairs he thought they were no taller than cribbage pegs. He could see himself going on and on into the bright misty future; he'd run the whole Northwest some day; and Pat Rafferty would still be tending bar.

"Boys," he said, "have another round. I'll own me a senator some day and feed him peanuts like a pet monkey, and you can tell people Jim Buckmaster bought you a drink."

The fancy girls flocked around him, but in that mood he didn't even want a woman.

When he left the saloon it was past midnight, but instead of going to his lodging house he went for a walk. It was a fine March night, crisp and clear, with frozen slush crusty in the streets and patches of black ice on the sidewalks; and he went striding all over town, working off his excitement, thinking how it would be to pilot a log raft. He didn't know the river as well as a pilot should, but that didn't worry him: he'd hire Greasy Dick Cassidy as linesman, and the Grease could give him advanced training. That was the advantage in having authority and money at your disposal; you could hire brains.

Striding along through the sleeping town, he thought a lot about Caleb McSwasey, but about Mrs. McSwasey almost not at all. He should have known better; any time there was a woman in a situation, she needed thinking about, for any woman was a pool of power; or, putting it another way, of trouble. But the women he had known left him unprepared for Mrs. McSwasey. They all had their whims and surprises, but compared with her they were direct and uncomplicated. In any case, his had been mainly a world of men, and he didn't know then that the higher you climbed through the intricacies of capitalism the more women you met who wielded great power, one way or another.

*

Next day he left for Camp Seven, but the rest of that spring he was only marking time till he could float down the Mississippi piloting a raft. The weeks crawled, he was so impatient, and with his head full of plans he seemed distant and withdrawn to his crews, wrapped in the remoteness of authority. He was twenty-two years old that spring, almost twenty-three, with the sinewy body and sharp eyes of a fencer, and the quick reflexes; and he carried a level head on his shoulders. His was the best-run camp in the McSwasey & Zumwalt organization, the bunkhouse spic-and-span, oxen sleek, tools sharp, everything in its place, and his outfit was banking a record number of logs, but that was the result of past discipline, for now his thoughts were elsewhere. In the woods during the day when he selected trees to be cut, and notched them to indicate for the choppers the direction they should fall, and in the bunkhouse at night, dipping a goose quill and keeping his neat records, he was working automatically, almost.

April came, the snow slushing and the Medicine River thawing; the drive began. Those were busy weeks, herding the logs down the Medicine to the Chippewa, where they mingled with logs from other McSwasey camps. He was river boss that year, overseeing everything for the company, a responsibility that kept him in bateaux from daybreak to dark, and that robbed him of sleep, for you had to drive logs on the crest of snow water or you might find yourself stranded with the river dropping and thousands of the season's cut hung up; so when the drive plugged, as of course it always did, constantly, in small jams and large, he was right there at the trouble spot, giving orders, and using a cant hook himself in places of uncommon hazard. That was one thing about him, those river hogs used to say; he never ordered you to do anything he was afraid to do himself.

McSwasey visited the drive that spring, and—of all things—Mrs. McSwasey. Jim didn't much like that, a woman to distract his men. Somebody like Molly Fitzpatrick was one thing, because the boys didn't have to stare at her and imagine how she would look without her clothes; they knew that already; but you take a woman like Mrs. McSwasey, all frilled out like a plush race horse, she took their minds off their work. A man riding a log down a rapids might feast his eyes on her one second too long, and next thing the log might throw him and a boulder would crack his skull. Jim couldn't figure what McSwasey was thinking of, bringing the Missus to a drive.

He was polite to the McSwaseys, but he didn't waste much time with them. McSwasey was the big push, sure; but the way Jim figured it, if he spent a lot of time making jaw music with those two, his drive might hang up, and if that happened McSwasey would never think to blame himself, he'd blame Jim. So Jim just said hello, glad to see you, make yourselves to home; and then he plunged back into work. Friendly, you understand, but a drive wasn't any pink tea party. McSwasey hired a river boss to get those logs down to the booms, not to stand chinning.

Funny how he didn't tumble to the fact that Esperanza McSwasey had visited the drive just to see him. Oh, sure, he caught the excitement in her eyes when she looked him over, and sometimes she stood closer to him than necessary, and touched his sleeve, but most women perked up when he was around; he was used to that and given to ignoring it, unless the woman was a piece that appealed to him especially. Mrs. McSwasey didn't. She was a tasty little dish all right, but for some other man—her husband, for instance—not for him. In his experience you either wanted to go to bed with a woman or you didn't; and if you didn't, why waste your time? Well, he didn't want to, with Mrs. McSwasey; if she had been a saloon girl he would have passed her up and saved two bucks. And because she didn't attract him, it never occurred to him that he might attract her so powerfully. He should have known better; he should have known she was trouble ahead, and he was floating toward it.

The McSwaseys spent the night in a crude hotel at War Bonnet, and damned if the Missus didn't invite him to come have supper with them. He almost laughed in her face, he was so busy. If she had been anybody but the big push's wife, he would have said listen, girlie, I've got logs to drive, I eat on the run, girlie. What do you think a log drive is, a church sociable?

But since she was Mrs. McSwasey, he was real polite, saying that's nice of you, ma'am, but I've got me a river full of logs to keep out of mischief. Business before pleasure, ma'am.

He remembered how her face clouded; she put him in mind of a pouty child, standing beside her husband there on the bank of the Chippewa. But then she changed tactics and acted sad; he half expected her to edge closer and start twisting a button on his shirt; he wondered what her husband was thinking. But McSwasey wasn't an easy man to figure, standing there gray and battered by the years, head forward, mouth full of false teeth, jaw blocky, eyes on his wife, who looked young enough to be his daughter.

Jim was glad when they left for New Empire; he wouldn't have wanted McSwasey to get ideas.

On that entire drive he didn't drown a single man or have to dynamite a single plug; and after the last log was herded into the McSwasey & Zumwalt booms, there in the sloughs at the mouth of the Chippewa, and all the river pigs went poling in bateaux toward Read's Landing on the west side of the Mississippi, Jim did something odd: he steered clear of all the saloons strung along the river front, going instead to a lodging house where he hired a room. Then he inquired the way to the home of Greasy Dick Cassidy.

By that time it was dusk, a fine evening, with fireflies winking as he followed a path toward the bluffs. He stopped once and looked back at the river, smooth as dark glass tonight and spattered with starshine. At the levee a couple of packets were tied up, their red and green lanterns mirrored in the water; and from the saloons and fancy houses he could hear singing and whooping. He regretted missing the good times celebrating the finish of the drive, but he had a career to think about. Another week and he'd be piloting a raft, and it scared him a little, for although he had bucked an oar for several seasons, an oarsman wasn't in it with a pilot, when it came to knowing the river. That river could be sweet one minute and mean the next; she could change tactics as fast as Mrs. McSwasey, that river could.

He walked on, coming to a sorry-looking cabin with a yard full of half-breed young ones chasing fireflies. On the stoop, Greasy Dick was a round-shouldered shadow.

"Grease," Jim said, "I'm a raft pilot now. How would you like to ship downriver as linesman?"

*

Greasy Dick Cassidy had one of those snap-turtle memories which never let go a fact; within his oval skull he carried knowledge about the Upper Mississippi which even the Almighty had forgotten. But the Grease had been stranded on shore for several years now, since Kelly told him he smelled like an Injun and beat him up.

"Jim," Greasy Dick said, that evening on the stoop, "I'd like to get off the bank, and that's sure. But how about Kelly? Will he be bucking an oar?"

"Maybe," Jim said. "That Kelly's a good rooster. But you ain't afraid of Kelly."

"Damned right I'm afraid of him, Jim. He busted me up something fearful. He told me to stay off the river. A good breeze come along, he said, and he could smell me ten miles away."

"Don't you fuss about Kelly," Jim said. "I'll cool him off. I want you for linesman."

As usual, he got what he wanted, and that very evening his higher education began. Next day it continued, and next week and next month and all through that season, and through the season following.

In the Grease, Jim had an accurate, tobacco-chewing reference library, and a tutor as well. No crotchet or whim of running water could surprise Greasy Dick; with the vagaries of log rafts he was well acquainted. Mile by mile, for the eight hundred odd miles between Read's Landing and St. Louis, he remembered every frog-pond and inlet, every crossing, every bluff, every crow's nest and dead cottonwood, every stretch where the river flowed among islands so sinuously and bewilderingly that a pilot might mistake a bayou for the main channel and end up with his raft in thin water. And he knew also what he didn't know, and what no pilot running eight hundred miles of river could ever know: how to navigate the Rock Island Rapids below Le Claire, and the Keokuk Rapids below Montrose. That was a specialist's job; and it was Greasy Dick's advice, earnestly given and scrupulously followed, that Jim should always hire a standing pilot to navigate those treacherous chains of rock and swirl. Elsewhere, the Grease and Jim pooled their experience and judgment, and floated countless feet of pine to St. Louis without losing a log. But it wasn't easy.

"A log," Greasy Dick said once, "has the disposition of an alligator, and a lady alligator at that. She wants to do what she wants to do, and it's never what you want. And a log raft is like harnessing ten thousand of them alligators together and swimming them down a river that's all woman with a knife in her stocking. The feller that thought of rafting logs should be swapped for a polecat, and the polecat shot."

Harnessing the logs took place in the network of sloughs clustered about the mouth of the Chippewa. Over there, in the McSwasey & Zumwalt rafting works, men shuttled the logs from the great storage booms into canal-like waterways enclosed by pilings and squared timbers. Using lash poles and lock downs and plugs, the fit-up crews stitched the logs together into units called strings, each sixteen feet wide and five hundred feet long, with a sweep at either end. Then the strings were floated into the Mississippi, lined up side by side, and coupled together with crosslines and diagonals; and after being equipped with a snubbing works, with shanties for the crew, with grub, with snatch poles, with endless coils of lines, with handspikes and axes and all the other tools of a rafting kit, the big float was ready to start south.

Jim never liked to think what might have happened, if he had set off downriver with his brains alone to pilot his first raft; they might have grounded that first day at Devil's Gut, for the channel narrowed there more than he had remembered, owing to the building up of a sandbar. But Greasy Dick advised getting a shore-hold, a mile upstream from the Gut, and splitting the raft into strings and floating those through one by one.

"You run the Gut with a full raft," he said, "and it would be like jamming a catfish down a minnow's throat."

It was Greasy Dick, too, who warned that the strings left above the Gut, and those which had run it and were moored below, should be closely guarded, for a rash of log piracy had been erupting along the river. It had started last fall, after Jim had gone back to the woods; Greasy Dick had been muttering about those damned pirates ever since he signed on as linesman. Now he was emphatic.

"On the eighth of last November," he said, "T. C. Howe lost a string right here at the Gut. He'd got three strings through, but then it turned dark and he waited till morning to run the last one. Well, sir, in the morning it warn't there."

Other thefts had occurred. Last December a full raft owned by Smith & Warburton had been caught by freezing weather and left for the winter in the Winneshiek Bottoms; this spring it had vanished. Ramsay & Company had lost two strings at the mouth of the Bad Ax. A small operator named Caswell, floating three strings downriver with a short crew, had lost a string in broad daylight when he left it unguarded. And there were other instances, all up and down the river.

The Grease didn't know who the pirates were; maybe Bulldog Ryan's old crowd; maybe renegades from the Wisconsin River or the Black; probably it wasn't one gang but many little ones. A few men, working fast, could float a string into a bayou and cordell it back among the islands where even a pickerel couldn't find his way.

"Leastwise I couldn't," the Grease said. "I know a little bit about the main channel of this old crick, but back there—"

He gestured at the vastness of the river bottoms and shook his head. Jim asked who milled the stolen logs; Greasy Dick didn't know. Likely those pirates collected several strings and sold them to some marginal operator glad to buy at a discount; once a log was sliced into lumber, who could tell its origin? Or maybe they altered the brand marks stamped on the logs and sold their rafts to honest mills.

"Anyway," he said, "we'd best watch our strings."

Jim nodded; and McSwasey & Zumwalt never lost a foot of timber from one of his rafts. The following year, however, pirates stole a string from a McSwasey raft piloted by Dave Howells. And Caleb McSwasey didn't like that so well; he fired Howells. A man had to be careful, working for McSwasey & Zumwalt. So Jim was very careful, although not careful enough.

*

There were times in a man's life when everything seemed to be swimming along like a raft down an untroubled reach of river, the sky cloudless and the sun bright; times when all the girls were golden girls; when nobody watered your whiskey; when your money belt grew heavier and your spirits lighter; when other outfits offered you jobs; when everybody wanted to buy you a drink; when it was hello, Jim, good old Jim, glad to see you, Jim. Those two seasons piloting always merged in his memory as one of those times.

Well, at a time like that he guessed you'd best watch out. There was always nasty water ahead. Watch it, or you'd be running the Keokuk Rapids without a standing pilot. A check line would snap and clout you into the river and you'd forget how to swim. Somebody—God or Caleb McSwasey or somebody—would put dynamite into your pot of beans. Your whole life would come crashing about your ears, if you didn't watch it; maybe even if you did.

He watched it, during those two seasons, and it was a fine time. Four hundred a month from McSwasey, regular as the new moon. A few weeks' hard work, floating a raft down from Read's Landing, but still work that was enjoyable, with the river swishing past your raft like a silk petticoat, with tall summer clouds floating overhead, with autumn mornings when you wakened to thick mist, the oar handles dripping, and then presently the sun broke through and it was another fine day.

From Greasy Dick you learned to stand at the bow and decipher the secret lingo of the river: how riffles meant a sandbar; how crinkled water that looked like bobbing ducks was shallow; how water that flowed smooth and dark was deep. You learned to watch for snags and breaks and sawyers, and for mighty trees that had crashed and been swept out into mid-river and stranded there, a tangle of scum and flotsam; and to follow with your eyes the long scribbles of foam that rode the current as it flowed close to shore, gnawing at the bank, and then swung in a long diagonal toward some island it was building up and some day would tear down. You learned to pilot through rain-slant when the river was the color of dishwater, and through squalls of early snow in November when the lines would freeze at night, and through the freshets of spring when the current was swift and whirling, and somebody's farmhouse went rotating down the wide flood with chickens perched on the roof. You memorized landmarks, such as bluffs that looked like barns or castles; and little by little, in your very bones, you developed a sixth sense about rafts and the river, so that the tug of the current sent messages up from the logs to your brain, and presently you could run at night, a moonless night preferably, without shadows to alter the familiar contours of shore.

After a day on the river your lips and eyes felt wind-burned, and your body had a fine outdoors tiredness, and you were ravenous; and after supper, standing with your boots apart and a cigar in your fingers, hearing the trickle and gurgle of the current; and watching a yellow moon peeking over the eastern bluffs, you had the odd feeling that you were longer-legged and broader-shouldered and deeper-chested than ever before, as if all the vastness of sky and channel had made you grow to giant's stature.

There were times when you felt like the boss of the universe, standing on your raft, watching the awkward water birds flapping up from the shallows, seeing an island drifting by to larboard, with its thick under-brush and huge grapevines weaving among the trees, or watching a Dakota village on shore with the dogs barking and young squaws waving, or passing the clay-yellow mouth of the Missouri and heading toward a sawmill with a big sign: "McSwasey & Zumwalt Lumber Company, New Empire and St. Louis." You'd done it again; you'd brought down a raft; and that sign made you feel part of something pretty important, a far-flung organization with logging camps a thousand miles away, and booms in the Chippewa sloughs, and retail yards along the river, and a blocky man named Caleb McSwasey directing it all from a New Empire office.

After delivering your raft to the mill superintendent, and gathering together all the gear of your rafting kit, so that it could be shipped back to Read's by an upriver boat, you always took an evening of pleasure in the fine little old town of St. Louis. In those days you could buy anything you wanted in St. Louis, even happiness, because your happiness was a simple thing then. A few rolls of the dice; a few shots of tanglefoot; a girl to finger your biceps and brag on how hard they were: that was all you asked. That, and to be known as Jim Buckmaster, the rootenest, tootenest pilot on the Upper Mississippi. When you came shouldering into Sally McGuire's bar, old Sally would take one look at you and yell: "Back from the bar! Back from the bar, you frill-shirted dandies! Here comes Jim Buckmaster!"

Those were sweet days, those days on the river.

After a night or two of pleasure, you rounded up your crew and loaded them aboard an upriver packet, maybe carrying some rooster over your shoulder like a grain sack, if he was too drunk to walk. Going back to Read's Landing, you lived high, eating in a gilded dining saloon, getting a shave and haircut and a dash of bay rum from the boat's Negro barber, walking the decks with a cigar, laughing at the river when the old boat steamed along through spots where your raft had had a bad time. But maybe you made a mistake there, laughing at the river; she was a woman. Still, it was not the river but another woman who got you tangled up in trouble; a woman named Esperanza McSwasey.

And you never knew what was happening to you, that was what galled you, later. You went along about your business, piloting rafts for two seasons, spending the intervening winter on a timber-cruising operation for the company, never once wishing that Esperanza McSwasey's pretty slippers were lined up under your bed; but all during that year-and-a-half trouble was gathering behind your back. You heard about it afterward when it was too late, and you were flabbergasted. Damn! A woman could get a man into more trouble than he could get out of.

*

When trouble hit he felt like a boy whipped for something he never did, for actually he saw Mrs. McSwasey only infrequently during those months piloting. Now and then, on his way upriver, he stopped in New

Empire between boats, to confer with Caleb McSwasey in his office, and sometimes she came there, moving gracefully in her summer gown of cool cambric, a sunshade dangling from her wrist, her smile a white flash in her Spanish-colored face, her voice musical, her handshake firm and warm, her French water and sweet powders and freshly-ironed petticoats filling that place of business with a scent delicate and alluring.

"Why, Mr. Buckmaster," she always exclaimed, "what a surprise!"

Only it wasn't a surprise. She knew he would be there. But she didn't know that her husband knew that she knew. It all came out later, after the deadfall had been sprung: how McSwasey had told the nigger woman, Lilith, to tell his wife, casually, that Jim Buckmaster was expected in town this morning. Looking back on those days, Jim could see that McSwasey had been a man with all the puppet-strings in his fingers. Half-sitting there on the table edge, gray hair rumpled, a cigar cocked up from his thick mouth, the wall-map of Wisconsin looming behind him in great squares of lake-blue and spruce-green, watching his wife and his raft pilot, he must have been smiling coldly to himself and thinking them simpletons. He had wanted to throw them together to see how they would act: it all came out.

Well, so far as Jim could remember, he never gave McSwasey any call for jealousy, except by being alive and young and wearing britches. He took Mrs. McSwasey's hand when she offered it, sure, but he never issued any bedroom invitations, by word or glance.

"Morning, ma'am," he said, keeping his handshake impersonal and his face expressionless.

She was always vivacious, there in the office, babbling sweetly, flashing swift and inviting looks with her eyes, patting her husband's shoulder as if he were some old bear that she had tamed, fingering the stacks of reports on the table; and sometimes when she moved toward the door she would halt abruptly and turn, so that her skirts swirled and rustled like a dancer's with castanets.

"Good-by," she would say winningly, to the room at large.

And for a fragment of time, as she turned again, languidly, her bright mouth would wear a smile like a riddle, and her glance would sweep toward Jim, standing there big and uncomfortable in his cheap store suit, bought ready-made in St. Louis.

How could he have known that such vivacity was not her normal behavior, and that it alone would have roused McSwasey's suspicions? He'd never seen her except when he was around to get her excited, had he?

And so far as that went, how could McSwasey have known she meant nothing to him? He could hardly have said, "Captain, that wife of yours is quite a stepper, but she leaves me dead as a wet firecracker. Hell, Captain, I wouldn't buy her kind at a dollar a cord delivered and stacked."

Being jealous and touchy where his wife was concerned, McSwasey might have been a little put out at talk like that.

During all his time as a raft pilot, Jim was never alone with the Missus except one afternoon; and even then, as it transpired later, you could hardly call it being alone, for McSwasey had set up a system of espionage among his servants. That was early in October during his second season piloting, a day of drizzle with the river as gray as the clouds. About two that afternoon Jim stepped ashore at New Empire from the northbound steamboat *Esperanza,* a fine swift packet, built at Cincinnati and put into service that summer, the first boat owned by McSwasey & Zumwalt. The big push was mighty proud of that boat, plying the river in the Saints' Trade, as the run between St. Louis and the Falls of St. Anthony was called; and Jim knew he would be questioned as to the behavior of her crew, and whether the coffee served in the dining saloon was too weak, and whether the Negro band played off-key, for McSwasey was a sharp-shooter for details.

Autumn was in the air that afternoon, as Jim walked north along Front Street toward the retail yard and home office of McSwasey & Zumwalt. A couple of more trips rafting and the season would be over, for McSwasey didn't like to run his floats so late as to be caught by a freeze. Jim's plans for the winter were uncertain, although he supposed McSwasey would want him to go landlooking again. Fine; for while the pay couldn't touch his salary as pilot, still it all added up to experience in the lumber industry. There were big opportunities in landlooking, if a man happened to forget about honesty being the best policy. Jim had never forgotten, and wasn't likely to; still, in idle moments, he couldn't help daydreaming about the killings to be made. You could, for instance, landlook a tract of rich pine but report to McSwasey that it was too measly for cutting. Then you could sell your minutes to another company, or buy in that pine yourself. But a man would be a deadhead to grab an easy ten or fifteen thousand, only to get himself blacklisted by every timber operator.

Reaching the corner of Front and Chicory Streets, he noticed a brougham pulled up outside McSwasey's office. And Dexter Yarlow, the coachman, all rigged out in a scarlet and yellow uniform, with glazed black boots and a plug hat, shuffled into the drizzle from the building entrance with the information that Mistah McSwasey was at home, sick in bed, and wished Mistah Buckmaster to come.

"What's wrong with him?" Jim asked.

"Caught himself a colt. Like I'm fixin' to do, out in this wet rain."

Jim had never ridden in a carriage as luxurious as that brougham, with its resilient springs and glass doors and goatskin upholstery; stretching out his legs in that snug interior, with the raindrops tapping the roof, he could see there were advantages in being as rich as McSwasey, with the money pouring in from logging camps and sawmills and lumber yards and now from a steamboat. A good thing, he guessed, he'd gone to work for McSwasey & Zumwalt at fifteen and had stuck with them, for whatever McSwasey touched turned to money, and he expanded his operations constantly: working for an outfit like that, a man learned all the quirks of the lumber business. And as the carriage crossed the bridge to the island, and followed the road among shining foliage, Jim wondered idly about the Zumwalt of the partnership: who the hell was he?

It was *Herr* Zumwalt's daughter, although he didn't know her as such, who greeted him at the front door, with a vivid smile and a rustling of silk.

"I'm *so* glad to see you," she said, prolonging the handshake. "It has been a long time and I have thought about you a great deal."

"Thank you, ma'am. How's the mister?"

"Ooo, he caught a very hard cold. He is upstairs in bed."

She didn't, Jim thought, appear much worried about her husband's condition. Gliding along the hall, smiling over her shoulder, she led him toward the back drawing room, where, she said, he must have hot tea, lest he too catch cold after the rain. Lady, he told her, he didn't catch cold that easy; besides, hadn't he better go upstairs and see the push? She shook her head emphatically and spoke in a low voice.

"Not now. He is asleep. It would make him very angry to be wakened."

Well, what could a man do?

The leaf-brown carpet cushioned his feet, and the drawing room with its gold wallpaper and rich blue draperies was snug and dry when he eased himself onto the gold sofa facing the marble fireplace. Flames crackled there, reflecting themselves in polished rosewood and in the sparkling crystal of the chandelier with its pendants shaped like grape clusters. Hands on knees, knowing how that bull felt in the china shop, Jim sat regarding two old acquaintances: those busts of Julius Caesar and Claudius perched on blue marble columns. Friends of Sophronicus Gentry, McSwasey had said, on that windy March evening a year-and-a-half ago. Jim wondered what kind of company Judge Gentry traveled in, to make friends with roosters like that.

After pulling a bell rope, Mrs. McSwasey rustled over and sat beside him on the sofa, and even though she wasn't his kind of sawlog, he could understand how a man with a different taste in women might find her attractive. She was wearing gold silk today, hued to her hair, the bodice tight, the skirt lavish. A blue velvet belt encircled her fine waist, and when, in defiance of ladylike etiquette, she crossed one knee over the other he could see a blue slipper and a pretty ankle in a gold silk stocking with blue clocks. As they talked, she kept twisting that foot in slow circles, so that the warm light from the fire shifted tantalizingly on the stocking.

Not a great distance separated them, there on the sofa; he could smell her fragrance and get a close look at her face. It was striking, he could see that, with its smooth coppery-beige skin, its black eyes thickly-fringed

611

with black lashes, its crisp and pretty ears with their turquoise earrings; but something in that face bothered him, as if the races that produced it were still at war there. She was part Injun, anybody could see that, and Jim distrusted breeds. The cheekbones were high, Injun-like; and the sweep of jaw could have been Injun; but he had never seen a mouth like hers on an Injun. It was wide and full and probably warm for kissing, but the ends were too long. Slyness lingered in those mouth-ends, and maybe cruelty. Bothered him. Give him a full-blooded Injun every time.

Still, he felt half apologetic about not wanting to bed down with the Missus, although he reckoned McSwasey would like it just as well that he didn't. But when you were a man, and a lady swished her skirts your way, you felt called on to do something about it. Ordinary politeness. But damn, he just didn't want to touch the Missus any more than he wanted to touch a glitteringly beautiful snake.

When the tea-tray came, and was placed on the buhl table inlaid with ormolu and mother-of-pearl, Jim looked over the maid, a big, healthy, blond-headed Swedish girl, and he thought she was like wind off a lake, brisk and clean, compared with Mrs. McSwasey. With a girl like that, he'd start logging at a minute's notice. He was sorry when she left the room.

*

The tea cups were eggshell-thin and held scarcely more than a swallow; Jim went back for several refills; and he couldn't help contrasting those cups with the big thick ones in logging camps. Up there in the woods, and on the river, everything was heavy, crude and uncomplicated, when compared with this room and this woman. But something warned him there were hazards here too; he'd better watch it. It would never do to give Mrs. McSwasey an inkling that he didn't like her. So he smiled, and when she chanced to brush against him, or touched his hand, he didn't yank back. In those days women were only recreation with him, and he didn't pretend to understand them, but one thing he did know: the unforgivable insult was to let a woman suspect you had no interest in bedding with her. Even with the sleaziest saloon girl he was courteous in that regard.

"Mr. Buckmaster," Mrs. McSwasey was asking, "would you do something for me?"

He smiled; and Molly Fitzpatrick had been right; it was a sweet smile.

"Would you let me call you Jim?"

The ice was thinning; next thing, God damn it, she would be fingering his ear or something, and piloting him toward bed. He said:

"Well, now, lady, that's my name."

"And would you call me Esperanza?"

"Sure," he said. "Sure I will, lady."

"You're sweet," she said, touching his hand.

"Thank you, ma'am."

Her voice took on a conspiratorial tone.

"But we must be careful, Jim. Never call me Esperanza when Caleb is around. He is a very jealous man."

"With a wife like you, I don't blame him."

The words slipped out of his mouth before he thought; and for a second, while she tested the cutting edge of that two-edged compliment, her eyes flashed dangerously. Jim smiled, and made his face look as if he didn't know a pike pole from a crank auger. Then her eyes softened, and her voice was a kitten's purr.

"Thank you, Jim."

"Don't mention it, lady."

"You were going to call me Esperanza," she said, with a mock pout.

"Yes, ma'am. That's what I meant to say. Esperanza."

"Ooo," she murmured, snuggling against him, "I like to hear you say my name. You have a wonderful voice, Jim. So deep."

The room was getting warm; he could feel sweat on his forehead; he ran a finger around under his collar. Damn it, women were worse than a shaking bog; take one step and you were in up to your ears. They were not human, women weren't, Greasy Dick Cassidy had said once; most of the world's troubles, he said, could be traced to the way men went around considering women human, when actually a man would be safer walking up to a timber bear unarmed.

"Jim," she was murmuring, "remember that afternoon you first came here? The wind was blowing and you were in such a hurry to find Caleb. That was a wonderful afternoon, Jim. And then you came to supper . . . I wish we could see each other oftener."

"Sure," he said, "sure. That would be fine."

"I wish . . . well, maybe I'd better not tell you what I wish."

He had known, damn it to hell, some fast workers, but this little hustler made them seem slow as a thaw on the north side of a hill. And sitting there with the sweat leaking from his pores, he had a strange notion that they were being watched, or at least listened to. The door to the hall stood open, and there were double doors in the east wall, leading to the front drawing room; somebody could be standing beyond them, listening. McSwasey? Hardly. He couldn't imagine the big push doing that. That feeling of eavesdroppers must be just his woods caution working overtime. But he wished he could get out of here.

Mrs. McSwasey was speaking again about the frightful jealousy afflicting her husband, telling how once in St. Louis she went to a museum to improve her mind, and he followed her, and accused her of flirting with two soldiers. She hadn't, she said, even spoken to them; she had hardly, really, been aware of their existence; but Caleb had flown into a jealous rage and threatened to firebrand her face if ever she were untrue to him. Had Jim ever heard of such a thing?

"Yes, ma'am, a few times. Injuns do it to their squaws, when a lodge-poling won't make them behave. But the usual thing, a Chippewa favors biting off the squaw's nose."

She laughed suddenly and said that was one thing she needn't fear, for Caleb's teeth were false. And Jim smiled, but he didn't like the way the conversation kept going. First she had managed to imply that they were in a conspiracy together, calling each other by their first names; now they were making fun of her husband. A man could ruin his whole future with McSwasey & Zumwalt, at the rate things were going.

He stood up, catching sight of himself in the mirror above the fireplace; it was framed in gold, and topped by an urn from which festoons looped to the beaks of pheasants. Within that artificiality, his face looked long-jawed and practical and not, he noted, the least bit flustered. He pointed to the gilt clock on the mantel.

"Is that the right time, lady?"

She supposed so; Caleb was a great one to go round winding clocks.

"I'd best be going up to see him," Jim said. "I've got to catch the six o'clock boat upriver."

* * *

Going with her along the lower hall and up the stairs, he felt as out of place as a stag in a palace, what with the population of statuary and busts, and the lush carpets, and the dark oil paintings in massive frames, and the sweeping tapestries, and the urns and lacquered vases. But he didn't let those tulipwoods and friezes and San Domingo mahoganies over-awe him.

At the top of the stairs Mrs. McSwasey clutched his arm.

"He will be jealous," she whispered, "if we go in together. It's that door. Good-by."

And she lifted her skirts and scampered down the stairs.

He thought her logic faulty and her play-acting silly. God damn it, she was a fool. And he remembered a woods adage about never going to bed with a fool. It should be expanded, he guessed, to include never sitting on a sofa with a fool.

Entering the door she indicated, at the southeast end of the hall, he found himself in a private sitting room pleasantly colored in lavender and soft French gray. McSwasey wasn't there; just more gold mirrors and gilded walnut and ormolu and crystal. Jim coughed.

"That you, Jim?" McSwasey called, from beyond a door in the west wall. "Come on in."

It was a bedroom of shell-pink and champagne-yellow, a woman's room, the dressing table of ladylike satinwood, with a shield mirror decorated with rosebuds. The silk draperies at the windows were candy-pink; the glowing fireplace was of cream-yellow Italian marble, with chiseled cupids. Propped up in bed, chewing a cigar, a two-days' growth of whisk-

614

ers frosting his face, maps of timberlands strewed about him, McSwasey looked like a grizzled old bear caged up in a silken crib.

"Where the hell you been?" he asked.

Jim thought it best not to lie.

"Downstairs. The Missus fixed me up some tea. She said you were asleep."

"Asleep, hell. When I caught this cold the doc gave me laudanum and I slept twenty-two hours. Haven't been sleepy since."

"How do you feel?" Jim asked.

"My nose is sore, from blowing it. It's just a hard cold. No worse than a dose of clap. Sit down, Jim, and make camp. Any trouble with the raft?"

"Smooth as a greased tomcat," Jim said.

"Come up on the *Esperanza?*"

Jim nodded.

"How'd you like her?"

That boat, Jim said, being sure to mention the word boat, was the sweetest-handling packet on the river; he had visited the pilothouse, and had taken the wheel for a minute. The food was first rate too; the waiters courteous; the barber expert; the band laudable; the schedule maintained to the minute, virtually.

"Did she do any racing?" McSwasey asked.

"No, sir, she just steamed along."

"Good. I won't have any damned racing. Your engineer gets excited and ties down the safety valve, and next thing your boilers go and your boat's in the air in a million pieces. That *Esperanza*'s a sweet one. I'd hate to lose her."

"I don't blame you."

"Any son of a bitch that tried any tricks with her, I'd . . . Well, we won't go into that."

Jim didn't say anything. McSwasey sat chewing his cigar, eyes slitted, hair belligerent. Finally he said:

"That boat's a gold mine, Jim. If you want to get rich, build you a boat and haul movers to Minnesota. And cut yourself a few trees and slice them into lumber and sell it to the movers. By God, it's better than freighting to Santa Fe and hauling back beaver plews. I'll have me another boat next year. She's building already, and I've named her the *Harmony*. That was my mother's name, back east. I was the black sheep of the family, Jim, and maybe I still am, but by God that black sheep has got gold fleece."

Jim smiled.

"Captain," he said, "that's the kind of talk I like. One of these days I'll have me a boat and race you to Pig's Eye Bar and come in first."

"Like hell you will," McSwasey said. "You start racing me and I'll

615

stoke the fires with lard. And if the engineer don't tie down the safety valve, I'll shoot the son of a bitch."

"That's a deal, Captain," Jim said.

McSwasey removed his cigar and sat regarding its soggy butt, then cast it into a spittoon by the bed. A shred of tobacco clung to his protruding lower lip.

"Jim," he said, "I'm working on a better deal than that. I can't talk about it now, but when it's cooked I'll let you know and cut you in."

"Landlooking?" Jim asked.

"Better than that. And bigger. It may surprise you, and you may not want in. It's the chance of a lifetime for a young fellow, but it's ticklish. It needs careful handling. You might end up with a bullet through your shirt pocket."

"And I might not," Jim said, smiling.

"I thought you'd say that, Jim. I figured you'd be the man to handle it. I'll let you know. Maybe I'll come up to Read's Landing, if the doc will let me. When will you tie loose from there with your next raft?"

"End of the week, I reckon, if the fit-up crews have her ready."

"All right, Jim, I may be up. I don't say it's a safe deal, but it's opportunity. It's a short cut to the big bank rolls, if you don't wake up dead."

"Dead?" Jim asked. "What's that?"

McSwasey grinned.

"I'll be up there, Jim. Now let's have a drink."

He got out of bed and went to the sitting room, returning with a bottle and glasses. In his nightshirt he looked faintly comic and a little pitiful, with his freckled legs and his bare feet with their skewed toes. Around the middle he had taken on weight; no longer did red pepper show in his salt-colored hair; on the back of his thick neck there were wrinkles like the cracks in dried mud. He looked domestic and settled deep into the rut of his fifties, not like a man who had adventured rashly in the South and the West. But his jaw was pugnacious, and when he poured the whiskey his hands were steady and strong-looking, with their thick palms and short heavy fingers.

"Good luck," he said.

But he didn't mean it.

＊

Against the windows the light had changed from pearly gray to taupe, and the drizzle had turned to a monotonous downpour, cold and autumnal, when Jim left that bedroom and made his way along the upper hall through pale candlelight and goblin shadows. He should have felt elated, after McSwasey's talk about a big, mysterious deal, but melancholy drifted through his mind, perhaps because of the heavy weather, or the sadness leaking from all those Florentine tapestries and objects of art, so old and loaded with memories of ancient intrigues.

Lamps burned in the lower hall and in the front parlor, but Mrs. McSwasey was not to be seen. Just as well. Better. Hell with her. It was her fault, likely, that he was in the dumps; fending off her advances had not been an ideal prelude to his meeting with McSwasey. Well, he'd feel better once he had another whiskey and a hot supper on the upriver boat and a night's sleep.

When he was in the vestibule, finding his hat, somebody called his name, and he saw a fat nigger woman waddling along the hall, a child in her arms. She said he'd best wait inside out of the rain, till Dexter Yarlow drove from the stable with the carriage. Suddenly he didn't want to spend another minute in this house; he wanted fresh air and solitude, so maybe he could figure why his talk with McSwasey had left him so unaccountably uneasy. But it would be a long walk to the levee through the rain.

"I'm Lilith," the woman said. "How you think Mistah McSwasey look?"

"He looked all right."

"I don't know, he look kind of peaked to me. Hope that cold don't go into his chest. He ain't as young as once. None of us is."

"He'll throw it off," Jim said.

"Sure hopes so. Mistah McSwasey mean a lot to me. Knowed him now getting on to twenty-five or thirty years. He took me to Taos once. We camped. I was a fine-looking gal in them days. Slim as a mink and just as lively. I ain't never been the same since he took me to Taos."

She cackled.

The child in her arms was blond and somber, but he smiled when Jim said hello.

"This here," Lilith said, "is young Mistah McSwasey. Heinrich von Zumwalt McSwasey, she name him, after his great-grandpa back there in Russia or somewhere. She say he a general. Me, I don't know. Never met the gentleman. But Mistah Zumwalt always say the same, that his papa was a general."

"Zumwalt?"

"That's right. Miss Esperanza's papa. He owned me, back there in Santa Fe. Bought me young and kept me bred, that's what he done. I give him the most scrumptious little niggers you ever did see. But they was all sold. Even the twins, all sold. I didn't mind so much, 'cepting that boy Wisdom. He was my first young one, and he was chuck plumb full of fine Virginia blood, same as me, but Mistah Zumwalt sell him. I cried like I was peeling onions. Never did know what happen to that boy. Mistah Zumwalt sell him, but I think Miss Esperanza put him up to it, that's what I think. I raised her up like my own daughter, only she wasn't. She used to take after me with a switch something awful. Twigged my naked meat, that's what she done. Man,

I can feel them whippings yet. But not for a long time now, 'cause I live in Wisconsin and I'm free. But all that freedom don't do me no good. I'd never leave Mistah McSwasey. I'd do anything for Mistah McSwasey. Mistah Zumwalt was all right, 'cepting he talk too much about chasing spiders. But Mistah McSwasey, he's my man."

The front door opened and Dexter Yarlow, wearing oilskins, said the carriage was ready. It was quite dark now; the carriage lamps were lighted. Dexter shuffled through the puddles and opened the brougham door. Jim turned up his collar and ducked through the rain. When he entered the carriage he found Mrs. McSwasey sitting there.

*

In his stateroom on the *General Taylor* he passed a restless night, his consciousness so thinly-coated with sleep that whenever the boat stopped at a landing he stirred and listened to the shouts of roustabouts and warehouse clerks coming through the darkness and the rain; and once about 3:00 A.M. at a wood landing he got up and stood looking out at the flaring light from basket torches gleaming on the skin of huge Negroes tossing chunks of hickory from the stacked cordwood on shore to the deck.

He hadn't touched her, except to take her hand when he said good-by. That brougham, intimate and secluded, fragrant with her perfume, had been designed for love, but he had refrained. It troubled the Old Adam in him, for the Old Adam had not only no conscience, as reputed, but no ambition in the lumber business, and although Mrs. McSwasey was not Jim's kind, yet ultimately nearly anything in skirts was the Old Adam's kind, and in a dark carriage all women looked alike. Still, he hadn't touched her, although she had touched him, with hand and silken leg and warm arm. A situation demanding tact!

As an excuse for being in the carriage she said she had an errand in town; did he mind if she rode along? Not at all, glad to have her. Had Caleb, she asked in a whisper, acted jealous? What could he say? Whether yes or no, the implication would be the same: that James Lorne Buckmaster and Esperanza Zumwalt McSwasey were in a lovers' conspiracy. Damn. Women managed those things as easy as breathing.

If she had been more his type, and some other man's wife, he might have enjoyed that sense of conspiracy, for the human race, although forever groaning about its troubles, was much given to seeking yet further troubles, provided they were interwoven with love or money; but as it was, after having listened to McSwasey hinting about a chance of a lifetime, he certainly didn't propose to ruin his career by ruining Mrs. McSwasey. Still, since women, unlike businessmen, enjoyed being ruined, he knew he must employ great tact in refraining from ruining her.

Had he succeeded? God knew. If not, he had made an enemy. But he believed he had succeeded; saying good-by, she had squeezed his hand.

He returned to his bunk, there in the stateroom, and lay listening to the throb of engines and the creaking of the walking beam, remembering that dark carriage with the rain tapping the roof. Not wanting to engage her in love, he had engaged her in that second great passion of women, talking: was it true, he had asked, that as Lilith had said she was the daughter of one Zumwalt, resident of Santa Fe? Oh, yes, it was true. And was this Zumwalt the same person who was a partner in McSwasey & Zumwalt? Yes, although Caleb had been talking lately about buying out his share of the business. And her grandfather was a general? Oh, indisputably! And where had she met Caleb? In Santa Fe; he had, it seemed, fallen madly in love, swept her off her feet, insisted that she return with him to St. Louis and marry him. She had been only fifteen; she had not known what she was doing. If she had it to do over, she would refuse to marry Caleb, except for one thing. Could he guess what that was? No, he was a poor guesser. Well, she said, by marrying Caleb and living in New Empire, she had met a certain man. And she had fallen in love. Desperately. Love was consuming her. Could he guess the man's identity?

"I reckon," he said slowly, "I'd best not try."

It could have meant anything. And women in love believed what they wished.

"Ooo!" she exclaimed, and squeezed his hand and snuggled closer.

Jim kept thinking of Caleb back there in the bedroom; it was time, perhaps, to change the subject. He said:

"Say, I met your son there in the hall. He's a fine boy."

"Thank you, Jim," she said, without enthusiasm. Maybe her son wasn't her type.

"He's got your hair," Jim said, "but I couldn't see much of his father in him."

"Couldn't you?"

Clearly, the love which was consuming her was not mother love.

"It sure keeps raining," Jim said.

She said she liked the rain; it was romantic.

At the levee, where the upriver boat was preparing to tie loose, he thought he'd never get away from her; she kept begging him to remain another few seconds. When would she see him again? What would he think if she wrote him a letter? This had been a wonderful afternoon for her; had it been wonderful for him?

The boat whistled; he reached the gangplank just as they were taking it up. He went directly to the bar and ordered whiskey and tossed it down neat and ordered more.

*

In New Empire the following Friday evening another man, Caleb McSwasey, boarded another boat, the *Greek Slave,* and passed a restless night on his way to Read's Landing. Contrary to Lilith's fears, and his wife's hopes, his cold had not turned into pneumonia, but it had drained his energy and left his feet leaden; his game leg ached. He couldn't sleep, there in his stateroom, till long after midnight; slumped in his chair, sometimes kneading the muscles of his right calf, he sat drinking whiskey and smoking cigars, rehearsing what he would say to that son of a bitch Buckmaster.

He would have preferred action to words; action with a knife or a derringer or a sock loaded with a rock. But America had grown namby-pamby, sheriffs having developed foolish prejudices against a man's protecting his wife from her own silly passions; and he had grown old —well, older, fifty-four last April—and he was not at all sure this rooster Buckmaster could be heaved into eternity as easily as another menace, that bastard Andrew J. Gentry. If you sneaked up behind Buckmaster, he might whirl and slug you.

Well, there were more ways than one to skin a bear. You could match your wits against his brawn. You could dig a pit and rig up a deadfall, baiting it with promises so extravagant that the ambitious son of a bitch could not resist.

For a long while now, ever since that evening Buckmaster had eaten supper in your home, and your wife sat there in a low gown, all titted out like a fifty-dollar whore, and hung on his words, you had known that sooner or later you would have to deal with the big rooster. You did not propose to father another son by proxy. Lilith, who was a good reliable nigger, had made regular reports on your wife's temperature, which had spurted upward as soon as she laid eyes on the bastard, and had remained high. She was, she had confided to Lilith, in love. Well, the little slut would get over it, once Buckmaster was put away: women had an admirable practicality in those matters.

All during the past year-and-a-half, you had been aware of a scheme for getting rid of the bastard trying to coalesce in your mind. Fire Buckmaster: that had been one such thought. Not good enough. If you fired him, he'd only get another job or strike out for himself, and he would be free to meet your wife in some hotel.

Finally, the other afternoon, when you lay sick, and downstairs the bastard was probably pawing her bare bosom, a really first-rate scheme floated into your consciousness. It had to do with log piracy, and its only drawback was a barefaced boldness: would the wife-stealing son of a bitch fall for it? Maybe, if you presented it skillfully enough. After all, there actually were a few log thieves on the Upper Mississippi. They were a pest and a nuisance, but certainly they did not even remotely threaten to turn the balance sheet of your company from black ink to red. But Buckmaster didn't know that. Tell him they were making alarming inroads into your profits and the profits of every other lumber operator; tell him there had been a meeting of all lumbermen to see what could be done to bag the thieves, and that the meeting had appointed you to clean up the gang, and that you were appointing him to do the job, and that if he succeeded you would reward him lavishly. If he accepted that commission, you would have him. There were details to be worked out, but you would have him.

Hire him killed, maybe, and let out word that he had been hunting log thieves and they had done the job? No; too risky; you didn't want to lay yourself open to blackmail from the hired killer. Kill him yourself? Better; but damn it, he was big and fast, and if your gun misfired or your flung knife missed its target he would be on you like a lynx. Damn it, this was going to take some doing.

But basically it was an excellent scheme, and after he left your bedroom the other afternoon, and rode to the levee with—and for all you knew, on—your wife, the ultimate refinement of that project came to you. That was why you were in a stateroom of the *Greek Slave,* traveling toward Read's Landing. You hoped you could present the matter in such a way that the bastard's mouth would water like a beaver's smelling castor, and that like such a beaver he would plunge toward the trap. If he didn't—if he saw through what you were up to and laughed in your face and announced he intended having your wife—you believed you would pull your derringer and put a hole through his heart. You could plead self-defense. But that would be troublesome as all hell, and you might end up dangling from a limb, for he was popular along the river and those roosters in Read's Landing would enjoy a lynching bee. If you escaped lynching, you could get out of it, probably, with a good lawyer and plenty of money. But you might not escape lynching.

You were a little drunk now, and pretty tired—your watch showed 1:00 A.M.—so you lay on your bunk and invited sleep by thinking pleasant thoughts, such as how he would look with a derringer hole in his shirt. Risky, though, risky . . . The other scheme was best. Well, one thing: you weren't going to have Buckmaster or any other son of a bitch tickling your wife. She was yours, by God, yours to take what you wanted despite her biting and scratching; that only roused you more; you owned the little spit-cat the way you used to own nigger gals and damn it to hell anything you owned no other man could tit-paw and get away with it.

*

Next morning his breakfast digested inefficiently, because of his anger, and along toward noon, when he stood on the hurricane deck of the *Greek Slave,* cigar in mouth and carpetbag by his side, his alimentary system felt bloated; not since his trouble with that wife-stealing Andy Gentry had food lain so hard on his stomach. Well, he had cured himself by turning Andy into worm-fodder, and he would cure himself again. Meanwhile, he reckoned he'd better skip eating this noon.

It was a fine October morning, the river flowing blue under a deep blue sky, and autumn was a witch girl who had walked the bluffs at night and left everything burned scarlet and orange and lime-yellow and salmon-pink. Standing there in his tall gray hat, his linen crisply ruffled and his waistcoat canary-colored, he was remembering another October long ago when he and his bride left a steamboat at Flannigan's Landing and went canoeing up the Chippewa. His eyes softened at that memory, and a little ache hovered about his heart; and when he thought how he had been nine years younger then, and in love, and how he used to call her honeychild, and how she used to say she loved him, he was filled for a moment with sadness. But only for a moment; he took hold of himself. And although he knew it was illogical, he found himself blaming Buckmaster for all his marital woes, all his wife's tantrums and cat-scratching and calculated cruelty when she said he was a lecherous old man and that no, she didn't love him, she never had. He carried wounds on his soul, veteran that he was of connubial wars.

Far ahead, after the packet rounded a bend, he could see the windows of Read's Landing glittering on the west bank, and steamboats tied up at the levee, their chimneys sending forth smoke. Within his memory Read's had been nothing but a wide place between river and bluffs; now it was a cargo-breaking point, where freight was shifted from steamboats to pole-boats and dispatched up the Chippewa. The whole Northwest was booming, and he had got in on the ground floor. He thought of his brother Paul, still running that dinky store back in East Bainbridge, and of Florence Abbott who had married Malcolm Penwick, the pudgy bastard. Well, justice was not dead: the Penwick bank had gone bust, and the last he heard Malcolm was clerking for Paul. Served him right; served Florence right too, refusing to let him walk her home from meeting. Even in his present jealous stew, he was capable of a twinge of anger at Florence and Malcolm, for jealousy, like love, was infinite.

Read's Landing was gliding nearer; he could see the gaudy false fronts of saloons and sporting palaces, and the new Mississippi House, three stories tall and built of red brick, with its wrought-iron fancy work running around the roof. He could see pole-boats and skiffs and—what interested him most—a huge log raft tied up to the west bank a quarter of a mile below town. The *Greek Slave* steamed past it, close enough for a knife-toss, and from the height of the hurricane deck Caleb could look down on that raft and watch the roosters unloading barrels of salt meats and flour from a grocery wagon and rolling them toward the cook shanty. In the bright autumn sunshine he could make out the cook, Mike Hogan, with his red mustaches; and the yellow-headed chore boy; and Greasy Dick Cassidy, round-shouldered in a dirty undershirt; and he saw Buckmaster. A lot of man, that Buckmaster. A lot of long-legged, booted, flat-bellied, big-shouldered, check-shirted male, damn his tomcatting soul to the devil.

622

Buckmaster looked at the packet and gave a wave. Caleb made himself smile and wave back. It nearly cracked his face, smiling, but he did it. But his eyes weren't smiling.

A few minutes later, when the gangplank was lowered, and he limped ashore and made his way along the wooden sidewalks toward the Mississippi House, he looked not unlike an old bull buffalo plodding along with head lowered and angry eyes. Clusters of men were standing on the sidewalk, and when they saw him coming they made way: he never swerved an inch. Not many men could have cleared a path for themselves in a town like Read's Landing by sheer prestige and inner toughness, but he was a big man in the Northwest.

His room in the Mississippi House was a cubby with walls of unpainted lumber, two hard chairs, a table, a bed with a shuck mattress. Pulling off his shoes, pouring himself bourbon and lighting a fresh cigar, he lay on the bed during the noon hour, deep in sullen meditation, asking himself whether he had underestimated Buckmaster's intelligence. Would the son of a bitch swallow all that bilge about log pirates? Well, he'd better.

Early that afternoon, somewhat rested but still troubled by an angry stomach, Caleb left the hotel and followed a tawny road south from town where milkweed stalks were tattered and burdock dusty. When he reached the raft he stopped on the bank, hearing the distant cawing of crows and the even more distant *hoo-hooing* of steamboat whistles; and when he picked his way down to the gangplank, where the lines were creaking as the raft swung gently with the current, he moved carefully, watching his footing, like any man not so young as he used to be. But damn it, he wasn't old; not in bed he wasn't.

Buckmaster saw him and came striding; and Caleb reminded himself savagely to act friendly; he smiled broadly, so that his eyes slitted nearly shut, and any pinpoints of hate were hidden.

"You don't look like you've ever been sick," Buckmaster said, when they shook hands. "How are you feeling?"

"I'm all right. Nothing wrong with me that being thirty years younger couldn't cure."

And as they stood talking, Caleb yearned as never before after his gone youth; if he were twenty-four again he wouldn't be piddling around with schemes to trap the bastard; he would pick a quarrel and kill him and be done with it. But he wasn't twenty-four; he was short of wind and his leg hurt; and Buckmaster's legs were long and hard-driving.

"Like to look over the raft?" the bastard was asking.

"I might," Caleb said; and he picked his way from log to log, watching sharp for Norwegian holes, those pockets of floating bark where the logs didn't fit tightly together and where a man might go into the water up to his crotch. Now and then, with his foot, he tested a crossline or an "A" line; once he said:

"Tight enough to play a tune on it."

"Thanks, Captain. When them fit-up crews coupled her together I was right on hand. I like to know how a raft I'm piloting is made."

Braggart!

"You're a good man, son," Caleb said. And then, with a dry throat, he added: "Remember what I mentioned the other day? Well, she's all set. It may surprise you. But if it's opportunity you want . . ."

Buckmaster smiled.

"I guess," he said, "me and you talk the same language."

Caleb looked deliberately around, as if making certain they were beyond eavesdroppers, but it was all part of the play-acting. In a low voice he said:

"Come to the Mississippi House and have supper. You'll hear about it then. It's big. It's the chance of a lifetime, for a young fellow. But for God's sake keep your mouth shut about it, or the fat will be in the fire."

"Why, Captain," Buckmaster said, "my tongue never knows what my brain is thinking, when I don't want it to. I'll be there."

Caleb nodded. "You poor simple bastard," he was thinking.

*

Throughout supper, Jim thought McSwasey seemed abstracted; he said little; and of course the big deal, whatever it might be, was not mentioned, for they ate boarding-house fashion at a long table with twenty pairs of ears ready to listen. They sat side by side, McSwasey wearing a napkin tucked under his blocky jaw, his burly shoulders sagging, his thick hands with their stubby fingers showing a few liver spots. After pouring his coffee into a saucer, and blowing on it, and quaffing it in one long draught, he rustled two cigars from his pocket, handed one to Jim, pinched the end off his, and lighted up from a nearby candle. Then he said:

"I've got a bottle upstairs, if you'd like a snifter."

Jim followed him through the lobby, noticing how coarse and unruly his gray hair looked, and how he was limping more than usual, and yet how powerful his body seemed, like a wrestler's. In his room, McSwasey uncorked a bottle of tanglefoot.

"Say when," he said.

"That should do," Jim said, when the whiskey had climbed to the glass-brim.

McSwasey filled his glass too, and lifted it.

"Luck," he said.

Then he sat on one of the straight chairs and kneaded the calf-muscles of his right leg.

"God damned leg's been giving me trouble tonight," he gruffed. "Sometimes I think that jackknife wasn't worth it."

624

He was scowling, his eyes looking like little blue marbles beneath their bushy and unwhitened red brows. His lashes had escaped graying too; they were reddish tan.

Finally he sat back, chewing his cigar, and his voice was low.

"These walls," he said, "ain't any too thick, and I don't want some son of a bitch listening. Can you hear me?"

"Sure," Jim said. "I've got ears like a rabbit."

McSwasey chewed his cigar some more; in profile his lower lip stuck out, and his nose looked bulbous and delicately-laced with violet veins.

"Jim," he said at last, "I've been watching you a long time. I've watched you chop and I've watched you bust jams. Your camps were always neat as a barracks, and your season's cut always went over quota. I took a chance and set you to piloting. Well, you never lost me a log, and from what I hear you're the meanest son of a bitch that ever floated a raft to St. Louis."

"Thanks, Captain," Jim said.

"Don't mention it, Jim. I wouldn't tell every rooster a thing like that, because it might go to his head, but a man as good as you are knows he's good, unless he's a damned fool, and you ain't. What I'm driving at is that I've got a whole passel of young fellows on my payroll, but not another mother's bastard of them is Jim Buckmaster. What do you want out of life, anyway, Jim?"

Jim didn't have to think long to find the answer to that one. He smiled.

"Money," he said, "that's what I want. Is there something else?"

"There might be," McSwasey said. "You never can tell, there just might. But nothing you can get your fingers into, like with money. Money's all right. I've never gone out of my way to dodge it, and I've tried not to dodge it in a lot of places. I've been on nigger deals in the South, and on fur deals in New Mexico. I've been on deals in Texas that scare me when I think about them now. Well, Jim, it was always the same. It was always money that made the mare go. It's muscle, money is, and the more you've got the more power you swing. A man can be ninety years old and ready for the wind to blow him away, but if he's got the money he's stronger than the Colossus of Rhodes."

"Who the hell is that?" Jim asked.

"Some rooster in the old country, I've never met him. It don't matter. What I'm saying is that a man with money can do anything. And there may be ways to make money faster than in the lumber business, but I don't know about them. You can buy one acre of stumpage for a dollar-and-a-quarter, and hook a hundred or maybe a thousand more. You can hire galoots to cut it who don't know a whore from a pork roast, and you can float them logs to your mills and sell the lumber at a whopping profit, because the prairies are filling up with stupid bastards who think they need a roof over their head. You can build steamboats and carry those bastards to wherever they're going, and next year you can haul their crop to market. You can buy up newspapers, like I bought me the *New Empire Chronicle* last summer, and the editors will sing your song because they're stupid bastards who think they're leading public opinion when all they're doing is crowing from on top of your manure pile. And when you've got the money and the newspapers, the politicians come wagging like pot-licking pups, and you give them your pot to lick. Pretty soon you can own the whole damned country, if you live long enough, and when you slip your lines some preacher who don't know a chicken's gizzard from a drumstick will say you did it all to build up Wisconsin and give jobs to the poor."

McSwasey made an uncouth noise with his lips, then took a long swig and reached over and kneaded his calf some more.

"God damned leg," he said. "Keeps this up and I'll chop off the son of a bitch." And he added, "Jim, I might as well come to the point. How would you like a quarter interest in McSwasey & Zumwalt?"

Jim always remembered that moment when he sat tipped back in his chair, glass in hand, staring at McSwasey. The room was quiet, but from outside he could hear a distant steamboat whistle and the sounds of Saturday night revelry in the streets. McSwasey had pulled up his pant leg now, and had crossed his right ankle over his left knee, and he sat kneading his calf deeply, scowling, his false teeth chewing his cigar.

"Did you hear me, Jim?" he asked.

"I reckon not, Captain. I reckon you didn't say what I thought. Maybe you'd best speak up."

McSwasey's stubby fingers gave his calf a final pinch. Then he thumped his right foot on the floor and shook down his pant leg.

"There, God damn you," he muttered. "That ought to hold you." And to Jim he said, "I'm offering you twenty-five percent of my company. What's the matter? Don't you want it?"

Jim gave a laugh then.

"Sure," he said. "Sure, I want it. But it looks like you've sized me up wrong. I've saved a few nickels, but not enough to buy in with you."

"It won't take money," McSwasey said. "Who said anything about money?"

Down the years it came back to him how he felt then, with McSwasey watching him with cold, shrewd eyes.

"I don't guess you mean it," Jim said.

"God damn it, Jim, of course I mean it. You think I'd shoot the breeze about a thing like that? I'm offering you a quarter interest in McSwasey & Zumwalt."

Things like that happened. Not often, but they happened. Not to you, but to somebody. You heard about them or read about them, how some big boss picked a likely young fellow and gave him stock in the business

Usually the big boss's daughter was involved, but McSwasey didn't have any daughters. Not any white ones, at least, or legal ones. Jim sat smiling, scratching his jaw.

"You heard all right, Jim. Twenty-five percent interest in the company. Just nod your head and it's yours."

All at once he believed his ears, it wasn't any joke, and he could remember how suddenly that room was a place of magic and dreams, everything better than life, like a saloon when a heap of money and chips lay on a poker table and you raised somebody and he threw down his cards and the pot was yours.

"Twenty-five percent?" Jim asked.

"Twenty-five, Jim. You heard all right."

"Make it thirty and it's a deal."

McSwasey broke out laughing.

"Son," he said, "you'll do. God damn it yes, you'll do. But it's twenty-five or nothing. Hell, you can cheat me out of the other five the first year."

Jim sucked in his breath and blew it out. Then he finished his whiskey. Then he said:

"All right, if you want to be small about it, I'm in. Now I need another snifter."

"Help yourself, son. When that's gone I've got more."

Jim remembered getting to his feet and refilling his glass and standing with one boot on a chair. The whiskey was working in his brain; he could see things in that room which weren't there. He could see pine forests and lumber camps and sawmills, and they looked small enough to pick up and tuck into his pockets, as if he were a giant. He could see his life stretching ahead like a reach of shining river, without snags or sandbars.

"Twenty-five percent," he kept saying. "Well, by God."

Smoke drifted in that room like clouds around a giant's head, and his brain was glowing. McSwasey's voice came from a long way off.

"Of course, Jim, there's a string attached. Twenty-five percent, but it's got a string tied to it."

The room was tipping gently, like a raft in quiet current, and through the smoke McSwasey was a squatty old man with a face that looked sifted over with brick dust.

"A string?" Jim heard himself saying. "That's all right. Tie a couple of strings to it. Hell, yes, tie as many as you want."

He took a deep drink and walked to the window and with a foot on the sill stood looking down at Read's Landing on a Saturday night: at red and green steamboat lanterns reflected in the water and at drunks reeling in the street. There was more to the world than these river towns, Sol Klauber had said once. Hell, yes, there must be. And he would see the world. Other roosters would go drifting like flotsam down

627

the years, kegging up in saloons and going under finally, kicked to death in brawls; but not him. He would be climbing and climbing up among the glittering dollar signs. Good-by, boys, he thought, looking down at those drunks in the street. I'm on my way, boys, he thought, smiling.

He heard McSwasey's voice.

"Come on back, Jim. Come on back and sit down and make camp. Sure there's a string, Jim. You're smart enough to figure that."

So he walked back and stood with his boot on the chair and took another drink.

"One string or a dozen," he said. "It's all the same to me."

"Just one, Jim. There has to be one. I don't go around every day giving away my company. Mine and Zumwalt's. We can forget him. He's a squarehead who's never heard there's a trail east from Santa Fe, and I'm buying him out anyway. For ten thousand dollars, Jim. A squarehead like him out there in Santa Fe, he don't know the business we're doing. So I'm buying him out. Half interest in the whole company for ten thousand. I'm his friend, Jim, that's why. Never deal with your friends, Jim."

McSwasey was laughing, and Jim laughed too, and although brass bands were playing in his mind, and flags were flying, and everything was dazzle, he could hear a cold voice saying, "Watch this son of a bitch or you'll lose the buttons off your pants, if he'll cheat Zumwalt he'll cheat you, watch him."

"Now me and you, Jim," McSwasey was saying, away off beyond the smoke and band music, "we're not friends. We'd slit each other's throats, only we won't. Maybe you hate me, for all I know, and I sure as hell hate you. Nothing personal, son, it's just you take an old buffalo like me and he'll hate any young bull. But I need you, son, so I won't slit your throat. Hell, no, I'll cut you in on my business. And you know why? Because I'm getting along. Fifty-four, son. Some days it feels like my shoulders are holding up the whole damned company. The money's pouring in, she's a gold mine, but I need me some help. Some young blood. Well, I've been watching you, Jim. And I've kind of liked what I saw."

Through the smoke McSwasey was grinning, and there was whiskey running in Jim's brain. Not enough to make him drunk, but the edges of things were softened. He didn't hate McSwasey; he didn't hate anybody. His feet felt miles away and he kept swallowing that tanglefoot.

"Sit down, Jim. Damn it, sit down and make camp and take it easy while I tell you about the fly in the soup. I've got a job of work cut out for you that not another son of a bitch on the river could handle. Maybe you can't."

Jim had to laugh then.

"Can't?" he said, easing his shoulders back against the chair. "What do you mean, can't? There ain't no such word, where I come from."

"It ain't the safest job in the world, Jim, but if you finish it off you can walk into my office as vice-president. I'll make you boss of all timber and river operations, that's what I'll do."

Those words were coming from far away, through tobacco smoke like clouds. Everything was dreamy; Jim could close his eyes and see himself out there in the years ahead, a giant standing astride the flowing river, with rafts and steamboats moving like toys.

"It'll say so right on the letterhead," McSwasey added. "Jim Buckmaster, vice-president."

"Let's make that James L. Buckmaster," Jim said. "What's the job of work?"

McSwasey pulled a surprise then, standing up and limping stealthily to the door. He yanked it open and peered into the hall, and when he returned his voice was low.

"This is the part," he said, "that's dead secret. They'd string you up, if word got out, and leave you for the herons to peck out your eyes. How much do you know about log piracy on the river?"

"Piracy? Not a hell of a lot. But I keep an eye on my rafts."

McSwasey nodded.

"Figured you didn't know the whole story, Jim. Some know about one string that's been stolen, and some about another, but nobody knows how bad it is. Or nobody did, till ten days ago. There was a meeting called then of all operators rafting on the Mississippi. Ramsay, T. C. Howe, Warburton, and all the rest. We didn't even hold it in a river town, Jim, for we wanted to keep it quiet. We met in Madison and every man read a list of his losses during the last year. It would have surprised you. It surprised me. Well, we decided the damned piracy has gone too far. But the law's no good. The law's been tried. Wouldn't surprise me to find a few sheriffs stealing logs. Well, everybody said we'd have to do something, but nobody knew what. Then I spoke up.

"The way I figured, that meeting should appoint one man to handle the cleanup. Collect a jackpot and furnish him funds and turn him loose. Then forget about the meeting. It never happened. See what I'm driving at? The fewer who know about that meeting the better. Appoint a man and let him handle it in his own way. Well, you know how meetings are. Since I was the old beaver who said we'd best appoint one man, damned if they didn't make me that man. I'm in charge of the cleanup, and there's not another son of a bitch in creation who knows how I'm going about it. When I tell you there'll be just two of us. Get the way my stick's floating, Jim?"

"Maybe," Jim said.

"All right, you leave here with your raft. Tie up somewhere near New Empire, and next Wednesday night me and you will rendezvous in Rafferty's Saloon."

"Rendezvous? That's a new one on me," Jim said. "What the hell's that?"

"It's like on the plains, Jim, or in the mountains. You tell some old coon you'll meet him on such-and-such a day at the forks of the Purgatoire River and the Arkansas, and even if it's a year later you meet him there. Unless, of course, some Arapahoe has lifted your hair. Him and you rendezvous, see? You meet and swap lies."

"Well," Jim said, "a man sure lives and learns."

"Some do and some don't. Learn, I mean. All right, Jim, me and you will make rendezvous in Rafferty's Saloon next Wednesday night at nine o'clock. We'll go to a table and put our heads together. Keep our voices down. But then we'll start arguing. Let our voices get louder, till everybody's listening. And we'll call each other crooks, Jim, and I'll tell you you're fired. I'll stand up and say look, you son of a bitch, you're fired and I'll blacklist you with every operator in the woods and on the river. Then I'll walk out mad.

"All right, Jim, word will get around. The boys will say Jim Buckmaster's through. Well, that makes sense. If you can't work in the woods or on the river, there's not much left except buying a nigger wench and whoring her out. You'll drift, Jim. You'll leave New Empire and drift up and down the river, cussing about me in saloons. And word will travel.

"Way I figure, those log thieves will hear about it and be looking you over. I mean the pirates, of course, not the operators. They'll figure you're sore-headed and ripe to steal a few logs yourself. Before long, somebody will likely sound you out, and invite you to join up with them. And if they don't come to you, you go to them and worm your way in.

"Every week or so drop me a line and keep me posted on how things are shaping up. And when the time is ready, tell me where you want one of my rafts left. Make it on the Wisconsin side and in Fox County. I'll have a raft moored wherever you say.

"All right, you tell those thieving bastards you've got wind of a rich raft moored along the Wisconsin shore. Make up some cock-and-bull story about why she's there unguarded. And you lead that crowd of thieves to the raft. Let me know when you'll be there, and I'll have a posse in ambush and we'll bag the whole outfit. Then I'll tell the sheriff you were my inside operator, and you'll be star witness for the state. Hell, you'll be a hero. How do you like it?"

Jim sat fingering his jaw.

"Could be better," he said finally. "I'd be sticking my head in a noose, for one thing."

"A noose, Jim? You think I'd cross you up?"

"Not if you could help. But look, Captain. Say I lead that crowd aboard the raft and about that time you drop dead. Before you could speak to the sheriff. That might be sort of embarrassing, Captain."

630

"See your point," McSwasey said, scowling and chewing his cold cigar. "And I wouldn't like it any better than you. But I don't figure to drop dead."

"It's been done," Jim said.

"But not by me, Jim. And I don't figure to try it. Well, let's say I write out what we're up to and how you're my inside operator. Say I seal it and put it in my office safe. Then if the Lord thinks he can't run heaven without me, why, that envelope will be in my safe and put you in the clear. Like that better?"

"Considerable," Jim said.

"All right, son, she's all yours. You've got a free hand to engineer it any way you like. It might take six months. All right, let it. Your wages will go right on, of course."

"Pilot's wages, or landlooker's?"

"Pilot's. The jackpot will cover that. The meeting gave me a free hand and I'm giving you one. Just get the whole gang together so we can bag them. After that, you can walk into my office as vice-president. Twenty-five percent interest in the company with an option to buy the whole shooting match on easy terms when I die."

Jim smiled.

"Looks like I might own the whole river at that rate."

"Hell, Jim, you'll own the river and Wisconsin to boot. You can't miss. And McSwasey & Zumwalt can't miss. I'll be frank with you, son. When that meeting in Madison dumped that basket of rattlesnakes in my lap, I balked. Way I saw it, I'd be doing the work and they'd be reaping the benefit. Well, Jim, they were reasonable. They saw my point. T. C. Howe said, 'Look here, Caleb. That stumpage of mine you've been wanting up at Oxbow Lake—if you bag them pirates I'll sell it to you. At government prices.' And Old Man Warburton offered me his upper mill at cost. The mill cuts more sawdust than lumber, but it's the mill site I'm after. That's how it went. Every man of them offered me a concession, if we bag the pirates. Hell, they'll wake up some morning and McSwasey & Zumwalt will hold first mortgage on their tonsils. Only it might be McSwasey & Buckmaster then. You pull this off, Jim, and I'll be generous. I can afford to be. Those operators are a slippery bunch, but their word's good with each other. There's honor among thieves, Jim. And with the concessions they offered, I can afford to cut you in on twenty-five percent. The company will be worth that much more, with those concessions."

Jim sat tipped back in his chair, legs stretched out, eyes on his whiskey. In some vague corner of his mind he was uneasy, but the sealed envelope McSwasey promised to leave in his safe should take care of any major risks. Anyway, no deal was without its drawbacks, and if you listened to the old men of caution yapping from their armchairs in your brain you would never get anywhere; there were times when you had to take chances. Twenty-five percent interest in the company; McSwasey & Buckmaster: words like that were dazzling.

"How about it?" McSwasey was asking. "Are you in?"

Jim tipped up his glass and drained it. Then he smiled.

"Why, yes," he said, "I'm in. But I still think I should have thirty percent."

"Damn you," McSwasey said, grinning. "You're a pirate already. Twenty-five or nothing."

That was smart: most men, selling you a deal that was all quicksand and bilge water, would have conceded that extra five percent.

*

Walking back toward his raft, Jim felt taller than a man on stilts; hell, taller than that. Taller than the tallest tree in the pinery; tall enough to pick that bright red star out of the heavens and wear it for a stickpin.

He'd been drinking, but it wasn't the whiskey that made him feel like a man with the whole river in the palm of his hand, flowing along his life line. Everything looked easy, everything possible. He was going on and on and up and up. He would own whole counties of timber, and a fleet of steamboats, and sawmills and lumber yards; newspapers and their editors would be his, and senators and bankers and all the silk hats and swallow-tailed coats in the legislature at Madison. Lew Fitzpatrick had been right: the meek might inherit the earth, but only after the strong were through with it. The way he figured it, he was one of the strong, maybe the strongest of the strong; nothing could stop him or hurt him now; that was how he figured it.

XII

WELL, McSwasey took him. He thought he was the biggest bullfrog in those waters, that night in Read's Landing, but McSwasey shriveled him down to tadpole size. Years later, after he headed a lumber company himself, and knew the world better, he used to marvel at what a lunkhead he had been, thinking McSwasey was on the square when he offered him a fourth interest in the business.

For a while everything went according to plan. Early Sunday morning the raft left Read's Landing, and on Wednesday evening, after a day of bucking wind, and of nearly saddlebagging on Turtle Island, it lay moored along the Iowa shore. He remembered how keyed up he had been that night, traveling toward New Empire in a skiff with Bobcat Pete and Noisy Swanson and Spaghetti Frank powering the oars, and that Danish kid, Rolfe Torkelsen, as passenger. Thinking back, he could close his eyes and hear the creak of oarlocks, and see the red and green lanterns on his raft growing smaller in the distance, and smell the river and the smoky autumn evening. He could see the star-spattered water, and the velvety bulk of islands and of bluffs; and presently, far away on the Wisconsin shore, the lights of New Empire. Sitting there in the stern, watching those lights coming closer, he could feel his heart beating with anticipation, for he was a man going toward a great destiny then. It was a fine thing, being young and knowing you were on your way.

When the skiff nosed onto the levee, and he stepped ashore, his watch showed only eight-thirty, so he told his crew to go on into the saloon while he took Rolfe Torkelsen to Judge Gentry's. The kid said don't bother, he'd find his way, but Jim always had a soft heart for young ones. So, with Rolfe carrying his carpetbag, they walked east along Winnebago Street and south along Gentry Avenue, through the smoke from leaf fires. Once Jim asked Rolfe if he felt homesick, getting into a strange town at night, and from the way the kid denied it, Jim knew he must be.

"You'll like it, I reckon," Jim said. "Once you get the drift. Me, I'm an honest man, and I never wanted the law. But a fellow like you with a crooked streak, you ought to make out real good."

The kid flared at that, as Jim had known he would; he was a peppery kid for sure.

"I'm not crooked," he said, "and I'm not going to be."

Jim had to laugh then, and after a moment the kid laughed too.

"Rolfe," Jim said, "you're all right. If the judge kicks you out, you come to me and I'll stake you."

"Why would he kick me out?"

"God, I don't know. Unless he finds out you're a Swede."

"I'm not a Swede. I'm a Dane."

Jim broke out laughing again; he was sure serious, that kid was.

Lights were burning in Judge Gentry's house, their rays shafting out onto the yellow leaves flecking the lawn. At the driveway Jim stopped and stuck out his hand.

"Rolfe," he said, "I'd lay my money on you, if I was a betting man. You'll make out. Whatever it is the judge wants you to do, you do it. You learn the law."

"That's why I'm here," Rolfe said.

"You study them books," Jim said, "and some day you'll be a lawyer, and this will be your town. It will be my town too, like as not. I won't always be a rooster, kid. Maybe I'll be a timber operator, and maybe I'll hire you to keep me out of trouble."

The kid thanked him for what he'd done, lending him money back there on the raft and bringing him to New Empire; and Jim stood watching while he rapped on the front door. A gray-haired woman opened it, and through the quiet evening Jim could hear her voice, a nice sweet voice with Kentucky accents. Rolfe Torkelsen went inside and Jim started back toward Rafferty's Saloon.

*

Down the years he remembered how he felt that evening, smiling to himself as he went swinging west along Winnebago Street. It all seemed adventure then, and he thought he would come through without a scratch. He remembered stopping there on the corner outside Rafferty's and drawing a deep breath, enjoying the rank smells from the river and the odor of roasting coffee from the Empire Wholesale Company down the street to the south. It lacked a few minutes of nine when he opened the door of Rafferty's; the saloon warmth and the beer fumes came flowing around him; he stood smiling at the haze of tobacco and the gleam of the cherry-wood bar and the bright dresses of the girls from upstairs.

Everybody liked him then; everybody called hello. It's Jim Buckmaster, they said; Jim's here; and a couple of girls came smiling, their skirts swishing, and said gee Jim, it's been a long time, how are you? He laughed and put an arm around each of their waists and told them they were prettier than ever and he'd buy them a drink; hell, he'd buy everybody a drink.

"Jim, me boy," Pat Rafferty said, from behind the bar. "It's good to see you, Jim."

He remembered standing there with a boot on the rail, inviting them all to wet their whistles; in the mirror he could see himself laughing, and he could see the crowd at the bar. The girls kept rubbing against him like affectionate cats, putting thoughts into his head, and he could smell their powder and fancy-house perfume.

"Pat," he told Rafferty, "have one yourself," and Pat said he didn't care if he did, and when he filled his glass he lifted it.

"Here's to you, Jim," he said. "Here's to the best damned raft pilot on the whole damned river. Long may you prosper, Jim, me boy."

Everybody yelled and lifted their glasses and drank to him, and he felt warm inside, loving them all, and he invited them to have another.

"You ain't stern-wheelers, boys," he said. "You're side-wheelers. And a side-wheeler can't run far on one paddle."

They laughed and whooped.

"But you take Sophie, here," Jim said, smiling at one of the girls by his side, "she's a stern-wheeler," and he swatted her rump.

Sophie yipped and stamped a foot, in mock outrage, and reached up and rumpled his hair, shoving his hat to a rakish angle; and the whole crowd was howling. In the mirror Jim caught sight of Bobcat Pete.

"Bobcat," he yelled, "how you feeling, rooster?"

The Bobcat looked down his nose and grinned sheepishly.

"I had to do it, Bobcat," Jim said. "I had to send your clothes to the washerwoman. No hard feelings, rooster?"

"Aw, shucks," the Bobcat said. "You know there ain't."

"Bobcat," Jim said, "pick you a gal. Pick you any gal you want, and I'll pay the freight charges."

The place really turned noisy then; somebody let out a hoot, and the girls were squealing.

Jim tossed a twenty to the bar.

"Pat," he said, "take the drinks out of that. And take out a ticket for the Bobcat. Hell, while you're at it, take out a third round."

He could always liven up a place.

By then it was after nine and McSwasey hadn't appeared but Jim wasn't worrying; McSwasey would come. He'd come and they'd pretend to quarrel and Jim would catch him a mess of log pirates and after that it would be McSwasey & Buckmaster, James L. Buckmaster, vice-president. His thoughts went dreamy as he stood there, smiling at the framed dollar bill hanging by the bar mirror and at the painting above it showing a languorous woman, nude save for open-work black stockings, lying among pillows with doves and posies.

Then all at once the racket subsided, the boys nearest the door falling silent, and after that everybody. Jim put down his glass and turned from the bar, facing the door, seeing a man standing just inside. A stocky man in a gray tweed topcoat, hands in pockets, a black hat on his head. Over there by the door, beyond range of the cones of light falling from hanging lamps, it was shadowy, but Jim saw that the man's jaw looked blockier than ever, and his mouth ugly.

"Well," he said, "Buckmaster. This is a surprise. Celebrating?"

So the play-acting was starting, and Jim got right into the swing, fingering his jaw and acting embarrassed.

"Not especially," he said.

"Where's your raft?" McSwasey asked.

"She's upriver. Up there by Turtle Island."

McSwasey didn't speak for a while; just stood looking Jim over. Finally he said:

"I'd like it just as well if my pilot would stick by his raft. But now you're here, there's a matter I'd like to take up with you."

Jim was laughing inside, but he tried to look worried, like a schoolboy about to catch it from a teacher, as he watched McSwasey striding back toward a table where the light was dim. Pat Rafferty, wiping his hands on his spotted apron, hurried from behind the bar and went to McSwasey, taking his coat and hat and hanging them on a hook. Jim followed, putting a roll into his walk, but he was cold sober.

"What can I do for you, Mr. McSwasey?" Rafferty was asking, standing by the little round table.

"A bottle of Split Ticket," McSwasey said, "and glasses. Clean ones. Then leave us alone. We've got business."

The theater, Jim remembered thinking, had lost a convincing actor when McSwasey went into lumbering; he sat there drumming his stubby fingers and looking sullen. But once he winked at Jim. When the whiskey came he poured a stiff one and tossed it down, and under his breath he said:

"All right, son, here we go. Don't be surprised if I take a poke at you, before we're through. I won't put much steam behind it and you can roll with my fist."

"You're the doctor," Jim said.

He certainly had to admire McSwasey's play-acting, the way he began rumbling in a low, angry voice, talking a lot of nonsense about how Jim had padded his payroll account last winter at Camp Seven, and had done the same with his rafting accounts. Presently his voice rose, drowning out Jim's protests, so that all those eavesdroppers in the saloon could hear.

"I paid you square wages, Buckmaster. But those accounts had a smell like a skunk. Well, I've got ways to investigate, and I investigated yours. And I didn't like what I found."

"Now just a minute," Jim said.

"I've got the goods on you," McSwasey said. "You were slick, and maybe it wouldn't stand up in court, but you crooked me out of better than a thousand dollars."

636

"Now wa-a-ait a minute, friend."

"Don't call me your friend, you crooked son of a bitch. You're fired. I'll blacklist you with every operator in the pinery. And by God I'll drive you off the river."

McSwasey had jumped up, so abruptly that his chair went over backwards.

"Now listen," Jim bawled, starting to rise. "No pug-nosed son of a bitch can call me—"

It was then that McSwasey's fist came blurting in a wild swing; Jim could have ducked it without trouble, but he figured McSwasey would hold to his promise and pull the punch; so Jim led with his chin, planning to roll with the blow and go down. But at the last moment, there in the dim light, he caught a metallic gleam from the knuckles; the fist smashed his jaw; and all the saloon lamps exploded and went black.

He thought he was breaking out rollways at the start of a drive; somebody yanked a trip-rope and the logs began moving; a log spurted up and shattered his jaw; he dropped into a hole and went rolling with the logs, over and over, toward the river. Maybe Sol Klauber would be waiting for him, out there in eternity, and a round-shouldered man named Lorne Buckmaster. But nobody was waiting; only blackness. Then, after centuries, he was back on a driving stream, pinioned under logs, water pouring into his face.

He was aware then of pain shooting up into his cranium; he opened his eyes; his face was drenched and he was lying in sawdust; he twisted and saw the curved iron legs of a saloon table. Then nausea hit the pit of his stomach and he lay there on his side, retching like a poisoned wolf. The floor was bobbing and the walls were whirling; his skull felt split open by an ax. Next thing he knew, without warning, a bucket of water was flung into his face. He groaned out a protest; he saw a pair of legs and an empty bucket dangling from a shirt-sleeved arm; he saw a concave chest and a thin-faced man with cold vicious eyes. The man drew back a foot and kicked him; the man said get up. Get up and get out, he said.

"Rafferty," Jim heard himself saying. "Say, Rafferty, what—?"

The man kicked him again and the saloon was tipping; the lamps burned yellow and then a peculiar blue and an odd green; Jim's head was throbbing and he needed a drink; he did for a fact.

"Get up, rooster. Get up and get out."

Jim closed his eyes; why couldn't they leave a man be?

Somebody kicked him again; somebody said up with you, I'll have no crooks in my place.

It took his strength, elbowing himself to a sitting position; he sat there in the sawdust with his head between his knees.

"Rafferty," he was mumbling, "did you see it, Rafferty? What did that bastard hit me with?"

"Up and out," Rafferty said. "I'll not be having you call Mr. McSwasey names in my place."

Everything was shadow and lamps with green flames; the air was thick as water; it was like swimming laboriously up from a river bottom, getting to his feet; he stood in vagueness, fingering his jaw; it was sore as a wasp-sting.

"Usual thing," he muttered, "a clip on the jaw don't put me to sleep. Hell, no. I've been hit plenty of times, Rafferty, and like as not it's busted the man's hand. Say, you don't suppose McSwasey wore knucks? You don't think—?"

He went reeling toward the bar where he saw himself in the mirror, hair wet and mussed, shoulders sagging. Pain ran from his jaw into his head, where it pulsated like the long streamers of the northern lights. His knees wanted to give way; his mouth tasted sour. Everybody was watching him, silently and contemptuously; he guessed he could have crumpled and cashed in, for all they cared. Their faces floated in the tobacco smoke, sometimes blurred, sometimes sharp; he saw a peculiar grin on Bobcat Pete's mouth, and the fancy girl, Sophie, had a curl to her lips. Nobody offered him a drink; nobody brushed the sawdust off his clothes. Well, it was a hard way to make a living, cutting logs in the woods and rafting them downriver.

"Boys," he said, "I don't know what's come over me. It's my jaw, boys, and this damned floor. Keeps tipping."

He stood with elbows on the bar, head in his hands. Then he heard Rafferty.

"All right, rooster, here's your hat. You're through, rooster. You've crowed and flapped your wings, but it took Caleb McSwasey to pick your feathers. Better go to Texas, rooster. Anyway, somewhere a long way off. For you're sure as hell through on the river, with McSwasey down on you."

And Rafferty jammed the hat on Jim's head.

He had a notion to make something of that, but his jaw and temples were throbbing. So, uncertainly, he moved to the door. Then he turned.

"Rafferty," he said, "I'll not forget. I'll own me the river yet, and I'll not forget."

Outside, he stood drawing in gulps of night air, and his thoughts cleared. But his head kept pounding and he needed a drink. Staggering a little, he crossed the street to the Pinery Boy Saloon and fumbled inside. Everybody was talking, but when they saw him they shut up. He stood weaving, looking them over, and through the haze he recognized a saloon loafer who had been in Rafferty's earlier this evening; after the fight, he must have hurried over to spread the news. Hell with him. Jim made his way to the bar and ordered whiskey.

Rattlesnake Bob Skellenger, who owned the place, stood behind the bar, a plump man of thirty-five with red hair and a gold tooth. Jim had given him considerable patronage, the past few years; when things were dull, Rattlesnake Bob would pull up his pant leg and exhibit the marks he said had been made by rattlesnake fangs. He was, he said, immune to rattlesnake venom, although rumor had it that he had punctured his leg with an awl and invented the rattlesnake story, to gain distinction. Tonight he made no move to reach for whiskey, and Jim repeated his order. The gold tooth gleamed in Rattlesnake Bob's sickly smile.

"Now look, Jim," he said, in his wheezy voice. "Look at it my way. You go crooking McSwasey and getting blacklisted and I can't serve you. He's too big a man in this town, Jim. I got to operate on a license, ain't I? He hear I been serving you and he'd have my license. He's a big man, McSwasey is."

Jim stood there gripping the bar, his head an agony. And he thought maybe he'd earn that fourth interest in McSwasey & Zumwalt, before he was through. It kind of got to a man, when everybody turned on him.

"I got my family to think about," Rattlesnake Bob was saying. "If it was me alone, Jim, I'd give you a drink. But I'm a family man, Jim. I can't get McSwasey down on me."

"He hit me with knucks," Jim said. "With brass knucks."

Everybody was silent; he could feel their eyes; Rattlesnake Bob stood there with arms folded, smiling that sickly smile. Jim wheeled slowly around, seeing them all watching, like timber wolves when a stag was hamstrung and sinking.

"Boys," Jim said, "I'll remember. Every one of you."

All the way to the door he felt their eyes; and on the street he stood uncertainly, wanting a drink because it might ease his headache, but knowing that if he went to another saloon it would likely be the same; news traveled.

*

At his usual lodging house the landlady must not have heard the news; leastwise she rented him a room; that same room he had sneaked out of years ago when he ran away from Sol Klauber. And she gave him pain powders, when he mentioned his headache; they put him to sleep.

Next morning his headache was still with him, although dull, and in the mirror he looked a sight, his jaw purple, the skin showing marks of brass knucks. At the wash bowl he sloshed his face, telling himself he would feel fine after breakfast; but all that day, when he went about town buying camping gear, and grub, and a bark canoe from a breed, his headache persisted. He kept thinking he would shake it, he would sleep it off; but that night, after going to bed early, he came awake about 2:00 A.M. with his skull feeling like a clubbed porcupine; he hated to do it, but he roused his landlady and got more of those powders. The pain left then and he overslept, so that it was midmorning before he loaded his dunnage into the canoe and started upriver.

His headache had not returned, and it was a fine October morning, the river smooth, the canoe's wake a widening V, glassy and undulating. On shore, the buildings of town stood out sharply from among masses of autumn-colored foliage, and when he passed McSwasey's Island he saw a man raking leaves in the garden. Somewhere inside the house Mrs. McSwasey was likely doing whatever Mrs. McSwasey did, to pass the days; but Jim gave her scarcely a thought. He was thinking of her husband.

Why would a man warn you he was going to punch you, but without much steam, and then sock you with all he had, his fist wearing knucks?

Your jaw was still discolored and sore. And you were sore too, a little. There had been no call for knucks, no call for so much power behind the punch. If you had known what was coming you could have got set; even with a hefty punch from knucks you could have ridden with the blow and faked being knocked out. But the way McSwasey had operated, pulling a surprise, you had stood with your jaw stuck out, just asking for it, like some greenhorn who had never been in a fight. Your stance had been all wrong for protecting yourself.

Knucks. The old bastard. Knucks and guns and knives were out of bounds, when you fought in the pinery or on the river. If you had a grudge against some rooster you stood up to him with your bare fists.

One thing, of course, old McSwasey had never been a pinery boy. Still, he must have known woods custom. But maybe he figured your jaw was hard, and he was an old man, damned near, and if he hit you with his bare fist, and you went down, as if knocked out, it would lack conviction. Maybe he had wanted that fight to look absolutely genuine, to the boys in Rafferty's, and he figured the best way for it to look genuine was for it to be genuine. And maybe he figured the only way to bring that about was to pop you with knucks. Sure, that must be it.

Well, you guessed not much actual damage had been done; your jaw felt as if porcupine quills had stabbed it and festered; but no real damage; you healed fast, usual thing. But damn, you still didn't like the idea of knucks, and after this whole thing was over, you sure as hell were going to take McSwasey aside and speak to him. Look, Captain, you would say, next time you take a notion to use knucks—don't.

*

That canoe bought from a breed wasn't much account. The seams were tight enough, and it took you up to Turtle Island without dumping you, but it was nowhere near as steady as a Chippewa canoe. It didn't have the right feel; the starboard gunwale was lower than the larboard; you felt you were fighting the gawky thing. If the weather turned choppy, a man would have to watch sharp, paddling through waves.

He nooned on Turtle Island that day, brewing tea and eating thick beef sandwiches and a slice of apple pie from his landlady in New Empire. Then, smoking his pipe, he stood looking across the water to the place along the Iowa shore where his raft had been moored. It had gone on downriver, of course, and he wondered who was piloting. "Leave all that to me," McSwasey had said, the other evening in Read's Landing.

It gave him an odd feeling, thinking of his raft sloshing along without him; a lonesome feeling, almost. At the tail somebody would be fishing for pickerel, for always under a raft minnows swarmed, and always pickerel swam along in the wake, to gobble them. Rafting was all right, a free and easy life; he was going to miss rafting, cooped up in an office as vice-president of the company.

He wished he might have been a minnow under the raft, the other night when the skiff returned from New Empire, to hear what was said when the boys told about his fight with McSwasey. But his ears might have burned. Still, some of the crew liked him. Didn't they? They had been afraid of him—that was one reason he had been a valuable pilot —but some of them liked him. Must have. Greasy Dick, certainly. He wished the Grease were here now; he would have liked a gab. But even to the Grease he wouldn't be able to tell what he was up to, trying to find log pirates and becoming one of them. Keep it dead secret, McSwasey had said.

Jim knocked out his pipe and set off again, paddling toward Iowa. Leaving his canoe pulled up on shore, he followed a path back into a ravine, that same path he had traveled the other afternoon when he smelled campfire smoke and went investigating. It had been nearly dusk then, but in the shadows he had made out a pike pole and a cant hook leaning against a tree, and he had seen three men around the fire. He had got a good look at only one of them, a young fellow with slick black hair and large white teeth. He would know that fellow, next time he saw him.

Not that he expected to find him here today, or the others. But they might have dropped something; he wanted to look over their bivouac.

Moving softly, he advanced along the path, through the bright tangles of autumn. Sometimes he stopped, hearing a bobwhite whistling off in the underbrush, and smelling the damp odors of humus and walnut hulls. His eyes kept moving over the thickets of catbriers and sumac, and wandering up the bluffs where the oaks were turning bronze and the maples were brilliant. When he came within sight of the camping place he saw at once that it had been abandoned; crossing the dry stream-bed, he poked among the cold ashes of the campfire, and went over the ground where the grass had been flattened by blankets, but he found nothing.

He hadn't expected to, actually. Men foxy enough to steal strings of logs and raft them downriver, without getting caught, would be unlikely to leave a back trail. Every timber operator on the Upper Mississippi was feeling the pinch, McSwasey had said; and that must mean a far-flung organization of thieves with maybe a sawmill of their own, and with brains and money at the top. It must mean too that they had operators planted among rafting crews, to smuggle information about raft movements. Could be, Jim thought, that somebody in his own crew had been working for the freebooters.

No wonder McSwasey had warned him to keep mum about what he was up to. And no wonder, when you looked at it that way, that Mc-Swasey had thought it necessary to sock him with knucks, to make the fight look genuine. Maybe one of those loafers in Rafferty's Saloon had been a freebooter; maybe Rafferty himself, even.

As he stood there studying the ground, he noticed a path, very faint, leading off north through the timber. After he had followed it a few paces the path forked, one branch twisting away toward the summit of the bluff, the other dropping toward the river. That branch interested him most; it took him through thickets of prickly ash and willow, down to a boggy shore where a stagnant bay was cut off from the river by drift-wood and dead trees. Coarse sedges grew there, and bulrushes; frogs heard him coming and plopped into the water, and a bittern went flapping over the cattails. The place had a marshy smell.

The mud had been tracked by boots, some calked, and at the water's edge he saw the impress of a bateau-keel. Well, the bay was large enough to have harbored several bateaux; an outlet to the main channel went winding among the flattened rushes.

He was thoughtful, returning along the path and following its loops to the summit of the bluff, a level place with oaks and elms but no evidence that anybody had been here before him, ever. A squirrel scolded; high overhead a blue-darter hawk was sailing. Where the limestone outcropping of the bluff dropped toward treetops and thickets, he stood looking out upon the river, vast and empty, flowing in various tones of blue when distance and shimmer altered its color. Miles to the east the Wisconsin bluffs looked like the coast of some never-never land, delicately tinted with lavender.

She was a big river, with a million places for raft thieves to hide. A man could spend a lifetime, just searching. McSwasey's scheme was best, of course: not to search. To be fired in disgrace and to go drifting, a down-and-outer, bitter against McSwasey. Then after a while the raft thieves would approach you; you were a good man with logs, and they would know it.

*

That night he pitched his tent on the Iowa shore, up beyond Catfish Bend, and next day he explored the Wisconsin backwaters, hunting a place to lay a trap for the raft thieves, once he found them. It should be on the Wisconsin side, McSwasey had said, and in Fox County, some spot where a posse could lie in ambush, watching a raft left as bait.

The weather turned warmer that day, and he was off early, crossing to the Wisconsin side and entering a slough wandering away from the main channel. It was all endless and intricate, back among the islands, with narrow passages where the current flowed swift and weeping willows brushed your face, and with winding tawny passages where the flow lay dead and carp sent up sluggish bubbles.

He put in a long day, exploring those backwaters. Sometimes his progress was barred by fallen trees, or by swampy savannahs of goose corn and wild rice; sometimes he paddled along broad avenues of water that mirrored stately trees; sometimes he felt his way through great oxbows, deep and ink-colored, choked with snags and derelict logs, teeming with pike and turtles and suckers. There were islands back there hardly bigger than daubs of mud, and islands many acres in extent with lagoons where lotus grew and with great old elms whose bark showed gray floodmarks. Those bottoms were like the slums of the river, with their stench of muck and decay and limitless fecundity. Muskrats lived back there, and deer and mink and crawdads; hairworms wavered through the water; there were swamp rabbits and wolves to eat them; there were funny-faced raccoons and slinking catamounts. And everywhere, in the silent sunshine, in the gurgle of the current, in the cries of terns and the screams of fish hawks, there was a loneliness such as he had never known in any wilderness; he didn't want to camp back there.

But he had to; sundown caught him; so he pulled his canoe up on an island, selecting an open place for his tent where tomorrow morning's sun would strike it, clearing the ground of sharp pebbles before unrolling his sleeping bag, chopping plenty of firewood, racking his fowling piece on crotched pegs inside the tent, putting everything in its place. His father had taught him wilderness housekeeping, saying that since a man was plagued by so many miseries on the trail, he might as well be comfortable in camp. After his fire was a mass of coals, with rocks for andirons and green butternut poles for a grill, he lifted from their bath of salt water a couple of squirrels he had shot earlier and laid them on to broil, with strips of bacon for basting. And he stirred up a batch of corn dodgers, baking them in the hot ashes.

Darkness fell, and the sloughs came alive with all the noises of night: the splash of a muskrat, the rustle of a marsh shrew in dead leaves. Sometimes from across the water he heard the cool laughter of a loon, and an owl was hooting. After supper he washed and stowed his dishes and buried his garbage, for a tidy camp was part of his code; and he sat watching the fire, thinking of his raft, far downriver by now, and wondering why, of a sudden, misgivings had stolen into his thoughts. Misgivings about this whole operation: about his fake fight with McSwasey; about becoming a log thief.

But it was a smart scheme McSwasey had cooked up, wasn't it? It was a way to get ahead fast. In the whole plan there wasn't a knothole, so far as he could figure. He still didn't like the way McSwasey had given him a sore jaw, but he'd been over that again and again: McSwasey wanted the fight to look genuine. Why else would he have used knucks?

No other reason unless—well—unless McSwasey hated him, and had seized the chance to give him a poke he'd remember. But that didn't add up; if McSwasey hated him, why would he have promised him a fourth interest in the company if he bagged the log thieves? And why would McSwasey hate him, anyway? He had always given McSwasey a full day's work for a day's pay.

Sitting there scowling at the fire, he cast about in his thoughts for all kinds of outlandish reasons why McSwasey might hate him, and once he thought of Mrs. McSwasey. She had said her husband was very jealous; could McSwasey be jealous of him? But that was a laugh. Why, hell, he and the Missus had hardly been alone together, except that afternoon in front of the fireplace and that evening in the carriage. He wouldn't take Mrs. McSwasey as a gift. And if a man like McSwasey, rich and powerful, got jealous of an employee, wouldn't he fire him outright and order him never to see the Missus again? Instead, McSwasey was giving him a chance to own a fourth interest in the company.

Jim touched his jaw; it was aching tonight, probably from the river damps, and there was pain at the base of his skull. And he was tired. That was a little strange, considering how he hadn't done any really heavy work today. Maybe it was this unseasonably warm weather; a night's sleep would smooth out his worries and leech away his aches.

*

He was right on one score: his worries had vanished by morning. But not, oddly, his aches. His jaw was sore and the ache at the base of his skull had spread into his cranium. It was enough to make a man think about seeing a doctor. But there weren't any doctors, back where he had camped.

During breakfast he kept massaging the back of his neck, and he ran his fingers along his jaw. The other day in New Empire, when he bought his outfit, he had forgotten to buy a razor, and already his beard was bristling. But even if he had bought a razor maybe he wouldn't have used it now, with his jaw so tender. Puzzlement was in his eyes as he sat eating, for this persistent headache was outside his experience, he had always been so healthy.

By noon that day he was back on the main river, paddling upstream, and the headache was still with him. The day was fine, and the warmth of sun on his neck and shoulders gave him some comfort, but not much. He'd best see a doctor; maybe something had been dislocated by that blow from knucks. Upriver a few miles, on the Iowa side, there was a town named Lanceport; maybe he'd put in there and look for a doc.

He sighted a log raft early that afternoon, in that wide reach below

Broken Ax Chute, and with spirits lifting he headed toward it. The raft was still far away and beyond identification, but he knew most of the pilots in these waters, and he wanted a gab. He'd been lonely the last few days; maybe he'd climb aboard and ride along for a mile or so; his boots itched to feel logs beneath them, and his ears yearned for the squeak of the big sweeps on their thole pins.

She was a five-string raft, and Jim watched her bow oars, flashing in unison. Then, as she drifted closer, he saw she was a Smith & Warburton raft, piloted by Nels Quist, the same Nels Quist who had been push of that first camp up on the Flambeau where Jim had started as bull cook. He let out a whoop of recognition and drove his canoe forward.

The bowsmen had shipped their oars and the raft was coasting along nicely, without navigation troubles, but Nels Quist stood on the logs staring straight ahead, as if puzzling out some deep problem of currents. Jim whooped again. And he saw Nels turn and watch the canoe coming; at last he lifted a hand in a half-hearted wave. The bowsmen all stood staring.

"By God, Nels," Jim called, "it's good to see you. How's that mess of flood trash behaving?"

Nels gave a faint—a very faint—smile, and crossed to the larboard edge of the raft, where Jim's canoe was bobbing.

"Hello, Jim."

"She's full of Norwegian holes," Jim said. "I can see that. And Number 2 logs. And rat-eaten lines. And a crew out of some old men's home. Typical Smith & Warburton stuff. Hell, Nels, you'll never get to St. Louis on that bunch of knotholes."

It was meant to be funny, of course, like always; and Nels should have taken his cue and come back with disparaging remarks about the canoe, and Jim's personal appearance, and his piloting ability. But Nels didn't. He just stood there at the edge of the logs, acting ill at ease. Jim asked what was wrong.

"Nothing," Nels said. "Everything's fine, Jim. Everything's dandy." And then, slowly, he added, "I heard you had some trouble, Jim. You and your push."

News traveled; yes, sir, it sure did.

"Why, yes," Jim said, "if you want to call it that. The son of a bitch took a poke at me with brass knucks."

"That's what I heard, Jim. I heard he told you to hit the hay trail, too."

"I was quitting anyway," Jim said. "He called me a thief, Nels. He said I'd padded my accounts."

"That's what I heard," Nels said. "Some feller got off a boat at Read's and was telling about it. He said McSwasey was blacklisting you."

"I don't doubt it," Jim said. "A bastard who will use knucks will do anything."

"It's none of my business," Nels said, "but I think you made a mistake, fighting McSwasey. He's a big man, Jim. He'll make it stick, if he blacklists you. I wouldn't mind having you in my own crew, but I couldn't touch you, Jim. Not if you're blacklisted. Old Man Warburton follows McSwasey's lead, Jim. They all do. He's a big man."

"No bigger than he thinks," Jim said.

"I don't know, Jim. He swings a lot of weight. You buck McSwasey and it will be like that time at Teal Feather. You were a hot-fisted kid, Jim, but I had to learn you. You buck McSwasey and maybe he'll learn you too."

"And maybe not," Jim said. "I aim to own me the river yet, Nels."

"I don't know, Jim. She's pretty sizable."

The raft and canoe were drifting apart; Nels Quist stood looking embarrassed.

"Anyway," he called across the water, "I wish you luck, Jim. You'll need it."

Jim watched him turn back to the center of his float, where he gave an order to pull to starboard. The oars dipped; the raft went sloshing past the canoe; and Jim's head was aching.

*

A few miles upstream from Broken Ax Chute the Wisconsin shore waded out in a point of land which ended in a tall limestone formation called Stovepipe Rock; and late that afternoon, when Jim sighted it, he had a hunch it might be a spot where a trap could be laid. On the map which he carried in his mind, the Stovepipe was well within Fox County, and it was a landmark known to everybody. If he wrote McSwasey to leave a raft as bait at the Stovepipe, there would be no danger of mis-understanding.

Looming high above him, Stovepipe Rock was red in the light from sunset when Jim reached it, the river lapping its base, a few scrub cedars and rock ferns growing from its crevices. On the downriver side a wide bayou, green in the fading day, went meandering into Wisconsin, its banks thick with tag alders and wool grass, and with a towering growth of river elms and swamp maples. Yellow leaves floated on the water, and when the canoe went whispering among them Jim took a sounding with his paddle and couldn't find bottom. Beyond its first curve, the bayou remained wide and deep; it could harbor two strings of a log raft with room to spare. He followed its winding course for several hundred yards, till it narrowed and ended where a rill came feeding in from the Wisconsin mainland. That was what he wanted to find out: that there would be no escape to the Mississippi at the far end. It was a pocket. A posse could find all the concealment a sheriff would want, in the underbrush, and the mouth of the bayou would be the jaws of a trap.

Dusk was falling when he left the bayou and paddled around Stovepipe Rock, to the north side of the point where the ground was higher;

he made camp there. And after supper, by firelight, he wrote his first report for McSwasey, telling what he had been up to the last few days, and describing the bayou as a fine place for a trap. Writing letters came hard for him; his thoughts seemed to log-jam, when they tried to flow through the pencil in his big hand; he kept wetting the point with his tongue. When the job was finished and the letter ready to mail, with the envelope marked Personal, his headache was worse. He swallowed a stiff drink, before turning in.

His sleep was fitful, with pain nagging him; and in the borderland of consciousness he kept remembering how Nels Quist had acted, tentative and cool. Nels was his friend, or supposed to be; an old friend. And Jim remembered what his father used to say, that when a man was down, there were always plenty of fellows to kick him. If Nels had been black-listed, Jim didn't think he would have treated him that way; he was loyal to his friends.

About five in the morning he came wide awake, pain shooting through his skull. Damn that McSwasey anyway, for using knucks. Jim crawled from his sleeping bag and dressed, stopping frequently to massage his head, and to swallow whiskey, which helped a little. Daybreak came but he wanted no breakfast; he wanted a doctor and some of those powders such as his landlady had given him. Lanceport should have a doctor, and it was only a couple of miles upriver, on the Iowa side.

So he set out for Lanceport, shortly after sunrise. A breeze was pulling up the river valley, and when it struck the heavy muscles anchoring his head to his shoulders the pain was all he could bear; his knuckles stood out as he gripped the paddle.

Lanceport looked like a haven to him that morning, when he saw it across the water. At the mouth of Lance Coulee, where the bluffs fell away from the Mississippi, the town stood on a wide alluvial plain with fine old trees. Running parallel with the river, the main street was lined with east-facing stores, their false fronts notched unevenly, their windows gleaming in the early sun. The levee was paved with cobbles, and on to the north Jim saw a large building with blank wooden walls and a pile of brown sawdust; it looked like a commercial icehouse. At the corner of the building a man was standing, watching the canoe.

Jim gave a wave and headed toward that icehouse, pulling his canoe up on shore beside the loading chute. The man came to meet him; he was about forty-five, with a lean body and shrewd eyes. Jim stood with his legs apart, braced against pain, but his voice was steady.

"Friend," he said, "I need me a doctor. I don't suppose you could tell me where to go."

"Why, yes," the man said. "We've got a doctor. One of these days we'll have two or three. This town, young man, is destined to be the greatest metropolis of the Northwest."

"I don't doubt it, friend, but where's the doctor?"

647

The man pointed toward a two-story building of red brick which stood at the southwest corner of the main street and a cross street. It had a sign which said Fansler House.

"You go ask for Dr. Wace Fansler," the man said. "He runs the hotel on the side. Tell him Alonzo St. Clair sent you. He fitted me with a truss."

Jim thanked him and started away, then turned.

"Friend, I'd count it a favor if you'd keep watch on my canoe. My outfit's in it, and I wouldn't like to lose it."

"Safe as with your own mother," Alonzo St. Clair said.

It was a pleasant-looking hotel, and when Jim came to the corner he saw a sign on the lamppost announcing that the main street was Promenade and that the other street, coming from the west and lined with shade trees, was Linden. He walked along Promenade to the south end of the hotel; glass doors led to the lobby. Inside, he made his way to the clerk's desk at the northwest corner, where a girl was sitting on a stool, working with a needle and embroidery hoops. Her hair was dark and lustrous, worn in a cluster of curls at the back of her head, and when she looked up her eyes were brown.

"Yes?" she said.

Seeing her sitting there, so clean-looking and composed, in a white muslin dress sprigged with tiny red flowers, it came to him that he must look like a regular river roughneck. And smell like one, with all that tanglefoot he had been drinking. He ran his fingers over his unshaved jaw.

"Miss," he said, his voice low, "I'm hunting a doctor. I need one real bad. A fellow named St. Clair said I'd find one here."

She sat there looking at him; at her throat she wore an onyx brooch framed in gold.

"I'm not drunk, miss," Jim said. "If I smell that way it's the whiskey I've swallowed, against the pain. I had a crack on the jaw the other night and it put me to sleep. Must have dislocated something, when I fell. Anyhow, my head is giving me—it's giving me blazes, miss."

"Dad's not here," the girl said. "He's out on a call. Would you like to wait?"

"Have to, I reckon," Jim said. And something made him add, "I know I look a sight, miss. I've been on the river. I guess a man should clean up when he sees a doctor."

"You could sit down, if you'd like," the girl said. She had a low voice, with shyness in it.

Everything was unsteady; he walked in pain, going to one of the rush-bottomed chairs by the front window. When he sat down he saw her watching, as if she had never seen the likes of him before; their gazes met, across the lobby, before she dropped her attention to the embroidery. The air smelled of breakfast coffee from the dining room, and of bacon and eggs; but Jim wasn't hungry. He sat with elbows on knees and with his head in his hands, eyes shut tight. Sometimes people walked through the lobby from the dining room; Jim wished the doctor would hurry back from his call. If anything, the pain in his head was worse.

Presently he heard a light, quick step and he looked up; it was the girl. She was young and pretty, about eighteen, and probably what people called a nice girl. But he wouldn't know. He had never had much to do with girls like that.

"You're in a good deal of pain, aren't you?" she said.

"Yes, miss, I am. I am for a fact."

"You could lie down," she said, "if that would help. Back in dad's office."

"It sure couldn't hurt none," Jim said.

He followed her through a door leading north from the lobby, along a hall carpeted in red. He remembered the gray-and-silver wallpaper sliding by, and how everything smelled clean, with a faint odor of furniture polish. The girl walked with a light tread; she had an attractive figure, and she was of a height he liked. The curls at the back of her head looked so elegant and symmetrical, like a cluster of dark grapes, that he wanted to touch them. At the end of the hall she opened a door on the right; it had a black-and-gold sign, small and glass-covered, which said Dr. Wace Fansler.

The office was dim, with the window shades pulled, and the air had a thin smell of chemicals. Over in the northeast corner a skeleton stood.

"Reckon I'm not in as bad a fix as that fellow, anyway," Jim said.

The girl smiled.

"You'll feel better," she said, "once you stretch out."

Against the west wall, between the door and a partition which reached part way to the ceiling, there was a leather couch; Jim lay down. When the back of his head touched the leather he could feel the pain streaking clear to his heels; he must have grimaced and caught his breath, for the girl said she was sorry he was suffering.

"Don't worry none about it, miss. Guess nobody's to blame but me. A fellow smacked me with knucks. I should have ducked."

"Knucks?" she said. "I don't believe I know what they are."

"No, miss," he said gently, "I don't guess you would," and while he explained, lying there with his eyes shut, he thought it was sort of appealing, to find a girl who didn't know about knucks and the sort of men who used them.

When she started to leave he propped himself up.

"Miss," he said, "I left my canoe there by the icehouse. Everything I own is in it. That fellow St. Clair said it would be safe, with him watching it, but I sort of wondered. I'd hate to lose my outfit."

She looked innocent, standing there, and puzzled.

"Don't you trust him?" she asked.

"Why, yes," he said, "I guess I do. Sure, I trust him. But I wouldn't want him stealing my outfit."

"Oh," she said, "he wouldn't steal. He owns the icehouse and the brick kilns, and he's superintendent of our Sunday School. He wouldn't steal."

"Well, thanks," Jim said. "I was just wondering."

After she had gone he had to smile, despite his pain, at a girl so inexperienced that she thought somebody was honest because he owned an icehouse and went to Sunday School. A man sort of had a hankering to stand between life and a girl like that, to protect her. And that was an odd feeling for him to have; most of his life he had been too busy watching out for himself to think of shielding others. The girls he had known had been quite able to take care of themselves.

He tried to sleep, but his headache got no better fast; finally he stood up and paced, the skeleton observing him with that sardonic grin the dead always give the living. On the partition, above a case of medical books, a mirror hung, and Jim saw himself. He looked a sight, hair rumpled and face unshaved; he wished he might have slicked up a little, before coming to see a doctor. At last he returned to the couch and sat massaging his head. Then a knock sounded; it was the girl.

"I've brought mother," she said. "Sometimes she helps dad with his patients."

Mrs. Fansler was a trim woman with brown eyes like her daughter's, and with gray hair; on her mouth she wore a professional smile, determinedly cheerful, and on her brow a beatific expression; but she had a willful little jaw.

"Where does it hurt?" she asked.

"It's my head, ma'am. It starts in my neck and goes up."

"Here?" she asked, fingering his neck.

The pain nearly lifted him, and he was about to exclaim, "God damn it, quit!" But just in time he remembered the girl; he wouldn't like to swear before a girl like that. She stood watching with sympathy in her eyes.

"That's the place," Jim said. "It's as sore as a bee-stung bear."

"It needs heat," Mrs. Fansler said, and she turned to her daughter. "Bonnie, fetch us some hot water and towels."

So her name was Bonnie. Even with his headache, Jim could admire the way her skirt flowed from her neat waist, and he liked the fit of her bodice.

"I do wish Dr. Fansler would get back," the woman was saying. "He's out to the Ashton place on Lance Creek delivering a baby. It beats all how many babies are born. You never realize it till you're a doctor's wife."

"I guess that's right, ma'am."

"But if the truth were known," she said, "I'll bet that baby's delivered and learning to walk by now." Her mouth still wore that smile, but she tossed her jaw and her eyes flashed. "I'll bet the doctor's sitting drinking cider with Sam Ashton. Or he's stopped at his spring. There's a spring somewhere in that coulee on the Lance Creek road, and he keeps a jug in it. I'd smash it, if I could find it. This was a temperance house when we bought it, and I said we'd keep it that way. You won't find a thimbleful in the Fansler House, Mr.—what did you say your name was?"

"Buckmaster. Jim Buckmaster."

"Mr. Buckmaster. Don't you think liquor's a great curse, Mr. Buckmaster?"

"Well, now, ma'am, I've heard tell it cures snake bite."

The woman snorted; she was telling her favorite cure for that when Bonnie Fansler returned, carrying towels and a basin and a tea kettle.

"Just sit where you are, Mr. Buckmaster," the woman said. "Bonnie, pour some water in that basin and hold it where I can reach."

While the woman wrung out towels and applied them to Jim's neck, the girl stood holding the basin. She had pretty hands, the skin smooth and warmly brown, the nails clean and pink. Sitting with his head lowered, he could see the toe of one slipper peeking from under her skirt, and he thought he could make out the contour of her leg beneath the dress; it set his imagination working. She was a slender girl but not skinny; her waist was maidenly and round. Once he shifted his head and Mrs. Fansler ordered him to hold still, but not before he had glimpsed the rise and fall of the girl's bosom as she breathed. A faint scent reached his nostrils of young flesh and starched muslin and sweetness. The hot towels didn't actually ease his pain, but he could bear it better with the girl so near.

Then footsteps sounded in the hall and the door opened, admitting a big man with an eminent nose.

"What's all this?" he asked.

"Wace Fansler, I declare," the woman said. "We thought you were never coming. Was it a boy or girl?"

"Both. Twins."

"Heaven help us! Did she have a hard time?"

"They always do," Dr. Fansler said. He took off his tall black hat, revealing a high bald head, brown as a buckeye, with a fringe of silky gray hair. Then he removed his black frock coat—he was wearing a waistcoat of yellow brocade—and rolled up his sleeves. And he asked Jim, "What are your complaints?"

"Headache," Mrs. Fansler said. "His name is Jim Buckmaster and he's off the river. Somebody gave him a crack in the jaw. It knocked him out and gave him head misery."

"The fellow wore knucks," Jim said. "That's how it happened. I've been hit plenty of times, with a fist, but knucks changes things."

"I should guess," Dr. Fansler said. And he told his wife and daughter that he would be examining the patient and they had better leave, lest modesty be affronted. When the door had closed behind them, he opened his worn leather satchel, found a bottle, shook out two pills, and went to a washstand where he poured a glass of water from a white china pitcher.

"Jim," he said, "the first thing is to drive out the pain. Then I'll look you over. Sounds like a fractured maxilla, but we'll see. I'd rather be kicked by a mule than hit with knucks. Like a drink?"

"Are you speaking of more water?" Jim asked.

"I am not."

"Friend," Jim said, "me and you talk the same language."

The doctor reached into his satchel and extracted a large bottle labeled Poison.

"Say when," he said.

"About four fingers should do."

Dr. Fansler found a glass for himself, poured it half full and lifted it. "To the human body," he said. "It's a damned poor thing at best, but it's all we have to house the soul, which may or may not be immortal. Let us hope not."

He sat down in a captain's chair and perched his big bluchers on a desk intricate with pigeonholes and snowed under with papers. He looked tired. Jim was thinking of the girl, and of how strange it was that this big-boned man with his homely face and shaggy brows should have fathered somebody so fetching. That girl was all right; he wouldn't mind knowing her better.

"Twins," Dr. Fansler said presently. "They'll live into the Twentieth Century, like as not, and listen to political windbags talk about the dignity of man. But getting born is damned undignified. Dying is more so, but less painful, I think. Lord, how they fought for life, out there this morning. It's always the same. They don't know a well from a hole in the ground, but they know it's good to breathe. How's the pain?"

"Easing off," Jim said. And he asked, "What was that thing you said I'd fractured?"

"Maxilla. I'll show you on Speedy here."

Dr. Fansler went to the skeleton and traced his forefinger along the lower jaw.

"You probably suffered a slight fracture, from what you've told me about those knucks. That would account for the headache. The whole face and neck are a network of nerves. I saw them when I dissected Speedy."

"You talk like he was a friend of yours," Jim said.

"Oh, he was. In a way. He used to work for me." Dr. Fansler refilled their glasses and sat down at the desk, and Jim had a notion he was talking to help his patient forget the pain. "I had a grist mill in western Maryland. A hill town called Elkader. Speedy drifted into town and hit me for a job. He was a gangling young man, a good enough worker, but slow. If he had a family anywhere, he never mentioned it. He was with me about a year, and then he took a bilious fever and died. I gave him a Christian funeral.

"I'd always wanted to be a doctor, Jim. When I was twenty-one I left my home in the Blue Ridge Mountains and went to Winchester, Virginia, where an old practitioner agreed to teach me what he knew. It wasn't much. And I supported myself by working as a hostler at Clark's Tavern. I might have become a doctor there in Winchester—it was a strong urge—but there are always other urges. A girl named Lottie Henderson worked at the tavern. She was from Lynchburg, Mrs. Clark's niece. I was a young man, and it was summer, and I had a room in the stables. Lottie used to visit me there. She was a fine figure of a girl, although her family wasn't of the best. Her mother lived in Lynchburg, and her father was Dick Stanger. Ever hear of him? No, probably not. Dick Stanger was a famous man along the Wilderness Trail. Infamous, perhaps I should say. A highwayman, back in the old days. He used to ride into Lynchburg in the dark of the moon and toss pebbles against Nan Henderson's window. Nan was Lottie's mother. Lottie was the fruit of that amour, so to speak. And by Godfrey, she was a girl, Jim. A real stunner.

"It was summer, as I've said. The happiest summer of my life. My room in the stables smelled of clover hay and oats and horse manure, an aroma sweeter than all the perfumes of Arabia, as Shelley has put it. Well, no summer lasts forever; the frost must come. We were married just in time. Just before the water broke, so to speak. Our son Max was born in April and a few days later Lottie died. Some people called it a judgment of heaven, although I called it puerperal fever.

"That was a low point of my life, Jim. By Godfrey, the things human beings go through! I'd smell horse manure and want to break into tears. And I smelled it all the time, of course, working in the stables. I got so I'd dread seeing a horse lift his tail. I was not quite twenty-two, and a widower with an infant son.

"Mrs. Clark was generous and gave him the best of care, but I must say my medical studies suffered. Then I met the present Mrs. Fansler, an estimable woman certainly. It came about because my son Max needed clothes. Mrs. Clark had no time to sew, with all her other duties, so I sought out Gwen Hawes. She lived with her parents there in Winchester—her father was a gunsmith—and she was a pleasant enough girl. A spinster, really; almost twenty-nine. She had been disappointed in love some years before, when her younger sister eloped with the man she was to marry, and she had taken up sewing for its therapeutic effect on a broken heart. I took Max with me to her home, so that she could measure him for clothes, and by Godfrey how she made over that baby!

It put ideas into my head, seeing her hold him. But she was petting the calf to get the cow.

"Max was fourteen months old when we were married. As a wedding present, Gwen's father gave us two hundred acres of land in western Maryland, and we moved there. So there I was, clearing land and begetting offspring. It seemed unlikely, in those days, that I'd ever be a physician, but in the evenings I kept studying. And when Mrs. Fansler presented me with children, I made the most of my opportunity to try my skill. You'd be surprised how much a man can learn about obstetrics right in his own family. And when a horse or pig fell sick, I had other opportunities. There is a great deal of medicine to be learned by practicing on the lower animals. Never feed an orphaned pig cow's milk, Jim. It will give him the scours. You must feed him sow's milk, which contains an acidulous substance that remains a mystery. There must be a connection between the scours in pigs and diarrhea in man, but I've never found it. But I will, and some morning like Keats—or was it Byron?— I will wake up famous.

"I never cared for farming, Jim, so after a few years I sold the land and moved to Elkader where I bought a grist mill. Not that I liked milling better, but in Elkader there was no doctor and I could hang out my shingle. A doctor must have practice, you know. Practice makes perfect. My fees were low so my practice grew, and the mill prospered tolerably. I had quite a family by then, three daughters in addition to Max. And I kept abreast of the latest developments in my profession. I studied. But there was one great lack in my training, Jim, and I felt it keenly: never had I dissected a human cadaver. Then Speedy came to town and died.

"I did what I did in the interests of science, Jim. Speedy had never benefited mankind greatly as he shuffled through life, but after he shuffled off this mortal coil, as Sir Walter Scott has so well said, Speedy became a specimen for the enlightenment of science. I had always shied away from robbing graves; it's a grisly business. But there lay Speedy. And he had no family. I gave him a beautiful funeral. And that evening I consulted my son Max.

"Max was eighteen by then and into everything. Wild as a hare. Sometimes I suspected that his stepmother curbed him too much when he was a child; she was always jealous of my first wife, of course. You can break the spirit of some boys, but not a boy like Max. And maybe he inherited a strain of madcap blood from Dick Stanger. Blood lines will tell, you know. Anyway, I reasoned that if Max was to be roistering into mischief, it might as well be mischief which would benefit science. When I put the matter up to him he was delighted. So the evening after poor Speedy was buried, Max and I betook ourselves to the necropolis. We carried spades and canvas. It was a beautiful September evening, when we exhumed Speedy.

654

"We carried him to a room in my grist mill and immersed him in a strong pickling solution. The room had a stout door with a heavy lock, and there, during the next weeks, I dissected poor Speedy. And from him I learned more about the human body than from all the books. Max used to help me, and I had hopes that he too would turn to the healing arts. But then Halloween came. Our town marshal, Ty Ransom, had vowed that no pranks should be played that night, and naturally that was a challenge to the young bloods. Max and his crowd had just succeeded in boosting a sheep into the belfry of the Baptist Church when Ty arrived on the scene. The boys ran. During the pursuit, Ty fell and broke his left tibia. There was talk of swearing out warrants against the mischief makers, so Max left for the West.

"And we left, my family and I, a few years later, in the spring of '46. By then I had strung poor Speedy together, and I knew my anatomy. And I heard the call of opportunity in the West. We went to St. Louis where Max was employed as a bartender. He had been a steward on river boats, and during his travels he had often visited this beautiful little city. He recommended it. So we came here and bought the hotel with the proceeds from the sale of my grist mill in Elkader. It was a fortunate move. My two elder daughters found husbands here, and my practice is successful. How is your head, Jim?"

"The pain's gone. And I'm getting sleepy."

"To be expected. Another drink, before we proceed with the examination?"

Jim held out his glass. Dr. Fansler's voice came from far away.

"You would have met Max, if you had been a day earlier. He left yesterday for St. Louis. Max is still restless. He spends the warm months with us, helping out at the hotel, but when the geese go south so does he. A bartender, he tells me, can always find work, in St. Louis or points south. And Max is lucky at cards. Now then, if you will sit in this chair, we will examine your maxilla."

*

Nothing bothered him now, except the desire to sleep. His body had gone away somewhere and his head was a balloon floating in river fog. Fingers were pressing his jaw but it didn't hurt; fingers pressed the base of his skull but still it didn't hurt. Through layers of fog came a voice belonging to a man named Dr. Wace Fansler, saying that the maxilla seemed unbroken . . . but perhaps cracked . . . and a vertebra had perhaps been dislocated . . . ah, yes, that should fix it . . . and now if Jim would lie down . . . and it might be well for him to remain here at the hotel for a day or two . . . under observation . . .

Sure, he thought, as the fog thickened, sure, I'll stay. Ought to get a shave, though.

He was thinking about a shave when he wakened, but he couldn't remember why it was so important. He elbowed himself up, there on the couch; then, with a sigh, lay down again. Sleep returned, but now it was thinner, and he thought his beard had grown till it was so long he tripped over it while being chased by a marshal on Halloween. Then he heard a door opening and he sat up.

"Oh," the girl said, "you're awake."

"Not quite. But I'm working at it."

"Dad's off on a call," she said. "He told me to keep watch. How is the pain?"

"Pain? Why, miss, the pain's all right. The pain's gone. What time is it?"

"Almost three o'clock."

He sat there feeling dreamy, thinking she was a pretty girl. He wanted to tell her so, the way he would have told a girl in a saloon, but something stopped him. He wanted to tell her she put him in mind of a doe deer in the woods, delicate and alert, standing among the lily pads at the edge of a shining lake, where everything was quiet and cool. He said: "I need a shave. I need a shave bad."

"You'd better lie down," she said.

With the shades pulled the light in the office was pleasantly green, like the underwater dimness of a millpond. An unaccustomed lassitude flowed along his arms and legs, but he felt fine, released from pain. He couldn't remember, right offhand, the day of the week or the month of the year, but it didn't matter; he was oddly contented to sit here doing nothing. Still, he ought to get a shave; the girl had never seen him clean-shaved.

"Miss," he said, "I don't suppose there's a barber shop in town."

"Oh, yes," she said, "there's a barber. But you'd better rest. Dad said you need it. He said you were lucky not to have a broken jaw."

He liked the sound of her voice, low-pitched and demure. He thought he could listen to it all afternoon without wanting it to stop. And he thought he could sit watching her all afternoon, but he didn't like to stare; that wasn't polite; so he just stole a glance now and then. In the dull light her hair had a dark luster, and her skin was evenly brown. She stood there unsmiling and almost somber, not looking at him.

"Miss," he heard himself saying, "you'll be hearing things about me. They'll say I was push of Camp Seven and the best raft pilot on the river, but that I padded my accounts. But don't you go believing all you hear, miss. There's a mistake somewhere. McSwasey said I'd padded my accounts and he smacked me with knucks, but it was all a mistake. Mistakes happen. You know that."

"Yes," she said, "of course. Of course mistakes happen."

"I would have been a fool, wouldn't I, to pad my accounts? I was headed for the top, miss. I was the best push in the woods and the best pilot on the river. I was going places, miss. It don't stand to reason, does it, that I'd pad my accounts and get blacklisted, with a future ahead of me?"

"No," she said, her voice so low it was almost a whisper, "of course not."

She looked bewildered by all he'd been saying, and he could understand that; he was outside her experience. Well, she was outside his, too. She wasn't a saloon girl. He didn't even want to take her to a bedroom, not right away. It sort of surprised him. Always before, that was all he had wanted from a girl. There was fire burning, he judged, behind the smoke of her somberness, but he wouldn't want to hurry things. Not with her.

"Miss," he said, remembering the letter he had written to McSwasey, "is there a post office in town? I've got me a letter to mail."

"In Winthrop & Marsh's store," she said. "You could mail it there."

She drew a breath and gave her head a little toss, to rearrange her curls. Then her eyes happened to meet his; she looked away quickly. It was odd, he thought, how it got right to him, when their glances met; it made it hard to breathe.

"Dad said you should lie quiet," she was saying. "You'd better sleep some more."

"Sleep?" he said, smiling. "Why, miss, I feel fine."

He stood up. And he did feel fine except for the hollowness in his legs, from missing meals. He went to the washstand and poured a glass of water; over the rim he saw her standing in the door, and he noticed that she had a good clean-cut jaw, long and firm. After draining the glass he reached down his hat from a hook.

"Mr. Buckmaster," she said, "dad wouldn't like it, your stirring around this way. He said for you to rest."

Hat cocked at an angle, he stood there smiling. She remained in the door, as if to block his exit, color working its way under the brownness of her cheeks. And she told him to lie right back down on that couch; he'd have another headache, getting up so soon. Her somberness had deepened; it was almost a sulkiness; almost, but not quite.

He had never been one to let a woman run him; no real good ever came of that. Even the handsomest filly, he guessed, needed a man's hand on the reins.

"Why, miss," he said, "I'm as good as new. I'm just going to the barber, miss." And when she remained standing in the doorway he added gently, "You wouldn't want me to pick you up and move you out of the way. I'll have to do that, miss."

She stepped aside then.

*

Outside the hotel in the bright afternoon he felt lightheaded from lack of food, but he was smiling, and the river had never looked bluer. It might have been a day in spring, the way he felt. He stood there on the

657

brick sidewalk, thinking Wace Fansler must be the best doctor in the world, to make a man feel so happy.

Through the years that afternoon shimmered like a dream. He remembered passing the livery stable south of the hotel, and a blacksmith shop where a smoky man in a leather apron was pounding red sparks from a horseshoe on the anvil. In the barber shop, where several loafers were ahead of him, but no customers, he stretched out in the plush chair and surrendered to the bliss of steaming towels and creamy lather. He could feel himself smiling, and he kept thinking that Bonnie was a very fine name. Bonnie Fansler. He had always been open-minded about the color of a girl's hair; brunette or blonde or redhead, it made no difference; but now he guessed he would take dark hair every time.

"Brother," the barber said, stropping his razor, "them whiskers of yours is tough. You must have been eating gravel."

"No," Jim said, "sawdust."

He didn't want conversation; he wanted to lie remembering. He could hear her voice, in memory, and see her walking along a hall, her curls the color of river nights. And he thought how it would be to muss up those curls, but that could wait. It could wait a long time, if need be. She was a nice girl, and he wouldn't want to hurry matters and spoil everything.

"Like a haircut too?" the barber asked, and Jim said yes; a man should slick up once in a while. When he got out of the chair and saw himself in the mirror he looked like a new man, his cheeks smooth and talc-dusted, his hair moist with that scented lotion the barber had sprinkled from a fancy lavender bottle.

The girl had said he could mail a letter in Winthrop & Marsh's store; it stood on a corner, a large brick building with a lodge hall above. It was cavernous inside, with iron pillars and hanging lamps and an acre of counters and cases. Going to the postal window, back by the golden oak and grillwork of the office, Jim passed through the smells of oilcloth and dress goods and new shoes, all mixed with the oiled-tool smell of hardware and acrid whiffs from the vinegar barrel. He felt a load slide from his mind, when he dropped the letter into the slot; reading it, McSwasey would know he was right on the job.

As he returned toward the front entrance, he saw a clerk coming along the aisle, a brisk young man of twenty-eight or thirty with a light, wiry build who asked if he could be of service.

"Well, now, friend," Jim said, "maybe you could, at that. Do you sell razors?"

Yes, the clerk said, they had a very good stock; and he led the way to a showcase with enough razors to arm all the black roustabouts on the Mississippi. He kept laying them on the case and passing compliments on their virtues; Jim wished he would hold his tongue so a man could think.

"Here's one of Sheffield steel. The very best. You'll want a strop too, and a mug and a brush."

Jim didn't much care for that clerk, with his high-powered tongue and his brown hair neatly brushed from a part on the side. His mouth and ears were small; his nose looked as if somebody had taken it between thumb and forefinger and squeezed it to a point; and his eyes were the size and color of little hazel nuts. When he leaned over the case you could see his shoulder blades trying to poke through his worsted coat.

"A newcomer, aren't you?" he asked once.

"Off the river," Jim said. "I'm staying a day or so at the Fansler House."

"That's where I live," the clerk said. "Cleanest beds and finest food this side of Bennington. But their prices are dear."

"The other fellow has to make a living too," Jim said.

The young man held out his hand. It looked lean-fingered from counting money, and when Jim took it, it felt bony and dry.

"My name is Hale Winthrop. Pleased to make your acquaintance."

Jim had a notion to give that shopkeeper something to remember by putting force into the handshake, but it would have been picking on somebody not his size.

"What else will you have?" Hale Winthrop asked, after Jim paid for the shaving equipment. "Some elastic galluses, maybe? A pocket knife? Spanish cigars?"

Jim said no.

"Ever play a harmonica? It's easy to learn, and we have some fine ones imported from Bavaria. No? Then how about a jew's-harp? You'd be surprised how easy—"

"I might take a pound of wooden nutmegs," Jim said.

Hale Winthrop laughed; he had small, even teeth, very white.

"Never stock them. That's for Connecticut merchants. I'm from Vermont. We do have the latest thing in Bibles though, the revised edition with the New Testament."

Jim shook his head, but then an idea came to him.

"I don't guess," he said slowly, "you'd have something a girl might like."

"Hundreds of items. Calicoes, silks, hosiery, shoes, stays, ribbons—"

"Nothing like that."

"Jewelry, maybe?"

"Maybe," Jim said, and unexpectedly he felt his ears coloring. He had never bought a present for a girl; he had never thought of such a thing before. Oh, drinks, of course, in a saloon; but this was different. This girl was different. It took him by surprise, wanting to spend money on a girl he hardly knew.

"Right this way," Hale Winthrop said, and Jim followed him to another showcase where all kinds of girlish do-dads were on display. Combs and bracelets and lockets; rings and watches and earrings; but none of them seemed fitting. Maybe it was too forward an idea anyway, buying a present for a nice girl he had met only this morning. But damn, it seemed he had known her longer. And he could always tell her the gift was in return for her kindness when he was in such pain.

"Is she somebody—ah—special?" Hale Winthrop asked.

She was, of course. But he didn't like this pipsqueak's prying into his affairs.

"Why, friend," he said, "maybe she is and maybe she isn't. I don't see what that's got to do with it."

"It's the matter of price. These are nice trinkets, but if she's somebody you'd be willing to lay out more cash for, I have a few really fine things back in the safe."

Again, Jim felt the blood in his ears. He said:

"I haven't been bellyaching about your prices, have I?"

"Let me get them," the shopkeeper said, and he hurried back to the office.

Waiting there by the showcase, Jim was aware of an odd self-consciousness, as if he were making a public spectacle of himself. He wondered what the other customers were thinking, seeing a full-grown man frittering his time at a case full of geegaws. But damn, it was his money; if he wanted to buy a gift for Bonnie Fansler, whose business was it?

When Hale Winthrop returned, and placed a half dozen small boxes on the counter, and snapped up their lids, Jim saw at once that their contents were not to be compared with those other gimcracks. These had a quiet richness, as if the craftsmen who fashioned them had been thinking of cool countesses and haughty princesses and all the fine women of the world; of handsome girls like Bonnie Fansler. Even their cases were splendid, with their smooth red or blue leather and their velvet lining.

There was a necklace of thin gold leaves dangling from a chain with infinitesimal links; there was a bracelet fashioned from the gold coins of Spain; there was a heart-shaped brooch set with fire opals. But what attracted him most was an oval sardonyx of carnelian red, carved with the fine profile of a Lydian girl in a tint of pale rosebud. He held it in his palm; it looked small and patrician, lying against his calluses. The girl of the cameo had flowing hair instead of curls, but her features might have been Bonnie Fansler's.

He knew he was going to buy it, no matter what the cost, for he felt flushed with a sudden prodigality he didn't understand. But he returned it to its case and examined the other merchandise.

"The prices run dear," Hale Winthrop said. "I won't pretend not. They don't rightly belong in a store like mine. Two years ago I was on a buying trip, and I picked them up at a bankrupt wholesaler's. When there's wildcat money afloat, the best place for funds is sometimes in jewels."

"What do you want for them?" Jim asked.

Hale Winthrop rearranged the boxes on the counter, his hands looking dry and thin-wristed.

"Less than they're worth," he said. "They may seem high, but they will still be bargains."

Then he named prices; the cameo was a hundred dollars

"I guess," Jim said, "you don't much want to sell."

And he made a move to leave.

"Hold on," Hale Winthrop said. "The time to grab a bargain is when you find it. Like with me and the toll bridge. I bought it for a thousand dollars and they thought I was crazy."

"A toll bridge for a thousand?"

"On the Wabash River in Indiana. That was in May of '43. I was twenty-two years old and I'd just come from Vermont with two thousand in cash I'd been ten years saving. Well, there was a freshet on the Wabash, and when I came to the town of Yardley the river was lapping the floor boards of the bridge. A banker owned it; he was standing by the tollhouse looking glum. I decided to gamble. A faint heart never won a fortune, you know. I told the banker there had been a cloudburst upstream and his bridge was sure to wash out, but that I'd pay him a thousand for the bridge as it stood so I could salvage the lumber. He made out the bill of sale so fast my head was swimming. Well, that was the crest of the freshet. The river dropped and I owned a valuable property. I operated it for a year and sold it for ten thousand. A man should never pass up a bargain."

Jim slipped a hand inside his shirt; from his money belt he extracted six gold eagles and spread them on the showcase. Winthrop started to reach, then pulled back his hand. But there was a gleam in his eyes.

"What are these for?" he asked.

Jim smiled.

"The necklace. Or maybe the brooch. It's all the same to me."

Winthrop shook his head, but he couldn't take his eyes off the gold pieces.

"Well, then," Jim said, pointing at the cameo, "how about this one?"

On the edge of the showcase Winthrop's hands looked twitchy.

"I'm losing money," he said.

But he took the gold eagles.

*

After Hale Winthrop wrapped the little box in tissue paper and tied it with ribbon, Jim dropped it into his shirt pocket and left that store forthwith, like a man retreating from a public indiscretion. He couldn't figure what had come over him, that he would squander sixty dollars on a trinket; he felt shamefaced. Yet he was oddly happy too, and outside the store he hesitated, wanting another look at the package. But there

661

were people on the sidewalk who might crane their necks; so, feeling queerly secretive, he crossed the street to the levee, empty in the sunshine, and leaned against a snubbing post, where finally he brought the package from his pocket. It looked festive, and he could imagine Bonnie Fansler untying the ribbon.

But maybe she wouldn't like that present, or maybe, being a nice girl, she would take it amiss, his giving it to her. Now that he thought about it, he seemed to remember some rule of etiquette that had trickled down from the polite world; something about a lady's never accepting gifts of a personal nature from a gentleman. A cameo, he guessed, might be of a personal nature, when you considered where she would wear it on her dress. But damn, he had spent good money for that cameo, and he sure as hell intended giving it to her, etiquette or not.

He returned the package to his pocket and stood looking toward the hotel, feeling like a man in some kind of pleasurable trance. Any minute now, he told himself, he would walk over to that hotel and go inside. She would be sitting behind the desk, working on embroidery, and he would cross the lobby and hand her the gift. Miss, he would say, you were mighty kind, when my head was bothering. Here's something I bought for you.

But he made no move; he remained there at the snubbing post, pulses beating, in his lungs a queer excitement, half fright and half anticipation. Minutes passed. He could feel himself smiling, at nothing in particular. Once he took off his hat—a pilot's hat of black felt, with an adventurous brim—and brushed off the dust with the edge of his hand. Then he paced back and forth along the levee, gazing out at the river. But always his attention returned to the hotel. In the dreamy afternoon it looked half-asleep, with soft sky overhead and autumnal trees rising behind it; the westering sun had left its façade in shadow, and the old red bricks were delicately overwashed with a bluish hue. Sometimes a pedestrian walked along the sidewalk, or a rig creaked down the street, the horses' hoofs muffled in the thick dust; and then everything would become hushed again, except for sparrows cheeping.

Well, hell, she couldn't eat him; the thing to do was take a deep breath and cross the street and give her the present. It wasn't like him, this fretting around. Usual thing, if he had a job of work to do, he did it. And girls had never scared him.

So he hitched up his belt and started, but after a few steps another thought struck him: suppose her mother was in the lobby. Her mother might not like it so well, having a strange man giving her daughter a present. It halted him. Feeling foolish, he retraced his steps to the levee. He hoped people weren't watching; they would think he had gone out of his mind. He turned his back, trying to act natural, and stared off downriver, as if watching for a steamboat; but before he knew it he was looking toward the hotel again.

Her mother! Damn! That was the drawback in dealing with nice girls: they had mothers. Allies, counselors, accomplices! Mothers were, so he had heard, notoriously suspicious, always taking the low view of a man's motives. That would mean, certainly, that Mrs. Fansler would be pretty dubious, when she learned that her daughter had received an expensive gift.

The afternoon was wearing on, and suddenly he remembered his canoe. Since morning he had given it scarcely a thought, and that too was unlike him, leaving his property where it might be snitched. So he left the levee and made for the icehouse, planning to get his calamity sack and return to the hotel. When he signed for a room, if the girl was alone in the lobby, he might give her the cameo then and there. And if Mrs. Fansler didn't approve, she would just have to lump it.

The canoe had vanished, when he reached the loading chute where he had left it, and that gave him a start; but then somebody called and he saw Alonzo St. Clair on the loading platform of the icehouse.

"Your outfit's inside," St. Clair said. "I saw you from the office and figured what you were after."

Jim walked up the incline to the platform.

"Friend," he said, "I've been sick. Usual thing, I don't walk out on my outfit like that. But I'm not myself today."

"Did the doc fix you up?" St. Clair asked.

"Yes, sir, he did. I had a headache, but it's gone now."

"We all have our miseries," St. Clair said. "With me it's hernia. I lifted too hard when we were cutting ice last winter. But Doc Fansler fitted me with a truss."

Jim followed him through a wide door into the icehouse, a vast dim place which smelled of musty sawdust. The canoe was there, and all his outfit. Picking up his calamity sack, he told St. Clair he would be staying all night at the hotel; if he could leave his outfit here, he would be glad to pay storage. Leave it as long as he liked, St. Clair said; there would be no charge; and he led the way through the building to an office at the front, where a cat was curled among the papers on the desk. It had also been a patient of Dr. Fansler, St. Clair said.

"He'd get chewed up fighting and I'd take him to Doc. Finally Doc said, 'Look here, this tom's going to get himself killed, courting all the time. Why don't we remove his temptations?' So that's what we did, and now he don't hate anybody. Nor love them either. I don't guess he gets too much out of life, but he's got his memories."

St. Clair picked up the cat and stroked it. And he asked:

"How long do you figure to stay in Lanceport?"

"A day or so. The doc wants to check me tomorrow."

"I was thinking," St. Clair said, "that if you're around next winter I might have a job for you cutting ice. You're a big strong fellow, and that's what it takes. Once the river's froze we cut a lot of ice, and ship it to St. Louis in the summer."

"Well, now, friend," Jim said, "I might take you up on that. We'll see." And he added, "That was white of you, bringing my outfit in under the roof when I was sick. I'd feel better if you'd let me pay storage."

Wouldn't think of it, St. Clair said. However, if Jim wanted to do him a favor, he could buy a ticket to a fish fry being held that evening in the basement of the Methodist Church.

"We're raising money to pay off the mortgage," he explained.

"Why, sure," Jim said, "I'll buy a ticket. How much?"

"Two bits."

Jim gave him a dollar. And he said, smiling:

"Hell, mister, you'll never pay off at two bits a throw. Keep the change. And put my ticket back in the kitty and sell it again. I'll be eating at the Fansler House and going right to bed."

He stayed in that office a little longer, guiding the conversation around to Dr. Fansler in the hopes that St. Clair would say something about Dr. Fansler's daughter. But all St. Clair wanted to talk about was his hernia and the operation on his cat. Jim could, he supposed, come right out and speak of Bonnie Fansler, but he shied away from that, as if she were a secret he would rather not mention. But he kept thinking of her.

There was a hint of early twilight sneaking out of Lance Coulee when he left the icehouse, and a smell of burning leaves. Somewhere in a barn-lot a cow was lowing, and a flock of blackbirds were clacking in the trees along Linden Street. Approaching the hotel, Jim was very much aware of the little package in his shirt pocket, and his heart began to pound; but when he entered the lobby Mrs. Fansler was behind the desk; her daughter was nowhere in sight.

*

In his room on the second floor of the hotel he stripped to the waist and spent ten minutes over the wash bowl scrubbing himself and toweling himself, till his skin glowed; and after selecting a clean flannel shirt, and smoothing it neatly inside his belt, he picked up the package containing the cameo and stood hefting it, smiling. Then he slipped it into his pocket and looked himself over, at the mirror. In the light from the single candle his skin was coppery dark, his hair and brows black, but his eyes were the warm gray of campfire smoke, and there were laughter-wrinkles around them, so that he looked a little like a genial rogue.

His watch said nearly six, and supper was served at six. Not for years —not since that evening long ago in Quickwater, when he had been invited to eat oyster stew with Mr. and Mrs. Lew Fitzpatrick—had he been so filled with anticipation about a meal. As he put on his jacket—

the best coat he owned—and renewed the crease in his pilot's hat, it occurred to him that he had been negligent about clothes, a roughneck for sure; he wished now for a well-tailored coat and trousers, and for a resplendent waistcoat. And he wished for the knowledge of decorum that went with a gentleman's clothes. Heretofore, he had dismissed as dandified the fine points of etiquette, but now he could see that such knowledge might come in handy. At the mirror again—and he had never been one to primp before a mirror—he was not entirely pleased with the fit of the coat; it looked too skimpy for his shoulders, the sleeves too short on his heavy wrists. And he thought his hands looked clumsy, with their broad palms and powerful fingers, and with the black hairs growing on their backs with so much vitality.

He left the room at last and descended to the lobby, where already the noise of crockery could be heard from the dining room. His heart was misbehaving and his nerves were tingling, as he thought he would be seeing the girl now, within a second or two. But she was not in the lobby. Nobody was there except that storekeeper, Hale Winthrop, standing at the table in the center of the room leafing through a magazine, looking dapper and cocksure. He said good evening and Jim replied, but he didn't linger there; he went to the open double doors of the dining room and glanced inside, where the air was scented with food and lamps were burning and two waitresses were hurrying platters to a long table populated by a dozen men bent in eating. The girl was not in the room. In the kitchen, maybe. She might not eat till after the first rush. Jim had tasted no food since last night, and his stomach was signaling for reinforcements, but he decided to wait. When he returned to the lobby Hale Winthrop looked up and said this was fine weather they had been having. Jim nodded, but his mind was otherwise occupied.

He drifted about the lobby, killing time, pausing to examine a long-case clock against the north wall, its face painted with flowers and medallions; looking at a picture above the pigeonholes behind the desk, which showed a lion peering from among palmettos; lighting a cigar finally and seating himself in a chair along the south wall. He felt restless, wishing the girl would appear. And he was baffled at himself for postponing eating on the chance that he might sit at the same table with her. Always before when he was hungry he had eaten, if food was available. Hell, he would be here a day or two; he would have plenty of chances to talk with the girl. What had got into him, anyway? He sat quietly, the ash lengthening on his cigar.

Then from the direction of Dr. Fansler's office he heard a door open and close—the Fansler family occupied those ground-floor rooms, he learned later—and he saw the girl coming into the lamplight, looking smart and striking in a flawlessly-fitted dress of black wool. Jim got to his feet.

"Am I late?" she asked, smiling.

665

But the question was not directed at him. She didn't even see him, so far as he could gather. She was speaking to Hale Winthrop, who had hurried to meet her.

On her arm she carried a light wrap, and while Jim watched she gave this to her escort and turned, her body graceful, so that he might arrange it over her shoulders. She had put up her hair tonight, and she wore a frivolous hat which was hardly more than a crisp little nosegay of ribbons and posies. Hale Winthrop said something and she laughed while she stood drawing on white gloves, which, like her white cuffs and collar, contrasted artfully with the blacks of her dress and hair. And although her bright glance kept moving about the room, she still didn't see Jim. It was remarkable.

Then Mrs. Fansler came from the dining room and the girl went over to her, looking so elegant and tempting that Jim's tongue was dry. He felt foolish, standing there staring, but he couldn't help himself; he had never, he thought, known such a bewitching girl. She and her mother were talking about the fish fry at the Methodist Church; apparently Hale Winthrop was taking her there; and Jim remembered the ticket he had bought from Alonzo St. Clair, and had not kept.

With Hale Winthrop by her side, with his hand, indeed, lightly guiding her elbow, the girl moved toward Jim on her way to the door. As she approached, he was aware of an elusive fragrance, and for an instant her glance met his, her smile coquettish, her eyes eloquent and a little self-conscious too. He could feel heat in his face and weakness in his knees. He watched her going through the door to the street, her step light as a young queen's. Then she was gone. He sat down, feeling he had passed through some extraordinary experience.

Somebody was asking him a question, something about his headache, and he looked up to see Mrs. Fansler.

"It's better, ma'am," he heard himself saying. "Yes, ma'am, it sure is."

She was glad, she said; and hadn't he better eat? Supper was on the table.

"Eat? Well, now, maybe I should, ma'am. But I don't feel hungry."

"You need food," she said. "Seems to me you still look sort of sick. Food will make you feel better."

So he followed her into the dining room; but food didn't make him feel better, much.

*

He couldn't remember what he ate. He couldn't remember the others at the table, or the waitresses, or whether he swallowed coffee or tea; everything was tasteless. But he remembered the girl; he had no trouble whatsoever in that respect. And he remembered Hale Winthrop.

Winthrop! A pipsqueak! Why would a girl like Bonnie Fansler go out with him?

If that hotel lobby had been a saloon, Jim guessed he would have brushed Winthrop aside and taken the girl for himself. Miss, he would have said, you don't want to fool around with that snap turtle. You string along with me. I'm going to own me the river, and I'll give you a handful of stars to sprinkle in your hair.

But in polite circles things were not done that way.

He finished supper and returned to the lobby, but without her it seemed an empty place. At the window he stood staring out at Promenade Street, although if his eyes picked up any interesting sights his brain never knew it; he was not even aware of his reflection frowning in the pane. A cigar found its way to his teeth, but he never thought to light it.

Feeling a vast restlessness, he left the hotel, thinking a walk might be good for whatever ailed him. He might even find his way to the Methodist Church. Not to go in—he wouldn't know how to behave—but it would be interesting to have a look at that church and know Bonnie Fansler was inside.

Next to the hotel, in the office of the livery stable, where a dim lantern cast a red glow, he was told the church could be found two blocks west of Promenade on Linden Street. He hurried, following those directions, as if fearful that the fish fry might be ended before he could get there. When he came to an intersection where a streetlamp burned, he cut across to the north side of Linden, passing dark houses and an alley and reaching a vacant lot. Beyond it he could see the church, the basement windows lighted. Buggies and wagons were tethered to hitching posts along the street, the horses stamping softly or shaking their harness. Jim hesitated, telling himself he had better go back to the hotel.

But something made him do otherwise; he was cutting across that vacant lot toward the church. The lighted windows were near now; he could hear laughter and girlish screams. When he reached the church he stood in deep shadow; and finally, wondering what he would say if somebody caught him, he stooped and peered through a basement window.

He saw a room with lamps and whitewashed walls. Tables and chairs had been shoved out of the way, and in the center of the room young people stood in what was probably a circle, although from where he watched he couldn't see its entire perimeter. Then he glimpsed Hale Winthrop scurrying around that circle, carrying a handkerchief; he passed from sight; there were shrieks; and when next he came into view he was being chased by Bonnie Fansler, who now carried the handkerchief. The laughter increased; pursued and pursuer vanished; and then they were in sight again, with Bonnie overtaking the young man and touching him with the handkerchief. She was laughing.

Drop-the-handkerchief! Well my God!

As he knelt there, a fine large scorn poured through Jim. So that was what went on in churches! He had an impulse to stand up and go tramping back to the hotel. But he kept watching. He couldn't take his eyes off the girl. And as he noticed how carefree she looked, he was aware of a mounting anger. He would have enjoyed busting into that party and cleaning house. Smashing all the young men's heads together. And then leading Bonnie by the ear out into the shadows and telling her a few things, such as how he didn't like it so well to have her leaving him at the hotel and going to parties with Hale Winthrop and smiling prettily at all the boys.

He stood up suddenly, sweating, and his fists were clenched. He made himself unclench them. He worked at calming down. And he told himself that giving way to anger must be an aftermath of his headache and of those pills he had swallowed. He would leave town tomorrow and forget the girl. She was a nice girl, that was the trouble; with her he was out of his depth.

All at once he realized that the fish fry was breaking up; he could hear voices outside the church and see people walking along the sidewalk. If somebody, the damned preacher or somebody, came snooping and discovered him here he would be in a fine pickle. So he struck out east across the vacant lot, intending to make a wide circle back to the hotel. But when he reached the alley with its deep shadows he decided to wait and watch for Bonnie Fansler. Not that she meant a thing to him, but she had, after all, been sympathetic when his head ached, and maybe he should keep watch over her in case that Winthrop tried getting fresh with his hands and she needed help.

Across the vacant lot he could see men with lanterns untying their teams, and hear the truckling of home-bound rigs; presently the hitching posts were untenanted. Everything was quiet, although lights still burned in the church basement. Bonnie must still be there; he would have seen her if she had left. He hurried back across the vacant lot and peered through the window where he had watched before, but the room was empty. He tried another window. And he saw her then in the kitchen of the basement, where, with a dozen others, she was cleaning up after the party, wearing an apron and drying dishes. And that apron, in its workaday contrast with her elegant dress, gave her a certain piquancy; she looked like a pretty young wife, somebody a man would like to come home to. When she turned, the apron strings tied in a big bow looked crisp and luscious and tempting; Jim could imagine reaching out and untying that bow.

Somebody else wore an apron—Hale Winthrop—and you could tell he thought it was a very funny thing to do. He kept clowning, pretending to drop a dish and then catching it, putting a polish on a plate and holding it up as if it were a mirror; the half-assed fool. Jim returned to the alley.

After what seemed a long time couples began leaving the church and the windows went black; Jim edged along the alley toward Linden Street. Presently, coming along the sidewalk. he made out two couples and heard

668

Bonnie Fansler's voice. He gave them time to proceed a safe distance before he fell in behind. At the intersection one couple turned north; the other—Hale Winthrop and Bonnie—crossed to the south side of the street. Jim followed.

Approaching Promenade Street they moved more slowly till they were nearly at a halt, and in the dull light Winthrop's arm encircled Bonnie's waist. Jim had all he could do to keep from breaking into a run and grabbing the fellow's collar. But that was unnecessary. Bonnie could take care of herself. As he watched, she took Winthrop's arm and removed it from where it had no business. They walked on.

And suddenly, a great surge of happiness poured through Jim. He wanted to dance a jig. By God, maybe nice girls were all right, at that.

*

Next morning Dr. Fansler examined his jaw and the base of his skull, and although pain lingered sullenly in both, it was the doctor's opinion that it would gradually leave.

"I won't promise you'll never have another headache," he told Jim, "but they shouldn't come as often. If you're bothered, take these pills."

Jim paid him, and in the lobby, where Mrs. Fansler was at the desk, he brought out his money to settle his hotel account.

"You're leaving today?" she asked.

That had been his intention. But he hadn't seen Bonnie all morning, although he had been watching. The cameo was still in his pocket. Somewhat to his surprise, he said:

"No, ma'am, I'll get an early start tomorrow. But I'll pay you now."

"We don't serve breakfast till six," she said. "Will you leave before that?"

Long before, he told her; he planned to be up at 4:00 A.M. In that case, she said, hadn't she better tell Guy, the night clerk, to knock on his door at four? He supposed so. And then, with a dry throat, he said he hadn't seen her daughter this morning; he wouldn't like to leave without thanking her for what she had done when he was sick.

"Bonnie is out in Lance Coulee," Mrs. Fansler said, "spending the day with her sister."

He felt at loose ends, wandering upstairs to his room and wandering back, eating his noon meal, drifting over to the levee. A south wind had come up; the sky was scummed with thin clouds and dust blew along Promenade Street; the river flowed in pale gray, with occasional whitecaps. He watched the waves lapping shore, feeling unaccountably weary and discontented. He might, he supposed, go for a walk into Lance Coulee, although if he met Bonnie she would probably think he had been tracking her. Maybe she wouldn't like that; maybe such things were not allowable in the polite world.

Finally he went to the office of the icehouse where he told Alonzo St.

Clair of his plan to pull out before daylight tomorrow; maybe, he said, he had better move his canoe and his dunnage outside now. No need for that, St. Clair said; the key was under the front mat.

"Any time you want your canoe, unlock the door and get it. There's no crime in Lanceport except drunkenness and fornication. Sit down—just move the cat. Have you thought over that offer about cutting ice?"

He had, Jim said; but maybe St. Clair wouldn't want him, if he knew he was the same Jim Buckmaster who had been fired by Caleb McSwasey. And he told what had happened in Rafferty's Saloon.

"I heard that story several days ago," St. Clair said. "Mate on the *Susie Kramer* was telling it. When you hit town I figured you were the fellow. Well, I know a little about judging men. I can pick the smart ones. You wouldn't fool around with picayune stuff like payroll padding."

"Thanks, friend," Jim said; and after a while, by degrees, he nudged the conversation around to the fish fry, mentioning how he had seen Bonnie Fansler and Hale Winthrop leaving the hotel to attend. Did they, he asked, go out together much?

"He's courting her," St. Clair said. "They would have been married before this, if she would have had him. But he'll wear her down, I reckon. Well, she'll have a rich husband some day, if she marries him. He's a hustler. I don't like him myself—he sold me a barrel of weevily flour and wouldn't make it good—that's a Yankee for you—but he'll end up owning the whole county."

"Who was it her sister married?" Jim asked. "The one in Lance Coulee, I mean."

"You mean Dorothy? She married Herman Dowd. He works for me cutting ice, when farming is slow."

"How far out does Dowd live, would you say?"

"Three or four miles. Let me tell you about the time I and Dowd was lifting this chunk of ice and it gave me the hernia. It was the twenty-third day of February, and—"

The wind was blowing harder when Jim left the office; the river was curdled with whitecaps; he wouldn't have wanted to be paddling a lopsided canoe through those waves. Maybe, he thought, going west along Linden Street, he'd better lay over in Lanceport several days. But McSwasey wouldn't like that; McSwasey expected him to keep moving; obviously, he wasn't going to run across log thieves in a village where the only crimes were drunkenness and fornication. Anyway, the weather pattern at this time of year was early-morning calmness; he could make a good many miles on the way to Read's Landing before the wind was likely to rise.

He passed the Methodist Church; the sidewalk petered out; hat pulled low, leaning into the wind, he followed a road that curved into a deep fold of the bluffs. In some places the valley was too narrow for farming, and the hills on either side rose steeply, wooded with hickory and oak and walnut, their branches heaving, their stripped leaves hurrying blindly like refugees trying to flee winter; in other places the coulee widened out in pastures and little patchwork fields of Indian corn, the wind-bent stalks pale gold. Fed by springs, Lance Creek came tumbling along the floor of the coulee, a talkative stream where trout were speckled like pebbles. When Jim sighted farmhouses he hurried on with hardly a glance. Even if he had known which house belonged to Herman Dowd he would not have stopped to lean on the fence and stare. Somewhere in his mind was a half-formed wish that Bonnie Fansler might be walking this road, but he didn't see her. Finally he lost track of how far he had walked, and he stopped where Lance Creek came frothing in a little waterfall and swirled in a clear pool. Sitting on a rock, he brought out his pocketknife and whittled, trying to figure why he would do a senseless thing like walking through blustery weather into a coulee and idling away the hours, just because a girl was somewhere nearby. Once he took the package containing the cameo from his pocket and stared at it.

Dusk was falling, he realized suddenly, and he started back toward town. The wind still blew. In farmhouses lights came on, looking yellow in the blue twilight; across the darkening sky ragamuffin clouds raced headlong. He would be late to supper; it didn't matter. The wind sniffed his boots and flapped his hat.

He must have been a mile from Lanceport when he heard something behind him; he made out shadowy horses and a buggy with a yellow lantern dangling from the rear axle. As it pulled up beside him a voice said, "Whoa. Give you a lift?"

Dr. Fansler's voice.

"Friend," Jim said, "this is nice of you. I—"

His boot was on the step when he saw that the doctor was not alone. "Climb on in," Dr. Fansler said. "It may be crowded but we'll manage. Move over, Bonnie."

Jim swallowed.

"I wouldn't want to crowd you," he said. "I can walk."

"There's plenty of room," Bonnie Fansler said.

He must have floated into that buggy; he didn't remember. But he remembered how intimate it was in there underneath the top. She was dim in the evening and sweet-smelling. But the notable thing was the warmth and softness of her leg smooth against his. Dr. Fansler was saying Bonnie had spent the day with her sister and he had called for her; and what was Jim doing out in this wind?

"Well, now," Jim said, "let me tell you. I like to look things over. A man never knows when he might see a piece of land he'd like to buy."

"Better buy in town, if it's real estate you're interested in. This town will be the greatest metropolis of the Northwest. We've got everything."

"I guess you have, at that," Jim said.

"Even wind," the doctor said. "This will blow up a rain before morning. When it stops at sundown, no rain. When it doesn't, rain sure."

"Yeah," Jim, "I guess you're right."

Once Bonnie shifted position and something round and alert and soft brushed Jim's biceps. For a moment only. It made his heart thump.

"My wife tells me you're leaving us in the morning," Dr. Fansler said. Jim said that was correct; the night clerk would wake him at 4:00 A.M. and he would start upriver.

"You're a better man than I am, starting before breakfast," the doctor said. "I'm no good till I've had coffee."

"I'll run for a couple of hours," Jim said, "and then stop and cook breakfast."

Lights of town came closer; the buggy reached Promenade Street and turned in at the driveway between the stable and the hotel. Jim got out and waited; Bonnie gave him her hand and he helped her down. The doctor drove on into the stable. Bonnie was a vague blur in the dim light and the wind. She started for the hotel.

"Miss," Jim said. And when she stopped he spoke slowly and with difficulty. "Miss—you were sure good to me, when I was sick. Here's a little something I bought for you."

And he handed her the package containing the cameo.

"Oh," she said, "thank you. Thank you very much. You needn't have."

"I wanted to, miss. I wanted to give you a present."

"Well, thank you," she said. "Thank you, Mr. Buckmaster."

And she hurried on into the hotel.

*

She must have gone straight to her room; leastwise he didn't see her when he walked through the lobby to the dining room. He wasn't sure he wanted to see her, for now that he had summoned his courage and given her the present he felt abashed, and he kept wondering whether he had offended her by giving her something so personal. He ate rapidly and went upstairs to bed. Lying in the dark, hearing the wind, he thought how it had been in the buggy with her so close. He carried those memories into sleep. Then somebody was pounding the door and the night clerk's voice said it was four o'clock. Lighting the candle, Jim noticed that the noise of wind had yielded to another sound, that of rain, steady and monotonous. Through the open window he could smell it.

He was tempted to crawl back into bed, it looked so warm and dry; but McSwasey was paying him to hunt log thieves. On a job like this you couldn't be choosey about weather, any more than you could when you cut timber and drove logs. All his life he had worked out in all weathers; he had never known anything else.

When he was dressed, and his calamity sack packed, he stood looking around the room, wondering if he would ever come back. And it struck him that he had been a wanderer, homeless and rootless, for a good many years. Bunkhouses, raft shanties, tents, hotels, lodging houses, river boats; since he was a kid those were all he had known. Maybe a man should settle down, some time or other. Find a good woman and settle down. All at once he felt bleak and nostalgic, but he didn't know why. Shouldering his sack, he blew out the candle and groped to the hall and the stair.

Well, life was full of surprises. Unpleasant ones, usually. But once in a long while a surprise of another sort came along. Such as now. When he came downstairs into the lobby, Bonnie Fansler was waiting there. He must have stood with his mouth open, he was so taken aback.

Coming to meet him, her hair in a cluster of curls, wearing a dark skirt and a white blouse, she said good morning, it was raining, and wouldn't he like a bite of breakfast before he left?

"Breakfast? Well, now, miss, I hadn't figured—"

"It won't take long," she said, "and you'll feel better."

He had never been happier than he was then, not in his whole life. He wanted to kick up his heels and let out a timber hoot. But he just stood smiling, looking at her, noticing she was wearing the cameo.

"Miss," he said, "you're up early. You're up before the roosters."

"Guy woke me," she said, indicating the night clerk. "I asked him to. I asked him to knock on my door before he knocked on yours. I couldn't see you leave without breakfast."

"Well, by God," he said. "Excuse my language, miss, but I didn't expect this."

She wasn't mad at him; that had been a silly worry; he could see that now. Etiquette or not, polite world or not, she was a girl; he should have known you never riled up a girl's anger by giving her a trinket. And she must like him, else she wouldn't have got up to see him off.

Carrying a candle, she led the way through the dining room and through a swinging door into the kitchen, a huge room where everything was clean and smelling of spices. He remembered how her body looked in her skirt and blouse when she reached up and lighted the lamps; he remembered the sound of rain spattering the sidewalk outside the door and pouring from the downspout into a rain barrel. She put on an apron, looking pretty enough to kiss, and asked him to kindle a fire in the cookstove. When he opened the back door, to fetch cobs and wood from the porch, the rain sounded louder and the air had that fresh, cool smell of a rainy October morning.

"She likes me," he thought, while the fire crackled and bacon sizzled and the aroma of coffee wafted through the room. "Maybe she liked me all the time. And when I gave her the present she knew I liked her."

She put him down at a big table in the center of the room, and served him bacon and eggs and fried potatoes and hominy grits and a slice of cold peach pie. The coffee when she poured it looked as black and shining as her hair. They might have been a married couple almost, with her getting him a big breakfast before he went to work.

"Miss," he said, "those are good victuals. You're a good cook."

Everything had a shine that morning; everything was better than he had known life could be. No matter what happened to him afterward, he could always go back to that morning and remember how snug that kitchen seemed with the rain falling outside, and how she looked like a pretty young housewife sitting across from him in her apron.

"Miss," he said once, "I see you're wearing what I gave you. I hope you like it, miss."

She blushed then, and her voice was low and shy.

"It's beautiful," she said. "I love it."

"I didn't know," he said. "I thought you might not like it. I'm not much of a hand at such things. It's the first present I ever bought for a girl."

"I love it," she said.

With his third cup of coffee he smoked a pipe of tobacco, putting off the time when he would have to leave; and then, seeing a lantern hanging from a nail, he had an idea.

"Miss, my canoe and my outfit are over in that icehouse. It will be darker than pitch. Do you reckon I could borrow that lantern?"

"Of course," she said.

"I'd borrow you too, if it wasn't for this rain. I'd ask you to come along and hold the lantern while I carry out the canoe, but it's raining."

She gave him a long straight look then, her eyes sober with their dark lashes.

"If you need me," she said quietly, "I'll go and help."

*

Wearing a shawl over her head and a long coat, she carried the lantern when they left the hotel; it cast a bright disk around their feet. It might have been midnight, everything was so black, and the downpour pelted them. He took her arm; it seemed the natural thing to do; and he wondered why he had ever been afraid of her; she was like somebody he had known for as long as he had known himself. They might have been man and wife—any man and wife—toiling along through the rain, with him big and setting forth on hazardous business, with her smaller and obedient and helpful. It gave him an odd feeling, thinking such thoughts.

At the icehouse he found the key under the mat and unlocked the office door; from its bed on the desk the tomcat blinked at the lantern light and opened its mouth in a mute meow. Back in the storage room, great shadows hulked; Jim had a strange sense of smallness and mortality, venturing into that place with the ceiling so high it was lost in darkness.

"Here we are," he said, when they came to his canoe, but his voice sounded hollow and sepulchral in the cold room with its echoes.

While Bonnie held the lantern he unbolted the wide doors leading to the loading chute; and then, his shadow gigantic, he hoisted the canoe to his shoulders and carried it inverted out to the platform and down toward the river. With his head inside the canoe, he could hear the rain tapping the birch bark. He set it down gently, then lugged out his dunnage. Bonnie was right beside him all the time, lighting his way.

"That does it, I reckon," he said. "I don't know how I would have managed, without you."

He took her arm again, walking up the loading chute; inside, he bolted the double doors, and they stood in that place of shadows. His heart was pounding and he wanted to put his arms around her, but something warned him not to hurry things; they made their way to the office. The cat, beyond the temptations now that afflicted men, blinked and formed another soundless meow. Outside, Jim locked the door and replaced the key.

"I'll take you back to the hotel," he said.

But Bonnie said no; she would light his way to the river.

They walked slowly, finding their way around the icehouse, stopping where his canoe waited.

"Well," he said, "I reckon I'd best be off. That was a good breakfast, miss. It was nice of you to get it for me."

She stood voiceless, a shadow in the rain.

"And lighting my way," he added. "I couldn't hardly have managed without you."

"I'm glad," she said. "Glad to be of help." And she asked, "Will you come this way again?"

"Well, now, miss, I might at that. Alonzo St. Clair has offered me work cutting ice. I might be back."

"They don't cut ice till January," she said. "That's a long time."

There was breathlessness in his lungs, but he wasn't afraid of her now. He had never felt so booted and male, taking the lantern from her hand and setting it on the ground. Then he took her in his arms and kissed her. For a moment she held back, then yielded against him, and it was better than he had ever imagined.

"Sure," he whispered into the fragrance of her hair, "I'll be back. Just you wait for me, miss."

He launched the canoe; she stood where he had left her; from out on the dark water he could see the lantern still on the ground. Then

675

she must have picked it up; through the rain he could see it describing an arc, as if being waved; then it went bobbing back toward the hotel.

*

There were times during those next weeks when the only reality was the memory of the girl; times when the actual world of brawling river towns seemed an apparition through which he shambled like a specter. He never liked to remember that period of his life, it was all so futile, so pointless, so askew. Acting the role of a down-and-outer, of a man blacklisted and disgraced, he found himself accepting the make-believe as the real; his old cockiness wilted. On the river front in Read's Landing, watching the packets steaming in, and the rafts being made up and provisioned, he felt as useless as a rusty boiler. Maybe some of that dark strain in Lorne Buckmaster's blood had been passed on to him; maybe his pretending to be a castoff of the logging industry was all the invitation that dark strain needed to seep into his brain.

He found no trace of log piracy, of course. All the way to Read's Landing, through days of rain, he kept exploring the backwaters, and stopping at river villages to hang around saloons, but it was time wasted. Years later, looking back, he wondered how he could have been such a deadhead, why he had ever swallowed that bilge McSwasey had fed him. Still, McSwasey had been shrewd, serving that bilge in a fascinating bottle wrapped in the silver foil of flattery and the gold foil of ambition; it would have been inconceivable to him then that McSwasey had been maneuvering him into trouble. When he discovered no log thieves, he remembered how McSwasey had said they were foxy and a long time might be required to trap them.

In Read's Landing he stored his canoe and took a room in a lodging house; the rainy weather continued; and every day he made the rounds of barber shops and livery stables and hotel lobbies and saloons, hoping that some contact man for the freebooters would sidle over and sound him out. It never happened. He was ignored, for the most part. Roosters he had known for years, pinery boys who had been his friends, barkeeps, crapshooters, steamboat men—all ignored him. Oh, they didn't refuse to speak; he was a dangerous fighter and nobody wished to insult him openly; they would nod and say hello and perhaps even make some comment on the weather; but after that they attended strictly to their own drinking. You might have thought he was a leper. Sometimes he felt like one. He used to stand hunched over one end of a bar, or slumped at a table in a corner, swallowing his tanglefoot and thinking his thoughts.

One thing he didn't do during those weeks: he didn't visit a single fancy house. And in saloons which kept a few girls to help with the overhead, he crawled out of invitations to visit any bedrooms. He was half sick, he told the girls; tomorrow maybe. He guessed he was being foolish; but damn, those saloon girls didn't look so alluring any more.

676

When one of them sat down at his table, and he saw her heavy make-up and heard her metallic voice, he would find himself thinking of Bonnie Fansler. Odd; but that was how it went.

Every few days he wrote a letter to Caleb McSwasey, reporting his lack of progress; and after a time the very writing of those letters, and the dropping of them into a slot, took on a kind of unreality, as if he were writing to somebody who didn't exist, like a kid sending letters to Santa Claus. But McSwasey existed all right; and he wasn't Santa Claus.

A couple of times he mustered his nerve and wrote to Bonnie Fansler, spending whole afternoons over those letters, wadding up what he had written and trying again and again, before he had something he could send; but the thoughts in his mind never came out on paper. "I am well," he would begin, "and hope you are the same," and after that he would chew the pencil. He wanted to tell her she was night and mystery and witchery, but those letters were always factual: he had suffered another headache but the pills had fixed it; he might return to Lanceport and cut ice for Alonzo St. Clair. But maybe that was only wishful thinking, that part about cutting ice. He might stop in Lanceport for a day or so, but common sense told him he had better go on downriver for the winter and try to pick up the trail of the log thieves there. If they had a sawmill, it would likely be downriver.

The rains drizzled themselves out at last; it was November by then, sharp and clear. Trees were bare now, and the river had that submissive look of waiting for the first freeze. And in that season when timber bears were thinking about hibernating, and mice were getting nicely settled in their winter homes between the walls of old houses, Jim knew what he wanted to do before starting south; he wanted to canoe up the Chippewa for a visit with Molly Fitzpatrick. He couldn't tell Molly—not even her—about McSwasey's great scheme to trap the log thieves, but otherwise he could talk to her with his defenses down. He might even tell her about Bonnie Fansler. He kept wanting to tell somebody about her.

He felt better, once he started up the Chippewa, for it was his home river. The noons were soft-aired now with the mildness of Indian summer, and a hush lay on the land. Squatting in his canoe, dipping the paddle, he kept thinking of Bonnie, remembering her somberness and her unexpected smiles when her whole face lighted; remembering her body against his when he kissed her. He wouldn't have traded those memories for all the fancy-house girls between Read's Landing and St. Louis.

At sundown, three days after leaving Read's, he nosed his canoe among the cattails along the west bank of the Chippewa and stood looking toward Molly's place. It had prospered with the years; the clapboards of the north wing glistened with white paint; there was a sloping lawn. Molly had been a shrewd business woman, plowing back some of her profits and investing the residue. She had never managed to get her revenge by ruining Dan Stoughton—he had died finally and a syndicate had bought his Quickwater Log & Lumber Company—but she had done well by running a place where loggers were never slugged and robbed and tossed to the wolves.

Several men were drinking when Jim opened the door, and Molly stood behind the bar rolling dice from a leather cup, playing her version of solitaire. She dropped everything when she saw Jim, and rushed to give him a hug.

"Jim," she said, "my God. Welcome home, Jim."

*

It was strange how when he was away from Molly for a long time he slipped back into thinking of her as she had been years ago in Quickwater, before she became a business and professional woman. She had been beautiful then, in a full-blown way. Now in her forties the voluptuous curves of her figure had expanded beyond all reason, and she had done things to her hair. It used to have warm coral tints in certain lights, and apricot tints in others, but when it began turning gray she must have dyed it, for now it was an unfortunate shade of orange. Her skin had coarsened too, and her faintly Roman nose had become more aquiline, suggesting a bird of prey. But her eyes were still the merriest of blues, and her voice had its old zip and twang.

"Jim," she said, "let's get the housecleaning done right off. Then we can talk."

He remembered his embarrassment, for all at once he realized that, for the first time since Molly had opened the White Water House, he had no wish to go with her to a bedroom. But he didn't want to offend her.

"Sure," he said, smiling and trying to act his old self, but avoiding her eyes. "Sounds fine. But I'm kind of tired. That's a long haul up from Read's. If it's all the same to you, I'd like a bite to eat."

He wasn't fooling her; he could tell that; he could feel her watching him. Then she called one of her girls to tend bar and took him to the kitchen where she put him down at the table. On the stove coffee was simmering, and there were beans baked with molasses, and brown bread, and cucumber pickles and cold ham and raisin pie. She sat opposite him, not putting out a plate for herself, but sometimes filching a strip of salt pork from the beans.

"Now," she said, "what's all this I hear about you and Caleb McSwasey?"

"The son of a bitch fired me. He said I'd padded my accounts."

"Had you?"

"No."

"Tell me about it," she said.

Elbows on the table, she sat frowning while he talked, her arms fat and jangling with bracelets, her fingers fat and aglitter with rings. Her eyes became cold and hard as she listened.

"He smacked me with knucks," Jim said, "and knocked me out. Like to have busted my jaw. So I set off upriver, and here I am."

Molly sat drumming her fingers. "Got a cigar?" she asked. After it was lighted she rolled it from one corner of her mouth to the other, and through the smoke her slitted eyes kept watching him.

"All right, Jim," she said finally, "now let's hear the straight of it."

"You've had it," he said. "That's it," but he knew he wasn't fooling her.

"God damn it," she said, "you make me mad. The man don't live that can get inside your guard and knock you out. And you're not a lunkhead. You wouldn't fiddle around padding payrolls. If you ever steal it will be millions. What are you and McSwasey up to, anyway?"

He smiled.

"All right," she said, "smile. Smile, God damn it, and see if I care. But let me tell you one thing. If you're mixed up with Caleb McSwasey in some damn fool scheme, you'd better watch. He may be the biggest man on the river, and the biggest in the woods, but I wouldn't trust him to clean out my backhouse, as it were. Want some more coffee?"

He watched her going to the stove, and when she poured the coffee, black and shining, he thought of Bonnie Fansler's hair. And he knew that he would not be making love to Molly again. She had changed or he had changed. He didn't like to offend her, but he would rather do that than take her in his arms.

She kept trying to pump him, and it might have been better if he had told the truth about McSwasey's scheme for trapping the log thieves, because she had a shrewdness that cut to the core of a problem; she would have realized at once that McSwasey was dealing cards from a stacked deck.

"Jim," she would have said, "wake up. A tough customer like Mc-Swasey ain't giving away a fourth of his business. He's using you, Jim. I don't know how or why, but he's leading you into a deadfall. Hell, Jim, you're half in it already. Try to get a logging job and you'll see. Everybody believes you padded your accounts, and nobody wants to hire a crook."

But he wouldn't give Molly an inkling of what he was about.

Business was quiet in the White Water House that evening, the roulette wheel motionless, the bar uncrowded. Jim went outside where in the darkness he breathed in the fragrance of balsam and pine; above the vastness of the timber, in the greater vastness of the heavens, the stars flashed with the brilliance of a sharp ax. He thought of Bonnie, and of how some day he would like to bring her up the Chippewa; he would like to take her to Quickwater and show her the spot where the Buckmaster cabin had stood.

The saloon door opened; in the lighted rectangle Molly was a bulky silhouette. "Jim," she called. And when he responded she came out to stand beside him, saying that since business was dull he might as well go on upstairs; she would be along in a minute.

"All right," he said, but he dreaded going.

Once her bedroom had seemed a lair of glamour and illusion. Tonight it seemed otherwise. Even the gondola bed with its carved ivory swans no longer delighted him; the paint, he saw, was chipping. The dressing table with its female arsenal of powders and sweet waters and heavy perfumes exuded a cloying scent. He lighted a cigar and sat in a rocking chair that squeaked.

"Jim," Molly said when she came in, "it's been a long time. I wish you'd stop in oftener."

She undressed, looking as fat and pink as a scalded sow, and came to sit on his knee. She took his cigar and tossed it into the slop jar where it sizzled.

"Jim," she said, "God damn it, what is it about you? You light me up like a lamp. I've known handsomer men, but they're not you. It's something . . . It's what you are inside, as it were. Maybe it's drive. Maybe it's sort of deadly. Maybe it's just man, all man. You'll get what you want in the world, and I wish it was me. I know it ain't, but I wish it was. You'll get what you want, and I hope you'll like it."

She kissed him; then she asked:

"What's the matter?" And when he didn't respond she said, "Don't just sit there staring at the rug. What's the matter?"

"I reckon I'll have to tell you," he said. "I reckon I'll have to."

He eased her off his knee and guided her to the bed; then he paced.

"Molly," he said, "something's happened to me. When McSwasey smacked me with knucks it did something. Cracked my jaw or dislocated my neck—something. I started having headaches, Molly. All the way up the river my head would ache. So I figured I'd best see a doc. Well, there's a town called Lanceport, Molly. I went there to a doc. He was a good doc too and he pretty well fixed me, but something happened. His name was Doc Fansler and he had this daughter. Girl named Bonnie. I thought I knew all about girls. I did for a fact. But this girl—I don't know—this girl—"

"She was different, I'll bet," Molly said.

"How did you know that? Yes. Yes, she was. She was different. I went right out and bought her a present. Fellow wanted a hundred dollars for it, and it wasn't much of a trinket either—a kind of cameo, he called it—but I got it for sixty. Then I was afraid to give it to her. Can you beat that? I was afraid. But I did give it to her, the night before I left. I was leaving at four in the A. M. the next morning, and I was living in the hotel this Doc Fansler runs. Well, sir, when I came downstairs at four in the A. M. there was this girl. She cooked my breakfast and helped me load my canoe. I didn't hardly touch her—just kissed her a time or two before I left—but—but—I don't know. I can't get her out of my head. She bothers me, Molly. She sticks to me like a bur in a fox's fur. Damn, I don't know. I never kept thinking about a girl so much before."

"Have you written her letters?" Molly asked.

"Sure I've written her. But how did you know? Yes, I wrote her a couple. But I couldn't say what I wanted. When I tried it was like I was using a broken jackknife to whittle punky wood. It all sort of crumbled and came to nothing. But I wrote her. And it's a funny thing. I never hardly touched her except to kiss her, but I keep remembering how it was. She was wearing a coat and it was raining, but I could feel her up against me. And it was just right. Our bodies fitted together just right. And I haven't wanted another woman since. That ain't like me, you know. Maybe it's what McSwasey did to my jaw, but I don't think so. I think it's the girl. I keep remembering her, and I don't want to do anything about the others. Not even about you, Molly. I just don't want to."

"And you don't know why?" Molly asked.

"No," Jim said, "I don't. I can't figure it."

Molly began to laugh, sitting there on the edge of the bed; she laughed so hard tears came to her eyes; and then she was really crying.

"Jim," she said, "oh, Jim. Why, you poor simple lunkhead, you're in love. You've fallen in love."

*

Up till then when he heard people talk about love he had thought they were deluding themselves; he had thought love was nothing but wanting to take a girl to a bedroom; but now he could see there was more to it than that. That was part of it, sure, but only a part; the rest was something mysterious. He tried to figure it, canoeing back down the Chippewa, but it was like trying to figure why grass grew or why a weasel had brown fur in summer and white in winter.

Molly had raised a ruckus when he refused to yield to her wheedling; she had suffered what he guessed you might call hysterics. He hated to disappoint her, but he had made up his mind, and he had a stubborn streak. Next morning her eyes were all swollen and red, but she was contrite, saying she was sorry to have called him all those names; she hoped he would stop by again, if only for a visit.

"Sure," he said, "I'll be back," but he was glad to get out of there.

Now that he knew what ailed him he wanted to do something about it, such as returning to Lanceport and telling Bonnie Fansler that he loved her, and asking her to marry him. Next summer should be about right for a wedding. By then, certainly, he would have rounded up the log thieves for McSwasey, and he would be vice-president of the company. Money would be coming to him in great bundles then; he would buy a house for Bonnie Fansler in New Empire, and she would be right by his side when he went soaring up among the dollar signs. That was a fine future when he thought about it, all misty and entrancing; he would buy her anything she wished and they would travel to some of the cities he had heard about. New Orleans and Cincinnati and New York; they would explore them together. It would be a fine thing to have your woman right with you; people would call her Mrs. Buckmaster. Mrs. James L. Buckmaster; he liked the sound of that. They would have kids some day, and their names would be Buckmaster too. He could see now there were things in life he had taken for granted: how, for instance, when a girl left her father's house she gave up her old name and took yours. When it happened to other people you thought nothing about it, but when it was going to happen to you it could bring a lump to your throat, almost. The way some husbands treated their wives, he guessed they didn't appreciate that enough, or appreciate how when a girl had only one life to live, a handful of years in all eternity, she chose you as the one to throw in her lot with.

In Read's Landing again, he wrote another letter to Bonnie, and now that he knew he was in love the words came more easily. Nothing fancy, of course; but as he sat in his lodging house gripping the pencil it occurred to him that he might as well tell her how he felt right now; it might be easier than popping the question in person. So he came right to the point: he loved her and wanted to marry her; he would arrive in Lanceport in a few days. He felt pretty fine after dropping the letter into a slot, and that evening, watching a downriver boat pulling out, and knowing it was carrying his proposal, he felt warm and happy. "I'm in love," he kept thinking. "By God, I'm in love."

Next day he wrote to McSwasey—the last letter, as events turned out, that he would send for a long while—telling how disappointing the thief-hunting business was in these parts, and reporting his intention to go downriver, even as far as St. Louis, to try his luck there. He said he hoped McSwasey wasn't becoming impatient; he was doing his best and he would catch those thieves yet; and in a roundabout way he reminded McSwasey of his promise to give him a fourth interest in the company, and to make him vice-president; Jim didn't want him to forget that part of the agreement.

When he left the post office that afternoon, after mailing the letter, he saw a round-shouldered man coming along the sidewalk, a man with dried tobacco juice outlining his mouth; Greasy Dick Cassidy.

"Jim!" the Grease said. "By God, it's you, Jim. Where you been?

I ain't seen you since I got back from downriver."

"Places," Jim said. "Up the Chippewa, and places. I'm not washed up yet."

"I got my troubles, Jim. I know you got yours, but I've got mine too. I'd like to talk to you, Jim. Some place where there ain't so many ears. Come on home with me."

As they left the river front, and followed a street that straggled up into the bluffs, Greasy Dick told of the trip downriver with Jim's last raft: how the morning following the fight in Rafferty's Saloon, McSwasey had sent a new pilot up to Turtle Island to take charge.

"A good enough trip, but I missed you, Jim. Everybody did. You used to make them step, but it's what a crew likes. They like to have a man with fists in charge. But I wish you hadn't fought McSwasey. Was it true you padded your payrolls?"

"No," Jim said, "the son of a bitch made a mistake about that. I never padded a payroll. He made a mistake and then hit me with knucks."

"That's how I heard it, Jim. Well, he's a hard rooster. Harder than a hard-shell turtle."

November had turned warm, but the sunshine was watery and the sky pale; from the bluffs you could see stands of bare trees on distant islands. The river looked glassy, flowing off into the obscurity of colorless hazes. Although the air was still, a vague uneasiness lurked in sky and water, as if Indian summer were living on borrowed time. If he wanted to outrun winter, Jim guessed he had better be on his way tomorrow.

A half-dozen children, breeds with Dakota eyes, were playing in the yard of Greasy Dick's cabin, and Jim caught sight of a shapeless squaw vanishing into the kitchen.

"I'd ask you in to set," the Grease said, "but the damned kids don't let a man think. Jim, you remember Kelly. Well, he's sent word to me. He's heard you're through on the river, Jim, and he's going to beat me up. He'll do it too, if I don't stay on the bank. Everything's going to hell, Jim, with you off the river."

"Don't you fuss about Kelly," Jim said. "I'll have a word with him. Is he in town?"

"He's left on a raft, Jim. But he'll be back. Season's almost over, but what about next year? If I try shipping out on a raft he'll beat me up."

"Next year? Why, hell, I might own the river, by next year. If I do, you'll be one of my pilots, with Noisy Swanson to keep the boys in line. I'll talk to Kelly. You send him word I'm not through. I'll take him aside and speak to him."

Jim was smiling, going back toward town. Tomorrow he would leave; in a few days he would see Bonnie; by spring—by summer at the latest—he would be vice-president of McSwasey & Zumwalt. Maybe by then it would be McSwasey & Buckmaster. He didn't feel a down-and-outer any more.

*

Canoeing downriver from Read's Landing, he should have pressed along faster; he could see that. Odd that he didn't, considering how Bonnie Fansler was waiting at the end of that journey. But maybe he half-dreaded seeing her; maybe he feared she had read his letter and was nettled by the abrupt and factual way he had proposed marriage. Girls were notional; just because she had let him kiss her didn't guarantee she would welcome a proposal scrawled in pencil on cheap gray paper. Being a nice girl, maybe she expected a man to kneel on the parlor carpet when he asked her to be his wife.

In any case, he took his time on that trip, smiling to himself, his thoughts full of Bonnie. And that was a bad mistake, thinking of anything but the river when you were traveling the river. He knew better than to do that; he knew the river was a woman. And she had her jealous streaks, that river did, and her treachery. She could storm at you and call you names, like Molly Fitzpatrick, and her curves could beckon you and her currents could whisper stories in your ears, but she never mentioned the dead men she had smothered with her love. She never told of the bones down on the river bottom and of the skulls where the chuck-suckers laid their eggs.

There were a thousand mistakes a man could make, in the woods or on the river, and the greatest of these was the one he made: to go paddling along like a man in a dream, not seeing what was taking place around him because he was thinking of a girl. If he had had his wits, he would have been suspicious of what the river and the sky were up to. The weather was like May and he never thought to question it, maybe because when a man was in love it was always springtime where his thoughts wandered. But it couldn't mean anything good, in late autumn on the Upper Mississippi, when the sun shone warm through haze and the river flowed like molten glass, flecked with bubbles and little whirl-pools. Everything was hushed, waiting for something, and the limestone bluffs showed through the branches of newly-naked trees, and the bluff sides were gold with fallen leaves. The sundowns were red and bloody, with flocks of long-necked loons hurrying south, flying high in V's.

By the end of the fourth day he could have made it to Lanceport, but he made another mistake; he stopped two miles short of the town and camped on an island. He had some fool idea that he wanted to arrive in the morning, just because the first time he put in at Lanceport and saw Bonnie Fansler it had been morning; when you were in love, you always wanted the nice things to happen over again in the same way. But he had needed a shave then, and this time he would be slicked up like a preacher on the way to church; first thing in the morning he

684

would douse the sleep from his eyes and lather his face and razor off the stubble. He would wear a clean shirt. He wouldn't look like a river roughneck, this time.

That night he slept heavily, which was another mistake. Usual thing, if he put his mind to it, he could wake when he wanted; he had learned that as a chore boy at Teal Feather. But so far as he could figure, there was no call to wake up at anything like 5:00 A.M. Give the girl a chance to get up and eat breakfast, before he walked in on her. Give her a chance to put on a crisp dress and perch herself behind the desk with embroidery, where he had seen her first. So, without any thought to the weather—although the stars were hazy blobs and the night too warm —he turned in and started logging.

He dreamed a school teacher named Alex Castleman was pouring ice water down his spine, and Molly Fitzpatrick kept shooting a pepperbox revolver to make him stop, only while he yelled Molly changed into Bonnie Fansler. Then he wakened; the dawn was wild and gray; and the shots were the sounds his tent made flopping in the wind: a northwest wind, colder than Spitsbergen. It cut like a knife when he came from his tent and saw leaves whirling in crazy dances; waves were lapping the island.

Looking back, he wondered what had got into him that morning; he should, of course, have battened everything down and holed in till the weather cleared. Even so, he might have had a bad time, but that course of action would have been best. But damn, he had planned to see Bonnie today, and maybe a man in love was like a moose in autumn when the smell of cow twitched his nostrils; nothing could keep him from crashing through thickets and swimming through torrents to where she was. But Jim guessed he should have forgotten love, till the weather stopped being so nasty.

Breaking camp took longer than usual that morning, because the gale kept grabbing his tent and engulfing him in canvas when he tried to fold it. But he was stubborn; no damned wind was going to interrupt his usual routine. But he didn't attempt to cook breakfast. Even in a tempest he could have got a fire going, but he didn't like the idea of sparks streaming into dry leaves and setting the island ablaze. There were limits to his stubbornness; he wasn't his grandfather; he wasn't Newcomb Dobner.

But he never should have set out in his canoe. It might have been the Dobner blood that made him do that. Trouble was, the wind roused his temper. He had finished loading his canoe when a gust lifted his hat and sent it sailing far out into the wild riot of the channel. Made him mad. He let loose with a string of pinery-boy oaths that would have skinned the bark off a log, and he wheeled around and glared at the wind. In a way of speaking; he couldn't see it. But he could feel it, ruffling insolent fingers through his hair and stuffing the words back down his throat. So he decided to show it. Fool thing to do, but he was good in a canoe. He was good in white water. It was another mistake though.

But one mistake he didn't make; he didn't leave that island wearing boots. The last thing before setting out he unlaced them and kicked them off, so that when he squatted in the canoe he was in his socks. That saved his life, probably.

Overhead great clouds came careening from the northwest like an armada under press of sail, and when the lookouts sighted him, a speck down there in the toss and foam, they must have screamed to the gunners that a lunatic had escaped a madhouse and taken to those running combers in a cockleshell; shoot the silly bastard, they must have yelled; for the canoe had traveled scarcely a furlong, leaping like a muskie, before the clouds let loose with a broadside of stinging sleet. That was when Jim began to jettison his cargo; ax and spade and fowling piece, calamity sack and skillet and his bagged tent; all went overboard. But that was a tired canoe, and lopsided; and the air was a whirling blur of sleet, blinding everything; and the river was a woman with the devil in her for sure, sending waves to swamp the bow and to come hissing over the gunwales.

But the river was a warm-legged woman too, lots warmer than the freezing air, when the canoe went away somewhere and Jim was left holding a paddle that didn't mean anything now because the canoe had gone away. Treading water, he let go the paddle, and after that he worked at getting out of his Mackinaw because it soaked up water and kept trying to drag him down into the deeps where the Johnny-darters weathered out the storm. But Jim didn't want to weather out the storm down there among the eel grass and come floating sluggishly to the surface next week and go drifting till somebody pulled him out and buried him. He would never get to marry Bonnie Fansler that way. So in the river that was bubbling like chowder he squirmed and threshed out of his Mackinaw and it too went away; the river was taking everything that morning.

After that he could swim better, but he didn't know where he was. Everything was curtained by sleet. Somebody had upset a gigantic salt-cellar and the salt came cascading, choking the air with white and stinging his ears and hissing into the water. His eyes were at water level only the water was not level for long; there were waves. He could see them gathering strength and hurling themselves at his head. Foam and bubbles, frothy as lace, came swirling around his ears and once he thought it was the lace of the river's petticoat when she flirted it at him because she wanted him. Sometimes the river put her hands on his head and ducked it under, playfully, and sometimes she flung water up his nose and he could feel it stinging way up where his brain lived and he would sneeze. And once he thought he would never get out of this because he was just keeping afloat without knowing which way to swim through the sleet which was turning to swarming snow.

But then an idea hit him and it was so simple he could have laughed. When the storm struck it had come from the northwest; all a man had to do was swim into the wind and he would be swimming northwest; that would take him to a place called Iowa. It was such a victorious idea that he felt strong again and struck out through the curdle of waters, and he never knew whether his lips yelled and laughed insults at the river or whether it was all inside his head. In either case, he told her. She was a harlot river with a knife in her stocking, and he told her. He had found him a nice girl named Bonnie and he was finished with whores and she would never get him now; that was what he told her.

Then he felt solid ground underfoot and he was lying on sand and the river kept spitting at him but he hadn't gone to bed with her even though she had grabbed and kissed and called him names. But maybe that was Molly. Anyway, he had best move. He was very cold suddenly; the whore's bed of the river had been warm but the air was freezing and the snow was flying thicker than Mormon flies around a summer street-lamp. He stood up. And damned if his head hadn't started aching again. And he felt as cold as a snowman and his legs were far away and brittle as icicles. By God, he'd better get a move on. A man could get the sniffles out in a storm like this without a hat or Mackinaw or boots.

Slipping on the snow, he climbed a bank and he was trotting through a timber and flapping his arms, trying to get warm; and he needed a doctor, he did for a fact, because his headache had come back. He kept stepping on stones and branches that hurt his feet through his German socks. His hands were hard as ironwood but not his feet; no logger's feet were; a logger wore boots all day and sometimes all night so his feet were what you might call protected, soft and smooth as a baby's un-less a man was deadhead enough to buy boots that gave him bunions, but Jim wasn't that kind of deadhead, he took care of his feet. But not now; not in this blizzard. They were getting all cut up, the way they felt, but let them, maybe that would promote circulation; he wanted to promote circulation because he wouldn't like to freeze his feet and have them mortify and turn ugly colors and have to be sawed off, he needed his feet. Better keep running; better never stop till you reached a warm place where a girl sat behind a desk with embroidery hoops.

Then he went crashing through bushes and came to a swampy place fringed with snow-coated cattails; through the whirling snow he could see a crust of ice. And for a moment it occurred to him that he was lost; maybe he had not swum to the mainland but to some island; maybe he had swum to Wisconsin or to nowhere at all. And he was touched by panic. But hell, he had never been one to panic in the woods; never panic, his father had told him, long years ago; there's always a way if you don't panic. So he didn't. And he thought he remembered hearing from Alonzo St. Clair about a swampy inlet that cut in from the river north of Lanceport. If he remembered right, and if this was the swamp, he was nearly where he was going. So he went plunging out among the cattails and through ice like thin glass; water rose to his thighs; his feet were slogging through muck; and on the other side he ran again and he was on a street. Dim through the snow, on his left, he made out a house, and after a minute a bulky building where a tomcat lived and a key was kept under the front mat. He could have stopped there. But he wanted the hotel. Man shouldn't stay in an icehouse, even if he felt like a pillar of ice; man should stay in a hotel.

He went groping through the racket of wind in branches, through whirlpools of snow, and his feet were getting heavier; he was plastered and armored in white. His head was in agony. All the time his legs felt thicker. He came to the wall of a brick building and nearly stopped, to lie and rest, but nobody except the town drunks slept on sidewalks, so he moved on, past windows all frosted over, to a glass door. He got it open, finally, and great waves of warmth rushed to engulf him. People were in that place, maybe a girl with embroidery hoops, but he didn't see, for his legs folded and the floor was coming up. He expected it to be hard, but it wasn't; it was soft and black and good for long sleeping.

*

There was a ceiling with wallpaper the color of cork, and when he noticed it first, lying on his back, he had the impression that many things had been happening about which he knew nothing. Not that it mattered. He couldn't guess where he was except that he was stretched out in a feather bed with a black-walnut headboard that towered up and up. He was weak; he closed his eyes.

His body didn't mean much any more because he could leave it whenever he wished, as if it were dead. He had always thought his body was the real Jim Buckmaster, but as things turned out his body was hardly more than a bateau which he had used for getting from place to place. The real Jim Buckmaster had learned the trick of leaving his body and sailing off into space where time was not a running river but a silvery lake that never went anywhere; in a million years it would be the same because it was not flowing the way a river flowed past a given point. He went away on many lovely voyages during those weeks when his body remained behind in a feather bed; once on the woodland trail to Injun Hollow he met a man with a pack whose name was Sol Klauber. Jim, Sol asked, what are you up to these days? And Jim said, I'm hunting for her, Sol. She's night and a doe deer and a wisp of fog and an echo. Sol said, I wish you luck, Jim, you'll need it.

A time came when he was strong enough to hold his eyes open and lie studying the wallpaper on the ceiling. There were cracks in its surface, so it looked like a map, and while he watched the cracks became trout streams flowing through pine forests. He would own it all some day. He would log it off and cut it into lumber. He could see how it would look when it was logged off, all slash and ravage, and he felt sad, but he knew that would never stop him from logging it off because it was beautiful and he was a man with a man's compulsion to stride across the world destroying everything and calling it progress.

Sometimes in the bleakness of night when the lamp was low people came to see him in that room, dead people who should have stayed in their graves. Dan Stoughton came with a monkey perched on his shoulder and Jim asked, Why does he scratch? And Dan said, If I knew that I'd know why you fell in love. Lorne Buckmaster came, round-shouldered and smelling of sawdust, and he said, Jim, you're lost. Climb the highest tree in the pinery, Jim, or follow the rivers to the sea and you'll never find your way. But Myrtle Buckmaster said, Bosh. Save your pennies and after a while you'll have a dollar, but don't you go signing notes for friends, Jim. Don't do that and you'll be a rich man.

But gradually the world of phantoms dissolved. It might have been the real world, for all he knew, or it might have been memory; anyway it was mist and voices and it vanished; and a big bald man named Dr. Fansler was saying, "Jim, you've licked it. Double pneumonia and pleurisy and river fever and I don't know what all, but you're pulling through."

"Sure," Jim wanted to say, "I figured to," but he was weak.

"It's the twenty-seventh of December," Dr. Fansler said. "You've slept right through Christmas. Most men would have died that first night. You had a fever like love in July, and I thought you were a goner, but you're a fighter. We'll start feeding you squirrel broth and you'll get your strength back."

Jim smiled and slept again.

Every day after that the actual world came back for a little longer; they used to prop him up with pillows and feed him steaming broth and poached eggs on milk toast; Mrs. Fansler spooned the food into his mouth because he was so weak; his biceps were flabby sacks and his ribs stuck out. He didn't see Bonnie. He asked about her, when he was strong enough to whisper, and he gathered that because of delicacy they had kept her out of the room; Mrs. Fansler had been his nurse.

Presently when he was able to observe such things he saw that this room was larger and better-furnished than the ordinary hotel room; there was a black-walnut dresser with a marble top and a long mirror; the cast-iron stove in the corner was embossed with vines and flowers, and it was fitted out with an urn on top; every morning Dr. Fansler filled this with water into which coltsfoot had been sprinkled, to release, as he put it, "the salubrious vapors so beneficial to man and beast." And when Jim asked what room he was in the doctor said it belonged to his son Max; it was one of those ground-floor rooms along the corridor leading from the lobby.

"That day of the blizzard," Dr. Fansler said, "we carried you in and undressed you and got you into one of my nightshirts. Then we popped you into bed and put hot bricks around your feet. I never knew a man to be so sick and pull through."

Jim wondered about his money belt but he didn't like to ask; the doctor might think he was accusing somebody of stealing. He might, of course, have unbuckled it when he was trying to keep afloat in the river, the way he had shed his Mackinaw; nothing—money least of all—had seemed important then except staying alive.

*

Sometimes he heard the wind howling along the street, and always the windows were opaque with frost. New Year's Day must have come and gone; he lost all count of days and nights. McSwasey would be wondering what had happened to him, but those schemes of trapping log thieves seemed to belong to another lifetime. And although he kept wondering about Bonnie and wishing she would come to visit him, he thought drowsily that she was a nice girl and the parents of a nice girl did not permit her to visit a man—even a man sick and weak—in his bedroom. He slept a great deal; even when he was awake he was half-dozing; he would lie with his eyes closed and go drifting downriver on long smooth currents, thinking how some day he would be strong enough to dress and sit in a chair and she would come to visit. But he gained strength slowly.

Then one morning after all those weeks he awakened feeling more his old self; he wanted to try getting up.

"Well," Dr. Fansler said, "maybe. For a minute."

He remembered that occasion: how willingly he swung his feet over the edge of the bed, but how when he tried to stand his legs were weak. He might have fallen, starting across the room, if Dr. Fansler hadn't grabbed him. He caught sight of that little drama in the mirror: the doctor holding up a strange man in a nightshirt with a black beard and long wild hair and sunken eyes. His forearms looked wasted.

"My God," he said, "I look awful."

"You should have seen yourself a month ago."

Bed was a wonderful haven to return to. His heart was laboring; he was desperately sleepy, suddenly.

"I need a shave," he muttered. "Shave and haircut. Need them bad."

"If you keep improving," Dr. Fansler said, "we'll call in a barber next week."

Jim was glad then that Bonnie hadn't visited him; he wouldn't have

690

wanted her to see him looking like a trapper after six months in the woods.

*

A few days later he tried walking again and made it to a chair where he sat for all of thirty seconds; and after that, every morning, he took regular exercise between bed and chair; he was improving fast, the doctor said; but it seemed slow. His appetite returned; presently he was ravenous all the time, like a bear just out of hibernation; the more he ate the stronger he became and the longer he could sit up; and one morning in early February Dr. Fansler brought in a barber. And Jim must have been a Samson in reverse, for once his hair was trimmed and his beard shaved away he gained strength faster, but that might have been because he looked like a human being again and could face Bonnie.

"Friend," Jim said, when the barber had finished, "you'll have to trust me for this. I don't guess I've got any money."

"You've got money, Jim," Dr. Fansler said. "It was in a belt when we undressed you."

He opened a dresser drawer and brought out Jim's money belt.

That was a relief; he had been worrying about how he was to pay the Fanslers for all they had done. He said:

"I didn't remember. I thought I might have shed it in the water."

Next day he dressed for the first time, and every morning the barber returned; Jim wasn't taking chances on having Bonnie mistake him for a porcupine. And one day a week or so after his first shave he hinted to the doctor that his recovery might be speeded if Bonnie could visit him.

The doctor smiled.

"I was wondering when you'd ask for her. We've had our hands full keeping her out."

*

He began to enjoy his illness when they permitted Bonnie to visit him. Out of respect for the proprieties the door was always left open and the bed always made, and usually Mrs. Fansler kept popping in and out, and Jim was dressed; but despite these deterrents to ripening friendship it was a fine time in his life. Although he tired easily, his strength was returning; presently he was able to take his meals in the dining room, and Dr. Fansler promised that when the weather moderated he could leave the hotel and get some fresh air; a modest enough promise certainly, for in that climate there was habitually six weeks more of hard winter after Ground Hog Day whether the ground hog saw his shadow or not.

Yet when he looked back on that period it had the feeling of springtime; the hotel was snug and when Bonnie was with him it made no difference whether a February thaw was followed by rain and a sudden freeze, to trick people into breaking their legs, and by heavy snow.

691

March came in not like a lion but like a herd of polar bears, and March limped out like a troupe of tatterdemalion snowmen; it made no difference. He was happy in those days. He was long out of touch with Mc-Swasey and doing nothing to ferret out log thieves; his career was a frozen river getting nowhere; but he was happy. He and Bonnie were never alone—not in the sense of being free from interruption—so for a long time he didn't so much as kiss her; but that was all right; spring would come some day and there would be evening strolls; meanwhile he was contented just to watch her and listen to her; if by giving up Bonnie he could have had a girl from a fancy house in his bed every night he would have said no thanks, I know when I'm lucky, I know when I've found the real thing.

At first they never mentioned the letter he had sent her proposing marriage, but he had a hunch she had received it and had not been offended. Little things told him: the look which sometimes came into her eyes and which could break a man's heart, it was so gentle and winsome; the way she treated that storekeeper, Hale Winthrop, with pleasant but distant politeness; the way, of an evening, she would become the least bit bossy, as if she had some claim on him, and tell him he must go to bed now and get his rest and regain his strength. But he couldn't put into words the principal thing that told him she was willing to become Mrs. Buckmaster. It was too subtle, a kind of intimacy that shimmered between them; nothing he could put his finger on, but unmistakable.

She must have shown that letter to her parents, and they must have approved, for in their attitude he sensed a quality just as indescribable but as manifest; instead of a patient and a hotel guest, he might have been a member of the family. Once he was well enough to smoke, Mrs. Fansler objected to his dropping ashes on the bedroom carpet, and she gave him regular lectures on the evils of strong drink, but she also asked about his favorite foods and saw to it that they were served in the dining room; and Dr. Fansler might have been his father-in-law, the way he would wink and bring a bottle labeled Poison from his bag and pour Jim a snifter. Jim liked the Fanslers; it would be nice to have a family again, something to tie to, he had been so homeless all these years.

Bonnie told him how alarmed she had been that morning of the blizzard when he came stumbling into the lobby and fell. It had, she said, been a terrible storm that raged for thirty-six hours; coming so early in the season, and so unexpectedly, it had caught many duck hunters out in the blinds; for several hundred miles up and down the Mississippi men had been frozen to death. Rafting crews had suffered and died from exposure; steamboats had run aground.

"You were lucky to save yourself," she said.

"And in more ways than that," he told her, and she flushed.

One evening in March when they lingered in the dining room after all the customers had gone, she told him she had done something terrible

—not once but several times—during the first weeks of his sickness.

"I knew I shouldn't," she said shyly, "but I couldn't help myself."

Sitting there at the table, the nail of her forefinger making nervous little marks on the cloth, her curls dark and elegant, her eyes lowered, she put him in mind of a child about to confess some dark crime such as passing notes in school; he felt gentle and amused and tender.

"What did you do, Bonnie?"

"You might not like me if I'd tell you."

He denied that.

"You might think I was too forward."

He denied that too, and he had a twinge of amusement and chagrin, thinking of the girls he used to know.

"Well," she said slowly, "I used to worry about you, lying there in Max's room. They made me stay out but I wanted to be there. My father said you were terribly sick. My mother would sit up with you, but she's a sleepyhead, and I was afraid she would nod in her chair and you would need something. My room is next to Max's, and I'd think of you on the other side of the wall. So some nights . . . well . . ."

She wouldn't look at him; her throat showed color; but she made herself continue.

"Some nights, very late, I would get out of bed and tiptoe along the hall and into your room. And it was the way I thought; my mother had dozed off in her chair. Everything was dim and silent and I was sort of scared. But I tiptoed over to your bed and looked at you. And you looked sick, Jim, you looked so very sick. Sometimes you lay like you were in your coffin, you were that still. And sometimes you tossed and moaned. I wanted to cry. You had always been so strong and in command of yourself, but now you were sick and it was sad. I wanted to nurse you, Jim, and I would have if they had let me. I would never have left that room. One night you talked in your sleep. That was when you were delirious. You kept talking to somebody named Molly. You even swore. 'I'll own it all,' you said, 'they'll never stop me. Wisconsin and the river,' you said, 'I'll own them all . . .' Then you seemed to be having a fight, Jim, with somebody called Bulldog. That's a funny name, but that's how it sounded. And then you were talking to Molly again, and crying. I don't mean there were tears, but you were sort of crying. Who is Molly, Jim? Is she somebody I ought to know about?"

He thought, "Good Lord!" And for a moment he even thought of explaining how it had been with him and Molly; how it used to be before Molly changed, or before he had. But something told him Bonnie would never understand. So he laughed.

"Molly?" he said. "Why, she was a kind of aunt to me. Up there in Quickwater when I was a kid, she used to be good to me. She and her husband. Once they had me over for oyster stew."

"I'm glad," Bonnie said. "I mean I'm glad Molly isn't somebody—you know—some girl or somebody . . ."

It was then that he kissed her. Right in a public place like the dining room of the Fansler House he kissed her, and be hanged to anybody who might catch them.

*

April came; April the lovely. The ice went out of the river; the robins returned. Out in Lance Coulee men were plowing; the prairie chicken sang his lugubrious song; in a thousand dens vixen foxes were suckling their puppies. On the sidewalks of town ants appeared, industrious as stockbrokers; bees hummed where old apple trees burst into blossom. Rains fell in quick-thrusting showers; in musical night-long downpours.

Time to set forth again, he told himself, and search for log thieves. He was strong again; he should buy another outfit and start downriver; yet he lingered, feeling drugged by springtime. He did, however, write McSwasey, telling how he had been caught in the November storm, how he had lain sick for months. Then he lied: he was still weak, he said, but making the most of his time here in Lanceport by worming into the confidence of a group of log thieves. He didn't mention Bonnie. His pencil kept wanting to, however.

She was always in his thoughts and much in his presence; he was bemused by her loveliness; he had eaten of the lotus. In a world more utopian, he would gladly have beguiled away his days at nothing more consequential than wandering with her where the spring beauties grew and the orioles whistled. He was not like himself in those days, with his ambition slumbering.

It was the best of youth and the best of life; he could see that, looking back. He was like a young god then, the way he felt. One afternoon when the sky was April blue he rented a rig from the livery stable, and Bonnie packed food in a basket. The rig was the most stylish the stable boasted, an elegant phaeton with a lavender body and yellow wheels, and the team were high-stepping sorrels; their silky coats looked almost gold in the sunshine of the Lance Creek road.

By then it was all settled; they were going to be married. In June, perhaps; anyway, just as soon as Jim could catch him some log thieves and become vice-president of the company. "I've a little business to attend to first," he told Bonnie, without explaining what kind. Not that he didn't trust her but her tongue might slip, secrecy was best. Besides, for some reason he couldn't understand, he would have been ashamed to tell her he was going to earn a fourth interest in McSwasey & Zumwalt by tricking and trapping other men. She was a gentle girl; she might have started feeling sorry for the wives and children of the thieves. She wouldn't understand that when a man got ahead—far ahead, fast—it was often necessary to step on a few faces.

"Bonnie," he told her, that afternoon as they drove along, "we're going places. You stick by me and you'll find out where the river goes. There'll be rings on your fingers and bells on your toes before we're through."

"I like it the way it is," she said.

"I've got plans," he said. "I've come up the hard way, but that's about over. I've been a river hog and a river rooster, but that's about over. We'll be rich, Bonnie. I can feel it coming. I'll buy me a plug hat and a swallow-tailed coat, and I'll have me a couple of senators for pet monkeys. We'll live in a house with so many rooms a man could get lost. When you want something you'll just yank a velvet rope and a Swede girl will bring it."

"It couldn't be any better than this," she said.

Well, maybe she was right, but it poked his ambition awake, talking that way.

"Bonnie," he said, "I might have to leave in a few days. I've got business; there's a big deal brewing. But I'll be back."

"Will you be gone long?"

"Two weeks, maybe. Maybe three or four. But I'll be back. You'll be surprised when this deal comes off. It's big, Bonnie. I'll be on the way to owning the river, when I come back. I'll own me Wisconsin too, before I'm done."

Talk like that disturbed her; he could see it in her face. So he laughed.

"Don't mind me," he said. "Maybe I'm still a river rooster crowing to hear the echo. Don't pay no attention—I know a man couldn't own the river—that's just the way I talk. I'm just telling you I'll take care of you."

She smiled then; her somberness went away. She looked beautiful sitting there in a crisp white dress, wearing a bonnet garlanded with flowers. A man wanted to muss her up, she looked so nice.

That coulee road took them deep into April; plum thickets were in blossom, and red-haw trees; they passed a meadow where a cow stood licking a wobbly calf, and Jim was reminded of how he had saved the life of Three-Cent Olson's calf back in Quickwater. He told her about that, and about Injun Hollow, and of how he had earned money singing in the Northern Saloon.

"We were poor," he said, "and I was out for the money. I saved me a pretty good wad, but I lost it all in the fire."

She wanted to know about that, and he found himself telling her things he would never have told a saloon girl; how the fire had snuffed out his family and how he had gone wandering with Sol Klauber.

"But I left him finally. Ran away. He had an idea that I should get educated in college, but I couldn't do that. I wanted the woods. I never saw him again till I saw him dead. That jolted me. It jolted me hard."

He felt bleak, telling her how Sol had drowned; he sat hunched forward with the reins in his hands. He must have looked bleak too, for

Bonnie patted his arm and sat closer; there was sympathy in her eyes. A saloon girl would have said, "Cheer up, you lunkhead. Wipe the funeral off your face and cheer up. You're alive, ain't you?" He had known a lot of hard girls, but this one was different. A man would want to be careful with a girl like this, not to hurt her.

Beyond the last farm, the road crossed Lance Creek and went wandering through a wildwood of sugar berries and butternuts; where a grassy bank sloped toward the creek Jim halted the team and tied up at a basswood tree; dandelions were scattered in the grass; and in secret moist places under the honey locusts and along the creek Bonnie found violets and Dutchman's-breeches and wild hyacinths. A faint fragrance hung in the air.

People had been here before; they must have, for somebody had built the road; but it all seemed new and untouched. Long afterward his memory would flash him pictures of that afternoon: Bonnie taking off her bonnet and giving her head that characteristic little shake, to rearrange her curls; Bonnie laughing and dodging a bee that came buzzing; Bonnie picking a single violet and contemplating it deeply, as if searching for some answer to tangled riddles.

The coulee was narrow here, the sides steep, so of course they wanted to climb it. In places where the going was sheer he went first, finding the way, holding out his hand and pulling her up. At the summit, among the old hickories and beeches, when they were standing side by side, they heard from far to the east the faint whistle of a river steamboat, musical and sad. Jim recognized the packet by its voice; it was a McSwasey & Zumwalt boat, the *Esperanza,* steaming upriver on her first voyage of the new season.

"What's the matter?" Bonnie asked.

"Matter? Nothing's the matter."

And he smiled.

"You were scowling," she said.

"Oh. Trying to make out what boat that is."

"What one is it?"

"I can't quite figure it," he said.

He didn't want to lie to Bonnie, and he wondered why he did. Maybe it was because that boat whistle brought him up short, reminding him he had better be on the move after those log thieves. But suddenly he didn't want to; doubts went ghosting through his mind. McSwasey hitting him with knucks; damn, he didn't like that. Molly Fitzpatrick's words came back to him: "If you're mixed up with Caleb McSwasey in some damn fool scheme, you'd better watch." Well, he was mixed up with McSwasey all right, and he had misgivings. But maybe that was because he was going to marry a nice girl who wouldn't like his doing anything underhanded. Yet he wanted that fourth interest in McSwasey's company more than ever, now that he would be a married man.

"You're doing it again," Bonnie said. "You're scowling."

"Trying to figure that whistle. But I've got it now. That there is the *Esperanza*. She belongs to the fellow who hit me with knucks. I should have ducked. But hell, let's forget that. When I'm married to you nobody will hit me with knucks. I'll be staying home nights behaving myself instead of helling around in saloons."

"Jim," she said, "you will marry me, won't you?"

"Marry you?" He laughed. "Why, hell's bells, that's all I'm living for. I should guess I will marry you. What made you ask that?"

"I don't know," she said. "Maybe because it seems too good to be true."

He kissed her then, and his doubts vanished. With her in his arms anything seemed possible.

Dusk was slipping into the coulee when they returned to the phaeton for the picnic basket and a blanket; Jim built a fire and they roasted wieners on green sticks. Afterward he lounged with his pipe while Bonnie tucked things back into the basket; he enjoyed watching her; the firelight brought shifting gleams to her hair. Sometimes she passed between him and the fire and he saw her figure in contour.

"There," she said, when the basket was packed. "We'd better be starting back. They'll wonder where we are."

He carried the basket to the phaeton, but something made him leave the blanket on the grass.

"You've forgotten the blanket," Bonnie said.

He said he guessed he had at that, and with her by his side he moved back to get it. He could feel her quivering when he took her into his arms.

"Jim," she whispered, "oh, Jim. It would be lonely here if it weren't for you. Lonely everywhere, I think."

In the dark the spring peepers were singing their humble little songs, and frogs were croaking. The evening had turned cool, but he knew that was not why she was trembling. I've got to be good to her, he thought, I've got to take care of her; but his hands were on the move.

"Jim," she whispered.

Everything was in his mind then, everything he ever wanted. The river flowed in all the glory of one of the great rivers of the world, rafts on its blue and gold waters, and he owned it all. The pinery was in his mind too, leagues upon leagues of virgin timber, redolent and dark, and he was a giant striding into it and ravaging it all. Everything was his. He was a booted figure stepping from the bluffs of Iowa to the bluffs of Wisconsin, and from up there in the sunny heavens he could look down and see his steamboats plying the river and his lumber yards and the capitol dome in Madison with the legislature he owned; and in a town called New Empire he could see a mansion with children playing on a green lawn and a lovely woman named Bonnie Buckmaster. He had it all then; there was nothing more that he wanted.

*

Always after making love to a saloon girl he was through with her till next time; he wanted to get the hell out of there; but with Bonnie it was different. With her, everything was right. It was going to be a fine marriage, he could see that. She lay quietly in his arms; he could smell the fragrance of her hair. In the shadows the peepers were cheeping, and a whippoorwill began to sing.

It kept on being fine. Some girls would have sobbed; some would have chattered; some would have become cross or scared; some would have asked that silliest of all questions, "Now why did you do that?" Not Bonnie. Returning to the phaeton, her arm through his, she walked with a kind of queenly pride, and when she spoke there was no rebuke in her voice.

"You mussed me up, Jim. I must look a sight. They'll know something has happened. But I don't care."

In the dimness he could see her giving her head a shake, to rearrange her curls; she put on her bonnet and brushed her dress.

"I don't care," she repeated. "I don't care what anybody thinks, so long as you love me."

He kissed her then.

Jim kept the horses at a walk, on the way back to town, because he wanted the evening to stretch out forever. His arm was around her, and her head was on his shoulder.

"I guess," she said once, "I chased you. That first morning when you came in with a headache and I was behind the desk—even then, Jim. When you looked at me something happened. I might have been asleep all my life up till then, but when you looked at me I woke up. And that evening when you gave me the cameo I went to my room and cried. I cried because I was happy, Jim, and I knew I had to see you before you left. That's why I got up so early to cook your breakfast. My mother didn't like it when she found out. She said you'd never be back. But I knew you'd be back. My mother said you were probably a drunkard—she had smelled whiskey that first morning—you reeked of it, you know—but I didn't care. She said you were probably wild like my half-brother Max, but even if you had been I would have loved you. Max is the black sheep of the family, Jim. Do you mind marrying into a family with a black sheep?"

He had to laugh at that; he told her he guessed his own wool had been a little dark around the edges, at times.

"But Max is goodhearted," she said. "You'll like him, Jim. My mother never did, though. He's not her son, you know. I think she used to be

698

glad, back in Maryland, when he got into scrapes. But I don't remember much about that. I was little. Max is ten years older than me, so I was only eight when he ran away west. He would do anything for you but he didn't like to work. He was supposed to weed the garden but he didn't like to. We lived in a nice house there in Elkader. The grist mill was on the bank of the river and our house was across the road with a garden in back and fruit trees and a pasture. Once when Max was supposed to dig the potatoes and store them in the root cellar he didn't want to, so he told my sisters and me that he would build us a road if we would dig them and load them into the wheelbarrow. It was a lovely little road too. It wound around through the garden and he even built us a little bridge. I used to be afraid of bridges because I thought trolls lived under them but this was just a little one. We girls dug the potatoes and piled them in the wheelbarrow and one of us would ride on top of the load when Max pushed that barrow along the road to the root cellar. He worked lots harder than if he had dug the potatoes himself in the first place, but that's Max. He'll work hard if it's fun. But you're not interested in all this."

He was, though. He said he wished he had known her then; he wished he had known her always.

"Oh, you wouldn't have liked me. I wore my hair in pigtails and when the boys at school yanked them I would fight and cry. But I was a fraid-cat too. Max used to go for the cow but after he ran away west we girls had to. Once I went to the pasture but the cow had got out. I could hear her bell in the timber beyond the pasture and I started after her. That was in the fall of the year and it was getting dusky. There was haze in the valley and I could see corn in the shock. It looked like Indian wigwams. I kept following the sound of the cowbell but then it was really dark and I was crying because I thought there were Indians behind the trees. A long time later men came with lanterns and found me. I remember how my father took me in his arms and kissed me. He always had that doctor smell. I felt safe in his arms. Just the way I feel safe in yours."

"You're safe," he said. "I should guess you're safe."

As Lanceport drew nearer he wondered what would be said at the hotel when he came bringing the Fansler daughter home with her clothes and hair mussed; she still belonged to her parents. But she belonged to him too in a way a girl never belonged to her father and mother. He guessed he would have to take a firm stand, if Mrs. Fansler made any trouble. She would have to learn who was head of the house, once he and Bonnie were married.

But they weren't married yet, and a thin depression went sneaking across his spirits. He wondered why, but then he had the answer: because he would have to be leaving Bonnie and hunting for log thieves. Suppose he couldn't find any thieves; what then? Yet, damn it, they existed—McSwasey had said they were the bane of all the operators on the river—and if they existed he would find them. But it might take months. McSwasey wasn't playing games with him, was he? Why would he do that?

Reaching the outskirts of town, the horses broke into a trot, and Jim didn't try to hold them back; if Mrs. Fansler thought her daughter looked mussed and wanted to raise trouble, it might as well happen sooner as later. But in the stable, when Bonnie stepped down from the phaeton, he couldn't see that she looked any different than you might expect in a girl who had been on a picnic in the woods.

"Jim," she said, on the sidewalk outside the hotel, "how do I look?"

"Wonderful," he said. "You look great to me."

But they need not have fretted that night about how Bonnie looked, for the Fanslers were too excited to spend any time examining her skirt for grass stains. When Jim followed her into the lobby, he saw Dr. Wace Fansler coming from the dining room, all smiles.

'Bonnie," he said, "I've got a surprise for you. Max is here. He came in on the *Esperanza* this afternoon. He's in the kitchen now."

Jim let Bonnie hurry on to greet her brother.

"Come along, Jim," Dr. Fansler said. "You'll like Max. We'll have to move you out of his room, but we can do that tomorrow."

When he went through the swinging door into the kitchen, just like a member of the family, Jim saw Bonnie turn.

"Jim," she said, "this is Max."

And Jim had seen him before. Last October. He had seen him camped in the bluffs near Weasel Creek Eddy, a man with slick black hair and big white teeth.

*

Long after midnight Jim left the hotel and went walking about the town. All the houses were dark now; the Methodist Church was a bulky shadow; he was the only pedestrian. Sometimes, passing a yard, he walked through streams of fragrance from lilacs or a fruit orchard, and once under a streetlamp he saw a toad waiting to gobble the insects that flittered there. When he returned to Promenade Street it had that empty, mournful look of a market place in the deeps of night when all the busy little money-getters are tucked into bed. Only the river was awake and on the move, flowing past the levee as it had flowed in La Salle's time, and in Marquette's, and in Perrot's.

For a long while he stood there on the levee, aware of the gathering of portentous events. He would need to search no further for river pirates; Max Fansler had returned from St. Louis. Already he had looked speculatively at Jim; already he had said, "Aren't you the rooster Caleb McSwasey blacklisted?" And already Jim had responded, "Yes, and I'll make him pay for it if it's the last thing I do."

He thought he understood it all. He could imagine a far-flung empire of thieves with Max Fansler in the upper councils, with Max coming north in the warm months to prod along the theft of rafts, with Max going south in the winter to oversee the contraband lumber moving from a contraband sawmill into the channels of legitimate trade.

He was in luck, great luck; things were coming his way; certainly Max Fansler would never suspect his future brother-in-law of being a secret agent for Caleb McSwasey.

And Bonnie? In the months ahead, when she learned he had led Max Fansler and a crew of freebooters into a trap at Stovepipe Rock, what would she think? Damn! He was scowling now; he could foresee appalling complications. Maybe he'd better write Caleb McSwasey to go jump in the river. The deal's off, McSwasey; I'm pulling out; I've found me a girl I love and I'm settling down; find somebody else to catch you your log thieves.

McSwasey would do just that, of course: he'd find somebody else. Some other rooster would trap the thieves; some other rooster would be given a fourth interest in the company.

And Jim Buckmaster? Would McSwasey welcome him back to the payroll? Would he revoke that blacklisting? Why, Jim, if you don't want to go through with it, that's all right. We've lost a lot of time while you made up your mind, but that's fine. Your old job's waiting, Jim. You've fizzled out on me, Jim, but think nothing of it . . . Would McSwasey say that?

Ha!

So he would marry Bonnie but where would he work? In logging camps? On drives? Rafting logs? Who would hire him? "I couldn't touch you, Jim," Nels Quist had said. "Not if you're blacklisted." Would any other operator touch him? Now that he had a reputation for payroll padding, would they all be scrambling to hire him?

He thought of the river-front loafers he had known, men nobody wanted, men like hollow shells and empty bottles, men who had missed somewhere, men dogged by bad luck, men who had been somebody once but were now nobody, men who had lived it up and drunk it up, men crippled in fights; all the has-beens, the never-weres, the failures. He thought of Greasy Dick Cassidy; he thought of Lorne Buckmaster.

And he thought of the wives of men like that, women who had been lovely once, and gay, and proud. Maybe as lovely, even, as Bonnie Fansler. But they had got the wrong pig by the ear. Life had slapped their faces and pushed them into mud puddles. They were the hollowed-out women, the bony women, the gaunt women; women who bedded with failure.

Max Fansler would be trapped in any case, some day, if he kept stealing logs. A man who had always been in scrapes and who stole logs on the river had to expect that some day he would be standing in court before a judge.

Jim left the levee at last. He would sleep on it. If she loved him she would marry him no matter what. Wouldn't she? But it had never been so good with a saloon girl. Crossing the street to the Fansler House, he was still scowling.

XIII

April came to New Empire also, in that fateful year, and there was progress. Down on Front Street, a man named Stahlknecht opened a magnificent brewery with the backing, so it was rumored, of Caleb Mc-Swasey; Rattlesnake Bob Skellenger exhibited several fresh ·fang-marks in the calf of his leg; Darrah's Lodging House, where Jim Buckmaster used to stay, sported a fresh paint job; and the Bank of New Empire, in a letter to its depositors, announced that a majority of its stock had been acquired by Caleb McSwasey, Esq., "thus strengthening an institution which has always been known as the financial Gibraltar of Fox County." Every morning a boy named Rolfe Torkelsen walked from Judge Gentry's house to the Gentry Block on Winnebago Street, where he studied his Blackstone; and Pat Rafferty imported two new girls from St. Louis. Farmers built barns; farmers built hog houses; the Baptists built a parsonage; and the nails and wood and cement all came from a business with a great new sign: McSwasey Lumber Company, New Empire and St. Louis.

Caleb celebrated his fifty-fifth birthday that April, although his wife, being so occupied with other matters, forgot to buy him a gift. Mr. and Mrs. Park Irwin, however, did not forget; they invited the McSwaseys to their home for supper; when Caleb and Esperanza entered, thirty or forty guests shouted, "Surprise! Surprise!" and sang Happy Birthday. "A great tribute to a great man," said the *New Empire Chronicle*, and it was probably correct, for all the county officials attended, and Judge and Mrs. Sophronicus Gentry, and even one of Wisconsin's United States Senators.

It was thoughtful of Park Irwin to give such a party, and it just went to show that gratitude was not dead in the human heart, for Mr. Irwin, a pleasant man in his late thirties, owed much to Mr. McSwasey and even more to the Bank of New Empire, which held a mortgage on his house. Mr. Irwin had been brought from St. Louis some years before, to manage the McSwasey retail yard; he had done an excellent job, and, being a fine mixer, was soon friends with everybody; and then last autumn, at Mr. McSwasey's urging and with his backing, financial and journalistic, he had run for sheriff of Fox County and had been swept into office with a handsome majority.

"It will not surprise us in the least," said the *Chronicle*, "if higher honors some day come to Sheriff Irwin."

*

On McSwasey's Island it had been a long, hard winter, but Esperanza endured it better than usual because she had convinced herself that when spring came Jim Buckmaster would return to New Empire, sweep her into his arms and carry her away. Like everybody else in town, she had heard about Caleb's encounter with Jim last October in Rafferty's Saloon; but not for a moment did she accept the explanation that the quarrel had concerned payroll padding; she believed it concerned her. How otherwise? On that rainy autumn afternoon when Caleb was sick, she had served tea to Jim Buckmaster, and when he left to board the up-river boat she had accompanied him in the carriage. That must have roused her husband's jealousy, for the very next Friday he had taken a boat for Read's Landing, doubtless to warn his raft pilot to keep away from his wife. What was said at that conference she had no way of knowing, but her imagination supplied the lack: Caleb's anger, Jim's denials, for he would not of course reveal to a jealous husband his intention of stealing his wife.

Brooding about that interview, Caleb must have found it unsatisfactory, so when he encountered Jim in Rafferty's Saloon, and discharged him and knocked him out, jealousy must have been goading him. It was understandable, she thought, that he would have spread the story that Jim had been padding accounts, for his pride would not have let him confess that he was jealous of an employee.

In April, about the time of that surprise party for Caleb, Esperanza began expecting Jim to return from the North, where fortunes came from, so every morning she tricked herself out in one of her new spring dresses, and when the doorbell rang her heart was in her throat. But it was never Jim. She grew restless, as the days passed, and she used to hold long conferences with Lilith.

"He'll come for me. Don't you think he'll come for me, Lilith?"

"Yes, ma'am. Reckon he will. You figure to run off with him, Miss Esperanza? You do that and Mistah Caleb ain't going to like it."

Esperanza smiled.

She daydreamed endlessly. She was a heroine from French fiction that spring, imagining herself and her lover fleeing Caleb's wrath and sailing away to Europe. She saw the Champs Elysées glittering with carriages, thronged with dashing officers, and herself a beauty strolling with a handsome man. She saw herself at the Opera, at society balls in the Faubourg St. Germain, at student balls at the Elysée Montmartre. She saw the skies of Italy, the olive trees, the radiant Mediterranean; she was white-gowned in a decaying palace reflecting itself in a Venetian canal;

and always Jim was with her, ready to protect her from Caleb, should he follow.

It never occurred to her that things might not work out as she imagined, for from her father she had inherited vast talents in self-delusion. She had no conception then of the forces at work behind her back; she never imagined that Caleb might be piling up redundant evidence of her infidelity, in the spirit of self-torture which leads a man to bite down on an aching tooth. She loved Jim and he must, he simply must, love her; wishing would make it so. Every week she wrote him a passionate letter, and these she entrusted to Lilith, who supposedly took them to Darrah's Lodging House to be forwarded. According to Lilith, she had gone to that lodging house last winter and had learned that the landlady was always kept informed of Jim's changing addresses up there in the North, where he was doing some hazy thing, such as estimating timber. Although replies to those letters never arrived, Esperanza was not discouraged; she had never discouraged easily, when she wanted something.

She had heard that a man who estimated timber often discovered opportunities to make a great deal of money fast, if he were not squeamish, so she convinced herself that during his winter's work Jim would amass a small fortune, more than enough for an elopement with Mrs. Caleb McSwasey.

"And I'll have my jewels," she told Lilith. "We could live in luxury for years, by selling my jewels."

The thought of doing that gave her a romantic thrill, for those aristocratic ladies in French novels, after fleeing incognito with their lovers, were forever selling their jewels.

April passed and May came to McSwasey's Island, but not Jim. Yet she could not doubt that he would come. Waiting for him, she retreated ever deeper into daydreams, and it was at that season when she began hearing those snatches of distant music.

One evening at supper in the dining room, when the windows were open and the candles burned with scarcely a flutter, she heard the music first.

"Listen," she said. "What's that?"

At the head of the table Caleb sat chewing, regarding her closely. "I don't hear anything."

"It's music," Esperanza said. "They're singing. Don't you hear it?"

"What are you talking about, Goldilocks?"

"It's a caravan," she said. "Listen."

From far away, off toward the river, the song came drifting with an elfin quality:

> *I jumped on a mule and started west,*
> *Started west, started west . . .*

"Can't you hear it?" she asked.

705

"Goldilocks," he said, "what's got into you?"

She jumped up and hurried to the back gallery and into the garden. The singing, accompanied by an accordion, seemed to be coming from some island in the Mississippi, or perhaps from the far Iowa bluffs.

I found me a gal in Santy Fee,
In Santy Fee, in Santy Fee . . .

The notes were very tiny, very sweet, like the notes of a music box. Caleb had followed her. He asked:

"What's got into you, Goldilocks?"

"You hear it," she said. "Of course you hear it. It's a trail song."

"You're crazy," he said.

"Listen! An accordion and men singing. Just as they did that evening in Pecos Canyon."

"I don't hear anything."

"You must be going deaf," she said. "Lilith hears it too. I'm sure she must. Let's ask Lilith."

And Esperanza hurried to the fountain, where Lilith and Heinrich were taking the evening air.

"You hear it, don't you, Lilith? You hear the men singing."

"What men?"

"Why, the bull whackers. They must have a campfire on an island. Listen!"

Sharp and sweet, the song came drifting:

She fed me corn and she fed me beans,
Fed me beans, fed me beans . . .

"No, ma'am. I don't hear nothing."

"You're crazy," Caleb told Esperanza. "There's no singing."

Arrgh! She stamped a foot and ran into the house and upstairs to the sitting room of the master's suite. The music followed her, growing louder. Suddenly she didn't like it, and she stuffed her forefingers into her ears. But the music persisted. She saw Caleb entering the room; he stood watching, head forward, in that listening attitude of a deaf man, a strange smile on his lips. He looked old and stodgy and practical. He exasperated her so much that she wanted to go to the vitrine and snatch the knife that had belonged to her great-grandmother. But then she heard him saying, "If you ain't fast with a knife you'd best not fool with it." Oddly, however, his lips were not moving, but she could hear the words as plainly as if he had spoken. She whirled and ran to the bedroom and flung herself to the bed, sobbing. After a while the music stopped.

*

During the next days when she heard the music she did not mention it to Caleb or to Lilith; they were growing old, she told herself, and their hearing was faulty. Sometimes the singing was loud as a church choir and she was surprised that the Scandinavian maids did not mention it, but usually it was far and faint like music from a magic forest in a fairy tale. There were days when she did not hear it at all, and other days when it was almost constant. It brought Santa Fe to mind; she thought of her father and of the man who wore yellow shoes. Fourteen years ago, nearly, since he had chased her. Bones in the earth now, eaten clean by ants. The dead were dead; he had not actually slithered from his grave and followed her east along the trail from Santa Fe.

And yet there were occasions when she could almost imagine that the dead were not dead at all but only metamorphosed, the way water changed to steam, and that they wandered at will among the living. One night after Caleb had made love to her, violently, she lay unable to sleep, thinking of Jim Buckmaster and wondering when he would arrive in New Empire to claim her. At last she slipped from bed and wearing slippers and a peignoir stole downstairs and out into the garden, wandering along the path to the river. It was late in May, the night warm with a half-moon shining. She stood staring upstream, thinking of Jim; but then all at once she forgot him because from an island in the river she heard the music.

> *The mule was neither horse nor mare,*
> *Horse nor mare, horse nor mare . . .*

Strange that nobody else ever heard that singing. Caleb and Lilith, she thought, were becoming odd. And then as she stood there by the river she heard something else, the merest whisper.

"*Zapatos y pelo.* Same color."

She went rigid, her scalp tingling, and she thought she felt fingers brushing her hair. She whirled then, but she saw nobody in the ghostly moonlight. Her knees were trembling, and from the island in the river the singing continued, faint and elfin. Slowly, telling herself she must not run or all would be lost, she started back toward the house. Her heart was pounding; her fingers were cold. And as she moved along she thought she heard footsteps following her. She broke into a run then, and a scream rose in her throat, but her vocal chords were unable to make a sound. Then the moon turned black and the night whirled. When she came awake she was lying on the path and there was no more singing. There was no more whispering.

"I've been staying home too close," she thought, "waiting for Jim. I must go into town more."

Next afternoon, dressed in her spring finery, she rode from the island in one of the family carriages and went to Dr. Washburn's office. But she did not tell him the whole truth.

"Doctor," she said, "it's something about my ears. There's a ringing in my ears."

"Wax, no doubt," he said, and he washed them out. "They'll give you no more trouble now."

Wax; yes, of course. She felt almost happy, leaving his office. Jim Buckmaster would be coming to New Empire any day now to snatch her away from Caleb, and it would be like beginning life anew.

When she reached the southeast corner of Winnebago Street and Gentry Avenue, she encountered a man leaving the Bank of New Empire. He lifted his hat. He was in his thirties, his light-brown hair pomaded, his brown mustache fashionably-trimmed; he wore a suit the color of brown sugar with an azure waistcoat; his shirt was frilled. He was Park Irwin, sheriff of Fox County.

They chatted, and Esperanza liked the way Sheriff Irwin looked at her.

"I could wind him around my finger," she thought.

Not that she wanted him, really; he was a married man with children, and in a snoopy town like New Empire an affair with him would raise a scandal; she wanted Jim. Nevertheless, it was rather jolly to flirt with Sheriff Irwin. Once she said:

"Park, would you do something for me?"

"Gladly, Mrs. McSwasey."

"Would you call me Esperanza?"

From the way his face lighted, you would have thought she had invited him to hang up his trousers in her boudoir. She was amused and pleased. It just went to show how much fun life could be, if one were not the wife of a jealous man.

"Why, yes, Mrs. McSwasey," Sheriff Irwin said. "It would be a privilege to call you Esperanza."

She lowered her voice and her eyes were intimate.

"But never call me that, Park, when Caleb is around. He is very jealous." She extended her hand. "It was so nice seeing you."

Feeling elated, she walked on, presently riding back to the island, and during the next days she heard no more singing. But one morning in the garden she underwent a queer little experience. Lilith had gone to town that morning, to attend to sending one of the love letters her mistress had written, so the care of Heinrich had fallen to Esperanza; she sat on a bench at that circular place where the fountain sparkled in the June sunlight. She wanted to daydream, but Heinrich, who had turned two last February, kept interfering with her thoughts. He would go toddling off to explore the brick paths till summoned by a waspish, "Heinrich! Come back here!" Then he would splash his hands in the fountain or poke into one of Ferdinand Vogler's flower beds. "Heinrich! Stop that!" And looking somber and blond, with his mother's long mouth with the thin ends, but at the same time looking very much like

Judge Gentry, Heinrich would stand staring at his mother. "Heinrich! Take your thumb out of your mouth!" Whereupon he would jump up and down and laugh and squeal.

She wondered why she did not love him. But that was a terrible thing to think. Of course she loved him. He was her son; certainly she loved him. But he annoyed her. He bored her. She loved him, yes, of course, but she would have loved him more if he were not such a little nuisance. When she took flight with Jim she would leave Heinrich behind. In Lilith's care. It would be a wrench, but she would do it. She wished Andrew J. Gentry had not been so careless.

Heinrich, as it turned out that morning, must have inherited his father's carelessness, for presently his interest was claimed by a tall stepladder which Ferdinand Vogler had left set up on the path leading away from the fountain. Watching, Esperanza could tell the exact moment when it occurred to her son that the ladder would be a fascinating thing to climb; but as he toddled toward it, and grasped its sidepieces, she did not call for him to stop.

It was great fun, that ladder. Heinrich pulled himself up to the first rung and looked around, as if expecting the cross beautiful lady to snap, "Heinrich! Stop that!" But the lady only sat staring with eyes that had turned flat and lusterless.

"I should stop him, he'll fall," Esperanza thought, but her tongue lay mute. And suddenly it came to her that she wanted him to fall. She was startled and a little horrified.

Now Heinrich had reached the second rung, and Esperanza told herself she should call out, but she sat as if in a wicked trance, watching the sunlight on her son's blond hair; thinking, with a sentimental pang, how tiny his hands looked, reaching, pulling himself to the third rung.

He squealed with delight then, jiggling up and down, and once he looked at the cross beautiful lady.

She could not speak; she could not move.

And then he reached the fourth rung, and after that the fifth, where, intoxicated with height, he screamed and laughed, his chubby little legs dancing.

"I can't move," she thought, "I can't watch him but I've got to—he'll fall—why can't I go to him?—what has come over me?"

Now he had gripped the sidepieces and was rocking back and forth; Esperanza's lips were parted, and her breathing had grown rapid; she had not thought he would climb so high; if he tumbled now he might really injure himself. He might strike his head on the brick path and die. She felt faintly sick; the sunlight was dazzling. The ladder itself was rocking now, back and forth, back and forth, its center of gravity high, almost tipping over but not quite; not quite yet.

Then she heard a shout, and she saw Ferdinand Vogler running from deep in the garden.

Esperanza sprang up and raced to the ladder and rescued her son. "I must have dozed off," she told *Herr* Vogler.

Then she spanked Heinrich.

*

The following Sunday was a crucial one for Esperanza, although it passed quietly enough on McSwasey's Island; things were happening behind her back. In the morning church bells sounded from town, calling the Scandinavian girls to Lutheran worship, and reminding Caleb to go to his office, for like a preacher he worked on Sunday, usually returning home for a huge dinner at two. Today, however, he did not show up, nor did he return for supper. Esperanza was unconcerned. During the evening she sat reading in the upstairs sitting room, finally going to bed. She was drowsily aware that Caleb came in very late, and evidently tired, for he did not rouse her to make love, and he was up and gone before she wakened in the morning. He was working, probably, on one of his big deals; she couldn't have been less interested.

Monday was likewise a crucial day for Esperanza, although, till evening, she had no intimation of this; everything went along as usual. When Caleb returned home for supper she sensed at once that things had been going well with him; his smile and his eyes radiated triumph; his hair bristled victoriously. He was wearing a white linen suit, wrinkled and limp, as if he had been working and sweating; and before supper, when he tossed down a couple of drinks, he kept watching her with a gaze so exultant that she thought he must have forced some competitor into a cul-de-sac and annihilated him utterly. He would have enjoyed that; he never, she knew, gave quarter. He kept drinking wine with his supper, and when the meal was over he said:

"Goldilocks, I want to talk with you."

"Yes?"

"Upstairs."

"All right," she said, thinking he wanted to strip her and top his triumph.

But in the upstairs sitting room, after locking the door, he lighted a cigar, and when she sat on the chaise he stood looking down at her.

"Have you heard anything?" he asked.

"What do you mean?"

"About what Park Irwin has been up to."

Park Irwin. Really! All she had done was to chat a few minutes with Sheriff Irwin outside the Bank of New Empire.

"Caleb," she said, "I'm not interested in Park Irwin."

"You will be," he said, "when you hear what he's done. Last night he took a posse up to Stovepipe Rock. He trapped a bunch of log thieves there. He brought them down here to jail. Fourteen of them. There were fifteen but one was shot. Killed. He tried to get out of the trap."

"Is that where you were last night?" she asked.

"I was in my office, waiting. Park Irwin came in about midnight and told me he had pulled it off. It will be a feather in his cap. Maybe I'll elect him sheriff again, if he behaves himself. Maybe I'll send him to congress. He knows how to follow orders."

Esperanza met his searching gaze, looking innocent, for her conscience was clear about Park Irwin.

"That's very nice," she said.

"Yes," he said, "very. This was a gang of thieves from Lanceport on the Iowa side. There will be no trouble about convictions. Park Irwin caught them red-handed. They were after one of my rafts. We left it in a bayou by Stovepipe Rock, as bait. And it worked. Slicker than a schoolma'am's leg."

"I knew you had been very busy," Esperanza said. "I thought perhaps you were at work on a big deal making money."

"This is better than money, Goldilocks. Hell, I've got so much money now I don't know what to do with it. I could buy and sell my brother Paul every day of the year with one of my bank accounts. I would, too, if the son of a bitch hadn't died last winter."

"Oh? I didn't know."

"I thought I told you. Well, it's not important. What's important is that we've cleaned up those raft thieves. They will all go to prison. I know a judge, Goldilocks, and he'll give them the limit. The bastards."

"I suppose they were desperate men," Esperanza said.

Caleb smiled.

"They just thought they were. It wasn't a real gang, strictly speaking. They had other work. One ran an icehouse and one was a shoemaker. They just stole logs on the side, for the fun of it, I suppose, and pocket money. I had an inside operator working with them, so I knew what was going on. He wrote me every move he made."

"You were shrewd."

"Damned right. I've been planning it almost a year. That's one reason I ran Park Irwin for sheriff. So I'd have somebody who would take orders. And I needed an inside man, so I picked somebody I could trust. Jim Buckmaster."

"Jim Buckmaster!"

"Sure, Goldilocks. You remember him. A big black-haired rooster."

"Oh, yes," she said. "Yes. I remember."

"An ambitious son of a bitch. I went up to Read's Landing last fall and pulled him in. Told him how the log thieves were cutting into our profits, and the profits of all the operators. Told him about a meeting in Madison when all the operators raised a war chest and appointed me to catch the thieves. I promised him certain things if he would go to work on it, and he was willing. And he pulled it off. Yes, sir, the bastard pulled it off."

"But that is wonderful! I mean how longheaded you were. But I thought—I heard—somebody said you had fought Jim Buckmaster in Rafferty's Saloon."

"A put-up job. We were just playing for the galleries. Those pirates wouldn't have trusted one of my men, Goldilocks. We had to put on a show. I fired him and knocked him out, and after that everybody knew we hated each other. When he smelled out those pirates they trusted him, knowing how I had done him dirt. And once he had wormed in with them, he wrote me to leave a raft at Stovepipe Rock. Then he took some girl on a picnic over there and found the raft. And he told the thieves it was there. He set up the business for last night and wrote me to have a posse waiting. I told Park Irwin I had a hunch the thieves would strike last night. He didn't ask questions. Knows better than that, dealing with me. He took a posse there and bagged them."

Esperanza sat with her hands loosely clasped in her lap, and she tried to make her face expressionless. So Jim was working for Caleb; he had been working for him all along. Would he continue working for him? Did this mean he no longer proposed to carry her away? She couldn't believe it. Perhaps Caleb would reward him for catching the thieves and he would use the money for the elopement. She said:

"I'm glad everything turned out well."

"You haven't heard the whole story," Caleb said.

Dusk had fallen and the room was in shadow; she couldn't see her husband's face. But his voice had an odd quality.

"Nobody has heard it all," he added. "But I'll tell you. Don't let it go any further. It's a secret. If you repeat it I'll deny it."

He was a shadow; he turned and cast his cigar into the cold fireplace, where it landed with a spurt of sparks. Then he lighted candles.

"I want to see your face when I tell it," he said. "I've been waiting a long time for this. Log pirates never were a problem. Not a big one. They were a nuisance, that's all. They weren't cutting into our profits. Not so you could notice. And there never was a meeting of timber operators. They never raised a war chest and they never appointed me to catch the thieves."

His face was flushed, his eyes fever-bright.

"I don't believe I understand," she said.

"No," he said, "but you will. You've underestimated me, Goldilocks. So has Buckmaster. He realizes it now, and so will you. I promised him a fourth interest in the company if he pulled this off. I promised he could be vice-president. He swallowed it. I told him to meet me in Rafferty's. I told him we'd pretend to fight. He swallowed that too. But I overstepped myself there. I hit the son of a bitch with knucks. I couldn't pass up a chance like that. If he'd been smart he would have pulled out then and there. It's a wonder I didn't kick him to death, once I'd knocked him out.

I wanted to. Get me started and it's hard to stop. But that would have meant complications. And he would have been dead. This way is better. This way he'll have a long time to think things over."

"I don't know what you're talking about," Esperanza said.

"Don't you, honeychild? You will, you will. And maybe it will teach you. I haven't told Park Irwin that Buckmaster was my inside operator. I haven't told anybody, except you. And you'll keep your mouth shut or I'll take it out of your hide. If you so much as squeak I'll firebrand your face."

"I think you're mad," she said.

"Maybe. So's a bull buffalo, honeychild, when a young bull goes after his cows. They play rough, Goldilocks, and so do I. Buckmaster knows it now. He's in jail, honeychild. They'll try him and they'll convict him. They'll give him the limit. He's trapped, and his life's all busted to hell. If he says I put him up to it they'll laugh. God! Everybody knows we fought in Rafferty's. Everybody knows I fired him for padding accounts. Park Irwin caught him red-handed. We'll make an example of the bastard. He'll be wearing stripes in the penitentiary, honeychild, and I'll get to the warden. They play rough, Goldilocks. If he ever gets out alive he'll be ready for a madhouse. But maybe he won't get out. Maybe he'll be shot trying to escape. Teach him not to tit-paw my wife."

She watched him pour a glass of whiskey; his hands were trembling and part of it spilled. He tossed it down and poured another. He's mad, she thought, mad, mad. He'll kill me, I suppose, some day.

"But why did you do it?" she asked. "There's nothing between Jim Buckmaster and me."

Holding his glass, he stood beside the chaise. His voice was low and amused, as if he were speaking to a child.

"Now, Goldilocks, you're all upset. Have you forgotten how much you love him, honeychild? Have you forgotten what happened in the carriage? Have you forgotten you were going to run away with the son of a bitch? I haven't, sweetheart. I remember it all. And I planned to trap him. Don't you believe me?"

She could feel the blood coursing up her throat; her eyes were lowered.

"I thought you might not," he went on, "so I brought his letters. You've got to know what you're up against, Goldilocks, married to me. I trapped him. Here's the proof, honeychild."

From his pocket he brought a packet of letters, neatly tied with tape, and dropped them into her lap. She saw the flowing, bold handwriting.

"Read them, Goldilocks. You'll learn how I handle men. You'll learn how I deal with a rooster who falls in love with my wife."

Her heart leaped.

"He told you he loved me?" she asked.

Jaw ugly, Caleb stood staring at her.

713

"He *does* love me, doesn't he?" she cried. "He told you he loved me, didn't he?"

Caleb laughed.

"Oh, sure, sure. What do you suppose we were talking about in Rafferty's? You little fool! Flirting your tail at anything in pants. Like you and Andy Gentry. Don't think I didn't know about that too. You weren't fooling me, Goldilocks. You never have and you never will. Sleeping with the bastard at the North Star Mill and getting yourself knocked up higher than a kite. You thought I didn't know. Well, I knew. I know everything you do, you little bitch. I know everything you think. Well, I killed Andy Gentry. Surprises you, don't it? You're white as a sheet, honeychild. I killed the bastard and threw him over the dam. Keep it under your bonnet or you'll wish you had. Nobody could prove a thing because I covered my tracks. I'm too smart for them, honeychild, and I'm too smart for you. I'm just telling you now so you'll behave yourself. You're mine, you little whore, and I propose to keep you. Next time think twice before you fall in love with some alley tomcat. Next time I'll take it out on you. You slut."

He finished his drink, and, wavering a little, set the glass on the mantel. Then he pocketed the packet of letters.

"Understand?" he said.

She couldn't speak; blood was pounding in her throat.

Then, unexpectedly, his open palm came swinging, slapping her face; his other palm swung also; tears sprang to her eyes; he kept slapping her; before she knew what she was doing she kicked at his legs. He moved in then; his fingers were at her throat. He's . . . he's . . . killing me, she thought; the room swung and grew dark.

But he wasn't. She lay on the chaise gasping.

"All right, honeychild," he said. "Behave yourself from now on. Don't start anything you can't finish. Just remember you're my woman and everything will be fine."

Then he left.

*

She stood up, finally, and saw herself in the mirror. She looked rumpled and abused. His woman. From now on she was his woman. Next year and the year after; five years from now; ten years from now; his woman. He would never die. He would be a man of ninety and she would be sixty, face ravaged by the years. She would never go driving in the Bois de Boulogne with Jim Buckmaster by her side; no marquis or count would ever kiss her hand. She would live on in New Empire hearing the steamboats wailing in the night. Jim Buckmaster would be a man in convict stripes and she would never fall in love again. Nothing was left.

She stood there, dry-eyed now, wishing she had never been born. Life was not worth the agony. At last she turned and went dragging

714

toward the door, but the vitrine happened to catch her gaze, and she stopped, staring at an object that had belonged to her great-grandmother. A weapon. She reached for it and stood balancing it on her palm, wishing she had the courage to unsheath it and sink it into her heart. Like those Roman generals in Shakespeare. Forever and forever farewell . . . Then she thought of something else.

And it was a course of action with a certain appeal. Her heart beat faster as she thought about it, and her muscles became supple and alive. Not that she would actually do what she was thinking of doing. It was too dangerous. Unless—

And there flashed through her mind a plan. A beautiful plan. Ooo, she thought, I wouldn't dare!

Yet why not? She could wind Sheriff Irwin around her finger. He was vain and she was subtle and intelligent. She could be a good actress if occasion required. Why not?

She slipped the knife inside her dress and left the sitting room, excitement racing through her veins. The more she thought of the plan the better she liked it. Some day he would lose all control and firebrand her face; some day he would misjudge his strength and kill her. He had killed before, many times, in battle and in a duel and on the plains. He had killed Andy Gentry. He was a killer and some day he would choke her to death. Was not self-protection justified? Was not self-preservation the first law of life?

She passed the nursery, there in the upstairs hall, and she heard Lilith singing a lullaby to Heinrich. Lilith would never know; Lilith was stupid. Nobody would ever know.

It would be simple enough, actually. She had proved that in dealing with the man who wore yellow shoes. Find a quiet spot and a means of knocking him out before using the knife: she would never dare to use the knife when he was conscious because he was so strong and fast. She was lighthearted now and she wondered why she had never used the knife on him years ago. It was very easy, really. It was not hard to kill a man. Not if you planned everything carefully.

In the lower hall she thought of something and went to the front drawing room, where, serving as doorstop, a little bronze dog of Chinese construction sat on its hind legs begging. She picked it up; it fitted perfectly into her palm. If Caleb could use brass knucks she could use a bronze dog. Perhaps, walking ahead of him, she could whirl and smash it into his jaw. Or better yet, contrive to get behind him and smash it into his skull. He had been drinking; it would be easy to trick him.

I can do it, she thought, I know I can. He will never know what hit him. It will be a kind death.

She felt very happy when she emerged to the back veranda. Through the darkness she thought she smelled cigar smoke from the garden, and among the fireflies she saw the end of his cigar brightening and dulling.

715

He had been frightfully upset, in the upstairs sitting room, and he must be strolling the garden paths to calm himself. She hurried to join him. He was standing by the fountain.

*

A short time later Esperanza moved through the starlight toward the stable, her step soft and elastic, like an Apache girl's. She was smiling.

Inside the carriage room of the stable she tiptoed to the surrey, where, on the floor of the back seat, she left a little bronze dog. Then, between the front seat and the upholstered back rest, she tucked a wallet and a sheathed knife which had been washed in the fountain. After that she mounted the stairs to Dexter Yarlow's quarters on the second floor of the stable.

"Who that?"

"Mrs. McSwasey," she called out gaily.

She heard Dexter shuffling toward the door, and after he opened it she told him to hitch up the surrey and drive to Judge Gentry's house.

"And don't stop in the judge's driveway, Dexter. I want you to turn in at the alley and stop behind the stable."

"Alley? Now let me git this right, Miss Esperanza. I recollect there is an alley along the north side of the judge's premises. I is to turn in there?"

"That's right, Dexter. And when you come to the north-and-south alley, turn south. Stop beside the stable and wait for me."

"You ain't coming along with me now?"

"No, of course not. I'll be there later. Do as you're told."

"Yes, ma'am."

"And hurry."

"Yes, ma'am, I'll hurry. I always hurry."

Maddeningly deliberate, he descended the stairs and hitched up a team to the surrey. At last he was ready to leave.

"Now what is it you are to do, Dexter?"

"I is to go to the judge's house and wait in the alley beside the stable."

"That's right, Dexter. When I meet you I'll give you ten dollars. I'll be along in an hour." And Esperanza added, smiling, "And don't tell Mr. McSwasey."

"No, ma'am. Won't say a word. Miss Esperanza, you reckon there is haunts in that alley? Seem I hear tell them haunts is mighty fond of alleys."

"Why, Dexter, of course not. Not in the judge's alley. Don't you know that haunts are scared of judges?"

"Yes, ma'am, seem I do hear that. Scared of judges. Just like the rest of us. Sure hope it's true."

After he had driven away, Esperanza stood in thought. Had she overlooked anything? Then it came to her: the letters! Jim Buckmaster's

716

letters. She would need them, not tonight but in a few days. After the funeral. And the letters were still in Caleb's pocket.

She would have preferred not returning to her husband, for that was all finished business, but there was nothing else for it. So, with no fear whatsoever—only with distaste—she stole back toward the garden, avoiding the light from the kitchen windows. Where the fountain splashed the shadows were deeper, but her eyes were used to the darkness now. Dead men couldn't hurt you. Sticks and stones could break your bones, but dead men couldn't.

He lay as she had left him, on his back, the way the man with the yellow shoes had lain. He had not moved; he would never move. It was wonderful to know that. He would never firebrand her now. She was free. She was a widow. A young and pretty widow.

Taking care not to brush against anything sticky, she found the letters and slipped them inside her bodice.

She had a start, when she stood up, for somebody was leaving the house. Lilith! And standing there in the darkness, Esperanza remembered that sometimes in the cool of the evening, after Heinrich was asleep, Lilith enjoyed sitting by the fountain, resting her feet. Now she was leaving the back veranda, and for a moment Esperanza couldn't move. Then just in time, or perhaps not quite in time, she whirled and fled deeper into the garden, stopping at a safe distance and crouching behind a hedge.

"Who's there?" Lilith was calling.

Esperanza wanted to giggle.

"Somebody out there. Who that out there?"

From her concealment, Esperanza risked a glance. Against the light from the house Lilith was a wary silhouette. Then, grumbling to herself, she advanced toward the fountain. Esperanza lifted her skirts and ran stooping through the garden, circling toward the road to town. When she reached the lawn south of the house she heard a long screech. The body of Caleb McSwasey, Esq., had been discovered.

And that was all right. Esperanza's beautiful plans were under way. She raced along the road toward town with that fleetness of foot inherited from Consuelo Delgado; faster and ever faster, as she used to run when she pursued that cowardly Wisdom; and her blood was champagne and her brain was a sparkling jewel. And she was free, free! And happy, oh, so very happy.

Across the bridge to the mainland. South along Front Street. East along Chicory Street, never pausing for breath. To her left she could see the vast shadowy piles of lumber belonging to Caleb McSwasey, Esq. Only now they belonged to her. Till now she had not considered the full significance of her husband's death; she had not thought of herself as rich. A young, rich, pretty widow. Money and power. Countless acres in the pinery; lumber camps, oxen; chains; cant hooks; rafts; real

717

estate; newspapers; lumber yards in St. Louis and a dozen other river cities; steamboats; notes; mortgages; bank accounts throbbing with power—all were hers.

"Park Irwin," she thought, "had better do what I want. He'd better take orders."

His house was lighted when she reached it; breathlessly, she flung herself up the steps and pounded the door.

"Sheriff," she called. "Sheriff Irwin! Caleb has been killed! Dexter Yarlow has murdered my husband!"

And she made herself sob, although never in her life had she felt less grief-stricken.

*

Leading news story in the *New Empire Weekly Chronicle,* issue of Thursday, June 12, 1851:

Dastardly Deed!

Terrible Murder!

Foul Play By a Servant!

Death of Mr. McSwasey!

Crazed Negro Runs Amuck!

Brave Deeds of Sheriff!

Last Monday was one of the most beautiful days we have enjoyed, in this land of beautiful days, and our thriving city went about its business, little dreaming that before another sunrise a horrible deed would be perpetrated in our midst, casting this happy community into sorrow of the deepest hues.

Many years ago a Negro named Dexter Yarlow came to New Empire, securing employment as factotum at the Commerical House, one of the most luxurious hostelries of this or any other city. This Yarlow, it was understood, had been manumitted by his master in the City of Baltimore, and to all appearances he was a harmless enough member of his race.

When Caleb McSwasey, Esq., one of our leading and best-loved citizens, constructed his lavish mansion on McSwasey's Island, he employed the black man as his butler and coachman. Yarlow has been a familiar sight on the streets of New Empire, dressed in fine livery, driving the many handsome teams and beautiful carriages of the McSwasey family. Always outwardly friendly, albeit of a somnolent nature, Yarlow gave no indication that beneath his black breast was beating the heart of a fiend.

But one may smile and smile and be a villain, as the great Bard of Avon (Shakespeare) has so aptly said, and on Monday evening the scoundrel showed his true colors. As reconstructed bv Sheriff Park Irwin, (whose handling of this case redounds to the credit of the voters of Fox County in electing him), Mr. McSwasey was sitting peacefully in his garden, musing upon the great future of this area, when Yarlow, miscreant that he was, sneaked up behind him and repeatedly struck him blows upon the skull. After rendering his victim unconscious by this cruel treatment, the rascal plunged a knife into Mr. McSwasey's heart, and the Soul of a great man went to join his Maker, whereupon the caitiff stole his wallet.

That Yarlow had been plotting the ghastly crime there can be no doubt, for the weapons he employed had been purloined from the McSwasey mansion, where, as a trusted servant he had been free to come and go at will. One was a small bronze dog, a costly and tasteful object of art from China, used as a doorstop in the front drawing room; the assassin used this to knock Mr. McSwasey unconscious. The other weapon was an antique knife, used by the McSwaseys for its decorative effect in the vitrine of the second-floor sitting room; with this the murderer concluded his bloody work.

As chance would have it, Mr. McSwasey's beautiful and talented wife, (now, alas!, his widow), left the mansion to join her husband in the garden just as the blackguard was leaving the vicinity of the fountain where the horrible murder took place. Thinking that Yarlow was acting strangely, Mrs. McSwasey addressed a question to him, namely, what was he about, whereupon the ruffian mumbled something to the effect that now he would even things up with Judge Gentry. Then he hurried to the family surrey, to which a spirited team was already hitched, and drove away with the speed of lightning.

Puzzled and not a little perturbed, and never dreaming that the lifeless body of her distinguished husband lay only a few feet away, Mrs. McSwasey strolled along the path toward the river, thinking that perhaps her spouse had gone there ahead of her, as was his wont on fine evenings. Intending to report to him the odd behavior of Yarlow, she was troubled not to find him, and she returned to the garden. And there—"Oh, that my head were waters, and mine eyes a fountain of tears"—Mrs. McSwasey discovered the corpse of her husband. Her feelings may better be imagined than described; let us draw a curtain across that lamentable scene.

Yet grief-stricken as she was, she recalled the words of Yarlow, namely, that his next victim was to be Judge Sophronicus Gentry, distinguished and long-time resident of New Empire, and dean of the Wisconsin bar. Acting with a dispatch and heroism amazing in one of the gentle sex, unless one remembers that she comes of valiant stock, her grandfather being a general in the Prussian army, and her father a famed Indian fighter in the South-west, Mrs. McSwasey, with characteristic generosity and public-spiritedness, suppressed her own grief and bethought herself of the impending danger to Judge Gentry, with a Negro madman on the loose.

Heartbroken though she was, she realized there was not a moment to lose, and she ran with express speed to the home of Sheriff Park Irwin, informing him of the evening's sorrowful events, and apprising him of the peril to Judge Gentry.

Acting with his usual dispatch and pluck, Sheriff Irwin armed himself, summoned his two deputies, Merle Gammerdinger and Clarence Durgin, and repaired to the Gentry residence, where he was much relieved to find Judge Gentry peacefully reading Cicero in his library. Next in order was an exploration of the premises, and when this took place Sheriff Irwin and his two gallant deputies discovered a surrey in the alley behind the Gentry stable, where the Nergo was lurking, doubtless plotting how, when the family was asleep, he would break into the house and plunge a knife into the heart of Judge Gentry.

Upon sighting the deputies coming along the alley, the murderer broke and ran, shouting something about "haunts." It is supposed that like Macbeth, who was tormented by conscience, the scoundrel was afflicted with some dim awareness of the enormity of his crime, and when he beheld those law officers approaching he mistook them for avenging spirits from another world. Thus conscience doth make cowards of us all. (Shakespeare.)

At any rate, when the miscreant ran, Sheriff Irwin ordered him to halt, and when he did not, the three officers fired at his fleeing figure. Two of the bullets found their mark and the murderer perished, thus saving Fox County the cost of a trial and a rope.

Investigation of the surrey revealed not only Mr. McSwasey's wallet, craftily hidden, but the two murder weapons, the bronze dog and the lethal knife. The latter had been washed clean of Mr. McSwasey's blood, probably in the fountain near which he was slain, and was ready for its horrible designs against the life of Judge Gentry.

Sheriff Irwin deserves—and is receiving—the profound thanks of our citizenry for his defiance of danger. That he is our best sheriff in years is incontrovertible; that he will continue to offer his services to his county— and perhaps his state—all are hoping. Coming as this does on the heels of his great feat in capturing a band of desperate log thieves, (for an account of which, see another column), his valor is doubly bright. We here and now predict that before his career is concluded, the name of Park Irwin will be not unknown to the Halls of Fame.

Meanwhile, New Empire and the State of Wisconsin mourn Caleb McSwasey. This is not the place to eulogize his countless virtues. Our poor pen would be a weak reed for such a task. For his life story, for a recital of his accomplishments, we respectfully direct the reader's attention to another column, where, along with an account of the obsequies, we are printing the funeral oration of the Rev. Ossian Wendell Benedict, pastor of the First Presbyterian Church.

Caleb McSwasey was a big man. His like will not come our way again.

Mortuary arrangements were handled with unusual efficiency by Hurlbut's Furniture & Undertaking.

*

News story from the same issue:

Caught in the Act

Thieves Apprehended

Log Pirates Bagged

Sheriff's Skill and Valor

Quick Conviction Expected

Growing boys of this community who in years past have raided watermelon patches and raised much mischief on Halloween would do well to ponder long and hard the fate of fifteen log thieves apprehended last Sunday night by Sheriff Park Irwin.

Boys, honesty is the best policy.

One thief lies cold and dead. Fourteen others are in the Fox County jail, behind bars. Long years in the penitentiary await them.

Be it said that Sheriff Irwin, a Godly man, deplores as much as anybody the necessity for acting on the Sabbath, but it must be remembered that Our Saviour Himself did not hesitate to cure the sick on the Lord's Day despite the sneers of Pharisees and others. Sheriff Irwin acted wisely, we think, and let only those who have never swatted a mosquito or killed a poisonous reptile on the Sabbath cast the first stones.

For the past few years, the stealing of rafts or parts of rafts has been a problem to logging operators on the Mississippi River. Officials have been lax in their attempts to stop this robbery, partly because the question of jurisdiction was so clouded. If a string of logs was purloined from its moorage at an island in mid-river, it was a moot point whether the crime took place in Wisconsin, in Iowa, or in territory belonging to the United States. Needless to say, the thieves took full advantage of this twilight zone.

But when Sheriff Irwin took office last January, he determined to bring the miscreants to book. In this determination, he enjoyed the full cooperation of the late lamented Caleb McSwasey, Esq.

Between them, Mr. McSwasey and Sheriff Irwin decided to lay a trap,

721

baiting it with some of the most tempting Number 1 logs from the McSwasey holdings in the Chippewa drainage. With this in mind, Mr. McSwasey, about a week ago, ordered his rafting crews to leave unguarded a fine raft in the slough to the south of Stovepipe Rock in the northern part of Fox County. It will be at once apparent that if Sheriff Irwin could surprise the thieves in the act of stealing that raft, no question of jurisdiction would be involved.

Last Saturday, having got wind that something was up, Mr. McSwasey suggested to Sheriff Irwin that he quietly assemble a *posse comitatus,* popularly called a posse by the unlettered, and on Sunday evening go to Stovepipe Rock and lay in ambush.

So great and unselfish was the late Mr. McSwasey's zeal and ardor for law enforcement that he offered Sheriff Irwin the use of more than a score of his employees, log raftsmen every one, to compose the *posse comitatus.* Moreover, in his generosity, Mr. McSwasey agreed to pay these men for their extra labor.

The *posse comitatus* was thus assembled, with great secrecy prevailing, the men being kept in ignorance of the purpose for which they were brought together, and of their destination.

Sunday afternoon, Sheriff Irwin, with his efficient deputies, Merle Gammerdinger and Clarence Durgin, departed by land for Stovepipe Rock, traveling in wagons, leading the *posse comitatus* of sixteen men, five less than the original number, owing to the fact that the demon rum in some mysterious manner found its way among the raftsmen, who looked upon the occasion as a celebration, and hence only sixteen were fit and ready for service, the other five remaining in the Fox County jail in a condition better imagined than described.

Arriving at Stovepipe Rock, Sheriff Irwin displayed a generalship of the highest order, placing his men at points of vantage in the undergrowth fringing the slough. A long wait ensued. But all good things are worth waiting for, and at about nine o'clock the thieves arrived. Waiting till they had manned the raft and were floating it toward the channel of the river, Sheriff Irwin gave a signal, namely, a whistle, whereupon the *posse comitatus* swarmed from hiding and overpowered the thieves. In the melee one tried to escape and was killed. He is identified as Max Fansler of Lanceport, Iowa, said to have been the leader of the gang. The body has been returned to Lanceport for interment.

The other fourteen thieves were brought to New Empire and lodged in jail, where they are now cooling their heels and awaiting arraignment. Most of them, owing to vigorous interrogation by authorities, have indicated an intention to plead guilty.

However, one of these red-handed thieves keeps insisting on his innocence. He is identified as James Lorne Buckmaster, a character of the lower order, not unknown along the Upper Mississippi, having been a frequenter of resorts of ill-repute. With unmitigated gall, this Buckmaster, it is understood, keeps maintaining that he was employed by the late Caleb McSwasey, Esq., for the purpose of locating the thieves and leading them into the trap. Thus is a cringing wrongdoer ever ready to defame the good name of the dead.

The story of this poltroon is easily demolished. He is the same Jim Buckmaster who for some years occupied a position of trust in the employ of Mr. McSwasey, having been foreman of logging camps and a raft pilot for the McSwasey interests. Last October, after thorough investigation, Mr. McSwasey collected evidence indicating that Buckmaster had betrayed his trust and pilfered thousands of dollars from his employer, by such underhanded means as payroll padding and expense account padding. Only Mr. McSwasey's kindness of heart prevented him from prosecuting Buckmaster on these charges.

It is common knowledge that one evening last October Mr. McSwasey chanced to encounter Buckmaster in the public house of Patrick Rafferty, Esq., of this city, where the motto has always been, "We Do Not Desire the Patronage of the Few Who *Abuse* the Right to Drink." At this meeting, Mr. McSwasey charged Buckmaster with padding payrolls, whereupon the latter, enraged at having been found out and made reckless by strong waters, struck out wildly with his fists, till subdued with Mr. Rafferty's assistance. Mr. McSwasey then and there discharged Buckmaster and told him he would inform all timber operators of his perfidy.

It is thought that Buckmaster joined the log thieves in a spirit of revenge, if, indeed, he had not been a member of the gang for several years.

As to Buckmaster's contention that he was an inside operator for his former employer, it need only be said that men of Mr. McSwasey's high caliber do not stoop to conquer. According to Sheriff Irwin, the mystery of how Mr. McSwasey knew that the thieves would strike Sunday night has now been solved. Mr. Rafferty, a businessman whose integrity has never been questioned, and whose reputation has never been impugned, is ready to take the witness stand and swear that one evening last week two strangers entered his place of business. He chanced to overhear their conversation, which indicated that the thieves intended to steal the raft in question on Sunday.

It is thought that these men were proprietors of some downriver sawmill on the Iowa side, in league with the thieves.

Mr. Rafferty, seeing his plain duty, at once communicated this information to Mr. McSwasey, who very properly acted upon it.

Rumor has it that no lawyer in this community would even consider defending Buckmaster, unless appointed by the court, for his contention is so ridiculous that wise men must weep.

We have always maintained that the theft of rafts had its origin not in Wisconsin, whose inhabitants are widely-known for honesty and industry, but from our Sister State across the river, namely Iowa, where the traveler does well to keep his hand on his pocketbook.

And thus again our alert and courageous sheriff, Park Irwin, has proved the wisdom of the axiom: honesty is the best policy.

*

From the issue of Thursday June 19, 1851:

The will of Caleb McSwasey, Esq., deceased, was filed for probate in district court this week by Judge Sophronicus Gentry, attorney. Mrs. Esperanza McSwasey was named by the testator as executrix.

Our readers will be glad to know that the instrument, which was drawn nearly ten years ago, bequeaths the entire estate to Mr. McSwasey's gallant widow, thus assuring this community that the McSwasey Lumber Company, which has brought so much prosperity and renown to New Empire, will remain intact in the McSwasey family.

Mrs. McSwasey has announced that the enlightened business policies of her husband will be continued.

*

From the same issue:

Correction!

In our issue of last week, a great injustice was done James Lorne Buckmaster, Esq., when it was erroneously stated that he was known as a frequenter of resorts of ill-repute. This is entirely incorrect, and the editor of this paper wishes to retract and hereby does retract that statement.

The error came about owing to a confusion of names. The person alluded to as a character of the lower order is one James Lane Ruckmaster, not James Lorne Buckmaster, whose character is of the purest. We apologize for this error and promise it will never happen again.

*

Leading news story from the same issue:

Public Service Rendered

Hero In Our Midst

Honors Due Mr. Buckmaster

Friend of Law and Order

New Empire Is Grateful

If unselfish devotion to the public good, combined with great physical courage and unflagging efforts to bring wrongdoers to justice—if, we say,

724

these qualities are the measure of a hero, then the citizens of this community have every reason to honor James Lorne Buckmaster, the Hero of Stovepipe Rock.

As we mentioned last week, the stealing of log rafts has for several years been a problem on the Upper Mississippi River. The late Caleb McSwasey, Esq., devoted much thought to apprehending the thieves, and it now comes out that with characteristic ingenuity and shrewdness Mr. McSwasey set about to trap the marauders.

Casting about for a man of unexampled integrity to aid him in this great task, Mr. McSwasey bethought himself of James L. Buckmaster, a trusted employee. Mr. Buckmaster, who is affectionately known by all as just plain "Jim," entered Mr. McSwasey's employ when a mere lad of fifteen, rising rapidly through the ranks till he capably filled the position of foreman of a lumber camp.

Thereafter, in the spring of 1849, Mr. McSwasey appointed Mr. Buckmaster to the post of raft pilot, than which there is no occupation demanding more courage, cool-headedness, and honesty. Jim—if we may be permitted to call him that—served so satisfactorily during the rafting season of 1849 that Mr. McSwasey reappointed him to serve in 1850, and meanwhile, during the winter, Jim was sent into the woods as a landlooker for the company, an occupation demanding the highest knowledge and probity.

Last October Mr. McSwasey gave Mr. Buckmaster his most delicate and difficult assignment, namely, the bringing to justice of a gang of rafting pirates. It was Mr. McSwasey's thought that if the miscreants could be convinced that Mr. Buckmaster had been discharged and blacklisted, and thus felt himself wronged, they would gladly admit him to their councils and avail themselves of his great skill in handling rafts. But how could the rafting thieves be convinced that Mr. Buckmaster, who was widely-known as the soul of honor, had fallen so low as to be willing to engage in unlawful activities?

It was then that Mr. McSwasey's genius as a businessman and public benefactor showed itself. In what must have been a flash of inspiration, such as comes to great poets like Shakespeare and Longfellow, and no less to captains of industry, (for is not business the true poetry of America?), Mr. McSwasey conceived the idea of publicly enacting a quarrel with Mr. Buckmaster, and apparently discharging and blacklisting him. A meeting was arranged to take place, apparently by chance, in the public house of Patrick Rafferty, Esq., and when this came about Mr. McSwasey and Mr. Buckmaster pretended to quarrel, although each felt only admiration and affection for the other. To lend realism to this little drama, Mr. Buckmaster permitted himself to be knocked out by Mr. McSwasey, and the word rapidly spread, Dame Gossip being what she is, that the two gentlemen had fought and that they hated each other bitterly.

It cannot be too strongly emphasized, however, that this quarrel was a sham and a hoax, designed to gull the rafting pirates, which it did.

Seemingly in disgrace, Mr. Buckmaster set off upriver, where, after many adventures, he located the gang of thieves at their lair in Lanceport, Iowa. Winning their confidence, he was able to lead them into the trap at Stovepipe Rock.

Mr. Buckmaster was arrested with the others and lodged in the Fox County jail, for Mr. McSwasey, believing that secrecy is everything in such an enterprise, had not even told Sheriff Park Irwin of his game, although he had hinted at it to his good wife, Mrs. Esperanza McSwasey, now, alas!, his widow.

According to Mr. Buckmaster, it was Mr. McSwasey's idea that the former should remain in jail a day or two, with the captured thieves, in order to use his influence to persuade them that the jig was up and that they had better plead guilty, thus saving Fox County the expense of a trial. It is a measure of Jim Buckmaster's devotion to duty that he was willing to associate himself with such miscreants after their capture, in order to serve the common good.

But alas! Before Mr. McSwasey could announce that Mr. Buckmaster had been secretly at work on the side of law and order, he was most foully murdered by his trusted servant, Dexter Yarlow. Upon hearing this, Mr. Buckmaster realized his position was an unenviable one, whereupon he told the whole story to Sheriff Irwin.

The sheriff, it seems to us, is scarcely to be blamed for not giving heed to Mr. Buckmaster's story, although now that we have the advantage of hindsight, it seems he might have listened more carefully. But jailed wrongdoers, of course, always maintain their innocence, so even when Mr. Buckmaster pointed out that Mr. McSwasey had promised to deposit in the company safe a written record of the thief-catching plan, the sheriff only laughed, in other words, he didn't take Mr. Buckmaster seriously. Nor did he believe Mr. Buckmaster's story that he had written a number of letters to Mr. McSwasey, reporting progress, directing that a raft should be left at Stovepipe Rock, and that the gang would go there to steal it at nine o'clock on the evening of Sunday June 8, and that a *posse comitatus,* (which is Latin for what is popularly called a posse), should be waiting in ambush.

Mrs. Esperanza McSwasey, however, upon hearing of Mr. Buckmaster's protests, remembered hints which her lamented husband had dropped, suggesting that Mr. Buckmaster was in reality engaged by him on a secret and important mission. Since her husband's unfortunate death, Mrs. McSwasey has taken charge at the company office in a manner quite unexampled for its efficiency and understanding of business principles, unless one remembers that her father is the leading merchant in Santa Fe, Territory of New Mexico, and that as a maiden Mrs. McSwasey was his assistant in operating his mercantile emporium.

Mrs. McSwasey, fearing that injustice was being done Mr. Buckmaster, looked in the company safe, and although she failed to locate Mr. McSwasey's statement about Mr. Buckmaster's innocence, she did find a packet of letters written by the latter. Upon reading them, she understood why her husband had neglected to write a statement. The letters in themselves were quite enough to prove the truth of Mr. Buckmaster's protests of innocence.

However, wishing to make assurance doubly sure, (Shakespeare), Mrs. McSwasey held her own counsel, merely requesting of Sheriff Irwin that Mr. Buckmaster should be brought to the company office, where she might question him. Mr. Buckmaster arrived under heavy guard. He and Mrs. McSwasey conferred alone for an hour, with Sheriff Irwin stationed outside the door and with deputies patrolling the lumber yard, in case Mr. Buckmaster should try to escape from the second-floor windows.

By his straightforward manner, and his honest answers to all her questions, Mr. Buckmaster convinced Mrs. McSwasey of his innocence, whereupon she sent for Judge Sophronicus Gentry, engaging him as Mr. Buckmaster's lawyer. Judge Gentry read the letters, questioned Mr. Buckmaster further, and he in turn was convinced of his absolute innocence. As a friend of the innocent Judge Gentry has no peer. Going into action at once, he conferred with Miles Schwebel, our popular district attorney, who immediately dropped all proceedings against Mr. Buckmaster.

"James Buckmaster is not a criminal," Mr. Schwebel announced. "He is a hero who deserves the gratitude of the better and law-abiding element of this community."

Upon Mr. Buckmaster's release from custody, a somewhat laughable incident took place. It seems that when he was being interrogated at the sheriff's office, his refusal to admit his guilt annoyed Deputy Merle Gammerdinger, who resorted to physical coercion of a mild sort. Therefore, once he was a free man, Mr. Buckmaster sought out Mr. Gammerdinger in the yard of the lumber company, and in the resulting fisticuffs Mr. Buckmaster decidedly was not worsted.

"Now you can arrest me again," Mr. Buckmaster told Sheriff Irwin.

But the sheriff, wisely, we think, preferred to treat the matter as a joke, and at Mrs. McSwasey's suggestion he discharged Mr. Gammerdinger.

"Gammerdinger has always been trigger-happy," Sheriff Irwin picturesquely phrased it.

So all is well that ends well, (Shakespeare), and this all goes to prove again the advantages of living in a free country like ours where an innocent man is considered innocent until proved guilty.

As Mr. Buckmaster's letters to Mr. McSwasey plainly showed, the latter had promised to make him vice-president of the company, and to give him a fourth interest in the concern, upon his successful trapping of the rafting thieves. Owing to legal complications involved with the estate, Mrs. McSwasey was unable to redeem this promise, but she has hired Mr. Buckmaster as general manager of the company, a post he is eminently suited to fill.

*

727

Editorial from the issue of Thursday June 26, 1851:

Falsus in Uno, Falsus in Omnibus

A copy of the *Dubuque Argus* has crossed our desk, protesting a statement in our issue of June 12 to the effect that thievery is a commonplace affair in the State of Iowa.

"How impudent of the *New Empire Chronicle*," sayeth the *Argus*, "to take a holier-than-thou attitude because a handful of rafting thieves from Lanceport, Iowa, were apprehended by a Wisconsin sheriff. If the sheriff wishes to discover robbery on a scale which would bring a blush to the Thief of Bagdad, let him look to the Wisconsin pineries. We hold no brief for the so-called rafting pirates, but it is pertinent to point out that the very logs which these picayunish pirates were purloining had doubtless been cut on the public domain without so much as a by-your-leave. It is common knowledge that great fortunes are being plundered from forests owned by the United States Government."

What humbuggery! What irresponsible hyperbole! What dangerous nonsense!

Our readers have probably never heard of the *Dubuque Argus*—few persons have, even in Dubuque, its circulation is so infinitesimal—and we would ignore this falsehood except that it is typical of the kind of Un-Americanism being maliciously spread by soreheads, knockers, ne'er-do-wells and treasonists.

The record of the *Argus* does not commend itself to the wise and thoughtful. It opposed the Mexican War. It has a taint of Abolitionism. It has calumniated the memory of the great Alexander Hamilton. It has maintained that freight rates on steamboat lines are too high. Although its masthead carries the slogan, "An Independent Newspaper," more than one person has suggested that it is probably the organ of His Satanic Majesty.

It comes as no surprise, therefore, that now it has chosen to attack the solid, honest, enterprising businessmen of this state, men who are building this Great Northwest by converting the raw material of standing timber into lumber to be used in building homes, schools and churches. If the *Argus* had its way, perhaps we would dispense with schools and churches, and dwell like red savages in crude wigwams.

Here is a thought for the *Argus*. If timber actually were being stolen, which it is not, would not the United States Government be the first to protest? Would not the senators and representatives from the states most affected, namely, such states as our own beloved Wisconsin, be demanding that public property be guarded? These distinguished men are serene, for they know that our timber, which is so abundant that it will last a thousand years, is not being illegally cut. The United States Government is not fretful. Only the mischief-makers, the disunionists, the bad-weather birds of radical ideas are screeching and moaning.

As Caleb McSwasey, the great empire builder, used to say, if the purpose of government isn't to foster and promote business, thus bringing prosperity to all, then, pray, what is its purpose? What is good for the McSwasey Lumber Company is good for New Empire, for Wisconsin, and, indeed, for all America.

*

News item from same issue:

Mrs. Esperanza McSwasey, widow of the late Caleb McSwasey, Esq., and Mr. James L. Buckmaster, newly-appointed manager of the McSwasey Lumber Company, were Dubuque visitors last Saturday, on business connected with the company.

*

From the issue of Thursday July 3:

Tragic Demise

———

Young Female Drowns

———

Body Recovered

———

When the noble Mississippi, Great Father of Waters, claims for her victim a female in the first flush of glorious youth, the hardest-hearted must drop a tear and muse upon the briefness of our stay in this Vale of Sorrow, namely, the Earth.

Such a tragic passing took place three miles upriver from New Empire last Friday afternoon, June 27, when a beautiful damsel of only nineteen summers, in a fit of despondency, threw herself from the main deck of the *General Taylor* and cruelly drowned.

Although the packet halted, when word reached the captain of the event, and boats were sent out, the body was not recovered till yesterday morning, July 2, when three urchins of this city, bound on a piscatorial expedition, in other words, going fishing, discovered the unfortunate female about a mile below this city, her dark tresses floating upon the water, her lifeless form entangled in the branches of a weeping willow.

Thus, alas, did Ophelia die, noble princess that she was, in the immortal Shakespeare's great tragedy, (*Hamlet*), and thus hath the river which ripples and purls past our fair city taken many a life, and will no doubt take many another, unless more of our citizens teach their sons and daughters to swim, and perhaps even then, for carelessness is a great fault among the young.

Tragedy had darkened the days of this pulchritudinous damsel, for it

729

has been learned that she was the half-sister of the rafting thief, Max Fansler, killed several weeks ago by some trigger-happy law officer in the great bagging of pirates at Stovepipe Rock. She was the daughter of Dr. Wace Fansler of Lanceport, Iowa, a man, it is understood, who is well-thought-of in his community, and who had no connection with the nefarious activities of his son.

Miss Bonnie Fansler, (for such was her name), arrived in our thriving city on Friday morning last, the day of the tragedy, having taken the downriver boat, the *Hawkeye State,* from Lanceport. She went at once to the McSwasey Lumber Company, where she requested an interview with the manager, Mr. James L. Buckmaster. This was granted.

Mr. Buckmaster tells us that he had known the young lady slightly last winter, when he lodged at the Fansler House in Lanceport and was treated for headaches by Dr. Fansler. He also knew her during his heroic activities, when, in the employ of Caleb McSwasey, he was tirelessly at work uncovering the trail of the desperate gang of rafting thieves, who were trapped and caught because of his herculean efforts.

Miss Fansler was very fond of her half-brother, Mr. Buckmaster tells us, and she came to New Empire to hear at first hand how the misguided young man met his "supreme day and the inevitable hour." (Vergil.) Miss Fansler and Mr. Buckmaster visited for something more than an hour, the tenderhearted young lady weeping copiously upon hearing the details of Max Fansler's death. When she left the McSwasey Lumber Company she was greatly distraught, although the possibility that she was contemplating taking her own life never occurred to Mr. Buckmaster, or he would have detained her and put her under the care of one of our three highly-competent physicians and surgeons.

But alas, who is to know the heart of another? Miss Fansler boarded the upriver boat, the *General Taylor,* shortly after 2:00 P.M., and, as we have already said, flung herself into the vasty deeps of the river.

Yesterday, upon finding her remains, the three urchins, Sammy Sharf, Robert Skellenger, Jr., and Teddy Friend, hastened back to New Empire and repaired to the Pinery Boy Saloon, where they told the news to Mr. Robert Skellenger, Sr., who at once informed Sheriff Park Irwin.

Guided by the urchins, and accompanied by a crowd of persons wishing to be helpful, Sheriff Irwin and his two deputies, Clarence Durgin and Vernon Sisson, proceeded to the scene of the discovery, bringing the body to New Empire, where it was taken to Hurlbut's Furniture & Undertaking.

Upon the request of Dr. Lester Fitch, county coroner, Mr. Buckmaster went to the Hurlbut establishment and viewed the body, for purposes of identification. Death was pronounced as due to drowning, and no inquest was held.

Mr. Buckmaster was much shaken by this experience, and he generously paid Hurlbut's Furniture & Undertaking for all expenses incurred, such as for a beautiful white casket; moreover, he personally superintended the sending of the remains back to Lanceport.

"I did it for her brother's sake," Mr. Buckmaster stated. "Max Fansler was not a bad fellow, just high-spirited and restless. As for Miss Fansler, she was one of the gentlest young women who ever lived."

In a family newspaper like ours, some things are better hinted at than stated, but the adults among our subscribers will understand when we mention that Dr. Fitch, after a post-mortem, let it be known that the young lady was in a delicate state of health, which, when it is remembered that she was neither maid nor matron, might help to explain her suicide. It is thought that perhaps one of the logging thieves, sentenced last week, might be as much responsible, in the eyes of God, for her suicide as she was.

But *de mortuis nil nisi bonum.* She was beautiful, she was young, and if she erred, then who among us has not? Alas—

> Golden lads and girls all must
> As chimney sweepers come to dust. (Shakespeare.)

O death, where is thy sting? O grave, where is thy victory?

*

News item from same issue:

Mr. James L. Buckmaster, manager of the McSwasey Lumber Company is confined to his room at the Darrah Lodging House with a severe headache which attacked him last evening. Dr. Otis Page, who is in attendance, expects Mr. Buckmaster to be up and around within a day or so.

*

News story from the issue of Thursday October 9, 1851:

McSwasey-Buckmaster Nuptials

Secret Marriage Revealed

Couple Wed Last June 21

Leave on Honeymoon

If we were believers in the pretty mythology of the Ancient Greeks, which we are not, this being a Christian country, we would say that there must be great rejoicing in the Halls of Hymen, the Hellenic god of marriage, because of an announcement made on Tuesday of the marriage of Mrs. Esperanza McSwasey to Mr. James L. Buckmaster.

The wedding took place nearly four months ago, on Saturday June 21, at the home of the M. E. pastor in Dubuque, Iowa. So well was the secret kept that nobody in this community suspected the same.

Mrs. McSwasey is the widow of Caleb McSwasey, who perished at the hands of a servant on June 9. She is respected and loved in this community because of her kindness, beauty, generosity, sweetness of disposition, graciousness and other fine qualities too numerous to mention.

Mr. Buckmaster, manager of the McSwasey Lumber Company, is widely-known not only in this community but all up and down the Upper Mississippi River. By his integrity, industry and ability he has attained the high position he now occupies.

The couple left on Tuesday for a belated honeymoon to St. Louis and New Orleans.

Every community, unfortunately, has a scattering of persons of a bigoted, narrow-minded, Un-American and treasonable disposition, in other words, kickers and whiners, and when the news of the marriage of this fine young couple became known it developed that New Empire, like all cities, has a few such scurrilous knockers, who, in their benighted and sacrilegious gossip, were heard to give as their opinion that the marriage took place too soon after the demise of Mrs. McSwasey's former husband.

We would remind such persons that when sorrow comes every minute is as an hour, every day is as a year, and by these calculations Mrs. McSwasey refrained from remarrying some dozen years, a longer period than the respected and beloved Martha Washington waited before marrying the Father of Our Country. As a distressed widow woman, helplessly faced with the problem of managing a vast enterprise like the McSwasey Lumber Company, a stranger to the complicated art and science of business, it is quite understandable that Mrs. McSwasey should turn to a man of strength like Mr. Buckmaster.

The leaders of this community feel otherwise about this splendid marriage than do the mischief-makers already referred to. Let the blatherskites read and ponder the sentiments of our really distinguished citizens, to wit, as follows:

Sheriff Park Irwin: "I am very happy at the news. Both the bride and groom are wonderful folks. This is really wonderful."

Patrick Rafferty, Esq.,: "The bride and groom are the two finest people I have ever known. By her beauty and charm, Mrs. Buckmaster has captivated the hearts of all. Mr. Buckmaster is a man of character, modesty, kindliness and spotless integrity. I count myself fortunate to have been his good friend for many years."

The Rev. Ossian Wendell Benedict, pastor of the First Presbyterian Church: "I see no reason for the unseemly comments by certain persons of Godless sects. I am delighted. God bless them both!"

Dr. Noah Washburn, M. D., popular physician and surgeon: "This is wonderful news. I congratulate the groom and felicitate (in other words, wish happiness to) the bride."

Guy Hurlbut, our wide-awake undertaker: "A marriage made in heaven if ever there was one."

Robert Skellenger, Sr.: "No matter what anybody does, there are always soreheads. Nothing could please me more than this splendid marriage."

Miles Schwebel, district attorney: "How anybody can doubt the desirability of this union is beyond me. I am very happy for both Mr. and Mrs. Buckmaster."

George Ragsdale, president of the Bank of New Empire: "I think it's fine, really very fine. May a long, prosperous life attend them."

Dr. Lester Fitch, coroner of Fox County: "I approve."

Judge Sophronicus Gentry: "It is important for all *aequam servare mentem*. A marriage *bonis avibus,* and besides, in the words of the sapient Ovid, *'si qua voles apte nubere nube pari.'* "

The *Chronicle* is happy to join these distinguished citizens in wishing Mr. and Mrs. Buckmaster all happiness and success.

*

Editorial from the issue of Thursday January 1, 1852:

A Great Company Looks To the Future

Our readers will find in another column an announcement by James L. Buckmaster of the change of name of the McSwasey Lumber Company to the Buckmaster Lumber Company, effective today. Mr. Buckmaster, who has been acting as manager of the company, will henceforth be known as president.

Mr. Buckmaster has also announced the establishment of a newspaper in the rapidly-growing city of Quickwater. This paper, in commemoration of the energetic rebuilding of the city after the fire which destroyed it a number of years ago, will be known as the *Quickwater Phoenix.*

Other stirring plans are afoot. Two new steamboats, being built in a Cincinnati boatyard, will be put into service this spring by the Buckmaster Packet Line, formerly the McSwasey Packet Line. These boats, which were tentatively called the *Yvonne* and the *Triphena Huckins,* will be called instead the *Bonnie* and the *Sol Klauber,* Mr. Buckmaster has announced.

Of more immediate interest to New Empire will be the erection of a new office building, four stories tall, which will be built during the coming year on the south side of Winnebago Street, on land now occupied by Hanopol's Billiard Parlor, the Sloan Carpenter Shop and the Jewett Block. With the coming of spring, these structures will be razed to make room for the imposing new building, which will house the offices of the Buckmaster Lumber Company, the Buckmaster Packet Lines, the Buckmaster Wisconsin Newspapers and the Buckmaster Development Company.

Since assuming charge of the erstwhile McSwasey Lumber Company, Mr. Buckmaster has evinced the energy and the vision which is rapidly

733

converting this state from a howling wilderness to a region of happy homes, contented workmen, sound banks, thriving industry and general prosperity. Empire builder is the phrase for Mr. Buckmaster; he is rapidly becoming the biggest man on the Mississippi River between St. Louis and St. Paul. Thus again do industry, energy, sobriety and plain hard work score.

On this first day of a glorious new year, we wish to take the opportunity to say to Mr. Buckmaster and all his enterprises, "Happy New Year!"

XIV

AND NOW for a time the lights blazed bright in the house on McSwasey's Island, which people were beginning to call Buckmaster's Island. Never had Esperanza been gayer, and never had New Empire enjoyed such brilliant social occasions. Jolly little game suppers; musical soirees; levees when the buffets were loaded with great bowls of punch and cold turkey and ham and saddles of venison; the *Chronicle* was rapturous. Before long, other chatelaines were emulating Mrs. Buckmaster; there were parties honoring St. Valentine and obscure visitors from St. Paul and St. Louis; there were lawn parties on summer evenings with Japanese lanterns festooned among the trees. At Esperanza's suggestion, during that first winter of her marriage, the Terpsichore Club was organized, with fortnightly dances in the Masonic Hall; even Judge and Mrs. Sophronicus Gentry attended, now and then.

If some persons had been startled—and more than a few had—at the briefness of Esperanza's widowhood, they vanquished their scruples fairly rapidly, for it was hard to stay mad at a million dollars, especially when it was personified in such a dashing young matron as Mrs. James L. Buckmaster. Except for Lilith, who didn't count, nobody grieved for Caleb. Out of sight, out of mind; and he was indisputably out of sight. The February snows might blow across his grave; the spring rains might fall there; nobody—nobody but Lilith—gave it a thought.

And nobody grieved for Dexter Yarlow either, except Lilith. But she had never loved Dexter, not as she had loved Mistah Caleb; she did miss him, however. He had been, after all, her lover, and not such a bad lover at that, more animated when he undressed her than ever he had been unhitching the horses. Now she slept alone. To replace Dexter as coachman, Esperanza had hired Hamar Hattlestad, a steady Swede of fifty who was unlikely to go berserk and start killing people.

There were times when Lilith considered leaving New Empire, during that first year or two after Caleb's death. Yet where would she go and what would she do? Besides, she could not bring herself to leave young Master Heinrich; she loved him as much, almost, as she had loved Wisdom; she sang to him and told him stories and comforted him when his mother, not always justly, punished him. So Lilith stayed on, at first resenting her new master, Mistah Buckmaster, then tolerating him, and

735

finally, little by little, growing fond of him. But he would never, she knew, visit her in her bedroom, the way she used to hope Mistah Caleb would; she was twenty years his senior and she looked it; her hair was turning gray.

As to Dexter's villainy in killing Mistah Caleb, Lilith was skeptical. This, however, she kept to herself, remembering the advice of her old mother, Panthea, who had warned her against mixing into the troubles of white folks. But Lilith had her thoughts; she brooded considerably.

*

Esperanza, however, never brooded any more, and she seldom thought of Caleb; nature seemed to have fogged over the memory of her first marriage, especially its abrupt termination. Not even in dreams did Caleb come limping through her brain; and the spells she used to suffer, when she heard distant singing, were banished. She was very busy, what with cotillions and oyster suppers and lyceum entertainments, sponsored by Judge Gentry, and magic-lantern shows; and she was very happy. Her girlhood had been cut short, she had married so young, and now it was as if she were in her teens again, with hardly a thought in her giddy head except of pleasure. She learned to skate, tutored by such experts as Park Irwin, for she was a modern young woman who laughed when old fogies said that girls who took to ice stood on slippery places. On fine winter evenings she and her new husband would go to the levee, where merry-makers thronged in the ruddy light of bonfires. Seating herself on a log, she thrust out her legs, her skirt pulled up farther than necessary, while Jim or Park Irwin or some other nice man knelt and fitted on her skates. She felt like a countess then, certainly a lovely feeling, and in the fire-light she looked bewitching, her smooth cheeks flushed with happiness, her golden hair in striking contrast with her dark velvet bonnet and her pert little jacket lined with rich black fur. A faint sweetness, like a halo of fragrance, hovered about her in the frosty air.

For skating she had a passion, loving it even more than dancing, per-haps because she soon became so expert. She had her share of falls, at first, but some gallant was always nearby to pick her up, and before long she went gliding over the ice with breath-taking grace, her skirt swinging, her willowy figure unconfined by stays. Of all the ladies in New Empire she was easily the most accomplished skater, by the second winter of her new marriage, and men were always choosing her as partner. Had she still been Mrs. Caleb McSwasey, this might have led to harsh words, but Jim was not in the least jealous; indeed, he was so broad-minded that when work called him back to the office in the evening, or when one of his headaches laid him low, he would urge Esperanza to run along without him, and to enjoy herself. With Sheriff Irwin as her partner, she sometimes went skating far from the bonfires, perhaps clear off to Iowa, and now and then they kissed, which was innocent enough probably;

at least, those kisses did not lead to anything more intimate, for the weather was nippy.

Oddly enough, however, Esperanza grew to prefer skating alone, not because she had lost interest in flirtations, but because she was so devoted to skating itself. Gliding over the ice, she felt victorious and free, magically released from the pull of gravity, as if her body had been changed into spirit, as silvery and unfettered as the breath from her lips. Sometimes on winter afternoons, leaving the house and passing the snow-heaped garden, she went to the river and skated for hours, flinging herself into the teeth of an Arctic wind, and blown by it at intoxicating speed. Then, when sunset was a red smudge behind the Iowa bluffs, and everything was cold green sky and lavender shadow, she would return home for a hot toddy and a steaming bath, feeling she had been consorting in far places with blond Northern gods.

She came and went at will; Caleb was dead; tyranny was routed. After the skating season, riding to town in a carriage, she felt no outer compulsion to check in at the lumber yard to inform her husband she was spending the afternoon shopping; Jim never held her to account. Yet usually she went to his office, driven by an inner compulsion, for his very lack of jealousy roused her contrariness, and now that she had a husband who gave her free rein she wished for the bit. She would find him, during that first spring of marriage, deep in reports from his far-flung empire, or poring over blueprints of the new Buckmaster Building, and she would go sit on his desk, her handsome buttocks, with a swish of silk, scattering the papers.

"Lover," she said, "you work too hard."

It was a charge he readily admitted, and he explained—as he had often explained before—that he had to work hard to get the hang of the business.

She would be perched on his knee, before the interview was over, fingering his hair and his ears. When she was near him she had to touch him. But she was never really near him, in spirit; something stood between them. Even in the marriage bed, when she was a woman with wind-flung hair, scaling Himalayas of ecstasy, or floating dimly among the lotus of warm lagoons, he was not actually with her; she could tell he was unpossessed. It bothered her.

"Kiss me, lover," she would say, there in the office, "and I'll leave."

So he kissed her, but something lacked. Or did she imagine it? In any case, she never wanted Caleb back.

Jim walked with her to the door, and before she opened it she stood admiring him. At her suggestion, when they stopped in St. Louis on their honeymoon, he had visited the best tailor, where he had been measured for suits of the finest fabrics, and he wore those clothes well; it was as if their elegance had smoothed down his rough edges and given him *savoir-faire*. And although he seemed as sure of himself as ever, it was a more urbane self-assurance; he never boasted any more; his voice was low and composed; something had quieted him down. And something—business cares, possibly—had thinned him down; there were faint hollows under his cheekbones, and his eyes looked deeper-set. They were, she thought, magnetic eyes, a warm and friendly gray, although she had seen them harden to the gray of nickel; and sometimes, when she caught him unawares, they looked troubled and even bleak, as if life had injured him.

That was how they had looked one evening soon after the honeymoon, when he told her about a letter from a firm of Boston lawyers, informing him he was sole heir to the estate of Sol Klauber.

"Who's Sol Klauber?" she asked.

"A peddler. A Jewish peddler. He was like a second father to me. But he was drownded up in Quickwater in the spring of '41."

There at the dining-room table, Esperanza couldn't understand why he should seem so cut up about the death, more than ten years before, of some old Jew who had never amounted to anything anyway; in the candlelight Jim's hair looked dead-black, and his shoulders sagged.

"He couldn't swim," Jim said, "and he drownded in Snowshoe Creek."

"You mean he drowned," Esperanza said. "The word is drowned, not drownded."

He gave her a quick look, and she had the feeling he had been talking to himself more than to her, and that her grammatical punctilio had brought his thoughts back from the villainous swirl of running waters that grabbed victims and dragged them down where the bullheads darted among the eel grass.

"What did you say?" he asked.

"Drowned, lover. Not drownded. You don't want to talk like a river pig all your life."

She smiled, to soften the rebuke, but she was determined that he should not only dress like a gentleman, and acquire a gentleman's decorum, but that he should talk like a gentleman as well.

"Drowned or drownded," Jim said, "he was dead when they pulled him out."

And slumped there at the table, toying with a fork, he told her about his life with Sol Klauber and how Sol had made out a will and left it with his Boston lawyers before his last trip to Wisconsin. The lawyers, according to their letter, had filed away the will and forgotten it; maybe out of sight was out of mind with them too; but then last summer a new clerk had come across it and asked the firm members who Sol Klauber was. They remembered, finally, and upon realizing they had heard nothing from their client in a decade they deduced he might have died, out in the Wisconsin wilderness. After making inquiries in Boston, and learning that his father-in-law and mother-in-law were dead, the lawyers inserted a notice in some legal publication or other, asking for information regarding Solomon Klauber, testator, and James L. Buckmaster, legatee. Rolfe Torkelsen, a student clerk in Judge Gentry's office, had called that notice to the judge's attention; the judge, after talking with Jim, had written the Boston firm; and so it was that upon paying fees and costs James L. Buckmaster would come into Solomon Klauber's estate.

"Is there much money, lover?" Esperanza asked.

"No money. Just an old I.O.U. from an officer in Washington's army, for ten thousand dollars."

"Can you collect?"

"Congress might come through. I may not even try to collect."

"Then why go to all the trouble?"

"Because Sol wanted me to have that I.O.U. It's something I'll have to remember him by."

Foolish man! She had her work cut out for her, Esperanza realized, in making him over.

"Why, that's silly," she said, laughing.

It was then his eyes hardened to the gray of nickel. And she knew she had gone too far; it alarmed her; in a showdown, she realized, he would be as tough-minded as Caleb. Hastily, she added:

"I don't mean *you're* silly, lover. I mean it's silly of the government to do business that way."

And she hurried around the table and kissed him.

*

Times were prosperous and the Buckmaster Lumber Company flourished. The new steamboats, the *Sol Klauber* and the *Bonnie,* were put into service; up in the North men yelled "Timber!" and the pine trees crashed; logs floated down the floods of spring; rafts floated to St. Louis, where the Buckmaster mills were operating around the clock. In New Empire, workmen razed Hanopol's Billiard Parlor and Sloan's Cabinet Shop and the Jewett Block, the March winds blowing clouds of plaster-dust; excavation for the Buckmaster Building began; and presently, when summer returned, the brick façade of the new building could be seen peeking over the wooden fence erected to protect pedestrians from the march of progress. The contract stipulated completion by December 1 and that would be none too soon, for with the business expanding so rapidly, and so many new employees, the old building was threatening to split at the seams.

Park Irwin announced he would run for re-election. A boy named Rolfe Torkelsen, sixteen years old now, went every day to Judge Gentry's office and studied. The Buckmaster Packet Company, reaping a rich harvest from the booming Northwest, ordered two more steamboats to be built, the *Quickwater* and the *Lanceport Belle*. The Buckmaster Development Company bought most of the weakly-held stock in the Bank of New Empire, and picked up such parcels of real estate as a hotel in

Dubuque, a business corner in St. Paul, a warehouse in St. Louis. With James L. Buckmaster in control, the New Empire Public Service Company was organized to build a gas plant, and a grateful city council granted a franchise in perpetuity. Jim Buckmaster, people said, had certainly taken hold of things in great shape; his business acumen, they said, went even beyond that of Caleb McSwasey; he was getting to be the biggest man on the river. Well, he was a hard worker, you had to give him credit; he was the first to reach the office in the morning, and often the lights burned there late at night. He took to work, they said, as some men took to drink, drowning himself in facts and figures. Too bad about his headaches, though.

You never saw him any more in the Pinery Boy Saloon or in Rafferty's; his days of sowing wild oats, people said, were over; he was a substantial member of the community now. Marriage, they said, had settled him; that, and the responsibility of great wealth. He used to be a regular rafting rooster, smiling and swaggering; but now, like any man at the head of vast enterprises, he was serious-faced and even, sometimes, moody. His clerks reported that occasionally when they entered his office they would find him with fists on his desk, scowling darkly; he had changed.

Not that his head was too big for his hat! He wasn't, people said, that sort; he wasn't one to forget his old friends. When some crony from his rafting days—somebody like Greasy Dick Cassidy—came to town, he unrolled the red carpet and passed the cigars and like as not, at noon, took the Grease to eat at the Commercial House. In ordinary circumstances the manager might have forbidden the Grease to enter the dining room, he looked so dirty and smelled so much like an Injun; but any circumstances in which James L. Buckmaster was concerned were not ordinary. The Grease was a raft pilot now, with a rooster named Noisy Swanson to enforce discipline; James L. Buckmaster, people said, didn't forget those he had known before he had grown so great.

Park Irwin triumphed at the polls, in 1852, as did one Franklin Pierce, and Mr. and Mrs. Buckmaster gave a party to celebrate the continuance of matchless law enforcement in Fox County. Keep your eye on Park Irwin, people said; he had something the voters liked.

During those busy months, letters used to arrive at the house on Buckmaster's Island from distant Santa Fe, bemoaning the passing of Caleb McSwasey, the best friend a man ever had; and bemoaning too the passing of Hod Kite, who, in these later years, had announced that life being what it was, any man was a fool who wished to outlive Methuselah; whereupon Hod had taken to drink and become quarrelsome, till finally he roused the ire of a trapper who shot him through the heart.

"It is what I have always said," Otto wrote, "he who lives by the sword shall die by the sword, which is why I have given up dueling already, although this does not mean I will forgive an insult so soon, or let same pass unchallenged, as they could tell you in New Orleans where I was known as One-Ball Zumwalt. After much thought, my dear little one, I have bought the property which formerly housed Kite's Saloon, and am remodeling it and will move there my fine store, for the business has been growing and I am somewhat crowded in the house with the fine board floor, still the best floor in the Territory if I do say so myself, although the cowardly ants have got under it and sometimes come marching up through the cracks, it keeps me busy chasing them, I have never liked ants or any other insects, especially flies and spiders."

Esperanza neglected to answer those letters, sometimes for weeks or months, she was so busy. Parties, skating, more parties, teas, receptions: what a whirl! When the Buckmaster Building was completed, the public was invited to an open house in what the *Chronicle* called the magnificent edifice, and that was a great success, with Kieckhefer's Bakery serving cakes and coffee, and with crowds trooping through the bright new offices, even peering into the walnut-paneled suite of James L. Buckmaster on the ground floor. Sheriff Irwin attended, along with a score of other statesmen; and Lilith brought Heinrich von Zumwalt McSwasey, looking like a chip off the old Gentry. He was nearly four now, and like his mother, devoted to Jim, who carried him pick-a-back through the building, telling him that some day he would rule the business there. Heinrich was quite the center of attention, for the *Chronicle* editor and all the politicians—even the governor from Madison!—wished to kiss him, or said they did, their reasoning being, perhaps, that when the little towhead ascended to the presidency of the company he would remember them favorably, if they were still extant, and in the meantime such homage would delight his mother.

But they couldn't have been more wrong; if there was going to be a center of attention, Esperanza wished to occupy it; the truth was that during the past months she had observed with growing uneasiness and jealousy the affection of her husband for his foster son. At the open house, however, she dissembled so successfully that none of the politicians dreamed she would have preferred they kiss her.

Late in the afternoon, when the crowd was at flood crest, Judge and Mrs. Gentry arrived, accompanied by Rolfe Torkelsen, a young man of medium height with an unruly shock of coppery blond hair. Jim flung an arm around his shoulders and asked the judge how he had been behaving.

"Why, sir, very well. Very well indeed."

"Let me know if he gets into mischief," Jim said, "and I'll toss him in the river."

At that, Rolfe and Jim squared off and shadowboxed, to the amusement of everybody in the office except Esperanza, who wished that her husband's roughneck past could be more successfully suppressed.

The *Chronicle* editor, his pad and pencil busy, asked Judge Gentry what he thought of the new building.

"Sir," said the judge, *"di novello tutto par bello."*

"Could I quote you on that?"

"I can find no objections, sir, to my opinions being promulgated *pro aris et focis.*"

"I didn't quite get all that," the editor said. "Would you mind writing it down?"

The judge acquiesced, and his wife smiled and sighed.

"He's *so* smart," she murmured. "I just don't see how he keeps all that old Greek in his head."

They were still a striking couple, although thinner and frailer; time had not spared them.

*

Upon marrying Jim, Esperanza had decided that children would be only a nuisance, ruining her figure and perhaps stealing her husband's love, so she spent many hours poring over a book she had bought in St. Louis, Dr. Charles Knowlton's *Fruits of Philosophy, or, the private companion of young married people.* Complete with beguiling illustrations, showing those parts of the human body which the Pilgrim Fathers thought God would have done better not to create, the volume, in addition to landing its author in jail, taught ways and means of implementing the theories held by the disciples of Malthus. The book, Esperanza thought, repaid all her study, for the months came and went with no patter of little feet in the Buckmaster house, except for those of an occasional mouse, and for Heinrich's.

And his were not so little any more; in another year he would start to school. Esperanza could hardly wait; he drove her to distraction sometimes; she wished she had studied *Fruits of Philosophy* before that evening at the North Star Mill. And although such thoughts were only those to be expected now and then in a normal mother, there were times when her feelings toward Heinrich went beyond unfriendliness.

His yips and his battles with a toy gun, when he yelled "Bang, bang," and slaughtered imaginary Indians, she might have endured, for after all warrior blood ran in his veins, and with a grandfather like Otto it was to be expected that he should begin early to exterminate the savages; but what she could not endure—at least without mistrust and nagging jealousy—was the way Heinrich attracted her husband's affections. She did not hold with the belief that freely-given love is inexhaustible; she believed rather that when her husband gave a portion of his love to her son, there would be that much less for her; and with her new marriage going into its second spring, she could not help contrasting Jim's casualness toward her with his fondness for Heinrich. Little by little, even, she began to suspect that her husband did not love her—he never so much as kissed her, unless she asked him to—so it was only natural for her

742

to fall into thinking of her son as a rival. Presently, even, she found herself believing he was scheming against her.

He idolized his foster father; on winter afternoons, as twilight gathered, he would go to the front drawing room and press his nose against the pane; and when at last the lamps of Jim's carriage shone through the evening, he would shriek with anticipation and scamper to the vestibule, to be picked up and kissed and boosted toward the ceiling amid shouts and merriment. And when Esperanza, hearing the commotion, came downstairs, she would find the two of them romping together, with Jim on his knees perhaps, teaching Heinrich to feint with his left fist and to drive his right to the jaw. Absorbed in the boxing lesson, neither noticed her arrival, till at last, in exasperation, she said:

"Well, lover, aren't you going to say hello?"

"Oh," Jim said. "Yes. Hello."

"Aren't you going to kiss me?"

"Sure. I'll—"

But before he could rise, Heinrich caught him in the ribs with a fist, and Jim yowled like a saloon rowdy and the boxing was resumed. And when Esperanza rebuked her son for hitting his foster father, Jim took his part.

"No, he did just right. He caught me offguard just like he should. When a man's in a fight he ain't got no business to let a gal distract him."

"Ain't!" Esperanza exclaimed. "You mean hasn't. And a double negative—"

But neither of those males, laughing and brandishing their fists, paid the slightest attention to what she was saying.

At such times, after she had been married long enough to backslide into her natural behavior, she would stamp a foot, exclaim "Arrgh!" and run upstairs where she lay sobbing and pounding the bed. But did her husband follow and apologize? Never. She could sulk all evening, for all he cared. He never told her he loved her. He never, for that matter, made the first advances in fulfilling his function as a husband. She had to do all the wooing. Once roused, he was the finest lover a woman could want, and she forgave him everything; but it was downright humiliating to be married to a man who seemed to believe the prime purpose of a hymeneal bed was restful sleep. Early in marriage she had supposed him bashful, and she was quite willing to finger him affectionately and lead him on, but now, after twenty months, it seemed odd that a man so indubitably male should take such scant interest in the most interesting part of holy wedlock. It was almost as if he despised her and could bring himself to love her only after he was sufficiently enkindled to be beyond caring about the identity of his bedfellow. Yet she couldn't believe that.

"Might be the man's got him another gal," Lilith said. "My experience, Miss Esperanza, a man's like a steamboat boiler. He let off steam with one gal and there ain't none left for his wife."

A chilling possibility! Instantly Esperanza opened her purse and gave Lilith twenty dollars. And there in the upper sitting room, the two women sketched out an espionage network: Jim must be spied upon day and night. If need be, the entire colored population of New Empire must be drawn into the conspiracy.

"Yes, ma'am! I'll talk with that no-good nigger that works in the Pinery Boy Saloon. He can wait outside the Buckmaster Building at night and see if some little whore sneaks in there when Mistah Jim's supposed to be working. And I'll hire that janitor at the Wisconsin House. And Mistah Ragsdale's yard man. Set 'em all watching. Going to take money though."

"There will be money," Esperanza said.

And so it was that during the second spring of Jim's marriage, and well into the summer, his movements were observed. But according to all secret-service reports, he never went near a fancy house; he never went slipping through the shadows to call on some mistress on a dubious street; women did not visit him at his new office. Late in the spring, Esperanza herself became an operative; on nights when Jim returned to his office, she would drop in unexpectedly. But never did she catch a woman in his arms. There in that richly-carpeted office, with its deep leather chairs and handsome spittoons, she would find him in his shirt sleeves at the desk, a green-shaded lamp casting a cone of light on the multitudinous reports from far outposts of his business. His hair was rumpled; he looked tired. At last, even Lilith—who had made a good thing out of her detective agency—had to admit that he appeared to be a faithful husband.

Thus, after two years of matrimony, Esperanza was forced back to her earlier conclusion: that Heinrich was blocking the spiritual consummation of her marriage. And he was so shameless about it! Esperanza almost hated him. She enjoyed sleeping late, but Heinrich, like Jim, was an early riser, and who knew what went on during those summer mornings? No doubt her son carried tales to her husband, telling how his mother punished him for nothing at all, and wounded him with her tongue. The little sneak! Sometimes she wished he would drown.

But he was unlikely to, for during that summer when he was four, Jim taught him to swim. Now and then Esperanza made herself get up early to see what was going on; wearing a peignoir, eyes swollen with sleep, mouth sullen, feet dragging, she walked through the dewy morning to the river where her husband and son were splashing and shouting. They gave her hardly a glance. In the early rays of the sun Jim's body gleamed; black hair grew on his forearms and chest and compact, muscular buttocks; his belly was flat, his calves and biceps sinewy; compared with him, Heinrich was blond small fry. And although prudery was one fault which had never afflicted Esperanza, she announced now that it was immodest for them to swim without their clothes. Anything to spoil their fun! But Jim paid no heed.

By August, Heinrich was a good swimmer, and there were mornings when, perhaps to escape the sound of her voice, the two of them would strike out through the water to a distant sandbar. And she couldn't follow; she had never learned to swim. Scowling, she would stand watching, wishing that a sudden cramp would seize her son. But even if that happened Jim would save him. When they reached the sandbar they lay stretched in the sun; now and then Heinrich's laugh drifted across the water. Esperanza glared. At last they swam toward shore, racing each other, and perhaps Jim would let Heinrich win. Fatuous! Disgusting! Then, wrapping themselves in towels, they would go trotting and whooping toward the house while Esperanza, fit to be tied, trailed in their wake. A fine way to treat American Motherhood!

Late that summer, at Jim's direction, one of his packets brought several pine logs downriver, leaving them at Buckmaster's Island, and after that those morning sessions were devoted to lessons in birling.

"I don't see why you're teaching him such nonsense," Esperanza said. "Heinrich will never be a river pig."

"That's where you're mistaken," Jim said. "Another ten years and I'll start him out in the woods. He'll learn to chop and he'll learn to drive logs."

"I won't have it," Esperanza said. "Heinrich is going to good schools and to Yale. He'll be a gentleman. Somebody in this family should be."

Jim stared at her, there on the river bank, till her gaze dropped. Then, quietly, he said:

"If you can't keep a civil tongue in your head, I reckon you'd best go back to the house. Heinrich is going to own the biggest business in Wisconsin, some day. Hell, it's almost that now. And if he's going to run the company he's got to know everything about it. I intend to see that he learns. Is that clear?"

She didn't reply.

"When I ask you a question," Jim said, "I expect an answer. Is what I said clear?"

Sulky as a child, she stood staring at the ground, and although she wanted to fly into a rage, something stopped her. His voice had been low and hard; perhaps she had gone too far; if she baited him too much, he might walk out on their marriage. She would never be able to bear that. She said submissively:

"Yes, lover. Whatever you think."

"All right," he said. "Now you know."

*

In October, when Jim left for the pinery on an inspection trip, Heinrich wished to go along, and so did Esperanza, for that matter. But he

745

refused them both. Heinrich, he said, was too young. As for Esperanza, the pinery was no place for a woman.

"Caleb used to take me," she said.

"And that was a great mistake," Jim said.

A mistake! Like all guilty consciences, hers needed no accuser, and she wondered whether he was referring obliquely to her evening with Andrew J. Gentry in the North Star Mill.

"Lover," she said, "please take me. I'll be good. I won't be the least trouble. I promise I won't."

"No," he said, "you're staying here."

They were seated at the dining-room table, and in the harsh glare of the new gas lights—for the New Empire Public Service Company was now a going concern—his face with its long jaw looked dark and stubborn. Esperanza kept arguing; at last she broke into tears. But it was all useless. Jim finished his meal and left the room, looking tired and troubled and a little gaunt-faced.

A few evenings later, when it was time for him to drive to the levee and take the boat to Read's Landing, Esperanza closeted herself in the upstairs sitting room, feeling much abused, determined to make him come to her and say good-by. Surely he wouldn't leave without a farewell kiss. Perhaps, even, at the last minute, he would relent and invite her to go along. She sat on the chaise, prepared to strike a pose of indifference when he came. But her ears were cocked for sounds from downstairs, and at last she tiptoed to the door and inched it open. From far away in the lower hall she could hear Jim's voice; Heinrich began to cry; then she heard the front door close, and presently, from the driveway, the sound of horses' hoofs. The carriage was leaving.

Anger surged through her, followed instantly by dismay. He would be gone two weeks and he hadn't even kissed her good-by. Tears sprang to her eyes and in a kind of panic she went racing along the hall and down the stairs and out the front door. Through the crisp evening she could see the carriage-lamps receding toward town; she lifted her skirts and ran in pursuit, calling Jim's name; but before reaching the bridge she tripped and sprawled headlong, scratching her knees; yet she was up in an instant, sprinting across the bridge through the pale moonlight and finally overtaking the carriage at the retail yard of the Buckmaster Lumber Company.

"Lover!" she cried. "Wait! Wait for me!"

The carriage stopped. But when she opened the door she saw that Jim was not alone in the dim interior; Lilith and Heinrich were there.

"Lover! How *could* you leave without saying good-by?"

Shivering, she squeezed herself into the seat beside him and sobbed on his shoulder, grief-stricken that he was going away from her and outraged that he had permitted Heinrich and Lilith to accompany him to the levee. But her sobs ceased when her son said that Jim had promised to take him to the pinery next spring for the drive.

746

"Well I like *that!*" she exclaimed. And she asked Jim, "Why did you promise him such a thing?"

"He'll be older then," Jim said. "It will be time for him to see a drive."

"And will you take me too?"

"I don't reckon I will. A log drive is no place for a woman."

"You will *too* take me, Jim Buckmaster! If you take him you'll take me."

"Not if I'm in my right mind," Jim said. "I'll take Heinrich to learn him how they drive logs. It will be a business trip for us both."

"You mean teach him, not learn him. I wish you'd watch your grammar. But I'll tell you this, lover. If Heinrich goes to the drive next year, so will I."

"Think so?" Jim said.

*

On their way back to the island after seeing Jim off, Heinrich babbled so much about going to the log drive next spring that Esperanza lost all patience, and in the upstairs sitting room she tried to excise her vexation by applying a hairbrush to her son's backside, but even his howls failed to soothe her; so after Lilith, looking daggers at her mistress, carried Heinrich away to bed, Esperanza poured a drink and rolled a cigarette and sat curled on the chaise, scowling at the fire, asking herself whether Jim no longer loved her, if he ever had. Yet he must have. He had married her. Still, he had not been precisely an ardent suitor. It was she who had proposed marriage. But he had accepted her proposal. Would he have done that if he had not loved her? He might have. His choice had been narrow: either marriage or prison. Tears welled into her eyes as she remembered that June morning more than two years before when she sent word to Sheriff Irwin that he should bring Jim to the office at the lumber yard.

In memory she could see herself sitting at Caleb's desk, which had become her desk; she was wearing a cool linen frock and a perfume of delicate hyacinth; she remembered how breathless she had been, waiting, and how she kept bringing out a mirror and admiring her face. At last she stood up and paced, sometimes stopping at a window to gaze out at the stacks of lumber in the yard, where a farmer and one of her employees were loading planks into a wagon; sometimes pausing at the wallmap which charted the vast holdings of the McSwasey Lumber Company. Now they were her holdings, or would be, when the estate was settled; she was rich. All of Caleb's scheming and marauding had ended in a rectangular hole in the ground, for him. He was dead, dead as Croesus in the earth of Lydia; and with a secret smile she remembered the Scriptural truism: he heapeth up riches, and knoweth not who shall gather them.

She had no regrets. What had to be done, she had done; he would never firebrand her now. Never again would he slap her around; never again would he rape her in her bed; never again would he kill one of her lovers, as he had killed Andrew J. Gentry. She was free.

And yet, being a woman not easily satisfied, she did not wish to be free. She yearned for sweet captivity, provided only that her captor might be Jim Buckmaster. Rich as she was, she could sail away to the ends of the earth, if the fancy struck her; she could winter in Havana and summer in Saratoga; she could take a house in Paris and buy silks and baubles in a thousand shops; but what would be the good of that, without Jim?

"I'm in love," she whispered, standing there in that workaday office, half closing her eyes and drawing a long breath. "Ooo, I'm in love."

She thought of other times when she had supposed herself in love; she thought of Gilberto Archuleta and of Andy Gentry; but they were as nothing to her now. She was callow then; now she was a woman. With Gilberto and Andy, she thought, she had been in love with love; now she was in love with Jim. She yearned for him with every cell; when she thought of him a pleasurable weakness stole through her; without him she felt as unfulfilled as an unplanted field ravening for the plow and the seed.

A knock fell on the door; she scurried to the desk and seated herself. "Come in."

"Madam," one of her clerks said, "the sheriff is here with Mr. Buckmaster."

"Show them in."

Her heart was pounding, her lips were dry. She could feel the blood in her throat and cheeks. She sat staring at the desk, fingering a rock about the size of two eggs which her husband had used for a paperweight. She was aware of footsteps; two men entered the office; the door closed.

"Good morning, Esperanza," Sheriff Irwin said.

"Good morning, Park."

"I got your note," the sheriff said. "It's a little irregular, bringing a prisoner here, but I can understand how you wouldn't want to come to the jail. Anyway, here he is."

She didn't trust herself just yet to look at his face. She saw two pairs of legs, Sheriff Irwin's in creased trousers, and another pair in scuffed boots.

"Oh, yes," she said, her voice sounding tight and strange. "You may wait outside, sheriff. I want to ask this man a few questions."

A momentary silence. Then the sheriff said:

"I don't know about that. I mean about me leaving him alone with you. Might not be safe."

"Park," she said, "don't be a goose. Of course it's safe. Wait outside, please."

Another silence. Finally Park Irwin said:

748

"All right, Buckmaster, if Mrs. McSwasey wants it that way I'll leave you here. But I've got deputies in the lumber yard and if you try to go through a window they've got their orders." And to Esperanza he said, "I'll be right outside the door, Mrs. McSwasey. If he gives any trouble, just call."

"He won't give me trouble," she said. "You may go, sheriff."

The door closed; with an effort of will Esperanza made her gaze travel up from his boots. She saw wrists that wore handcuffs; she saw a face dark with stubble and discolored by bruises. His eyes were defiant and cocky and oddly ironical.

"Hello," she said, and she smiled.

"Morning, ma'am."

"Sit down," she said. "You look terrible, Jim. What happened to your face?"

"Nothing much," he said, easing his long body into a chair. "They worked me over a little, that's all. Some roosters are pretty brave when a man's wearing cuffs."

"Which one hit you?" she asked. "I'll have his job."

He grinned then, a quirky little grin.

"You don't need to go that far," he said. "Just take off these cuffs and give me five minutes alone with that deputy, Gammerdinger."

"I'd like to see that," she said.

He nodded.

"So would I."

She laughed, and suddenly she was no longer embarrassed but only keyed-up and vividly aware of his exciting masculinity. She stood up, smoothing her skirt over her buttocks and pulling in her belly so that her breasts would stand out. Then, moving slowly and provocatively, she went to the door and turned the key. Jim sat with elbows on knees, cuffed wrists dangling, but he was watching her quizzically.

"Park Irwin," Esperanza said, "is a ninny. Some day I may send him to congress where it won't be noticed. He'd be popping in, if I didn't lock the door. I want to talk with you, Jim."

"Sure," Jim said, "go ahead. I've got plenty of time."

"What's all this nonsense about log piracy?" she asked. "I hear you've been saying you were working for Caleb. Is that true?"

"Sure," he said, "sure it's true. But nobody listens. There was a mix-up somewhere. Caleb never spoke up about it, like he promised to. Then he was killed by that nigger. He said he'd write it all out, what we were up to, and put it in his safe. You ain't come across any paper like that, have you ma'am?"

"There's no such paper," she said. "I've looked."

Jim lounged back in his chair, long legs stretched out. His lips were pursed and there were cool lights of irony in his eyes. His coarse black hair was rumpled—she wanted to smooth it—and his face with its bruises looked leaner than she had remembered. He kept rubbing his cuffed wrists together and flexing his fingers.

"I reckon the laugh's on me, ma'am," he said. "I had a through ticket to the stars. I had me a mortgage on the moon and an option on the whole damn river. Old Caleb promised me a fourth interest in the company and my name on the door as vice-president. Hell, ma'am, I figured to own me the river and everything she drains, in about ten years. Give me another ten and I'd own the earth. Well, she's all blowed now. It's all cigar butts and last year's bird nests. It's all flood trash for sure."

"Jim," she said, "I'm sorry," and she ran her fingertips over his hair.

"We set us a trap, I and Caleb did," he said. "And damned if I didn't get caught in that trap my own self. Seems funny old Caleb didn't speak up, as soon as I landed in jail. I've thought hard about it, and there's a lot of funny things. Take that night in Rafferty's. We'd planned he'd fire me and swing at my jaw, but easy like, so I could ride with the punch. But do you know what he did?"

"Yes," Esperanza said, "I know what he did. He hit you with knucks."

"He told you? Now why would a man do that to one of his friends? And why would he let me lay there in jail and never speak up?"

"He was trapping you," Esperanza said.

He looked up at her, his eyes gray as steel.

"Ma'am," he said, "you seem mighty certain of that. Did he tell you?" She nodded.

"Well, by God," Jim said. "Why, the damned old fox. When did he tell you?"

"The night he was—the night he died."

"Well, damn me for a whiskey-jack! Well, by God!" He got to his feet and took a turn around the office, scowling. "I guess I should have caught on, after he slugged me with them knucks, but hell . . . Say, why would he trap me, ma'am? I don't suppose he went into that."

"Oh, yes," she said, "he explained it all."

"But—why? Damn it, I'd shot fair with him. Why in hell did he—?"

"My husband," Esperanza said, "was a very jealous man."

"Well, sure, maybe he was, but—"

He must have seen it all in her face then, for she was staring at him and her eyes were swimming with tears.

"Oh, Jim," she said, and it was half a sob, "don't be such a dunce," and she went to him and snuggled her head against his chest. "I'd do anything for you, Jim, anything to get you. There's nothing I want, Jim, nothing in the world except you." She flung her arms around him, and she was crying now. "Ever since that afternoon you came to the house, Jim, looking for Caleb. It was March and windy and everything was drab. I was drab, Jim, I looked terrible in that old dress, and then I opened the door and you were standing there. If you'd crooked your finger I'd have followed you. I'd have gone anywhere you went and done anything for you. Something happened to me that afternoon, Jim, and I guess it's what they call love. I've never been the same since, Jim, and I'll die if you don't marry me."

Looking up at him was like looking through a rain-streaked window, her eyes were so wet with tears. His face was gaunt and haggard; he did not meet her gaze.

"Jim," she whispered, "oh, Jim, Jim. Marry me and everything will be all right. You'll own everything I own, Jim, I'll give it all to you. You'll be the biggest man on the river, Jim, and I'll be the happiest wife. And the best wife, darling, I'll do anything you want. If I do something bad you can beat it out of me darling, I'd like that, you can cuff me around, anything, just marry me darling, I've never wanted anything the way I want you. You'll own the river and you'll own the earth if that's what you want. Marry me, sweetheart, please, please, I know it's soon after Caleb's death and all, but we can be married secretly and nobody will know till we want them to, oh, Jim, marry me."

She seized his arms and shook him, as if trying to churn a confession of love from his lips.

"Why," he said, "why, ma'am—"

"Don't *call* me ma'am! Call me Esperanza!"

"Why, Esperanza, I don't reckon no good would ever come of it. Hell, ma'am, hell, I'm headed for the penitentiary. That's where they'll send me. You wouldn't want to be married to no jailbird, ma'am. They'll give me the limit."

"They won't!" she exclaimed, and she stamped a foot. "I won't let them. I'll tell them Caleb told me it was all a trap."

"You think they'd believe that? Why, hell, a smart lawyer would—"

"I know the smartest lawyer in the world," she said. "Judge Gentry—he'll get you off."

"Maybe. But maybe he wouldn't even touch the case. Hell, ma'am, I'm poison, these days. They've tried me and said I'm guilty in every saloon and livery stable in the county."

"He'll take the case," Esperanza said. "I've found proof. Caleb never wrote out what he promised, but you wrote him. You wrote him those letters about what you were up to. It's plain in those letters that you were trapping raft thieves for Caleb. Once Judge Gentry reads them he'll have those cuffs off your wrists in ten minutes. I'll send for him, Jim—I'll send right now—if—if you'll promise. Tell me you love me, Jim. Tell me you'll marry me. Then I'll send for the judge and you can beat up Gammerdinger. You can move in this office tomorrow as general manager. And we can go somewhere like Dubuque and be married and nobody need know till we're good and ready. Will you, Jim? Will you marry me?"

She remembered how he stood with boots apart, manacled wrists

751

dangling, black hair tangled, unrazored jaw bristly. She remembered his bleak eyes, and how he whispered something like, "Jesus God!" She knew a moment of despair then, and her bad old temper was a striking rattlesnake.

"You'd *better* marry me, Jim Buckmaster! If you don't I'll—I'll burn those letters. If I can't have you nobody can. I'll hire Judge Gentry to try the case against you. You'll rot in prison, Jim Buckmaster, and you'll never get out. I'll get to the warden just like Caleb said he would, and they'll bust every bone in your body. Do you hear me? Do you? They'll kick you into a cellar where you'll never see the sun, and the rats can eat what's left."

He stood staring down at her, his forehead ridged and shining with sweat.

"Now, ma'am," he said, "you're all upset—"

"And don't *call* me ma'am. God damn you, Jim Buckmaster, you've got to marry me. You've *got* to!"

And in her rage and despair she sprang toward him, her fists beating his chest. But that stopped abruptly when his hands came up, the cuffs jangling, and grabbed her by the throat and lifted her to tiptoe. His voice was low.

"You'd best calm down. You're acting like a two-cent whore. A man wants to think and you yowl like a catamount. Now shut up."

He shoved her away from him then, with such force that she went reeling and nearly fell. He turned his back and stood at the window, legs apart, as if bracing himself against some titanic manifestation of nature; his fists were clenched and his shoulders sagged. But when he turned he smiled.

"I never said I wouldn't marry you," he told her. "Hell, lady, you didn't even give me time to say yes. Sure I'll marry you."

"Ooo, Jim, Jim."

She flung herself against him, sobbing.

"Jim, Jim. You love me, don't you? You've got to love me. You've *got* to."

"Sure," he said. "Sure I do."

"I need you, Jim. You're strong and I need you so much. I need a real man, darling. I'm awful, I'm terrible, I know I'm bad and I can't help it, but you'll make me behave. You'll love me and make me behave myself, won't you?"

"Why, sure," he said.

"Kick me," she whispered, "and I won't care. Kick me all over the place and I won't care, just so you kiss me too."

She sank to her knees, her arms encircling his legs; then she grabbed his hands and pulled him down beside her on the carpet.

"Darling," she whispered, kissing his forehead and stubbled cheeks and

752

his mouth, "I wish we could make love now. I wish you weren't wearing those handcuffs. Ooo, I—"

*

A knock sounded on the door, quite some time later, and Sheriff Irwin called.

"Mrs. McSwasey. Esperanza. Are you all right in there?"

"Yes, of course."

"Well, I just wondered. It's been quite a while."

"Everything's fine," Esperanza called, through the door. "Everything's wonderful. And Park, I want you to do something. Send a man for Judge Gentry. Tell him it's important and to come at once."

"Judge Gentry?" the sheriff asked, sounding dubious.

"Yes, I want him immediately. Now do what I say."

"Certainly, Mrs. McSwasey."

At the desk, Esperanza propped her mirror against the rock which served as paperweight and touched up her appearance. Her face was flushed with happiness, her eyes dreamy.

"Darling," she said gaily, "I'm all mussed. I look a sight. It's written all over me. I suppose a widow should look sad, but I just can't. Ooo, I'm so happy."

Remembering something, she rummaged in a desk drawer and brought out a box of Cuban Pelions, those cigars that Caleb had liked.

"Lover," she said, "would you like to smoke? I'll light it for you. I'll do everything for you from now on. I'll make you happy. I'll make it all up to you that you've been in jail."

She snipped off the tip, struck a match, inhaled deeply.

"Ooo, it's strong. I like cigarettes better. I learned to smoke in Santa Fe. All the girls smoke there. My father didn't like to have me, but I did it anyway. He never made me behave myself. Caleb didn't either, although he tried. He wasn't man enough. But you'll make me behave, won't you?"

"I reckon so," Jim said.

He was sitting with legs stretched out. She carried the cigar over and put it between his lips.

"Will you be mad at me," she asked, "if I smoke after we're married?"

"Hell, no," he said. "Why should I be?"

"I just thought you might be. I suppose it isn't very ladylike. But I'll tell you what, darling. If you don't want me to smoke you can forbid it. Then I'll be a bad little girl and hide behind the barn and smoke. And you'll smell it on my breath. And you'll be furious I disobeyed you and you'll just cuff me and kick me good. You'll make me behave."

He had to smile at that.

"God," he said, "I don't want to kick you. I don't kick women. I don't give a damn if you smoke."

753

"Anyway," she said, "you'll make me behave. My father told me once I was like a Spanish burro. He said I couldn't be led and the only way to drive me was with a stick. But he never used a stick. Sometimes I'm just awful, lover, I really am, if I'd tell you some of the things I've done you wouldn't believe me."

"Nobody's perfect," Jim said.

"I know, lover, but I mean I've been really bad. You wouldn't believe I have it in me. I'd like to tell you some of the horrid things I've done but I guess I hadn't better. Maybe when we've been married fifty years I'll tell you."

"Jesus, but you're a talker," he said. "Sure, wait fifty years and tell me."

"If I talk it's because I love you, Jim. You get me all excited and I know I chatter. Now I'll kiss you and then I'll let Park Irwin in. I'll make him take off those horrible cuffs. Then after I've shown the letters to Judge Gentry we'll go downstairs and find that deputy who hit you and you can beat him up. Do you feel strong enough to do that, now?"

"Why, sure," Jim said, "I reckon I can handle him."

"Will you stomp him, lover? Will you kick him when he's down?"

"I shouldn't wonder."

She smiled.

*

Next morning James L. Buckmaster took over as general manager of the McSwasey Lumber Company, and a few days later, after that secret marriage in Dubuque, he became general manager of Caleb's widow. That was on June 21, the longest day in the year, and the most romantic Esperanza had ever known, blue-skied and hot. It was not yet seven when they met on the levee in New Empire and boarded the downriver packet. She had been up since four, too excited to sleep, for she considered getting married an interesting affair, as women often do, and with her Spanish love of intrigue she enjoyed the deception veiling the proceedings. To Lilith, and to others who might be curious, she had announced that she and Mr. Buckmaster were going to Dubuque to sign an important contract. This was certainly the truth, although not the whole of it, and the latent falsehood sent gay bubbles soaring through the champagne of her happiness when she thought of how she was duping New Empire, for like her father she had found lying a quick and easy means of attaining a sense of power.

The lie, of course, was necessary. With Caleb less than two weeks in his grave, not even Esperanza was willing to stage a gaudy wedding. She might have chanced it, if his death had been less unnatural, but as it was people would talk and some busybody might demand further ratiocination on Sheriff Irwin's part. They would talk in any case, when the marriage was at last announced, but more time would have passed and her back trail, if she had left one, would be cold. Not, so far as she could deduce, that she had left a back trail. She had been clever; the whole affair had come off beautifully; and she was grateful to her Apache ancestors for passing along their unmatched ability at leaving no sign. Even so, she supposed that strict prudence would have dictated waiting a year before marrying Jim, but she was afraid to chance that. He might change his mind. She was a great believer in the feminine proverb of never putting off till tomorrow the marriage that can be solemnized today.

The packet which carried them to Dubuque was the *Harmony Season-good,* and as Esperanza promenaded by Jim's side through the grand saloon, with its gilt and creamy walls, and its bewhiskered passengers with their fashionably-dressed women, she caught sight of herself and her groom-to-be in a mirror: she was a smiling young woman in a luscious summer gown of sea-green, the waist tight and the skirt flowing, her frivolous little bonnet crisp with jaunty flowers.

Compared with her, Jim looked like a roughneck out of the woods in his cheap, ill-fitting suit. She didn't mind; she wasn't marrying his suit; besides, she had faith in her ability to make him over. What did trouble her, however, was his gravity on this morning of his wedding day. He had led, she gathered, a pretty free and easy life; maybe he was suspicious of becoming a domesticated animal.

Traveling on the *Harmony Seasongood* had its advantages, for the McSwasey Packet Line owned the boat, and everybody treated Esperanza and her general manager with great deference. They climbed to the hurricane deck, where the captain invited them into the pilothouse; they could look for miles across that broad immensity of flowing water. Standing by Jim's side, Esperanza remembered another morning in a pilothouse more than a decade before, when she came to New Empire as a bride. She had wanted to take the wheel, but the pilot wouldn't permit it, nor would Caleb. If she asked to take the wheel today, probably this pilot would agree, but she decided not to risk it. She might run the big boat aground and hours would elapse before the crew could get it off the reef; that would mean running late into Dubuque, perhaps too late to buy a marriage license at the courthouse.

Out on deck, she stood with the light channel breeze in her face, her hand on Jim's arm, remembering how on her first trip up the river the boat had passed Indian villages with their dugouts and naked children. Now those settlements had vanished, supplanted by towns with stores and schools. Civilization had come to the Mississippi Valley; the whole Northwest was booming and bustling. And her company, the company that Caleb had founded and that her new husband would take over, would prosper enormously from that great influx of peoples. She was rich now, but she would become richer. The future stretched out all silvery and blue, like the river. Jim loved her—she was sure he must, in his taciturn way—and if he didn't love her now he would grow to. He was a strong man and he would protect her, if somebody should become suspicious about Caleb's death. But that wouldn't happen; she had covered her tracks. Even if it did happen, her money would rescue her; somewhere she had heard that they never hanged a million dollars.

*

Dubuque was booming too, a noisy young city hatched from the old French village where men had come nearly a century before to mine lead. Prominent on the river front was an extensive lumber yard with a sign saying McSwasey Lumber Company, New Empire and St. Louis; the lumber was now supplied by a steam sawmill Caleb had put into operation shortly before his death. When the *Harmony Seasongood* arrived at the levee, a dozen other packets were tied up there; and in the bright sunshine of early afternoon the debarking passengers were importuned by runners from various hotels to enter their omnibuses. A sign on the roof of the omnibus from the American House said: "Eat, Drink and Be Merry, For Tomorrow You Go to Minnesota." The levee smelled of sweat and horse dung and beer and river water and hot steam from the packets. Teamsters and roustabouts were shouting; the tires of drays rumbled on brick pavement; and fancy girls moved languidly through the crowd. One of these, whom Esperanza would have enjoyed shooting, gave a squeal of recognition and clutched Jim's sleeve. Smiling, he bent and whispered to the girl and pressed a bill into her palm; she giggled and said gee, honey, my mistake, but thanks anyway.

"Who was she?" Esperanza asked, after Jim had hired a hack and they were jogging toward the courthouse.

"Just a girl I used to know."

"She seemed to think you still knew her."

"Minnie's a good old wagon," he said, "always looking for a horse."

"Jim," Esperanza said, "I think I'm jealous."

"Don't be," he said. "At least not of Minnie."

"Of somebody else?"

"Oh, hell," he said, "forget it. You talk too much."

Her first impulse was to exclaim "Arrgh!" and to strike out with the two-edged rapier sheathed in her mouth, but she restrained herself; he was not yet her husband.

"Lover," she said, "don't be cross."

"I'm not cross."

Well, perhaps not; but he hardly looked happy. In the heat he had removed his coat; his straw hat was shoved back; his face looked defiant and sullen.

"Jim," she said softly, "when people buy a marriage license isn't there a record kept? And don't they publish their names in the paper?"

"I don't know. I've never been married before."

"I'm sure they do, Jim. I think the county publishes their names.

756

Maybe you could talk to the clerk. If you'd give him some extra money, maybe he'd help us keep our wedding secret."

"Ashamed to be marrying me?" he asked.

"Lover! You know I'm not! You're just a tease. But if we want to keep our wedding secret—you know, because of Caleb, and because it's so soon, and all—well—maybe you should talk to the clerk."

"Sure," Jim said. "I'll slip him a few dollars. He can always lose the records for a while."

"And maybe you should do that with the preacher too, Jim. Tell him we want to keep it secret till next fall. If anything came out about us in the Dubuque papers somebody in New Empire would be sure to read it. The talk would be terrible, this soon."

Jim nodded, but he seemed as disinterested in keeping the wedding secret as in going through with it.

"And lover, I've been thinking. We'd better stay in separate hotels tonight. We're supposed to be here on business. You go to the Iowa House and I'll stay at the Julien. Just in case somebody from home would see us."

"Suits me."

"But lover. You could come over to my room later tonight. After everybody's gone to bed. We wouldn't want to sleep apart on our wedding night. Will you come over to see me, Jim?"

"Sure, I'll drop in."

"Ooo!"

*

Dubuque was ever afterward a romantic town in her thoughts despite what happened on her wedding night. Looking back she could see it in the golden summer weather crowded between the green bluffs and the river, a market town on Saturday afternoon, its narrow streets thronged with farmers' buggies and wagons. She was a woman snatching at happiness then; her life had been a jumble of errors, but she told herself that from now on everything would be different. In memory she could see herself and Jim alighting from the hack and walking through bright green shade into the courthouse smells of tobacco spit and varnished wood and petty corruption and moldering documents. She remembered the cool gloom of the county clerk's office with its scarred wooden counter and its decrepit old man with a decrepit cigar. Esperanza stood waiting while Jim and the old man disappeared into a private office to arrange for secrecy; money, she thought, could buy anything. Pigeons were cooing somewhere; from a corridor a drunken voice was cursing the administration of Millard Fillmore; tall record books bound in red leaned against one another on the shelves of the office. This was the tollhouse at the frontier of Elysian fields; to this dingy cubbyhole must come all the hot young loves of summer; it was here that government, man's ancient and necessary enemy, exacted its cynical tribute from Aphrodite.

"Did you fix things up?" Esperanza asked, when they returned to their waiting hack. "Was he willing?"

"He said not. Against the law. But every man has his price. That old rooster's was pretty low. Ten dollars."

"You're wonderful," she whispered.

"I and the ten dollars," Jim said.

The hack moved from the curb, toward a preacher recommended by the driver. She remembered white dresses on summer streets and red brick buildings with flashing glimpses of the river at intersections; she remembered a residential street with maple branches meeting overhead and the stained-glass windows of the Methodist Episcopal Church with a modest parsonage beside it.

"Here we are," the driver said. "I'll wait if you say so."

Jim nodded; Esperanza stepped from the hack. Now that the ceremony was so near, her knees were quivering and she could feel a globule of sweat rolling down the valley between her breasts. She found herself remembering her first marriage in St. Louis so long ago, and she couldn't help thinking how furious Caleb would be if his ghost were watching here today. But he was dead, gone to his long home. There were no ghosts. She was a modern young woman: no ghosts, no heaven, no hell; just a few decades when something hot and mysterious burned in moist human clay, and then the everlasting dark. Less than two weeks dead, arms folded on his chest, lying as he would lie till the end of time in the earth of Wisconsin. How long till the damps rotted a coffin? How long till the worms discovered the new dead? Mustn't think such thoughts, she told herself; the past is nowhere, it is the vanished echo of a steamboat whistle, it is a wind that blew in Santa Fe long ago, it is the scattered ashes of a Spanish cigarette, it is not to be found save in the involuted byways of the human brain. Nothing exists but now, she thought, this moment when I am walking toward a parsonage in Dubuque, Iowa, and even that moment is a part of the past before I am aware of it. Less than two weeks dead but he would have died hereafter and look for me tomorrow and I will be a grave woman. All of us.

The parson's wife was a woman in her sixties with cracked red hands and a gentle smile. Yes, she said, her husband was in. Oh, yes, she thought he would be willing to perform the ceremony. Just come in, please.

The parson was tall and old and stooped; and he too was gentle, coming into that parlor with its shabby furniture; yes, he could perform the ceremony, and what a beautiful day you people have chosen for your wedding . . . Esperanza felt an odd embarrassment; she had known so few people like that, so few gentle people. Nearly everybody she had known had been driving hard toward something: toward money and power, like Caleb; toward a job as raft pilot, as Jim had been that first evening when he came to supper; toward furious proof of valor, like her father; toward command of all learning, like Sophronicus Gentry.

"But we'll need witnesses," the parson was saying. "Perhaps my wife, and your driver—"

"Just a minute, mister," Jim said. "Us two would sort of like to keep this marriage a secret, for a while. We've bought a license and all that, but we'd just as soon hold back the news for a spell. We're from upriver, and we've got our own reasons for waiting to announce it. I'll make it worth your while to keep your lip buttoned up."

The parson looked mildly startled; his smile was gentle and oddly innocent.

"I won't announce it," he said, "if that's what you mean. Of course, if anybody should ask me—"

"I don't reckon anybody will. I can see you're a square shooter, mister. Just keep it under your hat and we'll be much obliged."

A little later, when she was standing beside Jim facing the parson, Esperanza was trembling. Now that the moment had arrived, she felt a strange impulse to break away and go running from the house, as if some terrible retribution might befall her if she married again when she was less than two weeks a widow.

"Dearly beloved . . ."

And there was a part of the ceremony which she had forgotten. A part about if any person knows a reason why these two should not be joined in the bonds of holy matrimony, let him speak now or forever hold his peace.

But nobody spoke up. Not Caleb McSwasey, who would never speak again; not Bonnie Fansler, far away in Lanceport.

*

It was a night for love, balmy and humid. In her room at the Julien House, Esperanza waited in the dark. As she sipped bourbon and smoked cigarettes, ears alert for footfalls in the corridor, her nude body felt as full-blown and athirst for pollen as some golden spatterdock rooted in the mucky river shallows. Sometimes she lay on the bed, sprawling voluptuously; sometimes she stood at the open window, looking across a jumble of roofs and waste places toward the river, where moving packets cast rich reflections. Once in the darkness she made out the low bulk of a log raft with tiny figures jigging in silhouette against the cook's fire; she heard far singing and the strains of an accordion. A McSwasey raft, probably, traveling toward the St. Louis sawmills; next month that raft would be stacks of lumber; next year it would be figures on the credit side of a bankbook. It gave her a glow, seeing it, not because of the money but because it reminded her of Jim; he had been a raftsman. Thousands of things reminded her of Jim, and always with the pleasurable pang of one in love: the river, because it was his river; cigars, because he smoked them; the lavish scattering of stars in this blue night, because they had shone on him. She sighed. From a steeple somewhere, a great clock bonged out eleven strokes; he would be hearing that clock and thinking it was time to go to his bride. She began to tremble.

"Ooo," she thought, "I'm like a girl. I'm like a virgin tonight, nothing that happened with Caleb counts for a thing."

And nothing that happened with Andrew Jackson Gentry, for that matter; and nothing that didn't happen with Gilberto; she had brought to perfection the wonderful feminine ability of forgetting all others.

Something came buzzing through the open window and struck her cheek; something else struck her belly. Lighting a candle, she saw brown-winged insects, about the size of grasshoppers, crawling on the carpet. She smashed them with a shoe, and their dead bodies gave off a fishy stench. The lighted candle attracted several more; before squashing them she closed the window; and after that she could hear others of their kind plopping against the pane. The room had a rank swampy smell; she sprayed the air with French water, then blew out the candle. Yet the fishy smell remained, and with fresh air shut off other smells uncoiled from the carpet and woodwork and furniture: all the hotel-room smells of dust and mildew and stale chamber pots. She opened the window, then closed it almost at once, for more insects came buzzing. After lighting the candle and dispatching them, she decided to dress and go to Jim's hotel; perhaps he had fallen asleep; she would send a bell-boy to his room to rouse him.

A few minutes later, when she descended to the lobby, she found the clerk patrolling the place with a folded newspaper, swatting the grass-hopper-like bugs; they went shooting through the air; their corpses littered the terrazzo.

"Ain't it a fright, lady?" the clerk said.

"But what are they?"

"Just bugs. They won't bite. Some call them fish flies and some call them caddis flies. About once every summer they do this. They hatch out in the swamps and the lights of town attract them."

When she emerged to the street, she was assailed by that corrupt odor, as if the sweepings from a thousand fish markets had been dumped in the town. The insects swarmed around streetlamps in whirling plagues; bruised and burned they dropped to the sidewalk, crawling feebly; the air was thick with them, looping and spinning, so that the street looked like a blizzardy night. Going along the sidewalk, Esperanza crunched as if through snow; the gutters were long windrows of corpses; the bugs rattled around her face and coated her dress and buzzed in her hair. She felt unclean, as if Jehovah had hurled a Biblical plague at her poor mortality.

At Jim's hotel, the clerk and a bellboy were sweeping dead bodies from the lobby, and they reported that Mr. Buckmaster was not in; he had gone out about nine.

"Are you sure?" she demanded.

"Yes, ma'am," the clerk said. "He left a couple of hours before the bugs hit."

Esperanza gave the bellboy a coin.

"Go up to his room and knock. If there's no reply, unlock the door and go in, He might be asleep."

The bellboy hurried off; Esperanza explained to the clerk:

"I'm Mrs. McSwasey of New Empire. Mr. Buckmaster is general manager of my company. We're in Dubuque on business, and I've just heard of a matter requiring his attention."

"Golly, ma'am," the clerk said, "I never knew you were Mrs. McSwasey. I read in the paper how your husband was killed. You have my sympathy, ma'am. Your husband was about the biggest man on the river."

Less than two weeks dead, she thought. I could shock his shoes off if I'd tell him I'm Mrs. Buckmaster now.

The bellboy returned.

"No, ma'am, he ain't in."

Esperanza left. On the street the insects were thicker than ever. And still they came, infesting the town with the reeking stinks of the river underworld. The river was a beautiful harlot when you saw her sprawled silvery in the noonday sun, but she had her festering secret places, her greenish backwashes, her eels and leeches, her bloodthirsty lampreys, her water spiders, her obscene and fecund swamps. One of the insects struck Esperanza full in the mouth; she spat; she held a scented hand-kerchief to her nose.

And where was Jim? Gone more than two hours from his hotel; gone where? She had wandered vaguely down a side street, toward the river; now, through the blizzard of insects, she saw a great fenced commercial project; in the hissing illumination of lonely gas lights stacks of lumber towered; and as she moved along the fence she saw the lights of a steam sawmill and heard the screams of saws ripping through logs. McSwasey Lumber Company, a sign said, New Empire and St. Louis. Working twenty-four hours a day now, times were so prosperous; slashing into planks the logs looted from Wisconsin. Caleb, she thought, had planned this retail yard and this mill; within his tough old skull it had first come into being; now his brain was dank clay. Less than two weeks dead but the company lived on; it would live forever, probably, or until the forests were exhausted. Then perhaps it would move west, eating its way through pines of the Blackfoot Nation, leaving the slash; inching down the Columbia toward the Pacific littoral; less than a month ago he had been talking of that fine future; a longheaded man. Dead now in a cubby of dank Wisconsin soil; dead as Alexander and Charlemagne and Richard Coeur de Lion; as all the destroyers and empire builders of dusty ages; but Jim lived on; the empire builder was dead and long live his successor; and where was Jim?

She found herself at the levee, a place of high gas lamps and sleeting insects, of huge Negroes with purple torsos loading and unloading boats; they chanted barbarically as they worked; the reek of their sweat mingled with the fish stench of the insects, with the steamy, oily, smoky odors dribbling from the tied-up packets, with the rankness of the river. Then she smelled whiffs of beer; she had wandered to a street lined with saloons; fiddle music and singing exploded through the swinging doors in cacophonous blasts; men came reeling out, accosting her; hello, Goldie, hi ya, yellow-top, toodle-do, sweetheart.

She struck out across a street, wading ankle-deep in vanquished insects, and as she passed the Red Keg Saloon she glanced through the window and saw the object of her search. Big and smiling, hair rumpled, he stood with his back to the bar, cuddling a girl on either side, his strong voice lifted in song.

> *"Oh, drive the logs down, boys, drive the white pine,*
> *Drive 'em and ride 'em down to the boom . . ."*

She didn't fly into a rage; she surprised herself by not doing that. But tears came to her eyes and she thought: he's just a river roughneck. Maybe always will be. My wedding night.

And she pushed through the swinging doors.

He broke off singing, when he saw her, and let loose with a pinery boy howl. His eyes were glassy; he must have been pouring down the rotgut tonight.

"Look," he yelled, "look who's here. Well, by God! Boys, want you to meet my boss. Widow of Caleb McSwasey, the meanest son of a bitch that ever stole a log out of its bark."

The place had fallen quiet; Esperanza saw dozens of faces turned toward her; tough faces, river-front faces, pinery faces, hard painted faces of the girls who hustled for a living. The barkeep tapped Jim's shoulder.

"Take it easy, son," he said.

"Yes, sir, boys," Jim said, laughing, "the little puss herself. Hired me to run her business. And by God, boys, I'll do it. I'll own me the river, boys, and I'll own all your souls and sell 'em for sawdust."

"Jim," the barkeep said, "you've had too much. That there's Mrs. McSwasey, Jim."

"Sure it's Mrs. McSwasey. I work for her now, boys. I'm her pimp. Come here, puss."

The saloon was dipping and swaying; through bright tears Esperanza saw her bridegroom.

"Come here! God damn you, come here!"

"Yes, Jim," she whispered.

He put a hand on each of her shoulders.

"She's my push now, boys. My push and my puss. God damn her for a kettle of cat juice, anyway."

"Jim," Esperanza whispered. "Jim. Please, please—"

"Boys," Jim said, "I had me a headache. Damndest thing, boys, it was October. I went to a hotel, boys, upriver that was, and something happened to me, boys. You wouldn't understand it. Nobody but me would ever understand it, boys. I was alive then, boys. I'm dead now. The world's dead, boys, everything's dead. Ever hate yourself, boys? Ever look in a mirror and think you goddamned double-crossing bastard, how could you do a thing like this? Man will do anything, I reckon, to save his own hide. God! I'll own you all before I'm through, boys, and you'll hate me like poison, but not the way I hate myself."

"Jim," Esperanza whispered, "it's getting late."

"Puss," Jim said, "which one of these fine whores should I roll with? This here's Amy, puss, and this one's Francy. Flip a coin, puss, and tell me which one."

Esperanza was crying; she seized his biceps and shook him.

"Jim! You'll be sorry! Oh, Jim—"

Then suddenly her hands were torn from his arms, and, propelled by his strength, she went stumbling across the saloon and down into a heap in the sawdust and the dead insects.

"Puss," he was bellowing, "leave me be. Get back to your room and your beauty sleep."

She wavered to her feet; the girl named Amy snuggled against him and said:

"Gee, rooster, you treat 'em rough."

Everybody laughed.

"Hear me, puss?" Jim bawled. "You going to do what I say?"

"Yes, Jim, yes, yes, yes," she said, sobbing; and she fled through the doors and along the street of blizzarding insects, thinking perhaps it was all a dream and she would waken in her room with her groom kissing her. But it wasn't a dream. Next day, however, she pretended that it had been. Taking the packet back to New Empire, neither mentioned the Red Keg Saloon. Perhaps he had been too drunk to remember what had happened on his wedding night; she hoped so.

*

That was about his last fling; he settled down after that. In New Empire he stayed on at his lodging house till time for the marriage to be announced, and that was probably the most successful way he could have lived with Esperanza. She was always inviting him out to the island for supper and for games in the upstairs suite, but he was a reluctant partner; the games he enjoyed most were those he played with Heinrich. She didn't like that, having her groom pay more attention to her son than to herself, but she couldn't do much about it, except take it out of Heinrich's hide the next day. All in all, however, she was happier as Jim's wife than she had ever been, and on those hot summer evenings after Heinrich had been put to bed, she used all the tricks in French literature, and a few from Persian, to put her husband to bed also. What happened then was well worth the money; Molly Fitzpatrick had been right; he was a first-rate lover.

One evening early in July—the evening of the day when a young woman's body had been recovered from the river—Jim did not keep his supper appointment; more than a little piqued, Esperanza ate alone; and afterward she paced the garden paths, smoking furiously. In that season of long days, the sun had only just set; twilight was still an hour away; the river flowed smoothly past the island. Esperanza stood at the water's edge, frowning; Jim had no right to treat her this way. It was a perfect evening for love, the air benign and fragrant. Reaching a decision, she flipped her cigarette into the river and started on foot toward town.

South of the house, the grass of Ferdinand Vogler's lawn was spongy under her slippers; everything looked park-like. But beyond the lawn, in the woods of the island, Nature was her old savage self, a tangle of licentious vines and lawless underbrush and upthrusting saplings; following the sandy road, Esperanza was engulfed by the moist odors of leaf-rot and verdurous fecundity. And when she crossed the bridge to the mainland, the raw stench of life, of enthusiastic breeding in warm slime, of batrachian brides and crustacean bridegrooms, rose like a thick vapor from the green backwater, choked with its cattails and bur reeds.

The lumber yard was deserted, the watchman not yet on duty; she unlocked the retail office, which was full of silence and the day's trapped heat and the sterility of any business establishment when the automatons of commerce have briefly recovered their freedom and their manhood. Unlocking a second door, she climbed the stair to the counting room, that place of sloping desks and inkpots, passing through the gate and the stale air to Jim's office. He was not there. Only the desk with a rock the size of two eggs; only the wall-map of the pinery; only the memory of Caleb. But it was a memory only; not a ghost. There were no ghosts. She smiled, feeling utterly rid of him at last; it was a measure of her sanity, she thought, that she could come here in the beginnings of twilight and feel no apprehension.

"Caleb," she said aloud, with a strange smile, "how do you like it? You said I'd never get away from you, but I did. You said you'd follow me forever and firebrand my face, but you never can do that now.

You're dead, Caleb. This is a beautiful evening, but you'll never know it. You're dead and in your grave."

The sound of her words died away. There was no answer. His desk and his chair looked empty, inanimate. She felt she had been very brave, defying his shade in what had been the sanctum of his life; smiling, walking neither fast nor slow, never looking over her shoulder, she left the office.

Outside, she walked south along Front Street through the vanguard of dusk; the levee was empty of steamboats, but loafers were lounging against the Pinery Boy Saloon; even Rattlesnake Bob was there, wearing a soiled apron and his sickly smile. This wasn't Dubuque; nobody accosted her here. When she said good evening, to prove that democracy lived, the loafers touched their hats and replied politely; Rattlesnake Bob said, "Evening, Mrs. McSwasey."

Mrs. McSwasey. The secret of her new marriage had been well kept. She turned east at the corner and went to Jim's lodging house.

"Yes, ma'am, he's in," the landlady said. "But he ain't at all well. He went and got one of them headaches of his."

"Ooo? I'm so sorry. He was coming to supper tonight to talk business, and I thought something must be wrong."

"Yes, ma'am, he's sure suffering. He come in late this afternoon looking like a corpse."

"Could I go up and see how he is?" Esperanza asked.

"Why, ma'am, I don't guess no harm would be done. But you be quiet. He may be asleep."

The shades were pulled and the room was dark, when Esperanza tiptoed in. She sensed, rather than saw, a bed where a sick man lay, and she groped toward it.

"Jim," she whispered, "it's Esperanza. It's your wife."

He did not respond.

Moving softly, she found a chair by the bed; she reached out and touched his forehead, drenched with sweat.

"Don't!" he whispered furiously.

"Jim. I'm sorry, Jim. Does it hurt terribly?"

No reply.

"Jim. I'm sorry you're sick. We waited supper for you and when you didn't come I was worried."

"God damn it," he said, sounding agonized, "leave me be. You talk too much."

"It's because I love you, Jim. That's why I came here. Is there something I could do for you?"

"No. No, you can't do a thing."

"Maybe you should take something. Something to kill the pain, like laudanum."

"Already have."

765

"Do you think you could sleep, Jim? It would help if you could."

"What I'm trying to do."

"I'll be quiet," Esperanza said. "I'll be here if you need me, but I'll be quiet."

She sat there while he tossed and twisted; at last his breathing grew regular; she thought he was sleeping. But then, in a thick drugged voice, he said:

"Too much clothing . . . Pull you down every time . . . Like Sol . . . Like me on the Chippewa, spring of '45, at Dead Oak Pitch . . . Closed the door on myself . . ."

"Lover," Esperanza whispered, smoothing his damp hair, "try to sleep."

"Sleep?" he mumbled. "Sure, down where the bullheads wave their flippers across your eyes . . . I'm sorry . . . Sorry, sorry, sorry . . . Remember the icehouse? Raining . . ."

"Jim," she whispered, touching his cheeks, "you're crying, lover. You're out of your head and you're crying."

"Mean old bitch," he mumbled, "that river . . . Pull you out with waterweeds in your hair . . . Thought you'd be mad . . . Your brother . . . I . . . thought . . . you'd be mad . . ."

After that, he dropped into deep, deep sleep; a sleep as deep as the dark deeps of the river; his breathing was stentorian; the streaked tears dried on his face. Esperanza sat with him a long time, then kissed his forehead and tiptoed from the room and down the stair, as he had tiptoed from that same room so many years ago, when he ran away from Sol Klauber.

*

From then on she noticed a change in Jim; he was quieter; he lost weight that summer. When he came to the island for supper he picked at his food. And after the meal, smoking a cigar, he would sit staring with dead eyes while she chattered; she could tell he wasn't paying attention. Headaches afflicted him oftener.

"Jim," she said once, "is something bothering you? You could tell me if it is."

"Why, no," he said, with a pale smile, "hell, no, I'm all right. Just thinking about business."

Whatever his shortcomings as a husband, he was certainly an ardent businessman; the McSwasey Lumber Company couldn't have found a harder-working manager to step into Caleb's shoes. No matter how silent he had been, she could always get him to talk when she asked about company affairs. Having been brought up in the woods, he knew logging from stump to mill; he could estimate how much any given camp should cut, and how long it should take a log raft to travel from Read's Landing to St. Louis; his foremen were not likely to throw sawdust into his eyes.

He knew all the answers, when it came to logging and driving and rafting.

The retail end of the business, the management of the many lumber yards, was all new territory for him when he took over the company; he never pretended otherwise; but during that first summer he sent for the men in charge of the various yards and picked their brains; when Esperanza called at the office, she was forever finding him in conference with those managers, or with the director of the McSwasey Packet Line, or with his general superintendent of sawmills. And in October, on their belated honeymoon downriver, he spent more time at the St. Louis sawmills than in making love to his bride.

"You work too hard," she told him, as she used to tell Caleb.

"Got to. You wouldn't want me to bobble things and sink the company."

"I wouldn't care," she said, "so long as you still loved me."

She had hoped the packet trip from St. Louis to New Orleans would relax him. Well, it did, but not in the way she wanted. Instead of taking a vacation from business and becoming a full-time lover, he just took a vacation from business. And New Orleans was a city that would have felt quite at home in a French novel; a city existing for love and the fleshly pleasures; on Esperanza, its effect was powerfully stimulating.

"Do you love me, lover?" she asked a thousand times.

"Sure," he always replied. "I married you, didn't I?"

The leaves had been red, when they left New Empire, but down here in the capital of the South everything seemed to bask in perpetual April, the air moist and warm, the sunshine softened and diffused by the vaporous skies. The river which curved lasciviously around the city, and seeped into its cellars, and threatened always to spill into its streets, was not the river Esperanza had known in the North. Up there it was a wilderness river, sinuous and treacherous and feminine to be sure, but youthful. Down here it was a haggard old whore of a river, wide-loined, cynical, corrupted with sewerage; a sailor-town river; a river awash with the flotsam of a continent, with rotten fruit, with half-submerged crates and barrels. Along the levee, Jim and Esperanza saw deep-sea shipping from the great ports of the world, here to disgorge their spices and silks and coffee, and to ingurgitate the baled wealth of the cotton kingdom.

New Orleans had been Otto Zumwalt's city, for a time, and Caleb McSwasey's; Jim and Esperanza visited the Dueling Oaks, where One-Ball Zumwalt had so often defended the honor of a proud house; and on a warm drizzling morning, at the request of Judge Gentry, they went to the old battleground where General Andrew Jackson and Private Caleb McSwasey had upheld the honor of the Republic. Certainly, she thought, if Caleb's ghost intended ever to trouble her, it would do so here, but she saw only the rain-gray Spanish moss dangling from trees, and the holes of crawfish in the soggy ground, with the odd little chimneys they built from pellets of mud, and the ancient canal running from river to swamp where the crack shots from Kentucky and Tennessee had entrenched themselves. Remembering Santa Fe nights in years long past, when Caleb told of the battle, she wondered how her life would have gone if a red-coat bullet had pierced his heart. She would never have met Jim. She would never, she thought, have known real love. She took her husband's arm, snuggled against him.

"What are you thinking about, lover?"

"Why," he said, staring into the rain, "I guess I was thinking this would be a good lumber-yard site, except it's too low."

Several times during their New Orleans visit, they traveled in the steam cars out Elysian Fields Avenue to Milneburg, a pleasure resort on the shore of Lake Pontchartrain. At the bathhouse Jim rented a bathing suit and swam far into the lake while Esperanza, languidly twirling her sun-shade, waited on the beach. Finally his head was a speck on the dazzling water, and she was seized by a foolish little fear that he might drown. If that happened, she thought, she would want to die too. But he was a tireless swimmer. After he returned to shore and dressed, they sat beneath a vivid parasol at an open-air cafe, all very Continental, and Esperanza sipped subtle tropical concoctions in which rum was not absent. Jim stuck with bourbon, neat.

One afternoon he told her about that evening at the Northern Saloon in Quickwater when he was a boy and first met Molly and Lew Fitzpatrick.

"Lew surveyed for the New Orleans and Lake Pontchartrain Railroad," Jim said. "It gives me a funny feeling, to ride out here on the roadbed he surveyed."

And as he told how Lew Fitzpatrick had been killed by a breed, and how Molly had established a well-thought-of fancy house, Esperanza was invaded by a deadly feeling.

"Jim," she said, "I'm jealous. Did you ever—you know—go to bed with Molly?"

"Why," he said, "I reckon I did. Molly was a real woman, in them days."

"You mean in those days, lover. You're going to be a big man on the river and in the country—I'm so proud of you, lover—and when you go to Washington as a senator or something you'll want to talk correctly."

"Washington?" He laughed. "That's a good one. Why would I want to be a senator?"

"It would be a great honor. The president might invite us for supper."

He laughed again.

"Hell," he said, "I'll own me a couple of senators before I'm through. Maybe three or four. That's better than being one my own self. I'll own me the governor too, and the whole damn legislature. See that?" He pointed toward the railroad station, where, beyond the amusement-park concessions and the pleasure seekers, a fidgety little locomotive was sending up smoke from its balloon stack. "That's what they call the iron horse, puss. There's the future, right over there. It'll drive all the packets off the river, some day. Maybe I'll own me a whole stable of them iron horses, before I'm through. They tell me the legislatures are real generous, if a man wants to build a railroad."

"You talk the way Caleb used to," she said. "Don't you ever think of anything but making money?"

"Not if I can help it," he said.

*

"Did you see Molly Fitzpatrick?" Esperanza asked, when Jim returned from the pinery in the fall of 1853.

"Why, puss," he said, "what's it to you? Sure, I dropped in and said hello."

"Don't *call* me puss. And what's it to me!—I like that! You're my husband, that's what it is to me. Did you go to bed with her?"

"Just for an hour or so," he said, smiling.

"Arrgh!"

"Hell, puss," he said, "it didn't mean nothing. I and Molly are old friends. I didn't like to insult her."

"Oh, you didn't! You're a married man, but you didn't like to insult a whore!"

"She's more than a whore," Jim said. "She works with her head too. Molly's got a little gold mine, up there on the Chippewa, and she's saved her money."

"And since you're old friends," Esperanza said, "I suppose she gave you a cut rate."

"Better than that. She's never charged me a cent, and she's not starting now. Hell, puss, I said we're friends. We had a little fuss, a few years back, but that's blowed over now. Molly's all right."

Esperanza fled upstairs and lay pounding the bed.

Jim's reunion with his foster son was less stormy; Heinrich wished to hear all about the camps of the Buckmaster Lumber Company, so every evening Jim told tales of his adventures in the woods; Heinrich asked dozens of questions.

"Son," Jim would say, "you'll make a real logger. I can see that."

All that autumn and winter Heinrich talked of his trip next spring to the pinery with Jim, when they would follow the drive.

"You're not going," Esperanza said. "You might as well make up your mind to that. I won't let you."

Sometimes Heinrich disputed her, to his pain and sorrow, but one March afternoon in the upstairs sitting room Esperanza lost her rightful sovereignty over her son when Lilith came between them and seized the hairbrush.

"No, ma'am. You ain't a-going to whup that child no more."

A frightful scene ensued, Esperanza was so insane with rage; she accused Lilith of being an uppity nigger and told her she was discharged.

"Pack your things and get out. I won't have you in the house. You've gone too far this time, and you're through."

"No, ma'am. Ain't going."

"You are *too* going!" Esperanza screamed.

To Heinrich, who was hiding behind her skirts, Lilith said:

"Honey, you go downstairs and play. I got something to tell your mama."

"I won't listen," Esperanza said, after Heinrich had gone. "You're an uppity nigger and I can't trust you. Caleb knew about Jim and me, and I think you told him. I think you gave him my letters to Jim."

"Yes, ma'am. I thought a lot of Mistah Caleb. He set me spying on you and I spied. And he'd say, 'Lilith, Jim Buckmaster will be in town tomorrow. Tell the little slut,' he'd say, 'that her lover will be in my office tomorrow morning. I want to see them together,' he'd say. 'I want to see how they'll act.' Yes, ma'am."

Esperanza was white with anger.

"Get out," she said. "Pack up and get out. You're through in this house."

"Don't think I am, Miss Esperanza. I been thinkin'. I got me a big mouth, and if I was to tell what I been thinkin', I could make you a sight of trouble."

"Thinking! Niggers can't think. You're all animals. You've got wool on your heads."

"Yes, ma'am. That may be. But I been thinkin' nevertheless. I been thinkin' about the night Mistah Caleb was killed."

It was a thrust for which Esperanza was unprepared; her stomach felt hollow; she began to tremble; and when she spoke her lips were stiff.

"I don't see what that has to do with it."

"Got a lot to do with it. Yes, ma'am! I recollect how after supper that night old Dexter went right to the stable. Told me he was tired and going to bed. He never come back to the house to git that slicing-knife and that bronze dog. I'd have seen him."

"You're ridiculous," Esperanza said. "He probably *didn't* come back to the house. I think he stole the knife and the dog much earlier. Maybe that afternoon or the day before. I think he'd been planning for weeks how he'd kill Caleb."

"Huh-uh. Old Dexter never planned nothing more than a minute ahead, 'cepting how to git out of work. Besides, Miss Esperanza, that there slicing-knife was right here in that glass cabinet just before supper. Me and Heinrich was up here and I seen it. Then we went downstairs and old Dexter was in the kitchen eating his supper. You and Mistah

Caleb come up here right after supper and old Dexter went to the stable. That's how it was."

"You're mistaken about that," Esperanza said, but even in her own ears her voice sounded shaken and lacking in conviction.

"No, ma'am. Ain't no mistake about it. I recollect it like it was yesterday. Then after supper me and Master Heinrich was in the front parlor. And Heinrich had himself some fun playing with that dog. That dog was right there against the parlor door just like that knife was here in that glass cabinet. Then I brung Heinrich upstairs to put him to bed. I heard Mistah Caleb leave this room and go downstairs, and I heard you leave. But I didn't hear old Dexter coming up. He never did come up."

Esperanza was outraged at the way her body was betraying her. It shook; her cheeks burned; when she tried to speak her tongue could hardly form words.

"I—I think you're—you're just making this all up," she said, and she went to the chaise and tried to light a cigarette but her fingers were clumsy and shaking.

"No, ma'am. I been thinkin' it all out, and I know what I know. If I was to go to old Judge Gentry and tell him what I been thinkin', that judge would sure prance. He would say, 'Lilith, you pore old nigger, we got to look into this. Maybe justice ain't been done,' he would say. That there judge is always wanting justice done. Me and him could make a sight of trouble for whoever killed Mistah Caleb. It wasn't old Dexter, but it was sure somebody. Don't know exactly who, but it was somebody. I recollect how after Heinrich went to sleep that evening I went downstairs and out the back door. It was dark, but I seen a blond-headed woman out there by that fountain. Reckon that was you, Miss Esperanza, finding Mistah Caleb's corpse. Then you run. Always did wonder why you run instead of telling me Mistah Caleb was dead. Did you see anybody out there who could have killed him?"

"It was Dexter," Esperanza said.

"No, ma'am. Couldn't have been him. Must have been somebody who lived in this here house. Wasn't me, I know that. Wasn't Heinrich. Can't think who it could have been, but I am just a pore old nigger with wool on my head. Reckon the judge might figure it out, if I was to tell him what I know."

Esperanza wanted to say: "Go to the judge and see if I care. Do you think he would believe you instead of me? Do you think Park Irwin would dare arrest me?"

But she didn't say that. Judge Gentry prided himself on his integrity, and it would be just like him to listen carefully to Lilith's story and to insist that Sheriff Irwin reopen the investigation of Caleb's death. She would be questioned. She might go all to pieces and confess everything. Lilith was saying:

"You didn't really want to whup Master Heinrich with that there hairbrush. You just lost your temper with the child. I don't think, Miss Esperanza, you're going to have no call to whup him no more. And if he wants to go to that there drive with his daddy, why I reckon you'd just as soon he'd go. And you didn't mean what you say about me leaving these premises. You wouldn't throw out pore old Lilith. You wouldn't do that, would you, Miss Esperanza?"

She couldn't speak. In her lap her hands were clenched; an artery in her throat was beating like a second heart.

"Would you, Miss Esperanza? Would you?"

Through her tears the fireplace flames were leaping demons; Esperanza shook her head.

"Didn't think so," Lilith said. "Don't think you could git along nohow, without pore old Lilith. Lilith don't want to make no trouble for nobody, Miss Esperanza. No, ma'am, Lilith is a good old nigger and she don't want to git Judge Gentry to prancing. You just do what I says, Miss Esperanza, and I will keep my big mouth shut."

Esperanza lay for a long time on the chaise with her face in her arms.

*

After that she was no longer mistress of her own household, for it was necessary to defer to Lilith, to appease her, to give her money. Not again did Lilith threaten to go to Judge Gentry, but she was forever tormenting Esperanza with references to the night when Caleb died.

"Don't know who killed the man," she would say. "Wasn't old Dexter. Couldn't have been him. But somebody sure killed Mistah Caleb. Wish I knowed who. Reckon they'll find out who, some day, and then there'll be a hanging. Yes, ma'am!"

Esperanza felt sick with apprehension, as spring came on; her nerves grew raw and her temper short. Yet she didn't dare lose her temper with Lilith or with Heinrich; no matter how much her son prattled about his trip to the pinery, she had to spare the hairbrush. Her position was one of nearly unbearable frustration and humiliation, but it was preferable to a position at the end of a hangman's rope. Even in sleep she found no surcease, for she was always having terrible dreams and waking up with her fingers at her throat.

With Jim it was unnecessary to hold her temper, and the harsh words flew. Yet she loved him. And even when her tongue sprayed him with vinegar, she expected affection in return. He disappointed her in that. And in bed. And in the vestibule when he left for his office without kissing her. Everything was wrong with that marriage, it was disintegrating and unraveling, and she wondered why. Yet she thought she knew why. Heinrich was why.

Heinrich! He was, she kept telling herself, a little sneak, a trouble-maker, a spinner of plots, aligning himself with Lilith and Jim against her. She wished he would die. Other children caught scarlet fever or diphtheria and died fine natural deaths, but did Heinrich? Oh, no, not he! He was five years old now and healthy as a hussar. His legs were sturdy, his chest sound. Lilith adored him and Jim adored him. And who adored Esperanza? Nobody. It was enraging; it was heartbreaking. Strolling sadly through the garden on April afternoons, she pitied herself so much that tears filled her eyes.

She withdrew into herself that spring, daydreaming away the hours. No longer did she plan brilliant parties; seldom even did she put on her finery and ride to town; invitations to gay functions she refused. Under her eyes dark circles appeared; she neglected her hair and her clothes; her body felt thick-blooded and heavy, her feet leaden. Heinrich was stealing her husband's love and there was nothing she could do. If only her son would die then perhaps her husband would realize, in perspective, how insidious and unprincipled the little fellow had been. If only that would happen, then she might persuade Jim to sell the damned lumber company; with the proceeds they could sail away to foreign parts and live in luxury for the rest of their lives. Far from Lilith. Far from Judge Gentry and from sheriffs and prosecuting attorneys; beyond the jurisdiction of hangmen. But Heinrich would not die. Not without persuasion.

Persuasion! She recoiled, the first time such an idea darted through her brain.

"Oh, no," she whispered. "I couldn't do—that . . ."

Yet such a course of action had, without question, much to commend it, and after her first revulsion she considered it thoroughly. From experience she knew it was not difficult to kill a human being, and certainly such a perfidious little scoundrel would be better off dead. He carried tales; he was two-faced; he was wrecking her happiness. Give him another year and he would probably smash her marriage beyond repair.

But if she put her son out of his misery, Judge Gentry and Park Irwin might investigate, prompted by Lilith. Damn! Yet she could daydream, and daydream she did, as she wandered about the island on fine spring afternoons. Presently she was thinking of little else except ways and means of ridding society of Heinrich.

And oddly, the more violent her thoughts became, the gentler she grew with her son. If he could smile and smile and be a villain, she could dissemble also. She used to kiss him, that spring, and hold him on her lap and tell him stories, all the while thinking how soft and vulnerable his throat really was; it would be easy to press a thumb on either side of his windpipe. Yet, damn it, if her son died a violent death, she might be suspected. If only she could hit upon some way for him to die that would leave her conspicuously blameless. There must be such a way.

Early in May, Jim and Heinrich left for the pinery, and although that journey was not unexpected, it came as a blow to Esperanza; till the moment of departure she hoped Jim would decide against taking the boy.

Or perhaps he would relent and invite her to accompany them. But nothing of the kind! Off they went together, while Lilith cackled and complimented her mistress upon her change of heart in permitting Heinrich to go.

"'Spect they'll have them a high old time, up there in that pinery," Lilith said. "Yes, ma'am, I guess a log drive is mighty exciting. 'Spect they'll go to the drive every spring, from now on."

"Yes," Esperanza said serenely, "I imagine so," but her thoughts were black. Next spring and the next and the next; Heinrich was taking her place. As he grew older, he and Jim would doubtless go to the woods together on hunting expeditions and fishing trips; before long, Jim would be taking the boy on business trips to Dubuque and St. Louis, and leaving her in New Empire. And always when he was alone with his foster father, Heinrich would be undermining her, lying about her, turning Jim against her.

She was utterly restless and disheartened, the day after their departure; with Jim gone, the house was an empty shell; New Empire was a sterile town. She thought she couldn't stand it a minute longer; and then it occurred to her that she didn't have to stand it; if she wished, she too could take a trip. To New Orleans, to New York, to Cincinnati . . . anywhere. She had money; Caleb was dead; nobody was stopping her. When Jim returned he would find her gone; that might make him realize how much he really loved her. She decided, finally, to go to St. Louis; and so it was that two evenings after Jim left she boarded the *Sol Klauber,* southbound, accompanied by a trunk and bandboxes and valises. And on that journey she encountered adventure.

*

A change must have been what she needed, for when after a month she returned to New Empire the dark loops had vanished from beneath her eyes and her smile was flashing. Jim was waiting on the levee that evening, in response to her message that she would be arriving on the *Quickwater;* she came skipping to shore, smelling like a flower garden, looking like a Parisian spring in her new clothes; and when she caught sight of her husband she rushed to him and flung her arms about him.

"Darling! I've missed you so much!"

"Hello, puss," he said.

"And how is Heinrich?"

"Fine and dandy."

"I'm so glad. I was afraid he would fall in the river on that dreadful drive."

Jim laughed.

"He did fall in, a couple of times. He wanted to try his hand with a pike pole, of course. But hell, he's like a tadpole."

In the carriage, Esperanza snuggled against her husband.

"You aren't mad because I went to St. Louis?"

"Hell, no. Why should I be?"

"I spent a lot of money, darling. I bought a lot of new clothes."

"I reckon that's what money's for," he said. "The way it's pouring in I'd need me a harem to go broke."

She squeezed his hand.

"You don't want a harem, do you?"

"Great God, no," he said.

At the house, Lilith exclaimed, "Eee! Miss Esperanza!" and embraced her mistress, and Heinrich came laughing to kiss his mother. So it was a happy homecoming, and that night, owing to the prurient weather and a bit of urging by his wife, Jim made the reunion complete.

And as she went floating off to slumber, she told herself the visit to St. Louis had been a fine thing for everybody; she needed to get away oftener and have little adventures; happy as she was tonight, she could not imagine what had got into her last April, wishing her son would die.

The happiness lasted for several days after her return; sustained by memories of St. Louis, she wakened with a smile and sang as she un-packed her new clothes. After a week, however, the happiness wore thin; after a fortnight, it vanished. And it was all Heinrich's fault. He couldn't, she thought, let well enough alone; having won his victory and gone to the drive, he might have had the decency not to torture his poor mother by chattering about the fun he had had up in the woods. But did he consider her feelings? Oh, no, not Heinrich! All through the long June days he harped on that trip.

Again this summer, Heinrich and Jim arose early and went swimming in the Mississippi, and sometimes in late afternoon they set forth in a scow with a picnic lunch and fishing poles. A couple of times they even camped out all night on some island. And was Esperanza invited to accompany them? Never! Once when she hinted she would enjoy going along, Jim shook his head and said, "This is man stuff, puss. You stay here."

Well, a woman had a right to use any means to prevent her marriage from going to pieces, and by mid-June Esperanza would gladly have provided Hurlbut's Furniture & Undertaking with a young customer. Trouble was, however, that she simply could not dredge up a good, efficient, innocent-appearing way in which to shatter the sales resistance of Mr. Hurlbut's prospect. Heinrich was the liveliest member of the Buck-master household, glowing with health, as unlikely to die as Shakespeare's reputation. His mother in her daydreams thought of poisoning him, drowning him in the bathtub, breaking a vase over his head, choking him, hanging him in the stable, stabbing him, but each of those methods had the disadvantage of involving her in questioning by the authorities.

June 21 arrived.

"Lover," Esperanza said that morning, "do you know what day this is?"

"Sure," he said, "it's our third wedding anniversary."

"I didn't think you'd remember."

"How could I forget?"

"Lover," she said, "it's been a wonderful three years. We've had our spats, but it's been wonderful. I've invited a few people in for supper. You know, to celebrate."

"Oh, God," he said.

"Don't cry till you're hurt, lover. These are people you like. Sheriff and Mrs. Irwin, Judge and Mrs. Gentry, and that nice young man, Rolfe Torkelsen. I want you to fix all up, lover, so I'll be proud of you. And try to watch your language. Don't talk like a river pig, darling."

"Why, puss," he said, "if they don't like the way I talk, they can always leave. Park Irwin won't care how I talk. I'm going to run him for congress this fall. I'll elect the bastard, too."

"You're just the way Caleb used to be, lover. You push men around as if they were figures on a chessboard."

"Sure," he said. "A man either does the pushing or gets pushed. I'd rather do the pushing."

All that day Esperanza was on tiptoe with excitement, both because supper guests were coming and because she had decided to tell her husband, at bedtime, about her adventure in St. Louis. He would be very jealous; she was sure of that. The story would rouse all his male competitiveness; surely he would make violent love to her, to demonstrate he was still cock of the hen house; perhaps, even, he would realize he had been neglecting her for Heinrich.

It was a brilliant success, that party; before supper the company sat in the garden near the fountain, the men drinking bourbon, the ladies sherry cobblers. Esperanza was a charming hostess and a shapely one; her white gown of India muslin, with its full skirt and low tight bodice, emphasized the rich Spanish browns of her bare arms and enterprising bosom. All through the evening she was especially pleasant to Mrs. Park Irwin, a thin drab woman who would probably never amass much social seniority in Washington City no matter how often her husband might be returned to congress.

*

It was late when the guests left, and in the upstairs sitting room, at Esperanza's suggestion, she and Jim had a nightcap.

"Lover," she said, looking up at him from the chaise, "come and sit by me. I've got something to tell you. I think you'll be mad at me, but I can't keep anything from you. I'm a frank person, lover, and I'm sincere. I've been a bad girl, and I have to tell you."

He looked, she thought, uncommonly attractive tonight, in his well-tailored linen suit. When he sat beside her she saw his face in profile: the strong jaw and nose, the pleasant mouth, the black hair. She patted his arm and cuddled against him, basking in his masculinity.

"I don't know what you'll do to me, lover, when you hear. Maybe you'll give me a good hiding, that's what I need. I remember how you beat up that awful deputy sheriff, Gammerdinger, that day when I sent for Judge Gentry and Park Irwin took off those handcuffs. I'll never forget. We went down to the lumber yard and you said, 'Gammerdinger, give your gun to the sheriff. I'm going to clean your rudder for you, Gammerdinger, and you're the kind who'd pull a gun on a man.' Remember that, lover?"

Jim nodded.

"Gammerdinger had it coming," he said.

"Of course he had it coming! I remember how his face went white. His hand was trembling when he gave Park Irwin his gun. Then you moved in. You were just—just savage, lover. It was wonderful to watch. You never made a false move, lover, you were like a fighting machine. You looked as lean and hard as a rifle barrel, and I saw right away that you wanted to mark up his face. You hardly hit him any place, except in the face."

"I let him have a few in the belly," Jim said, "but that was just to knock out his wind. Hell, he was soft. He warn't no fighter, unless the other fellow wore cuffs."

"You were really vicious, lover. You were wonderful. I've never seen a man punished the way you punished him. He didn't land a blow, did he?"

"Not that I recollect."

"I remember when he went to his knees and threw his arms around your legs and tried to upset you. You brought your fist down on his head. It sounded like a rock hitting a barrel. Then when he let go your legs you kicked him in the jaw. I thought you'd killed him, for a minute. But then you grabbed him by the belt and yanked him up and worked on his face. It looked terrible. The blood was pouring from his nose and his eyes were swollen shut. Then you kind of turned him sideways and worked on one ear, and after that you swung him around and worked on the other. That was when Park Irwin wanted to stop the fight, but I wouldn't let him."

"Irwin's nothing but a half-grown chicken," Jim said. "He'll do better in congress than wearing a sheriff's popgun."

"And then Gammerdinger started yelling," Esperanza said. "He must have been in terrible pain. He must have thought you were going to kill him, lover. I remember how he was kind of sobbing and pleading for you to stop. But you kept right on smashing his face. It was just pulp when you were through, darling. Then you let him fall and he went down and lay still. You said, 'Next time think twice before you hit a man who's wearing cuffs.' I can't tell you how I felt. I was sort of sickish but at the same time excited. My head was swimming and I was sort of throbbing. I wanted you to grab me, lover, and fling me over your shoulder and carry me somewhere to bed. Your hands were all red from Gammerdinger's blood and I wanted you to hit me in the mouth till my lips bled. Jim, you heat me up so I think I can't stand it sometimes. You're more of a man than Caleb ever was, darling. You're so strong—I've never known anybody so strong. How did you get so strong?"

"Swinging an ax helped," he said.

"Lover . . . I have something to tell you, lover. You'll be mad. I know you'll be. But I have to tell you, anyway. Because I'm so frank. It's about what happened when I went to St. Louis . . ."

*

St. Louis . . . Early on that May afternoon, from the hurricane deck of the *Sol Klauber,* she could look far downstream and see the city taking shape, an extensive collection of warehouses and tied-up steamboats and stores and river-front shacks and skiffs and houses, all steeping in the heat-mists and smoke-hazes exhaled from this flourishing port. Off to starboard, the Mississippi flowed in a moiling hue of sewerage-yellow, for this was below the mouth of the Missouri, and that spleenish river from the Sioux Nation and the Blackfoot Nation had lugged to Middle America the wild raw colors of buttes and mesas and rattlesnake plains. Drift logs bobbed in the swift current, and uprooted young cottonwoods with their spring leaves still green. In the opalescent afternoon, the sunshine was pale, and beyond the steaming city the sky loomed gigantic with depths of pastel clouds.

The *Sol Klauber* was her boat, hers and Jim's; the captain himself had offered to make sure her luggage got ashore, and to engage a hack to carry her to the Virginia Hotel; so unlike the other passengers, who were bustling about below stairs with that ridiculous fretfulness of travelers approaching their destination, Esperanza was able to linger here on deck, twirling her sunshade. As the city came closer, she saw a great industrial enterprise on the river bank: a sprawling, smoking sawmill; heaps of slabs; mountains of sawdust; endless drying yards; runways slanting to the river where a raft was being broken up; and facing the Mississippi an imposing sign: Buckmaster Lumber Company, New Empire and St. Louis. Remembering how just below the city another Buckmaster mill was located, and ten miles farther downstream yet another, she had the cozy feeling of being sheltered by great wealth and influence, even when she went chasing off alone like this.

Steam blossomed in cotton-boll white from the *Sol Klauber's* whistle, and the palatial boat made a great sweeping curve—off toward Illinois, then downstream again, then upstream—so that it slanted against the current as it nosed along easily, with much bell-ringing and paddle-sloshing, to its moorage at the levee. Lines were hurled; the gangplank slammed down and passengers thronged ashore; and feeling as superior

778

as an entomologist observing an anthill, Esperanza watched them being absorbed by the crowd on the levee. She was in no hurry; the *Sol Klauber* was hers. So was the *Harmony Seasongood,* tied up beyond a half-dozen other packets. So was the *Bonnie,* taking on freight far up the levee.

When at last she went ashore, the captain doffed his cap and saw her to her carriage. Then he addressed the driver:

"This is Mrs. James L. Buckmaster. She's the wife of the biggest man on the Upper Mississippi. I want you to take good care of her."

"Yes, *suh,* Cap'n!"

Riding to the hotel, Esperanza was impressed, as always when she visited this city, by the almost frantic way it expressed its soul, as if under some materialistic compulsion, by throwing up buildings, using them for a while, then demolishing them and throwing up still larger ones. People, she thought, were busy little bastards. The levee had been jammed with boxes, crates, barrels, carts, drays; the street was choked with all manner of horse-drawn vehicles; vacant lots, with signs announcing the future home of this or that enterprise, were being excavated; in every block could be seen hod carriers and bricklayers and carpenters on the scaffoldings of half-finished buildings; stores were being remodeled and enlarged; prosperity was on the loose in the land, and St. Louis, a teeming supply depot for the roaring West and the Middle South, was bustling to keep pace. The sidewalks were crowded with Arkansas planters in wide-brimmed hats, with hurrying clerks and portly merchants, with roustabouts and raftsmen and steamboat mates and long, cool-eyed gamblers, with great ladies and pretty girls and leathery trappers and gaunt clay farmers and Injuns and river rats and sallow Frenchmen and red-faced Germans. And Negroes, of course—barefoot boys with cheeks of charcoal; mulatto girls in yellow dresses; wenches as fat as Lilith; grizzled old bucks as molasses-footed as Dexter Yarlow had been— for St. Louis was as Southern as Mobile or New Orleans, in spirit if not in latitude.

And as Southern in weather, at least on this spring afternoon; in her hotel room, at the mirror, Esperanza saw a mist of sweat on her forehead; her body felt sticky. She stripped off her clothes, bathed, and lay resting, moodily thinking of Jim and Heinrich in the woods. What lies, she wondered, was Heinrich telling about her? Presently she slept.

Thunder awakened her; at the window she saw lightning and a spring shower; down on the street people were running for the shelter of doorways. And because of her nap, or because the storm had cleared the atmosphere, Esperanza felt happier. She had come to St. Louis, she told herself, to escape her problems, and she might as well have fun: perhaps Heinrich would fall into the Chippewa and catch pneumonia, or perhaps the little Judas would go too far in his deceitfulness and Jim would realize his foster son was trying to break up the marriage. If not, when she returned to New Empire, perhaps she could hit upon some riskless way of eliminating Heinrich. Meanwhile, she was visiting an interesting city; the shops were crammed with fine raiment and her purse was heavy; and there were thousands of men in St. Louis. There must be many men, she thought, who would be delighted to engage in a flirtation with a beautiful young matron whose husband was far upriver. She smiled, standing there at the window, and her premonition was strong that adventure lay just ahead.

*

But adventure, like happiness, can be capricious. In the lobby of her hotel, in the dining room, in other hotel dining rooms, Esperanza saw many attractive men, but they were always with other women. Sometimes they looked her way and even smiled; if only they had been unencumbered . . . Now and then, of course, men approached her, as men will always approach a luscious little lady who is unaccompanied, but most of them were old, or young sports in the wrong clothes with dandruff and maybe worse; and Esperanza had no intention of picking up with just anybody; she was not that desperate, quite; besides she was a lady.

On her fourth afternoon in town, she hired a carriage and drove to the sawmill and retail yard of the Buckmaster Lumber Company, thinking the superintendent might be a personable fellow. He was sixty-three years old and active in the Zion Methodist Church. Next day his wife, who was president of the Ladies' Aid and far from tongue-tied, called at the hotel and invited Esperanza out for church and Sunday dinner. It was as dreadful as possible. In his sermon the minister said many complimentary things about Gawd and the very peculiar institution of slavery; the Nigras, he said, were descendants of Cain and hence condemned by Gawd to expiate the sin of fratricide; in proof of this contention the minister pointed out that the sons of Cain often dwelt in canebrakes and cultivated sugar cane. A good Nigra, he said, could expect to live in heaven when he died, providing he knew his place and didn't get uppity. Let us pray. After the noon meal at the superintendent's home, attended by numerous offspring and grand-offspring of the host, Esperanza coolly brought out her French cigarettes and lighted up. It was a moment. Piety struggled with economics and Southern hospitality, and piety lost the battle, finally, although it was a good fight. When Esperanza, at about 2:00 P.M., said she must return to her hotel nobody insisted that she stay. Nor did the superintendent's wife trouble her further. A couple of afternoons later, sated with buying clothes and bracelets and necklaces, she strolled through the sunshine to a Grecian temple with marble columns where a crowd was gathered about the porch observing the workings of the peculiar institution. On a marble block, wearing cottonade, a young field hand stood. The day was humid, the bidding apathetic, the auctioneer red-faced. Now, gentlemen, he said, this here is just ridiculous. I ain't never seed anything like this here.

780

This boy Pete belonged to Miz Higgins of Boone County, she never wukked him hard or had to whup him or nothin', this here is a good boy, gentlemen, and I'm a-tellin' you all one thing, I just ain't a-goin' to entertain them kind of bids you've been makin' and knock this boy down for no measly 'mount of money—

Somebody said, "Esperanza! Imagine finding you here!"

She saw a smartly-dressed man with a fashionable mustache. It was Park Irwin, sheriff of Fox County, Wisconsin.

*

Seldom had she been gladder to see anybody. He had arrived, he told her, only this afternoon, having come on official business. A month ago, he said, a Fox County farmer had been robbed by his hired man; the fellow had fled south and had been apprehended in St. Louis. Park Irwin was here to take him back to New Empire for trial.

"Will you be here long?" she asked.

"Several days. He refuses to waive extradition, so I'll have to wait to get the papers signed."

"But that's wonderful! Is Mrs. Irwin with you?"

"No, she stayed home with the kids. I'm alone."

"And so am I, Park. And very lonesome, at least till now. I came on a shopping trip while Jim and Heinrich went to the drive. I'm staying at the Virginia Hotel. Where are you staying?"

"The Western Exchange. Why don't we have supper together?"

"I'd love that, Park."

Her sense of romance returned.

At the door of the Virginia Hotel he removed his hat and took her hand.

"Shall I call for you at seven?"

"That will be wonderful, Park."

He gave her hand a little squeeze.

*

They ate in the dining room of the Western Exchange Hotel, that same dining room where Caleb had taken her one evening many years ago after buying her a string of pearls. But the Western Exchange was no longer new and fashionable; the terrazzo had become worn and chipped, the velvet draperies fusty. Most of the customers were traveling salesmen or middle-aged couples from drab little mule towns. Esperanza was easily the most spectacular woman there with her diamond bracelet and matching ear-pendants and diamond-studded comb in her upswept hair; she wore a summer gown of cool turquoise which brought to notice the elusive coppery glow in her brown flesh. With their drinks, when she produced her cigarettes, Park Irwin smiled at her across the linen and silver.

781

"Esperanza . . . Could I ask a tremendous favor of you?"

"Why, certainly, Park."

"It's about your smoking in public. I don't mind—you know I don't—but if somebody from home would happen in here and see us together, and you smoking, the news would travel all over Fox County. Everybody would say I approved of you smoking. When a man's in politics he can't be too careful."

She didn't know whether to laugh or pout. Then it came to her that if she wished this jolly flirtation to continue, tact would be best.

"Why, of course, Park, I'll do whatever you say. Maybe we shouldn't be seen together in public at all. You know, with both of us married. Maybe we should eat in a private dining room."

"That isn't necessary. Nobody from home is likely to see us, but if anybody does we'll make up some story. We'll say I just happened across you here in the dining room—something like that."

"Ooo, yes. We mustn't let anybody know that we really—well—like each other . . . Ooo, maybe I shouldn't have said that. Maybe you don't like me."

"You know I do, Esperanza."

So the evening was off to a propitious start; and Park Irwin's concern about her possible adverse influence on his political career gave her a dazzling sense of power and made her realize that like all women she was potentially the most dangerous hazard a man was likely to encounter. Smiling at her companion, seducing him with eloquent eyes, she felt wicked and gay and warmly confident that the evening was unlikely to end in a dull manner. Once she asked:

"Do people in New Empire think it's scandalous that I smoke?"

"I'm afraid they do, Esperanza. But they know they have to like it or lump it, with your husband such a big man."

She was delighted.

"Ooo, maybe they look on me the way peasants look on some chic countess. Maybe they think I'm warm-blooded and devil-may-care and hard riding. Is that what they think?"

"I shouldn't wonder."

"And what do you think of me, Park?"

"I think you're very sweet and conscientious. I think you're so true-blue you would never tell your husband we saw each other in St. Louis."

"Ooo, no, I would never do that. No matter how much we see each other or what we do, I would never breathe a word to a soul."

"It will be our secret," he said.

After the meal, when they emerged to the street, the evening was balmy and young and magical with all the possibilities for pleasure which habitually beckon a man and woman in a strange city when their spouses are far away. Park Irwin hailed a smart carriage, its top folded back.

"Where to, suh?"

"Anywhere. Just drive around for a while."

It was like the fulfillment of Esperanza's daydreaming: the humid air soft on her cheeks, the night sky violet with a slice of apricot moon hanging in the west, a forbidden man beside her in a luxurious carriage. They passed the levee with its dozens of slant-moored steamboats, some dark save for their red and green lanterns, some blazing with lights, their valves hissing, their chimneys throwing out sparks, elegant packets impatient to take off for Minnesota Territory or the sugar coast of Louisiana. Drays were on the move; there was a mingled hubbub of curses and shouts and the rumble of hogsheads; occasionally, when down in the vitals of a boat a firebox door was opened, a flame-red surge of light poured from the engine room, silhouetting heavy-shouldered roustabouts and lean mud clerks. Downstream from the levee, connected with shore by rickety catwalks, houseboats showed dim lights in a vast amphibious slum; off in those reeking shadows a child was wailing hopelessly, and there were drunken hoots and the music of a fiddler scraping away at "Possum Up the Gum Tree."

The carriage turned west, moving where fortress-like warehouses fronted the gas-lit street and long-shadowed alley cats tiptoed in search of mice and love. The air smelled of sewerage and roasting coffee and rotten fruit.

Later, on a fine avenue, the carriage reached a public park where people on benches listened to military music.

"Concert tonight," the carriage driver said. "Band comes in once a week from Jefferson Barracks."

Park Irwin, after consulting Esperanza's wishes, ordered the carriage to stop and wait; as they crossed the greensward they were approached by an old woman selling violets; Esperanza selected a bunch and pinned it to her dress. They found a bench in the shadows at the rim of the crowd; in the strong light of the bandstand, where moths flittered and dobson flies careened, a uniformed man with a baton extorted from trombone and drum the old stirring marches of the United States Army, the same pieces Frosty McSwasey had heard before Bunker Hill and Caleb McSwasey had heard when he fought with Old Hickory and Andrew Jackson Gentry had heard at Camargo. Beside her on the bench, Esperanza was aware of Park Irwin's leg close to hers; once he took her hand. And on that warm evening with its smells of grass and bodies in starched dresses and cheap perfume, with its genteel lubricity always evoked by band concerts on American summer nights, Esperanza found herself stirred by the naked clasp of his hand; her body felt like ripe fruit; and her thoughts drifted to her room in the Virginia Hotel.

"Park," she said, in the carriage after the concert, "would you do something for me?"

He said he would.

"I bought a necklace today and I'm not sure it's my type. Maybe I should take it back. Would you give me your opinion?"

"I'd be glad to, Esperanza."

"It's in my room at the hotel," she said. "If you'd come up for a minute I'd put it on."

"Why, yes," he said, "yes."

And he squeezed her hand.

If any eyebrows were lifted when they crossed the lobby and climbed the stairs she didn't notice; it was a time for boldness, and she carried herself with arrogance. In the room she locked the door and closed the transom.

"All right, Park, you sit over there and close your eyes. When I've put on the necklace you can open them, and you'll get the full effect of how I look. I want your frank opinion."

She removed the jewels she had been wearing, rummaged among her lavish purchases and found the new necklace, a plain gold chain with a diamond lavaliere. After it was in place, she glanced at Park Irwin; he looked, she thought, faintly comic and ineffectual, such a tidy and self-consciously stylish man, sitting with his eyes shut. And with a pang she remembered her husband. If only he were different, a more ardent votary of the great and somewhat peculiar institution of marriage, she would be, she told herself, a faithful wife. But Jim neglected her shamefully. Chasing off to the pinery and leaving her. It would serve him right to be cuckolded.

"Now you may look," she said.

He said the necklace suited her fine and dandy.

"Are you sure, Park? It's not too plain?"

"Not at all. Just right."

"I have to be careful in wearing gold. Gold dresses or even gold jewelry. It has to be the right tone or it clashes with my hair."

"You look beautiful to me," he said.

Smiling—flirtations were such fun—she lighted a cigarette and lay on the bed, propped by fat pillows.

"I'm sorry if my smoking bothers you, dear," she said. "I picked up the habit in Santa Fe. All the girls smoke there. New Mexico is so different from Missouri or Wisconsin. It's so free and easy, everybody does as he pleases."

"It doesn't bother me," he said; but she could tell it did. He looked uneasy, as if remembering his constituents and his career and thinking how he would be a ruined man if some voter from New Empire should catch him in Mrs. Buckmaster's bedchamber. And thoughts like that must have been ice water and saltpeter, for he made no move to join her on the bed. She thought of something.

"Park . . ."

"Yes?"

784

"Something happened to me at that band concert, Park. An insect of some kind bit me."

"I'm sorry, Esperanza."

"It hurt too. I didn't like to jump and make a fuss, but it hurt really bad."

"Where did it sting you?"

"It got under my dress, Park, and crawled up. It stung me up—here. And it still hurts. I'm afraid it left a stinger in my flesh."

"That's a shame," he said.

"Park . . ."

"Yes."

"I hate to ask this, but would you do something for me? Would you find the stinger and pull it out?"

"Why," he said, "why, yes, I suppose—"

"After all, if you don't I'll have to go to a doctor. It's no worse for you to pull it out than for a doctor to. Now you just kneel here by the bed and—"

She lay back voluptuously, her eyes closed, while his tentative fingers searched for the stinger.

"I'm afraid it's higher than that, Park," she murmured. "And more on the inside of my thigh."

But before he found it a heavy knock fell on the door. He was up like a jack-in-a-box and back in his chair. Looking cross, Esperanza got to her feet and shook down her skirts. Then she unlocked the door. In the hall stood a stocky man in a black suit.

"Mrs. Buckmaster," he said, "I'm sorry to trouble you, but I'm the houseman." He entered the room and gazed sorrowfully at Park Irwin. "Ma'am, I'm sorry to have to say this, but I'm just doing my duty, ma'am. It's against the rules for a lady to entertain a gentleman in her room."

"Why," Esperanza said, "I've never been so insulted in my life! Are you implying—?"

"No, ma'am, I sure ain't. I'm just doing my duty, ma'am. I seen you two come in and I waited, thinking maybe the gentleman would leave. But he didn't leave, ma'am."

"I think you're horrible," Esperanza said. "Of all the low-down, suspicious—"

"I'll go now, Esperanza," Park Irwin said. "If it's the rules, it's the rules."

"Thank you, sir," the houseman said. "I know you two ain't up to no harm or nothing like that. It's just that we've got a rule—"

"But when will I see you again, Park?"

"Tomorrow evening, if you'd like. I'll call at seven. Good night." And he hurried into the hall.

"Ma'am," the houseman said, "I never meant—"

"Get out!" Esperanza said. "Get out and stay out!"

He obeyed; Esperanza flung herself down and beat the bed with clenched fists.

*

Next day the weather changed; clouds shambled overhead; and that evening, when Esperanza sat with Park Irwin in Sharf's Oyster House, a warm spring rain, steady and copious, was drumming down outside.

"Esperanza," Park said, over the brandy, "I had a talk with the sheriff today and he told me about a place that's—well—a little off-color. I don't know whether we should go there or not, but—"

"Where is it?"

She had been moody this evening, eating mechanically and staring at the raindrops streaking the lozenge-shaped windowpanes, for last night's interruption had left her disconsolate, but now she brightened.

"It's a big barge," Park Irwin said, "and I'm afraid it's very sinful. There's gambling, and they have naughty shows and women. But the sheriff says it's safe. He says the best people go there for a lark."

"Will you take me?"

"I don't know whether I should. Still, the sheriff says some of the nicest ladies in town have been seen there. But it's wicked."

"I want to go. Please take me, Park."

He consulted his watch.

"There will be a yawl at the levee at nine. We might drop in for an hour. Nobody knows exactly where the barge will be moored on any given night. They call it the *Dancing Annie,* and sometimes they tow it to the Missouri shore and sometimes to the Illinois. Or they tie up at some island."

On the way to the levee in their hack, with its livery-stable odors brought out by the damp weather, and its coziness with the rain tapping the roof, Esperanza and Park kissed a few times, and her spirits rose. But presently she drew away. Not that she wanted to, but it was amusing and better tactics to tease a man along, unless the man chanced to be Jim. She would have been delighted to fritter away the rest of her life being kissed by her husband, but he treated her shabbily. She wondered what he was doing tonight, up there in the pinery. Giving ear to Heinrich's lies about her, no doubt. She was serving him right, she thought, going to a wicked place with another man. The wickeder the better! She felt reckless.

When the yawl came steaming to its moorage, Esperanza and Park Irwin were not the only persons who left carriages and went aboard; in the dim cabin, there must have been two dozen pleasure seekers, all very gay, mostly young couples. Some of the men were handsome and all were interesting-looking, Esperanza thought, and of obviously good breeding; there was much talk of fast horses and losses at cards and of

786

visits to Southern plantations and to New Orleans; one man even told an anecdote about his gambling at Monte Carlo! Park Irwin, by comparison, seemed a dull country sheriff.

The yawl steamed downriver, and once, through the rain, Esperanza saw the lights and furnace-glow of a mill on the Missouri shore; a great sign said Buckmaster Lumber Company, New Empire and St. Louis. With the demand for lumber so brisk it was working night and day, like all the Buckmaster mills. She thought of Caleb; he had been a shrewd man. But then, remembering how he had died, and Lilith's suspicions, a shadow crossed her brain, and she wondered whether it was raining in New Empire, and whether the downpour was seeping into the cemetery earth and dripping into his eye-sockets. Nearly three years dead; he would be noseless now, and fleshless, lying with bony fingers on bony ribs. A shiver cooled her spine. Mustn't think about Caleb. He was dead . . . dead; and ghosts never walked the earth. Nigger superstitions.

All the way to an island in midstream, where the *Dancing Annie* was moored, her clammy mood continued; but she threw it off when she boarded the barge and entered the main gambling saloon, a spacious place of mirrors and red wallpaper and cigar smoke and voices and the music of a piano from an adjoining room. Underfoot the carpet was deep; capacious spittoons gleamed; and there were Negro boys in scarlet uniforms. Customers thronged the place, strolling about or patronizing every type of gambling yet devised by that cunning little animal, man. Crap tables were islands of clamor from which came shouts of "Little Phoebe" and "Ada Ross the stable hoss"; roulette wheels hummed and glittered; a faro bank was doing thriving business; two poker tables, with chairs for ten men at each, and all filled, were silent, deadly battle-grounds. Hundreds of lamps were burning in ornate chandeliers, and the air was rich with the mingled odors of tobacco and costly fabrics and powdered shoulders and liquor and whiffs of rainy night and rank river water, when the doors opened to admit newcomers.

"It's quite a place," Park Irwin said.

"I love it!"

She edged toward a roulette layout where cold-eyed men and ladies of the evening in picture hats were placing bets. The smoothly-revolving wheel and the table with its bright black-and-red squares fascinated her, for this was the great traditional game of archdukes and czarinas; she felt as if she had stepped into the pages of Stendhal. At the far edge of the table, the fingers of the two croupiers—only in Missouri they called them dealers—hovered over stacks of silver dollars and stacks of red and white and purple chips. The little ivory ball pursued its cheerful course around the perimeter of the wheel, slowing finally and clicking into a cup. Twenty-three. If one had placed a thousand dollars on number twenty-three, one would have been paid thirty-six thousand dollars. Esperanza's fingers brought a cautious twenty dollars from her purse. A dealer shoved twenty purple chips across the board. Then a species of stage fright seized her; everybody, she thought, must be whispering that Mrs. James L. Buckmaster of New Empire, Wisconsin, was about to make a fool of herself. She held the chips back; the ball went spinning and tumbled again into cup number twenty-three.

"A repeater," the dealer said. And he gave the ball another fillip.

This time, feeling audacious, Esperanza placed five chips on different numbers. She lost. She placed another five, lost again. And then, on impulse, she dropped her ten remaining chips on number twenty-eight, because she was twenty-eight years old.

"I'll lose," she thought, "and I'll stop."

The ball slowed, dropped into a cup, bounced out and landed snugly in cup twenty-eight.

She experienced the bedazzlement and incredulity of sudden wealth. A bright wave of heat seemed to sweep her body; at her side Park Irwin murmured, "Golly." But nobody else seemed to think her winning remarkable. The dealer's fingers, swift and expert, clicked among the chips and shoved a great stack to her side of the table. She had won three-hundred-and-sixty dollars.

And now she felt she couldn't lose. Letting her original bet ride, she scattered chips with fine abandon. But it was possible to lose: the ball landed in cup one, and she had not bet on one. She placed more chips, this time with less abandon; number thirteen paid, and she had a chip on thirteen. She was in a fever now; nothing existed but the wheel and the table; the great cosmos of reeling suns and smoking godhead diminished and concentrated itself in an oblong of checkered red and black. She forgot where she was and the man at her side and the man in the New Empire graveyard. All the divinities perished, for her, save the goddess Chance. Her chips dwindled; a voice in her ear said:

"You're down to your original twenty, Esperanza. Better quit while you're even."

She seemed to waken as if from sorcery. She said:

"Yes . . . yes. But one more bet. I'll bet them all on—on five."

Heinrich was five years old; perhaps he would bring her luck.

The ball fell into cup ten.

Guided by Park Irwin's hand on her elbow, she left the table. Heinrich! Why had she been so mad as to believe Heinrich would bring her luck! Bad luck!—that was all he had ever brought. The lying little Judas!

"Too bad you lost," Park said. "Twenty dollars is a lot of money."

"Easy come, easy go," she said.

They passed into the adjoining room where a tremendous mirror glittered behind a long bar; there were little tables scattered about; a Negro boy was rendering "Oh, Susannah," on a white piano with the front removed; a stage with burning footlights stretched across one end of the room, the pink curtains closed. They sat at a table and ordered drinks; Park was explaining that soon there would be entertainment on the stage. She finished her drink; another arrived; the room was filling. Park asked the waiter if Hank was here tonight, and presently a swarthy man with gold teeth came to the table and there was a long low conversation; Park gave the man money in exchange for a key. When he left Esperanza asked:

"Who was he?"

"The manager. He was telling me about another entertainment in Parlor A. But it doesn't start till later."

"What was the key for?"

"That's a secret."

"Ooo, I love secrets. What is it?"

"It's a surprise," he said. "You'll like it better if you wait."

The piano struck up a piece with an African throb and the pink curtains swept apart; a company of blackface minstrels sang about the South of fantasy, that land of sweet-potato vines and whistling redbirds and river bends and sycamore bottoms and kind old masters cold in death; and then two comedians took over, the burden of their dialogue being that the natural functions of excretion and reproduction were not without humor. Everybody laughed, although they were the deathless jokes that had been repeated for generations in the horsesheds behind rural churches. And then a girl came onstage and sang.

She was young and brightly mulatto, with a shining mass of purple-black hair and a figure from an adolescent's dream; she wore a brief yellow skirt and a froth of cream and crimson underskirts; her shapely legs were clad in yellow silk stockings with purple clocks. And while the piano tinkled accompaniment, she strutted and slapped her thighs and cakewalked and sang, her voice rich and swampy:

> *"Oh, loaded my gun an' went a-huntin',*
> *Found me a yaller gal wearin' buttons,*
> *And oh, gee, you all should see*
> *What dat yaller gal done to me.*
> *But oh, good sir, you should hear her purr*
> *When I done what I done to her . . ."*

Applause was thunderous; the curtains swept shut; more applause; so the curtains opened and the girl reappeared and sang a comical number about the sexual embarrassment of a mule that fell in love. That ended the entertainment; another show in an hour, folks, the man named Hank announced; and presently in the bright unsteady room Esperanza saw the mulatto girl on Hank's arm, strolling among the tables. When they came closer, the girl glanced at Esperanza, and glanced again. Her face was serious now, and she whispered to Hank. He nodded and approached the table.

"Ma'am," he said, "my entertainer wanted me to ask you a question. I hope you don't mind, ma'am. She wants to know if you're Miss Esperanza Zumwalt."

Everything had become odd; Esperanza said:

"That was my maiden name. I'm Mrs. Buckmaster now."

"Well, ma'am, that gal of mine—and she's a two thousand dollar nigger and worth every cent of it—would like to speak to you, if it's all right. Would you do that, ma'am?"

"Of course. Bring her over."

The girl showed a certain diffidence, when she approached.

"Miss Esperanza," she said, "you don't remember me, but I'm Viola."

"You're who?"

"Viola Zumwalt. Remember Winola and Viola? We come to St. Louis with you and Mistah McSwasey and our mammy."

"Oh. Oh, yes," Esperanza said, "of course I remember. You're Lilith's daughter."

"That's right, ma'am. Mistah McSwasey sell us soon as we hit town. Sell us to Mistah Devereux. My, my, and wasn't *he* something."

She giggled.

"Yes," Esperanza said, "yes, I remember. And how is Winola?"

"Just fine, ma'am. Or was, last I heered. When Mistah Devereux died—and that was kind of a relief, ma'am—we was sold separate. Me, I went to Mistah Crocker. Mistah Henry Kozol buys me from Mistah Crocker. Pays two thousand dollars for me—yes, ma'am, I is very valuable. But Winola she was sold to a gentleman from New Orleans. She's living high down there, I hear tell, and has got three children. Me, I got just the two. One by Mistah Crocker and one by Mistah Henry here. Both girls, ma'am."

"And real lookers," Mr. Henry Kozol said. "Worth a thousand apiece on the hoof right now."

"But you're not *going* to sell them," Viola said.

"Ain't I?" Mr. Kozol said, chuckling, and he winked at Park Irwin. Esperanza said, "Lilith will be glad to hear news of you."

"Oh, ma'am, is she still alive? I was wondering, but I hated to ask."

"Very much alive. She speaks of you girls often. And of Wisdom."

"She always was a-speakin' of him, ma'am. Me, I don't remember no Wisdom. Guess your daddy sell him before I recollect such things. Is your daddy—is he still alive?"

"Alive and prosperous," Esperanza said.

They chatted a few minutes longer, and Esperanza was just as glad she had been fortified with drinks when Viola asked for news of Mistah McSwasey. He's dead, she said, and it was painful for me. Please, let's not talk about it . . . Presently Mr. Kozol said it was time he and Viola

790

left these good people to themselves, and Viola said good-by, ma'am, it was sure a great pleasure to see you, and if you ever bring my mama with you to St. Louis, why look me up, just ask anybody about Mr. Kozol and they will direct you to his home . . . Then they left. And Esperanza, feeling the melancholy which always attends such encounters, and something more besides, said:

"Park, I want another drink. I need one. I feel old, Park. I feel—I feel all the past is right here."

But when her drink came, it failed to dispel the thick *Weltschmerz* that had settled on her spirits; in her profuse Teutonic melancholy, she sat staring at the table, a couple of tears, fat as burgomasters, waddling down her cheeks.

"Maybe the past is always right here," she said. "We walk through life and we get muddy. Burs get matted in our hair. Maybe that's all growing old amounts to, getting weighted down with mud and burs. What do you think, Park?"

"I think we need fresh air," he said; and he guided her outside to the roofed deck running around the barge. Far away through the rain, St. Louis was a smudge of light against the low sky. Walking the deck, they came to a scarlet door where a lantern hung; silver letters said, "Parlor A."

"Do you want to see another show, Esperanza?"

"I don't care, Park. Anything you want."

"They say it's wicked," he said. "The sheriff told me about it. Black girls wearing nothing but white boots, and white men wearing nothing but black boots."

"I don't care. No, I don't think I want to see it, now. Let's walk some more."

Rain sounded dreary on the roof; a steamboat came plowing upriver, feeling its way through the nasty weather. For a minute they stood watching it; then Park Irwin led her to another door, fitting a key into the lock. Inside, a dim lamp burned.

"But whose stateroom is this?" she asked.

"Ours," he said.

*

That was the story, with excisions and heightenings, which she confessed to her husband late on their third wedding anniversary in New Empire.

"Next day," she said, "I moved from the Virginia Hotel and Park moved from the Western Exchange. We went to the Senate Hotel and registered as man and wife. And we lived together, Jim, till Park left St. Louis. I had to tell you, lover, because I'm so frank. It's the only time I've ever been untrue to you, and my conscience has hurt. I suppose you'll bust Park Irwin now. I suppose he's through in politics. But I had to tell you."

There in the upstairs sitting room, Jim had poured himself another drink; he stood watching the slosh in the glass.

"Will you bust him, lover?"

"You mean in the snoot? No. And not in politics, either."

"But—well—I thought you'd be so mad—"

"Irwin's a good man," Jim said. "He knows how to take orders. Hell, no, I won't bust him. I'll elect him. I need a man like him in congress. I never blame a man for piling into bed when it's offered."

"But lover—"

"How was he?" Jim asked. "A pretty good logger?"

"No, Jim, he really wasn't. It really wasn't worth it. He wasn't very good."

"That's how I'd figure him," Jim said. "Trigger-happy."

"I know you're furious at me, lover, and I don't blame you. I'm furious at myself. Sometimes an awful devil gets into me and I'm just—bad. I have to be wicked. Maybe it's my Apache blood. I'm part Apache, you know. I can't say I'm ashamed of it either, they're so wild and brave. But I suppose it's hard to live with a wife like that. Caleb was always so jealous of me. Not that I blame him, lover, he was a dear man, and sometimes I did awful things. You wouldn't believe me if I'd tell you."

"Sure," Jim said, sloshing the liquor, "I'd believe you."

"No, you wouldn't, lover. I've done things so bad I can hardly believe it myself. I have a tender conscience too, and that makes it hard to live with myself after I've been so wicked. I think there's just one cure for me, Jim, I really do. I think there's just one way to get the meanness out of me. I think I need a good hiding."

"Jesus, you're a talker," he said.

"It's not just talk, lover, I mean it. I've been a bad girl and I should be punished. I think you should treat me the way you treated Gammerdinger. Cuff me around, lover, and make me howl. Our marriage would be better, darling, if you would. I've always needed somebody to make me behave. But somebody I love the way I love you. Somebody I respect. My father never did—I wouldn't have had it—and when Caleb used to abuse me I'd just get the sulks because I didn't love him, Jim, not really, not the way I love you. You're so big and strong, lover, and so wonderful, sometimes I wonder how I ever got you. Sometimes I think I don't even deserve you. You're such a wonderful lover and I was so bad, going to St. Louis and being untrue. I've been just a wicked little squaw, lover, and the only thing for you to do is take it out of my hide."

"Oh, hell," Jim said.

He finished his drink, placed the glass on the mantel and yawned and stretched deeply. Esperanza jumped to her feet.

"Jim!"

"Yeah?"

"Don't you—care? Doesn't it make you horribly jealous that I let Park Irwin—?"

Chin on chest, smiling, he stared down at her.

"Lady," he said, "I reckon you're bad news. Any way you figure it, you're bad news. God Almighty, you picked up Park Irwin and wiggled it under his nose and then you tattled. Jesus! Where I come from, you stand by your friends."

"The only reason I told you, Jim—and I see now that was a mistake —was because I'm so frank. The only reason I went to St. Louis was because you and Heinrich went to the pinery. You haven't treated me right, Jim. You've neglected me for Heinrich. You know you have. Sometimes I think you like him better than you like me."

"What if I do?"

She broke into tears then, and her clenched fists beat her husband's chest.

"Jim! God damn you, Jim, you've *got* to be jealous. You've *got* to punish me for the way I've been acting. What kind of husband are you, anyway, not to *care* if your wife goes to bed with other men? A person would think you didn't *love* me."

He smiled, but his voice was deadly:

"Love? What do you know about love? I get sick of hearing you talk about it."

"You don't! You don't love me," she wailed; and she dropped to her knees, her arms encircling his legs. "Tell me you love me, Jim! Tell me or I'll do something—awful. I just know I will."

"Get up," he said. "You're mussing my pants."

"Jim!" She threw herself to the floor. "Tell me, Jim! Kick me or beat me—anything—anything so I'll know you love me."

And she lay there sobbing and pounding the floor. Meanwhile, her husband carried his nightshirt to the bedroom across the hall and locked the door; that same bedroom where Caleb had slept the night Heinrich was born.

*

From then on, night after night, Jim occupied that bedroom, despite the fuss it raised with his marriage. To win him back Esperanza tried everything. But it was no good; he was indifferent. She began to think he really didn't love her; yet not actually. It was a temporary estrangement, that was all. And she knew the cause of that estrangement. Heinrich! He and Jim were thicker than dandelions on the courthouse lawn, swimming together every morning and discussing the fine points of saloon fighting. On the Fourth of July—it was one of those periods when she was not speaking to her husband—Heinrich and Jim arose

793

early and shot off firecrackers; they spent the day together at the celebration down on Winnebago Street; and in late afternoon they watched when a balloon ascended and a parachutist jumped, landing, of all places, in a tree in Judge Gentry's yard; it was the greatest excitement New Empire had enjoyed since Caleb and Dexter Yarlow were killed. And poor Esperanza missed it all.

But for days afterward she heard about it from Heinrich; he thought it would be great fun to jump from a balloon and land in a tree and keep yelling, as the parachutist did, here I am, help, help, get a ladder, somebody, and for God's sake help me out of this goddamned tree. To rescue the parachutist, the volunteer fire department responded briskly, along with several hundred well-wishers, including Judge Gentry, who, when the fellow was safely grounded, said, "Sir, would you care to imbibe a little brandy?" "Damned right," the balloonist said, "but what I really need is your backhouse."

No matter how Esperanza treated Jim, she continued loving and motherly with Heinrich, for she had a pretty fair hunch his days were numbered, the little marriage-breaker! But ways and means kept eluding her. After the balloonist excitement, she considered sewing together a parachute and offering Heinrich its use, if he cared to try leaping from the roof; but her common sense told her the authorities would grow curious about where he had got the contraption, and might blame her, as everybody was always blaming her for everything. Then one July morning she wakened with a brilliant idea. After breakfast it still seemed excellent; during the day she examined it carefully and could find no flaw; she slept with the idea, and when she wakened it seemed better than ever. But to carry it out, she would have to send Lilith away. Well, that shouldn't be difficult. That very afternoon the two women were sitting in the garden, and Esperanza told of her encounter in St. Louis with Viola Zumwalt Devereux Crocker Kozol.

"You seen her? Eee! Why ain't you told me before?"

"I knew you'd want to go right to St. Louis, and I didn't think I could spare you. But I've been thinking, Lilith. You're a good nigger—you've been like a mother to me—and it isn't right not to tell you."

"Viola! My, my. You happen to see Winola too?"

"She's in New Orleans, happy as can be. Viola will tell you all about her. Winola has three children, and Viola has two darling little girls."

"Grandchildren! Eee! After all these years. Um-m-m! Sure would like to give them gals a hug."

"I think I could spare you, Lilith. You could go on one of our Buckmaster boats, and it wouldn't cost you a cent. And I could let you have fifty dollars to buy your grandchildren presents."

"Sure would like to. But I don't know. That there St. Louis is a slave state, ain't it? Maybe I step off that boat and some white man nab me and sell me off somewheres."

Esperanza shook her head.

"Not for six months. A free nigger can go into Missouri and stay six months before they can arrest him and sell him."

"You sure 'bout that, Miss Esperanza?"

"That's what I heard. You could ask Judge Gentry to make sure."

"Um-m-m! Viola! She say anything about my boy Wisdom?"

"Yes," Esperanza said, "as a matter of fact she did. But I was holding it back as a surprise."

"She mentioned Wisdom? You sure? What she say? Where that boy?"

Esperanza smiled sweetly.

"I'd been drinking when I met Viola, so I may have misunderstood, but I think she said he's living in Illinois right across from St. Louis."

"Illinois? Wisdom is in Illinois? That's a free state, ain't it?"

"Oh, yes, Wisdom is free. That rancher who bought him in New Mexico set him free in his will. And Wisdom came east to Illinois and is doing well. He's married to a free nigger and they have four lovely children."

Lilith began to cry.

"Oh, Miss Esperanza, you ain't never knowed how I done eat out my heart for that boy. When your daddy sell him I thought per'aps I git over it some day, but I never has. Account of he was my first, I reckon. He was the cunningest child. Oh, Miss Esperanza, I just got to go. If it was just Viola, maybe not, but Wisdom—"

So three days later Lilith boarded the packet *Bonnie,* southbound.

*

Early one hot afternoon, at about the time Lilith in faraway Missouri was learning that her mistress had been mistaken concerning Wisdom's living in Illinois, Esperanza left the house and hailed Ferdinand Vogler in the garden.

"I want to talk with you about some planting," she said.

"*Ja,* my gracious lady."

"Not now. First I must put Heinrich to bed for his nap. I'll meet you here in half an hour."

Herr Vogler promised to be there.

In the house, Esperanza told her son to put on his nightgown and come to the upstairs sitting room, where she would tell him a story.

"About the three bears?" he asked.

"No, I have a wonderful new story today. It's all about a little boy who went up in a balloon."

And she kissed him.

In the upstairs sitting room, at the long mirror, she looked radiant and happy and not at all wicked. Then, as if rehearsing a role, she practiced looking innocent and grief-stunned, making her eyes large and round. Turning her head from side to side, admiring her angelic hair, she was so deeply absorbed that she did not hear her son entering the room; it gave her a start to see his reflection in the mirror, a little blond boy in a white muslin nightgown.

"Ooo!" she exclaimed, whirling. "You scared me, honey."

They both laughed.

Sitting on the chaise, she took him on her lap and told a fascinating story about a little boy she had met in St. Louis whose father was a balloonist. One day the little boy heard about a magic substance which when rubbed on one's elbows and ankles gave one the power to float in the air. Having procured the magic substance and applied it, the little boy prevailed upon his father to take him aloft. Up, up, up soared the balloon, and when it was high over the city the little boy climbed to the edge of the gondola and dived. But instead of plunging headlong he went floating through the lovely afternoon; gently as a feather he drifted to earth; people were astounded and asked him many questions. When he told of the magic substance they tried it, but it would not work for them: only for little boys who were five years old and had blond hair.

"I bought a jar of the magic substance," Esperanza said. "But it won't work for anybody but little boys."

"Where is it?"

"In the other room. But you don't want to try it now, dear. Perhaps after your nap."

"Let me try it now, mama. Please."

"But we don't have a balloon, honey," Esperanza said, laughing. "All you could do would be to jump from the back gallery. That wouldn't be so much fun as jumping from a balloon."

"Yes, it would, mama. Let me try it."

Esperanza hesitated.

"Please, mama."

"Well, maybe. Maybe just once, if you'll promise to take your nap right afterwards."

Heinrich promised; so his mother brought a jar of cold cream from the bedroom and spread a thin film of the magic substance on his ankles and elbows.

"It takes a little while for it to work," she said. "I'll go downstairs and out to the garden. I want to see you float. It's almost like flying, they say."

She carried the cold cream back to her dressing table, and when she returned to the sitting room she knelt and took Heinrich in her arms.

"Now remember, dear," she said, "wait till you see me talking with Ferdinand Vogler out on the garden path. You'll be up on the second-floor gallery. Call to us and wave. Then climb to the railing and dive.

My, but Mr. Vogler will be surprised to see you floating out over the garden."

She kissed her son and hurried downstairs; when she emerged to the garden it was as if she had used the magic substance herself, for she had a sensation of floating. She was breathing rapidly. But when she saw Ferdinand Vogler she tried to make her voice casual.

"Ferdinand," she said, leading the way to the path which ran from the house to the river, "I was wondering about planting rosemary along here. We could let it grow till it's a couple of feet tall, and then clip it. It should make a nice hedge."

Ferdinand thought this a capital idea.

"It would make a nice scent in the garden," Esperanza said. "Or perhaps we should alternate lavender with the rosemary. Or we could—"

She talked on, deeply absorbed with the problems of horticulture. Then from the house she heard a joyous shout, and she saw Heinrich, his nightgown white as an apparition, waving from the second-floor gallery.

"Oh, Lord," she said. "He was sound asleep when I left him. Now what's he up to?"

Heinrich climbed to the railing, teetered a second, and plunged.

Esperanza screamed.

*

When the *New Empire Chronicle* stated that Mrs. James L. Buckmaster, upon viewing the tragedy, fell into a faint, it was strangely enough telling the truth. Likewise when it stated that the mother was prostrated with grief. Hardly a second passed from the instant Heinrich left the railing till he landed on the back of his neck, but in that watchtick regrets overwhelmed Esperanza. Her knees gave way and she crumpled to the path.

Beside himself with this onrush of non-gardening duties, poor Ferdinand Vogler made the welkin ring with Teutonic cries of distress; the coachman came running, and three housemaids. Cold cloths were applied to Esperanza's forehead, and smelling salts to her nose; and when, supported by the gardener and the coachman, she was led past a sheet-covered figure, her sobbing was not spurious.

"It's not true, it's not, it can't be," she moaned; but it was.

She was put to bed; when Dr. Washburn arrived, too late to give aid to Heinrich, he was at least able to give comfort to Esperanza by means of narcotics; he came to the house again that evening, and twice the next day. Upon the doctor's advice, Esperanza's husband and her good friends, the Park Irwins and the Gentrys, tried to dissuade her from attending the funeral, a semiprivate affair in the downstairs drawing room; but she insisted on punishing herself. Her shoulders drooped, her feet were leaden, and behind a heavy black veil her face was haggard.

797

It was a beautiful afternoon when the white child's casket was carried to the white child's hearse drawn by white fairytale horses; the cortege moved slowly along the sandy road of Buckmaster's Island, across the bridge and south past the vast stacks of redolent pine in the retail yard of the Buckmaster Lumber Company, New Empire and St. Louis. At Winnebago Street, where saloon-loafers stood with uncovered heads, the procession turned east, passing the Buckmaster Building where Heinrich would never now rule the biggest business in Wisconsin.

At the east edge of town, in the place of cypress and vine-dripping urns, the cortege reached its destination at a grassy plot with a tall carved stone bearing the proud name: McSwasey. There, beside the aging grave of Caleb, and not far from the older grave of Andrew Jackson Gentry, hero of Buena Vista, a raw new grave awaited the hero's son. It looked very small. Well, he had been a small boy.

*

Without the ministrations of Dr. Washburn she couldn't have lived with herself, during those next days. She ate nearly nothing; she lay inert with remorse; she walked the garden paths wringing her hands; she heard the bells at midnight; she heard the sad far voices of steamboats plying the river in the Saints' Trade.

"It was that balloon—that balloon on the Fourth of July," she kept saying, whether there were any ears save hers to listen. "Jim took him to the celebration and he saw that parachutist. From then on he wanted to try a jump."

Lilith returned; and the tears shed on Buckmaster's Island would have floated a packet off a bar. Sometimes the two women drove through the hot summer weather to the new grave, carrying futile flowers.

James L. Buckmaster never accompanied the women on those expeditions, and the tears he shed were dry and secret and bitter. He looked older, that summer, and he was a quiet man. But now and again, on evenings when he wasn't having headaches, he left the great empty house and walked alone, perhaps stopping in at Rafferty's Saloon for the waters of Lethe; and sometimes he was not so quiet, there.

In the Moon of Falling Leaves, the time of leaf smoke and hazes and south-honking geese, he boarded the *Sol Klauber* and traveled up the big river, past the village of Lanceport, where somebody else he had loved lay in the stillnesses of forever. At Read's Landing, rip-roaring old Read's Landing, he inspected his rafting works at the mouth of the Chippewa; then, by canoe, went up that lovely northern river to his vast holdings in the pinery where fortunes came from. And rumors trickled back to New Empire that he was somewhat his old self in saloons, hard-drinking and hard-loving and ready to fight. But nobody would fight him any more. He was too big a man for just anybody to take on. And rumor said also that he went to the White Water House on the Chippewa, and sought love and comfort from Molly Fitzpatrick; Molly who had known her own sadnesses; Molly who always understood the troubled hearts of men; Molly, forty-seven years old now, and fat as a hog.

*

Righteousness triumphed, at the polls in November, aided by Buckmaster money and Buckmaster newsprint: Park Irwin was elected congressman. And righteousness needed all the volunteers which could be marshaled, for something poisonous and strange was abroad in the Republic; far ominous sounds could be heard from beyond the hills of tomorrow, for those with ears of the wise. A great sickness was threatening the Republic, the sweet shining old Republic of Thomas Jefferson and Philip Freneau and Andrew Jackson; the American Dream was changing into the American Nightmare. Voices were lifted in anger, north and south; Kansas was to bleed, and more than Kansas. But perhaps Congressman-elect Park Irwin, that sterling statesman, would patch everything up, when he reached Washington.

Immediately after the election, the Buckmasters would ordinarily have given a party to celebrate Mr. Irwin's victory, but in this time of lingering grief the lamps burned low in the house on the island, and the music of fiddles and the laughter of ladies were never heard. Still, one could not grieve forever; life had a way of going on; Heinrich's toys had been gathered together and packed away; the winds of November had scoured the spot where he fell; he would never come back; the river where he used to swim was frozen. And in the month of the shortest days, when Christmas was no longer to be an occasion of joy, but a day to be dreaded and lived through as best poor mortals could, it was decided in the Buckmaster household that perhaps the prospect of a great party on New Year's Eve would somehow mitigate the pangs of Christmas Eve. It didn't; but one couldn't be blamed for trying.

In any case, a party for New Year's Eve was planned, both to celebrate the death of wicked old 1854, and to provide a stirring send-off for Congressman-elect Irwin. An orchestra was hired; invitations were dispatched; the governor promised to attend; likewise the mayor, the city fathers, the county officials and all their ladies. To make the occasion a joyous one, no expense was being spared, said the *Chronicle,* which had picked up the odd American habit of measuring spiritual values in terms of specie.

Snow fell, during the week after Christmas, but on New Year's Eve the skies were clear and frigid. All that day great excitement had prevailed in the Buckmaster house; odors of baking bread and pie and cake, of roasting beef and ham and venison, had wafted from the kitchen; by early evening the dining-room table and buffets were heaped and burdened; silver was laid out, gleaming in the gas light; bottles of champagne and bourbon and French wine were awaiting their rendezvous with the tonsils of statesmen; and the whole house had the air of a lighted theater just before the customers arrive. The buffet was planned for nine; guests would start coming at eight; and at seven-thirty, when James L. Buckmaster crossed the hall from his bedroom to his wife's quarters, the tuning-up sounds of the orchestra could be heard from the music room downstairs.

Looking at Mr. Buckmaster, nobody would have supposed that once he had been a boy in moccasins stuffed with deer hair, singing about Faithful Nellie in a north woods saloon. He wore evening clothes now, long tails and all, and very handsome and polished he looked too, with his black hair and black heavy brows, his smooth-shaved dark skin, his imposing features. He carried himself with the habit of authority, as befitted a man who owned a dozen steamboats and a half-dozen newspapers and heaven knew how many lumber yards and sawmills and acres of stumpage. But his eyes were gentle tonight, as if the memory of the dead lingered there.

He found his wife at the long mirror in the upstairs sitting room, wearing an opulent gown of turquoise silk, exceedingly daring, her flesh the color of New Mexican bad lands, her hair the color of a Heidelberg barmaid's, diamonds sparkling at her wrists and throat. Kneeling beside her, Lilith was coping with some esoteric problem concerning the hang of the skirt.

"How do I look, lover?" Esperanza asked.

"Fine," Jim said.

"I want to look nice, lover, and make you proud of me. I feel—I don't know—so strange." She frowned. "It seems so sad, having a big party, and Heinrich not here. I've been thinking of him all day, lover. Sometimes I feel so guilty, as if it were my fault that he died."

"Forget it," Jim said.

"I can't, lover. I think I've dreamed about him every night. It was my fault, I suppose, for not sitting by his bed when he took his nap. But how was I to *know?*"

She shivered.

"It wasn't your fault," Jim said. "It wasn't anybody's."

"It was both our fault," she said. "You never should have taken him to watch that balloon. From then on that was all he could talk about."

"Will you please shut up?" Jim said in a low voice.

"Lover. Don't be cross. Ooo, I'm going to be gay tonight, lover. But it's hard to be gay, on New Year's Eve. I don't see why people always want to celebrate when all it means is that another year has gone and we're that much older. Just think, 1854 will never come again, lover. Never, never. And where do the years go? That's what bothers me. We tear sheet after sheet off the calendar, and before we know it we're old. Do you think the dead are with us, lover?"

"God, how do I know?"

"Yes, ma'am, they sure is," Lilith said, getting to her feet. "They is all around us, *all* the time, 'cepting we can't see 'em."

"Some people see them," Esperanza said. "Some people see ghosts."

"Yes, ma'am, ain't no question 'bout that. Folks with kidney trouble that have to git up in the night, *they* see 'em. You take it 'long about two or three in the mornin', them ghosts is just perambulating all over the place. You ever see a ghost, Mistah Jim?"

He smiled.

"No. But I knew a fellow once who saw snakes."

"Eee! Serpents of the Lord! What kind of snakes, Mistah Jim?"

"Tanglefoot terrors," Jim said.

Esperanza frowned.

"I wish you wouldn't joke about such things, lover. It's bad luck. You have the oddest sense of humor, dear. Half the time I don't know whether you're serious or not."

"These were serious," Jim said, "to the fellow that seen them."

"Saw them, lover. I wish you'd watch your grammar. I don't know what the governor will think, if you get your tenses and pronouns all mixed."

"Hell, the governor won't care. I could talk Chippeway and it would be all the same to him, so long as I own six newspapers."

Esperanza took her husband's arm and they went downstairs.

*

That was really a brilliant party, attended by the very cream of New Empire; between eight and nine there was a constant jingling of sleigh bells from outside, and a constant influx of social, intellectual and political leaders. And the governor certainly must not have been worried about Jim's grammar or anybody else's; he was friendly to everybody, shaking hands right and left, just as common as an old shoe. After the buffet supper, the orchestra moved into the front drawing room, which had been cleared for dancing; and the governor, (whose lady had remained in Madison), claimed the first waltz with Mrs. James L. Buckmaster. Esperanza should have been gay, whirling around the room in the arms of all that integrity and power; surely she counterfeited gaiety; but her feet were heavy and her midriff, at this time of the month, acrawl with cramps; and she kept thinking of another social occasion in this room when Heinrich lay in a white coffin. Closing her eyes, she remembered every detail of that funeral, and her heart was a bag of buckshot.

Odd how grief had attacked her after her son's death. She had never grieved for Caleb. Or for Dexter Yarlow. Or for Andrew Jackson Gentry really, or for the man in yellow shoes. She had been, she supposed, not without responsibility for all their deaths, but she had shed few tears. With Heinrich everything had been different, possibly because he was her own flesh and blood. Moreover, his death had not after all cured the mortal ailment of her marriage; not since June had Jim slept in the master's bedroom. Sometimes she thought he hated her. Well, maybe not that, for hate presupposed passion; hate in a marriage was often only love turned inside out. Jim was just—well—indifferent. Completely impersonal. It was as if she held absolutely no allure for him. In her grief for Heinrich, she wanted—or thought she wanted—another child; perhaps two more, perhaps a half dozen; she was willing to toss *Fruits of Philosophy* into the wastebasket; but when she mentioned the matter to Jim he smiled wryly and regarded her with cool gray eyes.

"No, puss," he said, "I don't think so. If you want kids, go ahead. What's wrong with Park Irwin, puss? But when I have a kid I want to be sure it's mine. With you as its mother, I never could be sure."

Arrgh! She had never been so insulted. Or so man-hungry. But not man-hungry for Park Irwin or any other man except Jim. And he always locked his bedroom door. What a way to run a marriage!

The music stopped; the governor bowed and thanked her for the dance; and after that she went waltzing with the district attorney, the county clerk, the assessor, the treasurer, the newly-elected sheriff and several county commissioners. She smiled brightly, her skirts dipped and swished, but on the whole those politicians must have been more expert at public speaking than at dancing: her slippers, so it seemed, had been squashed by the whole weight of Fox County government.

Jim did not ask her to dance. Nor did Park Irwin, the coward! Ever since their indiscretions in St. Louis, he must have been living in terror lest his sins and his constituents find him out. Well, she didn't care. The hell with him. If she hadn't been a woman of conscience, she could have simply ruined his political career by telling around town what had happened in St. Louis. But she wasn't, she thought, vindictive; that was one thing about her, she had a forgiving nature.

By eleven o'clock, much champagne and bourbon had been consumed; the music was spirited, the dance floor crowded; and the editor of the *Chronicle,* the old goat, invited her to dance.

"Why, I'd love to," she said, smiling brightly, "but first I must go upstairs and touch up my hair."

"It looks beautiful the way it is," he said. "Let's dance first."

What a stupid man!

"In five minutes," she said; and she slipped through the crowd and climbed the stairs and visited the bathroom. Then, in the sitting room of her suite, she eased off her slippers and lighted a cigarette. Her feet ached, her midriff ached, her brain ached. From far away the music drifted; she wished Jim would open the door and join her here on the chaise and tell her he loved her. He never would. The long ends of her mouth turned down and her eyes were sullen; she wondered what would ever happen to her marriage; it couldn't go on like this. Suddenly she was crying, and she thought she had reached the end of her resources. How fine her daydreams used to be long ago when Caleb was her husband and she yearned for Jim. She remembered how once she had thought it would be lovely to travel by canoe with Jim far into a wilderness of unexplored forests and tranquil lakes and swift trout streams; to go on and on and never return. Well, that would never happen now; her husband cared so little for her that he wouldn't even take her to the pinery.

Downstairs the music had stopped; she could hear, from time to time, a polite spatter of applause. She remembered then the program that had been planned, with speeches by the governor and Congressman-elect Irwin. She supposed she should return to the party. Pulling on her slippers, she stood up and went to the mirror, where she rearranged a couple of gold hairpins inlaid with diamonds. Tears had left her eyes red, but that couldn't be helped. She stepped back and surveyed herself, and then her attention was attracted by something she saw reflected beside her in the mirror. Without thinking, she exclaimed, "Heinrich! You should be in bed!" But instantly she remembered that her son was dead and would never lie in a bed again; yet in the looking glass she saw him as plain as she saw herself, a little blond boy in a white nightgown, smiling sweetly.

"Heinrich! You—"

Her mouth hung open and a trickle of ice water streaked her spine. Her throat tightened; she began breathing hard. She threw a forearm across her eyes, then looked again. In the mirror the little fellow could still be seen. She whirled.

And she saw him not in the mirror but in the room; he had moved to the vitrine, still smiling sweetly; he waved gaily, then stretched out his arms and started toward her, as if for a goodnight kiss. Her lips went numb as she thought how his lips would feel, cold and clammy, and like a woman trapped she backed to the mirror. Heinrich kept coming.

Esperanza screamed, the long pealing screech of terror sometimes heard at midnight in the awful deeps of a madhouse. Blubbering, she worked her way behind the chaise and toward the door. Still he followed, not in accusation, not in anger, but in smiling affection.

Snatching open the door, she ran along the hall; at the stairs she glanced back. And she knew then that this sweet little boy who followed was not a ghostly figure of her imagination; he was real. He had come back; Heinrich had come back.

She plunged down the stairs to the landing and looked around again. And there he stood on the top step, wearing the very nightgown he had worn the afternoon he died, his mouth and eyes smiling, his arms outstretched. And distinctly she heard his piping little voice.

"Kiss me, mama. Kiss me goodnight."

She screamed, again and again, and pitched recklessly down the stairs; people clustered at the drawing room door were glancing around; she plunged and clawed among them, into the bright room, where Congressman-elect Irwin stood speaking.

"Park!" she screamed. "Jim! Park! He's back. Heinrich has come back."

And she fell to the floor where she lay moaning.

She heard Dr. Washburn's voice, ordering everybody to stand back and give her air, but she had not fainted; and presently she was able to tell what she had seen.

"You don't believe me," she said. "I can tell you don't. But he was there. Heinrich has come back . . . Yes! Look! There he is now!"

And she pointed to the figure of her son coming among the guests. "He's there! Right there! Don't you see him?"

People shook their heads; and she knew then that she was the only refuge of sanity in a world of mad people.

✳

After that he never went away. She was given sedatives, of course, and put to bed, but Heinrich remained, even sleeping with her; and in the morning he kissed her awake. And surprisingly, his lips were not clammy but warm; his body was warm with life when she embraced him; that afternoon she held him on her lap and told him stories.

Dr. Washburn kept coming to see her, every day for about a month, and she could tell he thought she had all but lost her mind, and she told him as much.

"You think I'm crazy," she said. "Well, I'm not. I'm as sane as I ever was. It's you who is crazy. How you can look right at Heinrich and never see him I'll never know."

After that Dr. Washburn stopped coming.

Spring came, followed almost at once, so it seemed, by summer and autumn and winter and another spring; one day she and Heinrich would be strolling through the garden in July, holding lovely conversations with the flowers and the elves, and the next day the windows of the upstairs sitting room would be crusted with rime and tremendous freezing winds would be howling. Next morning April would have arrived. Other people thought April was a month but Esperanza and Heinrich knew wonderful secrets, such as that April was a *Fräulein* herding beautiful white geese along the garden path; they used to talk with her, in German. They talked with the winds too. The North Wind was actually a Prussian military man named General Heinrich von Zumwalt, red-faced and bad-tempered and huffing; but the West Wind was a *señorita* from Santa Fe with flashing dark eyes whose real name was Consuelo Delgado. They had many friends, Esperanza and Heinrich did, among the Other People.

And that was just as well, because the poor, dull insane people who thought they were sane avoided Esperanza and her son. Parties were never held any more in the house on Buckmaster's Island; callers seldom came. Park Irwin never came and Jim Buckmaster slept in his own bedroom. The Scandinavian maids used to stare strangely, when Esperanza and Heinrich, hand in hand, went chattering and laughing along the halls; and even Lilith rolled her eyes and avoided her mistress.

"You is *in*-sane, that's your trouble," Lilith said once; and Esperanza laughed merrily.

So the seasons passed, and the years, but Heinrich never grew a day older, for on his elbows and ankles a magic substance had been spread which kept him forever young, a five-year-old in a summer nightgown. Occasionally, Esperanza overheard insane persons like Ferdinand Vogler and the coachman and James L. Buckmaster talking about events and men of the mad world they lived in. Fort Sumter . . . seventy-five thousand volunteers . . . Robert E. Lee . . . Fort Donelson . . . no terms except an unconditional surrender can be accepted . . .

The world had gone mad.

XV

For some persons it was a pretty good war. If your name was U.S. Grant, and if you had gone to West Point and after graduation had been stuck away in dull army posts, and had taken to the bottle, and had been cashiered, and had thereafter eked out a living chopping wood and peddling it in St. Louis, and finally had operated a stinking tannery in Galena, Illinois; if you were a nobody like that, trained for nothing except the science of killing your fellow human beings, it was a pretty good war for you. Or say your name was Robert E. Lee. You too attended West Point, educated at the expense of the Federal government, and in the Mexican War you tasted blood and excitement, liking them very much, because with your Puritan streak war was the only permissible outlet for your blood lust; and in 1861 you commanded a sun-baked post away to hell and gone in the horrors of Texas, and then the politicians bungled the country into civil conflict, and you hotfooted it back to Old Virginny, and talked about loyalty to your native state and about honor, and resigned from the army of the country which had educated you, and whose interests you had sworn to defend, and received a commission from the roses-and-moonshine government at Richmond, and before long commanded the Army of Northern Virginia: not bad; not bad at all.

Nor was it a bad war for one William Tecumseh Sherman, working for the street railway company in St. Louis; or for one Thomas Jonathan Jackson, teaching mathematics to dullards at a one-horse military academy; or for a two-bit lawyer in Indiana named Lew Wallace; or, so far as that went, for a politician in Illinois named A. Lincoln, who got himself elected president, an office which served as a magnificent sounding board for his English prose, at the composition of which he happened to be a genius. Messrs. Jackson and Lincoln got themselves killed, of course, but their newspaper notices were very good.

Manufacturers of worthless blankets and shoddy uniforms found it a fine war, as did the horse merchants who bought up thousands of creaky nags, ready for the glue-works, and sold them to the government at a splendid profit; and it was an excellent war for shipping magnates, who, at a great price, chartered decaying vessels to the government as troop transports, and sent them to sea loaded with human freight at thrice their capacity; and all sorts of businessmen thought it a wonderful war because there were so many opportunities, such as buying condemned rifles from one governmental agency and selling them to another at a stupendous markup: if the rifles exploded in the hands of those who discharged them, and blinded them, well, it wasn't the seller's fault, business was business and *caveat emptor.*

From slum ratholes and from the Indian frontier congenital killers rallied to the colors; whole pirate crews of adventurers and looters enjoyed themselves, raping and marauding and burning; and any number of fourth-rate lawyers went in as colonels and worked themselves right up to be brigadier generals and for the next forty years orated from the hustings about how they had saved the country and should be rewarded at the public trough. But for some persons the war was not so good. Take, for instance, Rolfe Torkelsen.

*

In those bad decades after the war people were always telling him he should write up his experiences; he owed it to posterity, they said; and besides, if he were to publish a pamphlet called something like *Thrilling Experiences Fighting For the Flag* it would help him with the voters. He never did though. But he used to think about such a pamphlet, sitting in the law offices of Gentry & Torkelsen on the second floor of the Gentry Block, wondering how with pen and ink you could evoke for posterity not the war, for wars were all alike essentially, but the feel of those ante-bellum years when everything was falling apart and the rats were preparing to leave the ship of state and go south for the duration. Such a pamphlet, he thought, might begin in 1850 when he came to New Empire to study under Judge Gentry and the Republic seemed as solid as a marble building; or it might begin on that day when, after he received his license to practice, Judge Gentry invited him to become a partner in the firm; or best of all, perhaps, it should open on that April morning in 1858 when, at the request of James L. Buckmaster, he went to the Buckmaster Building for a conference which would result in that long journey to Washington City.

Looking back on that April morning, he could see himself walking west along Winnebago Street, twenty-two years old, an unlicked fighting cock, his hat at a jaunty angle, his shoulders muscular and his belly flat, five feet, seven inches tall, a hundred and fifty-five pounds of bone and gristle and brain, an up-and-coming young lawyer with a promising future who could have slept with any girl in Fox County if he had married her first. That was a fine time of life for any man, with your glands working gladly and your juices flowing freely and pretty girls saying, "Why, hello, Rolfe," and their mothers baiting matrimonial hooks with invitations to fried-chicken dinners. You couldn't blame them: he was the best catch in town, what with Judge Gentry and James L. Buckmaster giving him buggy rides on the road to success. And if he was careless about his clothes, pants needing pressing and shoes unshined, and if his hair, five minutes after being combed, was an unruly copper-blond tangle, and if his closely-pared fingernails sometimes showed smudgelines, why a good wife could always nag him into more care about his personal appearance. But he thought he wouldn't marry till he was about thirty; he hadn't met Sue Hatfield then.

He had, however, met Nixie Auerbach—Mrs. Harold Auerbach—and if he had any worries on that fine April morning they concerned her. A lawyer—an officer of the court, sir—couldn't be too circumspect about his conduct, Judge Gentry always said; a bar which could bestow a license to practice could also take it away; and with Nixie Auerbach he had been indiscreet. He had, (in the language of God's best-known work of fiction), lusted after his neighbor's wife and lain with her. Not that Harold Auerbach was actually Rolfe Torkelsen's neighbor, for Rolfe still lodged at Judge Gentry's, (the house being commodious, as the judge always put it, beyond the needs of him and his wife), and Mr. and Mrs. Harold Auerbach dwelt in honest poverty a block north of the Buckmaster Lumber Company yard in a house not at all commodious. Mr. Auerbach, a strapping Nordic of thirty-five, had been employed at the lumber company where he helped build up the great Northwest by loading lumber onto the wagons of farmers. In the evenings, being industrious and eager to amass enough capital to open a butcher shop, he had worked as janitor on the second floor of the Gentry Block.

But one morning last February in the lumber yard a silly sort of accident had incapacitated Harold Auerbach: as he strode toward Shed Number Three he stepped on a patch of ice and slipped, striking his head on the frozen ground. It knocked him unconscious; after they carried him home he remained unconscious for a week; and when he recovered his senses he almost wished he hadn't, for he was paralyzed from navel to toes. "Mr. Auerbach," the *Chronicle* said, "finds it impossible to move his lower limbs."

Had he been employed by most companies, Mr. Auerbach would have been in a pretty pickle, for in those days before socialistic thinking had corrupted the country his name would have been stricken from the payroll at 10:17 A.M. when the accident took place, and while his employers would have been glad to pray for his recovery they would not have been so foolish as to continue paying wages to a square-headed loafer who spent all his time in bed, especially in 1858 when the economy was still suffering from the panic of the previous year.

But Mr. Auerbach was lucky, if you wished to regard it as such. He had worked for James L. Buckmaster. And although James L. Buckmaster was in most respects an excellent businessman, adept at applying the estrapade to rival firms, he had a queer weakness which led him to take care of his employees even when sickness or accident ended their usefulness. Cynics whispered that Mr. Buckmaster pursued this mad course for selfish reasons, because with that policy prevailing the most skillful laborers in Wisconsin were eager to work for his company. Others said Mr. Buckmaster was shrewd enough to realize that when he thus befriended a stricken workman he was sure to control the votes of that man and his friends, thus adding to the growing power of the recently-organized Republican Party, which Mr. Buckmaster had joined. Less cynical persons said that Mr. Buckmaster's father had suffered an accident as a young man, and that this had softened his heart toward unfortunates. Still others said that Mr. Buckmaster had uncommonly strong loyalties; he believed in standing by his friends. Perhaps all those deductions were accurate. In any case, Mr. Buckmaster's conduct toward disabled work-men was both Un-American and un-businesslike, and his rivals seethed, but they could do nothing about it, the Buckmaster interests had grown so powerful.

With Mr. Auerbach unable to stir from bed, his wife, Nixie, called on Judge Gentry and asked that she be permitted to take over the duties as janitor.

"Madam," said the judge, in his best courtroom manner, "I am grieved to learn of your husband's indisposition. But *ne cede malis.* Of you let it be said, *alis volat propriis!"*

"I know, Judge, but I sure need the work."

"Varium et mutabile semper femina, and I would prefer a man for such menial tasks. However, in your case, *cadit quaestio. Exitus acta probat."*

Mrs. Auerbach began to cry; she thought he had refused; and her weeping distressed the poor old judge so much that he took care to ex-press himself in English.

"Madam! Shed not another tear! Of course you may have the job."

And so it was that every evening Mrs. Auerbach left her children in the care of a neighbor and came to the Gentry Block to wield a broom and a feather duster. She was twenty-nine, a full-blown Ceres with a voluptu-ous bosom, a rather pretty face and thick coils of red-gold hair. Rolfe Torkelsen, that diligent young attorney, had formed the habit in his student days of returning to the office after supper for several hours of study, and now that he was a member of the firm he continued the custom. During the day, he was so busy interviewing clients and direct-ing the student clerks that often he had no time to brief cases; in the evening he could work without interruption. The truth was that since receiving young Torkelsen into the firm, Judge Gentry, who was now sixty-eight, had unloaded most of his work onto his junior partner. With the chess games the judge played by mail, with his reading of Homer and Vergil, with his coin collection and his memories, he was really too busy to devote attention even to the legal affairs of the Buckmaster Lumber Company, the firm's leading client. Oh, he still came to the office every morning, unless the weather was nasty or he overslept, and he was always available for consultation with Rolfe, who never ceased to marvel at the tons of jurisprudence within that Websterian head; but after all when you are pushing seventy and your investments are gilt-edged you might as well give the rising generation a chance to untie the hoodwink from Justice. Actually, the judge had never been too enthusiastic about legal minutiae; in his secret self, the best he could say for the practice of law was that, in his case at least, it wasn't stealing.

Back in February, the last thought in Rolfe's mind was that he might become involved with the janitor's wife. Leaving the Gentry house on a winter evening, striding along through falling snow or on crunchy slush, he was much too occupied with replevins and appeals and last wills and testaments to give thought to Nixie Auerbach. When he reached Winnebago Street, he crossed to the north side and made his way toward Maizeroy's Grocery on the ground floor of the Gentry Block. Bordering the Maizeroy display windows on the west, a wooden door under an octagonal lamp opened onto the creaky stairs leading to second floor. Your way was lighted, in the daytime, by a window set into the west wall at the half-landing, and at night by a gas flare burning fuel furnished by Mr. Buckmaster's New Empire Public Service Company. In the upper corridor, the smells of old wood and the ghosts of long-dead cigars were enriched by the cooking odors seeping from the living quarters of the Maizeroy family, who had an apartment in the northwest portion of the building above their grocery. They were French people with grandchildren scattered all over Fox County, some as old as Quentin, their last unmarried son, who lived with them and drove the grocery wagon. He was twenty, dark and personable; sometimes Rolfe encountered him going out for the evening, for he was a gay dog.

During February and early March, when Rolfe entered the reception room of Gentry & Torkelsen, he seldom spoke more than a few words to Nixie Auerbach; she was the cleaning woman, that was all. He would say good evening, ask about her husband, learn that his condition was unchanged, and go on through a door in the west wall of the reception room, to his private office, where he would light the Welsbach burners in the chandelier, stir up the fire in the stove—and in the fireplace too if the weather was bitter—and settle at his desk where he would fill his pipe and go to work. His powers of concentration were so intense, trained as they had been at the chessboard, that before he knew it the courthouse clock would be striking eleven. Usually he knocked off then, standing up and stretching, his eyes resting on the framed motto, in ornamental type, that hung on the east wall above a bookcase: "Where law ends, anarchy begins." It was his favorite maxim in those years; the law was his mistress and his passion. Occasionally, after resting on the black leather sofa along the north wall, he would return to his desk and work till midnight, while on the east bookcase the clock, with its portrait of George Washington, ticked off the flying seconds of his youth.

He wanted to get ahead; some day he might run for district attorney or for the legislature; he might be a judge, some day. In the meantime, while his clients slept, and rival attorneys played whist or themselves slept, he consulted the calf-bound books strewed over his desk, searching out forgotten decisions, marshaling his ammunition, preparing his briefs with that lucidity and thoroughness and irrefutable logic which so delighted Judge Gentry.

He was not the courtroom orator that the judge had been, in his active days. But he knew the law. And he knew his Chitty too: all the wiles and stratagems and concealed daggers of nomology; he knew how to concede unimportant points and lead his rivals deep along the primrose path of their ignorance. Then—wham! Without warning he would quote a decision that would throw his opponents into confusion and galvanize the bench. He was a good office lawyer and a good trial lawyer, and he had taken to heart the ancient precept that the practice of law is not so much a science as an art. In addressing a jury he was seldom rhetorical; he was a friend and neighbor talking things over in the light of common sense. Even his careless personal grooming had its appeal. The jury saw a pleasant young man with curly Viking hair, with a short nose scattered with freckles, with tobacco-stained teeth and thick-fingered hands, with sharp blue eyes that were sometimes earnest and sometimes almost impish, as if he were a small boy who had just played some prank; his grin was engaging; the jury liked him. They liked the way he stood with hands in the pockets of his baggy pants; the way his coat sleeves always seemed about an inch too short, exposing his unfresh cuffs and thick wrists; they liked, even, his slips in grammar, wholly intentional; and they liked his reputation for refusing cases where the client was at fault. If a Dane chanced to be on the jury—and quite a few Danes had settled in Fox County—it did Rolfe Torkelsen's cause no harm when, seeming to search for an English expression, he gave up and tossed off a few words in Danish. He would go far, people said.

Occasionally on those nights when he worked late, he would meet Quentin Maizeroy on the stairs, returning from some saloon or fancy house or from sparking somebody's hired girl. Once even, on a blizzardy night, Rolfe found Quentin reeking of whiskey and sound asleep on the lower landing.

"Hey, Froggy," Rolfe said, for that was Quentin's nickname. "Wake up."

"Go to hell," Froggy said.

Rolfe carried him upstairs and into the Maizeroy apartment, where he left him on the couch in the living room. Froggy Maizeroy, it was obvious, was not going far.

*

Rolfe enjoyed a snifter of whiskey as well as anybody, and with his racial capacity for hard liquor he could have drunk Froggy Maizeroy under the table, but for the most part he avoided saloons. A lawyer's reputation, he deduced, was not enhanced by helling around. He avoided fancy houses also, confining his association with what the *Chronicle* called—God knew why—the gentle sex to nice young ladies from nice old families who lived in nice houses in the nice section of town neighboring Judge Gentry's Lexylvania. Some of them were lookers too, and all of them, so far as could be ascertained, were virgins. And Rolfe Torkelsen, with his opportunities thus delimited, was a virgin. His wild oats were still in the bin. About this he was not overjoyed, for he was twenty-two and full of health. But he couldn't quite figure how to alter his deplorable condition; not so long as he was a rising young lawyer in a gossipy town like New Empire. Logic should have told him that God in his wisdom had apportioned the sexes into two roughly equal groups, and that each group spent an amazing amount of time dreaming of intimacy with its counterpart, and that sooner or later, even in New Empire, some nice girl would say, "Isn't it quiet here in the parlor with the folks all asleep in bed," or that some young widow would turn up. But Rolfe Torkelsen did not believe in God, perhaps because as a preacher's son he had heard too much about the old gentleman, or because, as a student, he had devoured many a heretical volume in Judge Gentry's library.

Whether the judge, having read those rational authors, believed in God was a moot point. Rolfe used to ask him, but the judge always answered in Latin or Greek, smiling benevolently. In any case, the judge believed in attending church, and he urged Rolfe to do likewise. Rolfe refused, for he possessed that rarest trait of man, intellectual honesty.

"No, Judge," he said, "I'll not pretend to be what I'm not. I'll stay out of saloons and keep out of mischief, because a client wants a dependable lawyer. But I don't think a man who wants to win a lawsuit gives a damn about his counsel's religion. If I keep winning cases the clients will come. My religion is my own business."

"Sir, you are a stubborn Dane."

"That's right," Rolfe said, with his impish grin.

"I must say," the judge said, "that I admire your integrity. But your common sense in this matter is open to question. Some day you will be running for public office, and—"

"If I do," Rolfe said, "they'll take me as I am."

"A stubborn Dane," the judge repeated. "You remind me, sir, of General Andrew Jackson. Willful and intrepid. Our greatest president since Jefferson. Once in the Executive Mansion, sir, I broke bread with him. I—"

And the judge was off.

The summer before Harold Auerbach's accident, a wild evangelist had come to New Empire and held camp meetings in a cow pasture adjoining the cemetery east of town. From the tales Rolfe heard in the barber shop, (corroborated by a spurt in the obstetrical business nine months later), the meetings offered fine opportunity for young persons wishing to enter the kingdom of heaven, but he stayed away. When the evangelist moved on to greener cow pastures, the sexton of the cemetery was much relieved, according to rumor.

So the state of Rolfe Torkelsen's love life, or lack of it, was highly unsatisfactory in the winter and early spring of 1858, but then an occurrence took place which changed everything. Years later he could call to mind that occasion in late March when, after supper, he left Judge Gentry's house and walked toward his office. The sun had set not long before and the street was imbued with that tender light which prevails in northern latitudes before the oncoming of dusk. Overhead the elms were venturing into bud with that unwise optimism of growing things in early spring, and through the mild air came shouts of children at play. From the river, so recently unclogged of ice, the whistle of a Buckmaster packet could be heard; robins trilled; the moist earth exuded impalpable vapors; at the corner of Gentry Avenue and Winnebago Street small boys were playing marbles. It was not an evening for poring over calf-bound books. Outside the door leading up to his office he paused, tempted to chuck work this evening. But he opened the door.

Pale light came through the window at the half-landing, and the gas flare was burning. And on the stair, with a mop and a bucket of scrub-water, Nixie Auerbach was at work, leaning over, her skirts caught up out of the wet. Her legs were bare. And in that moment before she turned and shook down her skirts, Rolfe was treated to a splendid view of those splendid legs, the calves boldly convex, the flesh behind the knees dimpled with womanly tendons, the soft curves above the knees seductive.

"Oh," she said. "Mr. Torkelsen. You gave me a turn."

Well, she had given him a turn too. He asked about her husband, (the poor fellow was no better), and for a minute he lingered there, commenting on the early arrival of spring.

"Yes," she said, "if it keeps up like this I'll be putting in garden soon."

He went on upstairs, but that evening his concentration was less complete. He kept thinking of those sturdy peasant legs of Nixie Auerbach. He remembered her coils of red-gold hair too, and how, there on the stair, she had brushed a strand away for her forehead with the back of her wrist. He remembered her full peasant bosom and the rich, earthy quality of her voice.

"Hell," he said, and tried to work. He heard the courthouse clock striking eight-thirty and nine and nine-thirty; he stood up and paced the room, from the tall walnut bookcases on the west to the low bookcase on the east; his pipe kept going out. And remembering how she had spoken of putting in garden he imagined her, barefoot perhaps, standing in the rich Wisconsin earth, her skirt caught up; and he imagined her leaning over to drop seeds into the loam.

At ten he left the office, but instead of going directly home he took a walk, west along Winnebago to Front Street, north past the yard of the Buckmaster Lumber Company, till he was passing the modest dwelling of Mr. and Mrs. Harold Auerbach, an L-shaped house behind a picket fence that needed paint. No lights showed there. In the shadows he stopped, staring at the house, imagining Mrs. Auerbach lying in bed.

"Hell," he said.

Next evening he did not return to the office, nor the next. But he kept thinking about Mrs. Harold Auerbach. Student that he was of the law, with its realism and cynicism, he told himself that a sure way to trouble was to become involved with a married woman. In the law library of Gentry & Torkelsen, a great many of the cases dealt with the entanglements resulting from the indiscretions of men who possessed what one old jurist had called "a lickerish nature."

On the third evening, after admonishing himself to control what indubitably was a lickerish nature, he nerved himself to return to his office. As he climbed the stairs his heart was pounding; he paused with a dry tongue outside the door lettered "Gentry & Torkelsen, Attorneys-at-Law." Taking a breath, he opened the door.

And he saw, there in the reception room, not Mrs. Auerbach but an old hag, toothless as a witch. She was, she said, a neighbor of Mrs. Auerbach, substituting for her tonight. Mrs. Auerbach was in bed with a cold; the grippe maybe. Rolfe experienced relief—and disappointment. That evening, he was able to concentrate better, although not so well as before he had glimpsed Mrs. Auerbach's legs.

Legs, he kept thinking. Not lower extremities; not lower limbs; but legs, bare and saucy. Legs were a hush subject, in those years when he had come to manhood; you deduced that girls must have them, because they managed locomotion; but they were not to be mentioned, not to be thought of, by pure men. Legs. Even the word had a breathless, aphrodisiac quality.

Next evening the hag substituted for Mrs. Auerbach again; for an entire week of evenings. Dutifully, Rolfe sat at his desk working, biting his pipe, while the juices of his manhood burbled. A couple of times, after work, he walked past the Auerbach house. Every evening he asked the hag about Mrs. Auerbach's health. She was getting better, the hag said.

And then, on the evening of April first, when he entered the reception room, he found that Mrs. Auerbach had returned. Her back was to him, when he opened the door, and she was reaching with a feather duster to destroy a cobweb hanging from the ceiling. She was on tiptoe, her dress wrinkled with the movement of her body. When he closed the door she looked around.

"Oh," she said, "Mr. Torkelsen."

He told her he was sorry she had been sick. She was sorry too. But she was feeling fine now.

"You certainly look fine," Rolfe said. And he added, "We've missed you around here."

For a moment her brown eyes—the rich brown eyes that go with red hair—met his; then her gaze dropped. She flushed. Rolfe's breath was coming faster; he thought of her husband, unable to move from the waist down. And he remembered a Danish proverb his father used to quote: drink your beer before it gets warm, kiss your love before she goes to sleep.

So he stepped forward, took Mrs. Auerbach into his arms and kissed her. Her lips were full and moist and clinging, her body willing.

"Why, Mr. Torkelsen," she said. "I—"

He led her into his private office and locked the door.

*

From then on he was involved, and he used to wonder how it would ever end. Not that he wanted it to end, actually. He was never in love with Mrs. Auerbach—her mind was banal—but certainly he was attracted by her earthy body. She too was of a lickerish nature, and with her husband incapacitated she was gladder than ever, now, to go in the evenings to the Gentry Block. All that spring, till Rolfe went away to Washington City with Jim Buckmaster, and all that summer and fall after he returned, he and Mrs. Auerbach had a pleasant time of it in his private office. He used to worry about the consequences of those evenings, not because he felt sinful—on the contrary, he had never felt better in his life—but because a lawyer, like a doctor and a preacher, was a public character; people expected them to behave. He remembered how it had been in his boyhood, back in Denmark; parishioners were always sniping at the Reverend Thorvald Torkelsen. Thor let them snipe. He was a long-legged, fiery, liberal preacher, independent and freedom-loving; if he wished to take his family to the street circus in Vordingborg, no gossiping members of his congregation were going to stop him.

Rolfe was nearly four then, and he remembered that journey into Vordingborg, a few miles south and east of the parsonage where he had been born in 1836. They traveled in a buggy pulled at a leisurely pace by an old mare, Thor and Rolfe and his baby sister, Jartrud, and his mother, Helsa. His mother, he thought, was a beautiful lady, and he was quite correct: a yellow-haired young woman with a fine figure and skin like Danish cream. Thor had met her when he was a divinity student in Copenhagen, her father being Peder Willemssen, proprietor of a *Boghandel* on the Frederiksberggade. Thor used to go to that shop, with its huge brass book hanging outside, and browse for hours. Peder Willemssen, a man with icy white hair and icy blue eyes and white skin, was somewhat irascible, his particular grudge being against customers who took a book from a shelf, examined it, and returned it to the wrong place. One afternoon he accused Thorvald Torkelsen of this crime.

Thor lacked the spurious humility of the ordinary divinity student; his father, who was an assistant curator of the National Museum in Copenhagen, always said that if the Danes were the Irish of the Scandinavians, (and he believed they were), then his son Thor was a prime example of this interesting ethnological peculiarity. So when Peder Willemssen barked at Thor, Thor barked right back. Hearing the commotion, Helsa Willemssen came from the back room and prevented bloodshed. Thor married her, after being ordained, and carried her off to that parsonage at the south end of Zealand, which was a good enough fate, Peder Willemssen said, for the bride of a man who would replace a book on the wrong shelf.

But Peder Willemssen was totally oppidan, so enamored of Copenhagen that he would hardly venture into the Dyrehaven of a Sunday; actually, the Zealand countryside was lovely beyond belief, at least in Rolfe's memory. The parsonage was a fairytale cottage, half-timbered and thatch-roofed, like something out of Hans Christian Andersen; surrounded by an ancient boxwood hedge, with daffodils and poppies in the front yard, it stood on the north side of a pastoral road in a landscape of slow-turning windmills of the Dutch type, and of milch cows knee-deep in lush pastures. Every May the storks returned, to refurbish their nest of sticks which topped the parsonage chimney, and when they departed in August, Rolfe's father, puffing his porcelain pipe, would open a huge atlas and with a long forefinger trace their flight to Turkey and the Holy Land and at last to South Africa. But Thor never told his son that storks brought babies; he told him the truth.

Nor did Thor hold with such nonsense as that the devil habitually visited the church at midnight when God-fearing persons were deep in their feather beds. The church, a white structure with a thick corbie-stepped gable, was located west of the parsonage beyond the churchyard. On summer afternoons, Rolfe used to squirm through the boxwood hedge and tiptoe among the old gravestones and cedar trees to the cat-door in the east wall of the church. The cat-door had been placed there a century before, for the convenience of the devil, and Rolfe scanned the grass hoping to find traces of the evil one's footprints. He remembered the deep country silence, broken only by the cooing of doves and the distant lowing of cows. When Thor heard what his son had been up to, he threw back his head and laughed, and then, with eyes flashing, spoke in his positive voice about the vulnerability of religion to superstition: he believed in neither hell nor the devil nor the wrath of the Old Testament Jehovah: Christ was his boy.

Most of the congregation, however, were convinced that the cat-door was regularly used; and the worldliness of their young pastor disquieted them. He was, they whispered, hardly better than a Grundtvigian. Nor were their suspicions wide of the mark, for ever since his student days Thorvald Torkelsen had followed with interest the career of Nikolai Frederid Severin Grundtvig, that black swan of the Danish National Church. Indeed, on the shelves of Thor's study were several volumes by the Rev. Mr. Grundtvig, not only *The Mythology of the North* but also that violent and bitter work, *A Short Sketch of the World's Chronicle.* A number of years before, the Rev. Mr. Grundtvig had attacked stuffy old Dr. Clausen, professor of theology at the University of Copenhagen, declaring him a heretic. Dr. Clausen promptly sued for libel, and Mr. Grundtvig was fined and booted out of the state church.

Mr. Grundtvig came up fighting. Becoming an itinerant preacher, he gathered about himself a band of disciples who shared his opinion that the state church was too rigid, too given to Pharisaism; like their leader, they believed that if one accepted the Apostles' Creed, the Communion Service and lived a moderately good life, one was an acceptable Christian. They gloried in the bloody old Norse myths; and they called themselves Happy Christians, believing that life should be lived joyfully. The state church was aghast. Then when King Christian VIII ascended the throne, he astonished everybody by appointing the Rev. Mr. Grundtvig chaplain of the Workhouse Chapel in Copenhagen, where he preached lustily, converting many persons to his sect. Thorvald Torkelsen had never heard the Rev. Mr. Grundtvig preach, but he intended to, next time he visited the capital.

Meanwhile, he enjoyed his pipe and his *geitost* and his fiery *aquavit,* which he washed down with lager; he loved the annual celebration on Midsummer Eve, with its bonfires and fireworks and dancing; and if he wished to take his family to the street circus in Vordingborg, the disapproval of his congregation could not stop him. And they certainly did disapprove; a few evenings later a delegation of parishioners called at the parsonage, and angry voices could be heard from the parlor. Pastor Torkelsen's voice was angriest of all; listening outside the door, little Rolfe could imagine his father, long and lean and vehement, his dark-blond hair rumpled, his jaw outthrust, standing in the midst of those thick-bodied peasants and laying down the law. He believed a pastor should run his church, just as he believed a husband should be head of the house. But he was a fine husband and father, never a tyrant, for he was convinced that one's wife and children were human beings with rights like anybody else.

So those were happy years in that country parsonage, with white geese stepping sedately in the farmyard and with whiffs of swine from the piggery and the good bovine odor of fat-uddered cows. One spring the whole family took an excursion to the island of Möen, where the anemones were blossoming in the great beech forest and the sea flung itself against the chalk cliffs. And occasionally Thor took his son to the public baths in Vordingborg, with their clouds of steam and smells of sweat and rubbing alcohol, for Pastor Torkelsen shared that ardent Scandinavian faith in the efficacy of steam cleaning, declaring that in creating sweat-glands the Lord had given man built-in physicians. As a youngster in Copenhagen, before entering the university, he had persuaded one Laust Nordentoft, who operated a bathing establishment, to teach him the craft of the masseur. Laust obliged, and during Thor's student days, between bouts with Greek verbs, he earned spending money by kneading the muscles of burghers obese from too much *røget aal* and *rejer* and *ryper* with sour-cream sauce.

During the winter when Rolfe became four, his father made a visit to Copenhagen, and while there, naturally, he looked in on his old friend Laust Nordentoft. And Laust, a jolly and not unworldly fat man, had become a convert to the sect of the Rev. Mr. Grundtvig. He invited Pastor Torkelsen to accompany him to the Workhouse Chapel.

Pastor Grundtvig must have been in especially good form that day, or perhaps Thor was ripe for Happy Christianity; in any case, he was impressed. Following the sermon, he enjoyed a long visit with Pastor Grundtvig in a nearby cafe, where the Lim Fjord oysters were especially tasty, and the Tuborg lager not bad; and after returning to the parsonage near Vordingborg he paced his study in self-examination. And the following Sunday, he tossed a grenade from the pulpit: he was resigning from the National Church and joining the Grundtvigians. Not since Martin Luther hurled the ink bottle had there been such ecclesiastical excitement. Following the service, women in black silk and men with silver watch-chains across huge bellies gathered in groups outside the church, talking angrily and even waving their fists; not many days later, the Torkelsen family left that land of green vistas and moved to Copenhagen.

Thor was an outcast now, a pastor without a pastorate. He preached on street corners, in lofts to sailors, in grogshops; and to support his family he returned to his old trade of masseur in Laust Nordentoft's bathhouse. The family—soon augmented by another son, Erik—dwelt above a bakery in an apartment overlooking the Nyhavn Canal. That was a section of sailors' cafes and lodgings; Rolfe remembered the huge cruller, twisted in bright brass, that hung outside the pastry shop; he remembered giants with blond beards and swarthy men with gold rings in their ears from the seas of the world. Things were not going so well with the family, now that Thor was off the payroll of the state church. Peder Willemssen was disgusted, but what, he asked, could be expected from a man who would replace a book on the wrong shelf? Thor's father, however, helped out with small sums. He was half a Grundtvigian himself, because of the sect's emphasis on the myths of Scandia, but in his position at the National Museum he dared not declare himself openly.

Still, they had their fun, the Torkelsens did; they always had fun. His father taught Rolfe chess, and there were excursions about the city, that enchanted fairytale city with its twisted spires and towers with golden balls and its roofs shining with copper. Years later, Rolfe could close his eyes and bring to mind the public squares with statues and fountains, the old women in the flower markets, the swans swimming in canals, the shop windows with their gleaming silver and crackle-glaze ware. Cobbled streets, narrow and winding, were in those memories, and the copper dragons standing on their heads atop the Børsen.

A few months after the Torkelsens moved to Copenhagen, Laust Nordentoft sold his bathhouse to a fellow Grundtvigian and set out for the New World; returning travelers among his customers had spoken of opportunities there. And he urged Pastor Torkelsen to follow. Thor was tempted but he hesitated; when one had a wife and three children such a move was formidable. But letters kept coming from Laust Nordentoft, full of enthusiasm for America; he had got wind of some excellent saline springs out in Indiana; and he said that if, after an investigation, he decided to set up in business there, Thor could always have a job in his establishment. Meanwhile, there were many watering places in the United States where Thor could find work. For instance, Laust had heard of a resort at Piedmont Springs in the upcountry of South Carolina; he was certain a Danish masseur, so superior to the American variety, could get work at Piedmont Springs.

So in March 1841, aided by a loan from Thor's father, the family set sail from Copenhagen, bound for Charleston, South Carolina, of all places. Perhaps the call of adventure, never really quiescent in Viking blood, contributed to Thor's decision; and then too the Rev. Mr. Grundtvig was enthusiastic about his disciple's going, for he had a dream of establishing a little Denmark in the United States where his doctrine of Happy Christianity could be proclaimed.

In Charleston, Thor lasted about ten days. He would have been urged to leave sooner, except his divinity school English was not readily understood. Trouble was, on his second day in town he attended a slave auction, and instantly became a full-fledged abolitionist. When the Charleston gentlemen at last understood that this wild Dane was advocating immediate emancipation of the slaves, he was advised to make tracks for the North unless he wished to be flogged, tarred and feathered, or subjected to even more vigorous methods of Carolinian argumentation. Thor could take a hint; and for the next year he and his family wandered about the tolerant North, where he was hired by various bathhouse owners and rather promptly fired for expressing the views he had discovered in the Constitution of the United States and in the Bible. He had lost touch with Laust Nordentoft. Then in the summer of 1842, while working at a Swedish Bath in Pittsburgh, he received a letter from Laust, many months old; it had traveled to Thor's father in Copenhagen and back to Pittsburgh. Laust had bought the Fountain House in Elysian Springs, Indiana; business was excellent; if Thor would join him there, he would give him a job and build him a log church where he could preach the gospel according to Grundtvig. A few days after the letter arrived, the Torkelsens boarded a river steamboat for New Albany, Indiana; from there they traveled by stagecoach through the tumbled hill country to Elysian Springs. And that was where Rolfe met Judge Sophronicus Gentry.

*

In those days Elysian Springs was not so much a town as a community in that limestone region of steep hills and haunted valleys and mysterious caves and lost rivers and tangles of briers and sassafras. After a day's travel northwest from New Albany, along the old Indian trail and the older buffalo trace, your stagecoach turned south and followed a narrow valley thickly-wooded with persimmon and tulip trees and jack oak, coming presently to a place where the valley broadened and sent one fork to the southeast and another to the southwest. Here, on the west side of the road, on a lawn among sugar trees and hickories, stood a rambling wooden hotel, three stories high and white-painted, with airy verandas. This was the Fountain House.

North of the hotel, a wooden bathhouse had been built to enclose artesian springs whose saline-sulphur waters came pouring forth, exuding steam and a stench of brimstone. Legend had it that for centuries the Indian Nations had declared this valley neutral ground where rheumatic warriors and constipated squaws could come and take the salubrious waters. Deer used to frequent the valley, and bear and panther, to lick the salty crust which formed around the springs.

By the 1840's, Elysian Springs was favorably known for hundreds of miles. Farmers drove for days to reach the place, whole families of farmers, and when they left, their lumber wagons were loaded with jugs of the medicinal waters. Southern planters and Southern belles came, their digestive systems coated with the greasy residue of old Southern cooking, their colons a-wiggle with tapeworms. Lumbago, misery in the joints, aching shoulders, lazy livers, sore muscles—all were said to be benefited by the waters. Laust Nordentoft was doing well.

Judge and Mrs. Sophronicus Gentry first visited Elysian Springs in the summer of 1844, on their way home to Wisconsin after a trip to Lexington, Kentucky. Like so many intellectuals, the judge was afflicted with a weak back and a languid colon, so every day in the bathhouse he took the cure, which included lying on a table and submitting to the pummeling of a steely-fingered masseur named Thorvald Torkelsen. One day as the judge lay there, he happened to mention he had been Kentucky born and bred. Thor, who was always glad to argue the merits of his favorite reform, assumed at once that his customer sympathized with the peculiar institution, so immediately he launched into a tirade upbraiding Sophronicus for owning Negroes and kicking them around

820

and separating families when he sold them and in general treating them almost as bad as if they were white men in prison.

"Sir," Sophronicus thundered, "you have fallen into egregious error! Never have I held in bondage so much as one hair from a blackamoor's head, and never have I lifted a hand against a hapless Ethiope!"

And even though he was lying there naked as Cupid, reeking with tincture of arnica, his voice rumbled with judicial dignity. Thor was taken aback. After translating blackamoor and Ethiope into lay English, he apologized handsomely, and the two became friends. Presently chess entered the conversation, and upon learning that his masseur enjoyed playing, the judge invited him to the hotel for a game that evening. After that they played often.

Once when Thor had been vanquished in a tight contest, he declared that the judge was the best player he had ever encountered, save for his son Rolfe. But why, the judge asked, didn't he bring his son to the lobby for a game? Thor said he would be glad to, except Rolfe was in the habit of retiring early. Whereupon the judge suggested an afternoon appointment.

Rolfe's age had not entered the discussion; the judge assumed he was in his teens; so it was with some astonishment, next afternoon on the veranda, that he saw Thor ascending the steps with an eight-year-old boy whose blue eyes held the satanic gleam so common to little fellows of that age and whose rumpled hair was like curly copper wire. A chessboard was set up, and Thor warned the judge to play cautiously, because Rolfe had learned the game at four and was possessed of the very devil whether playing chess or engaging in fisticuffs with his little friends. The judge said, *"Sauve qui peut,"* and with a smile he added, *"Vae victis,"* but he wasn't greatly perturbed about being defeated by this little Dane.

Winning the toss, the judge chose black instead of white, out of deference to the tender years of his opponent, but before many moves he realized his folly, for Rolfe attacked with all the derring-do of a Viking. Moreover, between moves, while the judge devoted deep study to the board, Rolfe scrambled from his chair and went romping along the veranda, searching for mischief; and once, till Thor bawled for him to stop that, he balanced himself on the veranda railing, weaving with outstretched arms as he walked. After the judge had finally moved a piece, Rolfe would scamper back to the board, make his move and be off again. This splendid psychological warfare shook the judge's confidence. During the middle game he was visited by an awful premonition of defeat, a foreboding that became actuality early in the end game.

"Well!" the judge said with a somewhat hollow laugh. "It looks as if I'm checkmated."

"You *are* checkmated," Rolfe said.

They played another and this time the judge wasn't giving odds: white was his to play and he played it. On Rolfe's twenty-second move he had the judge on the run, and on his thirty-fifth move he achieved checkmate.

"I've never seen the like!" the judge exclaimed.

"Just what I told you," Thor said, "he's a devil at chess. And," he added, smiling proudly, "at everything else."

They played another game with the same result.

"That boy," the judge announced, "is a genius! I've played for forty years. And he beats me three in a row."

He shook his head, torn between admiration and an impulse to turn the little imp over his knee.

"How long has this been going on?" he asked Thor.

"He got good about a year ago. Before that I could win most of the time."

"Remarkable! A genius! *Ecce signum!*"

"Rolfe!" Thor yelled. "Stop that!"

And his father had admonished him just in time, for Rolfe was about to trip a waiter carrying a julep to a gouty old planter from Tennessee.

"Come here," Thor called. "The judge wants to talk with you."

And when Rolfe obeyed, the judge stared at him contemplatively.

"Young man, what do you intend doing when you grow up?"

"Fight Injuns and help niggers into Canada."

"Sh-h-h!" Thor warned, glancing with some anxiety along the veranda, for Elysian Springs was too close to the Ohio River for underground railroading to be popular, except with Quakers and a few liberals like himself.

"Maybe we'll make a lawyer out of you," the judge said.

"Do lawyers fight Injuns?"

"Um-m-m. Only when they turn politician."

"I don't think I'd like it," Rolfe said.

At this juncture Lucretia Gentry came drifting along the veranda, fresh from her afternoon nap.

"My dear," Sophronicus told her, "this young man has just beaten me three games in a row. Ah, well, to the victor belong the spoils."

"Why, honey, I don't think he looks the least little bit spoiled."

And from that day forward, Lucretia maintained that Rolfe was *such* a sweet little boy; so good, too.

During the remainder of the Gentrys' visit, Rolfe and Sophronicus played a dozen games. By concentrating to the utmost, and secretly studying the book, *Fifty Famous Chess Games,* which he always carried in his carpetbag, the judge managed to win five. And before leaving, he had a serious conversation with Thor, offering to take his son under his aegis, when the time was ripe, and make a lawyer out of him.

"And it won't cost him a cent. He can live with us and study in my office. I'd like to take him with me now, but I don't suppose you want to give him up."

Thor said no, when you came right down to it, he was pretty fond of the boy, even though he was such a hell-raiser.

"The smart ones are always the hell-raisers," Sophronicus said.

And after returning to New Empire, he kept in touch with Thor by correspondence, and during the rest of the 1840's he managed a trip to Elysian Springs nearly every year, for trouncings on the rubbing table and on the chessboard. And in the spring of 1850, he sent Thor enough funds to cover steamboat passage and other expenses for Rolfe's journey to New Empire and a career in law.

*

To reach the Torkelsen place you left the hotel and followed the southeast branch of the valley till, after a furlong, you saw on the north side of the road a double log cabin with a truncated second story under its shake roof. Laust Nordentoft had donated the land for this parsonage, as well as for the small log church across the road to the south, and the whole community had turned out to help build the two structures. Now, after several years, the parsonage had a mellowed look, its snake fence entwined with Virginia creepers and morning glories, its grassy yard shaded by black walnut and maple trees. In the back yard stood a log barn where Thor kept a team; there was a fox-proof chicken house; and on spring mornings when the peony and snowball bushes were blooming you heard the clucking of hens and the ariettas of roosters. Helsa had given birth to two more daughters, Svanhild and Pintze, and all in all the Torkelsens felt lucky to have found such a snug haven.

In addition to his duties as pastor and masseur, Thor taught the village school, so the family received more cash income than was usual for a ministerial household. As for his congregation, it was slowly growing. Most members would have preferred a hell-fire preacher, but except for a Quaker meetinghouse in the next township Thor's church was the only one within miles, so persons of a spiritual bent made out as best they could with Happy Christianity. They didn't, however, much like it; and they liked even less the rumor that Pastor Torkelsen furthered his abolitionist beliefs by operating a station on the underground railroad. Slave chasers from south of the Ohio River had been heard to declare it was pretty goddamned peculiar how the spoor of a runaway was always leading plainly into this vicinity and then vanishing. If you asked their opinion, that long-legged preacher was in the underground up to his eyebrows.

Well, he was. And as time went on, so was his son Rolfe. Often an untroubled midnight would become exciting with a knock on the kitchen door, and Thor, in the northeast bedroom, would waken and come groping across the central hall, wearing his long nightgown and old-world nightcap.

"Who is it?" he would ask in a guarded voice.

823

"A friend with friends."

That was the password; Thor would unlatch the door and into the kitchen would come one or two or sometimes a half-dozen fugitives from dear old Massa in the old Kentucky home far away. Having drawn the curtains, Thor would light a candle, and about this time Rolfe would appear from his bedroom. Sometimes the Negroes had made the journey from slave territory with little difficulty, but more often they were starved and scared, tatterdemalions whose clothes had been torn in the brambles and whose shoes were disintegrating. They had been shot at; they had heard hounds baying and horsemen galloping; and in the kitchen they stood uneasily, always listening, eyes rolling and tongues licking dry lips.

Wearing a coat over her nightgown, Helsa Torkelsen would come from the bedroom, her yellow hair hanging in two braids to her waist; and while her husband tried to put the guests at ease she would fry eggs and side-meat and set the table. And while they ate, voraciously, and grew drowsy, Thor would decide where to hide the fugitives. Early in his activities with the underground, soon after three Quakers had called and suggested he help out, he would lodge the escapees in the barn or upstairs in the cabin. Rolfe remembered those nights: the huge shadows on the walls as his father lifted a candle and started up the open staircase from the kitchen, followed by the runaways who kept glancing around as if they feared the whole thing would turn out to be a trap. In the upper hall, Thor led his unlawful lodgers into a sparsely-furnished bedroom with a sloping ceiling. Throughout the night and all next day you heard nothing from that bedroom; it was silent with a silence almost palpable, the silence of hunted things; and the strain made itself felt downstairs among the family; even the children kept their voices low.

One day two rawboned men with guns came to the house and asked Thor if he had seen anything of three runaway niggers.

"If I had," he said, "I wouldn't tell you."

One of the men looked very ugly at that, and in his clay-hill twang said he had a good notion to come in and search the house.

"You'd better not try it," Thor said, standing there on the stoop with his jaw thrust forward. His face was flushed.

"We're two to your one," the man said. "We could come in if we'd a mind to."

"It wouldn't be worth it," Thor said. "You'd get hurt."

He didn't budge, standing there blocking the door; and presently the men left.

"They're getting on to us," Thor told Helsa. "We'll have to find another hiding place."

It was Rolfe who suggested the new hiding place. He knew those hills like a cottontail, and that afternoon he led his father south past the church and over a hogback ridge and down through the cockleburs and sticktight and wild honeysuckle, then up another ridge. Before reaching the top, he stopped where bull-nettles and buckthorns grew from the granulated detritus of a limestone overhang.

"There's a cave back there," he told his father.

That wasn't remarkable, in this region honeycombed with caves, but this was a special cave. It was haunted, or so Rolfe had heard from his schoolmates. People avoided it. Legend said that many years before a gang of outlaws had conducted a settler there at pistol point and had tortured him in the hope that he would reveal where his money was hidden. He died, during the process. The settler had been a recluse, one of those eccentrics common to the frontier, and when he vanished people supposed he had wandered on west. But a few years later small boys found a skeleton inside the cave, and they heard an odd moaning sound which might have been somebody's ghost groaning as it remembered torture. Men came and rescued the bones and gave them decent burial, and it was assumed they belonged to the vanished settler. After that nobody would go near the place except urchins who tiptoed to the entrance and listened, hoping to hear the ghost groaning.

Thor did not believe in ghosts, except the Holy Ghost, so now, stooping, he followed his son through the tangled buckthorns to the entrance, which was just large enough to admit a man.

"We'd go in," he said, "if we had a light."

"I thought you'd want to," Rolfe said, and he brought candles from his pocket.

Rolfe was hardly scared at all, following his father inside, but he was a little awed. Beyond the entrance, the passage was like an endless corridor with a ceiling so lofty that the candle-rays were lost in blackness; the walls glistened as if set with precious gems; now and then you saw a trickle of water. The passage curved, and then they heard a low continuous sound, like a man moaning, and Rolfe felt his short hairs lifting. After a minute Thor said:

"It must be an underground river. This place is big."

They moved on, even more cautiously, and when the passage forked they bore to the right, coming to a doorway opening into a vast chamber with jagged stalactites.

"This will do," Thor said. "It will do very well. We can stock it with food and handle any number of runaways."

And then Thor did an odd thing; odd because, even though a parson, he was not in the habit of pestering God with prayers, except in church and before meals and at bedtime. But now he dropped to his knees, there in that cavern.

"Heavenly Father," he said, in a tone almost conversational, "thank you for leading us to this place of refuge for your children who have been in bondage. Help us to conduct them here safely. Help us to alleviate the suffering of those less fortunate than ourselves. And Father, strike the scales from the eyes of our white brethren at the South. Cause them to repent and to end this awful practice of human slavery. And help all of us, North and South, black and white, to be more charitable one to the other. We ask this in the name of humanity, and of Our Saviour, Jesus Christ. Amen."

He stood up.

"Son," he said, "we'd better get a move on before our candles burn out."

*

Together Thor and Rolfe explored that cave, during the next years, finding that underground river with its blind fish, and finding thousands of feet of passageways and chambers there in the earth of southern Indiana. And as he grew older, Rolfe came to share his father's hatred of chattel slavery. But not of the South; not of slaveholders.

"Hate the evil, not the men who perpetuate the evil," Thor always said.

Once a fortnight, on average, runaway Negroes came knocking at the Torkelsen door, and Thor resorted to many subterfuges to deceive the men tracking them. These artifices were all basically the same: Thor would light a lantern and leave the parsonage with an air of bustle, sometimes hitching up his team and driving off in a hurry, sometimes striding to the schoolhouse half a mile away, sometimes vanishing into the timber northeast of the parsonage. If slave chasers were watching the house they would follow, for they were a stupid lot who were easily duped; meanwhile, Rolfe conducted the runaways to the cave, announcing casually, when they reached it, that once inside they would hear a distant murmur. That, he said, was the underground river. He wasn't taking chances that those Negroes would think it a haunt and refuse to stay hidden.

A few times, even, Thor carried his lantern to the church, while Rolfe hid in the bushes and waited developments. The church looked mysterious with its windows dimly lit; it looked as if strange business were going on inside. The slave catchers must have thought so too, for a couple of times Rolfe saw them materialize from the shadows and go to the church and tramp through the door. When that took place, Thor pretended anger that they had profaned God's house by carrying in firearms; he invited them to inspect everything; then he made them kneel while he prayed and asked that they might be forgiven their sacrilege. Meanwhile, Rolfe ran to the parsonage and told the Negroes to follow him. He wanted to laugh, leading them past the church where the slave catchers were kneeling.

By the time he was twelve or thirteen, the Torkelsen parsonage was about the most efficient station on the underground railroad between

Kentucky and Canada; only once did they lose a passenger. He was a boy of nine who somehow became separated from his companions when Rolfe led them to the cave; he wandered in the hills, lost, and next afternoon turned up at the Fountain House, hungry and scared and crying. Two slave catchers were on the veranda and they nabbed him. Thor came from the bathhouse and saw it all.

"They abused him," he told the family at supper. "And they tied him up and put him in a buggy and drove away. His cries were terrible. Sometimes I think some awful retribution will be visited upon this country for permitting such things to happen."

And that evening at prayers he beseeched God to enlighten the Southern Slavocracy. But perhaps that was asking the impossible even of God; at any rate, during the next decade, the Slavocracy ceased to admit that slavery was an evil, although in their opinion a necessary one; they began saying it was a positive good which should be permitted to spread and to augment itself by legalizing once more the slave trade with Africa. That was carrying things too far, of course, and in the North more and more persons thought perhaps those crazy abolitionists weren't so wrong, at that.

But in the late 1840's few respectable persons were abolitionists; certainly not Stephen A. Douglas or that conservative railroad lawyer, A. Lincoln. Dreamers, troublemakers, wild-eyed radicals, agitators, socialistic advocates of free love and heaven knew what all, enemies of the *status quo*—those were synonyms for abolitionists. Merchants and bankers, the great stodgy middle class, men of wealth and the men who licked the boots of men of wealth, preachers and lawyers and doctors, the smug men who believed in being practical and playing it safe—nearly all were opposed to William Lloyd Garrison and his likes. Trouble was, slaves were property. And property was sacred. Take one kind of property from one class of society and next thing you knew busybodies would be coming into your office and taking away your spittoons because they didn't approve of spittoons. Thus went the reasoning.

Not even Judge Sophronicus Gentry, who abhorred slavery, had sympathy with abolitionists.

"My dear young sir," he used to tell Rolfe, "violence is inherent in abolitionism. And violence is always inimical to the delicate political balances of a Republic. In a system such as ours, changes must come gradually, and with the enlightened consent of the governed. When the citizens of a free Republic resort to internal violence, Caesarism is likely to follow. It is not that I hate slavery less, but that I love the Republic more."

And so, little by little, after Rolfe moved to New Empire and studied under the judge, he grew to feel that the anti-slavery activities of the Reverend Thorvald Torkelsen had been rash and quixotic. Slavery, after all, was upheld by law in many states; the Federal government recognized the right of citizens to hold that kind of property, and to recover it when it fled toward freedom; the law was majestic; where law ended, anarchy began. If you helped a slave escape, were you not actually an accessory to theft? By the time he was twenty, he looked back with chagrin on his adventures with the underground railroad. He remembered his steamboat trip to New Empire and how he had been gulled out of thirty dollars by a swindler who pretended to be collecting money to buy a Negro out of slavery; he remembered how Jim Buckmaster had laughed at his credulity. His ears burned, and he came to regard his father as a visionary, a good man but impractical, a misguided sentimentalist who took the law into his own hands. He didn't want to be like his father, in those years; he wanted to be a lion of jurisprudence, like Judge Gentry, and a shrewd, humorous, skeptical, dashing buccaneer of finance, like Jim Buckmaster.

*

"One moment, Mr. Torkelsen," the clerk said, when Rolfe entered the outer office in the Buckmaster Building on that April morning in 1858. "I'll tell Mr. Buckmaster you're here."

While he waited, Rolfe glanced at copies of various newspapers published by the Buckmaster interests. Kansas had ceased to bleed; the Supreme Court, twelve months before, had decided that Dred Scott and all other persons of color were not really citizens; the Missouri Compromise was null and void; and Senator Stephen A. Douglas had invented a wondrous political device called Popular Sovereignty which was going to settle the slavery question forever. As for last year's financial panic, fiddle-faddle. Spring had returned, the papers said, and so would prosperity.

Rolfe smiled. Prosperity, wherever it had gone, seemed to be enjoying its trip; trade still languished. The smash had begun the previous August when the Ohio Life Insurance & Trust Company shut up shop, leaving the public poorer by seven million dollars. Railroads failed; the red on the books of brokerage houses was not red corpuscles; in great financial centers people queued up outside banks, wanting the cash which the bankers had long since spent. In factories, spindles and flywheels went on vacation; half-finished buildings lined city streets; even James L. Buckmaster, people said, was feeling the pinch, for sales had contracted at his retail yards and the price of lumber had dropped from twenty dollars to six dollars per thousand.

"Yes, Mr. Torkelsen," the clerk said. "Go right in, please."

Behind the counter, Rolfe passed through the door to the counting room where a score of high stools stood at sloping desks. Today, many desks were empty; the big room had an air of suspended activity. Opening the door marked "Mr. Buckmaster," he went into the private office.

"Hello, Swede," Jim said. "Have a cigar."

"No, thanks," Rolfe said, taking two.

Sitting there with his feet perched on the desk, Jim sighed.

"Lawyers," he said. "My God. I should have drownded you off my raft. Don't know why I didn't."

"Not man enough, maybe."

"Biggest mistake I ever made," Jim said. "Sit down, Swede."

James L. Buckmaster, Rolfe thought, hardly looked like a man feeling the pinch of stringent times. His black broadcloth suit and his flowered waistcoat were handsomely-tailored, his shoes polished, his linen immaculate; and when he stood up, stretching with the silky flexibility of a woods cat, and paced easily about the office, he looked as authoritative and sure of himself as in the old days when he maintained such hair-trigger discipline aboard his raft. Below black brows, his gray eyes were still sharp and humorous; and his hair, except for premature gray at the temples, was Indian black. Yet in some indefinable way his face had changed. It was not, perhaps, quite so coppery from the weather as when he piloted a raft, and although the bold profile was still strong, it was the subtle strength of refined steel, not the raw-ore strength of a hell-bent raftsman. It was the face of a man to whom things had happened. Well, heaven knew he had had his troubles, with his foster son killed in a fall and his wife deep in insanity.

"Swede," he said, standing with legs apart on the thick carpet, "what are they saying about me these days?"

"You know I never use bad language," Rolfe said.

Jim smiled, but it was gone in a moment.

"No," he said, "I'm serious. What are they saying about my bank and my companies?"

"About what you'd expect, after the panic. They say you've lost money, like everybody else. But nobody has any doubts about the Bank of New Empire. Hell, it's the financial Gibraltar of Fox County. It says so itself."

"All right, forget I asked you that. Sure it's sound. So are my newspapers and my packet line and my lumber company. So is my gas company. Everything I own is sound. Sound as a block of ice. And just as frozen. Fact is, Swede, I need ready cash."

"I could spare you a quarter," Rolfe said.

But James L. Buckmaster was serious now, pacing the carpet with a cigar.

"Remember old Caleb McSwasey?" he asked. "Well, Caleb was smart. Crooked as a jack pine, but smart. Once he told me how he got cleaned in the Panic of '37. 'Jim,' he said, 'it learned me. Expand in bad times and in good times hold on to your cash. A smash always comes, and then a man with cash can buy anything at ten cents on the dollar. You won't remember what I'm telling you,' he said, 'till it's too late, because no businessman is seasoned till he's gone through a panic his own self, but that's how it is.' Well, the son of a bitch was right. I expanded too fast, and now I'm left with my pants down and my assets frozen."

"I might even go to fifty cents," Rolfe said.

"God damn it, Swede, I should have drownded you when I had the chance . . . If I smash, so will New Empire. So will about half of Wisconsin. But you know something, Swede? I ain't going to smash. I've got plans."

He went to the big safe and pulled out a drawer from which he took an envelope. Opening it, he brought out a fragile-looking sheet of paper.

"Read that through, Swede, and see what you make of it."

Its chirography cramped, its ink faded, its grammar and spelling uncertain, the document was dated "In Camp Nere Savannah, Georga, Dec. 15, 1778," and signed by a paymaster of troops with the Continental Army. It acknowledged receipt of ten thousand dollars in gold from "Abraham Klauber, Jew Merchant of This Place, who with Commend'ble Patriotism has loaned this Summ to the Cause of Liberty so that our Troops may be Payed." It went on to urge repayment of this sum, along with "Satisfactory Int'st. Compoun'd Annually," by whatever government might be established upon "the Defeet of Tyranny & the Freedom of These Colonies."

"Well?" Jim asked.

"It looks genuine enough," Rolfe said.

"Hell, yes, it's genuine. I inherited it from Sol Klauber. Abraham Klauber was his grandfather. And I intend to see that congress pays this debt. It's run long enough."

"You might run into trouble there," Rolfe said. "Somebody will be sure to claim the receipt is a forgery."

Jim smiled.

"That don't worry me. I've had Park Irwin looking into this. The receipt was presented for payment before. On five separate occasions. It's all in the record. But congress never paid up."

Rolfe handed back the document; Jim returned it to the safe.

"Your claim ought to be pretty good," Rolfe said. "The muster-lists of the Continental Army should show that this Colonel What's-his-name was a paymaster with troops near Savannah in 1778. And there ought to be records showing that there was an Abraham Klauber in that area—"

"Park Irwin looked that up too. Abraham Klauber and his son Ben were in the militia that fought the British near Savannah. The old man was killed and his son was taken prisoner. The British raised hell with the Klauber interests—burned their warehouse and ruined them. Hell, Swede, they were patriots, and it would be pretty small of the government not to pay up its honest debt. Of course, I'm not a Klauber."

"But you're the heir and assignee of Sol Klauber. Send a certified copy of his will to Washington to prove it."

"Send it? Hell, I'll take it. And the receipt too."

"Take certified copies. The originals are too valuable."

"All right, Swede, whatever you say. And I want you to go to Washington with me. Park Irwin says we'll have to collar congressmen and talk them into voting payment. Well, I know how to soften up politicians. But I want you with me for advice. And I might get one of my headaches when the bill comes up—I want you there. I'll ask for ten percent interest on the loan, compounded annually. That's fair enough. We're getting twelve percent at the bank on short-term paper right now." Jim smiled. "I'll take all the cash the bank can spare," he went on. "Cash is a great little persuader, with politicians. If any of those congressmen should figure what ten percent of ten thousand amounts to, compounded annually, they might get real greedy. For your information, it amounts to quite a wad. Want to guess how much?"

"A couple of hundred thousand, maybe?"

Jim laughed.

"Hell, Swede, this is bigger poker than that. I had one of my clerks figure it. When he brought me the figures I didn't believe them. 'Oh, sir,' he says, 'compound interest is magic. It mounts up fast, sir. I had to make more than eighty calculations, sir, to figure how much.' Well, I still didn't believe it. So I had another clerk figure it. He got the same result. From December 15, 1778 to December 15 of last year the principal and compound interest at ten percent would come to—hold on to your chair, Swede—more than eighteen-and-a-half million dollars. And if we'd figure it till June 15 of this year, the total debt the government owes me would be—"

Jim picked up a paper from his desk and gave it to Rolfe.

"There it is, Swede."

The figure was $19,552,911.14.

"You're crazy," Rolfe said. "Congress would never pay that."

Jim smiled.

"Nobody's going to shoot me for trying, Swede."

*

Rolfe was walking on air when he left the Buckmaster Building; big things were stirring; and in anticipation the trip to Washington City seemed an odyssey of glamour and romance. As it turned out, realization was as fine as anticipation, perhaps because anything you did with Jim Buckmaster was tinted with adventure and fun; he made the world seem an exciting place.

They left New Empire in mid-April, traveling on the *Bonnie* to St. Louis, then going east by rail, changing cars several times, for in those days the gauges of various lines were of different width. Rolfe had never ridden the steam cars before; everything was new and fascinating.

Always when a Westerner goes east the journey is like a pilgrimage to the beginnings of the Republic; you see streams tumbling along valleys in the Pennsylvania mountains and remember the trek of young George

Washington from Virginia with Dinwiddie's letter to the French at Fort Le Boeuf; you see old towns looking like that greatest of all centuries, the Eighteenth; the very landscape brings to mind the bloody footprints at Valley Forge and Light-Horse Harry Lee and the Hessians throwing down their arms. For a while in your mind the Republic is young again and valiant; everything has a shine. Washington, District of Columbia, has a shine.

They arrived in Washington one spring morning when the redbud was blooming and the dogwood was white under a sky of faultless blue. Sight of the capitol, although its dome was unfinished, brought tightness to Rolfe's throat; he remembered George Washington laying the cornerstone; he thought of the great ones who had ridden along Pennsylvania Avenue to inauguration and destiny.

"Hell, Swede, it's just another town," Jim said. "Full of politicians with their hands out."

"Sure," Rolfe said, ashamed of his emotion; but he was under the capital's spell. Here John Quincy Adams had written those crabbed entries in his diary; here Andrew Jackson had gone horseback riding with Red Fox Van Buren; here Webster had eaten breakfast before beginning his reply to Hayne. Thomas Jefferson, Virginia gentleman, when the word gentleman meant something, had sent from here a couple of adventurous young men named Lewis and Clark, to explore unknown river valleys and mountain ranges; these streets had known the footsteps of Mr. Calhoun and Mr. Clay and John Marshall. This was the capital of it all: of Southern canebrakes and Northern forests; of gold diggings in California and lobster beaches in Maine; of card sharps in lusty young Chicago and of fiddlers in the Great Smokies. It was the essence of America, strong drink to a young man from New Empire, Wisconsin.

At the National Hotel they took a suite, two bedrooms and a sitting room, and during the next weeks all manner of statesmen and political hangers-on and lobbyists came to drink Jim Buckmaster's liquor and smoke his cigars and dip their snouts into the swill he had brought from the Bank of New Empire. First of these visitors was the Hon. Park Irwin, congressman from Wisconsin.

"Well, by God," Jim said, when he answered the knock. "It's a long time between drinks."

"Jim!" Park said, shaking hands with both hands. "And Rolfe Torkelsen! It's truly good to see you."

Serving in congress had agreed with Park Irwin; his belly had filled out, beneath his fawn-colored waistcoat; he had grown a pair of light-brown side-whiskers, carefully trimmed; and he wore a cutaway coat and striped dark trousers. His brow, however, still had that serenity of a man who has never been troubled by an original thought.

"And how did you leave your family?" he asked Jim, in a voice bland as an eel in oil.

832

"No better."

"Ah, yes, a great tragedy."

"What the hell," Jim said, "she's happy. Happier than the rest of us. She lives in a world of her own."

"Ah, yes, God is good."

"I wouldn't want to bet on that," Jim said. "Have a drink?"

Presently the conversation turned to the object of Jim's trip; Park Irwin had not, he said, been idle. Without exception, the senators and representatives from Wisconsin were willing to vote repayment of Abraham Klauber's loan, with compound interest; and the representative from the district containing Savannah, Georgia, was preparing a speech in favor of repayment.

"He expects—ah—a bit of compensation, of course," Park Irwin said. "And he tells me that if further compensation be available, he will line up the rest of the Georgia delegation to vote with us."

"There will be compensation," Jim said.

"Yes, I was sure of that. I made so bold, indeed, as to promise him as much. Then we have other support, scattered throughout the several states. Possibly it is not prudent to name names, but I can truly assure you that I have been rallying much support to our cause."

"Money makes the mare go," Jim said.

"Ah, yes, true, true. But not always. There are certain senators and representatives who are wealthy in their own right. Other levers must be found to move them. It's a delicate business, but it can be done. Certain members have bills which will benefit their constituencies without necessarily benefiting the country as a whole. With them, it will be tit for tat. They will vote with us if we will vote with them. These matters can be arranged. They are arranged at every session."

"Every man has his price," Jim said.

"And there are still other members," Park Irwin said, "who are left cold by such considerations. Neither money nor horse trading interests them. Some want appointments made which up till now have not been made. And some wish to meet members of the fair sex with whom to while away their evenings."

"Tit for tat, eh?" Jim said.

Rolfe laughed, but Park Irwin's face showed dull color at the roots of his handsome whiskers.

"It's truly the shame of congress," he said, "but the fact remains that often political ability is accompanied by carnal appetites. I could name you several influential members who are incorruptible except where the fair sex is concerned. Some of them—and more's the scandal—are old men."

"Hell," Jim said, "if they want whores, buy them whores."

"That's where the difficulty arises. They don't want ordinary fallen women. They want respectable young ladies who will be so overcome by their manly vigor that they will yield their charms freely."

"Jesus Christ!"

"Yes, it's truly a real problem. But even it can be overcome. With enough expenditure. I happen to know a gentleman who makes it his business to supply this demand, when important legislation is pending. His girls are beautiful and charming, possessed of all the social graces, and they are not, in the ordinary sense, whores. Actually, they're niggers. From New Orleans, mainly, but so light-fleshed they pass as Spanish or French. He buys them young and places them in charge of accomplished older women who teach them society manners and foreign languages. Some, I dare say, are virgins. Certain of our elder statesmen have a passion for inexperienced girls, and when an important bill comes up it is arranged for them to meet these lovely virgins at a social function, casually as it were. Usually the girl is introduced as the niece of some legislator who is eager for the bill to pass. Almost always the elder statesman finds, upon re-examining the bill, that it has virtues he had overlooked, and he votes for it. Occasionally some old gentleman becomes so enamored of a girl that he proposes marriage. I could tell you of one instance where such a marriage took place, and there were children. A well-known senator from a slave state. It's an expensive way to pass a bill, but it can be done."

Jim sat grinning through the cigar smoke.

"Park," he said, "when I sent you to congress I thought you were a horse's ass. I see I was mistaken, and I apologize."

"Thank you, Jim."

"You know your way around, I can see that. All right, I've brought plenty of money. When it's gone I can get more. I want this bill passed and the loan repaid. I don't care how you do it. Just do it. And when you do, I'll not forget you. I take care of my friends. I expect loyalty up to the hilt, and I give it. You stick by me and maybe you'll end up in the senate. Hell, even that's not the top of the ladder. Maybe you'll make it to the White House, with me behind you. But first we've got to pass this bill. Understand?"

"Yes, Jim," said Congressman Irwin.

*

Years later when he looked back on that Washington visit from the crags of his political rectitude, Rolfe Torkelsen was flabbergasted at his moral obtuseness. He should, he told himself, have picked up his carpet-bag and left that hotel as soon as he sniffed the taint of bribery. Judge Sophronicus Gentry would have done just that. So would the Reverend Thorvald Torkelsen. And so would Rolfe himself, later in his life.

But he was young then, thirsty for experience, and it seemed a great lark, this going up an alley and through the stage door of the Republic where behind the canvas flats you saw the great actors with their togas splotched and their laurel awry. It was amusing to discover that their swords were wooden and their shields only tin. After the curtain fell on a noble oration, it was somehow touching and funny to see Mark Antony hurrying to the toilet.

Even so, inexperienced as he was, he had a few nips of conscience when he saw how ruthlessly Jim Buckmaster was going about getting that loan repaid. Still, the loan was a valid obligation of the government. And congress had always ignored that obligation. Could you blame Jim for insisting that congress act? Could you say he was wholly culpable for using dynamite to blast that legislative jam?

Yes, Rolfe thought, years later, you could. The end never justified the means. Bribery was bribery, always ugly; in a free republic the public servants were only as honest as their masters; hence, every citizen must be scrupulous, for history had shown that of all forms of government a republic was most vulnerable to the ravages of corruption. A democratic republic was the nearest man had ever got, or ever would get, to a perfect government; it was the very flower of his civic imagination; and flowers needed more careful nurturing than weeds.

But that was the thinking of his middle years; at twenty-two, in something like rebellion against his father's decalogue, and even impatient at times with Judge Gentry's hair-splitting probity, Rolfe found himself swept easily into Jim Buckmaster's orbit. Compared with Jim, Thor Torkelsen was a moralizing country parson and Judge Gentry a stick-in-the-mud. Things happened, when you were with Jim, exciting things. Life was glamorous and romantic and filled with delightful surprises; he seemed a giant in a world of drab pygmies. Pretty girls and fragrant cigars and fine bourbon and laughter and deferential waiters—that was his world. He called senators by their first names; he handed a newsboy a quarter for the evening paper and told him to keep the change; when he gambled at the Rockendorff House on Pennsylvania Avenue he used gold pieces for chips and talked to the dice like a Dutch uncle; and always he smiled easily, or laughed, as if some part of him was amused at his antics. When you were twenty-two, it was easy to hero-worship such a fellow.

Actually, Rolfe was little more than a spectator at that business of persuading congress to repay Abraham Klauber's loan; Park Irwin and other representatives of the people of Wisconsin, along with several professional lobbyists, carried matters forward.

"Things are going fine, Swede," Jim used to say. "Why don't you run along and see the sights?"

There were many sights to be seen in that imperial city; the Republic of dreams—Judge Gentry's Republic—seemed very close when Rolfe went exploring. In the after-years he could remember Lafayette Square with its scented magnolias, its pigeons, its statue of Andrew Jackson on his charger; without thinking, Rolfe took off his hat when he saw it first.

Across the way, gracious on its lawn, could be seen the Executive Mansion where President Jackson had smoked his cob pipe and imposed on his era his own dream of a great Republic, not the aristocratic Republic of men like Hamilton, but the democratic Republic of Thomas Jefferson. That was one time his conscience bothered Rolfe, when he stood there in Lafayette Park, for it came to him that Mr. Jefferson and General Jackson had dreamed not of privilege for men like Jim Buckmaster, not of indulgences for a plutocracy; they had been remembering all the humble little people unknown to history, the private soldiers who coughed through the night at Valley Forge, the mechanics with greasy fingers, the women who followed their men through Cumberland Gap, the squatters on river bottoms and the rickety children in lonely hill cabins. They had been thinking of men like Lorne Buckmaster, not of men like his son Jim.

And they had been savagely hated, in their time, lambasted by journalistic mercenaries; indeed, the plutocracy had never forgiven them; polite historians, writing in the universities supported by great wealth, continually maligned and belittled them, for there were always scholars whose brains were located in their pocketbooks. Great wealth preferred to honor George Washington. Well, there was no contravening the integrity and capacities of George Washington. But nobody could argue that he had fought a revolution and established a government for the benefit of the common man.

Rolfe's thoughts returned to Andrew Jackson when he visited the capitol; there in the magnificent rotunda, President Jackson had attended the funeral of a representative from South Carolina. And without warning, at eight feet, an assailant had pulled a pistol. It misfired. Old Hickory was on him like a panther ... Rolfe told Jim Buckmaster about that, there in the rotunda, and Jim said President Jackson must have been a pretty good man.

"Yes," Rolfe said, "pretty good. He was nearly seventy at the time."

They moved on toward the senate, and while Jim went looking for some statesman in the cloakrooms, Rolfe slipped quietly into the gallery. Only a scattering of lawmakers were on the floor; the presiding officer kept yawning; page boys lolled on the steps to the rostrum, or carried glasses of water to members; there was much coming and going; the gentleman from Alabama spoke on and on, excoriating the enemies of chattel slavery, but nobody paid much heed. Under the dingy skylight it was a shabby little chamber, for the new senate extension was still being built, and everything was so unhurried and casual that it was hard to realize how much power dozed here. Yet suddenly it came to Rolfe that this was one of the most powerful rooms in the world. This was it; this was the sword-point of a mighty people; this was the forum where decisions with unimaginable consequences were made. Ever since arriving in Washington, he had been aware of a thought lingering in a corner of his mind, and now it took conscious shape: these men, these herculean buildings, were but the symbols of something bigger than any one of them, or indeed of all the men and all the buildings in the aggregate; they were but the embodiment of a tremendous and exciting dream, that man was a reasonable animal capable of governing himself. That was why in Washington City in the District of Columbia in the United States of America you felt always some lurking and unseen presence, dreamlike and alluring; here the shining ideal of self-government was being tested. And you felt too, even when chickens and pigs roamed the streets, that this was a capital destined for greatness; all futurity lay before it.

Jim Buckmaster had entered the gallery and seated himself beside Rolfe.

"How do you like it, Swede?" he whispered.

Rolfe smiled.

"Swede," Jim whispered, "some day you'll be down there making speeches. You won't always be in the gallery, Swede. Senator Rolfe Torkelsen, the gentleman from Wisconsin, that's what you'll be. They'll put your profile on a silver coin, some day. You stick by me, Swede, and I'll stick by you. I'll own the river and Wisconsin, and if this is what you want, why, hell, boy, I'll give it to you all wrapped up in a package."

*

That might be; but in the matter of the Klauber loan not all the money Jim Buckmaster had brought from New Empire, not all the promises of future money, not all the urging of Park Irwin and his cabal could persuade congress to move faster than its accustomed crawl. Days passed and weeks. There were evenings at the theater, suppers with wine at Fritz Reuter's restaurant, and, for Rolfe, afternoons in libraries and bookstores and on the capitol grounds. Along the north wing, still under construction, scaffolding had been erected; workmen were busy with cranes and buckets of hod; the capitol had an unfinished look, and Rolfe thought of the unfinished Republic.

And there were merry evenings in the Buckmaster hotel suite, with laughter and tinkling glasses and pretty women; several of the latter taught Rolfe that Nixie Auerbach was not the only member of her sex who knew how to make a man happy. Senators attended these soirees, and representatives, and cabinet members who would be influential in getting President Buchanan to sign the pending bill, once it was passed. None of them looked like schoolbook statesmen. They looked like insurance agents or small-town bankers or clerks or pettifoggers from the South. But once a man entered the suite who looked every jot and tittle a statesman. Tall, portly, his face like an old Roman's, his hair silvery and flowing, he looked ready for a pedestal. He was, it transpired, a lobbyist.

Of his sort there were many. All were ready to do business. If the Buckmaster bloc would promise to vote for the next tariff on pig iron or coal or woolens or whatever, they would swing the votes they controlled to pass the bill to repay the Klauber loan. So it went: endless talk, endless cigars, endless bourbon, endless dickering.

Tempers flared now and then, but those were evenings when by mistake anti-slavery and pro-slavery men had been invited to the same party.

"I'll tell you all one thing," declared a gentleman from South Carolina, "we ain't a-fixin' to stay in the Union and take it. We'll secede, that's what we'll do."

"Hell, Pete," said a gentleman from New Hampshire, "you Southern hotheads have been saying that for twenty years. You've used it as a club over our heads—"

"Now God damn it, you listen to me," said the gentleman from South Carolina.

"That's what we've been doing, listening to you—"

"Now God damn it, you listen. You listen to me. We ain't a-goin' up there to wherever you live and tellin' you all how to run your wooden nutmeg factories, and by God you ain't a-goin' to tell us how to run our rice plantations."

"We're not doing no such thing," said the gentleman from New Hampshire. "Keep your goddamned niggers, we don't give a damn about your goddamned niggers. All we say is you can't take your goddamned niggers into the territories and set up slavery there. And we're good and goddamned tired of your nigger catchers coming into our states and getting court orders—"

"You listen to me," said the gentleman from South Carolina. "Law's law and right's right, and if the *U*-nited States keeps treatin' us so poorly we'll secede right out of the Union and start us our own country. We got the cotton and cotton's king. We ain't a-fixin'—"

So it went, heat without light. Two years before, Representative Preston Brooks of South Carolina had entered the senate chamber and broken his cane over the head of Senator Charles Sumner, abolitionist from Massachusetts, and this had induced many lawmakers to carry pistols. More and more the South clamored about secession; not all Southerners, however; they were not all fools; but the North had heard that threat so often it had worn thin; few believed secession would ever be attempted. Rolfe Torkelsen didn't believe it. Neither did Jim Buckmaster, when he thought about it. But that was seldom indeed; he was too busy getting his bill passed.

*

And at last, after many delays, it did pass the house, going thence to the senate; and in the senate it encountered rough weather. Trouble was, some old senator from New England, who considered himself the watchdog of the treasury, grew curious as to how much ten percent of ten thousand dollars, compounded annually since 1778, would amount to; he spent an afternoon making calculations. Result of his mathematics brought a cry from the old tightwad, and after having his figures checked he arose in the senate and announced that he for one would never vote to pay James L. Buckmaster something like nineteen million dollars.

Immediately, several members of the Buckmaster bloc jumped up, wanting the gentleman to yield, and when he obliged, a senator from Georgia, where Abraham Klauber had lived, made a splendid oration about the patriotism of Mr. Klauber, and of Georgians in general, declaring it would be pretty small potatoes if a great country like the *U*-nited States of America refused to honor its just and honest obligations. There were, he declared, such things as principles, sir, and justice, sir, and a lot of other high-sounding words, sir, and when you considered how this Savannah merchant, Abraham Klauber, had given not only of his treasure but also his life in fighting tyranny, why, sir, it made one's blood boil, it sure enough did, and while he didn't know the habits of New England gentlemen, when it came to discharging obligations, he very well knew the honorable habits of Georgia gentlemen, and of all Southern gentlemen, for that matter, and he for one, sir, favored a course whereby the *U*-nited States of America would stand as an example before the world, (whose eyes were on this august body), and pay off a just debt which had run far too long.

The senator from the New England state, an abolitionist, now erred: he could not resist letting his argument stray from fiscal matters to slavery. It was well known, he said waspishly, that there were more gentlemen to the square foot in New England than to the square mile in the South, and he submitted that the average Yankee was more honest and honorable in paying off his debts than the average nigger-whipping slaveholder.

Pandemonium. Mr. President, Mr. President! Will the gentleman yield? Will the gentleman—?

"No, sir, I won't yield till I've had my say. The gentleman from Georgia, sir, talks about his blood boiling. Well, sir, my own blood boils when I remember how a blackguard from the house of representatives —a bully, sir, who called himself a Southern gentleman—came slinking into this chamber and brutally assaulted that great senator from the glorious old Bay State of Massachusetts, I refer, sir, to the great Charles Sumner, who—"

Bedlam. The president of the senate came close to breaking his gavel. Everybody was shouting. Both senators from South Carolina had to be bodily restrained from beating up the abolitionist gentleman. A senator from Alabama brought out a pistol and stood ready. Order, shouted the president; the senate will be in order; and after five minutes, with the aid of the sergeants-at-arms, things did calm somewhat.

"As I was saying," said the abolitionist senator, "the great Charles Sumner was attacked by a Southern bully—"

Pandemonium again. Somebody moved a recess and the president said you have heard the motion, all in favor say aye, the ayes have it—

From then on, so far as the Slavocracy was concerned, the bill for repaying the Klauber loan was sectional: if you voted against payment it meant you had sympathies with nigger-loving Yankees. This was manna for the Buckmaster lobbyists, and they consolidated their gains by whispering around that Abraham Klauber had held slaves and that James L. Buckmaster was absentee owner of a Georgia plantation with three hundred Negroes. To the abolitionist members of the senate, and to the middle-of-the-roaders, the lobbyists pointed out that there was no reason for dragging the slavery issue into a purely fiscal measure. When the bill came up again, one Southern fire-eater was so enthusiastic about its merits that he offered an amendment to repay the loan with fifteen percent interest; this was turned down; on the final vote, the senate agreed to repay at ten percent interest, compounded annually, from December 15, 1778 to December 15, 1857. Now, since the house had voted simply to repay with interest compounded up to the time of passage, the bill went to a joint house-senate committee, where it was agreed to accept the version passed by the senate. Next day the house concurred.

A final hurdle remained: to obtain the signature of President James Buchanan. But this, as it turned out, was a hurdle almost nonexistent, for President Buchanan was an old fuddy-duddy wholly in the hands of the Southerners around him; when they told him to sign he reached for his pen; and so it was that the treasurer of the United States drew a check payable to James L. Buckmaster for $18,621,820.13.

Nor did Mr. Buckmaster neglect to reward those who had brought this to pass; he always stood by his friends. Owing to Mr. Buckmaster's gratitude, a number of cotton senators that summer repainted ancestral mansions, and purchased more fair acres and more servants to work them; lobbyists bought new carriages and teams of blooded horses; throughout the land representatives celebrated the birthdays of their wives and mistresses with lavish gifts, and set their sons up in business; and Congressman Park Irwin purchased a fine home in Washington. Justice had been done and everybody was happy.

*

Neither Jim nor Rolfe had ever visited New York, so on the return to Wisconsin they circled northeast and spent a couple of weeks. In the unwritten autobiography of Rolfe Torkelsen, New York was as necessary as Washington in adding to his understanding of America. For New York was the capital of the United States, in all save government. Here came the men like Jim Buckmaster, the successful men, flush with winnings; here came the brains, legal, financial, artistic; here came the pretty girls from countless mud towns; here often enough, in Wall Street offices, were made the decisions which the congress in Washington would turn into law; here were floated the bond issues and the stock issues which would build the railroads and the railroad towns, which would gut a thousand mountains of their ore. Here could be read the newspapers, still damp with ink, which were stale and old when bought in the West; here were ships that had plied London River and the Indian Ocean; here were whiffs of salt water and the cries of gulls and the slosh of ferryboats; here were the opera and Appleton's Bookstore and Tiffany's and the St. Nicholas Hotel.

They took a suite in that lavish hostelry and sallied forth to see the sights: squads of Irishmen at work with mules and scrapers in what would be Central Park; the Crystal Palace in Reservoir Square; the wonders at Barnum's Museum. They strolled the Battery and omnibussed up Broadway; they dined at Delmonico's; and on several evenings they found their way to a second-floor gymnasium, mauve with cigar smoke, and watched bare-fisted pugilists slugging it out in a gas-lit ring.

New York was roaring in those years; it was the city of Fernando Wood and Alderman Tweed, of the Bowery Boys and Billy McGlory's Armory Hall; and even on afternoons of crushing heat it teemed with an energy which Rolfe found bracing and exciting. Yet it awed him at first: all those endless streets choked with traffic, all those swarthy men jabbering in outlandish tongues, all those tons of wealth and poverty; he felt very much from the country. But it didn't awe Jim Buckmaster, so far as could be observed.

"Sure," he seemed to be telling the city, by his manner, "you're big. But me, I'm big too. Eighteen million dollars big."

Reporters came to the hotel to interview the man who had struck it rich in Washington, and Rolfe had to admire the way Jim parried their questions. They were sharp and manifestly suspicious of the methods used to collect the Klauber loan, but Jim poured the drinks and passed the cigars and acted the role of a lunkhead from the country.

"I don't know what you slickers are hinting at," he said, grinning. "Hell, boys, I'm just a rooster off the river who don't know beans from onions. The panic left me strapped, till I thought about that note Sol Klauber left me when he cashed in. Well, I wrote my congressman. Wouldn't you have done that? He wrote back for me to bring the note to Washington. He took over then. What's wrong with that, boys? Ain't a congressman supposed to give a hand to the folks back home?"

"There've been rumors of bribery," somebody said.

"Bribery?" Jim scratched his jaw, looking bewildered. "No-o, there warn't nothing like that. Jeez, boys, do you think I'd have the gall to walk up to a senator and offer him money?" He laughed. "Jeez, I'd have been kicked out on my ear and never could have collected. No, it was just an honest debt the government owed. Ain't the government supposed to pay its bills? If you can't trust the U.S.A. to come through on its I.O.U.'s, who can you trust? If the old U.S.A. would start welshing on its bills, why, hell, boys, it would set what the fellow calls a bad example and every business in the country would go broke because of the deadbeats. Sure I was lucky. But my luck was in inheriting that note, not in getting it paid."

They asked him his plans.

"I thought I'd look over your town, boys, and maybe have me a spree. She's a nice town, I like it. Know what happened to me this noon? A lady winked at me, right out on the street in broad daylight. She was some punkins too, boys. Pretty as a schoolma'am. But hell, I'll never get the pine needles out of my hair, or the river sand out of my shoes. I've got me a little lumber yard back home, and I reckon after a week or so I'll go back and run that. You've got a nice town here, boys, but I wouldn't live in it if you'd give it to me."

New York smiled over the published interview, for here was just another yokel who had come into money and would lose it at Morrisey's on Twenty-Fourth Street.

But Jim didn't lose it, at Morrisey's or at any gambling house. Nor was that New York visit devoted entirely to pleasure.

"Come along, Swede," he said one morning, and a few minutes later, in a quiet office in the financial district, he was discussing with construction engineers the preliminaries of a railroad to be called the Madison, New Empire & Western.

"I didn't know you were planning a railroad," Rolfe said, later.

"Sure, Swede. I've got a few schemes on tap. I wouldn't want to get rusty."

And he went on to point out how the proposed railroad could connect at Madison with lines going to Chicago and how at New Empire it could receive from Buckmaster steamboats the wheat and hogs of the Northwest.

"I'll haul the immigrants out to new country, Swede, and I'll haul their supplies. I'll haul their produce back to market. I'll sell enough common stock to lay my track, and I'll own the construction company that builds her. Everybody wants railroads, these days, and the politicians know it. Look what they did in Illinois, Swede. The legislature gave the Central two-and-a-half million acres. Wisconsin ought to do as much for me. Hell, I'll organize a land company too, and sell farms and town sites. It's a bonanza, Swede, and I'll be in on the ground floor. And that's not all. Down there in Washington I kept my ears open. There's talk about a Homestead Act. They'll get around to passing it too, some time or other, and when that happens you can bet the U.S.A. won't forget the railroads. Free land, Swede, millions of acres. Timber rights and ore rights—everything. I'll own me the world, one of these days."

"And what will you do with it?"

Jim laughed.

"Hell, boy, I don't know. Give some of it to you, if you stick by me, and use the rest to stand on while I reach for the sun. I'm on my way now. They'll never stop me now, Swede."

But even James L. Buckmaster had his swamps of the spirit, as Rolfe learned toward the end of their New York visit. Late one afternoon the two men dropped in at Taylor's Ice Cream Saloon on Broadway, expecting to buy cocktails. But this was a saloon in name only; actually, it was a watering place for fashionable ladies who had been shopping at A. T. Stewart's.

"God Almighty, Swede," Jim said, laughing, "looks like we've busted into the Ladies' Aid. But I reckon we might as well stay, now we're here."

They ordered pineapple ices and sandwiches so diminutive that one of them, Jim said, would not have made a mouthful for a pinery boy. He was in fine fettle, sitting there at a dainty table, while waiters hurried and in the great ornate room could be heard the chirps and purrs and musical laughter of wealthy femininity. Dowagers, mothers with their daughters, young matrons, aunts and great-aunts, coveys of chattering girls as bright-eyed as quails: all were there, tipsy with that distaff intoxication which an afternoon of shopping induces. Scents of expensive powders and sweet Florida waters came to Rolfe's nostrils, and his eyes were beguiled with all the gay colors of summer frocks. Presently he noticed that Jim had fallen silent, and that his face looked bleak. He was watching, Rolfe saw, a girl several tables away.

She was nineteen or twenty, brown-skinned and dark-haired and dark-eyed, vivacious and winsome. Sometimes she laughed, chattering with her companions, and you saw her white teeth and red mouth. When she rose to leave, her figure was lovely; Jim watched till she disappeared. Then he sat deep in some mood Rolfe could not fathom.

The waiter asked if they wished anything else.

"No, no, nothing else," Jim said, and he stood up.

In the hot afternoon Broadway was an endless flow of carriages, drays, omnibuses, pushcarts; the sidewalk was a thick jostle.

"What's wrong?" Rolfe asked.

"Nothing, Swede. Nothing that can be helped. I'm getting a headache. And I want a drink."

In the vast bar of the Astor House, pleasantly gloomed after the sunny street, Jim drank his bourbon straight. It didn't reach him, seemingly. Finally he said:

843

"I'm getting a headache. God damn it, anyway. I'll have to go to bed and take that medicine."

In their suite at the St. Nicholas, he stripped off his clothes, poured whiskey into a tumbler, sifted in some powders, gulped it. Then, pillows behind his head, he stretched out on the bed with more whiskey. He wasn't drunk, but his voice sounded distant.

"Stay with me, Swede," he said. "I need you, boy. And you don't know why."

"Well, of course," Rolfe said, "when a man's sick—"

"Not that. Not this damned headache. I need you so I won't bust out crying. I couldn't do that with you around, could I, Swede? But if I was alone—"

He drank.

"You stick by me, Swede, now and always. A man don't make many friends. Not ones he can trust. Count them on the fingers of one thumb. Sol Klauber—and he died. Greasy Dick—and he died last year. Molly Fitzpatrick—and she turned whore. Don't you whore out on me, Swede, or get yourself drownded. You stick by me, and I'll push you up to whatever you want. They'll put your face on a coin some day, and you'll live in the White House."

Rolfe knew the liquor was in Jim's blood then, for he could never be president because he had been born a foreigner. He said as much.

"Hell," Jim said, "I'll tell them to change the law. They'll do it too, they'll do what I say, before I'm through. Eighteen million dollars, but it can't raise the dead. It can't bring a drownded man back to life, nor a drownded girl, neither. Name of Bonnie. Bonnie Fansler. Ever hear of her?"

"Bonnie Fansler," Rolfe said. "I'm not sure—"

"No, probably not. Long time ago. Seven years ago. I thought my life was going to be a stretch of river without a snag or sawyer, but it didn't turn out that way. Old Caleb framed me, see? Son of a bitch, I never trusted him, I should have been watching. Framed me, and I was in the clink. Then he died. And Esperanza said, 'Let's get married, Jim. Let's you and me hook up. You'll be out of jail slick as a schoolma'am's leg,' she said, 'and running this company.'"

He drank.

"What could I do, Swede? I'd promised to marry this girl from up-river, but what could I do? I couldn't have married her anyway, from prison. And her half-brother had been killed, and I thought she'd be mad at me. Nothing could ever have come from any of it. Still, I'd promised her. But Esperanza kept after me. And know what I did? I married her. I saved my own hide. I married her. Went to Dubuque and got married. And then one morning not a week later this girl from upriver comes to New Empire. Comes to my office, Swede. Jesus, I wanted to shoot myself. She was going to have a kid, Swede. My kid, hers and mine. It got right to me, Swede. It was a knife right through my guts, being twisted. She said—well—never mind—she was sweet, she was one in a million. Sad and sweet. She cried, sure, and guess I must have too. 'I'll think of something,' I said, 'there's always a way out. Come back this afternoon and I'll think of something.' She damn near smiled then, and that knife was twisting. 'No, Jim,' she said, 'there's no way out. It wouldn't be any good,' she said. 'You married her and saved yourself,' she said, 'and I'm not blaming you. But it would never be any good, after you did that.'

"Well, she left my office then, and I let her go. I blame myself for that, Swede, and for plenty else too. I let her go. Should have followed her and put her in a canoe and the two of us would have gone . . . somewhere. Way north, maybe. But I let her go. And that afternoon she jumped off an upriver boat and drownded herself. Jesus, Swede, that was . . . that was . . ."

He shook his head and heaved a breath and drank.

"Well, they didn't find her body, right away. Not for several days. Some kids found it below New Empire. The coroner needed somebody to identify her, and she'd been seen leaving my office. So he comes to me. I had to do it, Swede. I had to go to those funeral parlors and do it. God damn it, life shouldn't put a man through such things. Sol Klauber, he was drownded too, but they fished him out the same day. But after five days . . . Water weeds in her hair, Swede, that's the only part of it I like to remember, her hair . . . Gave me a headache . . . God damn it, Swede, we could have been happy. Everything was right, with us. Sometimes I think about it."

The medicine was taking effect, and the bourbon. He drained his glass and sank back on the pillows and presently he slept. And he cried then, even though Rolfe Torkelsen was there.

*

It was late June when they returned to New Empire, and the town looked insignificant, after the sights they had seen. But the river looked big. They hadn't seen any rivers back East that the Mississippi couldn't have swallowed.

The afternoon following their return Rolfe went to the Buckmaster Building, where he found Jim in shirt sleeves, his desk mountainous with accumulated mail.

"Sit down, Swede. Have a cigar."

As usual, Rolfe took two, and as usual they bickered about that, for like most businessmen they had developed certain comic rituals to make life bearable. Feet on the desk, Jim sat tipped back with hands hooked behind his head, sweat splotching the armpits of his shirt, a cigar cocked in his mouth.

"How did you find your family?" Rolfe asked.

"Same as ever. She doesn't even know me any more. How are the judge and his wife?"

"About the same. It gave me a start when I saw them, they've aged so much. I don't mean it happened while I was gone. I mean when I thought of them on the trip I thought of them as they used to look years ago. It brought me up short, seeing them as they are."

"He won't live forever," Jim said. "You'll be the whole firm, some day. Well, I'll keep you busy. I've got big plans. I'm ordering three more steamboats for next season, and there's this railroad thing."

He stood up and went to the huge map of Wisconsin on the wall, tracing a line with his forefinger from Madison to New Empire.

"I want to get started on this," he said, "while times are hard and costs are down. We'll need attorneys in Madison and in Chicago, and I'll leave it up to you which ones to pick. I'm making you chief legal counsel."

"You're a damned fool to do that," Rolfe said.

"Why?"

"Railroad law is highly specialized. I don't have the experience."

"You've got the brains," Jim said, "and that's what counts. You can pick up experience as you go along. Hire the best lawyers and learn from them. But I want you as top man. Know why?"

"Because you're a poor judge of character."

Jim laughed.

"No, Swede, it's because I trust you. You're on my side. I'm not on guard with you. I know you will stick with me. If I start making a fool move—and every man does that—you'll yell whoa. You're not afraid to tell me what you think. That's why I want you in there as chief counsel. I couldn't be sure of some Chicago lawyer I hadn't known."

"Have it your own way," Rolfe said.

"All right, better plan to go to Madison and Chicago next week and get the papers drawn. For three separate companies: the railroad, the construction company and the land company. I want to offer the public stock as soon as possible. But don't go buying any of that stock yourself, Swede. That's for widows and orphans. You might get a faster ride than you expected." He laughed. "Anyway, let's get off our asses and get started."

"I can take a hint," Rolfe said, standing up.

Jim squared away and shadowboxed.

"I ought to beat you up," he said. "I ought to toss you in the river."

"Any time you want to try."

Jim pivoted and picked up a slip of paper from the desk. His voice was serious but his eyes were humorous.

"Swede, I've made out a check in favor of Gentry & Torkelsen to

cover your fee on that trip east. I know it's small, but I'll be damned
if I'll pay you shysters more."

"We can always sue."

"Try it. By God, I'll drown you. A preacher's son ought to drown
awful nice. Preachers did, when I drownded me so many in the old
days. That was when they called me Preacher Drowning Jim, up on
the Flambeau."

He handed Rolfe the check. The sum was a hundred thousand
dollars.

"Jesus!" Rolfe said.

"No, Swede, the name's Buckmaster. Guess you've got me mixed with
some friend of your father's."

Rolfe's fingers trembled, holding the check. He sat down.

"You must have made a mistake," he said. "You meant to write a
hundred dollars."

"I meant no such thing. I meant a hundred thousand. Hell, what's
that? The government paid me almost nineteen million, Swede. And
you were right there standing by me, all the way through. I take care
of my pals, boy. And that's just the opener. You've got to raise your
sights. You'll be rich, boy, if you stick by me."

*

Rolfe could scarcely wait to show that check to Judge Gentry. But
when he returned to the Gentry Block, he learned the judge had gone
home for the day.

"Then I'd better follow him," Rolfe told a clerk. "If anybody wants
me I'll be there."

He remembered how he felt that afternoon, hurrying down the stairs
from the law offices and emerging onto Winnebago Street. Young men,
he supposed, were always dreaming of quick success and sudden wealth,
and he had achieved them when he least expected. At midafternoon on
that hot day the town was somnolent, the sun pouring down on teams
switching at flies along the hitching posts. On the sidewalk under the
awnings people kept stopping him to shake hands and ask about his
trip, but he never remembered what he told them; he was in a golden
daze. A hundred thousand for the firm; half of it his; he was rich.
At twenty-two. Worth fifty thousand. And that was but the beginning,
Jim Buckmaster had said.

He remembered how, in one corner of his mind, thoughts were sprouting which had never been there before: thoughts which astonished him
and which he did not welcome. Even while he shook hands with fellow
townsmen and cracked jokes, he was aware of those thoughts: they were
arrogant and supercilious, almost, telling him how he had already out-
distanced all the young fellows in New Empire and most of his elders,
how he would be wealthy and renowned while they plugged along be-

hind store counters. The future had never looked so fine. He understood better then some of Jim Buckmaster's elation in New York when he had talked of owning the world. Money could do that to a man, for money was an agglomeration of power, and power was man's second great lust.

"Easy," he told himself. "Damn it, you're the same person you were an hour ago. Don't get the big head."

But he was not the same person; he was that person plus half of a hundred thousand dollars. It made a difference.

"Why, Rolfe," Lucretia Gentry said, when he found her in the living room. "What are you doing home at this hour?"

"I wanted to talk with the judge."

"He's taking his nap. Is something wrong?"

No, he told her, quite the contrary. And he added:

"Don't wake him up. This can wait. I'll be in the yard."

He left the house and smiling to himself paced the old brick paths of the garden where, in the vegetable patch, tomato plants were in blossom and cabbage-butterflies flitted through the thick sunlight. In the orchard cherries hung in clusters; the lawn rippled away in green gold; everything looked pleasantly mellowed. But he was restless; passing the stable, he walked south along the alley to Blackhawk Street and west toward the river.

It was always that way, he thought: if you lived anywhere near the river you sought her out in your saddest or happiest hours, as men who lived near the coast sought out the sea. For the waters of the earth were the vast womb of mankind; from them, in bygone aeons, man had come groping and dripping, impelled by the itching nerve centers inside his cranium.

Crossing Front Street, Rolfe followed a weedy path between the tannery and the slaughterhouse to the cattail jungles fringing shore. Near at hand the water moved sluggishly, scummed with algae, but off toward midstream it was blue as Homerian seas. He watched a steamboat coming from the south, chimneys smoking; steam flashed and he recognized her whistle; she was the *Bonnie*. And he thought of what Jim had told him in New York about a girl named Bonnie.

When Rolfe returned to the house, Judge Gentry was awake, sitting in the library without a coat or collar. He looked almost feeble this afternoon, his throat ravaged by the years, his large hands bony and brown-specked, violet veins at his temples, his silky white hair damp.

"I can't read it without my glasses," he said, when Rolfe gave him the check. "And I don't know where I left them."

"It's our fee for my trip to Washington."

"You billed Mr. Buckmaster? You shouldn't have done that. You know we settle with him the first of the year."

"I didn't bill him. He wanted it this way."

848

"I see, I see." The judge's voice was edged with an old man's peevishness. "How much did he pay?"

"A hundred thousand dollars."

"How was that? How much?"

"A hundred thousand."

"But that's ridiculous."

"I know. It's a large amount of money. But that's how he wanted it. After all, he received nearly nineteen million from the government."

"And that's ridiculous too," Judge Gentry said. "The note should have been repaid, of course, but never with a sum like that. Congress has gone out of its head. It's this slavery question. It turns men crazy. Where it will end I don't know. I worry about it. Sometimes I can't sleep at night. I wish General Jackson had lived. He would have taken matters into hand. These persons like Stephen Douglas and James Buchanan. Pygmies, sir. Everything has been bungled. The Kansas question, everything. And these abolitionists. Men of violence. I have hated slavery all my life, but I do not want to see this Republic wrecked on that shoal. Do you?"

"No, of course not."

"When I was young," Judge Gentry said, "men were of larger natures. Some men. Not Mr. Clay. He disappointed us all. But men like General Jackson. Like Thomas Jefferson. He held Ethiopes in bondage, but he wished to abolish the institution when the Republic was formed. He looked ahead, sir, and foresaw what is coming to pass. It's a blessing he never lived to see it. Men can live too long, you know. Sometimes I think I have."

"That's nonsense," Rolfe said.

"Possibly. But this I know, sir. If this Republic ends in bloodshed and violence, I do not want to see it. If the Republic dies, let me die too. And if that sounds grandiloquent, make the most of it . . . Now about this bank draft. What was the amount again?"

"A hundred thousand."

"Absurd. That man Buckmaster has a great deal to learn. He has intelligence, sir, but it is untrained. Imagine asking nineteen million from the government! Life isn't a game of grab. Life is an exercise in self-discipline and moderation. And so is the law, which mirrors life. A hundred thousand! What folly! Do you suppose for one moment, my dear young sir, that your services to Mr. Buckmaster were worth any such amount? They were worth, perhaps, twenty-five hundred. Stretch a point and say five thousand. You'll return the check in the morning, of course."

*

"Swede," Jim said, next day in his office, "don't be a lunkhead."

849

"What else can I do? The judge says it's too big a fee. He's head of the firm."

"Horse manure. He's an old fogy."

"That may be. But he's still senior partner."

"Aren't you equal partners?"

"In theory. But I can't go against his judgment in a matter like this. It would rupture our whole relationship."

"Damn it, Swede, you earned the money."

"He says not. He says my services couldn't possibly be worth a hundred thousand."

"I'm the best judge of that," Jim said.

Rolfe shrugged. He had spent a sleepless night; his mouth tasted of stale tobacco; and for almost the first time since coming to New Empire he felt irked with Sophronicus Gentry. Damn it, there was no need for the old man to be so stiff-necked. And there had been no need for him to point out so bluntly that Rolfe's legal counsel could not have been worth a hundred thousand. It was true, but it hurt.

"If I want to pay you a good fee," Jim said, "that's my business. Maybe I didn't use you in Washington as much as I thought I might. What difference does that make? You were there if I did need you. When I back up a man, Swede, I back him the whole way. If he's in my camp, I believe in paying him good wages. I think you should bank this check. Once the thing's done, the judge may change his mind."

"He'll never change his mind."

"Oh, hell," Jim said, biting the end off a cigar. He lighted it, frowning, and stood up and paced the office, his face almost surly. "Damndest thing I ever heard of. Swede, why don't you cut loose from him? Start in business for yourself."

"I could never do that. Not after what he's done for me."

"No, I reckon you couldn't. Not the way you're put together. I remember that night on the raft, how you wanted to fight me when you thought I'd gone back on my promise not to beat up the Bobcat. God, you were a scrappy kid. And then you told me about giving money to that fake abolitionist, and how you'd have to work to make it up. You've got too much conscience, Swede."

"Maybe. But I couldn't leave the judge."

Jim smiled.

"I suppose it's one thing I like about you. Your word's better than most men's bond. So keep that conscience, Swede. And keep the check too."

But Rolfe shook his head.

"The judge would never touch it. You might as well tear it up."

"All right, Swede, if the judge won't he won't."

Jim took the check and tore it to bits. Watching, Rolfe felt a pang. At his desk, Jim picked up a pen.

"Five thousand dollars," he said. "Is that the top fee he'll take?"

"That's it."

Jim wrote, tore out the check, wrote some more. Then he leaned back in his chair.

"Tell you what I've done, Swede. I've drawn a draft for five thousand in favor of Gentry & Torkelsen. That's the firm's fee. But I've drawn another for ninety-five thousand, in your favor. And that's nobody's business but yours and mine."

Rolfe felt his heart jump, and for a second his elation of yesterday returned, but then he realized he couldn't take the check for ninety-five thousand. He said so.

"Why not?" Jim asked.

"It wouldn't be quite straight. I went to Washington as a firm member of Gentry & Torkelsen. I can't take a fee of five thousand on the firm's behalf, and another for myself."

"Well, I'll be damned," Jim said, sounding riled. "You'll never get rich that way, boy. God Almighty but you're green. You've got your way to make in the world, don't you realize that? It's all right for some old goat like Judge Gentry to go around with his nose up—he's made his and his race is nearly run—but God, Swede, you're just starting. Don't be a bigger damned fool than the Lord made you. What do you think life is, anyway, a debating society? It's a brawl, Swede. When you see a dollar rolling down the street you'd better grab it, and once you've done that you'd better hang tight for there are always six other roosters ready to take it away from you. And I'm sick of hearing how Judge Gentry might not like what you've done. How about me? Maybe I don't like it either, the way you act as if my money might give you smallpox. Damn it, I'll tear up this check for five thousand. Let the judge bill me in his own good time. But this one for ninety-five thousand, that's yours. If you don't take it I'm going to be mad, and when I get mad there's only one thing that'll calm me down and that's to skin alive the first Swede that's handy and eat him for supper."

"I'm not a Swede," Rolfe said. "Damn it, I'm a Dane."

Jim broke out laughing. And he stood up and ruffled Rolfe's hair and slapped his back.

"All right, boy, now get out of here. I'm busy. And take this check or I'll never speak to you again."

So Rolfe got out and took the check for ninety-five thousand. But he didn't, he told himself, have to deposit it. He could tear it up. This afternoon.

But when afternoon came he decided to wait till tomorrow, and when tomorrow came he still hesitated. That went on for several days and for several troubled nights. And he discovered that a great sum of money has a logic of its own, serpent-subtle, and a strength beyond the resolution of a young man starting out in life. So at last, reluctantly, he deposited the check to his own account in the Bank of New Empire. Nor did the sky fall. But absurdly, he felt uneasy in the presence of Judge Gentry. It was hard to meet the old man's straight gaze.

*

Long afterward he wondered whether James L. Buckmaster had tried to corrupt him. Probably not. At least not consciously. Could have been, of course, that Jim, looking ahead, had realized that the Buckmaster Lumber Company might find itself out on the windy side of the law, some day; perhaps he had wanted to make sure of his lieutenants. But Rolfe didn't believe that. He was not sure, even, that there had been corruption.

For several months after depositing the check, he could hardly believe the money was his; he had the feeling—and he knew it was absurd—that if he drew against that ninety-five thousand he would be called in by the bank and lectured for spending money he didn't possess. But gradually that feeling passed; presently it seemed right and natural that he should have an enormous balance at the bank.

He began investing the money the following autumn, tentatively at first and then with more confidence: a farm in Fox County; two farms in Illinois; a business building in Madison; a corner lot in Chicago. Traveling a great deal during the next year or so, on business for the Buckmaster interests, he kept his eyes open for the opportunities always so abundant in hard times, and by paying cash he bought at bottom prices. His affairs prospered.

And he grew in legal acumen and in knowledge of the world during those next two years, associating as he did with railroad lawyers in Chicago and political lawyers in Madison; his wits were sharpened. Bankers, engineers, merchant kings, company presidents, financiers, governors, landholders: he brushed elbows and bent elbows with them all. Twice he was offered partnerships in Chicago law firms, but he never seriously considered leaving New Empire. He was doing very well as it was, and besides, Judge Gentry had come to depend on him more and more.

He dressed better, but he would never be one of those impeccably-clad gentlemen of jurisprudence whose manners were courtly and whose voices were oil and honey. His weapon was a broadsword, not a cool stiletto. He was a good, hard, open fighter and he looked it, with his thick wrists and his impudent grin and his hair forever rumpled. Yet he no longer looked or felt like an untried lawyer from the country. He knew his way around.

Several months after his trip to Washington with Jim, construction began on the Madison, New Empire & Western Railroad, to the accompaniment of joyful hysteria in the counties through which it would pass. Even with money still tight the stock sold well; towns bonded themselves to pay the railroad to include them on its route; new towns were platted by the Empire Land Company, James L. Buckmaster, president, and the lots sold briskly. Telegraph wires were strung along the right-of-way; wires which would carry the news of John Brown's raid and Sumter's fall and Lincoln's assassination; progress, people said, was on the march. However that might be, James L. Buckmaster was indubitably on the march.

Construction of the railroad went ahead fast, with Mr. Buckmaster prodding the enterprise; labor and materials were cheap and plentiful, times were so hard; a dozen mule camps sprang up, tented cities that housed armies of workmen. Dynamite blasted the hills where the Kickapoos had buried their dead; rivers were bridged; track was laid at a furious pace. And if the Buckmaster Construction Company charged seven prices for this work, nobody could effectively protest, because the man who owned the construction company controlled the railroad. But scarcely anyone dreamed of protesting, actually, for a railroad builder was a public benefactor, in those days.

And so it was that in the autumn of 1859, a week before the old man of Osawatomie struck at Harpers Ferry, the first train, draped with bunting, chugged into New Empire from the south along rails that paralleled the river. At the new Front Street depot, still unpainted and smelling of pine, a great crowd had assembled and bands played. And Judge Sophronicus Gentry delivered the oration, the last public address in his long series of public addresses. On the platform, bareheaded in the sunshine, gripping his hickory cane, he looked like a forlorn plenipotentiary from the classical Eighteenth Century to the bustling Nineteenth. His voice was too weak to carry far; when he spoke of General Andrew Jackson tears filled his eyes; people couldn't hear; small boys giggled.

*

That was a dark autumn, in Rolfe's memory. The Republic had been in a bad enough way without old John Brown trying to start a slave revolt. He was a bloody-minded Puritan who belonged in a lunatic asylum, like all Puritans, and his outlook had been soured by the climate of New England and Kansas. In boyhood he had picked up the habit of reading the Bible, especially the Old Testament, and his God, made in Mr. Brown's image, was a bitter-eyed old sadist who never should have been put in charge of the universe in the first place. There was a twist of the masochist in Mr. Brown also; he must have wanted to be a martyr. So he and his silly friends seized the United States arsenal at Harpers Ferry.

It scared the South witless, of course. For years the South had been sleeping with a revolver under its pillow, afraid of a slave uprising, and old Brown's behavior convinced it that the North must be plotting dark deeds. So the South hanged old Brown higher than Haman, which was a good day's work except that it gave the abolitionists a martyr. While

Southern preachers cheered, Northern preachers moaned; in Northern cities meetings were held honoring the old murderer; and somebody made up a song about Mr. Brown's soul marching on, a peregrination which could not be substantiated.

But in any case, after those events at Harpers Ferry, the Republic was very sick indeed, and people felt in their bones that some black doom was impending. Meanwhile, one's own life went on.

News of Brown's raid reached New Empire late on a Sunday night; next day people kept going to the telegraph office in the new station for the latest word; Rolfe went there Monday evening on his way to his office. Twenty or thirty men were lounging about the place, their sympathies largely with old Brown. He had gumption, they said; he had done a fool thing and would doubtless be forced to surrender, but you had to admire a man who would stake his life on what he thought was right; most of these abolitionists did nothing but talk, but John Brown, he had gumption.

"Me, I don't hold with the niggers," one man said. "But I don't like the way the South's been trying to run us, neither. This Brown, he's a right smart feller. He's showing 'em. Don't know but what I'd as soon give the abolitionists my vote, if they've got many fellers like Brown."

The telegraph began clattering and everybody fell silent. Then the station agent announced:

"Brown's still holding out. The betting is they'll take him by morning. Colonel Robert E. Lee has gone to Harpers Ferry to take command."

"Who the hell's Robert E. Lee?" somebody asked.

Nobody knew.

After a few minutes Rolfe left; when he reached his office he found Nixie Auerbach at work with a broom; he told her about the latest telegraphic dispatches. She listened in silence; her physical equipment, he had long since discovered, was superior to her mental. Their affair had dragged on too long, outlasting his first excitement but not his uneasiness at being involved with a married woman. More than once during the past year he had thought it would be prudent to disentangle himself. Yet he needed a woman, and she was convenient. Tonight, as on so many other evenings, he led her into his private office and locked the door.

And it was good, as usual, but good only in emancipating him briefly from desire; ecstasy lacked; memory of ecstasy lacked. Afterward, lying beside her on the couch, he was almost disgusted. The whole affair seemed shabby. Illicit love: the very phrase had a hissing, sneaking sound. Some day he would meet a girl he wanted to marry, and what then? Would it be so easy to pull out of this relationship?

"Kiss me," she whispered in the dark, and he obeyed, although now that was the last thing he wished. Her lips were wet and loose.

He lay a little longer, his thoughts ranging far from that office, across the dark American land to a town called Harpers Ferry. Right now old Brown was beleaguered in his fortress, and a man named Colonel Robert E. Lee was giving orders. What would come of it all? Nothing good; events would move faster now toward—what? Civil conflict? That seemed inconceivable. Yet Judge Gentry was predicting that; all day he had looked grim as death.

"Mr. Torkelsen," Nixie Auerbach whispered.

Damn her, anyway. It made you feel odd to have a woman you had just made love to call you Mr. Torkelsen. Yet would he have liked it better if she had called him Rolfe? He said, "Yes."

"I'm afraid I have bad news."

"What kind?"

"About us."

He thought, my God. He said, "Oh? Well, let's hear it."

"I think I'm in the family way," she said.

"Are you sure?"

"I'm pretty sure. Yes, I think I'm sure."

The thing to do, he told himself, was to keep calm. But his thoughts raced. He asked banally:

"What makes you think so?"

"Well, you know."

"Yes," he said, "yes, of course. How long have you—?"

"I'm two weeks late," she said. "And I feel kind of funny. In the mornings I feel funny. I think I'm in the family way, all right. I've had three kids already. I know the signs. I'm sure I'm in the family way."

Damn it, why couldn't she say pregnant?

"And I don't know what to do," she said. "I don't know what I'll tell Harold."

Harold. Her husband, incapacitated from the waist down.

"I see," Rolfe said. "Yes, of course."

"Because Harold has never used me since his accident," she said. "He'll know some other man has been using me. I don't know what I'll tell him. It's going to be embarrassing."

Christ in heaven!

"He won't like it," Mrs. Auerbach said. "I know he won't. He'll be mad. What he'll ever do I don't know. I'll bet he'd take the kids and walk out, if he was well, but he can't do that on account of being sick. He'll do something though, with that ornery side of his. It worries me. Does it worry you?"

"Yes."

"I knew it would, but I thought I'd best tell you. Maybe you can think of something."

"Maybe I can," Rolfe said, "if you'll keep still for a minute."

He stood up, groped through the darkness to the window, his thoughts milling. "Gentry & Torkelsen," gold-leafed letters on the pane said,

"Attorneys-at-Law." Gentry & Torkelsen. Rolfe Torkelsen, the successful young attorney. He was thinking of nights when he was a boy back in Elysian Springs, studying by candlelight; of nights as a law student when he returned to this office to read the books till his eyes smarted. Damn. This needed handling. If he made a bad move, if there should be scandal, his career might be ruined; he might be disbarred. A lawyer, sir, is an officer of the court. A lawyer, sir, should be above reproach . . .

"I know you'll think of something," Nixie Auerbach was saying.

*

On his way home that evening he walked along Winnebago Street to the river and south to the railroad station where a few loafers still waited, hoping for excitement. But the situation at Harpers Ferry remained unchanged.

"He's got a lot of gumption, anyway," somebody was saying. "Yes, sir, that's how it appears to me."

Next week or next month would these same loafers be chewing over the great Torkelsen-Auerbach scandal? He could hear them, in imagination: Yes, sir, he wronged her. Been wronging her for nigh onto two years, so I hear. Well, it's a shame. That's what I said when I first heered it, and that's what I still say, it's a crying shame. Her husband flat on his back and her carrying on like that, and with three young ones too. But what I always say, when a woman goes bad there's a man to blame. Never did like that young Torkelsen. He thought he was *some!* Using all them long words a man can't understand, and all the time wronging a poor woman like that Mrs. Auerbach. They ought to disbar him, that's what, and I hear tell they may. Feller like that oughtn't be allowed to practice the law.

He left the station. The evening was crisp with a half-moon over the Iowa bluffs; fallen leaves rustled underfoot. When he reached the Gentry house a light was still burning; he couldn't face Judge Gentry tonight; so he walked on, north to Winnebago and beyond, through the frosty night. There must be a way out, he kept thinking; and of course there was, if he cared to risk it. He could give her money and send her to Chicago where shady doctors could be found. But he would never do that. Too risky. She might die. And even if the thing came off successfully, abortion was a crime, and he had not sunk so low he would become an accessory to that. Besides, it would be his child.

His child. In the vague way of bachelors he had thought how it would be, some day, to father children. But with a woman he could respect. Nixie Auerbach was a dullard. Yet for the rest of his life, if need be, he would give her money to rear such a child. But would her husband accept that as a suitable settlement? Lying ill, brooding against fate, wouldn't he be exactly the sort of person who would file a suit?

There seemed no solution; certainly there was none tonight. At last he returned home. A light still burned in the library.

"Is that you, Rolfe?" Judge Gentry called.

Rolfe went to the library.

"Have you heard any news?" the judge asked.

"They've sent troops to Harpers Ferry. Brown will be captured by morning."

"They'll hang him," the judge said. "They'll have to hang him. It's their legal right and duty, but they shouldn't. It will stir up the country. These abolitionists will make him their Christ. These are bad times."

"Very bad."

"If we had a man—a real man—for president. Buchanan is timid. Flaccid. The senate is full of scoundrels. This will divide the party, sir, mark my words. That will mean a Republican victory. Seward our next president. All the ragtag and bobtail rising to the top. Rolfe, I'd like a drink. Bring whiskey, will you, and join me."

Rolfe brought whiskey.

"To the Republic," Judge Gentry said. And after he drank he added, "It was a beautiful Republic, Rolfe. Always more a dream than reality, I fear, but beautiful. I fought for it, and I'd have gladly laid down my life. Twenty lives, if I had had them. And for a time it looked as if the dream might become reality. The Jeffersonian dream. Every man enlightened, and every man a statesman. Perhaps it was asking too much of human nature. Then this slavery thing, passions let loose. Anyway, I drink to it, Rolfe, I drink to it a thousand times. To the Republic."

"To the Republic," Rolfe said.

*

An attorney was his own worst lawyer: that was a maxim of the legal profession. When deep in trouble you lost objectivity. You needed the advice of somebody not emotionally involved.

Yet during the next week Rolfe tried to counsel himself, with pretty miserable results. He lost that mental poise, that detachment, so necessary in solving problems. Thinking back, he told himself that even in his indiscretion with Nixie Auerbach he had still been discreet, taking all necessary precautions.

Could she, then, be mistaken? She thought not.

"I'm in the family way, all right," she kept saying, night after night. "I can tell. I always get morning sickness early, and I've been having that. Gas, too. I always have a lot of gas when I'm in the family way."

She no longer seemed a seductive Ceres with coils of red-gold hair.

"Harold's getting suspicious," she said, one evening about ten days after John Brown's capture. "The way I'm sick every morning, he wonders. Just today he said to me, 'Bunny,' he said, (he always calls me Bunny), 'Bunny,' he said, 'you act like you've been knocked up.' I just laughed at that. But he's getting suspicious."

"Suppose you'd tell him the truth."

She looked dubious.

"I don't know about that, Mr. Torkelsen. I hate to say it, but Harold's kind of ornery. Being sick ain't helped his disposition, either. He'd raise a stink. He'd sue. He'd want to get even with you."

"I'll figure out something," Rolfe said. "Give me time."

"But time's kind of running out, Mr. Torkelsen. I always show it early. Take some women, they don't show nothing till they're four or five months along, but me, after about a month I look like I've been swallowing whole mushmelons."

So things were approaching a showdown; after she had gone that evening Rolfe paced his office. He couldn't, he simply couldn't, confide in Judge Gentry. The judge was a hard man to live up to. There was only one person he could turn to: Jim Buckmaster. He dreaded that, not because Jim was unworldly, but because he would feel like such a green young fool, getting caught like this. Yet he had to talk matters over with somebody. Two heads were better than one.

So he left his office and made his way toward Buckmaster's Island. Autumnal wind was blowing that night, driving last summer's leaves; they swirled round his ankles and danced madly; clouds kept racing. Winter was coming, the long bitter Wisconsin winter, and he wondered if he would be in disgrace and ruin before the geese flew north again. Crossing the bridge to the island, he trudged along the sandy road where the trees were already bare. When he reached the house he saw a light upstairs and another downstairs in a back room.

Nothing happened for quite a while, when he rang the bell, but then at last the door opened and Jim was standing there, a big muscular man in a dressing gown.

"Well, Swede," he said. "This is a surprise. Come in."

Rolfe followed him along the dim hall to what had been the back sitting room. Now it had been converted into an office. It was a man's room with two capacious spittoons, a shabby desk, old leather chairs. Against the wall, under a huge map of Wisconsin, stood a glass showcase; inside was a replica, in sand, of a stretch of river, with a miniature log raft.

"Greasy Dick whittled that out during his last sickness," Jim said, "and stitched it together. He wanted to give me a present. Could you use a drink?"

Rolfe could.

"Here's to you," Jim said. "I hope you live forever, pal, and I live to see you die. How's tricks?"

"Not so good. I'm in trouble."

"That's business," Jim said. "Leastwise that's what old Caleb McSwasey used to say. Business is trouble, he'd say. No trouble, no business. What's wrong?"

"I've got a woman pregnant."

"Congratulations, Swede."

"A married woman."

"That's the best kind to get pregnant," Jim said, "except a whore. If she's married, nobody can prove it wasn't her old man."

"Not with this woman. It's Nixie Auerbach."

"Who's she? Oh, yeah, I remember now. Wife of that careless square-head who got hurt. Yeah, I remember her. Not a bad-looking piece. How did it happen? Or maybe that's a hell of a question to ask."

Rolfe told how it happened. It was easy, unburdening himself to Jim Buckmaster, for Jim seemed to have gone beyond the common human temptation to judge one's fellow men.

"I can see how you've been worried," he said, when Rolfe had finished. "Well, your worries are over, Swede. Think no more about it."

"I can't help worrying."

"Sure, a man will, although it's foolish. But forget it. Let me handle it. I'll guarantee you'll hear no more about it."

A cloud lifted from Rolfe's brain.

"But I want every last fact you can think of," Jim said. "How often have you played around with her the last six weeks or so?"

"Not so often. I was in Chicago most of September. I came back the twenty-fifth. From then on, well, maybe six or eight times."

"Did you use anything?"

"Sure. I always did."

"Any reason to think it didn't work?"

"No."

"Good. She may be lying, Swede. You never can tell about a woman. Maybe she wants to get into you for some money. Or maybe that husband of hers figured it out. Maybe he figured if she'd tell you she was going to have a kid, and if he'd threaten suit, you'd cough up. Hell, if she is going to have a kid, maybe it's her husband's."

"But he's paralyzed."

"Love will find a way," Jim said, laughing. "Anyhow, don't worry. I'll call her in tomorrow and ask a few questions."

"You would have made a good lawyer," Rolfe said.

"There aren't any. Plenty of sharp ones, though, and you're one. But I might have been a lawyer, at that, if I'd gone to school like Sol Klauber wanted. Did I ever tell you how I ran off from him? Well, have another drink, and I'll—"

While Jim told the story a quality of tenderness came into his voice, as if he felt sorry for the waif he had been and even sorrier for Sol Klauber.

"Like a father to me," he said. "But I'm afraid I disappointed him.

859

I regret that. Well, a man picks up a lot of regrets. Here. Let me pour you another."

For the first time in nearly a fortnight Rolfe felt at peace. Jim had been good medicine; he was always that. As they sat there he told more about his childhood, how he had been a funny ragged kid with a determination to become rich.

"Well, I made it, Swede. And it don't amount to beans. You get a thousand and you want more. You get a million and you still want more. After while you can't stop, even if you wanted to, and you don't actually. But I'd trade it all if I could be twenty again, with my life to live over. I'd do different, Swede, on the second try. But that's the trouble, you don't get second chances."

Presently the door opened and a woman came in from the hall. Drifted in, really. It was Esperanza. Rolfe hadn't seen her for a long while; he scarcely knew her. Her hair that used to be so golden was now brownish and dull; her face was thin, her hands almost scrawny. But it was her manner that had changed most. She moved vaguely, and when she spoke her voice was gentle and vague and even sweet.

"We're looking for Jim Buckmaster," she said. "Have you seen him?"

"He's not around," Jim said.

"That's very odd. He promised to come back. We're engaged, you know."

"He's upriver somewhere," Jim said.

"We hope," she said, "he comes back soon, Heinrich and I." She smiled down at nothing whatever. "Say good evening to the gentlemen, Heinrich. That's the little man. Ooo, you are such a good boy. I don't know what I would do without you."

Jim was strangely gentle, putting his arm around her and guiding her into the hall, telling her to go to bed; perhaps Jim Buckmaster would return tomorrow.

"Tomorrow," she said. "Yes, tomorrow and tomorrow and tomorrow. I read that in a book once. In Santa Fe. Have you ever met my father? You would like him. His father was a general, you know."

*

Nixie Auerbach did not come to work the next evening or the next. It was November by then, the weather raw and wild; and at his desk, trying to concentrate, Rolfe could hear the wind screeching about the cornice of the Gentry Block. Despite Jim's reassurances, he was deeply worried. During the day, talking with clients, he found it hard to keep his mind on their problems.

"If I ever get out of this," he kept thinking, "I'll behave myself."

Far away in Virginia, John Brown had been tried and found guilty; in another month he would be hanged. And although New Empire had never been much concerned about slavery, those events hatched out a swarm of abolitionists; they held a protest meeting and passed angry resolutions. Those in attendance were not, in the main, leading citizens; they were humble persons whose lives had been dull and hard, the sort who welcomed a revival meeting or a medicine show or a funeral because of the novelty and excitement. John Brown gave them a cause and a chance to feel consequential. At the South their counterparts were the people who burned Negroes and bet on dog fights and were swayed by the rodomontade of William Lowndes Yancey.

"The canaille, sir," Judge Gentry said. "But they will do the country much mischief, before they are through. They've got the bit in their teeth and they mean to run with it."

Never had Rolfe seen the judge so dejected; national events had aged him; he looked frail. When he came to work he would forget to say good morning to the student clerks, he who had always been so courteous; and in his office he would sit by the hour, fingers peaked, mouth grim. He had lost interest even in chess; he wanted to talk of nothing but the fate of the country.

By the third afternoon following his visit to Buckmaster's Island, Rolfe was much too worried to accomplish anything useful, and he decided to go to Jim's office. He had been putting that off, mainly because he was afraid of hearing bad news. The sky was low and dull, the air gray, when he left the Gentry Block; the façades lining Winnebago Street looked drab and bleak. He was in the mood to avoid people, to seek out some wild, lonely place where he could brood over his problem, but his fellow citizens kept saying hello and cracking jokes; in a small town you were expected to be always friendly and cheerful. He wondered how many of those people would stand by him if he were disbarred and in disgrace. Judge Gentry would, and Lucretia, and Jim Buckmaster; who else? What was it Jim had said, in New York? That you could count your friends on the fingers of one thumb. He guessed that if Harold Auerbach stirred up a ruckus and branded him publicly as a seducer, he would go away somewhere. West, probably. That was where Americans always went, to escape humiliation and the complexities of a prudish civilization.

He crossed to the south side of Winnebago Street, and it was then that he saw Jim leaving the Buckmaster Building and coming toward him. Through the gray air he looked jovial and burly, and when you saw his woodsman's stride you thought of timber giants swinging their axes and raftsmen bucking their oars.

"Hello, Swede," he said. "I was on my way to see you."

"What's the news?" Rolfe asked, with a dry tongue.

"Everything's fine. Your worries are over, boy."

He was smiling; he clapped Rolfe on the back; and at that moment there was nothing Rolfe would not have done for Jim Buckmaster.

"I'd like to hear about it," Rolfe said.

"Sure, let's take a walk. I need fresh air."

They went to Front Street and south along the river, past wholesale houses and the new railroad station and the tannery and the slaughter-house. Jim talked of other things: of his plans to build a bridge, some day, across the river, and extend his railroad into the rich prairies of Iowa and on and on; of how he would lay rails up into the Wisconsin woods.

"Swede," he said, "I'm like a kid with blocks. I like to build. Hell, boy, there are places up there that are nothing but logging camps now, but when my railroad goes through they'll be towns and then cities. I'll put in steam sawmills and ship my lumber by rail. I'll build box factories and bucket factories and clothespin factories. I'll have the raw materials and I'll have the transportation. What's to stop me?"

"Nothing," Rolfe said. "Nothing ever will."

"That's the ticket, boy. Nothing will stop me. If any bastard gets in my way I'll stomp him. Business is like that, Swede. It's like a saloon after a drive. The rooster with the biggest fists wins. And the higher you climb the more like a saloon brawl it is. Only money's your muscle then, and lawyers are your fists. But you want to hear about Nixie Auerbach. It's all fixed, Swede. You're in the clear."

They had reached a waste place beyond the town where softwoods grew and dead leaves were ankle deep. Jim sat on a fallen log and stared out across the river, cloud-gray now.

"I called in this Auerbach woman," he said, "and had a talk. She was stubborn, but I wore her down. I had to make some threats, Swede, to get her to open up. Had to tell her I'd stop my monthly checks to her husband. She broke then, and cried. Damn, I didn't like that, but when you're after something—information or whatever—the way to get it is to get it. If you break a few heads, well, it has to be."

"Is she actually pregnant?" Rolfe asked.

"Oh, she's pregnant, all right, but you know what, Swede? It's not your kid at all. It's Froggy Maizeroy's."

Rolfe's jaw must have dropped, for Jim broke out laughing.

"Sure. He wears pants too, you know. And he wasn't as careful as you. It happened when you were out of town. She was working in your office one night with the door open, and Froggy was leaving his apartment across the hall. He said hello, and one thing led to another. From then on she was playing you both. How do you like that?"

Rolfe liked it, of course. But at the same time it irked his manhood to learn that Nixie Auerbach had shared her favors with Froggy Maizeroy. He had thought she was his woman only; his and her husband's.

"You'll hear no more about it, Swede. I put the fear of God in her good. She knows now if she drags in your name those monthly checks will stop. She turned white when I said that. She'll tell her husband it was Froggy. And Froggy's left town. I had him in yesterday, and when he heard what was cooking he left on a downriver boat. Your troubles are over."

Rolfe tried to put his relief and thanks into words.

"Don't mention it, Swede. That's what friends are for, to stand by you. Hell, maybe you can do me a favor some time. Besides, I came out all right." He laughed. "That Mrs. Auerbach is a looker, and yours ain't the only office with a couch."

*

In December they hanged John Brown and sent his body north where it was buried in a chilly New England graveyard and where it moldered, according to rumor. But his soul, people said, went marching on. That was too bad.

And as it marched the prospects of the new Republican Party rose. Former Whigs, free soilers, the sweepings of the old Know-Nothing Party, malcontents, intellectuals, moderate opponents of slavery: those odd bedfellows were the Republicans. They would win in the autumn, people said. They would nominate Senator Seward, very likely, or Salmon P. Chase, or N. P. Banks of Massachusetts. But out in Illinois an astute politician named Lincoln had other ideas; in his small-town law office, which was not unlike the law office of Rolfe Torkelsen, he sat writing letters and conferring and pulling a wire here and another there; and at the fag-end of winter he went east and spoke at the Cooper Union, an awkward rusty figure in the gaslight, but he had a knack with words.

Meanwhile the South was ravening, busting its britches to secede from something; so when the Democratic Convention met in Charleston the delegates from the Cotton States picked up their toys and went home, to foregather later and nominate John C. Breckinridge of Kentucky. And what was left of the Democrats nominated Stephen A. Douglas, and some ossified characters calling themselves the Constitutional Union Party nominated Bell of Tennessee, and at the Wigwam in Chicago the managers of the lawyer from Springfield horse-traded and made wild promises of cabinet posts and so secured the nomination of the Hon. A. Lincoln.

Compared with the campaign of 1856, when the Republicans ran a man on horseback named John Charles Frémont, the campaign of 1860 was apathetic. Lincoln would win, people said; how could he help winning, with the opposition so divided? Yet elections are never won till the ballots are counted, so the Republicans took no chances: there were campaign biographies emphasizing the ability to split rails as a prime qualification for the presidency, and deals were attempted with the abolitionists, who were having none of Mr. Lincoln; and there were torchlight parades and Wide-Awake Clubs. And to the irritation and sorrow of Judge Gentry, who would cast a reluctant ballot for Senator Douglas, Rolfe Torkelsen was president of the New Empire Wide-

Awakes. That was how he met Sue Hatfield.

He remembered that evening in late October when the Wide-Awakes sponsored a great pre-election rally and people flocked to New Empire from all over the county. Victory was in the air that night; the October states of Pennsylvania and Indiana had plumped for the Republicans; straw polls showed which way the gale was blowing; the South kept screaming about secession but few took that old threat seriously except the stock market which fell sharply in New York; Lincoln was as good as in; there would be no slavery in the territories and everything would end happily. Bands were playing that evening, down on the river front; a special train had arrived from Madison with state candidates and their well-wishers; now and then the locomotive tootled; and at last a great parade assembled and started east, filling Winnebago Street from curb to curb.

Never before, the *Chronicle* said later, had New Empire seen such a demonstration. Leading it rode the mayor on a charger, followed by a brass band uniformed in scarlet and gilt: that military music all but drowned out the huzzas of the sidewalk throngs, the squeals of children, the barking of dogs. Torches flamed boldly—an avenue of torches from Front Street to the Gentry Block—and in their red light the long procession took on a goblin quality, as if this were some pagan jubilee in the mad season of Halloween. Squads of pretty girls could be seen, costumed in tipsy hats and waving flags; there were prodigious banners carried on poles, bearing the names of Lincoln and Hamlin; there were candle-lit transparencies with campaign slogans. Carriages were in the line of march, draped in bunting and freighted with political dignitaries: you saw the dark flash of silk hats and the white flash of boiled shirts. And there were, of course, the floats, lumber wagons risen to glory, their wheel-spokes entwined with crepe paper, their Percherons wearing plumes, their platforms showing a log cabin or some travesty of Stephen A. Douglas. And always could be heard the music of bands or of a thousand voices singing about how Old Abe Lincoln came out of the wilderness.

At Court Avenue the parade wheeled north, swirling like a many-colored river into confusion and disbandment when it reached the courthouse lawn. Under the elms a speakers' platform had been built, and there were lumber benches for an audience of two thousand. These were quickly filled; people sat on the grass; small boys climbed trees; and the women's auxiliary of the Wide-Awakes, which had set up stands for the sale of coffee and doughnuts, did a thriving business.

"Let us pray," said the mayor; and a limber old man with a white beard reaching to his navel addressed the Almighty as one Republican to another. It was a lengthy prayer and well-reasoned, with humility and nagging in the exact proportions a good prayer should have, and with the proper amount of coughing from the audience. It said Mr. Lincoln was a good Christian, which would have been news to a Springfield lawyer named Herndon, and while it didn't exactly accuse God of voting wrong in 1856, thereby bringing about the present mess in Washington, it hinted that this was the case. It was not too late, however, for amends to be made: elect Lincoln and bygones would be bygones. Amen.

People sighed and finished their coffee, which had grown cold in the crisp air.

And now the mayor introduced the permanent chairman of this meeting, our good friend and neighbor, Rolfe Torkelsen. Applause. Away up there on the platform, across all those heads, he looked self-confident and personable, his hair rumpled and bright in the torchlight. When he spoke his voice was not a politician's; it was neither unctuous nor mellifluous; it was almost casual; people felt he was talking to them with the directness of a conversation on a street corner. But it had a carrying quality, and a suggestion of bite.

One after another, he introduced candidates for office on the Republican ticket. These were supposed to limit themselves to a few words, but they didn't, always. Even such lowly courthouse hacks as the assessor wished to point out how their re-election would halt the spread of slavery. People clapped, but this was not what they had come to hear. They had come to hear Senator Benjamin F. Wade of Ohio, who had been billed as the principal speaker. But where was Senator Wade?

"Ladies and gentlemen," Rolfe Torkelsen said, "it is now my painful duty to announce a disruption in our schedule. As you know, we had expected an address this evening by Senator Ben Wade. Unfortunately, the senator is not with us. Owing to circumstances beyond anybody's control, he missed the cars in Chicago which would have carried him to Madison in time to board the special coming here. But he sent us a telegram."

Rolfe read the telegram. It was flowery with regrets and with the hope that all Republicans everywhere would be successful, including the Hon. A. Lincoln and the Hon. Park Irwin.

After the applause Rolfe stood smiling.

"I know your disappointment will be the greater," he said, "when I tell you that much against my will I have been chosen to substitute for Senator Wade."

They laughed and clapped.

"I am reminded of a Danish story my father used to tell . . ."

He told it, throwing in a few Danish expressions, but not so many that the story would be lost on non-Danes.

More laughter and applause.

"And so ladies and gentlemen . . ."

And as he launched into his speech, he experienced for the first time the intoxication that comes to an orator who has reached the maturity of his powers and who is in complete rapport with his audience. He remembered that occasion always, when he helped elect the Hon. A. Lincoln. It would come back to him: the bright platform, the great dark throng, the torches in the night, the fine pitch of his mind. When the meeting opened he had known stage fright, but now he was keyed beyond that; his thoughts flowed lucidly; when he needed an exact word to express an exact idea, the word was on his tongue. He handled his body well; when he made a gesture it was the right one. And yet as he spoke, he was aware of some judgment chamber of his mind where another Rolfe Torkelsen sat listening with an ironic smile at a performance which was perhaps too slick and not without charlatanism. But the crowd liked it, except for one person.

Almost from the first he noticed her, down there in the third row, a girl of perhaps twenty-two with a plain intelligent face. Her hair—it was the color of cinnamon—had a gloss and shine in the torchlight. At first she smiled at his jokes, but as his speech went on, as he expressed the Republican Party's sympathy for the slave but its unwillingness to tamper with the sacredness of property by adopting abolitionist doctrines, the girl looked angry. He wondered who she was. Presently he found himself arguing directly at her: government was government, law was law, where law ended anarchy began, one's humanitarian impulses were all for righting the great wrong of slavery, but . . . but . . . all the usual straddles of politicians in that tragic autumn. She was unimpressed.

He made himself ignore her after that; he gave himself wholly to his peroration . . . the great Republic . . . a time of peril . . . a man of the people . . . a railsplitter . . . a man who . . . a man who . . . a man who . . .

Then he was finished and the applause was thunderous and on the platform politicians were pumping his hand.

"Rolfe," said Congressman Park Irwin, in his mushy-apple voice, "let me truly congratulate you. Truly a great speech."

"You did all right, Swede," Jim Buckmaster said. "A few more like that and we'll run you for president."

A great speech, Mr. Torkelsen . . .

You did the cause much good, Mr. Torkelsen . . .

Thank you, Torkelsen, for stepping into the breach. If you ask me, that goddamned Ben Wade must have got drunk in Chicago . . .

So it went while the crowd thinned.

Rolfe was one of the last to leave the platform. And at the foot of the steps, the girl was waiting. She was small in stature with a well-rounded figure, and she stood with her shoulders back and her head up.

"Mr. Torkelsen," she said crisply, "I waited to tell you that your speech was perfectly awful. I think you're a humbug."

Her face was flushed; her blue eyes were snapping.

Rolfe smiled.

"How did you know that?" he asked.

*

So Old Abe Lincoln came out of the wilderness and went to Washington, D.C., wearing a disguise in the best melodramatic tradition of American history, but before that happened the South realized it had to put up or shut up, and with all those windy orators it couldn't shut up. In South Carolina, where it was believed that Sir Walter Scott was a great novelist, that Negroes were mainly monkeys and that Abe Lincoln was mainly Negro, a convention was called; vast quantities of oratorical gas were released; and amid the ringing of bells and the cheering of belles that little old Palmetto State seceded itself right out of the U-nited States of America.

In Mississippi and Florida and Alabama the papers printed this news, and the few persons who could read spread the tidings among their cousins and half-cousins; whereupon many persons without the proper mental equipment tried to think, for the first time in their lives, and sent delegates to secession conventions; so out of the thick hot mists of ignorance the hurricane was born. The Confederate States of America was born.

And up in Washington President James Buchanan fumbled and doddered and bumbled, and in New York the stock market collapsed, and throughout the whole North money was tight and business floundered. Everything was going to pieces, the Republic of Thomas Jefferson crumbling. The worst fears of Judge Gentry had come upon him, as men's worst fears usually do; he was so sunk in gloom he could hardly eat or sleep; he lost weight and looked shockingly feeble. And he half blamed Rolfe Torkelsen for the whole sickness of the Republic, just because Rolfe had worked to elect A. Lincoln. No longer did the two men play chess in the library or engage in philosophical discussion. Indeed, their relationship grew so cool that Rolfe concluded it might be better for him to leave the household and engage a room somewhere.

But when he suggested this, Lucretia burst into tears and the judge looked stricken.

"Rolfe," he said, "don't leave us. You're the only son I have."

So Rolfe stayed on in the Gentry house, during that black winter and spring. Now and then the newspapers published some scrap of optimistic news, and hope surged through the North, but chiefly hope was bedraggled. March 4 came, Lincoln was sworn in, and when people read his inaugural address even his supporters were amazed, for it was apparent that those Euclidian arguments and pellucid sentences had been conceived in no ordinary mind. It looked as if the country might have a statesman on its hands; once again America, that lucky and amazing land, had found a first-rate leader when the need was great.

"Sir," Judge Gentry said, "I am surprised. I underestimated the man."
But the South curled its lip.

*

It was during that winter and spring of queasy peace that Rolfe grew
better acquainted with Susan Hatfield. She was, it turned out, a young
lady from Kingston, Massachusetts, in New Empire to visit her aunt and
uncle. He was Orlando Hatfield, a big, bluff pinkish-gray man who
owned the Empire Wholesale Company; the Hatfields lived in a rambling house only a block west of the Gentrys. Susan had arrived in
October, a few days before Rolfe's speech.

Soon after the election Mrs. Hatfield, who pursued matchmaking as
a hobby, invited the Gentrys and that nice young man, Rolfe Torkelsen,
to her home for the evening. It was a stormy occasion. For Susan was
an abolitionist of the purest breed. And she was more: an intellectual
girl, one of those astonishing blossoms which were forever popping forth
during the flowering of New England. She worshipped the memory of
Margaret Fuller; she regretted having been too young to have participated
in the Brook Farm experiment; her mind was lively, inquiring and ex-
asperating. Before the evening was well under way, in an argument about
slavery, Judge Gentry was thumping the floor with his cane, and Rolfe
was vowing never to get mixed up with *her*.

Yet she had her points. For one thing, the hotter the discussion the
cooler-minded she became. And the pleasanter. Other women, she
seemed to imply, might believe a difference of opinion meant you didn't
like them; not she. Never did she mix petticoats with logic. Her mind
was excellent, as tough as Rolfe's own and as quick as mercury. Then
the unforgivable happened. Somebody mentioned chess, and it seemed
Sue Hatfield enjoyed the game. Rolfe challenged her at once; she needed
a licking.

But amazingly, she didn't receive it. She played brilliantly, the skewer
being her favorite stratagem. An old skewer man himself, from way
back, Rolfe saw what she was up to and avoided most of her traps. But
not all. Trouble was, with all his politics and legal affairs, he had grown
rusty, and rust debilitates a chess player faster than it does steel. By the
middle game he knew he was trounced; she knew it too.

"You might as well concede," she said.

Concede? To this vexing female? Never!

So they played on and on, and on some more; Judge Gentry fell asleep
in his chair; Orlando Hatfield yawned behind his hand; and still they
played on, Rolfe retreating slowly and fighting every inch. Midnight
had struck before she achieved checkmate. It was too late to start another
game in which he might avenge himself.

He felt bedraggled but she looked as fresh as ever; when they said
good night she put out her hand; her palm was warm and firm. And

although her face just missed being homely, her figure was very nice indeed. But the hell with that. He'd never spend another evening with her. Nor did he, till three evenings later, when in reply to his note she wrote that yes, indeed, she would be very glad to have him call.

He was on his mettle then, and he won two games in short order. That gave him overconfidence, and she trounced him soundly in the third. Then she served cakes and coffee. He disliked her less. By midwinter he was calling once or twice a week, to play chess. Or so he thought. He didn't realize what was happening to him, for quite some time.

*

She told him about herself, little by little. In Kingston, Massachusetts, which was northwest of Worcester, she had been born in a fine big house on the east side of Forge River which ran through the town. Her father, Anson Hatfield, was the most consequential man in Kingston, self-made and mighty proud of his work. But Sue wasn't so proud of that. She loved him but disapproved of him. For her tastes he had been too smart, in the Yankee sense. Indeed, he had founded his fortune—and his fortune was huge, according to village standards—by a mighty clever stroke. As a young man he had worked as an apprentice in an apothecary shop owned by Kasper Driggs, a stodgy bachelor who lived with his sister Amanda and his sister Charity. And Kasper Driggs had a claim to renown: he made ink. Excellent, free-flowing, non-fading ink. People bought it and praised it; for fifty miles around it was famous. The formula was Kasper Driggs's own, kept under lock and key.

And it happened that one evening when Anson Hatfield and his employer were alone in the store, Kasper Driggs suffered a heart attack. In the back room. One instant he was alive and the next out like a candle. And Anson Hatfield, who had no reluctance to becoming rich, did some fast thinking. From his dead employer's pocket he filched his keys, unlocked the drawer where the formula was kept and appropriated it. Then he hurried to the Driggs home and informed Amanda and Charity that their brother needed a coffin.

Those maiden ladies knew so little about the apothecary business that they scarcely could tell a leech from a bolus, so they prevailed upon Anson to manage the shop. This he did, saving his money, and presently he went to Boston and worked for an apothecary, always saving. After a few years, when people had nearly forgotten about Kasper Driggs's wonderful ink, he returned to Kingston and opened a small factory, manned by himself alone. In a sizable vat he would mix up a batch of ink, bottle it, rent a rig and take to the road. Hatfield's Best Indelible Ink, his product was called. It sold well; reorders came. Before long peddlers were hawking that ink, and Anson remained in Kingston mixing fresh batches.

At twenty-nine he fell in love, supposedly, with Priscilla Sedgwick, a girl of thirty-two who had never attracted many boys. She had long thin hands and a sharp nose and a small repressed mouth: also a father, Nathaniel, who had founded a modest fortune during the War of 1812 selling barrels of salted and slightly-tainted beef to the government. After their marriage, aided by Nathaniel's capital, Anson Hatfield expanded his factory; he bought paper and made it up into copybooks; he manufactured pencils and rulers and slates. Everything he touched turned to money, people said, and while this was not quite the case it was still true that Anson Hatfield exemplified the best in American enterprise. By the time his daughter Susan was born, the Hatfield products were being made in a largish factory and sold throughout the land. And Anson had built his show place across the river from the village.

Susan remembered nothing of her older brother and sister, for she was only two when they drank wonderful country-fresh milk from a cow with *bacillus typhosus* and were, as Mrs. Hatfield said, taken from us. Susan drank the same milk and was ill for a while but she survived; she was the surviving type. Whereupon Mrs. Hatfield, who wept easily and frightened easily, vowed she would watch over and protect her remaining child. Smelling salts were always kept handy for Mrs. Hatfield.

But Susan, it turned out, was not the sort of child who enjoyed being protected. With her fine inquisitive mind and her ability to infer truth from any given data, she was something of a biological sport in that middle-class family. At four she sat on eggs to see whether they would hatch; they didn't, but her drawers got gooey. At seven she caught a garter snake to discover its method of locomotion; Mrs. Hatfield fainted. Not content to botanize like other girls, Susan was forever capturing bugs and climbing trees for birds' eggs and going to Forge River to seize minnows and frogs. When they told her she would get warts if she handled toads, she made it her affair to handle every toad she could find: she had to test things for herself.

And as if all that were not bad enough, Susan enjoyed reading. When Anson Hatfield built his house the architect, no doubt a subversive, designated one room as a library. Well, if you had a library you should have books: a practical man like Anson could understand that. So from a Boston bookseller he ordered books by the yard, to fill the shelves, and after Susan learned to read, (at a private school in Kingston conducted by the Episcopalian rector), she cut the pages of those books and read them through. Mrs. Hatfield could scarcely object to that, for after all Susan *was* quiet when she sat curled in a library chair, but at the same time the poor lady was vaguely uneasy, as well she might have been, for good books are time-bombs that set off explosions in keen minds.

When she was twelve Susan persuaded her father, who had scant sales resistance against his beloved daughter, to send her to Miss Cornish's School for Females in Boston. It was very polite. Susan, however, livened it up: it was correctly suspected that she was the transgressor who sneaked into Miss Cornish's bedroom and put Epsom salts in the chamber jar: when subjected to moisture, the salts foamed up enthusiastically; in her anger Miss Cornish very nearly forgot her gentility.

Susan spent only a few months at Miss Cornish's. Her father came one day to get her, explaining that her poor mother had fallen ill because of her absence. So with much protesting and many regrets—for she loved Boston—Susan returned to Kingston. Her mother promptly recovered her health.

"Baby," she said, "my baby," and burst into tears, when Susan entered the house.

Susan resumed her reading.

At fifteen, she launched a campaign to be sent to Miss Foster's Latin School in Cambridge. Her father readily gave his consent, but it took a great deal of doing to persuade her mother: tubs of tears were shed. But Susan got her way at last, and in the autumn of 1853 she matriculated at the school, determined this time not to let any illness of poor dear mama interrupt her education.

Miss Foster's was a pretty good school, everything considered; members of the Harvard faculty, who wanted to make a few extra dollars, taught some of the classes. And Sue was nearly a young lady now, quite beyond pranks. Those were years of intellectual excitement in the Boston-Cambridge area; books were being written; Margaret Fuller had been dead only a few years; ideas were in the air. Sue remembered that period as a time of intellectual intoxication, and also of her first crush.

His name was Donald Emery, a junior at Harvard who corrected the English compositions from Miss Foster's school. And for a couple of weeks, in the spring of 1854, he even taught the class in English, when the regular professor was down with influenza. After class, she used to go to his desk.

He was not the sort of young man her mother and father would have selected. Tall and stoop-shouldered, with a cowlick of brown hair falling across his high, narrow forehead, he peered at the world through a scholar's glasses. She thought him wonderful; he spoke her language; and she treasured those mornings when they left the recitation building together and emerged into the spring sunlight. Then the regular professor recovered, worse luck, and Sue was in despair. In her English compositions, which Donald Emery would correct, she tried to insinuate between the lines some of her feeling for him. She was nearly sixteen, and plain: regarding herself in her mirror, she faced up to that. Her glossy hair was attractive, her skin was fine-textured and well-scrubbed, her forehead was broad, her figure was very good, she looked virginal and healthy but . . . but . . . well, the total effect was not ravishing. Other girls were great beauties or nice sleek cats or blessed with eloquent bedroom eyes, but she was just plain, frank-eyed Sue Hatfield. She used to cry, secretly.

It was in May of that year when Anthony Burns, a black man who had escaped Southern servitude, was arrested in Boston in accordance with the Fugitive Slave Act. And Boston was angry. There was talk of a jail delivery. That didn't come off, but one evening a meeting of protest was held in Faneuil Hall. This was near the end of the term at Miss Foster's, and Sue's mother had come to Cambridge to help her pack and to accompany her back to Kingston. Sue received permission to spend the night with her mother at a boarding house. And she gave her mother the slip and took a hack to Boston.

She remembered the vast outraged throng crowding old Faneuil; she remembered the brilliant, passionate speeches; but best she remembered catching sight of Donald Emery nine rows away. The meeting over, she contrived to make her way among the people.

"Why aren't you in bed?" he asked.

She giggled and told of her escapade.

"Well," he said, "so long as you're here I'll buy you a dish of ice cream."

They went to a place called an ice cream palace on Tremont Street, and afterward they strolled on the Common. She linked her arm through his and wished he'd kiss her, but he didn't, either on the Common or in the hack back to Cambridge. She was suddenly languid; and all the following summer she read—and even tried to write—moonstruck poetry. And she said she was an abolitionist now, for somehow in her emotions the anti-slavery cause and the pro-Emery cause had become mixed.

She was sixteen and ready for marriage when she returned to Miss Foster's in the autumn, but for weeks at a time she never saw Donald Emery. Now and then a polite tea would be held at Miss Foster's, and she invited Donald; he drank much tea and ate many ladyfingers and discoursed about transcendentalism, but he didn't get around to asking her to marry him, perhaps because he was still an undergraduate with a thin purse. Occasionally she would slip away from school and stroll through Harvard Yard, hoping to encounter him, but he must have had his nose in a book.

Miss Foster taught the class in advanced Latin, and in the spring she assigned each member the task of composing a poem in that cumbersome language. At first Sue rebelled; a poem, she said, could not be written unless the Muse was lurking about; Miss Foster ordered her to fulfill the assignment or fail the course. Sue was outraged. But then one midnight the Muse or the devil visited her room, and she jumped out of bed and by candlelight composed a very fine poem in the spirit of Ovid; the setting was pastoral and the characters were a shepherd and a shepherdess who lost her maidenhead.

When Miss Foster read it she blushed and promptly expelled Sue

Hatfield. Her parents came, fully as chagrined as if she actually had lost what they considered her most valuable possession, but Sue was defiant. And back home in Kingston, she wrote a long letter to Donald Emery, justifying her literary endeavors and inviting him to pay the Hatfields a visit after his graduation. He accepted gladly, arriving in late June and remaining till late August, when he went away to Virginia and a tutoring job in a wealthy planter's household.

Neither Anson Hatfield nor his wife could imagine what their daughter saw in Donald Emery, for he was an impecunious scholar not at all attracted by the business of manufacturing ink. At the supper table he was likely to carry the conversation, for he was a facile talker, and if Anson Hatfield had only listened he would have learned about Chaucer's sources for *Troilus and Cressida,* and the probability that much of the cavern scene in *Macbeth* was written by a lesser poet than Shakespeare, and the virtues of Mr. Dryden's dramatic criticism. But Anson Hatfield did not listen, for after all he could not betray the middle class, of which he was a member in good standing, by evincing interest in ideas. He ate sullenly and shifted in his chair and now and then came forth with some off-the-subject comment about how many gallons of ink the dealers in Schenectady had purchased last week. But Sue thought Donald Emery wonderful. On summer afternoons they used to go for long strolls through meadows and woods, and one summer evening in the garden he kissed her at last. And that meant they were going to be married, some day, after he had paid his college debts and had got a job teaching somewhere. The future was all vague and rosy. And so long as they were going to be married, Sue reasoned there was no need to put off the act of marriage, for she was a young woman with advanced ideas and keen curiosity as well as her normal share of passion.

Donald Emery was as virginal as she, so they learned together, on many a summer evening in the deepest shadows of the garden or in some cow pasture. And although she did not become pregnant, she almost hoped she would, so she might go to the altar with a child in her arms as a gesture of defiance against mid-century culture.

Summer ended, he went away south to that tutoring job; her eyes were perpetually red. There were lugubrious autumn days of low clouds and rain when she tramped the countryside where they had strolled together; at supper she was mournful. And Anson Hatfield decided this had gone on long enough, so one evening he advised his daughter to forget that worthless young man who was frittering away his life in scholarly pursuits.

"Why," he said, "when I was his age—"

And he told how he had worked and saved and founded a business. Before he was through, warming to his subject, he even confided how clever he had been to filch the keys from Kasper Driggs's pocket.

"You did that?" Sue said. "You stole the formula?"

"I wouldn't call it stealing. Those Driggs girls never would have used it. I'd call it smart business. It paid off, didn't it?"

Without a word Sue left the house, hating the thing her father had done, hating the mercantile social order that applauded any sharp practice so long as it resulted in money without entangling you with the law. Yet she couldn't hate her father, for she saw him as the victim of that great American drive for wealth: get the money, get it fast, get it honestly or otherwise, but get it.

She lived for Donald Emery's letters, during that autumn and winter; he was planning to visit her again when summer came. But he didn't, the reason being that in May he married a Virginia girl. That was the end of everything; for several days she took to her bed; I'll never marry now, she thought. Gradually she came to terms with herself; when her father made business trips to Boston or New York she went along; and in Kingston she uncovered several abolitionists, and more in Worcester. If she couldn't have Donald Emery she could have a Cause, and she embraced it passionately.

Her parents didn't like that, for like most prosperous Northerners they shuddered at upsetting the *status quo;* abolitionists, Anson Hatfield said, were cut from the same cloth as atheists and anarchists and labor agitators and strumpets who wore bloomers; besides, the Hatfield Ink & Supply Company sold many products in the South; what would its customers think if they learned that the daughter of the company was an abolitionist? Sue didn't care what they might think, or what anybody might think. Then John Brown raided Harpers Ferry and was hanged; Sue addressed a meeting of protest in Worcester; she organized a similar meeting in Kingston; and during the summer of 1860, like all pure abolitionists, she went about urging people not to vote. Anson Hatfield had become a Republican; the party's platform and its candidate, he said, had taken a reasonable stand on slavery; he thought his daughter was making a common nuisance of herself.

So early in October he decided to make a trip west to visit his brother Orlando who was doing well in New Empire, Wisconsin, and he took Sue along.

And in New Empire Susan attended that Republican rally where Rolfe Torkelsen spoke. Her interest was snagged. His ideas, she told herself, were wrong as rain, but she sensed he had a tough, pounding mind; perhaps she could convert him to the Cause. And when her aunt told her Rolfe was unmarried, Sue decided to make a longer visit; her father returned east without her, in time to vote for the Hon. A. Lincoln.

*

Not without profit had the Hon. A. Lincoln read Aesop and sat in a hundred caucuses; he could be patient and foxy; and he understood the workings of the American mind. The South had left the Union; Civil

874

War was coming, probably; and if it did Mr. Lincoln as a minority president wished to be in the position of receiving, not striking, the first blow. He knew those Southerners; they would be like a small boy with a bunch of firecrackers, unable to keep their fingers away from the matches.

So while the South prepared for conflict things seemed to be drifting at the North. Anderson held Sumter and Mr. Lincoln would send him supplies; no he wouldn't; yes he would. Meanwhile in Charleston all the pretty ladies and handsome gentlemen were itching for action. So was General Pierre Gustave Toutant Beauregard; so in Montgomery was President Jefferson Davis. It would be necessary, he thought, to reduce Sumter.

"It is suicide, murder, and will lose us every friend at the North," said Confederate Secretary of State Toombs. "You will wantonly strike a hornet's nest which extends from mountain to ocean, and legions now quiet will swarm out and sting us to death. It is unnecessary; it puts us in the wrong; it is fatal."

So Sumter was cannonaded; and the hornets swarmed.

*

All over the country, North and South, the bugles were blowing that spring, as the young men prepared to go forth. Mr. Lincoln called for 75,000 volunteers, a reasonable request certainly, but it vexed the South no end, for the North had been expected to curl its tail and run. He got those volunteers too, and more, for the Union was closing ranks. Senator Douglas, after a visit at the White House, pledged himself to sustain the president. James Buchanan did the same. Yesterday's Southern sympathizers were today's patriots. Politics were all but forgotten; it appeared that the Americans of 1861 had the same gunpowder and vinegar in their veins as the Americans of 1776. For the flag had been fired upon, the United States flag, that lovely banner that had flown over the camps of General Washington and General Jackson; it was enough to make a man's trigger-finger itch. And when in mid-April Mr. Walker, the Southern Secretary of War, declared that by May 1 the Confederate flag would be flying over the capitol dome in Washington City, young men in Maine and Indiana and Iowa took a hitch in their belts and started for the recruiting offices. "At the darkest moment in the history of the Republic," wrote Ralph Waldo Emerson, "when it looked as if the nation would be dismembered, pulverized into its original elements, the attack on Fort Sumter crystallized the North into a unit, and the hope of mankind was saved."

Sumter had scarcely been evacuated before some young men in New Empire, Rolfe Torkelsen among them, subscribed their names to a proposed organization to be called the New Empire Rifles. They pledged money too, and ordered Enfield rifles, and held meetings all over the county, with a brass band and speeches, to enlist recruits. And they telegraphed the governor that the New Empire Rifles would be ready to leave for the front (only there wasn't yet a front) any old time; and after work they went to the cow pasture south of the cemetery and drilled, awkwardly and ignorantly, in the long spring dusk. Young ladies went to watch and admire; Sue Hatfield went. And when darkness fell she and Rolfe Torkelsen, who had been elected first lieutenant, strolled along streets that smelled of lilacs, and debated whether they should be married before or after the war, which would be a short one, because any Yankee could lick six of the Secesh singlehanded.

Sue favored a prewar wedding, Rolfe a postwar one. For he might, he said, be killed; that happened sometimes to a soldier. And if he were, it wouldn't be fair to leave a young widow.

"Pooh, pooh," Sue said, "you're not going to be killed."

That was reassuring; and so it was decided that they should be married early in June, not in a church or by a preacher, because both believed that showy weddings and funerals were barbaric, but in some place like Madison by a judge.

"But first I have to tell you something," Sue said. "Maybe you won't want to marry me, after you hear it."

He kissed her—it was a dark night on Orlando Hatfield's veranda—and said nothing could stop their marriage.

"I have to tell you," she said. "It happened years ago when I was a silly girl."

He remembered that May night with the tree shadows on the lawn and the fragrance of her clean-smelling hair and skin. Tree frogs were piping, and spring peepers, and from somewhere downriver far away came the melodious whistle of a Buckmaster packet named the *Bonnie*. New Empire had gone to bed, the houses dark, and the great dome of sky was dark and silent. The war, the war that had scarcely commenced, seemed distant and unreal. Yet somewhere perhaps, in the whippoorwill mountains of the South, or in camp by a languorous bayou, a Johnny Reb was cleaning a musket which would send a ball through Lieutenant Torkelsen's heart. Three months from now he might be lying in a shallow grave, the quickly-dug grave of a soldier. Those were the thoughts just below the threshold of consciousness as he listened to Sue's story. She told it honestly, how as a schoolgirl she had fallen in love with Donald Emery, and become engaged, and with him had performed the act of marriage. How he had gone away to Virginia and had married some other girl. How she had wept.

"But I didn't know what love was, then," she said. "Not till I met you. If you don't want to marry me, now that you know, you don't need to."

He wished she hadn't; a man always wished that. But against the backdrop of war and the fact of possible death all the petty morality of man, all the canting of society's witch doctors, all the rigmarole of what were called carnal sins seemed nonsense. He said so.

"Oh, Rolfe, Rolfe," she said, in a smothered voice; and when he kissed her he discovered her cheeks were running with tears.

*

But they weren't married early in June after all. That was Judge Gentry's fault.

Ever since John Brown's raid he had been failing rapidly, for he lacked the resilience of the young. Chaos might come and the young would live through it, but he was old. He had his loyalties—to the Democratic Party, to Kentucky, to the Republic—and the Democratic Party lay in ruins, Kentucky was convulsed in its own civil conflict, and the Republic was a marble statue that lay fallen and shattered. Americans had fired upon Americans; Americans had fired upon their own flag. Sumter, Sumter. The word was gall and wormwood in his mouth. And Virginia had left the Union. Virginia! Virginia of the lovely Shenandoah, of tidewater plantations beside broad rivers, of the Washingtons and the Lees, of Patrick Henry and Thomas Jefferson, of James Monroe and James Madison. Virginia that had been the mother of Kentucky, of statesmen, of patriots. Her very towns had names that fell on the ear like music, American music: Charlottesville and Norfolk, Richmond and Winchester, Fredericksburg and Roanoke and Staunton. She was the Blue Ridge Mountains and the Wilderness Road, she was Daniel Boone, she was Culpeper County and Bowling Green and Fairfax. And she had seceded, gone, tossed in her lot with the lower South; she was now an enemy of the United States; strange flags flew in her cities.

Small wonder, if you were in your seventies that spring of '61, that you felt like a man tottering amid earthquakes and volcanic dust.

"Rolfe," Lucretia Gentry said, "I'm worried about Sophronicus. He won't eat and he doesn't sleep and he looks so poorly. Why don't you get him to play chess? I think a good game of chess is just what he needs."

It may have been, but he wouldn't play. In the library or in his office he sat by the hour, staring. At the past, maybe? At a phantom Mr. Clay who was said to play brag for huge stakes, at a phantom General Jackson smoking a cob pipe, at a phantom Daniel Gentry who distilled the best drinking liquor in Bourbon County? Daniel Gentry who had been born in Frederick County, Virginia; whose father, another Sophronicus, had been named after a blooded race horse; Sophronicus Gentry the long hunter, friend of Daniel Boone and John Raines, of Uriah Stone and John Finley and Henry Skraggs.

Were those his thoughts, during those spring days when the bugles were blowing?

He was tired, desperately tired, and feeble, needing that Jackson hickory cane. People spoke to him on the street but they were phantoms too. The Republic itself was a phantom on a phantom globe whirling in the light-shafts of eternity.

"Eat something, honey," Lucretia said. "Don't you want a little broth?"

And she had been a young wife waiting in a Lexington house for her husband to return from another war. A war against the British and the Indians. Not a war of kin against kin.

It couldn't go on like that, with his not eating and hardly sleeping; and of course it didn't. One afternoon late in May he arrived home exhausted in the heat. And in the hall a shell seemed to hit him and burst; anyway, there was a moment of bright unbearable pain in his skull; and he fell.

*

And so Judge Sophronicus Gentry, attorney-at-law, scholar and gentleman, one of the biggest men on the big river, was the first New Empire casualty in the war of kin against kin. But he didn't die, right away, although he never regained consciousness. It was a stroke, the doctors said; he might die tomorrow or next month or next year. Meanwhile, make him as comfortable as possible.

Lucretia looked very old, as if she should be on her deathbed herself.

"Rolfe," she said, "I just don't know what I'll ever do, with you going to war, and all. I need you so much, Rolfe."

So Lieutenant Rolfe Torkelsen, with many regrets, did what had to be done: he resigned from the New Empire Rifles and told Sue Hatfield they had better postpone their marriage. She could not but agree, for no matter how advanced you were in your thinking there were old fidelities to be kept. Rolfe wouldn't have felt right about it, she knew, to be honeymooning while Judge Gentry lay dying.

Early in June the governor of Wisconsin ordered the New Empire Rifles to Camp Randall at Madison, and the whole town turned out to see them off. Sue and Rolfe were at the station that morning: he remembered the band music and the cheers, the bunting on the locomotive, the good-by kisses, the weeping, the excitement on the faces of those raw civilians who were off to adventure and war. He felt sick at heart, wanting to go too, as if he were a boy excluded from some thrilling game. He would never get into the war now, he thought; it would be all over before he could enlist. The locomotive whistled, the train jerked, the band played; and as the cars gained momentum heads and shoulders and waving arms could be seen along the line of windows. Girls waved handkerchiefs till the track was empty in the heat.

Rolfe worked alone in his office that summer, for his student clerks had gone with the New Empire Rifles. And the law seemed dull, stodgy, stale; nothing was of consequence except the war. And even the war stagnated; the newspapers cried for action; Lincoln should get a move on; would there never be a great decisive battle? Then rumors swept the country of a movement into Virginia; these were confirmed; the North was exuberant; any day now the South would be soundly thrashed and brought back into the Union. Congressmen and their ladies, with picnic baskets, followed the army toward Manassas Junction; the *New Empire Chronicle* flaunted a streamer head: On To Richmond!

Then the battle took place, in the July heat, but nothing worked out as planned. Back to Washington fled the congressmen with bullets chasing their pants; and the boys who three months before had been farm hands and grocery clerks and poolhall Lotharios threw down their guns and skedaddled. Not all the boys, however. Some stood and fired into the confusion, some lay with burning throats, some just lay. The New Empire Rifles took part in that battle, and the *Chronicle* printed the names of the wounded and the dead, along with an editorial, "This War Is Not Yet Won."

And in the house on Gentry Avenue, attended by nurses, Judge Sophronicus Gentry, protected by unconsciousness, never learned how Americans had slaughtered Americans at Bull Run. Perhaps he dreamed of other battles, or of magnificent orations in marble halls; perhaps not. August came, thick with heat, and still he clung to life. The house was hushed and portentous with something impending; outside, the katydids rasped and clattered. Then it was September; the doctors said he couldn't last much longer; nor did he; at 3:00 A.M. on the seventeenth he died.

Hundreds attended his funeral; a line of carriages several blocks long followed the hearse to the cemetery. They buried him beside his son, Andrew Jackson Gentry, in a plot not far from the grassy graves of Caleb McSwasey and Heinrich Zumwalt McSwasey. The afternoon was cloudy; the leaves were beginning to turn.

*

As a good lawyer should, but doesn't always, he left his affairs in apple-pie order, his last will and testament explicit, with each of his daughters provided for, and with Rolfe Torkelsen executor and Lucretia Gentry executrix. Lucretia, of course, that frail old lady, understood none of her duties; everything fell on Rolfe. There were a thousand details, the will to be probated, real estate to be liquidated, the partnership of Gentry & Torkelsen to be disentangled, the court's approval to be obtained on this decision and that. And Rolfe wished to enlist because the war was going badly, but he couldn't leave Lucretia to cope with that legal confusion. Without her husband she was a lost innocent; she needed taking care of; and she could be willful too in ways which complicated Rolfe's problems. After the funeral, she had moved from the house on Gentry Avenue and was staying at the ratty old Commercial House; she couldn't, she said, bear to spend another night in the house where Sophronicus had died; it must be sold. The court concurred, but who would buy it? Times were still hard, that early in the war.

"Why don't you buy it, honey?" she asked Rolfe.

879

"I can't afford it."

"But I'd give it to you cheap, honey. I want you to have it."

"You couldn't sell it cheap. You'd have to get the court's approval of the price."

"Oh, bother that old court!"

Well, why didn't he buy it? He had the money. Why not buy it and marry Sue Hatfield and set up housekeeping there? He discussed it with Sue, who liked the idea, and with the court, who was agreeable providing an independent agency—the bank, say—appraised the property and set the price.

And so it was that late in November Susan Hatfield and Rolfe Torkelsen were quietly married in Madison where they enjoyed a short honeymoon, although Rolfe felt a little uneasy—in that town full of soldiers from Camp Randall—at being in civilian clothes: he could tell that people were wondering why he wasn't in the army. And when the newlyweds returned to New Empire, they occupied the house Judge Gentry had planned and built and called Lexylvania.

And although perhaps he imagined it, he thought that even his fellow citizens of New Empire were whispering behind his back because he was of military age and not fighting to save the Union. Pretty soft, he could hear them saying, for Torkelsen. Resigned from the Rifles and lets the others get killed. Stays home and makes money hand over fist and buys the best house in town, except for Jim Buckmaster's. Sleeps in a clean bed with his bride while others are sleeping on the ground. Quite a patriot, that Torkelsen, when he makes a speech. But when it comes to holding a rifle—

"Pooh, pooh, let them talk," Sue said. "You know what you're doing."

Yes, he knew; he would straighten out his affairs, and Lucretia's, as best he could, well beyond the possibility of anybody's cheating her, and then he would request the court to appoint another executor so he could enlist. Sue used to go with him to his office that winter, to help cope with all the details of the Gentry estate; she could add a column of figures faster and more accurately than he; and she had common sense. It was she who suggested, during the endless untangling of the legal partnership, that he buy the Gentry Block; it would bring her income while he fought the Confederacy. The court approved; in February he acquired that property; the old partnership was dissolved; in March another executor was appointed, and Rolfe was free to enlist.

And reluctant, now that the time had come, because of leaving Sue. She was a good wife, it had been a good marriage, all three months of it. A man, he thought, was a fool who avoided marrying an intelligent woman. Even when they weren't making love—which was as seldom as they could manage—he enjoyed her: evenings of chess, of threshing over all the problems besetting the Republic. Little by little, she had swung him to her way of thinking: that slavery must be abolished; and she had

come to believe Mr. Lincoln was a good president, as good ⟨
man could be, in these times . . . No, he didn't want to leave h⟨
to war. But neither, probably, did those other thousands who h⟨
from North and South.

So on an evening of March wind, at the New Empire station, he kissed
his bride good-by and boarded the cars for Madison. No crowds were
there, no bands were playing, no bunting draped the locomotive; it was
very different from that sunny morning when the New Empire Rifles
departed.

*

Next day he enlisted in Madison, thinking of course he would be sent
to Camp Randall to drill, and Sue could visit him. But the ways of armies
are no less mysterious than the way of a man with a maid: the following
morning—it was Friday March 28—he and two other recruits, accompanied by a sergeant, were sent to Milwaukee where in a draughty
barracks at Camp Trowbridge they became members of the Eighteenth
Wisconsin Infantry. This was a newly-organized outfit, the officers and
men all perfectly green, and camp rumor had it that they would train
for weeks before seeing action. But on Sunday morning, March 30, looking more like civilians in uniform than like soldiers, for nobody kept
step and nobody had a rifle, they were marched to the station and loaded
aboard the cars.

And where were they going? Opinions differed. To Madison perhaps,
or east to the Army of the Potomac or to Chicago. Some place, the unmarried men hoped, where there were plenty of pretty girls. In any case,
to a camp where they would be issued rifles and taught how to load them.

Like all troop trains, this one was made up of cars ready for the junk
heap; it rattled and banged, made unexplained halts, jerked and creaked.
The air stank of smoky coal-oil lamps, of stale tobacco, of orange peel-
ings, of peanuts, of urine from the toilets. A crap game got going on
Sunday afternoon and lasted throughout the night; Rolfe lost five dollars
and sought a worn plush seat where he might sleep; and he did sleep,
in snatches.

Monday's sun rose on the left; they were clattering southward through
the flat fields of Illinois, through raw-looking villages with square houses
and bare trees. They ate from their haversacks and wished for coffee;
then, at a midmorning stop in one of those villages, a group of women
served free coffee and doughnuts on the platform, and wished them luck
and enjoined them to kill lots of Rebs. And for the first time Rolfe
began feeling like a soldier, in his travel-mussed uniform.

Their destination was known now: St. Louis. Well, fine. Probably
they would train at Jefferson Barracks and receive passes to visit the city
and Sue could travel downriver to spend a few days. It seemed a long
time since he kissed her good-by, and he thought pleasantly of the future:

how natty and military he would look when he met her boat, how they would stroll in the evening along a tree-shaded avenue.

Darkness had fallen when the train finally arrived at a woebegone station opposite St. Louis; they piled out and formed a ragged line of march; the air seemed warm, compared with Wisconsin; and after many delays they tramped to a low flat place with mosquitoes and lanterns and ghostly tents. Their arrival elicited many humorous remarks from soldiers already there: "Hi, greenhorns . . . Say, old Abe must be scraping the bottom of the barrel . . ."

Next morning, aboard ferryboats, they saw the St. Louis waterfront coming toward them, busy with war: barges and flatboats and smoking packets; a levee crowded with blue uniforms and cannon and heaps of shells and drays. Once on shore, they stood in the sun for an hour, waiting to go to Jefferson Barracks. But war, it appeared, was full of surprises: they didn't go to Jefferson Barracks at all. Instead, they were marched aboard a steam packet called the *John Warner*. Say, where in hell *were* they going, anyhow?

North to the Missouri and up that river to a camp? Or back north to Wisconsin, in some crazy zigzag of logistics?

They went south.

South down the Mississippi River, all nine hundred of them; south past cottonwood islands and dreary squatters' shacks and bobbing houseboats; south past St. Genevieve and Cape Giradeau; south in the early April sun. But at the tremendous watermeet near Cairo, where the Ohio, that big river from the east, pours into the Mississippi, that big river from the north, where the face of the waters is vast and swirling and treacherous and freckled with bubbles, the *John Warner* turned east. And they saw Cairo, its boatyards and warehouses and tented encampment; Cairo, that prodigious military depot for the war in the West. And travel-weary as they were, baffled and homesick as they were, they cheered. For it came to them then that the North was mighty, a workshop people that could build engines and more engines of war for her gathering armies. They felt a part of all that, corpuscles in the Northern giant. But where were they going?

Up the Ohio certainly, up *la belle rivière* of the *voyageurs,* with Illinois off to larboard and Kentucky off to starboard. And they stared at Kentucky, that mysterious land of chattel slaves. They had read Mrs. Stowe, most of them, and perhaps they half expected to glimpse poor Eliza wading out from shore, beseeching succor, while the bloodhounds bayed. But Kentucky looked the same as Illinois . . . or did it? Was not the sky softer, more misty and Southern, above the hickories? And those men they occasionally saw on shore: were they not lankier, more lantern-jawed?

At Paducah, when the *John Warner* pushed south into the Tennessee River, there was no longer any doubt that they were moving into the land of the Secesh. In February a tanner from Galena named U. S. Grant had given the Rebs a taste of Northern spunk, capturing Fort Henry and Fort Donelson. "No terms except an unconditional surrender can be accepted," he had told the Rebs. "I propose to move immediately upon your works." And the North had thrilled; here were victories at last. They nicknamed him Unconditional Surrender Grant and sent him cigars and loved the stocky little cuss even though, so it was said, he swallowed his whiskey neat. And Mr. Lincoln, who could be quite a card, was supposed to have told some busybodies who complained about General Grant's tippling that if he knew what brand of whiskey the general drank he would send barrels of it to his other generals.

Could it be, they asked themselves aboard the *John Warner,* that they were to serve under U.S. Grant?

Well, eventually, perhaps. But not this spring. They'd make a fine bunch of soldiers, wouldn't they, without rifles and without training. No, probably they were being sent to Fort Donelson or Fort Henry for garrison duty. Receive their training there. Hell, they didn't even know the manual of arms yet; they hardly knew how to salute. After they were trained, say in another three months, they might get in on some summer campaigns and really see the elephant.

So up the Tennessee River the *John Warner* steamed, deeper into Kentucky, into the South. The days grew warm; this was a lower latitude than New Empire, Wisconsin; this was it: the South. Uncle Tom and Little Eva: this was their land; the land of ashcake and honeysuckle, of cotton in the boll and firecrackers at Christmas; the land where cousins married cousins and fought duels and whipped niggers and rode to the hounds; the land of sandy bottoms and scented nights and hotmouthed women, of piney woods and cakewalking niggers and banjoes and persimmons and campmeeting preachers who shouted glory to Gawd. Yes, and of shouting orators and of cotton bales; of dangerous eyes and hot tempers; of sour gum and coffee trees, of swamps and mockingbirds: this was Dixie Land. And they had come to invade and subdue it, these young men of the Eighteenth Wisconsin Infantry, these Swedes and Danes and Germans and transplanted New Englanders: down from the ax-ringing forests, from the land of early freezes, from the North of the rippling aurora borealis. But first they needed rifles.

The weather changed and April rain was peppering the river when the *John Warner* steamed past Fort Henry; Rolfe could make out blurred redoubts, heaps of supplies under tarpaulins on the levee, drenched men laboring, steamboats moored to the bank. The *John Warner* whistled; the other boats answered; men on shore stopped work to wave. Rain in the upcountry had swollen the Tennessee River; twigs and scum and uprooted trees came rotating down its clay-colored water; and after passing Fort Henry the *John Warner* was but one of many boats plying that stretch of channel. Once through the downpour they saw a bizarre-looking craft, ponderous and shuttered and grim. Then suddenly they realized what it was: a gunboat. Back home in the papers Rolfe had read about these ironclads, wide-beamed and tougher than alligators, with their rifled guns; Grant had used them with withering effect in subduing Fort Henry; seeing this one brought the war close.

At midafternoon on Saturday, under clearing skies, the *John Warner* sighted her destination: a narrow strip of land on the west bank of the river from which rose wooded bluffs. Troop transports were tied up there, and supply boats were unloading; a heavy traffic of mule-drawn wagons could be seen straining up the muddy trail that led to higher ground, or waiting to receive boxes of cartridges, shells, solid shot.

"Men," said Colonel J. S. Alban, speaking to his regiment from the hurricane deck, "we are about to disembark on the soil of Tennessee and go into camp at this place called Pittsburg Landing. Under that intrepid general, U. S. Grant, a great army has been assembling here, the Army of the Tennessee, preparing for a campaign which will, I trust, crush Rebeldom forever. Upon reaching camp you will be issued rifles, and during the weeks to come you will be thoroughly trained in their use and in the warrior's way of life. Fresh recruits as we are, all of us, snatched by the gods of war from home and hearth, I feel we are fortunate indeed to be sharing a vast camp with veterans of those glorious victories at Fort Henry and Fort Donelson. By our association with these brave fellows, may all of us be imbued with their valor. This camp at Pittsburg Landing, I am told, is situated on high wooded ground, but interspersed with open fields ideal for drilling. Protected as it is by the Tennessee River on the east, by Owl and Snake Creeks on the north, and by nearly impassable forests on the south and west, it is indeed a well-nigh perfect camp for an army. I trust that all of you will work diligently to become soldiers worthy of our great state, and I want to say right here that this crap shooting has got to stop, I am a Christian man and I will tolerate no games of chance in my regiment. Also, leave the laundresses alone, if you so much as wink at one of them I'll have you in irons. And so soldiers of the Republic, we are arrived in the very homeland of the enemy. Do your duty, and God bless you."

They cheered; the *John Warner* whistled and nosed into shore.

*

Nothing went right on the levee because they were so green. Lieutenants and non-commissioned officers, all equally green, tried to muster them into marching order, but everything was a tangle of jostling uniforms and cursing mule skinners and mud. Finally they were told to march at will to the higher ground. This they did, an undisciplined mob, slipping in the mud and often nearly falling beneath the hoofs of the mules coming down the bluff with empty wagons. "Look where you're going, you clodhopping bastards," the mule skinners yelled. "Want to get run over, you galoots?"

They felt ludicrous, those civilians in uniform; they would be, they were sure, the laughingstock of camp. And they hoped that President Lincoln or General Halleck or General Grant or whoever was responsible for sending them among seasoned troops knew what he was about; it was lese majesty in the army to question the wisdom of one's superiors, but it did seem it might have been better if they had trained at Jefferson Barracks before joining the Army of the Tennessee.

A light wind had cleaned the sky and the sun was bright when they reached the top of the bluff. Back from the river what was evidently a broad plateau, broken by gullies, stretched off among hickories and elms. They milled and grumbled and laughed at themselves and cursed the day they had joined the army, up there among cannon and boxed rifles and endless stacks of grain and bales of hay, while fuzzy-cheeked boys from other outfits, veterans of all of two months, hooted and jeered and said you're in the army now and oh, man, they sure spoiled a lot of good farmers when they swore you in.

But at last they formed a line of march, of sorts, and went slogging along a sloppy trail leading southwest. Once, among the swinging shoulders ahead of him, Rolfe saw a man sitting a horse by the roadside; he was lean and sharp-eyed, with salt-sprinkled red hair and a stubbly beard. His uniform was rumpled. And it appeared he was somebody important, for suddenly everybody was saluting, awkwardly; and the man returned the salute easily and smiled.

"Don't worry, boys," he said, "you'll be soldiers in a week or two. You look like a bunch of scrappers to me."

And through the ranks went the whisper: know who that was? That was General William Tecumseh Sherman, that's who.

Sherman. Crazy Sherman, the newspapers had called him last autumn, in revenge because he had barred correspondents from his campaign in Kentucky when they printed information that would tip off the enemy. Crazy, they had called him, because he had said it would be a long hard war; and the government had relieved him of command and rusticated him. But he had a brother in congress who pulled wires, and of late he had been performing brilliantly; people said he was Grant's favorite lieutenant. And Rolfe thought: I like his looks. I wouldn't mind following him into a fight.

They kept marching, always southwest, the road winding among thickets and woods and past fields; when the lowering sun struck them they were accompanied by a file of shadows with legs long as stilts. They passed siege guns, batteries of 64-pound howitzers, of light field pieces, of rifled guns and 24-pound Parrots, of mighty Columbiads, all with their stacked shot and shell; they passed cavalry camps and infantry camps with tents beyond number; at some of these bands were giving concerts; and they passed wagons in park by the hundred, and rickety-looking ambulances. Colonel Alban had been correct: this was a vast camp; it stretched for miles; the word went through the ranks that fifty thousand soldiers of the Republic had assembled here, that a big push was planned on a railroad town named Corinth some twenty miles southwest. To Rolfe it seemed invincible, that Army of the Tennessee, on the afternoon of Saturday April 5, 1862.

And everything was oddly peaceful, despite all the accouterments of war. The air had a moist woodsy smell, sweetened with the scent of peach blossoms from some farmer's orchard, and with the fragrance of locust and dogwood; the redbuds were blooming. Robins and song sparrows caroled in the underbrush; wrens sang; mockingbirds could be heard everywhere. But high overhead turkey buzzards were circling; must be a dead horse somewhere.

Twilight had fallen when they reached a grassy site and pitched their tents on level ground which fell away east toward a stream called Locust Grove Branch; they heard marsh frogs and swatted mosquitoes. To the west they could see the campfires of the Sixty-first Illinois, the Eighteenth Missouri, the Sixteenth Wisconsin: maybe tomorrow they could go over and swap stories with those boys from the old home state. But now they ate a supper of crackers and cold ham—not much of a meal but their commissary supplies and personal baggage had been left at the landing; and then at last they were issued rifles and ammunition. By firelight they examined those muzzle-loading Springfields and practiced loading, clumsily. Then taps sounded, clear and melancholy in the spring evening, from regiments all over camp; they were bone-tired and glad to turn in; a week ago tomorrow they had left Milwaukee; it seemed a long while. They slept; the mighty army slept, except for sentries and men on picket duty off to the southwest who kept encountering Reb pickets and exchanging shots.

*

Rolfe was wakened by the urge to visit the latrine, for like everybody else he was suffering that chronic complaint of armies, diarrhea. On board the *John Warner* no meals had been served—upon leaving St. Louis the troops had been issued rations to last out the trip, and he had eaten from his haversack and filled his canteen with river water—and his intestinal tract felt raw. He lay there dreading to get up, for the pre-dawn air was chilly, but his body would not be denied; fumbling into the carpet slippers Sue had given him, he left the Sibley tent and the snores of his comrades and made his way through the thick dew.

He was wakeful, by the time he had attended to his needs, and he stood watching the first gray stain of a new day in the east. Off in the woods a whippoorwill sang drearily, and far away to the southwest he heard a half-dozen shots. Pickets, probably, discharging their rifles upon

886

being relieved. Dawn was breaking fast now, the stars fading and thrushes twittering; and he wished he were home in bed without any damned reveille to rout him out. Maybe Jim Buckmaster had been right; maybe he had been a fool to join the army. Yet somebody had to go; somebody had to bring the South to its senses. He remembered a line Judge Gentry had read aloud years ago from Chaucer: the Wife of Bath saying she had lived her life in her time. You had to do that, you had to live your life to the full in your own era, facing up to whatever came your way. He knew he would never have felt on good terms with himself if he had not enlisted. Patriotism was not band music and flag waving and highfalutin oratory; it was a secret thing of man's spirit; it was something better not talked about, because when put into words it sounded chauvinistic; it was, perhaps, something like Platonic love; it was knowing you belonged to a country and a country belonged to you, and when your country was in trouble you had to do something to help.

He yawned and returned to his cot, thinking he would only doze; but he must have slept hard because the next thing he knew he was hearing the awful racket of a drum being pounded. Somebody shook him.

"Get up, Torkelsen. It's the long roll."

"Reveille?"

"Hell, no. They want us out there with our guns. Must be a skirmish."

He snatched on his uniform, but he didn't believe a skirmish was impending. No officers in their senses would send troops as raw as the Eighteenth Wisconsin into a skirmish. It was probably another piece of army damned foolishness; they were always wanting to make you uncomfortable to toughen you up.

But when he emerged into the early sun he could hear firing off to the west, Colonel Alban was conferring with a man on horseback, and the company lieutenant kept pacing and gnawing his fledgling mustache and saying fall in, men, fall in, we may have a little work to do, fix bayonets and fall in, the Rebs seem to be making a reconnaissance, fall in, goddamn it, fall in.

So Rolfe fell in, and somebody was grumbling about no breakfast, and somebody else was saying he never would have joined the army if he had known they'd get you up like this in the middle of the night. Then came an order to load their rifles. It was ridiculous, how long it took, pouring in the powder and ramming home a ball. Rolfe's fingers were all thumbs when he tried to fit a cap on the nipple; he must have dropped two or three before he managed it.

Now fire low, just remember that, the lieutenant was saying. If we have a little action fire low. Get 'em in the guts, men, shoot off their balls. Remember your wives and sweethearts men, make them proud of you, fire low, blast off the bastards' nuts.

He's scared, Rolfe thought. He doesn't know what he's saying.

Fire low, men, they'll run, shoot 'em in their asses.

Off to the west the sound of guns was heavier now, as if a thunderstorm were brewing. But the sky was cloudless. You could also hear what sounded like bunches of firecrackers on the Fourth of July.

To the south of the camp an open field stretched, and the order was given to advance. Then it was countermanded; then given again; waving a sword, the lieutenant led the way. Presently the company was ordered to halt.

"For Christ's sake," somebody said, "when do we eat?"

And another: "I got to go to the can."

"Latrine, boy. You're in the army now."

"Well, I got to go."

"You're scared."

"Hell I am. I always go before breakfast."

"Cork your ass with a bullet and forget it."

They stood there ten minutes, fronting a heavy timber cut with ravines. Then the order came to about-face. They returned to camp, a ragged line, and about-faced again.

"By God, they're just giving us exercise."

"I'm hungry."

"Now you're talking! Bacon and eggs, boy, and flapjacks."

"I got a fat little wife back home who bakes me biscuits. Biscuits and honey, that's eating."

"I got to find a can somewhere."

"Use your cap."

"That fat little wife of mine, she sure can cook. You take biscuits and honey, that's mighty good eating."

An order came to advance.

So they advanced to where they had stood before. Artillery was thundering closer now, to their right; farther west, giants seemed to be bowling with iron balls.

"Hell," somebody said, "this ain't no skirmish. This here sounds like a battle."

"Battle, hell. The Rebs ain't that crazy."

"You take a thin woman now, and usual thing, she ain't much of a cook. But you take a fat little wife like that one of mine, she can cook. And I mean cook."

"My aunt Minnie, she's thin, and she can cook. Best doughnuts you ever et."

"That's what they call the exception that proves the rule. That fat little wife of mine—"

Off to the south, in a ravine, soldiers could be seen through the underbrush, carrying a flag.

Rebs, the lieutenant said. But somebody else said no, they weren't

Rebs, that was the Union flag. Colonel Alban considered the matter. Then he said:

"Must be our pickets being driven in. Hold your fire."

So the line held its fire, talking of fat little wives and latrines and saying if this weren't a battle it sure sounded like one, while the soldiers in the ravine worked their way around to the left of the regiment.

"Colonel, them's Rebs."

"No, no, for God's sake, hold your fire. Those are our men."

"You're the boss, Colonel. Hold your fire, men. Hold your fire."

Things were getting very hot indeed, to the west; above the angry obbligato of distant 64-pounders could be heard, near at hand, the boom of Parrot guns, the whistling and exploding of shells, the crackle of musketry. Then a new sound reached Rolfe's ears, from the woods in front and from the ravine on the left: a high, wavering scream. And suddenly, thick as bees from a hive, troops with butternut jeans came pouring from the woods and up from the ravine. The sun glistened on their musket barrels; then, snowy in the fresh morning, little puffs of smoke appeared at the musket mouths. And things came zinging waspishly.

"Ouch! Hey!" somebody yelled, and dropped clutching his stomach.

"Fire, men! Fire! It's the Rebs!"

Rolfe knelt and took aim and tried to fire low but his musket was swinging crazily. He pulled the trigger; the butt kicked his shoulder; he reloaded. The lieutenant was dancing like a cat on a hot stove, ordering everybody to reload and fire, but things were out of hand; smoke drifted across Rolfe's vision. Then something round and black came bouncing; Rolfe ducked; it missed him but took the lieutenant's head right off his shoulders; his neck spurted blood.

The noise was terrific; musket balls whining, everybody yelling; shells screeching overhead; artillery booming.

And Rolfe thought: I'm in a battle. So this is what it's like. And I'm not scared.

But next thing he knew he found himself running, along with everybody else, through the camp of the Eighteenth Wisconsin and on to the north, down through a ravine and up the other side.

"Men!" somebody in a lieutenant's uniform was yelling. "Halt! Make a stand! Men! Men! Halt! Halt, you goddamed cowards!"

So Rolfe halted, on a knoll, along with some others.

"Don't panic, men. That's the great thing, don't panic. We can whip 'em, and we will. Think of the Union, men! Reload, reload, reload. All right, now—"

Rolfe knelt and aimed into choking clouds of smoke and fired. But before he could load again men were dropping around him and from the acrid fog he heard that high, unearthly screech as of ten thousand banshees on the prowl. And he was running again, quite without volition; he stumbled, his musket jumped out of his hand, he scrambled up; somebody passed him; it was the lieutenant who had urged them to make a stand and had called them cowards; then all at once a great red explosion took place in the direction he was running. Instinctively, he threw himself flat, arms covering his face; when he stood up he was all over dirt and the lieutenant stood with his diaphragm blown away; with both hands he was holding up his viscera; his mouth hung open stupidly in his bloody face; then his knees sagged and he went down.

And again bullets were flying like hail and again came that wavering screech from the smoke and again Rolfe ran; everything was hazy as the kitchen of a cheap fry-restaurant; bursting shells had set afire last year's leaves on the forest floor and their smoke was added to the gunpowder smoke; cavalry troops thundered past, and riderless horses; and once in a thicket Rolfe saw a wounded horse threshing and screaming as the flames reached it. He was utterly done in now, and his diarrhea bothered him; he unbuckled his pants and squatted by a tree.

"Me too," somebody said, "only I did it in my drawers."

It was the young man who had a fat little wife back home.

"We wouldn't have run," he said, "if they'd trained us. But hell, what can you expect—?"

A look of amazement passed over his face; his hand started for his throat; but a bullet had severed his jugular vein; he died before long.

*

At night in dreams it would come back to him; it would come back to all of them, to all the boys in blue and the boys in butternut; it would come back. They would be old men in G.A.R. parades, old men at Soldiers' Homes dozing in the sun, old men yarning on the porches of country stores, but in bed at night the memory would come back, stark and raw, for it was the stuff of nightmare.

But when it was happening it was not so bad as it would be later in memory, because your consciousness blanked out. If you had been well trained and heard an order to rush into sheets of flame and capture a battery you obeyed because volition was absent; you acted as if under hypnosis. But if you had left Milwaukee one Sunday and gone into battle a week later, if your officers were scared and confused, if you had not been trained to obey orders, any orders, instantly and unthinkingly, then of course when your consciousness went blank you ran. Cowardice or valor had nothing to do with it, except in official reports.

In his memory those next two or three hours were smoke and hullabaloo, with now and then a picture sharp as a Brady photograph. The Eighteenth Wisconsin had been cut to pieces, scattered, and he was rootless as a ghost. He had lost his musket, he had eaten no breakfast and not much supper, his intestines burned and his tongue was arid, and he wandered. The ground trembled underfoot and the sky was full of endless bombination as if two thunderstorms had collided. Vicious little things sang past his ears; overhead other things screeched and whistled and sometimes landed in brilliant explosion; and always he could hear the high wavering shriek of the Rebels, sometimes far away and almost elfin beyond the whirling smoke. Wherever he walked bodies lay, some alive and moaning, some not. Once he was in a peach orchard where the ground was snowed with blossoms; more blossoms kept falling when something would go *z-z-zing*. And when he was in the orchard a cannonball came crashing through a rail fence, bouncing like a child's plaything; it smashed the trunk of a peach tree and the whole lovely bouquet of blossoms fell to earth.

After that he reached a gully where bodies lay piled like logs, mutilated in every imaginable way; a rich red rivulet trickled along the gully. He saw men's brains spilled over their faces; he saw men with their jaws shot away; he saw a booted foot that had become detached from its owner, and a stray arm or two. It was not like a battle in the history books; flies were buzzing. Picking his way across the gully, he heard a smothered voice, and when he looked around he saw an arm sticking from beneath a pile of bodies and waving. So he pulled off the bodies and underneath he saw a boy who looked as if he should be in school; the belly of his butternut uniform was scarlet. The boy kept moaning for water so Rolfe unslung his canteen and put it to the boy's mouth. But he couldn't drink worth anything; the water slobbered over his chin. And his eyes had a wild look and he began yelling for Ma. Ma, he would say, Ma, help, help, Ma, help. Rolfe said she's coming, she's coming right away; but the boy didn't hear: just kept yelling Ma, Ma, Ma. Then he heaved a big sigh and smiled and mumbled something about a sow that was going to have pigs; there seemed nothing more to do for him, so Rolfe left.

The sun was high and hot now; shade seemed cool; and in the shade he saw a funny thing: a Reb and a Yank lying face to face, each with his bayonet through the other. He had to laugh, that was so funny, only when he bent double to laugh he began retching and lost balance and lay on the moist earth, retching all the while, only nothing came up except phlegm because he had eaten no breakfast. And then he napped. But napping could be hazardous, on a battlefield: he was wakened by hoofbeats as a dozen cavalrymen went riding lickety-split on both sides of him; he saw the flash of horseshoes and the flying shapes of horses' legs; wonder he wasn't kicked. And he heard people asking: How was your husband killed, Mrs. Torkelsen? Oh, Rolfe? Why, he died a gallant death at Pittsburg Landing kicked by a horse while he was napping.

He stood up. The hell with this wandering about. If you were a soldier and found yourself in a battle you were supposed to fight. If the Eighteenth Wisconsin was all shot to hell and gone, you could attach yourself to another outfit. Maybe they'd have something to eat; he was hungry. So he went tottering through the woods, coming to an open place where a dozen corpses lay; he selected the best musket he could find; the fellow would never miss it. And inasmuch as he had left his canteen with that Reb who wanted Ma, he stole a canteen from another dead man and drank.

Remarkably, the canteen contained not water alone but water mixed with whiskey. It was nectar; it got right to him; he drank again. Man, he said aloud, you had the right idea. And he lifted the canteen for another drink, but something said *whin-n-n-ng* and the whiskey spilled from two holes, one on each side of the canteen; a ball had drilled right through it.

And Rolfe thought: If you're going to get it you're going to. If not, not. Damn, but it's hot.

When he reached a trail through the woods a lot of blue-clad troops came along on the double-quick, and a lieutenant yelled, Hey, you, why are you straggling?

And Rolfe said: Why, sir, I was with the Eighteenth Wisconsin, sir, and we saw some warm work and got cut up. I'm unattached, but I'd as soon fight with you as with anybody, who are you, anyway?

Eighth Iowa, the lieutenant said. Come along.

Afterward Rolfe wished he had attached himself to some other outfit, but if he had it might have turned out even worse; he supposed you shouldn't quarrel with your fate if you came through a war alive.

Through the midday heat and the floating smoke and the racket of musketry and explosions they made their way to a little rise where men stripped to the waist were swabbing out cannon and loading in shells. Then—pandemonium. The guns blazed, the explosion rocking them backwards, smoke pouring from the muzzles, and when you were so near to that unimaginable concussion your knees sagged and your ears felt as if somebody had blown a paper bag full of air and slammed it against the side of your head. And no sooner had you recovered than similar explosions sounded from right and left along a whole line of batteries. But maybe you got used to it, in time. The gunners seemed to be used to it. One was even telling a story, as he swabbed out the barrel, about an old maid who had a cat and one evening a bachelor called and—

But he couldn't finish the story because a minié ball pierced his medulla oblongata and crashed out through his mouth and buried itself in a tree.

Sons of bitches, a captain yelled. Give it to the bastards!

Things like that kept happening, all afternoon.

By then the Eighth Iowa and the New Empire representative of the Eighteenth Wisconsin were crouching behind some rude log fortifications along the crest of the rise; they faced an open field. And it appeared that this knoll was considered valuable real estate by the

Confederate command, worth five or ten or maybe twenty dead soldiers per square foot; anyway, they kept attacking. We are a salient, men, said the Iowa lieutenant, (before an enfilading bullet passed through his body from right to left, destroying both kidneys). We must hold, men, he said. They want to silence our batteries. Shoot low.

Rolfe thought it quite silly of the Confederate command to spend so much time on this salient; why didn't they flow around it like a river around an island? But no, they kept attacking, across that open field. Rolfe wouldn't have liked being in the boots of those Rebs; hot as things were where he lay, he still preferred being here.

Well, he had to hand it to those Rebs: they had what it took. Away off across that field he could glimpse them through the smoke, forming at the edge of a woods for the charge. Then with pennons and battle flags flying—maybe a white cross on a blue field, or a blue cross on a red field—with bayonets flashing, with knees pumping high, they came yelling, although in the racket you couldn't hear their voices: you just saw their mouths open and knew they were screeching. What happened to them then shouldn't have happened even to Rebels, for the Union batteries poured a withering blast of grape and canister and shrapnel into their ranks, and the Union muskets added their bit. They died in all sorts of curious ways—once Rolfe saw a severed hand go sailing through the smoke—and they lay in piles. Trouble was, they were meeting what a professional military man would likely call obstinate resistance. Our gallant troops charged spiritedly, a military man would likely write, in his report, but met obstinate resistance. Military men and writers of history were great ones to dress up a battle in resounding prose; they loved words like gallant and brave and courage and audacious; and they preferred telling about some cool-headed officer who perished facing the enemy with a bullet through his heart rather than mentioning the shattered thoraxes and testicles and punctured bladders.

You would have thought those Rebs might have grown discouraged, after a charge or two, but no, the bastards kept coming. And once they wore blue uniforms: somebody said God alive, those are Union men. But the lieutenant—another lieutenant, the first one had died by then—said no, those are Louisiana troops—see that Pelican flag?—they just happen to wear blue.

And to Rolfe that seemed an encouraging tidbit. He had been despairing of any ultimate triumph for the Union, so long as its leaders were such damned fools as to send men without training into battle. But it would appear that the Rebs must have plenty of simpletons commanding their forces too, or they wouldn't have let a regiment wearing Union blue enter a fight where they would probably be fired on by their comrades. In a war you were likely to suppose the other side had all the brains and tricks, but perhaps bungling and thick skulls were inseparable from any army command.

The Rebs kept charging and the butchery continued; nor was it all one-sided butchery, either. Sleet-storms of bullets swept the knoll where the Eighth Iowa lay; a lot of talented grocery clerks and hog-callers ended their careers that afternoon. And for all Rolfe knew a lot of future senators and judges and college professors. He thought about it, as he lay there loading and firing: in another twenty or thirty years, he thought, the country might find itself with nothing but fifth-rate ability in public office and in university chairs, the first-rate having been eliminated at places like Pittsburg Landing. And if the North should win and bring the South back into the Union, perhaps it wouldn't be worth bringing back with most of its best men gone to worms and glory. And there would be a lot of queer old maids, North and South, the men they would have married being no longer around, and a lot of children never born who might have grown up to invent things and paint interesting pictures and perhaps discover cures for piles and cancer. Maybe Judge Gentry had something, when he fretted about Americans slaughtering Americans.

Along about midafternoon it must have occurred to some genius on the Southern side that there was a better way to capture that real estate where Rolfe lay. Why not, he must have thought, shell it first and then attack? So off in those woods artillery was massed and the solid shot and the shells loaded with rusty nails and scrap iron began lobbing over, falling short at first and then falling long but at last falling very nearly right, from the Reb viewpoint. And when the Union artillery deduced what Mr. Davis's boys were up to more guns were brought up and wheeled into position, and there followed what a military writer might call a spirited artillery duel.

How any of them lived through it Rolfe couldn't imagine, unless they had not been born to die in battle. The noise was worst; he lay face down with forefingers plugging his ears, but even so he thought his hearing would be ruined. Lying there like that, in what was without doubt an unsoldierly attitude, he expected some lieutenant or sergeant to kick him, but they must have been occupied with their own affairs. Presently he got used to the racket and was almost comfortable, and weakened as he was by diarrhea and lack of food his thoughts went drifting far from what journalists would call the bloody field of Shiloh, (named in honor of a meetinghouse which Rolfe never did see). He thought how it was Sunday afternoon and how Sue might be reading a letter he had sent from St. Louis; and for some reason he thought of his trip to Washington City with Jim Buckmaster and remembered those muttonheaded statesmen like Park Irwin and those fire-eating Southerners with that singular Southern ability to take an extreme and wrongheaded stand and defend it with vehement ignorance. And then, oddly enough, right in the middle of a spirited artillery duel, he went to sleep.

What wakened him was a cessation of noise. The artillery had fallen silent, on his part of the line. He rolled over and sat up. And a rangy young man in butternut broke out laughing.

"Thought you was dead, Yank. Playing possum, I reckon."

"No, I went to sleep."

"Christ, that's a good one. Well, stand up. You're what they call a prisoner of war."

So Rolfe stood up; his musket was appropriated.

"How did it happen?" he asked.

"Don't ask me, I ain't no general. If I was I'd resign. God Almighty, man, they told us you Yanks wouldn't fight. Well, looks like we've licked you, but I'd rather go after a painter barefisted."

For a sleepy moment Rolfe thought he was the only captive; then he saw others in Union blue without their muskets. And he learned that General Prentiss, commander of the sixth division of the mighty Army of the Tennessee, had found himself flanked and surrounded; he had surrendered with some three thousand men; and the Eighth Iowa of the second division had surrendered at the same time.

It was late afternoon; off to the northeast, toward the landing, guns were still thundering; but for Private Rolfe Torkelsen the battle was over. Along with the other prisoners he was herded into a line of march; and guarded by Texas cavalrymen—lanky, humorous-tongued men with distances in their eyes—he left the field of Shiloh.

*

They shambled through havoc; a man might, Rolfe guessed, spend a long and honorable career as a civilian undertaker without seeing a tenth as many corpses. They lay in windrows, in niggerpiles, in ditches, in brambles; they strewed the rutted trail; sometimes they drooped from trees: sharpshooters who had been killed. They lay in long grass gazing blindly at the sky; they sat propped against trees; they lay heaped around artillery pieces. In some places you could have walked for a hundred yards across a field, stepping from one corpse to another, without touching foot to earth. They wore Union blue and Confederate gray, but they were all Americans.

And they, of course, were the lucky ones. They had died fast. Others not so lucky—countless others—lay waiting to die tonight or tomorrow. You heard their groans or their feeble cries as they called out for water, but there was nothing you could do to help, not if you were a prisoner of war marching along guarded by Texans on horseback.

Sometimes you met men hobbling on improvised crutches with a dangling shredded leg, or men lacking arms, or men with bandaged eyes led by comrades. Or you saw stretcher-bearers loading the wounded into an occasional ambulance; but there were not enough ambulances.

Dead horses lay everywhere, and dead dogs that had been mascots, and dead Negroes who had been body servants, and dead women who had been laundresses. Now and then, even, you saw a dead bird, a huddle of bright feathers that had been singing up the sunrise this morning.

They passed what had been Union camps, but now the tents were bullet-ridden or just sprawled canvas on the ground. Pots and pans lay scattered, and decks of cards and letters, and stray boots and socks and haversacks and knapsacks. You saw wagons with broken wheels and dead mules, upset caissons, bedraggled battle flags. You saw so much your brain went numb.

Presently they were marching through the supper bivouacs of the Confederate Army, the great Army of the Mississippi, and Rolfe expected jeers and catcalls and hate. There were none. Most of the boys were pretty fagged out, their mouths smudged from tearing open cartridges with their teeth. They looked like soldiers who had had a busy day; they were too tired to pay attention to prisoners of war. But now and then somebody would look toward Rolfe and say something like boy, you sure gave us hell, you sure fought like tigers.

The sky had turned cloudy and with dusk a cold rain began to fall. Where in hell they were being taken Rolfe didn't know: southwest somewhere. Rain filled the ruts of the road, they slopped and slogged, passing through the Army of the Mississippi. Men lay sleeping in the downpour, which seemed a good way to catch your death of cold, although perhaps no better way than stumbling through mud with wet feet and drenched clothes. Along the road, occasionally, they passed a sputtering pine torch, and sometimes their guards ordered them to leave the road to give thoroughfare to caissons and supply wagons and fresh troops marching toward the battlefield.

The rain fell with no letup; somebody said there was always rain after a battle because the concussion of the guns disturbed the atmosphere. Somebody else wondered aloud whether Grant was holding, back at the landing. Piss on Grant, somebody else said, it was his fault we were caught with our britches down. That started a discussion as to what had happened; there was general agreement that the Army of the Mississippi had stolen a march and caught the Army of the Tennessee unprepared.

"We should have fortified," a voice in the rainy darkness said. "Hell, we was there a month just scratching our asses, we should have fortified. But old Grant and old Sherman, they thought the Rebs would be nice and polite and wait for us to attack them at Corinth. God damn, I said all along we should have dug in."

"They should have put you in command," somebody said. "You'd have learned them how to lick the Rebs."

"Well, by God, I wouldn't have sat in no headquarters ten miles away like Grant did. I wouldn't have been caught a-sittin' on the pot the way he was."

Far away now, off to the northeast, they could hear the occasional reverberation of artillery; but for the most part they heard only the spatter of rain and the soupy, sucking sound of boots in mud.

They marched for hours, with now and then a rest period; their guards, surprisingly enough, treated them like human beings, like fellow soldiers who had fought as best they knew how and who had surrendered honorably. When Rolfe asked where they were being taken, one lantern-jawed fellow replied in a Texas twang that he reckoned there was no hurt in telling him: Corinth, Mississippi, that was where.

"And not much of a burg, if you ask me. Nothing but niggers and frilly-dilly ladies and soft-handed clerks. Boy, what I wouldn't give to be in Texas tonight. I don't like Mississippi nohow, nor Louisiana neither. I was borned in Texas, and I reckon I never should have left. All this damn rain. Why, man, where I come from it don't rain for six months at a stretch, and the cows got tits bigger than rainbarrels, and the gals got tits bigger than the cows. Damn, I should have stayed. But they told me there was a fuss being raised about niggers—where I come from you never see a nigger—first time I seen one I thought he was a Mexican who'd gone to sleep in the sun—anyway, they told me there was some fighting up here, and they needed us Texans to settle it. So I joined up. Well, the fighting's right good—I like a squabble myself—but there's too much horsing around between fights. That ain't no way to run a war. If you're going to fight, why, goddamn it, fight, that's what I say."

Midnight was long past when they sighted Corinth, a smudge of lights in the rain. They marched along streets where tree branches intertwined overhead; most houses were dark. But once the column halted before a dwelling ablaze with lights; two of their guards dismounted and went to the veranda. They returned, after a long time, and said something to the other guards, and a prisoner overheard and so the word traveled: in that house lay the corpse of General Albert Sidney Johnston who had commanded the Army of the Mississippi; he had fallen on the field of Shiloh. And they were cheered—little things always cheered them—for if the Rebs had lost their commander didn't it mean they would lose the battle and maybe the war? Why, hell, by tomorrow morning the forces of Grant and Sherman might be capturing Corinth.

The column moved ahead, through residential streets and a business district with oil streetlamps, into an area where railroad tracks branched in all directions and locomotives were panting and hooting. In a space of cinders they halted; a Texan with whiskers addressed them from horseback.

"Get some sleep, if you can," he said. "It's not up to the St. Charles Hotel in New Orleans, but it's the best we've got. I know you all are hungry, and I'm right sorry, I'm hungry myself, but maybe in the morning we can rustle up some victuals. You all are prisoners of war, and as such are entitled to the same treatment as our own troops, and so long as I'm in charge you'll get it. But don't none of you try to escape or you'll get shot."

The rain continued, and the cinders in the railroad yard of Corinth, Mississippi were no softer than cinders anywhere, but Rolfe was so tired that he slept.

*

Daybreak was gray and weepy, the air sultry. Rolfe's mouth felt like a rat's nest, and his bones ached, his muscles ached. He was catching a cold too, and no wonder, dressed as he was in a sodden, mud-smeared uniform. When he stood up his feet in their drenched socks felt squashy inside his boots; he needed a shave and a hot bath and breakfast. He had eaten nothing since Saturday night and not much then; he was weak. Other prisoners were stirring now, and in the gray air they were a sorry-looking lot with their begrimed faces and bleak eyes.

By and by, off to the northeast, the guns started rumbling again as Americans resumed killing Americans. There would be more corpses today and more wounded, but already the war seemed far away; let the crazy bastards fight; what Rolfe wanted was breakfast. He kept thinking of steaming coffee and toast and bacon and eggs; nothing fancy; just a good solid breakfast to start off the day right. Standing there on wobbly legs under the ragged gray sky, he could understand what that Texan had meant when he said Corinth, Mississippi, wasn't much of a burg; everything looked sodden and bedraggled; the railroad station, up the track a piece, was painted a hideous mustard color; locomotives kept clanging and hooting; and although constipation was not Rolfe's trouble —indeed, quite the reverse—he felt the way you do when you're constipated: that poisoned, draggy feeling. Finally he sat down with his head between his knees; finally he slept.

Somebody—another prisoner—nudged his ribs and said, "Come on. They're moving us." So Rolfe creaked to his feet and with several hundred others shambled toward a string of boxcars. "Get in, pile in," their guards ordered. They obeyed, about sixty men to a car, and the waiting began. In a war, it seemed, you were always waiting for something, and the usual thing what you waited for turned out to be not worth it. Cattle or pigs or some sort of animals with careless personal habits had occupied those cars before them; the floor was filthy. A half hour passed; an hour; the sun broke through the clouds and cooked down on those cars. Then at last their teeth were jarred and those who were standing were knocked off their feet when the locomotive backed into the train. Son of a bitch, somebody said, that goddamned engineer did it on purpose.

More waiting. Still no breakfast. But finally, with a jerk, the train started moving, puffing west along the Memphis & Charleston Railroad. And some amateur strategist explained that at Corinth the north-and-south Mobile & Ohio Railroad crossed the east-and-west Memphis & Charleston: that was why Grant had wished to seize Corinth, so that he might stop traffic on two lines important to the Confederacy.

"He'll have 'em by the balls—see?—once he takes Corinth."

"Yeah, if he ever does."

Wooden bars had been nailed across the boxcar doors, and Rolfe watched the country flying past, a hilly land of woods and brush, good for foxes and not much else, except in the bottoms where woebegone stalks from last year's corn crop could be seen. Likely no crop would be planted this spring, with the men off getting themselves killed. When the train crossed creeks on rickety trestles the water was high and reddish-brown; in the railroad cuts the earth's flesh was red.

Now and then the train screeched to a halt at lost little court towns, where on the platforms old men squirted tobacco juice and yelled things like hey, Yanks, you're licked and don't know it, bet you're sorry now you voted for old Black Abe.

Breakfast time was long past, noon came with no food or water; jerking and swaying, the cars clattered west, past country sawmills with meager piles of lumber; and during the afternoon, when stops were made, crowds were waiting to catch sight of the Yankee prisoners; word must have been telegraphed ahead. The sun was bright and hot now; the cars stank of manure and urine, human and animal, and of uniforms that had dried on sweaty bodies; the throngs on the platforms, women and old men mostly, looked clean and starched. And unlike the soldiers of the Army of the Mississippi, who were eager to kill you but willing to call it quits once you surrendered, these Rebs were unfriendly, especially the women. That didn't hurt Rolfe's feelings for he didn't see any real beauties—none of those luscious belles for which Dixie was famous; these were underfed girls with hatchet faces or matrons whose figures had gone to rump and ruin.

Maybe the girls were put out at the Army of the Tennessee for coming South and killing off the marriageable young men; in any case they didn't act like daughters of a self-proclaimed aristocracy. At one town, eyes mischievous, the girls had plates of sandwiches which they held out toward the boxcars, but when the hungry prisoners reached, the sandwiches were drawn back and the girls laughed and ate them themselves. And they said things like my, my, but I sure do favor a juicy roast-beef sandwich, sorry there aren't enough for you Yanks. And they said, why didn't you stay home, we weren't fixing to do you no harm, why did you want to come down here and invade us?

All this made some of the prisoners mad, and they engaged the young ladies in argument, but they were Rebs for sure, there was no reasoning with them, they lost their tempers. One scarecrow of a girl worked herself into a real frenzy, as if she were a convert at a camp meeting getting right with Christ; she jumped up and down and pointed an accusing finger at the boxcar and screamed, nigger-lovers, nigger-lovers, nigger-lovers!

"I'll show you all how a nigger needs treating," she screamed. "Lulu! Come here!"

Lulu came, a black girl of twenty with the whites of her eyes showing.

"I'll show you, I'll show you, you nigger-lovers," the Southern belle screamed. "I'll show you what a nigger needs."

And whack, whack, whack, she slapped the black girl's cheeks, again and again; whack, whack, whack.

"That's for niggers and that's for you, you nigger-loving Yanks," the Southern belle screamed.

The crowd on the station platform was laughing; Rolfe felt slightly sick in that baking boxcar. And he thought: They're madbrained on the subject of niggers, they're twisted and lunatic; mention niggers and they're raving; they're a whole people the gods have made mad. And he knew then it would be a long, grinding, bitter war.

*

Evening came before the train staggered into the Memphis yards; the prisoners were unloaded, and, guarded by men too old or unwell to fight, they were marched to the City Hall. Crowds lined the streets, calling them cowards for surrendering and telling them the South had won a glorious victory at Shiloh. Maybe so, but if that were true Rolfe knew the North would assemble more armies; he remembered the limitless capacities of that workshop people, his people. Never had he loved the North so much as on that evening in Memphis: redheaded Sherman and cigar-smoking Grant and old Abe Lincoln cracking jokes at cabinet meetings and the banner that was star-spangled and New Englanders with faces from steel engravings and with cool, logical minds and warm hearts: he loved them all. Perhaps there had—yes, certainly there had—been bungling at Pittsburg Landing, but the North would learn from its mistakes; victories would come. You'll find out, he thought, when the gentility jeered. Life isn't a novel by Sir Walter Scott, it isn't gimcrack heroics; you'll find out.

About half the prisoners were conducted into the City Hall and the rest, Rolfe among them, were marched downhill into an area that smelled of river water and catfish; they halted at a stone building whose walls rose high and blank in the dim light from streetlamps; a guard unlocked huge iron doors and they went inside and up steps to the second floor and then the third. It was a tobacco warehouse, judging by the smell; the third floor was a bare loft with a skylight showing blue night and dusty stars.

"Reckon this will hold you," a guard said. "If it don't, there'll be men with guns downstairs."

"How about grub?" somebody asked.

The guard laughed.

"We're plumb out. Besides, the cook's gone off to fight some abolitionist bastards who come down here to rape our wives and daughters."

A door slammed; they were alone and hungry and thirsty; they whispered about how maybe they would be exchanged or paroled, eventually, or how they might escape; they slept.

Next morning tubs of drinking water were brought in, but no food; that was Tuesday; most of Rolfe's strength had drained away; he lay half asleep, thinking of the way bread tasted and of thick steaks running with juice. The evening before, mosquitoes had invaded the warehouse where panes were broken in the high windows; he was covered with bites; and lice had traveled among the prisoners. One pastime was to strip and fumble with dirty fingers along the seams of your clothing, searching for those lice.

Breakfast was served at last, on Wednesday, and although it consisted only of hardtack it tasted delicious; you wished for a second helping. After the meal, somebody managed to stand on somebody else's shoulders and peer out a window; there were, he reported, a lot of people outside, just loafing around to stare at the building where the Union prisoners were confined; he yelled and told them this was no way to treat captives, more food was needed, they had a right to more food, according to the articles of war. But the crowd laughed and said why, hell, this warn't no war, old Black Abe hisself had said it warn't no war but an unlawful rebellion, so the articles of war didn't count. And one of the crowd, unable to deny himself the self-importance of passing on news, even bad news, asked if the Yanks had heard about what had taken place upriver. No? Well, you give us a whupping upriver, he said, up there at Island Number 10, you whupped us right good and captured the island; and somebody else said the battle at Pittsburg Landing, after the second day of fighting, had just pooped out; Beauregard had led the Southern troops back to Corinth; old Grant had been saved by the arrival Sunday night of the Army of the Ohio; old Grant still held Pittsburg Landing; the goddamned battle was nothing but a draw.

But the prisoners knew better; when they heard that news they gave three cheers—somewhat weak cheers, they were so tuckered with hunger, but still cheers—for old U. S. Grant, and three more for old General Don Carlos Buell, commander of the Army of the Ohio, and three more for the ironclads that had captured Island Number 10. For they were not illiterate Southern hill boys or swamp boys; they had been newspaper readers before their capture, and strategists by avocation: they knew it was a Union victory, if Grant came out of the battle still holding Pittsburg Landing; and they knew that Island Number 10 had been the western anchor of Albert Sidney Johnston's line across the Upper South. With Island Number 10 in Union hands, the gunboats would be steaming toward Memphis next.

Their guards must have known that too, for along toward noon they were marched from the tobacco warehouse to another freight train. And now the crowds watching them weren't so perky; the crowds must have known Memphis couldn't stand, with Island Number 10 gone; and perhaps the casualty lists from Shiloh had been coming in. People no longer jeered them as cowards; people just stared, sullenly.

The freight cars into which they were jammed were no better than the freight cars which had carried them to Memphis, and the engineer wasn't worrying about stopping and starting suddenly, lest some passenger have a boil on his hind end. On Rolfe's freight car there was a flat wheel which blatted continually as the train chugged south along the Mississippi Central Railroad into a flat land where Negroes were plowing with mules; through the bars across the door you saw unpainted shacks on lopsided foundations with pickaninnies spilling out onto the stoops; you saw scrubby timber and towns with courthouses and the usual crowds on the station platforms to catch sight of Yankee prisoners. And the crowds became cockier as the train made its way into the lower South, and their accents broader. And although Rolfe watched sharp he didn't see any persons who resembled those gallant young Southern gentlemen and those re-fined young Southern ladies that orators were always boasting about; the ones he saw looked as if they had been eating all the wrong fried foods, and hating too much, and catching the hookworm disease which the Negroes had brought to Dixie from Africa. And to while away the time, of which he had plenty, and to forget about food, of which he had almost none, he wondered if the whole Southern tradition were only a myth dreamed up so people could escape the realities of smothering summers and Negroes who might revolt and wormy stools and chills and fever and copperheads and mildew and chiggers and the fact that if your slave was chained to your wrist you were also chained to the slave.

It must have been Saturday when the train dumped them off at Mobile, although by then time was growing hazy. They were divided into three groups, there in the railroad yards under a withering sun; and Rolfe's group was marched to the Mobile River, the color of tobacco spit in the heat, and loaded aboard a steamboat. Mobile had been an important port before the war, but now with the Union blockade choking the Confederacy ships lay rotting at the wharves; there were endless bales of cotton shading dozing Negroes; everything was melancholy and comatose, although one of the guards bragged how last month a ship had run the blockade and fetched in supplies; a few more feats like that, he implied, and the Yanks would wish they hadn't driven the poor trembling South out of the Union. And Rolfe, thinking of the great port cities of the North, open to commerce with the whole wide world, connected with every roaring inland city by networks of rails, experienced sudden elation: the North would win, Yankee hardheadedness and organization and willingness to face storms of lead would triumph.

After much waiting, the steamboat headed up the Mobile and then into the Alabama River, through heat and past swamps and infested bottoms. The engines wheezed and broke down once, causing a delay of hours, while two men in a scow went back to Mobile and returned with a Negro who understood mechanics; a free Negro, so it was said, who because of his ability with engines had prospered and bought himself four wenches. If he warn't a nigger, a guard said, I'd call him smart, yes, sir, the black bastard would be smart if he was a white man, them four wenches of his have made him a lot of babies.

Repaired at last, the engines turned the stern wheel creakily and the steamboat made her way through mosquito dusk and night and day, up the winding Alabama with its clay banks, arriving finally at Montgomery where once upon a time Jefferson Davis had been sworn in as provisional president of the Confederate States of America. And as could be expected in the first Secesh capital, the crowds lining the river bank had left their Southern hospitality at home; but Rolfe was used to hate and jeers now. Some of the girls, he guessed, might be called belles; at least, they were good-looking in a dark, languid way; but from the things they yelled their tongues must have been dipped in vinegar. It didn't matter; all that mattered was wanting a square meal and a shave and a bath and clean clothes.

All things considered, he didn't care for Montgomery; he never wished to return. His home there was a cotton warehouse with a yard surrounded by a high brick wall; the weather grew hotter; meals consisted of corn bread, half raw with the ground-up cobs included, and salt beef or mule meat which your stomach usually sent back up in a hurry, after you had swallowed it; and the guards were gangling clay-eaters, rejectamenta of the Confederate armies, whose education had stopped once they had mastered the technique of chewing tobacco. Everybody was gaunt and sick and dirty; beards and hair lengthened and grew tangled; Rolfe's diarrhea gave him misery. Every afternoon, which the guards called evening, four men were detailed to leave the compound and lug buckets of water from a well in the yard of a cabin where a war widow dwelt with a horde of ragged children; and even though you were so weak you spilled half the water that was enjoyable because it broke the monotony. One afternoon—it must have been in late May or June— Rolfe and three others were assigned this task. Heavily-guarded, they dragged themselves to the widow's yard and pulled up buckets from the open well. One of the prisoners, a lieutenant from a Michigan battery, stumbled and went sprawling on his way back to the compound, spilling the water, some of which splashed on the pant legs of a guard; whereupon the guard broke into profanity and fired point-blank, putting a bullet through the lieutenant's heart.

Well, it was a hard climate, hair-triggering tempers, and Southern gentlemen were notoriously touchy about the dignity of their persons: the

Yankee never should have spilled that water. Still, the punishment seemed extreme to the prisoners in the compound, once Rolfe and his companions told what had occurred; so the prisoners, with the strength of anger, tore up bricks from a sidewalk and let fly at the guards, who got out fast and spread the tidings of a riot. All over town church bells began ringing, and men came running with shotguns and knives, surrounding the prison; the prisoners heaved brickbats over the wall and the townspeople heaved them back.

Then somebody sent for soldiers and an artillery piece, which was loaded with grapeshot and aimed at the tall doors in the wall; and the prisoners were told they could either behave themselves or be annihilated; they chose to behave themselves, and for reward they received no food or water during the next forty-eight hours.

Summer came on hotter and more humid; men died; it seemed they had been here always and would be here always; but then one morning a captain came and announced that General Beauregard had ordered all private soldiers taken prisoner at Shiloh to be paroled. This meant they would be sent home, if they were willing to sign an oath not to take up arms again against the Confederacy; they were willing. So a few days later they were marched to boxcars, which were no better appointed than any other boxcars, and the train jerked away from Montgomery and took them north to a town on the Tennessee River called Bridgeport, where they were loaded onto a steamboat. Frail as they were, dirty and ragged and unshaved and unshorn, they were in high spirits now, thinking of how it would be to soak in hot baths and sleep between sheets and eat again and go to a barber shop; the war was nearly over, for them; Rolfe could scarcely wait to tell Sue what war was really like; he had never received a single letter from her.

He remembered the morning when that Reb steamboat, flying a white flag, approached the north bank of the Tennessee River where another white flag hung limp above neat tents and men in blue uniforms. It had, then, all been arranged: this was the Union camp set up to receive paroled prisoners. The steamboat tootled and nosed into shore; Rolfe could scarcely wait for a square meal. But then a Union major came strutting toward the landing, holding up an arm with his palm toward the prisoners; Rolfe never forgot how well-fed he looked, how clean, how neatly-brushed were his brown whiskers.

"I can't let you land," he said. "General Mitchell in Chattanooga has decided no paroled prisoners are to be received."

There were, naturally, outcries of disbelief, and much argumentation there in the blazing sunshine; the commander of the Confederates guarding the prisoners asked the major where his humanity was, and the major couldn't exactly say; and the prisoners were beseeching the major in the name of God to accept them; but old Brown Whiskers was adamant: General Mitchell had given the order, and old Brown Whiskers had not become a major without learning that when a general gave an order you had damned well better obey it.

So at last the steamboat backed away from that Union camp and retraced its way upstream toward Bridgeport, Tennessee, where the prisoners were once again loaded aboard freight cars and taken for no good reason to Atlanta, Georgia, where for two weeks they waited in the railroad yards, some dying; and after that the train took them back to Montgomery, Alabama, which was hot as Africa, and more dreadful, because several escapees had been apprehended and staked out in the prison yard, spread-eagled and facing the Southern sun, from 10:00 A.M. to 2:00 P.M. daily for ten days; one went blind; but of course the French proverb was correct, there were no beautiful prisons, north or south or anywhere there were no good ones.

*

Time was a stagnant Southern bayou, green-scummed and torpid; it seemed never to pass but that was crazy, it did pass, the sun did come up now and then, there were noons and midnights, although you lost all count. But it must have been early September when once again they were marched forth and loaded aboard more freight cars and taken to a town in Georgia called Macon and conducted to a prison camp in the fairgrounds on the southeast edge of the city. And that was an improvement over the cotton warehouse in Montgomery. For one thing, trees grew in that park; for another, a creek flowed through on its way to empty into the Ocmulgee River bounding the park on the east. And once a day all five hundred of you were permitted to strip and bathe in that creek. It was a shocking thing to see the bodies of your comrades, ribs protruding and muscles wasted by starvation; for that matter, it was shocking to see your own body. No wonder you were weak as a kitten; no wonder you always felt lightheaded; no wonder, before you made any move with your body, you thought it over carefully first, because if you didn't you were likely to misjudge your strength or misjudge distances and fall down.

And the food at Macon was better than it had been at Montgomery; not much, but some. Also, the guards were several cuts above the Montgomery guards: soldiers who had been wounded and who had recovered enough to watch over Yankees. And even though you and the guards were enemies, even though they'd shoot fast enough if you tried to escape, still you had all served in armies and stood in battle; there was a certain freemasonry among soldiers. You had all, as the saying went, seen the elephant; you knew secrets the civilians back home could never know, even though they were told.

Upon being captured at Shiloh, and not knowing what was coming, Rolfe had never thought to hide money in his mouth or his boots; when they searched him they cleaned him. But some of the boys had been more

905

foresighted; they had United States money. And United States money, even though it had a Yankee accent, talked with much authority in the South; the guards were delighted to accept it in exchange for baskets of fruit and loaves of bread or even a ham bone. That would have done Rolfe no good if he had not struck up a friendship with a funny-faced little Jewish boy from Cincinnati named Izzy Weinberg. Like Rolfe, Izzy had been detached from his command at Shiloh and had fought with the Eighth Iowa, but unlike Rolfe he had not fallen asleep during the artillery duel, nor had he forgotten that money is not the least important thing in the world, come war or peace.

Izzy was a good friend; when a guard brought him peaches or cold round steak he didn't sneak off and eat alone; he shared with Rolfe. Then he would tell how at sixteen he had lied about his age and enlisted, thus forsaking a bright future in his father's pawnbroker business; and once he told how his father and mother had happened to meet. Seemed they were both enthusiasts about Laurence Sterne's *Tristram Shandy;* when a mutual friend learned this he introduced them; and they must have decided *Tristram Shandy* was a book that needed a lifetime for discussing; anyway, they married. And Rolfe reflected that if an Eighteenth Century parson had not written that baffling novel, Izzy's parents would never have met; there would have been no Izzy and no cold round steak for Private Rolfe Torkelsen.

In one way, at least, Yankee prisoners in the South had it better than Reb prisoners in the North: the winters were milder. Autumn was gentle and reluctant that year, a time of soft afternoons with far hazes, with red leaves floating languidly to earth, while at a great distance the war went grinding along, Americans killing Americans at Perryville and Antietam and in engagements so inconsequential that the press never mentioned them. Lincoln discharged McClellan and issued the Emancipation Proclamation mainly as a war measure; my paramount object, he wrote Horace Greeley, is to save the Union, and is not either to save or to destroy slavery; and in the autumn elections the Republicans lost many states, for with the war dragging along inconclusively people were disheartened, they wanted action, they wanted a quick, clean, neat victory. Fredericksburg came along in December, with General Burnside, one of God's errors, sending wave after wave of Union troops against the Reb fortified positions; the Rebs mowed them down, mowed them down; and General Lee, watching, told General Jackson it was well war was so horrible lest we would grow too fond of it; and in camp after the battle General Burnside pointed across the Rappahannock and cried out, "Oh, those men! Those men over there! I am thinking of them all the time," which was a nice sentiment although it might have been better if he had done his thinking before the battle. The new year came; days were short and cloudy, night came early; and a member of congress from Ohio wrote in his diary, "All is confusion and doubt . . . How striking the want of a leader! The nation is without a head . . . All faith and confidence in everybody seems to give way . . . The people are bewildered and in a fog."

And all this offered fine opportunity for persons at the North whose Southern sympathies had been squelched but not extinguished; you began hearing about Copperheads; and bad-weather birds like Congressman Vallandigham went about the country making speeches to the effect that a peace should be made at any price. The lower house of the Illinois legislature passed a resolution urging an armistice; a secret society sprang up, called the Knights of the Golden Circle, whose objectives were dubious; in congress Vallandigham made a speech saying, "You have not conquered the South. You never will . . ." And President Lincoln panicked; arbitrary arrests were made and the writ of habeas corpus suspended; free speech and a free press all but vanished; it was just as well Judge Gentry had died, he would have been so mournful; but it was war and civil war at that; it was men coming home blind or legless or armless; it was waiting for letters that never came, and receiving ominous telegrams from the War Department; it was sending boxes of food to the boys at the front and having them intercepted and the cookies gobbled by officers; it was troops invading the office of the *Chicago Times* and suspending its publication; it was fear and suspicion and hate and doubt; it was prices going up and some men getting richer and some men sleeping without blankets in a prison camp at Macon, Georgia, when a norther blew down from Yankee land.

Rolfe never heard from Sue; she might have died, for all he knew. He wrote her letters, when he could lay hands on a scrap of paper, and gave them to the guards to mail, although he realized it would require a succession of miracles for those guards actually to mail them, and for even one letter to make its way through smoke and ruin to New Empire, Wisconsin. Sometimes when he lay shivering at 4:00 A.M., hearing the moans and the coughs of his comrades, it would seem that New Empire had no existence, that he had dreamed it all; that a prewar young man named Rolfe Torkelsen, well-fed and cocky and healthy, had never existed, had never stayed in a suite at the St. Nicholas Hotel in New York and addressed a political rally urging the election of A. Lincoln. He was nothing now, a name listed missing on the rolls of the Eighteenth Wisconsin Infantry, a bundle of rags, a bundle of skin and bones.

Spring came early, that was one thing you could say for the South; and he had survived the winter; many hadn't, but he must have inherited a tough body from the Reverend and Mrs. Thor Torkelsen. And on warm afternoons he and Izzy Weinberg, who came of a people that had learned about surviving the hard way, used to lie whispering about the possibilities of escape. Escape: that was what prisoners always dreamed of; getting the hell out and being on their way. Now and then somebody managed it and was never heard from again; but usually the bloodhounds tracked them and they were brought back and staked out and required to wear an iron ball chained to their ankles. Still, Rolfe and Izzy kept wondering if it could be managed; they even had returned escapees draw them maps in the dust of the country thereabouts: of the Ocmulgee River that flowed southeast to join the Altamaha; of the Altamaha that made its way to the Atlantic Ocean. But what then, what if they did reach the sea? They would still be deep in the swamps of Rebeldom. Yet it would be worth a try, if opportunity offered.

Meanwhile, as the first anniversary of Shiloh came and passed, as new campaigns opened on battlegrounds of the Republic, the prisoners took to carving out trinkets, and the guards sometimes paid for these in Confederate paper money whose value was sinking so rapidly it might as well be spent. Rolfe was no good at carving out anything, except a career in the law; but those trinkets gave him an idea. Why not prevail upon somebody to carve out chessmen and to make a crude chessboard? In return he would teach them the game of kings. The idea caught on; nothing like a good game to take your mind off your nagging stomach, and the last deck of cards had disintegrated; so presently about half the prisoners were learning chess: the rest were too wasted in body and spirit to give a damn about anything. And by midsummer a chess tournament was organized there in camp; it was something to do. The guards watched incuriously; they were nearly as morose as the prisoners now, what with Vicksburg fallen to Grant and with Lee thrown back from Gettysburg. Rolfe won the first tournament, and the second and third as well, although he gave rook odds. And one afternoon during the third tournament—it was autumn again—the new commander of the camp, making a tour of inspection, stopped to watch. He was a colonel who had lost his right arm at Chancellorsville; Macon was his home town and the Confederate command, with a lucidity rare in high commands, had returned him here to run things. Colonel H. W. K. Devoe, that was his name; and he was thin and mild-seeming with a straw-colored mustache that drooped sadly.

"Chess, eh?" he said. "Let me know the winner's name."

The winner, of course, was none other than Private Rolfe Torkelsen, despite those rook odds and his intentional blunders; he had wanted to encourage the more promising novices, such as Izzy Weinberg; but an expert chess player had a deep-grained integrity that made it nearly impossible for him to throw a game. Anyway, a couple of mornings after the tournament ended, a guard told Private Torkelsen he was wanted in the guardhouse at the gate; it sounded ominous. In the guardhouse, however, he found Colonel H. W. K. Devoe.

"You're Torkelsen?" Colonel Devoe asked. "Sit down, sir. I understand you're a chess player."

"More or less."

"I'm told you won the tournament. Have you played long?"

908

"As long as I can remember."

"Yes, um-m-m, yes, a royal game. I learned when I was seven, myself. What was your occupation before the war?"

"Lawyer."

"And the Yankees put you in the ranks? Why weren't you an officer?"

Rolfe told why.

"I see," Colonel Devoe said. "Yes, of course. A waste of good material, though. A week in the ranks and you fought at Shiloh. Well, I'm glad to learn all the blockheads aren't in the Southern command. I could tell you instances ... but no matter. We did surprise you at Shiloh, though."

Rolfe nodded.

"Yes, sir, we surprised you. If Albert Sidney Johnston had lived things would have turned out differently. The battle was won and Beauregard threw it away. Gettysburg should have been ours too. If Stonewall Jackson had lived ... Well, it's a hard war. I suppose they all are. We thought we'd lick you in three months."

"And we thought we'd lick you."

Rolfe smiled and Colonel Devoe smiled. Out among the October foliage a mockingbird was singing.

"Sir," Colonel Devoe said, "I'd deem it a pleasure to cross swords with you at chess. We had a chess group here in Macon, before the war. Life was pleasant in those days. Our group is scattered now. Dead, most of them. I've missed those evenings. I'd deem it a pleasure to play with you."

"Any time."

"Yes ... But not here. Perhaps you could come to my home this evening."

"That's for you to say."

"Why, so it is. One forgets. We must agree, however, not to discuss the causes of this war. If you're an abolitionist I don't wish to know it. The war itself we can discuss, but not the causes. Our tempers might give way. And I should like your word of honor that you would make no attempt to escape."

Rolfe was remembering how Jim Buckmaster had play-acted in New York, when the reporters interviewed him.

"Escape?" he said vaguely. "Do you think I'm a fool? Look at me. Look." He held out a hand. "See how it shakes? That's weakness. I'm so weak I cave in if I'm on my feet five minutes. I'd do fine, wouldn't I, trying to escape?"

"Yes, um-m-m, I'm sorry about conditions, Torkelsen. I'm doing my best, but there are vast problems. Your blockade. And England has let us down. We're staggering, Torkelsen. I hate to say it, but we're staggering. Logistics is the problem. There's food in the South—there must be, we're an agricultural people, sir—but where is that food? Our troops are living on parched corn. Logistics, that's the answer. There has been bungling beyond imagination, and swindling too, I fear. Our railroads are rust. Half the locomotives have fallen to pieces. We are not a mechanical people, sir. We are a soldierly people but not a mechanical. And we're staggering."

"Yet you keep fighting," Rolfe said.

"What else can we do? We're soldiers . . . Tonight, then. You will come under guard, I regret to say."

Rolfe stood up and saluted, weakly. Using his left hand, Colonel Devoe returned the salute. And he said, as Rolfe was leaving:

"Um-m-m, Torkelsen."

Rolfe turned.

"Something I want you to know, Torkelsen. Those stories that were circulated in the North about our treatment of our servants—I hope you didn't believe them all. The servants in my family were never punished, Torkelsen. I loved my wet nurse like my own mother. My body servant and I played together as boys. He followed me to the war. When I was wounded at Chancellorsville he crawled between the lines and carried me back. And a bullet got him. I loved him, Torkelsen. We never whipped our servants."

"I'm sure you didn't."

"It was not a good system, Torkelsen. I mean slavery. Some of us realized it and were looking ahead to gradual emancipation. But events moved too fast. Our politicians were rascals. And so were yours, if I may say so. We found ourselves born into a system we didn't devise. Patience was needed, to alter it, and a largeness of mind. Then secession came. I opposed that, as best I could. But when Georgia left the Union I had to follow. You would have done the same, in my place. And I would have done the same in yours. Chess is a better game than war, Torkelsen."

"Yes," Rolfe said, "much better."

*

He was taken to the guardhouse again that afternoon where he found a Negro barber sent by Colonel Devoe.

"Look at yourself, suh," the barber said, holding up a mirror. "Like old Samson in Holy Writ. Yes, suh, just like."

In the mirror Rolfe saw a stranger with a coppery beard and a wild tangle of hair; the stranger's eyes were sullen and burning.

"Clip it close," Rolfe said, "and shave my beard."

"I don't know, suh. Beards is mighty fashionable these days. Hard on the barber trade too, but mighty fashionable."

"I want it off," Rolfe said.

When the barber had finished and held up the mirror again, the face Rolfe saw was still a stranger's. Over the cheekbones the skin was taut; beneath the cheekbones there were deep hollows; it was a face gaunted and drawn, the face of a man who had had experiences. All boyishness, all cockiness had left it; the owner of that face was only twenty-seven, but the face looked older than that, with its pallid skin and colorless lips.

"Somethin' else the colonel sent," the barber said, handing Rolfe a package.

It contained gray pants, a white shirt, a gray jacket, all well worn but clean. Rolfe changed at once; they nearly fitted him. But oddly, instead of being grateful, he found himself thinking sure, sure, he wouldn't want me coming to his house looking like a Yankee prisoner, he's so goddamned aristocratic I probably offended his gentility in those rags, he wants me to look like a gentleman, the son of a bitch.

But then he brought himself up short: that kind of thinking was prison thinking; prison made a man surly; you built up endless grievances, in prison.

"If you see the colonel," Rolfe said, "please thank him. I appreciate his thoughtfulness."

"Oh, yes, suh, he's thoughtful. So was his daddy. His daddy manumitted me and set me up in the barber business. I'm a free nigger, yes, suh, free as a bird, 'cepting I never done learned to fly." The barber laughed. "No, suh, never sprouted no wings, but I'm free. Some folks says Colonel Devoe's daddy and my daddy was one *and* the same. I don't know 'bout that. Some things is best not thought about."

But Rolfe thought: We never whipped our servants, Torkelsen. We loved our servants.

That evening, guarded by a soldier who had caught the rheumatism in the Army of Northern Virginia, Rolfe left the fairgrounds and walked through the streets of Macon. The air was warm as August in Wisconsin, and perfumed by flowers; fireflies were winking; moths flitted around streetlamps. But most of the streetlamps were dark, for streetlamps needed whale oil and that came from Yankee seas. Houses were dark too—people were saving candles, maybe—and the whole town seemed melancholy and dying in a cause that had been lost at such places as Shiloh. Somewhere off in the country hound-dogs were yelping, as if mourning the expiring Confederacy.

"Don't try nothin' smart," the guard said. "My back's a misery with the rheumatics, but I can still shoot."

"Hell, man," Rolfe said, "I'm not a fool. If I'd run a hundred feet I'd be done in."

"Just thought I'd give you fair warning," the guard said. "I was the sharpshootingest bastard in Lee's army. It warn't the Yanks that done me in, it was the winters. Never seen so much snow as after Fredericksburg. We went into quarters, but one blanket ain't enough for twelve men. Cold? My God, everybody's snot was icicles."

Beyond the business district, with its bare display windows and empty store shelves, they shuffled along a street shadowed by tuliptrees and live oaks, turning in at an opening in a tall boxwood hedge. Under the stars the house was a glimmering ghost, spacious with a gallery and Greek Revival pilasters; Rolfe had an impression of formal gardens and shrubs long unclipped. Somebody stirred on the veranda and came to the steps.

"Good evening, sir," he said. "Welcome to Crestwood."

"Good evening, thank you, sir," Rolfe said.

Colonel H. W. K. Devoe addressed the guard.

"You will wait here on the piazza. Private Torkelsen has given me his word of honor as a soldier and a gentleman that he will not attempt escape."

That was not wholly accurate, but Rolfe let it go.

"And now, sir—"

Colonel Devoe gestured toward the door.

It seemed odd being in a house for the first time in a year-and-a-half; everything was dim and princely. Rooms with double doors opened off the long central hall; a staircase swept graciously upward; mahogany furniture gleamed; there were massive paintings framed in gold. In the library, where a single candle burned on a chess table, the walls were bookshelves, loaded with rich bindings, climbing toward the high ceiling.

"Sit down, sir," Colonel Devoe said. "My wife and daughter ask you to accept their regrets, under the circumstances."

"Thank them for me," Rolfe said, "and tell them I quite understand. And I wish, sir, to express my gratitude for your favors of this afternoon."

He wondered if he were overdoing it. In his mind a plan had been forming, but before he could effect it Colonel Devoe must be put off guard.

"It was my pleasure," the colonel said. "If I can't make a Confederate out of you, at least I have the satisfaction of seeing you in butternut."

They tossed to see which would play white; the colonel won. And he was a chess player. He opened with a Ruy Lopez, sending his bishop to knight 5 on his third move; Rolfe countered with a pawn to queen's rook 3. The colonel smiled and said he was glad the Yankees hadn't made a general out of Rolfe. He took Rolfe's knight; Rolfe took his bishop; they fell silent, concentrating on that playing board, while the lace curtains at the tall windows stirred languidly and moths fluttered around the candle and far away in the Tennessee mountains the armies of a sundered Republic maneuvered toward what men would remember as Lookout Mountain. But in Colonel Devoe's library, the Confederacy triumphed, after an hour-and-a-half.

"Shall we try it again?" the colonel asked.

This time Rolfe played the white pieces, using a queen's gambit opening; the colonel accepted the gambit without, however, trying to hold on to the gambit pawn; yes, he was a chess player. An hour later, when doom seemed certain, he even managed to achieve perpetual check. On the chessboard you learned how your opponent's mind worked, and Rolfe knew that a man like that would never risk bringing a prisoner to his house with only one guard; probably another was stationed outside the window. Any attempt to escape must be planned weeks and perhaps months in advance; he would need a companion too, Izzy Weinberg probably; he must find a way for Izzy to be invited here also; it would all take patience and time. Well, time was what he had the most of.

"How about another go tomorrow evening?" the colonel asked.

"I'd like it."

"Capital. And now a bite to eat?"

Food. Just like that, if you were not a prisoner of war, you said it: how about a bite to eat? Why, yes, Rolfe said, yes I would. He was annoyed at how he was trembling. Colonel Devoe pulled a bell-rope; a pretty mulatto in a tignon shuffled in with a tray of peaches and cold fried chicken. Rolfe's tongue was running with saliva; it was all he could do to keep from falling on that food like a starved wolf. But he was a soldier and a gentleman, guest of an officer and a gentleman; if he ate like an unmannered Yankee he might not be invited here again. He took a drumstick, a knife and a fork; oh, eat it with your fingers, the colonel said, that's the only way to get at a fried chicken; Rolfe made himself chew slowly, and he refused a second piece. He did, however, accept a peach.

And he said colonel, there's a dog at camp, a kind of mascot, mind if I take this bone to the dog? Why, no, the colonel said, I like dogs myself; take my wing-bones too; Minnie, wrap these for Private Torkelsen.

The fairgrounds were silent and shadowy when Rolfe returned; in the makeshift hut where he slept he wakened Private Izzy Weinberg, and they gnawed those bones dry, chewing up the cartilage and sucking out every speck of sweet marrow.

And Rolfe whispered: "I think I'm on to something, a way to escape. It may take months, but we can work it. Are you with me?"

"All the way," Private Weinberg said.

*

And it did take months; nearly a year of months. First, it was necessary to convince his guard that never under any conditions would Private Torkelsen break for it and run. Night after night, several times a week, and week after week, he was the best-behaved prisoner in Dixie, walking to and from Colonel Devoe's. The routine, so unusual at first, of a Yankee prisoner being conducted to the commander's home, must be established in his guard's mind as the usual, the ordinary, the humdrum. One evening in January as they were walking toward the colonel's, they were unexpectedly and unintentionally assailed by a dozen colored children who, playing some such game as Run, Sheep, Run, came bursting from an alley; in the ensuing collision the guard was tripped and he fell; his curses scattered the children in all directions; Rolfe helped him to his feet.

"Goddamn niggers," the guard said. "Never know what they'll do. Only two places a nigger's any good: a buck in his grave and a wench in your bed." And he added: "Say, you could have skedaddled, Yank."

"I know it."

"Say, when I was there on my ass you could have made a break."

"Sure," Rolfe said, "and how far would I get? I'm no fool."

"Well thanks, anyway, Yank. If you'd get away it would be our asses."

"Yours and who else's? That guard outside the library window?"

"Say! How did you know about him?"

"Heard him cough once."

"Well, I'll be damned. Anyway, thanks, Yank."

That was not a good winter anywhere, North or South; frigid rains drenched the prisoners encamped at Macon; in Northern Virginia the armies of Lee and Meade floundered in slush; in New York, despite the draft riots of last July, fighting Irishmen who had no wish to fight were snatched from their pigs and impressed into service; wounded filled the hospitals; rumor had it that Mr. Lincoln was mainly ape and Mrs. Lincoln mainly crazy; and always the Yankee blockade was a pair of thumbs at the windpipe of the South: salt lacked; buttons lacked; paper and matches lacked; everything lacked; and prices kept soaring and it was a long, long war. Already the South was whipped, defeated, ruined, but that stubborn Scotch-Irish and dogged British blood wouldn't admit it; more would die in the campaigns of spring and summer, many more; and no longer after an evening of chess at Colonel Devoe's was Rolfe invited to have a bite to eat.

Those games, however, had improved his chess; he was winning half the time; and he had taken the colonel's measure: the colonel was a knight player. Rather than surrender a knight he would sacrifice, say, a bishop and a pawn; knights were his strength, (because he used them brilliantly), and his weakness, (because no chess player should fall so in love with any piece that he would risk his game to protect it).

Using this information, Rolfe spent long hours tutoring Izzy Weinberg in the employment of bishops. Knights were the dashing Southern cavalry of the chessboard; bishops were the long-range Yankee artillery; they were equal in power, roughly, at the beginning of a game, but toward the end a bishop could be deadly. So Rolfe devised cunning traps and ruses, and Izzy was an apt pupil; by March, he could probably, Rolfe thought, give the colonel an interesting time.

So one evening at the colonel's Rolfe mentioned a fellow-prisoner whose chess had improved phenomenally: he's been licking me, Rolfe said, and he might even lick you.

"What's his name?"

"Private Weinberg."

"Jewish?"

"Yes."

914

"Jews are sharp-dealing. Wouldn't trust one as far as I'd trust a nigger. Never could understand how President Davis could stand having Judah Benjamin in his cabinet. I've never had one inside my house. They're not gentlemen."

Rolfe shrugged.

"Private Weinberg," he said, "is a shrewd player. I can't blame you for fighting shy of a game with him."

"Who says I'm fighting shy? I didn't say that. By God, sir, I'll play chess with anybody. Bring him along some night."

"When?"

"Tomorrow will do. I'll issue the order."

And so it happened that next evening, and on many evenings, both Izzy and Rolfe went to Colonel Devoe's. Their guard was suspicious again, at this change in routine, but Izzy behaved as circumspectly as Rolfe; little by little the unusual became the usual. Fighting on the chessboard for his freedom, Izzy played wittily, with many a crafty trap; several times, benefiting from a code of signals he and Rolfe had devised, he won; and Colonel Devoe was always eager for return engagements. Meanwhile Unconditional Surrender Grant, appointed lieutenant general, went plodding bloodily toward the Wilderness, Spotsylvania, Cold Harbor; the fighting was murderous; Grant plodded on; casualty lists were appalling and people called him Butcher Grant; he plodded on; and in the West a lean, high-strung redhead, (whose hair was more gray now than red), maneuvered like a fencer past Ringgold and Resaca and Kennesaw Mountain, slicing toward Atlanta in the Dixie heartland. That was William Tecumseh Sherman; Crazy Sherman, they had called him, long ago; once he had managed the street railway company in St. Louis; now his men were tough as Caesar's legions and as savage in battle; he slept badly, writing voluminous letters and planning tomorrow's fighting through insomnious nights; and at the end of August he dispatched a telegram to A. Lincoln: Atlanta is ours, and fairly won.

And so they burned Atlanta, which annoyed many Southern ladies and gentlemen, it was so unlike the Waverley novels; war had grown vulgar and total and earth-scorching; the governor of Georgia issued stinging proclamations, but the time for words was past, shot and shell could give you hell but words could never hurt you. And in Macon many a brave heart beat faster, and many an intestinal tract suffered speedier peristalsis, because Atlanta was only a few dozen miles away; Sherman might come here next, brandishing a torch; children woke from nightmares crying.

Rumor of all this trickled through the fairgrounds prison, along with rumor that the inmates were to be taken elsewhere. The number of guards was reduced, for the reeling armies of Dixie needed every tatterdemalion who could be mustered; and Rolfe told Izzy the time was at hand to make a break for freedom. Throughout the spring and summer they had planned it; now, on an evening in September, they would act.

"Torkelsen," Colonel Devoe said that evening, when the playing was over, "I regret to say that this will probably be our last night at Crestwood together."

"How is that, sir?"

"Orders have come to move. We'll march tomorrow. I've been holding off, hoping for freight cars, knowing the condition of the prisoners, but we can't wait longer."

"If it's a long march, sir, I'm afraid not many will survive."

"Yes, regrettable. But Sherman is forcing our hand."

Colonel Devoe accompanied them to the door; their guard stirred. And as on numberless evenings, Izzy and Rolfe left the gallery and marched side by side toward the gate in the boxwood hedge, their guard close behind. On the street they turned toward camp, well-behaved prisoners of war. But after about a block, Rolfe caught his breath and said, "Ouch!" And he rubbed his left knee.

"What's the matter?" the guard asked.

"I don't know. All at once my knee—Jeez!—it hurts. I can't put my foot down."

"Let's see," the guard said, and he bent.

And at that carefully-rehearsed moment, Rolfe crashed his fist down on the back of the guard's neck; Izzy dived and tripped him; his musket went clattering; Rolfe was at his throat and Izzy kicked him in the groin. He threshed, but Rolfe's thumbs blockaded his breath. Presently he became quiet, although he wasn't dead; they stripped off his shirt and gagged him; they tied his wrists and ankles; they dragged him into a thicket on somebody's lawn. And Privates Izzy Weinberg and Rolfe Torkelsen were free.

*

On a hundred afternoons they had planned it, studying crude maps sketched in the dust, and Izzy had exchanged his last Yankee dollars for the Confederate dollars other prisoners had earned carving out trinkets. Now, keeping to alleys and vacant lots, they worked their way south through town, crossing the right-of-way of the Georgia Central Railroad, wading through cattail sloughs, till they reached a road leading south. Low in the west a red slice of moon hung like a lantern, faintly lighting their way. Back in town dogs were barking, and when they passed thick-shadowed cabins they sometimes heard chains rattling and the deep-throated baying of hounds. They scooted on, remembering that in these parts there were men who made a living tracking fugitive Negroes and Rebel deserters and escaped Yankees.

They passed an orchard and risked snatching apples from the grass; they snitched corn from a field, although the kernels were hard; and presently they cut off toward the east, through a pasture that became a

916

bog and then a swamp. The moon had gone now; they groped and fumbled in slime, stopping to rest when they encountered a grassy mound. In New Empire, Wisconsin, away off there under the North Star, this night would be tangy with frost, but here the air was warm. They ate the apples and gnawed the corn and even dozed, till the eastern sky turned the color of a Confederate uniform; then, wading to their waists sometimes, and trying to forget such creatures of God as cottonmouth moccasins, they slithered toward the dawn, coming finally to a sluggish river that looked like green glass; thin mist hung above it.

"The Ocmulgee, it must be," Rolfe said. "We'd better get across."

Their shoes were not much—battered, broken things—but they might need them; so they took them off and tied the laces together and held the laces in their teeth when they swam the Ocmulgee. It was hardly wider than a slough along the Upper Mississippi, but weak as they were after prison food that swim tuckered them; on the east bank they rested. But before long, remembering bloodhounds and men spread-eagled in the sun, they were on the move again, following the river downstream, hoping to come across a moored scow and carry out their plan of floating down the Ocmulgee to the Altamaha and down the Altamaha to the sea. Once they reached the coast, they hoped to catch sight of some Yankee warship blockading the Confederacy, and signal it, or they might tramp on to Florida whence vague rumor had blown of Yankees invading. It was playing hide-and-seek with death, this break for freedom; the odds against them were staggering; but other prisoners had managed it, and what man had done man could do, sometimes.

Winding and snaggy, choked in places with driftwood, its muddy water reflecting sweetgum and cypress and festooned vines, the Ocmulgee was their guide that morning. Sometimes the bank was so soft they sank in mud; sometimes their progress was barred by an inlet, or by jungles of cane or Bermuda grass; they kept going, although they sighted no boat to be stolen. And always they cast glances over their shoulders, or stopped to listen. Along toward noon, the river flowed past a rich bottom where corn grew; that meant a plantation nearby; they inched along, ears alert, and halted to whisper, seeing the gleam of sun on the sword-shaped leaves of that Indian corn, and the sky milky-blue with humidity, and off in the distance above a timber the leisurely circling of turkey buzzards. And hungry as they were, they sneaked among the corn, higher than their heads, and broke off ears and ate. When they left the field it was by a circuitous route which took them into a dense cane-brake; the stalks rattled noisily; and they emerged at the river to find themselves face to face with an old Negro whose gray hair was like a close-fitting cap.

Rolfe's impulse was to take to his heels, but he brazened it out. He asked, What's your name? Me, suh, the Negro said, I'm Chester. Belongs to Mis' Melbourne.

"What are you doing here?" Rolfe asked.

"Lookin' for de cow. She done got loose. Mis' Melbourne think she might be headin' for de corn."

"Do you know who we are?"

"Yes, suh. Soldiers, I reckon. Plenty soldiers round here last three-four years. Took all our hosses off to fight de Yanks. Stole de chickens right off de roosts. Times is awful hard."

"We're Yanks," Rolfe said.

Chester swallowed.

"Them pants ain't Yank pants," he said finally. "Hear tell Yanks wears blue pants."

"We're from the Macon prison. My other pants wore out."

"Pants does that. Yes, suh. Nigger's pants wears out at de knees. Master's on de seat. But Master Melbourne he was killed. At place called Chickenmagga. That was Old Master. Young Master, he done fell at place called—well, I forgits—somewhere up North. Times is awful hard."

"You'll go back to the house and tell Mrs. Melbourne you saw us," Rolfe said. "That's what you'll do, isn't it?"

"No, suh."

"You'll tell her, and she'll send somebody to Macon. They'll come after us with bloodhounds. They'll catch us too. And we'll remember old Chester did it. The Yanks are coming, Chester. Thousands of Yanks. They'll set us free and we'll say Chester snitched. Get old Chester, we'll say, and—"

"No, suh, no, suh! Ain't goin' to snitch. Me, I don't know nothin' about nothin'. No, *suh!*"

"Maybe not," Rolfe said. "Maybe you'll be a smart nigger."

"Sure will try. Bein' smart never come easy, but sure will try."

"Maybe you'll be smart and earn a dollar. Bring us some food and earn a dollar."

Chester thought that over.

"Might fetch you a little pig. Ain't much else, but a two-month pig is sweet meat."

"And a knife to skin him, Chester. That would be two dollars."

"Yes, suh. I can fetch a knife."

"And salt—"

"Ain't no salt. Yankees got a lot of ships and keep de salt from comin' in. Ain't had no salt for years. Mis' Melbourne, she done had us dig under de smokehouse. Dig up de dirt where de salt used to drip. Got some salt from that dirt, but it's all been et."

"And a boat, Chester. We need a boat."

"A water boat? Yes, suh, I understand. But there ain't nothin' like a water boat round here."

"Five dollars for a boat, Chester. That would be seven dollars."

"You rich? You don't look it. Say I fetch de pig and de knife and de water boat—only there ain't none—and you say, all right, Chester, that will do, Chester, run along you black bastard—where do that leave me?"

Rolfe turned to Izzy.

"Show him the money."

Izzy produced seven dollar bills. Rolfe took them, rustled them.

"Think hard, Chester. Where there's a river there's always a boat."

"Yes, suh. Where there's a river there's a boat. Only Master used to keep his in a pond back yonder, so no trash would steal it. I goes fishin' sometimes, Mis' Melbourne admires a mess of catfish, and I drags it to de river. For five dollars reckon I could help you drag it, and I could look de other way when you steals it."

"And we'll want matches, Chester."

"Ain't no matches. Ain't been no matches for years."

"Ten cents for a match, Chester. A dollar for ten."

Chester scratched his head and sighed.

"Yes, suh. My old woman take a few from de kitchen, back when they is gittin' scarce. Got 'em hid away somewheres. Ten for a dollar, you say?"

"Ten for a dollar. That will make eight dollars."

Chester smiled.

"I'm goin' to be rich," he said. "Yanks is comin' to set me free, and I'll be rich."

*

But Rolfe wasn't trusting Chester wholly; he wasn't trusting anybody except Private Izzy Weinberg; Chester just might be one of those faithful old retainers the South liked to talk about.

"Night will be best," he told Chester. "Go look for that cow, and come back after dark. Bring the pig and the matches and the knife, and we'll get the boat then."

"Don't know 'bout that. How's we goin' to see what we's doin', in de dark?"

"There'll be a moon. Now do what you're told."

"Yes, suh."

"And Chester—"

"Yes, suh."

"If you snitch we'll tell the Yanks. The Yanks will come and get you and—"

"Ain't goin' to snitch! No, suh! I ain't got no woman's tongue."

He shuffled away north along the river bank and into the corn. Noon was hot and still.

"He'll never come back," Izzy said.

"I think he will. He wants the money. But he might tell his mistress and they might lay a trap. We'll hide out now and when night comes

919

we'll separate. That way, they won't trap us both."

Downstream along the river Rolfe and Izzy moved warily, through the smells of fishy water and swamp honeysuckle and green fecundity, slipping in black mud, crawling among briers and cockleburs. After a quarter-of-a-mile they came opposite a place where a broad inlet drained phlegmatically into the Ocmulgee from what appeared to be a cypress swamp; they saw Spanish moss bearding the forlorn trees, and tall rank bulrushes. It looked like a good hiding place for fugitive prisoners as well as bull alligators and copperheads and muskrats. So, taking off their shoes, they swam across the Ocmulgee and slopped their way into the swamp, through ooze and chartreuse water and rot, while dragonflies whirred in the hot sun and salamanders fled and a white ibis stretched its snaky neck to observe these intruders before it flapped away crying.

On a squishy island, tufted with willows, they found a cottonwood that had been uprooted in some ancient storm, its trunk incrusted with moss and toadstools. They waited a while in the willows, listening and watching, before perching themselves on the cottonwood; a water locust gave them shade. Gradually, the swamp resumed its wonted ways. A limpkin flew by calling *cre-e-e-e,* bitterns cried, a turtle came lubbering from the gumbo to sun himself on a log, and Rolfe was reminded of that Federal gunboat he had seen on the Tennessee River a thousand years ago. They talked of the war, in whispers. It seemed unbelievable that Union troops held Atlanta, less than a hundred miles away. And what would Sherman do now?

"What can he do," Rolfe said, "except dig in and build up supplies? The railroad down from Ringgold is his only life line. He'll have to guard that. It will be spring before he'll be ready for another push. My guess would be he'll head for Mobile. Cut up the South like you would a pie. This war's not over yet. The Rebs are licked but they won't yell enough."

"Rolfe," Izzy said, "I've been wondering. Maybe we should have tried it for Atlanta."

"Through the Reb lines? That country will be alive with cavalry. We'd never make it."

"Do you think we'll make it this way?"

"We can try. I've decided one thing. I'm not going back to prison. If they take me they'll take me dead."

"Me and you both. It's funny, thinking we might be dead tomorrow. Do you think there's a life after death?"

"I hope not," Rolfe said. "Once is enough."

"Do you think there's a God?"

"I wouldn't know. I hope not, but I wouldn't know."

"Why do you hope not?"

"Because the question comes up as to whether he's good. And the weight of the evidence is that he isn't. And there's additional evidence that he's a bungler. And vain. Either you go down on your knees and salaam, or you get tossed into hell. I won't go down on my knees to anybody."

"I used to think there was a God," Izzy said. "I thought the rabbi was personally acquainted with him. That was before Shiloh. I went into Shiloh thinking there was, and I came out thinking there wasn't."

"The beginning of wisdom," Rolfe said, "is to stop fearing the Lord."

The afternoon dragged on; once in the distant northwest they heard hounds baying. Hounds and chains and bullwhips and shotguns: that was also Dixie. And turkey buzzards circling and snakefeeders flittering and the dark old crime of a people in bondage. After a while the hounds bayed out of hearing; Izzy stretched out on that cottonwood trunk and slept. But the slaveships from the Gold Coast, Rolfe thought, had been owned and manned by Yankees. And there had been slavery in the North till it was found to be economically unsound. And early in the war, on the way to Pittsburg Landing, he had heard plenty of the boys say they were fighting to save the Union, that they wouldn't lift a musket for no damned niggers. It was an odd kind of war that had started to halt secession and now had been twisted into a crusade for emancipation. You could say it was the South's fault for leaving the Union and firing on Sumter, but you could also say those events would never have taken place if Yankee fortunes had not been founded on the middle passage. You could also make out a good case for the South's right to leave the Union. Yes, an odd war, fought not for territory or plunder or for some ruler's personal glory, but to keep intact a dream Republic which would never be the same again with half of it gutted and ravaged. The afternoon was somnolent: Rolfe lay back against a crotch and closed his eyes, thinking of Sue, wondering if he would ever see her again, if he would ever sleep again in a bed and do sane things like eating breakfast and going to the office and preparing briefs.

Sundown was near, the mosquitoes humming and the frogs tuning up, when he wakened. Well, he had business to do. Izzy was already awake, and Rolfe sketched out his plan: Izzy to wait on the west side of the river while Rolfe swam across and reconnoitered before meeting Chester. If Chester showed up alone, fine; if he brought men with shotguns, Izzy Weinberg would still be free. Izzy protested, but Rolfe was ten years older and he pulled rank on him.

Cumulus clouds were gold-edged castles in the northwest, but the sun had gone and the mosquitoes were ravenous when Rolfe and Izzy toiled back through the swamp; on the west bank of the Ocmulgee, south of the inlet, Rolfe went over their plans once more.

"Wait here and I'll meet you with the boat. We'll travel at night and hide out during the day. If you hear anything—anything like shooting— don't peep. Lie low for a while and then follow the river south. Is that clear?"

Izzy nodded; he looked close to tears.

"Rolfe," he said, "I wish you good luck."

"I'll be fine."

"And Rolfe. I've been thinking. If I pull through and you don't, I'll go to Wisconsin and see your wife. I'll tell her how it's been."

"I'll pull through," Rolfe said.

"And if you do but I don't, would you go to Cincinnati and see my folks? Isadore Weinberg—my father's name is the same as mine. They wondered why I lied about my age and enlisted. You tell them, Rolfe. Tell them—tell them it was the kids at school, Rolfe. They always called me a Hebe. Shylock Weinberg, that's what they called me, because my father ran the pawnshop. And when war came they said no Hebe would fight. All the Hebes would be sutlers, they said, but they wouldn't fight. But I fought, Rolfe. I fought like a wildcat, at Shiloh. I shot low, and I fought. I even—I even ran my bayonet through a Reb. That was when my regiment broke and ran. Everything was smoke and the Rebs were yelling and then this Reb came out of the smoke. He wasn't much older than me, and before I knew it I had run him through. It was just like they taught us at camp. Only he was alive, he wasn't a bag of sawdust. And you know something, Rolfe? He was a Hebe too, a Reb Hebe. I remember his eyes when he looked down and saw the bayonet and then looked at me. It was all over in a second, just like running a bayonet through a dummy at camp. Only he didn't leak sawdust. He died pretty fast. That's a long time ago but I can't get it out of my mind. I dream about it. Do you ever dream about Shiloh, Rolfe?"

"Yes," Rolfe said.

"Do you think we'll ever forget it, Rolfe?"

"No."

"Well, anyway," Izzy said, "I fought."

He seemed like a schoolboy there in the greenish dusk with his funny homely face; Rolfe patted his shoulder.

"Izzy," he said, "I ran at Shiloh. At first. But then I fought too. They'll never give us medals, but we'll know. We'll know it's our country because we fought for it. Now stop this goddamned mooning and keep your wits."

So once again Rolfe swam the Ocmulgee and moved like a shadow through the thickening twilight to his rendezvous with Chester. Nobody was there. After a minute, ears straining, he worked his way along a dim path leading inland from the river, and presently, in the faint light from the young moon, he made out stables and the black shape of a plantation house. And he heard the voices of Negro children at play in the slave quarters; they would never be sold now; Old Master was dead and Young Master was dead and Sherman was in Atlanta.

Somebody was plodding along the path; Rolfe crouched in the grass and saw Chester going by, a gunny sack over his shoulder. The Negro children kept laughing and screeching till a woman's voice called them to bed. No men with shotguns had followed Chester; Rolfe stood up and went toward the river.

At the rendezvous everything was deep shadow; Rolfe said, "Chester."

No response.

"Chester. I'm the Yank in gray pants."

"Yes, suh." A shape stirred from the canebrake. "I done got you de shoat in this here poke. Had to cut his throat and bleed him, he was so squeally. And here's de knife and here's de matches. I done brought you more than ten. No charge for de extras. I got to thinkin'. I got to thinkin' how you come down here from where de big drinkin' gourd is." Chester pointed at the Big Dipper. "You comes down here to set us free. So I brought you de extra matches. De boat's back this way."

They returned a few paces along the path and cut over through high grass to a pond where the moon was silvery.

"Old Master had this here dug," Chester said. "Called it de fish pond. Us niggers used to seine up fish by de hundred and put 'em here. When Old Master want a fish fry for supper, here was de fish. Don't do that no more. Most of de field hands has lit out to find Sherman. Everything's gone to wrack and ruin. Times is awful hard."

The boat was an old hunting skiff; they dragged it through the grass to the river.

"That fixes you, I reckon," Chester said. "There's lines and fishhooks aboard. No extra charge. Some say Sherman is de son of God. You hear 'bout that?"

"No."

"That's what they say, de son of God, come to load de niggers into a gold chariot and take us to Canaan. But Mis' Melbourne say he de devil."

Rolfe paid Chester.

"Uh-h! De days of milk and honey is come upon us. Thank you, suh, thank you. I wish you good luck."

"We'll need it."

"Yes, suh, you sure will. You best keep out of sight in de daylight. Always soldiers around. And you wants to watch sharp at that town they call Hawkinsville. Never been there, but I hear tell it's 'bout thirty-forty miles down de river. There's a ferry crossing at that town, so I hear, and lots of soldiers guarding it. Hear tell they hanged up three niggers at Hawkinsville last Friday. By de neck till they was dead. Don't know what them niggers done, neither, but white folks is gittin' mighty touchy, with old Sherman so close . . . I sure do thank you, suh. Good luck and good-by."

"Good-by," Rolfe said. "I hope you find the land of Canaan."

"Uh-h! Yes, *suh!* Milk and honey and de women got no tongues. That what a preacher man tell me once."

Chester laughed softly and Rolfe pulled out into midstream, sculling along till he picked up Izzy Weinberg. They traveled till midnight when they risked a halt and a fire; even without salt, those slices of pork, roasted on sticks, were the best food Rolfe had ever tasted. Then they doused their fire and traveled till daybreak.

*

Hawkinsville. It had a portentous sound. And it was a word they spoke often during those next days and nights, while they drifted with the current or sculled along with oarlocks muffled by Southern moss. Always at dawn they concealed themselves and their skiff, on islands or in swamps or bayous, and before sleeping they pondered ways to slip past the heavily-guarded ferry crossing at Hawkinsville. They had no map and no certain means of knowing how far ahead that town might be, for the river meandered everlastingly, doubling back on itself, all but losing its identity in wide listless marshes, befuddling itself with bayous that looked like the main channel but that petered out in mud soup. Some nights they must have traveled only four or five miles, as a heron would fly it; they lost count of time.

There were drizzling days when they turned the boat upside down and slept beneath it, and stormy nights, black as a Congo Negro, when sudden lightning revealed a lilac-colored riverscape of rain-slant and whirling water and dense vegetation on shore. There were brilliant nights as the moon waxed full when a sharpshooter could have picked them off like bottles on a fence, and windy nights with scudding clouds when every tree and bush whispered of the world's madness.

By comparison with their prison fare they were eating well, for this was the season of ingathering; sweet potatoes were theirs for the stealing, and field corn and apples and possum grapes; sometimes they smelled out patches of cantaloupe and watermelon. They pulled in fish and wrapped them in green leaves and roasted them in coals; but a fire was dangerous. Late in the afternoons, they used to sneak along the river bank watching for Negroes in adjoining fields; if no overseer was visible, they would call softly and beckon; and thus they bought or were given an occasional ham bone, corn pone or a live chicken.

And those Negroes had all heard of Hawkinsville. Yes, suh, many soldiers there. Yes, suh, hear tell three niggers was hanged there for helping some 'scaped Yanks.

And how far away was Hawkinsville? Opinions varied. Down the river a piece.

Well, there were two ways to deal with Hawkinsville: by land or by water. They might, Rolfe said, abandon their skiff and make a wide circle around the town. That would be risky—although what wasn't?—because they would likely get lost, not knowing the country, and it would be sheer luck if they missed encountering patrols. Below the town, at the river again, they would have to steal another boat. As they considered that course, it seemed the risks multiplied faster than slaves on a thriving plantation.

They liked the other possibility better: to stick with their boat and sail her right past the town down the middle of the river. That way, there would be but one big risk, if you ignored all the ever-present little risks of men out fishing and of soldiers canoeing with girls and of Negroes who might snitch. So at last they decided to accept the one big risk and run the ferry crossing; but it was a decision nearly untenable owing to their ignorance of Hawkinsville's whereabouts. Piloting by hope and hunch, they might find themselves swept by the current around a bend and right spang in the middle of that ferry crossing. If that happened at daybreak the game would be lost.

They wasted much time, on those nights above Hawkinsville, searching the horizon for lights bespeaking a town. They started later and stopped earlier. Meanwhile the moon waned and blackened and was born again; it must be, they thought, October by now; and they wondered what had happened to their comrades left behind at Macon. And how was the war going? And the autumn campaigns in the North? This was a presidential year: would Lincoln be re-elected? Four years ago a rising young attorney named Rolfe Torkelsen had addressed a rally on the courthouse lawn, and people were saying the South would never secede. What were they saying now? That the South would never be defeated? That Rolfe Torkelsen would never return, that he must have been one of the anonymous dead at Shiloh? Well, he never would return: not the same Rolfe Torkelsen. He had been young then, and now he felt ageless; the young warrior had gone forth and misplaced his youth in the Confederate States of America. His hair was snarled with burs, his face a tangle of beard; he was a ragamuffin the dogs of New Empire would have barked out of town. Maybe Sue wouldn't want him now, if he ever got back. Maybe she had given him up for dead and had married again. And if he did return to find her waiting, what about his law practice? Years away from his office: his clients would have found other lawyers. He would have to begin again. Thus went his thoughts as the soft Georgia autumn was a breath of mist at dawn and a whiff of leaf smoke at twilight and a sun-yellowed wench through the long warm noons.

At last they had definite word about Hawkinsville; a Negro told them. Yes, suh, know dat place well. Been dar oftentimes of a Saturday. How far? 'Bout five-six miles, by road. By river? Well, a little farther. Per'aps eight-nine miles.

And that night, floating with the current, they saw the lights of town faint on the horizon. They pulled over to an island, dragged the skiff among the willows. And slept fitfully, knowing that in another twenty hours they would run the ferry crossing.

It was sleep that gave Rolfe a notion of how to get past Hawkinsville. He was a boy of fourteen, in sleep, working on a raft piloted by Jim Buckmaster. It all came back: the Upper Mississippi flowing in majesty, a cook named Mike Hogan, a linesman named Greasy Dick. And Jim Buckmaster looked as he had years ago, big and hell-bent and laughing, before his headaches and his marriage to Esperanza McSwasey. The raft was floating through a stretch of channel cluttered with driftwood; you saw whole trees, uprooted by flood, revolving in the current. And Jim was saying, Swede, I've never seen so much driftwood, there must have been a storm upriver, I've never seen so much. Then Judge Sophronicus Gentry was standing on the raft, looking as he used to before he failed so badly, and he was saying, *Auspicium melioris aevi,* so it was written in ages past, Birnam Wood must come to Dunsinane . . . Whereupon the driftwood was metamorphosed into bateaux, carrying persons Rolfe knew, all waving and laughing. Truly a beautiful war, Congressman Park Irwin was saying, truly an inspiring sight, the field of Shiloh, where so many patriots made the supreme sacrifice . . . And Susan Hatfield Torkelsen said you're nothing but a humbug, and Park Irwin said truly, truly, truly, while the bateau carrying Sue drifted far down the river.

Rolfe came awake on an island in another river, thinking there would be a moon tonight, a just-right moon, about half full. He lay smiling. And presently he said:

"Izzy, never let them tell you a classical education isn't practical. If it fooled Macbeth it will fool the Rebs."

Izzy wished to know what Rolfe was talking about. Rolfe explained. And they spent the rest of that afternoon selecting the proper sort of branches, leafy branches, and knifing them from the island trees.

It was late, the gibbous moon within an hour of setting, when they pushed away from the island, the skiff bedecked with branches. Across dim water the skiff would look like only a drift log, or so they hoped. They sculled along with hardly an oar-sound, keeping to midstream. Then, swinging around a wide bend and floating toward them, they saw the lights of Hawkinsville. They shipped oars and crouched. Through the foliage they could see the red and green lanterns of a ferry; on shore a sentry paced with his musket. Otherwise the town looked wrapped in sleep, in dreams, perhaps, of a glorious slave Republic; but the bonnie blue flag was battle-tattered now.

They had a bad few minutes when some vagary of current seized the skiff and turned it; they floated broadside and then stern first. And from rafting days Rolfe remembered what he never had known he knew: that a current would always carry a floating object toward the inner curve of a bend. The next bend, so far as he could make out, was below Hawkinsville and on the opposite shore.

"Lie down," he whispered. "Let her go."

They lay on their backs watching a sky that slowly revolved; presently the boat was running bow first again, then stern first, then bow first. Well, that was how a drift log would behave; if they tried to set a straight course somebody might notice. There was a soft bump after a time as the skiff nudged the bend; it hung in the current, then drifted on. When they permitted themselves to look, Hawkinsville was only a shimmer of light against the upriver sky.

*

They took it as a lucky omen, their getting past Hawkinsville; and when Negroes warned them of an important bridge, heavily-guarded, some thirty miles beyond, they repeated all their precautions: stopping early on those nights when the bridge was coming nearer, making inquiries, and at last cutting more fresh foliage. But running a bridge, Rolfe said, could be more dangerous than running a ferry crossing; they waited till the moon was black. It must have been about 2:00 A.M. when they finally saw the lights on that bridge; they lay flat. And again the skiff turned end to end, and as the current took it under the bridge it bumped an abutment. Overhead on the bridge floor they could hear the miniature thunder of horses' hoofs and the creak of wagons, and when they floated into the clear they could make out the dim silhouettes of soldiers with muskets marching across the bridge, looking like the moving dummies in a shooting gallery.

Autumn was well advanced by then, and from Negroes they had heard rumors of General William Tecumseh Sherman. Atlanta was in ruins; he had left it and his columns were crossing Georgia in a wide swath toward—could it be the Atlantic Ocean? Rolfe doubted that; few generals in history had dared to cut loose from their supply lines and cross enemy territory in force. Still the rumors persisted, as the mornings grew crisper and the leaves fell.

The Ocmulgee was a broad river now, making a great loop southeast and then east and then northeast, toward its meeting with the Altamaha, and the land through which it flowed was vast and lonely with loblolly pines; turpentine orchards, the Negroes called those forests. Spanish moss drooped in subtropical luxuriance from the live oaks; and sometimes for days the river was beleaguered by cypress swamps, rank with decay. Mosquitoes bred by the million, in those backwaters, and there were outlandish, slow-flapping birds with stilted legs and forlorn cries; the noon sun was like July in Wisconsin; and the nights, with the moon full again, were rippling quicksilver and India ink. And so, sleeping by day and traveling by night, living on fish and scratching mosquito bites, they floated down that Southern river, rejoicing when it joined the Altamaha and the combined waters carried them toward Darien on the Atlantic coast and a destiny sprigged with question marks.

Vast plantations appeared once more, to larboard and starboard, and when they crept along shore and summoned Negroes from cotton picking they kept hearing news of General Sherman; he was coming, he was coming; across the state word of his columns had traveled by tarheel telegraph; yes, suh, sure is coming, to set us niggers free. Presently it became necessary to take those rumors seriously. And then one afternoon on the north bank of the river they came upon three Negro men, two dozing and one fishing, while in the field beyond the cotton sunned itself unpicked. The cotton, the Negroes said, belonged to a plantation called Halifax Acres; it remained unpicked because three days ago the owners had fled in fear of General Sherman.

"Yes, suh, dey hitched up and runned. Nobody left but us niggers. Dey took de house servants and left us all. Fifty-sixty of us. We is restin' and waitin' for de general."

Rolfe stared across the cotton; a half-mile away in the shimmering afternoon he could see orchards and stately shade trees.

"Dat's it," one Negro said. "Dat's de mansion. Runned away and left it. Go see for yourselves."

Rumor insisted on being accepted as fact by then; Sherman must have done the inconceivable and marched from his supply base.

"Ain't nobody goin' to grab you," the Negro said. "White folks is all gone away. Go see."

"All right," Rolfe said. "Let's try it."

So he and Izzy and the Negro made their way through the cotton, the cotton no longer king. And after those fugitive weeks it gave him a queer feeling, walking along in broad daylight through enemy country; his reason told him it was safe but his nerves disbelieved; he kept looking over his shoulder; he felt vulnerable.

But is was no trap; in the slave quarters men lay sleeping or sitting against magnolia trees, peeling oranges and cracking pecans; in the shade of an oleander hedge a black boy and a black girl lay kissing; women sat on cabin stoops; children romped.

These here are Yanks, their guide told anybody who would listen.

" 'Scaped Yanks. 'Scaped from de Macon jailhouse and floated down de river. Dey is General Sherman's men."

A woman who must have been a hundred took a cob pipe from toothless gums and stared with rheumy eyes.

"He's a-comin'," she declared, and cackled. "Day of deliverance is at hand. Day of jubilee."

Rolfe saw some six-year-olds using a silver service for mud pies; a four-year-old boy without pants was lugging a tooled-leather volume of Byron; on a stump somebody had perched a bust of Washington.

In the orchard oranges were ripe; they ate their fill; and for supper a granny served them mustard greens with ham and cornbread. But that was after they had explored the plantation house.

Halifax Acres: it was the quintessence of the dream South, of Dixie

Land where young blades bent over the hands of beautiful ladies. It was Greek Revival, of course, with the galleries and white pillars of numberless sentimental ballads; and amid its live oaks and lemon trees and China trees and green bay it was a great white specter in the late afternoon of the Confederacy. It was tradition materialized in soft red brick and white wood; the tradition that had shaped the South: the magnificent paradoxical tradition of cavaliers from the time of Charles the Second, of pink-coated gentlemen riding to the hounds through English shires, of a new Hellenic state complete with slaves and laurel and warriors and oratory; of lawless Byronic romance and a Scottish clan culture and Sir Galahad forgetting the Grail to mate with hot-legged dark girls; of a yeomanry grown suddenly rich from the fertile soil of a subtropical land; it was ludicrous and grandiloquent and transient and pitiful; a dreamy, in-debt-to-your-London-factor, God-fearing, gassy tradition; and to uphold it the boys in butternut had flung themselves into withering gunfire at Shiloh. And now Sherman was coming.

*

That night Izzy and Rolfe slept in beds; and for breakfast, sitting outside a slave cabin, they ate side-meat and grits and molasses. Further rumors of Sherman had come during the night; his right column was a scant dozen miles away; his bummers, those boys from the practical North, whence through all history came the pillagers of soft cultures, were putting the torch to proud houses and stealing everything in sight; Negroes by the thousand danced in the wake of his army.

So Rolfe and Izzy decided to leave the river and strike out to make contact with those Union columns. They should watch sharp, a granny told them, for units of Confederate resistance were skulking here and there; but Rolfe had guessed that would be the case: he intended to watch sharp.

Mockingbirds were singing and the leaves of magnolia trees gleamed in the sunshine of a fine day when he and Izzy left Halifax Acres and followed a road which took them past idle fields and a crossroads cotton gin, also idle, and past an occasional plantation house with shades drawn. In the noon sunshine, off to the northwest, they saw a thread of smoke rising; the thread became a tall white column with gleams of flame; Georgia was burning. Old books were burning, and rosewood pianos and portraits of hawk-nosed men; it was war. Presently as they watched another column smoked upward in the northeast; wars were easier started than stopped; listen long enough to frothy-mouthed orators, send one of your sons into a sacred civic chamber to break a cane over a Bay State cranium, secede yourself right out of the U-nited States of America and fire on Sumter, and first thing you knew you might lie mangled at Shiloh and your ancestral mansion might be rising smoke.

929

"Let's eat," Rolfe said; and they lounged on the banks of a little stream and munched the cold ham and johnnycake and oranges they had brought from Halifax Acres. Mourning doves were calling; a thrush sang. The stream and the green grasses were dappled with sun and shade. Izzy asked if they would reach Sherman's army by evening.

"Patrols, maybe," Rolfe said. "The main army must be moving in a path several counties wide."

"What will you do first when they take us in?" Izzy asked.

"Find a barber. And write my wife."

"I'll write my folks," Izzy said. "They likely think I'm killed. Do you suppose Lincoln was re-elected?"

"Nobody knows what a jury will do," Rolfe said, "or a voter with a ballot. The army may have news of the election. I hope he made it. He's a better man than I thought when I voted for him. When peace comes the country will need all the brains it can muster."

"Will they hang Jeff Davis and General Lee?"

"Not if they're smart. The war was everybody's fault. We sent the wrong men to congress and so did the South. War is what happens when diplomats are stupid. And civil wars come when politicians fail. I hope the country's learned a lesson. Let's go."

The sun was hot on their shoulders and the road, thick with dust, absorbed the sound of their footsteps; everything was quiet. They passed fields of fine cotton, but no Negroes worked there; the lush pastures were untenanted by cows. Sometimes they heard a woodpecker tapping, and once a meadow lark poured out its crystal melody. And Rolfe remembered his boyhood in Elysian Springs and how people asserted the meadow lark was saying, "Laziness will hurt you." He remembered too those nights when a knock fell on the door. Who is it? A friend with friends. Then the Negroes shuffled into the kitchen. He had helped them and years later Negroes had helped him. Working for the underground railroad, he had done his mite, he supposed, to bring on war. Everybody's fault. Slavery had been the Republic's Gordian knot; war had cut it. With that question settled, perhaps the Republic could go on toward that bright misty destiny of which Judge Gentry had dreamed.

"I'm thirsty," Izzy said.

Rolfe was thirsty too. A quarter-of-a-mile away, he saw what looked like a plantation grove; they could stop and drink. His body felt sticky; a mixture of dust and sweat begrimed his face. He ran his fingers through his beard and over the hair shaggy on his neck: needing a shave and haircut always made him feel seedy.

The plantation was close now; maybe there would be a springhouse, and Negroes to feed them. Then unexpectedly, when they had nearly reached the avenue of live oaks leading toward the house, they heard a sharp exchange of shots; there were yells; and a moment later four or five mounted men came lickety-split toward the road, waving carbines. They were Rebs: at least they wore the conglomeration of rags which passed for Reb uniforms this late in the war. Rolfe and Izzy flung themselves into a ditch. But the horsemen, instead of turning into the road, went galloping across it and over a fence and on through a field. Rebs could ride.

Rolfe and Izzy jumped up in time to see a half-dozen infantrymen in Union blue legging it along the avenue, chasing the Rebs. Sherman's men. Rolfe and Izzy shouted and waved and ran toward them. Then something astonishing happened. Several Union soldiers lifted their muskets for a quick aim.

"Hey," Rolfe yelled, "don't shoot, we're—"

The rifles cracked; something hot and shattering struck Rolfe's left kneecap; he fell.

And he yelled, "You fools! You goddamned fools! We're Union!"

Izzy didn't yell; a minié ball had gone cleanly through his heart.

*

Somebody said how do we know he ain't a Reb, hell, boys, kick him in the ditch and let him rot, I'll bayonet him first, but Rolfe yelled you goddamned fools, I was Eighteenth Wisconsin, I fought at Shiloh and was captured and Izzy and I escaped, and somebody said who's Izzy, oh, you mean the dead kike, and Rolfe yelled oh, goddamn you, you fools, you bastards, you thick-headed bumbling bastards, and somebody said Wisconsin, you say, what part, I'm from Milwaukee myself, and Rolfe said New Empire I was sworn in in Milwaukee, Eighteenth Wisconsin, and you've shot Izzy and—

A debate ensued, while Rolfe lay with the strength bleeding out of him and the sky swung back and forth. One voice said we can't take him with us, hell, we ain't got no way to take him, but another voice belonging to the Milwaukee soldier said by God, we'll find a way, get a cart or something, he's from Wisconsin and we'll find a way to get him where there's an ambulance.

About then the debate was interrupted by a ten-year-old girl calling them damned Yanks and scalding them with her tongue, they just laughed, but then a sad-eyed, long-eared hound came snuffing toward Rolfe and licked his face, Rolfe whispered hello, boy, hello, but then the hound yipped as if kicked and the little girl was screeching oh, don't, please, please, please don't, but a musket barked and the girl broke into hysterics, and the voice from Milwaukee said hell, Hank, why did you have to shoot the kid's hound, and the voice of the man who wanted to leave Rolfe rotting said I don't like their goddamned hounds, they track our boys when they escape.

Somebody was doing something to Rolfe's leg, to stop the bleeding, and a voice from darkness said well, I'm staying with him, you'll stay too, won't you, Dave, and Dave said, yup, reckon so; and the Milwaukee voice said hell, there must be a cart or a wagon, we can pull it ourselves if we can't steal a mule; and the voice of the soldier who disliked hounds said oh, well, have it your own way, you pissants, but first we'll burn the house.

Then everything went away, beyond the darkness, and presently even the darkness went away, only to return when the world became a heaving, bone-jolting place as if assailed with perpetual earthquakes; and after that there was quiet and then dim voices talking about a leg that had mortified, and suddenly hot pain streaked from Rolfe's knee and he yelled and men held him down on something hard till everything went away again.

He must have dreamed, although he never could remember what; next thing he knew he was lying weak as a piece of string on a cot staring up at canvas; the place had a vile medicinal smell; must be a field hospital; and for a time Rolfe thought he had been wounded at Shiloh and had dreamed all the rest. Then gradually he remembered and it occurred to him that it was very queer that while he could wiggle his right foot he couldn't wiggle his left; the truth came to him then; and he asked a bare-armed young man did they amputate my leg, and the young man said sure did, had to, it had mortified.

For a while Rolfe envied Izzy.

Later still, after he was eating a little, he heard a brisk voice saying hello, son, and he opened his eyes to see a man with sharp eyes and a lean face with grizzly stubble and a dusty uniform; Rolfe had seen him before, aeons before, sitting a horse beside a road at Pittsburg Landing on a Saturday afternoon.

I heard what happened to you, the man said. Sorry, son.

And Rolfe said, I saw you, I saw you at Pittsburg Landing. I was the Eighteenth Wisconsin and we were green. You said we looked like scrappers.

Did I, son? And were you scrappers?

I got detached, Rolfe said, but I fought. With the Eighth Iowa. They captured us.

Yes, the man said, I know.

That was 1862, Rolfe said. I've got a wife. If she's alive. I've never heard. Mrs. Rolfe Torkelsen of New Empire, Wisconsin ... Was Lincoln re-elected?

But the man had gone away; Rolfe could hear him saying Mrs. Rolfe Torkelsen to somebody; and then Rolfe went away.

He was always going away; coming back and going away; and sometimes he was lying naked in snowdrifts, shivering, and sometimes lying spread-eagled under a blazing Southern sun; once a bare-armed man

932

told him he had the ague. That was when the world jolted and heaved again; then it just heaved, up and down, and there was a smell of salt water; and a long time later in a barnlike place with rows of cots where he was always shivering and sweating he heard a voice say here's somebody to see you, and he opened his eyes and it was Sue.

Hello, he said. Was Lincoln re-elected?

Evidently not, for Sue began to cry.

XVI

In June they dismissed him from that York State hospital, complete with an army discharge, a wooden leg and the doctors' assurances that he was as good as new, nearly. But that wasn't quite true. The wooden leg was the least of his troubles, for a lawyer's job is a sitting-down job mainly, and he had plenty of company in misery: in those postwar years America was populous with wooden legs and empty sleeves and worse; nor did he fret too much about the malaria which would come upon him every autumn; it was another kind of sickness that bothered him. In those days there was such a word as shell, and such a word as shock, and there was a well-known word, combat, and a common word, fatigue; but no doctor had yet conceived of putting the words together and getting shell shock and combat fatigue: Sigmund Freud was still a boy playing with toys, and Carl Jung was unborn. So no doctors would have understood his symptoms: it's all in your head, they would have said. Well, it was.

But Sue understood, as well as anybody could who had not gone through Shiloh and thirty months in Southern prisons; he guessed the best thing he ever did was buying a license to marry Sue. Through dreary midnights he unburdened himself to her, telling how when you were a young man who had never stood in battle or lain it out in prison you thought the world was a pretty fine place in which you would carve out a brilliant career and end up rich and esteemed; you accepted people at face value, on the whole, except when trying to dispel the fog of lies from a witness; you rejoiced in being alive. Then you went to war. And war stripped the surfaces from life; you witnessed cruelty in ten thousand forms. And if you were a young man of average sensitivity, you couldn't forget; shadows lay on your brain. Seeing people on the street—pleasant-looking men and women—you wondered whether in the right circumstances they would slap a Negro girl or stake prisoners out in the sun or shoot a friendly hound-dog. And presently you found yourself thinking that civilization was nothing but a conspiracy on everybody's part, to cover up the wolf in man's nature, the tiger, the jackal, the serpent.

And if you decided to pick up your normal life where you had dropped it, back in 1862, your nerves took their revenge. They wouldn't let you.

934

They were still too raw. They kept you awake all night while the memories came back; they whispered doubts into your ears, such as if you start practicing law again maybe you'll go all to pieces when you're charging the jury, and you'll lose the case and some poor devil who didn't after all murder his neighbor will hang. Or worse, lay it out in prison.

Those were bad years, after the war.

*

Discharged from the hospital, he dreaded returning to New Empire. In prison he had dreamed of going back, but now he thought he never could. Well, he didn't have to, right away. He had funds; in that he was luckier than the average returning soldier. Sue had managed his investments well, while he was gone; and in 1863, knowing he was going to die, her father had sold the Hatfield Ink & Supply Company at a war-inflated price; half his money had been willed to his only living daughter and half to his wife; when she died Sue would receive the rest. They were well-to-do people, Mr. and Mrs. Rolfe Torkelsen; he didn't have to return to a law office.

So they went to New York, living at the Fifth Avenue Hotel, but the memories came sneaking along the corridors of even that fashionable place. Whiskey and tobacco were a help; they got him through many a stark midnight; but Sue was better even than whiskey. She listened and asked questions and drew him out, as if knowing intuitively how memories of that sort fester. He told her how he would be lying in bed almost asleep, and then without warning his nervous system would jerk and he would sit bolt upright, wide awake and trembling. He felt, he said, as if the cells of his body might suddenly go berserk and fly off in all directions; he felt like a shell just before it explodes. On especially bad nights they used to dress and take to the streets, tramping to the wharves or to Central Park; occasionally policemen questioned them. And when Rolfe explained that he had been off to war and couldn't sleep, the policeman would sometimes say, I know what you mean, sir, I fought at So-and-So, but this is a bad part of town.

A bad part of town? Rolfe smiled. He had seen worse. That was one thing, the war had left him without physical fear. He would as soon have tramped the Five Points and Carey's Alley, except for Sue. It was as if his body had encountered so many physical dangers it had grown calloused. His troubles were all inside his head. There were times during those New York months when he thought he might be going insane.

Another dreary thing: the war had left him incapable of performing man's most important work. Maybe that was partly physical, starved as he had been; maybe his body knew it wasn't yet in shape to reproduce its kind. But the trouble was chiefly nerves. Sue had a desirable body—

935

girls with plain faces often had—but when he took her into his arms he would start thinking the death thoughts. She is only mud, he would think; put a bullet through her heart and in three days she would be swollen with corruption and the blowflies would be swarming. Thoughts like that unmanned him. At the nadir of those postwar years he used to tell her she had better leave him and find a real husband; but Sue was a remarkable woman; Sue always understood. She didn't, she said, want another man; she wanted Rolfe Torkelsen who was going to become his old self again, some day.

They went to Massachusetts and visited Sue's home town for a long while; now and then on a street corner Rolfe would fall to talking with some veteran; and thus he learned he was not the only ex-soldier with problems. That helped. And when he attended meetings of the Grand Army of the Republic, there in Kingston, Massachusetts, he had a feeling of homecoming and odd peace; they had all been through it together; many lacked legs or arms or hands or eyes; they understood one another. They told how it had been at the Bloody Angle or at Cold Harbor; he told them about Shiloh; everybody understood. In public memory the war was beginning to recede; boys and girls were growing up who had been babies when John Brown raided Harpers Ferry; sure, the war had been bad, but let's talk about something else for a change; but the veterans talked of little else. Maybe that was why the Grand Army of the Republic flourished; maybe its real purpose was not to agitate for pensions but to give persons like Rolfe Torkelsen a chance to spend an evening with those who had been there.

*

Boss Tweed ruled New York and Thad Stevens ruled Washington and acidulous cartoons by Thomas Nast appeared in *Harper's Weekly* and a good president was bespattered with rotten ink and nearly impeached because he attempted to carry out what would have been A. Lincoln's program of generosity to a fallen foe. Frothy hate like hydrophobia raged among the sons of bitches in congress; the South, they snarled, must be punished; and punished the South was. They called it Reconstruction. Under the protection of Federal bayonets shifty men carried carpetbags into Dixie and rigged elections, filling the legislatures with morons and scoundrels; and enormous bond issues were passed for needless public works, and the carpetbaggers swindled and stole. Meanwhile, at the North, men like Jay Gould and Jim Fisk and Jay Cooke plundered and stole everything that was not nailed down, and some things that were, such as railroads, while the cyclonic postwar inflation roared on and the country thought itself prosperous. In the carcass of war millionaires had hatched out like maggots, and now they erected preposterous wooden castles which they filled with bad paintings and grotesque furniture and statuary, while tutors labored to teach their daughters to avoid saying ain't.

Prosperity, Rolfe used to think, was something America could never endure with equanimity; it swilled it down till its head swam; it scattered greenbacks like an Irishman on Saturday night; and it dozed off while vile men picked its pockets. In times of danger and crisis America was a cool-headed frontiersman; adversity brought out all that was gallant and sagacious in the American temper; but when prosperity came America lost its wits and did ridiculous things like taking to itself a general for president. That happened in 1868; Ulysses S. Grant was elected. And the thieves rejoiced.

By the time Grant was inaugurated Mr. and Mrs. Rolfe Torkelsen had returned to New Empire, after a few days in Cincinnati, Ohio, where in living quarters above a pawnshop Mr. and Mrs. Isadore Weinberg asked sad quiet questions about the last days of Private Izzy Weinberg, warrior of the Republic.

"He was so young," Mrs. Weinberg said.

It helped Rolfe extirpate those ghosts of war, telling that tale of escape and suffering; and on the cars to New Empire he thought he was well again, that he would be practicing the law. Certainly he was much better physically; he had learned to walk with a wooden leg almost as efficiently as with one of flesh and bone; and gradually, owing to Sue's patience and understanding, and to his own sincere ambition, he had once more become a bedfellow any wife would have been pleased to have. But he was not yet ready for the law.

Their house had been rented but now it was home again, and he remembered that March morning when he walked toward his office, carrying the hickory cane which had been Judge Gentry's and which Mrs. Gentry, before her death, had told Sue she wanted Rolfe to have. He dreaded that walk; since returning to town two evenings before he had remained at home; but as a student of R. W. Emerson he knew man must do what he fears.

And what did he dread? Was it the wraith of that younger Rolfe Torkelsen lingering in his office? Was it man's common dread of opening graves better left undisturbed with the sweet grass growing? Was it stopping to shake hands with townspeople and being asked where on earth have you been, why didn't you come home, aren't we good enough for you any more? He didn't know. Or was it because he had been wounded not in a great battle but in what people might think a serio-comic engagement with Sherman's bummers? Was it because he remembered the thing he had been in prison, a bundle of rags and lice and gaunt ribs, man at his lowest common denominator, scarcely a man at all, except for man's quenchless spirit?

Anyway, he walked to his office. And people he had forgotten, men who looked older, men who looked different with fashionable beards, women who had been pig-tailed girls and who now were shepherding children of their own, stopped him and said why, it must be Rolfe Torkelsen. We expected you home sooner, they said. What happened? Where have you been?

"I've been sick," he said. "I've been in hospitals."

"Bet it seems good to be back."

It didn't, but in America it was part of the social ritual to say travel was all very well but after all there was no place like home. Rolfe equivocated.

"Can't you imagine?" he said.

"Yes, sir, I sure can. Best town in the country, New Empire. Seen the new bridge?"

Rolfe hadn't.

"You ain't seen the bridge? Buckmaster built it, clear across to Ioway. Guess his railroad's pretty near reached the Missouri by now. He's a big man, that Buckmaster is. Biggest man on the river. He's sure put this town on the map."

"Yes," Rolfe said, "a big man."

He hadn't yet looked up Jim Buckmaster, and he dreaded that too. He didn't know why.

At last he reached the building still called the Gentry Block and pulled himself upstairs to his office; up those stairs where one evening years ago he had caught sight of Nixie Auerbach's legs. He wondered if she were still in town. If so, would he meet her some day on the street, and would she be leading a child who looked like Rolfe Torkelsen? No, of course not: she had told Jim Buckmaster that Froggy Maizeroy was the father. But suppose she had been mistaken.

He unlocked the outer office door and ventured in, for some reason locking the door behind him. The place was cold; it had a shut-up smell of dust and calf-bound books. With the shades drawn the light was dim. He kindled a fire and stood looking at the room where as a stripling he had first opened the law books. At that long mahogany table he had briefed cases. Nearly twenty years ago.

He went into what had been Judge Gentry's office; it was just a room now, stripped of its books and pictures and coins from the ancient world; the stuffed owl had vanished. And he thought if the dead ever rose from their graves, this of all rooms would be the one Judge Gentry's ghost would seek. It wasn't there.

Finally he forced himself to cross the reception room to his own office; he hated to open the door. But he made himself go in. It looked smaller than he had remembered; the couch where he had made love to Nixie Auerbach was shabby. Dust lay on the desk; the clock had stopped; there were cobwebs; the calendar was turned to March, 1862. That gave him an odd feeling.

*

Next morning and the next he returned to his office, dreading every step, and he always locked the door and left the shades pulled. And for hours at a stretch he would sit at his desk thinking I ought to make a start, I ought to read some law just to get my hand in; but he did nothing. He was tired; he felt like the shell of a burnt-out building; he had been off to war and had left a leg and his youth in Dixie. I'm through, he thought; I'll never try another case; I'm through at the great age of thirty-three.

He avoided reading the papers because what was happening to America should never have happened to any country, least of all to the Republic of Jefferson and Jackson and Judge Gentry. In the White House sat a man who as a boy had decided to take up killing as a profession—a general could be other things, but first he was a killer—and when peacetime army life had driven that man to whiskey he had been kicked out, a failure. He had failed as a farmer and as a wood chopper and as a tanner; he was a killer by trade. Then came the Civil War and of course he succeeded. And because he was such a fine killer America had elected him president, after the war. But the war was not over for the South, for the proud foolish South which had paid the price of its folly on a hundred battlefields and now was being made to pay twice and thrice. They would come back into the Union, some day, those tobacco states and cotton states, those states of the mockingbird and the hot pride and the magnificent folly; and they would not forget. Knock a man down in a fair fight and he might be willing to shake hands; kick him when he was down, spit on him, and he would remember.

Rolfe didn't much like his own country any more, that country for which he had been willing to die.

Sometimes with the shades pulled he lighted the gas and read Shakespeare, everything from the hot young works like *Venus and Adonis* through the turbulent despairing plays of the middle period to the serenity of *The Tempest;* and he read Defoe and Fielding and Thackeray and Thomas Jefferson; but he didn't read the law. He didn't read the *New Empire Chronicle* or Horace Greeley's *Tribune.* He wanted to forget the Nineteenth Century.

Then one morning a tremendous knocking sounded on the door of the outer office; some client maybe; but he wanted no clients. The knocking persisted till at last, grudgingly, he dragged his wooden leg through the reception room and unlocked the door.

"Swede!" the man said. "Well, my God! Why haven't you been to see me?"

"Come in," Rolfe said.

Jim Buckmaster grabbed his hand and shook it.

"Swede. What's the matter? Are you mad at me?"

"No, of course not."

"Then why didn't you come to my office? I didn't know you were back. I've been up in the woods. But my clerks told me you haven't been near."

"Come in," Rolfe said. "Come in and sit down."

He felt oddly ashamed walking with a wooden leg as he led the way into his private office.

"What the hell's going on?" Jim asked. "Sitting here with the shades pulled and the gas burning. My God! Let's let in some sun."

He went to the windows and put up the shades, and in the daylight Rolfe could see he looked older. He had grayed prematurely, or was it prematurely? He must be in his forties. But his eyebrows were still black, and with his weather-burned skin that gray hair flattered him; he looked like a handsome executive with tons of power at his command. His suit was gray too and beautifully-tailored, and his manner was smoother than it used to be; the calluses had long since vanished from his hands; you might never have guessed he had been a rough-tough raftsman.

"My God, Swede," he said, "you look awful. You look haggard."

"I feel haggard."

"Tell me about it, boy."

"You wouldn't understand."

"Hell I wouldn't."

"It's hard to talk about," Rolfe said.

"I don't doubt it, but I want to hear. You'd best get started. I'll stick with you till you tell me."

"I can't tell you," Rolfe said. "You weren't there and you wouldn't understand."

"Well, by God!" Jim said, and then he appeared to get angry, but Rolfe knew it was play-acting. "We're friends and you won't even tell me how you lost your leg."

"I said I didn't want to talk about it."

Jim stood up and paced the office, moving easily, as always, like a woods cat. His shoulders were still broad, his belly flat; he looked trained down to bone and sinew, like a fighter.

"Old Peg-leg Torkelsen," he said. "The damn fool enlisted. I told him not to, I told him even if they'd put through the draft I could fix him up, but oh, no, the goddamned silly fool enlisted."

Rolfe felt the blood in his ears. He knew Jim was play-acting, but it made him mad.

"Will you leave off that?" he said.

Jim stood with legs apart, big and well poised, and now he was smiling; the laughter-wrinkles around his eyes gave him that look of a genial rogue.

"No, Swede," he said softly, "I won't leave off. If you won't tell me I'll tell you. You goddamned opinionated Swede."

"I'm not a Swede. I'm a Dane."

940

"What's the difference? You all chew the same snuff. You're all useless. And you were so dumb you went to war. A private, for Christ's sake! I could have pulled wires and started you out as a colonel, but oh, no, you had to do it in your own goddamned blockheaded way. You wanted to be a little soldier boy. Strut around in a blue uniform and show off. You worthless son of a bitch."

Play-acting, all play-acting, but Rolfe's fists clenched.

"Stop it! Get the hell out and leave me alone!"

But Jim stood smiling.

"Well, you found out, Swede. You went to the army and it wrecked you. Old Peg-leg Torkelsen, no good for anything. Sits on his cry-baby ass in a dark office and moons. You'll never amount to a damn, you dunderhead. You're through. Lost your leg and lost your gumption. A peg-legged Swede. Don't even dare to hit me. Man talk to me like I'm talking to you and I'd pop him. But not you. No brains and no guts."

"I told you to shut up," Rolfe said, rising.

"Peg-leg Torkelsen. He had a future once. Now it's all shot to hell. A deadheaded little weasel that not even a whore would have for a pimp."

"God damn you, Jim Buckmaster, I told you—"

And Rolfe limped around the desk and drove a fist into Jim's jaw. Jim laughed.

"You little baby, Swede. Think I felt that? Hell, I've been hit by men, Swede. You've got a fist like a feather."

Rolfe lost all control and struck out again and again, but Jim dodged and laughed; the blows went wild. Then Rolfe's wooden leg betrayed him and he fell; and for an instant, tumbled in a heap there on the carpet, he hated Jim Buckmaster and all men who had come through the war sound in wind and limb; something gave way and he was crying. Slowly, he dragged himself up and limped back to his chair where he sat with his face buried in his arms. After a long while he looked up. Jim was smiling.

"You'll feel better now, Swede. I went to your house and Sue told me you were here. She told me how you've been. I wanted to make you mad. Sometimes it helps a man to hit somebody."

"I'm sorry," Rolfe said.

"It's what I wanted, Swede. I wanted to bring you out of it. Now tell me about it."

So Rolfe told the story of Private Torkelsen, defender of the flag and prisoner of war. He told how when a man had been in prison, even in the cause of patriotism, he felt tainted and unclean. Jim sat tipped back in his chair, blowing cigar smoke at the ceiling; now and then he asked a question. Rolfe's mind had been a blood-soaked sponge but Jim Buckmaster squeezed it dry.

"Swede," he said finally, "I've always liked you. A man don't make many friends, not after he gets rich. Plenty of bastards come kissing his ass, but you can't trust them. I can trust you. You're right out what you are. You always were, even when you were a kid on my raft and wanted to fight me. I know just where I stand with you. Some day I'm going to make you president."

"You can't. I was born in Denmark."

"Just leave it to me, Swede, let me worry about that. I'll send you to the legislature and to congress and to the White House, if that's what you want. But not yet. You're tired. You're tireder than you know. And you're a damn fool to come back and try to practice law. You've got to get away, you and Sue. You've got to get your health back. You've got to stay away till you want to start trying cases."

"I'll never try another case."

"A sick man's words, Swede. Tell you what I'll do. I'll put you on a retainer basis and send you to New Orleans. A rooster there owns half the timber lands in the South, and I want to buy. People up here think the pine will last forever. Well, it won't. Not the way we're cutting. I'm picking up stumpage out in Washington and Oregon, and I want those Southern forests. So you go to New Orleans and see this rooster, you and Sue, and then you take a ship. Go somewhere. Somewhere like the West Indies. Look those islands over for me. There must be investment opportunities, and I want a report. I don't mean timber. I mean banana plantations and sugar plantations; I've got some loose cash that wants to go to work. If you find something that looks good, write me about it. If not—well, I'll know there's nothing worth fooling with."

The West Indies. Robinson Crusoe and pearl-like islands such as Shakespeare wrote about in *The Tempest*.

"I'll do it free," Rolfe said. "You needn't put me on a retainer."

"God damn it, Swede," Jim said, "when will you let me run my own business? I know what I'm doing. Hell, boy, I'm rich, I cleaned up during the war. The money's pouring in so fast I can't find bins to keep it in. And when a man's my pal I stand by him. I don't ask him to do me a favor. I pay him for his work. Now let's you and me go down to Rafferty's and swallow a few."

*

So once again Rolfe journeyed south, this time with Sue. In New Orleans the business of those timber lands took only a couple of mornings; Jim had exaggerated the extent of the seller's holdings; there were no legal complications; the whole affair could have been settled by mail; and Rolfe knew then what he had suspected before: that out of friendship Jim had dispatched him on a needless errand in the hope that a change would restore his health.

Perhaps he should have revolted against such coddling, even though it was well-intentioned, for if you had an independent nature it was never wise to run into debt to a friend; a man had to stand on his own two feet. But Rolfe had only one foot now, and he was tired. Besides, Jim Buckmaster was hard to resist, in generosity or anything else. Actually Rolfe did write a protesting letter; he would, he said, sail to the West Indies, but he refused to do so on a retainer basis; yet when he received his bank statement he discovered that Jim had deposited the retainer fee to his credit. But that was many weeks later; mail ships to the West Indies were slow and infrequent.

They stayed at the St. Charles in New Orleans, and on fine hot mornings they tramped across Canal Street to the Quarter where in Jackson Square the Union flag reigned once more. They sat in the sun; pigeons came waddling for crumbs; the air had that unique New Orleans scent of oleanders and river water and magnolias and sewerage; brown women shuffled past; and in the fine restaurants there were wine and watercress and the witchery of Gallic cooking; but the city was impoverished and melancholy; Reconstruction hung over it like a pall. A nasty, spiteful man named Major General Phil Sheridan had been appointed commander of the Department of the Gulf, and a former Union soldier was governor, a financial genius named Warmoth who in four years saved a million dollars from a salary of eight thousand. Everywhere it was the same in those years, North and South: a thieves' festival. Lincoln was dead, Jackson was dead, John Quincy Adams was dead, honor was dead; men like Park Irwin were running the country. Rolfe was glad to board a ship with Sue and go drifting down the big river, past Chalmette where General Andrew Jackson and Private Caleb McSwasey had fought, down through the flat delta lands, Acadian but not Arcadian now, and out into the wide blue Gulf where porpoises greeted them with humor and exhibitionism.

Elbows on the rail, watching those porpoises, he found himself smiling; he slept better; his appetite returned. The seas of the world were vast; in the sea you could have drowned all the battlefields and all the politicians waving the bloody shirt; he liked the swish of foam at the bow, the broad wake; he came of a seafaring race. They put in at Havana where Spanish dandies with cruel nostrils swaggered in uniform; they sailed into the harbor of the white tropic city of San Juan, with its memories of Sir Francis Drake and its teeming poverty; they disembarked at the Danish island of St. Thomas. And to the throngs on the Dronningensgade in Charlotte Amalie—throngs black and blond and golden mulatto—the American Civil War was something long ago in the newspapers, but that was in another country and besides the wench was dead. In St. Thomas there were no opportunities worth the attention of an empire builder like Jim Buckmaster; Rolfe hadn't expected any, nor had Jim, probably. They ate of the mango and the papaya; they drank rum punches and the milk of green coconuts; they heard the trade winds in the mahogany trees; and one blue tropic evening Sue wore a hibiscus in her hair.

"You look beautiful," Rolfe said.

"Pooh, pooh. You know I'm homely as a mud fence."

But he meant it; Sue looked beautiful to him.

Danish was spoken in the island, and before long word reached the old families of an American traveler who knew the language like a native, so they were invited to dinners and teas in official circles, meeting persons who had known Rolfe's Grandfather Torkelsen at the National Museum in Copenhagen, and others who had bought books from Grandfather Willemssen. It was a sparkling little society there in the colony, with golden-haired women and vivacious conversation; they stayed a long while in St. Thomas, letting the raw old memories heal.

At last, by schooner, they went on to St. Croix, whose only claim to infamy was that it had sent Alexander Hamilton to America: the handsome, brilliant Hamilton with the secret shame of being a love child; he had dreamed passionately of a Federal government by great wealth, of great wealth, for great wealth; and he had nearly brought it off too, for President Washington was easily hoodwinked; but a redheaded Virginian named Thomas Jefferson outmaneuvered him. In Christiansted, visiting the store where Hamilton had worked, Rolfe and Sue talked of the early Republic; otherwise, America seemed nonexistent. He remembered the hot tropic light at noontime and cool rum on a gallery; he remembered the pretty Negro girls and Negro men like black Apollos; Denmark had not needed to go to war with itself to abolish slavery. Those Caribbean islands were the best of the tropics; they seemed outside time; the weeks dreamed by.

Antigua, Nevis, Martinique, Guadeloupe, Grenada: each was different and each was lovely; they saw cocoa growing and bananas and tall rank cane; they saw the Union Jack against halcyon sky; and in Port-of-Spain they ate the tasty little oysters that grew on the roots of mangrove trees.

In Barbados, on that stretch of matchless beach north of Bridgetown, they took a house, complete with five servants, all at a ridiculous tariff; and in Barbados, little by little, the wounds on Rolfe's spirit healed. Winter was warm as summer, within a few degrees; month after month Rolfe lay in the sand and became brown and almost mahogany; on Saturday mornings, when the whole island flocked to Bridgetown for shopping, they rode there in a victoria with a Negro coachman whose vowels were broad as a lord's. The Civil War in America? What was that, sir? Shiloh? Never heard of it, sir. In Bridgetown they spent hours along the careenage, where schooners loaded and unloaded, and Negro women walked with baskets on their heads; or they went to the esplanade for band concerts, or to colonial hotels for lunch in dining rooms open to the trades; sparrows fluttered in and stole sugar.

Now and then a ship brought mail: letters from Jim Buckmaster in New Empire, who was growing richer and richer; or from Rolfe's mother in Elysian Springs, Indiana, with the news that Thorwald Torkelsen had died. Rolfe sent her a check—he had been sending money to his parents for years—and one melancholy morning while the trade winds whispered in the palms he told Sue about Pastor Torkelsen's work on the underground. He had, of course, told her all that before, many times; but that was a wonderful thing about a good marriage: you could tell the same stories again and again, reliving your childhood, and your wife never stopped you.

They might have stayed in Barbados forever, and sometimes they wished they had. But at last there came a time when ambition, that glamourous bitch, whispered tales in Rolfe's ears. He had been trained for the law: was he going to fritter away his best years? He began remembering how it was when you tried an important case; how you got up early and paced your office rehearsing what you would say in court; the law could be exciting; and he remembered the intoxication of American politics, the torches in the night. America was his country; she had taken to streetwalking, as so many women did in war; but perhaps he should return and tell her of her great past and of the great future that could be hers.

So he and Sue began talking of leaving the tropics; they remembered gentle spring mornings in Wisconsin, and October with its hazes and shocked corn and pumpkins orange in the blue swirl of dusk. Then Sue became pregnant; they wanted the child born on American soil; so they left those dream islands and sailed through pirate seas back to New Orleans and traveled by steamboat up the big river to New Empire, Wisconsin.

"Does it seem good to get back?" somebody asked.

"You bet it does," Rolfe said.

*

It was like beginning his career all over again, except with his investments and Sue's money he was no starving young lawyer. So far as that went he was no longer very young; he had turned thirty-seven his last birthday. He looked all of thirty-seven too, with crow's-feet around his eyes and a face that had known hard usage. His hands were heavy, his jaw squarish; in rough clothes he could have passed for a Danish seafaring man, one of those intelligent common sailors who had made the best of his hours off watch and had puzzled out the mathematics of navigation and had passed his examinations and now had his master's papers; you would have trusted yourself to any vessel under his command; he looked dependable. He had gone into his own valley of shadows and had wrestled with his own peculiar dragons and had come forth triumphant and tough and resourceful; clients wanted a lawyer like that.

But he made no effort to get clients for a time, not while he was so rusty. He read Blackstone and Chitty; he whetted his mind on the cases in the law reviews that had piled up during his absence. And now that he was working again he went to his office early and stayed late and sometimes returned to burn the gas till midnight, for after those years of idleness he was making up for lost time.

"Swede," Jim Buckmaster said, "you're a work horse. You could work any three men under the table, except me. Have a cigar."

Rolfe took two.

"I'll make you president yet," Jim said. "When do we start? Would you like to go to congress?"

"How about Park Irwin?"

"Well, what about him? If he hasn't filled his pockets by now he never will. Besides, a work horse is better than a horse's ass any day."

But Rolfe shook his head. First things first, he said. He might go into politics eventually—in another five or ten years, say—but before that he wanted to build a solid practice. Maybe he would never enter politics; the smartest lawyers didn't; a client disliked coming to your office and learning you were off campaigning or spouting in the legislature; a neglected law business went to seed fast.

"Where would the country be," Jim asked, "if all the best lawyers thought like that?"

"Just where it is today," Rolfe said.

And that was nowhere good: panic had come again. Poor old American capitalism, it seemed, would never get the facts of economic life through its fat head; during a boom it always supposed that all which went up stayed up. Now the wonderful postwar prosperity had collapsed; Fisk & Hatch had failed; Jay Cooke & Co. had failed; most of the busy little war millionaires had discovered they had been only paper Midases, and their daughters could go back to saying ain't because they were not going to marry Italian counts after all. As usual in such doleful times, the stock market had become an *enfant terrible*, thumbing its nose at horrified bankers; soup lines were forming again, and employment offices dusted off their No Men Wanted signs; and the people who had thought U. S. Grant a great little president and had re-elected him now went to the polls in the off-year elections and turned out the ins, most of them Republicans.

But Jim Buckmaster laughed at that panic of 1873.

"I learned my lesson, Swede, in '57. I've got reserves. This had to come. People had to get back to earth. When the Atlantic Bank failed last April I figured what was going to happen. And do you know what I did?"

"Switched to cheap cigars," Rolfe said, "judging by this one."

"No, Swede, I sold my own stock short. Yes, sir, I went short of the old Madison, New Empire & Western. And it's dragging its tail in the cellar today, along with all the others, and I'm covering. It's sound— I've seen to that—and it's bound to climb again. And I'll have a profit both ways. Hell, I'll make a fortune out of the panic."

946

Scandals kept breaking that autumn and winter and during the remainder of President Grant's dismaying administration; those were the days of the Whiskey Ring and the Sanborn contracts and the Freedmen's Bureau and Honest John Patterson; Boss Tweed was jailed in New York; the Emma Mine scandal exploded in the hands of Secretary of War Belknap; Senator James G. Blaine swam in the corruption of bonds for the Fort Smith & Little Rock Railroad. "Let no guilty man escape," said President Grant, but most of them did. Reconstruction buzzards flapped home to roost under the White House eaves; Federal soldiers invaded the Louisiana legislature and removed the duly-elected speaker of the house; exposé followed exposé; it was too much; the North gagged. And so at last a great exodus took place from Dixie, the men with carpetbags returning North: the buttock-faced men, the men with the wolf eyes and the jackal teeth, the fat-pratted men, the loose-lipped, thick-pawed men.

But those were events you read about in the newspapers; in New Empire life went on and people died and babies were born, among them, on a March midnight, a daughter to Mr. and Mrs. Rolfe Torkelsen. They named her Margaret Fuller Torkelsen and like all new parents hoped that her world would be clean and noble, that the Republic would become shining again.

*

By then Rolfe was back in his legal stride, working too hard but thriving on it, always going somewhere to take care of the Buckmaster interests. The Madison, New Empire & Western Railroad—known as the New Empire Line—was no longer merely a Wisconsin carrier; its eastern terminus was Chicago where its head offices were located; its western terminus was a town on the Missouri River; and between those points it was a parabola with feeder lines from the tall corn and the tall timber: on a map it looked like a many-branched tree limb. Its president was a man who had come up the hard way, from a locomotive cab, and who understood railroad operations; but as chairman of the board Jim controlled everything; the place to make big money in the railroad business, he always said, was the New York stock market; you used your road as a club or a snare. His horizons had expanded; in awed voices people said he knew such giants as Jim Hill and E. E. Harriman and J. P. Morgan and a praying Baptist in Cleveland named Rockefeller; but Jim laughed and said it was nothing to boast about. He traveled a great deal, on one of his steamboats or in his private car, and gossip had it that he had been seen in city lobster palaces with vivid ladies wearing hats with ostrich feathers. Well, people said, perhaps you couldn't blame him, with his wife the way she was.

The main office of the Buckmaster Lumber Company remained in New Empire, and presently Rolfe Torkelsen was head of its legal staff and Mr. Buckmaster's personal counsel. If he had wished, he might have stepped into his old position as top attorney for the New Empire Line, but that would have meant moving to Chicago; he preferred Wisconsin. But he worked closely with the legal brains of the railroad, and when a case came along involving the New Empire division he usually handled it.

Rolfe must have been making up for lost time in ways other than jurisprudential, for a second daughter was born a year-and-a-half after the first; they called her Susan and nicknamed her Kitten; a dear child, Rolfe said, quoting the Danish proverb, has many names. They were, of course, the most beautiful daughters in all the world, with their flaxen hair, and mightily in danger of being spoiled by James L. Buckmaster who brought them presents from New York; they called him Uncle Jim. "Swede," he used to say, "you're the ckiest man alive, with a wife like Sue and two such daughters."

The words of a lonely man, Rolfe thought; when Jim said that his eyes had the bleak look Rolfe had noticed years ago in a suite at the St. Nicholas Hotel.

Hard times persisted, in the wake of the panic, but not for James L. Buckmaster or his legal lieutenant, Rolfe Torkelsen. It looked, however, as if the Republican Party, with Grant's record to defend, must lose in 1876. And it did lose, despite an ex-general for candidate and a bloody-shirt campaign; Samuel J. Tilden of New York was elected, although he never took office, for the politicians had grown so brazen and skillful that they managed to steal even the presidency: Rutherford B. Hayes was sworn in. And although Rolfe was a Republican—you could scarcely be anything else in Fox County, Wisconsin, so soon after the Civil War—he objected to that barefaced theft. But Jim Buckmaster did not object. "Hell, Swede," he said, "politics is war. Anything goes."

But politics wasn't war, Rolfe said; the analogy was false. In a free Republic politics was supposed to be, in addition to the art of governing, the art of presenting issues to the electorate so that the best men with the soundest ideas could be chosen. Sometimes your party deserved to lose; sometimes it ought to lose, for the good of the country.

Jim laughed.

"Still the same old Swede. You're an idealist, boy, that's your trouble. Don't know where you ever would have got, if I hadn't taken you in tow."

That rankled, just a bit.

It must have been about then, as Rolfe remembered it, that he began to question the rough-and-ready business methods of James L. Buckmaster. There was the matter of his railroad giving secret rebates to certain shippers, thus bringing bankruptcy to rival shippers he might wish to ruin and gobble. There was the matter of his building branch lines into unpopulated areas only in order to receive the governmental largesse of rich public lands. There was the way he handled the strike of 1877, when thugs from city slums were hired to shoot down his own workers and the governors of three states called out the National Guard, tax supported, to starve brakemen and section hands back to their underpaid jobs. There was the way when he wanted something from the legislature—something like a charter to throw a logging dam across a navigable river—he always got it. Always. And one day in the office of the Buckmaster Lumber Company, going over some old figures about steamboat operations to gain general background on a damage suit, Rolfe was troubled to learn the prices Jim had received from the Federal government during the war when he leased his boats as troop and supply transports. They were outrageously high. Business was business, of course; business was not patriotism; and yet—well—

So far as he could learn, from any record, Jim Buckmaster had never operated outside the law. The man-made law. Ethics was something else again. He had never heard of ethics, apparently. Fist fights in saloons had taught him to be ruthless, and he believed the end justified the means. When he wanted something he grabbed it. When a man got in his way he knocked him down and stomped him. He was an individualist. He was, even, an anarchist.

For a long time Rolfe hesitated to face it: that he and Jim Buckmaster had completely irreconcilable ethical standards. And when he faced it at last, he found himself extenuating the man who had been his good friend. After all, Jim was a child of his era and in step with his era; America was the land of the pragmatist and the materialist; not to be expedient was not to be a businessman; America might grudgingly tolerate a philosopher like Emerson but it acclaimed enthusiastically a thundering old fraud like P. T. Barnum; to boggle at fraud was Un-American; Rolfe was the one out of step.

So their friendship drifted along without a break; and Rolfe wanted no break. Jim was tremendously good company, you liked him, you laughed a lot when he was around. And he liked you and had helped you in countless ways; he would have given you his last dollar, probably, or at least fifty cents of it. And it was hard to censure a friend who was lonely and basically unhappy, a friend who had shown you the old scars from the deaths of Sol Klauber and Bonnie Fansler, who had told you how a forest fire had left him a frightened orphan. As you grew to know him better you even pitied him. He still suffered agonizing headaches, and in some curious fashion, despite his successful drive toward power and money, he seemed adrift and rootless; he depended on you. He had no family life; at times such as Christmas Eve he was always turning up at your house, like some homeless old dog who yearned to be where a cheerful fire crackled and children were laughing. One June toward the end of the Hayes administration he even invited you and your family to take a trip to the North Woods in his private car. The car was, according to the *New Empire Chronicle,* a palace on wheels, the pride of the bustle epoch, with its gilt and red plush and deep carpets and Negro servants; and Jim was a cordial host.

"It's my home, this car," he said, sitting in a deep chair with an aromatic cigar. "I can't very well entertain at the house."

No, naturally not, with a mad wife: there were tales she had grown worse, a gray woman with flying tangled hair who sometimes ran screaming down the stairs because a phantom named Caleb McSwasey was chasing her with a firebrand.

The car had a name—Quickwater—and with the Torkelsens aboard it clattered from the New Empire yards toward the north, crossing the Chippewa River and following the Whiskey River through a valley scraggly with brush and no-account popple.

"This used to be all pine through here," Jim said, waving a cigar on the observation platform. "This was where Caleb McSwasey first started cutting. I went to work for him in a camp up beyond Noggin Lake."

And he went on to tell how after the pine was cut, the land had been hawked to immigrants from Europe who hoped to establish prosperous farms. But things had not worked out that way, exactly. These farms were beggarly, the houses unpainted and the barns dilapidated; some had been abandoned.

The train stopped at a station called Millville.

"Caleb had a mill here once," Jim said. "Cut a lot of pine too. The North Star Mill, he called it. One spring in high water Judge Gentry's son fell off the dam and drownded."

Mill and dam had vanished now, and the Whiskey River had silted up.

Beyond Millville, the tracks reached Noggin Lake and followed the shore toward Lake City.

"You wouldn't believe how pretty all this used to be," Jim said. "The water was so clear you could look right down and see rock bass, and the pine was thick. See that point over there? Used to be a Chippewa village there. I moved in on them and lived one summer. That was before I went to work for Caleb. Must be forty years ago. Lot of changes."

Summer cottages cluttered the lake front now, sad things with names like Dew-Drop-Inn; and Lake City was a town of twelve hundred where they manufactured clothespins. Buckmaster clothespins.

Jim wanted to inspect the factory, so the car was switched to a siding for the night; next morning, it approached a Chippewa River town called Fitzpatrick.

"Hope you folks don't mind," Jim said, as the train slowed, "if we pick up an old friend of mine here. I didn't know whether to ask her, on account of your girls, but she's an old lady and she'd be hurt if I didn't. She was good to me, when I was a kid. Well, I've done her a few favors in return. I ran my railroad through here and called the town Fitz-patrick. After her. I tipped her off what would happen, and she cleaned up on town lots. She used to run a place here called the White Water House."

Jim swung off the observation steps when the train stopped, and on the station platform Rolfe saw him embracing a woman who wore on this summer morning an amazing gown of parrot-green velvet and a matching hat with a wide brim and feathers. Age had rounded her shoulders and brought into prominence her shoulder blades, but her step was spry when she climbed aboard.

"Pleased to meet you, I'm sure," she told the Torkelsens. "Jim Buck-master and I are old friends, as it were."

She elbowed his ribs and laughed.

"Now, Molly," Jim said, "behave yourself."

"You can't teach an old dog new tricks," she said, in a voice like brash metal. "My, Mrs. Torkelsen, what pretty daughters you have."

"Thank you," Sue said, and her eyes were twinkling.

"Me, I never had no kids. Always wanted them too, and nobody can say I didn't try. Would you mind if I smoked, Mrs. Torkelsen?"

"Not at all."

"It's a bad habit," Molly said, laughing, "but most habits are if they're fun. Give me a cigar, Jim."

She took off her hat, after she had lighted up, and Rolfe saw that her hair had been dyed red. Time had ravaged her throat and crisscrossed her face with a thousand wrinkles. Her lips were painted and she wore two necklaces of imitation jade and many bracelets.

"You wouldn't believe it," she said, when the train left the station, "but when I come down here from Quickwater this was all pine woods. Pinery boys and Injuns and little else. My, but it was nice though, I've always loved nature myself, and I must say I always had fun, as it were. The Injuns are cleaned out now, and good riddance, I say. A breed killed my husband when I wasn't as old as you are, Mrs. Torkelsen. I went to pieces after that. A lady needs a man to look after her. If I had one drink too many when Mr. Fitzpatrick was alive, he'd say that's enough, Molly. A lady needs a husband."

The tracks were following the Chippewa River through forests of spindling popple and scrubby jack pine; now and then you saw a tam-arack swamp. There were no white pines.

"It's a poor country through here," Molly said. "Always was, except for the pines. The soil's so thin and sandy you can't hardly raise a fuss. The Injuns got along on it fine though, till Dan Stoughton come in. After that it was a scramble to chop the pine, and then that awful fire come along. I wouldn't give you nothing for this damned birch."

"I'm using it," Jim said. "It makes paper."

Molly slapped her thigh and laughed.

951

"Wouldn't you know it! Put Jim Buckmaster down in the middle of the ocean and he'd catch sardines and sell them to whales."

Presently the train crossed to the east side of the Chippewa and entered a bright little city with a courthouse and some sort of industrial enterprise on the river bank. Jets of steam rose white in the sun, and a mountainous slab heap could be seen. A sign said Buckmaster Lumber Company.

"My paper mill," Jim said. "Right on the site of Dan Stoughton's mill where my father worked. I supply my newspapers from here."

"Quickwater's a city now," Molly said. "Used to be nothing but a trading post and saloons. I've seen changes in my time, and I can't say they're for the better. Not when I look in the mirror. I used to be a fine figure of a woman. Plump as a pigeon. I'd walk into a saloon and you should have seen them prick up their ears, as it were. Well, they were good boys. They liked me and I liked them. No harm in a little fun as you go along. Better grab it while you can because you'll get the grief. Jim, this was nice."

The train was pulling alongside a station; Molly put on her hat and rose.

"Aren't you staying?" Sue asked.

"Not me. I don't like Quickwater. Too many memories, although you wouldn't know the town, the way it's grown. I'm going back on the down local." She pointed to a train on a siding. "I'm pleased to have met you folks. And thanks for giving me the ride, Jim. I'd do as much for you any day, as it were."

She slapped her thigh and laughed.

After Jim had escorted her from the car, Rolfe said to Sue:

"Obviously a retired whore."

"What makes you think she's retired?" Sue asked.

*

The car remained overnight in Quickwater, and in a rented rig Jim drove the Torkelsens about the town, pointing out spots of interest. But they interested him more than they interested his guests; he must have been seeing things they couldn't see. The streets were paved now, not with sawdust but with brick, and a good bridge crossed a muddy stream called Snowshoe Creek; Jim stopped the rig and pointed.

"Right down there Sol Klauber was drownded. Now I'll show you where he's buried."

He was buried, of all places, on the courthouse lawn; an iron fence enclosed the monument above his grave.

"This land was my father's," Jim said. "The house stood about there. I kept a cow in a shed out back. I gave the land to the county for the courthouse, and they agreed not to disturb the grave. I thought Sol would like having people around where he's buried."

Driving east along Shin-Tangle Street, (now sedately marked Yew Street), Jim pointed at a drugstore.

"That's about where Vonnie Olson lived. She was a midwife and a fortune teller. Once she predicted all of us Buckmasters would die in a forest fire. She was right too, except for me. The burn came but I pulled through."

The path to Injun Hollow was a pleasant residential street now; everything had changed.

Next morning the car was coupled to a northbound train, and by afternoon, after hours of thin farms and stump lands and waste places where gullies had eroded, they entered the white pine forests. Sunlight slanted among monumental trees where the earth was clean of underbrush, and the crisp air had a sweet piney smell.

"All of it used to be like this," Jim said. "And some day all of this will be like what we've been through."

He looked older and even melancholy, sitting there on the observation platform, his face no longer that of a man prematurely gray. But his brows were still black and his profile vigorous; there was a lot of power in his jaw.

*

One evening the following March a distinguished-looking old gentleman traveled toward New Empire on the cars from Chicago. He was of medium height with a snowy mustache and imperial; beneath white brows his eyes were blue; and although he carried a cane and couldn't have been much under eighty, his shoulders were erect in that bearing known as military. When the train reached New Empire he descended the steps, where he was greeted by Jim Buckmaster. And the next Thursday the *Chronicle* carried the following story:

Old Indian Fighter
Arrives in City

———

Mr. O. V. Zumwalt Visits
In Jas. Buckmaster Home

———

It is not often in these civilized times that we have the pleasure of interviewing one of the genuine old pioneers who trekked into the Far West in the early days and opened the Great Plains to the march of progress. Such a man arrived on Monday evening last in our bustling little city, to visit his son-in-law and daughter, Mr. and Mrs. James L. Buckmaster.

Mr. Otto V. Zumwalt is the name of our distinguished visitor. When pressed upon the point of what his middle initial stands for, Mr. Zumwalt will tell you his full name is actually Otto von Zumwalt. As everybody knows, or should know if they don't, the prefix "von" in Prussia indicates noble birth, and none who meets Mr. Zumwalt will doubt that in his case this is true. However, upon coming to America as a youth, he dropped the "von" out of consideration for our democratic institutions.

And what a life Mr. Zumwalt has led! World traveler, duelist, Parisian boulevardier, artist, explorer, plainsman, successful businessman—he has been them all. Born in East Prussia in 1801, son of General Heinrich von Zumwalt, a brave soldier who was wounded at the battle of Jena while leading a charge, Mr. Zumwalt early showed his courage and quick-thinking when he plunged into the Baltic Sea and rescued his brother from drowning.

"That was nothing," Mr. Zumwalt says with characteristic modesty. "I was an expert swimmer as a young man."

Sent by his doting father to the University of Göttingen, Mr. Zumwalt led the gay, dashing life so typical at that time of young men from aristocratic families. Not only was he an expert duelist, receiving and inflicting many a wound, but he was also, as he now confesses with a smile, something of a beer drinker and a hand with the fair sex.

"*Ja,* the girls always liked me," he told us. "A pretty little barmaid at Göttingen fell in love with me, but she was nothing but a peasant."

But lucky at love and unlucky at cards! Mr. Zumwalt now ruefully admits that his gambling debts mounted while at Göttingen, so at last, after paying them all, he left for Paris and struck out for himself.

Having early shown a talent in art as well as in languages, Mr. Zumwalt spent about a year studying painting in the gay, wicked capital of France, where he was a leader in the bohemian set. But alas, he fell ill, and upon his recovery he fulfilled a lifelong ambition, namely, to come to America. In New Orleans he secured employment with a firm of importers, rising rapidly in the business, but after several years the call of adventure whispered to him, and he traveled upriver to St. Louis. There, he made arrangements with an important hardware concern, Proudfoot & Sons, to travel into the Great West with a train of freight wagons along the Santa Fe Trail.

"It was on that journey," says Mr. Zumwalt, "when I made the two best friends I ever had."

One of these was a youth named Billy Proudfoot, son of the owner of Proudfoot & Sons. The other was Caleb McSwasey, whom old-timers in New Empire may remember, although Mr. McSwasey passed away somewhat violently about a quarter of a century ago.

It was on the journey to Santa Fe when Mr. Zumwalt's prowess as an Indian fighter first showed itself. One night Billy Proudfoot stole from camp and went out to hunt buffalo.

"And the cowardly Comanches killed him," says Mr. Zumwalt, with some feeling. "I vowed then and there that vengeance must be mine."

Leaving the wagon train, Mr. Zumwalt courageously set forth to track the murderers of his friend. There were, he says, seven in all, and one by one with the resourcefulness and bravery of a Prussian warrior Mr. Zumwalt tracked them down and avenged himself.

Comanches, he tells us, are basically cowardly, and when the word spread among the tribe of his deed, he was much respected by the savages. In fact, they went so far as to call him the Blond Comanche.

"It was a fine lesson I gave the cowards," Mr. Zumwalt says. "After that they knew better than to bother our wagon train."

Arrived in Santa Fe, Mr. Zumwalt, as could be expected in such a red-blooded fellow, abandoned the trifling life of an artist for the noble pursuit of business. Although his paintings had been praised by many discerning critics and fellow artists, he felt dabbling in oils was no way for a grown man to spend his time, and he established a Santa Fe branch of Proudfoot & Sons.

The business prospered, under Mr. Zumwalt's expert management and Prussian efficiency, and before long he found himself invaded by a tender passion for a beautiful young lady of Santa Fe, daughter of the most aristocratic family in New Mexico. Mr. Zumwalt was now the leading and most popular merchant of that ancient capital, and his union with the young beauty was blessed with a daughter, Esperanza, now Mrs. James L. Buckmaster of this city. But his wife, unfortunately, forfeited her own life in giving to the world this daughter.

Mr. Zumwalt never remarried, preferring to revere the memory of his Lost Love, whose name was Consuelo.

The aforementioned Caleb McSwasey, after some years, bought out Proudfoot & Sons, and for a time he and Mr. Zumwalt were partners in the Santa Fe branch of the firm. Then, when Mr. McSwasey decided to enter the lumber business in Wisconsin, he and Mr. Zumwalt were partners in that. And Mr. Zumwalt's daughter, after a charming courtship, became Mrs. McSwasey.

"Mr. McSwasey was the best friend a man could have," Mr. Zumwalt declares. "I was delighted to have him for my son-in-law. Honest and upright, he was a fine example of the men who came into Wisconsin when it was a howling wilderness and built it up till it is the thriving, civilized state we know today."

Presently, owing to the demands of his Santa Fe affairs, Mr. Zumwalt withdrew from the partnership, and devoted himself entirely to retail business in Santa Fe, now and then, however, like Cincinnatus of yore, dropping routine affairs and seizing the warrior's sword to teach various Indian tribes of the Southwest to behave themselves.

When pressed for details, Mr. Zumwalt will recount how he killed many Apaches in battle, as well as Pueblo Indians, most of whom, he says, are cowards of the most arrant sort. In the Pueblo uprising of the 1830's, Mr. Zumwalt was the staunch right arm of the governor and played a leading role in subduing the savages.

Often during the years Mr. Zumwalt contemplated a trip back east, for despite his living there he has not a high opinion of New Mexico, it being populated, he tells us, by a lazy, shiftless race lacking in any sense of time and of valor. However, business prevented such a trip.

Last February, however, the Santa Fe Railroad completed a branch from the main line to the capital, whereupon Mr. Zumwalt sold his business and traveled by the safety and convenience of rail to New Empire, where he will make an indefinite visit. In addition to the welcome he has received from many new-found friends, he was warmly received by the colored servant Lilith, who has served faithfully in the Zumwalt-McSwasey-Buckmaster families for more than half a century.

Mrs. Buckmaster, who has been in delicate health for many years, did not, unfortunately, at first recognize her father, but after a day or two she remembered him and father and daughter have enjoyed many a long conversation in the Spanish and German they both know so well.

Next Wednesday evening, Mr. Zumwalt will be guest of honor at the monthly supper of the German-American Singing Society. The evening has been designated as Von Zumwalt Night. Mr. Zumwalt has consented to recount some of his experiences as an Indian fighter, and all who enjoy stirring tales of manly adventure are urged to attend.

*

In many ways Rolfe Torkelsen was as happy as a man ever is, during those years of brocades and tight bodices and lawn croquet and the brass spittoon. While neither wealthy nor famous, he was certainly comfortably-fixed, and in Fox County he was thought of as a leading citizen. His law practice thrived; he was active in the G.A.R.; always on Memorial Day his name appeared on the program as principal speaker; and he had become chairman of the Republican Central Committee of Fox County, a position of power, for without his endorsement nobody could hope to be appointed janitor at the courthouse or deputy sheriff. In party councils on the state level, and even on the national, he was favorably known, for elections are won in the precincts, and it was said Rolfe Torkelsen had Fox County in his palm. Rank and file Republicans would have felt easier, doubtless, if he had been a churchgoer or in any case a church member, and if his wife had been less outspoken about her belief in woman suffrage; but after all the most important qualification of a county chairman is his ability to deliver the vote, and Rolfe did that.

His health had improved. Seldom were the nights when he awakened in a sweat after dreaming of boxcars on Southern railroads or the guns of Shiloh; the war was a long time ago. He got around splendidly on his artificial leg, and although the ague returned every autumn that was a common ailment; most persons had it, sooner or later, its cause being the gasses which rose from newly-plowed land or the vapors from swamps, so it was thought.

His marriage could hardly have been better, with a wife who enjoyed chess and reading aloud and ideas, no matter how advanced, and with two sweet daughters. He lived in the finest house in town, except for one; there were sleek horses in the stable and Shetland ponies for the girls and money in the bank. His investments were sound. He had everything, it appeared, worth having.

And yet . . . well, something kept troubling him, while the sands of the 1870's ran out and the 1880's began. At first it was only an infrequent uneasiness which he shoved from his thoughts; but it persisted, becoming a pretty basic doubt. He shoved that from his mind too, or supposed he did, but it must have grown in the dark, for presently he found himself given to irritation about nothing at all, as if he were living at war with himself. And at last, during his annual attack of ague in October 1880, the doubt stalked into his consciousness and had to be dealt with. It concerned a most important part of his law practice, his representing James L. Buckmaster.

The incident which ushered the doubt into his thoughts was trivial enough: his receiving a tear sheet from a newspaper called the *Franklin County Independent*. Sick in bed with the fever, he asked Sue to go to the post office, and the tear sheet, sent anonymously in a long envelope, was among the mail she brought back. Franklin County was northeast of Fox County, and the *Independent* was edited by one Preston Neal, a state senator. And Mr. Neal was neither Republican nor Democrat; like his newspaper, he was an Independent. An outlaw, both Republicans and Democrats called such men. And Franklin County was an outlaw county, which was to say that the Granger movement of the 1870's had thrived vigorously there: Granger votes kept electing Preston Neal.

Men like James L. Buckmaster were the natural enemies of the Grangers. And decidedly vice versa. For the Grangers were small farmers who had bought cutover land and nearly starved; they were the Lorne Buckmasters of this earth, the luckless men whose oats were flattened by wind and rain a week before harvest, whose wheat was eaten by grasshoppers, whose corn was washed out, whose horses caught the heaves and whose pigs caught the scours, whose cows ate wild garlic and whose barns were struck by lightning, whose wives were always pregnant and whose children had adenoids. And in recent years their numbers had been swollen by farmers who would have been prosperous, normally, but who found the grade too steep from the bottom of the depression; and by small-town merchants who couldn't collect. The Grangers had elected a Wisconsin governor, back in the mid-seventies, and a legislature that had passed a law to regulate the railroads. Two years later the law was hastily repealed, not without urging by Mr. Buckmaster, and the governor defeated; since then they had been a minority in state politics, although a mighty vocal one. Mention the Grangers and conservative citizens purpled.

In that tear sheet from the *Franklin County Independent* sent to Rolfe, Senator Preston Neal devoted his editorial page to the coming election. The railroads were his *bête noire*. And he had a talking point, so far as that went. For without regulation, the railroads could—and did—charge what the traffic would bear. If a farmer harvested a good crop, the expense of hauling it to market drained off his profit. Storage charges for grain were exorbitant. Freight rates hiked the cost of machinery. And while the farmer paid taxes on the value of his land, the railroads were taxed by a complicated and easily-juggled system based on earnings per mile.

Boxed on the editorial page was a quotation from Chief Justice Ryan of the Wisconsin Supreme Court:

"There is looming up a new and dark power. I cannot dwell upon the signs and shocking omens of its advent. The accumulation of individual wealth seems to be greater than it has ever been since the downfall of the Roman Empire. The enterprises of the country are aggregating vast corporate combinations of unexampled capital, boldly marching, not for economic conquests only, but for political power. For the first time really in our politics money is taking the field as an organized power . . . The question will arise, and arise in your day, though perhaps not fully in mine, 'Which shall rule—wealth or man; which shall lead—money or intellect; who shall fill the public stations—educated and patriotic free men, or the feudal serfs of corporate capital?'"

In commenting on Justice Ryan's words, Senator Preston Neal wrote that for the past twenty years in Wisconsin wealth had been ruling. "The timber crowd," he wrote, "the railroad crowd, nabobs like James L. Buckmaster and his chore boy, Rolfe Torkelsen—they are the actual lords of our destiny."

That last sentence had been heavily underlined, presumably by the anonymous sender of the tear sheet.

Lying in bed, Rolfe examined the envelope. It was postmarked New Empire and addressed in block letters.

"What's the matter?" Sue asked.

Rolfe handed her the tear sheet.

"Pooh, pooh," she said, after reading the underlined sentence. "You're not Jim Buckmaster's chore boy. Are you?"

"I don't know. Maybe."

She gave him a searching look.

"If you are," she said, "you'd better stop it. You're not the sort to be happy as anybody's chore boy."

While she read the rest of the tear sheet, Rolfe lay wondering who had sent it, thinking that an anonymous letter made you feel like a man hit with a stone from ambush; you knew you had an enemy, but you couldn't fight back. If the sender of that tear sheet thought of him as Jim Buckmaster's chore boy, how many other persons thought the same?

"This Preston Neal is nobody's fool," Sue said. "His pen is sharp. Who is he?"

"State senator from Franklin County. Probably the most brilliant man in the legislature. Certainly the most fearless."

"How about Justice Ryan? Is what he says true?"

"It's true, all right. He said that seven years ago in a graduation speech at the law school in Madison. It was true then and it's truer now."

"If it's true, why do people stand for it?"

"The Grangers don't. They're hungry, and when you're hungry you begin thinking. They're well organized and they get out the vote. But their funds are limited."

"And Jim Buckmaster's aren't?"

"It's more than that. He and his crowd have most of the newspapers. They've smeared the Grangers as wild-eyed radicals. Month in and month out people read doctored news and editorials by Buckmaster's hired men. People swallow what they read and before long they think the editors' opinions are their own ideas. Most men won't change their minds, once they believe something. A man will always vote for what he thinks is his own interest. The trick is to convince him that your interests are his. The best time to do that is when he reads a newspaper in his carpet slippers and elections are a year away. His mind is wet cement then, and you're scratching on it what you want him to believe. When election time comes, the cement has hardened and he'll have a fist fight at the polls if somebody says his ideas—which are really your ideas—are wrong."

"You've been doing this?" Sue asked.

"I haven't had to. The editors do it. A county chairman's job isn't to convince Democrats to vote Republican. Not primarily. His job is to maintain party discipline and see that his crowd goes to vote."

"A chore boy's job?"

Rolfe smiled.

"If you want to call it that. But Preston Neal meant something else."

"What?"

Rolfe laughed.

"Don't look at me like that. I haven't been up to anything crooked. But of course—"

He was facing it then, all the doubt, all the uneasiness of the past few years.

"You might as well tell me," Sue said. "You know what a nagger I am."

"You're not a nagger. You're just a woman with a very honest mind."

"Tell me about it."

It wasn't easy, probing into the deeps of his mind and snagging a doubt and dragging it up into daylight. But there had been a lawsuit known as the Larimer Case. Sam Larimer, rheumatic and sixty-ish, had worked for the Madison, New Empire & Western as a switchman in the New Empire yards. One January night a couple of years before he had slipped during a sleet storm and had died beneath the wheels of a locomotive. His widow sued and Rolfe defended the railroad.

"I advised Jim to settle out of court," Rolfe said. "Larimer's widow was destitute, and the railroad could have pensioned her without missing the money. But Jim wouldn't. That surprised me. He used to be generous with his employees. He's grown harder. Even since the strike in '77, he's had a grudge against his workmen. Sometimes it seems he hates them. Anyway, he told me to fight it out in court. Well, I'm his lawyer, so I did. We lost in district court, of course. Any jury would find against the railroad. But I appealed, and we won. It bothered me. We deserved to win, strictly according to law. But it bothered me."

"What happened to Mrs. Larimer?"

"She's in the county home."

"Why didn't you tell me this?"

"Because a man should leave his business in his office. If he brings it home he'll take it to bed, and then he won't sleep."

"And you were able to sleep?"

"Not too well, for a while."

"What else has been bothering you?" Sue asked.

Well, Rolfe said, there was the way Jim Buckmaster had put out of business a railroad known as the Medicine Bluff & Northern. It had been a prosperous little road on the west side of the river with about fifty miles of track, built and owned by local capital. From Medicine Bluff on the Mississippi it slanted northwest to the town of Dixon.

"Jim wanted it. Well, that's the trend. You know how it was in the early days of railroads: two towns would raise money and lay track between them. When the big systems came along, those local roads were consolidated into the main lines. Usually it was better. Usually the small lines were bankrupt anyhow. But the Medicine Bluff & Northern was different. There's coal at Dixon, and the local outfit hauled it to Medicine Bluff on the Mississippi. And from Medicine Bluff, the road carried freight from river boats into the back country. It made money, and the stockholders didn't want to sell.

"Jim made up his mind to have it. First, he refused it a connection with his line at Medicine Bluff. Then his river boats wouldn't carry freight to Medicine Bluff if it was bound for Dixon. That put a crimp in the little line. But it limped along. Jim was in a hurry—he's always in a hurry about such things—so next he slashed his steamboat rates on any freight bound for a landing called Woodman. It's on the Mississippi due east of Dixon. Next, he slashed rates on freight outbound from Woodman. That was the *coup de grâce*. People could order goods sent to Woodman and haul them by wagon to Dixon at low rates. Coal from Dixon was hauled to Woodman instead of going by rail to Medicine

Bluff. The railroad lost heavily. Jim bought its bonds, and when they defaulted he threw it into bankruptcy. Then he bought the line at ten cents on the dollar."

"And you had a hand in that?"

"No, the legal department in Chicago engineered it. But I knew what was going on."

"What else?"

Plenty else, it seemed. There was, Rolfe said, the matter of the Catfish Boom.

"It's a technical device used in driving logs. I'm no mechanic so don't ask me how it works, but it's a simple mechanism, I'm told. When you're driving logs you may want to hold back some of your crop, or to herd them into a sawmill pond. A boom is used. It's a string of logs chained together. In the old days, men in bateaux had to haul the boom from one side of the river to the other. That took time and labor. Then some river hog up on the Chippewa invented this automatic boom. His nickname was Catfish Harry, so they called it the Catfish Boom. By placing fins at the proper angles he devised a method of opening and closing the boom so that the river current worked it automatically. You can imagine how valuable that would be to a big operator.

"Catfish Harry wasn't even a Buckmaster driver. But when Jim heard about the boom, he had me make out papers buying all rights to the invention 'for valuable considerations now in hand.' Then he went upriver and found Catfish Harry. Paid him a hundred dollars and bought him a drink, and Catfish Harry signed away all rights. After that, Jim patented it.

"All the other operators were hopping mad. Catfish Harry had been working for the Northern Lights Log & Lumber Company when he invented the boom, and they claimed it should be theirs. They sued Jim. Well, we licked them."

"And what about Catfish Harry?"

"Jim hired him the next season and he was killed breaking a jam."

"What else has been bothering you?" Sue asked.

He told her other instances of Jim's using his railroad or his steamboats to crush rivals; he told her about secret rebates; about logging dams, built with permission from the legislature, which had flooded out small farmers; about abuses under the Homestead Act such as the Buckmaster Lumber Company's paying a pinery boy to file on a quarter-section of fine timber in return for a deed to the land.

"Then there's the way he got Chippewa lands in Minnesota. The government made a treaty with the Chippewas which entitled every head of an Indian family to free land. Jim sent his agents into the Chippewa Nation to help them fill out the governmental form. Then they bought the land for a jug of whiskey. And here in Wisconsin he's got Indian lands for a song. If there's an honest Indian agent, he uses Park

Irwin in Washington to get him removed. An agent who is ready to do business is appointed. He'll recommend that certain tracts of Indian timber be sold. A crooked appraiser looks over the land and values it low. And Jim sends several men to the public auction. One buys the land for what he has to pay, but after the auction he forfeits his bid. Then another Buckmaster man buys it at its appraised valuation, which is low. I could talk all afternoon about things like that. But I'd rather not. I'd rather forget it."

"You'll not forget it," Sue said. "How long have you known these things?"

"I've known some of them ever since we came back from Barbados. I knew he sailed close to the law sometimes, but I didn't think he was crooked. But the last year or two I've found out things which changed my mind. It's bothered me. Maybe he's right. Maybe I'm an idealist."

"Did you think you weren't?"

"I knew I used to be when I was a kid. Anyone who worked on the underground was. But I thought I'd got over it."

"Do you think I'd have married you," Sue said, "if you hadn't been an idealist? Of course you're an idealist. That's why you enlisted as a private. That's why the war cut you up so horribly. You may not have inherited your father's religion, but you inherited his conscience. No wonder you've been so testy lately. You have a bad conscience. You've been living against your fundamental nature. You've been living two lives. In the daytime you're Jim Buckmaster's chore boy, and at night you brood over Emerson. You'll have to become one thing or the other."

"You may be right," Rolfe said.

"A woman's always right about a man, when she loves him. And if I'm right about you, Jim Buckmaster is going to lose a chore boy."

"You think I should cut loose from Jim?"

"You know what I think. But it's your decision."

"It will cut into our income."

"All right, it will cut into our income. Does that mean the sky will fall?"

All at once Rolfe had a sense of release.

"Did I ever tell you," he said, "that I think you're wonderful?"

"Yes. But pretend you haven't and say it again."

*

Cutting loose from Jim Buckmaster, however, was easier decided upon than accomplished.

"Swede, you damned fool, what's got into you?" Jim said, a few days later in his office. "We can't get along without each other. You know that."

"I've been working too hard," Rolfe said.

"Well, then, goddamn it, kick out your other clients. Use your head, boy. I'm the biggest man on this river. Shystering for me gives you a lot of prestige."

"I've never shystered for you or anybody else."

Sitting at his desk, Jim had been scowling and chewing a cigar, slitted eyes hard and gray. But now he threw back his head and laughed.

"The same old Swede. The same old rafting chore boy you always were. Just as soon fight me as look at me. Should have tossed you in the river and been done with it." He stood up, came to Rolfe's chair. "All right, Swede, out with it. You're mad at me, and I don't know why. What have I done?"

In that mood when he chose to use good humor and all the force of his personality he was hard to resist. He could be like the river in flood, sweeping everything before it. He was well into his fifties now; deep lines ran from his dominant nose to his mouth; puffy places showed under his eyes, and the flesh beneath his long jawbone had a hint of flabbiness; liver spots could be seen on his hands; his shoulders sagged a little; but he was still a powerful man; a big man.

"You might as well tell me, Swede. What's eating you?"

If you had known him since rafting days, how could you deal with him? I think you're a crook—could say that? You've grown harder, you're ruthless, you've plundered your state and your nation, you've gouged and kicked competition in the groin, you've grabbed more than you could ever use, you've laid waste to the forests and left the land to be gutted by torrents, you've cheated and bribed and bullied your way to the top—could you say those things?

Not if you were Rolfe Torkelsen; not if you'd been his friend for thirty years; not if you liked him and damned near loved him; not if in the man standing there you saw the tatterdemalion kid in the smoky ruins of Quickwater.

"There've been things I haven't liked," Rolfe said.

"Don't I pay you enough?"

"More than enough."

"Then I don't understand," Jim said; and Rolfe saw that he didn't understand, he really didn't: if somebody paid you enough that should fix everything.

"I didn't like the way you ruined the Medicine Bluff & Northern," Rolfe said.

"Jesus, Swede, did you own some of their stock? I didn't know that. I'd have tipped you off—"

"Of course I didn't own their stock."

"Thank God for that. You had me scared for a minute. Well, if you didn't own any, where's the skin off your nose?"

"I just didn't like it."

"You didn't handle the legal end, did you? I thought the Chicago crowd took care of that."

"They did. I wasn't in it."

"Then why in hell—?"

"It was a prosperous railroad, minding its own business. And you wrecked it."

"Sure I wrecked it. But I warned them. They had their chance. I'd have bought them out at a fair price. They wouldn't listen to reason, Swede. So I had to get a little rough."

"I don't see why."

"God damn it, Swede, a blind man could see why. I needed that line. And I wanted that coal up at Dixon. That's all there was to it. Plain as a mink's tracks. They wouldn't sell so I had to put on the pressure. What's wrong with that?"

"Do you think it was honest?"

"Honest? Hell, I don't know. It was legal. Nobody's come to arrest me so it must have been. It was just a business deal, Swede. Happens every day. I don't understand why it's got your wind up."

"And I didn't like the Larimer case either. I won it for you, but I didn't like it."

"Why not?"

"You should have settled. Sam Larimer was hurt on the job, and you should have taken care of his widow."

"I disagree," Jim said, "and so did the court. That makes it my opinion and the court's opinion against yours."

"You should have settled. She's an old woman."

"And Sam Larimer was an old troublemaker. In the strike of '77 he was with that crowd that burned a string of boxcars. I never should have taken him back. But he came in here and begged, so I weakened. Then the damned fool fell under a locomotive. Hell, Swede, if I'd made a settlement every bastard on the line would have started suit every time he got a sliver in his ass from sleeping on the job. You can't give in. What else don't you like about the way I run my business?"

"There's no use going into it," Rolfe said. "We're so far apart in our thinking it's no use."

"Well I'll be damned," Jim said. He was scowling again, and his lower lip protruded; he looked troubled and sullen. Going to the window, he stood with his back to the office, shoulders sagging. His gray hair looked dead and old.

"So I'm resigning," Rolfe said.

Jim's fists clenched, but then he swung from the window and his face was jovial again.

"Swede, Swede—for God's sake. Let's cut out this damned foolishness. You've been sick, that's your trouble. Look, boy. Have I ever asked you to do anything crooked?"

"No."

"And when you've run your raft aground haven't I always got you

964

afloat again? Didn't I handle Nixie Auerbach for you?"

"Yes."

"Have I ever done you a bad turn?"

"No."

"See there? Hell, we've been friends for thirty years. I need you, Swede. You're the only rooster I can trust, damned near. You've been sick. Rest up a while. Think things over. And now get the hell out of here so a man can do a little work."

*

At his office, Rolfe wrote a letter to Jim, withdrawing as attorney for the Buckmaster Lumber Company; the letter came back with a penciled notation: "Request refused." In January Rolfe received his quarterly retainer fee from the company; he returned the check; Jim sent it again; Rolfe tore it up and sent the pieces to Jim, who thereupon deposited the amount of the fee to Rolfe's credit in the Bank of New Empire.

"What will you do now?" Sue asked.

"Tell the bank I refuse to accept the deposit. I won't work for him."

Several times Jim sent word for Rolfe to come to his office to discuss legal matters; Rolfe did not go. Finally Jim came tramping up the stairs of the Gentry Block, angry and hurt, but Rolfe would not budge from his decision. After that a period of coolness ensued between those old friends. They still spoke when they met on the street, but Jim looked wounded and guarded, and months passed without his dropping in at the house on Gentry Avenue.

"He'll get over it," Rolfe told Sue. "It's just that he's used to having his own way, and he doesn't know what to make of it."

Meanwhile, the retainer checks stopped coming, but Rolfe scarcely missed them, for his practice had grown and his income was sizable. He had a habit of winning cases and a habit of refusing questionable business; people said he was a keen lawyer and an honest one; clients came from all over that part of the state. His colleagues respected him— one year he served as president of the bar association—and now and then he was appointed referee in bankruptcy, always a basket of plums in any law office. His position seemed impregnable. He got along without Jim Buckmaster very well.

Then he entered politics.

That came about in the spring of 1882 when the state senator from Fox County, a furniture merchant from a neighboring town, was kicked in the head by a horse. Everybody had liked him, except possibly the horse; he had been a good vote-getter; and thus his death was genuinely mourned in Republican circles. Early in June the party nominating convention was to be held in New Empire, and the delegates were eager to put up a man for state senator who could win, for the Granger movement had gained strength, and no longer was Fox County a certain

Republican stronghold: the bloody shirt had passed into its twilight years. As early as May, the party fathers were saying Rolfe Torkelsen would be the strongest candidate, and one morning a group of politicians called at his office to sound him out. Spokesman was George Appleton, president of the recently-organized First National Bank, a brisk man of forty with a Roman nose who likely thought of himself, correctly, as a hard-hitter.

"We understand," said Mr. Appleton, "that you are no longer attorney for the Buckmaster interests. Is that correct?"

"Yes."

"Good. There's been a ground swell of feeling against Buckmaster. The farmers don't like him and neither does labor. If you're free of him you're a sure winner. We could count on those Danish townships a hundred percent. If you will accept, I can pretty well assure you of nomination on the first ballot."

Rolfe said he would think it over.

He not only thought it over; he talked it over with Sue, for he realized the wisdom of the Chinese proverb that a woman's advice may be worthless, but a man who doesn't listen to it is a fool. She thought he should run. The legislature, she said, could do with a few more brains. The campaign would last only a few weeks, and the legislative session never lasted more than a couple of months; he could afford to take that much time from his practice. Besides, he could pass on to the lawmakers some of the enlightened ideas he had hatched out after reading that best seller, *Progress and Poverty,* and Edwin L. Godkin's *Nation.*

So he agreed to run.

"There's just one thing," George Appleton said, "that bothers me. That's your religion. Some people say you're an atheist."

"They're wrong. I'm an agnostic."

"My God, what's that?"

"I neither affirm or deny the existence of a Supreme Being. I simply don't know."

Mr. Appleton looked dubious.

"It would look better if you'd join a church," he said.

Rolfe smiled.

"I'm afraid I can't oblige you. My religion is exactly what Abraham Lincoln's was. He wouldn't join a church. When they urged him, he said he couldn't quite see it. If the party doesn't want me on those terms, it can find somebody else."

"Oh, the party wants you! You're the best speaker in ten counties and the G.A.R. would be behind you. We want you, all right."

Thus things stood when the county convention met. It nominated Rolfe Torkelsen by acclamation. He resigned as chairman of the county central committee, and George Appleton was appointed.

Next morning, one of Rolfe's student clerks told him that James L. Buckmaster was waiting in the outer office.

And he was good old Jim, jovial old Jim, striding into Rolfe's office and thrusting out his hand.

"Congratulations, Swede. I'm just back from Chicago and heard the news. That's wonderful."

"I'm not elected yet."

"You will be, with me behind you. I've told the *Chronicle* to go all out. And if you need campaign funds, just yell for Uncle Jim."

"Thanks," Rolfe said, "but we're fairly well fixed in that line."

"State Senator Torkelsen," Jim said. "It's a beginning, Swede, and your best years are ahead. How old are you?"

"Forty-six."

"Lord, what I'd give to be forty-six again! Hell, you've got a good quarter-century ahead of you. In two years if you want to go to congress I'll get Park Irwin kicked upstairs. And after that there's the United States Senate. Remember what I told you that time in Washington? We were in the old senate gallery and I said you'd be down there some day, making speeches. You will too, only in the new senate. And then there's the White House. Sure, you were born in Denmark, but I can get that changed. I've pulled off bigger jobs than that. President Rolfe Torkelsen. You'll sleep in the White House, Swede, and I'll be there to lick you at poker. They'll put your face on a coin, some day. I told you you'd never regret it if you hooked up with me."

That was all nonsense and pipe dreams, of course, but Jim Buckmaster's enthusiasm was always infectious. For a moment Rolfe permitted his imagination to range into that future which was brighter than life could ever be. Then he smiled.

"I'm still not elected."

When it assembled the following week, the Democratic convention nominated a token candidate in the person of Darrell Pfister, a young lawyer with pimples, few clients and the personality of a weasel. Nobody —not even Mr. Pfister—believed he had a chance. In November, Rolfe was elected by a thumping majority.

*

Although the site for Wisconsin's capital city had been chosen many years before so that some speculating politicians could dispose of marshy land, those early patriots had builded better than they knew: Madison was a lovely town, snow queen of a winter state, engirded by lakes where skaters and iceboats could be seen, seat of a thriving university, canopied by blue northern sky, modern with horsecars and newfangled telephones, well-provided with those two essentials of successful law-making, saloons and fancy houses. Downtown in the principal square the capitol stood, looking pristine as new snow and classic as an Athenian temple, its great dome reaffirming the interest of mankind in things mammillary. At the southeast corner of Capitol Square, in the very shadow of this symbol of a dairying state, stood the Park Hotel, a brand new hostelry of cream-colored brick, four stories tall, with an elaborate mansard roof and spacious piazzas, with an ornate lobby and reading rooms and dining rooms and a grand ballroom, all steam-heated by clanking radiators. Brussels carpets cushioned the feet of the mighty and the beautiful; oiled walnut furniture was provided throughout; and in January 1883 when Senator Rolfe Torkelsen took a room there the place buzzed day and night with politicians and lobbyists and reporters and ladies with seductive busts, bustles and eyes.

Sue had come down to Madison for a few days, to sit in the senate gallery and watch when he took the oath of office, and James L. Buckmaster was there too; that evening they all attended the reception in the governor's mansion, a brilliant social occasion: Rolfe remembered the glittering carriages discharging guests, the blaze of gas lights, the stringed music, the scent of cigars and perfumes, the swish of silks and satin, the powdered arms and billowing skirts and snug bodices in shades of tea rose and crocus and absinthe and peach. James L. Buckmaster, wearing evening clothes, was easily the most distinguished-looking man there, with his eyebrows black as broadcloth and his hair white as his boiled shirt; not even the butler had better manners. He had come a long way since the nights when he brawled in saloons.

And more guests, so it seemed, wished to greet him than wished to greet the governor; assemblymen and senators shook his hand and told him jokes; railroad lobbyists and timber lobbyists, genial men with handsome women, hovered nearby; judges looked pleased when he called them by their given names. He was getting on toward sixty but you would hardly have guessed it, from the lean virility of his body; only his face and hands betrayed his age. He looked as if, in a pinch, he might still have been able to ride a log through rapid water.

One group of guests, however, ignored Jim Buckmaster. They were the representatives and senators from outlaw counties: half-breeds, they were beginning to be called. Most of them wore ordinary business suits, ill-fitting garments with shiny elbows and pants that could have stood a press job; their faces were raw from sun and wind; and they lacked the social graces. Their hands, often enough, looked as if they had labored with monkey wrenches and shovels and plow-handles; they were men who had come to Madison directly from the people. Among them was Preston Neal, who had once written that Rolfe Torkelsen was Jim Buckmaster's chore boy.

Senator Neal was a long, stoop-shouldered man of sixty, narrow-faced and brown-skinned, with a shock of iron-gray hair and suspicious hazel eyes; his lips formed an "O" around a perpetual cigar. He looked cold-minded, dry-humored, deadly; but for some reason Rolfe thought he would enjoy knowing that man and hearing his ideas about the love affair between great wealth and politics. But Senator Neal obviously wanted none of Senator Torkelsen; he didn't so much as nod, when their glances crossed.

The half-breeds kept to themselves, at the reception and in the halls of the capitol; some were Independents, some Democrats, some Republicans, but they thought alike and voted alike. The *Madison Star,* a Buckmaster newspaper, assailed them unmercifully, of course, not only on the editorial page but in the news columns as well, but they seemed to thrive on abuse and to be proud of the enemies they made. The *Star's* cartoonist lampooned them as men with forked tails, with bombs ready to be tossed, as Samsons about to bring down the temple of stable society; but the half-breeds went their way, refusing railroad passes and invitations from lobbyists to jolly suppers with wine and girls.

During those opening weeks of the legislative session, they interested Rolfe more and more. The best speeches were made by half-breeds, and they were demons at parliamentary stratagems; they understood how to make the most of their tight little bloc. From their comments in debate, Rolfe deduced that they too had read *Progress and Poverty,* and now and then the *Nation* could be seen in Senator Neal's coat pocket. Rolfe knew he belonged with them, the way his thinking had been running the last few years, rather than with the railroad senators and the timber senators; but of course the half-breeds had no intimation that he was no longer Jim Buckmaster's chore boy.

One evening in January when snow was riding a stinging wind, Rolfe left the hotel and went to the east side of the square, climbing steps to a second-floor restaurant called the Madison Oyster House, a plain place where the food, so he had heard, was good. He had not, however, heard that the Madison Oyster House was a half-breed hangout—an informal club, really—where they could eat cheaply and lay their plans. Twenty or thirty of them must have been there that evening, laughing and talking, but when he limped in and brushed the snow from his overcoat the place fell silent. He was watched, when the plump German proprietress conducted him to a lonely table back by the door to the kitchen, and it came to him that the half-breeds must suspect he was dining here to eavesdrop. He felt embarrassed.

Conversation was gradually resumed, as he ate his oyster stew and drank his beer, but it was carried on in low tones unless it concerned something like the wintry weather. The ragout of beef was delicious, the coffee the best he had found in Madison, but he would not be eating here again. He would have given a good deal to walk over to Senator Neal and be welcomed into that group; they were his kind and Sue's kind; they were, he told himself, far better Americans than the men who sold their votes for a mess of Buckmaster dollars. In their limited field they were the Jeffersons and the Jacksons and the Philip Freneaus of

American politics; the men who had dreamed dreams of a working democracy, who hated not wealth but wealth used as a political bludgeon to plunder and ravage; they answered to that word which was always a sneer-word in the mouths of heavy-necked politicians: idealists. Their ideal was a self-disciplined commonwealth, and they wished only that political power should remain where the Constitution delegated it: in the people. And because such were their ideals, they were besmeared by the railroad press and the timber press; they were called radicals, crackpots, irresponsible men with dangerous opinions.

Rolfe left his table and put on his overcoat, and as he descended the stairs, holding the rail lest his wooden leg trip him, he imagined that the conversation would have a freer tone back in the restaurant, now that Buckmaster's chore boy had departed.

The wind was higher and the snow thicker, on the square, and when Rolfe emerged he encountered a plump man in a fur coat, one of Jim Buckmaster's lobbyists.

"Well, Senator," the man said. "Didn't expect to ever see you coming from that nest of wild-eyed buzzards."

Rolfe had a notion to say, "Are you referring to the duly-elected representatives of the people of Wisconsin?"

But the man's mind was as fat as his belly; it would be wasted breath.

*

During his first weeks in the senate, learning his way about, Rolfe kept his ears open and his mouth mainly shut, but his brain was in a ferment. All his liberal thinking ripened during that period, and something told him that before the legislature adjourned he would toss in his lot with the half-breeds. That would amount to risking his political future, but it was something he knew he must do, if he expected to live comfortably with himself. Sitting at his desk in the senate chamber, he used to think how appalled the majority leader would be if he knew the contents of Senator Rolfe Torkelsen's mind. And it occurred to him that his position was not unlike that of the Reverend Thor Torkelsen many years ago when he decided to go over to the Grundtvigians. He had, he supposed, inherited a wild, storm-loving, Viking streak from his father.

And would Fox County re-elect a senator who voted with the kittle-kattle, who associated with Grangers and half-breeds? He didn't know. If not, so be it. But he hoped to return to the senate, for he loved it. The chamber was small and even intimate, when compared with the house of representatives; there were many page boys to bring coffee or copies of pending bills; and Rolfe used to muse how it was all part of the shining tradition of self-government, going back to Washington, D. C., and the English Parliament and to dim beginnings in the Roman forum and in Greece. The tradition was greater than the men who participated in it, at least here in Madison; but it was there; and he liked the dignity imparted by the parliamentary rules. In that dignity and formality there lingered an assumption: that here in this quiet control center of a sovereign state the representatives of the people would reach decisions by intellect alone; the senate was a hopeful symbol of man at his best. He liked the ideal of senatorial courtesy, that convention which presupposed the members were gentlemen; he liked the easy atmosphere and the undercurrent, sometimes, of humor; and he even enjoyed the sense of security given by the sergeant-at-arms and his deputies, for you felt that with the doors guarded and everything under control the business of the state could proceed in an orderly manner, no matter how many pressure groups thronged the corridors.

Sessions were held in the mornings; afternoons were spent in committee rooms, listening to arguments for and against pieces of legislation; and nearly every evening, in his hotel room overlooking Capitol Square, Rolfe briefed himself on the next day's agenda and replied to letters from his constituents. He tried to be a good senator, although as a freshman his influence was limited. Greatest nuisance were the lobbyists, professional and amateur, who buttonholed him in corridors and accosted him on the street and in the hotel dining room: everybody wanted something. Once, even, he was offered a thousand dollars for his vote.

That was early in February, and the issue concerned the granting of a bridge-building charter to the Milwaukee & Lake Superior Railroad, which wished to cross the Wisconsin River. So far as Rolfe could determine, the state would be justified in granting permission to build the bridge. He was not anti-railroad, so long as the public interest was not impaired. Many of the half-breeds, he knew, were opposed on principle to granting anything to any railroad—in that they erred as much as the conservatives, who wanted to grant everything to all railroads—but Rolfe had a judicious mind: he refused to think in clichés, even liberal ones. One evening in his room, pondering the matter, he decided to vote to grant the charter when the bill came up next morning; and then a knock fell on his door. Two men stood in the hall. One was the great-bellied lobbyist he had encountered when he left the Madison Oyster House, a man named Craddock. The other was vice-president of the Milwaukee & Lake Superior Railroad, a dark Irishman named O'Fallon.

"Senator," Craddock said, after the amenities had been disposed of, "we're counting noses. Mr. O'Fallon has come to Madison in the interests of the Wisconsin River bridge. You are voting with us, of course."

Rolfe disliked that phrase, "of course."

"What makes you think so?" he asked.

Craddock's brows lifted.

"Well, naturally, Senator, we assumed . . . I suppose you know Jim Buckmaster is a stockholder in the Milwaukee & Lake Superior."

"No," Rolfe said, "I didn't know."

"Oh, but he is, Senator. Isn't that true, Mr. O'Fallon?"

"Ten thousand shares," Mr. O'Fallon said.

"So you'll vote with us, of course," Craddock said.

There it was again: "of course." Jim Buckmaster held stock in the line so of course his chore boy would vote correctly.

"I haven't decided how I'll cast my vote," Rolfe said.

"But Senator. Jim Buckmaster wants the bridge built."

"What has that to do with it?"

Mr. Craddock and Mr. O'Fallon exchanged glances. And Mr. Craddock said smoothly:

"I hope, Senator, you haven't been listening to the half-breeds."

"I don't know what you mean," Rolfe said.

"In plain English, Senator, I mean bastards like that son of a bitch Preston Neal. Do I make myself clear?"

"Perfectly."

"After all, I *did* see you leaving the Madison Oyster House one evening not long ago."

Rolfe felt his Viking blood rising.

"Let's understand each other," he said crisply. "I was sent to Madison by the people of Fox County. As their representative I am free to eat where I choose and to associate with whom I please. And it is my privilege and my duty to vote as I think wisest on any measure."

"I agree, Senator, but with one emendation. On any measure in which the interests of James L. Buckmaster are not involved."

"To hell with James L. Buckmaster. He's a citizen of Fox County, neither more nor less important than any other citizen, so far as my voting is concerned."

"Senator Torkelsen," Mr. Craddock said, "I'm sorry to find you taking this attitude. But I've had much experience with the legislature, and if you will pardon my saying so your attitude is rather common among freshman members. Sometimes being elected to public office goes to a man's head. He needs a hat of a larger size, if I make myself clear. He sometimes forgets his sponsor. My business is to remind him that without Jim Buckmaster's support he would not be here at all."

Rolfe's brain was a stormy Viking sea.

"Get out," he said. "Get the hell out."

Mr. Craddock laughed, his belly and full-moon face those of a jolly fat man.

"Senator, please. Don't you know I was joking? Of course you'll vote as you think best. Now if you'll excuse me, I'll leave you gentlemen alone. I have business down the hall."

And Mr. Craddock left. When the door had closed, Mr. O'Fallon said:

"I hope you'll overlook what Craddock said, Senator Torkelsen. He's had too many beers. I'm not here to argue with you, Senator. You'll vote as you think wisest. But I will say that if you find it is to the public interest for the bridge charter to be granted, the Milwaukee & Lake

Superior will be very grateful. And when we are grateful, Senator, we express our appreciation in more than words. I am not trying to influence you, but if you vote for the charter you will find a plain envelope in your key-box at the lobby desk. It will contain a thousand dollars in currency. But make up your own mind. If you vote against us, there will be no hard feelings."

"Well, thanks," Rolfe said. "It's a relief to know that."

"But no friendly feelings either, Senator. By the way, our line is expanding its legal department. We are appointing legal representatives in various cities, on a retainer basis. We have not yet decided on our attorney in New Empire. Any suggestions, Senator?"

"Yes," Rolfe said. "Take the Milwaukee & Lake Superior Railroad and stick it up your ass."

*

Alone, he stood at the window looking out at the snowy square. Through bare trees he could see the statehouse, its dome looming vast against the stars. His anger was ashes now, but his jaw was set. Finally he went to bed, where he tossed with insomnia, and when he slept he dreamed of Shiloh. It was no longer a battlefield, but an immense cemetery where skeletons had risen and were marching in endless parades, carrying Confederate flags and Union flags, all bullet-ridden and tattered. He wakened when the winter dawn was black, and he did not sleep again.

And that morning in the senate, Preston Neal took the floor and attacked the bill granting a bridge charter to the Milwaukee & Lake Superior Railroad. Why, he asked, should the people of Wisconsin bestow favors on an industry which had consistently robbed them? Outside the sky was dark and snow was falling, big feathery flakes, and Senator Rolfe Torkelsen knew he was going to make a speech.

He stood up, when Senator Neal had finished, and he was immediately recognized by the president of the senate, for it was assumed by everybody that Jim Buckmaster's chore boy would engage in rebuttal. The half-breeds watched him with sullen eyes or smiled sardonically.

"Mr. President," he said, "I cannot agree with the distinguished senator from Franklin County. I have studied this question, and on its merits I believe the charter should be granted. When the roll is called, I intend to vote aye."

That was no surprise to anybody. The president of the senate settled in his high-backed leather chair and prepared to endure a routine speech; at their table newspaper reporters looked bored; members were whispering to one another; and Rolfe could see Senator Neal at his desk, chewing a cigar as he rustled through papers.

"However," Rolfe went on, "I am voting to grant the charter despite the efforts of the Milwaukee & Lake Superior Railroad to influence me to do exactly that. Last evening in my room I made my decision to vote for this bill. That decision was reached, as I have said, on the merits of the case. A new line from Milwaukee to Superior will benefit the northern counties of our state. After I had made my decision, however, two gentlemen came to my room. They represented the railroad, and they are not, I imagine, unknown to you. One was Vern Craddock and the other Francis O'Fallon."

A ripple of interest and uneasiness passed over the senate. Preston Neal stopped rustling papers. At the press table reporters looked at one another.

"These gentlemen," Rolfe said, "endeavored to sway my thinking. If I may use an ugly word, they tried to bribe me. I was offered a thousand dollars for my vote, and a legal retainer from the railroad."

Outside, the snow fell; inside, there was the silence of deep shock. Then three or four senators—railroad senators and timber senators— jumped up. Would the senator yield?

"I will yield in good time," Rolfe said, "but first I must finish. I refused the compensation offered by these gentlemen. My vote is not for sale. I hope and trust that no vote in this distinguished chamber is for sale. It is my belief that the charter should be granted, although it is a temptation to vote against it simply to teach the railroad interests that such tactics are of no avail. To that temptation, however, I shall not succumb. A railroad is needed in the area of the proposed line, and my vote will not prevent its being constructed even though corporation hirelings break the law by offering bribe money."

Senator Neal had removed his cigar; he sat watching Rolfe. Newspaper reporters were whispering; the president of the senate wore a sickly smile. Members kept urging the senator from Fox County to yield.

"There is no reason for me to yield," Rolfe said. "This is my first speech of the session, and in this body where full and open debate is permitted, I intend to express myself fully. There will be ample time for rebuttal."

"The senate will be in order," said the president, using his gavel. "The gentleman from Fox County has the floor. Other members will resume their seats."

"Mr. President," Rolfe said, "I had hoped that the days of 1856—of the LaCrosse & Milwaukee Railroad scandal—had passed into bad memory. You will, I am sure, recall the details of that gigantic bribery. In case you do not, let me remind you. In the legislature of 1856—"

And Rolfe sketched out that shame of nearly thirty years before, when the governor, the lieutenant governor and most members of the legislature, according to sworn testimony, had been bribed with railroad bonds in return for land grants.

"As I say, I had hoped those days were gone. Patently, they are not. The people of this state, wishing for modern transportation, did everything in their power to foster our early railroads. A favorable tax system was devised, thousands of acres of the best timber were given the fledgling carriers, they were permitted to fix their own rates. Naturally, they prospered and waxed fat. They became powerful. And today, Mr. President, the people find they have hatched out a brood of dragons. Arrogant with great wealth, drunk with mastery, fat with privilege, the railroads of Wisconsin are serpents coiled around our windpipes. Business must pay them the tribute of banditry, farmers must ship at preposterous rates or see their crops rot in the field. Leagued with the lumbering interests, the railroads have plundered our forest wealth. And where is the Beowulf to scotch this serpent, where is the St. George to slay this dragon?"

At the press table reporters were writing furiously; sometimes one of them hurried out, presumably to the telephone. Word of Senator Torkelsen's speech must have traveled along the corridors, for the gallery was filling. The president of the senate sat glaring at his desk; members who owed their seats to lumbermen and railroads were red-eared; the half-breeds were smiling broadly.

And now that his vocal chords had warmed, Rolfe found himself casting all prudence behind him, and he launched an attack on the business methods of James L. Buckmaster. He did not mention Jim Buckmaster by name, but everybody knew. He told how a powerful railroad magnate had clubbed rivals to their knees and robbed them; he told of the unneeded miles of track laid only to get land grants; he emptied his mind of its vexations with Jim, its contempt of Jim. At such heresy the conservatives looked flabbergasted beyond protest; they slumped in their chairs. Outside the snow kept falling, the light was dull, and Rolfe talked on, piling fact upon fact, committing political suicide in what amounted, almost, to a public confession, for he had been Jim Buckmaster's attorney once. He spoke easily, standing there at his desk, sometimes making a grim joke; his hair was rumpled, his tie awry, his coat wrinkled; more than ever he looked like a Danish sailing master who had known rough weather in his time.

"And what is the solution, Mr. President? How are the people of this once free state to regain their birthright? How are we to draw the fangs of this dragon called railroads? How are we to use this power in the public interest?

"The solution is there for all to behold. The state is sovereign and supreme. The state granted charters to the railroads to operate within its borders. The state financed their construction. They are a business, to be sure, but a particular sort of business. Quasi-public in nature, they could never have laid a mile of track without permission. The people permitted their inception, they operate under franchise from the people, and the people have the right to control their excesses.

"In 1874, this legislature passed what was known as the Potter Law. It was feeble, but it was a start. As you know, Mr. President, the carriers cried out in anguish at this law, and secured its repeal. Now the time has come to pass another such law, only stronger. A railroad commission should be established, its members appointed without regard to politics, and this commission should have the right to fix rates. Rebates should be prohibited. Rate discrimination should be abolished under severe penalties. And the entire system of railroad taxation should be overhauled. Railroads should be assessed taxes on the actual value of their property, like other businesses and like private citizens. Till the lower house of this legislature and till the senate are prepared to take those steps, we shall have the dragon in our midst. His scaly tail will thresh and blight our fair land. His fiery nostrils will annihilate all who oppose or censure him. His fangs will leave their mark on the throats of businessman and farmer. The trail of the serpent will scar our state, even unto the day of our children's children. It is for us in this generation—in this session of the legislature—to face up to that challenge a great Wisconsin jurist issued years ago: 'Which shall rule—wealth or man; which shall lead—money or intellect; who shall fill the public stations—educated and patriotic free men, or the feudal serfs of corporate capital?' "

Rolfe sat down; the hubbub defied the president's gavel; and Senator Preston Neal came beaming with outstretched hand.

*

And so he became famous, in Wisconsin, between 11:00 A.M. and 5:00 P.M. on a snowy day. In cities large and small newspapers published extras, for the simple truth is always sensational; he had scarcely stopped speaking before Jim Buckmaster's *Evening Star* was being hawked on the streets of the capital. Telegraph wires hummed; even in Chicago and Detroit the press devoted space to what editors called the stormy petrel of Wisconsin politics; reporters searched for Vern Craddock, who could not be found, and interviewed Mr. Francis O'Fallon, who would have a lot to account for next time he attended confession. And other reporters hung on Senator Torkelsen's words and coattails during the rest of that day, acting on the old journalistic theory that a volcano which erupts once is likely to erupt again.

Senator, they asked, who was the railroad magnate you referred to? Was it James L. Buckmaster, Senator? Didn't Mr. Buckmaster support you, Senator? Why have you broken with him? Will you introduce a bill for a railroad commission, Senator? Has anybody else tried to bribe you?

"No comment," Rolfe said. "No comment. Sorry, boys, no comment."

What are your plans, Senator? People are saying you intend to run for governor—is that true, Senator? Have you made a deal with the Grangers?

No comment. No comment, boys. Sorry.

Biographical sketches of Senator Torkelsen appeared in the afternoon

976

papers, read by persons going home on horsecars, by cashiers in restaurants, by drummers in hotel lobbies, by shut-ins, by locomotive engineers at railroad lunch counters, by everybody.

He was, of course, the darling of the half-breeds, welcomed into their group with the joy and bonhomie always shown to any convert. He lunched with Senator Preston Neal and a half-dozen others; he was invited to a powwow that evening at the Madison Oyster House.

"There was but one subject of conversation here at the capital today," wrote a political commentator for a Milwaukee paper, "and that was the amazing speech of Senator Rolfe Torkelsen. Compared with it, a thunderbolt from fair skies would have been unremarkable. Nothing in Senator Torkelsen's career had prepared the capital for his outburst. He is a Republican of long standing. For several years he served as his party's chairman in Fox County. He has been a regular of the regulars. A well-known attorney in the river counties, he has been untainted with Grangerism and for many years he devoted much of his time to the legal interests of James L. Buckmaster. As a senator serving his first term, he was considered safe in the conservative fold.

"In view of his background of party regularity, Republican leaders at the capital are especially outraged by his address. They feel betrayed. One party chieftain, who wishes to remain nameless, has issued to this writer the following statement: 'Torkelsen's charges are so patently fabrications that they need not be answered. And his proposal for a railroad commission is absolutely unworkable, the vaporings of a daydreamer. Some years ago Wisconsin tried a railroad commission with disastrous results. Business cannot prosper if shackled with governmental controls. If business does not prosper, workers lose their jobs. Torkelsen's crackbrained scheme would throw thousands of men out of work.'

"This leader went on to charge that Senator Torkelsen has been bitten by political ambition. 'Instead of being content to rise slowly but surely like other men,' the speaker said, 'Torkelsen has chosen to ignore the state leaders of his party and to make a demagogic appeal to irresponsible elements among the electorate. It is plain he is aiming for the governorship. He has degraded his office and the senate chamber by using them as a sounding board in this opening speech of his campaign. But the voters are wise. They will not be duped by such tactics. Wild accusations against honest men and upright corporations, insane proposals to put business in chains—these the voters will reject, along with the man who made them.'

"This statement gives but an inkling of the resentment of Republican leaders. They feel that by implication Senator Torkelsen has charged them with accepting bribes. Many assemblymen and senators of both parties who had honestly decided to vote for the bridge charter now hesitate to do so, lest their constituents suspect them of accepting under-the-table money.

"Only the insurgents—the so-called half-breeds—rejoice. By his speech, Senator Torkelsen has unquestionably become one of the most prominent insurgents in Wisconsin. If he has his eyes on the gubernatorial mansion—and most observers feel he has—he will be a formidable candidate, either as a Republican or an Independent. He was born in Denmark, and this will count heavily in such Danish settlements as Racine. He has resided in Fox County for more than thirty years, and was elected last autumn by the largest vote ever given a candidate for state senator in his county. He is well-thought-of in his own profession, having served as president of the state bar association. And last but not least, he is prominent in G.A.R. circles. As a private in the ill-fated Eighteenth Wisconsin Infantry, he fought at Shiloh, and after being captured there he endured more than two years in Southern prisons. He lost his leg in the war. We have not heard the last of Senator Torkelsen."

Rolfe had not seen that comment when he went to the Madison Oyster House for supper with the half-breeds; not till the morning papers would the guns of conservatism blast him; everything was shining that night, the way the world looks to a bridegroom. The restaurant was crowded with his kind of people—men who loved America more than they loved their bank accounts or any corporate power; men who wanted the great American experiment in self-government to operate successfully; men too proud to accept bribes; men who had seen crippled workers abandoned by their employers, who had heard the rifles of state militia firing on strikers, who had seen the homeless children in Chicago and New York, barefoot in January, men who hated police brutality and money brutality, men who had watched the forests stolen and butchered, men who realized, if only dimly as yet, that with the industrial revolution new strange forces had been let loose, forces so greedy and cyclonic that they could be controlled only by government.

"Bob," said Senator Preston Neal, "I want you to meet Senator Torkelsen. Senator, this is Bob La Follette, the best district attorney Dane County has ever had."

And Rolfe was shaking hands with a hard-jawed young man who congratulated him on a great speech.

"It was hardly that," Rolfe said, "but it told the truth."

"And isn't the truth always great?"

He was introduced to a bearded man with a New England accent, John Bascom, president of the University of Wisconsin.

"What I liked about your speech," said President Bascom, "was its point of view. The fact, indeed, that it had a point of view. An ethical point of view. Expediency is the curse of American politics. It's refreshing to find a man who speaks from an ethical base and lets the next election take care of itself."

Most of those present were politicians, but such politicians as Rolfe had never sat with before. The usual hog faces were absent, and the hog bellies, and the hog necks slopping over collars; these were lean men with rapier minds. They were not timid of ideas. And because they loved America, they did not hesitate to criticize her; it was assumed that only fools love blindly.

Snow was still falling when the gathering broke up and Rolfe dragged his bad leg back toward the Park Hotel. His brain was on fire; not for years had he felt so stimulated. Everything seemed possible that night: a progressive movement gathering strength; all the rottenness cleaned from the statehouse and from county courthouses; intellect and ethics in high places. What was it Bob La Follette had said, back at the restaurant? "We must stop the encroachment of the powerful few upon the rights of the many."

Outside the hotel he paused and drew the cold air into his lungs. It felt clean and he felt clean; he had made a speech and cleansed himself. Then he entered the hotel. And in the lobby he found James L. Buckmaster.

*

He looked older than Rolfe had ever seen him, sitting there chewing a cigar, his hat shoved back, his overcoat across his knees, his profile bitter in the thin gaslight. The evening paper was in his fist. At that hour the lobby was nearly deserted, and he looked peculiarly alone. When he saw Rolfe he dropped his cigar into a spittoon and stood up, a big man, unsmiling.

"Hello, Swede."

"Hello, Jim."

"Is it still snowing?"

"Yes."

"God damned weather. Gives a man a headache. I'd have been here sooner, but Number 389 bucked snow all the way from New Empire. I want to talk to you."

"All right," Rolfe said.

"I've been waiting an hour. Where've you been?"

"At supper."

"Took you long enough. Let's go to your room."

They climbed carpeted stairs and made their way along a corridor where gas jets wavered and threw big shadows. Inside his room Rolfe turned up the lights; Jim tossed his overcoat to the bed.

"Have a cigar?"

"No thanks."

Jim bit the end from his and struck a match, eyes gray and truculent.

"Got anything to drink?" he asked.

"Bourbon."

"Let's have some."

Rolfe brought a bottle, tumblers. a carafe of water. Jim poured a glass half-full of whiskey, emptied in some powders, drank it down, poured more.

"Damned headache," he said. "They keep coming oftener. I've paid a fortune to doctors. Sons of bitches are all quacks. I've never kicked about their bills. Just cure these damned headaches, I've told them. I don't care what it costs. But none of them know a peavey from a cross-cut saw. Caleb must have busted something when he hit me. It's no wonder either. Bastard wore knucks."

"Here's to your health," Rolfe said.

Jim nearly smiled then.

"Thanks, Swede. I'll drink to that."

He sat in a deep chair, watching the ash on his cigar.

"You know why I'm here," he said.

"Yes."

"You might have picked better weather, Swede, to have diarrhea of the tongue. I'd have been here sooner. Snow's heavier up toward New Empire. Had to use a plow in front of Number 389. I didn't like that speech, Swede."

"I didn't expect you to."

"Craddock wired me about it. Said you'd gone crazy. I got here as soon as I could. When I read it in the paper I couldn't believe it. Did the boys get it right? Is that what you said?"

"It's a stenographic report," Rolfe said. "Yes, they got it right."

"Jesus! Well, a man's tongue can get him into a lot of trouble. You say something and it's said. Never can pull it back. Put it on paper and you can tear it up. You can't do that when you say it . . . Swede, I've always thought a lot of you."

"And I've thought a lot of you," Rolfe said.

"Damn it, Swede, you've always been in my camp. You've been one of my crew. I could trust you. One of the three or four people I've known that I could trust. Sol Klauber and Molly and a girl I used to know named Bonnie—and you. That about says it. And they trust you back in New Empire too, Swede. People think a lot of you."

"I'm glad to hear that."

"You've got influence, Swede. They know you're honest. If you take a case they know you won't shyster out on them. And a jury knows if you're handling a case you think your client's right. It's kind of like it used to be with Judge Gentry. They trusted him and they trust you. That's a good reputation for a man to have."

"Yes," Rolfe said, "it is."

"Hell, Swede, those Danes in Einar Township would give you their last cow. It's like money in the bank, the way they like you. And people think a lot of Sue too. At first they didn't. All that talk about votes for women—they thought she was a strange one. But they like her now. They know she speaks her mind, just like you, but she's no damned gossip. They like you both. I'd say you're about the leading family in New Empire."

Jim poured more whiskey.

"But Swede," he said, "that speech of yours was a mistake. You got off on the wrong foot in that one. You never should have told how Craddock and O'Fallon offered you the sugar."

"Why not?"

"Politics ain't a Sunday School, Swede. You know that. It's got its good side and its bad side, like everything, but it's no Sunday School. But that's no reason for taking to the pulpit like some goddamned preacher and start throwing mud. If a man goes into a game he accepts the rules. He takes it as he finds it and beats the other boys at their own play. Hell, I've gone into poker games I've known was crooked. I've flashed a roll and acted like the biggest sucker you've ever seen. Same with craps where the dice are switched. They'll always let you win a time or two, as a come-on. So I've taken their money and dusted out. Said I had a sick friend I had to see. Get what I mean, Swede? If a man sells you a dozen rotten eggs you don't have to bust them over his head. Instead, dress like a farmer and sell them back to him. Use your head, boy. If a game's crooked you don't have to make a god-damned speech about it. All you need to do is learn the marked cards and clean the house. You've ruined Craddock's usefulness here in Madison for this session. Every damned politician in town will be scared to be seen with him. I'll have to send him to Illinois or Des Moines. And Francis O'Fallon. He's an all-right mick, he was just going along doing what he thought had to be done. So you make a speech about him. God, you've embarrassed him, Swede. You don't have to make a speech about it, every time you catch some kid jacking off in the barn. Things like that ain't done. Have a cigar?"

"No, thanks."

Jim threw his half-smoked one away, bit the end from another. And he emptied more powder into his glass.

"Damndest thing how these headaches hang on," he said. "Just like a beaver biting my skull. And all the doctors can do is give me a pain-killer. Old Caleb must be sitting in hell laughing. Gave me a headache and a wife I didn't want. She's getting worse too. Has to wear diapers just like a baby."

He tossed down the whiskey and the medicine, refilled his glass.

"Now about this speech, Swede. All that crap about a railroad com-mission. Jesus God! And about a new tax system. You really poked us where it hurt then. I've had wires from every railroad in the Middle West. They blame me, Swede. They know you're my sawlog, and they blame me for letting you get out of the boom."

"What makes you think I'm your sawlog?"

"Well, aren't you?"

"No," Rolfe said, "I'm not anybody's sawlog."

"Let's put it another way, Swede. We've been pals for thirty years. I've thrown you a lot of business and paid you a lot of fees, and I've helped you bust a jam or two. All I've asked in return is loyalty. If a man can't give me loyalty, he can't give me nothing. If he's not loyal, he's no damned good. If he's not in my camp, he's out of it, and if he's out of it he's my enemy. That's how I've always figured it, and it's worked pretty well. If he's in my camp, if he backs me to the hilt, why, hell, then I'll back him. Take Park Irwin's seat in congress, Swede. You can have it, if you'd like. I'll send you to Washington next term, if you want to go. But I won't let Park Irwin down. I'll get the bastard appointed ambassador somewhere. And he's not even been loyal to me, always. Years ago he even screwed my wife. Not that I cared, but he didn't know that. If I'd loved her, I'd have operated on him with a jackknife. A dull one. His crowing would have been high-pitched, after that. But he's been a pretty good congressman, he's done what I told him, and I won't let him down. I'll send him as ambassador to Arabia. With all those horses they've got, they won't notice one more horse's ass. And I'll send you to Washington. How about it?"

Rolfe was smiling, but he shook his head.

"Well then, goddamn it, Swede, if you don't want to go to congress, what do you want?"

"I'd like to be a judge, some day."

"Hell's bells, why didn't you say so? All right, it's a deal. You'll be on the bench within thirty days. We'll kick some fat ass upstairs and get the governor to appoint you. Nothing to it. You'll have to make another speech first, of course, withdrawing your remarks. You're good at shooting off your mouth, that won't give you any trouble. Just say you guess you misunderstood Craddock and O'Fallon, and that after further study you've decided you were wrong about a railroad commission. Run in some patriotic stuff about how the railroads have opened up a great state to commerce and industry, you know, the usual crap. And I'll make you a judge. A few years on the bench and you might want to go to congress. Or the White House. That's a nice little place for a man to live. How about it?"

"No thank you."

"What do you mean? You just said you'd like to be a judge."

"Not on those terms," Rolfe said.

Exasperation showed in Jim's eyes.

"Damn it, Swede, you're a hard bargainer. Well, all right, here's what I'll do. I'll hoist you up to the bench, and I'll give you a thousand shares in the New Empire Line. And another thousand in the Buckmaster Lumber Company. Like that better?"

"No."

Jim sat chewing his cigar, eyes slitted and granite-colored.

"I have enough money," Rolfe added.

"What kind of talk is that, Swede? A man never has enough money."

"I'm not interested," Rolfe said. "Offer me the whole New Empire Line. Offer me all your timber and all your mills and all your steamboats. I still wouldn't retract a word of that speech."

"Well I'll be damned. You mean it, don't you?"

"Yes."

Jim sat staring, his mouth ugly. Then he jumped up and paced.

"I didn't want to get tough about it, Swede. You're forcing me to it, just remember that. Hell, who do you think you are? God damn it, I'm the biggest man on the river. I'm the biggest man in this state. Do you think you can stand up against me?"

"I can try."

"I'll bust you, Swede, if you won't listen to reason. I've got the newspapers and I can do it. I'll knock you down and stomp you, with my newspapers. I'll kick you in the teeth and I'll kick you in the nuts. You'll be sneaking down alleys picking up rags, before I'm through. Nobody will give you a vote for whorehouse janitor, by the time I'm finished."

"That suits me," Rolfe said. "Go ahead. Try to bust me."

Jim's fists clenched; his jaw was sticking out; in his temple a vein was beating.

"By God, I'll do it. I will do it. I'll turn the dogs loose. I'll sic my editors onto you. There won't be anything left, after that. They'll gnaw your bones."

He flung his cigar savagely into the spittoon, jammed on his hat, grabbed up his overcoat. But after jerking open the door, he turned back.

"Sorry I got mad, Swede. We shouldn't fight like this. Hell, we're old friends."

"I'm not fighting," Rolfe said.

"That's the checker, boy. No need to fight. Let's have another drink." He poured whiskey into both glasses. "Damn it, boy, you got under my skin. That speech. You never should have done it. It was a knife between my shoulders, boy. You were in my camp and you knifed me. But hell, I can be big. I can overlook it. You didn't mean it, I know that. Something you ate for breakfast likely. We need each other, boy. With me behind you, you'll go to the top. Nothing you can't have. I don't want to break with you. And I'll bet you don't want to break with me, when it comes right down to it. Do you?"

"No, of course not."

"There you are," Jim said, smiling. "Damned fool way for old friends to act, fighting like a couple of bobcats. Why don't you do what I said? Make another speech. You're good at stringing words together. Get you on a platform and you can make a man believe black is white. You don't need to take back what you said about Craddock and O'Fallon. Hell with them. Or what you said about me. But that stuff about a railroad commission, Swede, that's dangerous. It starts people to thinking. That was a low punch, boy. Just say you've thought it over and decided you were wrong. Won't you do that?"

"No, Jim," Rolfe said, "I won't. I meant what I said and it will have to stand."

For a long moment Jim stood there, not looking angry so much as bewildered and melancholy. He heaved a breath.

"All right, Swede. You've had your chance. God, boy, I feel sorry for you. You don't know what you're in for. You can expect the business, Swede. Get me started and I'm a hard fighter. Always was. Where I grew up you fought for keeps. Well, I'd best get over to the paper."

Coat over his arm, hat pulled down, he went to the door.

"No chance you'll change your mind?" he asked.

Rolfe shook his head.

"I can't figure you, Swede," Jim said. "Never could, very well. Like that time you wanted to fight me about Bobcat Pete. Crazy kid. Me and you are different, that's all. You won't like me much, by the time my papers are through with you. But remember I gave you your chance. Just remember that, Swede."

Then he left.

*

Next morning the desk clerk handed Rolfe a telegram. It was signed Sue. "So very proud of you," it said. "Happy birthday and much love."

He looked at the calendar: it was Thursday February 8. In the rush of events he had forgotten about his birthday; he was forty-seven. He felt about ninety-seven.

After the snow the morning was bright and freezing; on the way to the statehouse he felt like a man waiting for an avalanche to destroy him. In the corridor he encountered Senator Neal.

"Torkelsen," he said, "I heard Jim Buckmaster came to town last night. Did you see him?"

"Yes."

"I hope you held firm."

"I didn't budge."

Senator Neal smiled.

"I didn't think you would. Some of our crowd were worried, when they heard Buckmaster had come, but I can pick a man with iron in his spine. Well, you'll need it. He'll attack you."

"He promised to."

"He's got the press," Senator Neal said, "he and his bunch. It's not easy to stand up and let them shoot at you. I know. I've been through

984

it. He wanted you to withdraw your speech, I suppose."

Rolfe nodded.

"And made you all kinds of promises?"

"Nothing but the world on a string," Rolfe said.

Senator Neal smiled.

"Don't I know. Sometimes a man's tempted. Politics would be a picnic, if a man would go along with the timber crowd and the railroad crowd. I could be in congress today. Sometimes a man's tempted."

"I wasn't tempted," Rolfe said.

Senator Neal patted his shoulder, the way a father pats a son of whom he's proud.

"Politics is mainly crow-stew and choke cherries," he said, "if you buck the money crowd. Sometimes I wonder why I keep running. But then a young fellow like you comes along, and it's worth all the ashes in your mouth. Ever read Plato?"

"Sometimes."

"He said it better than I can: 'Those having torches will pass them on to others.' I'm getting old. I may not live to see it, but we'll take over the state, some day. We'll clean out the muck and put the house in order. There'll be a railroad commission, some day. I may be in my grave, but you'll live to see it. You and young fellows like Bob La Follette. And you'll pass on the torch . . . By the way, you'd better plan to eat supper with us again tonight. You may need cheering up, after you see the papers."

And Senator Neal was quite correct; the papers from Milwaukee and Oshkosh and even Chicago fired the opening salvos in what would be a long bitter war. Worst of all was Jim Buckmaster's *Madison Star*. The cartoon on page one pictured Senator Torkelsen as a snake accusing upright-looking gentlemen of being dragons. The leading editorial was one long piece of scurrility. It said, among other things, that Senator Torkelsen had been posing as a war hero when actually he ran away at Shiloh, surrendered as soon as he could, spent the war in safety and comfort well behind the lines, and was shot by a Union provost guard when he refused to stop looting the home of a Northern sympathizer in Georgia. A news story quoted Francis O'Fallon as saying that Senator Torkelsen had approached him asking a thousand dollars in return for his vote; Mr. O'Fallon indignantly refused; whereupon Senator Torkelsen, cloaked with senatorial immunity, had his revenge by charging that Mr. O'Fallon had tried to bribe him.

"American business," Senator Neal said, "does not easily forget, and it never forgives."

*

The attacks continued. Whenever a half-breed made a speech or voted against big money, the press contrived to drag in Senator Torkelsen's name. Senator Torkelsen and his gang of outlaws; Senator Torkelsen and his bunch of wild jackasses: those were favorite gibes. In the headlines he became "Tork." The *Star* cartoonist wallowed in derision; by early March, Rolfe had been pictured as a schoolboy in a duncecap, as a spider, a skunk, a donkey, a bull, a wolf and, of course, a snake.

"One of our favorite American myths," said Senator Neal, at the Madison Oyster House, "is that the press is free. There's just enough truth in the myth to keep it alive. Our press is free of governmental control. But it's not free of money control. Try telling the truth in a paper and see what happens. I know from my experience with that little sheet of mine. Your advertising evaporates, that's what happens. I make out because I'm small and my advertisers are small merchants depending on the farmers. But a paper with big overhead either gets big advertising or it dies. It's dependent on business, and business knows that if the public learned the truth about its shenanigans, liberalism would sweep the country. So the press is a wet nurse, feeding pap and lies. If somebody makes a speech telling the truth, the press attacks him. Him. Not his ideas alone: it tears into him. *Ad hominem* reasoning. The average voter is not a reasoning animal. He's an emotional animal. Bad reasoning impresses him as much as good. Sometimes more. That is not to say he's a fool: he's only without experience in reasoning. If he acts like a fool at the polls, it's because he's accepted the bad reasoning of editorial writers, and because his information has been half true or false. He knows the world is round because he has been given that information. The press—that is to say, business—has no objection to his knowing that. But if suddenly it would help business to have him believe the world is flat, the press would convince him of that. Any teacher or map maker who said otherwise would be attacked as an anarchist and seducer of virgins. Any half-wit who said the world is flat would be praised as a fount of wisdom. Man is a conventional animal—he must be, being gregarious—and he wants to think like everybody else. Before long he would believe the world flat simply because everybody else believed it. If a world traveler made a speech to the contrary, the press would charge that he once kicked his mother downstairs. And that would settle the matter for the average man."

"You're a cynic," somebody said.

"*Ad hominem* reasoning. My ideas startle you. They are not as your ideas. Therefore, they are wrong. If they are wrong, they must be born of a cynical mind."

"Are you saying," somebody else asked, "that all newspaper men have sold out?"

"Not consciously. But experience has taught them that a certain sort of news story goes into type and another sort into the wastebasket. A man who writes for the wastebasket is not kept on the payroll. So after a while reporters and editors acquire what is almost an instinct in such matters. And they keep repeating that the press is free. They must believe that. If they saw themselves as they are—as the pimps of big money—they'd take to drink. Some, of course, do. Those who don't are exceedingly touchy on the point of a free press. It's their Achilles' heel."

"Are there no honest papers, then?"

Senator Neal smiled.

"I recommend to your attention the *Franklin County Independent.* But let us say a story came to my desk praising James L. Buckmaster. He must have good qualities. Everybody has. Perhaps he was good to his mother. Maybe he has sent coal to poor families. All right, hand me such a story. It would go into the wastebasket. Does that answer your question?"

Everybody laughed.

Rolfe's bill for a railroad commission never reached the senate floor; it was smothered in committee. And a bill introduced by a half-breed in the assembly, providing for revision of railroad taxation, likewise went to committee and died the death. In the last hours of the legislature, however, the bill granting a bridge charter to the Milwaukee & Lake Superior Railroad was passed *viva voce.*

*

When Rolfe returned to New Empire in March, he expected to find his constituents hostile. But nothing of the kind. Among those who knew him, the attacks in the press had little effect, or an effect quite opposite to that intended. He had been lampooned as a dunce, but those who had heard him speak on Memorial Day or in court realized he was anything but that. His comrades in the G.A.R. were outraged at the slurs on his war service; some of them had also been in Southern prisons. The Danes of Fox County remained loyal; and railroad workers loved him for the enemy he had made. Most persons discounted the editorials and were only amused at the cartoons; indeed, they were proud that their freshman senator had stirred up so much notice in Madison.

Senator, he was told, in barber shops and on the street, you sure poked up the animals. Gave the rest of the state something to think about. Let 'em know we're alive, here in New Empire. Let 'em know Jim Buckmaster ain't the only big fish in the river. I hear he's pretty mad at you. Well, he's like that, if he can't run things he don't like it a little. Thinks he's so big in the britches he can tell us how to vote. Well, he's got another think coming.

One of Rolfe's first moves was to transfer his account from the Bank of New Empire to the First National Bank. That pleased its president, George Appleton, who was still chairman of the Republican Central Committee.

"Senator," he said, "your speech was a smart political move. I'll admit it startled me at first, but I believe it will work out for the best. You've picked up a lot of Granger support, and farm support in general. Some of the businessmen on Winnebago Street were calling you a radical, after that speech, but I calmed them down. 'Torkelsen knows what he's doing,' I told them. 'He's sound on the goose. He's no more a radical than I am.' And—um-umm—you aren't, are you?"

"Only as radical as the founders of the Republic," Rolfe said.

"That's just what I told them, Senator. Exactly. 'Torkelsen's sound on the goose,' I said. 'As conservative as a four percent bond.' They all oppose a railroad commission, of course. I do myself. It was something of a shock when you introduced that bill."

"Why do you oppose it?"

"It's a half-breed measure. Anything those outlaws are for I'm against."

"Are you against a fair—not an exorbitant but a fair—profit for railroads?"

"Certainly not. I'm for a fair profit for everybody."

"Are you against farmers shipping at reasonable rates so they can make a reasonable living?"

"You know I'm for the farmer. Our business depends on the farmer."

"Are you against the merchant receiving goods at a freight rate which will enable him to lower prices and still make a fair profit?"

"Of course not, Senator."

"Then you're for a railroad commission, whether you know it or not."

"I never thought of it like that, Senator. No, sir, I never—"

And thus Rolfe began the political education of Fox County. And of Wisconsin, so far as that went, for during the next months he was always responding to invitations to speak all over the state at such things as banquets and farm fairs. As a political notoriety, he could draw a crowd. And he kept pounding away at railroad banditry and forest freebooting. The newspapers crucified him, but he rose from the dead. The *New Empire Chronicle* was especially nasty. Office holding, it charged, had gone to his head; ambition had pilfered his reason; he wanted to be governor. Every brickbat hurt, but he kept speaking. Sometimes Sue accompanied him on those trips; his cause was her cause.

And did he want to be governor? He wasn't sure; he refused to look that far ahead. He knew only that he wanted to be re-elected state senator so he could wage effective battle for enlightened government in Wisconsin. He wanted to save the forests, what was left of them, and to put a bit into the mouth of the iron horse. He wanted what Senator Neal wanted, what District Attorney La Follette wanted, what awakening liberalism all over America wanted.

Seldom did he see James L. Buckmaster any more, and then only at a distance on the street. Jim never dropped in at the Torkelsens'; those days were gone. Now and again, however, busybodies brought Rolfe news of some remark Jim had made about him; he was very bitter.

"You crossed him, Senator. He'll give you trouble for that. He'll get you, one way or another. He thinks he's God any more. Anybody who crosses him regrets it."

"I may be the exception," Rolfe said.

Those were times of ferment on the national scene too, while big money consolidated its loot from the Civil War and went prowling for more. Men like Jim Buckmaster bought up little companies in basic industries and merged them with other companies; corporations were formed from these moneybag marriages, and corporations were adjudged persons—bloodless, heartless, brainless persons with all the rights of citizens but none of the responsibilities; and the corporations were amalgamated into bigger corporations called trusts. The press applauded. It was progress. America was the land of bigness. And because the Republican Party had been in power during the war, and hence was popular in the North, it was seized and used by big money. The fat cats waxed fatter. Yet more and more persons—clerks with detachable cuffs, mechanics with wrenches, farmers, ordinary people in ordinary towns like New Empire—grew uneasy: times were changing, America was changing. The Granger movement would not die. Populism was just over the horizon. Farmers burned corn in their stoves because it did not pay to ship it to hungry cities, with the high railroad rates. And in 1884, when the Democrats nominated a beefy man named Grover Cleveland, the Republicans grew worried; he might win. It would be necessary for the party to nominate the strongest local candidates to help the national ticket.

In New Empire, the convention of Fox County Republicans nominated Senator Rolfe Torkelsen to succeed himself. Not by acclamation, however, for James L. Buckmaster had worked deviously to pick up delegates for another man. But Senator Torkelsen won on the first ballot, and it was thought he would lead the ticket and swing the county for James G. Blaine, the same Senator Blaine who years before had picked up a little quick cash on a deal in bonds of the Fort Smith & Little Rock Railroad: he was called the plumed knight of Maine. Fox County did not favor Senator Blaine; there was too much Granger sentiment there. As practical politicians, however, the convention realized that often at the polls persons fearing to cross party lines lest they ruin their ballots would vote a straight ticket in order to elect, say, Rolfe Torkelsen. So in the county Republican councils it was decided to spend money and concentrate attention on Senator Torkelsen. If they ignored the national head of the ticket, perhaps he would go away from voters' minds.

The Democrats of Fox County nominated Darrell Pfister to run again against Rolfe Torkelsen. They too were practical politicians. Nobody, they reasoned, had a rat's chance against Senator Torkelsen anyway, so they might as well honor that squeaky rat Pfister, for after all he had drudged along for the party: in such matters there is honor among politicians as among thieves.

The local campaign got off to a slow start that year, for during the dog days voters are always more interested in getting drowned on Sunday and drinking cold beer than in choosing their rulers. The Republicans established headquarters in a vacant store on the north side of Winnebago Street, a half block west of Rolfe's office; they hung out red, white and blue banners and filled the windows with campaign posters, but not much happened. In September, however, with the first frosts, interest perked up, for a front-page story in the *New Empire Chronicle* carried an interview with James L. Buckmaster who declared for Darrell Pfister.

"I have talked at length with Mr. Pfister," said Mr. Buckmaster, "and have found him a man of sterling character and sound ideas."

Then he blasted Senator Rolfe Torkelsen.

Said County Chairman Appleton: "The best thing that could have happened, Senator. Buckmaster may be the biggest man on the river, but people hate him."

Said Sue Torkelsen: "Pfister! If Jim Buckmaster ordered him to climb a pole like a monkey he'd do it."

Said Margaret Fuller Torkelsen, aged ten: "Why did Uncle Jim get mad at Daddy?"

Said Susan (Kitten) Torkelsen, aged eight: "Daddy will win, won't he?"

Said Congressman Park Irwin, in a statement issued to the *Chronicle:* "As a Republican since the inception of the party, and as your representative for more than a quarter of a century, the last thing I would ordinarily do is to urge the voters of Fox County to send a Democrat to the state senate. However, after talking with Mr. Darrell Pfister, and finding him a young man of unimpeachable character, profound mind, and upright religious beliefs, I truly believe he is a better man than his opponent."

Said the Rev. Clarence Duane Sonnabend, Methodist pastor, to whose church, in July, Mr. Buckmaster had contributed a pipe organ: "I am grateful for this opportunity extended to me by the *Chronicle* to endorse the candidacy of Darrell Pfister. As a member of my flock for many years, Mr. Pfister is known to me as a young man of Christian upbringing and Christian practice. In this age of heresy masking under the guise of 'reason,' it is wonderful to be able to cast a vote for a real red-blooded Christian. Mr. Pfister's wife, Gwynne, has long been active in our Ladies' Aid, and his son, Erwin, has the enviable record of being neither absent nor tardy at Sunday School for three years, except last winter when he was stricken with the mumps. A vote for Mr. Pfister is a vote for God. If Christ were among us today, He would vote for Mr. Pfister."

Said County Chairman Appleton: "Damn it to hell, they're bringing up religion. Senator, why don't you and your family start attending church? Just during the campaign. Will you do that?"

Said Senator Torkelsen: "No."

By mid-October it was quite apparent that Mr. Pfister was getting nowhere rapidly. Trouble was, he was a pinhead and looked it. His pimples reminded the voters of the seamy side of adolescence. His light squeaky voice was all wrong for the hustings. His smile was a smirk. His handshake was batrachian. The cakes his wife baked for church sociables always fell. His son, Erwin, although indeed a regular attendant at Sunday School, was a little sneak who had been apprehended, the previous spring, peeking through a knothole in the ladies' backhouse at the church.

"I think you'll make it," Chairman Appleton told Rolfe. "If Cleveland weren't heading the Democratic ticket, you'd be a shoo-in. Only thing I'm afraid of, folks who vote for Cleveland won't scratch for you. So keep plugging."

Rolfe kept plugging. By horse and buggy, often with Sue, he traveled into every township, during that season of red apples and morning mists from the river and golden leaves and golden afternoons. He crawled through fences and limped into fields where farmers were shucking corn; he entered dairy barns at lantern light and talked about a railroad commission while milk squirted into buckets; he shook hands with section workers eating from dinner pails; and in the Danish townships he spoke the language of his early childhood.

"I'm for Cleveland, myself," people told him. "First time I've ever voted for a Democrat since the war. But I'll scratch for you, Senator. I liked that speech you made."

And in the evenings—the frosty, smoky evenings of American politics—he addressed meetings at country schoolhouses, at Grange Halls, at G.A.R. posts. He went to the people, the little people unknown to fame, and talked of the land America had been once, that Republic of Jeffersonian dream and flintlock rifle and hound-dogs ambling in the shade of wagons lumbering west along the Wilderness Trail. He told of the power in the people when the people got their dander up and elected somebody like Andrew Jackson or A. Lincoln of Illinois. Standing there looking tired and rumpled-haired and older, he evoked that great dream America that had beckoned across the seas to the adventurous, the rebellious, the audacious. His words had the beat of fife-and-drum music; they had a sharpness like the crack of farmers' rifles at Concord; they took you to the gun stations on frigates in the War of 1812. People wanted to smile and to cry just at being Americans, when they listened to him.

And he told them about the Civil War, although most of them remembered that well enough already. He told of the boys who went to

991

the army, and of the boys who stayed behind; of the boys who pinned their names to their shirts before the charges at Cold Harbor, knowing they must die, and of the boys who hired substitutes; of the boys who sat it out in Southern prisons, and of the boys who sat in countinghouses, scheming ways to dip their fingers into the stream of cash flowing from the war government. He told of the fortunes founded on selling condemned rifles, on chartering rotten ships, on selling shoddy blankets; and he told how those fortunes had come between the people and their elected representatives till presently the representatives heard only the clink of coins and not the voices of their constituents. And he told of the vast amalgamations of money power, defrauding the people of their public lands, their forests, their lovely streams turned into factory drainage ditches, their franchises, their sites for valuable dams and bridges and wharves. He told of railroad rates that amounted to barefaced robbery, of railroad arrogance, of railroads that derived their right to run from the people and that looted the people, of taxes too low for corporate wealth and too high for individual poverty.

He was dreadfully in earnest, during those speeches; no longer did one part of his mind sit listening and smiling. He wanted to return to the senate—wanted that so badly it was an ache—and he wanted the people to understand what had been done to them.

And did they understand? Did they respond? Of course they did. He felt their understanding flowing up to those schoolhouse platforms, and his brain sang with the realization that the people, the little people with chapped hands and patched trousers, were not stupid. If they did not have knowledge, they had wisdom. They had sagacity.

He knew he was winning the campaign; victory was in the autumn air.

*

Election that year would be held on Tuesday November 4; on the afternoon of Thursday October 30 Rolfe left his office and walked toward Republican headquarters. It was a fine sunny day and he would remember it always: he was happy then. Pumpkins and apples were piled in grocery windows, and one merchant had even rigged up a display of a witch and broomstick, for tomorrow was Halloween. That reminded Rolfe of the party his daughters were giving tomorrow evening; for the past week they had been working on costumes and carving jack-o'-lanterns.

Across Winnebago Street, from Republican headquarters to a building opposite, a great banner stretched: Re-Elect Senator Rolfe Torkelsen. No mention was made of electing James G. Blaine president, for in Fox County the less said about Blaine the better. Rolfe was quite aware of the irony of his running on the same ticket with Blaine; it was, he supposed, a compromise; or was it? Not once had he asked the voters to support the national ticket. And the whole strategy of the half-breeds was to work within the established parties; to leaven them with new ideas; to put liberals into county chairmanships; to send liberals to county and state conventions; to remake the old parties into what by tradition they should be: political instruments of the people.

As he entered county headquarters, Rolfe expected to find the usual buzz and stir: volunteers stuffing literature into envelopes; bewhiskered satraps from outlying townships smoking cigars and discussing the situation; precinct chairmen laying plans for getting out the vote; the usual scattering of alcoholics with no influence asserting they had great influence in such-and-such a district and would deliver it if only the party would give them a few dollars expense money.

Instead of all that, he found headquarters oddly quiet: people sat absorbed in newspapers.

Then somebody looked up, hurriedly dropped his newspaper, attempted a smile.

"Oh, hello, Senator. Have you seen the *Chronicle?*"

Rolfe hadn't.

"Look at it, Senator. This will need answering."

When he saw the banner headline, Rolfe felt kicked in the stomach, and his lips went stiff with anger. His whole body flushed.

"Yes," he said, "yes. I'll want to study it. If I could take this with me—"

He folded the paper and tramped back to his office, moving along with his gaze on the sidewalk, not wanting to talk with anybody. He could feel the sweat on his forehead; he was trembling. Damn that Buckmaster, he was thinking, damn him, damn him. Furiously he pulled himself up the stairs of the Gentry Block and told his clerks he was not to be disturbed. In his office he spread out the paper on the desk. It said:

WRONGED WOMAN ACCUSES SENATOR TORKELSEN

———

"Father of My Child," Says Mrs. Nixie Auerbach

———

Heart-Rending Tale of Woe

———

"Seduced and Abandoned."

———

Fox County voters will be as stunned as we were, we believe, at the startling accusation made today by Mrs. Nixie Auerbach of Dubuque, Iowa, formerly of this city.

In a sworn statement before Notary Public Arthur Scott of New Empire, Mrs. Auerbach declares that State Senator Rolfe Torkelsen seduced her in his office when she worked there as janitress. Then, according to Mrs. Auerbach, when her need was greatest, Senator Torkelsen turned a calloused ear to the poor woman's pleas and left her to shift for herself.

As the Great Bard of Avon says, let those of you who have tears prepare to shed them now. Here is Mrs. Auerbach's affidavit *in toto*:

"My name is Mrs. Nixie Auerbach. I am the widow of Harold Auerbach who passed on to his Reward in 1867. Till my husband's death, I lived in New Empire, Wisconsin, but thereafter I moved to Dubuque, Iowa, where I found employment as a seamstress. I have returned to New Empire of my own free will to make this statement, because I do not believe the voters of Fox County should be represented in the senate of this great state by a man of the low moral character of Rolfe Torkelsen. If by my confession I can help replace Senator Torkelsen with a fine Christian gentleman like Mr. Darrell Pfister, I will feel I have done God's work. Although once a sinner, I am now a member of the United Brethren Church of Dubuque, where I attend two services on Sunday as well as Wednesday evening prayer meetings, weather permitting, because I am somewhat crippled up with rheumatism.

"In 1858 I was a happily-married woman, being the wife of Harold Auerbach, a sweet-natured man of German descent. Harold and I were the parents of three lovely little ones. Harold was employed in the New Empire yard of the Buckmaster Lumber Company. In the evenings, being of an ambitious nature and aspiring to become a butcher, Harold worked as janitor in the law office of Judge Sophronicus Gentry, a man whom older residents of New Empire may remember.

"But alas! One wintry morning while at work my husband slipped and fell, an accident which paralyzed him from the waist down. From then until his death he was bedridden. Our humble little family would have been in dire straits indeed, except for the generosity of Mr. James L. Buckmaster. Mr. Buckmaster, whom Harold often said was a saint in disguise, continued paying my husband's salary up to and including the day of his death, and since then he has paid me a small but helpful pension. God bless James L. Buckmaster, I say, as I have often said throughout the years.

"After Harold's accident, hoping to augment the family income, I persuaded Judge Gentry to let me continue Harold's work as janitor in the Gentry Block. This was a step I have often bitterly regretted, the devil was guiding me when I asked to become janitress, I am sure.

"Junior partner in Judge Gentry's firm was a young man calling himself Rolfe Torkelsen and laying claim to be of Danish descent, although I always doubted this. Scarcely had I begun my duties as janitress before Mr. Torkelsen launched out in a campaign to wean me away from the religious training of my girlhood. He scoffed at God and laughed at Our Saviour and Lord Jesus Christ.

"Horrified as I was at such blasphemy, I was no match in argument for Mr. Torkelsen, who with a pettifogger's cunning and a mind and tongue guided by the devil kept trying to rob me of my faith. I prayed nightly that he might see the Light, but none is so blind as he who will not see.

Moreover, I feared that if I argued too vehemently with Mr. Torkelsen, he would discharge me, for he had attached himself to Judge Gentry and exercised great influence over the old gentleman, who was not one to suspect a viper in his own legal household.

"After a short time, Mr. Torkelsen began a campaign of another kind to rob me of my other precious possession: my virtue. As I look back I am persuaded that the two campaigns were interlocked: that he hoped first to rob me of my faith, thus leaving me Godless and without the will to repel his advances.

"In the first campaign he did not succeed; I kept my faith. But in his second purpose, I regret to say, he triumphed brutally. In his private office I surrendered my virtue on the leather couch which clients of Mr. Torkelsen will remember. Little have they thought, probably, as they sat there, that on that very couch a poor young woman was brought to shame. In those days Mr. Torkelsen was a husky young man—he had not yet lost his leg in dubious circumstances during the war—and I was no match for him.

"Such wickedness always results in disaster, and in the autumn of 1859 I learned I was 'eating for two,' as the saying goes. I reported my condition to Mr. Torkelsen, who became very ugly, maintaining the child was doubtless my husband's. As anybody who remembers poor Mr. Auerbach's condition will testify, this would have been a physical impossibility. Delicacy restrains me from saying more. Mr. Torkelsen would do nothing for me. I was seduced and abandoned. Moreover, upon learning of my plight, he discharged me from my position as janitress.

"The scene which occurred when I confessed all to my husband is better imagined than dwelt upon. Harold, as I have said, had a sweet nature, except as he used to say when his Dutch was up.

"In June 1860 Mr. Torkelsen's daughter, Maybellene, was born. He never so much as came to see this pretty little baby. My friends and acquaintances, knowing Harold's condition, were somewhat surprised at my giving birth to a child, but a few little white lies, which I hope God will forgive me, convinced them that my husband was the child's father.

"After my husband's death, as I have said, I moved to Dubuque, where Maybellene passed away when she was thirteen, having contracted the summer complaint, a judgment of God if there ever was one.

"The years passed and I am now a broken old woman, poor as a church mouse. Meanwhile, the man who seduced me has prospered. Never once has he written me or sent me money. When Maybellene passed away he remained silent. Although a pretender to compassion and humanitarianism on the public platform, he is in reality the hardest man I've ever known.

"It is not for me, a resident of another state, to tell the voters of Wisconsin how to cast their ballots. But my conscience would have given me no peace if I had not returned to New Empire to tell this story. I hope and pray Fox County will send Mr. Darrell Pfister, a real Christian, to the state senate.

"Nobody asked me to make this statement. I have received no money for doing so. I have acted only in the public interest and for the glory of God."

Thus ends Mrs. Auerbach's moving story.

We would remind our readers that this is no idle accusation. It was made in affidavit form, sworn to in the presence of a Notary Public. It is as much sworn testimony as the statement of a witness at a trial. Any departure from truth would be punishable as perjury.

As a sample of public reaction to this horrifying story, we recommend to our readers the statements in this issue of the Hon. Park Irwin, United States Congressman, and of the Rev. Clarence Duane Sonnabend, pastor of the First Methodist Church. Also, our leading editorial dealing with the qualifications of Rolfe Torkelsen and Mr. Darrell Pfister will be of interest.

To help Fox County choose the best man to represent it in the state senate, this issue of the *Chronicle* is being sent to every registered voter, whether a subscriber or not.

*

Till reading Mrs. Auerbach's affidavit, Rolfe Torkelsen had never felt the itch to murder. Now he thought he would gladly go to Jim Buckmaster's office and shoot him. He wouldn't—he was a civilized citizen of the Nineteenth Century—but he understood why the duel had always been so popular.

For the affidavit, of course, was the handiwork of Jim Buckmaster and his attorneys. Probably Jim had offered Mrs. Auerbach a good sum of money to come to New Empire, sign the statement and then hurry back to Iowa. There were holes in her story wide enough to drive a brewer's wagon through; put her on the witness stand and any competent lawyer could tangle her in lies and tears; but a political campaign was not a trial. "Politics is war," Jim had said once. "Anything goes."

Yes, even libel. In politics you surrendered your right to recover for defamation of character. Not your legal right but your practical right. It wasn't done, according to the unwritten rules of American politics. Voters resented a candidate who filed suit. They felt he was a spoilsport.

A knock fell on the office door; Rolfe said, "Come in." It was a student clerk.

"I know you said not to disturb you, Mr. Torkelsen, but Mr. Appleton is here and he—"

"Send him in."

George Appleton was purple.

"You've seen the *Chronicle?*"

"Yes," Rolfe said.

"What are we going to do about it?"

"Nothing."

"Nothing! Great God! This will cost you the election, Senator! This will cost us Fox County."

"I know it."

"And you sit there and say we'll do nothing! We've got to cook up a reply. The woman must be a whore. Say so, anyway. Say it's a pack of lies. And maybe we can dig up something on Darrell Pfister. Is the woman's story true?"

"Part of it."

"Which part?"

"I never discussed religion with her. Or anything else, very much. We did have sexual relations. When she became pregnant, I went to Jim Buckmaster for advice. We were friends then, and I was only twenty-three. He talked with her. She admitted having relations with a young man named Maizeroy who used to live in the apartment across the hall. When he heard what was happening he left town in a hurry. The child was probably his. It might have been mine, although I doubt it. I'd taken precautions. And I'd been in Chicago during the period when she was impregnated, so far as could be determined."

"The voters will never understand all that," George Appleton said. "They like things all black and all white. Deny everything, that's the best line."

"I'll deny nothing," Rolfe said, "and I'll admit nothing."

"But why? My God, if we issue a denial maybe we can save something—"

"A blanket denial would be untrue," Rolfe said. "I'm peculiar about the truth. I respect it. Perhaps it's because I'm without religion. I have to live by a code of ethics. A religious man can lie and lie, yet hope that God will forgive him if he prays hard enough. I have no God to lean on. I believe man is alone in a savage universe. I have nothing to lean on but ethics. If I start departing from ethics, I will have nothing left."

"Lawyer talk. You should have joined a church like I told you."

"Which one?"

"What do I care which goddamned one! Any church. Then you would have had a preacher on your side. It's too late now, anyway. Every preacher in the county will be against you. They'll read that you scoffed at God and played snuggum with Nixie Auerbach and they'll skin you alive next Sunday. But maybe it's not too late, at that. Issue a statement that you're a deeply religious man. Say that you read the Bible every night—"

"But I don't. It would give me bad dreams. And I'd feel I was intellectually slumming. It has always seemed to me a very savage and childish book."

George Appleton pounded the desk.

"Stop it! Stop it, Senator! I won't listen to that sort of talk even to carry Fox County for the Republican Party."

"I apologize," Rolfe said. "A man should not discuss religion and I'm beginning to think he shouldn't discuss politics."

"And I'm beginning to think," Appleton said, "that we made an awful mistake to nominate you, Senator. I'm not sure a man with your ideas should sit in the legislature. And you should have tipped off headquarters about this Auerbach woman. That way, we could have dug the dirt on Pfister. Had it ready to throw back. I think we're licked."

"We are," Rolfe said, "if the voters let themselves be influenced by *ad hominem* arguments."

"Ad who?"

"To the man. In other words, mudslinging. Buckmaster and Pfister can't answer my arguments. So they attack the man who put forth the arguments. It's the oldest trick in logic."

"Then you won't issue a denial?"

"I won't issue anything except a no comment."

"You damned fool," George Appleton said, and he left.

Rolfe sat at his desk alone, thinking that the way of the transgressor was easy compared with the way of the independent, for man was a herd animal, and he resented the insurgent who refused to abide by the pack ideas, by the lowest common denominator ideas. Yet the race's only progress had come from men who refused to be ordinary, who refused to abide by absurd tribal taboos, who were unimpressed by ludicrous dogmas, who insisted upon being themselves and hence being different. In the outer office he could hear his clerks leaving; silence fell; twilight was falling over the town and sneaking through the windows. The clock with its portrait of George Washington ticked diligently, counting off the seconds toward election day. He would not return to the senate. As he had sensed victory so now he sensed defeat. Darrell Pfister would be senator from Fox County. He would never make a speech that would offend James L. Buckmaster and the railroads; he would never eat supper at the Madison Oyster House; he would vote right; the cartoonist on the *Madison Star* would never lampoon him. There would be no railroad commission. The forests would continue to be slaughtered. America would continue to be looted while the press applauded.

In the dusk he could see the sofa where a quarter of a century ago he had made love to Nixie Auerbach. Scientists said the cells of man's body were replaced every seven years: he was thus three times removed from that other Rolfe Torkelsen, the young man who had glimpsed a pair of bare legs and had responded as nature intended. And even though that young Rolfe Torkelsen had got this middle-aged Rolfe Torkelsen into trouble, he could not censure him; he had been going with nature. He could only censure his middle-aged self for having ventured into politics. He should have known better, with his religious ideas and his insurgence and with Nixie Auerbach in his past.

The office was dark; streetlamps had been lighted; and then it was he heard a distant door opening and footsteps in the reception room. A knock sounded on his office door.

"Rolfe?"

It was Sue's voice; she always knocked, at home or at his office; and he always knocked; it was part of the etiquette of a good marriage.

"Yes," he said wearily. "Come in."

"Sitting in the dark," she said.

"Yes."

"Brooding?"

"I suppose. You've seen the *Chronicle?*"

"Yes. And what a trite mind that Auerbach woman has." There was humor in her voice. "I'm surprised you took up with her. Your pants must have been sizzling, darling, in those days."

"They were."

"So were mine," Sue said.

"You're not mad at me?"

"Mad at you? Rolfe Torkelsen! You're getting me mixed with some of the whores you used to know. I'm Sue. Remember? I have a brain cell or two. Do you think I'd be absurd enough to be mad because twenty-five years ago you relieved the congestion of your glands with some little tart?"

He smiled.

"It's Jim Buckmaster's game," he said. "He's won. Or will. This will lick me."

"Pooh, pooh. So it will lick you. Does that mean your life's ruined? You're an attorney, not a politician."

"It will hurt my practice."

"I hope so. You work too hard anyway. But it won't hurt it for long. Wait till somebody gets into deep trouble and wants a good attorney. They'll come to the best one in town, and I don't mean Darrell Pfister. Aren't you getting hungry? I am. Let's go home to supper."

"All right," Rolfe said, and he wondered again, as he had so often wondered in the past, why intelligent men ever married any but intelligent women.

*

He was able to feel objective and even cheerful, that evening and the next morning, for a good marriage was a citadel against the world; the county might defeat him and the town might blabber, but with Sue on his side he would be invulnerable. He should have known better. He had read Francis Bacon. He had read about hostages to fortune.

His were particularly lovely little hostages, with their Danish blond hair and flower faces. Friday noon they walked home from school with chins high and lips compressed, but once inside the house they burst into tears. The playground at recess, it seemed, had been their ordeal by ridicule. Other girls had scratched them with little cat claws and tittered at their discomfiture; bad boys had yanked their braids and shouted naughty words beyond their comprehension. Now they wanted no food, and they thought they never could return to school.

All of Rolfe's anger came back then.

"Don't make us go to school again," they pleaded. "Let us stay home just for this afternoon."

Rolfe and Sue looked at each other. Then Sue said:

"You'll have to go back."

"No, mama, please—"

"Monday would be worse," Sue said, "if you'd stay home today. Some things you can't run from. Some things you have to face. You're going back with your heads high."

They thought they couldn't. And they kept asking what it was that their father had done.

"Something you wouldn't understand now," Sue said. "But it wasn't bad. Your father's the best man I've ever known. He's the bravest. And he needs us. He needs us to help him face down this nasty town. You'll be helping him when you go back to school. Hold up your heads and pretend you don't care. Give them as good as they send."

So they returned to school, to the jeers of dullards, to the derision of unwashed freckles, to the raillery of nasty-nice daughters of conformity, to the refined cruelty of spinsters with itching groins and sterile brains.

Rolfe wouldn't have had the heart to make them return—his daughters were his weakness—but Sue was right, of course: they couldn't stay away from school forever. And probably she was right in insisting that they go ahead with the Halloween party that evening. It was a droopy affair. Thirty children had been invited; only six came. The attendance at the party, he thought, was like a straw poll of his chances next Tuesday. Five of the guests were sons and daughters of railroad workers; the sixth was Mark Appleton, son of the Republican chairman, a well-behaved boy of nine. Apples were bobbed for, the guests ventured through darkened rooms where perfectly terrible ghosts waited to scare them, games were played and prizes awarded, but a party like that needed more children.

About mid-evening, when ice cream and cookies were served, a throng of ruffians came noisily along Gentry Avenue, boys and girls of high school age. They soaped windows, they smeared the door-knob with molasses; and on the lawn they chanted a variation of the campaign doggerel the Republicans had been using against Grover Cleveland:

> *"Ma, Ma, Ma, where's my Pa?*
> *Running for the Senate! Haw, haw, haw!"*

*

Next evening on the courthouse lawn, at the great Republican rally, Rolfe heard that doggerel many times. He never should have attended that rally and tried to speak; he was an open target for the catcalls and shouts from the horde of riffraff that came from nowhere and packed the meeting. They were not even Fox County voters, so it was said; Jim Buckmaster, according to rumor, had brought them to town on a special train from Chicago or somewhere; likely the same detective agency which supplied him with strikebreakers had found them in flophouses; they were very drunk, very foul-mouthed and abusive. That was quite a different rally from the one twenty-four years before when Rolfe helped elect A. Lincoln.

During the brief speeches of candidates for courthouse offices they were fairly quiet, but when Rolfe stood up to make the principal address they yowled and shouted things like "Oh you Nixie!" and "Maybellene wants Daddy," and "Ma, Ma, Ma, where's my Pa? Running for the Senate! Haw, haw, haw!"

"Citizens of Fox County," Rolfe said, but that was as far as he could get.

Jim Buckmaster had his innings that night. Bona fide voters left in disgust. It never paid to get Buckmaster down on you, people said. When he set out to destroy somebody, he stopped at nothing. He had the money and he was willful. Republican or Democrat—it made no difference to him. He'd as soon back one party as the other; he zigzagged like a steamboat on a crooked stretch of river; he just wanted the men elected who would vote as he wished. He was a big man.

Even preachers opened and shut their mouths the way he wanted. At least many preachers did in Fox County, on Sunday morning. Some merely hinted, in their prayers, that it would be to God's advantage to elect a state senator who believed He existed; but the Rev. Clarence Duane Sonnabend gave a regular old time, pulpit-pounding, Bible-waving sermon.

Monday and Tuesday, on the school playground, Margaret Fuller Torkelsen and Susan (Kitten) Torkelsen heard that campaign chant often. Ma, Ma, Ma, where's my—

With God and Jim Buckmaster against him, Senator Rolfe Torkelsen should have been snowed under so deeply they wouldn't have found him till the thaws next spring. It didn't, however, happen quite that way. Amazingly, he led the Republican ticket in Fox County. He polled more votes even than the Hon. Park Irwin. The Danish townships never wavered. With a decent candidate running for president, he would have won easily. But James G. Blaine was running. And Grover Cleveland headed the Democratic ticket. He swept Fox County like a broom. The farmers were discontented and they voted mad. For the first time since the Civil War the Democrats took the county courthouse. And Darrell Pfister was elected state senator by a margin of ninety-eight votes. On the recount that margin dwindled to sixty-three votes. But they were firm votes; he was elected. Senator Rolfe Torkelsen was returned to private life and railroad stockholders could sleep.

*

Studying the returns, he saw that the town of New Empire defeated him. He lost New Empire and the farming townships couldn't save him. With their worries about making a living, the farmers hadn't much cared about his long-ago affair with Nixie Auerbach. But New Empire cared. Trouble was, he had sinned and been found out. And had refused to issue mealymouthed, sanctimonious statements of penitence. Fellow like that needed a lesson. Show him you couldn't scoff and blaspheme and get away with it.

"There'll be a reaction, two years from now," George Appleton said. "You'll lick Pfister hands down."

"I'm through with politics," Rolfe said.

"Now, listen, Senator. A vote-getter like you! Why, you led the Republican ticket."

"If I'd run again," Rolfe said, "they'd throw the same old dirt."

"Let them. It's an axiom of politics, Senator, that the same dirt never sticks twice. They've shot their wad. It will be old stuff, in two years."

"They'd throw it just the same," Rolfe said. "I have two daughters to think about."

He might have forgiven Jim Buckmaster anything else, but he couldn't forgive him what he had done to Margaret and Kitten. They had been sunny girls, protected girls, and they had learned abruptly, the hard way, that life was not all a tale by Hans Christian Andersen. For weeks after the election they dreaded going to school. Gradually, of course, the scandal wore itself out; by and by they were laughing once more; but they had gone through something no father had the right to put them through again.

"Under no circumstances will I be a candidate for any office," Rolfe told the county convention in 1886.

*

For several years during the mid-1880's other men than Rolfe Torkelsen were invited to deliver the cemetery speech on Memorial Day. And for several years when parties were held by the grade-school set the Torkelsen girls were not asked to attend. The town was doing its best to discipline that family. At the post office when that Christly man, the Rev. Clarence Duane Sonnabend, encountered Rolfe he refused to speak. And when Rolfe went to a barber shop the loafers were likely to say, "Hello, Senator. Been working nights much lately?"

But the town got nowhere; in the Torkelsens the town had met its match. Like it or not, they were a leading family. They drove fine carriages and read fine books and took trips to Chicago and New York. They never so much as stepped foot inside a church, and the town could put that in its pipe and smoke it. Rolfe turned away as much business as he accepted, for Sue had been right: a man in trouble wanted the shrewdest lawyer available, and to hell with his religion and night life.

In 1886 the voters returned Senator Darrell Pfister to private life and elected a liberal Republican from the south end of the county who threw in his lot, in Madison, with the half-breeds. Robert M. La Follette, fighting the bosses over in Dane County, was sent to congress; the political climate was changing. In 1888, tired of starving, Darrell Pfister packed up his family and moved to Dakota for a fresh start. That same year the Methodist conference transferred the Reverend Mr. Sonnabend to some town over near Oshkosh. But Rolfe Torkelsen remained in New Empire. He might be a freethinker, but he was New Empire's freethinker. He was theirs.

You kind of have to admire him at that, people said. Lot of brains under that hat of his. He's no hypocrite, that's one thing. He's right out what he is. And he's a scrappy cuss. Never walked away from a fight. Big or little, he'll take 'em on, *he* don't care. Went right up to Jim Buckmaster and spit in his eye. Guess there were a lot of lies in that campaign back in '84. All that about how he lost his leg looting a Northern sympathizer's house in Georgia, that just don't stack up. Not like Torkelsen at all. He went to the Civil War, you have to give him credit, and went as a private, and he lost a leg for his pains. Lot of fellows paid substitutes and stayed home, but not Torkelsen, he was right in the thick of things. And all that stuff about his wronging that Auerbach woman, that was just more politics, I guess. Maybe he did diddle her, but it was a long time ago, he was young then, and a young blood will ride any mare he can catch. Seems kind of funny, the way she turned up and swore out that affidavit just before election. Something smelly there. Somebody must have paid her, and wouldn't doubt but what it was Buckmaster. Torkelsen's never been much of a ladies' man, true as a die to that wife of his. And you have to say one thing for him, he never opened his trap to answer that Auerbach woman. He wouldn't fight a woman, wouldn't call her a liar or no bad names, just swallowed his medicine and kept still. I kind of like that. Sort of think he'd get my vote, if he'd run again.

The Memorial Day Committee for 1889 decided that after all Rolfe Torkelsen was the best speaker in the river counties and it was silly not to use his talents; he was invited to deliver the address at the cemetery. And that was Appomattox in the long war between town and Torkelsen. People said it was his best speech ever, and perhaps it was: he was fifty-three and at the height of his powers. Standing hatless in the hot sunshine, within earshot of the graves of Caleb McSwasey and Sophronicus Gentry and Andrew Jackson Gentry, those forgotten warriors of the Republic, he evoked his favorite dream: a mighty, self-disciplined America, untrammeled by the chains of great wealth.

"Call me a dreamer," he said, "and I will not deny it. Call me a visionary, and I will reply that where there is no vision the people perish. I see new times and a new century. I see a shining land. I see great libraries open to all who thirst for knowledge, I see slums demolished and replaced by sunny habitations, I see the labor of children in factories prohibited, I see the ugliness and shame and degradation of poverty only a wretched memory, I see intelligence in public office, I see the vast agglutinations of wealth made to obey the same laws which you and I obey. I see, if you please, the dragon slain, the serpent scotched. No longer will the barons of great finance levy their toll on farmer and shopkeeper and laborer. I see man walking free in the sun and wind, free to doubt, free to inquire, free to criticize, free to be different, free to speak. I see laws passed to compensate injured workmen and their widows, I see commissions to regulate railroads and other public utilities, I see government for the benefit of all, not for the few alone. Call all this socialism or communism and you will not disturb me. Calling it such does not make it such. But call it Americanism and I will agree. The land I see is the land seen in their great dreams by the Jeffersons and the Tom Paines and the Andrew Jacksons, by the Monroes and the Madisons and the Lincolns, by the men who insisted on their right to think freely, to worship as they saw fit or not to worship or to deny the existence of Providence, by the men united in one thing, their love of America."

His ideas had not changed one whit; nothing could change them. And as he spoke he seemed to grow in size till he looked big; a big man. No longer was his hair bright and coppery; it was dull blond and gray; around his eyes the wrinkles were deep in his weathered skin; more than ever he looked like some old Norse sea dog. He had fought his fights and suffered his wounds and survived triumphant.

Sitting on front row his women listened with shining eyes: his wife and his daughters. Margaret Fuller Torkelsen was fifteen; Kitten would be fourteen in the autumn; they were young ladies, almost, with their hair up and their skirts lengthened. And sitting beside Margaret Torkelsen somebody else listened as if to the voice of the Republic itself: a good-looking young man of high-school age, Mark Appleton, son of County Chairman Appleton.

After the speech, after the applause, after the congratulations, Mark Appleton edged through the crowd.

"Gee, Senator," he said, "that was a wonderful speech. I enjoyed that. It was—it was sort of like hearing a band playing the Star-Spangled Banner."

*

The town knew it was licked, after that Memorial Day address; the Torkelsen family had been too much for it. And it must have figured that if you can't lick 'em, join 'em; for when high school took up in September Margaret Torkelsen was elected president of the junior class. New people kept moving to town; other people kept dying or moving away; and once more the Torkelsen girls were invited to parties; parties were held again in the house on Gentry Avenue. And as in any household with two attractive daughters of mating age, there were always young men about. The nineties came and they were gay indeed, in the Torkelsen household, what with young people playing the piano and singing and pulling taffy and gathering on the lawn for Fourth of July fireworks. One young man was there especially often: Mark Appleton.

"He's sweet on Margaret," Sue told Rolfe.

"Seems like a nice boy," Rolfe said. "What does she think?"

"Girls of her age don't think," Sue said. "She's keeping him dangling. Him and three or four others."

Then suddenly she was graduated from high school and off to the university at Madison, preparing herself for an odd new career called Social Service, for she was an admirer of a young woman named Jane Addams.

"We won't see much of Mark Appleton now," Sue said, but she was wrong; he kept dropping in. And not to pay court to Kitten; Kitten had her own followers; he came to visit with Rolfe. After high school he had gone into his father's bank, but he was finding it dull. He enjoyed reading and not books on finance either; he liked such things as the Federalist Papers and biographies of Revolutionary figures. Rolfe lent him these and many others, and he told Sue:

"Young Appleton has character. Lend him a book and he brings it back."

But the nineties were not so gay as rumored, in much of America; workmen could never make ends meet somehow, and hard times dogged the farmer. Dust blew across the midlands from earth that never should have been plowed; and so many swamps had been drained and so much timber cut that when rain fell nothing held it in the soil; it runneled the land and flooded the rivers, and a few months later droughts came: the pioneers, it appeared, had been not only noble but damned fools. Plagues of grasshoppers swarmed across middle America; the corn borer appeared; in the South people began worrying about the boll weevil. And on verandas at Saratoga Springs and at Newport poor rich old ladies and poor frightened old gentlemen worried themselves sick about such organizations as the Knights of Labor and the Populist Party, and for that matter about the growing strength of the half-breeds out in Wisconsin.

Changes, changes. Fewer steamboats plied the Mississippi River, except to carry freight; passenger traffic was always in a hurry; it took the trains. Packets such as the *Bonnie* and the *Sol Klauber* were seen no more. And instead of log rafts and lumber rafts that floated with the current, logs and lumber went to market in enormous tows, with a steamboat pushing and a bow-boat guiding. Year after year millions of feet of forest wealth slid past New Empire; the north woods were being stripped. And people began to say that perhaps after all the pine wouldn't last forever. Rolfe Torkelsen said it, in speeches all over the state, to graduating classes and farmers and to such organizations as the Wisconsin Horticultural Society. And always after such speeches he was attacked by the Buckmaster newspapers.

Out of politics though he was, Rolfe kept in close touch with the half-breed movement, for he was a leading liberal; sometimes during a campaign he went into doubtful counties and spoke for progressive candidates, and he could be counted on for contributions. And in Fox County his influence remained considerable in Republican councils; usually he managed to maneuver the nomination of candidates with progressive ideas. Over in Dane County Bob La Follette, who had been retired from congress, was Rolfe's friend; and La Follette was a fighter; his star had set but people said it would rise again. Progressive ideas and progressive government would prevail, they said; the Old Guard— men like Jim Buckmaster—were making a last-ditch stand. But meanwhile, up in the woods, the pines kept crashing. Laws might be passed some day against the ravages of the lumber barons, but it would be too late then.

Rolfe had an urgent letter, early in 1893, from old Senator Neal.

"We need your help here in Madison," it said. "Come armed with petitions and bring along your fellow citizens. Here's what is happening:

"Up in the Indian Head country is one of the last magnificent stands of white pine in Wisconsin. There are several hundred thousand acres of the stuff, and it's prime. Till two months ago it was United States Government land, but Buckmaster finagled things in Washington and had it transferred to the state. So now he's up to the old dodge of proposing to run a branch of his railroad through that virgin timber. A railroad is needed there about as much as a foot warmer in hell. But if we can't stop this deal, the legislature will grant him the usual bonanza for every mile of track he lays. This land has never been open for entry; it's the biggest lumber prize in Wisconsin today.

"The cloakroom rumors are that the big boys have reached an understanding. They have stopped quarreling among themselves about what's left of the pine, and have decided to stand together. The logging crowd from the eastern counties will back Buckmaster's play for the Indian Head land. So will the crowd from the Lake Superior counties. And he'll throw his weight to give them Indian reservation pine in their areas. When thieves agree, honest men must weep; but let's fight first. We've got to act fast."

Within a couple of hours after reading that letter, Rolfe had petitions circulating. Next day he hired small boys to deliver handbills to every house in town, announcing a Saturday evening mass meeting at the high school. He pulled every wire, tossed into the fight every ounce of political weight he could muster.

The turnout at the mass meeting surprised him; people were waking up. His years of political education were having their effect. Even George Appleton, gradually, was leaning toward progressive ideas, although his thinking may have been swayed by the fact that the Buckmaster bank—the Bank of New Empire—was his competitor. In any case, when Rolfe took the cars to Madison fifteen other residents of Fox County accompanied him.

Madison in January. Snowy Capitol Square and the Madison Oyster House. It all looked much the same as back in the days when Rolfe Torkelsen was senator from Fox County. His room in the Park Hotel looked much the same as that other room where men had tried to buy his vote and where Jim Buckmaster had promised him the world. The senate chamber looked much the same: a little grimier, perhaps, but much the same. It gave him a pang, to think that he might have been sitting there through all the legislative sessions since 1883.

The battle of the lobbyists—that was what the press called the struggle of those days in Madison. It didn't, however, point out that the lobbyists from Fox County and many other counties were amateurs, unpaid, people who had come to the capital at their own expense to pack the galleries, to accost senators and assemblymen in the corridors and in hotel public rooms; people who wanted to save what was left of the pine because they loved their state.

It was a good battle but not a victorious one for Rolfe and the progressives. A majority in the assembly and a majority in the senate voted as might have been expected. Whose bread they ate his song they sang.

And yet Rolfe couldn't feel that the defeat was overwhelming: it held a promise of future victories. The progressive cause was gaining. Ten years before people from towns all over the state would never have thrust personal affairs aside and have come to Madison on an altruistic mission. It was possible to believe that in another ten years the half-breeds would take the statehouse; a man like Bob La Follette might sit in the governor's office.

On his last noon in Madison, Rolfe ate in the dining room of the Park Hotel. A stringed orchestra was playing, and on the other side of the busy room Rolfe caught sight of James L. Buckmaster. He was a tall, straight old man, leaner than he used to be, in a beautifully-tailored gray suit. His mouth had changed, owing to false teeth. His silvery hair had thinned, but it was carefully brushed across his brown skull. He must have been within shouting distance of seventy, but you had the feeling he was not through yet, not by a long shot. He handled himself with a certain resilience, like an old Indian. His brows were still coal black. His jaw was still purposeful. He looked flushed with triumph.

And with something more, perhaps, for across the table sat a lovely woman, not more than thirty-five. Her hair was dark, her figure enchanting in a gown of black velvet ornamented with jet. She looked regal, almost; a distinguished woman; not at all like the easy girls any man of wealth could pick up. Rolfe wondered who she was.

XVII

HER NAME was Mrs. Adrienne Purcell. And Rolfe had been correct: she was decidedly not an easy woman. Although engaged in business, it was not the business of Molly Fitzpatrick: she operated a photographic studio out near the university. Her husband, Warner Purcell, had died two winters before, leaving her with an eleven-year-old son and a nine-year-old daughter and various cameras, glass plates and photographic chemicals. Also ten thousand dollars from insurance. Knowing nothing of the photographic craft, Mrs. Purcell hired a man who did; herself, she set out to get business. And in the studio she was receptionist. That was how James L. Buckmaster met her; he had gone there with a senator he was bribing. While the senator sat for a saving-the-country portrait, James L. Buckmaster remained in the reception room. And it was as if the years had rolled back, bringing him his youth again. For Mrs. Adrienne Purcell resembled Bonnie Fansler.

When he left the studio with the senator, James L. Buckmaster was abstracted; he couldn't get her out of his mind; so two days later he returned and arranged to have his portrait taken. And when he called to look over the proofs, he summoned his courage and invited her to lunch at the Park Hotel; he had a business matter to discuss with her, he said.

"Mrs. Purcell," he told her, there in the hotel dining room, "I'm more than pleased with the work of your studio. It so happens that I've been planning to have pictures taken of all the officials of the New Empire Line. And of all the executives of my lumber company. These will go into our archives, so that posterity may see the kind of men who opened the Northwest to civilization. I've looked over the work of other studios, but I like yours best. I'm inclined to give you the business."

Her smile was sorcerous.

*

"What in hell," officials of the New Empire Line asked themselves, "is the old man up to? Why go to Madison just to have a picture taken? What's wrong with our photographers here in Chicago?"

But if they wished to remain with the company as vice-presidents and traffic managers and superintendents, it was necessary to follow Buckmaster's orders. So during the following months, many a bewhiskered or mustachioed countenance was recorded for eternity on photographic plates at the Purcell Studios in Madison. And James L. Buckmaster always accompanied these dignitaries to their sittings. Several times he took Mrs. Purcell to lunch. Twice he took her to the theater. People began to notice and to talk.

After the railroad officials had been photographed, sittings were arranged for executives in the Buckmaster Lumber Company. Summer came—one of those sweltering, drought-plagued summers of the 1890's—and Mrs. Purcell looked bewitching in picture hats and crisp airy gowns. And James L. Buckmaster knew that for the second time in his life he had fallen in love. The sixties are the adolescence of old age, and his courtship had a tentative adolescent quality; he daydreamed much about her night-colored hair and eloquent eyes and Lillian Russell bust; he remembered her shapely hands, so feminine and yet capable-looking; and gradually it came to him that the ultimate prize life could give him would be marriage to Mrs. Adrienne Purcell.

There were obstacles. Well, all his life he had skinned his nose against obstacles. When you were young you kicked obstacles aside; when you were older you paid for their removal. It would be necessary to divorce Esperanza von Zumwalt McSwasey Buckmaster. All right: his attorneys could attend to that. And it would be necessary to convince Mrs. Purcell that marriage to a man twice her age could be agreeable. She would inherit a railroad, for one thing, and a lumber empire, for another. She would inherit eleven newspapers. She would inherit stocks, bonds, mortgages, farms, town lots, city lots, checking accounts in a dozen banks. Her children would be wealthy. He would take her to Europe on their honeymoon, or around the world: anywhere. In return she would permit herself to be made love to by a man who could still give a good account of himself in a bedroom. That was all. He wouldn't even require that she fall in love with him; he would be well enough pleased if she only pretended to love him.

He turned sixty-seven that July, and how time raced in your sixties! When you were young life stretched ahead of you in meadows of forever, but at sixty-seven you were much aware that the timber was mainly cut and the drive was nearly finished. If you intended to mention marriage to Mrs. Adrienne Purcell you had better be about it.

Yet he procrastinated, and that was unlike him. Usual thing, when he wanted something he went after it. Bought it. Lord, the merchandise he had bought in his time! Senators and governors and smaller political fry; mistresses in Chicago, ladies of the evening in New York, railroads and steamboats. Everything was for sale, he had found. The price tag might be high, but it was all for sale. Except somebody like that goddamned Swede Torkelsen. Stubborn bastard. Refused to deal and ruined his life. Could have been in the U.S. Senate by now. Could have been a rich man: really rich. James L. Buckmaster couldn't understand the workings of such a man's mind.

Early in September, a dusty, dry September, he boarded his private car in the New Empire yards and traveled toward Madison. Sitting with a cigar, on edge with apprehension but bemused with enchantment, he reached a decision: this would be the day. This very afternoon he would ask Mrs. Purcell to marry him. On his hands there were spots—old-age spots—as brown as his cigar.

*

At four-thirty that afternoon when he left the Purcell Studios his face was flushed and his eyes were the hard gray of steel rails in winter. His Panama hat was jerked low. Blotches of sweat showed at the armpits of his linen suit. Instead of hailing a cab he went tramping angrily along State Street toward Capitol Square. The sun was blistering. People made way for him: a lean old man striding purposefully. But he had no purpose, now.

Capitol Square. The statehouse dome gold against the hard blue sky. Shoppers swirling around him; students who had returned early to the university; laughing dark girls, bright blond girls; and young men. He hated the young men. Once he could have knocked them all down and kicked in their teeth.

He found himself in a dark cool bar; he ordered whiskey. Drank it straight, jigger after jigger, with a water wash. Two young men came in, students likely; one stuck a cigar into his mouth and searched his pockets for a match. Then he turned to James L. Buckmaster.

"Got a light, Gramp?"

James L. Buckmaster nearly—very nearly—let him have a fist in the jaw. But his bones were brittle. He was getting along in years, that was his trouble. And he was an old fool. Might have known a stuck-up bitch like that Adrienne Purcell would just play him along for a sucker, getting all that portrait business, and then refuse to marry him.

When he left the saloon he knew what he wanted: he wanted the woods. His compass needle had always pointed north and he wanted to go there now. Standing in the blazing afternoon he had a vision of tall pines and foaming trout streams and still lakes; he wanted the woods. To hell with Madison; he hated Madison. Madison was Bob La Follette's town and Bob La Follette was not for sale. Rolfe Torkelsen and Bob La Follette and Mrs. Adrienne Purcell: none of them had a price tag. Give them the world and they wouldn't sell. Damned fools.

A cab took him to the railroad yards; that evening his car was coupled to a northbound train. He sat with a bitter cigar and a glass which his Negro servant kept refilling. The car wheels said clickety-clack, clickety-clack, taking him through the night toward the Big Dipper and Polaris.

"Mistah Buckmaster, suh, ain't you gettin' sleepy? It's past one in the morning, suh."

Sleepy? No, he wasn't sleepy. Hell, no. Go to bed, Stephen. Didn't mean to keep you up. Go to bed. Leave the bottle.

He drank and smoked and drank. An old man didn't need so much sleep. Three years and I'll be seventy. My God, seventy. Maybe you can't blame her. Only thirty-five. Jesus, though, what a body. But no price tag. She needn't think she's so goddamned high and mighty. Should have seen me forty years ago: she'd have been glad enough to have me then. Bonnie wanted me. If Bonnie had lived . . . Damn, I'd have found a way. I'd have got rid of Esperanza and married Bonnie. But she jumped overboard. Jesus. Waterweeds in her hair. And I'm getting a headache. Have to take those powders. Three years and I'll be seventy. And then? I hope it's quick. When it comes I hope it comes quick. Struck by lightning, something like that. Not one of those diseases that eat out your insides. Rats in your guts. Not that.

*

At daybreak he wakened in his chair; the train lurched and hooted, heading north. And he needed more of those headache powders. But first, another drink. Whiskey for breakfast; a pinery boy for sure.

The sun rose over Wisconsin, but this was not the woods. The woods used to extend clear down here, but no longer. They had been cut and shipped down the little rivers to the bigger rivers, and down the bigger rivers to the Mississippi. To the big river and the St. Louis sawmills. Swede Lena's place where the coffee was so good and Noisy Swanson jabbered a blue streak; and a saloon where some two-fisted wench whose name he had forgotten used to yell, "Back from the bar, you frill-shirted dandies, here comes Jim Buckmaster." All the whiskey he had swallowed, the girls he had loved, the sunrises he had seen.

This sunrise was blazing hot; he was sweating; and cinders from the locomotive speckled his skin. He slept again, despite his headache; then the Negro man was shaking his sleeve.

"Mistah Buckmaster, you should have went to bed, suh."

"Where are we?"

"Just pullin' into Quickwater, suh."

He stared out the window.

"You'd never know the place," he said. "It was beautiful once."

"Don't doubt it, suh."

"Dan Stoughton had a monkey. And I had a cow once. And Molly Fitzpatrick never had kids."

"Who is she, suh?"

"Dead. And Dan Stoughton—dead. And Lew Fitzpatrick—dead. And Sol Klauber—drownded. Drownded in a freshet. Pulled him out dripping. Long time ago."

"You should go to bed, suh. Get yourself some rest. I'll undress you."

"And Noisy Swanson—he's dead too. And Greasy Dick. And Bulldog Ryan—he was going to gouge out my eyes. Well, he didn't."

"Just bet he didn't, suh! No man ain't goin' to gouge you nohow."

"And Bonnie Fansler—she drownded. And Rolfe Torkelsen—he whored out on me. Thought I could trust the bastard. I put him on his feet. Did everything for him. He was in my camp, and when a man's in my camp I take care of him. But the son of a bitch whored out on me. Know who you can trust?"

"No, suh. Sure don't know that."

"None of them. They're all slippery as cedar logs. Caleb McSwasey— the bastard used knucks. And he's dead too. They're all dead."

*

That afternoon when he wakened in his stateroom the train was still lurching north, and he still had a headache. He poured whiskey, dumped in the powders and swallowed the mess. Then, wearing a bathrobe, he went to the observation platform. Heat-devils danced above the cinders of the right-of-way, and the land on both sides of the track stretched off in man-made desolation. It was cutover land. White pines had grown here once; there had been cool trout streams and swamps that were natural reservoirs. Now it was all ruin and devastation. The streambeds were choked and arid; the swamps were deserts. In the dry September heat he could see hillsides that had been slashed and gutted by long-ago rains; he could see nettles and thistles flourishing in that vast graveyard of dead forests; he could see beggarly stands of no-account tamaracks and oc-casional clumps of jack pines, those bitter pimplike trees. Nothing worth cutting was left. Nothing worth anything was left. It was all rubbish now; all trash. Pinery boys had come and gone; empire builders had come and gone; nothing was left.

Presently the train pulled into a town called Stoughton. Not much of a town; not so much of a town as Dan Stoughton had been a man. Facing the railroad, the façades of the main street were ramshackle wooden things, saloons mainly. Most of them had been abandoned; windows were boarded over or smashed. On the map in his mind he could see his railroad stretching north to Lake Superior, and he wondered testily why his private car was being switched to a siding in this Godfor-saken place. Then he remembered. Yesterday in Madison he had given orders that his car should be dropped off here. A branch line wandered northwest from the town of Stoughton to Oxbow, and beyond Oxbow track was being laid into the virgin pine the state had granted him last winter.

He had told the division superintendent he wanted to inspect that new track. But now he realized he had wanted more than that. He had wanted to go deep into the woods, clear to railhead. There would be high old times at railhead: there always were. There would be saloons and fancy houses thronged by men from the mule camps. There would be tinny pianos and chesty talk and whores. Dice would be rolling, roulette wheels spinning. He wanted to plunge into that life again as if into his youth. A roaring town in the woods: that was what he wanted.

A locomotive came chuffing along the siding and backed into his private car. Steam and smoke drifted from the locomotive. And as the car began rolling, out of Stoughton along the branch line, through the cutover land strewed with slashing left by his loggers, he noticed off to the south and west a strangeness in the sky. Zenith was blue, but as his gaze moved toward the horizon he saw haze, smoke haze, which deepened to the color of mustard, almost. Fires burning somewhere, likely. There always were. Men like that bastard Rolfe Torkelsen said that sparks from locomotives set fires in the woods. All right, so his locomotives dropped a few sparks. What was Rolfe Torkelsen going to do about it? What were the goddamned half-breeds going to do about it? Set up a railroad commission to regulate the way he ran his affairs? Make him put spark arresters on his locomotives? Not while he had any fight left. No bunch of visionaries—men who had never met a payroll in their lives—were going to boss him around. He went inside.

"How you feeling, Mistah Buckmaster?" the Negro man asked.

"I'm all right, Stephen. A little headache, that's all."

"I don't know, suh, seem to me you look kind of sick-like."

"Me sick? I'm never sick. Except for these damned headaches. But I'm fine. Know what I'm going to do tonight?"

"Sleep, I hope, suh."

James L. Buckmaster laughed.

"I'm going to have me a woman, Stephen. That's how I feel. I want a woman."

"Yes, suh."

"You think I'm too old, don't you? You look at me and think what does that old goat want with a woman? That's what you think."

"No, suh, no, suh. Nothin' like that, suh. My old daddy, he's goin' on eighty-nine and he done got married again last June. I say, 'Daddy, what you goin' to use for love?' He say, 'Son, you 'tend to your own affairs.'"

Stephen chuckled.

The car was rocking: not much of a roadbed on this branch line. That was because the roadbed had never been built in the interests of efficient transportation. It had been built only so the Buckmaster Lumber Company could grab the timber land bestowed by a generous legislature. Five years ago, that was; and then last winter the legislature had granted him more timber land, beyond Oxbow. He stared out the window; everything had been logged off. There were stumps, thousands of stumps, and they looked like gravestones. Weeds and desolation. The sun was lower now and red as a hot penny when seen through the atmospheric murk; the light on the ruined land was sulphur-colored.

"Think you can shave me, Stephen, with this car rolling?"

"Reckon so, suh."

"All right. But bring whiskey first. I want to get drunk, Stephen."

"Ain't never seen you drunk, Mistah Buckmaster. Seen you swallow a powerful lot, but never drunk."

"It takes a lot," James L. Buckmaster said. "And bring those head-ache powders."

"Yes, suh. What's in them powders, anyhow?"

"Damned if I know. Morphine, maybe."

He drank and lay back in the special barber chair the car carried, surrendering to the pleasure of hot towels and creamy lather. And with his eyes closed he thought of Mrs. Adrienne Purcell. The bitch. Offered her everything . . . Why, Mr. Buckmaster, I never dreamed . . . Oh, no, I'm sorry, I'm terribly sorry, but I'm afraid I—I couldn't . . . Jesus. God damn, God damn! Built like a brick backhouse. Built like a little red wagon. Could have been wonderful. Diamonds, emeralds—any of that junk women liked—she could have had them all. A dozen bank accounts. Lumber yards, sawmills. You might have expected her to jump at mar-riage. For the sake of her children, if for no other reason. She would have inherited everything and her children would have been rich. But oh no, not Adrienne Purcell . . . But Mr. Buckmaster—you see, well—I don't love you. I was happily married and I was in love. Don't you think a woman should marry for love?

God damned fool.

"Have to hold still, suh," Stephen said, "else I'm like to cut you."

Well, he would show her. He would get slobbering drunk, he would find the prettiest, juiciest whore in the woods, he would show her . . . I like you very much, Mr. Buckmaster. As a friend. But of course there's the difference in our ages . . .

"If you could just hold still, suh. Way you double up your fists and sort of jerk, I am like to cut you."

"All right, Stephen. All right. All right."

The car swayed on, toward Oxbow. Clickety-clack, clickety-clack.

"There we are," Stephen said. "Smoothest job of razor-shaving a man ever had."

James L. Buckmaster went to the mirror. Yes, a very smooth job. But those damned liver spots on his face. Old, old.

*

Beyond Oxbow the locomotive and private car crept along the newly-laid track at hardly ten miles an hour. The sun had set but the air remained oppressive; the scent of the sweet white pines was all but smothered by that other smell of fires somewhere. James L. Buckmaster kept swallowing whiskey, trying to get drunk, but he had always had a good head for liquor. Well, the evening was young. He'd manage, before the evening was old. He'd swallow bourbon and get roaring and happy. He'd forget Mrs. Adrienne Purcell. Find him a whore and forget.

He had eaten, by the time the car halted at railhead. End of the line; there wasn't any more. Deep woods ahead; deep woods on either side; deep woods behind, except for the tenuous single line of track. From the observation platform he could see the dim white tents of the mule camp. And there was another tent, brightly-lighted. The walls were rolled up; he could see a bar built of planks laid across barrels; he heard a piano.

"Stephen," he said, "go find me the construction boss."

A few minutes later a burly young man came into the car.

"Yes, Mr. Buckmaster."

"What's your name?"

"Finnegan, Mr. Buckmaster. Denny Finnegan."

"I came up to look things over," James L. Buckmaster said. "But it's too dark to see much now. So I'll have a little fun."

"Yes, sir."

"Are there girls over in the saloon tent?"

"Yes, sir."

"Young ones? Pretty ones?"

"Well—you know how it goes, sir. The usual crop. There's one though that ain't bad. Sophie. Sophie ain't bad."

"Sophie," Jim said. "I knew a whore years ago named Sophie. In Rafferty's Saloon. But this couldn't be the same Sophie. She died. Well, introduce me. And pass the word I'll set up drinks for the house. For the whole damned camp, all anybody wants to drink. Let's go."

"I don't know, sir. If the boys get to kegging up they ain't going to be no good tomorrow. Lose a day."

"Hell with tomorrow. This is tonight. When Jim Buckmaster hits town things whirl. Always did, always will. Tell them Jim Buckmaster's here. Tell them the drinks are on him."

Outside the car Denny Finnegan said:

"Smell that smoke, sir? It's been getting worse."

"Nothing but God's cigar," James L. Buckmaster said. "He always smokes foul ones."

Finnegan crossed himself.

The tent was not so good as a wooden saloon, not so good as rivertown saloons when a drive was finished, but it would have to do. Entering, James L. Buckmaster let out a pinery boy hoot.

"Here I am, boys. Jim Buckmaster's come and he's on a tear. Anything you want, boys, it's all on me."

The construction workers looked at one another. Their voices were subdued, when they told the barkeep what they would have.

"Hell, boys, it ain't a funeral," James L. Buckmaster said. "Liven it up, liven it up. And let's have some fast music over there."

The piano player did his best, but that was a constrained crowd. It wasn't the way it used to be, when a drive was finished. Maybe they felt uneasy, having the biggest man in Wisconsin in their midst.

"This here is Sophie," Finnegan said.

"Hello," she said.

She was not young. Thirty, maybe. A hard thirty. But her hair was dark. Like Mrs. Purcell's, like Bonnie's. When she smiled you saw she had neglected her teeth. But her rump and boobies were all right.

"Sophie," James L. Buckmaster said, "have a drink. Forget your troubles."

"Take more than one to make me do that," she said.

"All right, goddamn it, take two. Take a dozen. Won't cost you a cent. I'm paying for everything tonight." And to the crowd in the tent he shouted, "God damn it boys, liven it up. Keg up, boys. It's all on me."

They obeyed, they did as he ordered, they kegged up. But nobody was gay.

"Jesus Christ!" James L. Buckmaster shouted at last. "What's wrong with you galoots? Don't you know how to have fun? Why, when I was your age I—I sang. Hell, I'll sing now. Old pinery boy song. My father taught it to me. Friend of his made it up right out of his head. Here's how it goes, boys."

And in a voice that was always threatening to crack with the adolescence of old age, James L. Buckmaster sang. He was feeling the liquor at last; he could imagine he was a boy again, singing to a crowd in the Northern Saloon while Molly Fitzpatrick listened:

"Oh, drive the logs down, boys, drive the white pine
Drive 'em and ride 'em, down to the boom ..."

When he finished hand-clapping spattered. There were no cheers. No enthusiasm.

"Hell with this crowd," he told Sophie. "Come on."

As they groped toward the private car she sneezed.

"It's this smoke, Mr. Buckmaster."

"Call me Jim."

"It's this smoke, Jim. Makes me sneeze. Makes my eyes water."

"Nothing but a smudge," he said.

In his stateroom he turned off the lights; she was a silhouette undressing. He stripped too. Then he kissed her, hungrily, and ran his dry old man's hands over her body with an old man's lasciviousness. Her breath was bad.

*

He must have achieved drunkenness or perhaps he swallowed too many headache powders because he slept at last, deeply. And he dreamed he was on the river again, on the big river on a big raft. Wind was blowing and the raft kept threatening to drift into Weasel Creek Eddy and saddlebag on Turtle Island. All hell would be to pay, then. Jim, Caleb McSwasey would say in his quiet voice, maybe you're not such an able rooster as I thought. That little deal we talked over in Read's Landing—let's forget that, Jim. You can go to hell, Jim.

But he would save the raft. He and Noisy Swanson would save her, with the help of Greasy Dick.

And the river was all mysterious and misty and veiled with soft promise, like the future. Maybe that was the future down there, waiting; New Empire was there.

Then he heard Stephen's voice.

"Mistah Buckmaster! Mistah Buckmaster, suh! Wake up!"

"Go to hell," James L. Buckmaster mumbled.

"Wake up, suh! You got to! Wind's come up, suh, and there's a fire."

He sat up; he heard a gale howling; he smelled smoke.

"What's we goin' to do, suh? I'm scared."

"We'll go to the river," James L. Buckmaster said.

"What river?"

James L. Buckmaster was yanking on his trousers.

"Why, goddamn it, the Chippewa."

"Ain't no river. Ain't no Chippewa. We's miles from the Chippewa. Ask me, suh, and I think we's trapped. I am scared, suh."

No, of course there was no Chippewa. This wasn't Quickwater.

He pulled on his shoes, laced them, strode into the corridor and through the car to the observation platform. The wind was tremendous. To the southwest the night sky was bright as sunrise. Firebrands went sailing overhead; there was roaring. He stood there gripping the car rail, still stupefied from bourbon and headache powders, thinking of his pine. Burning, burning. The best stand of pine in Wisconsin.

Then he saw a tree a hundred yards away turn to a torch. One moment it was standing dark and monumental and the next it was seething.

He whirled, stumbled down the car steps and ran. His eyes smarted, his nostrils were full of smoke, he coughed. Thing to do was scoot along low. But his legs hurt.

Get to the Chippewa, that was what to do. Quickwater was burning but he would save himself, once he reached the flowage above the mill dam. It would be all right, he would reach the river and swim to the other shore. And the future was all waiting, clean as new paper. It was his to live all over again. Only this time things would be different. He wouldn't let Bonnie Fansler get away, this time.

He stumbled and fell, waiting for somebody named Sol Klauber to pick him up. But Mr. Klauber didn't come.

XVIII

ONE MORNING the following spring a student clerk knocked on the door of Rolfe Torkelsen's private office.

"George Appleton to see you, sir."

"Send him in."

Rolfe leaned back in his chair, stretched, inhaled the warm May air flowing through the open window. He had been working too hard, as usual; his desk was piled with briefs and calf-bound volumes. But hard work had always agreed with him; he looked very fit. In these harvest years of his career much of his business came from beyond the little river city of New Empire; when people in Madison or Milwaukee or even Chicago needed a good lawyer they often sought him out.

Looking affable, George Appleton came in, and after it was agreed that the weather was sublime he said:

"Two things I want to talk about with you, Senator. Since Judge Mason's death, I've been sounding out opinion. This will be a Republican year. You know that."

"Looks that way," Rolfe said.

"So the man we nominate to succeed Judge Mason will go to the bench."

Rolfe nodded.

"I've been in every county in the judicial district," Appleton said. "I've talked with the chairmen and with the men who will be delegates to the judicial convention. Ninety percent of them are agreed on the nomination of one man. If we can get him."

"And who is that?"

"You."

Rolfe smiled.

"I thought," he said, "it was understood I'm out of politics."

"It is understood. But a judgeship is hardly politics. At least it shouldn't be. I don't like to see a man campaigning for the office of judge. A judge should be above that. Well, I've been asked to sound you out. If the convention nominated you, would you accept?"

Rolfe sat looking at his desk, at a hickory cane leaning against the desk. Once that cane had belonged to Sophronicus Gentry. To Judge Sophronicus Gentry.

"I don't know," he said.

"I know what you're thinking," George Appleton said. "You're remembering the campaign of '84. You're remembering the mud. There wouldn't be any mud this time, Senator."

"How do you know that?"

"Do you think William Millet of Franklin County is the sort to throw mud?"

"What has Bill Millet got to do with it?"

"He's slated for the Democratic nomination for the judgeship. Do you think he'd throw mud?"

"No," Rolfe said, "Bill Millet wouldn't throw mud. He'd fight clean."

"There you are, Senator. It would be you against William Millet. A Republican year like this will be, you'd win hands down. I'll bet you wouldn't need to campaign at all and still you'd lead the ticket. Hell, you even led it here in Fox County in '84. You're a vote-getter. Will you consider the matter?"

"Yes," Rolfe said, "I'll consider it. I'll talk it over with Sue and consider it."

"How old are you, Senator?"

"Fifty-eight."

"Fifteen good years ahead of you, Senator. Go to the district bench and you can't tell what would happen after that. You've been a leader for years in the progressive movement. Everybody knows exactly where you stand. You've never shilly-shallied. You've said what you thought and you've meant what you said. Well, progressivism is going to take this state, some day. It's in the cards. They won't be able to stop men like Bob La Follette. Or men like you, Senator. Go to the district bench and after that—well—it's anybody's guess. I hope you'll consider the matter favorably."

"I'll consider it," Rolfe said.

"Favorably?"

"I shouldn't wonder."

George Appleton smiled.

"There's one other matter," he said. "It's more personal. It's about my son, Mark."

Mark. Mark Appleton and Margaret Fuller Torkelsen. Rolfe thought it somewhat old-fashioned of George Appleton to believe that future fathers-in-law should discuss the matrimonial plans of their children.

"Yes?" Rolfe said.

"He's not happy in the bank," George Appleton said. "I thought he'd grow to like it, but I doubt if he ever will. He wants to be a lawyer."

"If he wants to be, he should be."

"Exactly. I've come to believe that too. And if he should—well—marry while he's still studying, I could give him financial assistance. I believe a young man should do what he wants. Well, Mark would like to enter your office and study under you."

Rolfe remembered the books he had lent Mark Appleton, the books that had always been promptly returned. He said:

"I'd like to have him, of course. He'd be very welcome. But he might do better to go to the university law school at Madison."

"He's considered that," George Appleton said, "but he prefers studying under you. We talked about it last night. And Mark said, 'Senator Torkelsen could teach me more than I'd learn at Madison. Senator Torkelsen,' he said, 'is the biggest man on this river. I'd like to study in his office.' That's what he said."

Rolfe started to reply, but he found it hard to speak.

"And you know," George Appleton said, "I think he hit the nail on the head, Senator. I agree with him. You're the biggest man in Fox County and the biggest man on the river. Lots of other people think so too. Run for judge, Senator, and you'll find out. You're the biggest man we've got."

*

After George Appleton had gone, Rolfe couldn't concentrate; he sat fiddling with the hickory cane that had belonged to Judge Gentry. At last he stood up and went to the window, looking down at Winnebago Street, bright in the spring sunshine. Fifteen good years ahead of him; perhaps more, with luck. And Mark Appleton reading law in his office.

And he remembered the line from Plato old Senator Neal had quoted many years ago. Those having torches will pass them on to others.

Progressivism was on the march. Liberalism was on the march, all over America. James L. Buckmaster was dead, and the men like him—the men whose captive press had called them empire builders—were dead or dying. And they passed on no torches because they had none to pass. Materialism was never a torch. Greed never flamed up like a beacon in the night. Expediency was never a torch.

But the Bob La Follettes, the Senator Neals—yes, and the Rolfe Torkelsens—they had torches. They spoke their minds and their words struck fire in the young men coming on. In the Mark Appletons. The torch of liberalism would never fall and gutter out in the dust. The young men would seize that torch and carry it proudly into the new century.

On the door a knock sounded.

"It's Mrs. Torkelsen, sir," a student clerk said.

"Send her in," Rolfe said; and he was smiling, the way a man who loves his wife always smiles when he has good news to tell her.